MARY ELISKA GIRL AVIATRIX

Mary Eliska Girl Detective Girl Aviatrix Air Mystery Stories
18 Chapters Girl Detective Girl Aviatrix Air Mystery and Romance
Chapters 1 - 6 © 2022 Case No. 1-11371703511 and Chapters 7 - 18 © 2022 Case No. 1-11376521721

WILLIAM A. STRICKLIN

Olympus Story House

CONTENTS

About the Book:

This is a book about a girl and her marvelous accomplishments in the air. Fictional Mary Eliska Girl Detective Girl Aviatrix is a heroine of modern times. The book concentrates on the efforts of the girls and women who, like their male counterparts, have obtained wonderful results in the air. She wins an airplane by means of her remarkable air feats, and keeps the reader tense with excitement from cover to cover.

About the Writer:

William A. Stricklin is a Phi Beta Kappa scholar who earned his AB with honors at the University of California, Berkeley. He was Cal student body president and selected as the outstanding cadet of the United States Army ROTC program at UC Berkeley then trained at Fort Lewis, Washington, then Infantry Officer Training School at Fort Benning, Georgia, cloak-and-dagger training at Counterintelligence School, Fort Holabird, Maryland, learning Cold War spy-craft, hence six years active and reserve military service -- followed by his earning a doctor of laws JD degree at Harvard Law School in Class of 1964. He is a member of the Bar Associations of California, Washington and Hawaii. Mary Eliska was his third daughter, whose life was cut short, for whom he has created a longer, fictional life as Mary Eliska Girl Detective Girl Aviatrix.

Writer's Preface Foreshadowing

Real-life female detectives emerged in the mid-19th century through the young widow Kate Warne, then a Pinkerton Agency detective who helped smuggle Abraham Lincoln away from would-be assassins in Baltimore. In 1856, Kate met with Allan Pinkerton, the founder of the famous Pinkerton Detective Agency, to make an important point: a woman detective could go places that his male detectives could not. The first true girl detective made her debut in The Golden Slipper and Other Problems for Violet Strange (1915). The author, Anna Katharine Green, was an American friend of Conan Doyle's, and had a string of best-sellers featuring female detectives. One of the major selling points of those books was Green's fact-checking every legal detail in her bestselling mysteries. Green created the first famous female sleuth in fiction, the curious spinster Amelia Butterworth, in That Affair Next Door (1897), sketching the original pattern for Agatha Christie's Miss Marple. Our heroine in these two volumes of 18 chapters, Mary Eliska, Girl Detective Girl Aviatrix is a well-off young lady whose grandfather Albert Stricklin is a newspaper publisher in Piedmont, California, who supports her as a reporter for his paper *The Piedmont Star*, aware that she likes to dabble in detective work. Flying in her airplane and driving her jalopy "Calamity Jane", Mary Eliska joins with her three best friends: nieces Jacqueline Gray ("Jax") and Marlow Ray, and nephew news photographer Liam McAdam to solve the occasional case out of curiosity and sometimes to earn money separately from her family. Mary Eliska Girl Detective Girl Aviatrix gives life to my daughter born sixty years ago, March 10, 1963, whose life was cut short in Clifton Springs New York September 12, 1963. She has charming manners, oscillates between tomboyishness and a feminine ideal. She knows law and manifests moral righteousness. Often she wears enviable dresses. Mary Eliska's detective stories and unsolved mysteries I have re-written from the public domain tales by Carolyn Keene (always a pseudonym), Anna Katharine Green, Mildred Augustine Wirt Benson, Frances Crane, and anonymous writers about Penny Parker, Mary Louise, Nancy Drew, and others. Please enjoy reading "Mary Eliska Girl Aviatrix."

Dedication:

Amelia Mary Earhart
Attribution: https://en.wikipedia.org/wiki/Amelia_Earhart

Amelia Mary Earhart beneath the nose of her Lockheed Model 10-E Electra, March 1937 in Oakland, California, before departing on her final round-the-world attempt prior to her disappearance

Born	Amelia Mary Earhart July 24, 1897 Atchison, Kansas, U.S.
Disappeared	July 2, 1937 (aged 39) Pacific Ocean, en route to Howland Island from Lae, New Guinea
Status	Presumed dead[1] January 5, 1939 (aged 41)
Other names	• Lady Lindy (after Charles Lindbergh) • Meeley (childhood)
Alma mater	• Ogontz School • Columbia University (did not graduate from either)
Occupation	• Aviator • author
Known for	Many early aviation records, including first woman to fly solo across the Atlantic Ocean
Spouse	George P. Putnam (m. 1931)
Parent(s)	Samuel Stanton and Amelia Otis Earhart
Awards	• Distinguished Flying Cross • Légion d'honneur • National Aviation Hall of Fame • National Women's Hall of Fame
Website	www.ameliaearhart.com
Signature	

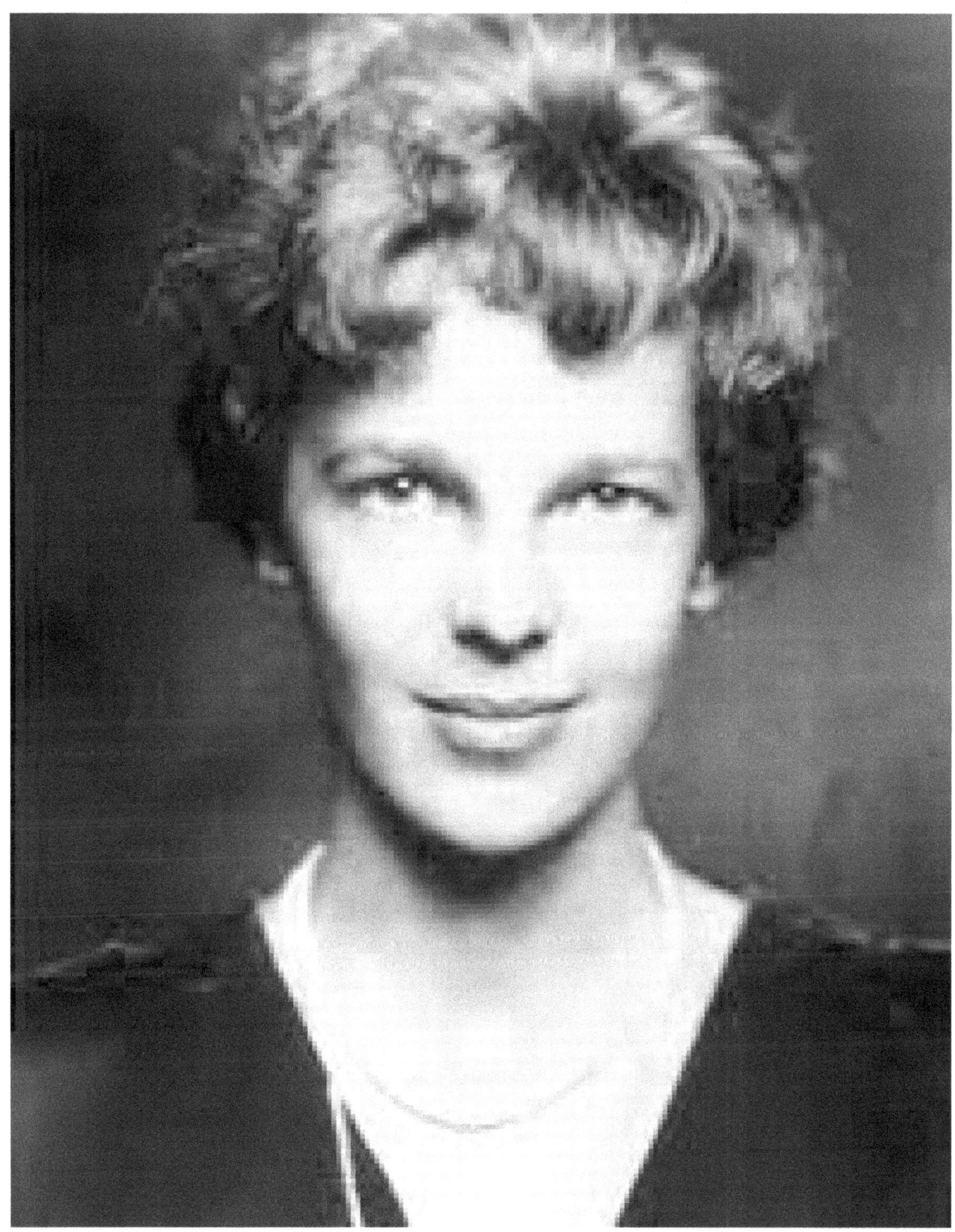

Amelia Mary Earhart (/ˈɛərhɑːrt/ *AIR-hart*, born July 24, 1897; disappeared July 2, 1937; declared dead January 5, 1939) was an American aviation pioneer and writer. Earhart was the first female aviator to fly solo across the Atlantic Ocean. She set many other records, was one of the first aviators to romote commercial air travel, wrote best-selling books about her flying experiences, and was instrumental in the formation of The Ninety-Nines, an organization for female pilots. Born and raised in Atchison, Kansas, and later in Des Moines, Iowa, Earhart developed a passion for adventure at a young age, steadily gaining flying experience from her twenties. In 1928, Earhart became the first female passenger to cross the Atlantic by airplane (accompanying pilot Wilmer Stultz), for which she achieved celebrity status. In 1932, piloting a Lockheed Vega 5B, Earhart made a nonstop solo transatlantic flight, becoming the first woman to achieve such a feat. She received the United States Distinguished Flying Cross for this accomplishment. In 1935, Earhart became a visiting faculty member at Purdue University as an advisor to aeronautical engineering and a career counselor to female students. She was also a member of the National Woman's Party and an early supporter of the Equal Rights Amendment. Known as one of the most inspirational American figures in aviation from the late 1920s throughout the 1930s, Earhart's legacy is often compared to the early aeronautical career of pioneer aviator Charles Lindbergh, as well as to figures like First Lady Eleanor Roosevelt for their close friendship and lasting impact on the issue of women›s causes from that period. During an attempt at becoming the first woman to complete a circumnavigational flight of the globe in 1937 in a Purdue-funded Lockheed Model 10-E Electra, Earhart and navigator Fred Noonan disappeared over the central Pacific Ocean near Howland Island. The two were last seen in Lae, New Guinea, on July 2, 1937, on the last land stop before Howland Island and one of their final legs of the flight. She presumably died in the Pacific during the circumnavigation, just three weeks prior to her fortieth birthday.[10] Nearly one year and six months after she and Noonan disappeared, Earhart was officially declared dead. Investigations and significant public interest in their disappearance still continue over 80 years later. Decades after her presumed death, Earhart was inducted into the National Aviation Hall of Fame in 1968 and the National Women's Hall of Fame in 1973. She now has several commemorative memorials named in her honor around the United States, including an urban park, an airport, a residence hall, a museum, a research foundation, a bridge, a cargo ship, an earth-fill dam, four schools, a hotel, a playhouse, a library, multiple roads, and more. She also has a minor planet, planetary corona, and newly-discovered lunar crater named after her. She is ranked ninth on *Flying*'s list of the 51 Heroes of Aviation.

Acknowledgement of the Original Authors of Chapters 1-18 of this volume; all currently in the Public Domain

- Acknowledgement of the Original Author of Chapter 1: Noel Everingham Sainsbury Jr.
- Acknowledgement of the Original Author of Chapter 2: Noel Everingham Sainsbury Jr.
- Acknowledgement of the Original Author of Chapter 3: Noel Everingham Sainsbury Jr.
- Acknowledgement of the Original Author of Chapter 4: Noel Everingham Sainsbury Jr.
- Acknowledgement of the Original Author of Chapter 5: Edith Harper Lavell
- Acknowledgement of the Original Author of Chapter 6: Edith Harper Lavell
- Acknowledgement of the Original Author of Chapter 7: L. Frank Baum
- Acknowledgement of the Original Author of Chapter 8: L. Frank Baum
- Acknowledgement of the Original Author of Chapter 9: Edith Lavell
- Acknowledgement of the Original Author of Chapter 10: Bess Moyer
- Acknowledgement of the Original Author of Chapter 11: Edith Lavell
- Acknowledgement of the Original Author of Chapter 12: Harrison Bardwell
- Acknowledgement of the Original Author of Chapter 13: Margaret Burnham
- Acknowledgement of the Original Author of Chapter 14: Margaret Burnham
- Acknowledgement of the Original Author of Chapter 15: Margaret Burnham
- Acknowledgement of the Original Author of Chapter 16: Margaret Burnham
- Acknowledgement of the Original Author of Chapter 17: Edith Lavell
- Acknowledgement of the Original Author of Chapter 18: Bess Moyer

CHAPTER 1

Mary Eliska Wins Her Wings

Chapter 1.1
OUT OF THE NORTHEAST

"Hi, there, young lady!" "Hi, yourself,--what d'you want?"

At the water's edge, a girl of sixteen stopped in the act of launching a small skiff. She straightened her lithe figure and faced about, her blond hair blowing in the breeze, turning a pair of snapping blue eyes inquiringly upon the young man who walked down the beach toward her. "Mary Eliska, isn't it?" asked the stranger, his deeply tanned features breaking into an engaging smile. "I'm not sure I recognized you at first in the bathing suit--"

"No matter how you were dressed I'm sure I wouldn't recognize you," returned Mary Eliska, shortly. "I've never laid eyes on you before--that's why."

The young man laughed. "Quite right," he said, "you haven't. But I happen to be a near neighbor of yours, and I've seen you."

"Up at New Canaan?"

"Yes. Dad has taken the Hawthorne place,--bought it in fact."

For a full minute the girl stared at this tall young man with the blonde hair and the jolly smile. Surprise left her speechless.

Then--"Why--why--" she gasped. "Y-you must be the famous Bill Bolton!"

"Bolton's the name, all right," he grinned. "But that famous stuff is the bunk."

Mary Eliska was herself again, and a little ashamed of her burst of feeling.

"But you *are* the aviator!» She went on, more calmly. «My father told me the other day that you and your father were coming to live across the road from us. And I don›t mind telling you we›re simply thrilled! You see, I›ve read about you in the papers--and I know all about the wonderful things you›ve done!»

"I'm afraid you've got an exaggerated idea--it was all in the day's work, you know," protested the blonde-headed young man, his eyebrows slanting quizzically, "I'm Bill Bolton, but I didn't barge in on you to talk about myself. You're starting out for a sail in that sloop that's moored over there, I take it?"

"Why, yes, I am. Want to come along?"

"Thanks a lot. I've got a business matter to attend to down here in a few minutes." He hesitated a moment, then--"I know it's none of my affair, but don't you think it's rather risky to go for a sail just now?"

Mary Eliska shrugged. "Oh, I don't know. There's a two-reef breeze blowing out beyond the Point, but that's nothing to worry about. I've sailed all over Long Island Sound since I was a kid, and I've been out in worse blows than this, lots of times."

"Maybe," countered Bill. "Storm warnings were broadcast about an hour ago. We're in for a northeaster--"

She broke in scoffingly--"Oh! those weathermen! They're always wrong. It's a perfectly scrumptious afternoon. The storm, if it comes, will probably show up sometime tomorrow!"

"Well," he retorted, "you're your own boss, I suppose.--If you were my sister," he added suddenly, "you wouldn't go sailing today."

"Then it's a good thing I'm *not* your sister. Thanks for your interest,» she mocked. There was a hint of anger in her voice at the suspicion that Bill Bolton was trying to patronize her. «Don›t worry,» she added, resuming her usual tone, «I can handle a boat--Good-bye!»

Their eyes met; Bill's gravely accusing, hers, full of defiant determination.

"Good-bye--sorry I spoke." Bill turned away and walked up the beach toward the club house.

Mary Eliska chuckled when she saw him throw a quick glance over his shoulder. She waved her hand, but he kept on without appearing to notice the friendly gesture.

"A temper goes with that blond hair," she said to herself, digging a bare heel into the loose shingle. "I guess I was pretty rude, though. But what right had he to talk like that? Bill Bolton may be a famous aviator, but he's only a year older than I am."

She ran the skiff out through the shallows and sprang aboard. Standing on the stern thwart she sculled the small craft forward with short, strong strokes, and presently nosed alongside the *Scud*. As she boarded the sloop and turned with the skiff's painter in her hand she caught sight of Bill getting into an open roadster on the club driveway. "I guess he meant well," she observed to the wavelets that lapped the side of the *Scud*, "but just the same--well, that's that."

Making the painter secure to a cleat in the stern, she set about lacing a couple of reefs into the mainsail. Having tied the last reef-point, she loosened the skiff's painter, pulled the boat forward and skillfully knotted the rope to the sloop's mooring. Then she cast off the mooring altogether and ran aft to her place at the tiller.

The *Scud's* head played off. Mary Eliska, as she had told Bill, was no novice at the art of small boat sailing. With her back bracing the tiller she ran up the jib and twisted the halyard to a cleat close at hand.

Then as the sloop gained steerageway, she pulled on the peak and throat halyards until the reefed-down mainsail was setting well. The *Scud*, a fast twenty-footer, was rigged with a fore-staysail and gaff-topsail as well, but Mary Eliska knew better than to break them out in a wind like this.

As it was she carried all the canvas her little boat would stand, and they ran out past the Point, which acted as a breakwater to the yacht club inlet, with the starboard gunwale well awash. The wind out here stiffened perceptibly and Mary Eliska wished she had tied in three reefs instead of two before starting. Her better judgment told her to go about and seek the quieter waters of the inlet. But here, pride took a hand.

If she turned back and gave up her afternoon sail, the next time she saw Bill Bolton she must admit he had been right. No. That would never do. Although the wind out here was stiffer than she had imagined, this was no northeast gale; a good three-reef breeze, that was all. So lowering the peak slightly she continued to head her little craft offshore.

The *Scud* fought and bucked like a wild thing, deluging Mary Eliska with spray. She gloried in the tug of the tiller, the sting of the salt breeze, the dance of her craft over choppy seas. Glistening in the clear summer sunlight, flecked with tiny whitecaps, the landlocked water stretched out to where the low hills of Long Island banked the horizon in a blur of purple and green.

Now and then as she luffed into a particularly strong gust, Mary Eliska had her misgivings. But pride, confidence in her ability to handle her boat and the thrill of danger kept her going.

She had been sailing for about an hour, beating her way eastward with the Connecticut shore four or five miles off her port quarter, when all at once, somehow, she felt a change. The sunshine seemed less brilliant, the shadows less solid, less sharply outlined. It seemed as if a very thin gauze had been drawn across the sun dimming without obscuring it. Mary Eliska searched the sky in vain to discover the smallest shred of cloud.

At the same time the breeze slackened and the air, which had been stimulant and quick with oxygen seemed to become thick, sluggish, suffocating. Presently, the *Scud* was lying becalmed, while the ground swell, long and perfectly smooth, set sagging jib and mainsail flapping. Except for the rattling of the blocks and the creaking of the boom, the silence, after the whistling wind of a few minutes before, was tremendously oppressive.

Then in the distance there was a low growl of thunder. In a moment came a louder, angrier growl--as if the first were a menace which had not been heeded. But the first growl was quite enough for Mary Eliska. She knew what was coming and let go her halyards, bringing down her sails with a run. Now fully alive to the danger, she raced to her work of making the little craft secure to meet the oncoming storm.

She was gathering in the mainsail, preparatory to furling it when there was a violent gust of wind, cold, smelling of the forests from which it came, corrugating the steely surface of the Sound. Two or three big raindrops fell--and then, the deluge.

Mary Eliska rushed to a locker, pulled out a slicker and sou'wester and donned them. Returning to her place by the tiller, she watched the rain. Rain had never rained so hard, she thought. Already both the Connecticut and Long Island shores were completely blotted out, hidden behind walls of water. The big drops pelted the Sound like bullets, sending up splashes bigger than themselves.

Then suddenly the wind came tearing across the inland sea from out the northeast. Thunder crashed, roared, reverberated. Lightning slashed through the black cloud-canopy in long, blinding zigzags. The wind moaned, howled, shrieked, immense in its wild force, immense in its reckless fury. A capsized sloop wallowed in the trough of heavy seas rearing a dripping keel skyward--and to this perilous perch clung Mary Eliska.

Chapter 1.2
TAXI!

The black brush of storm had long ago painted out the last vestige of daylight. Crouching on the upturned hull of her sloop, Mary Eliska clung to the keel with nerveless fingers, while the *Scud* wallowed in an angry sea laced with foam and spray. She knew that in a little while the boat must sink, and that in water like this even the strongest swimmer must quickly succumb. Cold, wet and helpless, Mary Eliska anxiously scanned her narrow horizon, but in vain.

For another half hour she hung on in the rain and darkness, battered by heavy combers that all but broke her hold. She was fast losing her nerve and with it the willingness to struggle. Phantom shapes reached toward her from the gloom. Strange lights danced before her eyes....

With a rolling lurch the *Scud* sank, and Mary Eliska found herself fighting the waves unsupported. The shock of sudden immersion brought back her scattering wits, but the delusion of dancing lights still held; especially one light, larger and brighter than the others. Surely this one was real and not the fantasy of an overwrought imagination!

Half smothered in flying spume, the drowning girl made one last frantic effort to keep afloat. Above the pounding of the sea, a throbbing roar shook her eardrums, a glare of light followed by a huge dark form swooped down as if to crush her--and she lost consciousness.

Mary Eliska awoke in a darkness so complete that for a moment she thought her eyes must be bandaged. Nervous fingers soon found that this was not the case, and reaching out, they came in contact with a light switch.

The sudden gleam of the electrics half blinded her. Presently she saw that she lay on a narrow bunk in a cabin. Presumably she was aboard a vessel, still out in the storm, for the ship pitched and rolled like a drunken thing, and the roar of a powerful exhaust was deafening.

Someone had removed her sweater, had tucked warm blankets about her body. Her throat burned from a strong stimulant which apparently had been administered while she was unconscious.

For some minutes she lay there taking in her surroundings. The charts tacked to the cabin walls, the tiny electric cookstove, hinged table and arms rack opposite. Listlessly she counted the weapons, four rifles, three shotguns, two automatics--and fastened in its own niche was a machine gun covered with a waterproof jacket. A complete arsenal.... The shotguns bespoke sportsmen, but this was neither the season for duck nor for snipe. Men did not go shooting in Long Island Sound with rifles, revolvers and a machine gun.... *Bootleggers!*

It came to her like a bolt from the blue. She was on board a rumrunner, no less, and notwithstanding the exhaustion she suffered from her battles with the waves, she found exhilaration in the exciting discovery.

Mary Eliska threw off the blankets, sat up and swung her legs over the edge of the bunk. Her bathing suit was still wet and clung uncomfortably to her skin. With a hand on the side of the bunk to support her, she stood up on the heaving floor to catch sight of her face in a mirror screwed to the opposite wall.

"Gracious! I'm a fright," she cried. "I don't suppose there's a vanity case aboard this lugger--and mine went down with the poor little *Scud!*"

Then she spied a neat pile of clothing at the foot of the bunk, and immediately investigated. A dark blue sweater, a pair of trousers, heavy woolen socks, and a pair of boy's sneakers were seized upon and donned forthwith.

Mary Eliska giggled as she surveyed herself once more in the little mirror. "Just a few sizes too large, that's all. But they're warm, and *dry*, and that's something!"

She rummaged about on a shelf, found a comb and with dexterous fingers smoothed her short damp hair into place, then with a sigh of satisfaction, muttered again to herself, "Much better, my girl."

Her makeshift toilet completed, she decided to leave the cabin and continue her explorations outside.

There were two doors, one on the side and one at the end which evidently led forward. After a moment's hesitation, Mary Eliska chose the latter. With some difficulty, for the ship still pitched unmercifully, she stumbled forward. Then, summoning up her courage, for she was not without trepidation at the thought of facing her desperado rescuers, she laid a hand on the knob and turning it, swung back the door.

Mary Eliska found herself in a small, glassed-in compartment, evidently the pilot house. She had hardly time to glance about, when an oddly familiar voice spoke from out the darkness. It was barely distinguishable above the motor's hum.

"Please, Mary Eliska, snap off the light or shut the door. I can't possibly guide this craft in such a glare."

"Why, it's Bill Bol--Mr. Bolton, I mean," she cried in surprise, and closed the door.

"Himself in the flesh," replied that young man.

She could see him clearly now, seated directly before her. His back was toward her and he did not turn round. So far as she could see he seemed very busily engaged, doing something with his feet.

"Then--then it must have been you who picked me up," she stammered.

"Guilty on the first count, Mary Eliska."

"Please don't be funny," she retorted, now mistress of herself once more. "I want to thank you--"

"You are very welcome. Seriously, though, it is the boathook you have to thank. Without that we'd both have gone to Davy Jones' locker long before this."

Mary Eliska was nearly thrown off her feet by an unusually high sea which crashed over the pilot house and rolled the vessel far over on her side.

"Whew--that was a near one!" the girl exploded as the ship righted itself.

"We'll weather it, don't worry," encouraged Bill, though he did not feel the confidence his words proclaimed.

"It looks to me," said Mary Eliska soberly, "as though we'll be mighty lucky if we reach shore at all--and I guess you know it."

"Never say die, Mary Eliska!"

"Suppose we drop this miss and mister stuff, Bill. Sounds rather silly at a time like this, don't you think so?"

"Right you are, Mary Eliska. I'm not much on ceremony, myself, as the Irishman said when--"

"Look here, Bill!" Mary Eliska tossed her head impatiently, "I wish you'd omit the comedy--it really isn't necessary. I'll admit I was in a bad way when you dragged me out of the briny deep--and I appreciate your coming to my rescue. But you needn't expect me to faint or to throw hysterics. That sort of thing went out of fashion long ago. Girls today have just as much nerve as boys. They don't very often get a chance to prove it, that's all."

"Please accept my humblest apology, mademoiselle." Bill's eyes twinkled though his tone was utterly serious. "I can assure you--"

Mary Eliska's merry laugh rang out--her mood had passed as suddenly as it had come. "Don't be absurd. Tell me--why are *you* piloting a rumrunner?»

"Rumrunner? What do you mean?"

"If this isn't a rumrunner, why do you carry that machine gun and the rifles and revolvers in the arms rack?"

"Just part of our equipment, that's all."

Mary Eliska's impatience flared up again. "Why do you talk such nonsense?"

"Nonsense?" "Certainly. You don't mean to tell me that you took a boat of this size on long cruises!"

Bill grinned in the darkness. "But you see," he chuckled, "this isn't a boat."

"Well, what is it then?"

"A Loening amphibian. Not exactly the stock model, for Dad and I had quite a few changes made in the cabin and this pilot's cockpit."

"*What?*" shrieked Mary Eliska. "An airplane--one that can land either on water or on land?"

"That's right. The old crate has the hull of a boat equipped with retractable wheel landing gear which operates electrically."

"You're too technical for me," she said frowningly, and balanced herself with a hand on the back of the pilot's seat. "But if this is an airplane, why keep bouncing along on the water? I'd think you'd fly to land and have done with it."

"My dear girl--" began Bill. "Don't use that patronizing tone--I'm not your dear girl--not by a long shot!"

Bill laughed outright. "My error once more. However, Miss Spitfire, when you learn to fly, you'll find out that air currents are very like water currents. When it is blowing as hard as it is now, flying a plane is fully as dangerous as sailing a boat--more so, in fact. When the wind reaches a certain velocity, it is impossible to balance your plane. You have to land--or crash."

Mary Eliska was beginning to understand. "Then you must have taken some awful risks coming out after me."

"I was lucky," he admitted. "But you see, even if we were able to fly in this gale, now, it's quite impossible to take off in such a heavy sea. If I gave the old bus enough gas to get up a flying speed, these combers would batter the hull in--I'd never be able to get her onto her step. Someday, when it's fine, and the water's smooth, I'll show you what I meant by that. Now all we can do is to taxi."

"Taxi?--This is the first seagoing taxi I've ever been in!"

"In air parlance," he explained, "to taxi is to run a plane along the ground or on the water--just now, it isn't all it's cracked up to be."

"I should think it would be easier than flying."

"Not on water as rough as this. Your legs go to sleep with the strain you have to put on the rudder pedals."

"Oh--you're steering with your feet?" "Yes."

"Well, why don't you let me help you? I'll drive her for a while," offered Mary Eliska.

Bill shook his head. "It's terribly hard work," he demurred.

"What of it? I'm as strong as an ox."

"Thanks a lot. You're a real sport. But the difficulty is in shifting places with me without swamping the old bus. She isn't equipped with dual controls. There's only one set of pedals, and as soon as I release them she will slue broadside to the waves, the wings will crumple, and she'll simply swamp and go under."

"And you must taxi either before the wind, or into the wind as we are now, in seas like these?"

"You've guessed it," he nodded.

"But there must be some way we can manage it," argued Mary Eliska. "You can't keep on much longer. Your legs will give out and then we'll go under anyway."

Bill hesitated a moment. "Well, all right, let's try it--but it's no cinch, as you'll find out."

"That's O.K. with me. Come on--orders, please--and let's go!"

Chapter 1.3
A WILD RIDE

"Hey, not so fast," laughed Bill. "First of all, will you please step into the cabin, and in the second locker on your right you'll find a helmet and a phone-set. Bring them out here. This shouting is making us both hoarse and we'll soon be as deaf as posts from the noise of the motor."

"Aye, aye, skipper," breezed Mary Eliska, and disappeared aft.

In a minute or two she returned with the things he had asked for. Bill showed her how to adjust the receivers of the phone set over the ear flaps of her helmet. Then reaching for the head set at the other end of the connecting line, he put it on and spoke into the mouthpiece which hung on his chest.

"Much better, isn't it?" he asked in a normal tone.

"It certainly is. I can hear you perfectly," she declared into her transmitter. "--What next?"

"Come over here and sit on my lap.--I'm not trying to get fresh," he added with a grin, as she hesitated. "I've had to make a shift like this before with Dad. There is only one way to do it."

Mary Eliska was a sensible girl. She obeyed his order and placed herself on his knees.

"Now put your feet over mine on the rudder pedals. And remember--to turn right, push down on the right pedal, and vice versa. Get the idea?" "Quite, thanks."

"Fine. Next--grab this stick and keep it as I have it. Now, I'm going to pull my feet from under yours--ready?"

"Let her go!"

Bill jerked his feet away, to leave Mary Eliska's resting on the pedals.

"Good work!" he applauded. "The old bus hardly swerved. Keep her as she's pointed now. We can't change her course, much less take off until we hit one of those inlets along the Connecticut shore, and smoother water. Brace yourself now--I'm going to slide out of this seat."

Mary Eliska was lifted quickly. Then she dropped back into the pilot's seat to find herself fighting the tenacious pull of heavy seas, straining her leg muscles to keep the plane from floundering.

"How's it going?" Bill's voice came from the floor of the cockpit where he was busily engaged in pounding circulation back into his numbed legs and feet.

"Great, thanks. But I will say that this amphibian of yours steers more like a loaded truck in a mudhole than an honest-to-goodness plane! How are your legs?"

"Gradually getting better--pretty painful, but then I'm used to this sort of thing."

"Poor boy!" she exclaimed sympathetically, then gritted her teeth in the effort to keep their course as a huge comber crashed slightly abeam the nose.

Bill grasped the side of her seat for support. "You handled that one nicely," he approved when the wave had swept aft. "But don't bother about me--you've got your own troubles, young lady. I'll be all right in a few minutes."

"What I can't understand," said Mary Eliska, after a moment, "is why this plane didn't sink when you landed and picked me up. How *did* you keep from slewing broadside and going under?»

"Well, it was like this. When I left you on the beach, I motored back home to New Canaan. The sky was blackening even then. I was sure we were in for the storm, so after putting up the car, I went out to the hay barn in that ten-acre field where we house the old bus. She needed gas, so I filled the tanks, gave her a good looking over and went back to the house and telephoned."

"You mean you phoned the beach club about me?"

"Yes. The steward said you weren't anywhere around the club, and your sloop wasn't in the inlet. It was pretty dark by then and the wind was blowing a good thirty-five knots. I made up my mind you must be in trouble. Frank ran after me on my way out to the plane--he's our chauffeur you know--"

"Yes, I know--" broke in Mary Eliska--"he drove you and your father to the movies last night. I saw him."

"That's right. Frank's a good scout. He wanted to come along with me, but I wouldn't let him."

"I s'pose you thought you'd save *his* skin, at least?»

"Something like that. A fellow doesn't mind taking responsibility for himself--it's a different thing with someone else. Well, before Frank and I ran this plane out of the barn, I rigged the sea anchor (nothing more than a large canvas bucket with a couple of crossed two-by-twos over the top to keep it open) with an extra-long mooring line. The sea-anchor I brought up here in the cockpit with me. The other end of the line was fastened to a ring-bolt in the nose, of course. Well--to get through with this yarn--I took off alone and flew over to the Sound."

"But wasn't it awful in this wind?"

"It was pretty bad. As soon as I got over water, I switched on the searchlight, but it was a good half-hour before the light picked you up. Then I landed--"

"Into the wind or with it?" interrupted Mary Eliska.

"Getting interested, eh?" commented Bill with a smile. "Well, just remember this then, never make a downwind landing with a seaplane in a wind blowing over eighteen miles an hour."

"Why?" "Because the wind behind your plane will increase the landing speed to the point where you will crash when you strike the water--that's a good reason, isn't it?"

"Then you landed into the wind when you came down for me?"

"That's right. And as soon as I struck the water, I shut off the motor, opened one of these windows and threw over the sea anchor. Then I fished you out with the boathook."

"It sounds sort of easy when you tell it--but I'll bet it wasn't." She gazed at him admiringly. "You surely took some awful chances--"

"Hey there!" called Bill. "Pull back the stick or you'll nose over."

"That's better," he approved as she obeyed his order. "Keep it well back of neutral. Sorry I yelled at you," he grinned.

Bill got to his feet. "I'm O.K. now," he went on, "and you must be pretty well done up. I'm going to take it over."

Seating himself on her lap, as she had sat on his, he placed his feet upon hers. A minute later, she had drawn her feet back from the rudder pedals, slipped out from under and was seated on the floor, rubbing life back into her feet and legs, as Bill had done.

"Why is it," she inquired presently, "that the plane rides so much smoother when you're guiding her?"

Bill smiled. "When I give her right pedal, that is, apply right rudder, I move the stick slightly to the left and vice versa. In that way I depress the aileron on the side I want to sail. It aids the rudder. You got along splendidly, though, and stick work when taxiing needs practice." Mary Eliska got to her feet, rather unsteadily. "Look!" she cried. "Lights ahead. We must be nearing shore, Bill."

"We are. There's a cove out yonder I'm making for. And better still, the wind is lessening. Just about blown itself out, I guess." In another ten minutes they sailed in through the mouth of an almost landlocked inlet and with the motor shut off drifted in comparatively smooth water. "Any idea where we are?" inquired Mary Eliska, when Bill, after throwing out the anchor, came back to her.

"Somewhere between Norwalk and Bridgeport, I guess," he replied. "There are any number of coves along here. I'll take you ashore, now. We've got a collapsible boat aboard. Not much of a craft, but it'll take the two of us in all right. We'll go over to one of those houses, and get your father on the phone. He can come down and drive you back to New Canaan."

"Drive us both back, you mean!"

"Sorry--but it can't be done. I've got to take this old bus home as soon as the wind dies down a little more."

"How long do you suppose that will be?" asked Mary Eliska quietly.

Bill glanced up at the black, overcast sky and then turned his gaze overside and studied the water toward the inlet's mouth.

"Oh, in about an hour I'll be able to take off."

"Then I'll wait and fly back with you."

"You certainly are a sportsman," he applauded and looked at his wrist watch. "It's only ten to six--though anyone would think it was midnight. I'll tell you what--suppose I shove off in the dinghy. I'll row ashore and telephone your Dad from the nearest house. He will be half crazy if he knows you were out sailing in that blow and haven't reported back to the club. In the meantime, you might scare up something to eat. There's cocoa, condensed milk, crackers and other stuff in the cabin locker nearest the stove. You must be starved--I know I am!"

They were standing on one of the narrow decks that ran from amidships forward to the nose of the plane below the pilot house.

"The very thought of food makes me ravenous," declared Mary Eliska, starting for the cabin door. "Give Dad my love and say I'm all right--thanks to you!" she threw back over her shoulder--"Tell him to put back dinner until seven-thirty--and to have an extra place laid. In the meantime I'll dish up a high tea to keep us going."

Within the cabin, she set water on the two-burner electric stove to boil. While it was heating she let down the hinged table and set it with oilcloth doilies, that she found, together with other table necessities in a cupboard next the food locker. She discovered some bread and a number of other eatables stowed away here, as well as the things Bill had mentioned.

Twenty minutes later, Bill returned to find the table set with cups of steaming cocoa and hot toasted sandwiches spread with marmalade.

"I'll say you're some cook, Mary Eliska!" He pulled up a camp stool, and seated himself at the table. "This is a real party!"

"There isn't any butter--" began Mary Eliska doubtfully. "Don't apologize. It's wonderful--do start in or I'll forget my manners and grab!"

Mary Eliska helped herself to a sandwich and handed the plate across the table. "Were you able to get Dad?"

"Yes. Just caught him. He'd only got home from the bank a few minutes before. One of the maids told him you'd spoken of going sailing, so he phoned the club about you. He was just leaving the house to drive down there when I rang him up."

"Did he say anything else?"

"Oh, naturally, he was glad you were all right. He didn't seem so pleased when I told him I was flying you back. He asked me if I was an experienced pilot."

"He would." Mary Eliska chuckled. "What did you tell him?" Bill laughed as he helped himself to another sandwich. "I wanted to get out here to your high tea, you know, so I asked him if he smoked cigarettes."

"*Cigarettes?*" "Yes. 'If you do, Mr. Stricklin,' I said--you know the old slogan, 'Ask Dad--he knows--' and I'm sorry to say I rang off."

"I'll bet he goes over and asks your father!"

"Very probably. Dad's rather touchy when anybody questions my rating as a pilot. I'm afraid your father will get an earful."

Cocoa and toast had disappeared by this time so the two in the cabin set about clearing up.

"You must'nt mind Daddy's crusty manner," she said with her hands in a dishpan of soapsuds. "He's always like that when he's upset. He doesn't mean anything by it."

Bill, who was stowing away cups and saucers in the locker, turned about with a grin. "Oh, that's all right. I had no business to get facetious--my temper's not so good, either. But there's no hard feeling." He held out his hands. "If you're finished with the dishpan I'll throw the water overside. The storm has broken and there's practically no wind. So if you're ready we'll shove off for New Canaan--and I'll give you your first hop."

Chapter 1.4
THE FIRST HOP

"How about giving me my first flying lesson now?" Mary Eliska suggested as Bill hauled in their anchor.

"You really want to learn?" "Of course I do--I'm crazy about it!"

Bill coiled the mooring line, looping it with practiced skill. "And I'd be glad to give you instruction. But you're a minor--before we can start anything like that we must get your Dad's permission."

"Oh, that'll be all right, Bill," was the young lady's cool assurance. "But how about right now--"

"Every student aviator is a watchful waiter the first time up. You stand behind me this trip and I'll explain what I'm doing as we go along."

"That'll be great! I'm just wild to fly this plane!"

Bill smiled. "But you won't get your flight instruction in this plane, Mary Eliska."

"Why not?"

"This amphibian is too big and heavy, for one thing; for another, she isn't equipped with dual controls."

"But what does that mean?"

"I see we'll have to start your training right now, Miss Student Pilot--Controls is a general term applied to the means proved to enable the pilot to control the speed, direction of flight, altitude and power of an aircraft.--Savez?"

"You sound like a text book--but I get you."

"All right. Now, unless we want the bus washed up on the beach, we'd better shove off."

Fastening the door to the deck after them, they passed through the cabin and into the pilot's cockpit where head-phone sets were at once adjusted. The amphibian bobbed and swayed at the push of little waves. The sun's face, scrubbed clean and bright by wind and rain was reflected in the rippling water; whilst wet surfaces of leaves, lawns, tree trunks and housetops bordering the inlet gleamed in a wash of gold. Little gusts of fresh air blew in through the open windows filling the cockpit with a keen sweet odor of wet earth.

Mary Eliska drew a deep breath. "My! the air smells good after that storm!"

"You bet--" agreed Bill. "But I'll smell brimstone when your father comes into the picture, if we don't shove off pronto for New Canaan."

"Oh, that's just like a boy--" she pouted.

"Shush! student--Listen to your master's--I mean,--your instructor's voice, will you?"

"Instructor's better," she smiled.

"Here beginneth your first lesson." Bill slid into the pilot's seat. "Stand just behind me and hold on to the back of my seat," he ordered.

Mary Eliska promptly did as she was told. After all, was not this the real Bill Bolton the famous ace and midshipman she had read about?

"All set?"

"Aye, aye, sir."

"Good enough! Here we go then. I'll explain every move I make, as I make it. Look and listen! First--I crack the throttle--in other words, before starting the engine, set your throttle in its quadrant slightly forward of the fully closed position. Next, I 'contact'--that's air parlance for 'ignition switch on.' After that, I press the inertia starter to swing our propeller into motion--" the engine sputtered, then roared.

"It is most important," he went on a moment later, "to see that the way ahead and above is clear at this point. Safety first is the slogan of good flying."

"Yes. But really, Bill, you don't have to explain everything you do. I'm watching closely. When I don't understand, I'll ask--if it's all the same to you?"

"Good girl. Don't hesitate to ask me, though."

"I won't."

With that she saw him widen the throttle and with his stick held well back of neutral to prevent the nose dipping under the waves, he sent the big seaplane hurtling through the water toward the inlet's mouth. The wind had changed since the storm and now, as they raced into the teeth of the light breeze, Mary Eliska tingled with that excitement which comes to every novice with the take off.

Six or eight seconds after opening the throttle, she saw him push the stick all the way forward.

"Why do you do that? Won't that raise the tail of the plane and depress the nose?"

Bill shook his head. "In the air--yes. But we're moving at some speed now on the surface--and the bow cannot be pushed down into the water. Our speed is gradually forcing it up until--now--we're skimming along on the step, you see."

Mary Eliska nodded to herself and watched him ease the stick back to neutral and maintain it there while they gathered more and more speed.

"Now I'm going to talk some more," said Bill. "Don't blame me if it sounds like a text book.--In order to fly, certain things must be learned--and remembered. Do not take off until you have attained speed adequate to give complete control when in the air. Any attempt to pull it off prematurely will result in a take-off at the stalling point, where control is uncertain. Understand?"

"I think so--but how does one know when to do it?"

"That comes with practice--and the feel of the ship. As flying speed is gained, I give a momentary pressure on the elevators (like this)--and break the hull out of the water--so-- easing the pressure immediately after the instant of take-off. Now that we are in the air our speed is only slightly above minimum flying speed. Any decrease in this would result in a stall. That is why I keep the nose level for six or seven seconds in order to attain a safe margin above stalling point before beginning to climb."

"There's certainly a lot more to it than I ever dreamed!"

"You bet there is. I haven't told you the half of it yet. One thing I forgot to say--you must always hold a straight course while taxiing before the take off. Also, never allow a wing to drop while your plane is on the step.--We've got enough speed on now, so I'll pull back the stick and let the plane climb for a bit."

"But you're heading for the Long Island Shore directly away from New Canaan--" she protested, "why don't you bring her about--not that I'm in any hurry, but--"

"This is an airplane, not a sailboat, Mary Eliska. All turns must be made with a level nose. If I should try to turn while in a climb like this, a stall would probably result, and with the wing down the plane would most likely go into a spin and--"

"We'd crash!"

"Surest thing you know!"

"*Oh!*"

"But the altimeter on the dash says one thousand feet now. We're high enough for our purpose. So I push the stick forward, like this--until the nose is level--so! Now, as I want to make a right turn, I apply right aileron and simultaneously increase right rudder considerably."

Mary Eliska saw one wing go up and the other go down. She was hardly able to keep her feet as the plane's nose swung round toward the Connecticut shore.

"Isn't that called banking?"

"Right on the first count," replied Bill.

"Why do you do it?"

"Because in making a turn, the momentum of the plane sets up a centrifugal force, acting horizontally outward. To counteract this, the force of lift must be inclined until it has a horizontal component equal to the centrifugal force. The machine is therefore tilted to one side, or banked, thus maintaining a state of equilibrium in which it will turn steadily. No turn can be made by the use of the rudder alone. The plane must be banked with ailerons before the rudder will have any turning effect.--Get me?"

"I get the last part. Guess I'll have to do some studying."

"Everybody has to do that. But I'll lend you some books, so you can bone up on the theory of flight. What I said just now amounts to this: if you don't bank enough you send your plane into a skid."

"Just like an automobile skids?"

"Yes. But of course the danger doesn't lie in hitting anything as in a car. A skidding plane loses her flying speed forward and drops into a spin. On the other hand, if you bank her too sharply, you go into a sideslip!"

"And the result in both cases is a crash?"

"Generally. But I think you've had enough instruction for today."

"Oh--but I want to know how you ended that turn. We're flying straight again now--and I was so interested in what you were saying, I forgot to watch what you did!"

"Well, after I had banked her sufficiently, I checked the wings with the ailerons and at the same time eased the pressure on the rudder. Then I maintained a constant bank and a constant pressure on the rudder pedal throughout the turn. To resume straight flight, I simply applied left aileron and left rudder: and when the wings were level again, I neutralized the ailerons and applied a normal amount of right rudder.”

“My goodness!” exclaimed Mary Eliska--”and that is only one of the things I have to learn. I thought that flying a plane wouldn’t be much more complicated than driving a car.”

“Oh, it’s simple enough--only you have to balance a plane, as well as drive it.”

“Do you think I’ll ever learn?”

“Of course you will. It takes time and practice--that’s all.”

“I wonder how birds learn to fly?” Mary Eliska glanced down at the wide vista of rolling country over which they were traveling. The dark green of the wooded hills, the lighter green of fields, crisscrossed by winding roads and dotted with houses, all in miniature, seemed like viewing a toy world. And here and there, just below them, there was the occasional flash of feathered wings, as the birds darted in and out among the treetops.

“Birds have to learn to fly, too. They get into trouble sometimes.”

“They do?”

“Certainly--watch gulls on a windy day--you’ll see them sideslip--go into spins--and have a generally hard time of it!”

“Oh, really? I’d never thought of that. But of course they can fly much better than a plane.” Bill shook his head. “That’s where you are wrong. No bird can loop, or fly upside down. Reverse control flying and acrobatics--stunting generally is impossible for them.--But look below! Recognize the scenery?”

“Why, we’re almost over New Canaan. There are the white spires of the Episcopal and Congregational churches--and there’s Main Street--and the railroad station!”

“And over on that ridge is your house--and mine across the way,” he added. “Well, here’s where I nose her over. Hold tight--we’re going down.”

Chapter 1.5
TROUBLE

After releasing the retractable wheel landing gear, which turned the big amphibian from a seaplane into one which could land on terra firma, Bill brought his big bus gently down to the ten-acre lot behind the Bolton residence.

As the plane rolled forward on its rubber-tired wheels and came to a stop, two men came walking in its direction from the trees at the edge of the field.

“Here come our respective fathers--” announced Bill, stripping off his headgear. “Remember--I take all responsibility for bringing you back in the plane.”

“You--do nothing of the kind!” Mary Eliska’s tone was final. She handed him her headphone and running back through the cabin, vaulted the low bulwark to the ground.

Bill hurriedly made things secure in the cockpit and followed her.

"And so you see, Dad," he heard her say, as he approached where they stood, "Bill not only saved my life--he took all kinds of chances with his own, flying in a gale like that. And--oh! I forgot to tell you that he warned me *not* to go out in the *Scud* this afternoon!» she ended with a mischievous look toward Bill.

Albert Stricklin was a tall man, whose tanned, rugged features and searching gaze suggested the sportsman. He turned from his excited daughter, with a smile and an outstretched hand.

"I'm beginning to realize, young man, that I owe you an apology for my shortness over the phone. Judging from Mary Eliska's story, I can never hope to express my gratitude for what you've done today."

Bill mumbled an embarrassed platitude as he shook hands, and was glad when Mr. Bolton broke into the conversation.

"The Boltons, father and son, were probably born to be hanged," he chuckled. "It's a family trait, to fall into scrapes--and so far, to get out of them just as quickly. Now, as nobody has been polite enough to introduce me to the heroine of this meeting--I'm the hero's fond parent, Mary Eliska. We are about to celebrate this festive occasion by a housewarming, in the form of a scrap dinner at the hero's home--what say you?"

"But I thought you were coming to our house--" cried Mary Eliska. "I--"

"But me no buts, young lady. Your father has already accepted for you both and we simply can't take no for an answer."

Mary Eliska glanced at Bill, who stood rather sheepishly in the background. Then she laughed. "Why, of course, if you put it that way--I'd love to come; that is, if the *hero* is willing!» «Say, do you think that›s fair!» Bill›s face was red. He didn›t think much of that kind of kidding. «I think it would be great, that is, if you mean me,» he ended in confusion. Amid the general laughter that followed, Mary Eliska uttered a cry of disgust. «But I can›t come like this--» she pointed to her clothes, which were the things that Bill had laid out for her in the big plane›s cabin.

"You look charming--" Mr. Bolton bowed, and Mary Eliska blushed. "However--"

"Make it snappy, then, dear." Mr. Stricklin drew out his watch. "You have just fifteen minutes. And Mr. Bolton won't keep dinner waiting for you, if he's as famished as I am!"

"Oh, give me twenty!" she pleaded.

"All right--hurry, now!"

With a wave of her hand, Mary Eliska darted away.

"I'll look after the plane, Bill," said his father, as she disappeared among the orchard trees. "I want to show Mr. Stricklin over it, and that will give you time for a slicking-up before dinner."

It was a jolly, though belated meal that was eventually served to them in the cool, green dining room of the Bolton's summer home that evening. Mr. Stricklin, with the finesse of an astute business man, drew out Mr. Bolton and his son, and the two told tales of adventure by land and sea and air that fascinated the New England high school girl. It all seemed unreal to her, sitting in the soft light of the candles. Yet the Boltons made light of hairbreadth escapes in the world's unmapped areas--just as if these strange adventures were daily occurrences in their lives, she thought.

"It certainly is a shame!" she burst out suddenly. Coffee had been served and they had moved to the comfort of low wicker chairs on the terrace. The air was filled with the perfume of June roses.

"What's a shame?" Bill, now spick and span in white flannels, settled back in his chair.

"Why, all the wonderful times you and Mr. Bolton have had--while Dad and I were sticking around in New Canaan. I'd love to be an adventurer," she finished.

"I dare say you'd find it mighty uncomfortable at times," observed her father. "How about it, Bolton?"

"Like everything else, it has its drawbacks and becomes more or less of a grind when one 'adventures' day in and day out--" that gentleman admitted. "I'm only too glad to be able to settle down in this beautiful ridge country for a few months--to rest and be quiet."

"There you are, Mary Eliska." Her father smiled in the darkness. "And who would there be out in the wilds to admire that smart frock you're wearing, for instance?"

"Gee, Dad! You know I don't care half as much about clothes as lots of the girls--and that hasn't anything to do with it, anyway."

"I think we ought to break the news to her," suggested Bill, a white blur in the depths of his chair.

Mary Eliska sat up eagerly. "What news?"

"But perhaps we'd better wait until tomorrow. Tonight, she wants to become an explorer--and give away all her best dresses. She might not take kindly to it." This from Mr. Stricklin, between puffs of aromatic cigar smoke.

"You're horrid--both of you. Don't you think it's mean of them to make such a mystery of whatever they're talking about, Mr. Bolton? Won't you tell me?"

"Of course, I will, my dear. What do you want to know?"

Mary Eliska choked with vexation. "*Oh!*"

"Let's tell her now--right now--" said Bill, his voice brimming with laughter.

"I don't want to hear."

"Yes, you do--all together: one--two--three! You--are--going--to--learn--to--fly!"

Mary Eliska sprang to her father's chair and caught his arm. "Will you really let me, Dad?" she cried in delight.

"Mr. Bolton says that Bill is an A-1 instructor--and he claims that flying is no more dangerous than sailing twenty-footers in a nor'easter, so I suppose--"

"Oh--you *darling*!" Mary Eliska flung her arms about his neck.

"Here--here--" cried Albert Stricklin. "You're ruining my collar, and my cigar--"

"Have another," suggested Mr. Bolton. "I'd willingly ruin boxes of cigars if I had a daughter who'd hug me that way!"

"Aren't you nice!" She turned about and bestowed a second affectionate embrace on that gentleman. "That is because you aren't quite as mean as your son--he's the limit!"

"Never slang your instructor," sang out Bill. "That's one of the first rules of the air."

"Seriously, Mary Eliska," her father interposed. "This is a big responsibility Bill is taking--and I want your word that you'll do just as he says. No more running off and smashing up a plane as you did the *Scud* this afternoon!»

"All right, Dad. I promise. But what am I to learn in? Bill says that the Amphibian is too heavy--and she's not equipped with dual controls."

Mr. Stricklin lighted a fresh cigar. "I see that you've already started your flight training."

"Bill explained the procedure to me on our way up here this afternoon. But what are we going to do for a plane?"

"Bill has some scheme, I believe."

"Oh, I know," she decided. "Bill shall pick me out a nice little plane and--"

"I shall pay for it," said her father grimly. "Nothing doing. When you have won your wings--well--we shall see. Until then, you and Bill will have to figure without financial help from your fond parent."

"That's fair enough," agreed Mr. Bolton.

"O.K. with me, too," echoed Bill. "I happen to have an old *N-9*, a Navy training plane, down at the shipyard near the beach club, that will do nicely. I was down there this afternoon having her pontoon removed. I want to equip her with landing gear so I can house her up here. The Amphibian uses up too much gasoline to go joy-hopping in."

A maid appeared on the doorstep.

"Mr. Stricklin wanted on the phone, please," she announced, and waited while that gentleman preceded her into the house.

A moment later Mr. Stricklin was back on the terrace.

"The bank's been robbed!" he cried. "Sorry, gentlemen, but I've got to hustle down there just as soon as possible." "This way!" called Bill, springing down the steps to the garden. "My car's out here--come on!"

"That young chap can keep his head," thought Mr. Stricklin as he ran beside his daughter and Mr. Bolton. "It would take a lot to fluster him." Then they came upon him, backing slowly up the drive, both doors swinging wide so they could jump in the car without his stopping. "Which bank, Mr. Stricklin?"

Bill had the car in the road now and was racing toward the village.

"First National Montecito Bank and Trust—Coast Village Road, next the Town Hall. I'm president, you know."

"I didn't know. But I'm glad to hear it."

"How's that?" "You should have a drag with the traffic cops. We are doing an even sixty now--and it would be a bad time to get a ticket."

Mr. Stricklin grasped the door-handle as Bill skidded them into a cross road with the expertness of a racing driver. "Just get us there, that's all," he gasped. "The chief himself phoned me. I didn't wait to hear details--but from what I gathered, the hold-up men got clean away before the police discovered the robbery. But time is always a factor in a case of this kind, so don't worry about traffic rules."

"I won't," said Bill and fed his powerful engine still more gasoline.

Along the straight stretch of Oenoke Avenue they sped, with Bill's foot still pressing the accelerator. They flashed past the white blur of the Episcopal Church and on down the hill into Main Street and the little town. The car's brakes screamed and Bill brought them to a stop on the edge of the crowd of pedestrians and vehicles that blocked further progress.

"D'you want us to wait here?" asked Mr. Bolton. "No--come along," returned his friend, jumping to the sidewalk. "We'll learn the worst together."

Chapter 1.6
THE HOLD UP

With Bill at her right and Mr. Bolton at her left elbow, Mary Eliska pushed her way through the crowd behind her father to the entrance of the Bank. The policeman at the head of the short flight of steps to the doorway stood aside at a word from Mr. Stricklin. The four passed inside and the heavy door swung shut behind them.

"Rather like locking up the barn after the sheep vamoosed, isn't it?" Bill nodded over his shoulder toward the police guard.

"Never mind, son--this isn't our party," rebuked his father.

A fat man in a dark blue uniform, rather tight as to fit and much be-braided, came bustling up. "Who are these men, Mr. Stricklin?" he inquired pompously. "Can't have strangers around the bank at this time--"

"From what I hear, Chief, you and your men let some strangers get away with about everything but the bank itself a little while ago." Mr. Stricklin's tone showed his annoyance. "These gentlemen are friends of mine. What's actually happened? Give me some facts. Anybody hurt? Anybody caught? Just what has been taken?" Questions popped like revolver shots.

"Well--it's like this, sir--" The Chief seemed pretty well taken down.

"Thunderation! You and your sleuths are enough to tempt any man to law breaking. There's Thatcher Allen! Perhaps I'll learn something from him."

Mr. Stricklin strode toward the rear of the bank.

"You mustn't mind Dad," Mary Eliska said consolingly. "Just now he's half-crazy with worry, Chief.--These gentlemen are Mr. Bolton and his son. They've bought the Hawthorne place, you know."

Chief Jones mopped his perspiring face with a red bandanna and then shook hands all around. "Terrible warm tonight--terrible warm. Well, let's go over and find out what's what. I was over to a party at my daughter Annie's--only just got in here myself. Annie--"

"Yes, let's find out what has happened." Mary Eliska cut in on this long-winded effusion, and led the way behind the tellers' cages to where her father and several other men were standing before the open vault.

"Ah, here's the watchman now!" cried Mr. Stricklin as a man, his head completely covered with bandages, came toward them and sank weakly into a chair. "Now, Thompson, do you think you can tell us exactly what happened, before Doctor Brown drives you home?" "Yes, sir. Glad to." The man's voice, though feeble, betrayed excitement. "He sure knocked me out, that bird did--but I'd know him again if I saw him. I c'd pick him out of a million--"

"That's fine," Mr. Stricklin interrupted gently. "But start at the beginning, Thompson, and we'll all get a better idea of him."

"That I will, sir, and 'right *now!*' as that French guy says over the radio.... Well, it was about eight o'clock and still light, when the night bell buzzed. I was expecting Mr. Thatcher Allen. He'd told me he'd be back after supper as he had some work to do. I'd been readin' the paper over there by the window, so I got up and opened the front door. But it wasn't Mr. Thatcher Allen. A young fellow in a chauffeur's uniform stood outside."

"'I'm Mr. Stricklin's new chauffeur,' he said. 'Here's a note from him. He tried to ring you up, but the phone down here seems to be out of order. He said you'd give me a check book to take back to him. Better read this.' He passed over a letter--"

"Have you still got it?" asked Mr. Stricklin.

"I think so. Yes, here it is, in my pocket." Thompson handed the missive to the bank president, who read it aloud:

> "'Dear Thompson:
> 'Please give the bearer, my chauffeur, a blank check book and oblige
> 'Yours truly,
> 'Albert Stricklin.'"

"Looks like my handwriting," sighed Mr. Stricklin when he had finished, "but of course I didn't write it!--What happened after that?"

"Well, sir, he asked me if he could step inside and take a few puffs of a cigarette, seein' as how you didn't like him to smoke on the job. So I let him in. Then I goes over to one of the desks for a check book and--I don't remember nothin' about what happened next, until I found myself in the far corner yonder, with Mr. Thatcher Allen near chokin' me to death with some water he was pourin' down my throat--and a couple of cops undoin' the rope I'd been bound up with. I reckon that feller must have beaned me with the butt of his revolver just as soon as I'd turned my back. Doc here, says as how the skull ain't fractured--but that bird sure laid me out cold. If I hadn't had my cap on, he'd of croaked me sure. Of course, I shouldn't of let that guy inside, but--"

Mr. Stricklin's tone was abrupt as he silenced Thompson with a word. "Thank you, Thompson," he said. "You are not to blame. If you hadn't let him in, he might have shot you at the door. Doctor Brown is going to take you home now. Lay up until you feel strong. And don't worry."

He patted the man on the shoulder and Thompson departed, leaning on the doctor's arm.

"I guess you're next on the list, Thatcher Allen." Mr. Stricklin nodded to Thatcher Allen. "How did you happen in here tonight?"

The cashier, a slender young man, prematurely bald, and dapper to the point of foppishness, removed his cigarette from his mouth and stepped forward.

"Had that Bridgeport transit matter and some other work I wanted to finish," he said crisply. "Told Thompson I would be back about eight-thirty. Matter of fact, it was twenty to nine when I rang the night bell. I rang it several times, no answer; then tried the door and found it unlocked. I thought something must be wrong--and was sure of it when I stepped in and saw Thompson lying on the floor, his arms and legs bound. Saw that he was breathing, and went to the phone. It was dead--couldn't raise Central. I didn't waste much time then, but ran out and hailed Sampson, the traffic cop on the corner. Told him there'd been a holdup here, so he blew his whistle, which brought another policeman and we three raced back here."

"You brought Thompson to and cut his bonds--then what?"

"I went to the vault. The door was ajar, with books and papers scattered all over the place. Haven't had a chance to check up, but it looks as though everything in the way of cash and negotiable securities has been taken."

"But the door hasn't been damaged--they couldn't have blown it open!"

The cashier shook his head. "No," he admitted, "they opened it with the combination. Must have used a stethoscope or the Jimmy Valentine touch system--"

"Not with that safe, Thatcher Allen. But how about the time lock?"

"It is never put on, sir, until we have no more occasion to use the vault for the day. I notified the Protective System people that I would be working here tonight and would set it when I was through."

"Humph!" growled the president in a tone that boded ill for someone. "So the time lock wasn't set!"

"It is the usual practice, sir," explained Thatcher Allen nervously. "I--"

"Never mind that now. Anyone else know anything about this robbery?"

"Yes, sir. Sampson, the traffic policeman saw the car."

"Well, let's hear from Sampson, then, if he's here."

The officer came forward rather sheepishly.

"I was directin' traffic at the corner of Main Street and East Avenue, sir, when I seen your car run down Main and stop in front of the bank here."

"*My* car!» exploded Mary Eliska›s father.

"Yes, sir--least it was a this year's Packard like you drive--and it had your license number on it--AB521--I ought to know, I see it every day."

"Yes, that's the number--but--well ... did you notice it further?"

"Yes, sir, I did. That was about eight o'clock. The chauffeur got out and rang the bell at the entrance to the bank. Then I seen him speak to Thompson and pass inside."

"Did you investigate?"

"Why, no, sir. The man came out almost directly and the door swung shut behind him. Then he jumped into the car and drove up the alley at the side of the bank. You always park your car there, sir, so I thought nothin' of it. About twenty minutes later, out he drove again and up Main Street the way he'd come. And that's the last I've seen of him."

"There was only one man in the car--the chauffeur?"

"I only saw one. If there was anybody else, they must've been lying down, in the bottom of the car."

"Very likely." Mr. Stricklin turned to the chief of police. "And what has been done toward catching the thieves--or thief?"

"Nothing, as yet," the Chief confessed. "But I'll get busy on the wire with descriptions of the man and the car right away. You see, I only just--"

"Never mind that--get along now and burn up the wires. That car has had over an hour's start on you. I'll look after things here for the present."

The head of the local police force waddled off with much the air of a fat puppy who had just received a whipping, and Mr. Stricklin walked over to Mr. Bolton.

"You can do me a great favor, if you will," he said.

"Name it, Stricklin."

"Thanks. Go to the drug store down the block and call up the Bankers Protective Association in the city. You'll find their number in the directory. Tell them what's happened--that will be enough. I want you to call their New York headquarters. That will start them on the job through their branches in short order."

"Right-oh!" his friend agreed. "And when I get through with New York, I'll see what New Canaan can do to fix your phone here."

"Thanks. I'll appreciate it."

"Anything I can do, Mr. Stricklin?" inquired Bill.

"Nothing here, thanks. But if you will take my daughter home and see that she doesn't get into any more trouble today, I'll be much obliged to you."

"Oh, *Dad!*" Mary Eliska, threw him a reproachful look, then stood on tiptoe and kissed her parent's cheek. "There, there. I know you're worried. Phone me when you want the car. I'll have sandwiches and coffee waiting when you get home."

Mr. Stricklin gave her an affectionate hug. "You're a good little housewife," he praised, "but run along now--both of you. There are a million-odd things to be done before I can leave."

He beckoned to the cashier and disappeared with him into the vault. "Not that way, Bill--" Mary Eliska's voice arrested Bill as he started for the door. "Come out the back way."

"What's up?" "I don't know yet. But I've found something that the rest seem to have missed. It may be important--come and see."

"You're on, Miss Sherlock," he said. Catching her arm, he hurried with her toward the rear of the bank.

Chapter 1.7
GROUND TRAILS

Bill unlatched the back door of the bank, pushed it open and stood aside for Mary Eliska to pass through.

"Wait a minute." She put out a restraining hand. The full glare of the arc light in the alley fell on the damp ground at their feet. "Right over there are the tire marks of the holdup car. It's lucky it rained this afternoon. The prints are perfect in this mud."

"Well, that's interesting, but--"

"Oh, no. Of course they won't solve the mystery. That's what you were going to say, isn't it?" Mary Eliska's voice was mocking as she looked up at Bill. "But here--see these footprints? From this door to the car?" Her tone was triumphant now. "They ought to help just a little, don't you think?"

But Bill seemed unmoved at her discovery. "Probably hoofmarks of the cops," he said rather disparagingly.

Mary Eliska laughed. "If those footprints were made by policemen I'll eat them. Where are your eyes, Bill? The cops in this town wear regulation broad-toed shoes. When I heard the traffic cop tell Dad that he'd seen the robbers' car go up the alley, I dashed out here to have a look around. And as soon as I saw these prints I knew they were not made by broad-toed boots. Let's examine them closer."

Taking care to avoid stepping on the well-defined trail that led from the door to the tire marks of the car, the two studied the line of footprints.

"One fellow wore rubber soled shoes--I guess you're right, Mary Eliska," acknowledged Bill, squatting on his heels. "The pattern on this set of prints could have been made by nothing else. But what do you make of these tracks here? Just holes in the mud with a flat dab right ahead?"

"High heeled shoes, Bill. One of this gang is a woman, that is clear enough. What bothers me is the third set--look!"

Bill stared at the footprints to which she pointed. "The right-hand one was made by a long, narrow shoe, but I'll swear that boot last was never made in America. It's too pointed," he said finally. "The shoe that made that imprint was bought in southern Europe, I'll bet--Italy, probably. But those queer looking marks to the left are beyond me," he frowned. Then he cried--"No, they're not! I have it--the man who made those prints was club-footed!"

Mary Eliska disagreed with him. "A club-foot couldn't make that mark. It is too symmetrical--straight on both sides and kind of rounded at the back and front. It wasn't made by a wooden leg, either, Bill!"

"No. That would simply dig a hole in the mud."

"Oh, I know! Why didn't I see it at once!" she exclaimed excitedly--"The man was lame!"

Bill snorted. "And he had long pink whiskers which he tied round his waist with a green ribbon!"

"Don't be silly--I know what I'm talking about."

"How so?"

"I *know* that a lame man made that set of marks.»

"Very well. May Doctor Watson inquire on what Miss Sherlock Holmes bases her astounding deduction?"

"On those queer marks, of course, stupid!"

"Thanks. The clouds have vanished. You make everything so lucid." Bill stood erect once more.

"But, Bill--did you ever see a lame man--whose left leg was shorter than his right?"

"Maybe I did. But I can't swear at this distant date which leg was the shorter."

"Well, I can tell you that in this case, the left was!"

"Maybe--"

"Maybe nothing! Why am I sure of it? Because the man wore a lame man's boot--the kind with a very thick sole. My grandfather wore one. He twisted his hip when he was a boy and that leg didn't grow as long as the other. What is more, he always walked on the *sole* of his big boot--the heel never touched the ground!»

"I believe you *are* right,» mused the young man, studying one of the queer footprints again.

"I know I am, Bill. That kind of a shoe would make exactly that print. Not such a bad hunch to take a look out here, was it?"

"You're a swell sleuth, Mary Eliska. Let's see. Now we know there were three in the gang this evening. The chap who played chauffeur and wore sneakers, a woman, and a lame man-"

"Yes. But that doesn't solve the mystery, does it?"

"No, but it helps a lot. How about the tire tracks?"

"Not our car. Daddy uses Silvertowns and those were made by some other kind."

"Goodyears, I should say. How about going in now and telling your father what we've learned?"

"I'd rather not, if you don't mind?"

"Why!"

"Well, you see, Bill, Dad hasn't much confidence in girls' views on what he calls 'the practical side of life'--mine especially. There'll soon be a bunch of detectives on this case. If they find out for themselves, it's O.K. with me--but I shan't tell them."

"You want to work up the case yourself?"

"That's exactly it. If you'll help me?"

"Certainly I will. But we may get into trouble--I mean it is likely to be dangerous work."

"Does that bother you?"

"I'd hate to have you get hurt--"

"I won't do anything on my own without telling you first. We'll work together. Does that suit your highness?"

"You bet! Where do we go from here?"

"Back to my house. We'll go down the alley and hop in your car. I want to ride up to our garage. I've got another hunch."

"The kid's clever," remarked Bill admiringly. "Want to tell me? I haven't a glimmer."

They turned out of the alley into Main Street before Mary Eliska answered.

"Suppose you guess," she suggested teasingly as she stepped into the car. "Or, better still, now that you've become my aviation instructor, I'll even things up and give you a short course in sleuthing."

"That's a go, teacher," grinned Bill. The car rolled up the hill past the white Memorial Cross on the village green. "But to a mere amateur in crime it looks as though you had barged into a pretty good mystery, no kidding."

"Sh--" commanded Mary Eliska. "Sherlock Holmes is thinking."

"Don't strain anything," Bill advised as he stepped on the accelerator.

Mary Eliska did not retort to this thrust, but remainder wrapped in her thoughts for the remainder of the ride. Bill turned the car into the Stricklin's drive before she spoke again.

"Keep on to the garage, please."

"Right-oh! Still sleuthing, I take it?"

"Yes."

"What *is* the big idea?»

"Wait and see." He drew up under the arching elms with the glare of their headlights focused upon the closed garage doors. Mary Eliska sprang out and ran forward.

"Locked," she affirmed, giving the handle a tug. "Wait a minute, Bill. I'll be right back." She disappeared in the direction of the house.

Bill shut off the engine and clambered down to the ground. Presently he saw her coming back, accompanied by a woman in maid's cap and apron.

"All right, Lizzie," her young mistress said, "I want to look at something first. Then you can tell us exactly what happened. That's right, give me the key."

She swung open one of the wide doors.

"The Packard's there, just as I told you, Mary Eliska," volunteered Lizzie as the three stepped inside the garage. "It's your car that's missing."

"I left it at the beach club--" Mary Eliska cut herself short. "The license plates are gone from the Packard!"

"Wasn't that to be expected after what the cop told us in the bank?" There was a hint of mockery in Bill's voice.

"Of course. But the point is--were they taken this afternoon while Daddy had the car parked behind the bank--or later this evening after he drove home? He would never remember whether he drove from the bank with the plates still attached or not. He never notices details like that."

Bill seemed amused. "Perhaps not--but what's the difference?"

"Wait a minute. You'll soon get another slant. Now, Lizzie--start from the very beginning."

Lizzie spoke up eagerly. "Yes, miss. Cook and me was havin' our supper in the kitchen, miss--"

"Where was Arthur?--He's our chauffeur-gardener," explained Mary Eliska to Bill.

"It's Arthur's night off, miss. He went to the movies--said he'd get a bite at the lunch wagon on Coast Village Road though why a man should want to eat hot dogs and such trash with honest-to-goodness vittles waiting for him at home is more than--"

"Never mind that now, Lizzie.--You and cook were eating supper--?"

"Yes, miss. We was just finishin' when we heard a car pass the house on its way out to the garage. I thought it might be Arthur, back in the Ford for some supper. Cook said--"

"Oh, Lizzie, please! What happened then?"

"Why, a man came to the back door and asked for the key to the garage. Said as how he had orders to fix the Packard."

"What time was that?"

"About five minutes after we heard the car drive out here, miss."

"No--I mean the time of day."

"I couldn't rightly say, Mary Eliska. The kitchen clock is down to Whipple's being mended. But it was just after you'd gone over to Mr. Bolton's for dinner."

"What did the man look like, Lizzie?"

"Like any young man, miss."

"But was he tall or short?"

"Kind of medium-like--"

"Dark hair or light?"

"I can't seem to remember--he had a chauffeur's cap on and was in his shirt sleeves, that I do know."

"Did you notice if he limped?"

"No, he didn't, miss--but the other fellow did--him with the big boot."

"Bull's eye!" cried Bill. "You're sure some detective, Mary Eliska!"

"Keep still?" ordered Mary Eliska. And then to the housemaid: "We'll take up the man with the big boot in a minute, Lizzie. Now then, you gave the other one the garage key, I s'pose?"

Lizzie snorted. "That I didn't, miss. I took the key off the hook and walked out to the garage with him. Mr. Stricklin wouldn't be thankin' me to let strange men fool round in the garage by theirselves!"

"Then how in thunder did they cop the license plates without your seeing them?" exploded Bill.

"Do shut up and let me talk!" Mary Eliska stamped her foot impatiently. "Now, Lizzie, what happened next?"

"Well, miss, I unlocked the doors and he started tinkerin' with the engine of the Packard there. Then all of a sudden he went out to the other car and spoke to somebody inside."

"What car was that?"

"The one he'd drove up in. It was parked out on the drive where the young gentleman has his'n now."

"Another Packard, was it?"

"I couldn't say, miss. I didn't pay much attention to it, except that it was a closed car--and there was a man and a woman in back."

Mary Eliska exchanged glances with Bill. "And then?"

"Then the young feller comes back and says as how the lady in the car was feeling sick, and could I fetch her a glass of water with a teaspoonful of bicarbonate of soda in it. I knew we had some in the medicine chest upstairs, so--"

"So you went back to the house and got it?"

"Yes, miss."

"And *that's* when they copped the plates!» declared Bill, the irrepressible.

"Bull's eye!" derided Mary Eliska. "How'd you guess it?"

"Form of genius some of us have."

Mary Eliska ignored this last and turned again to the maid. "What happened when you brought back the bicarb, Lizzie?"

"I give it to the young lady in the car, miss."

"Young, was she?"

"I couldn't get a good look at her face, for she was dabbin' her eyes with a handkerchief like she'd been cryin'. But she was dressed in some of those new-fangled pajamas like you wear to the beach, they was--sort of yellow-green color--and a wisp of her hair that had got loose from the bandanna she wore was red--the brightest red hair I ever see. She turned her head away when she drunk the medicine, but she thanked me prettily enough when she handed back the glass."

"Have you washed it yet?"

"No, miss. You see, I--"

"Then don't. I want that glass, just as it is. Was the lame man sitting beside her?"

"No. When I brought her the soda he was comin' out of the garage with the other fellow. He was carryin' a package wrapped in newspaper and he says as how he was takin' some part of the engine back to the shop. He spoke kind of funny, like a foreigner, I thought. And all dolled up in a light suit and a cane. Why, he'd even got lemon-colored gloves on for all his lameness and the big boot he wore!"

"Did the girl and the other man wear gloves?"

"The man put them on when he started to tinker with the car, I remember. But the girl had no gloves on."

"You're sure?"

"Oh, yes, miss, because I noticed her shiny pink finger nails, particular. I thought at the time that washin' dishes couldn't be no part of her life."

"That's fine, Lizzie. You make a splendid witness."

"Thanks, miss. I got a good look at the lame man, too. He had a funny little black mustache like they wear in the movies and little gold knobs in his ears--what do think of *that*!" Lizzie paused dramatically as she gave this choice bit of information.

"Earrings?" "Earrings, miss--and--"

"Thank you, Lizzie. You may go now."

"Remember those earrings, miss. And I'll keep the glass for you, and won't let cook touch it either, never fear!" Lizzie's slight figure faded into the darkness.

"So you've got pretty good descriptions of the gang *and* the lady›s fingerprints!» Bill summed up. «I›ve got to hand it to you, kid. Reckon you›ll have to let your father know about it though. Those fingerprints will have to be examined by the police.»

Mary Eliska nodded. "Guess you're right. I'll tell him what we found out."

"What *you've* found out, you mean. As I think I told you before, when it comes to detective work, I›m a ground hog!»

"Nonsense! But that reminds me, Bill. Do I get a lesson tomorrow?"

"Do you think you can take time enough from your life work?"

"Don't be ridiculous. You may think I've finished fooling with this robbery when I turn over the dope to Daddy--but I haven't. I want a flying lesson, just the same, in the morning. Shall we go up in the *Loening* again?»

"No. I'll drive you down to the shore and we'll take the *N-9* out. Don›t wait for your father tonight. Tell him what you want to at breakfast.»

"But I've got to--"

"This is your flight instructor speaking, Mary Eliska. No lesson in the morning for you, young lady, unless you go straight to bed now and get a good night's rest. A clear head and steady nerves are the first requisites for flying."

"All right then. I'll turn in directly. Good night."

Bill was already seated behind the wheel of his car. "Good night, Mary Eliska. By the way, *I've* got a hunch about this bank business. After you›ve had some flight training we›ll investigate together--and the plane will be a great asset,» he added mysteriously. His foot pressed the self-starter.

"Don't be so vague--spill the news like a good fellow."

"Sh--" mocked Bill. "'Sherlock Holmes is thinking!'" His laugh rang out and the car disappeared in the deep shadows of the drive.

"He's not so dumb as he pretends," mused Mary Eliska. "What can he have up his sleeve?"

Slowly she moved off toward the back door of the house.

Chapter 1.8
NEXT MORNING

"You've done splendidly, my dear. I'm proud of you. This information you've dug up will be a lot of help in tracing that gang, I'm sure."

Mary Eliska and her father were seated at the table, taking their morning meal in the breakfast porch, just off the dining room. Although the bond of affection uniting father and daughter was a strong one, especially since the mother's death some years earlier, neither was particularly demonstrative. And Mary Eliska was not used to receiving unstinted praise of this sort from her father. The color in her cheeks deepened, and she said off-handedly:

"I'm awfully glad, Daddy. You haven't had your second cup of coffee, have you?"

Mr. Stricklin smiled, and passed his cup to her. His shrewd glance took in her evident embarrassment.

"No need to dissemble, daughter. Fact is, I keep forgetting you're no longer a child; and I don't mind telling you how valuable you are to me."

Mary Eliska smiled back at him. "Thanks a lot, Dad." She returned his filled cup. "Did the gang get away with much?"

"Plenty. A number of easily negotiable bonds, what currency we had on hand, and so forth. Of course, we're well covered by insurance--but the worst of it is, they took Mrs. Hamberfield's diamond necklace!"

"What! The Hamberfields, of Canoe Hill?"

"The same. They bought the old Adams place two years ago and keep it for a summer residence. More money there than--er--taste, I believe. Mrs. H. goes in for jewels on a big scale."

"Wears diamonds at breakfast, I'll bet, Daddy. She came to the Astoria Golf and Country Club last Saturday night, dressed up to the hilt and beyond it. I've never seen so much jewelry! Doug Parsons suggested that she'd been robbing Tiffany's. A regular ice-wagon with her diamonds!"

"Well, she's lost a lot of them, now. That gang evidently knew she had a habit of keeping some of them in her deposit box at the bank, for it was the only one they raided."

"That's interesting."

"In what way?"

"Never mind now. Tell me some more."

"Well, naturally, I phoned the lady last night--and well--she was most unpleasant--"

"The nasty cat! Serves her right to have them stolen!"

"Hardly that, dear. But the bank is responsible for her necklace and other gewgaws. And her husband is a power in the financial world."

Having breakfasted sufficiently for one day, Mary Eliska was busy with an orange lipstick.

"More unpleasantness for you, Daddy?" she asked through pursed lips, her eyes on the small mirror of her compact, open on the table before her.

"He is in a position to do the bank considerable harm--By the way, Mary Eliska, are you as efficient at manicuring as you are at making up your mouth?"

"P-perhaps. Why?"

"Good. Then, after this I'll get you to do my nails while I have my second cup of coffee each morning!"

"Aren't you horrid!"

"Aren't you the cheeky kid, using that thing in front of me?"

"You really don't mind, Daddy?"

"Do you think it an improvement over nature?"

"I know it isn't."

"Why use a lipstick then?"

"But--why do you wear that curly mustache?"

"More cheek?"

"Not at all. But it adds dignity to your face--what's more, your mustache is becoming and you know it."

"Nonsense!" Mr. Stricklin's tone was derisive but there was a twinkle in his keen gray eyes.

Mary Eliska nodded decisively. "While my lipstick, properly used, is also becoming," she went on. "And it gives your daughter a sophisticated appearance otherwise lacking--" she broke off with a giggle as she saw her father's expression.

Mary Eliska snapped her compact shut and rose from the table. Going round to his side, she gave her father a hug and kissed him lightly on his mustache. "There!" she laughed. "Now I've added sophistication to your dignity, Daddy. You'll be able to run both the bank and that ritzy

Mrs. Hamberfield like a charm today. So long! Bill is coming for me and we're going down to the beach. I'm to have my first real flight instruction this morning, you know."

"From all accounts you did pretty well yesterday, young lady. Don't you think you'd better come down to the bank and tell the story of your sleuthing to the Bankers' Association detectives? They'll be up here from New York this morning."

From the doorway, Mary Eliska shook her head. "Nothing doing!" she cried. "I love you a lot--but you have the story down pat yourself--and I've got a date I can't break. That glass with the fingerprints on it, you'll find nicely wrapped up on the hall table. 'By--" She was through the door and across the lawn before Mr. Stricklin could reply.

He folded his napkin and laid it on the table with a sigh. "Heigho!" he murmured. "I wonder what her mother would say to that? Still, Mary Eliska grows more like her every day. The youngster has brains if she only uses them in the right way. She certainly has been a help on this robbery-- and she is a comfort to me--but a great responsibility at that."

Then, carefully lighting his after-breakfast cigar, Mr. Stricklin walked into the house.

Shortly after Mr. Stricklin had left for the bank, Bill's horn honked in the drive.

Mary Eliska appeared presently, wearing a boy's outing shirt open at the neck and a pair of fawn-colored jodhpurs. She noticed as she approached the car that Frank, the Bolton's chauffeur, was seated in the rumble.

"I've got to run into New York and buy some flying clothes," she announced as she seated herself at Bill's side.

"Don't bother about clothes, for heaven's sake. They won't help you to fly. I've got several extra helmets and some goggles and those things you're wearing now will be just the thing. All you need are overalls--and I bought you those in the village this morning."

"Aren't you nice," she beamed. "But I do need a leather coat, don't I?"

"What for?" "Didn't you tell me the cockpits of your N-9 were open--that they didn't have windshields?"

"Yes--but what of it?"

"Won't it be cold?"

"Not at this time of year. We're not out for an altitude record. Of course, when you get a couple of miles or so above the earth you have to bundle up--but the old OXX motor in my N-9 would never get you there. She's not built for that kind of work. Later on, you can order a monkey suit or a leather coat from the city."

"Yes, I'll get one of those sporty knee-length coats--" decided Mary Eliska gleefully.

"Not if I know it!" "But why not? They're so good looking!"

"And more dangerous than a broken strut!"

"They are?" Mary Eliska's tone was horrified.

"Certainly. If you buy a coat, get a waist-length model. Anything longer not only hampers a pilot, it catches the wind and is likely to get caught around your stick or other controls and crash the plane."

"Oh!" said Mary Eliska disappointedly.

Bill slanted his eyes from the road and smiled at her. "Not everyone who wears a yachting cap is a yachtsman! You'll have plenty to think of during your flight training without bothering about such things."

"I guess you're right," she agreed. "How long will it take to teach me to fly, Bill?"

"It all depends upon your aptitude, Mary Eliska. Ask me again after ten hours of dual instruction. But no matter how apt you prove to be, flying is not learned in a day. I've mapped out a forty-hour course for you. Want to look it over?" He handed her a typewritten sheet.

She studied the paper interestedly. It was titled.

"Course of Flight Training.

I. *Dual Instruction.*

First hour	Taxiing
	Straight flying
	Turns
	Glides
Second	Take-offs
	Climbing
	S-turns
	Breaking Glide and leveling off
	Slow motion landings by instructor
Third	Flying at leveling-off height
	(seaplanes only)
	Slow motion landings
	Normal landings, use of elevators only
Fourth	Cut-gun landings, under three feet,
	elevators only
Sixth	Normal landings
	Cut-gun landings
	Spirals
	Use of ailerons, rudder, throttle
	Approaches
	Elementary forced landings
Ninth	Stalls and spins

II. *Elementary Solo Flying.*
First solo: Five-minute flight, necessary turns, one landing
First 5 hours: Take-offs, turns, landings
Instruction flight: Instruction as necessary, including spins; power stall landings (seaplanes only)
5 to 10 hours: Take-offs, turns, spirals, landings
Instruction flight: Instruction as necessary, including spins
10-15 hours: Same as 5 to 10 hours

III. *Advanced Flying.*
Instruction flight: Reverse control turns and spirals, side-slips, power spins
15-20 hours: Take-offs, turns, spirals, landings; reverse control turns and spirals
Instruction flight--Acrobatics
20-25 hours: Acrobatics, with 20 minutes of each hour on elementary work
Instruction flight: Precision landings, forced landings, figure-eight turns, wing-overs
25-30 hours: Precision landings, forced landings, figure-eight turns, wing-overs
Final instructions flight: Review; instruction as necessary."

"Looks pretty complicated to me," sighed Mary Eliska, handing back the paper. "Gee, but there's a lot to learn!"

"More than the average novice has any idea of. But don't imagine that this course will make you or anyone else an experienced pilot. Additional time must be spent in the air before you can get an interstate commercial pilot's license. But after the instruction I've outlined here, your knowledge of flying should be sufficient to enable you to go on with your training yourself."

"I hope so," said Mary Eliska, but there was little confidence in her tone. Bill brought the car to a stop beside an open field. "Cheer up!" he encouraged. "Flying is like anything else worthwhile--troublesome to learn, but easy enough when you know how. Hop out, kid. There's the N-9, with her new landing gear, over there. Frank will take the car back. We'll fly up to my place now and I'll give you your first real instruction over our own flying field!"

Chapter 1.9
AIR TRAILS

Mary Eliska donned her overalls while Bill spoke to the mechanic who was waiting by the plane. Then the man got into a car and drove away, and Bill beckoned her to him.
"All set?"
"All set."

"Then we'll begin. First of all, you must know the names of the different parts of the plane. Some you know already, but we'll go over them just the same. That hinged movable auxiliary surface on the trailing edge of the wing is an aileron. Its primary function is to impress a rolling movement on the airplane. Got that?"

"Yes."

"Then repeat what I just said."

Mary Eliska did so.

"Good. Now this is a drag wire."

After twenty minutes of this kind of thing he asked her to point out an aileron and explain its use.

"K.O." he said at last. "We'll go over parts each day for a while and the book work you must do at home will help to refresh your memory. Now nip into the forward cockpit and I'll explain the working of the controls."

He gave Mary Eliska a hand up and when she was seated, swung himself on to the cowl of the cockpit.

"First of all--and let this become habit--" he ordered, "adjust your safety belt. Yes, that's the way. Now we'll go ahead. That's the stick there. Take hold of it. You'll notice it is pivoted at its base. Forward movement of the stick increases the angle of attack of the elevators and depresses the nose. Backward movement decreases angle and raises the nose. Lateral movement of the stick operates the ailerons, movement to the right depressing the right wing, and to the left, the left wing."

When she was sure she understood the functions of one thing he explained the next.

"Now tell me just what I have told you--" he commanded.

Fully an hour had gone by before he was satisfied that she understood thoroughly.

"Tired?" he asked at last.

"Not a bit," she smiled. "I'm afraid I'm kind of dumb--but all these gadgets, as you call them, arc a little confusing at first."

"Oh, you're catching on in first rate order," he told her. "Nothing but practice will make you letter perfect. And that comes soon enough when you handle the plane yourself. Now I'll fly us home. All I want you to do is to fold your arms and listen. Keep your eyes in the cockpit and watch the movements of the stick and rudder bar. My cockpit aft is equipped with similar controls. When I move my stick--yours moves--and vice versa. All right?"

"You bet."

He reached in his pocket and drew forth a small leather-bound book which he handed her.

"Here's your Flight Log Book, Mary Eliska. Write it up after every flight. There are columns for the date, type of plane, duration and character of flight, passengers or crew carried (if any) and remarks. A commercial pilot should have his log book certified monthly by an official of the company. For a student it is a good thing to commence during training. Stick it in your pocket," he advised as she thanked him. "And put on this helmet. It's a Gosport, with phones in both ear flaps, connected by a voice tube to this mouthpiece. I'll use that end of it to coach you through during flight."

"But this helmet is hard and stiff," objected Mary Eliska. "I'll bet it isn't nearly as comfortable as that nice soft leather one you're wearing."

"Possibly not. But until you're through with your instruction I want you to wear a 'crash' helmet. They're a lot of protection for the head in case of minor accident. No instructor worth his salt permits a student to use a soft leather helmet until you've had a lot of experience."

"Oh, very well then," she said, adjusting her heavy headgear, "you're the boss!"

"You bet I am when it comes to this kind of thing. If I weren't sure you were willing to give me strict obedience, I'd never propose teaching you. And please remember that this isn't a joy hop. The more attentive you are to instruction--the quicker you'll learn."

"I'm your willing slave, sir," she mocked good-humoredly, and drew the helmet strap tight beneath her chin.

Then as the engine roared and the plane rolled forward she felt the same thrill she had experienced the afternoon before when she and Bill had taken off in the amphibian. The same tightening of her muscles and beating throb of the pulse in her neck. They were soaring upward now and the sensation of smoothness became apparent after the jars and bumps of taxiing over the rough field. The sting of the wind on her face was exhilarating, but her eyes were streaming. Realizing that she had forgot to adjust her goggles, she pulled them down from the front of her helmet.

"I've been wondering how long it would be before you did that," came Bill's voice through the headphones. "Never mind--it's a grand thrill while it lasts--you'll lose it soon enough."

Mary Eliska, for the first time in her life, found a retort impossible to make.

"Now that we've got enough air under us," Bill's voice continued, "I'm going to fly straight for home. Remember what I said about watching your stick and rudder bar. Also keep an eye on the bank-and-turn indicator as well as the fore and aft level indicator and inclinometer."

Mary Eliska shifted her gaze to the instrument board before her. Unconsciously she ticked off the other instruments. There were the two Bill had just mentioned; a magneto switch, oil pressure gauge, earth inductor, compass indicator, altimeter, 8-day clock, primary pump and tachometer. It pleased her that she could so readily recall their names and uses. Then she heard Bill's voice in her ear again:

"The reason that I keep pulling the stick back slightly so often, Mary Eliska, in level flight, is because the old bus is a bit nose heavy. You'll notice it when you handle her later on. It's nothing to worry about. Very few planes are perfectly balanced."

Mary Eliska turned her eyes guiltily on the stick again. She had been caught napping that time! One really needed half a dozen pairs of eyes for a job like this. And--how different Bill's manner aboard an airplane, she thought. He was certainly all business. But she respected and admired his knowledge and his ability as an air pilot which left no opening for argument.

"You can look overside now," came his voice again interrupting her thoughts. "We're going to land."

Below them she saw the Bolton's house. The nose of the plane dropped suddenly as the stick went forward and they shot down to land on the field near the Bolton's hangar.

Bill spoke again from the rear cockpit. "If you're ready for more flight instruction, hold up your right hand."

Mary Eliska held up her right hand.

"Good. Then we'll practice taxiing," came back the even voice. "Remember that a land plane with engine idling will remain at rest on the ground in winds of normal force. That means that all movement of the plane must be made by use of the engine. When your bus begins to move you control it primarily by using the rudder. In a wind as strong as the one blowing now, you'll notice the plane's tendency to turn into it. That's due to the effect on the tail. It tends to swing like a weathervane until the nose is headed directly toward the point of the compass from which the wind is blowing. Your experience in sailing is going to be a great help.

"Now, just one thing more and we'll shove off. While taxiing, you must hold the stick well back of neutral. That will prevent any tendency of the tail to rise and cause the plane to nose over. Grasp the stick lightly with your fingers. Never freeze onto anything. If you feel me wiggle the stick sharply--let go at once. I may or may not have my hands and feet on the controls, but you cannot know that. Act just as if you were alone in the plane. Got all that?"

Mary Eliska raised her hand again.

"Then snap on the ignition and get going."

For the next hour she taxied the *N-9* around the field while Bill issued commands from the rear cockpit. So interested was she in her lesson that it seemed no time at all before he told her to shut off the engine.

"Take off your helmet and get down," he said as the plane came to a stop. And he helped her overside.

"Gee, Bill, it's wonderful!" she cried, jumping lightly to the ground beside him.

"You did splendidly," he encouraged. "This field is pretty rough in spots--makes it bumpy going. How are you--stiff?"

"Not a bit!"

"You need a rest, just the same."

"But I'm not in the least tired. Can't I go up now?"

Bill looked at her and shook his head. "Nothing doing," he said with pretended sternness. "That is--not for the next fifteen minutes. Here comes Frank with something cold to drink on his tray--horse's neck, probably. There's nothing like iced ginger ale with a string of lemon peel in it when you're real thirsty!"

"My, you're thoughtful!"

"Don't thank me--it's all Frank's idea."

They sipped their drinks in the shade of the old barn that had been turned into a hangar for the Bolton's planes.

"While you're resting, I want you to study this paper, Mary Eliska. It's a routine I want you to follow in preparing for every flight you take--with me, or soloing," he explained, handing it over. "When you've got it by heart, repeat it to me and then we'll carry on. Your first job for the next hop will be to do exactly what I've written there."

For perhaps ten minutes both were silent and Bill closed his eyes and turned over on his back.

"Asleep?" asked Mary Eliska presently.

"No--just relaxing. Got that dope down pat?"

"Sure. I mean, yes, instructor."

"Give me back the paper then, and shoot!" he said, sitting up.

"Preparations for flight:" recited Mary Eliska. "First, inspect the plane and engine as necessary. Second, observe the wind direction. Third, observe the course direction (if a course is being flown). Fourth, set the altimeter. Fifth, see that helmet, goggles and cushions are properly adjusted. Sixth, see that cloth to wipe goggles is handy. Seventh, give the engine a ground test. Eighth, see that the gas valve is properly set. Ninth and last--Buckle the safety belt!"

"One hundred per cent! Good work, Mary Eliska. Now come over to the plane and show me how you do it." He grinned, awaiting a quick retort--but Mary Eliska, intent on the business of learning to fly, walked at his side in a fit of concentration.

"She sure is keen," he said to himself. "I never got a rise--and 'Mary Eliska,' to Mary Eliska, is like waving the American flag at a Mexican bull!"

Mary Eliska continued to prove her aptitude for she went through the flight preparations with but one mistake. She entirely forgot the matter of the cloth to wipe her goggles!

Presently he took her up again and started in with his coaching.

"You now have thirty-five hundred feet registered on your altimeter," he announced through her phone. "Enough air below to get us out of trouble if we should happen to get into it. The higher one flies, the safer one is. Now you are going to get straight flight instruction. I am moving the stick backward--now forward--now backward--now forward. See how the nose of the plane rises and falls in response? Watch closely--I'm going to do it again. There, now--take the stick and do it yourself."

Mary Eliska did as he bade her. It was thrilling to feel the huge plane respond to her will.

Then followed instruction in moving the stick successively right and left by which means the right wing and then the left are correspondingly depressed. After that came rudder instruction. First Bill pushed the right and left sides of the rudder bar successively, forward, thereby swerving the nose first to the right and then to the left. Mary Eliska, of course repeated these movements after him. Then he explained that to hold a steady course, to fly straight, constant right rudder must be maintained to overcome the torque, or drag of the propeller blades tending to swing the nose to the left. While to fly level longitudinally, some point on the engine is kept in line with the horizon. That to fly level laterally, up aileron and opposite rudder are applied whenever a wing drops. He told her numerous other things, such as that when flying straight, the nose should frequently be dropped momentarily, or the course changed a few degrees in order to look ahead. Otherwise, an approaching plane may be hidden by the engine.

"Good night!" thought Mary Eliska as she strained her ears to catch every word, while she watched the controls and saw how the plane reacted to their manipulation by her instructor. "If it takes all this detail to fly straight and level, I'll get the heebie-jeebies when it comes to acrobatics!"

"Take over controls," came Bill's voice. "Fly straight for that white church tower on the horizon."

Mary Eliska's body stiffened, but she took hold of the stick again bravely enough, and placed her feet on the rudder bar at the same time. She could feel her temples throbbing, and her heart was beating faster than the clock on her instrument board. At last she was actually flying an airplane--all by herself. But was she? Suddenly there came a check in the forward speed of the plane and Mary Eliska felt it start to slew off sideways as the nose dropped.

Then before she knew exactly what was happening, the stick in her hand seemed to spring back, then to the right, while right rudder increased considerably without help from her foot. Up came the nose, followed by the left wing, and down went the right. The slewing stopped as suddenly as it had begun. Then she felt left aileron and left rudder being applied--and once more the N-9 was flying straight and level.

"Forgot what I said about checking a skid just now, didn't you?" said Bill's voice in her ear. "Here's the news again. Any swinging of the nose to the left can be promptly recognized and checked--but,--and here's where you went wrong--the nose cannot be swung back to the right without applying a small bank. Any attempt to do so will cause your plane to skid. That naturally results in a loss of flying speed forward and the heavier end drops. If not checked at once, it means going into a spin. Carry on again now, and please try to keep your wits about you. This is not a kiddie-car. Mistakes are apt to be costly!"

Mary Eliska bit her lips in anger. More than ever did she regret the lack of a mouth piece on her head phone. Her temper flared at his sharp tone, and what seemed to her unfair criticism so early in the game. But she took over again as he ordered and gradually her vexation disappeared in her effort to concentrate every faculty on the job of flying the plane and keeping to her course. She was gradually gaining confidence. She made the same maneuvers which had caused the skid before, and carried through perfectly.

Bill told her so in no stinted terms, and the last shreds of her anger disappeared.

"The man who put *me* over the bumps," he added, «always said: ‹when a student aviator makes a mistake, give him blazes--make him mad. He›ll remember what he should have done all the better--and live longer!› That advice applies to either sex, Mary Eliska. Naturally, I hope you›ll live to a ripe old age.»

Mary Eliska liked him for this apology. She wanted to thank him but of course that was out of the question.

"I'll take her over now." She heard his even tones once more, above the engine's roar. "Time for lunch. This afternoon, if you like, we'll take up another end of this business. And you can get even by teaching me how to become an honest-to-goodness sleuthhound!"

Chapter 1.10
THE MEETING

After lunch Mary Eliska and Bill established themselves comfortably in the shade of the terrace awning back of the Bolton's house, and Mary Eliska's ground training began.

"First of all," said her instructor, "you must learn the signals for maneuvers, such as when the stick is shaken laterally, one hand held up, it means control of the plane is resumed by the instructor. Opening the throttle in a glide means resume level flight. There are eight of these signals to memorize. Then there are eight correction signals as well."

"I'll get them down soon enough," his pupil assured him. "Is that all?"

"I should say not. That's just a starter. Your ground training will consist of three parts: theoretic training, which takes up principles of flight; aircraft construction, aviation engine construction; and the elements of meteorology. Next, practical training, which embraces the maintenance and repair of aircraft together with maintenance and repair of aviation engines. Then comes aviation procedure, which takes up air commerce regulations; instruction procedure (signals come under that) and precautions and general instructions."

"Whew!" whistled Mary Eliska in dismay. "It *is* a business!»

Bill laughed at her forlorn expression. "Cheer up--the first hundred years are the hardest. But seriously, to become an efficient air pilot, it is essential to know thoroughly this ground work and all of the maneuvers I listed under elementary flying. None of them can be safely omitted. Of those I included under advanced flying, acrobatics are not required for a pilot's license, but they're a grand help in developing ability to handle a plane with confidence. Proficiency in reverse control flying, precision landings with power, forced landings and cross-country flying is required for an interstate commercial license--and vital for every pilot."

"Is *that* all?» asked Mary Eliska, with diminished enthusiasm.

"No. To become a real flyer, you must understand aerial navigation and pass off formation flying and night flying. It sounds like a lot--but it really isn't so difficult. Of course, if you don't *want* to go the whole way--»

"Oh, but I do, Bill," she said earnestly. "It's only that I never dreamed there was so much to be learned. It kind of takes my breath away--"

"You mustn't let that bother you. I'm glad you're going to do the thing up right, though. It will take a lot of your time--but you'll find it worth your while. Let's get busy now. We'll start on signals. Then later this afternoon you can go up again if you feel like it."

For the next two weeks Mary Eliska worked daily with Bill. By the end of that time she had completed her elementary solo flying and was now engrossed in mastering the difficulties of reverse control.

Bill realized after giving her two or three lessons, that his pupil showed a high degree of aptitude for flying. Their trip home in the amphibian after the wreck of the *Scud*, had proved pretty conclusively to him that this sixteen-year-old girl had an unusually cool and stable temperament. Ordinarily, flight training is inadvisable for anyone under eighteen years of age, and Bill knew that twenty years is preferable. For, ordinarily, the instinctive coordination between sensory organs and muscles, which is necessary toward the control of a plane in the air, does not develop earlier. An airplane must be kept moving or it will fall; and the processes of reason are far too slow to keep up with the exigencies of flight. Flying cannot be figured out like a problem in mathematics. Calculation won't do the trick--there isn't enough time for it.

Of course there are exceptions to this rule. Bill Bolton was one himself, and Mary Eliska, he knew, was another.

When Mr. Stricklin questioned him as to Mary Eliska's progress, he gave him a list of the maneuvers that had already been mastered, and the approximate length of time she had taken to satisfy him in performance.

"But that doesn't mean a thing to me--" objected the older man. "Look here--I was talking to a friend of mine who is an old Royal Flying Corps man. He said that Mary Eliska should wait several years before training. How about it? I know your reputation as a flyer, and I've proved my confidence in you by trusting you with my daughter's life. Why is it better for her to start now, rather than later?"

"Do you play the violin, sir?"

"No ear for music." Mr. Stricklin shook his head in reminiscence. "My father played well. It was his ambition that we play duets together. But after wasting money for two years on lessons for me, he gave it up. My! the sounds I made when I practiced! It must have been torture to him. I can't tell one note from another--but I remember how awful it was. But what has *that* got to do with Mary Eliska›s flying?»

"A good deal. You couldn't play the violin because you are not musical, and only a musical person can learn to play it well. In some respects, mastery of the violin and mastery of flying, have a common bond. With both the one fundamental requirement is natural or instinctive aptitude. Flying is an art, and without natural ability it is useless to attempt it. And if it isn't inherent, Mr. Stricklin, it just can't be acquired. Moreover, the only way to find out if that aptitude exists, is by trial. If Mary Eliska had the natural ability for the violin that she has for flying, practice and experience would make her a second Kreisler!"

A smile crept along the corners of Mr. Stricklin's mouth. "Ah, but Kreisler is a *man*!"

"I know, sir, but honestly, sex has nothing to do with it."

"So you think she should keep on with her flight training?"

"I *know* she should, Mr. Stricklin, if you want her to fly at all. She has all the qualifications that go toward making a really *good* air pilot.»

"Well, I'm glad to hear you say it, and glad you're so enthusiastic."

"Of course I am," declared Bill. "She's fearless and alert and she loves the work-- she'll do well."

And so Mary Eliska continued her flight training.

She came down one afternoon from a solo flight and Bill, who had been watching her maneuvers from the shade of the hangar, walked over as the plane rolled to a stop.

"Not so good--" she called out as she sprang to the ground. "I nearly overshot my landing."

"So I noticed," returned her young instructor rather grimly. "Carelessness, you know, that's all. Keep your mind on the job. And here's something else. Remember, when you are making a flipper turn, the nose must first be dropped to level. Otherwise you'll get into serious trouble. Also don't forget that until the wings pass an angle of bank of 45 degrees your controls are not inverted and must be handled as in a normal turn."

"O.K. skipper," she sighed. "I'll remember in future."

"One thing more. Those two 360-degree spirals with an altitude loss of about 1000 feet were well done. But you must bring your plane out of reverse control spirals above 1500 feet altitude--Now we'll put your bus away and call it a day."

Work finished, they strolled over to the terrace where Frank as usual had iced drinks awaiting them.

"You've certainly taught me a lot in fourteen days," observed Mary Eliska after sipping her ginger ale. "But it's kind of put a crimp into our detective work. By the way, you never have told me what you had up your sleeve with regard to the robbery--something to do with an airplane coming in handy, wasn't it?"

"Your memory is better on the ground than in the air!"

"Pish! likewise, tush! You don't intend to wait 'til I finish training or anything like that, before coming across with that clue that will help us land those birds in jail?"

"Why should I?"

"I don't know. Thought maybe you might figure my interest in landing the gang would take my mind off flying--"

Bill took a long, refreshing drink of the iced liquid at his elbow. "You're on the wrong track. I'm simply biding my time and keeping a finger on the pulse of the robbery, as it were."

"Do you mean that?"

"I'm in deadly earnest," he assured her, although his eyes twinkled mischievously.

"Then all I can say," exclaimed Mary Eliska, "is that you're one up on everybody else who is working on the case."

"How come?"

"Why? you know as well as I do that when the Packard rolled out of the alley by the bank, in all probability carrying three people and the loot, it disappeared completely. And it's stayed that way ever since, hasn't it? That's two weeks ago tonight."

"Any new clues lately?"

"Nary a one. The police traced the red-headed girl's finger prints to Sarah Martinelli, better known as Staten Island Sadie. They sent Dad her record--I saw it--believe me, that lady is a ripe egg!"

"How beautifully expressive."

Mary Eliska raised her eyes from her compact's tiny mirror.

"Well, she must be!--Are you trying to kid me?"

Bill finished his ginger ale. "Come on, tell me the rest."

Mary Eliska grinned. "That's all there is, there isn't any more, my child. Don't imagine those police are efficient, do you? None of the missing bonds have been found, and as for the money, those chaps have probably spent it by this time. I feel awfully sorry for Daddy, though," she continued in a changed voice, "--that Mrs. Hamberfield is still raising the roof about her diamond necklace. Serves her right for being such a mutt, I say."

"Tough on both parties, I should think."

"Nothing of the kind. Daddy says that her husband, Stonington Hamberfield, made his coin profiteering during the war. What do you think his name really is?"

"You tell me."

"Steinburg Hammerfeld--isn't that a hot one?"

"A Hun, eh?"

"Well, if he isn't--I'm President Hindenburg, San Francisco Harbor and the Statue of Liberty all in one!"

Bill smiled appreciatively at this sally, then changed the subject. "Let's go to the movies this evening?"

"Can't. It's Pen and Pencil Club night."

"What on earth is that?"

"Oh, about a year ago, a bunch of us at high school, girls and fellows, started a club to write short stories. We meet every other Tuesday night at some member's house. Everybody has to write a story at least one a month, or they're fined a quarter. We read aloud and discuss them at the meeting. Come with me after supper and pay my quarter."

"Nothing doing. That kind of thing is my idea of a perfectly terrible evening."

Mary Eliska slipped the compact into a pocket of her jodhpurs and got to her feet.

"That's where you're all wrong, Bill. Noel Sainsbury, the writer, is our adviser. He makes it awfully interesting--we have lots of fun. He was a naval aviator during the war. You two should have lots in common. Do come along and meet him."

"Why I dined at his place, Little Windows, last night!"

"Oh, you do know him?"

"Naturally. Where would I be if it weren't for him? Look at the books he's written about me. Noel Sainsbury brought Dad and me to New Canaan. We're awfully fond of him and his wife and little girl."

"Yes, Winks is a darling and Mrs. Sainsbury is a peach--" Mary Eliska agreed. "She comes to our meetings, too. I'm named for her, you know."

"Really? That's interesting."

"You bet. Then you'll come tonight?"

"I'd like to, very much."

"All right. The meeting is at Betty Mayo's, in White Oak Shade. I'll be here about eight in my car and drive you down there."

"I'll be ready--so long!"

"So long!"

It was nearly quarter to nine before they got started, as things turned out. Mr. Stricklin had gone to New York for the day on business, had been detained in town, and Mary Eliska waited dinner for him.

"Well, we won't have missed much," she explained to Bill as her car breasted the Marvin Ridge Road. "The first half hour is always taken up with the minutes of the last meeting and all that parliamentary stuff. I love driving in the twilight, anyway. Next place on the left is where we're bound. We'll be there in a jiffy."

They rounded a bend and came upon a Packard parked at the roadside. The hood was up and a man looked up from tinkering with the engine as their lights outlined his figure. "Pull up! pull up!" Bill's tense whisper sounded in her ears. "Where are your eyes, girl?" But Mary Eliska needed no second warning. She shot home the brake, for she too had seen the great, misshapen boot that the dapper little motorist wore on his left foot.

Chapter 1.11
FOLLOW THE LEADER

"Need any help?" inquired Bill, as Mary Eliska drew up opposite the Packard.

"Thanks! This thing has got me stumped. I'm not much of a mechanician," returned the lame man ruefully. "Do you know anything about motors?"

"Making them behave is my long suit," was Bill's glib retort as he alighted from the car and crossed the road. "Let's see if I can locate your trouble. Got plenty of gasoline?"

"Lots of it. I just looked to see."

"Then let me have your flashlight while I give her the once over."

"Wait a minute--" called Mary Eliska, "I'll swing this car round and put my lights on the engine. There--is that better?" she ended, trying to keep the excitement out of her voice.

"Nothing could be sweeter!" sang out Bill without turning his head. "Hold her as you are."

Mary Eliska's offer had not been quite so altruistic as it sounded, for now her lights brilliantly illuminated the two figures bending over the Packard's engine. While Bill went over the motor with the sureness of an expert, keeping up a desultory conversation with the stranger, Mary Eliska used her eyes to good advantage.

But after a while she grew impatient. Why didn't Bill capture the man at once so they could haul him off to the police station? Why did he continue to go on with his pretended inspection of the engine? He couldn't really be in earnest, for if he found the trouble and fixed it, the lame man would simply get in his car and drive away. Could it be that Bill wasn't sure of his quarry? Of course, he was clean shaven, although Lizzie had described him as having a

42

small mustache. Naturally, he'd shave it off. By this time he must know that his description had been broadcast. And so far as she could see the earrings were missing too. But that was to be expected. And he spoke good English with a slight Italian accent.

What was the matter with Bill! He was big enough to take care of the man with one hand, when all he did was tinker and jabber. What was the use of that?

"Your engine seems to be in A-1 condition," Bill was saying. "Doesn't look as if you'd been running the car lately."

"I haven't," replied the lame man. "She ran like a charm when I drove down here earlier this evening. Then all of a sudden she stops--and won't go on."

"Ah! here we are!" Bill exclaimed a moment later. "You've got a choked jet. I'll fix that in a jiffy."

"You are very kind," beamed the Italian. "Is that a serious trouble?"

"Not so bad. Buy better gas and have your carburetor well looked over. I'll fix it so the car will move, though."

"Do you think she will run fifty miles?"

"Sure--but there are plenty of garages nearer than that if you want to fix it."

"I'll wait until I reach home. My friend--he will give the engine a thorough going over. He understands very well such things."

"Good enough." Bill straightened his back and closed the hood. "You're O.K. now. She'll run."

"Then thank you so much. You have been very kind."

"Don't mention it." Bill waved farewell and crossed the road as the lame man climbed into his car and drove off in the direction of New Canaan village.

"Whatever *is* the matter with you?» Mary Eliska broke out in a fever of angry disappointment. «Why didn›t you nab him while you had the chance? Now he›ll get away and--»

"Hush, sister! Likewise calm yourself," cut in Bill. "Move over. I'm going to drive. This business isn't finished by a long shot. It has only just begun."

Mary Eliska, flabbergasted by his high-handed manner, slid across the seat as he directed, and Bill sprang in behind the wheel. The tail light of the Packard disappeared around the bend of the road.

"What's the idea?" she fumed.

"Wait 'til we get going, Mary Eliska." Bill threw in the reverse and started to turn the car in the direction from which they had come a quarter of an hour before.

"*Don't* call me ‹Ecker›! You know I won›t stand for it. Aren›t you the limit--Going to try to trail him, I suppose, when you could have nailed him right here!»

"Don't get peeved!" Bill swung the little car onto the road and switching off his lights brought his foot down on the accelerator. "I know what I'm doing." "*Well, maybe* you do.» Her voice was full of sarcasm. «But we might just as well go back to the Pen and Pencil meeting. You›ll never catch up with his bus.»

"Shan't try to. There's his tail light now!" They rounded the turn and Bill sent the car streaking along the black road like a terrified cat up a back alley. "There's no need to get snippy," he added. "You heard what our friend said about *his* friend--who understands all about engines? On a bet, that›s the lad who wore the chauffeur›s cap and beaned the night watchman. He said he›d let him look over the carburetor when he got home, didn›t he? And like as not that ripe egg lady--the one with the red head--will be there too!»

"Staten Island Sadie?"

"Sure thing."

"Perhaps," admitted Mary Eliska. "The lame man *was* alone in his car. But you stand a good chance of losing him, even if he doesn›t see us. We›ll have to switch on the lights going through towns.»

"But, you see, I'm pretty sure I know where he's bound for."

"You do?" Her surprise drove all petulance from her tone.

"That's what I've kept up my sleeve. If he takes the Ridgefield Road, out of New Canaan, then I'm certain of it."

"Better switch on the glims again," she advised. "We'll crash or get a ticket running without them in this South Main Street traffic--we're nearly in the village now. I can spot the Packard ahead there." Then, contritely, she continued: "Sorry I was peeved, Bill, old thing. I didn't understand. Forgive me--and let's hear all about it."

"Of course--hello!" he cried. "He's slowed down. Confound it, anyway. That comes of talking and not keeping my mind on the job. I'll bet he has his suspicions. Wants to see if we're following--nothing dumb about that bird. I shouldn't have driven so close. He'll tumble to a certainty if we slow up too."

"What are you going to do?"

"Give me time--" he answered grimly. "Confound again! There goes the red light on the Library corner! Now we're in for it."

"P'raps he won't notice us," said Mary Eliska hopefully as they drew up behind the Packard.

"Not a chance. But we'll fool him yet. Let me do the talking," he whispered as the lame man thrust his head out of the car and looked back at them.

"Hello, there!" cried Bill cheerfully. "I see you've got this far without another breakdown!"

"Good evening, my friend," replied the Italian. "This is a surprise. I thought you were going the other way."

"Oh, no. Just ran down there to leave a message." Bill's tone was affability itself. "You must have come pretty slowly. How's the car running?"

"Nicely, thank you."

"Don't be afraid to let her out. Well--there's the light. Excuse me if I pass you," he said airly. "We're in a hurry. So long."

"Au revoir ..." Mary Eliska added gaily and waved her hand as Bill swung to the left, then headed up Main Street in advance of the Packard.

"Aren't you smart! You'll get us into a heap of trouble yet with your 'au revoirs'!"

"Hey, there"--she cried. They were rolling swiftly up the hill past the bank.

"You should have turned right then left, for Ridgefield--back at the last corner!"

Bill laughed. "Old Angel Face did just as I figured," he informed her, still chuckling. "I spotted him making the turn, in the glass."

"Where are we going? Sure you haven't lost him?"

"Listen. That chap is heading for Ridgefield. From there he will run another ten miles up to Danbury. Unless I'm completely wet, his objective is a certain house in the hills on a back road, over toward the New York borderline about twenty-five miles north. It's a rough, wild stretch of country, with Pawling, N. Y., to the west and New Milford, Connecticut, on the east, that he's heading for. Nice riding too, dirt roads, mere trails that haven't had a scraper on them since the Revolution. That house I just told you about is a good ten miles from a railroad as a plane flies--probably twice as far by road."

"Interesting--but why are we heading this way?"

"Simply because it is too dangerous to follow that lad just now. He smells a rat and is sure to park in some dark spot along the way to make certain he's not being followed."

"Then what *are* we going to do?»

"I'm going to run west over to Bedford, New York. Then north from there through Golden Bridge and Croton Falls to Brewster. From Brewster I'll keep to the same state road north toward Pawling. But just before I get to Patterson, there's a dirt road that turns off into the hills to the northeast. That's the one I'll follow. Eventually, I'll get to the house. Angel Face's route is shorter--but I'll get there soon after he does, if he stops along the way to see if anyone's after him. First of all I'll drop you at your house and get myself a gat."

"You'd better get two--for I'm coming with you."

"Sorry, my girl--this is a man's job."

Mary Eliska turned and stared at him. "Well--of all the consummate nerve--" she began.

"Sorry, Mary Eliska--it just can't be. I've got no right to let you run the risk."

"Don't you *dare* to ‹Ecker› me again!» Mary Eliska was distinctly irritated. «And what›s more, if you try to ditch me, I›ll phone the police station and spill everything. They›ll pick you up at Bedford and horn in, of course--and like as not, they›ll gum it all.»

"If you talk that way, I suppose I'll have to take you."

"Of course you will. Say, Bill, that was only a bluff, wasn't it?"

Bill smiled. "Perhaps. But it's a risky business."

"No worse than learning to fly, is it?" "Fifty-fifty, I should say." "That's settled, then. What I can't understand is why you didn't corral that gang long before this--or at least put the police on to them, if you knew where they were all the time."

"But that's just it--they haven't been in the house since the robbery. I've driven up there several times and reconnoitered from the air as well."

"Then what makes you think you'll corner the gang at the house now?" The car turned in the Stricklin's drive and came to a stop by the side entrance. "You'll have to wait 'til the next chapter for that," he laughed. "Time is worth more than money now. I'll tell you all about it when we get going again. Beat it upstairs now and change that light dress for breeches and a dark sweater or coat. I'll run across the road for something more suitable and less conspicuous than white flannels."

"O.K." Mary Eliska sprang out of the car. "Don't forget our armory."

"Not a chance. Now forget the prinking and make it snappy," he sang out, backing down the driveway.

Chapter 1.12
THE HOUSE IN THE HILLS

"Don't tell me it takes a girl long to change her clothes!" was Mary Eliska's salutation, as Bill drove up to the side entrance again. "You've kept me waiting here exactly three minutes and a half."

"Sorry," he said in mock contrition. "Fact is, I thought we'd better use my own bus tonight and I had to go out to the garage to get it."

"What's the big idea?" Mary Eliska sprang in beside him, looking very trim and boyish in jodhpurs and dark flannel shirt over which she wore a thin brown sweater. "Isn't my car good enough for you?"

"This boat has a full tank," he replied tersely. "Can't waste time tonight picking up gas."

They had reversed the car down the drive and were now speeding along the tree-lined road in the direction of Bedford.

"Got my gun?" she asked.

"Surest thing you know!" Bill passed over a small revolver in a holster. "Tie yourself to that! It's a Colt .32 and it's loaded. Know how to use it?"

"Certainly. What do you expect me to do--release the safety catch and pull the trigger to see if it works?" Her tone flared hotly with indignation.

Bill whistled a tuneless air, but the whistle developed into a laugh and the laugh continued until Mary Eliska snapped:

"*Don't* cackle like a billy goat!»

"Billy goats don't--" he began but broke off, changing his bantering tone. "Then why do you tie the leg-strap around your waist?" he asked seriously enough.

She swallowed hard.

"Because--well, because I've never used this kind of a holster before, smarty. But I can shoot--Daddy taught me--I can box, too, and I've had lessons in jiu jitsu. Oh, I can take care of myself, if that's what's worrying you!"

"Glad to hear it, Mary Eliska. Excitement kind of stirs you up eh?"

"It's not excitement that does it, Bill--it's suspense. But I'm sorry I bawled you out."

"Don't mention it. My humble apologies for being so rude--"

"Imbecile! You weren't. But never mind that--tell me about this house in the woods and what it has to do with the gang who robbed the bank."

The car ran into Bedford and taking the turn to the right, he swung on to the northbound turnpike.

"Go ahead with the story," begged Mary Eliska as they left the picturesque village behind.

"Right-o! Here goes. On our way back from the South last month, I dropped Dad at New Orleans. The old *Loening* needed a thorough overhauling, so Dad left me there with the plane and went north by train. After I saw him off at the L. and N. station, I went back to the St. Charles Hotel and slept for nearly twenty-four hours. I got a touch of jungle fever when I was down in the cypress swamps and was still feeling pretty rocky.

"So for the next ten days I loafed while the amphibian got what was coming to her. When she'd been made shipshape again I flew her north. I was in no hurry to reach New Canaan and stopped off at Atlanta, and at Philadelphia, where I have friends.

"A couple of days before I met you I started on the last leg of the hop. It was raining when I left Philly--a filthy morning, with high fog along the coast. That is why I decided not to follow the New York-Philadelphia-Hartford air route, but cut straight north over eastern Pennsylvania and northern New Jersey, hoping for better visibility inland. Instead, the old bus ran me into even worse weather. The fog grew lower and denser and flying conditions became even rottener than before. You haven't run into fog in a plane, yet, Mary Eliska--and, believe me, it's no fun.

"I expected to cross the Hudson at about Haverstraw and fly east to New Canaan. I know now that I must have overshot that burg; that the plane was probably nearer Newburgh when we crossed the river and headed east. To make matters worse, a few minutes later, the engine commenced to skip. I began to realize then that I didn't know where I was."

Mary Eliska had been listening intently, her eyes on the grotesque shadows cast by their headlights upon the stone fences along the road; now she turned and stared at him in astonishment.

"That's a good one! You've flown pretty much all over the country and get lost in dear little Connecticut!"

"Oh, I don't know--parts of the state are as wild as the Canadian woods! And just remember that the visibility at five hundred feet was so poor I could hardly see the nose of my plane. And worse luck, I knew that with the engine cutting up the way she was, I'd soon be forced to land."

"What did you do?"

"Nosed over until I got almost down to the trees on the hilltops. Visibility was better there, but for the life of me I couldn't spot a landing place.--Nothing but one chain of hills after another, all covered with trees. The sides of these foothills of the Berkshires are steep as church roofs--and they run down to narrow, densely wooded valleys. Well, for some time I circled about with the engine acting worse every split second. Then, in a valley a little wider than any I'd come across so far, I saw the glint of water--a little lake. Fifty yards or so away, there was a good-sized farmhouse with a fairly level hay field behind it. I chose the lake, although it wasn't much better than a duck pond--and landed.

"The house was a ramshackle affair, but some smoke rose from the chimney, so I figured someone lived there. While I was fixing my engine, a girl--or rather I should say a young woman--came out of the house and walked down to the little dock near where the plane was floating."

"Of course she had red hair and wore yellow beach pajamas?" said Mary Eliska.

"She did--I mean, she had. Anyway, when Lizzie described the girl in the car who wanted bicarbonate of soda and got it, I was sure that my er--lady of the lake and she were one and the same."

"Did you talk to her?"

"I did. I told her I was lost and asked her where I had come down. She told me, after a while. That is, she gave me a general idea in what direction Danbury lay and about how far away from town we were. But I thought at the time that she was awfully cagy and tight with her information."

"In other words, she didn't seem especially glad to see you?"

"That's it. Instead of inviting me ashore and up to the house for a meal, she wanted to know how long I was likely to be on the lake--and then she beat it back to the house. Naturally, I thought it queer she should be so inhospitable and stand-offish. People are usually interested anyway, when a plane arrives unexpectedly in their neighborhood--too darn interested, if anything. Still, I didn't think much about her, then. I had the information I wanted, and after changing a couple of sparkplugs, I took off and made New Canaan via Danbury without any more trouble."

"Did you see anyone besides the girl with the red hair?"

"Not a soul."

"And you've been back since the robbery, I think you said?"

"Several times. But the place has been deserted and the house locked up tighter than a drum."

There was a long pause.

"Why do you think the gang are there now?" asked Mary Eliska. "Simply because we saw the lame man take the Ridgefield road?"

"This is the way I figured." They had passed through the little town of Brewster, heading north, some minutes before. Now Bill turned the car off the state highway and on to a winding dirt road full of deep ruts that he knew ran far into the wooded hill country to the northeast. "It is my idea," he continued, slowing down to a bare twenty-mile pace, "that after the robbery, that gang scattered and laid low for a while. They didn't go to the house, that I do know. After you went to bed that night, I drove up here to have a look-see. Nobody home, as I've told you. But they couldn't have a better place for headquarters. There isn't a house anywhere round that neck of the woods. Sooner or later, they're bound to meet there. The loot has got to be divided. Seeing our lame friend headed in that direction this evening makes me doubly certain. I've kept it to myself, because if that army of detectives who are on this case started camping out near the house on a watchful waiting spree, those crooks would be sure to spot them and never show up."

"I guess you're right," she said.

For some time neither spoke, while their car bumped slowly along the uneven road.

"What do you suppose that lame man was doing on Marvin Ridge?" she inquired presently.

"Search me. How should I know? You certainly love to fire questions at a guy."

"He told us the car hadn't been used lately," she mused, ignoring his remark.

"That only goes to prove we're right in thinking he has been in hiding somewhere."

"But where?"

"Merciful heaven! Another question! That road runs down to Noroton, doesn't it? And from there the Boston Post could bring him from all points east and west. There's no telling where he'd come from."

"But I drove up from the Post Road that way yesterday. It has been freshly oiled to within a half mile of where we met him. Yet that Packard hadn't run through oil. If she had, I'd have seen it with my headlights smack on her."

"Perhaps he came down a side road?"

"Not between that point and the oil--there isn't any."

"Maybe he'd been calling in the neighborhood--"

"Don't be silly--I know everyone who lives along that road."

"You think it out then--I've got enough to do trying to navigate this road. I'm going to switch out the lights, now. We're not more than a couple of miles from the house."

"Do you think they'll put up much of a fight?"

"Good Lord! You don't think I've any intention of trying to capture them?" Bill exclaimed. He was very busily engaged in keeping the car in the middle of the grass grown trail as it rolled, down a steep hillside at a snail's pace. "I'm not taking chances with you along. It would be foolish to attempt anything like that. You'll get into no battles tonight, miss. This is just a scouting party. If the gang have arrived, we'll beat it back to Brewster and get the cops on the job."

"Oh, *dear*!" sighed Mary Eliska. "And I thought this was going to be the real thing!"

"No grandstand plays for you tonight, young lady. What's more--I'm running this show. If you don't promise to behave, you'll warm a seat in this car, while I mosey up to the house. How about it?"

Mary Eliska's voice betrayed her disgust and disappointment.

"Oh, I'll promise. But if we are leaving all the fun to the police, why did you bring the guns?"

"Because you seemed to expect them, little bright eyes. But we might as well have left them home, for all the use they'll be--I'll see to that. It's bad enough to be forced into bringing you up here. Your father will certainly raise the roof when he finds it out. I shan't tell him, that's flat."

"You believe in being candid!" with cutting sarcasm.

"You bet. And please remember that if you try to pull off anything you'll probably crab the show. And get us into a good old-fashioned mess besides."

He stopped the car and slipping into reverse gear, backed off the trail.

"There!" He switched off the ignition. "We're all ready for a quick getaway if need be."

"How far are we from the house?" she asked in a tense whisper.

"About a mile. I'm afraid to drive nearer--sound carries a long way up these quiet valleys. Let's get started now. I want you to walk just behind me. Be careful where you place your feet. We'll follow the trail a while farther, but it's pretty rough going. Above all else--don't talk--and make just as little noise as possible."

"What if they have sentries posted?" she asked, coming to his side.

"Aren't you the limit!" Bill seemed really annoyed. "There you go talking again! For your satisfaction, though--if we have the bad luck to come across anyone, I'll naturally do my best to scrag him. You, of course, will act as you think best. My advice is to beat it to the car, as fast as you can. Come along now--and quiet!"

"Aren't you horrid tonight!" she breathed, swinging up the overgrown trail behind him.

But Bill didn't hear her. Anyway, he didn't answer, and she followed in his footsteps while a pleasurable thrill of excitement gradually took the place of her disappointment. It was nearly pitch dark, walking along in the shadow of tall trees that lined the twisting path. Now and then the cry of a night bird came to her from the woods, but except for the dull sound of their steps on the damp earth--the occasional snapping of a twig underfoot, all was quiet in the forest.

Bill was only a blur in the gloom ahead. But she was glad to know he was there just the same. This creeping through the still night to reconnoiter a gang of bank-thieves held a kick all its own. Yes, she was glad that Bill was close by.

There came a movement in the underbrush behind them. Hands of steel caught her arms, pinning them to her sides.

"Sentries, Bill!" she screamed, struggling frantically to free herself. "Look out! *Look out!*"

She heard Bill mutter angrily. Heavy feet crashed in the brush and she heard the sharp impact of a solid fist meeting soft flesh. Several men were shouting now and someone groaned.

Bending suddenly forward and sideways, Mary Eliska managed to fasten her teeth on the wrist of the man who held her. With a howl, he let go her right arm and at the same time a gun went off. The night was torn with a scream of anguish. But before she could use her free arm someone dropped a bag over her head, a rope was knotted about her wrists and a muffled voice spoke to her through the folds of the sack. "*Be*have, sister! *Be*have, I say, or I'll crack yer wid dis rod. I ain't no wild cat tamer. Quiet now, or I'll bash yer one!"

Inasmuch as it was no part of Mary Eliska's plan to get "bashed" in a bag, that young lady kept quiet. "That's the girl!" he applauded. Swinging her over his shoulder as though she were a sack of flour, he walked away from the scuffle on the trail.

Chapter 1.13
TRAPPED

The burlap sack was stiflingly hot. Moreover it seemed impregnated with fine particles of dust which burned her throat and nostrils and set her coughing. Mary Eliska was frightfully uncomfortable. Breathing became more and more difficult.

"Let me go--I'm smothering!" she gasped.

"And get another piece bit out of me arm?" snorted her captor. "Nothin' doin'."

"But I'm choking to death in this filthy bag! It's full of dust!"

"Keep yer mouth shut, then," gruffed the man. "And stop that wrigglin'. I'll tap yer one if yer don't. What do ye think this is, anyway--a joy ride?"

"But--" she began again.

"Shut up!" he growled. "Behave, will yer? Say, sister, if I had me way youse'd get bumped off right now. Give me more of yer lip and I'll do it, anyway!"

There was a grim menace in the gangster's tone that frightened Mary Eliska more than his words. Thereafter she spoke no more. She even refrained from struggling, although her head swam and his grip of iron about her knees had become torture.

What had happened to Bill, she wondered, and cold fear entered her heart. She was almost certain that it had been a blow from his fist she had heard directly after her warning shout. But the shot and the scream immediately afterward? Had that been the sound of his automatic--or another's? The thought of Bill lying in the woods wounded--perhaps dead-- drove her frantic. Yet she was powerless, with her wrists lashed behind her back. While the man who carried her lurched forward, stumbling now and then over the uneven ground, each step causing his victim fresh agony, Mary Eliska's conviction of hopelessness assailed and overwhelmed the last shreds of her fighting spirit. She wept.

Presently,--it seemed an age,--she sensed that the gangster was mounting a flight of steps. There came the creak of a board underfoot. Then she knew that he was fumbling with a doorknob. A glow of light appeared through the burlap.

"Here we are, sister!" he grunted, with evident relief. Swinging her from his shoulder, he placed Mary Eliska on her feet and pulled off the sack. "Gosh!" he exclaimed, steadying her as she would have fallen, "I thought it was a Mack truck I was carryin'. But you're only a kid! Nobody'd think you weighed so much. Did I make you cry?"

He placed an arm under her elbow and led her to a chair. It was of the hard, straight-backed, kitchen variety, but Mary Eliska was only too glad to sit down and rest. She kept her eyes closed, for the light, after the dark confines of the bag, was blinding. Her breath came in convulsive gasps.

"Feelin' kind of woozy?" The man's tone was callous, but at least it evinced a slight interest in her condition and she took advantage of that at once.

"Yes, I am," she admitted, keeping her eyes closed, but drawing deep breaths of air into her lungs between words. "You nearly smothered me in that filthy bag. If you want to make up for it, you can bring me a drink of water now."

"You certainly have some noive! Y' don't happen ter want a couple of ice cubes and a stick in it too?"

"Plain water, if you please."

"Dat's all you'll get, kid. But I'm dry myself, so I'll bring you some."

She heard him cross the room, jerk open a door and tramp over an uncarpeted floor beyond.

Mary Eliska opened her eyes.

A wave of faintness swept over her and the room seemed to whirl before her. As she tried to struggle to her feet she found her roped hands had been securely fastened to the back of her chair. She sank back wearily, her thoughts in wild confusion.

After a moment she turned her attention to her surroundings, conscious of the futility of any further effort to free herself, and resolved to bide her time.

The long, narrow room evidently ran the width of the house for shuttered windows broke the bare expanse of walls at either end. Behind her chair, she knew, was the door through which she had been carried into the room, with shuttered windows flanking it. Facing her were two other doors, one open and one closed. Through the open door came the sound of a hand pump in action, where her captor was drawing water.

The room in which she sat was dimly lighted by an oil lamp, its chimney badly smoked and unshaded. It stood on an unpainted table amidst the debris of dirty dishes and an unfinished meal. Chairs pushed back at odd angles from the table gave further evidence of the diners' hurried exit.

"They must have posted someone farther down the road," she mused. "I wonder how he got word to the house so quickly?"

Then she caught sight of a wall-phone in the shadows at the farther end of the room. "Telephone, of course! They must have planted one somewhere this side of the turnpike. The man on watch saw our car pass and immediately sent word along the wire!"

It suddenly occurred to Mary Eliska that she herself might find that telephone useful. For a moment she contemplated dragging her chair across the room, but gave up the idea almost at once, for the sound of the pump in the room beyond had ceased and she heard the gangster's returning footsteps.

He appeared in the doorway almost immediately. A broad-shouldered, narrow hipped, sinewy young man, with a shock of sandy hair falling over his ferret-like eyes. The white weal of an old knife scar marred the left side of his face from temple to chin. An ugly, though not bad humored countenance, she summed up--certainly an easy one to remember.

"Here yer are, sister!" was his greeting. "Get outside o' this an' yer'll feel like a new woman!"

He held a brimming glass of fresh water to her lips.

Mary Eliska gulped eagerly.

"Hey, there! Not so fast," he cautioned. "You'll choke to death and Sadie'll swear I done yer in." He pulled the glass out of her reach. "Tastes good, eh?"

"It certainly does. Give me some more."

"Take it easy, then. I don't want yer to get sick on this job." He grinned and allowed her to finish drinking. "I guess yer ain't used to a dump like this--" he waved his hand toward the litter on the table and included the peeling wall-paper.

"Still, it's a heap better than a hole in the ground out in the woods. You certainly are the lucky girl!" He grimaced, then laughed heartily at his joke.

Mary Eliska's tone was stern, "What have they done with Bill?"

"Who's Bill? Yer boyfriend?"

"Is he hurt?"

"I hope so. He sure gave Tony a nasty crack. A rough little guy, he is--some scrapper. It looked like a battle royal to me when I left an' brung yer up here. But don't get the wrong idea, kid. By this time, one of the bunch has slipped a knife into him--pretty slick at that sort o' thing, they are."

Mary Eliska said nothing, but he read her feelings in her face.

"Cheer up, sister," he said, heaping a plate with baked beans and sitting down at the table. "Pardon me, if I finish supper. That lad ain't so hot. You've got me now, haven't yer? I'm a better man than he was, Gunga Din!"

"Yes, you are--I *don't* think!»

"How do yer get that way?"

"Well--" Mary Eliska eyed him uncompromisingly--"why are you afraid of me, then?"

"*Afraid?* You little whippet!» He paused, his knife loaded with beans half way to his mouth. «Say--that›s a good one! What are yer givin› us?»

"You keep me tied up, don't you? Why? You're twice my size and you've got a gun--"

"Two of 'em, little one--my rod and yourn."

"Yet you're afraid to loosen my hands."

"No, I'm not--but--"

"Please," she begged, changing her tone. "My face itches terribly from all that dust and I--"

"Well, what do yer think I am? A lady's maid?"

"Don't be silly--I just hate to sit here talking to you, looking such a fright!"

"So that's it," he laughed. "Don't try yer Blarney on me! I'm as ugly as mud and yer knows it. Though I'll say yer need a little make-up--and I'll let yer have it. But just get rid of that idea that you've got me buffaloed--yer haven't!"

He pushed back his chair and coming around the table, untied the rope that bound her wrists.

"Thanks." She began to rub her hands, which were numbed and sore.

"Don't mention it," he leered. "Now yer can doll up to yer heart's content while I shovel some more chow into me. I sure am empty an' that's no lie!"

"Hey, Mike!" called a man's voice from the doorway behind her. "Where do they keep the wheel barrer in this god forsakin' dump?"

"In the shed out back," returned Mike, sliding his chair up to the table again and picking up his knife. "What yer want it for? What's the trouble?"

"Trouble enough!" grumbled the other. "There's a couple o' guys messed up pretty bad down the line. Need somethin' to cart 'em up here in. Sling me a hunk o' bread, will yer? I ain't had no chow."

"Tough luck!" Mike replied callously, his mouth full, and tossed him half a loaf. "So long."

"So long--" sang out the other, and Mary Eliska heard him cross the porch and thump down the steps.

She was busily engaged in flexing her stiff fingers. She began to feel better, stronger, quite like her old self again. But the news that two men were badly hurt was anything but comforting. Was Bill one of them? she wondered.

With an effort, she thrust the thought from her, and drawing forth a comb and a compact from a pocket, she commenced the complicated process of making herself presentable. If she were to make her escape before the rest of the gang arrived she must work fast. But not too fast, for every second brought back renewed strength to her cramped arms and fingers.

"How's that?" she asked a few minutes later, replacing comb and compact in her pocket and getting to her feet.

"Say! You're some looker! I'd never have thought it!"

Mike pushed back his chair and came toward her, wiping his mouth with the back of a hand. "Say! You've got Sadie lashed to the silo!"

"Who's Sadie? Your steady?" she asked, playfully pointing a forefinger at him.

Mike leaned back against the table. "Never mind Sadie," he retorted. "I've got an idea."

"Spill it."

"You wanta breeze--get outa here, don't yer?"

"What a mind-reader!"

"Cut it, kid!" Mike's tone was tense with earnestness. "That guy you been travelin' with is either dead or a cripple. Sposin' you pal up with me. Tell me yer will, kid, and we'll hop it together, now."

"How about the rest of the gang?"

"What about 'em. I ain't a regular--just horned in on this deal to make a coupla grand extra."

"But I'm expensive--" she laughed.

"I'll say you are! What of it? I make good money. I'm no lousy crook. I've got a real profession."

"What is it?"

"I'm a wrestler, kid, and I ain't no slouch at it, either."

For a moment Mary Eliska paled. For some reason she seemed taken aback.

"What's the matter?" he asked.

Mary Eliska straightened her lithe figure.

"Not a thing," she shrugged. Then musingly, "So you're a wrestler, eh?"

"Sure--what did yer think I was--a gigolo?"

Mary Eliska giggled. "Know this hold?" she asked casually.

And then a startling thing occurred--especially startling to the unsuspecting Mike. There was a flash of brown-sweatered arms, a swirl of Mary Eliska's hair and Mike felt himself gripped by one elbow and the side of his neck. He knew the hold, had practiced it in gymnasium, but not for some years. To be seized violently thus aroused the man and it brought an instinctive muscular reaction which was assisted by a stab of pain as Mary Eliska's thumb sank upon the nerve which is called the "funny bone."

Yes, Mike knew the hold, and how to break it and recover; so as Mary Eliska swirled him backward onto the table with uncanny strength, he pivoted. Then, clutching her under her arms, he clasped his hands just beneath her shoulder blades, bearing downward with his head against her chest. It was a back-breaking grip, but her slender form twisted in his arms as though he had been trying to hold a revolving shaft. An arm slipped over his shoulder, a hand fastened on his wrist and began to tug it slowly upward with the deliberate strength of a low-geared safe hoist. Then the other hand, stealing around him, encircled the middle finger of his clasped hand and began to force it back--a jiu jitsu trick. If he resisted, the finger would be broken. To release his clasp would mean a probable dislocation of the other arm.

Mike realized that he had to do not only with a phenomenally strong girl, but with a skilled and practiced exponent of Oriental wrestling tricks. He was by no means ignorant of this school, and countered the attack in the proper technical way--with utter relaxation for the moment--a supple yielding, followed by a swift offensive. Though he was broader of shoulder and heavier, the two were nearly of equal height, possibly of equal strength, but of a different sort. Mike's was slower, but enduring; Mary Eliska's more that of the panther--swift, high of innervation, but incapable of sustained tension.

Such maneuvers as immediately followed in this curious combat were startling. Mike felt that he was struggling with an opponent far more skilled than himself in jiu jitsu, one trained to the last degree in the scientific application of the levers and fulcrums by which minimum force might achieve maximum results in the straining of ligaments and paralysis of muscles.

And to give him his due, for all his bluff about striking her with the gun on the way up to the house, Mike had some decent instincts beneath his roughness. Whereas he was striving to overcome without permanently injuring the girl, Mary Eliska had no such qualms. She was fighting with deliberate intention of putting him out of the running, for at least such time as would permit her to carry out her plans for escape. But for a time Mike's efforts were purely defensive, his object to save himself from disgraceful defeat. What would the gang say if she bested him, a professional wrestler, and make her getaway? They fell across the table, shattering the crockery, then pitched off on to the floor with Mike underneath. He writhed over on his face and offered an opening for an elbow twist which was not neglected. There was an instant when he thought the joint would go; but he broke the hold by a head spin at the cost of infinite pain.

Mike had seen the state in which jiu jitsu wrestlers left their vanquished adversaries. Defeat at this girl's hands would probably leave him helpless and crippled for three or four hours. It was not a pleasant thought. He would have to hurt her--hurt her badly, if he could. He was flat on his face again when suddenly he felt his automatic jerked from its holster and she sprang to her feet.

"If you move an eyelash," said Mary Eliska, rather breathlessly, "I'll pull the trigger!"

"If you don't drop that rod at once, I'll blow the top of your head off," declared a dispassionate voice from the doorway.

Mary Eliska dropped the gun.

Chapter 1.14
THE DOCTOR

"And now, Mike," continued the voice, "I'd like to know how you happened to be caught napping." Mary Eliska swung around to see another young man standing in the doorway. With a gasp of consternation she found herself staring down the barrel of a revolver. For a fraction of a second her heart turned over with a sickening thud. Then she recovered her poise.

"Well, I guess *my* trick›s over,» she exclaimed as cheerfully as possible.

Mike scrambled to his feet, catching up his automatic as he did so. Instead of answering the man who leaned against the door frame, he stared at Mary Eliska in a sort of amazed wonder. She met his gaze, a malicious little smile at the corners of her mouth. Aside from a flush on her cheeks, she showed not the slightest sign of the ordeal she had just passed through, nor the exhaustion it must have produced. His eyes fell rather stupidly to her feet. If Mike had not so recently staggered under Mary Eliska's material weight, he would not have believed her to possess any at all. He drew a deep breath.

"Who taught you jiu jitsu?"

"A woman professional in New York. She had a class--the others went in for it in a lady-like way. But I took it up seriously because I thought I might need it someday."

"Have you--ever?" He had dropped his east side argot, she noticed.

"Once or twice--but never like this," she smiled.

"I should hope not." Mike was rather pale. He frowned. "Where do you get your appalling strength?"

"Heredity--and training. I come by it honestly. It's not so extraordinary as some people seem to think." Her smile widened. "My father Albert Stricklin is the strongest man I've ever known. Although you'd never guess it by looking at him. He can do all sorts of stunts. He's trained me—marathon running, boxing, fencing, swimming--"

"I'll say he has! I wouldn't have believed it possible--and you only a kid!"

Mary Eliska nodded and looked at him with a curious light in her blue eyes.

"Perhaps I'm not so strong as you think--I know a little more about Oriental wrestling than you do, that's all."

"Yes, that's all!" said a woman who had joined the man by the doorway in a mocking tone. She stepped across the threshold and came toward them. "Go over there and sit down." She motioned Mary Eliska to a chair. "And not another peep out of you--understand?" Her eyes gleamed at Mary Eliska through narrowed lids with a light more metallic than the reflection from the barrel of her automatic. It was a strange look--combined of ruthlessness and malicious amusement.

"Interesting--very interesting, indeed!"

She turned to Mike, as Mary Eliska obeyed her and sat down.

"And now that you and your little lady friend have finished your heart-to-heart, perhaps you'll tell me what it's all about--why I find you flat on the floor covered by her gun?"

"Jealous, Sadie?" Mike's tone was tantalizing. "You *fool!*"

She took a step forward. The expression on her face underwent a startling change. Mockery gave way to an exasperated ferocity. Her eyes opened to their full size. Then the volcano of her wrath erupted. Words poured forth with the sharp regularity of a riveting hammer. Mike was given a description of his characteristics, moral, mental and physical, that brought the angry blood to his forehead.

Whereupon he retorted in like spirit and soon they were going it hammer and tongs, while the fury on Sadie's face froze into livid hate.

It was a wicked face, yet beautiful, Mary Eliska thought as she watched from her chair in the corner; a strangely beautiful face beneath a crown of glorious red hair. But its beauty was distorted, devilish. Her lips were scarlet, slightly parted, showing the double rim of her even teeth as she hurled insult after insult at the man before her. Like some evil goddess, she stood motionless, the rise and fall of her bosom the only token of the deadly emotion she felt as her voice poured forth vituperation.

Presently Mary Eliska's ears caught the sound of footsteps thumping on the porch. The lame man limped into the room and sized up the situation at a glance.

"Stop that scrapping, you two!" he commanded. "Stop it, Sadie! Do you hear me? Stop it at once!"

The red-haired girl glared at him, but she obeyed. There was a dangerous finality in his tone that debarred argument. She swept over to the table, and deliberately turning her back upon the others, poured herself a cup of coffee.

"Mike!" barked the Italian. "Go out and give the others a hand. We've got a couple of invalids with us. I've already administered first aid, but they will have to be carried upstairs and put to bed. Hustle, now!"

Mike disappeared through the door without a word. This little lame person seemed to brook no opposition. He was probably the brain and the leader of this gang, thought Mary Eliska--but he was speaking to her now.

"Good evening again, Mary Eliska! I felt somehow certain we were fated to meet a third time tonight!" His glance snapped from her to Sadie and back again. "Sorry we had to 'bag' you, as it were--hope you suffered no great inconvenience?"

"Oh, I'm all right," she replied coolly.

"But I notice that your sweater is torn in several places. You will excuse me?--but you look rather rumpled. I got the impression that you and the young lady who is at present drinking coffee might have had--a difference of opinion, shall we say?"

"No. These tears in my sweater were caused by accident. Miss Martinelli had nothing to do with it."

"So you know her name! But, of course you would. That bicarbonate of soda proved a boomerang. Too bad she really needed it at the time. It's a lesson to us, to remember that servant girls are likely to be lazy."

"Oh, it wasn't Lizzie's fault," smiled Mary Eliska. "I caught her before she had had time to wash the glass, that's all."

"You are a very clever young woman."

"Well, I don't know about that--" she drawled. Then she left her chair and took a step toward him. "Tell me--is Bill Bolton very badly hurt?"

"Just a bit frazzled, that's all." Her aviation instructor limped into the room. His coat was gone and his soft shirt, once white, hung from his shoulders in dirty, tattered streamers. One eye, half-closed, was rapidly turning black. Blood streaked his cheeks. Just above his left knee the trouser-leg had been cut away and a blood-soaked bandage was visible. Mary Eliska saw that his wrists were handcuffed behind his back. At his elbow, a man whose jaw was queerly twisted to one side, stood guard with drawn revolver.

The lame man grinned. "Here's your young friend now. You can take him in the kitchen if you like and wash him off a bit. I'll come in later with some bandages. You'll find matches and a lamp on a shelf just inside the door.--Stick that gun in your pocket, Tony," he added to his henchman. "Come over here. Now that we've proper light, I'll snap that jaw of yours back into place."

Mary Eliska put an arm about Bill without speaking and led him slowly into the dark room. Then as her hand groped for matches on the shelf, there came a loud click from the other room, followed by a scream of anguish. Mary Eliska felt her hair rise on the back of her neck. There was a momentary silence, then low, breathless moans.

"What is it, Bill?" she whispered fearfully. "What's happened?"

Bill chuckled. "Tony's dislocated jaw is back in place, now, that's all. Too bad I didn't knock it clean off while I was about it. He's the bird who knifed me a while ago. No fault of his that he only got me in the leg, either. I'm glad to hear he's getting his, now."

"Goodness--" Mary Eliska found the matches at last and struck one. "Here I stand--and you're badly hurt--don't say you aren't--I know it. Where's that lamp? He said it was on the shelf. It isn't. There it is on the table. *Dash*--there goes the match!"

"Take it easy, kid!"

"Oh, I'm all right. That man's scream kind of set my teeth on edge."

She struck another match, then lit the lamp and carried it to a dresser by the sink.

"Come over here and sit down," she said, drawing out a chair. "I want to swab out that cut in your leg. The rag is filthy--" She pulled out the drawer in the dresser. "Here's luck! Towels--clean ones! Who'd have thought it!"

With deft fingers she unfastened his bandage, then cleaned the wound with fresh water from the pump, using every precaution not to hurt him.

"You're certainly good at this kind of thing," was Bill's sincere tribute as she turned her attention to the bruised cut on his head.

"Part of my high school course, you know. I'm better at this than at Latin," she admitted with a smile. "Tell me what happened in the woods after I got scragged and Mike carted me up here?"

"Who's Mike?"

"I'll tell you about him in a minute. Get along with your story first."

"Not much of a story. I didn't last long enough to make it interesting."

"Tell me about it, anyway."

"Well--I heard you yell and half turned when Tony and another lad jumped me. You know what happened to Tony--"

"Yes, but the shot right afterward? Oh, Bill, I was scared silly they'd killed you! Whose gun *was* that?»

"Mine. I'd got my gat loose by that time and drilled him through the shoulder. It turned out later that he tripped over a log when he fell, came down with his leg under him and snapped the bone. When I learned the horrid truth, I wept!"

"I'll bet you did! Couldn't you break away then?"

"I could not. Several others had joined the rough-house by that time. For a while--not very long--we played a lively little game of tag, blind-man's-buff, post office, dilly-dilly-come-and-be-killed, with me as dilly, until another chap jumped out of a Ford on to the middle of my back and rubbed my face in the cool, wet soil! At that bright moment old Limpy, they sometimes call "Doctor", clinched these handcuffs on my wrists and read me a lecture on the error of my ways.

"He's a physician when he isn't bank-robbing, I think. Anyway, the gang call him 'Doctor.' He seems to be running the show. Not such a bad lad if he could be made over again. Tony, you must know, has developed an almost uncontrollable penchant for sheathing his pigsticker in my carcass once more. Strangely enough, I can't see it Tony's way. And fortunately for me, neither can the Doctor! Now, young lady, if you're finished squeezing cold water into my sore eye, I'll sing the doxology!"

Mary Eliska giggled. "Aren't you funny! I don't believe more than half of that tale is true. I'll wager things were a whole lot worse than you've painted them, sir!"

"Well, you've proved to be a good little guesser quite often--what I'm interested in is what happened to you."

Mary Eliska told him.

"Nice work!" Bill complimented her as she finished talking. "I know a few jiu jitsu holds, but you must be a wonder at it. It's too bad Staten Island Sadie had to butt in and spoil your show. The more I see of that lady, the less I like her. She was in the woods when the gang jumped us--barged off in a huff later, because the Doc wouldn't let her croak me then and there. She's a nice little playmate. Every one of this gang is a cold-blooded thug--but she's a fiend! But, to tell the honest truth, it's our lame friend who worries me most."

"Yes," agreed Mary Eliska. "That suave manner of his gives me the creeps!"

"So sorry--" purred the Doctor's voice directly behind them. "But if I were in your position, my young friends, I should undoubtedly be worried about me, too."

Bill and Mary Eliska swung round to see him coming toward them. In his hand he carried a small, black bag.

"How is our invalid, nurse?" he inquired, feigning ignorance of their startled surprise, and placing his satchel on the table. "Those who live by the sword--but you are familiar with the quotation, I'm sure?"

Opening the bag, he produced bandages, adhesive tape, a pair of surgical scissors and a large tube of salve.

"Lay these out, so I can reach them easily, please," he ordered as he unwrapped the temporary bandage Mary Eliska had bound about Bill's leg.

"Ah! I see you have cleansed the wound, but it is safer to be more thorough. Hand me one of the swabs you will find wrapped in cellophane in the bag, please. Strange how the professional spirit will dominate--even though the patient's life may not be a long one!" He glanced smilingly at Mary Eliska.

"Don't tell me the knife was poisoned?" she cried in horror.

"Hardly anything so melodramatic, my dear. You don't quite grasp my meaning."

"He means," said Bill grimly, "that after he has had the fun of patching me up, I'm to be taken for a ride. But don't let him bluff you. He's only trying to scare us."

"Too much knowledge is dangerous at times--entirely too dangerous," returned the lame man. "Hand me another swab, nurse. But you put it rather crudely, young man--and I am perfectly in earnest, I assure you."

"Oh, you couldn't do *that!*" Mary Eliska blenched and her hand shook as she passed him the swab.

"Well, you see, it is not entirely up to me," he replied, carefully cleaning the wound. "The matter of your friend's future, shall I say?--as well as your own, will have to be put to vote presently. Of course, if Miss Martinelli has her way--but why anticipate the unpleasant?"

To Mary Eliska's surprise, Bill chuckled.

"They hang in this state, for murder," he remarked coolly. "It's a nasty death, I've heard. What's more, Doctor, a man of your mentality does not deliberately stick his head into a noose!"

"Perhaps not, my young friend. But you forget that in order to prove murder, there must be a body--or bodies, as the case may be." The Doctor looked up at Bill and smiled again.

Chapter 1.15
STATEN ISLAND SADIE HAS HER WAY

"I believe that I have done all that is necessary," said the Doctor after a few minutes--"and I think the patient will be more comfortable now." Then, with a sardonic gleam in his eye, he added, "Also, I have enjoyed our conversation very much!"

He walked to the sink where he washed his hands and dried them carefully on a clean towel. "And so, if you young people are quite ready, we'll adjourn for that voting contest I mentioned a little while ago." He motioned them to precede him, and brought up the rear with his bag as Mary Eliska helped Bill limp into the front room.

Politely, the Doctor placed chairs for them and bade them be seated. Never once had this black-eyed little man's manner betokened anything but courteous consideration. But his suavity troubled Mary Eliska far more than bluster would have done. She sensed the venom behind his smooth tones, the purring growl of the tiger before it springs.

Mary Eliska knew she was losing her nerve. But she looked at Bill and smiled bravely as they sat down.

Bill smiled back at her then shifted his glance with hers to the table, where the members of the gang were seated. The little Doctor headed the board, the others at the side facing the room. Next to the lame man sat the red-haired girl; then came Mike, Tony, who was nursing his jaw, Johnny, the man who had fetched the wheelbarrow, and another whom Mary Eliska had not seen before. Tony, she fancied, had played the part of chauffeur at the bank.

Then Bill broke into the low-voiced conversation that was going on at the table.

"How about unlocking these handcuffs, Doctor?"

The Doctor shook his head. "No, no, my young friend. Even with your honorable wounds of combat, you are far too active for us to take any chances."

"But what could I do? You are six to one, counting Miss Martinelli--and all armed," insisted Bill. "These things are darned uncomfortable."

Tony shot him a deadly glance. "I'm glad to hear it," he muttered through clenched teeth. "You'll be a lot more uncomfortable by the time I finish with you."

"Shut up, you two!" snapped Sadie. "Now, Dad," she went on in a different tone, addressing the Doctor, "let's finish this business. We can't sit here gabbing all night."

"That's what I say!" This from Johnny. "Bump off the pair of 'em--they know too much. Then we can divvy up and be on our way!"

"You forget that it is our custom to put such matters to vote," interposed the Doctor. "Two of our company are upstairs and unable to attend. Also, another member is expected at any time now. Without his help our little *coup* would have been extremely difficult.»

"Chuck and Pete are too ill to vote," argued Miss Martinelli. "As for Thatcher Allen--that sap is scared to death! I doubt if he shows up at all."

"Oh, he wants his share," declared the Doctor. "He'll come. We shall give him five minutes--and then continue our business."

He tapped a cigarette on the back of his gold case, struck a match and lounged back in his chair, inhaling the aromatic smoke with evident enjoyment.

Mary Eliska's eyes met Bill's in astonishment.

He smiled but said nothing.

It was interesting enough that Sadie should turn out to be the Doctor's daughter. But the news that Thatcher Allen, Mary Eliska's father's trusted lieutenant at the bank, was mixed up in this robbery was simply dumfounding to Mary Eliska. That was how things had been made easy for the gang--that was how they knew just when Mrs. Hamberfield's necklace would be in her deposit box. And another thing--Thatcher Allen' home was on the Marvin Ridge Road, just beyond the Mayo place where the Pen and Pencil Club were to meet! The Doctor had been coming from the Thatcher Allen' house when she and Bill had met his car. And that explained the absence of road oil on the Packard's tires!

Johnny's voice interrupted her train of thought.

"How are we goin' to make our getaway tonight with them two lads down and out upstairs?" he grumbled. "Our plan was to separate after we'd divvied up the loot--but them fellers can't be moved."

"Supposing you stay and look after them--" derided Sadie. "When we've made the divvy, as you call it, this bunch breaks up for the time being. We all go our own sweet ways. It's a case of each for himself. If you want to stick here and nurse those boobs upstairs, nobody's going to stop you."

"Not me! I don't know nothin' about--"

"Then keep your mouth shut. Whatever we do, we'll decide later on. How about the time, Dad?"

"Time's up," decided the Doctor with a glance at his watch. "We'll wait no longer for Mr. Thatcher Allen. Now, concerning our two young friends who were so unwise as to join us tonight--what is your pleasure?"

"Bump them off, of course, as Johnny so prettily puts it," yawned Sadie languidly. "I'll attend to the job, if the rest of you are squeamish."

"We will put it to vote," announced the Doctor. "Those in favor will raise their right hands and say 'aye'."

Five hands, including his own, sprang into the air.

"Contraries, 'no'."

"*No*," said Mike in a firm voice, holding up his right hand.

"The ayes have it," declared the Doctor dispassionately.

"What's the matter with you, Mike?" sneered Sadie. "Got a crush on the girl?"

"No," retorted Mike. "Just trying to stop you from making an even bigger fool of yourself than you are usually!"

"I'm afraid you'll have to pipe down, Mike." The Doctor's eyes gleamed balefully. "Sentence has been passed on Mary Eliska and Mr. Bolton--and that is all there is to it."

"That's where you're dead wrong."

"What do you mean? Don't you realize that these two know too much about us to permit them to live?"

"Have I said they didn't? But Sadie should not be allowed to be their executioner."

"Oh--aren't you considerate!" Sadie's tone was pregnant with sarcasm. "Want the job yourself?"

"Not particularly--none of us should do it."

"Who then, may I ask?"

"Why, Thatcher Allen, of course."

"You're crazy! He hasn't the nerve."

"Maybe not--make him do it anyway."

It was the lame man's turn to take a hand. "And why should Thatcher Allen be so entrusted?"

"To keep his mouth shut."

"I'm afraid I don't understand you."

"And I didn't think you could be so dense. Look here, Doctor. I haven't been one of your crowd long, but I'd never have joined up at all if I'd known I was getting in with such a bunch of nitwits!"

"You are forgetting yourself, I think," the Doctor's tone was cutting.

"No. I ain't. Listen--Thatcher Allen only came into this because he was up against it proper. How you found out he had speculated, first with his own money and then with the bank's, is none of my affair. What I do know is that when Wall Street put him into a tight place, you put up the extra margin with his brokers upon an assurance from him that he would do--just what he's done!"

"You are very well informed, Mike. And what then?"

"Just this: the bank has been robbed, but it was a crude job at best. Why the bulls haven't fastened on Thatcher Allen already on account of that time-lock business, is beyond me. Then, for once in your long and successful career, you were careless, Doctor. You allowed your paternal feeling to out-weigh your natural caution. The result is that the cops got Sadie's fingerprints and a description of you, of her and of Tony. I am simply bringing all this up to show you that we are not out of the mess yet--not by a long shot."

"In other words, you think we have a fifty-fifty chance with the police?"

"Better than that, perhaps. I think, though, that if we do get nailed, we should stop Thatcher Allen from blabbing--and stop him effectually."

"I see," said Sadie. "Let him bump off the pair over there--then take him for a ride?"

"Be still, carissima!" Doctor Martinelli was interested. "I see what Mike is driving at. He fears that if things should by chance go wrongly, Thatcher Allen would try to save his precious skin by turning state's evidence. And that if he were forced to--er--place these two young people where they will do the least harm, Mr. Thatcher Allen will not be in a position himself to turn state's evidence--that is, of course, should it become necessary. That is your reason for not voting with the rest of us?"

"It is, Doctor. Do you wish to vote on it again?"

"Not necessarily. I consider your plan adequate."

"But why make the biggest mistake--of murdering us?" Bill entered the conversation.

Mary Eliska leaned toward him. "It's no use, Bill," she whispered steadily. "They've made up their minds--and you heard what the Doctor said in the other room!"

Bill did not attempt to reply, for Doctor Martinelli was speaking again.

"And why, in your opinion, are we making a mistake in putting you and Mary Eliska out of the running?" he inquired affably. "Take your time, young man, answer carefully. We are in no hurry--until Thatcher Allen arrives."

"He won't arrive," rejoined Bill. "The authorities have got him by this time."

"Bluff!" shot out Sadie and turned fiercely on her father. "What's the use of all this?" she cried. "It makes me sick. Why do you stand for it?"

"Because he knows Bill *isn't* bluffing!» Mary Eliska›s raised voice silenced the woman. «We knew that you had been visiting Thatcher Allen this evening, Doctor. And we passed word to the police on our way through New Canaan. The only reason you weren›t arrested on the way up is because they want to catch the whole gang together. If you hadn›t shown up here, the rest of your people might have got wise and left before the police could make arrangements to surround the place.»

"But, you see, my dear," said the Doctor, "I wasn't visiting Mr. Thatcher Allen this evening. I had just motored up from the Post Road, and--ah--points east, when I ran into you and your friend Bill." Mary Eliska laughed. "Oh, no, you hadn't, Doctor. The road beyond Thatcher Allen' place was freshly oiled. There was no sign of oil on your car."

"She got you that time, Doc!" exclaimed Mike. "D'you mind saying why you were foolish enough to drop in on Thatcher Allen and put us up a tree this way?"

Doctor Martinelli was irritated. "Because the safest place to park that loot was in Thatcher Allen' house," he snapped, "and as he refused to bring it up here himself, I had to fetch it."

"Then all I can say is that you and Sadie have made a pretty mess of things."

"Is that so?" retorted the red-haired young woman. "Was it *my* fault that that fellow over there landed his plane on the lake? That was before the New Canaan deal. He had nothing at all to go on then!»

"That's where you're wrong," broke in Bill. "Your hair and those beach pajamas make a combination not easily forgotten. You wore them once too often, Miss Martinelli."

"And you seem to forget," added Mary Eliska, "that you've been finger-printed both in this country and in England. The police know all about you and your father and Tony. They probably have the records of the rest of your gang. If anything happens to Bill or me, you are bound to pay the penalty."

"Say, Doc!" Johnny's excited voice sounded shrilly, "I don't like this--not a little bit I don't. Tie up that pair and let's vamoose. Them cops is likely to be here any minute. I'm tired of all this fool talk. Come on--this place is gettin' too hot fer me!"

Mike got to his feet. "I don't stir from this place until I get my share of the divvy," he declared firmly. "What's the matter with you, Johnny? If Doc lights out with the bag full of kale, it ain't likely the rest of us will ever get what's coming to us."

"But I can't afford to get pinched--" Johnny faltered. "Not after that Jersey City job, I can't. It means the hot seat for me." The gangster shivered and moistened his lips.

"It is my candid opinion that you are all exciting yourselves unnecessarily." The Doctor's voice betrayed no emotion whatsoever. "Mary Eliska and Mr. Bolton are clever young people--but not quite clever enough. They're throwing a gigantic bluff to save their lives. The police won't be here tonight. Why? Simply because if they knew anything about this house, we would have been raided long before this. Those two haven't told the police or anyone else a thing about it. They wanted to pull off their job all by themselves!"

"And how, may I ask, do you figure that?" Bill endeavored to make his tone sarcastic. "For this reason: if you had reported what you had learned--and guessed--the authorities would never have permitted you to come here tonight. And this proves it!"

There was a light step on the porch and Thatcher Allen came in through the open door.

Chapter 1.16
WHAT HAPPENED IN THE WINE CELLAR

"Sorry to be so late," greeted the bank's cashier. "My car broke down. I've had to walk five miles, at least--" He broke off, catching sight of Mary Eliska and Bill for the first time.

"Hello!" he exclaimed, "what are you two doing here?"

"They are waiting for you to bump them off," replied Sadie with a sneer.

"Why, what do you mean?" Thatcher Allen gazed breathlessly around the room.

"Just what I said. You are going to stop their mouths for good--and do it right now. We've been shilly-shallying over this business long enough!"

Thatcher Allen' glance took in the others seated at the table.

"Has she gone nuts?" he asked.

"We have decided that you are to do what my daughter has just mentioned," said the Doctor smoothly.

"And I," retorted Thatcher Allen angrily, "tell you here and now that I will be no party to murder!"

Sadie drew her revolver.

"Well--if he won't, I will!" she began when her wrist was caught in a grip of steel, then twisted up and backward.

"Drop it, little one--drop it--or I'll break your arm," said Mike.

Sadie shrieked with pain, but she dropped her revolver and Mike pocketed it.

"I'll get you for that!" she screamed.

Her father leaned forward in his chair. "Shut up, you idiot!" he said coldly and deliberately slapped her across the mouth with his open hand. "We've had enough from you for one evening. Mike was perfectly right to stop you. Thatcher Allen is going to do this job, and you know *why* he is going to do it. I'll have no more argument from you. Keep still now, until you have my permission to speak.»

"But I tell you I'll have nothing to do with it," repeated Thatcher Allen, and attempted to light with trembling fingers the half-burned cigar he was chewing.

Doctor Martinelli swung around in his chair. "You'll do as you're told," he said through clenched teeth. "A little persuasion of the kind I have in mind has been known to make braver men than you change their opinions, Thatcher Allen!" He glared at the cashier, who dropped his eyes--and the cigar--at one and the same moment.

"That's the way, Doc," applauded Mike, getting to his feet. "We've been sittin' round this table so long we're all getting stale. What we need's a little excitement."

He pointed to Mary Eliska and Bill.

"I'll take these two down stairs and stick them in the old wine cellar. They'll keep fine and dandy down there. Later, when Mr. Thatcher Allen sees reason he can run down and finish them off. While I'm gone, Johnny, you beat it out to the woodshed and fetch in a length of garden hose." He guffawed--"I guess you know that trick--the bulls have made it pretty popular?"

The lame man smiled and nodded. "O.K. Doc?"

"It's a good plan, Mike. Go ahead with it."

Mike took a flashlight from his pocket and beckoned to the prisoners.

Sadie pushed back her chair and jumped up. "Tie that girl or she'll get away!" she ordered.

"Pipe down!" thundered the gangster and there was an ugly gleam in his eyes as he glared at her. "Give me any more of your lip, Sadie, and you'll take a trip downstairs yourself. Some day when you ain't got a thing to do fer a couple of weeks, try gettin' outa that place with the door locked. Run along now--murder yourself, if you have to--you red-headed bag of hot wind!"

He turned his back on the furious woman and motioned Bill and Mary Eliska to walk before him into the kitchen.

"Well, of all the nerve--" Mary Eliska heard Sadie cry sharply as Thatcher Allen broke in with--"Look here, Doctor Martinelli, do you really mean to--"

Mike shut the door, cutting the argument in the front room to a mere mumble of voices.

"Down those stairs to the right and then straight ahead, you two," he directed, pointing the way with his flashlight--"No tricks, either, unless you want your buddie hurt worse than he is now, Miss Wildcat!"

Mary Eliska, with her arm about Bill's shoulders, stopped at the head of the cellar stairs.

"I think you told me you were getting two thousand dollars for your share in the New Canaan robbery," she murmured.

"That's right--a coupla grand," he acknowledged. "Not much, but when I made the deal, I wasn't as strong with Doc as I am now."

"If you let us go, my father will pay you ten thousand!"

"Nothing doing!"

"And I promise you he'll use his influence in your behalf, as well. It seems to me a mighty easy way to make a lot of money--"

Mike shrugged his shoulders.

"Maybe it is," he admitted. "But then you see, I've never double-crossed a pal yet, and I'm not going to start at this late day. Cut the chatter now--there's nothing doing."

"You won't regret it, Mike."

The door behind them opened slowly, revealing Doctor Martinelli's slight figure.

"My judgment of human nature is rarely at fault," the little man went on rather pompously. "I believed I could trust you--now I know it. There's a full share coming to you on this deal, Mike. Cut along now, but hurry back. As soon as you've locked them up, I'll need your help with Thatcher Allen."

The door closed once more and Mike waved toward the gaping black of the cellar stairs.

"You heard what Doc said--down you go!"

"Over there to the left," he directed when his two prisoners reached the bottom and Mary Eliska helped Billy to hobble across the damp, earthen floor, in the shifting rays of Mike's torch.

Ahead in the wall of native stone that formed the foundation of the house, they could see a door of heavy wood, at least six inches thick. Mike pushed it fully open. For a moment Mary Eliska thought of jumping him, but now she saw he carried a revolver in his free hand.

"In you go!" he said roughly, elbowing them over the threshold. But instead of locking them in, he stepped over the sill and gently pulled the door shut behind him.

Bill, anticipating the end, stepped between Mary Eliska and their captor.

"Let her go, Mike. Her father and mine will give you anything you ask. Shoot me if you must--but let her go. Use two shots, and the others will think--tell them--"

"Quiet, please," whispered Mike fiercely, and Mary Eliska started, for he spoke now with the voice of a well-bred Englishman.

"Neither of you will be shot tonight, if you do as I tell you. Here--take this automatic, Mary Eliska. And listen carefully, both of you. I've only a minute. You'll find a few useful articles under the pile of sacking in that far corner," he went on, pointing into the gloom behind them. "Then, get out of the window as quickly as you can--the bars are sawn through. Your car is still parked where you left it. Go straight home. That, I think, will be all at present."

Bill and Mary Eliska stared at him in wide-eyed amazement.

"Who are you, anyway?" the girl whispered, peering up at him.

"To ease your minds," he smiled, "I'm not exactly what I pretend to be. And I want to apologize to you, Mary Eliska, for the exceedingly crude game I was forced to play with you. The Doctor had his suspicions of me, until just a few moments ago, I believe, and he has had us watched ever since I brought you here. But now he has proved his judgment to be sound--" he chuckled to himself--"and has ceased his strict surveillance."

He paused a moment then went on, more seriously. "My name is Michael Conway. I am a detective-inspector in the Criminal Investigation Department of New Scotland Yard. I've trailed certain members of the Martinelli gang all the way from London. My plans seem to have miscarried this evening; otherwise, you need not have been put to all this inconvenience. Remember that the house has ears, and be as quiet as possible. Good night--and good luck!"

The door swung shut behind him. They heard him turn the key in the lock and he was gone.

"Gee Whiz!" muttered Bill, "and I thought--"

"Sh--Bill!" cautioned Mary Eliska. "Never mind now. Stand where you are, or you'll break your neck in this darkness."

Her voice came from farther off now. He knew she was feeling her way across the room toward the corner.

Presently a light appeared and she spoke again.

"I've found the things," she told Bill. "Besides this flash, there's another automatic, a small ax, and a chisel."

"Thank heaven for that," said Bill. "Now I've a chance of getting these handcuffs off!"

"But we can't do it in here," Mary Eliska objected. "Remember what Mike said about making a noise. We'll have to wait 'til we get outside. There's the window. It's going to be a tight squeeze."

Her light showed them they were standing in a narrow room, walled like the cellar in native stone. Along the sides, piled one on top of the other were wine casks, which proved to be empty. The damp air was heavy with the fumes of evaporating lees. High to one side was a small barred window.

"Lean against this barrel, so it won't slip," whispered Mary Eliska, and clambered up to the window. "Yes, the bars are loose!"

She removed the short lengths of rusty iron from the open frame and carefully laid them on the ground outside.

"Now the paraphernalia--" She placed ax, chisel and revolver beside the bars on the grass and descended to Bill's side.

"Guess I'll have to go first," observed Bill. "We'll never make it, otherwise. Give me a boost, will you?"

They were both breathless and nearly exhausted by the time Bill had been pushed up and out of the window. Mary Eliska was so tired it took every ounce of her waning strength to drag herself through the narrow aperture after him. They rested for some minutes in the long, dewy grass, gathering strength and courage for the waiting ordeal.

As soon as they began to move away from the house, Mary Eliska realized that Bill was near collapse. Even with her supporting arm, he lurched and stumbled through the tangled undergrowth.

"It's that old hole in my leg," he grumbled in answer to her question. "It's opened up again--been bleeding pretty freely. You'd better leave me here."

He sank wearily to the ground behind a cluster of elder bushes, about two hundred yards from the house, the weight of his body pulling Mary Eliska to her knees beside him.

"I'll do nothing of the kind!" she whispered fiercely.

"But you must--I can't go any further," his voice trailed off weakly.

With a quick movement she felt for his wound in the darkness and tightened the bandage.

"We'll wait here 'til you're strong enough to walk, that's all. If I try to run the car up here, they'll hear it from the house. There's no use to try to cut off your handcuffs, either. The least sound will bring that gang down on us."

"Not the car--" he mumbled. "The amphibian--beat it for the Loening--and bring help."

Mary Eliska bit her lip. With Bill delirious there was nothing she could do but remain with him.

"That's all right," she said, trying to calm him--"We'll stay here 'til you feel stronger, Bill. Then I'll help you down to the car."

Bill had been lying on his side, his head pillowed on her knees. Now he wriggled into a sitting position.

"I'm pretty well all in," he admitted, "but I'm not off my head--not yet--if that's what you're thinking.--Didn't I tell you about the amphibian?"

"You certainly did not----" Mary Eliska's tone was relieved, yet excited.

"Well, here's the dope, then. She's parked in the next valley--over that hill behind the house. You'll find her under the trees at the edge of a wood lot. I flew up here several nights ago. Wanted a means of quick getaway, if it became necessary. Frank met me over there and drove me home. It's a rotten landing place. You'll find it worse for the take off. You'll be taking an awful chance to do it."

Mary Eliska got to her feet. "You certainly are the one and only life-saver," she breathed joyfully. "Every time we get really up against it--you've a plane up your sleeve or something. Don't worry--I'll fly it all right!"

"Hop it for Danbury, then. When you get there, land in the fair grounds. Phone the police and tell them to run down in a car and that you'll fly them back here. You can land on the lake. The bus has a searchlight--"

He broke off as the sharp detonation of an automatic came from the direction of the house. This was followed by shouts and the sound of a scuffle. Presently all was quiet once more.

"Something's up!" said Mary Eliska. Bill nodded gravely. "I wonder if they haven't found we're not in the wine cellar--if they've charged Mike Conway with our escape?"

"Well, I'm going over to see."

"No, you're not--I'll go."

But by the time Bill had struggled to his feet, Mary Eliska had run to the house and was peering between the shutters of the side window. She stood there for a moment, then ran back to him.

"The Doctor has been shot," she gasped. "Not badly hurt, I think--evidently took it in the shoulder. But they've got Mike. He's tied hand and foot and bound to a chair!"

"That's bad," said Bill slowly.

"It's awful! They'll surely shoot him before I can get the police here!" Bill hobbled back toward the shelter of the bushes with Mary Eliska's arm about his waist. "Some break!" he said disgustedly, as he sank to the ground. "I'm out of the running and you can't hold up that bunch single handed--"

"I can try it though, Bill."

"Not if I have anything to say, Mary Eliska, you won't. There are too many of 'em--it's impossible. But what we're going to do now, I haven't the slightest idea!"

Chapter 1.17
THE LOENING

"One thing is clear--" said Mary Eliska firmly--"and that is, we can't let Michael Conway be butchered by that band of cut-throats. He saved our lives--we've got to save his."

Bill, his head in his hands, did not reply.

"If you were only in better shape so I could get those handcuffs off--and if there weren't so many of them in the house," she went on, speaking her thoughts aloud, "one of us might be able to hold them up from the window while the other went round through the door and took their guns away. But we can't afford to wait 'til you can walk alone and I can free your hands. What's to become of Mr. Conway, in the meantime? Oh, Bill, you're generally so fertile with ideas--*can't* you think of anything?»

Bill lay motionless, and still did not answer.

Mary Eliska stooped over him.

"Bill! Bill!" she called in a tense whisper. Then, daring greatly, she flashed her light on his face, held it there for an instant, then snapped it off.

"Down and out, poor chap," was her summing up after a glimpse of his closed eyes and dead white features. "Loss of blood, probably. He'll come around after a while--but when?"

Her heart sank. For several minutes she knelt beside his quiet form, lost in thought. Then she began to act.

"Sorry, Bill, old thing, but I've got to leave you. It's the only way." Her murmured tones were muffled by the sweater she pulled over her head. Stripping free her arms, she rolled it in a ball and placed the soft pillow beneath Bill's head. She gave him a little pat, then started off toward the hill back of the house.

Mary Eliska crossed the field beyond the farm's overgrown orchard in darkness. It was not until she reached the woods at the foot of the hill that she dared to snap on her flashlight.

Even with its help the climb was no sinecure. The hillside, steep as a church roof and densely wooded, was, moreover, thick with underbrush, which hindered her progress. Rocky outcroppings and huge boulders made frequent detours necessary.

By the time she struggled to the top she was winded and pretty well done up. Her vitality had suffered considerably from strain and worry and violent exercise during the course of the evening. She was quite ready to drop down and have a good cry, and to admit to herself right then that she was beaten. Only the knowledge that a life, possibly two, hung upon her efforts, kept her going. Stopping only long enough to tie a broken shoelace, she hurried over the crest of the hill and plunged down the farther side.

Here, her progress became even more difficult, for she floundered into a berry patch whose thorns tore her clothing and badly scratched her face and hands. Determinedly, she pushed her way through, gritting her teeth in pain.

Presently, after several bad falls over hidden rocks and tree stumps, she found herself on a narrow, grass-grown wood road at the foot of the hill. So far as she could see, the trail wound along the middle of the valley. But she hadn't the faintest idea in which direction lay the field (Bill had called it a wood lot) where the *Loening* was hidden.

Mary Eliska was totally at a loss. *Why* hadn't she taken more precise directions before tramping over here? This trail *must* lead to the wood lot or near it. Bill said Frank had driven there in the car....

"What a fool I am!" she exclaimed suddenly to the night at large and pointed her flashlight toward the ground at her feet.

There were the tire marks of a car, plain enough. Brewster and Danbury lay far to the left beyond the mouth of this valley which paralleled that of the gang's headquarters. Therefore, Bill's car must have come up the trail from the left. The tracks kept on up the road to her left--the wood lot must be in that direction.

As she trudged on, watching carefully for any deviation of the tire marks, she forgot her weariness for the time being. The winding road ended and she saw an open space ahead. It must be the wood lot. Hadn't Bill said it was the only possible landing place in the valley!

Mary Eliska hurried across the field, through a tangle of knee-high grasses and wild flowers. She pointed her light higher now and tried to pierce the black of the night for a glimpse of the airplane. Then she saw it parked at the forest's edge, directly ahead, and sprang forward with a delighted cry.

As she came close, she saw that it faced the open lot, and silently thanked Bill for his foresight. With a plane the size of the amphibian it would have been impossible to swing around the tail unassisted.

Her preparations for this flight would probably not have met with her instructor's approval. But knowing that time was more important than detail, she cut them to a minimum.

A quick glance at the retractable landing gear sufficed to satisfy her that the wheels were securely blocked. Then she sprang aboard and gave the engine a short ground test. It was acting splendidly and she shut it off almost directly.

A hurried trip aft to the cabin and she came back to the pilot's cockpit, dragging the airplane's machine gun, which, after some trouble, she managed to set up on its tripod which she fastened to cleats in the decking.

Certain now that the gun was secure, she adjusted the ammunition belt as Bill had instructed her. Then she raced aft again and overside. When she returned, she brought the wheel blocks with her. These she dropped in the cabin, saw to it that the door was properly fastened, then took her place at the controls forward.

The night was overcast and starless; the ceiling unusually low, and so far as she could judge there was not the slightest breath of wind. She switched on the plane's searchlight and started the engine.

The trees at the far end of the wood lot were uncomfortably near and high. Yet Bill had judged a takeoff from such a place to be possible, or he would never have parked there.

The big Loening was moving now--rolling drunkenly over the rough ground, yet gaining speed with every foot. She widened her throttle, steadily, fully--at the same time pushing the stick well forward. Then as the amphibian gained still more speed and she felt the tail lift clear, she eased the stick steadily back to neutral.

They were racing over the field now. She gave the elevators a slight upward pressure. The wheels lifted clear, but the trees at the edge of the lot were perilously near. She knew that when a plane leaves the ground its speed is not far above stalling point. And with these trees so close, to stall now would precipitate a bad crash--and failure.

Mary Eliska, therefore, kept the nose level for an instant or two, a dangerously short instant, she feared. Back came her stick again. The plane was climbing at last but at a frightfully precipitous angle. Would they make it? Would the throbbing engine continue to function under the unaccustomed strain?

Mary Eliska bit her lip. She eased off slightly as the motor coughed; but pulled the stick back almost immediately.

They were abreast the treetops now.--They were over. But with a margin so small that Mary Eliska was certain the wheels had brushed the branches.

She eased their angle of ascent, but still continued to climb. Then when she was sure they were well above the crest of the hill, she leveled off and banked to the left.

Once more she leveled off and turned on the electrical mechanism which raised the plane's landing gear.

Below her she could dimly make out the gangster's farmhouse, the lake and the stretch of ground between them. She closed her throttle, pushing the stick forward as she did so, and at the same time applied right aileron and hard right rudder.

As the plane shot downward she neutralized the elevators. Then did likewise with her ailerons as the proper bank was reached. Left aileron and hard left rudder were next applied until the wings became laterally level. Having completed a beautiful half spiral, Mary Eliska landed the amphibian on the little lake.

Her next move was an unusual one, but on it depended the success or failure of her plan.

With the airplane headed toward the lake's low shore beyond which lay the farmhouse, she turned the switch which propelled the retractable landing gear downward and into the water. Then she opened the throttle for the last time.

There came a bump and a jar. The tail tilted to a dangerous angle as the plane's wheels struck the shallows. Would they mire in the soft ground at the lake's edge she wondered, and cause the big bus to nose over and crash? But no--the plane, after a sickening wrench, rolled free. It glided over the sandy bank and on to the grass.

Shutting off her engine, Mary Eliska permitted her amphibian steed to come to a stop at the porch steps, its ugly snout poked almost up to the open doorway of the house.

Mary Eliska had been too busy guiding her bus to pay any attention to the reception accorded her arrival. A shot or two had been fired from the porch and she had caught a glimpse of dark figures silhouetted against the open doorway.

But now, as the slowing wheels struck the steps, the porch was empty. The way was clear for Mike's release. Together they would find Bill and make a clean getaway in the amphibian. What did it matter if the gang made their escape? Her life and the lives of her two friends were all that counted now.

To speed the departing company she turned the Browning into action and sent half a belt of bullets whipping through the door. But Mary Eliska aimed high. She had no desire to play the part of executioner.

From her place in the cockpit she got a good view of the front room. Mike, the Scotland Yard detective, still sat bound to his chair, but the others were streaking for the back of the house. She could see them tugging at the doors, which for some reason, seemed to give them difficulty of exit. Huddled at the far end of the room, they clamored and struggled to get out of range.

Mary Eliska stopped firing and Bill Bolton hobbled up the porch steps.

"Jumping Jupiter! girl, you're a wonder!" he applauded. "Hold the Browning on 'em. They can't get away. I locked those doors from the outside. Crawled through the wine cellar window to do it," he panted. "Thought it might embarrass them some--but this stunt of yours makes it perfect."

He took a step forward and raised his voice.

"Stick 'em up!" he cried. "Stick 'em up--every one of you--that's better. Now line up, facing the back wall--and remember--just one bad break is all Mary Eliska wants to rip off another belt--aimed right, this time--" he added significantly.

As the gangsters scrambled to obey his orders, Bill walked into the room and Mary Eliska saw that his wrists were still handcuffed behind his back.

"Who's got the handcuff key, Mr. Conway?" he inquired.

"Johnny, I believe," returned Mike quietly.

"Johnny, have you the key?" This from Bill.

"Y-yes, I got it." "Got a gun?" "N-no, sir, it's on the table."

"I'll take your word for it. Throw the key over your shoulder, then stick up your hands again."

Johnny complied with these demands, and Bill picked up the key by sitting on the floor and worming over to where it lay.

"Think you can turn this with your teeth, Mr. Scotland Yard?"

Mike nodded. Bill swung round and lifted his hands as high as his bonds permitted. The detective lowered his head and got his teeth on the key. A moment later there sounded a slight snap--and Bill was free. "Good job!" He worked his cramped shoulders. "That certainly is a relief!"

He limped to the table, snatched a knife and a couple of seconds later Mike was on his feet. Without more ado they turned to, and roped the gangsters one by one.

Mary Eliska got down from the plane and came into the room. "Who's going to stand guard while the plane goes for the police?"

"Nobody," was Bill's answer. "We'll pile the bunch in the bus and take them to New Canaan ourselves. Gosh, there'll be some big time in the town tonight, when we arrive!"

"This morning, you mean," yawned Mary Eliska. "It's getting light. And you two may not know it, but I could go to sleep standing up--and right now!"

"Brace up, kid! You're some aviatrix, even though I did train you!"

"I'll second that--" beamed Mr. Michael Conway, grasping her hand. "I had a splendid view through the doorway--and when that big bus hurled itself out of the water like a hippo--and began to charge the house, I--"But Mary Eliska interrupted him with a shake of her head and an involuntary glance at Bill. "All I did was to take some awful chances with Bill's property, Mr. Conway."

"Ah--incidentally--saving my life, and making the capture of this gang possible?" smiled the detective. "You're a modest young lady, indeed. But I suppose we'd better be getting along--" and with a wave of his hand, he added, "it may interest you to know that the loot is in that kit bag under the table."

"O.K. We'll attend to that," said Bill. Then turning to Mary Eliska--"I'll say you took some chances, young woman! How about getting a plane of your own to fool with from now on?"

"Oh, Bill! Do you think Daddy will let me?"

"I know he will." Bill was serious now. "After what you've done tonight, you've certainly won your wings!"

CHAPTER 2

The Mystery Plane

Chapter 2.1
AT THE BEACH CLUB

"Here he comes again, Mary Eliska!" Liam McAdams balanced on the edge of the beach club float and pointed upward toward the approaching airplane. Mary Eliska bobbed up beside the raft, blew the water from her nose and reached a long-tanned arm for the young man's ankle.

"Here *you* come into the drink, you mean!" she gurgled.

Liam McAdams yelped, lost balance, and recovering desperately, dived over her head. His departure rocked the float, so that Sean Hall's lanky figure poised on the diving board, lurched and fell awkwardly into the water.

Jax Gray, hugging her damp knees on the middle of the float, shrieked her approval of this double exploit.

"Swell work, Mary Eliska!" she laughed as that young lady pulled herself aboard. "You'll catch it in a minute though!"

Mary Eliska stood up. Her scarlet bathing cap flamed against the ash blue sky and her wet suit clung to her slender form like a sheath of black lacquer. "Maybe!" Then, in quite a different tone: "Goodness, Jax Gray, he's missing!"

Jax Gray sprang to her feet. "You're crazy—" she retorted as she caught sight of Sean Hall and Liam McAdams knifing their way back to the float. "Why'd you try to scare me? Those boys are all right."

But Mary Eliska was staring skyward.

"Not the boys! I mean the plane, Jax Gray. Over there beyond the club house. His engine's missing. Bet you an ice cream cone he'll have to land!"

"No, you won't," Jax Gray flashed back. "I don't know a thing about airplanes, and I'll take your word for it. Ooh, Mary Eliska—do you think he'll hit the roof?"

"Oh, he's all right—"

"Yes, he's over the roof now—but *look*!" Jax Gray's voice rose to a shriek. "He's aiming the plane straight for us—it'll hit this float—"

The last word was no more than a gurgle. Jax Gray had dived overside.

Mary Eliska did not trouble to turn her head. With her bare feet firmly planted on the timbers, her straight body balanced easily to the float's gentle rocking, she gazed interestedly at the big amphibian sweeping down toward her.

On came the plane, losing altitude with every split second, and sailed over her head a bare thirty feet above the water. Then as she faced about to watch it land, the tail of her eye caught sight of Liam McAdams hauling himself over the edge of the float.

"Get you for that last one!" he cried, and scrambled to his feet. "'Who laughs last,' you know!"

"I know—" mocked Mary Eliska, evading his grasp and running up the springboard. She dived and her body entered the water with scarcely a sound.

As she rose she turned lazily on her back.

"Come and get me!" she tantalized. Then as she saw him start in pursuit, she rolled over and headed out toward the seaplane which now floated two or three hundred yards away toward the mouth of the inlet and Long Island Sound.

Liam McAdams knew the speed developed by her flagrantly perfect crawl, and did not attempt to follow her. He chuckled as he watched the bob of scarlet and the flash of a brown arm that was all he could see of Mary Eliska.

"Hey, where's Mary Eliska?" called Jax Gray as she and Sean Hall clambered on to the raft.

"Halfway to Boston, I guess. Race you to the beach for the cones!"

All three cut the rumpled surface of the water with a single splash.

Mary Eliska's interest in the airplane that had just landed was twofold. Since qualifying for her private pilot's license earlier in the summer, she had met most of the owners of planes living in or near New Canaan. To the best of her knowledge the Loening Amphibian which her father had given her for rounding up the Martinelli gang was the only one of that model privately owned in that part of Connecticut. That the plane lying just ahead on the water was a duplicate of her own meant that the owner was not a local person.

Mary Eliska was a keen aviatrix and proud of her airbus. She wanted to compare notes with the owner of this amphibian. She was also curious to learn where the plane came from; and why every day for the past few weeks it had appeared over the Club at about this same time of an afternoon. At five-thirty sharp the crowd of young people on the beach would see it, a speck in the north, coming from over the ridge country back of the Sound. Flying at an altitude of not more than five hundred feet, it would swing over the beach club and cross the Sound, to disappear in the ether toward the dim line of the Long Island shore.

Liam McAdams jokingly termed it the Mystery Plane. He told Mary Eliska that its owner made these daily flights in order to show her how a plane should be managed in the air. She usually returned his good-natured teasing with interest, but each time she saw the amphibian, her curiosity increased.

As she swam nearer it was plain that this airship was actually the same stock model as her own. With the retractable landing wheels drawn up, the spoon-shaped hull of the biplane, with its two open cockpits aft of the inverted engine, floated easily on the water. The aviator, she saw, was busily engaged in going over his engine.

Mary Eliska stopped swimming when she was a few yards from the amphibian.

"Hello, there!" she called, treading water. "Need any help?"

The man looked up from his work, evidently perceiving her for the first time. Mary Eliska was surprised to see that the face below the soft helmet and goggles was bearded to the eyes.

"No, thank you," he answered and went on tinkering with the motor. The words, although courteous enough, were spoken in a tone that showed plainly that he wished to end the conversation then and there. Mary Eliska was persistent and not easily discouraged. "Located the trouble?" she asked.

"Not yet," replied the man without lifting his head.

"Looks like loose manifold, or gasoline connection, to me."

There was no reply to this helpful suggestion.

She began swimming toward the plane again. "Mind if I come aboard?" she called. The bearded aviator straightened his back and faced her again, his right hand grasping a monkey-wrench.

"No. I do not wish it," he flared. "Why for do you bother me? Keep off, I tell you."

For the first time, the girl in the water noticed his strong foreign accent. "Aren't you polite!" she mocked. "I don't suppose you'll mind if I come alongside and rest a moment?"

"You stay where you are, young woman." As the man's anger grew, his accent became stronger. "I haf no time to bodder wid you. Go away—and stay away!"

"But I just want—" "I don't care *what* you want. Come alongside, and I'll use this wrench on you!" "Oh, no you won't!"

Liam McAdams slipped around the engine and tripped up the aviator. Before that irate person knew what was happening he found himself flat on his back with a hundred and sixty pounds of young American kneeling on his chest, menacing him with his own monkey-wrench.

"That's not a nice way to talk to a young lady!" Liam McAdams remarked dispassionately eyeing his victim. "Ask her pardon like a good little boy. Do it quickly, my friend, or I'll plant this wrench in the middle of that bush you call a face!"

"I didn't mean nossing," the man grunted.

"Try again!" Liam McAdams whacked his captive's shin with the wrench. "Also try to cut the double negatives. Our English teacher says they're bad form and—"

Liam McAdams's banter stopped with a yelp of pain as the man's head jerked upward and his teeth snapped on the hand which held the wrench.

Mary Eliska, who had swum to within a few feet of the amphibian, saw Liam McAdams thrown to one side. Like cats, the boy and the man seemed to land on their feet—but now it was the strange aviator who held the monkey-wrench.

"Look out, Liam McAdams!" shrieked Mary Eliska as she saw the man's arm swing upward.

The small deck forward of the lower wing section was far too narrow to permit dodging. Liam McAdams did the only thing possible under the circumstances to save himself. Three seasons on the football team of the New Canaan High had made that young man a quick thinker. He dove below the swinging blow and tackled the aviator just above his knees. It was a well-aimed tackle and the two went hurtling overside to disappear with a splash.

Liam McAdams's blond head was the first to appear. Then as the aviator's came popping up, facing the other way, Liam seized him by the shoulders and sent him under once more. "Let the man alone, Liam McAdams!" commanded Mary Eliska. "Can't you see he's swallowed half the Sound?"

"But he'd have brained me with that wrench, Ecker—"

"I'll 'Whack' you if you take liberties with my first name!" Mary Eliska shook her fist above her head, "Anyway, it's my fault. I butted in. That man and his airplane are none of our business."

They were swimming back toward the float now and a glance over her shoulder told Mary Eliska that their late antagonist was pulling himself aboard the amphibian.

Liam McAdams saw him too, and waved a hand. But the foreigner, occupied in wringing water out of his clothes, disregarded them.

"I've had enough of the water for one day," declared Mary Eliska between strokes. "How's the wrist? You might have been badly hurt, Liam McAdams." Liam McAdams motioned toward the float. "But I wasn't, Mary Eliska," he chuckled. "Come over to the raft a moment, before we go ashore. I've got something I want to show you."

"Make it snappy, then," she rejoined. "You and I have got to be at Silvermine by seven-thirty, you know. Curtain up at eight-thirty—and you remember what Mr. Watkins said about any of the cast being late?"

Liam McAdams swung himself up on the decking and gave a hand to Mary Eliska.

"I'm only a chorus man," he grinned. "We'll both get to the Sillies in time. Look at this—"

He opened his hand and held it out, palm upward.

"I'm not interested in seaweed!" Mary Eliska's tone was full of disgust.

"Seaweed, nothing! That's a piece of your friend's beard!"

"You don't mean to tell me you pulled it out?" "Not out, dearie—off. That wasn't his own hair that lad was wearing."

"A *false beard*?" "What else?"

Mary Eliska pursed her lips. "Well, that amphibian and its pilot are two of the most mysterious things I've ever run into." "I wonder what he is up to, Ecker—I mean, Mary Eliska?"

"I wonder, too. By the way, how did you happen out there—and just at the right minute? I thought I saw you start a race for the beach with Jax Gray and Sean Hall?"

Liam McAdams nodded his wet head and laughed. "That was only a bluff to make you think I wasn't coming after you. As I saw you were having an argument with him, and I didn't like the way he was acting, I swam around the tail of his plane and got aboard on the farther deck—and—well, you know the rest. Why did you want to go aboard?"

"Curiosity, pure and simple. Have you any idea why he flies over the Club nearly every afternoon, and always at the same time?"

"No—have you?" "Not the dimmest. But now that I know friend pilot wears false whiskers, I'm certainly intrigued."

"Come again," frowned Liam McAdams. "I didn't get that last one. Did you say *intrigued?*"

"Cut the clowning. This is serious, Liam McAdams. That fellow is up to some mischief, or he wouldn't disguise himself."

Behind them the amphibian's engine sputtered, then roared.

"I've got an idea," said Liam McAdams as the two watched the plane taxi out toward the takeoff. "Why don't you get your bus and follow that bird some afternoon?"

"I'd already decided to do it tomorrow. Want to come?" "You bet! How do you expect to work it?"

"Look here, if we're going to make that show on time, we'd better go right now. We'll make our plans later. Come along." Their bodies cut the water with hardly a splash as they raced for the beach. Out in the inlet the amphibian rose gracefully into the air and headed into the mist which was creeping up Long Island Sound.

Chapter 2.2
THE THREE RED LAMPS

In the wooded valley of the Silvermine, some three miles from the village of New Canaan, lies the famous artists' colony which bears the name of that rippling little river. In the midst of this interesting community, the artists have built their Guild House, where exhibitions of paintings and sculpture are held. And here it is that once a year they give that delightful entertainment known as the Silvermine Sillies.

The casts of the Sillies invariably comprise the pick of local talent from the two communities. Mary Eliska had starred in the musical show given by the New Canaan High School the previous winter. She had a lovely voice and a natural talent for acting. She loved amateur theatricals. But that she should have been assigned a part in the Sillies while yet in High School was a compliment beyond her expectations. She had worked hard at rehearsals and under an assumed calm was wildly excited on this, the opening night of the show. She left Liam McAdams on the beach, after cautioning that young man again not to be late, and ran up the shingle to the Stricklins' cabana, which, together with its gaily painted counterparts, flanked the long club house at the top of the beach.

A surprisingly few minutes later, Mary Eliska reappeared, her bathing suit having been discarded for an attractive linen sports frock, and jumped into her car.

The distance between Tokeneke on Long Island Sound and New Canaan back in the hills of the Ridge Country is slightly under eight miles. Luckily, on her drive home, Mary Eliska encountered no traffic policemen. Notwithstanding summer traffic and the narrow, winding roads, she pulled into the Stricklin garage on the ridge a mile beyond the village, a bare ten minutes later.

Another change of costume and she ran downstairs to the dining room. Her father and a friend were about to sit down at the table.

"Sorry to be late, Daddy," she apologized, slipping into her chair. "Good evening, Mr. Holloway."

"Good evening, Miss Mary Eliska," returned the gentleman with a smile. "You seem a bit blown."

"Some rush!" she sighed, "but I made it!"

"Youth," remarked her father, "is nothing if not inconsistent. We dine early, so that Mary Eliska can get to the Sillies at some unearthly hour, and—"

His daughter interrupted.

"Please, Daddy. I had an awfully exciting experience this afternoon. I'd have been home in plenty of time, otherwise."

"At the Beach Club?"

"Yes, Daddy."

"Well, suppose you tell us the story, as penance." He turned to his guest. "How about it, Holloway? This should interest you, one of the club's most prominent swimming fans!"

Mr. Holloway nodded genially. He was older than Mr. Stricklin, between fifty and sixty, tall and rather thin. He had the brow and jaw of a fighter, and his iron-grey side-whiskers gave him a rather formidable appearance. But Mary Eliska liked him, for his eyes, behind his horn-rimmed spectacles, beamed with friendliness.

"The Beach Club, eh?" He leaned back in his chair. "Yes, I take a dip most afternoons. Wonderful bracer after mornings in the city in this hot weather. You ought to get down there more often."

"Well, there's a pool at the Country Club, and I'd rather play golf," argued his host. "I haven't been to the Beach Club this summer, but Mary Eliska tells me that the cabana you've built is quite a palace—much larger and more 'spiffy,' I think was the word, than those we ordinary members rent!"

"I like to be comfortable and have some privacy when I entertain my friends down there," Mr. Holloway admitted. "But I'm interested in hearing Mary Eliska's story. I was there this afternoon, but I didn't notice anything unusual."

"Did you see the airplane that landed in the cove?"

"Why, no. What time was that?" "A little after five-fifteen."

"I had already left for home. I'm rarely at the club after five o'clock. I like a bright sun when I'm in the water. What about the plane?"

While Mary Eliska told of her experience with the bearded pilot, the two gentlemen continued their meal in silence.

"A nasty customer—that!" snapped her father when she had concluded. "But then, my dear, you shouldn't allow your keenness for aviation to over-excite your curiosity. Let it be a lesson to you not to interfere with other people's private business."

"You say that he wore a false beard?" interjected Mr. Holloway. "Now I wonder why the man wants to disguise himself? And why he was so standoffish about his plane?"

"He's probably in training for some test or endurance flight and wants to keep his identity secret for the time being," suggested Mr. Stricklin. "There's often a lot of hush-hush stuff about such things—that is, until the stunt comes off—and then the secretive ones become the world's worst publicity hounds!"

Mary Eliska remarked the change that came to their guest's face: the eyes narrowed, the mouth grew harder; something of his levity disappeared.

"Perhaps," he said slowly. "But whatever his reason for wishing privacy, we can't have club members insulted by strange aviators in our own cove. I shall take it up at the board of governors' meeting tomorrow. In future we will see to it that no more airplanes land on club waters. Do you think you would recognize the man without his beard, Mary Eliska?"

"I don't think so—but Liam McAdams, who was nearer to him, swears he could spot him anywhere."

"If he should do so, ask him to report the matter to me, and I'll see that the man at least offers apology."

"Thank you, Mr. Holloway." Mary Eliska was pleased at this interest. "I'll tell him."

"You three had better leave well enough alone," her father declared bluntly. "The plane is probably being flown over a set course which happens to take it over the club. That aviator seems to be a surly customer. My advice is to forget it...."

Mary Eliska pushed her chair back from the table.

"You'll excuse me, won't you?" she smiled. "I've got to run, now." She went to her father and kissed him. "Please don't be late, Daddy. I come on the first time right after the curtain rises—it will spoil my evening if you two aren't there!"

Mr. Holloway's kindly eyes twinkled behind his glasses.

"Nice of you to include me. I wouldn't miss the first number for anything. I'll see that we're both there in time."

"Don't worry, sweetheart." Her father patted her hand. "We've got a small matter of business to go over and then we'll be right along. Success to you, dearest." "'Bye!"

A fine rain was falling when Mary Eliska stepped into her car. As yet it was more a heavy mist than a downpour. But with the wind in the east she realized that this part of the country was in for several days of wet weather. She drove carefully, for the winding wooded roads were slippery. Upon arriving at the Guild House, she changed at once into costume. The Silvermine Sillies, like Mr. Ziegfield's more elaborate Follies, is invariably a revue, consisting of eighteen or twenty separate acts. As Mary Eliska stood in the wings, waiting for her cue, shortly after the first curtain rose, she was addressed by the stage manager: "Have you seen Liam McAdams?" "Not since this afternoon. Why?" "He's not here."

Mary Eliska was fighting back the stage fright that always assailed her while waiting to "go on," but which always disappeared as soon as she made her entrance. She turned her mind to what the manager was saying with an effort.

"You mean he hasn't shown up?" she asked a bit vacantly.

"Your perception is remarkable," returned the harassed stage official with pardonable sarcasm. "No, Liam McAdams isn't here. Do you know whether he had any intention of putting in an appearance at this show tonight when you last saw him?"

Mary Eliska was wide awake now. "Of course he had!" "He didn't mention some more important date, perhaps?"

"Of course not. Liam McAdams wouldn't do such a thing!"

"Well, he goes on in less than two minutes. Who in blazes am I to get to double for him? Deliver me from amateurs! There's your cue, Mary Eliska—better take it!"

"Hey, you, Bill!" she heard him call to a stage hand, as she made her entrance. "Duck into the men's dressing room and bring me Liam McAdams' overalls and wig. Here's where I do his stuff without a makeup!"

Liam McAdams failed to show up during the first part of the program, so during the intermission, Mary Eliska slipped out front and sought the delinquent's father and mother in the audience.

"Why, my dear, I'm quite as surprised as you are," gurgled Mrs. Walters. "Isn't this rain disgusting? You looked perfectly lovely Mary Eliska—and you did splendidly, splendidly, my dear. I thought I'd die when your rope of pearls broke and you went hunting for them—a perfect scream, my dear—the funniest thing in the show!"

"Those were Jax Gray's pearls," said Mary Eliska. "I wasn't in that act. You say Liam McAdams left the house in plenty of time, and he expected to drive straight down here?"

Mrs. Walters had said nothing of the kind, but Mary Eliska had known the lady for years, and had long ago devised a method of securing information from her.

"He didn't even wait for dessert, my dear. He probably went to the movies or remembered some other date. Boys are like that!"

"Liam McAdams isn't." His father spoke up. "He must have been going to pick someone up and give them a lift down here—then blew a shoe or something. Still, I don't like it. I hope the boy hasn't met with an accident."

"Oh, don't say that, Reggie! You make me feel positively faint. I know he has gone to the pictures." Mrs. Walters was nervously emphatic. "Don't be so silly, dear—I know he has."

"You know nothing of the kind," declared her husband.

"But, Reggie dear—"

Mary Eliska hurriedly excused herself and went back stage. But by the time the final curtain was rung down, no Liam McAdams had appeared. Mary Eliska was really worried.

Jax Gray was giving a party to a number of the cast at her house in White Oak Shade, but despite protests, Mary Eliska made her regrets and went to look for her father.

"I think I'll beat it for home, Dad," she announced, buttonholing him near the door. "I'll be along in a few minutes, darling. I certainly am more than extra proud of you tonight. I never realized what an actress you are. But you look troubled—anything the matter?"

"I'm worried about Liam McAdams. I know he wouldn't deliberately put us all in this hole. He's not that kind."

"Probably had a break-down," consoled her father. "Excuse me, dear, I want to speak to the Joneses over there."

Mary Eliska drove a six-cylinder coupe whose body had seen better days, though she claimed for its engine that the world had not seen its equal. With her wind wiper working furiously, she came cautiously along Valley Road, her big headlamps staring whitely ahead. The rain was pelting down now, and since she must have a window open, and that window was on the weather side, one arm and part of the shoulder of her thin slicker were soon black and shining.

"Something he couldn't help—that's what made Liam McAdams let us down," said her subconscious mind, and she wondered how any of the cast could have expressed contrary opinions. She was glad she had refused Jax Gray's invitation. She liked Liam McAdams and was deeply concerned about him. He wasn't the sort to default unless something unforeseen and unusual occurred. Mrs. Walters said he had been full of the show at dinner and had spoken about getting to the Guild House early. Something had come up, that was certain. And that something, after he had started for Silvermine in his car. The more she thought about it, the more mysterious it seemed. She would phone the Walters again as soon as she reached home. Maybe he would be back by that time.

The car skidded round the turn into the Ridge Road that ran past the Stricklin place. A mile farther on, Mary Eliska decided it would be well for her to keep her mind on the road ahead. A few minutes before, a lumbering truck had almost driven her into the ditch, and now, with a mile to go, she saw ahead of her three red lights. She slowed her engine until she came within a dozen yards of them. They were red lamps, placed in a line across the road, and if they meant anything, it was that the road was under repair and closed. Yet she had passed the truck going at full speed just beyond the corner. From its lights, she was sure it had come along this stretch of road.

She peered through the open window and saw on her left a dilapidated stone fence, the top of which was hidden under a blanket of wild honeysuckle. She saw by her headlights a gap where once she knew a five-barred gate had blocked the way to the open field. All this she took in at a glance, for Mary Eliska knew exactly where she was. Then she turned again to her scrutiny of the road and the three red lamps.

"Well!" said Mary Eliska to herself. She switched out all the lights of the car, and taking something from her pocket, she opened the door quietly and stepped into the rain. She stood there for a while, listening.

There was no sound except the swish and patter of the storm. Keeping to the center of the road she advanced slowly toward the red lights, picked up the middle one and examined it. The lantern was old—the red had been painted on the glass. The second lantern was newer, but of entirely different pattern. Here also, the glass pane had been covered by some red, transparent paint. And this was the case with the third lamp.

Mary Eliska threw the middle light into the ditch and found satisfaction in hearing the crash of glass. Then she came back to her car, got inside, slammed the door and put her foot down on the starter. The motor whined but the engine did not move. The car was hot and never before had it failed. Again she tried, but without success.

"This looks suspicious," she muttered to herself.

She sprang out into the rain again and walked to the back to examine her gasoline tank. There was no need, for the indicator said, "Empty."

"I'll say suspicious!" she muttered again, angrily, as she stared down at the cause of her plight.

She had filled up just before dinner, but notwithstanding that fact, here was a trustworthy indicator pointing grimly to "E"; and when she tapped the tank, it gave forth a hollow sound in confirmation.

Mary Eliska sniffed: the air reeked with fumes. Flashing her pocket light on the ground she saw a metal cap and picked it up. Then she understood what had happened. The roadway, under her light, gleamed with opalescent streaks. Someone had taken out the cap and emptied her tank while she was examining the red lamps!

She refastened the cap, which was airproof, waterproof, and foolproof, and which could only have been turned by the aid of a spanner—she had heard no chink of metal against metal. She did not carry reserve fuel, but home was not more than a mile down the road, round the turn. And she knew there was a path from the gap in the stone wall, across the field and through a belt of woods that would halve the distance.

She sent her flashlight in the direction of the open gateway. One of the posts was broken and the rotting structure leaned drunkenly against a lilac bush. In the shadow behind the bush, she was certain that a dark form moved.

Mary Eliska lingered no longer, but switching off her light, she turned on her heel and raced up the road.

Chapter 2.3
WHERE'S LIAM MCADAMS?

Behind her, Mary Eliska heard a shout, and that shout lent wings to her feet. Scared as she was, she grinned. For she was probably doing the only thing her would-be assailants had not counted on. She was running away from the red lights and home, sprinting down the road the way she had come. Overhead, tall elms met in an archway, and from the darkness at her back came the quick patter of footsteps. Suddenly they stopped.

Mary Eliska gave a sigh of joyous relief, for around the bend in the road she saw the double gleam of headlights, shining through the wet. Stopping short in the middle of the road, she switched on her flashlight again and waved it frantically from side to side. "Daddy!" she cried as the big car drew up. "I was sure you weren't far away. Gee! but I was glad to see your lights."

Mr. Stricklin snapped open the door and Mary Eliska slipped in beside him.

"Why, what are you doing out here? Have a breakdown?"

"H-holdup," she panted. "My car's down the road. Step on it, Dad—maybe we can catch them."

"An ounce of discretion is sometimes worth forty pounds of valor," he began, throwing in the clutch.

Mary Eliska cut him short. "Look!" she cried excitedly, and for all Mr. Stricklin's cautious announcement, the car jumped forward with a jerk. "See, Daddy! There's my tail light! They've turned it on again. And the red lights have disappeared."

"What red lights?"

"Tell you in a minute. Better slow down. My car's out of gas. I've got a piece of hose in the rumble. We can siphon enough from your tank into mine to get me home."

Mr. Stricklin brought his car to a stop directly behind Mary Eliska's coupe. "Before we do anything, I want to hear exactly what happened, dear. You scared your fond parent out of a year's growth when I caught sight of you waving that light in the middle of the road!"

"Poor old Daddy." She threw an arm about his neck. "You weren't half as frightened as I was. Those men were pelting down the road behind me and—"

Her father broke in. "Well, they seem to have disappeared now. Let me hear the beginning."

In a few short sentences, Mary Eliska told him.

"So you see," she ended. "There's nothing more for us to do about it, I guess, except to put some gas in my tank, and go home."

"Wait a minute. Hand over that flash, please." He opened the door and with an agility surprising in so large a man, sprang into the wet road and ran toward the gap in the wall.

As he ran, Mary Eliska saw a light flash in his hand. Then he went out of sight behind the wall but she could still see the gleam through the bushes. Presently he came back to where she was standing beside the car.

"Vamoosed!" He tossed the flash onto the seat. "As there's no car on the road ahead they must have beat it over the field. I wonder why they didn't hold you up when you'd stopped for those red lanterns? Strange. Also, why do you suppose they switched on your lights?"

"It's beyond me. Well, Daddy, if you'll pull alongside we'll siphon the gas. This place and the rain and everything gives me the shivers. Let's talk it over when we get home."

Soon they were under way, and they continued on to the Stricklin place without further incident.

"Your shoes are soaking wet, Mary Eliska. Go up to your room and change them, my dear," decreed her father. "While you're doing that, I'll phone Walters."

When Mary Eliska came downstairs her father was in the living room.

"Come over here and sit down," he said, making room for her on the lounge beside him. "Liam McAdams has not come home yet. The family pretend not to be worried—and that's that. I said nothing about what happened to you on your way back from Silvermine."

His daughter groaned. "Oh dear—if we could only figure out—but those three red lights seem to cinch things, Daddy."

"Hardly that. But they do make it look as though this disappearing business is pretty serious—"

Mary Eliska interrupted him eagerly: "Then there isn't any doubt in your mind but that our experience at the club this afternoon is accountable for Liam McAdams's disappearance, and my holdup?"

Mr. Stricklin, who was filling his pipe, struck a match and puffed contemplatively.

"We can't jump at conclusions, my dear. My first idea about that plane may be the right one. On the other hand, this business tonight certainly forces one's suspicions. If Liam McAdams doesn't show up by morning, we'll turn the matter over to the police and start a thorough search. But I do think it wise to keep the story of the amphibian and its pilot to ourselves."

Mary Eliska nodded. "You mean that if we spread our suspicions to the police, they'd let the cat out of the bag and the man would be on his guard?"

"That's just it. And then you must remember that we really have no facts to go on as yet."

"Well, I think I'll go to bed," yawned Mary Eliska. "Do you mind if I try to trail that plane with my own?"

"Not if you'll promise to be careful, dear. In fact, I think it's a good idea. But one thing I must insist upon and that is—you're to keep me posted. No more of this taking things into your own hands, as you did with the Martinellis. It's too dangerous. Confide in your old Dad, girl, and we'll do a lot better."

Mary Eliska was half way across the room, but here she turned and ran back to her father and kissed him. "Of course I'll tell you everything. Isn't it too bad, though, that Bill Bolton is away? He'd have been a wonderful help. Have you any idea what he is doing?"

"All I know is what his father told me—that he's off on some government job. It may be Secret Service work, again. Anyway, he's to be away indefinitely, I understand. Now, just one thing more." "Oh, *Daddy*! *More* instructions to take care of myself?"

Mr. Stricklin laughed at her outraged expression, and relit his pipe.

"Not exactly—you seem to have the luck to generally land on your feet. But, I want you to consider this: if the bearded aviator or his associates *are* behind Liam McAdams's disappearance, they kidnapped him because they thought he would recognize the man. And they tried to do the same thing to you tonight."

"Why on earth should they fear being recognized?"

"Haven't the slightest idea. It depends on what they're up to. There must be a strong motive behind it. You don't strike a match unless you want a light. But unless we're chasing moonbeams, something illegal is going on and if there is a hunt for Liam McAdams tomorrow, I don't want you to take part in it."

"You think they'll try to get me again?"

"It is highly possible." Her father got to his feet and put his hands on her shoulders. "So promise me you won't go running about country byroads in your car, even during daylight hours. If you must go out at night, either I or Arthur must be in the car with you." (Arthur was the Stricklins' chauffeur-gardener.) "There's no use trying to pretend I'm not worried about this mysterious business. Be a good girl and don't make it harder for me, please."

"I'll be good, Daddy. If I find out anything tomorrow, I'll report at dinner."

"That's my girl," he beamed, and kissed her good night. "I shall nose about, myself, a bit. I'm sure that you and Liam McAdams know that bearded aviator or some of his friends. Otherwise, he wouldn't be so perturbed about recognition. Unless we're all wet, Mary Eliska, this affair is made up of local people. Mind your step—and we'll see. Go to bed now and get a good rest—I'm coming upstairs as soon as I've locked up."

Chapter 2.4
THE THUNDERHEAD

Mary Eliska telephoned the Walters next morning, to learn from a maid that Liam McAdams was still missing, and that Mr. Walters was down in the village, putting the matter in the hands of the police. "May I speak to Mrs. Walters?" she asked.

"I'm afraid not, miss. Mrs. Walters has been up all night. Doctor Brown has given her a sleeping powder and issued orders that she is not to be disturbed."

"If there is anything that I can do," said Mary Eliska, "telephone me." "Thank you, miss. I'll tell Mr. Walters when he comes home."

Mary Eliska rang off and went about her household duties with a heavy heart.

Later on she motored to the village to do her marketing, and upon her return found that her father had telephoned. She immediately called up the New Canaan Bank, of which he was president.

"Any news, Daddy?" she inquired anxiously, as soon as she was put through to him.

"That you, Mary Eliska?" she heard him say. "Yes—Liam McAdams's car has been found." "*Where*, Daddy?"

"On a wood road in the hills back of the Norwalk reservoir. The car was empty. A farmer driving through there found it early this morning and phoned the license number to the police."

"But what in the world could Liam McAdams have been doing way over there? I know that road. It's no more than a bridle path—the reservoir is three or four miles beyond Silvermine."

"My opinion is that Liam McAdams was never anywhere near the place," explained her father. "He was undoubtedly held up, removed to another car and his own run over to the spot where it was found."

"No sign of him, I suppose?" "No. I've talked with Walters. The poor man is nearly off his head with worry. We're getting up searching parties to cooperate with the police. I'll see you at dinner tonight. It will be impossible for me to get home at noon."

"I'll hope to have some news for you, then," said Mary Eliska. "Going up in spite of the rain?"

"I've got to. We can't afford to waste time—the weather's not so bad." "There are storm warnings out all along the coast."

"I'll be careful, Daddy." "All right. Bye-bye 'til dinner time. "Bye."

She hung up the receiver and for the rest of the morning, busied herself about the house, determined not to let her mind dwell upon the darker side of this latest development. After lunch she changed into flying clothes and went out to the hangar. Unlocking the doors, she set to work filling the amphibian's gasoline tanks. Then she went over the engine carefully and gave it a short ground test. After that, the instruments came under her inspection. Altogether, she gave her plane a thorough overhauling, which was not entirely necessary, but kept her from thinking and helped to kill time.

About twenty minutes to five she ran the amphibian out of the hangar and took off into the teeth of a fine rain. It was no part of her plan to fly in the neighborhood of the Beach Club until the plane she was seeking should put in an appearance. Her self-imposed duty was to spot the mysterious amphibian and to follow it to its destination without allowing the pilot or an understudy to spot her.

So instead of banking and heading for Tokeneke, when her bus had sufficiently topped the trees, she continued to keep the stick back so as to maintain a proper climbing angle. Back in her first thirty hours of early flight training, it would have been difficult for her to keep *Will-o'-the-Wisp* (more often termed Willie or Wispy) at the correct angle safely below the stalling point, unless she could first recognize that angle by the position of the plane's nose relative to the horizon. On a wet day like this with an obscured horizon it would have been well-nigh impossible: at best, a series of bad stalls would have been the result. But now her snapping gray eyes sparkled with exhilaration; she no longer needed the horizon as a guide. Between leveling off every thousand feet or so, to keep the engine from overheating, she shot *Will-o'-the-Wisp* up to six thousand, maintaining the proper angle of climb by the "feel" of the plane alone.

With her altimeter indicating the height she wanted, she leveled off again; then, executing a sharp reverse control or "flipper" turn to the left she resumed straight flight again by the application of up aileron and opposite rudder. The plane was now headed south, several points to the west of the Beach Club.

The visibility was even poorer than at a lower level, but the young pilot knew this part of the country as she knew her own front lawn. Either dropping or swerving her plane's nose at frequent intervals so as to get an unimpeded view ahead, she passed over the wooded ridges toward the shore, over the city of Stamford and out over the slate grey waters of Long Island Sound.

That body of water is some six or eight miles wide at this point, and upon reaching the opposite shore, Mary Eliska commenced a patrol of the Long Island shore line from Lloyds' Neck, which lies just west of Oyster Bay, to the farther side of Smithtown Bay, a distance of fifteen or sixteen miles. And as she flew, she kept a sharp lookout for planes appearing out of the murk toward the Connecticut shore.

Since she knew it was the bearded aviator's practice to fly at a comparatively low altitude, Mary Eliska chose to keep *Will-o'-the-Wisp* at this greater height for two reasons. An airplane flying far above another plane is much more unlikely to be noticed by the pilot of the lower plane than one flying at his own level or below him. Then again, by keeping to the higher air, Mary Eliska, under normal weather conditions, was bound to increase her range of vision proportionately. Her plan was a good one. But weather is not a respecter of plans. The visibility, poor enough when she started, gradually grew worse and worse. Although what wind there was seemed to have died, long curling tongues of mist crept out of the east, while above her head she saw black thunder clouds, sinking lower and lower.

Now one of the first things any aviator learns is that fog must be avoided at all costs. Any attempt to land in it is attended by considerable danger. Mary Eliska knew only too well that in case of a fog bank cutting the plane off from its destination, the flight must be discontinued by a landing, or by return to the point of departure.

She glanced overside again. Long Island Sound was no longer visible. "He's late now, unless I've missed him," she said to herself. "I'll finish this leg of the patrol and if he doesn't show up by the time I'm over Oyster Bay, *Willie* and I will head for home."

Pushing her stick slightly forward to decrease her altitude, she continued along her course.

Three minutes later, she realized her mistake. The wisps of fog seemed to gather together, and *Will-o'-the-Wisp* sank into an opaque bank that blinded her.

"Gee, but I'm stupid!" she mumbled. "What was it that text-book I read only yesterday said? 'In the event of general formation of fog below, an immediate landing must be made before it becomes thick enough to interfere seriously with the approach.' Heavens, what a fool I am! Now that we're in it, though, I might as well see if it thins out nearer the water."

Her compass told her she was flying almost due west. Throttling down the engine, she pushed her stick still farther forward, at the same time applying right aileron and hard right rudder. As the proper gliding angle was reached, she neutralized her elevators and held the nose up as necessary. Next, she checked her wing with the ailerons and eased her rudder pressure. Then having made a quarter-spiral with a change in course of 90 degrees, she applied left aileron and hard left rudder until the wings were level laterally, and with her stick still held forward, continued to descend in a straight glide until she was within fifteen hundred feet of the water. The plane was heading directly back across Long Island Sound toward the Connecticut shore.

But each moment the fog seemed to grow more dense. To land blindly meant a certain nose-in and was out of the question. And even if the mist did not hold to the water's level, to fly lower meant the chance of striking the mast or spar of a ship, a lighthouse, perhaps, or anything else that came her way.

"We're up against it, *Wispy*," she murmured, opening the throttle and pulling back her stick. "If we can't go down, at least we can 'go above,' as they say in the Navy. Beat it for the heavens, my dear. This beastly fog can't run all the way to Mars!"

Mary Eliska was not frightened, although she knew how serious was her predicament. No pilot likes flying blind in a fog. With the knowledge that what one sees, one hits, it is a nerve-wracking experience.

But Mary Eliska's nerves were good—none better—and she sent her plane into a long, steady climb, hoping for the best and keeping her vivid imagination well within control.

Headed into the north, she continued her climb, leveling off every few thousand feet to ease the strain on her engine. When the altimeter marked thirteen thousand she began to worry, for the service ceiling of her plane was but two thousand higher. The cold damp of the thick mist penetrated like a knife. Hemmed in by the dank grey walls, she could barely distinguish the nose of her ship. The active needles of the altimeter and rate of climb indicator were the only visible signs that *Will-o'-the-Wisp* was moving at all.

Fourteen thousand feet—intense physical discomfort, added to the nervous strain, were becoming intolerable. Mary Eliska clenched her chattering teeth in an effort to retain her control. Then with a suddenness astonishing, the fog parted and she sailed into clear air.

Below her the heavy mist swirled and rolled like a sluggish sea, grey-yellow streaked with dirty streamers, while directly ahead loomed a towering mass of cotton-like clouds rising tier upon tier as far as she would see.

A quick glance over her shoulder and to the sides, brought forth the fact that this small pocket of free air was entirely surrounded by similar cloud formations. There was no time for thought. Automatically, her hand clasping the stick shot forward, bringing down the nose to the position of level flight, and she drove the amphibian straight at the thunderhead. Immediately afterward the plane passed into the cloud, and like a leaf caught in an inverted maelstrom, it was whipped out of her control.

Gripped by tremendous air forces, the amphibian was shot up and sideways, at a speed that burned Mary Eliska's lungs. Tossed about like a rag doll, with her safety-belt almost cutting her body in two, she was thrown hither and yon with the plane, blind, and without the slightest idea as to her position.

Never in her wildest nightmares had she dreamed that a heavy plane, weighing close to four thousand pounds when empty, could be tossed about in such fashion by currents of the air.

For a space of time that seemed years, she was entirely away from the controls. But gradually, with infinite effort and in spite of the whirling jolts of her air steed, Mary Eliska managed to hook her heels under the seat. A second later she had caught the stick and was pushing it forward into the instrument board.

Will-o'-the-Wisp reared like an outlawed bronco, then dived until the airspeed indicator showed one hundred and sixty-five miles per hour. Still her downward speed was less than the rate of the upward draft, for the rate of climb indicator told the frenzied girl that the plane was being lifted fourteen hundred feet per minute. Still diving at 45 degrees, the phenomenal force of the updraft carried the plane to the mushroom top of the cloud, where with a jar like an elevator hitting the ceiling, it was flung forth into the outer air.

Chapter 2.5
HIDE AND SEEK

The strong air current which spread horizontally over the thunderhead blew Mary Eliska's plane sideways and away from the cloud. An instant later it was roaring downward in the thin air, quite beyond her control, a self-propelled projectile rushing to its doom.

While shooting upward in the cloud, the violent and intensely rapid gyrations of the airship caused her safety belt to become unclasped, and had her parachute not caught in the cowling, she must have been flung clear of the plane to a horrible death far below.

With her heels still hooked beneath the pilot's seat, she wrenched the parachute loose. Then she closed the throttle and half-suffocated by the force of the wind and lack of breathable oxygen, she commenced to pull the stick slowly backward.

A glance at the altimeter showed a height of eighteen thousand feet—three air miles above earth—and three thousand feet above *Will-o'-the-Wisp's* service ceiling.

Notwithstanding the shut-off engine, the speed of the diving plane was terrific. Mary Eliska felt the grinding jar of the wind-strained wings as the nose began to rise in answer to the pull of the elevators; and wondered helplessly if they would hold.

The air pressure was agony to her eardrums. Her head reeled. She was well-nigh exhausted. She no longer cared very much what happened.

The plane dropped into a blanket of fog. She felt the wet mist on her face, refreshing and reanimating her. Suddenly she realized that her parachute was starting to fill and would shortly pull her out of the cockpit. With her free hand she reached under the seat and brought forth a sheath knife. A frenzied second later she had rid herself of the flapping bag. As it flew overboard, she tightened her safety belt and placed her cramped feet back on the steering pedals.

Though still fog-blind, she could at least breathe comfortably now as the plane lessened speed in descent. *Will-o'-the-Wisp* still shook and groaned, but no longer fought the pull of the stick. Up came the nose, slowly but surely and with her ailerons functioning once more, Mary Eliska gained control and sent the plane into a normal glide. The altimeter marked five thousand feet. The dive had been over two miles long.

Another fifteen hundred feet and gradually the mist lightened until it became mere wisps of smoky cloud. Long Island Sound had been left behind. Below lay the wooded hills and valleys of the Connecticut ridge country, cloaked in multi-shaded green. As she still headed north, Mary Eliska knew now that she had been blown beyond New Canaan. She gave the plane hard right rudder and right aileron and sent it swinging into a long half spiral, which, completed, headed her south again. Almost directly below, she recognized the Danbury Fair Grounds, with home just twenty miles away.

Again her hand sought the throttle and as *Will-o'-the-Wisp* snorted, then roared, Mary Eliska breathed a thankful sigh. Fifteen minutes later she had housed her plane in its hangar, and was limping up the porch steps of her home.

Lizzie, the Stricklins' servant, met her in the hall.

"Whatever is the matter, Miss Mary Eliska? You've had an accident—you're half-killed—I know you are! There's blood all over your face—"

Her young mistress interrupted, smiling:

"You're wrong again, Lizzie. No accident, though I know I look pretty awful. I feel that way, too, if you ask me—"

"But the blood, Miss Mary Eliska?"

"It's from a nosebleed, Lizzie. I assure you I'm not badly hurt. If you'll help me out of these rags and start a warm bath running, I'll be ever so much obliged. A good soaking in hot water will fix me up. Then," she added, "I think I'll be really luxurious and have my dinner in bed."

When the solicitous Lizzie brought up the dinner tray three-quarters of an hour later, a tired but decidedly sprucer Mary Eliska, in pink silk pajamas, was leaning back against her pillows.

"My word, I'm hungry!" She seized a hot roll and began to butter it. "I'm off bucking thunderheads for life, Lizzie. But you can take it from me, that kind of thing gives you a marvelous appetite!"

"Yes, miss, I'm glad," returned Lizzie, who had no idea what Mary Eliska was talking about. "You certainly look better."

"By the way, what's become of Daddy? Hasn't he got home yet?"

"Oh, Miss Mary Eliska, I'm so sorry. Sure and I forgot to tell ye—Mr. Stricklin won't be home for dinner."

"Did he telephone?"

"No, miss. He came home about quarter to five and packed his suitcase. He said to tell you he'd been called to Washington on business and he'd be gone a couple of days. Arthur drove him to Stamford to catch the New York express—he didn't have much time."

Mary Eliska helped herself to a spoonful of jellied bouillon. "Any other message?"

"Yes, miss. He said that Mister Liam McAdams hadn't been found yet. I asked him b'cause I thought you'd like to know. That was all he said. I'm sure sorry I forgot it when you came in, but I—"

"That's all right, Lizzie, I understand. You come back for the tray in half an hour, will you? And if you find me asleep, don't wake me up. I'm tired to death. I need a long rest and I'm going to take it."

When Lizzie came back she found Mary Eliska deep in the sleep of exhaustion. She lowered the window blinds against the early morning light and picking up the tray from the end of the bed, tiptoed from the room.

Morning broke bright and clear with no sign of yesterday's mist and rain. Mary Eliska remained in bed for breakfast and it took but little persuasion on the part of Lizzie to keep her there 'til lunch time. She still felt stiff and bruised and was only too content to rest and doze.

Toward noon she rose and dressed in her flying clothes. Immediately after lunch she went out to the hangar. She slipped into a serviceable and grubby pair of overalls, and spent the afternoon in giving *Will-o'-the-Wisp* a thorough grooming. At quarter to five she was in the air and headed for Long Island Sound.

Half an hour later, with an altitude of ten thousand feet, she was cruising over yesterday's course above the Long Island shore, when she spied a biplane coming across the Sound. In an instant she had her field glasses out and focused on the newcomer.

"That's him!" she murmured ungrammatically, though with evident relief. "Now for a pleasant little game of hide-and-seek!"

The *Mystery Plane* was flying far below, so continuing on her course at right angles, she watched it with hurried glances over her shoulder. When she reached the Long Island Shore line, it was a mile or so behind and below Mary Eliska's tailplane. So waiting only long enough to be sure that her quarry was headed across the Island, she banked her plane and sent it on a wide half circle to the right. Long Island, at this point, she knew was about twenty miles wide.

Mary Eliska's plan for trailing the *Mystery Plane* and doing so without being seen, was as simple as it was direct. The farther end of her circular course would bring her over Great South Bay and the South shore of Long Island at approximately the same point for which the other plane seemed to be bound. She would arrive, of course, a minute or two behind the other aviator. And as she planned, so it happened.

From her high point of vantage, Mary Eliska, swinging on her arc a mile or so to the east, was able to keep the other amphibian continually in sight. She watched him pursue his southerly course until he came over the town of Babylon on Great South Bay. Here her glasses told her that the bearded aviator turned his plane to the left, heading east and up the bay in her direction.

Below her now lay the Bay, hemmed in from the Atlantic by long narrow stretches of white sand dunes. For a second or so Mary Eliska thought they would pass in the air, her plane far above the other. But before she reached that point, she saw the other make a crosswind landing and taxi toward a dock which jutted into the Bay from the dunes. Just beyond the dock an isolated cottage stood in a hollow on the bay side of the dunes. There was no other habitation in sight for over a mile in either direction.

"Aha! Run to earth at last!" muttered Mary Eliska contentedly. Maintaining her altitude, with Babylon across the bay to her right, she continued her westward course above the dunes.

A few miles past the cottage she flew over Fire Island Inlet. When she was opposite Amityville, she came about. Shutting off her engine, she tilted the stick forward and sent *Will-o'-the-Wisp* into a long glide which eventually landed her on the waters of Babylon harbor. Mary Eliska stripped off her goggles and scanned the waterfront. Slightly to her left she spied a small shipyard, whose long dock bore a large sign which carried the legend: "Yancy's Motor Boat Garage."

"Good. Couldn't be better!" exclaimed Mary Eliska in great satisfaction. "Atta girl, Wispy! We're going over to have a talk with Mr. Yancy."

She gave her plane the gun and taxiing slowly over the smooth water, through the harbor shipping, presently brought up at the Yancy wharf and made fast. "Hello, there! Want gas?"

sang out a voice above her, and Mary Eliska looked up. A smiling young man, dressed in extremely dirty dungarees was walking down the wharf toward her.

"Hello, yourself!" she returned as he came up. "No, I'm not out of gas, thank you. I want to hire a boat."

"Better come ashore, then." The man wiped his palms on a piece of clean cotton waste and gave her a hand up. "We've got plenty of boats—all kinds, lady. Got 'em fast and slow, big and little. Just what kind of a craft do you need?"

"Something with plenty of beam and seaworthy, that I can run without help. I'm not looking for speed. I may want to take her outside—I don't know."

The young man pointed down the wharf to where a rather bulky motor boat, broad of beam and about thirty feet waterline was moored head out to a staging.

"*Mary Jane*—that's your boat," announced Mr. Yancy. "She's old and she ain't got no looks, but she's seaworthy and she'll take you anywhere. You could run over to Paris or London in that old craft if you could pile enough gas aboard her."

"She looks pretty big," Mary Eliska's tone was dubious. "Think I can handle her by myself?"

"She is big," he admitted readily, "but she runs like a sewing machine and she's all set to be taken out this minute if you want her."

"I'll look her over anyway," she declared and led the way to the landing stage.

Stepping aboard the *Mary Jane*, she peeped into the small trunk cabin which was scarcely bigger than a locker, but would give shelter in case of rain. She observed that there were sailing lights, compass, horn and a large dinner bell in a rack, and two life preservers as well. In one of the lockers she came upon a chart. Stowed up in the forepeak were an anchor with a coil of line and three five-gallon tins of gasoline. A quick examination showed the fuel tank to have been filled.

The motor was a simple and powerful two-cylinder affair, with make-and-break ignition, noisy, but dependable; the sort of engine on which the fishermen and lobstermen along the coast hang their lives in offshore work. It seemed to Mary Eliska that it ought to kick the shallow old tub along at a good ten-knot gait. The boat itself though battered and dingy, appeared to be sound and staunch so far as one could see.

"I'll take her," decided Mary Eliska. "That is, if she's not too expensive?"

"I guess we ain't goin' to fight about the price, mam," asserted Yancy. "How long will you be wantin' her and when do you expect to take her out?"

"Not before nine tonight—and I'll hire her for twenty-four hours." "O. K. mam. You can have her for a year if you want her. How about your air bus?"

"She'll be left here. I want you to look after her. I don't think there'll be any wind to speak of. She'll be all right where she is."

"We're going to get rain in a couple of hours, so if you'll make her secure, I'll have her towed out to that buoy yonder. I'll rest easier with her moored clear of this dock."

"I'll pull the waterproof covers over the cockpits and she'll be all right," returned Mary Eliska. "Then we can go up to your office and fix up the finances."

Chapter 2.6
THE HOUSE ON THE DUNES

Having come to agreeable terms with Mr. Yancy and having secured the name and location of Babylon's best restaurant, Mary Eliska left the waterfront and walked uptown. A glance at her wrist-watch told her it was not yet seven o'clock. She was in no hurry, for she had more than two hours to wait before it would be dark enough to start. So she strolled along the bustling streets of the little city, feeling very much pleased with the way things were progressing. Arrived at the restaurant, she ordered a substantial meal and while waiting for it to be served, sought a telephone booth. She asked for the toll operator and put in a call for New Canaan. A little while later she was summoned to the phone.

"Is that you, Lizzie? Yes. I—no, no, I'm perfectly all right—" she spoke soothingly into the transmitter. "Don't worry about me, please. I've had to go out of town, and I wanted to let you know that I won't be back 'til morning. Never mind, now. I'll see you tomorrow. Good-by!" She replaced the receiver and went back to her table, a little smile on her lips at the memory of Lizzie's distracted voice over the wire.

"Poor Lizzie! She's all worked up again at what she calls my 'wild doin's'," she thought. And with a determined glint in her eyes, she proceeded to eat heartily.

When she had finished, she asked at the desk for a sheet of paper and an envelope. She took these over to her table, ordered a second cup of coffee, and began to compose a letter. This took her some time, for in it she explained her maneuvers during the afternoon, and gave the exact location of the cottage on the dunes, where she believed the *Mystery Plane's* pilot had been bound. She ended with a sketch of her plans for the evening and addressed the envelope to Liam McAdams' father. With her mind now easy in case of misadventure, she paid her bill and walked back to the water front.

"Good evening, Mary Eliska," greeted Yancy as she stepped into his office. "I've done what you asked me to. You'll find a pair of clean blankets, some fresh water and eatables for two days stowed in the *Mary Jane's* cabin. I know you don't intend to be out that long, but it's always wise to be on the safe side with the grub."

"Thanks. You're a great help. Now, just one thing more before I shove off. Although I've rented your boat for twenty-four hours, I really expect to be back here tomorrow morning at the latest. If I don't turn up by noon, will you please send this letter by special delivery to Mr. Walters in New Canaan?"

"I sure will, Mary Eliska. But you're not lookin' for trouble, are you?"

Mary Eliska shook her head and smiled. "Nothing like that, Mr. Yancy. I just want Mr. Walters to know where I am and what I'm doing."

"Good enough, M'am. Anything else I can do?"

"Not a thing, thank you. Don't bother to come down to the wharf with me. I've got several things I want to do aboard before I set out."

"Just as you say. Good luck and a pleasant trip." Yancy's honest face wore a beaming grin as he doffed his tattered cap to Mary Eliska. "Thank you again. Good night."

Mary Eliska went outside and found that Yancy's prediction of rain earlier in the evening had been justified.

"Lucky this is drizzle instead of fog," she thought as she hurried down to the landing stage. "I'd be out of luck navigating blind on Great South Bay!"

She dove into the *Mary Jane's* cabin and after lighting the old-fashioned oil lamp in its swinging bracket, put on her slicker and sou'wester. Then she fished the chart of the bay out of the locker and spent the next quarter of an hour in an intensive study of local waters. Having gained an intimate picture of this part of the bay, she plotted her course, and checked up on the blankets and food. That done, she blew out the lamp, picked up the anchor and left the cabin, closing the door behind her.

Outside in the drizzle, she deposited her burden in the bow, making the anchor rope fast to a ring bolt in the decking. Then she put a match to the side lights and coming aft, cast off from the staging. Next, she started the motor, a difficult undertaking. At the third or fourth heave of the heavy flywheel it got away with a series of barking coughs. She slid in behind the steering wheel and they headed out across the bay.

Night had fallen, but notwithstanding the light rain, visibility on the water was good. The tide, as Mary Eliska knew, was at the flood, so she cut straight across for the dull, intermittent glow of the Fire Island Light. The boat ran strongly and well and Mary Eliska gave the engine full gas. She knew from experience that one of its primitive type was not apt to suffer from being driven, but on the contrary was inclined to run more evenly.

It had been at least two years since she had sailed on Great South Bay, but she remembered it to be a big, shallow puddle, where in most places a person capsized might stand on bottom and right the boat.

"No danger of capsizing with the *Mary Jane*," she reflected, "she's built on the lines of a flounder—I'll bet she'd float in a heavy dew!"

The two and a half feet of tide made it possible for her to hold a straight course and presently she could see the dim outline of sand dunes. The faint easterly draft of air brought the roar of the Atlantic swell as it boomed upon the beach outside. It was time to change her course.

A quarter turn of the wheel swung the *Mary Jane* to port and straightening out, she headed across the inlet. Five minutes later she had picked up the dunes on the farther side. With the dunes off her starboard quarter, Mary Eliska made the wheel fast with a bight of cord she had cut for the purpose, and going forward, extinguished her side lights.

Back at the wheel again, she steered just as close to the shore as safety permitted. For the next couple of miles she ran along the shallows. "Thank goodness!" she muttered at last. Swinging the *Mary Jane* inshore, she cut her motor and headed into a small cove, to ground a moment later on a pebbly beach.

Springing ashore, Mary Eliska dragged the anchor up the beach and buried it at its full length of rope in the sand. Then with a sigh of satisfaction, she straightened her back and took a survey of her surroundings.

The little beach ran up to a cup-shaped hollow, encompassed by high sand dunes. She had noticed the inlet on the large-scale chart, and chose it because she figured that it lay about a mile on the near side of the cottage she sought. And since she had decided to use the motor boat instead of the plane because she wanted to cover her approach, this spot seemed made to order for her purpose.

Her eyes scanned the skyline, and for a moment her heart almost stopped. Surely she had seen the head of a man move in that clump of long, coarse grasses at the top of the incline! Standing perfectly still, although her body tingled with excitement, she continued to stare at the suspicious clump.

Then with characteristic decision, she drew a revolver from her pocket and raced up the side of the dune. But although she exerted herself to the utmost, her progress was much too slow. Her feet sank deep in the shifting sand until she was literally wading, clawing with her free hand for holds on the waving sand grass.

Panting and floundering, she pulled herself to the top, only to find no one there. Nor so far as she could see was there any living thing in sight. The deep boom of the surf was louder here, and peering through the rain, she made out the long stretch of beach pounded by combers, not more than a couple of hundred yards away. Some distance to the right, facing the ocean twinkled the lights of a row of summer cottages. To her left nothing could be seen but tier after tier of grass-topped dunes, a narrow barrier of sand between Great South Bay and the Atlantic Ocean, bleak and desolate, extending farther than the eye could reach. Despite this evidence to the contrary, Mary Eliska still retained the impression that she was not alone. She had an uneasy conviction that she was being watched. She shivered.

"My nerves must be going fuzzy," she thought disgustedly. "I can't risk using a flash, and if there were any tracks this stiff breeze from the sea would have filled them in while I was climbing up here. Well, get going, Mary Eliska, my girl—this place is giving you the creeps— good and plenty."

The Colt was slipped back into her slicker, and she trudged through the loose sand to the black stretch of ocean beach. Here, walking was better, and turning her back on the lighted cottages, she set out along the hard shingle by the surf.

Several times during that walk, Mary Eliska stopped short and scanned the long line of dunes above her. Try as she might, it seemed impossible to rid herself of the idea that someone was following. When she judged the remaining distance to the cottage to be about a quarter of a mile, she left the beach and continued her way over the dunes.

Although Mary Eliska had no tangible fact to connect the *Mystery Plane* with her holdup in New Canaan and Liam McAdams's disappearance, she approached the lonely cottage with the stealth of a Native American. And even if this night reconnoiter should prove only that the bearded aviator had a sweetie living on the shore of Great South Bay, or that he was making daily trips to visit friends, she had no intention of being caught snooping. No matter what she should learn of the cottage's inmates, if anything, she proposed to return with the *Mary Jane* to Yancy's wharf and spend the rest of the night aboard. She had no desire to tramp about Babylon after midnight, looking for a hotel that would take her in.

As she slowly neared the cottage, taking particular pains now not to appear on the skyline, she wished that this adventure was well over. She still felt the effects of her adventure with the thunderhead. The tiny cabin of the motor boat seemed more and more inviting to the weary girl. Trudging through the rain over sand dunes was especially trying when one was walking away from bed rather than toward it.

Then she caught sight of the house roof over the top of the next dune and her flagging interest in her undertaking immediately revived.

Mary Eliska skirted the shoulder of the sandy hill, using the utmost precaution to make not the slightest sound. Then she squatted on her heels and held her breath. Directly ahead, not more than thirty or forty feet at most, gleamed the light from an open window, and from where she crouched, there was an unobstructed view of the room beyond.

There were three men sitting about an unpainted kitchen table which held three glasses and as many bottles. All were smoking, and deep in conversation. One man she knew immediately to be the bearded aviator with whom she had talked on the Beach Club shore. But although Mary Eliska strained her ears to the bursting point, the heavy pounding of the surf from the ocean side prevented her from catching more than a confused rumble of voices.

For a moment or two she waited and watched. The other two men wore golf clothes, were young, and though they were not particularly prepossessing in appearance, she decided that they were American business men on a holiday. They certainly did not look like foreigners.

Mary Eliska, crouching beside the sand dune, felt vaguely disappointed. She did not know exactly what she had expected to find in the cottage, but she had been counting on something rather more exciting than the tableau now framed in the open window. But since she had come this far, it would be senseless not to learn all that was possible. Taking care to keep beyond the path of the light, she crept forward on her hands and knees until she was below the window. Here it was impossible to see into the room, but the voices now came to her with startling distinctness.

"Why?" inquired a voice which Mary Eliska immediately recognized as belonging to the aviator, though oddly enough, it was now without accent. "You surely haven't got cold feet, Donovan?"

"Cold feet nothing! The man don't live that can give me chills below the knee," that gentleman returned savagely. "But I won't be made a goat of either, nor sit in a poker game with my eyes shut. Why should I? I've got as much to lose as you have."

"Those are my sentiments exactly," drawled a third voice, not unpleasantly. "Listen to that surf. There's a rotten sea running out by the light. Raining too, and getting thicker out there by the minute. By three o'clock you'll be able to cut the fog with a knife. What's the sense in trying it—we're sure to miss her, anyway."

"Perhaps you chaps would prefer my job," sneered the aviator. "You make me sick! But you'll have to do what the old man expects of you,—so why argue?"

"How come the old man always picks days like this to run up his red flag?" Donovan was talking again. "There's just as much chance of our picking up that stuff tonight as—as—"

"As finding a golf ball on a Scotchman's lawn," the third man finished for him. "I know there's no use grousing—but it's a dirty deal—and well, we've got to talk about something in this God-forsaken dump!"

"I don't blame you much," the aviator admitted, "but look at the profits, man. Well, I must be shoving off, myself. We'll have another bottle of beer apiece and—" But Mary Eliska did not hear the end of that sentence. Her vigil was suddenly and rudely interrupted. Someone behind her thrust a rough arm under her chin, jerking back her head and holding her in an unbreakable grip. The sickly-sweet odor of chloroform half suffocated her. For a moment more she struggled, then darkness closed in about her.

Chapter 2.7
SHANGHAIED

Mary Eliska came slowly back to consciousness. She was vaguely aware of the chug-chug of a small engine somewhere nearby. Her head swam and there was a sickly sensation at the pit of her stomach. She tried to move, and found it impossible. She heard the splash of waves but could see nothing except the boarded wall of her prison a foot or so away from her eyes.

After a while she became accustomed to the gloom and her sight was clearer. She decided that the rounded wall was the side of a boat. Turning her head slightly she saw that she lay on the flooring of an open motor sailor, beneath a thwart. It had stopped raining. Now the sound of the engine and the gurgle of water against the hull told her that the craft was moving.

She hadn't the slightest idea where this cabinless craft was bound, or how she came to be aboard. Gradually there returned to her a confused memory of the cottage on the dunes, voices through the window. Someone's arm about her neck, forcing her head back—she remembered, now, and groaned. Her body was one stiffness and ache.

Again she tried to heave herself into a sitting position, only to find that her ankles were bound with a turn or two of cord, and her wrists whipped together behind her back. She was trussed like a fowl, and by the feel of her bonds, the trusser was a seaman. She wriggled and writhed, consumed by rage at her own helplessness. The only result was to restore her circulation and clear her faculties, allowing her to realize just what had happened.

"Shanghaied!" Mary Eliska muttered thickly. "Oh, if I'd only had a chance to let loose a little jiu-jitsu on that beast who scragged me!"

Why had they brought her on board this boat and tied her hand and foot? Where was the motor sailor bound? What was going to happen to her next? Mr. Walters would probably get her letter during the afternoon. Yancy seemed a dependable sort of man. Without doubt a raid on the beach cottage would follow, but by that time the birds would have flown, and what good would the raid do her! Her thoughts ran on.

Those men in the cottage were not fools. Their conversation, as they sat around the table, had meant little to Mary Eliska, but she no longer doubted that the gang was interested in an undertaking that was illegal and fraught with considerable danger to themselves. Could it be bootlegging? Possibly. But Mary Eliska did not fancy that idea. The *Mystery Plane*, (she had got in the habit of calling it that now) hadn't enough storage capacity to carry any great quantity of liquor. Where did that amphibian come into this complicated scheme?

This night's work had turned out a failure so far as she was concerned: she should never have undertaken the job of ferreting out the truth alone.

If only Bill Bolton were not away. He would never have allowed her to get into this mess!

Suddenly she heard the creak of a board and the sound of footsteps approaching. Mary Eliska realized that she lay huddled in the bow of the craft, with her head aft and her feet forward. That was why she had not been able to see anything of the crew. She shut her eyes again as someone flashed a torch in her face.

"She's not much better," said a voice she recognized as belonging to the man called Donovan. "Doesn't look to me as if she'd be out of it for a long time. I think you must have given her an overdose of the stuff, Peters." He stirred her none too gently with his foot. "I hope I did!" answered a new voice. "That little wildcat got my thumb between her teeth while I was holdin' the rag to her face. She bit me somethin' terrible, I tell yer."

"Never mind your thumb. We've heard enough of that already. How long did you hold the chloroform to her nose?"

"I dunno. I gave her plenty. If her light's out, I should worry."

"You're right, you should. I'm not handling stiffs on the price of this job." Donovan's tone was biting.

A hand pressed Mary Eliska's side.

"No stiffer than you are," affirmed Peters matter-of-factly. "I can feel her breathe."

"She looks pretty bad to me," Donovan insisted. "The old man will raise the roof if you don't get her over to Connecticut O.K. You know what he said over the phone!"

"Then why not ask Charlie? He used to be a doctor before he did that stretch up the river." He raised his voice. "Hey, there, Charlie! Leave go that wheel and come here for a minute."

"Can't be done," replied Charlie, and Mary Eliska knew that the third man on the beach cottage group was speaking. "What do you want me to do—run this sailor aground in the shallows?"

"Well, Donovan thinks the girl's goin' to croak."

"That's your worry. You're the lad who administered the anesthetic. You probably gave her too much."

"Say, Charlie, this is serious," Donovan broke in anxiously. "Quit high-hatting and give us your opinion."

The steersman snorted contemptuously. "She'll come out of it all right—that is, unless her heart's wobbly. If it is, I couldn't do anything for her out here. You're supposed to be running this show, Don, and Peters did your dirty work. I'm only the hired man. If she goes out, you two will stand the chance of burning, not me. Cut the argument! There's shipping ahead. What are you trying to do—wake the harbor?"

Donovan and Peters stopped talking and went aft. Presently their voices broke out again but this time came to the girl in the bow as a low, confused murmur.

So she owed this situation to Mr. Peters. Mary Eliska was feeling better now and despite her discomfort she spent several minutes contemplating what she would do to Mr. Peters, if she ever got the chance.

The motor sailor's engine stopped chugging and soon the boat came to rest.

"I'll carry her in myself," spoke Donovan from somewhere beyond her range of vision. "Peters bungled the business when he was on watch at that dump across the bay. I want no more accidents until she's safely off my hands."

Mary Eliska was caught up in a pair of strong arms as if she had been so much mutton.

"Think I'd drop her in the drink?" laughed Peters.

"You said it.—Sure this is the right dock, Charlie?"

"No, Donny, it's the grill room of the Ritz—shake a leg there, both of you. We've got a long boat ride and a sweet little job ahead of us. We can't afford to be late—hustle!"

Donovan did not bother to reply to this parting shot. He slung Mary Eliska over his shoulder, stepped onto a thwart, from there to the gunwale and on to the dock. They seemed to be in some kind of backwater from where a set of steps led up from the dock to a small wharf yard, shut in on three sides by high walls and warehouses. Donovan shouldered open a door and ascended a narrow flight of rotting stairs. It had been dark in the yard, but inside the warehouse the night was Stygian. At the top he waited until Peters came abreast. "Where's your flash, Peters?" he growled.

"Haven't got one, Cap."

"Here—take mine, then, and show a glim. It's in my side pocket. My hands are full of girl!"

"Got it," said Peters, a moment later.

The light came on and Mary Eliska, between half-shut eyelids saw that they were in a long, dismal corridor.

"I'll go ahead," continued the man, "I've got the key."

Down this long corridor they passed, then into another narrow passage running at right angles from the first.

Peters eventually stopped at a door which he unlocked and flung open.

"Here we are," he announced and preceded them over the sill.

Mary Eliska caught a glimpse of a small room that smelt of rats and wastepaper with a flavor of bilgewater thrown in. Then she closed her eyes as Donovan dumped her on the bare floor, propping her shoulders against the wall.

"Well, that's done," Donovan said with great satisfaction. "Are you going to wait here for the car, Peters, or out in the yard?"

"The yard for mine, Cap. This joint is full o' spooks. It's jollier outside."

"Right. We'll get going then."

Peters paused and looked at the girl. "There might be some change—maybe a bill or two in the lady's pockets, Cap?" He winked at Donovan hopefully.

"You leave the girl's money alone. The boss distinctly said not to search her. He wants her delivered just as she is."

"Well, what if she passes out on me hands, Cap?"

"Deliver her just the same. And mind—you obey orders or you'll bite off a heap more trouble than you can chew. Come along now!"

The two men left the room. The bolt in the door shot home, then the key turned in the lock; As the sound of their footsteps over the bare floor died away, Mary Eliska opened her eyes. Summoning all her strength, she wrenched at the bonds that held her, but she accomplished no more than lacerating her wrists.

She was to be shifted to some safer place, presumably in Connecticut, where she was to be taken by car. Meanwhile, there was no escape from where she was, even if her limbs were free. Should she show signs of consciousness, the best she had to hope for was another dose of chloroform or a gag when that enterprising thug, Mr. Peters, returned. He was not the kind to leave anything to chance.

Almost before she had got her wits to work, Mary Eliska heard steps in the passage and let herself go limp again, her knees drawn up, her head and neck against the wall. The bolt was drawn, and Peters entered the room. He flashed the torch over his prisoner.

"I don't think there'll be any harm in me takin' a dollar or two," he muttered. "What's the use of money to a stiff? And you sure do look good and dead, young woman!" he chuckled as he bent down to begin the search.

"Guess again!"

Mary Eliska's bound feet shot upward with the force of a mainspring uncoiling. Her neck was braced against the wall and the whole strength of her thighs was behind the kick that drove her boot heels smashing under her captor's chin. The gangster sailed backward. His head hit the base of the opposite wall with a resounding crack and he lay like a log.

The electric torch trundled over the planks and came to a standstill, throwing its pencil of light across the floor. For a couple of seconds, Mary Eliska peered and listened. Then with intense exhilaration of spirit, she rolled and wriggled herself across the intervening space until she was underneath the window. Here, after a little straining and wobbling, that nearly cracked her sinews, she got on her knees. Then she heaved herself upright so that she leaned sideways against the sash. With a thrust she drove her elbow through the pane. There was a crash and a tinkle of falling glass.

Two more thrusts shivered the pane until there remained only a fringe of broken glass at either side. Turning her back to it, she felt for the broken edge with her fingers and brought her rope-lashed wrists across it. Splintered window glass has an edge like a razor. Mary Eliska fumbled the cord blindly to the cutting edge, sawed steadily and felt one of the turns slacken and part.

It was enough. In a few seconds her wrists were free and she stooped and cast loose the lashings from her ankles. She staggered a little and collapsed on the floor. After chafing her arms and legs, she turned to attend to her companion.

There was no need. Mr. Peters showed no further sign of animation than a ham. To insure against interference or pursuit, Mary Eliska turned him over, untied a length of cord from her ankle-bonds, and cast a double sheet-bend about his wrists.

Picking up the flashlight, she hurried out through the door which that canny seeker of "pickings" had left open. She hurried along the two passages and down the rickety stairs. The door at the bottom was closed, so snapping off her light, she pulled it open and stepped into the yard.

But here she was certain there was no egress except by swimming unless she could find a way through the other side of the house. Somewhere out in the darkness she heard the lap and plash of water and the faint creak of rowlocks. Instantly she ducked behind a pile of empty barrels.

A boat skulled stealthily through the gloom and fetched up alongside the dock. A tall figure made the little craft fast, climbed the steps and peered around the yard.

At that very moment, a water rat dropped from the top of the wall to the ground by way of Mary Eliska's shoulder. It was impossible for her to suppress the exclamation of fright that escaped her. The figure in the middle of the yard swung round and an electric torch flashed over the barrels.

"Come out of that or I'll shoot!" ordered the stranger. "And come out with your hands up!"

Chapter 2.8
THE CORK CHAIN

With the white sabre of light blinding her vision, Mary Eliska walked out from behind the stack of barrels, hands above her head. "*Mary Eliska!*" exclaimed the tall figure in astonishment. "What on earth are you doing here?"

There was an instant's pause; then Mary Eliska giggled. "Gee, what a relief—but you scared me out of six years' growth, Bill Bolton!"

As her arms dropped to her sides, she staggered and would have fallen if Bill had not stepped quickly forward and placed his arm about her. He led her to an empty packing case and forced her to sit down. The surprise of this meeting coming as a climax to the strenuous events of the evening had just about downed her splendid nerves. "Oh, Bill—" she sobbed hysterically on his shoulder—"you can't guess how glad I am to see you. I've really had an awful time of it tonight."

"Take it easy and have a good cry. Everything's all right now. You'll feel better in a minute," he soothed.

"What a crybaby you must think me," she said presently, in a limp voice. "Do you happen to have a handkerchief, Bill?"

"You bet. Here's one—and it's clean, too."

Mary Eliska dried her eyes and blew her nose rather violently.

"Thanks—I do feel much better now. Do you mind turning on the light again? I must be a sight. There—hold it so I can see in my compact."

Bill began to laugh as her deft fingers worked with powder, rouge and lipstick.

"What's the joke?" she asked, then answered her own question. "Oh, I know! You think girls do nothing but prink. Well, I don't care—it's horrid to look messy. Is there such a thing as a comb in your pocket, Bill? I have lost mine."

"Sorry," he grinned, "but I got my permanent last week. I don't bother to carry one anymore."

"Don't be silly!" she began, then stopped short. "We've got to get out of here," she said and snapped her compact shut. "They are coming after me in a car. Donovan or Peters, I forget which, said so."

"Who are Donovan and Peters—and where are they going to take you?"

"Not that pair—other members of the same gang. D. and P. are two of the crew over at the beach cottage who chloroformed me, then tied me up and carted me over here in an open motor sailor."

"Well, I'll be tarred and feathered!" Bill switched off his torch. "Here I've been following you for over two hours and never knew it *was* you! Never got a glimpse of your face, of course—took you for a man in that rig! Well, I'll be jiggered if that isn't a break!"

"So *you* were the man I thought I saw in the grass clump?"

"Sure. You led me to the house. I knew the gang had a cottage somewhere along that beach, but I didn't know which one it was. By the way, I've got your *Mary Jane* tied to a mooring out yonder—Couldn't take a chance on running in closer. That old tub's engine has a bark that would wake George Washington." Mary Eliska sprang to her feet. "That's great! We'll make for the *Mary Jane*, Bill, right now. If those men in the car catch us here there'll be another fight. Mary Eliska has had all the rough stuff she wants for one night, thank you!" Bill took her arm.

"O.K. with me," he returned. "Think you're well enough to travel?"

"I'm all right. Hanging around this place gives me the jim-jams—let's go."

Together they crossed the yard and hurried along the narrow planking of the dock to the dinghy. Bill took the oars and a few minutes later they were safely aboard the motor boat. It began to rain again and the dark, oily water took on a vibrant, pebbly look.

"Come into the cabin," suggested Mary Eliska, watching Bill make the painter fast. "We'll be drier there—and I've got about a million questions for you to answer."

"Go below, then. I'll join you in a minute."

Mary Eliska slid the cabin door open and dropped down on a locker. Presently Bill followed and took a seat opposite her. "Better not light the lamp," he advised, "it's too risky now. By the way, Mary Eliska, I'm darn glad to see you again." Mary Eliska smiled. "So 'm I. I've missed you while you were away, and I sure do need your help now. Tell me—where in the wide world am I?"

"This tub is tied up to somebody else's mooring off the Babylon waterfront,—if that's any help to you."

"It certainly is. I hate to lose my bearings. Here's another: I don't suppose you happen to know what this is all about?"

Bill crossed his knees and leaned back comfortably. "There's not much doubt in my mind, after tonight's doings. Those men in the beach cottage are diamond smugglers and no pikers at the game, take it from me!"

"Ooh!" Mary Eliska's eyes widened. "Diamonds, eh! That's beyond my wildest dreams. How do they smuggle them, Bill?"

"Well, these fellows have a new wrinkle to an old smuggling trick. Somebody aboard an ocean liner drops a string of little boxes, fastened together at long intervals—the accomplices follow the steamer in a boat and pick them up. And now, from what I've found out, there's every reason to believe that this gang are chucking their boxes overboard in the neighborhood of Fire Island Light."

Mary Eliska sat bold upright, her eyes snapping with excitement. "Listen, Bill! Those men in the cottage—I heard them talking, you know—couldn't make anything out of their conversation then, but now I'm beginning to understand part of it."

"Didn't you tell me they were arguing against going somewhere—or meeting someone—in the fog?"

"That's right. It was the man they called Charlie—the one who'd been a physician. Let me see ... he said that there was a rotten sea running out by the light. That must mean the Fire Island Light! Then, listen to this. He was sure that by three o'clock the fog off the light would be thick enough to cut with a knife—and that they would probably miss her anyway!—Don't you see? 'Her' means the liner they are to meet off the Fire Island Light about three o'clock this morning!"

"Good work, Mary Eliska—" Bill nodded approvingly. "And that is where Donovan and Charlie headed for when they parked you with Peters," he supplemented. "On a bet, they're running their motor sailor out to the light right now."

Mary Eliska glanced at the luminous dial of her wrist watch. "It is just midnight. Think we have time to make it?"

"Gosh, that's an idea! But, look here, Mary Eliska—" Bill hesitated, then went on in a serious tone, "if we run out to the lightship and those two in the motor sailor spot us, there's likely to be a fight." Mary Eliska moved impatiently. "What of it?"

"Oh, I know—but you'll stand a mighty good chance of getting shot. This thing is a deadly business. They're sure to be armed. Now, listen to me. I'll row you ashore and meet you in Babylon after I've checked up on those guys." Mary Eliska stood up and squeezing past Bill, opened the cabin door.

"And my reply to you is—*rats!*" she flung back at him. "Of course I'm going with you. There'll be no argument, please. Get busy and turn over that flywheel while I go forward and slip our mooring."

Bill made no answer, but with a resigned shrug, followed her out to the cockpit. They had known each other only a few months, but their acquaintance had been quite long enough to demonstrate that when Mary Eliska spoke in that tone of voice, she meant exactly what she said. Bill knew that nothing short of physical force would turn the girl from her project, so making the best of things as he found them, he started the engine.

Bill was heading the boat across the bay when Mary Eliska came aft again. She went inside the cabin and presently emerged with a thermos of hot coffee, some sandwiches and hard-boiled eggs. "We may both get shot or drowned," she remarked philosophically, "but we needn't starve in the meantime."

"Happy thought!" Bill bit into a sandwich with relish, "One drowns much more comfortably after having dined."

"Hm! It would be a cold wet business, though. Doubly wet tonight." She looked at the black water pock-marked with raindrops and shook her head. "Hand me another sandwich, please. Then tell me how *you* came to be mixed up with this diamond smuggling gang, Bill."

By this time they were well on their way across Great South Bay toward the inlet. From the bows came the steady gurgle and chug of short choppy seas as the stiff old tub bucked them. Holding a straight course, the two by the wheel were able to make out the grey-white gleam of sand on Sexton Island.

"Well, it was like this," began Bill. "You remember the Winged Cartwheels.[1] Well that was a Secret Service job for the government."

"I know," nodded Mary Eliska.

"Well, as I was saying—because of that and some other business, Uncle Sam knew that I could pilot a plane. Six weeks ago I was called to Washington and told that an international gang of criminals were flooding this country with diamonds, stolen in Europe. What the officials didn't know was the method being used to smuggle them into this country. However, they said they had every reason to believe that the diamonds were dropped overboard from trans-Atlantic liners somewhere off the coast and picked up by the smugglers' planes at sea. My job was to go abroad and on the return trip, to keep my eyes peeled night and day for airplanes when we neared America."

"Did you go alone?"

"Yes, but I gathered that practically every liner coming over from Europe was being covered by a Secret Service operative. I made a trip over and back without spotting a thing. On the second trip back, something happened."

"When was that?"

"Night before last. The liner I was aboard had just passed Fire Island lightship. I stood leaning over the rail on the port side and I saw half a dozen or more small boxes dropped out of a porthole. They seemed to be fastened together. Once in the water, they must have stretched out over a considerable distance. Of course, there are notices posted forbidding anyone to throw anything overboard: and there are watchmen on deck. But they can't very well prevent a person from unscrewing a porthole and shoving something out!"

"Did you report it?"

"You bet. The skipper knew why I was making the trip. We located the stateroom and found that it belonged to three perfectly harmless Y.M.C.A. workers who were peaceably eating their dinner at the time. Somebody slipped into their room and did the trick."

"Did you hear or see any plane?" "I thought I heard a motor, but it didn't sound like the engine of a plane. I couldn't be sure."

"The motor sailor, probably?"

"It looks like it, now. Well, to continue: I landed in New York and took the next train to Babylon. Then I got me a room in one of those summer cottages on the beach. I was out on the dunes for a prowl when the *Mary Jane* put in at that little cove. That in itself seemed suspicious, so I followed you to the house and saw Peters scrag you. Although, at the time I had no idea who you were. Then when they tied you up and went off with you in the motor sailor, I knew for certain that some dirty work was on. So I beat it back to the cove and came along in this old tub."

Mary Eliska finished the last of the coffee. "Did you see the amphibian tied up to the cottage dock?" she asked.

"Yes. It took off just before the motor sailor left." "Just how do you figure that it comes into the picture?"

"I think these people have a lookout stationed farther up the coast—on Nantucket Island, perhaps. When a ship carrying diamonds is sighted off the Island, the lookout wires to the aviator or his boss and the plane flies over to let the men in the cottage know when to expect her off the lightship. Then when they pick up the loot, he flies back with it to their headquarters next day. Of course, I don't know how far wrong I am—"

"But he's been doing it every day for weeks, Bill—maybe longer. Surely they can't be smuggling diamonds every day in the week?"

"He probably carries over their provisions and keeps an eye on them generally. I don't know. What he is doing is only a guess, on my part, anyway." Mary Eliska smothered a yawn. "Do you suppose the red flag those men spoke of is a signal of some kind?"

"Guess so. But look here, you're dead tired. I can run this tub by myself. Hop in the cabin and take a nap. I'll call you when we near the lightship."

"You must be sleepy, too." "I'm not. I had an idea I might be up most of the night, so slept until late this afternoon. And after those sandwiches and the coffee, I feel like a million dollars. Beat it now and get a rest." Mary Eliska yawned again and stretched the glistening wet arms of her slicker above her head.

"Promise to wake me in plenty of time?" "Cross my heart——"

"Good night, then." "Good night. Better turn in on the floor. We're going to run into a sea pretty soon. Those lockers are narrow. Once we strike the Atlantic swell you'll never be able to stay on one and sleep!"

"Thanks, partner, I'll take your advice." She turned and disappeared below.

Chapter 2.9
DEEP WATER

The ebb tide soon caught the *Mary Jane* in the suck of its swift current and the boat rushed seaward. Presently she struck the breakers and floundering through them like a wounded duck, commenced to rise and fall on the rhythmic ground swell.

Mary Eliska came out of the cabin rubbing the sleep from her eyes.

"You didn't take much of a rest," said Bill from his place at the wheel.

She yawned and caught at the cabin roof to steady herself.

"*Mary Jane's* gallop through the breakers woke me up. Sleeping on a hard floor isn't all it's cracked up to be—and the cabin was awfully stuffy."

"Are you as good a sailor as you are a sport?"

"I don't know much about this deep-water stuff, but I've never been seasick. Thought I might be if I stayed in there any longer, though."

"Feel badly now?"

"No, this fresh air is what I needed. Is that the lightship dead ahead? I just caught the glow."

"Yep. That's Fire Island Light. I wish this confounded drizzle would stop. The swell is getting bigger and shorter. Must be a breeze of wind not far to the east of us."

"D'you think we're in time, Bill?"

"Yes, I think so. The weather is probably thick farther out and up the coast, and the ship will be running at reduced speed. It's likely she'll be an hour or so late. There is a ship out yonder, but it's a tanker or a freighter."

"How do you know that?"

"Why, a liner would be showing deck and cabin lights. Here comes the breeze—out of the northeast."

"It's raining harder, too. Ugh! What a filthy night." Bill nodded grimly in the darkness. "You said a mouthful. It'll be good and sloppy out here in another hour or two. Jolly boating weather, I don't think! And we can't get back into the bay until daylight, I'm afraid."

The big boat continued to pound steadily seaward and before long the lightship was close abeam. Bill ran some distance outside it, then stopped the engine.

"No use wasting gasoline," he said, and emptied one of the five-gallon tins into the fuel tank.

He went into the cabin again and reappeared with two life preservers.

"It's lucky the law requires all sail and motor craft to carry these things. Better slip into one—I'll put on the other."

Mary Eliska lifted her eyebrows questioningly. "Think we're liable to get wrecked?"

"Nothing like that—but a life preserver is great stuff when it comes to stopping bullets."

"Gee, Bill, do you really expect a scrap? There isn't a sign of the motor sailor yet."

"I know—but they're out here somewhere, just the same. Neither of us is showing lights, so in this weather we're not likely to spot each other unless our boats get pretty close. And if they do, those hyenas won't hesitate to shoot! Here, let me give you a hand."

Having put on the life preservers over their dripping slickers, they sat down and waited. The wind was freshening. A strong, steady draft blew out of the northeast and it was gradually growing colder. The rain had turned into sleet, fine and driving, but not thick enough to entirely obscure the atmosphere. "Good gracious, Bill—*sleet!* That's the limit, really—do you suppose we'll ever sight the ship through this?" Mary Eliska's tone was thoroughly disgusted. "Oh, yes," he replied cheerfully, "this isn't so bad. Her masthead lights should have a visibility of two or three miles, at least."

Mary Eliska said nothing, but, hands thrust deep into her pockets and with shoulders hunched, she stared moodily out to sea. For about an hour they drifted, the broad-beamed motor boat wallowing in the chop which crossed the ground swell. Twice Bill started the motor and worked back to their original position. He did not like the look of things, but said nothing to Mary Eliska about it. The wind grew stronger and seemed to promise a gale. The low tide with the line of breakers across the mouth of the inlet would effectually bar their entrance to Great South Bay for the next ten hours. And he doubted if they would have enough fuel for the run of nearly fifty miles to the shelter of Gravesend Bay.

Then as they floundered about, he heard the distant, muffled bellow of a big ship's foghorn. Again it sounded; and twice more, each time coming closer. Bill started the engine and headed cautiously out in the direction from whence it came.

Suddenly there sounded a blast startlingly close to the *Mary Jane*. This was answered from the lightship, and through the flying scud and sleet they saw a vivid glare. Bill put his helm hard over and when the steamer had passed about four hundred yards away, he turned the motor boat again to cut across the liner's wake. Faint streams of music reached their ears emphasizing the dreariness of their position.

Directly they were astern of the great ship, he swung the *Mary Jane* into the steamer's course. Running straight before the wind, it was easy to follow the sudsy brine that eddied in her wake. He was by no means certain, however, that he could keep the dull glow of her taffrail light in sight. That depended upon the liner's speed, which might be more than the *Mary Jane* could develop. But he soon discovered he had either underestimated the power of the motor boat or, what was more probable, the steamer had reduced her own. Before long he was obliged to slow down to keep from overhauling.

And so for nearly an hour they tagged along, astern, keeping a sharp lookout on the band of swirling water. Little by little their spirits sank, as no floating object appeared to reward their perseverance. The weather was becoming worse and worse, but the sea was not troublesome; partly because the *Mary Jane* was running before it and partly because the great bulk of the liner ahead flattened it out in her displacement.

"If this keeps on much longer, we're going to run short of gas," said Mary Eliska, still peering ahead. "Any idea how long it *will* keep up?" Bill shrugged and swung the boat's head over a point. "Not the dimmest. I'm beginning to wonder if we'll have to follow her all the way to the pilot station and then cut across for Gravesend Bay."

"We'll sure be out of luck if we run out of fuel with this wind backing into the northwest. It will blow us clean out to sea!"

"Take the wheel!" said Bill abruptly. "I'm going to see where we stand."

Mary Eliska, with her hands on the spokes, saw him measure the gasoline in the tank and then shake his head.

"How about it?" she called.

"Not so good," he growled, and poured in the contents of another tin. "This engine is powerful, but when you say it's primitive, you only tell the half of it. The darn thing laps up gas like a—"

"*Bill!*" Mary Eliska raised her arm—"there's another motor boat ahead!" Both of them stared forward into the gloom. For a moment Bill could see nothing but the seething waters and the faint glimmer of the liner's taffrail light. Then in an eddy of the driving sleet he caught a glimpse of a dark bulk rising on a swell a couple of hundred yards ahead. At the same time they both heard the whir of a rapidly revolving motor distinctly audible between the staccato barks of their own exhaust.

"The motor sailor, Bill!"

"Sure to be. It must have cut in close under the steamer's stern. Let me take the wheel again, Mary Eliska."

"O. K. Do you think they've seen us?"

"Not likely. They'll be watching the ship and her wake. To see us, they'd have to stare straight into the teeth of the wind and this blinding sleet."

"But they'll hear us, anyway?"

"Not a chance. That motor sailor's got one of those fast-turning jump-spark engines. They run with a steady rattle. There's no interval between coughs. Ours are more widely punctuated. Anyhow, that's the way I dope it. They've probably signaled the ship by this time, and the contraband ought to be dropped from a cabin port at any time now."

"Got a plan?"

"I think I have."

He gave the boat full gas, then a couple of spokes of the wheel sheered her off to starboard.

"What's that for?" Mary Eliska thought he had decided to give up the attempt. "Not quitting, are we?"

"What do you take me for? Get out that gun of yours and use your wits. I'm goin' to loop that craft and bear down on them from abeam. If they beat it, O. K. If they don't, we'll take a chance on crashing them!"

"You tell 'em, boy!" Mary Eliska had caught his excitement. "If they shoot, I'll fire at the flashes!"

Bill was working out his plan in detail and did not reply. He felt sure his scheme was sound. The *Mary Jane* was heavily built, broad of beam, with bluff bows and low freeboard. The motor sailor was a staunch craft, too, but she was not decked and with a load of but two men aboard she would have no great stability. He was certain that if he could work out and make his turn so as to bear down upon her from a little forward of the beam, striking her amidships with the swell of his starboard bow, she would crack like an egg.

Bill did not dare risk a head-on ram. That might capsize them both. To cut into her broadside at the speed she was making would possibly tear off or open up his own bows. The *Mary Jane* must strike her a heavy but a glancing blow at an angle of about forty-five degrees. Such a collision meant taking a big chance with their own boat. But the *Mary Jane* was half-decked forward and the flare of her run would take the shock on the level of her sheer strake.

Quickly he explained his project.

"I'm taking a chance, of course, if I don't hit her right," he finished.

"Go ahead—" she flung back. "I'm all for it!"

Bill grinned at her enthusiasm, and with the engine running full, he started to edge off and work ahead. But he could not help being impatient at the thought that the contraband might be dropped at any minute and hooked up by the others. He took too close a turn. As the *Mary Jane* hauled abreast about two hundred yards ahead, the smugglers sighted them. Their motor sailor swerved sharply to port, and with a sudden acceleration, it dived into the gloom and was lost to sight. "Bluffed off!" he shouted triumphantly.

He turned the wheel and was swinging back into the liner's wake when Mary Eliska gave a cry and pointed to the water off their port quarter.

"Look! There! *There!*" she screamed.

Staring in the same direction, Bill saw what at first he took to be a number of small puffs of spume. Then he saw that they were rectangular. The *Mary Jane* had already passed them and a second later they disappeared from view. Bill nearly twisted off the wheel in an effort to put about immediately. The result was to slow down and nearly stop their heavy boat. Gradually the *Mary Jane* answered her helm and presently they were headed back in the ship's path.

And then as the *Mary Jane* was again gathering speed, the motor sailor came slipping out of the smother headed straight for the contraband, her broadside presented toward her pursuers.

"Stand by for a ram!" yelled Bill and pulled out his automatic.

Not fifty yards separated the two boats. Bows to the gale, the *Mary Jane* bore down on the motor sailor. If those aboard her realized their danger, they had no time to dodge, to shoot ahead, or avoid the ram by going hard astern. They swerved and the *Mary Jane* struck full amidships with a fearful grinding crash.

Bill caught a glimpse of two figures and saw the flame streak out from their barking guns. He felt a violent tug at his life preserver. Then a yell rang out and the two boats ground together in the heave of the angry sea. Steadying himself with a hand on the wheel, he reversed and his boat hauled away. As she backed off he heard the choking cough of the other craft which had now been blotted out by the darkness and driving sleet.

Bill turned about with a triumphant cry on his lips, then checked it suddenly as he saw that Mary Eliska had fallen across the coaming and was lying halfway out of the boat.

Chapter 2.10
WRECKED

The engine gave a grunt and stopped. But Bill scarcely noticed it. Hauling desperately to get Mary Eliska inboard, he thought his heart would burst. Suddenly he heard her cry:

"Don't pull! Just hold me by my legs."

She squirmed farther across the coaming and he gripped her by the knees. "That's it," she panted. "There—I've got it! Now haul me in." Bill gave a heave and just then the boat, caught by a huge wave, rolled far over and landed Bill on his back with Mary Eliska sprawled across him. As they struggled to their feet he saw that she was laughing.

"Aren't you hurt at all?" he asked, rubbing a bruised elbow.

"Only—out of—breath," she gasped. "They—are all—fastened together. Haul them in."

Glancing down, he saw that she was holding one of the white boxes toward him. He made no motion to take it, but stared to windward, listening.

Mary Eliska could hear nothing but the wind and the waves and the swirling sleet.

"What is it?" she jerked out, striving to regain her breath.

"Wait a minute." Suddenly Bill snatched up his electric torch and dove into the cabin.

Mary Eliska dropped down on a thwart with the box in her hand. After a short rest, she renewed her endeavors to get the remainder of her haul overside. When Bill clambered out of the cabin she was tugging at the strong line to which the boxes were tied. "It's jammed, or caught, or something," she announced.

Bill looked overside.

"Yes, dash it all!" he growled. "We fouled the line and wound it round the tail shaft when I backed off just now. That's what stopped the motor, of course. Let me see what I can do. You're blown."

He picked up another box bobbing alongside and started to haul in the line. One end of this he found was jammed under the stern, while on the other length a box appeared every thirty or forty feet.

"Ten, in all," he told her and drew the last aboard.

"Hooray! We've done it!" cried Mary Eliska exultantly.

"We sure have. You just said it all—" His tone was sarcastic. "The boat is leaking like a sieve. That lateral wrench started it. The propeller's jammed. It's beginning to blow a gale and there isn't enough gas to run us out of it. Three cheers and a tiger! Also, hooray!"

Mary Eliska's enthusiasm evaporated. "Gee, I'm sorry. I'm always such a blooming optimist—I didn't think about our real difficulties."

"O. K. kid. I apologize for being cross. That water in the cabin kind of got me for the moment. Let's see what it looks like here."

He wrenched up the flooring and flashed his torch.

Mary Eliska gave a gasp of dismay. The boat was filling rapidly.

"I'll get that bucket from the cabin," she said at once.

"Good girl! I've just got to get this coffee mill grinding again, or we'll be out of luck good and plenty."

Mary Eliska fetched the bucket and began to bail. She saw that Bill was trying to start the engine.

"The shaft wound up that line while we were going astern," he explained. "It ought to unreel if I can send the old tub ahead."

Switching on the current, he managed to get a revolution or two. Then the motor stopped firing.

"No go?" inquired Mary Eliska.

"Not a chance!"

He ripped off his life preserver and slipping out of his rubber coat, pulled forth a jack-knife and opened it. "What are you going to do?" Mary Eliska paused in her bailing.

"Get overboard and try to cut us loose. Don't stop! Keep at it for all you're worth. It's our only chance of safety!"

Wielding her bucket in feverish haste, she watched Bill lower himself over the stern. The water pounded by this unseasonable sleet must be freezingly cold. She wished it were possible to help him. Fortunately, the *Mary Jane* was light of draft. He would not have to get his head under, but that tough line must be twisted and plaited and hard as wire. What if his knife broke, or slipped from his numbed fingers? Mary Eliska shuddered. Meanwhile, the storm was getting worse and the heavy boat drifted before it.

"Hey, there, Mary Eliska! Give me a hand up!"

She dropped the bucket and sprang to his assistance. Then, as his head came in sight, she leaned over and gripping him under the arms, swung him over the stern.

"My word—your strength's inhuman—" he panted.

"Don't talk nonsense. Get busy and start the engine. The water's gaining fast."

"Confound!" he exclaimed. "I'd no idea the cockpit flooring was awash. Another six inches and it will reach the carburetor."

While Bill talked he was priming the cylinder. A heave of the crank and the motor started with a roar. Then he flashed his light on the compass and after noting the bearing of the wind, laid the *Mary Jane* abeam it.

"Take the wheel," he said to Mary Eliska. "And steer just as we're heading now."

"What about the bailing, Bill?"

"My job. You've had enough of it."

"But I'm not tired—"

"Don't argue with the skipper!"

"But you're soaked to the skin!"

"Of course I am—what I need is exercise—I'm freezing!"

"Oh, I'm so sorry—here—turn over the wheel, skipper."

Mary Eliska grabbed the spokes and Bill hastily slipped into his rubber coat and adjusted the life belt over it.

"How are we headed?" she inquired. "I can't see the compass without a light."

"Straight for shore, and we'll be lucky if the old tub stays afloat that long. The whole Atlantic Ocean's pouring in through her seams."

"Maybe the pump would be better?"

"No-sir: not that pump. I've seen it!"

"Mmm. That's why I chose the bucket. Say, I hope you won't get a chill."

"I'll hope with you," returned Bill and kept his remaining breath for his labors. A heavy wave broke against the *Mary Jane's* bow and swept them both with a deluge of water. Mary Eliska paid off the boat's head half a point.

"Lucky that didn't stall the motor for good and all," she observed grimly. "One more like it, and we'll be swimming."

"Tide's on the ebb," grunted Bill. "Wind's barking around—it'll be blowing off the land in half an hour, I guess."

"Do you think the old tub will last that long? She's getting terribly sluggish. Steers like a truck in a swamp!"

"Listen!" he cried. "There's your answer."

From somewhere ahead came the unmistakable booming roar of breakers. As they topped the next wave Mary Eliska saw a white band on the sea. She steadied the wheel with her knee and tightened her life preserver. She knew they could not hope to reach the beach in the *Mary Jane*. Low and open as she was, the first line of breakers would fill her. The motor was still pounding away when she leaned forward and raised her voice to a shout.

"Stop bailing, Bill! Stand by to swim for it!"

"O. K., kid."

Bill dropped the bucket and dove for the cabin. A second later he was back in the cockpit with a three-fathom length which he had cut from the anchor line. He fastened one end about Mary Eliska's waist and took a turn about his own body with the other. Then, catching up a bight of the line which secured the boxes he made it fast to his belt with a slip hitch.

The *Mary Jane* was forging strongly ahead, her actual weight of water being about that of her customary load of passengers. The swells began to mount, to topple. Searching the shore, Mary Eliska could see no sign of any light or habitation.

"If I'd known we were so nearly in, we might have raised the coast guard with the flash light." Bill groaned his self-contempt. "I ought to have kept an eye out—and the Navy said I was a seaman!"

"Don't be silly! It was my fault, if anyone's. You were busy bailing. Chances are the light couldn't have been seen from shore, anyway. Gosh, what weather! Who ever heard of sleet in August!"

"Look out—behind you!" yelled Bill.

A moment later she felt herself snatched from the wheel and was crouching below the bulwark with Bill's arm around her waist. Then as a brimming swell lifted them sluggishly, its combing crest washed into the boat. The next wave flung them forward and crumpled over the gunwale.

The *Mary Jane's* motor gave a strangled cough and stopped. The boat yawed off and came broadside on her stern upon a line with the beach. "This is what I hoped for," he shouted in her ear. "Gives us a chance to get clear." She saw him gather up the boxes and fling them overboard.

"Keep close to me. We'll need each other in the undertow!" she yelled back at him, as he pulled her to her feet.

Then as the next big comber mounted and curled, they dove into the driving water and the wave crashed down upon the sinking boat. Mary Eliska felt her body being whirled over and over, sucked back a little and driven ahead again. The water was paralyzingly cold, but she struck out strongly and with bursting lungs reached the surface. A second later, Bill's head bobbed up a couple of yards away. Blowing the water from her nose, she saw they were being washed shoreward. Her life preserver, new and buoyant, floated her well—almost too well. She found it difficult to dive beneath the curling wave crests to prevent another rolling.

Bill was swimming beside her now and as a great wave caught them up and carried them forward he grasped her under the arm.

There came a last crumbling surge and the mighty swirl of water swept them up the beach and their feet struck bottom. Fortunately, the beach was not steep. The tide was nearly at the last of the ebb and there was but little undertow. Together they waded out and staggered up the shingle to sink down on the sand breathing heavily.

The boxes were washing back and forth at the water's edge and Bill's first act was to haul them in. "Well, the government's precious loot is safe," he said grimly. "Are you able to walk?"

"I—I guess so." "Then, let's get going. We'll freeze if we don't."

He gathered up the boxes and looped them from his shoulders, rose to his feet and held out a hand. Mary Eliska took it, scrambled up and stood for a moment swaying unsteadily.

"The end of a perfect d-day—" she tried to grin, her teeth chattering with cold.

"I *don't* think!" replied Bill unenthusiastically, and helped her to get rid of the heavy life belt.

"Know where we are?" she inquired when he had dropped the belts on the sand. "Not precisely. But if we keep going we ought to strike a lifesaving station or something—come on."

Mary Eliska groaned. "I suppose I must, but—gee whiz—I sure want to rest."

Bill, who knew that physical exertion was absolutely necessary now, got his arm about her and they started unsteadily down the beach assisted by the gale at their backs.

They had walked about half a mile when he felt her weight begin to increase and her steps to lag. He stopped and peered into her face. As he did so, she sank to the sand at his feet. Bending over her, he was surprised to see that she was asleep—utterly exhausted.

The outlook was anything but pleasant. They had apparently struck upon a wild and desolate strip of sand—an island, he thought, cut off by inlets at either end and flanked by the maze of marshes in the lower reaches of Great South Bay. Without doubt they were marooned and to make matters worse, Bill knew he had just about reached the limit of his own strength.

Chapter 2.11
FROM OUT THE SEA

Bill stared down at Mary Eliska sleeping the sleep of exhaustion on the cold, wet sand. Her clothes, like his, were soaked with sea water and with rain. He realized that something must be done at once, or they would both be in for pneumonia. So stripping off his rubber coat and covering the unconscious girl, he started for the dunes.

Day was breaking as he left the shingle and commenced to plow through the loose sand. The storm was abating somewhat. Although the wind still blew half a gale, the sleet had turned to a fine, cold rain which bade fair to stop altogether once the sun was fully up. By the time Bill Bolton worked his painfully slow way to the top of the dunes it was light enough to see for a considerable distance.

At first glance the prospect was anything but alluring. His point of vantage was in the approximate center of an island of sand and shingle, a mile long, perhaps, by half a mile wide. Inlets from the white-capped Atlantic effectually cut off escape at either end of the outer beach on which a fearsome surf was pounding. Along the inner shore of this desolate, wind-swept islet a complicated network of channels intertwined about still other islands as far as the eye would reach. Nor could Bill make out any sign of human habitation.

"Water, water, everywhere, and not a gol-darned drop to drink," he misquoted thoughtfully and wondered if by chewing the eel grass he would be able to get rid of the parched feeling of his mouth and throat. He pulled a broad blade and chewed it meditatively. Then spat it out in disgust. The grass was as salty as the sea. It made him thirstier than ever. Turning seaward he swept the pale horizon with a despondent gaze.

Not a sign of a craft of any description could be seen. Wait a minute, though. Bill caught his breath. What was that—bobbing in the chop of the waves, just outside the bar of the eastern inlet? Could it be a boat? In this gray light a proper focus was difficult. It was a boat, open; a lifeboat, by the look of it. Waiting no longer for speculation, he hurried down the low hill toward the sea.

Once he struck hard sand, Bill raced into the teeth of the wind, with the boom of the surf on his right, and dire necessity lending wings to his tired feet. Forgotten were his thirst, the clammy cold of his wet clothes and his weariness. Every ounce of strength, the entire power of his will centered in the effort to come close enough to the boat to signal her assistance.

With his heart pumping like a steam engine, he passed Mary Eliska, who was lying exactly as he had left her. Then he got his second wind and running became less of a painful struggle. He could see the boat more plainly now. Surely it was an open motor sailor. Could it be the one belonging to Donovan and Charlie, he wondered. What irony!—to be rescued by the smugglers—and to lose liberty and the diamonds after all this storm and stress! But the motor sailor was drifting—into the surf off the bar—without a soul aboard. Coming to a halt at the inlet, he watched the tide pull the boat through the breakers on the bar to the smooth water. Off came his jacket and flinging it behind him on to the sand he waded into the water and swam for the boat. He reached her at last and with difficulty pulled himself aboard.

For a moment or two he rested on a thwart in a state of semi-collapse. As he had thought, it was the smugglers' boat. But there was no sign of Donovan or Charlie. However, except for six inches or so of water that sloshed about his feet, the motor sailor seemed to be in good condition.

When he felt better, he started the engine and ran her ashore on the island. Then after inspecting the boat's lockers, he buried her anchor in the sand and trudged back along the beach to Mary Eliska.

She was still sleeping, tousled head pillowed on her right arm, and it was some time before he could bring her back to consciousness.

"Let me alone," she moaned drowsily, "I'm too tired to get up this morning, Lizzie. I don't want any breakfast—go away and let me sleep!" Bill raised her to a sitting position. "Wake up—wake up! You aren't at home. And this isn't Lizzie—it's Bill—Bill Bolton! We're still on the island."

Mary Eliska opened her eyes, and looked at him wonderingly. "The island—" he reiterated. "We were wrecked—had to swim for it. Don't you remember?" Suddenly she gained full control of her waking senses. "I know. I know now, Bill. Guess I've been asleep. Ugh! I'm soaking. What did you wake me for? At least, I was comfortable!" "Come to breakfast and dry clothes. You'll get pneumonia if you stay here. Do you think you can walk? You're a pretty husky armful, but I guess I can carry you to the boat if I must." He grinned at her.

Mary Eliska was stiff and weary but she fairly jumped to her feet. "What boat? Where is it?" Bill told her.

"But you said 'dry clothes and breakfast'—"

They were hurrying along the beach.

"That's right. She's got plenty of food aboard—and one of the lockers is packed with clothes. There are even dry towels, think of that! Those guys had her provisioned and equipped for a long trip."

"What's happened to them, do you think?"

"I can't make it out. The boat has shipped some water, but nothing to be worried about. The motor's O.K. and there's plenty of gas. They may have got into the surf, thought she was going to founder, perhaps, and swam ashore like we did."

"But they're not on the island?"

"No. If they made the beach, it was somewhere else along the coast."

"We should worry," said Mary Eliska. "If they don't want her, we do—and she certainly looks good to me."

They walked down the shingle and Bill got aboard the boat.

"You wait on the beach," he directed. "It's pretty wet underfoot. I'll pass the things overside. I think the best plan is for you to go up in the dunes and change there. Meanwhile, I'll start in with the handpump and get rid of the water. I'll have her good and dry by the time you get back. Then you can rustle a meal while I put on dry things. Catch!"

Mary Eliska found herself possessed of a bundle knotted in a large bath towel. Upon inspection it proved to contain dungaree trousers, a jumper, a dark blue sweater, woolen socks and a pair of rubber-soled shoes.

"They may be a trifle large," said Bill. "But at least they're dry and the clothes seem to be clean."

"Nothing could be sweeter," was Mary Eliska's comment. "See you in ten minutes—so long!"

"O.K.," replied Bill and turned to the handpump.

Quarter of an hour later he was completing his labors with the aid of a large sponge when he heard footsteps on the shingle and looked up to see a young fellow in blue dungarees and sweater coming toward the boat, carrying a bundle of clothes.

"Mary Eliska! Gee—what a change! For a minute I thought you were a stranger."

"Somebody's younger brother, I suppose," she laughed. "These things are miles too big for me—but they're darned comfortable and warm. You go ahead and change your own clothes. I'll finish bailing." Bill stepped overside and on to the sand, carrying his dry rig and a towel. Mary Eliska was spreading her sodden clothing on the sand.

"Bailing's over for today," he told her, "don't forget about breakfast, though. I could eat a raw whale."

"Don't worry, young feller," she retorted. "Your breakfast will be ready before you are. Just let me get these things drying in the nice warm sun that's coming up now, and you'll see!"

With a wave of his hand he disappeared over the brow of the sand hills, and Mary Eliska clambered aboard the beached motor sailor. Much to her delight she found a small two-burner oil stove, already lighted, standing on a thwart. Nearby had been placed a coffee-pot and a large frying pan. The lid of the food locker lay open, as did the one containing the water keg.

"Bright boy," she murmured approvingly. "You're a real help to mother! Now let's see what smugglers live on."

She had set a collapsible table that hinged to the side of the boat and was busy at the stove when she heard Bill's halloo.

"Breakfast ready?" he called from the beach. "Will be in a jiffy," she answered without looking up. "How do you like your eggs?"

"Sunny side up, if it's all the same to you."

"O.K. Spread your wet clothes on the sand and come aboard."

She was serving his eggs on a hot plate when Bill's head appeared over the side.

"My, but that coffee smells good," he cried, and swung himself aboard. "How did you manage to cook all that food!"

"Come to the table, and see what we've got."

He sat down and inspected the various edibles, ticking them off on his fingers.

"Coffee, condensed milk, bread and butter, the ham-what-am, fried eggs, marmalade and maple syrup! Say, Mary Eliska, those guys certainly lived high. Some meal, this!"

Mary Eliska turned about from the stove, smiling. "And here's what goes with the maple syrup!"

"A stack of wheats!" He shouted as she uncovered the dish. "You're a wonder, a magician, Mary Eliska. How in the world did you manage it?"

Mary Eliska laughed, pleased by his enthusiasm.

"Found a package of pancake flour in the locker. They're simple enough to make. Now dig in before things get cold. Help yourself to butter—it's rather soft, but this lugger doesn't seem to run to ice."

Bill set to work as she poured the coffee.

"Like it that way," he replied, his mouth full of ham and eggs, while he plastered his pancakes with butter. "Well, we've sure put it over on Messrs. Donovan and Charlie this trip, not to mention your friend Peters. Got their diamonds and their boat and their clothes. Now we're eating their breakfast,—the sun is shining once more—and all is right in the world."

"Where are those diamonds, by the way?" exclaimed Mary Eliska suddenly, having taken the edge off her ravenous appetite.

Bill laid down his knife and fork. For a moment he looked startled, then burst into a great roar of laughter.

"We're a fine pair of Secret Service workers!" he cried derisively. "But it's my fault. You were all in."

Mary Eliska's jaw dropped. "Don't tell me you left them on the beach!"

"Surest thing you know. I left them beside you on the sand and forgot all about the darn things when I spotted the motor sailor. Never thought of them again until this minute!"

Mary Eliska nodded sagely. "Which only goes to show that diamonds don't count for much when one is tired and wet and hungry, not to mention being marooned on a desert island!"

"Ain't it the truth! Another cup of coffee, please. I'll fetch them when we've finished eating."

"After we've washed up?"

"O.K. with me."

Bill drank his third cup of coffee and leaned back with a sigh of content.

"Well, the old appetite's satisfied at last," he admitted comfortably. "And I don't mind telling you that was the best meal I ever ate."

"Thank you, kind sir. Though I think it is your appetite rather than the cook you should thank." Bill shook his head. "When it comes to cooking, you're a real, bona fide, died-in-the-wool, A-1 Ace! How about it—shall we wash the dishes now?"

"I can't eat any more, and if I don't get busy soon, I'll go to sleep again."

"Pass the dishes and things overside to me. I'll sluice 'em off in the water. We should worry. This will be our last meal on this boat. I'll bet a rubber nickel those smuggler-guys wouldn't have done this much if they'd got the *Mary Jane*."

"Poor *Mary Jane*," sighed Mary Eliska as they tidied up. "She was a staunch old thing. I wonder what Yancy will soak Dad for her?" "Nothing. Uncle Sam pays for that boat. She went down on government service, didn't she?"

"That's good news," smiled Mary Eliska. "Now, that's the last plate. Let's go along the beach. I'm getting worried about those boxes of diamonds. Do you think they'll be there, all right?"

"Sure to be. Unless somebody has landed on this island while we were busy with the eats. Come along and we'll see."

Chapter 2.12
THE NOTEBOOK

"Do you really think they'll be where we left them, Bill?"

"Why sure! You're not worrying, are you?"

The two were hurrying along the beach toward the spot where Mary Eliska had dropped to the sand and fallen asleep.

"Yes, I am." "Well, it's Uncle Sam's loot, not ours. And I reckon he cares more about knowing how the smuggling was done than the contraband itself, anyway."

"I know. But that's only half of it. The gang has got to be rounded up. We don't know where they have their headquarters or who is in back of this business. So I'd hate to have to admit I'd lost the diamonds, after all." Then, as Bill began to reply, she went on: "And don't forget that Liam McAdams is still missing—or was, when I flew over from New Canaan yesterday!"

"You're right, pal. I just didn't want you to take it too soberly. But that bearded aviator has got to be checked up. No easy matter, either, after what happened last night." He broke off sharply. "There are the old boxes—just where I dropped them—so you see you've had your worry for nothing." "Just the same, we've been terribly careless!"

"Don't rub it in," said Bill, looping the line and its dangling load over his shoulder. "These things go to a bank for safe keeping just as soon as I can get rid of them."

Mary Eliska caught his arm. "Let's pry open one of the boxes, and make sure there really are diamonds inside."

"Nothing doing," Bill answered decisively. "They're going to be turned over to the authorities—as is!"

"Well, you needn't be so snooty about it. But I am crazy to see the sparklers—especially after all we've been through to rescue them!"

"Of course,—I'm sorry," apologized Bill with a grin, "I'm kind of jumpy this morning, I guess. Me for bed as soon as I can find one. But you know, we really can't open those things up, because we'd then be held responsible for contents—or no contents—as the case may be. See?"

"I didn't think about that, Bill. But let's forget the old boxes. I'm all in myself. Any idea what time it is? My watch has stopped."

Bill glanced at his wrist. "Just seven o'clock. Seems like noon to me. This nice warm sun is a wonderful help—I was chilled to the bone." "Me too," said Mary Eliska. "Well, here we are at the motor sailor. Nothing to keep us longer on this island. I vote we shove off." "Second the motion. Hop aboard and go aft. Your weight in the stern will help to raise her bow so I can push her out without breaking my back."

"How's that?" called Mary Eliska a minute later.

"Fine! Stand by for a shove!"

A heave of his shoulder against the bow loosened the boat's keel from the sand and Bill sprang aboard as she glided into deep water.

"Don't suppose there's a chart of the lower bay stowed in one of those lockers?" he remarked as he started the engine. "The shallows are going to be the limit to navigate without running aground. Do you mind seeing what you can find, Mary Eliska?"

"Not at all—seeing I've already found one," she laughed. "Came across it when I was looking for food."

"Good." Bill took over the wheel. "Let me see it, will you?"

Mary Eliska passed over the map. Bill studied it with a hand on the wheel.

"Thank goodness the deeper channels are marked," he ruminated, "that's a help, anyway."

Mary Eliska peered over his shoulder.

"That island must be one of those in Jones Inlet. I had no idea we'd gone so far west."

"All of fifteen miles as a plane flies to Babylon. No chance of making any time until we get into South Oyster Bay which is really the western end of Great South Bay. If we make Babylon by noon, we'll be lucky."

"No reason why we should both try to keep awake," observed Mary Eliska. "I'll skipper this craft for a spell. Make yourself comfortable somewhere and go to sleep. You'll be called at ten o'clock."

"But you need rest more than I do," began Bill.

"Oh, I had a snooze on the *Mary Jane*," she interrupted, "and got another on the sand this morning. Pipe down, sailor! This is your master's voice what's speaking. Excuse the ungarnished truth, but you look like something the cat brought in and didn't want!"

Bill's laugh ended in a yawn.

"Aye, aye, skipper. Call me at four bells. Night!"

He went forward and lay flat on the flooring, his head pillowed on his arms. He was asleep almost immediately.

For the next couple of hours Mary Eliska steered a winding course among low sandy islands and mudbanks. It was impossible to make any speed in these shallow, tortuous waters and she was taking no chances on running aground. It was monotonous work at best. She was deadly tired. There was little or no breeze and the sun, unshaded by the faintest wisp of cloud, fairly blistered the boat's paint with its fierce heat.

At ten she roused Bill, and as soon as he was sufficiently alert to take over she went to sleep on the flooring in the shadow of a thwart.

It seemed as though she had but closed her eyes when Bill's voice called her back to wakefulness.

"We're almost in," he reminded her. "Better run forward or I'm likely to ram the dock."

Mary Eliska jumped to her feet and ran her fingers through her rumpled hair. She was astonished to see that the motor sailor was closing in on the dock of Yancy's Motor Boat garage.

"We must have made wonderful time—" she yawned, stumbling toward the bow.

"Only fair," Bill said. "It's almost noon. Snap into it, kid, and fend her off with the boathook."

Presently they were tied up to the dock and Mary Eliska was making a sketchy toilet with the aid of her compact.

"How about it, old sport?" she looked up from her mirror, busy with damp powder and lipstick. "What's on the program now? Thank goodness *Wispy* is still at her mooring over there. I s'pose after we settle with Yancy for the *Mary Jane*, we'd better take the plane and fly home."

"Eventually, yes," decided Bill. "I'll go up to the office and fix things with Yancy. I've got to do some long-distance telephoning, anyway, and park these boxes in a bank. It will save a lot of time if you'll go over this boat with a fine-tooth comb while I'm gone. I don't expect you'll find anything much, but there's no telling."

"All right," she nodded. "And while you're about it, get hold of that letter I wrote Mr. Walters and phone Lizzy we will be home for a late lunch. The sooner we can get back to New Canaan and Little Mary Eliska can crawl between clean sheets, the better she'll be pleased!"

"Yep. I'll work as fast as I can."

Bill clambered on to the dock and made off in the direction of the boat yard.

For the next hour Mary Eliska worked manfully, overhauling the motor sailor. Fierce rays of the noonday sun beat down on the open boat. She was worn out and dizzy, but stuck pluckily to her job, turning out the contents of lockers and investigating every nook and cranny of the smugglers' craft. Except for an old coat and those odds and ends which accumulate aboard any boat as large as the motor sailor, she found absolutely nothing. Tired and hot and crazy for sleep, she decided to call off this unprofitable search, when Bill's voice hailed her. "Hello, there, pardner," he sang out, stepping aboard. "How are things going?"

Mary Eliska straightened her back and wiped the perspiration from her forehead with a sodden handkerchief. She noted the deep circles below Bill's eyes and the tired droop of his shoulders. He looked on the verge of collapse, but his voice still held its hearty ring.

"Not so good, old timer. There isn't a blessed thing worthwhile aboard this scow. Finish your business?"

"Reckon so. Got Washington on the phone and the big chief is tickled silly with all we've done. Tell you more about it later. Yancy will be recompensed for the *Mary Jane* and will look after this motor sailor until the government men take her over. I got Lizzie on the wire. She expects your father home tonight."

"Thanks. Did you get my letter, too?"

"It's in my pocket. I put the diamonds in a safe deposit box at a bank uptown. And I guess that's pretty much everything."

"You look done up, Bill."

"I've felt sprucer. But you look pretty rocky yourself."

"Feel like a wet smack, thank you. The heat is terrible."

"Wait 'til I collect my duds and yours," he suggested, "and we'll beat it for New Canaan and Home Sweet Home!"

"They're rolled up in a sea bag," she told him. "Here it is."

She started toward him with the bag in her arms, stumbled and would have fallen had not Bill's steadying hand prevented.

"Kind o' wobbly, eh?"

"Not as bad as all that, Bill. Caught my toe in that floorboard. It's loose."

"Have you had them up?"

"Why, no, I never thought of that."

Bill took the sea bag from her and tossed it on to the dock.

"Hop on a thwart," he prompted. "I don't suppose there's anything but bilgewater under the boards but we might as well have a look."

"Need a hand?" asked Mary Eliska, looking down at him. "No, I guess not. These sections aren't heavy—" He broke off with a sudden exclamation and fished up something from the wet.

"What is it?"

"Seems to be a notebook. Probably dropped out of either Donovan's or Charlie's pockets and got kicked under that loose flooring in the gale last night. But it's soaking wet and its pages are stuck together. Wonder if we'll be able to get anything out of it?"

Mary Eliska held out her hand.

"Give it to me. I'll dry it out on the dock while you look some more."

For the next few minutes Bill continued his search while Mary Eliska after placing the notebook on the decking of the dock watched it carefully, lest the light breeze blow it into the water. At last he joined her and lifted the sea bag over his shoulder.

"How's it coming?" "Not so good. It's going to take a long time to dry the book all the way through even in this sun."

"Then let's take it along to New Canaan. I'll get Dad to put it in our oven as soon as we get home. That'll do the trick. Get aboard that dinghy and I'll row you over to the plane."

Mary Eliska picked up the notebook and slipped it into her pocket. "That's the best thing you've said today," she beamed, "I'll be home and asleep in twenty minutes! Come along."

Chapter 2.13
THE WARNING

Mary Eliska and Mr. Stricklin were finishing breakfast next morning when the Boltons, father and son, dropped in. "Good morning, stranger," was Mr. Stricklin's greeting to Bill. "I understand you've been to Europe and back a couple of times since we saw you last. We've missed you, boy."

"Thanks," returned Bill. "I'm glad to be home again."

"Which home?" asked his father with an amused smile. "When in New Canaan you seem to spend most of your time across the way here."

"And why not?" protested Mr. Stricklin. "Mary Eliska and I return the compliment often enough. Since you people moved here two lonely widowers have acquired another child apiece. It's fine—both Mary Eliska and I are the happier for it."

"And that goes two ways," asserted Bill. "How about it, Dad?"

"Yes, of course," Mr. Bolton assented heartily. "The intimacy is one I enjoy immensely. But I'm afraid that Bill has begun the habit of leading Mary Eliska into all kinds of dangerous adventures. This diamond smuggling business, for instance."

Mr. Stricklin chuckled. "If you ask me, I don't think Mary Eliska needs any leading."

"Well, I should say not!" exclaimed his daughter. "If it weren't for Bill, I'd never be able to get out of half the messes we drift into together!" Mr. Stricklin pushed his chair back from the breakfast table. "This meeting of the mutual admiration society is all very nice," he announced with a twinkle in his eye, "But it is high time the ways and means committee got together on this last Bolton-Stricklin hair-raiser. I vote we adjourn to the porch and learn what the subcommittee on the smugglers' notebook has to report."

"Second the motion," chirped Mary Eliska. "I'm just crazy to hear what you've found out, Daddy Bolton. I suppose Bill has been hitting the hay, like me?" "He put in nearly sixteen hours of uninterrupted slumber," Mr. Bolton answered as they found chairs for themselves on the shaded porch, where the air was sweet with the scent of honeysuckle.

"Well, I guess it was a dead heat," she laughed. "I woke up less than an hour ago, myself."

Mr. Stricklin passed his case to Mr. Bolton and when their after-breakfast cigars were well alight, Bill produced the notebook.

"While you're busy with that stogie, Dad, I'll start the ball rolling."

"Humph! That—er—stogie happens to be a fifty-cent Corona!" snorted Mr. Stricklin who was touchy about his smokes.

"Means nothing to me," replied Bill blandly. "Don't use 'em myself and—"

"Say, will you please pipe down on cigars—" broke in Mary Eliska, "and get to the notebook?"

"Oh, what a pun—" groaned Bill, "you certainly—"

"Be still!" ordered his father. "She's right. Let's get down to business. Now, here's the book," he went on, opening the little volume. "I dried it in our oven and although the writing is blurred, it is still quite legible. As you see, only a few pages have been used, and they show a simple set of flag signals. The red flag means: 'Meet Steamship.' The yellow flag stands for 'A.M.'; the white, 'P.M.' Then there are twenty-four flags to designate the hours and half-hours from one to twelve."

"Is that all?" asked Mary Eliska, disappointedly.

"Absolutely. The rest of the pages are blank."

"I remember hearing the men speak of the bosses' red flag when I was listening outside the cottage," she said slowly, "and that meant, of course, that Donovan and Charlie were to meet the steamer."

"Quite. But until we are able to locate the spot where these signals are displayed we won't accomplish much."

Bill nodded. "And now that they know we have discovered their method of smuggling, they'll probably shift their operations from Fire Island Lightship to some other point along the coast."

"Very likely," his father acquiesced. "Although it is my opinion they will discontinue, temporarily, and lay low for a while."

"Still there must be other shipments in transit right now," suggested Mr. Stricklin. "But I suppose they could manage that by sending radios in code?"

Mr. Bolton carefully knocked the ash from his cigar.

"I think that's beyond the point," he argued. "We can only surmise what they may or may not do. The government men will watch the ships and the coast. Both Bill and I talked to Washington over the phone just before we came over here. And the officials there believe that the bearded aviator's plane is a most important factor in the operations of the smugglers. And the Chief wants Bill to find that plane—"

Mary Eliska snorted derisively. "Well, he doesn't want much! That airplane won't fly over the Beach Club again, after this—" Mr. Bolton smiled at Mary Eliska's vehemence. "But you see, my dear, the Washington gentleman thinks that if Bill is able to follow the mysterious amphibian, it will eventually lead him to the headquarters of the gang."

Bill burst out laughing. "It's just like telling me to take a handful of salt—and if I can put it on the birdie's tail, I will eventually catch the birdie! But it isn't really the Chief's order, he knows what we're up against. It's that assistant of his who wants to cover himself with glory. I asked him if I hadn't better disguise my plane like a string of white boxes so they'd take me for a diamond necklace!"

"What'd he say?" giggled Mary Eliska. "Oh, he spread on the soft soap until I got even more disgusted and turned him over to Dad!" Mr. Stricklin chuckled. "It's a pretty large order. I don't suppose your Secret Service friend gave you any valuable suggestions?"

"He did not," sneered Bill. "That, as he explained, was entirely up to me!" For several minutes no one spoke. "We sure are up against it," sighed Mary Eliska at last.

"You mean I am," was Bill's reply. "The only thing I can do is to start a series of patrols."

"*We* will start a series of patrols," she corrected. "Two planes will be better than one."

"Just as you say." Bill showed no enthusiasm. "My idea of something uninteresting to do is to fly around all day, hunting another plane, that's probably safely housed in its hangar all the time."

"Oh, don't be such a wet blanket! If none of us have brains enough to think of a plan to trap that fellow, there's no use grouching over it!"

"That's all very well. But where are we going to patrol? You told me, I think, that those lads planned to take you from the warehouse to their headquarters in Connecticut. This state's not so big when you compare it with Texas or California—but when it comes to locating a single plane—"

"Listen!" cried Mary Eliska and ran to the porch steps. "Come here—all of you—quick!"

The deep drone of an airplane increased to a giant roar as a smart two-seater swept down toward the house.

"It's the *Mystery Plane*!" she shrieked. "The nerve of him!"

On came the amphibian with throttle wide open, just topping the trees at the edge of the lawn. Then the four on the steps saw the pilot drop something overside and zoom upward missing the roof of the house by inches. "I should say he has nerve—" Mr. Stricklin pointed out on to the lawn. "Run out and get that parcel he dropped on the grass, Bill. This business is getting more interesting by the minute!"

Bill brought the package back to the porch.

"Oh, what do you think it is?" Mary Eliska grabbed Bill's arm in her excitement.

"Calm down!" said her father, as Bill held out a small box covered with brown paper and sealed with dabs of red wax. "Handle it carefully—there may be explosive in it."

"I don't think so—" said Bill, "those things generally run by clockwork. There's no tick in this box."

"Come on—let's open it," exclaimed Mary Eliska impatiently. "I'll bet it's nothing dangerous. Couldn't have been dropped from a plane without going off!"

"Wait one minute," commanded her father. "We'll be on the safe side, anyway. Don't touch the thing 'til I come back."

He ran into the house.

"Any address on it?" inquired Mary Eliska.

"Not the slightest bit of writing. If there is any, it's underneath this outside wrapping." Mr. Stricklin came out of the house carrying a pail of water, which he brought down to the lawn, where they were waiting. "Drop that package into the water," he ordered Bill. "A good soaking will take the sting out of any explosive."

Mary Eliska burst out laughing.

"Maybe—but not in this case, Dad. Look, the thing floats!"

She snatched up the package and ripped off the outside paper, disclosing a white cork box, similar to those used for carrying the contraband.

Bill took a knife from his pocket and opened a blade that proved to be a small screwdriver. He took the box from Mary Eliska and removed the screws from the lid.

"Gee, do you think they've sent us a diamond?" she asked jokingly.

"Not a chance. This is a message of some kind, I'll bet!"

The box was filled with jeweler's cotton, from the center of which he drew a revolver cartridge. Around it, fastened by a rubber band, there was a small sheet of note paper. The others gathered close as he smoothed out the paper.

Blocked in capitals with a red crayon was the smugglers' message.

"LAY OFF! THIS MEANS BOTH OF YOU."

"Aha! And if we don't lay off, we'll be plunked with a bullet from a cartridge like this!" Mary Eliska summed up. "This affair is likely to get exciting before we finish it."

Mr. Bolton studied the paper then returned it to the box with the cartridge.

"Has it struck you oddly," he said quietly, "that these people should know that Bill was mixed up in this? That message, of course, is for Mary Eliska and Bill."

"Yes, I was thinking of that," admitted Bill.

"Strange—" cogitated Mr. Stricklin. "You two flew from Babylon back here without a stop—and you both went straight to bed. Neither you, nor I, Bolton, have spoken to anyone about their exploits, I'm sure."

"Somebody must have found out from the servants that our offspring flew back together," his friend decided. "It could not have happened any other way. Then that fact, added to the glimpse they must have caught of a young man in the *Mary Jane* with Mary Eliska, when they rammed the smugglers' motor sailor off the lightship, gave them a simple line of reasoning. And the joke of the matter is that their warning has done just the reverse from what they figured it would do!"

Mr. Stricklin looked puzzled. "I don't quite see what you mean?"

"Why, it has given us the only real clue we have to the gang's whereabouts," smiled Bolton senior.

"Dad's one up on me, too," grinned Bill. "How about you, Ecker?"

Mary Eliska stamped her foot. "You'll get a whack you'll remember for the rest of your life if you murder my perfectly decent name that way, Bill! You ought to know by now that I won't stand for it."

"So sorry, Mary Eliska!" he apologized with mock politeness. "Will Miss Sherlock Holmes, the famous lady sleuthhound who solved the New Canaan Bank mystery, deign to say whether or not she also spots a clue in the villain's message?"

"Aren't you the bunk! Yes, I think I know what Daddy Bolton is talking about."

"Well, Miss Cleverness, what is it then?"

"Oh, you make me tired! But just to prove that I'm not as dumb as you act, the clue is this—"

"Give me a chance," begged Mr. Stricklin, entering into the spirit of the game. "Your idea, Bolton, is to find out from the servants who they've been talking to and trace the smugglers from—"

"Cold as an iceberg," broke in Mr. Bolton. "I'm sorry to admit it, but you and Bill don't seem very quick on the uptake this morning. What do I mean, Mary Eliska?"

Mary Eliska made a face at Bill.

"We know that these men have headquarters somewhere in this state," she began airily. "Why? Because Donovan said they must get me over to Connecticut. And later, in the warehouse, he told Peters not to rob me because the boss wanted me delivered just as I was. Daddy Bolton believes that because these men have been spotted so quickly that *you* are mixed up in it, Bill, their headquarters are much nearer to this house than we figured: that the chances are, it is only a very few miles from here that they're to be found—or their system of spying on us couldn't be so perfect!"

"That's right," concurred Mr. Bolton. "This smuggler boss or his accomplices over here must live in the neighborhood. Some of his servants know ours—have known them for some time or they would not have been able to ask questions without causing suspicion."

Mr. Stricklin looked suddenly serious. "You can't mean that our neighbors along this ridge are mixed up in it? The Clarks, old Holloway, the Denbys, Miss Cross—and ten or a dozen others—are all old friends and eminently respectable people! Why, it's preposterous to think—" "I'm not trying to pin it on anybody yet," countered Bill's father. "But mark my words—when this business is cleared up, you'll find that some eminently respectable New Canaan household *is* mixed up in it!"

Chapter 2.14
UP AGAINST IT

It was finally decided that Mary Eliska and Bill should make a series of circular patrols, centering above New Canaan.

"We'll each take a plane," said Bill, "and keep each other in sight."

"What's the use of doing that?" Mary Eliska asked. "Why not make the patrols separately? When I come down, you go up. In that way we can stay in the air twice as long on the same amount of gas, and take a rest once in a while."

"Too risky. These smugglers are desperate. We've already thrown a good-sized monkey-wrench into the works of their organization. That *Mystery Plane* is quite likely to pack along a machine gun—and use it if the pilot finds out we're trying to follow him."

"Are we going up unarmed?"

"You are—but I'm not."

Mary Eliska raised her eyebrows in surprise.

"Well, that's nice of you!"

"Look here, young lady," cut in her father. "I don't know what Bill's plans are, but if you're going on these patrols, just remember that he is the captain of the outfit and must have obedience. Otherwise, I'll not consent to your going at all."

"Oh, I'll be good, Daddy. But I do think—"

"But you mustn't! Your job is to do what you're told and let your captain do the thinking."

"You see, Mary Eliska," explained Bill, "in order to use a gun in the air, a pilot must have training and practice. Otherwise, all you do is to draw the enemy's fire. If we meet up with this bird you'll have plenty to keep you busy—a very important part to play. But if there's any gunning to be done, I'll do it. Before we go up, I'll outline exactly what we're to do in the event we sight the gang's airplane." Mary Eliska got out of her chair.

"How about getting busy, then?" she suggested. "The longer we're up, the more we are likely to accomplish."

"Hold your horses," laughed Bill. "Don't think for a minute we're going to patrol all day long."

"Why not?"

"Waste of time."

Mary Eliska plumped herself down in her chair again.

"Oh, all right. Have it your way. Personally, I can't see doing a thing at all, unless one does it properly. You and your plans make me tired."

"Don't get peeved," he bantered. "These won't be endurance flights."

"They won't be anything at all unless we find that plane and you can't expect it to take the air just when you want it to!"

"Stop quarreling, children," admonished her father. "Bill knows what he is talking about."

"Well, maybe he does. He can catch the old plane by himself. I'm through."

"What you need is another nap, young lady. You're tired and cross."

"I'm not. Men always club together."

"And what can a poor girl do?" supplemented Bill with a grin.

"Stop teasing, Bill!" commanded Mr. Bolton. "Apologize to Mary Eliska and tell her why you mean to take short hops. I can't see the sense in such procedure myself—any more than she can. And just remember that an overdose of excitement puts anybody's nerves on edge. She's been through a lot more than you have during the last few days."

At his father's words, Bill's face wore such a look of honest contrition, that Mary Eliska's conscience smote her. They both began to speak at once.

"Gee, I'm sorry, Mary Eliska—"

"I'm an idiot, Bill—"

They burst into laughter simultaneously.

"Now we can get on with our discussion," smiled Mary Eliska. "Go ahead, Bill."

"Well, the smuggler's pilot has been taking most of his flights—or I ought to say, the flights we know about—during the late afternoon. I haven't the slightest glimmer why he chooses to fly at that time. But, as I see it, if he has done it day after day in the past, the chances are he'll continue to leave his hangar at about the same time. My plan is for us to take off at about four each afternoon. We can remain in the air until six. If he comes from around here, we'd catch him shortly after he takes the air. That's how I figure it."

"Maybe you're right." Mary Eliska was still unconvinced. "But how about the warning we got a little while ago?" "What's that got to do with it?"

"Well, we hadn't had lunch yet—he dropped the message from his plane in the morning— not during the late afternoon!"

Bill yawned unblushingly and got to his feet.

"Cuts no ice," he asserted. "That wasn't a regular hop."

"What then?" This from Mr. Stricklin.

"A grandstand play, pure and simple. Those lads haven't the brains I gave them credit for, if they really think they can steer us off with tripe like that!"

Mr. Bolton ground the butt of his cigar on an ashtray, and rose.

"Perhaps that wasn't the idea," he suggested.

Three heads were turned sharply toward him.

"What do you mean, Bolton?" asked Mr. Stricklin.

"A come-on," returned his neighbor.

"A come-on?" echoed Mary Eliska in a puzzled voice. "Just that—nothing more nor less."

"I get you," Bill nodded. "Get us in the air, by that teaser—rely on us to go after the *Mystery Plane* as a matter of pride—and then fill us full of machine gun bullets. If they start anything like that—well—two can play the game and if that lad with the beard can't shoot any better than he handled his plane when he zoomed the house just now—it is, as the French say, 'to laugh'!"

"That's all very well," argued Mr. Stricklin. "I don't mind Mary Eliska flying, but I do draw the line at machine guns. That's no game for girls. You keep your two feet on solid earth until this business is over, my dear."

"Oh, Daddy!" Mary Eliska's voice was full of disgust. "Sorry, daughter, but I simply can't let you take the risk."

Mr. Bolton placed his hand on his friend's arm. "You know, I don't think that Bill would have countenanced Mary Eliska's going on patrols with him unless he felt assured she would run no danger. How about it, son?"

"If she does get into trouble, it won't be with my consent," he smiled. "But seriously, sir," he turned to Mr. Stricklin. "There will be a minimum of danger if Mary Eliska does as I tell her. In the first place, machine gun fire in the air is not nearly so potent as it is on terra firma. Try and hit a small object flashing by when you're traveling like a bat out of—ahem!—Harlem. Try it and see how many planes you don't hit! And in the second place, that bearded guy won't get a chance to turn his gun in her direction."

"Well, I'm no flyer and I haven't the slightest idea of the technicalities that must arise in aerial combat work," Mr. Stricklin made this statement slowly and thoughtfully, "but still—"

"Daddy, *don't* be ridic." Mary Eliska's tone was tolerantly amused. "Do you really think I'm foolish, my dear child?"

"Oh, pigheaded is a better word, at times, if you insist on the truth!" All four burst into roars of mirth.

"That's one from the shoulder, Mr. Stricklin," choked Bill. "You'd better go the whole hog, now she's a licensed pilot!"

Mary Eliska's father shook his head in pretended sorrow. "You're all against me, that's obvious. And there's much too much pig in this conversation to suit a conservative parent." He threw an affectionate glance at Mary Eliska. "Ever since this tomboy daughter of mine was able to grip my finger when I leaned over her crib, she has pulled her old Dad hither and yon to suit her fancy. So I suppose I'll have to give in again—acknowledge I'm wrong, and so forth. Run along, children, and see to it your airships are in apple-pie order."

"You're a darling!" His daughter bestowed a hearty kiss upon his left ear. "Beat it—you scamp!" Mr. Stricklin's voice was gruff, though his eyes sparkled with merriment. "If you bother me much longer, it will be lunch time before I get down to the bank—and I'm likely to change my mind. Shoo!"

"Ogre—I defy you!" With a laugh, she beckoned to Bill and ran down the steps. "Well, what shall it be?" she inquired when he joined her. "Your ship or mine, first?"

"Mine, I think. None of the three has been off the apron of the hangar since I left for Europe. Frank has been looking after them. He's a great old feller, you know. When we brought him back from New York he didn't know a fork from a gadget. Now he's chauffeur, general factotum around the house, and practical mechanic for me. He knows his job all right, but my boats will need more overhauling than yours."

"Which plane shall you use for this work?"

"The Ryan M-l, that the bank gave me after that Martinelli business. She certainly is a smart little bus—can fly rings around anything in this neck of the woods. Hello—" he broke off as they came down the drive, "somebody's had a breakdown."

Drawn up at the side of the ridge road stood a green coupe of the type motor car manufacturers advertise as "deluxe model." As they came in sight, a young man crawled out from beneath the body.

"Why, that's Mr. Tracey," said Mary Eliska. "Do you know him?"

"Yes, I met him at Mr. Holloway's house one night. Isn't he the old boy's secretary?"

"Yes, he is. He's quite nice. Dad sees a lot of Mr. Holloway, you know."

The secretary, tall and sleekly blond, was looking ruefully down at his grey flannel trousers, now streaked with the dirt of the roadway.

"Good morning, Miss Mary Eliska," he greeted, clipping his words in a precise manner. "Afraid I'm not exactly presentable." Then for the first time, he appeared to notice Bill. "Hello, Bolton," he said affably. "You're quite a stranger around here."

"Got back a couple of days ago," returned Bill casually. "Need any help?"

"Thanks, no. Loose nut, that's all." He patted his monkey wrench with a grimy hand. "This fixed her. Doing much flying, Miss Mary Eliska?"

"Yes, I go up quite often. Bill taught me, you know."

"Yes, I remember. I'd like to take lessons, myself. How about giving me instruction—that is, if you're not too expensive?"

"I'm really not in the business," parried Bill. "You'd do much better at one of the schools. Glad to give you a hop, though, if you'd like to go up?"

"Thanks so much. I'll be glad to take advantage of your offer. What about this afternoon? It's a perfectly lovely day."

"Sorry, but today I'm overhauling my planes. Been away some time, you see. I'll probably take them up on tests about four. But of course I don't want the responsibility of a passenger until I know they are running O.K."

Mr. Tracey nodded and got into his car.

"I understand perfectly. Thanks for the invitation, though. I'll give you a ring later in the week and allow myself the pleasure of going up with you. Goodbye. Goodbye, Miss Mary Eliska."

With a wave of his hand the car moved off and Mary Eliska turned to Bill. "Why did you tell him you were going to take the air about four?" she asked.

"Because if the smuggling gang know what I'm going to do it will save time if we pull off our little scrap this afternoon."

Before this admission Mary Eliska had looked puzzled. Now her eyebrows went up in startled astonishment.

"Good Heavens, Bill! You surely don't think that Mr. Tracey has anything to do with that! He's as prim and prissy as a pussy-cat!"

"Just my opinion. Of course he knows nothing about the diamonds. But your prissy boyfriend has the reputation of being the worst gossip in New Canaan. When he takes those gray bags of his to be cleaned, it will be all over the village that Bill Bolton is back and intends to test out his planes late this afternoon.—And that is just what I want."

"Oh, I see," Mary Eliska nodded thoughtfully. "But I'll tell you one thing. If we are going up today, it's high time we quit talking and got busy on the planes."

With four airplanes to groom, the next few hours proved busy ones for both Mary Eliska and Bill. But by four o'clock everything was ready for their flight.

"Got your instructions down pat?" he inquired as Mary Eliska got aboard the *Will-o'-the-Wisp*. The airplane was resting on the concrete apron of the Stricklins' hangar, preparatory to the take off.

"Know them backwards," she flashed with a smile.

"Good luck, then."

"Good luck to you, Bill."

He stepped swiftly to one side as she switched on the ignition. For a moment or two he stood there watching her amphibian taxi away from the hangar, gathering speed as it went. Then when the wheels left the ground and the big bird of wood and metal soared upward, he turned away and made off in the direction of his father's property.

As *Will-o'-the-Wisp* climbed in great widening circles, Mary Eliska at the controls knew she had plenty of time to gain the position agreed upon before Bill could get under way. The air was smooth and still, without the slightest breath of disturbing wind. Perfect flying weather and wonderful visibility with a clear blue horizon unmarred by the smallest shred of cloud.

The Boltons had turned the ten-acre pasture behind their house into a level flying field. The old hay barn had been enlarged, partitions removed and a concrete floor laid. It now made a large roomy hangar, for their three planes.

Looking down as she kept on circling higher and higher, Mary Eliska saw Bill cross the ridge road and appear a moment or two later on his own flying field. She watched him hurry down to the hangar and could see Frank busy about the Ryan before its open doors. Then she saw Bill get aboard. When she looked again, his small monoplane was already in the air.

By this time the indicator on *Will-o'-the-Wisp's* altimeter marked a height of between eight and nine thousand feet. According to instructions, Mary Eliska leveled off and bringing right rudder and right aileron simultaneously into play, she sent the plane into a wide circular turn. Far below, the Ryan was pursuing the same tactics, so that both planes were cruising over the township of New Canaan.

Mary Eliska and Bill continued to maintain the same relative positions for the next fifteen or twenty minutes. Then as *Will-o'-the-Wisp* swung round toward the west, Mary Eliska spied a third plane, streaking toward New Canaan at an altitude of some three thousand feet.

The fact that Bill had also spotted the intruder was evident, for he began to climb. "Bill's advertising plan worked," muttered Mary Eliska with satisfaction. "If that amphibian over there isn't the *Mystery Plane*, I'll eat my ailerons!"

Chapter 2.15
RUN TO COVER

Mary Eliska reached beneath her seat, brought forth a pair of field-glasses and clapped them to her goggles. Focused through the powerful lenses, there was no mistaking the *Mystery Plane*. And although at this distance it was impossible to see the pilot's face, she could plainly distinguish the barrel of a machine gun that poked its wicked muzzle over the cockpit's cowling.

"So the bearded aviator means mischief!" She returned the glasses to their case. "That guy must be a cold-blooded dog to try anything like that over a populated township. He's likely to bite off more than he can chew if Bill and I have any luck. If he cracks up, I shan't weep."

At first sight of the smuggler's plane, she brought *Will-o'-the-Wisp* back on an even keel, but now in order to get an unimpeded view directly below, she sent the plane into a steep bank.

Bill, in the Ryan, with an altitude of some twenty-five hundred feet and its nose slightly raised was streaking toward the smuggler.

Most air battles are fought in the higher ether, because combat flying often necessitates acrobatics and the ordinary pilot wants plenty of air below for such work. The smuggler being the aggressor in this case, naturally started to climb when he spotted the Ryan. He hoped, no doubt, not only to increase his altitude but to gain greater ascendency over Bill before diving at the monoplane with his machine gun going full blast.

It was time for Mary Eliska to act. As the smuggler's plane began to ascend, she sent her amphibian diving toward him at a tremendous spurt of speed. The *Mystery Plane* nosed over and dove in turn at the Ryan, some five hundred feet below. "Ha-ha!" Mary Eliska shut off her motor and brought *Will-o'-the-Wisp's* nose gradually back to the horizontal. "Our scheme worked! That bird either doesn't know his business or he's lost his nerve!" A fighting plane attacking has as its objective a position directly behind the hostile plane at close range. A position either above or below the tail is equally good. From these positions the enemy is directly in the line of fire, and in sighting no deflection is necessary.

The smuggler's maneuver showed Mary Eliska that he was a novice; for instead of going into a climbing spiral which would have eluded her dive and made it possible for him to attain a superior position over both planes, he dove at the Ryan. This might have been a proper fighting maneuver if Bill's plane had not been nosing upward toward him; and had the Ryan not been the faster of the two.

By this blunder he put himself in the direct line of fire from Bill's machine gun. And had that young man been minded to use it the battle would have been over—almost before it started.

Seeing his mistake almost immediately, the bearded aviator broke his dive by zooming upward. Again Mary Eliska's plane dove for his tail and right there he made his second error.

Instead of gaining altitude and position by making an Immelman turn, which consists of a half-roll on the top of a loop, he pulled back his stick sharply, simultaneously giving the *Mystery Plane* full right rudder. The result was an abrupt stall and a fall off, and his amphibian emerged from the resultant dive headed in the direction from which he had first appeared.

Mary Eliska sent her bus spiraling downward, while Bill simply nosed his Ryan into a steeper climb. By the time the *Mystery Plane* levelled off from its split-S turn it had lost over a thousand feet. Granted he was headed for home, if that had been his intention; now he was placed in the worst possible situation with regard to his opponents. For instead of one, both planes had attained positions above him.

For the next few minutes the man in the smuggler's plane did his best to out-maneuver the elusive pair whose motors roared above his head like giant bees attacking an enemy. Never was he given a chance to better his position or to gain altitude. Every time he maneuvered to place one of the planes within line of fire from his machine gun, the other would effectually block the move; the menacing plane would sheer off at a tangent and its partner, crowding down upon his tail, would hurl forth a smoke bomb. By the time he floundered through the cloud, his antagonists would be back in their relative positions, again, the one directly above his tail plane, the other slightly behind him to the right.

The bearded aviator knew that he was being outclassed at every move, that gradually they were forcing him down to a point where he must land or crash.

Both Mary Eliska and Bill knew exactly when the man in the plane below guessed their purpose. For with a sudden burst of speed he shot ahead, streaking in the direction of North Stamford like a ghost in torment.

"We've got every advantage but one," mused Mary Eliska, widening her throttle in pursuit. "He knows where he's going—and we don't. He's up to some trick, I'll bet."

That her thoughts were prophetic was made apparent almost immediately. By shutting off his engine and by kicking his rudder alternately right and left with comparatively slow and heavy movements, the smuggler pilot sent his plane's nose swinging from side to side. This evolution, known as fish-tailing, he executed without banking or dropping the nose to a steeper angle. Its purpose is to cut down speed and to do so as rapidly as possible.

The *Mystery Plane* slowed down as though a brake had been applied, sideslipped to the left over a line of trees and leveled off above a field enclosed by a dilapidated stone fence.

"Confound!" exclaimed Mary Eliska, with a glance behind. "He's going to land and both Bill and I have overshot the field!"

Nose depressed below level, a lively flipper turn to left brought *Will-o'-the-Wisp* sharply round facing the field again with its wings almost vertical. Immediate application of up aileron and opposite rudder quickly brought the amphibian to an even keel once more. Then Mary Eliska nosed over, went into a forward slip, recovered and leveled off for a landing.

As the wheels of her plane touched the ground, she saw the Ryan come to a stop on the grass some yards to the right. Just ahead and between them was the *Mystery Plane*. It lay drunkenly over on one side, resting on its twisted landing gear and a crumpled lower wing section.

Mary Eliska stood up in her cockpit when *Will-o'-the-Wisp* stopped rolling and saw the smuggler-pilot vault the wall at the far corner of the field and disappear into a small wood. Bill was walking toward the disabled amphibian. She got out of her plane and hurried toward him.

"Pancaked!" she cried, pointing toward the wreck as she came within speaking distance.

"You said it—" concurred Bill. "That guy was in such a hurry he leveled off too soon. Usually I don't wish anybody hard luck but that bird is the great exception. Too bad he didn't break a leg along with his plane. Now he's beat it and—"

"We are just about where we were before," she broke in.

"Not quite, Mary Eliska. The *Mystery Plane* is out of commission.—I wonder where we are?"

"Somewhere in the North Stamford hills."

"I know—but whose property are we on?" "Haven't the least idea."

"I can't see any houses around here. Did you notice any as you came down?" Mary Eliska shook her head and laughed.

"My eyes were glued on this field," she admitted. "I was too busy trying to make a landing myself to take in much of the landscape. Wait a minute, though—seems to me I caught a glimpse of the Castle just before I put *Wispy* into that reverse control turn. Yes, I'm sure of it."

"The Castle?" Bill frowned. "What in the cock-eyed world is that?"

"A castle, silly!"

"Make sense out of that, please." "Sorry. You're usually trying to mystify me—I just thought I'd turn the tables for a change."

"Oh, I know—I'll say I'm sorry or anything else you want. Only please tell me what you're talking about."

"Well, it seems that about fifteen or sixteen years ago, somebody built a castle about two or three miles from North Stamford village. It's less than five miles from where we live. Not being up on medieval architecture I can't describe it properly, but Dad says it is the kind that German robber barons put up in the fourteenth century. Anyway, the Castle is built of stone with a steep, slate roof, which spouts pointed turrets all over the place. I wouldn't be surprised if it had been built by a German—it certainly looks as Heinie as sauerkraut!"

"Who lives there?" asked Bill. "Nobody, now. During the war, Dad told me, the place was suspected to be a spy-hang-out or something like that. Anyway, there was a lot of talk about it. What became of the owner, whoever he is, I don't know. The place has been rented several times during the past few years. It is quite near the road. I drove past it just the other day on my way to and from Nance Wilkins' tea and the old dump looked quite empty and forlorn."

"Well, that's that," said Bill. "This bearded guy may have been heading for your Castle, but I doubt it. Fact is, he probably decided to land at the first convenient place when he found we were too much for him, and decided to trust to his legs for a getaway."

Mary Eliska had been swinging her helmet by its chin strap in an absent-minded manner. Now she raised her eyes to his.

"What are we going to do about it?" she inquired. "We can't try to break into the Castle in broad daylight."

"Hardly. And after our experience with the bank gang, we'll do no more snooping around strange houses on our own. I am going over to that little wood where our friend ran to cover. Maybe I can find some trace of him. You stay here with the planes."

"Why can't I go with you, Bill?"

"Because that smuggler may simply be hiding in the woods in hopes that we'll come after him and that we'll leave these airbuses unguarded. Then when we're gone, he'll come back here, grab one of them and fly quietly home."

"All right. I see."

"Have you got a gun?"

"That small Colt you gave me is in *Wispy's* cockpit."

"Get it and keep it on you—and if that guy shows up, don't be afraid to use it."

Mary Eliska shook her head. "I never shot at anybody in my life—"

"Don't shoot *at* him—*shoot* him. You might have to, you know."

"But surely, Bill—"

"Oh, I don't mean for you to kill the guy. Plunk him in the leg—disable him. If you have any qualms about it, just remember that machine gun in his bus here. The man is as deadly as a copperhead and twice as treacherous. Look out for him."

"I will. But su-suppose you get into trouble, Bill. How long do you want me to wait here before I come after you?"

"My dear girl," Bill was becoming impatient. "I'm just going to try to find out where that lad is headed. I won't be gone more than ten or fifteen minutes."

"Yes. But suppose you *don't* come back here!"

"Wait for half an hour. Then fly back home and tell Dad what has happened. He'll know what to do. Don't get nervous—I'll be all right. So long. See you in a few minutes."

With a wave of his hand, he ran across the field and Mary Eliska saw him hurdle the low wall and disappear between the trees of the wood where the bearded aviator had run to cover.

Chapter 2.16
THE TUNNEL

Mary Eliska walked slowly back to *Will-o'-the-Wisp* and climbed into the cockpit. From the pilot's seat she had an unobstructed view of the field and the two other airplanes. Overhead, fluffy wind clouds began to appear from out of the northwest. Near the stone wall, three small rabbits sported in the sunshine; and presently a groundhog waddled across the field.

She glanced at her watch. The hands marked five past five. Bill had been gone twenty minutes.

"And he told me not to get nervous," she thought indignantly. "This waiting around is enough to set anybody off—I'll give him just ten minutes more!"

Mary Eliska counted those ten minutes quite the longest she had ever experienced. Fifteen minutes past five and still no Bill. He had told her to wait half an hour and then to fly home for help! But she was not the sort of girl who permits herself to be quietly wiped off the picture by an order from a boyfriend! She just wasn't made that way. Bill might be worried about the safety of the planes; it was his safety that worried her.

Determinedly she transferred the small revolver from its holster to a pocket of the jodhpurs she was wearing. Should she pack a flash light, too? No need of that, she decided. Figuring on daylight saving time, it wouldn't be dark until after eight o'clock. Without more ado, she got out of the plane and crossed the field toward the wood.

After she had climbed the wall at the spot where she had seen Bill disappear on the trail of the bearded aviator, she came upon a path. Narrow it was, and overgrown, yet certainly a path, leading through the trees at a diagonal from the stone fence. Without hesitation, Mary Eliska followed it.

She was soon certain that her idea of the wood from the air was correct, and that it covered no great acreage. Hurrying along the winding footpath, she began to catch glimpses of blue sky between the tree trunks, and less than three hundred yards from the wall she came into the open.

The trees ended at the edge of a broad gully, apparently the bed of a shallow stream in the spring or after a shower; but now, except for a puddle or two, it was dry. On the farther side, cows were grazing in a meadow.

"Nice pastoral landscape," she said aloud. "Doesn't look like much of a spot for mischief—"

In spite of her bravado, Mary Eliska felt a lump in her throat. If Bill were missing, too, and she could not find him....

The pasture sloped gently upward over a hill, perhaps a quarter of a mile away. And on the horizon above the hilltop, the Castle reared its pointed turrets skyward. For a little while she watched the huge, grey pile of stone, whose narrow leaded windows reflecting the late afternoon sun, winked at her with many mocking eyes. What a dreary-looking place it was, she thought. Ugly and forbidding, it was entirely out of place in this New England countryside. The Castle seemed utterly deserted. It probably was. At least the path ended at the gully; there was no sign of it across the meadow.

Where was the bearded aviator—and above all, where was Bill?

"Bill distinctly said he would not snoop around the Castle," she thought. "I wonder if he really came this far?"

So eager had she been to reach the edge of the wood that she had paid very little attention to the ground she was covering. As this new thought struck her, she turned and gazed back over the way she had come. There were her own footprints clearly defined in the damp earth—but there was no sign that either Bill or the smuggler had passed that way.

Back along the path she trudged, walking slowly this time.

"I'm a pretty poor woodsman," she told herself. "They must have turned off somewhere."

Her eyes searched the soft earth of the narrow trail and the thick bushes through which it wandered. But it was not until she had gone half way back to the stone wall that she discovered traces of footprints. And where the prints left the path, a ragged remnant of a handkerchief swung from a twig near the ground.

"There!" she pounced upon it joyfully. "How could I have been so stupid as to miss it—I might have known!"

The initials, "W. B." embroidered in one corner of the dirty fragment of linen banished any doubt she may have had as to its ownership. Leaving it tied to the bush, she struck into the wood.

Now that she was intent upon her stalking, there was no mistaking the trail left by the other two. A broken twig, heel marks on the soft mold, a trampled patch of moss; all these signs bespoke a hasty passage through the brush.

She had not gone far, when suddenly in a clearing she came upon the end of the trail. The earth here was bare of undergrowth and sloped sharply down into a marshy ravine. In the center of the little clearing a pile of brush was heaped with dead grass and rubbish,—tin cans, old shoes, automobile fenders, rusty bed-springs, boxes and weathered newspapers.

For a moment Mary Eliska stared at the rubbish dump. Then she noticed footprints circling the heap and followed them down to the ravine. Here, as if to bulwark the miscellaneous junk and to keep it from sliding, was a buttress of boxes and barrels.

Mary Eliska got down on her knees and examined these carefully. At the very bottom, almost on a level with the tussocky surface of the marsh, a barrel lay on its side, its depth leading inward. A sudden inspiration made her pull a long stick from the pile and run it into the barrel. She gave a little gurgle of astonishment. The barrel had no bottom.

Still on her knees she peered inside. Just beyond the rim lay a scrap of paper. She picked it up and scrawled upon it were the words "This way".... "Another message!" she whispered jubilantly.

She tried to move the barrel but found that it was securely nailed to the bulwark of packing-cases. The soft earth about its mouth was heavily marked with footprints.

"Well, there's no doubt about it now—'this way'—" she murmured and without further waste of time wormed her way into the barrel.

As she crawled through the other end, she found herself in a narrow tunnel. The daylight appearing through its ingenious entrance was strong enough to show her that the rubbish had been built over a frame of two-by-fours and chicken wire, which formed the roof and sides of the tunnel under the dump.

Mary Eliska got to her feet. A short distance ahead the tunnel led straight into the high ground over which she had come from the wood path. Here the sides were timbered with stout posts, and ceilinged with cross beams to prevent the earthen roof from falling.

"Gee, if this isn't like Alice in Wonderland! Why, I might meet the White Rabbit any minute now." She giggled, then shivered as she remembered why she was there.

For a moment she considered returning to the plane for her flash light, but decided it would take too much precious time, and passed on cautiously, stopping now and then to listen. She could hear nothing but the squashy sound of her footsteps on the marshy floor of the tunnel.

After proceeding about fifteen feet, the dark passage turned slightly in its course. Just beyond the turn, as Mary Eliska was groping to find which way it led, her hands touched a wooden surface. This proved to be a heavy door, standing partly open. As she shoved it back with her shoulder, she tripped over a heavy object which lay across the sill. Mary Eliska reached down in the darkness and picked up a crowbar.

She advanced, dragging the crowbar after her. The floor of the passage at this point began to slope up hill. But after a few paces ahead, she found it went abruptly downward at a considerable angle, took a sharp turn to the right, then began to slope gently upward again.

By this time she had lost all sense of direction. She progressed slowly, feeling along the wall with her left hand, resting it on one timber until she had advanced half way to where she supposed the next would be. In this manner she crept on for nearly a quarter of a mile without meeting any obstruction. The air, though cold and lifeless, was breathable; but the darkness and the horrid feeling of being shut in began to get on her nerves. Once more she stopped to listen. Absolute stillness. Mary Eliska could hear nothing but the beating of her heart as she strained her eyes to pierce the black passage. She seemed completely shut off from everything on earth. Feeling that inaction was even more unbearable than running head-on into danger, she recommenced her slow advance. Presently, she came to a place where the tunnel widened out. Here, even with outstretched arms, she could not reach both walls at once.

As she swung to follow the left-hand wall, her right arm struck a free timber which seemed to have no connection with either side of the passage. From this she deduced that she was now in a sort of subterranean chamber, and that this free post was one of the supports of its roof. Continuing along the left wall, with her right arm outstretched, she soon reached another post. The heavy crowbar which she was endeavoring to carry at arm's length, struck against the base of the upright and made a loud, cavernous sound.

"Bloomp!"

Mary Eliska was prepared for the next timber, some three feet farther on. She took the crowbar in her left hand and extended her right to grasp the post, with the intention to discover the size of the chamber.

Suddenly she recoiled in horror. She could feel a chill rush up and down her spine. For she had touched, not the splintered wood of the post, but, unmistakably, human flesh.

Dodging quickly to one side, she dropped the crowbar and drew her revolver. Holding it straight before her, ready to fire at the first sign of a hostile advance, she listened breathlessly.

To her amazement, there was no sound; not the slightest indication of movement in the awful darkness. She supposed the enemy must be maneuvering to take her from some unexpected quarter. But she could not understand how it could be managed in that inky blackness without giving her some audible sign.

Feeling that she must have something firmer than mere space behind her, Mary Eliska retreated, keeping her pistol leveled. With her left hand she groped behind her and when she felt the solid timber, she leaned back against it, waiting.

Seconds dragged like hours and still there was no sound. Gradually, Mary Eliska's nerves were beginning to quiet down.

"Well, this is darned queer," she thought, "maybe that person is making tracks out of here. I can't just stand still and do nothing, anyway."

She began to move forward very cautiously. When she had covered ten short paces, she stopped and listened again. Absolute stillness everywhere, stillness pervaded by the strange, dank smell of unsunned earth and the musty rot of roots and wood.

But this time Mary Eliska fancied she could hear a faint, very faint sound of breathing. At first she thought it was her own, reechoing from the walls of the dark cavern. Then she held her breath and listened once more. *There* was someone else in this subterranean chamber. "Well, here goes," she said with closed lips. "It's now or never. I can't stand this much longer!"

But she had only taken a single step when the same chill of horror and fright raced over her again. Her revolver muzzle had touched something apparently alive and yielding, the clothed body of someone who stood motionless as before.

"Hold it! hold it!" she cried, her teeth chattering. "Don't move or I'll plug you!"

With her gun firmly pressed against the body, she raised her other arm to ward off any blow that might be directed against her. As she did so, it became evident that the body still had not moved, that the breath was coming regularly and faintly, but there was no stir of limbs, no shift of muscle or of weight.

Such mysterious behavior filled Mary Eliska with terror. She bit her lips and dug the mouth of her Colt forward into the body.

"Stick 'em up—do you hear? Over your head!" she said viciously between her teeth.

The figure remained motionless and as silent as before. Mary Eliska felt her heart beats mount to a violent thunder. She felt she could stand the strain no longer.

Still holding her pistol against the flesh of this mysterious being, she lowered her arm from her forehead and reached slowly forward. She touched something. Her whole body was convulsed with horror, anguish and surprise.

Her trembling fingers had descended upon the smooth, cool softness of a leather helmet. They slipped, cold and damp, from the helmet to the face and over the warm cheek.

In that moment everything was changed. Now Mary Eliska understood why the figure was motionless and quiet. She touched a fold of cloth that bound the mouth and slipping her hand to the shoulder, she felt a twist of thin rope.

She slipped the pistol into her belt without hesitation. Bill always carried several packets of matches in his pockets. She found one and struck a light.

When the little puff of smoke and the obscuring haze of the first flash settled down to a fitful flame, Mary Eliska got a glimpse of her friend. He was gagged and bound to one of the upright supports. His eyes were closed and his head drooped to one side. In less than a second Mary Eliska had flung away the match and was cutting the young fellow's bonds with her knife, groping for them in the dark and supporting his released body against her own as she worked. At last she was able to lift him out of the loosened loop that had held his feet and stepping back, laid him on the earthen floor.

Then she knelt beside him, rubbing his wrists and cheeks with her grimy palms. For some minutes her ministrations seemed of no avail. But presently, under her fingers she felt his head move. At first she could only catch groans and sighs. Then, as consciousness began to assert itself, Bill raised his head a little and said faintly:

"Who's that?"

"It's me—Mary Eliska."

She lifted his head into her lap. As she did so Bill gave a start and struggled feebly.

"Let me go!" he muttered. "Let me alone!"

"Just keep quiet, Bill," she soothed. "You'll be better soon."

Bill lay back in her arms and was still.

"Who are you?" he asked again and this time in a firmer voice.

"It's Mary Eliska, your pardner!"

"Mary Eliska? Thank Heaven for that." He caught at her hand and squeezed it. "We're in the tunnel, aren't we?"

"Yes—where it widens out into a kind of room."

"I remember now—that guy slugged me when I was making for the candle on the table over there."

"Who slugged you? The bearded aviator?"

"That's right. I was coming along, lighting matches to see by when he stepped from behind one of the uprights—and that's all I remember. Knocked me out, I guess."

"He certainly did! You've a bump on your head like an egg. The helmet probably saved your life. Feel pretty rotten, don't you?"

"You said it! Dizzy as blazes—and my head's as sore as a boil. But I guess I'll be all right in a minute if I can just lie still. Do you mind?"

"Of course not, silly. Take your time. I suppose you followed the footprints to the barrel, like I did." "Yep. But how come you went after me?" he chuckled. "I thought the idea was to beat it home in the plane."

"Oh, Bill, I just couldn't!"

Bill sat up. "Well, I suppose I was crazy to ever think you would—but I honestly didn't think I'd get into such close quarters with that fellow. As it is, I'm mighty glad you didn't take my fool suggestion," he admitted. "Where would I be now, if you hadn't shown up? By the taste in my mouth and the feel of my wrists, that galoot must have tied me up and gagged me!"

"He did that. You were bound to an upright. Have you any idea where this tunnel comes out?"

"Ten dollars to counterfeit two-cent piece, your Castle is the answer to that question," he said, and lit a match. "Oh, there's the table, Mary Eliska. Do you mind lighting that candle? I'm too dizzy to stand up yet or—"

He stopped short and Mary Eliska saw his eyes widen in startled surprise. "*Look out!*" he yelled and the match went out.

Mary Eliska felt a hand grip the back of her neck and immediately afterward its fellow clutched her throat. In a fierce frenzy of terror, she shot to her feet, gasping and choking and flinging her arms wildly backwards as she rose.

Chapter 2.17
"THE TOMBS"

Mary Eliska's vigorous motion forced her assailant to relax his grip upon her throat, and as she felt his weight upon her shoulders, she lunged down and backward. There was a dull, cracking thud, and the sound of a body falling. The back of her head struck one of the timbers that supported the ceiling of the tunnel. The place seemed to whirl round and round and glittering sparks danced before her eyes. When this sensation ceased, Mary Eliska leaned back against the post into which she had flung herself in her apparently successful effort to shake off her opponent.

With the realization that the attack had halted and that her assailant had either made his escape or was incapacitated, she fumbled in her pocket for a match.

"Where are you, Mary Eliska?" Bill's voice called from the dark void.

"Right here, old thing—by the wall."

She struck a light.

"All right?"

He looked pale and shaken in the flicker of the tiny flame. She saw that he grasped the crowbar.

"A bit woozy," she replied, and lit the candle on the table. "Cracked my head on a beam or something."

"That bearded guy didn't hurt you?"

"He didn't get a chance. Which way do you think he went?"

Bill laughed softly. "You put him out of business. Look!"

He pointed toward an upright and Mary Eliska saw a crumpled figure lying huddled at the base of the post.

"Goodness! You don't think I've finished him?" she breathed in horrified alarm.

"No such luck," he affirmed callously and bent over the man's body. "Sit down until you feel better. This chap is only stunned. I'll take care of him."

Mary Eliska stumbled over to the table. Near-by was a chair. She dropped into it.

"He bumped his skull on this post," Bill went on. "No great damage, I guess. Funny—whenever there's a rough-house in the dark, somebody invariably gets a broken head. The three of us are even now."

"What are you going to do with him?" Her dizziness was passing.

"Oh, I'll give him as good as he gave me, and lash him to this upright."

He busied himself tying up the unconscious smuggler. When he had finished, he looked up and beckoned to Mary Eliska.

"Come over here. He's plenty secure now. This rope held me, I guess it'll hold him."

"What are you going to do now?"

"Find out who this chap really is."

His fingers peeled off the false beard and Mary Eliska cried out in astonishment.

"Mr. Tracey!" she gasped.

"It's Tracey, all right!"

"But who'd have thought that sleek pussy cat was mixed up in this? Aren't you surprised, Bill?"

"Not very. When his car had the breakdown this morning I began to suspect. The whole thing was too darn opportune. He was part of their system of watchers, of course. Probably wanted to find out how we'd taken their warning."

"But surely Mr. Holloway can have nothing to do with it! He's such a sweet old man."

Billy transferred two revolvers from Tracey's belt to his own.

"If you want my candid opinion," he said, "Old Holloway is the leader and brains of the gang. Only it's going to be the dickens and all to prove it in a court of law."

Mary Eliska stared at him incredulously. "Why, Bill—are you *sure*?"

"Why not? He's just a double-dealer, that's all. That wise old bird is certain to have a flock of cast iron alibis up his sleeve. He must have made more than enough money out of this diamond smuggling to keep Tracey's mouth shut—and the mouths of any others who may be corralled."

"I've got a hunch," said Mary Eliska.

"Let's have it."

"Not yet. I want to chew it over a bit. Let's go back now and get help."

"That's for you to do. I'm going on to the Castle and surprise whoever's there. I don't think they have a suspicion of what has happened down here. Tracey never got that far, I'm sure of it."

"Well, you can take it from me that you're not going alone. I'm coming with you."

Bill hesitated.

"Well, perhaps that's the best way, after all," he admitted at last. "It will take some time to get the proper people over here—and by then somebody in the Castle might spot the crumpled plane and start to investigate. Time's more than money now—let's go."

"But do you think you can make it?"

"Can do," he said grimly. "I've got a sweet headache, but it might be worse. How about you?"

"Ditto," she smiled. "Are you going to drag that heavy crowbar?"

"Think it might be wise. Lucky I found it by that camouflaged dump. I had to bash the lock of the door to the main tunnel with it. And there may be another door farther along."

"Then I'll take the candle," she said. With the light held well over her head, she followed him out of the chamber.

The tunnel from here on was concreted, walls, roof and floor. Passing quickly along for possibly a hundred yards, they approached a steep flight of steps. At the top they found a closed door. Bill turned the handle and it swung inward.

"Guess I won't need this anymore," he said and braced the door open with the crowbar. "If they're too many for us, we may have to leave in a hurry. Just as well to keep the way clear."

By the feeble light of the candle they saw that they stood in a small whitewashed cellar. Leading off this to the left, was an open corridor, and from some distance down this passage came the glow of electric light. A large safe, painted white, was built into a corner of the cellar wall.

At a nod from Bill, Mary Eliska blew out the light and placed the candlestick on the stone floor. Then as she straightened up he brought his lips close to her ear.

"I'll bet that's where they keep the loot! Follow me, and hold your gun handy."

One after the other, on tiptoe, the pair crept across the cellar, their rubber-soled shoes making not the slightest sound. When they came to the corridor, Bill slackened his pace but continued to stalk steadily forward. On their left the whitewashed wall led straight on in an unbroken line. In the right wall, they saw the iron grills of cells. They passed the first, which was dark, and evidently empty. From the second came the glow of light.

Bill turned and placed a finger on his lips. Then he got down on his hands and knees and crawled forward to the door.

"Good heavens!" Mary Eliska heard him gasp. "So that's where they had you!"

He stood up and she hurried toward him.

"*Liam McAdams!*"

Her cry was one of absolute amazement. Through the grating she saw her long-lost friend, starting up from his cot where he had been reading when Bill's exclamation caused him to look around. Liam McAdams advanced to the door and greeted them.

"Well, by all that's wonderful! Mary Eliska! Bill Bolton! What—"

"Are you all right? You're not hurt or anything?" Mary Eliska's excited whisper broke in upon his incoherent surprise.

"No, I'm safe and sound, except that I'm pretty tired of reading—cooped up in this hole. But say, how did you two manage to get down here?"

"Through the tunnel," replied Bill with a grin.

"Gee, is there a tunnel, too? Never heard of it. How about that lad Peters and the others— you didn't see them?"

"No, we came through the cellar. Have you any idea where they are?"

"Upstairs, probably—in the house—playing cards. Since Peters came here a few days ago he's been bringing me my grub. He's quite chatty; likes to boast about how he trims those others at poker."

"How many men are there altogether, do you know?" asked Mary Eliska.

"I've never seen more than three at a time, unless you count their be-whiskered pilot I mixed it up with at the beach club. Remember him, Mary Eliska? But he doesn't come around much, so Peters says. He doesn't like him—thinks he's high-hat."

"Well, he's out of the picture, now," declared Bill. "We got him in the tunnel."

"Yes—and Liam McAdams, do you know that he is Mr. Tracey?" Mary Eliska could not contain the exciting news any longer.

"Great grief! You don't say so! I never could stand that fellow—didn't think he had sense enough to come in out of the rain. But then, you never can tell which way a cat will jump." He stepped closer to the grill and looked anxiously from Bill to Mary Eliska. "Say, do you think you two could find a way of getting me out of here?"

"We left a grand crowbar in the cellar! Don't you think we could bash the lock with it, Bill?"

"Might pry it open. But I'm afraid the noise would give us away—"

"Not a chance of that—if you mean it might disturb the poker players," Liam McAdams interrupted. "There's a perfect whale of a sound proof door at the head of the stairs. I was brought down that way. They always keep it shut."

"Good!" Bill hurried off to get the crowbar.

"What's all this about, Mary Eliska?" asked Liam McAdams. "All I know is that these lads held up my car the night of the Sillies. Some bird in a mask drew a gun on me—my eyes were bandaged and I was popped into another bus and brought over here. Where am I, anyway?"

"Why, you're in that old stone Castle—near North Stamford. This is a diamond smuggling gang we're up against. The local and the state police, not to mention Secret Service agents, have been scouring the country for you. Wait 'til you see the newspapers! You're nationally famous! But your mother and father and the rest of us have been terribly worried."

Liam McAdams nodded. "I've been thinking of that," he replied. "But diamond smugglers, eh! No wonder—" he whistled softly. "You've no idea what it was like to be caged up here— thinking of the family and how terrible it was for them—not knowing why I was here, or if I'd ever be set free. Yet they've not tried any rough stuff. Gave me plenty of books and magazines, and enough decent food, thank goodness!"

Bill reappeared, carrying the bar.

"Now get back from the door, Liam McAdams," he cautioned. "I'm going to have a go at it with this."

He placed the end of the crowbar through the grating and behind the steel disk which held the lock. Then he shoved it forward and sideways until that end was jammed between the inner edge of the door and the frame.

"Lend me a hand, please, Mary Eliska, and we'll see what a bit of leverage will do."

Together they seized the crowbar and pulled. There was a sharp snap and the door flew open.

"Good enough!" cried Liam McAdams. He sprang into the corridor and grasped their hands.

"You said it," laughed Bill. "That's the second time this bar has come in handy since we started this job. If we ever get out of here I'm going to keep it as a souvenir."

"I'll take the diamonds," Mary Eliska added enthusiastically.

"What's on deck now?" inquired Liam McAdams.

Bill grew suddenly serious.

"Have you any idea where they keep themselves above?"

"It's ten to one they'll be playing poker in the kitchen. They've nothing else to do now, except to feed me—or so Peters says."

"Where's the kitchen? I mean, how do we get to it from here?"

"It's along this passage and up the staircase at the end. The door at the top—the sound proof one—opens into the kitchen."

Bill handed Liam McAdams a gun. "Don't be afraid to use it," he commanded. "They won't hesitate to shoot if they get a chance."

Liam McAdams looked at him in great disdain. "Say, just because I appear to be my cheerful self and so on, don't get the idea that I've enjoyed this rest cure. All I've been thinking about for days—and nights too—is the chance to get even with them. Now I have it." He patted the revolver. "O.K. then, come along, both of you." It was but a step to the turn in the passage. Directly ahead lay a steep flight of stairs. And at the top was the silent menace of the closed door.

Chapter 2.18
THE FLAGS

"Do you think it will be unlocked?" Bill dropped his voice to a whisper. The three were standing on the landing at the head of the stairs, facing the door.

"Sure to be," returned Liam McAdams. "That is, if we can take friend Peters' word for it. He spilled all this dope when he'd had an argument with the rest of the gang."

"Then let's go—" said Bill. "You stand to one side, Mary Eliska."

"Shucks!" With a twist of the handle, that young lady threw the door wide and jumped into the room. "Hands up! Stick 'em up!" she cried. Two of the three men seated at the table complied at once with her command. Their hands shot above their heads with the rapidity of lightning. The third reached for a revolver that lay amongst the scattered cards.

"*Bang!*"

The man gave a cry of pain and caught at his shattered wrist with his other hand. Startled by the sudden detonation just behind her, Mary Eliska almost dropped her gun.

"Dog-gone it!" Liam McAdams seemed annoyed.

"What's the matter?" Bill still covered the men.

"Matter enough! Too much rest cure, I guess. Forgot to remove the safety catch on this gat you gave me. Lucky you fired when you did."

"Well, never mind that now," Bill's words were crisp and to the point. "Grab that clothesline and tie their hands behind their backs. That's right! Mary Eliska, will you give first aid to that fellow's wrist? I'll see that they don't play any tricks."

After securing the men, Liam McAdams searched their clothes and produced two revolvers and a wicked looking knife. He also took a ring of keys from Peters.

"Gee!" exclaimed that gentleman. "If it ain't the girl what blame near kicked me teeth out I'll eat me bloomin' hat!"

"You'll eat skilly in Wethersfield Prison, or Atlanta, before you get through," Liam McAdams promised. "Shake a leg—both of you. Down to the cells for yours. Did you ever realize what a swell difference there is between the titles of jailer and prisoner? March!"

"Wait a minute!" Mary Eliska cut in. "I'll help you take this man along, too. I've done all I can for him. It's a clean hole through his wrist. Bone's broken but the bullet missed the artery. He might be worse off."

Bill spoke from the doorway that led into the rest of the house. "While you're gone I'll search this place for any other members that might otherwise be overlooked!"

After housing the smugglers in cells, Mary Eliska and Liam McAdams returned to the kitchen and were surprised to find Bill speaking over the telephone.

"And that's that, Dad," they heard him say. "Spread the good tidings in proper places and make it snappy, please. Bye-bye!"

He placed the receiver on its hook.

"I guess you got that," he smiled. "Dad will phone the police and Washington. Then he's driving over here with Frank. And he will also let Mr. Walters and your father know, Mary Eliska."

"Fine—I'm glad he thought of that!" Mary Eliska laughed in excited approval.

"Didn't take you long to search the place," said Liam McAdams.

"No—only a few rooms on this floor are being used. The staircase is thick with dust. Nobody up there—no footprints."

"Well, what's to do now?"

"We'll wait for Dad, of course," said Bill, "and then Mary Eliska and I can fly our respective planes home. How about it, pal? Feel able to do that?"

Mary Eliska lifted her eyebrows in derision. "Well, I should hope so! I suppose I do look pretty frazzled—but you don't seem in the best condition yourself. However—I've another plan."

"What's that?" Liam McAdams had taken over the phone and was talking in low tones to his mother.

"Do you remember I told you I had a hunch, Bill?" "Yes, I do. What about it?" "We're going to follow my hunch."

"Where to?"

"Well, we'll start out of this house—by the front door this time, if you please—then across the meadow and through the wood to the field where our planes are parked."

"And—?" "And then you're going to get into the rear cockpit of *Will-o'-the-Wisp* and take a little hop with me."

Bill looked surprised. "What about my Ryan?"

"Oh, Frank can pilot her home."

"Yes? And then where are we going?"

"That's my secret. Tell Liam McAdams, and come along now. We're in a hurry, even if you don't know it."

"Well, I'm evidently not supposed to know anything of this new mystery!"

"Don't be stuffy! Come on, now. This is serious, Bill, really, I'm not leading you on a wild goose chase, I promise you."

"Humph! It must be hot stuff—not!"

Mary Eliska made a face at him. "I want to tell you it's the hottest stuff of the whole business. And I just want you to be in at the finish, don't you see, stupid?"

"All right. As you insist—"

"That's right. Of course I do. And when we've done this thing up brown, I'll cart you back home to dinner—and if you are very good you can sit next to me!"

Bill grinned. "You may be New England Yankee, but that line of blarney you hand out spells Ireland in capital letters! Come on then, we'll leave Liam McAdams to guard the fort."

After they had put that young man wise to their plans, the two left the Castle. They were both pretty nearly exhausted after their experiences in the tunnel, but the success of their adventure was elating, and more than made up for its bad effects. "Well, here's the field just where we left it," announced Bill as he helped Mary Eliska over the stone fence. "And there's that *Willy* plane of yours, too. Whither away?" "Hop in and you'll see."

Five minutes later, Bill looked down from his seat in the rear cockpit and saw that she was going to land near the tennis courts in the broad parking space behind the cabanas at the beach club. The members had become used to seeing her land *Will-o'-the-Wisp* on the club grounds. Their descent therefore caused little or no notice. The plane stopped rolling and a man in the club uniform of a beach attendant ran up.

"Hello, Jeffries," waved Bill. "I thought you might be here. How are things?"

"We caught Donovan and Charlie Myers over at Babylon. But they're small fry. Anything new, Bolton?"

Bill got out of the plane and helped Mary Eliska to descend.

"I should say there is! Tell you about it in a minute. Mary Eliska, let me present Mr. Arthur Jeffries, one of the very big men of the United States Secret Service. Arthur, this is the famous Mary Eliska!"

Arthur Jeffries said some polite things which caused Mary Eliska to blush modestly, and in a few pithy sentences Bill told the story of their afternoon.

"So you see, old man," he ended. "You won't have to wait around this club any longer disguised as a goldfish or what have you—because the bearded aviator won't fly the *Mystery Plane* over here anymore—that is to say—not for twenty years or so at the soonest."

"He'll get all that or more," Jeffries commented crisply. "But the man he worked for—sunning himself over there on the sand—old Holloway, I mean—he's the nigger in the woodpile! The boss of this gang of diamond smugglers—but I can't arrest him on that evidence!"

Mary Eliska made an eager gesture. "Will you come with me—I want to show you two something. We'll go around the far side of that big cabana on the end of the boardwalk. We're going inside."

"Holloway's bath house?" This from Bill.

"Exactly. I don't want him to see us, though, so be careful."

The three rounded the gaily painted cottage and ducking under the red and black striped awning, entered the front room which was fitted out with the usual wicker furniture and bright rugs.

"I wonder where he keeps them," Mary Eliska murmured to herself. "Ah—this looks like it!"

She lifted the hinged lid of a handsome sea chest and pulled forth a dozen or more colored flags.

"By jove! The goods!" cried Bill. "How did you ever guess it, Mary Eliska?"

Mary Eliska was so pleased by her find that she passed over his use of the despised diminutive.

"I just happened to remember that he generally decked out his cabana with a flock of these things. And though the club runs up flags on special occasions, Mr. Holloway did it nearly every afternoon. It came to me when you pulled off Tracey's beard back there in the tunnel."

"Precisely," said Arthur Jeffries. "Holloway would get word in New York at his office, probably, when a liner carrying contraband was expected off Fire Island light. Then he'd come out here and signal the time to Tracey in his airplane, by means of these flags. I'll bet the old boy never went near that Castle. Some alibi! He and Tracey probably never saw each other from the time he went to the city in the morning until he came home for dinner at night."

"Are you going to arrest him now?" she asked breathlessly.

"As soon as I can get out on the beach. I'll do it as quietly as possible, of course. No use in causing a disturbance with his friends around. So long, Bill. Glad to have met you, Mary Eliska—and many thanks. See you both later on." They left the cabana with him, but turned back toward the plane as he went down the beach.

"That ties it, I guess," she smiled.

"It certainly does!" agreed Bill.

"Now—didn't I tell you it would be hot stuff?"

He looked at her and they both burst out laughing.

"And the best of it is that the government will probably pin a medal on you for it!" he declared.

"Oh, Bill! Do you really think that?"

Bill grinned at her excitement. "You get into that plane and take me home to dinner. That was the bargain, and I'm famished!"

"Dinner!" exclaimed Mary Eliska in disgust. "My word! We've caught those diamond smugglers when the whole of the Secret Service couldn't do it—and all you think of is food! Gee, I'm glad I'm not a mere man. Hop aboard. I'll give her the gun and fly you home to your dinner."

CHAPTER 3

Mary Eliska Solves the Conway Case

Chapter 3.1
OUT OF LUCK

Above the speeding airplane, lowering black of approaching night and storm; below, the forest, grim and silent, swelling over ridges, dipping into valleys, crestless waves on a dark green ocean.

"We can't make it, Jax Gray." Mary Eliska, at the controls, spoke into the mouthpiece of her headphone set.

Jacqueline "Jax" Gray, in the rear cockpit, glanced overside and shuddered.

"But you can't land on those trees!" Jax cried shrilly. "We'll crash—you know that!"

"Maybe we will—and maybe we won't!" returned Mary Eliska, gritting her teeth. "Keep your eyes peeled for a pond or a woodlot—anywhere you think we can land."

"What—what's the matter?" called back her friend, steadying her wobbly nerves with an effort.

"Matter enough. We're nearly out of gasoline—running on reserve fuel now. When the rain starts, it'll be pitch dark in no time."

"Oh, Mary Eliska—do try to stay up! We can't crash and be killed—that's what it will mean if you try to land here!"

"Jax Gray, behave, will you? This is my funeral." The pilot in her anxiety, had struck upon an unhappy choice of words.

"Oh, you must do something—this is terrible—" the frenzied girl in the rear cockpit almost shrieked.

Mary Eliska ripped off her headphone set. She could no longer allow her attention to be distracted by Jax Gray's excited whimpering.

The small amphibian, flying low, topped a crag-scarred ridge. At the foot of the cliff she saw a tiny woodland meadow.

Action in the air must be automatic. There is never time to reason. With the speed of legerdemain the young girl pilot sent her airplane into a steep right bank and pushed down hard on the left rudder pedal. The result was a sideslip, the only maneuver by which the amphibian could possibly be piloted into the woodlot. Tilted sideways at an angle that brought a scream from terrified Jax Gray, the heavy mass of wood and metal dropped like a plummet toward the earth.

This was too much for little Jax Gray. Convinced that her friend had lost control of the plane, she closed her eyes and prayed.

With uncanny accuracy, considering the rainswept gloom, Mary Eliska recovered just at the proper instant. Hard down rudder brought the longitudinal axis of the plane into coincidence with its actual flight path again. At the same time she brought the up aileron into play, thereby preventing the bank from increasing. Then as the amphibian shot into a normal glide, she leveled the wings laterally by use of ailerons and rudder.

Their speed was still excessive, so for a split second or two, Mary Eliska leveled off and fishtailed the plane. That is, she kicked the rudder alternately right and left, thereby swinging the nose from side to side, and did so without banking and without dropping the nose to a steeper angle.

Taking the greatest possible care that her airplane was in straight flight prior to the moment of contact with the ground, she gave it a brief burst of the engine, obviating any possibility of squashing on with excessive force. The airplane landed well back on the tail, rolled forward over the bumpy ground and came to a stop at the very edge of the little meadow, nose on to the line of trees and underbrush.

Mary Eliska switched off the ignition, snapped out of her safety belt and turned around.

"Hail, hail, the gang's all here," Mary Eliska said cheerfully. "Wake up, Jax! We've come to the end of the line."

Jax Gray opened her eyes and looked about in startled amazement.

"Why—why we didn't crash, after all!"

"Certainly not," snorted Mary Eliska. "D'you think I'd let *Wispy* mash up my best friend? Come on, dry your eyes. Good thing it's so dark and your twin brother Liam McAdams and none of the other boys are with us. You'd be a fine sight," she teased.

"I think *Will-o-the-Wisp* is a silly name for a plane." Jax Gray's remark was purposely irrelevant. She wanted to change the subject.

"Then don't think about it. Turn your mind upon the answer of that dear old song, 'Where do we go from here?'"

"Where are we?" Jax Gray could be practical enough when her nerves were not tried too severely.

"Mmm!" murmured Mary Eliska. "That's the question. I'm not quite sure, but I think we're on the New York State Reservation over on Pound Ridge. A good ten miles or more from home, anyway."

"If we're on the reservation we're certainly out of luck," sighed Jax Gray. "It's a terribly wild place—nothing but rocks and ridges and woods and things. They keep it that way on purpose."

"Nice for picnics on sunny days, I guess," affirmed Mary Eliska. "But not so good on a rainy night, eh? Here, put on this slicker before you're wet through. Then get down. We've got to move out of here." Jax Gray stood up, caught the coat Mary Eliska threw into the cockpit, and after slipping into it, she stared fearfully about.

"What are you waiting for?" Mary Eliska inquired from below. "I'm going to stay where I am," announced Jax Gray in a quavering voice. "It's safer."

"How safe?" Mary Eliska turned on her flash light. Its moving beam brought into bold relief the jungle of scrub oak and evergreens that walled the little pasture.

"Listen, Mary Eliska! I remember my poppa John saying that they preserved game on the Pound Ridge reservation. There are sure to be bears and—and other things in these woods. Turn off the light—quick—they'll be attracted to us if we show a light—"

"Bears—your grandmother!" said Mary Eliska's mocking voice and the light flashed full on Jax Gray. "Don't be so silly. Come down here at once!"

"No, I won't. I'm going to stay up here. I—I'm sure it's safer."

"Then you can be 'safer' by yourself. If you think I'm going to stick around this woodlot all night, you've got another guess coming. Snap out of it, won't you, Jax Gray?"

"But you wouldn't leave me all alone out here!"

"Watch me." The light began to move away from the airplane.

"I'll come—I'll come with you, Mary Eliska—wait!"

The light came back and Jax Gray scrambled to the ground in a fever of haste.

"Now, then, stop being a goop and take this flashlight," directed Mary Eliska. "Hold it on the plane so I can see. We've got to make *Wispy* secure, before we get under way."

"I s'pose you get that Navy lingo from Bill Bolton." Jax Gray felt rather peevish now. "You talk just like him ever since he taught you to fly."

"I wish he were here now," retorted her friend, and climbed into the cockpit. "Here—take these wheel blocks and stop grouching. And for goodness' sake, please don't wobble that light! I want to get these cockpit covers on before everything is flooded."

A few minutes later she climbed down again and after adjusting the wheel blocks, took the flashlight from Jax Gray.

"All set?" she inquired briskly. "Got your knitting and everything? 'Cause it's time we were moving."

Jax Gray began to cry.

"I think you're mean—of course I want to get out of here, but—but you n-needn't—"

Mary Eliska put her arm about the smaller girl's shoulders.

"There, there," she comforted, "cheer up. I won't be cross any more. Here's a hanky, use it and come along. Gee, I wish this rain would stop! It's coming down in buckets."

"I'm sorry, too, for sniveling," said Jax Gray meekly. She made a strenuous effort to be brave as they walked away from the dark shape of the plane. "But don't you think you'd better get out your revolver, Mary Eliska? Honestly, you know, we're likely to run into anything out here in these woods."

Mary Eliska burst into a peal of laughter. "Bless you, honey," she chuckled. "I don't carry a gun when I go calling—or any other time if I can help it. We'll get out of this all right, don't worry. I should have looked at the gasoline before we left home, but I thought there was plenty to take us over to Peekskill and back. *Wispy* eats the stuff—that's the answer!"

They stumbled along on the outskirts of the woodlot, Mary Eliska keeping her light swinging from side to side before them. "But I thought you *always* carried a gun—" insisted Jax Gray, her mind still on the same track—"you ought to, after all you went through with those bank robbers and then the gang of diamond smugglers!"

"Well, you've got to have a license to tote a revolver—I'll admit I've carried 'em now and then—but not to a tea!" replied Mary Eliska. "Do try and help me now, to find a way out of this place."

"But maybe there is no way out. We can't climb those cliffs, and this meadow's hemmed in by the woods. Oh, dear, I wish I knew where we are!"

"I'm not certain," mused Mary Eliska, more to herself than to her companion, "but I think I caught sight of the fire tower on the ridge just before we sideslipped. That would mean that this meadow is on the eastern edge of the reservation—and that there's a road on the hill across from the ridge. There must be a trail of some kind leading in here. They could never get the hay out or the cattle in, otherwise; this place must be used for something."

They trudged along, keeping the trees on their left until the farther end of the meadow was reached. As they rounded the corner the light from the flash brought into view a narrow opening in the trees and undergrowth.

"What did I tell you?" sang out Mary Eliska. "There's our trail! This certainly is a lucky break!"

"Where do you suppose it goes?" Jax Gray's question was lacking in enthusiasm.

"Oh, it's the tunnel from the Grand Central to the new Waldorf-Astoria," said Mary Eliska, squinting in the darkness. "I'm going to take a room with a bath. You can have one, too, if you're good!"

Jax Gray stumbled into a jagged wheel rut and sat down suddenly. "Oh, my goodness!" she moaned. "My new pumps are ruined—and these nice new stockings are a mass of runs from those nasty brambles!"

"Humph! Just think how lucky you are to be alive," suggested Mary Eliska callously. "Look—we're coming into another meadow. Yes—and there's a light—must be a house up there on the hill."

"What if they won't let us in?" wailed Jax Gray.

They were heading across the meadow, now, toward the hill. Mary Eliska stopped and turned the flashlight on her friend.

"You certainly are a gloom!" she declared angrily. "Do you think I'm enjoying this? *My* shoes and stockings are ruined, too, and this ducky dress I'm crazy about has a rip in the skirt a yard long. It will probably be worse by the time we get through the brush on that hillside. But there's absolutely no use in whining about it—and there's not a darned thing to be scared of.

Is that clear to you, Jax?" She paused, and then went on more gently. "Come on, old thing, you'll feel much better when we've found a place to get warm and dry."

"I know you think I'm an awful baby." Jax Gray tried her best to make her voice sound cheerful, but her attempt was not a brilliant success. "But I'm just not brave, that's all," she went on, "and I do feel perfectly terrible."

"I know. You're not used to this kind of an outing, and I am, more or less. But I can see how it would upset you. Here's a stone fence. Give me your hand, I'll help you over. Fine! Now save your breath for the hill. We've got a stiff climb ahead of us."

For the next fifteen or twenty minutes they fought their way up the steep slope through a veritable jungle of thickets and rock. In spite of frequent rests on the boulders that dotted the hillside, both girls were exhausted by the time they came to another dilapidated stone wall that acted as a low barrier between the brush and an over-grown apple orchard. Through the gnarled trunks, they could dimly see the shape of the house whence came the light.

Mary Eliska sat down on top of the wall, and pulled Jax Gray to a place beside her. Then she switched off her flash.

"Some drag, that!" Her breath came in labored gasps. Jax Gray was too weary to make any reply. For a time they sat, silently. Then Mary Eliska slid painfully off the wall into the orchard. "You stay here, Jax Gray. I'm going over to the house and reconnoiter."

"Say! You don't go without me!" Jax Gray sprang down with sudden determination.

"Then walk carefully and don't make any noise."

A tone of startled surprise came into Jax Gray's voice.

"What—what are you afraid of, Mary Eliska?" she whispered excitedly.

"Not a thing, silly. But there may be watch dogs—and I want to get some idea of the people who live in that dump before I ask 'em for hospitality. I've got myself into trouble before this, going it blind. I know it pays to be careful. If you must come with me, you must, I suppose. But walk behind me—and don't say another word."

She stalked off through the orchard with Jax Gray close at her heels. As they neared the house, which seemed to be badly in need of repair, it was plain that the light came from behind a shaded window on the ground floor. Mary Eliska stopped to ponder the situation. A shutter hanging by one hinge banged dully in the wind and a stream of rain water was shooting down over the window from a choked leader somewhere above. She felt a grip on her arm. "Let's don't go in there," whispered Jax Gray. "It's a perfectly horrid place, I think."

"It doesn't look specially cheerful," admitted Mary Eliska. "But there may not be another house within a couple of miles. There's a porch around on the side. Maybe we can see into the room from there."

Together they moved cautiously through the rank grass and weeds to the edge of the low veranda. There was no railing and the glow from two long French windows gave evidence that the floor boards were warped and rotting. The howl of the wind and driving rain served to cover the sound of their movements as they tiptoed across the porch to the far window. Both shades were drawn, but this one lacked a few inches of reaching the floor.

Both girls lay flat on their stomachs and peered in. Quick as a flash, Mary Eliska clapped her hands over Jax Gray's mouth, smothering her sudden shriek of terror.

Chapter 3.2
TO THE RESCUE

The cold, wet wind of late September howled around the house. Mary Eliska wished she had brought a revolver.

"Stop it! Jax, stop!" she hissed and forced her friend to crawl backward over the rough boards to the edge of the porch. "Stay here, and don't make a sound. Do you want them out after us? For goodness' sake, take a grip on yourself! I'm going back to the window and—not another peep out of you while I'm gone!" With this warning, she slithered away before Jax could voice an objection.

Lying flat before the window once more with her face almost level with the floor, she stared into the room. The scene had not changed. Nor had the three principals of the drama being enacted on the other side of the pane moved from their positions. A sudden gust tore loose the shutter at the back of the house, sending it crashing down on some other wooden object with terrific racket.

"Must have hit the cellar doors," thought Mary Eliska. The man with the cigar, who stood before the cold fireplace stopped talking. She saw him cock his head to one side and listen. The bald-headed man in the leather armchair kept his revolver leveled on the room's third occupant, and snapped out a question. With a shrug, the man by the fireplace went on speaking. He was a dapper person, flashily dressed in a black and white shepherd's plaid suit which contrasted disagreeably with the maroon overcoat worn open for comfort. Mary Eliska took a dislike to him at first sight. Notwithstanding his mincing gestures, the man had the height and build of a heavyweight prizefighter. Now he leaned forward, emphasizing with a pudgy forefinger the point of his oratory which was directed toward the third member of the party.

Mary Eliska uttered an impatient exclamation. She could not hear a word. The roaring storm and the closed windows prevented her from catching even the rumble of their voices. She continued to gaze intently upon the prisoner, a well set up youth of eighteen or nineteen, curly-haired and intelligent looking. Her sympathy went out at once to this young fellow. He was bound hand and foot to the chair in which he sat. A blackened eye and his shirt, hanging in ribbons from his shoulders, told of a fight. Then she spied an overturned table, books and writing materials scattered over the rumpled rug.

"Whew!" she whistled softly. "He staged a little battle for 'em, anyway, I'll bet!" She smiled as she noticed that the youth's opponents had likewise suffered. For the bald-headed man held a bloodstained handkerchief to his nose, while the other's overcoat was ripped from collar to hem and he nursed a jaw that was evidently tender. The room which lay beneath her scrutiny offered a decided contrast to the unkempt exterior of the house. The walls were completely lined with bookcases, reaching from ceiling to floor. The shelves must have held thousands of volumes. Essentially a man's library, the furnishings were handsome, though they had evidently seen better days.

In reply to a question barked at him from the dapper prize fighter, the young prisoner shook his head in a determined negative. The big man spat out an invective. This time the boy smiled slightly, shook his head again. With a roar of fury that was audible to the watching girl outside, the prize fighter-bully strode over to his victim and struck him across the mouth.

That brutal action decided Mary Eliska. She wormed her way backward off the porch. Jax Gray was still crouched where she had left her. She sprang up and caught her friend's arm.

"Isn't it terrible?" she whispered tensely. "He's such a good-looking boy, too—don't tell me they've killed him or anything?"

Without speaking, Mary Eliska led Jax around to the back of the house.

"No, they haven't killed him," she answered when they had reached the shelter of the apple orchard. "This is no movie thriller. But something pretty serious is going on in there. Now tell me—are you going to pull yourself together and be of some help? Because if you're not, you can climb one of these trees and stay there until it's all over. That's the only safe place I know of—and even up there you'll get into trouble if you start screaming again!"

"Well, I really couldn't help it, Mary Eliska. He was such a darling looking boy and—"

"My goodness—what have his looks got to do with it? He's in a peck of trouble—that's the principal thing. I want to help him."

"Oh, so do I!" asserted Jax eagerly. "I'll be good, honest I will."

"Obey orders?" "Do my best."

"O.K. then. I'm going around front. Those blackguards must have come in a car—and I'm going to find it."

"But you can't leave me here alone—"

"There you go again, silly! I'm not going to drive away in the car. I've got another plan. Listen! There's a cellar door, somewhere back of the house I guess. It's one of the flat kind that you pull up to open. I heard that shutter slam down on it."

"I suppose you want me to open it?"

"Bullseye!"

"You needn't be so superior," Jax Gray's tone was aggrieved. "What'll I do if it's locked?"

"Oh, people 'way out in the country never lock their cellar doors," Mary Eliska's tone was impatient, her mind three jumps ahead.

"But suppose this one is?"

"Wait there until I come back. Hurry now—there's no telling what's going on in that room. So long—I'll be with you in a few minutes. If you hear a crash, *don't scream!*"

She raced away and as she reached the corner of the side porch, a quick glance over her shoulder told her that Jax Gray was marching resolutely toward the cellar door.

This time Mary Eliska skirted the porch and toward the front of the house she came upon a weed-grown drive which swept in a quarter circle toward the road some fifty yards away. A limousine was parked before the entrance to the house. It was empty.

Mary Eliska breathed a sigh of relief. She hurried past the car and found that the drive ran around the farther side of the house, out to a small garage at the back. The garage doors were open, and inside she spied an ancient Ford. For some reason the sight of the Ford seemed to perturb her. She stood a while in deep thought.

Then as an idea struck home, she drew forth her flash light and sent its beam traveling over the interior of the garage. She did not take the precaution of closing the doors. The library was on the other side of the house and there was little danger of her light being seen. Suddenly she uttered a cry of satisfaction. Her light had brought into view about a dozen gasoline tins stacked in a corner. She lifted them one by one—all were empty. She hunted about and presently unearthed a short piece of rubber hose from under the seat of the automobile.

"First break tonight!" she said to herself. "Here's hoping the luck lasts!" A few minutes later, if anyone had been watching, they would have seen a girl in a slicker, her dark curly hair topped by an aviation helmet, leave the garage carrying two gasoline tins. These she took to the orchard and deposited them behind a couple of apple trees.

Her next movements were more puzzling. She walked back to the garage and around that little building to the side away from the main house. Again her flash light was brought into play. This time she focused it on the land to the side and rear and saw that the low wall which partly encompassed the orchard ended at the back of the garage. There was no obstruction between the drive at the side of the house and a rough field that sloped sharply down the valley whence she and Jax Gray had come. Then she realized that the house and orchard lay on a plateau-like rise of land which jutted out into the valley from the main ridge, the ground dropping steeply on three sides.

"Well, the scenery couldn't be sweeter!" remarked Mary Eliska. "Now, I hope to goodness they've left the keys."

It was blowing half a gale now, and rain in crystal rods drove obliquely through the flash light's gleam. She switched off the light and stuffed it into a pocket of her dripping slicker and beat her way against the storm toward the house. Here she found the limousine, and hastened on toward the side porch.

Lying flat at the window once more, she saw that a fire had been started in the fireplace. The dapper person crouched before it, holding an iron poker between the burning logs.

Mary Eliska realized on the instant the fiendish torture those beasts were planning. She jumped to her feet and tiptoeing over the boards, raced for the car.

Her hand, fumbling on the dash, brought a faint jangle from a bunch of keys—

"Break number three!" she cried and slipped behind the steering wheel. As she switched on the ignition she brought her right foot down on the starter and when the powerful engine purred she fed it more gasoline and let in the clutch.

The car rolled forward and she swung it around the corner of the house toward the garage, with her thumb pressed down hard on the button of the horn.

"That'll bring them out!" she chuckled and slipping into high sent the car hurtling off the drive, headed for the field beyond the garage. An instant later she dropped off the running board while the limousine raced into the field and down the steep hillside to the valley below—and destruction.

At the same moment Mary Eliska heard shouts from the house and footsteps pounding on the gravel. She wasted no time peering after the car. Turning on her heel, she flew around the garage and over to the rear of the house. The cellar door was open, Jax Gray was standing on the top step.

"Down you go!" panted Mary Eliska. "Take this flash and switch on the light—quick!"

A slight shove sent Jax Gray stumbling down the stone flight and Mary Eliska followed more slowly, bringing down the wide door over her head.

"The light, Jax Gray, the light!" she cried.

"B-but we can't go into the house—those men—"

"Never mind the men—do as you're told. I can't find the lock on this door in the dark. Where are you, anyway?"

"Right here," said a small voice and the flash light gleamed.

Mary Eliska shot home the bolt and took the torch into her own hand. "Come on!"

Without waiting to see if her order was obeyed, she ran to the stairs that led up to the first floor. At the top of the short flight, she found a closed door. She opened it and stepped into the kitchen, with Jax Gray at her elbow. Locking the door behind them, she flashed her light about the room, then walked over to a table and pulled out the drawer. "Here—take this!" Jax Gray stepped back as a large kitchen knife was thrust in her direction.

"Take it!" commanded Mary Eliska and again the smaller girl unwillingly did as she was told.

"But—but you can't mean we're going to fight them with knives," she spluttered, "why, Mary Eliska; I just couldn't—"

"Don't talk rot!" Mary Eliska's tone was caustic. "Please cut the argument, now—I know what I'm doing!"

Jax Gray trotted at her heels as she crossed the kitchen toward the front of the house, passed through a swinging door into the dining room. An arched doorway to their right, brought the hall into view, and beyond it, another door stood open, leading into the lighted library, where they saw its single occupant still tied to his chair.

"Go in there and cut him loose," directed Mary Eliska. She pushed Jax Gray into the room and raced for the open front door. She heard the sound of voices from the drive as she neared the end of the hall. She could see the figures of two men just beyond the front steps. Just as her hand reached the door handle, they turned in her direction and the black night was seared with the sharp red flash from an automatic.

Chapter 3.3
IN THE CONWAY HOUSE

With the detonation of the gun in her ears, Mary Eliska flung herself against the door and slammed it shut. Her hand fumbled for the key, found it and sent the bolt shooting into place. About the house the rain-lashed wind howled and moaned like some wild thing in torment. Her heart was pumping and her breath came in choking gasps. Leaning against the solid oak door she pressed her ear to a panel. The noise of the storm muffled all other sound, but she thought she could detect the mumble of men's voices just outside the door. It was impossible to catch the words, of course, but the mere sound told the girl that they were standing on the small front porch. To her right was a sitting room. She hurried into it.

A quick flash of her torch showed two windows facing the drive. She tried the catches. They were unlocked. She fastened them and ran out of the room, down the hall to the rear. The light from the library threw the staircase into silhouette. Mary Eliska started for the dining room, but stopped short as the young man whom she had sent Jax Gray in to free, bounded into the hall.

"Hello!" he cried. "Do you know where they are?"

Mary Eliska pointed toward the front door.

"Right out there!"

"Good! I'll fix 'em!"

He raced up the stairs and she heard him running toward the front of the house.

"Jax Gray!" she called. "Come here!"

"What is it?" answered that young lady's voice from the library. "George told me to stay in this room."

"*George?*" exploded Mary Eliska. She ran to the door and looked in. Jax Gray was toasting her soaking pumps from a chair before the fire. She turned her head when Mary Eliska appeared and beckoned toward the blaze.

"Yes—George Conway," she explained smilingly. "He owns this house, you see."

Mary Eliska's fingers pressed the wall switch and the electric lights went out.

"Well, you *are* a fast worker—" was her comment. "Dash over to those windows and see that they're fastened. Then pile some of these chairs and tables in front of the French doors—anything will do, just so it's heavy. Hurry—and when you've finished, go into the hall and stay there." Jax Gray stared through the darkness. "But George says—" "I don't care *what* George says! The hall is the safest place right now."

"Well, why can't you help me?" grumbled Jax Gray. "Suppose those awful men come before I've—" "They won't if you snap to it. I'm off to fasten the windows in the rest of the house."

This last was thrown over her shoulder as she tore across to the dining room. After making the rounds in there she went into the kitchen. Here she found a window open and the back door unlocked. It took her but a moment to remedy this, and she was passing back to the dining room when there came a terrific crash and reverberation from the floor above, followed by screams and curses from outside. She went out into the hall and another report from above shook the windows in their frames. Jax Gray, wild-eyed with fright, rushed into the bright arc of Mary Eliska's flash light. "What on earth is it?" she cried in very evident alarm.

"Shotgun," said Mary Eliska tersely. "If those yells meant anything, I guess we can take it that somebody's been hit."

Then she noticed that Jax Gray's left hand held an open compact, while in her right she clutched a small rouge puff. Her ash-gold hair which she wore long had become unknotted and hung halfway down her back. Her petite figure drooped with weariness.

"Gracious, Jax Gray! How in the wide world did you ever get rouge on the end of your nose? You're a sight!"

"Well, you turned out the light—" Jax Gray's tone was indignant, as she rubbed the end of her nose with a damp handkerchief. "I think I'll run upstairs and spruce up a bit." Mary Eliska looked at her and laughed. "Come on up with me," suggested Jax Gray. "You don't look so hot yourself." "No, you run along and pander to your vanity, my child. When you've finished, why don't you go into the kitchen and make us a batch of fudge—that would be just the thing!"

"Why so sarcastic?" Jax Gray raised her delicate eyebrows.

"Well—what do you think we've run into—a college house party or something?" "Oh, I think you're mean," Jax Gray pouted.

"But you do choose the queerest times to spiff up!"

"Do you think those men will try to get in again!" Jax Gray's blue eyes widened.

"If I didn't know that your head was a fluffball—But what's the use. Run along now. It sounds as if George were coming down. Hurry up—you might meet him on the stairs!"

"Cat!" said Jax Gray and flew. Mary Eliska went to the door and listened. If the two men were still outside, they gave no sign of their presence. Nothing came to her ears through the panels but the howl of the storm.

Then she heard footsteps running down the stairs from the second story and switched her flashlight on George. He carried a double-barreled shotgun in the hollow of his arm.

"Howdy!" he greeted her enthusiastically. "You know, I can never thank you girls enough for all you've done. Gosh! You're a couple of heroes, all right—I mean heroines. When I saw Jax —I mean, Jacqueline Gray," he amended quickly with an embarrassed grin, "come sprinting into the library and begin to cut me loose, why I just couldn't believe my eyes!"

"Some wonderworker, isn't she?" Mary Eliska contrived to look awestruck, but there was no malice in her amused tone.

"You said it—she's a whizbang! And she told me you two came in an airplane. I've never met a girl aviator before. I guess she's a second Mary Eliska—you must have read what the newspapers said about that girl!" He shook his head admiringly. "Jax Gray sure has nerve!"

"She has, indeed!" Mary Eliska kept her face straight with an effort. "But tell me—what did you do to that crew outside?"

"Plugged 'em—clean. Got a bead on them through a front window."

"What? You—killed them? Buckshot, at that distance?"

George chuckled. "Not buckshot—rock salt. Use it for crows, you know. It stings like the dickens."

"I'll bet it does!" Mary Eliska's laugh was full-throated and hearty.

"What's become of them?" she asked when she could speak.

"They beat it around the house to the garage. Do you know what happened to their car?"

"Yes. It ran away—down the lots to the bottom of the valley. And between you and me and the hat rack, I don't think it will ever run anymore."

"Gee whiz!" chuckled George. "Who'd ever think a little thing like Jax would have the pluck to pull a stunt like that!"

"Who would?" said Mary Eliska and joined in the laugh. "Well, as long as their car is out of the running, they'll probably try to steal my flivver 'Calamity Jane'." George tapped his gun significantly, "But I'll put a crimp in that. They've got to pass the dining room windows to get out of here."

"You needn't bother—the Ford won't move."

"Sure it will." George stopped short in the doorway and turned toward her. "That car of mine runs like a watch."

"But not without gasoline," explained Mary Eliska. "I drained the tank into a couple of tins." "You did?"

"Sure thing. Parked the tins in your orchard. They'll never find 'em." "Say!" exclaimed George. "You must be almost as good as Jax Gray that is, I mean—"

"Who's taking my name in vain?" Jax Gray was tripping blithely downstairs. "You two seem to be finding a lot to talk about."

George stared at her. "Say, you certainly look swell when you're dolled up."

"Well, it's the best I can do now," deprecated Jax Gray. "I borrowed a pair of your slippers though—woolly ones. That is, I s'pose they're yours?"

"Glad to have you wear 'em." George's eyes were still glued to Jax Gray's pretty face when Mary Eliska broke in.

"Look here, we'll have to get down to business. George—listen to me. Jax Gray won't melt, you know—"

"Oh, I think you're terrible—" interrupted Jax Gray.

Her friend paid no attention, but kept on talking to George. "Do you really think they've gone?"

He nodded. "I'm pretty sure they have—that is, for the present. You can't do a whole lot when your hide is full of salt. I'll bet they're kiting down the road right now. Maybe they'll stop in at the Robinson's or somewhere and get a lift to Stamford or Ridgefield or wherever they came from. They may have some pals about here, of course. I sort of gathered that they weren't working on their own—that there was somebody in back of them."

"Well, at least we can count on a breather. Let's go in the library and turn on the light. I'm tired of standing about in this hall and I want to dry out by the fire."

In the library, George pushed a couple of easy chairs before the comforting blaze. Mary Eliska cast aside her slicker and helmet and dropped into one of them. She kicked off her sodden shoes and stretching her legs toward the warmth, drew forth a comb and proceeded to make herself neat. George perched on the arm of Jax Gray's chair, and the two stared at the flames without speaking.

At last Mary Eliska put her comb away, turned to George and broke the silence.

"It's none of my particular business, of course, but would you mind telling me the reason for all this rough house? Why did those men attack you and tie you up—what were they doing around here?"

George shook his head slowly. "Hanged if I know," he said.

"You don't know? But they seemed to be asking you questions—from what I could see through the window, it looked that way."

"That's right. But—but—well, you two girls are real sportsmen. You've pulled me out of an awful mess. Heaven knows I appreciate what you've done, but I just can't have you running any further risk on my account, Miss—"

"Stricklin," supplied Jax Gray. "I forgot you hadn't been introduced."

George leaned forward. "Do you come from Jackson Hole?" he shot out.

"Of course, we live there," said Jax Gray. "And I want you to know that Mary Eliska is my best friend. We're seniors at the Jackson Hole High—if that interests you."

"So *you're* Mary Eliska, the flyer!" he exploded. "Suffering monkeys! I didn't know I was entertaining a celebrity. Why, you're the girl I was talking about—who—"

"Here, here—don't make me blush," laughed Mary Eliska.

"But don't you see? Your being Mary Eliska makes all the difference in the world."

Mary Eliska's eyebrows drew together in a puzzled frown. "I don't get you," she said. "I really don't know what you're talking about."

"Why, if what the newspapers say is true, you simply eat up this gangster stuff—a whiz at solving all kinds of mysteries."

"Nice lady-like reputation, what?" she mocked.

"Well, that's all right with me. Because now—I have no hesitancy in telling you all I know about this queer business. You'll probably know just what to do—and you'll be a wonderful help."

"How about me?" Jax Gray was a direct little person and seemed at no pains to disguise her feelings. "I don't think you're a bit polite, George!"

"Oh, I feel differently about you—" stammered that young man, then stopped short and looked painfully embarrassed. Mary Eliska thought it time she took matters into her own hands.

"Don't be silly, Jax Gray, George knows how clever you are!" She flashed a mischievous glance at her friend, then went on in a serious tone. "And of course we're keen to hear all about it, George, and we'll do anything we can to help you. But your story will keep a while longer. I hope you don't mind my mentioning such a prosaic thing—but do you happen to have anything to eat in the house?"

"Oh, my gosh! Of course I have—" he threw a glance at the clock and jumped to his feet. "It's nearly eight o'clock. You girls must be starved! Sit right here and I'll bring supper in a jiffy. I was just about to eat mine when those two thugs dropped in and put an end to it for the time being."

"I'll help you," offered Jax Gray, hopping out of her chair.

"That's a good plan," decreed Mary Eliska. "While you're starting things in the kitchen, I'd like to use the phone, if I may."

"There it is, on that table in the corner," said George. "Hop to it. I'll drive you home later in the flivver."

"Thanks, but I've got to have gasoline for my plane. We'll talk it over at supper, shall we?"

She took up the telephone and the others hurried from the room.

Presently she joined them in the kitchen.

"I called up your mother Dee, Jax Gray, and told her you were spending the night with me," she announced. "Poppa is away, so I got hold of Bill Bolton and he'll be over here in about twenty minutes."

"Oh, fine—" began Jax Gray and stopped short as an electric bell on the wall buzzed sharply.

For a moment they stared at it in startled silence. Then George spoke. "Somebody's ringing the door bell," he said slowly.

Chapter 3.4
VISITORS

"You girls stay in here—I'll go," continued George, his hand on the swinging door to the dining room.

"No, you shan't!" Jax Gray sprang before him, blocking his way.

"Don't make such a fuss," said Mary Eliska. "Somebody's got to go. Come here!"

Her long arm shot out and Jax Gray was held in a light embrace that seemed as unbending as tempered steel.

"Stop wriggling," she commanded. "This is George's job. Did you leave your gun in the library, George?"

"Yes. I'll pick it up on the way."

"Better not do that. Maybe it's one of your neighbors."

"Haven't any. None of the people around here come to see me."

The bell buzzed loudly again, and continued to do so. Someone was keeping a finger pressed on the button beside the front door.

"I have a plan," Mary Eliska announced suddenly. "Jax Gray, you stay here, and—"

"And have them break in the back door while you two are in the front hall? No thanks—I'm coming with you, that's all." Mary Eliska did not stop to argue. She hurried into the dining room and across the hall to the library, followed by the others.

"Look here," she whispered, picking up the shotgun. "Slip on your jacket, George. That shirt will show anyone you've been in a fight. Jax Gray and I will go into the front sitting room. It's dark in there. Turn on the hall light and open the door as though everything were all right, and you expected a friend. If it is someone you know, they won't see us in the sitting room. If it isn't—and they try to start something, jump back so you're out of line from the door to that room … and I'll fill 'em full of salt!"

"Swell idea! A regular flank attack!" enthused the young man, struggling into his coat. "All set?"

He switched on the hall light. The girls ran into the sitting room. Mary Eliska stood in the dark with the shotgun pointed toward the hall and saw him turn the key and pull open the door.

"Good evening, George," whined a high-pitched voice. "Mind if I come in for a minute or two?"

"Walk in, Mr. Lewis. Bad night, isn't it?"

George's face showed surprise but he swung the door wide and closed it with a bang as a tall figure, leaning heavily on a cane, shuffled into the lighted hallway. The man's bent back, rounded shoulders and the rather long white hair that hung from beneath the wide brim of his soft black hat, all bespoke advanced age. Immensely tall, even with his stoop, the old man towered over George, who was all of six feet himself. Although the night was not cold, he was buttoned to the chin in a long fur coat. Mary Eliska caught sight of piercing black eyes beneath tufted white eyebrows. The long, cadaverous, clean-shaven face was a network of fine wrinkles.

"What say?" He cupped a hand behind his ear.

"I said it was a bad night to be out in," shouted George. "What can I do for you?"

"Yes, that's it, my lad—there's something I—Yes, it's a bad night—bad storm. Listen, George!"

"Yes, sir."

"What say?"

"I'm listening, Mr. Lewis."

"Well, listen then."

The sharp eyes peered up and down the hall. Mary Eliska moved farther back into the dark room.

"Your father had a lot of books, George—a very fine library."

"Yes, he had."

"What say?"

"I said he had."

The old man shook his head. His high voice became querulous.

"I know he's dead," he snorted. "I'm talking about his books."

"They are not for sale," said George.

"Bless you—I don't want to buy 'em. But there's one I want to borrow."

"Which one is that?"

"What say?"

George's reply *sotto voce* was not polite. He was getting impatient.

"I want to borrow a book called *Aircraft Power Plants*; it's by a man named Jones."

Mary Eliska pricked up her ears.

"All right," shouted George. "I'll try to find it."

"What say? Listen, George! Speak distinctly, if you can. I'm not deaf—just a little hard of hearing. Don't mumble—you talk as though your mouth was full of hot potato. That's a bad eye you've got—been in a fight?"

George ignored this last. "Listen—" he said, then stopped, controlling a desire to giggle as he realized his plagiarism. "Come into the library, Mr. Lewis. I'll try to find the book for you." He took the old man by the arm and led him down the hall.

Jax Gray crept over to Mary Eliska.

"Do you know who he is?" she asked in a low tone.

"Mr. Lewis, I gathered," said Mary Eliska, straining her ears to catch the muffled sounds coming from the library. "*He* talked loud enough,—quite an old gentleman, isn't he?"

"Old skinflint, you mean."

"You've seen him before?"

"Certainly. I've seen him at our house. Daddy knows him—says he's made a fortune, foreclosing mortgages and lending money at high rates of interest. He's terribly rich, though you'd never know it by his looks."

"That's interesting—wonder what he wants with George?"

"Came to borrow a book—that's plain enough."

"Almost too plain, if you want my opinion," Mary Eliska said thoughtfully. "There's no use guessing at this stage of the game."

"What are you talking about?"

"Oh, nothing much. Can you hear what they're saying in the next room?"

"They seem to be having an argument—but it's not polite to listen—" "Polite, your grandmother! I'd listen if I could—but all I get is a mumble-jumble. I vote we go back to the kitchen. I want my supper. I'll feel better when I've eaten. This house gives me the jim-jams for some reason."

"Me, too," Jax Gray admitted ungrammatically. "Fancy being alarmed at the sound of a doorbell!"

"My word—and likewise cheerio!" Mary Eliska turned the flash on her friend. "How do you get that way, Jax Gray? Been reading the British poets or something?"

Jax Gray blinked in the glare. "Turn it off. No, I haven't. Don't you remember the movies last night? The English Duke in that picture—" She broke off suddenly and caught at Mary Eliska's arm. "Listen—Ecker, listen!" she whispered.

From the rear of the house came a muffled pounding.

Mary Eliska shook her off. "I'll ecker you a couple, if you take liberties with my name," she snapped. "And for goodness' sake, don't hold on to me that way, and stop that listen stuff! This isn't an earthquake—somebody's at the back door, and I'm going to see who it is!"

"But suppose those men have come back?"

"They're too well salted down," Mary Eliska flung back at her. "I *fancy* you'd better stay in here—if you're *alarmed*!" She crossed the hall to the dining room again and hurried through the kitchen with Jax Gray close on her trail. That young person apparently preferred to chance it rather than be left alone.

Mary Eliska went at once to the back door.

"Who's there?" she called, as the knocking broke out again.

"It's Bill Bolton," returned a muffled voice. "Is that you, Mary Eliska?"

She drew back the bolt and flung the door open.

"Hello, Bill!" she hailed. "You're just in time for supper."

A tall, broad shouldered young fellow wearing golf trousers and an old blue sweater which sported a Navy "N" came into the room. He was bareheaded and his thick, close-cropped thatch of hair was brown. When he smiled, Bill Bolton was handsome. A famous ace and traveler at seventeen, this friend of Mary Eliska's had not been spoiled by notoriety. His keen gray eyes twinkled good-naturedly as he spoke to Mary Eliska.

"Well, I should say you look pretty much at home," he grinned. "But then you have a faculty of landing on your feet. And how's Jax Gray tonight? Thought I'd find you girls in a tight fix and here you are—getting up a banquet. Liam McAdams was over at my house when you rang up, so he came with me. He's outside, playing second line defense. All sereno here, I take it?"

"Quiet enough now," Mary Eliska admitted, "though it was a bit hectic, to say the least, a while back. Call Liam in, will you? I'm going to do some scrambled eggs and bacon now."

She reached for a bowl and began to crack eggs and break them into it. Bill stuck his head out the door and whistled. A moment later, a heavy-set, round-faced lad of sixteen made his appearance in the doorway. Under his arm he carried a repeating rifle.

"H'lo, everybody," he breezed, resting his rifle against the wall. "This is some surprise,— Bill and I were all set to play the heavy heroes and we find you making fudge!"

"Not fudge," corrected Jax Gray. "Honest-to-goodness food! Mary Eliska and I haven't had a single thing to eat since lunch, except a lettuce sandwich and some cake at Helen Ritchie's tea over at Peekskill this afternoon. We're getting supper now."

"*We?*" Mary Eliska's tone was richly sarcastic. "Then, old dear, suppose you do some of the getting. I think I heard the front door shut just now, so that means that old Mr. Lewis has shoved-off. You can go into the dining room and set the table.—Bill, you're a good cook—

how about starting the coffee? Liam, be a sport and cut some bread—you might toast it while you're about it!"

"Whew!—some efficiency expert!" Liam winked at Bill. "Where do they keep the bread box in this house, anyway?"

"Barks her orders like a C.P.O. doesn't she?" laughed Bill, opening the coffee tin. Then he drew forth a wax-paper wrapped loaf from an enameled container, held it up: "Here's your bread, Liam—catch!" The door from the dining room swung open and George came in. "Well, George!" Mary Eliska turned to the others. "Here is our host," she explained and introduced him all around. "It's certainly wonderful of you fellows to hustle over here," he said as he shook hands. "I appreciate it."

"Oh, don't mention it," grinned Bill. "We seem to be rather late for the excitement."

"Well, if it hadn't been for Jax Gray and Mary Eliska—" began George.

"You'd have pulled yourself out all right," interrupted the latter young lady. "Look here, supper's nearly ready, and since I've set everybody else to work, suppose I give you a job, too? Take Jax Gray into the dining room and show her how to set the table, and you'll be a fine help."

"Say, it's great, the way you've pitched in here—did you have a hard time finding things?"

"No, not at all. Except—" here Mary Eliska looked stern, "I don't approve of your housekeeping methods—I had to scour the frying pan twice, sir, do you realize that?"

George hung his head. "Gee, I guess I'm pretty careless, but—"

The cook giggled: "Mercy, you look downcast. I was only kidding, George. I think you're a fine housekeeper, honestly, I do. Now you get a wiggle on with the table, please. These eggs are nearly finished. They'll be ruined if we have to wait."

When the two had disappeared, Mary Eliska dished the scrambled eggs into a warm plate and turned to Bill and Liam.

"He thinks Jax Gray ran this job," she informed them. "They've got a crush on each other, I guess. So don't put him wise, will you?"

"Mum's the word," smiled Bill, while Liam nodded. "Far be it from me to mess up love's young dream."

"Don't be silly," retorted Mary Eliska. "But you know, Jax Gray's a darling. I had to be terribly cross with her all the time, just to keep her bucked up. But she's my best friend and I'm crazy about her."

"She is nervous and high-strung, I know," supplemented Liam. "I'll bet you had a sweet time with her."

"Not so bad. Have you boys had supper?"

"Oh, yes, some time ago," answered Bill.

"That's good. I didn't want to use up all George's food. I'll let you have some coffee, though—that is, if you're good and don't kid those two in the other room."

"Cross-my-heart-hope-to-die-if-I-do." Bill's face was solemn.

"Likewise me," declaimed Liam. "I must have my coffee."

"Table's set," announced Jax Gray, popping in to the kitchen, closely followed by George.

"Eggs are finished and the bacon's fried," returned Mary Eliska. "How about the coffee, Bill?"

"Perfect—though I sez so."

"*And* the toast!" Liam was busy buttering the last slice. "You know, lovers used to write sonnets on their lady's eyebrows—now, if they'd seen this toast!" Mary Eliska shook her head at him. "That will be about all from you. Come along, all of you—everything smells so good, and I'm simply ravenous."

It was a merry party that gathered about the old mahogany dining table. Bill began by teasing Mary Eliska about her lack of foresight that sent her up on a flight without enough gasoline. She returned his banter with interest: the others joined in and for a time everybody was wisecracking back and forth.

George was the first to bring the conversation back to current events. "I don't know Mr. Lewis very well," he replied in answer to a question of Jax Gray's. "He was a friend of my father's—at least father had business dealings with him. I thought I'd never get rid of the old boy tonight."

"Did you find the book he wanted?" asked Mary Eliska. "Jones' *Aircraft Power Plants*, wasn't it?"

"Some book, too!" affirmed Bill. "Have you read it, Conway?"

"Didn't know I owned it. The book—in fact, the whole library, was my father's. About all he saved from the wreck. When I couldn't find the book for old Lewis, what do you think he said?"

"'Listen!'" Mary Eliska's voice mimicked perfectly the old gentleman's querulous tones. Everyone burst into laughter.

"Yes, he said that," George told her, "and a whole lot more."

"I hate riddles," cried Jax Gray. "Do tell us—"

"Why, he wanted to buy the entire library—and when I turned him down, he made me an offer on the house providing entire contents went with it!"

Jax Gray laughed. "A good low price, I'll bet. Mr. Lewis is a terrible old skinflint."

"I thought so, too, until he made me this offer."

"Do you mind saying how much?" Mary Eliska never hesitated to come to the point.

"Twenty-five thousand dollars!"

"Seems like a lot of money to me!" was Bill's comment.

"A lot of money! I should say so." George cried excitedly. "Why, this place isn't worth more than eight—possibly ten thousand dollars at the outside."

"I smell a rat," said Liam, "or to put it more politely, the old boy's offer has something doggoned stinking crooked mixed up in it."

"To add to Jax's cultured twin brother's oratory," said Bill, "There certainly seems to be something pretty darned putrid in the kingdom of Denmark!" "A whole lot nearer home, if you ask me," broke in Mary Eliska.—"That old man—" "Just a moment," begged Bill. "Your deductions, Mary Eliska, are always noteworthy. In fact, at times, the press of our glorious country has frequently referred to you as Miss Sherlock Holmes, but—" "Cut the comedy, Bill!" broke in the object of this effusion. "What is it you're driving at?" "Simply, as I was saying when so rudely interrupted, that your deductions and ideas on this business may be Aland a yard wide, but except for what you shot at me over the telephone, both Liam and I are wading about in a thick pea soup fog, so to speak. Suppose you give us your account of these mysterious happenings. That should put us 'hep' to the situation, and then George can tell us his end of the story, why he got tied up by these blokes and all that." George did not appear cheerful. "But I don't know—" he protested. "Haven't the slightest idea."

"So Mary Eliska said over the phone. But perhaps if you start far enough back—give us the story of your life, as it were—we may be able to dig out a motive." "At times you show positively human intelligence, Bill!" Mary Eliska yawned, without apology. "Well, here goes! Maybe if Bill will let me get a few words in edgewise, I may forget I'm so sleepy!"

Chapter 3.5
THE MOTIVE

"And then I opened the back door and found you standing there, Bill. Phew!" Mary Eliska ended with a sigh. "It's almost more of an effort in the telling than it was in the doing!"

"I wouldn't believe it if I didn't know it was true," declared Liam solemnly. "You've the great gift of stating things clearly, Liam," remarked Bill Bolton. "In other words, why must you put in your foot every time you open your mouth? Mary Eliska, my girl, you said your piece nicely."

"I'm not your girl, thank heaven! If I was at all interested, I'd certainly burst into tears. Please don't try to be humorous—it's painful, positively painful."

"I guess I'd better begin my story," George decided diplomatically. "Or somebody's likely to start throwing things. Where do you want me to start?"

"Like this," volunteered Liam, setting his empty coffee cup on its saucer. "'I was born an orphan at the age of four, of poor but dishonest parents....'"

"'And until the age of thirteen and three-quarters, could only walk sideways with my hair parted in the middle,'" came George's quick follow up.

"He's all right," decreed Bill. "Let him speak his piece, gang—this is going to be good."

"Of all the conceited nerve!" exclaimed Mary Eliska.

"Do shut up and give George a chance," broke in Jax Gray heatedly. "I want to hear about it—and this is a serious matter, I—"

"Now you're the one who's stopping him," accused her chum. "For goodness' sake, get going, George—we've got to drive to Jackson Hole some time tonight."

"All right," said George. "If you people don't find it interesting, well, you've brought it on yourselves. Surprising as it may seem, I was born at the usual age at 'Hilltop,' that big white house on the ridge, overlooking the other side of the reservation. Father, you know, was an inventor. He was always an extremely reticent man and I realized as I grew older that he was very much of a recluse. He never spoke to Mother and me about his inventions, but they must have brought him a good income. We kept up that big place and had plenty of servants, although we entertained very little. After I got through the nursery stage, I had a French governess and later a tutor. Mother and I were great pals. She must have been a busy woman, for she superintended the running of our model farm and dairy, but she was never too occupied with her duties but what she had time to romp and play with me. I know now that she must have led a very lonely life.

"My father spent nine-tenths of the time in his laboratory and workshop. He did not encourage friends or acquaintances and he never went anywhere with Mother. He had but one hobby, his work, and although I know he was very fond of us, the work came first. Even later, when I grew up, he never seemed like the fathers of other fellows I knew. It was his reticence and absolute absorption in those inventions of his that kept us practically strangers.

"Five years ago last spring, when I was twelve, Mother died. Her heart had never been strong—her going took the only person I really loved away from me." George was unable to go on for a moment, and Jax Gray caught his hand under the table and held it. The tenderhearted little girl was very near to tears. George smiled manfully, then went on with his recital.

"Sorry," he apologized for his show of feeling, "I never quite got over losing Mother. My governess had been replaced by a tutor a couple of years before this, but now Father decided I was to go to boarding school. So I was packed off to Lawrenceville, a homesick, lonely little kid if there ever was one. I'd never been thrown with boys of my own age before—I guess I was pretty much of a young prig—but as the poet says, 'I soon learned different.'

"During the holidays I used mostly to come back to Hilltop. Father never made a kick if I brought fellows back with me. We had the run of the place, which he kept up just as it had been when Mother was alive. One thing was understood though: he must not be annoyed by my guests. There were saddle horses, for he rode regularly every morning before breakfast; cars to drive, and he also belonged to the club over at Bedford, although I don't think he had ever seen the place. He gave me plenty of money to spend and always allowed me to accept invitations from other fellows to visit at their homes. Altogether I had a pretty good time. The only trouble was that Father never took any real interest in me. I was lucky enough to get my 'L' at football, but he never came down to Lawrenceville—not even to see a game."

"I've got your number, now!" cried Liam, interrupting him. "You're Stoker Conway! I thought I'd seen you before. Say, Bill, this guy is too modest. 'Lucky to make his letter,' I don't think! Conway captained the Lawrenceville team last season. My cousin, Ed Durham (they call him Bull Durham down there) played left tackle. I went down with Dad and Uncle Harry last fall to see the Princeton freshman-Lawrenceville game."

"I remember your telling about it," said Mary Eliska. "Somebody, I think, made a sixty-yard run for a touchdown."

"I'll bet George did it," piped up Jax Gray.

"He certainly did! And let me tell you, Angel-face, that your boy-friend was the fastest halfback Lawrenceville or any other school has seen in years. All American stuff—that's what he is. Hard luck you didn't get to college this year, old man."

"Can't always have what we want," remarked George philosophically.

"Who won the game?" asked Bill. "The one you saw, Liam?"

"Why, Lawrenceville, of course. Smeared 'em—outplayed those freshies from start to finish and did it with a lighter team. Thirty-three to nothing—think of it!"

Mary Eliska turned toward George.

"Stoker Conway—I like that name, 'Stoker.' How did you get it?"

George grinned. "I was a grubby little mutt—my first term at Lawrenceville. Somebody pasted the name on me, and it stuck."

"Three celebrities at one table," sighed Liam. "I knew we had two with us tonight— but a third! It's just too much. Jax Gray, you and I have just got to do something to make ourselves famous. There's practically no hope for me, I admit, but you will probably become a movie queen, when you're old enough—ash-gold hair and a baby doll face are all the rage on the screen!"

"Oh, I don't know," hit back Jax Gray, ignoring the laughter caused by this left-handed compliment. "How about the fame you won in the diamond smuggling case? You got plenty of newspaper publicity then."

This sally turned the laugh on Liam, for as the three others knew, he had played anything but an heroic part in that episode.

But Liam McAdams was a jolly soul and his hearty laugh at his own expense joined with the others.

"Lay off, Jax Gray!" he cried, "that was one below the belt. What do you bet I spot the motive in this mysterious case of Stoker's?"

"See here, will you pipe down?" Bill expostulated. "All you will spot is your clothes. Keep quiet and quit waving your arms—you nearly upset my coffee. How can any of us learn anything unless you give Stoker a chance to get on with his story?"

Liam suppressed a retort and George hurried into the breach.

"Here goes on the second installment, then," he said. "And it will probably interest you all to know I'm pretty near the end. Let's see—where was I?"

"Last fall, at Lawrenceville," prompted Mary Eliska. "You couldn't get your father to come down there."

George nodded. "Yes, that's right. He never would come—not even when I graduated last June. I wrote him specially about it, but, well, he was having his own troubles about that time. Before I came home I passed my finals for Princeton. It was on the books that I'd go there this fall.

"Only I didn't," continued young Conway rather solemnly. "Father met me at the Bedford station in the flivver when I came back. On the way up here he told me that reverses in business had forced him to sell Hilltop. I knew, of course, that business conditions were pretty bad all over the country. But he looked ill and he had aged terribly since I'd seen him during the Easter holidays. I was much more worried about his physical condition, he seemed so played out, so feeble. But when we drove into the yard and I saw this down-at-the-heels old house—well, I certainly got another shock."

"It must have been terribly hard," sympathized Jax Gray. "Especially after living all your life in the big place on the hill."

"A bit of a comedown," acknowledged George, "but I don't want any of you to think I was ashamed of the place. If Father had to live here, it was good enough for me. I felt so sorry for him, though. He'd never been much of a mixer, as I said, but when he did talk to a fellow he was certainly interesting, full of pep and vitality—and a sure hog for work. Now all that was changed. He had no workshop or laboratory here. All day long and half the night he would sit reading in the library across the hall. If I spoke to him, he would answer 'yes' or 'no' to a question—but never volunteered anything on his own account. He seemed more like a man stunned—a man who realizes his life is a failure and no longer cares to go on.

"The woman down the road who cooks and keeps the house clean told me he had moved in here the early part of April and that during the time before I came back, he had been exactly as I found him.

"I wanted to get a job in the city. Even though I couldn't get him to talk about his affairs, I knew he couldn't have very much money, living in a ramshackle place like this. But though I wanted to get out and earn some money, I realized I must stay with him for the time being—and I'm glad I did. Father passed away in his sleep the night of July fourth. The doctor said it was his heart—like Mother.

"Well, I guess that's about all of it. When the will was read I found that he'd left me everything. It amounted to two thousand dollars in cash, and this house and the sixteen acres that go with it. I stuck on here for the rest of the summer, trying to get the place in better shape; gave the house a couple of coats of paint, re-shingled parts of the roof, and have done as much as I could. I'm trying to sell the place, you know, and the agent told me I could never do it unless it was put in better condition. It looks pretty bad still, but I've worked like a dog.

"And I forgot to say, that Mr. Lewis bought Hilltop from father. He drops in here every once in a while for a chat. I know he's got a reputation for being a skinflint, but I sort of like the old man, anyway."

Mary Eliska, who had been absent-mindedly rolling bread pills on the table cloth, threw him a sharp glance.

"What happened tonight, before we came?" she asked.

"Why, I was just about to get my supper, when the bell rang. I opened the door and those two guys jumped me."

"Not very subtle, were they? What do you suppose they were after?" Bill looked inquiringly at George.

"Well, this is the funny part of it all. They said they'd come for the letter Father had left for me to read after his death—" "And you didn't give it to them?" "I'd never even heard of such a letter. I told them so." "And they wouldn't believe you, eh?"

"They thought I was bluffing, of course."

"But how on earth—did they say anything about the contents of the letter?" This question came from Mary Eliska.

"No. Simply that they wanted it—and they knew I must have it. What I can't understand is how they could be so sure that a letter exists—even if I'd known about it, I wouldn't have given it to them—but it's all as clear as mud to me."

"Has Mr. Lewis ever spoken to you about it?" "Never."

"Have you any reason to suppose that your Father might have left a letter for you—any idea that he might have had an important message to convey to you in that way?" "Not the slightest. You see, I—" "Look here," broke in Liam. "Do you think it possible that old Lewis knew that your Father wrote you that letter—and believes that it's in this house? He might have hired those thugs to get it from you, then when he found out they failed, he hopped over here himself and made that offer to buy your place, in order to get hold of it? There may be something valuable contained in it, and he wants to get it at any cost." "Too crude," declared Mary Eliska with a shake of her head. "Perhaps he does want to buy it—but I doubt if he has anything to do with those holdup fellows. Mr. Lewis may be close but I'm sure he's a clever man. The very fact that he came here so soon after the fracas clears his skirts of trying to hold up Stoker. As I say, he may want to get hold of the letter himself, but I'm dead sure he's not the nigger in this particular woodpile." "Then who is?" Liam wanted to know. "Tell us that, and you'll win the fame you're after," chuckled Jax Gray. "Just a moment," Bill was speaking again. "If old Lewis is as clever as you think he is, Mary Eliska, then the smart thing for him to do would be exactly what he *has* done!" "How's that?" "Well, if he did hire those lads, he might figure that by coming over here, Stoker'd begin to believe he was the man behind the gun. *But*, he might have realized that on second thought, Stoker would discount the idea, for the very reason you have done so." "Gosh!" exploded Liam. "That's a stumper, Bill. What are we going to do about it?" "That's the question—*can* we do anything?" Mary Eliska flicked a bread pill across the table.

Chapter 3.6
CORNERED

"There's one thing about it," Bill Bolton told the others seated at the supper table. "This letter that Mr. Conway is supposed to have written to Stoker is at the bottom of all this queer business."

"But that doesn't get us anywhere, does it?" objected Liam. "We must find out what that letter's about. Get hold of the underlying motive, you know."

"Say, you got that out of a detective story—'underlying motive'—I know you did." Jax Gray shook an accusing finger at him.

"Well, what of it? That's the thing we've got to do—and I guess it doesn't matter how you say it."

"Enter Doctor Watson!" Bill grinned and winked at Mary Eliska. "Look out for your laurels, Miss Sherlock Holmes!"

"Oh, come on—this isn't any jazz number," she returned with spirit. "What's your big idea, Liam?"

"Why, hunt for the letter of course. When we find it, we'll have the—ahem!—underlying motive as well."

"Maybe. Who's going to do the hunting?"

"All of us. We'll each take a room, and—"

Mary Eliska laughed. "You're some organizer. Suppose you start in with the library. It won't take you more than a week to go through all the books in that room!"

"But listen, Mary Eliska—" "Don't be absurd. We'll have a hunt tomorrow, if you want. But Jax Gray and I have got to get home now—and anyway, I know where that letter is."

The four about the table stared at her in unfeigned amazement.

"*Where?*" they cried in chorus.

"I'll give each of you three guesses," she went on mischievously.

"Oh, don't be horrid," pleaded Jax Gray.

"You know we're absolutely up a tree—" chimed in George.

"Come on and tell," invited Bill.

"How did you find out?" added Liam.

"Simply by keeping my eyes and ears open," retorted the object of this wordy bombardment, "and by knowing that two and two make four, not sometimes, but all the time. Every one of you has heard as much about this as I have tonight, and every one, excepting Stoker, has kidded me because I found out some things about the bank robbery and that smuggling gang this summer. Now you won't even take the trouble to think for yourselves. The whereabouts of that letter is clear enough; to be able to put our hands on it, is something quite different."

"Well, I apologize for us all," Bill leaned across the table, "we were only kidding you—weren't we, Jax Gray?"

"Why, of course—she knows that, she's only trying to—"

"Come on, Mary Eliska," Liam coaxed her with a grin. "The letter is—?" George asked soberly.

Mary Eliska pursed her lips, then smiled.

"In your father's copy of Jones' *Aircraft Power Plants*," she replied calmly. "Find that book, which Mr. Lewis was so keen to locate that he offered to buy this house in order to get it—and you'll have the letter."

"I believe you're right," conceded Bill, "you generally are—but that book is going to take some finding, or I've got another guess coming."

"If there really is a letter and it's in the book," said George, "Mr. Lewis must have hired those men."

"Not necessarily," returned Mary Eliska, "but I'll admit it's possible."

George's face wore a puzzled frown. "What I can't understand is why outsiders should know about this letter, when I have never heard of it."

"And if your father really wrote a letter to you, and they knew it—why did they wait nearly three months before they tried to steal it?" Bill shook his head. "It's beyond me."

"And why did they start in using strong arm stuff right off the bat?" Liam propounded this question to the table at large.

"Well, I think it is the most mysterious thing I ever heard of," said Jax Gray, struggling to stifle a yawn.

Mary Eliska stood up.

"Well, we can't talk about it any longer tonight. Jax Gray and I must be getting home." She turned to Bill. "Did you bring some extra gas for *Wispy*?" she asked. "From the sound of things outside, the storm seems to be pretty well over. I don't want to leave the airplane in that woodlot all night. Some tramp might come across her and bust something."

"I've brought enough gasoline to fly back to Jackson Hole and then some. I'll go with you in the airplane."

"How about me?" Jax Gray looked surprised, yet oddly hopeful.

"Liam'll drive you home," said Bill.

George looked disappointed, but voiced no objection to the plan, and Jax Gray merely shrugged.

Mary Eliska spoke up quickly. "No, I think you'd better stay here tonight, Liam. Somebody ought to stay here with George ... pardon me, Stoker! But as it's Sunday tomorrow, there's no school to get up early for, and Stoker can drive Jax Gray over to my house and come back here. Bill and I will bring her over after breakfast and we can see what we can do to locate that letter."

"Good plan," agreed young Conway enthusiastically. "I'll be back in less than an hour."

"But who's going to wash all these dishes?" grumbled Liam.

"Not afraid to stay here, are you?" said Mary Eliska.

"Oh, if you put it that way I'll wash them," he retorted.

"You do 'em tonight, and we'll do 'em tomorrow—but we really must be going now."

Ten minutes later, Jax Gray and George chugged out of the drive in his flivver 'Calamity Jane'. Liam parked Bill's car in back of the house, then he helped his friend to lift out the three large tins of gasoline they had brought with them from Jackson Hole.

"I'll take two," announced Bill, "and you'll have to tote the other one, Mary Eliska."

"Hadn't I better carry it down the hill?" suggested Liam. "It's kind of heavy."

"No, thanks, I can manage it all right." She lifted the can by its handle. "It's not so heavy. Your job is to stay in the house. As it is, I hate leaving you here alone."

Liam waved them off.

"I'll be all right," he scoffed. "I think we've got those guys buffaloed—for the time being, anyway."

"Keep your rifle handy," advised Bill, "and don't open up to anyone except Stoker."

"You bet I won't."

"Good night, then—"

"And good luck," added Mary Eliska, switching on her flash.

"Good night, both of you—see you in the morning."

He watched their light travel into the orchard and turned back to the empty house.

Mary Eliska and Bill reached the rear wall of the orchard and came to a stop. Although the storm had passed and with it the driving rain, heavy cloud formations obscured the stars.

"Better hop over the fence, Mary Eliska," said Bill, "then I'll pass these containers across to you. Gee whiz! It sure is some black night. You came up this way, didn't you?"

"Yep." Mary Eliska's voice came from the other side where her light was flashing. "Hand over the cans. That's right." Bill joined her and picked up his load again.

"The ground slopes down to the valley from here," she said. "Drops would be a better word, I guess. It goes down like the side of a roof. Watch your step! This wet grass is slippery as ice."

"I've found that out," said Bill, sitting down suddenly. "Which way is that woodlot trail from here?" He got to his feet. The tins had saved him from a bad tumble. "Off to the right— down in the valley." "Then let's steer off that way. Take this hill on the oblique. It's easier walking. By the way, which side of the river have you got the bus parked?"

"River? What river? I didn't know there was one."

"Well, there is. Stone Hill River, it's called. If you didn't cross it going up to Stoker's house, the plane must be on this side."

"You've got a master mind," she retorted and her light went out.

"What's the matter?" "Followed your example, and sat down."

The light flashed on again. "Aren't hurt, are you?"

"Don't be personal," she laughed. "How did you know there was a river down in the valley?" "Why, I brought a map of the Reservation with me—studied it on the way over while Liam drove. We'd never have found that dirt road Stoker's house is on otherwise. Part of it is really in the Reservation, you see. The concrete road from Poundridge Village that runs to South Salem parallels it about a quarter of a mile to the east."

"Route 124," said Mary Eliska, walking carefully for fear of slipping again. "I know that road. Ever been in the Reservation, Bill?" "No—have you?" "When I was a little girl, we used to drive over, for picnics sometimes. I don't remember much about it, though, except that it's a terribly wild place—all rocks and ridges and forest. It covers miles. The state has cut trails and keeps them open, otherwise the woods have been left in their virgin state."

"There are cabins, too, the map calls them shelters," Bill informed her. "The state rents them to camping parties. Well, it's quite wild enough to suit me right here. How are you making out?"

Mary Eliska was leading the way with her light.

"Fine, thanks. I'm on the level again."

"Glad to hear that you are," chuckled Bill. "Silly! I mean I'm on fairly level ground again. And look what I've found." Her light flashed to the left and came to rest on the wreck of a seven-passenger closed car. "Good enough!" exclaimed Bill. "Those thugs won't do any more riding in that bus. See how the car smashed that big tree—it must have torn down the hill like greased lightning!"

They deposited their gasoline tins on the grass and inspected the mass of twisted metal more closely.

"Hello!" ejaculated Mary Eliska. "Someone's been here before us."

"How do you figure that?"

"The license plates have been removed. I know they were on the car when I sent it down here. I was in such a rush I forgot to take the number, worse luck!"

"Too bad—now we won't be able to trace the owner."

"Oh, yes, we will. Unless we've got an unusually clever mind bucking us, I'll bet we can trace it through the factory number and the number of the engine. Give me a hand, Bill. Let's get the hood up."

"Master mind number two," grunted Bill when Mary Eliska's flash was turned on the motor. "Him and me both, eh? The number plate has been removed, and the one on the engine chiseled off. Those lads must have had a lovely time doing it, with their hides full of salt."

Mary Eliska switched off her light with a click.

"*They* never came down here, in their condition," she said decisively. "It must have been somebody else—probably the man who is back of them—or others of that gang."

"Old Lewis?"

"I don't know. Of course, he himself couldn't have done this—"

"Yes, he's a bit too old to come traipsing down to this valley all alone in the dark."

"Too bad we've showed our light on the hill and around here just now," she said slowly.

"You think they may still be in the offing?"

"I hope not. Chances are they don't know about the plane."

"You'd better go back to the house," he advised. "I can lash two of these tins together and sling them over my shoulder. If there's going to be a shindy, you'll be better off up the hill with Liam."

"Thanks a lot," said Mary Eliska. "If there's going to be trouble, we'll go it together. Anyway, you'd never be able to find the trail to the woodlot in the dark. It's great of you to suggest carrying on without me, but it just can't be done."

"You sure are a good sport, Mary Eliska." Bill picked up his tins. "Where do we go from here?"

"Follow me. And the less noise we make, the better."

With Bill close on her heels, she led across the clearing toward the dark line of trees on their left, winding her way around rocky outcroppings and stunted bushes that made traveling in the dark a difficult proceeding.

"Think you can find the cart road?" she heard him whisper. "It's black as your hat without the flash."

"Sure can," she replied cheerfully. "All we have to do is to turn right at the woods and follow them up the valley until we come to it. Quiet, now—if anybody's, watching, we may be able to get by them in the dark."

They had gone another twenty yards or so, when Mary Eliska stopped suddenly and caught at Bill's arm.

"There's somebody behind that big rock to the left!" she whispered fiercely. "I'm sure I saw something move."

"You sure did, young lady," announced a gruff voice close to their right. "Tell your girlfriend not to make a fuss, Mr. Conway. My men are all around you." A tall figure, hardly more than a blur in the darkness, stepped from behind a tree and came toward them.

Chapter 3.7
RAVEN ROCKS

Bill Bolton dropped one of the gasoline tins he was carrying and grasping the other with both hands, hurled its heavy bulk at the stranger. The tin caught the man full in the chest.

As he staggered back, Mary Eliska felt herself seized from behind. A quick twist and pull sent her antagonist hurtling off to the right. It was not for nothing she had put in long hours mastering the complicated throws and holds of jiu-jitsu, that strenuous art of Japanese wrestling. She freed herself in time to see Bill crash his fist into the face of a third man.

"Come on!" he yelled, and they raced for the line of trees.

But their troubles were not over yet. Straight ahead and directly in their path, another dark figure was leaping toward them. There was no time to dodge—to swerve. Bill dove at the man, stopping him short and bringing him to the ground with a clean tackle just above his knees. The force of contact was terrific. For the fraction of a second neither the tackler nor his opponent moved. Then as Mary Eliska, trembling with excitement, bent over them, Bill scrambled to his feet.

"Are you hurt, Bill?" The girl's voice was breathless with concern.

"No—only winded—" he gasped. "Be all right—in a minute."

Mary Eliska gripped him by the arm and they trotted forward again, gradually increasing their speed as Bill regained his breath. From behind them came the calls and angry shouts of their pursuers.

All at once, the inky black blur of the woods loomed before them.

"Keep along the edge of this pasture toward the wood road," Mary Eliska whispered quickly. "I'm going to start a false trail. Maybe we can fool them. You get your breath—join you in a minute or two."

She sprang into the underbrush, crashing over low bushes, snapping dead twigs and branches under foot with all the clatter of a terrified cow in a cane brake. Then the noise stopped as suddenly as it started, and Bill was surprised to hear her light footsteps at his heels. "I want 'em to think we're hiding in there," she explained hurriedly. "Can you run now?" "You bet!"

They sped along the edge of the wood, spurred by the thought that the ruse would delay their pursuers and perhaps throw them off the trail altogether. From their rear came the sound of a rough voice issuing commands. Men were beating the underbrush, cursing in the darkness. Both Mary Eliska and Bill had got their second wind and were running much more easily now. Then Mary Eliska tripped on the uneven ground and would have fallen had not Bill thrust out a steadying hand.

"Thanks," she said jerkily as she ran. "Look over my shoulder. Lights back there."

"Wonder they didn't use 'em before," was Bill's only comment.

Mary Eliska slowed down to a fast walk and Bill also slackened his pace. "We must be nearly there," she panted, "though since we had to drop the gasoline, there doesn't seem much use hiking over to the plane."

Bill nodded in the darkness. "Think we'd better get back to the house?"

"Yes; they'll never see us, especially now that they've got their flashlights going—that glare will blind them. I vote we keep on along the valley until we pass the wood road, then swing across this pasture again and up the hill 'til we strike the road. That will take us back to the Conway place and—" "Look!" Bill's exclamation arrested her, but his warning was unnecessary. Far above, a sudden rift in the clouds brought a full moon into view. The woods, the open pasture and the steep hill down which they had traveled almost blindly a few minutes before were now bathed in clear, silvery light as bright as day. As they dashed forward again, a shout from behind told them they had been seen.

"Stop or we'll fire!"

"There's the trail, Bill—it's our only chance!"

Men were calling to each other behind them and she caught the sound of heavy feet pounding along in their wake. As she and Bill turned into the wood road and sped down its winding stretches under the arch of intertwining boughs, a revolver cracked several times in quick succession. Overhead, the bullets went screaming through the branches.

"Shooting high to scare us," wheezed Bill. "'Fraid we're running into a dead end."

"Maybe not—this moonlight won't last—clouds too heavy."

Mary Eliska wasted no more breath in speech. Her every effort was centered in keeping up with the long-legged young fellow who seemed to cover the ground so easily and at such an amazing rate of speed.

Presently they swept out of the wagon-trail and into the glaring moonlight of the woodlot. Shouts and calls from their pursuers but a short distance behind now, lent wings to their feet. At the far end of the open space, Mary Eliska's amphibian lay parked where she had left it.

"Not that way!" warned Bill and caught her arm as she started to swing toward the airplane. "Straight ahead!"

There was no time for argument. Mary Eliska swerved and dashed across the lot, following his lead. Straight ahead lay a narrow belt of woods which ended abruptly in precipitous cliffs towering upward almost perpendicularly for several hundred feet to the top of the ridge. What Bill's plan might be, she could not guess. Those sheer palisades certainly could not be scaled. What could his objective be? If they turned up or down the valley the enemy would be sure to hear them tracking through the thick underbrush. And there would be no chance of outflanking the pursuit, for the men were between them and the Conway house.

She and Bill were trapped at last—trapped by walls of rock and the encompassing passing ring of the enemy.

They reached the farther edge of the field where a hurried glance behind showed them that the men were plunging out of the wood road. Then the moon, perhaps ashamed of the trouble he had brought them, swam away behind another cloud formation, and once again the world was sunk in darkness.

Bill's fingers gripped her hand.

"Follow me. Walk carefully and hold your arm before your face. It's a case of feel our way 'til we get used to the gloom—and there's no sense in losing an eye."

He led onward through the wood and although Mary Eliska could see nothing but an opaque blackness before her eyes, Bill never hesitated in his stride. With his hand behind his back, he pulled her forward as though guided by an uncanny knowledge of invisible obstructions in their path.

"How do you do it?" she marveled. "Don't tell me you can actually see to dodge these branches and tree trunks?"

She heard him chuckle.

"Not *see*—feel. I learned the trick in the Florida swamps last summer. Osceola, chief of the Seminoles, taught me."

"Oh, yes! He's a wonder in the woods. How is it done?"

"Tell you sometime. Here we are—at the Stone Hill River. You'll have to get your feet wetter, I'm afraid, but it's only a small stream, not deep. We turn right, here."

"Golly, it's cold!" Mary Eliska splashed into the water behind him.

"Brrr—I know it. Lift your feet high or you'll fall over these boulders. And please try to make as little noise as possible."

From the direction of the woodlot came a prodigious crashing and threshing. The pursuit had gained the woods.

"Noise!" she said scornfully, floundering along in his wake. "Those thugs can't hear me—they're making too much racket themselves. I suppose, Bill, you're working on a plan, but what it can be is a mystery to me."

"You mean—where we're bound for?"

"Yes. We can't get back to the big pasture and the hill up to Stoker's house. They'll head off any play of that kind."

"I know that. Stand still a minute, I want to listen."

"But Bill—" "Sh—yes, that must be it!"

"Must be what?" There was impatience in Mary Eliska's tone. "The waterfall I was trying to find."

"You don't mean to tell me you're planning to crawl behind a waterfall and hide! Honestly, Bill, I—"

"Oh, nothing like that," he answered coolly, "the fall isn't big enough."

"Look here, will you *please*—"

"All right, calm yourself. We haven't much time but I guess they've lost our trail for the time being. On the way over here in the car, Liam told me something of the lay of the land. He's crazy about hiking, you know, and mountain climbing. He's walked all over the reservation and he knows it like his own back yard."

"Yes, yes, what of it?"

"Well, Liam told me that there is just one possible way to get out of this Stony Hill River Valley on this side. That is, unless one goes a mile or two up or down the valley. There are entrances to the reservation at either end—dirt roads that cross from the concrete turnpike over to this ridge above us."

"But there is a way out?" "Yes. A sort of trail up the cliffs. It's not marked on the map of the reservation. Liam found it last summer. Pretty tough going even in daylight, I guess."

"But how on earth can we find it in the dark?"

"Liam told me that a smaller stream flowed into this creek at just about this point, and that it drops into the river gully by way of a low waterfall. It was the sound of that fall I was listening for. Hear it just over there to the right?"

"What's the next move?"

"We turn our backs on the waterfall, and cross this stream. The trail starts in a kind of open chimney in the foot of the cliffs. The map calls these young precipices Raven Rocks, by the way. If you think it is too dangerous, we can let those chaps catch us. They'll probably let us go soon enough. They're trailing the wrong party, though they haven't realized it. What do you say?" Bill's tone was non-committal.

"I know, they took you for Stoker Conway. But don't you see, Bill—" her tone was firm, "they must not find out their mistake. While they're tracking us, they will leave the Conway house alone, and that'll give Liam and Stoker a chance to hunt for the book and the letter."

Bill's reply was flippant, but there was a note of relief in his voice. "Chance to get a good night's rest, you mean!"

"They're not going to bed—" Mary Eliska pulled her companion toward the opposite bank of the stream. "Liam told me so."

"Thank goodness we're out of that," she exclaimed a moment later as they climbed the steep side of the gully. "If there's anything colder than a trout stream, I've yet to find it. I'm soaked nearly to my waist—how about you?"

"Ditto. We'll be warm enough presently—just as soon as we hit Raven Rocks."

"Wish we had raven's wings—we could use 'em!"

"Listen!" Bill stopped suddenly in his tracks.

"Don't *say* that," she whispered—"reminds me of old man Lewis!"

"They're coming this way. I guess they got tired of beating the woods for us. Take my hand again. We've got to find that chimney."

They went perhaps ten paces more when Bill brought up short again.

"Here's the cliff—wait where you are—be back in a minute."

He drew his fingers from her clasp and she heard him move off. Standing in utter darkness she could hear the men splashing toward them along the shallow river bed, and still others tramping through the woods with flashing lights that moved nearer every second.

Not once did her alert mind question the advisability of trying to scale Raven Rocks on a coal-black night. Not once did she waste a thought on the danger of that perilous enterprise. Mary Eliska never counted the cost when it was to help a friend. Her entire attention was centered on their pursuers. Who they were, or why they sought George and his letter were points of little consequence now. All that mattered was that they be kept on their search for as many hours as possible. Presently they would come abreast and their lights would pick her out at the foot of the cliff. The sopping skirt of her frock sagged about her knees, dank and clammy beneath her slicker. She gathered it in her hands and squeezed what water she could from it, more for want of something to do than for any other reason. No longer could she hear Bill stumbling about. What could have happened to him? The lights were only a dozen yards away now. In another minute or two their glare would pick her up for a certainty. For the first time that evening, Mary Eliska became fidgety. Bill had told her to remain here. That was an order, and must be obeyed. But—oh! if Bill would only come!

Chapter 3.8
THE CHIMNEY

Then on her right she heard a soft rustling, immediately followed by a low call: "Mary Eliska, where are you?"

The words brought her joyous relief. "Coming!" she replied in a cautious whisper, and with her left hand feeling the almost sheer wall, she hurried toward Bill's voice.

From the darkness he grasped her hand and spoke close to her ear. "I've located the chimney, Mary Eliska."

"Good! I was getting worried. Is it far away?"

"No. Only a few steps."

"What kept you so long, Bill?"

"Had to find the rope."

"What rope?"

They were moving now in the direction from which he had come.

"The one Liam hid in a niche of the rocks. Talk of hunting needles in a—"

"But do we need it?"

"Couldn't risk the climb without it. You've never done any mountain scaling—I have."

"Well, what's the dope?"

They had stopped and Bill took her arm. "Here—let me knot this end around your waist. First, ditch the slicker, though. You won't be able to climb in that. I'll take care of it for the present."

He took her coat and she felt him make the rope secure.

"I'm tied to the other end," he told her.

"But what'll you do about my slicker, Bill? If we ever get to the top of the ridge, I'll need it."

Bill was busy and didn't answer for a moment. Then—"Your coat and mine are rolled up and lashed to my back," he explained. "I'm going first. I know more about this kind of thing than you, and my reach is longer. May have to pull you up the hard places. Don't be afraid to put weight on the rope when I give the word. But if you slip—yell."

He did not say that a slip on her part would in all probability pull him with her to crash on the rocky ground below. Bill Bolton did not believe in being an alarmist, but she understood just the same.

"Thanks, I'll do my best, Bill."

"Start climbing." His voice came from above her head and she felt a jerk on the rope. "This chimney is a fissure in the cliff, and it slants slightly upward, thank goodness. Reach above and get handholds on the rock projections first. Then pull yourself up, until you find a foothold. When you put your weight on your feet, press your legs against the side walls. That will keep you from slipping. Take it easy and rest as much as you like. This kind of thing can only be done slowly."

"I'm coming," Mary Eliska said quietly and she pressed her body into the niche she could not see.

"That's the stuff! I'll rest while you climb. And while you're doing it, I'll keep the rope taut and out of your way."

Mary Eliska was silent. Groping in the darkness above her head, her fingers came in contact with a rough projection. It was little more than a small knob in the rocky side of the chimney, but she managed to get a firm grip on it with her right hand. Her left found another projection slightly lower on the other side. She exerted all her strength and slithered upward.

Drawing her knees up she sought rests for her feet on the sides, but the rock seemed absolutely smooth. For an instant she was at a loss. Then remembering Bill's advice, she pressed her legs against the chimney walls and pushed.

That her body moved upward so easily came as a surprise. It was hard to realize that sheer walls would give such a purchase. Almost at once her shoulders were above the hand holds and she could raise herself by pressing downward until her left knee was planted on the same projection that she had gripped with that hand.

Braced firmly against the rock, she looked for higher hand holds, found them and soon was able to get her left foot on to the place where her knee had been. With her weight on that foot, it became a simple matter to plant her right in the opposite niche. Straightening her body, she lay forward against the slanting cliff and rested.

"Go ahead, Bill," she called in a low voice as soon as she could speak.

"O.K., kid," came the prompt reply from overhead. "On my way."

Pressed against the wet rockface she could hear the scrape of his boots and the heavy breathing of muscular strain. Her own thin-soled shoes were sodden from the wet of the woods and pasture. Worse still, the leather was bursting at the sides. And this climb would probably complete their ruin. By the time she reached the top, they would be beyond walking in at all. Never again would she board her plane shod in pumps.

"Come along!"

Bill interrupted her soliloquy, and using the same tactics as before she continued to climb.

The first drops of rain she had felt at the bottom of the cliff now increased to a steady downpour. Mary Eliska became soaked to the skin. Water from her leather helmet ran down her forehead, forcing her to keep her eyes closed most of the time.

The cliff, wet and slippery from the preceding storm, was soon slick as a greased slide. Twice she lost her foothold and would have fallen had not her sharp cry warned Bill in time. How he managed to stick to his precarious perch and bear her weight on the rope until she found a grip on the rock again was more than she could fathom. Each time she slipped her heart almost stopped beating. And the horrible emptiness at the pit of her stomach made her feel deathly ill. But she never wholly lost her nerve. Climbing, then resting, she kept steadily on.

But her strenuous exertions and the almost continuous strain on muscles ordinarily little used was wearing down her vitality. Would this terrible climbing in the dark never end, she thought. Her whole body ached, her arms and legs felt heavy as lead. Wearily she raised her right hand seeking another hold. When she felt Bill's fingers grasp her own, she started. The shock very nearly caused her to lose balance.

"Now your other paw," said his well-known voice somewhere above in the gloom. "That's the way—up you come."

Then before she really understood what was happening, Mary Eliska was dragged higher until she was seated beside Bill on a narrow ledge. His right arm held her tightly. He was puffing like a grampus. She wriggled and wiped the water and perspiration from her eyes with a wet, clammy hand.

"Sit tight—old girl," Bill's words came in little jerks. "I know you're used to altitudes in a airplane, but this is different. I guess you'll get a shock when you look below, so—steady."

Mary Eliska opened her eyes and was glad of his supporting arm. Far below, at the foot of the cliff, pinpoints of light moved hither and yon, puncturing the darkness.

"They know we're somewhere up here," he said softly. "Heard you when you slipped, I dare say. Well, we'll take some finding—and that's no lie," he chuckled.

"Why—I—I—had no idea we'd come so far," she stammered. "Those lights look miles away."

"Three or four hundred feet, that's all."

"Funny—it makes me almost dizzy to look down there. You're right—it is different from flying altitude. Bill, do you think they'll find the chimney?"

"Maybe. But they're not likely to try to use it—not tonight, anyway."

"Why not? We did it."

"We were sure of a way up—they aren't. And I don't imagine they bargained for any blind climb up cliffs like these in the rain and darkness. They wouldn't mind slugging one of us with a sand bag, but when it comes to real danger, they'd count themselves out."

"Gee," Mary Eliska giggled nervously. "I wish I'd been able to!"

"Count yourself out? Well, I don't blame you, kid. Nerve-wracking isn't the name for it. But you certainly stood up well. Do you feel able to go on now?"

"Yes, I suppose so." Her reply was rather weak.

"Then we'd better get under way. Liam said the chimney was the worst of it and we are through with that now. It ends at this ledge." He helped her to her feet. "Brrr—that wind is cold on wet clothes. If we don't get moving, we'll cop a dose of pneumonia, sure as shooting!"

"You're a nice, thoughtful fella, Bill," Mary Eliska smiled grimly in his direction. "Trouble is your thoughtfulness is oddly strenuous at times. Is there much farther to go?"

"We're more than half way," he assured her, "and from now on you'll get more walking than climbing." Mary Eliska wanted to laugh but was too tired to do so.

"Lead on, MacDuffer," she cried gamely. "I'm lame, halt and blind, but I'll do my best to follow my chief!"

"Atta girl," he commended. "Give us your paw again, we can travel better that way."

"We'll travel, all right—that is, unless our friend Liam is a dyed-in-the-wool fabricator."

"Hopefully not, as they say in the Fatherland," he chuckled. He caught her hand in his and they started on a climb up the steep hill that ran back from the ledge.

As Bill had predicted, the going here was not nearly so difficult as it had been in the chimney. So far as Mary Eliska could tell, the cliffs, which were covered with a grass-grown rubble, sloped in at this point, and at a much easier angle of ascent. Whereas the chimney was almost perpendicular, here, by bending forward and aiding progress with occasional handholds on bushes and rocky outcroppings, it was possible to do more than merely creep forward.

A slip, of course, would be dangerous. It would be hard to stop rolling, once started down the incline; and unless a bush or a boulder were conveniently in the way, a bound over the ledge would be inevitable—and then oblivion.

She did not like to think about it. Bill guided her up the incline and did so with uncanny accuracy, considering the darkness, and the fact that he had not travelled this trail before. She came to the conclusion that the worst was over, when he stopped abruptly.

"Sit down and take it easy," he advised. "This is where I've got to see what we're doing."

"Surely you're not going to show a light?" she asked in alarm, and sank down on the rocky ground.

"Have to," was his quick reply. "Those guys below us know we're up here, so what does it matter?"

"But I thought we were almost at the top."

"Almost, but not quite. Look at that!" A beam of light shot upward from his torch, and turning her head, she saw a sight that sent her heart down to the very tips of her ragged, soaking pumps.

They had indeed come to the top; but merely to the top of this steep hillside of bushes and rubble. Where this ended, a few feet away, the naked rock towered almost perpendicular. Forty feet or more from its base this wall jutted sharply outward, half that distance again.

She sprang to her feet, an exclamation of dismay on her lips.

This rock canopy above their heads, this absolutely unscalable barrier to their hopes extended in both directions so far as the eye could see. Bill, who had moved several feet downhill, was flashing his light back and forth along the rugged edge of this roof of rock beneath which she stood. "How far does it go?" she asked in a small voice. "According to Liam," he replied, "right to where the cliffs end—both ways—and without a break or a tunnel. But you can't walk along underneath very far, because this slant we are on is only forty or fifty yards wide. Beyond it in either direction there's a sheer drop."

"Then—we're out of luck." Her tone was entirely hopeless.

Bill laughed shortly. "Where Liam got down, we can get up—but it's not going to be easy—and that's sure fire!"

Chapter 3.9
OVER THE TOP

"Well! If you know the way out, why don't you say so?" Mary Eliska flared in exasperation. "What?" returned Bill vaguely. He was walking across the side of the hill, keeping beneath the end of the rocky overhang forty feet above his head. The light from his electric torch swept along the edge of this seemingly unsurmountable obstruction. Then it darted out and upward as if to pierce the dripping night above.

"Did you speak?" he amended, looking back at her. "Thought I heard you say something, but couldn't quite catch it."

His voice was as sincere as the words he had just uttered, but Mary Eliska's reply was caustic.

"I said why keep the secret to yourself? All this stuff about how Liam got down and we are supposed to get up is keeping me on pins and needles. If Liam left a rope ladder or something hanging over the edge last summer, it must be gone by now."

"No, he didn't use a rope ladder—"

"Well, it looks to me as if we'd have to fly up if we ever want to get to the top of this ridge! I don't know whether you're *trying* to tantalize me—but you're succeeding, all right. For goodness' sake, Bill, if you know the answer, tell me."

"I'm sorry, Mary Eliska," he called repentantly. He ran up the incline toward her. "I didn't mean to leave you in the soup—I ought to have realized—Look, I'm awfully sorry," he repeated in sincere contrition.

"Oh, that's all right, Bill." She was embarrassed now. "I had no business to get so shirty." Under the light of the torch, their eyes met in a smile of friendly understanding.

"But please tell me what it is you're trying to find?"

"Why, the tree—I honestly thought I'd told you about it before."

"What tree?" she asked patiently.

"The one that Liam used to get down here. It's our only hope."

"But I don't see any tree. If there is one, how is it going to help us?"

Bill took her hand and gave it a little pat. "Come over here with me," he said, and led the way toward the spot where he had been standing. "But Bill—there's no tree up there—"

"Wait until I get the light on it. There you are!"

And there was a tree, after all. But instead of pointing toward the heavens like any other tree she had ever seen, this Colorado spruce grew sideways out from the top of the cliff. With the exception of a few tufts on the top, its branches grew only on the upper side of the horizontal trunk, giving it more the appearance of a ragged hedge than an honest-to-goodness tree.

"I get you," she said slowly. "The tree—and the rope."

"Aha! young lady, you're not so dumb as you'd sometimes like people to think!"

"But is the rope long enough?"

"Hope so. Liam claimed he used it double."

"Yes?" she said doubtfully. "But will the tree hold us both? You've been a sailor, but I don't think I'm up to climbing a swinging rope, hand over hand after coming up that chimney." She thought for a moment, then went on. "There's only one way I can get up there. You'll have to tie one end of the rope to a stone and sling it over the trunk. When that end drops, we can take out the stone, I'll stick my foot in the loop and—"

"Bill Bolton pulls you up," he ended for her. "That listens well, Mary Eliska, and if the rope was running through a pulley up there, everything would be hunky-dory. As it is, she'll be chafing against a hard, uneven surface. I'd probably pull the tree down, even if I was able to get you off the ground."

"But my arms feel dead—right up to my shoulders."

"I know, kid. But you can do it, after I fix the rope and you have lashed your end to this big bush here. It's going to be a case of shin for you, not hand over hand climb. Although that's not so hard when you know how. Like most things, there's a knack to it."

"All right. I'll do my best."

"You'll make it," he assured her. "If you'll untie that end of the rope from around your waist, I'll hunt up a rock and we'll get busy."

Presently a heavy stone was fastened to the rope end.

"Stand clear," sang out Bill. Then as she stepped back, he swung the stone round and round in a vertical circle, much as a seaman heaves the lead for a sounding. Up went the stone and the rope, and Mary Eliska watched with bated breath while she pointed the torch for guidance. She saw it swing over the tree trunk and drop to earth on the farther side.

"Snappy work, Bill," she applauded. "Who goes first? You or me?"

"This is a case where gentlemen take precedence. I'll go first—and show you a little trick they teach midshipmen at Annapolis."

He untied the knot which held the stone and bringing the ends together pulled the rope until the lengths on both sides of the trunk were even.

"So long," he breezed, "see you anon!"

With a hand on either rope he swung himself upward, seemingly without effort. It was as though he were lifting a penny-weight rather than one hundred and seventy-five pounds of solid American bone and muscle. Then with a quick movement he twisted the slack ends about his thighs, and the girl was amazed to see him let go both hands and wave.

"It's a way we have in the Navy," he laughed. "Quite a comfortable seat—if you know how. Skirts are rather in the way, so I don't advise you to try it. Although I must say in parting that you have already parted with the greater part of your skirt."

Mary Eliska giggled. "What of it? There's a perfectly good pair of bloomers underneath." She was amused by his fooling, though she suspected he was trying to put heart into her.

Bill coughed. "Finicky persons of British extraction might claim that your last statement was a decided bloomer itself—but I digress—" he went on, in the manner of a barker at a side show. "Laydees and gen-tel-men—I wish to state that William Bolton, late tiddledywinks champion of the Nutmeg State, is about to give his famous impersonation of a monkey on a stick!"

His hands grasped the ropes above his head. Up came his body, the turns about his thighs providing an apparently comfortable seat or purchase, while his hands shot upward again. The speed with which he went through these movements was remarkable, the swiftness of his passage up the ropes only comparable to an East Indian running up a cocoanut palm. Before Mary Eliska could believe her eyes, he was sitting astride the tree trunk, hauling up the rope.

"That was marvelous!" she called up to him. "Someday you'll have to show me how you do it."

"O.K.!"

She saw now that one end of the rope was coming slowly down again. As it sank nearer, her torch brought to view the fact that it was knotted every few feet. Soon she was able to catch the swinging end.

"Make it fast to that bush," he commanded. She did as she was told and turned to him for further orders. Bill pulled the rope taut, then lashed his end about the trunk close to the point where the tree jutted out from the rock. That done he slashed the loose half free with his knife just above the knot. "That gives us a hauling line," she heard him say. "I'll hang on to this end—you knot the other about your waist."

She caught the end that he threw down and after fastening it securely about her, peered up at him again.

"All right for me to shin up?" she asked, with a hand on the knotted rope that was to act as her ladder to the dizzy height above.

"Wait 'til I get back on terra firma—this tree won't stand our combined weights."

Perhaps a minute elapsed. Then she heard his voice again, though she could no longer see him.

"Come ahead!" he directed. "Sing out when you start and let me know if I pull too hard."

Mary Eliska switched off the light and slipped the torch down the back of her frock where it was caught in the blouse made by the line about her waist. "Ready!" she called and grasping the taut rope, she started to shin up.

Almost immediately she was helped on her way by a steady pull on the line Bill was holding. The going was difficult but the knots held her and kept her from slipping. Notwithstanding aching arm and leg muscles, it was surprising how easily she was able to hoist herself upward with the added pull from above. The actual distance to be climbed was not so great, but it seemed unbelievably soon when her hands touched the tree trunk.

Bill called a warning. "Get a good purchase around the rope with your legs, then lift your arms—take hold of the branches on top of the trunk and heave!"

She felt a stronger pull on the rope; her hands grasped two upright branches and she was dragged upward and on to the tree. Bill caught her under her arms and swung her on to the rock. Then he picked her up bodily and carried her back a few yards from the edge of the chasm.

"Hurray! We're up!" he gasped and let her down on solid ground.

Mary Eliska did not reply. For a moment speech was beyond her. She sank down on a boulder. After a little while she untied the rope that belted her and producing the electric torch, handed it to Bill.

"Snap on the light, will you?   while I take stock of the damage. I know I'm a wreck, but it's just as well to learn the worst at once."

"Rather rumpled," he pronounced as he complied with her request. "Good night! You've only got one shoe!"

"Lost the other coming up the rope. This one is no good either. What's left of it is just a mass of soaking pulp."

Then she laughed softly as she brushed some spruce needles from her knees and picked a malicious little bit of flint from the palm of one hand. Her wet skirt was in ribbons. She saw that her stockings were a mass of ladders now, and she had a suspicion that her knickers were torn. But what did such trifles matter when one was bent upon a great achievement?

"Pretty bad," she admitted and stood up on one foot. "Hand me my slicker, please. This rig is beyond repair—that will keep some of the wind out. Gee, it's chilly!"

"And wet," he added grimly, as he helped her into the coat. "Sorry to have to remind you, Mary Eliska, but we've got to be on our way, again."

"I don't think I can go any farther, Bill."

He knew this to be a candid statement of fact, not a complaint.

"But we must, Mary Eliska. They are coming after us, you know."

"Not up this cliff! Unless, you mean—" her voice was troubled, "the rope! Could you slide down ours and untie that from the bushes, then shin up again?"

"I could, but it isn't necessary. They aren't coming that way."

"Is there another way?"

"Yes, for them. By the road across the valley and around by either of the entrances to the reservation." "Why are you so sure?"

"Because while I was out on the tree trunk, I saw lights going up the hill. Then a car which evidently had been parked down the road from Stoker's house, started off toward the Boutonville entrance. Which means, of course, that they'll motor in on the Boutonville road. That crosses the reservation. Then all they've got to do is to leave the car at the mouth of the Fire Tower trail and hike down here along the top of the cliffs. They've cut off any retreat down the cliffs on our part, too. Those birds intend to catch us—or rather, they want to get hold of Stoker pretty badly. They've left men down in the valley, I saw their lights."

"Well, it will take them some time to walk over here from the Boutonville road," Mary Eliska said wearily. "I'm going to sleep. I've got to."

"You can't—not in this rain. And you're soaked through into the bargain." Bill's tone was firm. "Wait a minute—I've got an idea."

Mary Eliska, who was half dozing with her back to the boulder, opened her eyes with an effort. She saw him draw forth a paper from his pocket, unfold it and study it with the aid of the lighted torch.

"This is a map of Poundridge Reservation," he explained. "Here's a trail that leads back from Raven Rocks to the Spy Rock Trail. This end of it must be about a hundred yards along the cliffs to our left, if I've got my bearings right. Listen, Mary Eliska! These two trails meet about a mile and a half from here—and close by is a cabin. It's marked Shelter No. 6 on the map. Once in there we'll be under cover. These shelters are rented to campers during the summer, you know. There's sure to be a fireplace. I'll find the dry wood and we can dry out and get warm."

Mary Eliska yawned and shut her eyes again.

"No use, Bill. I hate to be a short sport—but I'm just all in. Chances are we'd find the cabin locked when we got there."

Bill put the map back in his pocket. "I don't blame you," was what he said. "I'm used to roughing it and I don't feel any too scrumptious myself. But we've got to do something. The gang will be here in less than an hour. But I must admit that I don't see how you're going to walk a mile and a half with only one shoe." He looked down at Mary Eliska. She was fast asleep.

Chapter 3.10
OL' MAN RIVER

"Poor kid! She certainly is all in," Bill muttered in a tone that was close to despair. What on earth was he going to do now?

The wind had stiffened and heavy rain slanted out of the east in an unremitting deluge. Both of them were soaked to the skin under their slickers. Despite his vigorous cliff-climbing, Bill was chilled to that Mary Eliska, huddled against the boulder, was shivering in her sleep. He himself was weary and heavy-eyed. His vitality was at low ebb. But with a sudden exertion of latent will power he got painfully to his feet. He bent over the sleeping girl and taking her by the shoulders shook her back and forth.

"Wake up, Mary Eliska!" he called. "Wake up!"

Deep in oblivion, she made no answer. Bill shook her harder.

"Leave me 'lone," she murmured drowsily. "Want sleep—go 'way!"

Putting forth his full strength, Bill lifted her until she stood leaning against him still sound asleep. Bringing her arms up and over his shoulders, he pivoted in a half circle. Now that his back was toward her, he bent forward, and catching her legs, drew them over his thighs. Mary Eliska, still oblivious to all that went on, was hoisted up into the position called by small children, "riding piggy-back." Though slender, she was well-built and muscular, and he was surprised at her dead weight. With his forearms beneath her knees, clutching the lighted torch with one hand, he moved slowly off with her in the direction of the Raven Rock Trail.

After some little trouble he found it, a narrow swath cutting back through the forest at right angles to the top of the cliffs. Without hesitation he began to follow the path.

Overhead the twisted branches met in a natural arch. It seemed even darker below their dripping foliage than in the open on the cliffs, and the feeble ray from his flash light penetrated but a few feet into the yawning black ahead. It was heavy going with Mary Eliska's solid weight on his back. The uneven ground, sodden with rain, was slippery where his feet did not sink in the muddy loam. And at times he was near to falling with his burden. The trail followed a snakelike course. For a time it wound over comparatively level ground, then dipped steeply into a hollow. The girl was becoming heavier by the minute. Bill stuck it out until they topped the opposite rise, then let her down.

Mary Eliska awoke with a start.

"What are you doing?" she cried. "Where am I?"

"So far as I can make out, we're about half a mile down the Raven Rock trail," he said slowly.

"And—and you carried me all this way?"

"Piggyback," he replied laconically.

"Why, Bill! You must be nearly dead—"

"Well, there have been times when I've felt more peppy—"

"How could you, Bill? Why didn't you wake me up?"

"Tried to—but it just wasn't any use. You couldn't have walked it, anyway—with only one shoe."

"Oh, yes, I could. But you were sweet to do it, only—"

"Better climb aboard again," he suggested, ignoring her praise, "we've got all of a mile to go before we get to the cabin."

Mary Eliska made a gesture of dissent.

"Thanks, old dear. I'm going to walk."

"Well, if you feel up to it—you take my shoes—I'll get along fine without them in this mud."

"I'll do nothing of the kind. I've got a better plan. Stupid of me not to think of it before. Hand over your knife, please."

Mary Eliska cut two long strips, six or seven inches wide, from the bottom of her slicker. "I'm going to use these to bind up my feet," she explained and handed back the knife.

"Wait a minute!"

Bill seized his own raincoat and cut two wider strips, which he folded into pads.

"Sit down on that stump, and hold up your hoof," he ordered. "I'll show you how it's done."

Mary Eliska hopped to the stump and after seating herself, kicked off her remaining shoe.

"There goes the end of a perfect pump," she chuckled.

"Think I'll keep it for luck," declared Bill.

She raised her eyebrows and laughed.

"Some girls might think you were becoming sentimental—you, of all people!"

"Well?" "Well, I know it's only because you were born practical. You want that shoe so as to prevent anyone else from finding it, the men who are chasing us, for instance?"

"I never argue with members of the opposite sex—that's why I still enjoy good health."

He grinned and pocketed the shoe.

"Hold up your foot, young lady. It's a lovely night and all that, but we're going to get out of it as soon as possible."

He placed one of the folded pads beneath the sole of her foot and wound a strip of slicker about it and the foot bringing the ends together in a knot about her ankle.

"Now the other," he prompted, and dealt with it in the same way.

Mary Eliska stood up and took a trial step or two.

"Wonderful!" she said. "I could walk to New York in these. They're a lot more comfortable than the shoes I ordinarily wear."

"We'll have to patent the idea."

"That reminds me, Bill," Mary Eliska spoke slowly. They were moving along the trail again. "Do you think the letter Mr. Conway is supposed to have written Stoker could possibly have had anything to do with patents?"

"What patents?"

"Oh, I don't know exactly—patents belonging to Mr. Conway."

"You mean—which he left to Stoker?"

"Why, yes. Mr. Conway was an inventor. He must have patented things."

"Very probably. But Stoker told us that his father's entire estate amounted to the place he's living in and a few thousand dollars. If Mr. Conway still owned patent rights on his inventions, why weren't they mentioned in the will?"

"You think, then, that he sold them before his death?"

"Looks that way," summed up Bill. "Anyway, if there were patents, they'd be registered in Washington. It wouldn't do anyone any good to steal them."

Mary Eliska tramped along beside him. Except for the sound of their footsteps squishing in the muddy path and the drip of the rain from wet leaves and branches, the woods were very still.

"What can those people be after if it isn't the patents on Mr. Conway's inventions?" she said in a puzzled tone, after a pause.

"Search me—whatever it is, the thing must be very valuable. They'd never take all this trouble otherwise."

"Give us all this trouble, you mean. And here's another riddle, Bill. Why was Hilltop sold?"

Bill threw her a glance and shrugged.

"Ask me something real hard," he suggested, "You're the Sherlock Holmes of this case. I'm only a mighty dumb Doctor Watson. And I'm no good at problems in deduction, even when my thinkbox is moting properly—which it isn't at present."

"But there must have been some good reason for the sale of that property," she persisted. "When Stoker went back to Lawrenceville after the Easter holidays last spring, everything at home was going on just as usual—a big place, servants, cars, horses, plenty of money— everything. Then he came back from school in June, and all that everything just wasn't!"

"And father had moved into that dump on the Stone Hill River road with a part-time maid-of-all-work, and that 1492 flivver.... Deucedly clear and all that! By the way, do they teach English or just plain Connecticut Yankee at the Jackson Hole High? Your use of words at times is more forceful than grammatic."

"Grammatical for choice. You're not so hot on the oratory yourself, Bill. People who live in glass houses, you know—?"

"Wish we were in one," was his reply. "Anything with a fire and a roof that sheds water would suit me just now!"

"What are you trying to do, Bill, evade my question?"

Mary Eliska's nap had done her good. Though still weary and stiff, she felt tantalizingly argumentative for all that she was wringing wet and horribly chilly. Talking helped to keep up her spirits. Just ahead their torch revealed a branching of the path.

"The map says we keep to the right," announced Bill. "It's only a step over to the Spy Rock trail now."

"Glad to hear it—but it seems to me you *are* trying to evade my questions!"

"Questions?" He chuckled. "They come too fast and furious. And to be honest, how can you expect me to guess the right answers when you don't know them yourself? You certainly are the one and only human interrogation point tonight."

"And you're so helpful," she retorted. "This is the most mysterious affair I've ever been mixed up in."

"Here we are at the other trail, praise be to Allah."

"Turn to the right?" she asked.

"That's it. In about a hundred yards we ought to run on to a path leading off to the left. That leads to shelter No. 6. The cabin's quite near now, if this map in my pocket's any good."

They trudged along the trail and a couple of minutes later in the dim glow from the flash they saw an opening in the trees.

"Come on," he said, quickening his pace. "We'll be under cover in a jiffy."

"We'll probably have to break in." Mary Eliska caught up with him as the path swung round in a quarter circle to the left. "No, we won't," he replied, catching her arm and coming to a halt. At the same time he shut off the electric torch.

Straight ahead in the darkness they could make out the blur of a small building. Through a chink in what they took to be a closed shutter came a thin ray of light.

"Somebody's got there ahead of us," Bill observed more to himself than to Mary Eliska.

"What are we going to do?"

"Do? What can we do but knock them up and ask for shelter?"

"I guess you're right," she admitted. "Neither of us can go on until we've had rest and a drying out."

"That's how I look at it."

"We've got to go easy, though. Remember what I trotted into with Jax Gray at Stoker's house?"

"Where do you get this 'we' stuff?" he said rather gruffly. "Here, take this gun and get behind a tree. I'm going over there. If they get nasty when they open up, I'll sidestep—and you can use your own judgment."

"I'll use it right now, Bill. I'm going to the house with you. Don't argue—" She started on along the path.

Bill caught up with her. "Take the automatic, anyway," he shoved the gun into her hand. "Shoot through your pocket if you have to. Better keep it out of sight. Stand to one side just out of the line of light when they open. All set?"

"Go ahead."

Mary Eliska's right hand gripped the revolver in her pocket. She slipped off the safety catch, pointed her forefinger along the snub-nosed barrel and let her middle finger rest lightly on the trigger.

Rat-tat-tat—rat-tat-tat. Bill's fist pounded the cabin door. There came a pause. She felt the quickened beats of her heart. Rain pounding on the gutter-less roof dripped in a steady trickle on her bare head and down her neck. From somewhere nearby came the mournful cry of a hoot owl.

Bill knocked again. Within the little house they heard the sound of footsteps. Mary Eliska stiffened. The bolts of the door were withdrawn, the door opened and Mary Eliska stepped up beside Bill. Framed in the lighted rectangle was an ancient, white-haired man. He peered out at them from beneath the cotton-tufts of his eyebrows, blinded for the moment by the night.

"Good evening, Uncle. Can we come in out of the wet for a little while?" Bill's tone held gentle camaraderie.

"Lordy, Lordy—you nice folks, an' drippin' wet!" exclaimed the old fellow, straightening his bent back and smiling pleasantly. "Walk right in, Capt'in—and you, too, Missy. Ol' Man River ain't got quarters like you is prob'ly useter—But it's dry and it's warm, an' yo-all's sho' is welcome!"

Chapter 3.11
MR. JOHN J. JOYCE

"Thank you, Uncle," said Bill and motioning Mary Eliska to go first, he stepped across the threshold.

The old man slammed the door shut behind them blotting out the storm, and sent the bolt home.

"Yo'all go over ter the fire an' drip," he beamed, pointing to the blazing logs in the fireplace of native stone. "Lordy, Lordy, you chillen is sho' 'nuf half drown'. But we's gwine ter fix dat sho' nuf in a jiffy." While the two warmed their hands at the hearth, he bustled off towards the rear of the cabin and disappeared through a doorway that led into another room.

Mary Eliska looked at Bill and smiled delightedly.

The cabin was primitive though there was a cozy and homelike air about it. The chinks between the bark of the logs which formed the walls were stuffed with dry moss and clay. There was no ceiling to the room. One looked up through the cross beams clear to the gable of the slanting roof. From these sturdy four-by-fours hung half a ham, several bunches of onions, a pair of rubber boots and other oddments. Wide boards had been laid across them in a couple of places, evidently to provide hold-alls for other paraphernalia.

The small room's principal article of furniture was a rustic, handmade table. Three stools without backs and an armchair of like manufacture completed the furnishings if one did not count several shining pots and pans that hung on nails driven into the logs and a huge pile of kindling that took up an entire corner. A steaming kettle hung from a crane over the fire and the floor of the room flaunted a large mat woven of brightly colored grasses.

"He keeps everything as neat as a new pin," Mary Eliska whispered. "Isn't he perfectly sweet?"

"Wonder how he happens to be here," said Bill. "This shelter is state property."

"Shush—he's coming." The old man ambled into the room again, grinning from ear to ear. Ol' Man River, as he called himself, quite evidently enjoyed bestowing hospitality. Over one arm he carried a bundle of clothes.

"Ise mighty thankful dat yo'all come 'long dis evenin'," he exclaimed. "It sho' do get mighty lonesome up in dese hyar woods—speshally on a night when de rain come an' de wind howl roun' dis cabin. I brought you all some clo's. 'Twant much I could find, jes' overalls and shirts, like what Ise got on. But dey is dry and dey is as clean an' sweet as soap and rainwater can make 'em."

Mary Eliska took the faded blue flannel shirt and overalls he held out to her. "Thank you, Uncle. You certainly are kind and thoughtful, but it's a shame to use your clean clothes this way."

The old man's grin grew wider, his even white teeth gleamed in the wrinkles of his kindly face.

"Don' you menshun it, Missy. Dese clo's ain't nuffin. Dey ain't no tellin' what's gwine ter happen ef you don' hop inter de back room an' take off yo' wet things. While yo' gone, de young genneman can change. An' Ol' Man River, he's gwine ter dish up supper. Now, Missy, run away or yo'll sho' catch yo' death in dose wet things."

Mary Eliska hurried into the back room and closed the door. On a little table she saw an old-fashioned oil lamp with a glass base and an unshaded chimney, which cast a cheerful glow of light over a home-made bed which filled one side of the cubicle. As she sat down, she found that instead of a mattress, the bed boasted fir and hemlock boughs, scented and springy to the touch. Several khaki-colored army blankets were neatly rolled at the foot of the bed. A row of hooks behind the door and rudely fashioned shelves which extended the breadth of the partition between the two rooms, completed the appointments of Ol' Man River's bedroom.

Mary Eliska saw that the partition did not rise all the way to the peak of the roof, but ended at the crossbeams. The sound of Bill's voice and the old man's came over the top, and a most appetizing odor of coffee and frying ham. It was just then that Mary Eliska realized how famished she was. A glance at her wristwatch showed that it was a quarter past midnight.

She continued to strip off her wet clothes and the wrappings from her feet. Picking up a couple of flour sacks from the stool by the shuttered window, she gave herself a thorough rub down. The home-made towels had been washed until they were soft as linen, and they sent a pleasant glow of returning circulation throughout her tired body. Warm and dry once more, she donned the overalls and shirt and drew on a heavy pair of gray wool socks. Though the overalls needed turning up and the shirt was too long in the sleeves and more than a trifle wide across her shoulders, it was on the whole a warm and comfortable outfit.

She rubbed her lovely blond hair dry, then combed it into place before the cracked mirror which stood on the wall shelf. A deft application of powder and rouge from her ever-present compact completed her simple toilet. There came a knock on the door and Bill's voice told her that supper was ready.

"Coming!" she called.

Picking up the sodden heap of clothes from the floor, she blew out the light, opened the door and marched into the other room.

"Transformation!" Bill saluted her gaily. "How about it, Uncle? You'd never take her for the same person, would you?"

The old man, who was bending over the hearth, turned his head toward her and smiled.

"Roses," he said, "roses in June!"

Mary Eliska laughed outright. "Thanks for the compliment, Uncle, but I'm afraid these roses came out of a compact."

She hung her wet clothes over a chair, near to Bill's.

"Den I should'a said, fresh as a rose," the old man chuckled.

"And not half as dewey as when you let us in," added Bill. "By the way, Mary Eliska, let me introduce our host, Uncle Abe Lincoln River—known to the world at large as Ol' Man River, but to his friends he's Uncle Abe. And the young lady who is parading around in your clothes, Uncle, is Miss Mary Eliska of Jackson Hole! She looks kind and gentle, but if you value your life, never take her on in a wrestling bout. She's Sandow, the Terrible Greek and the Emperor of Japan all in one."

Mary Eliska waved him aside.

"Get out of my way, slanderer!" she cried. "I want to shake hands with Uncle Abe. Dry clothes seem to have gone to his head, Uncle."

The aged man stood up and took her outstretched hand between his horny palms.

"Why, I'se read about yo'all when I worked fo' Misteh Joyce, Missy. Dey uster let me hab de papers after de folks up dar ter de big house done finished wid 'em. Airplanes, robbers, ebbryt'ing!" Ol' Man River shook his head. "Sho' wuz tuk back some ter see what ladies kin do dese days, ma'am!"

"Well, then you must have read about Mr. Bolton, here, too? Bill Bolton, the flyer—?"

"Dat's so, ma'am. I done heard tell o' dis genneman, too!" He turned his rolling eyes in unfeigned admiration upon Bill.

Bill glared at Mary Eliska. "Oho! so you put the spotlight on me, do you?" He cried in pretended anger.

But Ol' Man River motioned toward the table which was set with tin cups and plates and a very much battered metal coffee pot.

"Supper's ready, Missy. I'se sorry I ain't got a cloth. 'P'raps yo'all won't mind dis time. Now if yo' an' Marse' Bill will tak' yo' chairs, I'll serve it up quicker dan whistlin'."

"But you've only set two places," protested Mary Eliska. Put another cup and plate on the table, Bill, and another knife, fork and spoon. Uncle Abe's going to eat with us, or I won't touch a thing—and believe me, this food looks tempting!"

"Well, if yo' puts it thataway, ma'am, I will take a bite." Uncle Abe gave a mellow chuckle. "I sho' duz love ham. De smell of it in de pan fair do make my mouf water!"

Mary Eliska took up the hot skillet from the hearth. "I'll put the ham on the plates, Uncle Abe, if you'll bring over that pan of hot bread you've got warming in the ashes."

"Not hot bread, Mary Eliska," corrected Bill, "—corn pone—real honest-to-goodness corn pone!"

"Mmmm—" she exclaimed with eyes dancing, "hurry up, Uncle Abe, I just can't wait!"

"Dey ain't no butter," explained Uncle Abe, "but if yo'all puts some o' dis ham gravy over it, I reckon yo'll fin' yo' kin eat it."

"Ho, that's the best way to eat it!" cried Bill. "Used to have it that way when I lived at Annapolis. If there's anything that tastes better, I've yet to find it. And look, Mary Eliska, we've got molasses to sweeten our coffee! Uncle Abe sure does set a real southern table."

The old man chuckled happily as the three sat down to the meal.

"Marse Johnson done give me dat 'lasses," he said as he filled the coffee cups from the battered pot. "He de big boss o' de reservation. I don't mind tellin' yo'all, ma'am, if Marse Johnson didn't wink at Ol' Man River a-livin' in dis hyar cabin, I sho' would be in a bad way. But dese reservation folks knowed 'bout Marse Joyce turnin' me loose after I'd worked fo' him all dese years. I did odd jobs for 'em dis summer, an' a while back, Marse Johnson, he 'lowed I could have de cabin, now it's gettin' kinda chilly fo' de ol' man to sleep in de barn."

"That was pretty decent of him," remarked Bill, with his mouth full of fried ham and hot corn pone. "But who is this Mr. Joyce you speak of, Uncle?"

Ol' Man River wiped his mouth with the back of his hand.

"Dat man's name ez John J. Joyce, Marse Billy. He's got dat big place on de ridge over yonder nexter Hilltop, Marse Conway's ol' home. I worked fo' Marse Joyce fo' 'bout ten years—eveh sence I come up no'th from Virginny where I was raised."

"And he let you go after you'd worked for him all that time?" cried Mary Eliska, setting down her coffee cup. "I call that rotten mean!"

"Yaas, ma'am—John J. Joyce is sho' a hard man. I wuz one o' de gard'ners on de' 'state. One noon he calls us all up ter de big house. 'Men,' he say, standin' on de gall'ry steps, 'times is hard an' they's gwine ter be harder. I'se got ter do my bit fer dis 'ere depresshun like eve'y one else. Dat is why I'se a-cuttin' you down from six ter three. De three what am de oldest can clear out. Dey ain't wu'th as much ter me.'"

"The dirty dog!" Bill's face was hot with anger.

"I should say so!" Mary Eliska's tone matched Bill's in vehemence.

Uncle Abe shook his head. "De Good Book say, 'Him what has, gits, and him what ain't got nuffin' gits dat nuffin' tuk'n away'," he remarked a bit sadly. "But I ain't got no complaint, ma'am. Ol' Man River has sho' got a warm cabin. He ken trap Brer Rabbit in de woods, and 'times he gits Brer Possum. Marse Johnson pays fer a spell o' work once in a while and dat pays foh things I haster buy over to de store. I kinder git de idee, Missy, dat dis hyar ol' man is livin' on de top o' de worl'."

"Well, maybe," answered Mary Eliska, "but I call it doggone mean, just the same. Tell me, Uncle, outside of being mean and heartless, what sort of man is this John J. Joyce?"

"Waal, you see'd how he done me, Missy. Jes' git up an' go—didn't say he wuz sorry or nuffin'. He's rich and he's sharp. Maybe he's honest, I don't know, but I'se allus thought as how Marse Conway 'ud done better if he'd er hoed his own 'taters. But I reckon I hadn't oughter be crit'sizin' de quality."

"Quality, nothing!" exploded Bill. "Mr. Conway was all right—at least, George is—but the other fellow is the worst kind of a polecat!"

"Den yo'all knows Marse George?"

"Yes, Uncle, he's a friend of ours," said Mary Eliska. "And he is right up to his neck in trouble just now. Anything you can tell us about his father will be a big help."

Uncle Abe pushed his plate away and leaned his elbows on the table. "Dey ain't much I kin tell," he announced, "but I'se knowed Marse George since he wuz a l'il boy. He wuz allus nice an' friendly with Uncle Abe."

"You say that his father and Mr. Joyce were friends—that they had dealings of some sort together?" Mary Eliska inquired. "Yaas, ma'am. Dey wuz pardners in bizness, I reckon. Leastways, like you said, dey had dealings togedder."

"But if Joyce was in business with Mr. Conway, why didn't Stoker mention that?" asked Bill of Mary Eliska.

"Perhaps he didn't know about it, Bill. He was away at school, remember, most of the time. And he told us that his father never spoke of his affairs or encouraged him to ask questions."

"But it doesn't sound reasonable, Mary Eliska. A fellow must know the name of his father's firm."

"That's true, in a way. But maybe there was no firm—of Joyce and Conway? Isn't it possible that Mr. Joyce may have acted as Mr. Conway's agent—sold the inventions for him, perhaps? Mr. Conway was not a business man. He was always too occupied in his laboratory or in his workshop."

"Dat am de way it wuz, Missy," broke in the old man eagerly. "'Times, de gennemen 'ud walk in de garden an' talk while I done de weedin' or plantin' or wotnot—neveh done pay 'tenshun ter Ol' Man River. He don't count fer nuffin' atall. Marse Conway done make his 'ventions—Marse Joyce done what he call 'put 'em on de market.' Is dat what yo'all wanter know, ma'am?"

"Yes, thank you, Uncle. I believe I'm beginning to see light at last."

"Blest if I do," commented Bill. "Joyce couldn't try to steal patents registered in Mr. Conway's name, could he?"

Mary Eliska smiled. "That can wait. It's time we helped Uncle Abe wash up. Then maybe he'll let us have a couple of blankets to spread before the fire. We're dead for sleep and we're keeping him up too." The old fellow started to answer, then cocked his head and lifted a warning hand. "Is folks a-follerin' yo' chill'un?" he asked suddenly.

"Yes," said Mary Eliska, "and they mustn't catch us!" "Dey's someone a-comin'," he whispered. "Don' yo' say nuffin'. Jes do like Uncle Abe tell yo'all and he fix it so nobody can't find nuffin' hyar!"

Chapter 3.12
VOICES FROM BELOW

"Take dose clo'es by de fire yonder," directed the sharp-eared old man, "an' go in de back room an' shin up de wall shelves to dese fo'-by fo's oveh our heads. Tote de clo'es 'long wid yo' an' lay flat on dem boards. 'Times I trap somefin' out er season—I got ter eat—dat dere's mah hidin' place. Nobody can't see yo'all, nobody can't fin' yo' dere!"

While he talked and the others snatched their half-dried things from before the fire, the old man was clearing the table of dishes. He flung the remains of the meal onto the blazing logs and scooping up the cups and plates, stacked them, dirty as they were, on a shelf.

Mary Eliska and Bill ran into the back room and scrambled up to the crossbeams. As they crawled along the boards which were laid close together in threes, they saw Uncle Abe light an ancient corncob, then pick up a tattered newspaper and sit down by the fire. No more had they laid themselves flat on their airy perch with their bundles of damp clothing, than there came a pounding on the cabin door.

"Who dat?" called out Ol' Man River without moving from his chair. "Open up, do you hear, River? I want to speak to you," barked a voice from out the night.

"Yaas, suh—comin'!"

Peering through the cracks between the boards, his guests saw him rise slowly and shuffle to the door. Stretched out over the little bed chamber, with their heads close to the partition, they had an unobstructed view of the lighted room beyond. As the boards were laid over the middle of both rooms and ran nearly the length of the cabin, they realized with satisfaction that unless someone stood close to the side wall, it would be impossible to spy them out. Uncle Abe's oil lamp sent its gleams but a few feet, and the rest of the room and the crossbeams lay in deep shadow which was an added protection to the hidden two.

Ol' Man River drew the bolt and swung open the door.

"Walk right in, Marse Joyce," they heard him say. And without waiting for a reply, he hobbled painfully back to his chair before the hearth. Three men stamped into the cabin and banged the door shut on the storm. "You're keeping late hours, River," the leader of the party snapped out without preamble.

From the tones of his voice, Mary Eliska and Bill knew him to be the same man who had spoken to them in the valley meadow, and who Bill had downed with the gasoline tin. He was a short, stocky person with a bulldog face and a scrubby toothbrush moustache. He and his companions looked tired and angry. They were also very wet.

The speaker walked over to the fire, leaving a track of little pools across the floor. Putting his hands over the blaze, he scowled down at Uncle Abe.

"Well," he contended disagreeably, "I said you were up late. Answer me, can't you?"

"So yo' say, Marse Joyce. So yo' say."

Uncle Abe continued to gaze unconcernedly into the fire as though he had no idea the heavy-set man was becoming angrier by the minute.

"You!" he thundered, "What do you mean by bandying words with me?"

Uncle Abe remained silent.

"Are you deaf?" cried Joyce. "Tell me what you're sitting up for!"

"I'se takin' a warm, suh."

"Taking a—*warm?*"

"Yaas, suh. I'se a mis'ry in der feet—rhumytizzem. Can't sleep nohow. So I sets an' reads de paper by de fire—an' takes a warm."

"Oh, you do, do you?"

"Yaas, suh, I sho' do."

"Don't answer me back that way, do you hear?"

The old man continued to puff calmly on his corncob.

Mr. Joyce thrust his hands in his pockets and glowered at him. His companions stood silently by, watching Uncle Abe.

"Where are your visitors?" he asked suddenly.

Bill released the safety-catch on his automatic.

Uncle Abe puffed steadily on his pipe, but said nothing.

"Answer me! Where are they?" snarled John J. Joyce.

"Yaas, suh!" The old man removed the corncob from his mouth and looked up at his late employer.

"Well, why don't you speak?"

"Kase yo' done tell me not ter answer a while back."

"I tell you to answer me now." Mr. Joyce glared threateningly into his face. "Are you just stubborn, or in your dotage? *Where are your visitors?*"

The old man spat with great precision on to a glowing cinder. "Dey right hyar, Marse Joyce," he said.

"Right here? Where?"

"Hyar in dis room, suh. All three o' yo'."

"Say, are you crazy, or am I?" Joyce flung at him.

"No, suh, I ain' crazy," returned the old man, and Joyce's companions broke into a roar of laughter at this none too subtle gibe.

John J. Joyce turned on them furiously.

"Shut up, you two! Go into that back room and pull them out!"

Still guffawing, the men disappeared through the doorway in the partition.

"Nobody in here!" a voice sang out after a moment.

Joyce looked bewildered. Then he picked up the lamp, walked to the open door and looked into the room.

"Yank that bed apart!" he ordered.

The two lying on the boards above his head heard the men dragging the evergreen boughs off the couch. Joyce said not a word when their search was ended, but turned on his heel and returned to the front room, followed by his henchmen.

"Didn't think yo'd fin' nobody," remarked Uncle Abe mildly, "If yo' had, I'd sho' bin supprised!"

"So you'd been surprised, eh?" John J. Joyce had an unpleasant way of repeating words. Now he stood over the old man belligerently. "Yaas, suh," replied Uncle Abe with an unconcern he probably did not feel. "I could o' tol' yo' dat dey's nobody in dere. Who yo'all a-lookin' fo'?"

"What business is that of yours?" The old man remained silent.

"If you must know," snarled Joyce, "we're looking for a young fellow and a girl."

"What dey doin' uphyar in de woods at dis time o' night?"

"Tryin' to get away from us, I guess," said one of the men.

"You keep your trap shut, Featherstone," barked Joyce. "I'm not paying you to talk. This is my show, not yours."

"Well, if you talk that way, you can run it by yourself. I'm not your slave. Keep a civil tongue in your head, Joyce—or I'll go back to the car—and go right now."

"That goes with me, too," broke in the second man gruffly. "What d'you take us for—a pair of fools? I wasn't hired to do a marathon the length and breadth of the forest on a soakin' wet night. Those kids ain't here—let's go!"

"Oh, is that so? Well now you've had your say, and you'll go—when I get good and ready," sneered Joyce in his disagreeable, domineering voice.

"But what's the use of hangin' round?" argued the first man. "I'm tired and I'm hungry and I'm soaked to the skin—"

"And if I say the word to certain parties, the two of you will be taking a longer journey," snapped their employer, "—a little trip up the river that ends in a chair—a red hot one. Shut up, both of you."

He turned to Uncle Abe again. "Come, River—out with it," he commanded. "Where have that boy and girl gone to?"

"How should I know?" Uncle Abe knocked his pipe out on the hearth. "What fo' yo'all chasin' dese hyar chillun in de woods?"

"That's my business. There are fresh tracks leading along the trail right up to your door."

"Dat may be, suh. Day may be. I ain't sayin' dey isn't, Marse Joyce." He wagged his head solemnly. "I wuz out myse'f e'rlier in de evenin'."

"Huh! You wouldn't leave two sets of tracks!"

"Yaas, suh, Marse Joyce—goin' an' comin'."

Mary Eliska, from her perch above, smiled at the old man's astuteness. Their tracks were on the trail, of course, for those who followed to read; but the rain had long ago blurred the outlines. Their pursuers could not know in which direction the footprints led.

"So you think it was your tracks we followed?"

John J. Joyce continued to speak in the harsh, bullying tone that made Mary Eliska want to kick him. She realized, nevertheless, that the old man's last statement was proving a serious facer to his inquisitor.

"I ain't a-gwine ter say jes' dat," returned Uncle Abe. "All I knows is dat I made tracks on de trail. If dey's more'n two pair, dey ain't mine."

"What trails were you on?" came the sudden question, and Mary Eliska tingled with excitement as Uncle Abe hesitated.

"Lemme see, suh—why, I wuz down de Spy Rock Trail, an' de Cross Trail. And den I wuz 'long de Overlook and de Raven Rock Trails—"

"A nice long walk you had on a wet night," sneered Joyce.

Uncle Abe was imperturbable. "Yaas, suh."

"I don't believe a word of it."

"Dat yo' priv-lige, Marse Joyce."

"Well, it doesn't sound likely to me, especially when you say you've rheumatism in your feet."

"I'se gotter eat, suh."

"What's that got to do with it? There are no stores on these trails. What do you pretend you were doing, anyway?"

Ol' Man River chuckled gently. "Baitin' traps."

"Catch anything?" Joyce sneered. "I don't suppose you did."

"Den you's a mighty bad 'sposer, suh. Kaze I done cotch dat der rabbit yonder!" Following the direction of his pointed finger, Mary Eliska saw for the first time that a large jackrabbit hung from a crossbeam in a corner.

"It's no go, Joyce," broke in one of the henchmen. "He doesn't know where those kids are. Let's beat it."

Joyce, who had unbuttoned his coat, fastened it up again.

"For once you're right," he admitted truculently. "It's time we got back to the car. That pair have holed in for the night somewhere else. We'll watch the reservation entrances in the morning."

"Good night, suh, and a pleasant walk!"

Mary Eliska had hard work to repress her laughter. She loved this spunky old man.

Joyce turned angrily upon him. "You keep a civil tongue in your face, River!" he menaced. "In the first place, this is a state preserve, and poaching is severely punished; and secondly, you have no right to be squatting in this shelter, I—"

"Pick on someone your size, Joyce," advised the man who had spoken before. "This old man ain't doin' you nor anyone else any harm. Leave him alone."

"It's two to one, Joyce. Come on!" said the other.

For a moment Mary Eliska thought there would be a row. Joyce looked as though he would burst with rage. But evidently thinking better of it, he turned his back to the fire and strode over to the door. Without another word, he opened it and disappeared into the black night.

He was followed immediately by the two men. The one who had spoken for Abe swung around in the doorway.

"I know you're a good-hearted old liar, Uncle," he whispered. "And if you think a minute you'll know why I know it! Don't blame you. Joyce has a nasty temper and no matter where those kids are, we'll round 'em up in the morning, anyway. Good night!"

"'Night," returned Ol' Man River. "Pleasant walk, suh!"

"Yep. The joke's on us," grinned the other and shut the door behind him. Bill and Mary Eliska were about to move from their cramped positions when they saw the old man raise a finger to his lips in warning as apparently he studied the glowing embers of the fire.

The door suddenly opened and the same man stuck his head in.

"You're a sly old fox," he said. "I know you've got those kids hidden somewhere. Maybe they're listening for all I know, and I can tell you, Uncle, they are getting a rotten deal. Joyce calls me Featherstone. Here's my card. Give it to them. G'd-night."

A bit of white pasteboard fluttered to the floor as the door slammed. Uncle Abe got stiffly off his chair, shuffled over to the door and sent the bolt home. Then he picked up the card.

Bill pushed the pile of damp clothing off the boards, then swung himself down to the floor. Mary Eliska was beside him as he turned to catch her.

"Uncle Abe," she said, taking the old man's hand, "you are kind and you're good, and you are very, very brave. Bill and I can never properly thank you for all you've done for us tonight."

"Say no mo' 'bout it," protested Uncle Abe, when Bill put his hand on his shoulder.

"Look here, Uncle Abe," he broke in, "you're one of the grandest guys I know. Someday perhaps we can even up things a bit. You ran a big risk for us, you know."

The old man smiled and blinked at them for a moment. "Then, yo' all must be sleepy—I sho' is. You kin take the back room if you will, Missy. Marse Bill an' me's gwine ter hit de hay in here."

"Who was that man, Uncle Abe?" asked Mary Eliska, stifling a yawn with the palm of her hand. "What did his card say, I mean?"

"Spec' he's a deteckative, Missy. De card say 'Michael Michaels, Private Inquiry Agent'."

"Evidently he's got his eye on Joyce," summed up Bill. "Wonder who he's working for?"

"What interests me more just now," said Mary Eliska, "is how Mister Michael Michaels knew we were hidden here."

The old man chuckled. "He's sho' 'nuf a smart man, Missy. It wuz de tracks on de trail. He know'd I done never make dem tracks. He know'd dey wan't nobody else's but yourn."

"How come, uncle?" asked Bill.

"Dat jackrabbit a-hangin' yonder done it, suh."

"But what's that rabbit got to do with our tracks?"

"Marse Michaels, he must o' touched dat bunny. Den he know'd it wan't never trapped today. Dat bunny's stiff ez er hick'ry log!"

Mary Eliska and Bill burst into laughter.

"Bet you were scared silly for fear Joyce might examine it and realize that you hadn't been out tonight!" said Bill.

"Dat's right, sho' nuf, Marse Bill."

"You know, Mr. Michaels may be a big help to us," remarked Mary Eliska, yawning unashamedly in their faces this time. "Well, I just can't hold my head up any longer. Good night, both of you."

"Good night," returned Bill and Uncle Abe in unison. Mary Eliska took herself off to the back room and bed.

Chapter 3.13
THE WAY OUT

The gray light of early morning crept into Shelter No. 6 through the open shutters. It brought to view two forms rolled in blankets, sleeping soundly before the dying embers of last night's woodfire. In the back room, Mary Eliska was curled up on the fragrant bed of evergreens, deep in a dreamless slumber. The storm of the evening was gone, leaving in its place a fine, steady drizzle. The air was chill and damp. It bade fair to be another unpleasant day. The hands of a battered alarm clock that stood on the chimney shelf marked quarter to eight, but the sleepers were motionless. Then suddenly Uncle Abe sat up and knuckled the sleep from his eyes.

"Lordy, Lordy!" he grumbled, catching sight of the clock. "Dose chillun wuz ter git 'way early an' dis hye'r ol' man sleepin' lak de daid. I speck de young Missy an' Marse Bill need der sleep—an' we'll fool Marse Joyce jus' de same."

He got stiffly to his feet, stretched his ancient arms above his head and set about building up the fire.

Presently Bill opened his eyes and yawned. Then he threw off his blanket, sat up and sniffed.

"Bacon—eggs—coffee," he murmured. "Good morning, Uncle, you sure are an A1. up to the minute chef!"

Hovering over a sizzling frying pan, the old man turned his head and smiled at Bill.

"Mornin', Marse Bill. Yaas, suh, I 'low dat eatin' brekfus' an' gettin' it, too, is de bes' fashion what is."

"You said it," grinned Bill. "Say, I guess we all overslept! Well, no use crossing our bridges 'til we come to 'em. Any place in this hotel where I can wash and slick up a bit, Uncle?"

"Sho' is, suh. De soap an' de towel an' de bucket an' de basin is over yonder by de do'. When yo'alls done wid dem, p'raps yo'll wake de young missy, an' carry de bucket in yonder?"

"Sure will," returned Bill, "but I'll wake her up first."

He went to the door in the partition and banged his fist on the panels.

"First call for breakfast in the dining car ahead—"

"Ummm—" responded a sleepy voice from the back room.

"Time to get up, Mary Eliska. Hop to it, kid!"

"I'm awake!" called back that young lady.

"O.K. When you're ready, there'll be a pail of water outside your door."

"Thanks. Be with you in a jiffy."

Bill crossed the room, sloshed water into the tin basin and carried the pail back. While he was immersed in his morning ablutions Mary Eliska's door opened and her hand withdrew the pail.

Bill had no more than taken a seat at the table, when she put in her appearance. Dressed in the overalls, flannel shirt and heavy wool socks of the night before, she looked particularly bright and cheerful.

"Morning, everybody!" she smiled. "That bed of yours, Uncle Abe, is the most comfortable one I ever slept on. Too bad I had to turn you out of it."

"Reckon neither Marse Bill ner me knowed what we wuz a-sleepin' on, Missy. I sho' wuz daid ter ebbryt'ing all night long. De flo' ain't discomfertubble, when yo' knows how ter lay on it."

"I'm kind of stiff," admitted Bill. "But I feel fifty million per cent better. Bet I never moved from the time I turned in until the smell of breakfast woke me up."

"My!" exclaimed Mary Eliska, peeking into the frying pan. "Where did all these swell eggs come from, Uncle?"

The old man chuckled.

"Dat's one o' de two things a pusson mus'nt never ask no other pusson, Missy."

"And what's the other?" Mary Eliska inquired with twinkling eyes.

"Where I gits my chickens."

All three of them laughed this time and sat down to breakfast.

During the meal there was little conversation. Both Mary Eliska and Bill were frankly hungry and each was silently puzzling a way out of their predicament. Uncle Abe, always affable, nevertheless, rarely if ever volunteered advice unless called upon. In his mind, to do otherwise would have been a breach of good manners. Bill drained his second cup of coffee and met Mary Eliska's look.

"Got any ideas?" he asked her.

She shook her head and pushed her chair back from the table. "No, I haven't," she confessed gravely. "But if I'm any judge of bad character, Mr. John J. Joyce will keep his promise. Too bad we slept so long."

"Maybe," said Bill. "But without that good rest, we'd have been dead ones today. The tough part of it is that Joyce's men will be posted at all the reservation entrances now—"

"And on the trails around this shelter."

"Very likely. If we could ditch those guys and hike over to a road, we might get a lift out in somebody's car. Lots of people drive in here on Sundays."

"Not in weather like this, Bill. No, even if we did persuade someone to give us a lift, we'd be soon seen and stopped."

Bill suddenly brought his fist down upon the table.

"We're a pair of idiots," he declared. "Joyce's men won't stop us. They'll be looking for Stoker Conway and a girl. Keep those clothes on you're wearing, and with my old hat, all they'll see is a couple of fellows on a tramp. Nobody'd take me for George Conway. Why, we've got nothing to worry about!"

"That's where I differ with you. We most certainly have plenty to worry us."

"But how come, Mary Eliska?"

"How do we know that friend Joyce hasn't got hold of Stoker and possibly Liam, too?"

"Then—if he has, he won't want us."

"Oh, yes, he will. You can bet your boots, Mr. Joyce isn't letting anyone go whom he may think was mixed up in last night's affair."

Bill looked surprised. "But Joyce can't go on kidnapping people," he argued. "Or rather he can't keep on trying to kidnap the whole bunch who were in Stoker's house last night, and then hold them indefinitely. Even if he caught us all, he couldn't hold us long."

"Long enough to get what he thinks Stoker has got—and make his getaway, if necessary. At least that's how I figure it. If he catches any of us we're not likely to come in personal contact with him. He's too smart to give himself away like that."

"Possibly you're right. But if he did catch any of us, he'd soon find out that Stoker and the rest of the bunch know less about this mysterious something he's after than he does himself!"

Mary Eliska smiled. "Rather involved, but I think I fathom your meaning. You seem to forget, Bill, that when Jax Gray and I butted into this thing up at the Conway house, a couple of strong-arm men were starting to heat a poker. I don't think Mr. Joyce's hospitality will prove a pleasant experience if we are caught by him or his men."

"Well, we've got to get off this reservation—how are we going to do it?"

"Blest if I know," she admitted candidly. "But we've just got to find a way. And look here, Bill—I know you think I'm all steamed up over a trifle—but I honestly believe that whatever Joyce is trying to steal from Stoker is so enormously valuable that he's determined to risk pretty nearly everything short of murder to gain possession of it!"

"I wouldn't put murder past him, either," said Bill.

"His actions prove he's in deadly earnest," Mary Eliska went on, and then turned to Ol' Man River, who was peacefully puffing his pipe. "You've heard what we were saying, Uncle Abe. Have you any suggestions to give us?"

That ancient gentleman removed the corncob from between his teeth and pursed his lips. "Waal, yaas, m'am. I reckon Marse Johnson is de answer to yo' question," he said thoughtfully.

"Oh, he's the reservation superintendent—you're right, Uncle Abe—he can do it if anyone can. Why didn't we think of him before?"

"Dat am so, Missy. Der ain't a-gwine nobody ter stop yo'all long wid Marse Johnson."

"That's a great idea, Uncle," applauded Bill. "The super's house is right across the reservation from here, if I recall rightly?"

"Yaas, suh, it am. Right down yonder where de Boutonville road come out far side ob de reservation t'ard Cross River."

"Think you could pilot us down there and give those guys in the woods the miss?"

"I speck dese men ain't gwine ter git familious wid us if yo' foller Ol' Man River. I'se boun' we-all sho' give 'em de bestes' game er hide an' seek dey ez ever had. It ain't a-gwine be easy, Marse Bill. But I'll git yo'all down yonder and den you kin carry de young Missy home in a kyar. Marse Johnson, he's got three automerbiles."

"I hope it'll be as easy as you say," grinned Bill, amused by the old man's earnestness. "I'll make a bundle of Mary Eliska's clothes and then the best thing we can do is to get started."

"I'se got a pair er sneakers dat you kin wear, Missy," Uncle Abe announced. "Dey ain't no count nohow, but dey's got sol's an' dat sho' am better dan walkin' in dose socks."

"Thanks a lot, Uncle, you're such a grand help to us—" She smiled at the old man and he fairly beamed. "I'll love wearing them. But first of all, we'll heat some water and wash dishes. Don't look so annoyed, Bill. We've got plenty of time, now, and there's nothing more slovenly than letting the dishes go after a meal. We did it because we had to last night, but I intend to leave Uncle Abe's cabin just as spick and span as we found it. You fetch some water and heat it while Uncle Abe scrapes the plates. In the meantime I'll straighten up the back room and sweep out the house."

Mary Eliska was as good as her word. By the time the dish water was hot, her bed had been made, the cabin swept and generally put to rights. Then she brought out the dishpan and washed both the supper and breakfast dishes while Bill and Uncle Abe dried them. "Some swell housekeeper," said Bill to Uncle Abe with a grimace, "and she knows how to make the men folks work, too!"

"An' dat am ez it should be," declared the old man solemnly. "De Good Book say, 'what am food fo' de goose am good eatin' fo' de gander'...."

"I don't know whether that's a compliment, or not, Uncle," laughed Mary Eliska. "But you see, it didn't take long, and I feel better knowing everything's clean."

"Is your ladyship ready to go now?" asked Bill.

"Quite ready—thank you so much."

"Then let's shove off. What you said about Stoker and Liam a while ago has got me worried, I must admit. I want to get to a telephone just as soon as possible."

Uncle Abe left the cabin first. After scouting about in the cold drizzle for a few minutes, he came back and declared that the way was clear.

"I gen'rally goes 'long Overlook Trail an' down de Cross River Road ter git er Marse Johnson's house," explained the old man, once they were outside the cabin.

"But dis mornin' we ain't gwine dat-away—t'aint safe. Yo' all stick close behin' Ol' Man River, an' sing out ef he's a-travelin' too fast. Dis ain't no easy trail we'se takin'."

He struck directly into the woods and for the next hour Mary Eliska never even sighted a path. She soon found out that when Uncle Abe described this as 'no easy trail,' he was telling the unvarnished truth. Mary Eliska was no Alice-sit-by-the-fire. She had been on some stiff hikes before this, but the ancient man led them up hill and down dale, through the tangled undergrowth or virgin forest dripping wet with rain. And he led them through this wilderness of trees and rocks at a perfectly amazing rate of speed. Until Mary Eliska caught her second wind, she was hard put to keep up. If Joyce had men out, they never saw them. In fact, except for an occasional bird or small forest animal scuttling away in their advance, they neither saw nor heard any living thing. Eventually they climbed the steep side of a wooded ridge and stopped.

Below them, through the trees Mary Eliska made out woodland meadows, stretching down to a road which ran along their side of the valley. Lower down and paralleling the highway, a winding river ran down the vale. Lying in broad fields near the river to their left was a large farm house and barns.

"Cross River Road, Cross River, and Marse Johnson's house," announced Uncle Abe, using a hand and forearm for a pointer. "Dat highway yonder what runs inter de Cross River Road near de house ez de Honey Holler Road. Right dar am de Cross River entrance, an' right dar ez 'zackly de place whar ol' man Joyce's gang am hangin' out."

"It's going to be a job to get down there without being seen," remarked Bill.

"Der ain't nobody gwine ter see us," protested the old man, "kaze soon ex we git ter der open, you an' me an' Missy am gwine ter ben' down low an' hug de far side er de stone fences. But we'alls stayed hyar confabbin' long 'nuf. Got ter git goin' ag'in."

He moved off down the slope, the others following. By dint of doing exactly as he advised, fifteen minutes later found them ringing Mr. Johnson's doorbell.

"Dese young people am fren's er mine, Miz Johnson," Uncle Abe told the motherly person who opened the door.

"Step right in," she invited with a smile. "Lands sakes, you're drippin' wet. Come in by the kitchen range and get dried out. You must be perishin'—"

"Thanks. May I use your telephone?" inquired Bill as he spied a wall instrument in the hall.

"Of course you can," beamed Mrs. Johnson. "There's a book on the table there."

"Thank you, I know the number."

"Going to call up Stoker?" asked Mary Eliska in a low tone. "Yes. You and Uncle Abe go into the kitchen and get warm. I'll be with you in a minute or two."

But it was not until a good five minutes later that Bill put in his appearance. "Everything all right?" demanded Mary Eliska from her seat on a kitchen chair close to the coal range. "I'm afraid not," Bill looked worried. "They don't answer the phone."

Chapter 3.14
THE LION'S DEN

"No answer at all?" Mary Eliska inquired anxiously.

"That's what I said." Bill's tone was a bit gruff. He walked over to the range and warmed his hands at the glowing coals.

"What I mean is, could you hear the bell ring in Stoker's house?"

"Oh, yes, the bell rang. But nobody came to the phone."

"That's what I wanted to know."

"Why? I can't see that the ringing of the phone bell makes any difference—"

"All the difference," declared Mary Eliska. "Never mind why, now. I've just told Mrs. Johnson that I had to park *Wispy* on the other side of the reservation last night, and that some men over there were very disagreeable and we were forced to accept Uncle Abe's hospitality for the night."

"We think a heap of Uncle Abe on the reservation," affirmed the superintendent's wife. "And don't you worry about your airplane, Mary Eliska. We'll see that it don't come to no harm. My husband had to drive over to Katonah this morning, but I'll get Sam Watson on the job. He's in the office right now. Sam!" she called, "come in here."

A stalwart, broad-shouldered young man walked into the kitchen. His natty uniform marked him a member of the Reservation force.

"Did you want something, Mrs. Johnson?"

"This is Miss Mary Eliska of Jackson Hole, and Mr.—" she hesitated.

"Bolton—Bill Bolton," supplied that young man.

"The flyers!" Guard Watson's honest face wore a broad grin. "Heard about you both—who hasn't? Pleased to meet you, I'm sure." He shook hands with them and nodded to Uncle Abe.

"It's like this, Sam," explained Mrs. Johnson. "Mary Eliska ran out of gasoline last night and her airplane is down to the woodlot just below Raven Rocks in the Stone Hill River valley. Get Eddie, that's his beat anyway, and keep an eye on the airplane until these young folks pick it up this afternoon. They had trouble with some tramps over there last evenin' and put up to Uncle Abe's for the night. Pass the word on to the rest of the boys about them dead beats that's botherin' people on the Reservation, will you?"

"I sure will, Mrs. Johnson. If they're still around, we'll run 'em off quicker'n greased lightning."

"You're very good," smiled Mary Eliska. "We saw a couple of suspicious characters hanging around the Cross River entrance when we came over here to headquarters just now."

"I'll rout 'em out," Sam Watson promised. "If they kick up a fuss they'll put in thirty days behind the bars. Well, I must be hoppin' it. Glad to have met you folks, I'm sure. So long, everybody!"

With a stiff salute and a broad smile he was gone. They heard him tramp down the hall and then the front door slammed.

"Checkmate to J. J. J.," murmured Bill.

Mary Eliska played chess with her father—"Not checkmate—check," she corrected. "By the way, Mrs. Johnson, I wonder if we can trespass on your good humor still further?"

"Land's sakes alive! I haven't done nothing for you yet!" The superintendent's wife was busy with hot water and a teapot.

"Do you happen to have an extra car that we could borrow for a few hours?"

"Why, sure I have, my dear. But there's no hurry about your leavin', is there? A cup of tea, now, to warm you up and some of these nice crisp crullers I made yesterday? Then I'll get you and Mr. Bolton some dry things to put on and after dinner you can take the car and ride home. How'll that be?"

Mary Eliska laughed and shook her head. "You're awfully kind, really, Mrs. Johnson, but we can't stay. We've got an appointment that just can't be broken."

"But your wet clothes, Mary Eliska?"

"Thanks for your offer, but we aren't so wet now. I will have a cup of tea if I may, although we only finished breakfast a little while ago."

"And don't forget those crisp crullers," protested Bill with a grin. "I certainly do love homemade crullers, ma'am."

"An' dey ain't nuffin' better 'an de ones Miz Johnson makes," chuckled Uncle Abe. "I'se tasted 'em befo' an' I knows!"

Mrs. Johnson beamed delightedly.

"Even if I do say so who shouldn't," she remarked modestly, "this batch came out pretty good. But are you sure I can't tempt you to stay for Sunday dinner? We're having fish chowder, chicken friccassee, with dumplin's, and a pumpkin pie!"

"You sure do make my mouth water," groaned Bill. "I only wish we could stop, and meet your husband, Mrs. Johnson. If you'll keep the invitation open, we'd love to take advantage of it some other time."

The good lady passed them their tea and a plate heaped with golden brown crullers.

"We'll make it next Sunday noon then. Our children are all married, with homes of their own. Mr. Johnson and I miss not having young folks around the house. It'll make it seem like the good old times again, if you come. Don't forget now, next Sunday."

"We'll be here with bells on, Mrs. Johnson," promised Bill.

"And we'll try not to look like a couple of tramps then," added Mary Eliska.

"You'll always be welcome, no matter what you wear," declared their hostess. "I'll make another pumpkin pie for you."

They chatted for ten minutes or so and then bade Mrs. Johnson goodbye.

"Uncle Abe will take you out to the garage," she said in parting. "Take the Buick. You'll need a closed car on a day like this."

When the kitchen door had shut out the smiling, motherly figure, and they were following Uncle Abe along the drive, Mary Eliska turned to Bill.

"And they say that New Englanders are not hospitable! Why, they're the most hospitable people in America if you really know them!"

"Country people, no matter what part of the United States they live in, are generally friendly. Living in cities, where your next-door neighbor is a stranger, makes a person suspicious. But I've found that most honest-to-goodness Americans will do a lot for a person in trouble."

"Dere's de kyar, Missy," Uncle Abe interrupted apologetically. "Reckon I'll wish yo'all goodbye an' mo' comferble beds ternight."

Mary Eliska caught the old fellow's hand and held it between her own.

"Uncle Abe," she said, looking straight into his shining eyes, "do you really like living up there in the woods, all by yourself?"

"Waal, I ain't used ter much, Missy," he said slowly, "an' de cabin am a heap better 'an a barn er no roof at all. But, it sho' do get mighty lonesome, 'times."

"I bet it does. How would you like to live in quarters over our garage and work for my father? He was saying only a day or so ago that what with driving the cars and all Arthur has too much to do around the place. We need a gardener and general handy man. The job is yours if you'll take it—and I don't mind saying I'll feel badly if you don't."

Ol' Man River winked back the tears with a brave effort, although the little wrinkles at the corners of his mouth puckered in a smile.

"Yo' sho' is good ter me, Missy!"

"And you want to come? I won't take no for an answer—"

"It do me good fer ter hear you sesso, Missy. Kaze yo' sho' is de qual'ty and I never get no real fambly 'time."

Bill winked at Uncle Abe.

"And if Mary Eliska's nocount Stricklin family don't treat you right, you come right across the road to my house."

"Spect I'll git 'long tollerbul well on Mary Eliska's side," he chuckled.

"Well, what's the good word now, Mary Eliska?" Bill motioned toward the Buick. "It's about time we beat it over to Stoker's, don't you think?"

"I do think," returned Mary Eliska. "And that's why we aren't going over there."

"But surely—"

"But nothing. The boys aren't there or they'd have answered the phone. If you hadn't heard the bell ring we could be fairly sure the wire was cut and that they were holding the house in a state of siege, so to speak. Now we know they aren't there." Bill did not seem impressed.

"If that line of reasoning is logical, I'm as cold on the right answer as a water tank in winter. How do you know Joyce's men haven't got them tied up in the house?"

"Because at this stage of the game, Joyce would hardly do that and leave them there for their friends to find. And if his men were still in the house, they'd be sure to answer the telephone. You and Uncle Abe get right into that Buick now. We are going to take a run up to Mr. John J. Joyce's place."

Bill did not attempt to hide his astonishment.

"Gee, whiz, Mary Eliska?—you've got a whale of a lot of nerve!"

Mary Eliska shrugged and looked steadily at Bill. "Well, are you game?"

For answer he followed her into the car.

"Pretty much like jumping feet first into the lion's den," he commented, "but considering your middle name is Daniel, or ought to be, I dare say we'll have a roaring good time of it!"

"Stop talking jazz, Bill. How about you, Uncle Abe?"

The old man already lounged back on the rear seat.

"Reverse dis hyar injine inter de drive, Mary Eliska an' when yo'all turned round I'se gwine ter show yo' where we'se a-gwine."

Mary Eliska, smiling over the steering wheel, backed out of the garage and got the Buick headed toward the road.

"Well, Uncle?" she prompted.

"D'reckly in front of us, way over yonder on de far hill ez er big house."

"The white one in the trees?" asked Bill.

"Yaas, suh, de only one any pusson kin see from hyar. Dat am Hilltop, Marse Conway's ol' place."

"Where Mr. Lewis lives now!"

"Eggzackly so, ma'am. Marse Joyce's place ez jus' back er yonder."

"Bet he calls it, 'The Den,'" said Bill.

Uncle Abe cackled, "No, suh, Marse Bill—hee-hee—dat house done called 'Nearma'."

"Near ma?" repeated Mary Eliska in a puzzled tone. "There are some queer Native American names in this part of the country, but that's a new one on me."

"'Tain't Injun, Missy. Dat dere hones' ter goodness 'Merican. Marse Joyce's ol' Ma uster lib cross de ridgeroad. Dat how he come ter name de house 'Near Ma'."

"That old scurmudgeon! I don't believe it!" cried Bill in an explosion of laughter. "Dat am de spittin' trufe, Marse Bill. De ol' lady am daid, but he still call de place Nearma jus' de same."

"How do we get to it, Uncle?" Mary Eliska asked after a moment. "Run out de entrance 'til we come ter de turnpike, Missy. Den right, long dat road to Cross River. From de village yonder we follers de road ter Lake Waccabuc, but we don't hafter travel dat far." "Good enough." The car swung round the side of the house and into the road. "I guess Sam got rid of the Watchers by the Gate—there's nobody at the entrance."

They swept into the highroad and on through the pre-revolutionary hamlet of Cross River. Half a mile farther, as they were speeding along the top of a wooded ridge, Uncle Abe spoke again.

"Dat stone fence long de road ter de right b'long ter Hilltop," he pointed out. "De house am set way back from de road behin' de trees. Round de bend ahead yo'all gwine ter see 'nother higher wall, dat starts by three white birches. Yonder am where Marse Joyce's land begins.""And what's on the farther side of the Joyce property?"

"Dere ain't nuffin, Missy, 'cept jes' mo' dese hyar woods."

"Fine! And I suppose, after being up here for nearly ten years, you can find your way about in those woods?"

"Sho' can, Missy. Ef dere's er rabbit hole I va' missed in dem woods, I wanter know."

"Better and better. You're a marvelous help, Uncle Abe."

"What do you plan to do? Park the car near the road, hike back through the woods and cut over toward the house from that side?" Bill was not enthusiastic.

"Just about that." "And when you sight the historic mansion?"

"I'm going into the house." "Oh, yes, you are..." "Oh, yes, I am!"

"And how do you expect to do that without being nabbed right off the bat?" "Last night you told me I asked too many questions, Bill. And Uncle Abe says 'what's food for the goose is swell eating for the gander...'!"

Chapter 3.15
IN THE TOILS

"Ef yo'll pahdon my sayin' so, Mary Eliska," volunteered Uncle Abe as the car was run into the underbrush beyond the Nearma wall and parked behind a clump of scrub oak and evergreens, "I 'lows as how it sho' would er bin better ter 'proach de house from de odder side. We could er traveled down Marse Lewis' place and come in dat-a-way. Dere's mo' lan'scapin' on dat side."

"Thanks for the suggestion, Uncle," Mary Eliska locked the ignition. "But I think we'll keep just as far away from Mr. Lewis' property as we can, for the present."

"Do you think he really is mixed up with J. J. J. in this business?" Bill asked her. "Can't say—it certainly looks like it—and we'll take no unnecessary chances."

"How about the chances we'll take in breaking into Nearma?" "I said unnecessary! Anyway, I'm the one that's going in there."

"But look here, Mary Eliska! Do you think I'm going to let you walk into that place alone?"

"Not alone, old dear. Uncle Abe is coming with me."

"Oh, is he? And what am I to do while you're in the house mixing it up with those thugs? Do you expect me to stick out here with the car and see that somebody doesn't steal the tires?" Mary Eliska looked amused. Bill was annoyed with her and she did not blame him. "You'll have plenty to do, Bill." She gave his shoulder a good-natured pat and sprang out of the car.

"Come on, both of you. I'll explain my plan as we go. Lead the way, Uncle Abe. I want to get to the kitchen door without being seen from the house if possible."

Uncle Abe got out of the car. Bill was already beside her.

"Yo'all foller Ol' Man River!" said the old man and led into the woods away from the road.

"Well, what's the dope?" Bill's tone was less exasperated now, and side by side they swung in behind the old man.

Mary Eliska took his arm. "I guess you think I'm a brainless idiot," she began, "with all my wild schemes—"

"Well, I don't quite see your idea in going in there alone—but it's your show, so go ahead and explain."

"Attaboy! Now this is the point. I want to do some scouting inside and I'll need you to cover me as it were. Uncle Abe knows Joyce's servants. And Mr. Joyce is looking for you and me. Well, don't you see, if Uncle Abe brings a stray *boy* into the kitchen for a bite to eat, it won't seem anything out of the way. In these clothes, I'll never be taken for a girl."

"But you won't stay in the kitchen—I know you!" Bill was not quite convinced. "Perhaps not—what I do inside will depend on circumstances as I find 'em."

"Humph! And what is my important work to consist of?"

"I want you to watch this side of the house. If I need you, I'll open a window and wave. If it happens to be a window on the ground floor, you can get in that way. If I open a second story window, come in through the kitchen. You've got a gun—that ought to be a help."

"But—suppose you aren't able to get to a window?"

"Oh, then wait half an hour; when the time's up run down to Cross River in the car and phone the state police and get them up here just as soon as possible." "Why not get them up here now?"

"Because we really haven't got anything to go on. Chances are they wouldn't come and I want to be able to pin something good and definite on Mr. John J. Joyce before we get the police on the job."

Bill seemed impressed by her reasoning. "I guess you're right. If Stoker and Liam are in Nearma and we can prove it, J. J. J. will have a nice little charge of kidnapping to face." "And I want to get him for grand larceny and conspiracy as well," she returned. "That may sound ambitious, but I want to land that gentleman and his friends on a bunch of counts that will send them to Sing Sing for a very, very long time."

"You and me both. I don't know what Joyce's plans are, but after listening to his bark last night, I'll bet they're something pretty rotten. Hello!—There's Uncle Abe beckoning."

They caught up with Uncle Abe who was peering through the woods to their right. "Yonder's de stone fence, Missy," he announced, "an' beyon' am Marse Joyce's prop'ty. De house am 'bout fifty yards from de fence."

"Good. Bill, you go ahead and lay low behind some of the bushes near the house. Uncle Abe and I will be along in a minute."

"Aye, aye, skipper. Take care of yourself."

With a wave of his hand he climbed the low stone wall and disappeared into the shrubbery on the Joyce grounds.

Mary Eliska turned to Ol' Man River. "I suppose you know the cook over there, Uncle?"

"Oh, yaas, ma'am. Liza an' me's bin frien's fer ten years."

"That's fine. Now listen to what I say, because you've got your part to play in this affair and there mustn't be any slipup."

For several minutes she talked earnestly to Uncle Abe.

"Is that all clear?" she ended presently.

"Yaas, missy. I'll do what yo' all tells me to—but I ain't 'zackly hankerin' fer you to do all dis."

Mary Eliska laughed. "Neither am I, Uncle. But it's just got to be done, you know."

They climbed the fence as Bill had done and set off in the direction of the house, which soon came into view through the shrubbery and trees. As they drew nearer, Mary Eliska saw that Nearma was a large white frame house with green shutters in the conventional New England style. A wide veranda ran along the front of the house and on the far side a massive fieldstone chimney broke the expanse of clapboard between the rows of windows. The drive swung around the front of the building and turned sharply to the rear cutting the wide lawn on the near side. The grounds were beautifully landscaped. On a bright summer's day it must indeed be a lovely spot. Just then it looked bleak and drear in the steady autumn downpour. They reached the drive without sighting Bill, and followed it to the back of the house. Presently Uncle Abe was knocking on the kitchen door. His second knock was followed by the sound of footsteps and the door opened to disclose an enormously fat woman whose head was bound with a bright red bandanna. The angry glare on her face changed to a delighted grin as she recognized her visitor. "Lord, lordy," she exclaimed. "If it ain't Uncle Abe River hisself. Come in outer de wet. You sure is a sight fer sore eyes. Ain't seen you nohow fer a month er Sundays!"

Liza bustled her callers through an outer pantry into a spacious kitchen. "I wuz over ter Cross River," said Uncle Abe, seating himself in a proffered chair. "An' you is allus so good an 'commydatin', Liza, I 'lowed I'd drop in an—"

"Find out whedder Liza would ask you t' dinner," chuckled that good natured person. "Reckon you ain't livin' so high now'days in dat der cabin."

"Yo' sho' is a good guesser," grinned Uncle Abe. "But I likes ter see ol' frien's an' I wanted speshul ter ax if Marse Joyce could gimme a spell o' work rakin' leaves er sump'n."

Liza pursed her lips an shook her head vigorously.

"'Tain't likely dat man'd give you nothin'," she said darkly. "De goin's on hyar lately is sure terrubul. Wat wid all dese strange men in de house an' de young gemmun dey brought in han'cuffed las' night—an' right froo dis hyar kitchen too—I'se jes' 'bout ready ter give notice. But I mustn't say nothin'! Who is dis hyar boy wid you, Uncle?"

Mary Eliska made a quick decision. "Not a boy, Auntie—a girl," she said quietly. "—And a friend of the young man who was brought here last night."

"Sakes alive!" exploded the stout cook. "Wat's all dis I'm a-hearin'?"

"Yo'all hearin' de spittin' trufe, Liza," chimed in Uncle Abe earnestly. "Miss Do'thy am de qual'ty. Jes' yo' listen ter wat she say."

Mary Eliska waited for no more comment. With a few deft word strokes she painted a vivid picture of last evening's happenings at the Conway house. Then having aroused a wide-eyed interest in her story, she went on to tell of the adventure in Uncle Abe's cabin and the morning's experiences.

"I am not trying to make trouble between you and Mr. Joyce," she ended, "but if you will help me to free that young gentleman—he must be either George or Liam—you'll be doing a very fine thing and my father Albert Stricklin will see you come to no harm."

"I'se 'spected fo' some time Marse Joyce wuz er bad man," said Liza, "but I ain't askeert of him. Wat you want I should do, Mary Eliska?"

"I just want you to tell me some things, Liza. Then you go on getting dinner and I'll see what I can do for my friend."

"Hadn't I better call in Marse Bill?"

"No, not yet. If anything goes wrong in the house I want to have someone on the outside to phone for the police." She turned to Liza. "Do you know where Mr. Joyce and his men are now?"

"Yes, ma'am. Marse Joyce an' most of 'em done gone somewheres in de big car—left de house 'bout 'n hour ago."

"How many are still here?"

"Two o' dose no-count men is somewhere in de front part of de house. An' let me tell yo'all if dey comes a-bustin' inter my kitchen agin, dey a-gwine ter git a rollin' pin bounced offen dere skulls!"

"If you can't do it, Liza—I will—" added Uncle Abe.

"Ho—how come I can't do it, Abe? You jes' watch. I'll bust 'em an' bust 'em good!"

Mary Eliska giggled. Liza had upset her gravity for the moment.

"I can see you're both going to be useful. But tell me, Auntie—do you know where they're keeping this young man?"

"He's in de blue room, Missy. I done tote up his breakfas' to de do'. Marse Joyce give de odder two girls de day off, so I'se cook an' waitress an' chambermaid today. You run along, Mary Eliska an' if dose cheap rollers try ter git fresh—jes' holler fo' Aunt Liza—she'll bust 'em!"

Mary Eliska had started for the pantry when Uncle Abe sprang out of his chair and caught her arm. "'Scuse me," he apologized then went on eagerly—"I'se got er idee."

"Yes? What is it, Uncle?"

"Dey's logs an' dey's kindlin' in der entry, missy. I done seen 'em when we come in. Well, Mary Eliska, you tote some kindlin'—an' I'll carry a couple er logs an'—" "Fine! We'll do it!" Mary Eliska's alert mind had grasped the plan before Uncle Abe's tongue could give utterance to it.

"An' de bes' part of it is, honey," grinned Liza, "dat all de rooms on dis flo' has fireplaces an' mos' of dem upstairs too. Marse Joyce, he's a crank on open fires."

Mary Eliska chuckled. "Lucky break for us." She took a small armful of kindling that Uncle Abe held out to her.

"Yo'all better foller me," said Uncle Abe, "I knows de way 'bout dis house."

He pushed open a swinging door and they slipped into a dining room, paneled in white pine. It was an attractive room and Mary Eliska decided that despite his criminal traits, John J. Joyce was a man of taste. Uncle Abe tiptoed across the room and paused in the doorway to the hall.

"We better see who's downstairs befo' we goes up," he whispered, and trotted off along the corridor.

He stopped at a closed door near the foot of the staircase and lifted his hand to knock. But before his knuckles had touched the panel, the heavy oak swung inward and they were confronted by the prizefighter whom Mary Eliska had last seen heating a poker in the Conway house. "'Scuse us, suh. We'se bringin' wood fo' de fire." The big man glared at them for a moment. Then apparently satisfied, he stepped aside. "O.K. Thought I heard someone snoopin' around. Dump those logs in the box and then get out." He paid no more attention to them. Slouching stiffly in a big chair before the fire, he became immediately engrossed in the Sunday paper. Uncle Abe dropped the logs into the wood box, and Mary Eliska knelt on the hearth and piled her kindling beside it. In rising to her feet her head brushed Uncle Abe's arm, knocking off the soft felt hat Bill had lent her. Quick as a flash she retrieved it and thrust it back on her head. "A boy with a girl's bob!" Mary Eliska turned sharply and found herself staring into the muzzle of an automatic.

"Stand right where you are," barked the big man, as he got up out of his chair. "And you too —" The revolver swerved for a second in Abe's direction. "Ol' Man River and the girl, of course—we expected you to show up. The laugh's on you, all right. Where's your boyfriend?"

"Right here!" Bill Bolton stepped from behind the heavy window draperies, his revolver trained on the gangster's stomach. "Drop that gun—drop it, or I'll drill you!" Then as the automatic crashed to the floor, a smile spread over his tanned face. "And this time the laugh is on you, my friend," he added softly. "Oh, *yeah*?" came a rasping voice from the hall doorway. "You drop *your* rod, bo'—and stick 'em up! Don't move—you're covered. Now laugh that one off—ha-ha!" Bill's gun fell to the floor and his hands rose slowly upwards. In the doorway stood the bald man—the other member that Mary Eliska had spied on in the library of the Conway house.

Chapter 3.16
THE BOOK

The newcomer limped a couple of paces into the room. His left arm and one leg were swathed in bandages.

"What price rock salt?" remarked Bill pleasantly, still reaching toward the ceiling.

Despite her qualms, Mary Eliska could not help smiling. The bald man's face became scarlet with fury.

"Another crack like that and I'll give you a taste of something harder than rock salt," her roared. "And when I get through with him that guy who was so free with his shotgun last night will wish he'd never been born!"

Bill ignored this outburst. "That gat was my only weapon," he announced without rancor. "This house is in New York State, so if you want to burn in Sing Sing, shoot—I'm tired of holding up my arms."

He lowered his hands and thrust them into his trousers pockets.

The bald man looked daggers but he did not pull the trigger. Instead he turned on his partner.

"Why don't you do something, Chick?" he growled. "You know I'm laid up—oughta be in bed right now, for that matter."

"Say, Eddie," complained the burly fellow, "I'm stiff as a board myself—I got peppered all down my back and you know it."

"Aw, quit yer grousin'. You can still move around. Tie 'em up and we'll dump 'em somewhere 'til the boss gets back."

"Yeah? An' what do we use fer rope?"

Eddie scratched his head with the butt of his revolver and hobbled over to an armchair. "Stick that gat in yer pocket, Chick," he ordered as he lowered himself carefully into the deep cushions. "I've got 'em covered. Beat it into the kitchen—that fat cook in there's got plenty of clothesline. Help yerself and tell her I'll come in an' bump her off, if she gets nasty!"

Chick pocketed his revolver and started to walk stiffly across the room when Liza's ample figure appeared in the doorway. In her hands she bore a wooden mixing bowl, brimming with cake batter. The whites of her eyes gleamed dangerously, as she glared at Chick; then she waddled into the room and halted just behind Eddie's chair.

"I done heard what yo'all said jes' now, bald man—" She shook her head slowly from side to side and stared down at the gangster's hairless pate. "Seems ter me you was talkin' 'bout bumpin' some buddy!"

With his gun covering the three prisoners, Eddie was unable to look up at her. Chick undoubtedly hailed Liza's appearance as relief from the painful necessity of a walk to the kitchen. He sat down on the edge of a chair opposite Eddie and scowled at her sourly. Eddie took up the conversation with the angry woman behind him.

"That's right, fatso," he chuckled hoarsely. "We want some clothesline, to tie up these here nuisances—an' if you don't cough some up right now—I'll bump you off, see?"

"Reckon you got your names mixed—" Without warning Liza brought the solid mixing bowl down upon his unprotected skull.

Eddie collapsed beneath the forceful blow and as he crumpled to the floor, Liza flung the bowl and its contents in Chick's face. Then with an agility surprising in one so cumbersomely made, she catapulted herself at the astonished ruffian. Over went his chair and they crashed in a tangled heap of broken furniture, waving legs and cake batter.

Bill broke into a roar of laughter, but Mary Eliska wasted no time in being amused at this spectacle. She dove for Bill's gun which Eddie had not bothered to retrieve. She ran over the struggling pair on the floor and held the muzzle to Chick's head.

"Stop fighting!" she commanded. "Stop it at once—"

Chick sat up and tried to scrape the batter out of his eyes. "I ain't fightin'," he growled, "I'm half blind and I'm fair smothered. An' if me back ain't broke it oughter be! Take that Mack truck offen my legs—I can't move, much less put up a scrap!"

"Get up, Liza!" Mary Eliska had to smile at the fellow's plight. With Bill's help she got Liza planted on her feet again. Uncle Abe stood guard with a poker over Eddie. That glum gentleman was heralding his return to consciousness with the most remarkable series of coughing grunts.

"This sure is the craziest rough house I ever got mixed up in," laughed Bill. "Baldy over there sounds like a French pig rooting for truffles—" Mary Eliska grinned absent-mindedly, her thoughts on the next move to be made.

"We'll let dese two pigs burrer an' grunt down cellar," declared Liza, straightening her turban and smoothing down her apron. "Dere's a empty storeroom down dere—it's got a strong door an' a good bolt, too. Gimme a gun, please Mary Eliska. Me an' Uncle Abe can 'tend ter dis."

Liza walked over to Eddie, who stared about the room, a dazed expression on his face.

"Git up an' come along."

Then as Eddie continued to look at her vacantly, she picked him up as if he were a baby and draped him over her broad shoulders.

"Yo'all go first, Liza," said Uncle Abe. He prodded Chick with the gun he had taken from her. "Him an' me'll be right behin'."

Mary Eliska and Bill watched the odd procession pass from the room.

"Whew!" she exclaimed. "That was a hectic five minutes. But how did you happen to be in here?"

"Got tired of sticking round outside, so slipped in by that window. Eddie was asleep at the time, but he woke up right afterward. Then you and Uncle Abe walked in—and you know the rest. Say, it must be Liam these guys nabbed. Wonder what's become of Stoker and Jax Gray?"

"Heaven only knows," said Mary Eliska wearily. "I'll go up and let Liam out and I think the best thing you can do is to phone the state police. With Liam here, we've got enough on Mr. John J. Joyce to hold him, now."

"We sure have. Wonder what the J in John J. Joyce stands for?"

"Well, it will stand for Jay, Jonah, Jailbird and Jinx all in one, *if* you get the police here before he comes back and sets his men free. By the way, I may be going coo-coo with all this, but it seems to me that I keep hearing shots every now and then. There's another—hear it?"

"Somebody's probably potting bunnies in the woods." Bill seemed unconcerned. "I noticed it just after I got in here. Beat it upstairs now, and I'll hunt up a telephone."

Mary Eliska found the room where Liam was held prisoner by the simple expedient of opening each door as she came to it. The fourth door was locked, but the key was on the outside. It was no surprise to her, upon opening it, to see her friend Liam lying on the bed. A quick glance showed Mary Eliska that both windows were barred.

Liam sprang up with a glad cry. "It's sure good to see *you*!" He gave her a good-natured hug. "How in the world did you manage this?"

Mary Eliska told him as briefly as possible. "What I want to know," she said in conclusion, "is how they happened to catch you napping—and what's become of George Conway and your twin sister Jax Gray?"

"They didn't catch me napping," Liam retorted. "You and Bill had been gone about an hour and I expected Stoker back from taking Jax Gray home any minute. A Ford drove into the garage, there was a bang on the door and a voice sang out—'Let me in. It's George.' Well, I opened up and—"

"It wasn't George—" supplied Mary Eliska, as usual going straight to the point. "Joyce and his men nabbed you, of course. That's plain enough. But where are Jax and George?"

"Search me."

Bill burst into the room and stood breathless before them.

"Did you get the police?" asked Mary Eliska.

"Got headquarters all right. But what do you think's happened?"

"Spill it, Bill. This is no guessing bee," said Liam.

"The sergeant told me they'd had a phone call from Lewis. The old man was frantic. Joyce and his gang were trying to break into his house. The whole caboodle from headquarters are up there now, rounding up John J. Joyce and Company."

"That accounts for the shots we heard," cried Mary Eliska. "Get on your rubbers, Liam. We're going to hike over to Mr. Lewis's place right now. I want to be in at the finish."

"And I," added Bill, "want to find out what this mess is about!"

They raced downstairs and stopping only long enough to tell Liza and Uncle Abe of this new development, set off for the Lewis property adjoining. Following hasty directions given them by Uncle Abe, they hurried along a path which led them to a gate in a high wall. The gate was not locked and they continued along the path which crossed the Lewis estate. Presently the dim shape of a large white house appeared through the mist.

"Halt!" A gruff voice arrested them as they were about to ascend the steps at the side entrance. A state trooper barred their way. "Who are you—and what do you want?"

"We are friends of Mr. Lewis," said Mary Eliska. She explained the circumstances of their arrival.

"Well, we've just sent Joyce and his men to the lockup. The whole crew of 'em. We corralled 'em proper. They'd busted into the house, you know, and it sure would have been a mixup if this fly cop that horned in on the Joyce bunch hadn't clapped his gat to Joyce's head and held up their game until we got here."

"Oh, that must have been Michael Michaels—the private inquiry agent who came to Uncle Abe's last night," said Bill. "We'd like to go in the house, officer."

"O.K. with me. There's some kind of a pow-wow goin' on in the living room. I'll take you in there."

He opened the door and led them across the square hall into the living room. Here they found a surprise awaiting them.

"Jax! George!" cried Mary Eliska. She flew across the room. "I'm so glad you're safe. How did you get here?"

"Oh, darling! It's too exciting for words!" gurgled Jax Gray as they hugged each other. "And George was so brave—he—"

"Mr. Lewis and his chauffeur stopped our Lizzie last night," broke in Stoker. "Told us Joyce and his men were likely to hold us up down the road. So we left the Ford and came over here with Mr. Lewis. And we've been here ever since."

"Listen, George!" said that old gentleman, and both girls giggled. "Hadn't you better introduce your friends? This young lady in overalls is Mary Eliska, I take it?"

"She certainly is," smiled Stoker and performed the necessary introductions.

The other men in the room proved to be Michael Michaels and an inspector of the state police. For a few minutes everybody seemed to be talking at once. Bill told George and Mr. Lewis of his adventures with Mary Eliska, while Liam explained his capture by the Joyce gang to the inspector and Michaels.

"Listen!" said Mary Eliska and threw a reproving glance at the others' unsuppressed smiles—"Will somebody please tell me what Mr. Joyce has been trying to steal from Stoker?"

"Why, that's so," interjected Mr. Lewis, "you have no idea, of course—"

"No, except that it's probably mixed up with that book, *Aircraft Power Plants*, I think it's called—"

The old gentleman looked at her in unfeigned astonishment. "Listen, Michaels!" he cried. "She says this business is connected with that book. Pretty good guess, eh?"

"Certainly is," returned the detective. "But the book is a mystery in itself, and one we haven't yet solved."

"But what *was* Joyce after?" interrupted Bill with a show of impatience.

"The plans, of course," said Stoker Conway.

"But what plans?"

"The plans of my father's new aircraft engine. I knew nothing about it until Mr. Lewis told me last night."

"Where are the plans, and what has the book to do with them?" broke in Mary Eliska.

"Listen, young lady," began Mr. Lewis, when Michaels the detective stopped him with a gesture.

"Better let me tell them, sir," he suggested. "These young people have a right to know."

The old gentleman nodded approval and the detective, after biting off the end of a cigar, continued to talk while the others grouped about him. "About two weeks ago," he said, "Mr. Lewis called at my New York office. There he told me the following story. Six weeks before his death, Mr. Conway came over here and told Mr. Lewis that he had perfected plans for an aircraft motor which would develop very high power on a very small consumption of gasoline."

"That's just what all the inventors are after now," interposed Bill.

"Why, I should say so!" cried Mary Eliska. "If *Wispy's* motor didn't lap up the gasoline like a thirsty camel, I'd never have been forced to land in that woodlot yesterday afternoon!" "All very interesting, I'm sure—" Liam's voice was sarcastic. "But do let's hear what Mr. Michaels is trying to tell us!"

"That's all right," smiled the detective. "Let's see—where was I? Oh, yes, the motor: well, the inventor told Mr. Lewis that his partner and sales agent had ruined him financially, and that now he was convinced that he'd been swindled, and that Joyce was a crook. Mr. Lewis suggested Mr. Conway take the matter to the courts, and offered to advance money for legal expenses. Mr. Conway said he hadn't sufficient evidence for a case; that Joyce had covered his tracks too well. Then he spoke about the plans for this new motor he'd just completed. He said that Joyce knew about it and was trying to get control of the thing; but that outside of stealing the plans outright, Joyce could do nothing, as the partnership had been dissolved. And at the same time he told Mr. Lewis that he knew he was suffering from an incurable disease and could live but a few months longer at most."

"Listen, Michaels—let me tell it," interrupted old Lewis. "You are wandering all over the place.... Your father, George, said that should he have the new motor built, Joyce would undoubtedly make trouble, and he, Conway, wanted to die in peace. He told me he was going to entrust me with the plans and would send them to me after he had made some slight changes in them. And he said that he would send me his check to cover the expense of building and exploiting the engine. 'After I'm gone, you attend to it for George,' he said. 'That boy has no mechanical ability, and he's too young to market a thing like this motor. Joyce or other wolves like him would rob him of it in twenty-four hours.' And that, was the last time I saw John Conway alive."

The old gentleman pulled out a handkerchief and blew his nose violently. "He wouldn't see me when I called, nor would he mention the plans over the phone. He died while I was in Boston on business. When I got back the next day, I found a package from him waiting for me. Of course, I thought it would contain the plans and his check. When I opened it up I found nothing but a book—*Aircraft Power Plants*, by a man named Jones. I was naturally surprised, and searched its pages from cover to cover, but found no papers of any kind. I've even read every word of it since then. And its pages have been tested for invisible ink. But I've had my trouble and pains for nothing."

"I wonder why Father didn't tell me of those plans?" George remarked rather wistfully.

"That I can't explain, my boy. As you know now, I thought you had them. Either that you had removed them from the book before it left your house, or that your father had changed his mind and given them to you. Anyway, I decided to await developments. Nothing happened until Joyce, who had been in Europe since Conway's death, returned home a couple of weeks ago. He came to see me and asked me outright if I knew anything about Conway's airplane motor plans. I never liked nor trusted Joyce, but I saw no harm in telling him the truth. For of course I figured that George must have set the wheels in motion for the sale of the motor long before. Joyce could do nothing about it at this late date."

"But to my astonishment, the man told me the motor had not been marketed—that he would have heard if any company had bought it. 'Either that boy's got the plans,' he said, 'or Conway had two copies of the book and sent you the wrong one—' I didn't understand how the book came into it and told him so. 'Conway always sent important papers through the mail by placing them between the pages of a book,' he assured me. 'Thought they would travel safer that way.'

"Well, he changed the subject then, and left. I got nervous about what I'd told him, and hired Michaels to watch the fellow. Michaels dug up a lot of things about Joyce, and managed to get himself placed on his staff of roughnecks. If he could have been in two places at once, all this trouble over at the Conway house last night would never have come off."

Mary Eliska spoke from her place on the couch beside Jax Gray. "How did you happen to go there last night?"

"I wanted to find out if George really had another copy of the book. Later I learned from Michaels that Joyce's men had tried to torture the boy into telling them where the plans were—and that then he intended to kidnap him. I was on my way over there to warn him when we met on the road. He wanted to put young Walters wise, but I was sure the Joyce gang wouldn't hurt his friend. I had promised Michaels not to go ahead on my own hook until I saw him. Perhaps I was wrong, but I did what I thought was best for George's interests. I've heard since that they just about tore the house apart, looking for the other copy of that book!"

"Do you happen to have the copy that was sent you, here in the house?" asked Mary Eliska.

"Yes—right here, on the table." Michaels handed it to her.

Mary Eliska pored over the book for a few minutes, then laid it down. "Mr. Lewis, do you mind if I take it home with me?"

"Why, of course not—keep it as long as you wish."

"Thanks," she smiled. "Now, you gentlemen want to plan about what to do with Joyce and Co., and Bill and I have some gasoline to buy and an airplane to fly home. So I'll say *au revoir* for the present!"

Chapter 3.17
THE TEST

One morning some three months later, the private flying field on the Bolton place was the mecca of a considerable portion of Jackson Hole's population. The ridge road and the surrounding meadows were jammed with cars that flaunted license plates of a dozen different states. Although the December sun shone brightly in a cobalt sky, the crowd shivered and stamped on the frozen ground for the winter air was icy. All eyes were turned upward toward an airplane, high above their heads, which swept the sky in immense, horizontal circles.

A small group of people bundled in heavy fur coats stood and chatted by the open doors of the hangar.

"I almost wish they'd come down," said George Conway. "They must be half-dead for want of sleep, and they've already beaten the world's record by hours. It must be a terrific strain, especially for Mary Eliska."

"Oh," cried Jax Gray. "Isn't she marvelous?—and Bill, too!"

"They're a pair of young idiots!" growled old Mr. Lewis, whose false teeth were chattering. "But I must admit they're first-class sportsmen to stay up all this time for a friend!"

"You said it." declared Liam McAdams, and glanced at his wrist watch. "In exactly one minute, they'll have been up one hundred and one hours, without refueling. Gosh, it's wonderful! That motor of your father's is some humdinger, Stoker!"

"Why, it's simply adorable!" Jax Gray was brimming over with excitement. "And I just can't help being glad that that horrid Mr. Joyce and his men are being sent to Sing Sing for years and years and years! It's too—"

"Here they come!" The crowd yelled and roared and swarmed toward the roped-off enclosure.

Sure enough—At last the big airplane was spiraling downward. It landed lightly on the frozen ground and bowled across the field. The crowd surged in, but there was no sign of life, no movement about the plane. Mechanics jerked open the door, and there, side by side, grimy, worn, unkempt, were Mary Eliska and Bill Bolton, sleeping like children!

Somehow they were taken into the Bolton's house and put to bed, where they continued to sleep for twelve hours, while certain anxious gentlemen waited about, impatiently demanding interviews.

The pair eventually looked up from quantities of ham and eggs in the dining room, to greet their visitors.

"Now, I want to talk business," said the portly man who led the van. "Mr. Conway will not discuss the matter. He refers me to you."

"Oh, you can talk to her," said Bill. He motioned to Mary Eliska. "She's run this show from start to finish."

"And what," asked the portly gentleman, coming at once to the point, "will you take for that motor, Mary Eliska?"

"Hmmm—A hundred hours, without refueling," remarked Mary Eliska, thoughtfully buttering a slice of toast. "I hope you've given that some thought."

"I have given it several thoughts. Name a price."

"A million," said Mary Eliska. "Dollars?" Bill kicked her under the table.

"Pounds, certainly," said Mary Eliska. "I went to England last year, and after I learned how to figure their complicated money, I've never been able to unlearnit!"

She smiled benignly upon the company.

Bill nodded. "Mary Eliska's some little bargainer, ain't she?" he said delightedly, with his mouth full.

"Give you a million dollars," said the portly gentleman.

"Give up your place," said Mary Eliska, "and let some of these other gentlemen into the game."

"A million and a half," said the portly gentleman, edging closer to the table.

"Make it two million and you win." "Done!" "Thank you," smiled Mary Eliska. "Now please make the check payable to George Conway."

The gentlemen filed out of the room. "Gee, you're a whizbang, Mary Eliska!" Bill exploded as soon as they were alone. "Some Christmas present for Stoker!"

"You're not so bad yourself," laughed the girl. "That kick of yours was worth just a million dollars!"

Five minutes later, the kitchen door of the Bolton's house was flung open and a happy face peered in. "Has yo'all heard de news, Liza?" panted Uncle Abe in great excitement. "G'wan home, I'ze busy makin' waffle fo' de chilluns," retorted the Bolton's cook. "Golly, but dey sure is hungry!"

"Mary Eliska done sol' dat motah fo' two million dollars. I wuz stickin' roun' outside an' done hear de gen'men talkin' 'bout it."

"Lan's sakes, but dat a pile er money," said Liza pouring batter on to the hot waffle iron. "How come Marse Bill was able ter build dat engin'? I thought dat de plans was lost?" "You sho' has a one-track mind, Liza," Uncle Abe observed contemptuously. "And dat track spells nuthin' but kitchen. My young Missy *found* dem plans! She beat all dose big detecatives to it!"

"Do tell! Whar was dey?"

"In er book, Liza." "Shucks, I done heard 'bout de book. Dey warn't no plans inside it."

"Huh! Dey sho wuz, too!" "Whar dey at?"

"Mary Eliska done took er knife an' ripped dat book erpart! Dat little lady is de quality, an' she sure am smart. De plans was on thin paper, pasted in de back whar de leaves o' de book am sewed togedder."

"Do tell!" Liza shook her head. "But what I nevah did un'erstan' wuz why Marse Joyce tried ter kidnap de other boys and girls."

"Liza, you sho' is dumb. It all come out in de trial. Firs' Marse Joyce think Marse George know 'bout de plans, so his men try ter make him tell. Den when Mary Eliska busted up dat party, he know dat de other chilluns would sho' crab his game if dey wuz let loose ter tell 'bout it."

"Abe, you is crazy! How dat man goin' ter keep all dose young folks locked in his house while he try to sell dem plans? De police sure find dem befo' he's able ter do dat!" "No. Liza, you's wrong agin. Marse Joyce knew a lot about dem plans. Marse Conway had done tol' him consider'ble about dem, and Marse Joyce done tell de Rooshians what Marse Conway tell him. De Rooshians say dey give him a heap of money jes' as soon as he build dat engine."

"An' Marse Joyce figured he'd beat it to Rooshia jes' as soon as he could put his han's on de plans?" said Liza.

"Dat's right—" nodded the old darky. "You ain't quite ez dumb ez yo' looks. An' de way Marse George is a-hangin' roun' Miss Jax Gray—"

"Yo'all talks too much," Liza cut him short. "Lan' sakes! Gossipin' at yo' age! Tote dis hyar plate of hot waffles inter der dinin' room. De young folks am hungry!"

CHAPTER 4

The Double Cousins

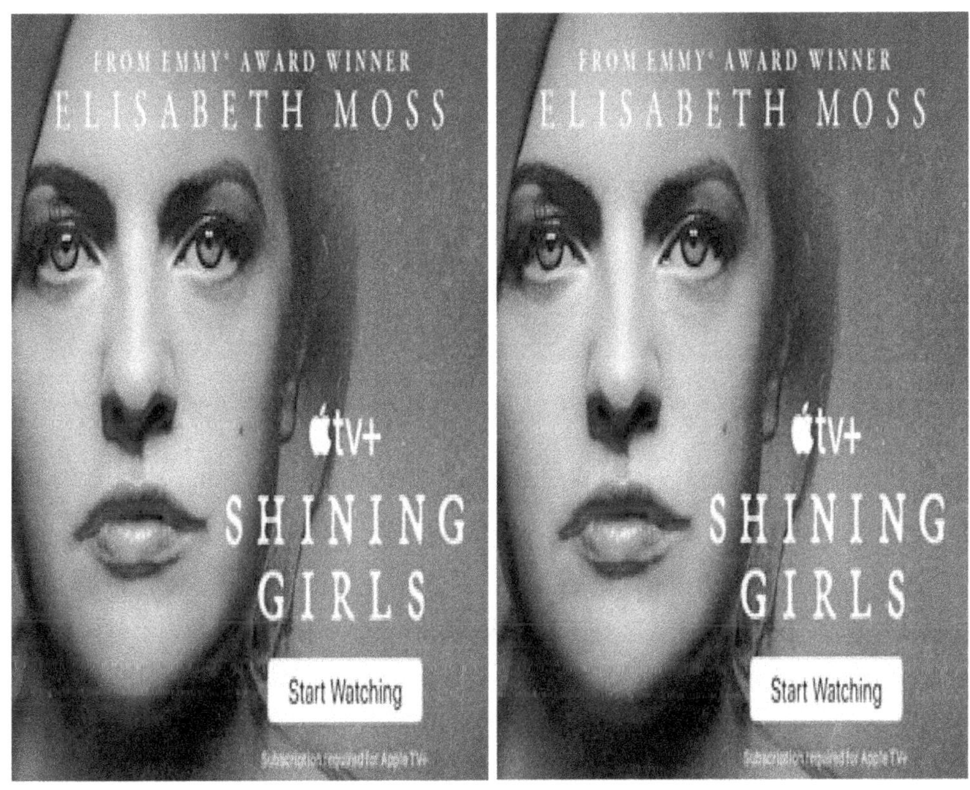

Chapter 4.1
THE ENCOUNTER

"Why—good heavens, girl! How in the world did you escape?"

Mary Eliska heard the low, eager whisper at her elbow but disregarded it. She was intent on selecting a tie from the colorful rack on the counter before her. She spoke to the clerk:

"I'll take this one, and that'll make four. I hope Daddy will approve my taste in Christmas presents," she smiled, and laid a bill on her purchases.

"But—please, dear, tell me! Don't you know I'm worried crazy? Who let you out?"

This time Mary Eliska felt a touch on her arm. She wheeled quickly to face a tall, slender young fellow of twenty-two or three. As she stared at him, half indignant, half wondering, she saw sincere distress in his brown eyes, and in the lines of his pleasant face. Hat in hand, he waited anxiously for an answer to his question, while the crowd of holiday shoppers poured through the aisles about them.

Mary Eliska's eyes softened, then danced. "It seems to me," she said, "that you have the wires twisted—it's not I who've escaped, but you! Run along now and find your keeper. You're evidently in need of one!"

"Your change and package, miss," the impersonal voice of the haberdashery clerk intervened and Mary Eliska turned back to the counter.

"But why on earth are you acting this way, Marlow Ray?" The strange young man was at her elbow again.

Once more Mary Eliska turned swiftly toward him but when she spoke her eyes and voice were serious. "Do you really mean to say you think you're speaking to Marlow Ray? Because—"

"My dear—what are you trying to tell me?" He broke in impatiently. "I certainly ought to know the girl I'm going to marry!"

Mary Eliska nodded slowly. "I agree with you—you ought to—but then, you see, you *don't!*"

The young man crushed his soft felt hat in his hands and took a step nearer to her. "Look here—what *is* the matter with you? I know you've been through a lot, but—" He broke off abruptly, a gleam of horror and suspicion in his honest eyes. "Marlow Ray! What have they done to you?" Mary Eliska laid a firm hand on his arm. "Sh! Be quiet—listen to me." Then she added gently—"I am *not* Marlow Ray, your fiancee." "You're not—!"

"No. My name is Mary Eliska—and I'm Marlow Ray's first cousin." The young man seemed flabbergasted for a moment. Then he stammered—"Wh-why, it's astounding—the resemblance, I mean! You're alike as—as two peas. If you were twins—"

"But you see," she smiled, "our mothers, Marlow Ray's and mine, *were* twins, and I guess that accounts for it. I've never seen Marlow Ray, but this is the third time, just recently, that I've been taken for her by her friends, Mr.—?"

"My name is Bright," he supplied. "Howard Bright. Yes, now I can see a slight difference, Mary Eliska. You're a bit taller and broader across the shoulders than she is. But it's your personalities, more than anything else, that are altogether unlike. I hope you'll forgive me, Mary Eliska, for making a nuisance of myself!"

"No indeed—that is, of course I will!" Mary Eliska laughed merrily. "You're not a nuisance, you know, but," and her tone became grave, "I can see that you're in trouble. Is there—" she hesitated.

"Not I, Mary Eliska—that is, not directly. But," he lowered his voice, "Marlow Ray is—is in very serious trouble. And for a moment, when I saw you, I thought that in some miraculous way she had escaped."

Howard Bright's face suddenly became almost haggard and Mary Eliska's sympathy and concern for her cousin deepened into resolve.

"Look here, Mr. Bright," she said abruptly, "we can't talk here, in this shopping crowd, it's a regular football scrimmage. Let's go up to the mezzanine. A friend of mine is waiting there for me now, I'm a little late as it is, and—"

"But I can't bother *you* with this," he protested, "and especially—"

"Oh, come along," she urged, "Bill is a grand guy when it comes to getting people out of messes. I insist you tell us all about it. After all, Marlow Ray's my cousin, you know, and you'll soon be a member of the family, won't you?"

"There doesn't seem much hope of that now." Young Bright's tone was despondent. "But Marlow Ray certainly does need help, and she needs it badly—so—"

Mary Eliska caught his arm. "I'm going to call you Howard," she announced briskly. "So please drop the formalities. And come on—let's push our way over to the elevators."

The mezzanine floor of the department store was arranged as a lounge or waiting room for customers. Comfortable arm chairs and divans invited tired shoppers to rest. Writing desks and tables strewn with current magazines gave the place a club-like appearance.

Mary Eliska and her newly-found acquaintance stepped out of the elevator and looked about. The place seemed especially quiet after the rush and bustle on other floors, and was almost deserted, save for two elderly ladies conversing in low tones near a window, and a young man, who rose at their approach.

As the good-looking youth moved toward them with the lithe, easy grace of a trained athlete, Howard Bright saw that he had light brown hair, and blue eyes snapping with vitality and cheerfulness.

"Hello, Mary Eliska!" He greeted her smilingly, "better late than never, if you don't mind my saying so. I'd just about figured you were going to pass up our date."

"Sorry, Colonel," she mocked. "Explanations are in order I guess, but they can wait. This is Howard Bright, Bill—Howard, Mr. Bolton!"

The two young men shook hands.

"Bolton—Stricklin?" Howard's tone was thoughtful. "Why!" he exclaimed suddenly. "You two are the flyers—the pair who won the endurance test with the Conway motor! I'm certainly glad to meet you both. The papers have been full of your doings. Well, this is a surprise! But you know, I'd got the impression that you were both older—"

"I'm sixteen," smiled Mary Eliska. "Bill has me beat by a year."

"How about lunch?" suggested Bill. He invariably changed the subject when his exploits were mentioned. People always enthused so, it embarrassed him. "You'll join us, of course, Mr. Bright?"

"Thanks, Mr. Bolton. I really don't think I can butt in this way—"

"There's no butting in about it," Mary Eliska interrupted. "Howard is engaged to my cousin, Marlow Ray, Bill. And Marlow Ray's in a lot of trouble. I've promised we'd do everything we can to help."

Bill, after one look at Howard's worried face, sized up the situation instantly. "Why, of course," he said. "And we can't talk with any privacy in this place. I can see that whatever the trouble is, it's serious."

"Marlow Ray's in desperate peril," Howard said huskily.

"You said something about her escape when we met," Mary Eliska reminded him. "Has somebody kidnapped her? Have you any idea where she is?"

"Yes, she's a prisoner. A prisoner in the Rays' apartment on West 93rd Street."

"Then her father is away?"

"No. He leaves tonight, I believe."

"But, my goodness!—a girl can't be kidnapped and made a prisoner in her own home. Especially if her father is there. It doesn't sound possible."

"I know it doesn't," admitted Howard desperately, "it sounds crazy. But it's the truth, just the same. She's in frightful danger."

Mary Eliska looked horrified. "You mean that my uncle and Marlow Ray don't get on together—that they've had a row and you're afraid he will harm her?"

"Oh, no, they're very fond of each other."

"Then Uncle Michael is a prisoner, too!"

"No, he is free enough himself, but he can do nothing—it would only make matters worse."

"Well!" declared Mary Eliska, "I don't think much of Uncle Michael if he can't protect his own daughter."

Bill stepped into the breach.

"What about the police—can't you call them in?"

Howard Bright shook his head. "They would only bring this horrible business to a climax," he explained. "And that is exactly what must not be done. It is more a matter for Secret Service investigation—but I don't think that even they could be of any real help."

Bill and Mary Eliska exchanged a quick glance.

"Have you ever heard of a man named Ashton Sanborn, Mr. Bright?"

"Yes, I have, Mr. Bolton. Wasn't he the detective who helped you unearth that fiendish scheme of old Professor Fanely?"

"Bull's eye!" grinned Bill. "Only Ashton Sanborn is quite a lot more than a mere detective. And it so happens that he is over at the Waldorf right now, waiting for Mary Eliska and me to lunch with him. Let me tell you, Bright, it's a mighty lucky thing for Marlow Ray that he is in town. Come along. We'll hop a taxi and be with him in ten minutes."

Howard hung back. "But really—"

Mary Eliska caught his arm. "Don't be silly, now," she urged.

"But I can't call in a detective, Mary Eliska. I know I'm rotten at explaining, but if these devils who have Marlow Ray in their power are interfered with, they will kill her out of hand!"

"But you spoke of the Secret Service just now. This is not for publication, but Mr. Sanborn is the head of that branch of the government. If anyone *can* help Marlow Ray, he can do it."

"I doubt it. I admit I'm half-crazy with worry, but Marlow Ray is going to be removed from the apartment tonight, and heaven only knows what will happen then. It takes days, generally weeks, to get the government started on anything."

"Not Sanborn's branch of it," interrupted Bill. "We're talking in circles, Bright. If Sanborn can't help Marlow Ray, he'll tell you so. At least you can give him the dope and find out. He's an expert and you'll get expert advice."

"All right, I'll go with you. But I'm afraid it won't do any good. Please don't think, though, that I'm not appreciating the interest you're taking. I don't mean to be a wet blanket."

"Of course you don't, and you're not." Mary Eliska led toward the staircase. "You'll feel a whole lot better when you get the story off your chest."

"And when you've got outside a good substantial lunch," added Bill. "I know I shall, anyway."

"That," said Mary Eliska, "is just like a boy. I believe you'd eat a good meal, Bill, an hour before you were hung, if it were offered to you." "I'd be hanged if I didn't," he laughed and followed her down the steps onto the main floor.

Chapter 4.2
"FAMILY AFFAIRS"

"Just—one—moment, please!" Ashton Sanborn's keen blue eyes twinkled as he surveyed his young guests. His heavy-set body moved with a muscular grace as he placed a chair for Mary Eliska and motioned the two boys to seats on a divan nearby. "Now then, Mary Eliska and Bill—I want you two chatterboxes to keep quiet while I ask Mr. Bright some questions and get this matter straight in my own head. Your turn to talk will come later." His quizzical smile robbed the words of any harshness, and the culprits grinned and nodded their willingness to comply with his request.

"Mr. Bright," he went on, "if you'll just answer my questions for the present, I'll get you to tell the story from the beginning in a few minutes."

"It's mighty decent of you to take all this interest, Mr. Sanborn."

The Secret Service Man shook his prematurely grey head—"It's my business to ferret things out. Now, as I understand it, you mistook Mary Eliska for her cousin, Marlow Ray, to whom you are engaged. The likeness must be amazing?"

"It is, sir." "Yes—well, we'll get back to the likeness after a while. You say that Marlow Ray is a prisoner in her father's apartment, and is in danger of her life?"

"Yes, sir." Howard, tense and taut as a fiddle string, his hands gripping the edge of the cushioned couch, gazed steadily back at his questioner.

"Do you know for certain that she is in actual danger at the present moment, Bright?" Ashton Sanborn's quiet tone and unhurried manner of speaking was gradually gaining the young man's confidence. Bill and Mary Eliska noticed that Howard's strained look was beginning to disappear, and he had started to relax.

"She has been in great danger," he replied, "but now, they've decided to test her. There isn't a chance, though, that she will pass the test, Mr. Sanborn. The poor girl is so worn out and nervous she's bound to fail."

"Do you know what time she is to be taken away from the apartment?"

"Yes, sir. Lawson told her to pack her clothes today, so as to be ready to leave at midnight."

"Mmm!" Sanborn glanced at his watch. "It is now one-thirty. That gives us exactly eleven and a half hours in which to get her out of their hands. Now just one question more, Mr. Bright. What made you say that this is a matter in which the so-called Secret Service of the United States should be called in, rather than the police?"

"Well," Howard's brows knit in a puzzled frown, "you see, Marlow Ray is being taken to Dr. Tyson Winn's house near Ridgefield, Connecticut, tonight. As I understand it, Dr. Winn has a big laboratory up there where he is experimenting on high explosives for the government. Lawson, the man who told Marlow Ray she was to go there, is Dr. Winn's secretary. It all looks so queer to me—I thought—"

"That *is* interesting!" Ashton Sanborn's tone was serious and for a little while he seemed lost in thought. Then abruptly he looked up from an inspection of his fingertips, and rose from his chair. "I ordered lunch for three before you young people arrived," he said with a return of his cheerful, hearty way of speaking. "Now I'll phone down and have lunch for four served up here instead." He looked at Mary Eliska. "By the way, the menu calls for oyster cocktails, sweetbreads on grilled mushrooms, O'Brien potatoes, alligator pear salad, and cafe parfait—any suggestions?"

"Oh, aren't you a dear!" Mary Eliska, who had been using a miniature powder puff on her nose, snapped shut the cover of her compact. "You have ordered all the things I like best. No wonder you're a great detective—you never forget a single thing, no matter what it is."

Sanborn laughed. "Thanks for the compliment—but those dishes happen to be favorites of my own, too. Now get that brain of yours working, Mary Eliska. When I've finished with the head waiter, I want you to tell us all you know about your uncle and cousin. Before we can go further I must have every possible detail of the case at my fingers' ends."

He took up a phone from a small table near the window, and Mary Eliska turned toward Howard.

"You probably know more about the Rays than I do," she said. "I have a picture of Marlow Ray that she sent me a couple of years ago. We always exchange presents at Christmas—but we've never seen each other."

"I really know very little about the Rays, myself," protested Howard. "You see, Marlow Ray and I saw each other for the first time just five weeks ago. It was on a Sunday afternoon, I'd been taking a walk in Central Park, when one of those equinoctial downpours came on very suddenly. Marlow Ray was right ahead of me, so naturally, I offered her my umbrella. She's—well, rather shy and retiring, and at first she wasn't so keen on accepting—"

"So there *is* a difference between the cousins!" Bill winked at Howard. "If it had been Mary Eliska, she'd have taken your overcoat and rubbers as well. Nothing shy or retiring about Marlow Ray's double!"

"Is that so, Mr. Smarty! It's a good thing Howard met her that rainy Sunday. If it had been you, Bill, the poor girl would certainly have got a soaking!"

"You mean she wouldn't have accepted my umbrella?"

"I *mean* you never would have offered it!"

"You win—one up, Mary Eliska," said Ashton Sanborn when the laughter at this sally had subsided. "What happened after you and Marlow Ray got under your umbrella, Bright?"

"Oh, nothing much. We walked over to Central Park West but there were no taxis to be had for love nor money. So then I suggested taking her home and we found we lived in the same apartment house. I asked if I might call, but she said that was impossible—that Mr. Ray permitted no callers."

"Well," said Mary Eliska, "that didn't seem to stop you. I mean you are a pretty fast worker, Howard, to get engaged with a tyrant father guarding the doorstep and all that."

"Cut it out, Mary Eliska," broke in Bill, who had been waiting patiently for a chance to get even. "You can't be in the center of the stage all the time, and your remarks are out of order, anyway."

"I'll whack you one, if you take my name in vain, young man!"

"Silence, woman! Go ahead, Howard, and speak your piece, or she'll jump in with both feet next time."

Mary Eliska said nothing but the glance she shot Bill Bolton was a promise of dire things to come.

"Oh, I don't mind," grinned Howard, and Mary Eliska immediately put him down as a good sport. "Well, to go on with it—we used to meet in the lobby, go for walks and bus rides, sometimes to the movies or a matinee. Two weeks ago, Marlow Ray, who is just eighteen, by the way, said she would marry me. She seemed to have no friends in New York. I've seen her father, but never met him. Except for this horrible business, which came up a few days ago, all that I know about Marlow Ray is that her mother died when she was five, her father parked her at a boarding-school near Jackson Hole, Wyoming, and she stayed there until last June when she graduated. Her summer holidays were spent at a girls' camp in Wisconsin. She was never allowed to visit the homes of the other girls, so Christmas and Easter holidays she stayed in the school. During her entire schooling, she saw her father only five times. Last summer he took her abroad with him. They traveled in Germany and in Russia, I believe."

"Gosh, what a life for a girl!" exploded Bill.

"I should say so!" Mary Eliska made no attempt to hide her disgust. "The more I hear about Uncle Michael, the less I care about him."

"Tell us what you do know about him," prompted Sanborn. "I want to get all the background possible before Bright explains the girl's present predicament. I know a good deal about Dr. Winn and his secretary. If those men are threatening her, there must be something very serious brewing. Go ahead, Mary Eliska—luncheon will be up here any minute, now."

"All right, but I warn you it isn't much. My mother, who as you know died when I was a little girl, had one sister, my Aunt Eliska, who was her twin. They looked so much alike that their own father and mother had trouble in telling them apart. Aunt Eliska fell in love with a young Irishman named Michael Ray, whom she met at a dance. He seemed prosperous, and my grandfather gave his consent to their engagement. Then he learned that Michael Ray made his money by selling arms and ammunition to South and Central American revolutionists. Grandpa, from all accounts, hit the ceiling. He was a deacon of the church, very sedate and all that, and he said he wouldn't allow his daughter to marry a gun-runner. And that was that. To make a long story short, Aunt Eliska ran away with Michael Ray. They were married in New York, sent Grandpa a copy of the marriage certificate, and then sailed for South America. For several years there was no word from them at all. My mother, whose name was Marlow, by the way, loved Aunt Eliska as only a twin can love the other. But she couldn't write to her because the eloping couple had left no address. Six years later, mother had a letter from Uncle Michael. He was in Wyoming then, and he wrote that Aunt Eliska had died, and that he had placed little Marlow Ray at the Pence School in Jackson Hole. Mother and Daddy went right out to Jackson Hole, to see Uncle Michael. They tried to get him to let them take Marlow Ray home with them, and bring her up with me. I was only three at the time, so naturally I don't remember anything about it. But what I'm telling you Daddy told to me years later. Well, their trip to Wyoming was all for nothing—Uncle Michael refused to let them have Marlow Ray. It almost broke my mother's heart. Well, and that is the reason Marlow Ray and I have always given each other presents at Christmas and on our birthdays, although we've never even met. Two years ago, she sent me her photograph, and both Daddy and I were astounded to see the resemblance to me. Twice, since then, I've been taken for Marlow Ray by girls who were at school with her at Jackson Hole. Perhaps, if we were seen together, you'd be able to tell us apart—I don't know."

"I do, though," declared Howard, "you may be slightly broader across the shoulders, Mary Eliska, but otherwise you might be Marlow Ray, sitting there. You've the same blond hair, blue eyes, your features are alike—"

"How about our voices?"

"Exactly the same. You have a more forceful way of speaking, that's all. I keep wanting to call you 'Marlow Ray' all the time." Howard turned his head away, and Mary Eliska could see the emotion that again overtook him as he thought of his helpless fiancee, a prisoner in the hands of unscrupulous men.

She glanced at Bill, and shook her head in sympathy. Just then there came a knock on the sitting room door.

"Ah! lunch at last!" Ashton Sanborn rose and put his hand on Howard's shoulder. "Come, no more of this now. The subject of the double cousins is taboo until we've all done justice to this excellent meal!"

Chapter 4.3
THE SLEEPWALKER

"Mr. Sanborn," said Mary Eliska, "when you're tired of fathoming mysteries for people, come out to New Canaan and help me order meals. That was the most scrumptious lunch I've had in a month of Sundays." She dropped a lump of sugar in her demitasse and threw her host a bright smile across the table.

"Thank you, my dear," the detective smiled back. "I may take you up on that one of these days. But speaking of mysteries reminds me that now the waiter is gone, it's high time we busied ourselves again with the affairs of Marlow Ray. Now that I understand something of the young lady's background and her family, I want to hear all there is to tell about her present position." He pulled a briar pipe and tobacco pouch out of his pocket and commenced to fill the one with the contents of the other while Mary Eliska lighted her own tiny pipe. "All ready, Howard. Start at the beginning and don't skimp on details—they may be and they generally are important."

"Very well, sir. I'll begin with a week ago today." Howard pushed his chair away from the table, thrust his hands into trouser pockets and jumped into his story. "Marlow Ray had a date to meet me last Thursday at two p. m. at the Strand. We intended to take in a movie—but she never showed up."

"Then you aren't a business man—?" This from the detective.

"Oh, but I am—a mining engineer, Mr. Sanborn. With the Tuthill Corporation. But I am free on Thursday afternoons, instead of Saturday. It is more convenient for the office staff."

"Hasn't your concern large mining concessions in Peru?"

"It has, sir—silver mines. To make matters worse—but no—I'll tell it this way. I particularly wanted to meet Marlow Ray last Thursday, because I had been told the day before by the head of our New York office that I was to be transferred to Lima, Peru. The boat that I'm scheduled to sail on, leaves this coming Saturday. I was fearfully pepped up about it. I'm going down there as assistant manager of our Lima office, the job carries a considerable increase in salary, and, if I make good, a fine future with the firm. My plan was to get Marlow Ray to marry me, with or without her father's consent, and to take her to Lima with me. I couldn't bear to think of leaving her to the kind of existence she'd had before I'd known her—and with no way of correspondence—Well, I waited for over an hour in the lobby of the theater but she didn't come. At last I went up to my apartment."

"Why didn't you phone her?" asked Mary Eliska, who was nothing if not direct.

"Because Marlow Ray had asked me never to do that. She said if her father knew she had a boyfriend, he'd pack her off somewhere, and we'd never be able to meet again."

"Nice papa—I don't think!" observed Bill Bolton.

"No comments now, please," said Sanborn. "Go on, Howard. If you couldn't talk to Marlow Ray, how did you find out that she was a prisoner?"

Howard smiled. "But we *were* able to talk to each other, Mr. Sanborn. About the time we became engaged, I fixed that. My small flat is on the ninth floor of the building, the Rays' on the seventh. My three rooms have windows on an air shaft. The Rays' back bedroom and bath overlook the same airshaft and are directly opposite my sitting room, two flights below. The shaft is only twenty feet wide, so I bought one of those headphone sets that are used in airplanes for conversation between the cockpits of a plane while it is being flown. I lengthened the wires of course, and got a long, collapsible pole. After dark, Marlow Ray would come to her window, I'd pass her headphone set down to her, hooked on to the end of the pole, and we would hold long conversations across the court without anybody being the wiser. When we were through talking, I'd pass the pole over to her and draw it back when she'd attached her headset."

"By Jingoes!" cried Bill. "I'll say that's clever!"

"It sure is, Howard!" Mary Eliska was quite as enthusiastic. "You certainly deserve to get Marlow Ray after that."

Howard shook his head. "We'll have to do something really clever to get her away from the bunch who are holding her prisoner. Well,—as I say, when I got to my flat, I sat down by my sitting room window, and pretended to read a book. In reality, of course, I was watching Marlow Ray's window. Presently she appeared. Even at that distance, I could see that she had been crying. She held up a slate, for we never dared to use the headphones in the daytime, and slates are a good medium for short messages. On it she had written, '*After dark.*' Well, that was one of the longest afternoons I'd ever put in. About five-thirty, she came back to her window and I passed over the headgear. When I heard her story, I went half crazy, and I guess I've been pretty much that way ever since.

"You see, Mr. Sanborn, Marlow Ray has told me that occasionally she walks in her sleep, especially when she isn't feeling very well. The evening before, that was a week ago Wednesday night, she had a headache and went to bed early. When she awoke, she was terrified to find herself seated on the floor of their living room, behind a large Chinese screen. There seemed to be seven or eight men in the room, including her father. Of course, she could not see them, but she could hear every word they said. By the clock on the wall above her head, she saw that it was one in the morning. She soon realized that this was a meeting of the heads of some large society or organization and that these men had come there from all parts of the world. There was an air of mystery about them and their talk. No names were mentioned but they addressed each other by number. Mr. Ray was Number 5; Number 2, who spoke with a foreign accent, was evidently conducting the meeting, in place of the absent Number 1, whom they all seemed to hold in great awe. Marlow Ray realized that she must have entered the room before the meeting started, while she was still asleep. She saw that so long as the meeting lasted, there would be no way of escape. Gradually she became terrified at her predicament, and—"

"Just a moment," interrupted Ashton Sanborn. "Has Marlow Ray ever told you anything of her father's business?"

"She really knows nothing about it, Mr. Sanborn. I asked her myself some time ago, and she said then, except that he seemed to travel a lot, she hadn't the slightest idea what he did for a living. Once when she asked him outright what is was, Mr. Ray flew into a rage. He said it was his own affair, and that so long as it brought them in enough money to live comfortably, he did not wish her to bring up the matter again. The one thing she does know is that he doesn't go regularly to an office. Men frequently come to see him at the apartment, but their conversations are invariably held behind locked doors."

"I see. Go on now, with Marlow Ray and the meeting."

"Well, sir, as I've said, she was behind that screen, listening to what the men said—and in fact, she couldn't help listening. Not that she understood much of what they were saying. Number 2 made a long speech and the gist of it was that now they were agreed upon the use of Formula X, the demonstration (whatever that was) must be made in their respective sectors at the same time on the same day. He also proposed that Number 5 (Marlow Ray's father) interview Number 1 and learn from him when the demonstrations should be made. This motion was carried unanimously. Then Number 3 asked the chairman if they could not in future hold their meeting in some safer place than the Rays' apartment. 'For all we know,' he said, 'someone may be secreted behind that screen!' Mr. Ray laughed at this, and told Number 3 to close up the screen if it made him nervous. So the first thing Marlow Ray knew, the screen was dragged aside and she was staring into the face of a Chinese. Seated in a circle behind him were the others, her father among them."

"Gosh!" exclaimed Mary Eliska. "I'll bet that scared the poor kid silly."

"It did," admitted Howard. "She was absolutely petrified. And then there was the dickens to pay. All the men started talking at once. The Chinese pulled a revolver and pointed it straight at her, yelling that she had heard their secrets and must be immediately executed!"

"'She has heard nothing!' her father told them. 'She frequently walks in her sleep. She was asleep when she wandered in here before the meeting, and she is sleeping now—look!' Then he lit a match and held the flame before Marlow Ray's eyes. 'You see,' he said, 'she doesn't even blink. Marlow Ray has heard nothing, gentlemen.'"

"Of course Marlow Ray had taken her father's hint, and followed it. She knew that he was doing the only thing he could to save her life, so she kept right on staring in front of her without moving, while the Chinese held the automatic within a foot of her head. But the strain she was under nearly broke her nerve. She knew that the slightest sign on her part that she was conscious would mean a bullet through her brain. A furious argument followed. Most of the men—there were eight of them including Mr. Ray—wanted her put out of the way at once. But at last, her father and Number 2, a big man with a long beard who seemed to be more humane than the rest, prevailed upon them to let him lead her back to her bed. Her father was forbidden to hold any intercourse with her whatsoever. She was locked in her bedroom, afraid even to cry, for fear she would be heard, and not knowing what moment the door would open and they would drag her to her death."

"Horrible!" Mr. Sanborn's pipe had gone out but he didn't seem to notice it. "That experience was enough to unhinge a person's mind. Marlow Ray may be shy and retiring, but she evidently doesn't lack grit. By the way, did she say she recognized any of the men at the meeting?"

"No. She said that without exception she was sure she'd never seen any of them before, although they were all on good terms with her father. Each one seemed to be of a different nationality. One was a dark man who wore a turban—an East Indian, probably. Another, also pretty dark, wore a red fez. The others were apparently Europeans, but as they all spoke English together she had no way of guessing what they were. Number 2, the man with the long brown beard, she thought might be a Scandinavian. She was sure, though, that her father was the only American or Anglo-Saxon in the group." "Tell us what happened next morning," proposed Mary Eliska. Her coffee, now cold, remained untasted in the cup.

"I'm getting to that. At eight o'clock her door was unlocked and a woman, a stranger to her, came into her bedroom with a breakfast tray. She put the tray on a table and went into the bathroom and turned on the water for Marlow Ray's bath, then left the room and locked the door after her. At nine this same woman came back, brought some books and magazines to her, made up the bed and put the room straight. Whenever Marlow Ray spoke to her, she shook her head and put her finger to her lips. But Marlow Ray said that even now she doesn't know whether the woman is actually dumb or only acting under orders. She has brought and taken away her meals ever since, but she has never been able to get her to speak."

"But how did she find out about going to Dr. Winn's house?" asked Bill Bolton, who had shown an interest quite as keen as Mary Eliska's or Sanborn's.

Howard Bright drank a glass of water. "I'm getting to that part now," he explained. "I'm not much of a story teller and I seem to be taking an awful time to get through this one—but I'm doing my best just the same."

"Of course you are!" Mary Eliska motioned Bill to keep quiet. "You're doing nobly, Howard! Pay no attention to that goof over there."

"O.K., Mary Eliska." Howard replaced his empty glass on the table. "At about noon of the first day of Marlow Ray's imprisonment in her room, the door was unlocked and Mr. Lawson came in. She knew him as a friend of her father who had dined with them two or three times. She had always thought him quite a jolly sort of chap and knew that he was private secretary to Dr. Winn, the celebrated chemist. Naturally, she felt rather relieved to see him, and she opened up on him at once. She still felt that her only hope for life and freedom was to pretend absolute ignorance of the happenings of the night before. And she managed to keep up that pretense before Lawson, though what he had to do with the affair she hadn't any idea, nor does she yet know where he comes into the picture. Anyway, he wasn't at the meeting. She let him know, though, that she was very indignant and astonished to find herself kept a prisoner, and demanded to see her father. Lawson, she told me, was most affable and kind to her. He said that she of course did not realize that she had been very ill during the night and that she was now under doctor's orders. He also told her that her father had been called away on business, so he had come to her as an old friend of the family, to be of any help that he could. Marlow Ray said that his sympathy almost undermined her suspicion—she almost confided in him. But luckily, she didn't. He has been to see her every day since, and she is now convinced that his part in this devilish scheme is to gain her confidence, and to find out whether she actually did hear or see anything at the meeting. Yesterday he told her that it had been decided she should visit him and his wife at Dr. Winn's house while her father is away, and that in order to occupy her mind, she should act as secretary to Mrs. Lawson, who assists Dr. Winn in his work."

"Maybe they don't really mean to harm her after all," said Mary Eliska hopefully.

"Marlow Ray is certain," said Howard, "that they want her at the Doctor's for close observation. She took a secretarial course at school, so that part of it is all right, but I believe with her that one slip, one sign that she is deceiving them, will mean that she will simply vanish and never be heard of again. She knows that Lawson lied about one thing: her father is still living in their flat. She has heard his voice several times."

"But what I can't understand," said Mary Eliska, "is why, just as soon as you knew all this, you didn't go to the nearest police station and have that flat raided!"

"Because, Marlow Ray won't hear of it." Howard's tone was thoroughly wretched. "I worked out some other plans to release her, but she refuses to budge."

"Is the girl crazy?" This from Bill.

"No—she's as sane as any of us—maybe saner. She says that if the police are called in or I help her to escape, that crew will believe her father knew all the time that she was faking—as of course he does. And she says she is sure they will have him killed out of hand, once they discover that. To make matters worse, if possible, my firm thinks I'm going to sail for Lima the day after tomorrow! If I turn them down, I'll lose my job here and ruin my future. I've been hoping against hope that something would turn up so Marlow Ray could sail with me. I certainly shall not sail without her. I was buying some clothes for the trip when I ran into you this morning—" Howard's voice trailed off hopelessly.

"Gee!" It was evident that Mary Eliska was not far from tears. "You poor dears are in an awful fix! I do wish I could help you. Do *something*—so that you two could get married and sail for Peru!"

"Perhaps you can." Ashton Sanborn knocked the ashes from his pipe into an ash tray.

"*How?*" shouted three voices simultaneously.

Chapter 4.4
MEET DASH!

"Mary Eliska, have you ever done anything in the way of amateur theatricals?" Ashton Sanborn stroked the bowl of his pipe reflectively.

"Why—er—yes, a little." She looked a bit bewildered. "I've been in the Silvermine Sillies for the past two years."

Sanborn nodded. "How is it you're out of school on a Thursday?" The question seemed irrelevant. He was leaning back in his chair now, surveying the ceiling rather absently, but there was nothing lackadaisical about his crisp tones.

"Christmas holidays. Why?"

"Because, if you're willing, I may want you to work for me for a few days. I suppose I can reach your father by telephone at the New Canaan bank?"

"No, you can't—Daddy is down in Florida on a fishing trip. He's on Mr. Bolton's yacht, somewhere off the coast. They won't be back until Christmas Eve."

"That," said the Secret Service man, "complicates matters. Who, may I ask, is looking after Mary Eliska while her father Albert Stricklin is away?"

"I'm looking after my own sweet self, sir." Mary Eliska grinned roguishly.

"Then who is to take the responsibility for your actions, young lady?"

"Why, you may—if you want to!"

For a moment or two the detective studied her thoughtfully. There was a certain assurance about this girl's manner, a steely quality that came sometimes into her blue eyes, an indefinable air of strength and quiet courage—

"Do you think you could impersonate your cousin, Mary Eliska?"

"Why—of course!" Mary Eliska showed her surprise. "We look exactly alike. Didn't Howard take me for Marlow Ray?"

"He did—but from what he has told us about her, your natures are entirely different. Marlow Ray, from all accounts, is a rather meek and demure young lady. Remember, that in order to convince anyone who knows her you would have to submerge your own personality in hers. And nobody would ever describe *you* as a meek, demure young lady!"

"An untamed wildcat—if you ask me," chuckled Bill.

"Why, thanks a lot, William!" Mary Eliska's hearers were abruptly aware of the changed quality of her voice as she continued to speak in melting tones of pained acceptance. "But nobody *did* ask you, darling, so in future when your betters are conversing, be good enough to button up that lip of yours!" She finished her withering tirade in the same quiet tones and with a positively shrinking demeanor that sent the others into shouts of laughter.

"Say, you're Marlow Ray to a T!" cried Howard. "Her voice is always like that if I happen to hurt her feelings."

"How about her hair, Howard? Is it long or short?"

"Oh, she wears it bobbed like yours."

"I suppose," Mary Eliska said to Mr. Sanborn, "that you want to smuggle me into the flat and have me change places with her?"

"That's the idea exactly," admitted the detective. "And I don't want you to make your decision until I explain my plan in detail—or, rather, the necessity for the risk you will be taking."

"Shoot—" said Mary Eliska, "but I can tell you right now, risk or no risk, I'm going through with it. Marlow Ray, after all she's been through and from what Howard has told us, is bound to flop once she gets to Dr. Winn's. Nervous, and probably high strung, the chances are against her being able to hold up under the strain."

"I think you are right about that. But although Marlow Ray is in serious danger, she could be rescued and her father guarded without bringing you into the picture, Mary Eliska, if it were not for one thing. These men who hold Marlow Ray in their custody are in some way mixed up with Dr. Winn, who has undertaken to make some very important experiments for the United States government."

"I make a bet that he is Number 1 of the gang!" ventured Bill, the irrepressible.

"Very possibly. That has yet to be discovered. But what I want you young people to realize is that this is no ordinary gang. Quite evidently we are up against an international organization. Their treatment of Marlow Ray is concrete evidence of their cold-blooded ruthlessness when they believe their plans to be in jeopardy. If you take your cousin's place, Mary Eliska, of course we will see that you are well guarded, but even so, your part in clearing up this mystery will entail a very great element of risk."

"I'm willing to take the chance." Mary Eliska met his inquiring eyes steadily. "Naturally, I'm sorry for Marlow Ray and I want to help her. The only thing is, I've got to be back at Jackson Hole High School by January fourth."

"I think I can promise you that this job will be cleaned up within a week."

"I reckon," smiled Bill, "that you haven't told us all you know about these lads with numbers instead of names." "Not quite all." Sanborn smiled back at him. "But that is neither here nor there just now. By the way, Mary Eliska, how are you on shorthand and typewriting?"

"Oh, not so worse. It's part of the course I'm taking at Jackson Hole High."

"Good enough. Frankly, young lady, I would not consider using you, had not the Wyoming Bank robbery, the affair of the Mystery Plane and the Conway Case proved conclusively that you have a decided flair for this kind of thing."

"Thank you, sir," said Mary Eliska with mock coyness. "Them kind words is a great comfort to a poor workin' goil. Do I pack a gat wid me, Mister?"

"You do not. In fact, you will take nothing except what belongs to your cousin. If I am able to get you into the Ray flat and they carry you up to Ridgefield in her place, just being Marlow Ray, who never woke up when she was sleepwalking last week will be your best protection. Of course, I'm not deserting you. Either I or some of my men will find means of keeping in touch with you constantly."

"And when the villains scrag me, the secret service boys will arrive on the scene just in time—to identify the deceased! No thank you. If the gun is out of orders, Dash will have to go. Of course my jiu-jitsu may help at a pinch, but Dash is more potent and ever so much quicker."

"What are you talking about, Mary Eliska?" Ashton Sanborn looked puzzled.

"It's a cinch you can't drag a dog along if that's your big idea," declared Bill.

"It is not the big idea, old thing." Mary Eliska grinned wickedly. "Dash and I have got very clubby this fall. He's really quite a dear, you know. We travel about together a lot."

"The mystery of this age," observed Bill, "is how certain females can talk so much and say so little."

"Then," said Mary Eliska cheerfully, "I'll let you solve the mystery right now. Catch!" She tossed him a macaroon from a plate on the table. "Go over to that bedroom door," she commanded. "Stand to one side of the door and throw that thing into the air."

"But, I say, Mary Eliska!" interposed Ashton Sanborn. "This is no time for fooling, we've got—"

"This is not fooling, you dear old fuss-budget," she cut in. "It's—well, it's just something that may save you from worrying so much about me. Now, Bill, are you ready?"

"Anything to please the ladies," retorted that young man wearily. He got up and walked to the far end of the room and took his stand beside the closed door. "Is Dash a cake hound? Will he jump for the cookie?"

"He sure will—toss it in the air."

The small cake went spinning toward the ceiling, and at the same instant Mary Eliska's right hand disappeared under the table. With the speed of legerdemain she brought it into view again and her arm shot out suddenly like a signpost across the white cloth. There was a streak of silver light—and the three male members of the quartet stared at the bedroom door in open-mouthed wonder. Quivering in the very center of its upper panel was a small knife, and impaled on the knife's blade was the macaroon. "Meet Dash!" said Mary Eliska.

"Great suffering snakes!" exploded Bill, plucking out the blade, and examining it. "The thing's a throwing knife."

"Six inches of razor-keen, leaf-shaped blade," said Mary Eliska, "and three inches of carved ivory hilt, beautifully balanced—that's Dash. How do you like him, fellers?"

"You," declared Howard, who was still goggle-eyed with surprise, "you are the most amazing girl I've ever met, Mary Eliska!"

"And you don't know the half of it," said Bill with unstinted fervor.

"Think I can take care of myself at a pinch, Uncle Sanborn?" Mary Eliska was laughing at the expression of astonishment on the detective's face. "You win, young lady." He chuckled softly. "After this I'll keep my worries for Doctor Winn and his friends. Who'd have thought you had anything like that up your sleeve!" "Not up my sleeve, old dear. A little leather sheath strapped just above my left knee is where Dash came from."

"Regular Jesse James stuff, eh?" remarked Bill as he handed back the knife. "Oh, yeah?" Dash disappeared as quickly as he'd come, and Mary Eliska stood up. "What's on the boards, now, boss?" she asked sweetly.

"Howard—" said Ashton Sanborn, "will you let me have the key to that apartment of yours? Thanks. Bill and I will need it this afternoon, and even if things go according to Hoyle, we'll be powerful busy. In the meantime, I've got a job for you and Mary Eliska." He took out his pocketbook and extracting a sheaf of bills, handed them to the girl.

"You and Howard are going to have a busy afternoon, too. See that you're back here in time for dinner at seven, and—"

"But what under the sky-blue canopy is all this?" Mary Eliska was thumbing the bills, counting them. "Why, I've never seen so much money—"

"Use it to buy your cousin a trousseau. Have the things sent to Mrs. Howard Bright's apartment at this hotel. And remember, that when she arrives here, Marlow Ray will have nothing but the clothes she is wearing. You don't mind doing this, do you?"

"Mind! Why, I'll love it!" Mary Eliska turned a dazzling smile on Howard, who was simply tongue-tied by the detective's announcement. "Isn't he swell, Howard? Isn't he some guy?" Ashton Sanborn laughed. "Don't thank me. Uncle Sam is paying, so you needn't bring back any change."

Mary Eliska thrust the money into her purse. "Don't worry, old bean, I won't. So long, you two. Come on, Howard, we're going to have a beautiful afternoon!" She caught young Bright by the arm and whirled him across the room to the coat-rack. She jammed a bright green beret over her right ear and slung her leopard-cat coat onto her shoulders. "All set for Fifth Avenue!" she called out merrily as she preceded Howard out of the room.

Chapter 4.5
ON SECRET SERVICE

To say that Mary Eliska enjoyed her afternoon's shopping would be putting it mildly. Give any girl plenty of money and tell her to go out and buy an entire trousseau for herself—or even for somebody else—and watch her jump at the chance!

Howard trailed along in more or less of a daze. This sudden change in his outlook; being drawn from the depths of despondency to the hope of a future with the girl he loved, and all in the space of a couple of hours, was a little too much for him to realize at once. Ever after, he had but a hazy recollection of that shopping tour. The afternoon seemed but a whirling maze of lingerie, stockings, street dresses, party frocks, coats, hats, shoes and accessories, upon which his advice was invariably asked, and never taken.

They were bowling hotel-wards in a taxi, jammed with cardboard boxes and packages of various shapes and sizes, before he returned to normal.

"Whew!" he looked at Mary Eliska. "I should think you'd be dead!"

She shook her head and laughed. "No girl ever gets tired of shopping," she told him gaily. "Wait 'til you're married—you'll find out."

"But what's the idea of bringing all these things back with us? I thought Mr. Sanborn said to have them sent."

"He did—but I have a better idea. This is part of it. I'll tell you all about it when we get to the hotel. Keep still now—I want to go over the lists and see if I've forgotten anything!"

Howard sighed in resignation.

At the hotel desk they learned that Ashton Sanborn had not returned as yet, but had left word that they should go to his rooms. With the assistance of three bellboys, they piled themselves and their packages into the elevator.

"Gee! This looks like the night before Christmas!" Howard dropped his hat and overcoat and stared at the boxes and bundles piled along the wall of the sitting room. "Marlow Ray certainly will be surprised when she sees all those things!"

Mary Eliska pulled off her close-fitting little hat, and tossed it with her purse and coat onto the table. Then she sank into an easy-chair. "Well, I only hope she'll approve. My, this was a strenuous afternoon. You'd better sit down."

Howard followed her advice. "You said it. But I know Marlow Ray—she'll be crazy about the things you've bought."

"Oh, you boys are all alike." Mary Eliska yawned unashamedly.

"I don't get you.""What I mean is that as soon as a fellow goes around with a girl for a while, he invariably says 'Oh yes, she'll like this,' or, 'she won't like that'."

"And—?" "Ninety-nine times out of a hundred you guess wrong."

"Why?"

"I think it's because girls like to do their own choosing. Especially when it comes to buying clothes. Well, anyway, I think the things are darling, and they'll be becoming, too. At least they look well on me."

"Don't worry—those clothes will make her look like a million dollars."

"I know they will. I'm tired, I guess." Mary Eliska yawned again and closed her eyes.

Howard started to say something, thought better of it, yawned, and let his head pillow itself on the soft upholstery.

Three quarters of an hour later, Ashton Sanborn and Bill Bolton marched into the room to find the two shoppers sound asleep in their respective chairs. The detective coughed discreetly and both the young people awoke.

"I see that you've brought your spoils back with you," he smiled, pointing to the boxes and bundles. Mary Eliska stared at him, only half awake, then sat upright in her chair as she realized where she was.

"Looks to me," said Bill, getting out of his overcoat, "as if she thought Marlow Ray was going to start a shop of her own. Why did you cart all the stuff back here instead of having it sent?"

"Because, Mr. Inquisitive—well, just because. You and Howard run along now and prepare your handsome selves for dinner. The principles of this piece are going into conference now."

"My *word*—" began Bill, but at a shake of the head from Sanborn, he took the still drowsy Howard by the arm and together they disappeared into the bedroom.

"Pretty tough time you've had, I expect?" Mr. Sanborn's eyes twinkled, though his tone was grave. "Oh, but it was lots of fun," cried Mary Eliska. "Thanks to Uncle Sam, and Uncle Sanborn! And look here, I've got a great idea."

"Which has to do with your bringing back the packages yourself?"

"Quite right, it has. Do you think those boys can hear what we're saying?"

"I doubt it, Mary Eliska—but Bill, as you probably guessed at the end of the affair of the Winged Cartwheels, is a full-fledged member of my organization and—"

"Oh, I don't mind Bill," she interrupted in a low tone. "But Howard mustn't get wind of it. He might make a fuss."

She rose from her chair and going over to the detective, began to whisper in his ear.

"But that's impossible, Mary Eliska!" he protested, although he allowed a smile to come to his eyes. "And what's more, my dear, I'm afraid it would be illegal."

"Oh, no, it wouldn't! Not if you—" And again she brought her lips close to his ear.

"You're a young scamp!" he laughed as she ended. "But—well—you're doing a great deal for me, so—"

"So you'll go downstairs and start telephoning right away!" she prompted eagerly.

Ashton Sanborn held up his hands in mock despair. "Nieces," he declared, "should not badger hard-working old uncles. But since this niece has been a good girl today, Uncle will do as he's asked."

"I shall never call you anything else but Uncle Sanborn, now," Mary Eliska cried delightedly.

"Thanks, my child, and I'll do my best for you."

"Angel uncles can do no more," she laughed.

"Right-o. I'll be on my way, then. Come along in about fifteen minutes with Bill and Howard. I'll arrange for a table for dinner and meet you three in Peacock Alley." The detective caught up his hat and hurried out of the room.

Although Mr. Sanborn was a perfect host, and did all he could to make that dinner entertaining, he confessed later that he would always consider it one of the few failures of an otherwise unblemished career.

Notwithstanding the delicious food, the charm and beauty of the huge room with its lights and music and scores of well-dressed men and beautifully gowned women, the dinner was not a success. All three of the young people were too excited by thoughts of what would happen later to do justice to the meal. Mary Eliska, moreover, had the added annoyance of feeling that her tailored frock, smart enough for luncheon or shopping, was definitely not the thing to wear at dinner in a fashionable hotel. Each endeavored to be sprightly and at ease. But since they knew that the one thing they wanted to talk about was forbidden in public, conversation flagged. Upstairs at last in Mr. Sanborn's sitting room, he came directly to the point.

"Now I know you're just rearing to go," he said. "And perhaps the sooner we get under way, the better." He turned to Bill. "You go ahead with Howard," he ordered. "Mary Eliska and I will follow you in about ten minutes. Go straight to the apartment. We'll meet you there."

"O and likewise K, boss," Bill returned. "Get into your rubbers, Howard. And don't look so gloomy. You're on your way to meet your best girl, remember."

When they had gone, Mary Eliska turned at once to the detective. "How about it, Uncle Sanborn?" she asked eagerly.

"To quote Bill, 'O and likewise K,' niece."

"Gee, you *are* a dear!" Mary Eliska clapped her hands. "And now that that is that—I don't care what happens."

"But I do, Mary Eliska." Ashton Sanborn was serious. "Listen to me, young lady. From now on you're working for the U. S. government, under me, and I must have my orders obeyed to the letter."

"Yes, sir, I understand." Mary Eliska's tone was crisp and business-like.

"Good. I let those chaps go ahead of us as there is no need of having us all arrive at that apartment house at the same time. This afternoon, Bill and I made all arrangements, so that you can change places with your cousin shortly after you arrive."

Mary Eliska felt secretly proud that this keen-eyed secret service man took her at her word, and did not ask her again if she were really willing to go through with it. "May I ask you a question?"

"Certainly."

"Well, suppose that after you manage to get me into Marlow Ray's room, she refuses to leave it. Do you want me to force her?"

"Heavens, no." Sanborn laughed. "That has all been taken care of, Mary Eliska. I talked to your cousin by means of Howard's headphone set shortly after dark this afternoon. I explained the whole thing to her and when she understood that her father would be brought into no extra danger because of our plan, and that I had drafted you into becoming a secret service operative, she consented."

"I'm glad of that," said Mary Eliska fervently. "She could easily have misunderstood and spoiled everything."

"Well, we'll have a lot to do to put it over, even though Marlow Ray is willing. I persuaded her that by doing exactly what you told her, once you arrived, she would be serving her country like a loyal American. You, of course, will use your own judgment, when you see her. The principal thing is to change clothes and get her out the way you came just as soon as possible."

"But how am I to get into the Rays' apartment?"

"Good soldiers, Mary Eliska, do not ask questions. There's no secret about it, but I've other things to tell you now. Lawson will probably come for you—or for Marlow Ray, as he will believe you to be. He is a tall, slender man, about thirty, rather good-looking, dark curly hair and a small mustache. Your Uncle Michael, if you should run into him, is heavy set and rather short. He has reddish hair, turning grey, and is clean shaven. Marlow Ray has never met either Doctor Winn, or Mrs. Lawson. Now just a word about the lady. She is a very beautiful and a very clever woman. Be on your guard with her, continually. I believe that the principal reason that you, or rather, Marlow Ray, will be taken to Ridgefield, is so that you may be studied at first hand by this woman. There is no need for me to tell you to keep up the Marlow Ray personality day and night. Incidentally, you will have only a very short time to study your cousin, so make the most of it. Well," he concluded, "I guess that's about all. You will receive further orders within the next day or two. In the meantime, simply carry on as Marlow Ray. I am taking a great responsibility in letting you go, my dear. For I won't hide the fact that you'd probably be safer in a den of rattlesnakes than in the same house with Mr. and Mrs. Lawson."

"I'm not afraid, you know," said Mary Eliska simply and smiled up at him.

"I know you're not. But it would really be better if you were. For then you'd be much more careful, and you must watch your step every minute until I get you out of it. Here's your coat. Slip into it and we'll get going. The sooner I get you safely into Marlow Ray's room, and that young lady out of it, the easier will your Uncle Sanborn feel."

Chapter 4.6
WHO'S WHO?

The December evening was cold and wet as Mary Eliska and Ashton Sanborn crossed the sidewalk and entered their taxi-cab. The day had been a dreary one, and now a dense, drizzling fog lay low upon the great city. Dun-colored clouds drooped over a muddy Park Avenue as they were swept up town. On the side streets the electrics were but misty splotches of diffused light which threw feeble circular glimmers upon the slimy pavements. The yellow glare from shopwindows streamed out into the chill, vaporous air, and threw a murky, shifting radiance across the crowded thoroughfare. To Mary Eliska there was something eerie and ghostlike in the endless procession of faces which flitted across these narrow bars of light. She was not in any respect a timid girl, but the dull, heavy evening, and the prospect of the strange venture in which they were engaged, combined to make her feel nervous and depressed.

At 59th street the taxi turned west and rolled steadily along the shining black asphalt, stopping now and then for the red lights. They crossed 5th Avenue and swung into Central Park. Mary Eliska caught glimpses of the gaunt shapes of trees in silhouette against the cold fog. She closed her eyes and resolutely turned her thoughts to the events of the afternoon.

So engrossed had she become in the contemplation of her delightful buying orgy that she was surprised when their cab pulled up with a jerk and Ashton Sanborn opened the door.

"Muffle up in your fur collar, Mary Eliska," he said. "The fewer people who see your face, the better."

Now that the ordeal had arrived, Mary Eliska's nervousness vanished. She buried the lower part of her face in the soft fur collar and walked at Mr. Sanborn's side into the lobby of the apartment house.

A man in brass buttoned uniform stood by the elevator. Two shining rows of white teeth flashed in a smile of greeting for the detective.

"All the way up, George." Mr. Sanborn gave the order as the car started upward.

"Yaas, suh, boss, I understand." George smiled again, and presently the elevator stopped.

With Mr. Sanborn in the lead, Mary Eliska walked along a corridor and up a narrow flight of stairs. The detective opened a door at the top and the damp cold of the night swept in upon them. A moment later they were crossing the flat roof of the apartment house toward a small group who stood near the parapet at the roof's edge. As they drew nearer, she saw that the group awaiting them was composed of Bill Bolton, Howard, and a stranger. They were standing beside a small crane. The secret service man nodded a greeting and turned to Mary Eliska. "We are directly above Marlow Ray's window, which is three flights below," he said quietly, and glanced at the luminous dial of his wrist-watch.

"And you're going to let me down with the auto-crane?" she asked with just a tremor of excitement in her voice.

"That's the idea. It's perfectly safe. Bill tested it this afternoon."

Mary Eliska gave a little laugh. "Oh, I'm not scared, Uncle Sanborn."

"I know you aren't, my dear."

"When do I take off?"

"Whenever you're ready."

"All set now, then, please."

"Good. You'll go in a minute. Here are last instructions. You will seat yourself in that swinging seat that Bill is holding. The cable to which it is attached runs through the pulley at the end of the crane's arm. This building is nine stories high. The Rays' flat is on the seventh floor, you remember, so Marlow Ray's window is the third one down." He moved to the low parapet and leaned over. "The window is dark, so everything is O.K.," he said, coming back to her. "Pull your seat in with you when you enter, Mary Eliska, and pull down the shade, of course, when the light is turned on. When Marlow Ray is ready, switch off the light again and have her give a couple of pulls on this guide rope." He placed the rope in her hand. "Then we will hoist her up. Ready for your hop now?"

"Yes, thanks."

"Good luck, then. And remember that although you may not see us, I or some of my men will be near you all the time."

Mary Eliska shook hands with her three friends and stepped into her swinging seat. She sat down, steadying herself with a grip on the cable.

"All serene?" asked Bill.

"Shove off!" said Mary Eliska.

Bill motioned to the stranger, there came the low whir of an electric motor. Her feet left the roof and she felt herself swung upward. Then the ascent stopped, the arm of the crane swung outward and with it her pendant seat. Her feet cleared the parapet and she was over the narrow airshaft. Blurred lights from closed windows of the various apartments gave her a glimpse of many empty ashcans in the small courtyard far below. But the crane was lowering her now close to the wall of the building. She was facing the wall, and looking upward she made out four heads leaning over the parapet at the edge of the roof. The descent was slow, but at last she passed two windows and came to rest beside the third, whose lower sash she saw was open. Then two arms caught her about the knees and she was pulled into the room. "Mary Eliska—oh, Mary Eliska!" sobbed an excited voice so like her own that Mary Eliska gave a start.

"Well, here I am, Marlow Ray." It was a prosaic reply, but her own heart was beating quickly, nevertheless. "Gee, it's dark in here! Be a dear and shut down the window on this cable—and draw the shade, then turn on the light. I'm busy getting out of this thing."

She heard the window and shade come down with a rush. As she stepped free of her conveyance, the lights flashed on, and the cousins flew into each other's arms. "Marlow Ray!" "Mary Eliska!" For a long moment the girls hugged each other and Marlow Ray, the more over-wrought, sobbed on her cousin's shoulder. Mary Eliska was herself deeply touched, but managed to control her feelings. "Come, dear," she said at last. "We'll just have to get going, I guess. They're waiting for you on the roof—and somebody is likely to come to the door. We mustn't be caught together, you know."

"I know it." Marlow Ray released her and again Mary Eliska gasped, for she heard her own voice speaking although the words came from Marlow Ray.

"Look, Mary Eliska!" Marlow Ray pointed to a long mirror in the corner of the room. "I knew that we were a lot alike, but I never could have believed—"

"Well, talk about two peas in a pod!" In the glass Mary Eliska saw herself standing beside her cousin; and had it not been that she wore a coat and hat, while Marlow Ray was dressed in a wine-colored silk frock, she would have had difficulty in knowing which was her own reflection. "Maybe I'm half an inch taller, or hardly that," she said after a bit. "Lucky we both have had our hair shingled. You wear a bang, though—but that's easily fixed."

She whipped off her small hat and went over to the dressing table where she picked up a pair of nail scissors. Two minutes of snipping and Marlow Ray's bang was duplicated on her own forehead. The hair she had cut off had been carefully placed on a magazine cover and opening the window a trifle she dropped the ends into the night.

"Now," she said, closing the window. "You and I had better change clothes, Marlow Ray. And we'll have to make it snappy."

"Yes—and oh dear—" Marlow Ray was slipping off her dress—"I've got so much to talk about. You can't realize what a horrible time I've had—and then to find you, only to lose you again!" Marlow Ray was very near to tears.

"But you won't lose me long," Mary Eliska flashed her a comforting smile as she got out of her own dress. "Meanwhile, you'll have Howard. He's waiting on the roof, now. And Ashton Sanborn says he can clear up this business in a few days."

"You certainly are wonderfully brave to do this for me," sighed her cousin. "If Mr. Sanborn hadn't insisted that by changing places with you I'd be really helping the government, I couldn't allow you to do it. As it is, I feel I'm cowardly to go through with it—"

"Why, you're nothing of the sort," Mary Eliska protested. While Marlow Ray talked and they both undressed, she watched her cousin's mannerisms, storing away in her memory, for future use, every gesture, and inflection of the voice so like her own.

"Who's who?" she giggled, and now her tone was softer, an exact duplication of Marlow Ray's manner of speaking.

Her cousin smiled. "In our undies," she admitted, "even I am beginning to wonder if I'm not seeing double and talking to myself. How about shoes and stockings, Mary Eliska?"

"Chuck 'em over, Marlow Ray, we'd better do it up right. I sp'ose most of your things are packed in that wardrobe trunk over there?"

"Yes. I packed it this afternoon. You'll find some handkerchiefs and gloves in the top bureau drawer. I left the trunk open on purpose. When Mr. Lawson comes, you might be putting them in—it would help to make things natural." "Right you are—that's a good idea."

"My arctics and my hat and coat are in the closet. Your coat is much better looking than mine. It's a shame to take it from you."

"What's a coat between cousins who love each other?" laughed Mary Eliska and put on Marlow Ray's dress.

A few minutes later, the change of clothing had been made, and the girls regarded each other in awed wonder.

"I'll bet," Mary Eliska declared, "that when Howard sees you he'll think I've come back again." Marlow Ray blushed. "Well, he'll soon find out different. But it's a shame to leave you here, darling. If there were *only* some other way!"

"But there isn't. So cut along now, and just remember that this kind of thing is my stuff—I love it."

"Someday I'll make it up to you—if I ever can!"

Mary Eliska hesitated for a moment, then smiled. "You can do it tonight, if you want to." "Why—what do you mean?"

"Just follow any suggestions that Mr. Sanborn may make."

"But, what does that—you're hiding something from me!"

"Perhaps I am." "What is it?" "Never mind, now."

"But, Mary Eliska—"

"No time for that, Marlow Ray. Get into that swing arrangement with your back to the window."

"All right, but kiss me goodbye, first."

They held each other close for a second. Then as Marlow Ray took her place on the seat attached to the steel cable, Mary Eliska switched off the light. "I'll—I'll do as you ask, I mean, about Mr. Sanborn," whispered Marlow Ray.

"Thanks, darling, I—" began Mary Eliska, her hand on the window sash ready to raise it. Then suddenly she stopped.

Somebody was unlocking the door into the hall.

Mary Eliska ran to the door and caught hold of the knob. "Who's there?" she cried.

"It's I—Martin Lawson, Marlow Ray. May I come in?"

"Oh, please, Mr. Lawson, not right now." There was a soft tone of pleading in her voice. "You see, I've been lying down and I'm not quite dressed." "But I thought I heard you speaking."

"You did." The real Marlow Ray, shivering by the window, caught her breath and heard Mary Eliska's tone sharpen slightly. "To myself. Being cooped up like this for hours on end, I'm glad to hear the sound of my own voice. I often read aloud. But I'll be ready shortly, if you want me."

"All right, then. I'll be back in five minutes. Your father is here and he wants to say goodbye."

The key turned in the lock and with her ear close to the panel Mary Eliska was sure she could hear the faint tread of footsteps retreating down the hall. With her heart pumping sixty to the second, she dashed back to Marlow Ray and carefully raised the window. "Heavens! that was a narrow squeak—" her cousin whispered shakily. "What nerve you've got! I nearly fainted—"

"Never mind," Mary Eliska whispered back, "you've got to get out of here—and right now!"

"Oh, but I can't, Mary Eliska. I'm afraid!"

Mary Eliska gave the signal rope two savage pulls. Almost immediately the cable began to tighten. "Close your eyes and hang on with both hands," she ordered.

"But Mary Eliska—I'll scream—I'm going to—I know it!"

"No, you won't!" Quickly Mary Eliska clasped the frightened girl's fingers around the taut cable. A dive into the pocket of Marlow Ray's coat brought forth her own handkerchief which she hurriedly crumpled into a ball and thrust into her cousin's mouth. The seat, with Marlow Ray in it, was rising slowly. She caught the paralyzed girl below the knees, steadied her as the crane drew its burden clear of the sill and pushed her carefully into the outer darkness. When Marlow Ray's feet were on a level with the upper sash, she pulled down the window and shade and switched on the light again.

"Skies above!" Her breath came in short gasps and she leaned against the end of the bed to steady herself. "Talk about your thrills! That was worse than my first solo hop, by a long shot." She ran her fingers through her short hair. "Let's see—what next? Oh, yes—I was supposed to be lying down."

She caught up a book from the table and tossed it open onto the bed. Then she lay down, rumpled the coverlet, made sure that the pillow showed the impression of her head, and sprang up again. An adventurous past had taught her the need of being thorough.

She went to the window and raising it, looked out and upward. Neither Marlow Ray nor the crane were in sight. Thankful that her cousin was safe at last, she pulled down the sash.

Chapter 4.7
PLAYING A PART

Two or three minutes later, when the door was unlocked, the two men who entered surprised her in the business of packing the contents of the top bureau drawer into Marlow Ray's wardrobe trunk. And now came as pretty a piece of acting as has ever been seen upon the stage; acting that Mary Eliska's audience of two must not realize was acting, and furthermore, one of these men was the father of the girl she impersonated. Why hadn't she remembered to ask Marlow Ray what she called that mysterious father of hers? Father, Papa, Dad, Daddy—which should she use? A mistake now would be fatal. Even her uncle must not become aware of her real identity. There was no time for hesitating. He was speaking now. "Marlow Ray, my dear—" he began.

Mary Eliska ran to her uncle and throwing her arms about his neck, buried her head on his shoulder. "How could you leave me like this?" she wailed. "Why do you let these people keep me locked in my room? And now they are going to take me away!" Her voice grew louder, almost hysterical. She sobbed pathetically and clutched him a little tighter.

"My dear child—you mustn't cry this way—you really mustn't!" Mr. Ray patted her back in the silly way men do when they want to be comforting. "Mr. Lawson and his wife will look after you in the country, while your Daddy is away."

She released the embarrassed man, and pulling a handkerchief from his breast pocket, dabbed her eyes with the cambric until she felt certain they looked bloodshot enough to pass inspection. "But I don't *want* to go, Daddy. Please don't let them take me," she begged, her voice trembling as though she was using all her will power to gain self-control. "If you can't take me with you, why can't I go back to school?"

"But that's impossible, Marlow Ray. You are going to be Mrs. Lawson's secretary. Don't be foolish. All arrangements have been made."

"Well, I'm eighteen," said Mary Eliska with a show of temper. "My mother was a year younger than that when she ran away and married you. I am no longer a child. I don't like being packed off like—like a bag of potatoes."

"Are there any other reasons why you don't want to come to Ridgefield with me?" Mr. Lawson spoke for the first time. His words fairly dripped with suspicion.

"Yes, there are." Mary Eliska turned on him angrily. "Daddy goes off on a trip, and for reasons which appear to be a secret, you keep me locked in my room for more than a week, Mr. Lawson. And you seem to wonder why I resent it."

"But you have been ill, my dear Marlow Ray."

"If I'm so ill, why has no doctor been to see me?" Her voice was full of scorn. "I have been keeping you under observation myself."

"Quite possibly. I've been allowed to see nobody except that maid who acts as if she were deaf and dumb. If you are trying to tell me that I'm mentally deranged, I won't stand for it! The mere fact that you now propose that I act as your wife's secretary proves that you consider me capable. What right have you to keep me a prisoner in my own home? Who are you, Mr. Martin Lawson, to take upon yourself the regulating of my life?" Mary Eliska burst into angry tears. "But my *dear* child—" protested Mr. Ray. "I've never seen you behave like this—"

"No! And up to now," she stormed, her eyes flashing, "you've never given me cause. In the first place I'm no longer a child—you forget that—and then—what kind of a life did you give me as a child? You are my father and you say that you love me, but can you expect deep affection from a daughter whom you ship to boarding school at five? You wouldn't even let me visit friends during the holidays. For years at a time you never took the trouble to come and see me. How can you expect love and obedience after years of neglect?" She drew a sobbing breath, then went on: "For a while we traveled—you were nice to me—I enjoyed it. We settled down here. I forgave what you'd done to my childhood. I tried to make this flat a home for you, even though I was kept like a cloistered nun and you allowed me no friends. But this is going too far."

"And what, may I ask, are you going to do about it?" inquired Lawson with a disagreeable smile.

"What can a defenseless girl without friends do to stop two big bullies? I shall go with you, Mr. Lawson, because I can't help myself. But don't expect me to like being used as a slave, even though I may be of some comfort to that long-suffering wife of yours. Oh, that makes you angry, does it? Well, let me tell you, that you are not half as angry as I am. You can practice your strong-arm methods on defenseless women and get away with it—someday you'll try it on a man—and by the time he gets through thrashing you there won't be enough left for the boneyard." She flashed a smile of contempt on the furious man, and turned to Mr. Ray who was speaking again.

"What has come over you, Marlow Ray?" he was saying. "I've never heard you speak so rudely to anyone before. You've always been such a quiet little mouse—"

"And you've taken advantage of it," she interrupted. "What you forget is that even a mouse will turn and fight when it's cornered. If you really loved me—if you had a spark of manhood in your selfish body, you'd thrash this man to within an inch of his life and throw him into the street. Get out of here—both of you!" she cried hysterically. "And please—no more silly arguments—I don't want to be forced to say before outsiders what a contemptible person my father is proving himself to be."

This last tirade seemed to stun Mr. Ray. From the almost agonized expression on his face, she saw that at last conscience was at work. The man was utterly miserable. He could not hide it.

"Will you—will you be ready to leave in half an hour, Marlow Ray?" His voice was a mere whisper and shook with suppressed feeling. "Yes, I'll be ready. Go now, please—both of you!" She turned her back on them and walking over to the window, she threw up the shade and the sash. As she stood there staring into the night, she heard them leave the room.

This time the door shut without being locked. Mary Eliska streaked across the floor and pressed her ear to the keyhole. Just outside the men were talking.

"You're a fool, Lawson, if you still think that Marlow Ray wasn't asleep during the meeting," she heard her uncle say. "Tonight proves it. And let me tell you this. From now on, my business and my home shall be kept separate and distinct. Never again will I allow myself to be placed in a position to be dressed down by my own daughter. There was no comeback either. Every word she said was gospel truth. It's a terrible thing when a daughter makes her father realize what a low, cowardly creature he is at heart. Well, how about it? Aren't you now convinced of her innocence?"

"I am." Lawson clipped off the words, and as he went on speaking, there was insolence as well as a hint of nervousness in his tone. "But when it comes to giving me a thrashing, Number 5—well, I shouldn't try it if I were you—not if you value your—er—health!"

"Stop talking like a fool!" retorted Marlow Ray's father. "Is the girl to be sent to Ridgefield or not?"

"Now you're talking rot, yourself," snapped Lawson. "You know quite as well as I do that Laura won't take our word for it. She told me this morning that any clever woman or girl for that matter, could twist a man around her finger without half trying. Laura wants to study your daughter herself—and that's all there is to it."

"I hope Mrs. Lawson has a pleasant time of it." Mr. Ray said sarcastically. "But I'm afraid my hope will not be granted."

"Laura," answered that lady's husband, "can be rather disagreeable herself when she's roused. Let us hope for Marlow Ray's sake, that she doesn't try her tantrums on my wife. By the way, what are you doing now?"

"Getting away just as fast as I can, thank you. No more scenes for me, tonight. I wouldn't meet Marlow Ray on her way out of here for a million dollars!"

They moved farther along the hall and Mary Eliska went slowly back to the window. Across the narrow court, two flights up, the shaded windows of Howard Bright's flat shone a dull golden yellow in the black wall. For several minutes she stood watching the windows, her thoughts upon what she had done and what she had just heard.

Suddenly, shadows appeared on one of the yellow rectangles. The shade was raised and framed in the window were Marlow Ray and Howard. Just behind them stood a stranger who wore the round, conventional collar of a clergyman. The young couple were smiling happily. Both waved, and Marlow Ray held up her left hand. Mary Eliska knew the significance of that gesture, and threw them a kiss. Then she saw the shade roll down, and she turned away.

"And so they were married and lived happily ever after." She sighed. "Uncle Sanborn kept his promise, like the fine old sport he is."

She stuffed the last of Marlow Ray's belongings into the trunk, slammed it shut and locked it. "Now for the dirty work—and Laura Lawson." She smiled grimly and went to the closet for Marlow Ray's hat and coat.

Chapter 4.8
"WALK INTO MY PARLOR"

The sedan, with Martin Lawson driving and Mary Eliska beside him, purred smoothly through the dank, cold night. Now that they were past the realm of traffic lights, it lopped off the miles between them and Ridgefield with the regularity of an electric saw cutting planks from a log. During the entire journey, now nearly over, Mary Eliska had spoken no word to the man beside her. She wanted him to believe that she was still furiously angry. As a matter of fact, she had felt antagonistic toward him from the first moment she laid eyes upon him;

his smug overgrooming, the highly polished fingernails, the small waxed moustache and too immaculate clothing, all repelled her. She knew at once what it had taken Marlow Ray some time to realize: Martin Lawson might be and probably was a very clever man; he was, on the other hand, a man to be wary of. His manner was just a little too complacent, too smooth. Notwithstanding the forewarning she had received regarding his character, Mary Eliska knew instinctively that he was not genuine and not a trustworthy person in any respect. She detested him thoroughly.

He was a careful driver, she gave him credit for that. They found little traffic to impede their progress along the Boston Post Road, once the long tentacles of the great city were left behind. But the black swath of highway leading out and on from their moisture-coated headlights glistened wetly in their reflection. After they turned into the hills behind Stamford, heading for the Connecticut Ridge Country, the road for a mile or more at a stretch was covered with wet leaves. They crawled along at a snail's pace to prevent skidding and a crash into the New England stone fences that rambled along the roadside dividing woodland from the rolling meadows.

Just beyond New Canaan, they drove past Mary Eliska's home and Bill Bolton's, for the properties faced each other across the ridge road. Before they reached Vista it was raining dismally, and Lawson had the windshield wiper going. Mary Eliska was thankful that the sixty-mile journey from New York was nearly over. At last they reached the outskirts of Ridgefield, and the car swung into a driveway between high pillars of native stonework. In the glow from the electric globes on the gate posts, the blue stone driveway curved and twisted like a huge snake, winding through landscaped lawns and gardens as formal and precise as a public park.

It was raining harder now, and Mary Eliska could see nothing beyond the path of their headlights. Although she had never been in the grounds before, she had driven past the Winn place numbers of times. Finally, she made out the bulk of a great stone house. Martin Lawson stopped the car beneath a porte-cochere. They had arrived. Massive doors of wrought iron and glass swung open. A butler and two footmen in livery ran down the steps. The butler, a tall, important-looking individual, snapped open the car door. "Good evening, Mr. Lawson," he said. "Good evening, Miss."

The voice with its high-pitched Oxford drawl still smacked of Whitechapel. Mary Eliska, who had traveled in England, was sure that under stress, the cockney in this personage would come out. She knew he was careful of his aitches.

"Good evening, Tunbridge," Lawson returned briskly, and Mary Eliska smiled pleasantly. "Is Mrs. Lawson still up?"

"Madam is awaiting you in the library, sir." Tunbridge helped Mary Eliska to alight and handed Marlow Ray's overnight bag to a footman. "Jones," he said to the other flunky, as Lawson stepped out of the car, "drive around to the service entrance. Marlow Ray's box is in the back of the car. See that it is taken up to the Pink Bedroom and have Hanley garage the motor-car."

"Very good, sir," returned the man, and he got into the automobile.

Tunbridge ushered them up the broad stone steps. Mary Eliska caught a last glimpse of a leafless, dripping hedge across the drive, and the giant skeleton arms of a tree that seemed to menace earth and sky; then she entered the house, wondering what the next act of this strange drama would bring forth.

She found herself in an enormous hall, furnished with objects such as she had never seen outside a museum. Elaborately carved oak, suits of armor, stone urns, portraits, a wide stone staircase mounting upward to surrounding galleries, stained glass windows, tigers' and lions' heads, antlers of tremendous size, strange and beautiful weapons, all ranged in confusion before her eyes and suggested a baronial castle rather than the home of an American scientist, in the Connecticut hills.

Tunbridge led to a door on the right, where he knocked, then opened, as a muffled "Come in" was heard.

"Marlow Ray and Mr. Lawson, Madam," announced the butler, and he stood aside to let them pass.

Mary Eliska walked into a room whose walls seemed built of books. The furniture was richly attractive and looked luxuriously comfortable. A fire blazed in a fine chimney and a table near it was set with a glitter of splendid silver and hot water plates below shining metal covers.

A tall, superbly beautiful woman, with dark eyes and coal-black hair that grew in a widow's peak on her brow, rose from a chair on the wide hearth and came toward them. Her clear, white skin, and a broad streak of silver across the black hair gave her a strangely ethereal appearance, as though she might have been a being from another planet. The hand she held out to Mary Eliska was exquisitely formed, the fingers long and tapering.

"How do you do, Marlow Ray," she said pleasantly. "Welcome to Winncote. You are later than we expected. The Doctor has gone to bed, but he left his greetings."

"Thank you," Mary Eliska returned formally and shook hands. "You are very kind, Mrs. Lawson."

Laura Lawson gave her a smile, but the girl saw that it was a smile of the lips alone, her dark eyes remained somber. "Did you have a breakdown?" she asked her husband, taking notice of him for the first time.

"Slippery roads—it was impossible to do much more than crawl, Laura." He lifted a dish cover on the table and inspected its contents. "Glad you thought to order supper—I'm famished."

"So am I," admitted his wife and her words seemed to carry a double meaning. "It's long after three. Come over here by the fire and get warm, Marlow Ray. Now Tunbridge—if you'll please serve us?"

Tunbridge seated them at the supper table and uncovered the dishes.

"Just a light meal," announced the hostess, "scrambled eggs, toast and cocoa, but it will warm you up and help you last until breakfast."

"It looks delicious!" said Mary Eliska, who discovered at the sight of food that she was starving. In fact all three were hungry, and for some little time conversation was dropped while the soft-footed Tunbridge waited upon them.

"We will have a chat tomorrow, Marlow Ray," Mrs. Lawson said presently. "Tonight you are tired and so am I. We take breakfast in our rooms. Ring for it when you're ready, but don't hurry about getting up, I'll see you down here about eleven-thirty. Have you had enough to eat and drink, my dear?"

"Plenty, thank you, Mrs. Lawson." Mary Eliska thought it would be just as well if she played the demure mouse until she had a chance to size up her employer.

"Then I think we'll go upstairs, Marlow Ray, and I'll show you your room." She looked at her husband. "You'll be coming up soon, Martin?"

"Just as soon as I finish this pipe, and get a bit warmer."

"I think," said Mrs. Lawson, "that both you and Marlow Ray had better take a hot lemonade before you go to bed. I don't want to have you both laid up with colds tomorrow." She smiled solicitously at the girl.

"I hate the filthy stuff," protested her husband.

"Don't be ridiculous," she answered coldly and turned to the butler. "Tunbridge, have hot lemonades sent to Marlow Ray and Mr. Lawson in about twenty minutes, if you please."

"Very good, madam."

Laura Lawson slipped her arm through Mary Eliska's. "Don't be long, Martin."

"I won't. Good night, Marlow Ray."

"Good night, Mr. Lawson." Mrs. Lawson seemed lost in thought as they slowly mounted the stone stairs. Suddenly she began chattily: "Men are such stupid creatures, Marlow Ray. So stupid about taking medicine or anything else that may be good for them. Martin and that hot lemonade is a case in point. I hope that you haven't any foolish ideas like that?"

"Oh, no, indeed. I'm rather fond of it."

"That's fine. Now promise me you'll get into bed and drink it just as hot as possible. There's nothing better to ward off a cold, and you'll sleep like a top into the bargain. Well, here's your room, my dear. It's late, so I won't come in, but I think you'll find all you need to make you comfortable. If you want anything, ring. Good night, Marlow Ray. Sleep well."

"I'm sure I will, Mrs. Lawson. Good night."

The older woman passed along the gallery and Mary Eliska entered her bedroom. It was a good-sized room, attractively furnished with everywhere evidence of a woman's taste. Pink-shaded electric candles gleamed from the walls papered in cream and scattered with tiny pink rosebuds. The small grey-painted bed displayed pink pillow cases, sheets and blankets. A dainty writing desk in one corner of the room was also painted grey as was the chaise longue and the chairs, where the upholstery carried out the note of pink. A soft grey rug, pink-bordered, covered the floor, and Mary Eliska's feet sank into its thick, warm pile as she investigated her new quarters. She saw that the room was nearly square, and opposite the door a rounded alcove sheltered a bow window, hung with pink taffeta, and the window seat below it was cushioned in pink. In a corner against the wall stood Marlow Ray's wardrobe trunk, and near it was a door that led into a spacious closet. Mary Eliska hung her coat on a padded hanger, and then looked into the rose and onyx tiled bath.

As she re-entered the bedroom she stopped short in surprise. A small piece of white paper protruded from beneath the door to the gallery. Quickly she stooped, snatched the paper and opened the door. The gallery was empty. Crossing to the balustrade she looked down upon the great entrance hall. That also was deserted and nobody was to be seen on the staircase.

She turned back, closed and locked her door. Then she spread out the paper she had crumpled in her hand. Printed on one side in pencil she read the words:

"BE ON YOUR GUARD. DO NOT DRINK THE LEMONADE. DESTROY THIS AT ONCE."

"Now I wonder..." Mary Eliska muttered softly, "who sent me this note?"

Chapter 4.9
IN THE NIGHT

Mary Eliska turned over the piece of paper to find as she expected that the other side was blank. No signature. Nothing but the double warning, and the admonition to destroy the missive and to do so at once. Evidently the writer either believed or knew for certain that she would shortly be disturbed. There was no fireplace in the bedroom. Even though she tore the note into bits, some of the scraps might be found and pieced together should she throw them out the window; and her room might be searched at any time. How could she make way with it? For a moment or two Mary Eliska was at a loss. Mechanically her fingers tore the paper into fine shreds. Then she smiled. "I guess we'll let the plumbing take care of you," she said, gazing down on the little pile of paper on her palm, and she disappeared into the bathroom.

When she returned, Mary Eliska opened Marlow Ray's over-night bag, took out a pair of green silk pajamas, bedroom slippers and toilet accessories, among which was a new toothbrush in a case. This, and the underwear she had on were the only belongings of her own that she had retained.

From Marlow Ray's purse, she extracted the trunk key. After some rummaging in that large traveling wardrobe, she found a quilted bathrobe of pale pink satin on a hanger toward the back. It was too late to unpack entirely, and she was about to close and relock the trunk, when she decided to leave it open. The Marlow Ray she was portraying had never waked up at the famous meeting of last week. That Marlow Ray would feel outraged at her imprisonment, her father's seeming callousness and would naturally be furious at being packed up here willy-nilly: but she would have no cause to be suspicious of these people in this big stone house. If she had locked the trunk—Mary Eliska realized she had almost made a mistake, although a minor one—and in her present position mistakes were dangerous affairs.

Although it was very late and the day had been a strenuous one Mary Eliska did not feel tired. While she undressed, she went over in her mind the new vistas opened up by this mysterious note she had just destroyed. As she dissected it word by word from memory, she was astonished to find that the scrap of paper carried much interesting information between the lines.

Undoubtedly, Ashton Sanborn had planted a member of his organization in the house, but how that had been possible, she could not imagine. First of all, there was the warning to be on her guard. That Mrs. Lawson was indicated she had no doubt. Her hostess, while seeming most charming and courteous, had nevertheless suggested the hot lemonade which the note told her not to drink. It was quite likely that her unknown adviser had reason to think that the lemonade would be drugged. And then these people could hardly mean to poison her so soon after her arrival. For their whole idea in bringing her to Winncote, as she understood it, was to make sure whether the real Marlow Ray had heard their secrets or not. No—they merely wanted her to sleep soundly. But why?

Mary Eliska pondered on this for several minutes. There could be only one reason, she decided. Somebody was planning to enter her bedroom tonight, and wished to do so without her knowledge. What their purpose might be she could not guess and she did not bother about it. To a girl of a nervous temperament, such as Marlow Ray, the knowledge that such a visit was planned and success arranged for by means of a drug, would have been torture. But Mary Eliska, who could feel "Dash" in his holster just above her knee was merely worried for fear that lemonade or no lemonade she would fall asleep. The arrival here had been uneventful enough after what had happened at the Rays' apartment. At least, to all outward appearances it had been smooth sailing. She was beginning to realize that nothing with these people was what it seemed to be. She had climbed her Vesuvius and was standing at the crater's edge. Already the first rumblings of the eruption had been heard.

Her position, though seemingly secure, was nothing of the kind. The sooner Ashton Sanborn gave her the orders he had promised, and she could carry them out and get away from this place, the better for Mary Eliska. And yet she could not help a feeling of exhilaration.

There came a gentle knock on her door. Wearing her quilted wrapper and slippers she turned the key and opened to—the imposing Tunbridge. He bore a small tray on which stood a steaming tumbler, a bowl of sugar, two spoons and a napkin. "Your hot lemonade, Marlow Ray," he announced in his pompous voice and rather as though he were offering her a priceless gift. "Mrs. Lawson's instructions are to drink it after you get in bed, Miss. May I mention also that it is very hot?"

Mary Eliska took the tray. "Thank you, Tunbridge, I'll be careful. Good night!"

"Good night, Miss."

The butler departed in the direction of the stairway, and Mary Eliska closed the door and locked it again.

She set the tray on a chair beside her bed and put two spoonsful of sugar into the tall glass. It was too hot for anyone to drink yet, so she went into the bathroom to get ready for bed.

Five minutes later she switched off all the lights except the one on the head board. Then she got into bed, picked up the glass and stirred her lemonade, making sure that the spoon tinkled against the glass. If anyone were listening outside her door they would naturally think she was drinking the stuff.

After waiting a moment or two longer, she set the glass down on the tray with a thump that might have been heard on the gallery. But the glass remained in her hand. Off went her light now, and still holding the lemonade she got quickly and quietly out of bed. A silent trip to the bathroom in the dark and she emptied the lemonade into her washbowl. Then she came back and placed the empty glass on the tray. She hurried over to the bow window, opened a sash, turned off the heat in the radiator and crawled into bed again.

The bed was to the left of the door as one entered the room. By lying on her right side, Mary Eliska held the entire room within her view. After the soft glare from the shaded electric lights, it seemed inky black, but soon her eyes grew accustomed to the gloom. In the wall just beyond the foot of the bed was the closed door of her closet. The trunk stood beyond that in the corner. The alcove and window seat took up a large section of the farther wall and in the corner, diagonally across from where she lay was a dark spot—the writing desk. Opposite her bed was the half open door to the bathroom. The dressing table, the door to the hall but a few feet from her head—mentally she had completed her tour of the room.

Then for a long while, or so it seemed to the excited girl, she lay there waiting. Of course her door was locked, but the affair of the Winged Cartwheels a few months before had taught Mary Eliska that keys may be turned from the outside with a pair of small pincers. Her mind now set itself on the key in the door. In vain she listened for the warning click that would come when it turned in the lock. Now that she was lying in bed she began to discover how tired she was. It became harder and harder to stay awake.

She knew that she must have dozed, for without warning a light appeared, a golden circle on the center of the rug. Instantly she was wide awake and her hand beneath the blankets drew her throwing knife from its sheath. Through half-closed eyelids she made out a dark figure holding a flash light pointed toward the floor.

Then the glowing circle moved to the empty glass beside her bed, and Mary Eliska closed her eyes. For a moment it rested upon her face and she heard a low chuckle. Mary Eliska knew that voice. Her visitor was Laura Lawson.

The light swept away from her face. Mrs. Lawson touched the wall switch by the door and the bedroom sprang into light. The drug in the lemonade must have been a strong one, for it was evident that the intruder had no fear of her awakening. Without wasting another glance on Mary Eliska, Laura Lawson went to the wardrobe trunk and commenced a detailed inspection of its contents.

The woman's back was turned, so Mary Eliska had no difficulty in watching her movements. Everything in the trunk was taken out, glanced at and put back exactly as it had been. This took some time, and it was fully half an hour before her hostess finished with the trunk. Next she overhauled the small traveling bag and the purse. Then the empty drawers of the dressing table and desk came under the woman's eye. The pillows and cushions of the window seat were lifted. The rug was turned back. Every nook and cranny of the room and closet came under observation. Then she went into the bathroom.

"What under the shining canopy can she be looking for?" Mary Eliska marveled. "It can't be the note I got tonight. She proposed the lemonade before that could have been written. I wonder if she'll search the bed? She mustn't find Dash—"

When Laura Lawson returned to the bedroom, she saw that the sleeper had turned over and was now facing the wall. For a moment she gazed down on the girl, then her hand crept under the pillow. Finding nothing there, the covers were pulled back to the foot of the bed.

Mary Eliska felt the cold breeze from the open window blowing on her pajamaed body, but she did not move. Presently sheet, blankets and silk comfort were replaced and the woman left the bedside. Mary Eliska chuckled inwardly. Dash was still safe. She was lying on him.

Off went the light. Mary Eliska knew that Mrs. Lawson's slippered feet would make no sound on the thick pile of the rug. She waited to hear the door open and close, but heard nothing. With her face to the wall, she could see nothing. The strain of lying motionless became nerve wracking. What was the woman doing anyhow? Slowly she rolled over again. So far as she could tell, the room was empty.

For what seemed an age Mary Eliska lay, listening. Except for the wind sighing through the bare trees outside her window, there was no other sound. She felt nervous and unpleasantly excited. She must know if the door had been left unlocked. Slipping out of bed she tiptoed across to it and tried the handle. The door did not give.

Suddenly she froze against the panels. A dim glow appeared on the opposite wall as the closet door swung slowly back, and outlined in the opening was the tall figure of Tunbridge.

Chapter 4.10
SURPRISES

Mary Eliska's experiences, since she had shopped for neckties for her father that morning had been quite enough to lay up the average girl for a week, and to wreck her nerves into the bargain. Laura Lawson's appearance in her bedroom had strained tightened nerves to the breaking point.

The arrival of this second intruder was just too much. As the butler stepped out of the closet and started to close the door, Mary Eliska's self-control snapped like a rubber band. She forgot that she was playing a part; that it might be suicidal to show her hand so early in the game. Fear gripped her throat. Had this man been sent to kill her? If not, then what was he doing, stealing into her room through a secret entrance like an assassin of the middle ages? Self-preservation bade her act. The consequences could take care of themselves.

"Stop!" The harsh whisper, as her hand dove for Dash, sounded like the voice of a stranger. "Move another step, and I'll pin you to that door!" Dash was in her raised hand now, the extended blade reflecting the light in the closet as though the polished steel were glass.

She saw the man start in surprise and turn his head in her direction. As she was about to hurl the knife, Tunbridge found his voice.

"Ashton Sanborn sent me, Mary Eliska. Please don't throw that knife."

Gone was the English accent, and the pompous intonation of the British man servant. Tunbridge, if that were really his name, spoke the American Mary Eliska was accustomed to hear, the accents of the cultured New Englander. For the second time in her life, Mary Eliska fainted.

She awoke to find herself in bed. Tunbridge was beside it. She could just make out his tall, powerful figure in the darkness.

"Goodness—did I faint?" she said weakly.

"You certainly did, Mary Eliska." His tone was little above a whisper. "Please don't raise your voice—and drink this. I found the aromatic spirits of ammonia in the bathroom. You need something to steady you. No one is cast iron—you've been through a frightful lot today."

Mary Eliska took the glass and drained it. Then she lay back on her pillow. "I got the scare of my life just now. Why didn't Ashton Sanborn tell me about you, Mr.—"

"Tunbridge is really my name, Mary Eliska. John Tunbridge, and very much at your service. I was afraid my rather abrupt appearance would startle you, and especially coming so soon after Mrs. Lawson's—er—visit. I got a shock myself when I saw your white figure by the door just now, and all ready to split me with that knife, like—like a macaroon." He chuckled, and removing the tray, sat down on the chair beside her bed.

"Oh, then you've seen Ashton Sanborn this evening, Mr. Tunbridge?"

"Heard from him, Mary Eliska. As you must know by now, I am a secret service operative and I am working under Mr. Sanborn. There isn't time to go into detail now, but a couple of months ago, our department received an anonymous letter saying that Doctor Winn would bear watching. Shortly before that the Doctor had engaged Mrs. Lawson, who is an expert chemist by the way, to take charge of his laboratory. Her husband has been Doctor Winn's secretary since last spring. We thought at that time that Mrs. Lawson might be the mysterious letter writer. Since then we've altered our opinion. Mr. Sanborn decided that inasmuch as Doctor Winn was working for the government it would be well to have a secret service man in the house. We prevailed upon the butler here to resign and I took his place."

"Then Doctor Winn knows you're a government detective?"

"No one in this house knows that, except you, Mary Eliska. The whole matter was arranged through an employment agency. Doctor Winn and the others here have no idea that I, like you, am simply playing a part."

"Well, you're certainly a splendid actor, Mr. Tunbridge."

"Thank you, Mary Eliska. As you've no doubt discovered, acting, convincing acting, often plays a large part in our profession. You are doing brilliantly in that respect yourself. Mr. Sanborn thought, however, that it would be better if you did not know about me until the necessity arose. Mrs. Lawson, he knew would be watching you like a hawk when you arrived. If you had been aware of my identity, your position would only have been more difficult. She might have had her suspicions aroused in some way, which would have given you a wrong start from the beginning. I think you will realize tomorrow how hard it will be to treat me as though I were merely Tunbridge the butler."

"Oh, I think you're right. Tell me, how did you find out about the lemonade?"

"I overheard the Lawsons talking, yesterday. Made it my business in fact. It seems that Mrs. Lawson has had the idea that if Marlow Ray were only shamming sleep at that meeting, she would do her best to communicate with her father in some way. The natural thing to do would be to write a note and slip it in his hand or his pocket, when he came to see her. Martin Lawson was sure he would detect anything of the kind when he brought Ray to say goodbye to Marlow Ray tonight at the flat. If not, the plan was to drug the girl with hot lemonade so that Mrs. Lawson could search her belongings for the note tonight."

Mary Eliska nodded. "I watched her closely while she was in here, and so far as I could make out she didn't find anything that interested her particularly. The Lawsons must have guessed wrong about Marlow Ray writing her father."

"Well, no, they didn't," declared her new ally. "Marlow Ray wrote a letter, just as they surmised."

"But where could it be?" asked Mary Eliska in a startled whisper, and sat bold upright in bed.

"Probably destroyed by this time," Mr. Tunbridge chuckled. "There's no need to worry on that score, Mary Eliska. When Ashton Sanborn spoke to your cousin this afternoon by means of Howard Bright's headphone set, he learned that Marlow Ray proposed doing just what this clever pair here figured upon. Of course she had already written the note, and as there was no safe way to get rid of it in her room, he told her to take it with her when she left. And now if you'll be good enough, I wish you'd tell me what happened after you took her place in the flat." Mary Eliska gave him a short sketch of her encounter with her uncle and Martin Lawson in Marlow Ray's room, and of the conversation between the two men in the corridor afterward. "All the way up here," she ended, "I pretended I had a grouch. Mr. Lawson tried to start a conversation several times, but he soon found it wasn't much fun talking to himself and he gave it up as a bad job."

"Excellent," applauded the secret service man, "and quite in keeping with your behavior in the flat. You have done most remarkably well, Mary Eliska. Only—you won't mind if I warn you not to let first success make you careless."

"Do you really believe that these people mean to do away with me if they discover I am not what I appear to be, Mr. Tunbridge? It sounds a bit too melodramatic, don't you think?"

"These Lawsons, husband and wife, are playing for gigantic stakes." The detective's voice, though barely audible was extremely grave. "They will stop at nothing. When crooks have at least two murders behind them, they're not likely to stop at a third."

"Then—then they are *not* what they pretend?"

"Certainly not. They're a pair of high-class European crooks named du Val."

Mary Eliska shuddered. "And *murderers!*"

"Undoubtedly. They're wanted both in England and in Austria for their crimes."

"How did you find that out?"

"Oh, you see I recognized them when I arrived here, Mary Eliska."

"But—but I can't see why—why you didn't arrest them then and there! You knew that they were after the secret of Doctor Winn's new explosive, or whatever it is he has invented."

"Yes, we realized that the formula for Doctor Winn's explosive gas was the magnet that drew the du Vals to this house; but until today we had no idea how they proposed to dispose of the formula after stealing it."

"I see. And now you realize that they probably intend to sell it to the organization of which my uncle is a member?"

"You are right, Mary Eliska."

"Then why can't you arrest the Lawsons now?"

"We can take the Lawsons at any time," Tunbridge explained. "But we want to catch the ringleader of this organization. We know the group exists and for no good purpose, but what their definite object may be we still have no means of telling. We can't arrest them on suspicion alone. Once they actually buy the formula from the Lawsons, it will be quite a different matter."

She shook her head slowly. "But why hasn't the formula been stolen before this? They've had plenty of opportunity, surely—"

"Because it is not completed. At dinner tonight I heard the Doctor say that by tomorrow afternoon the work would be finished, and that he expected to take the formula to Washington the day after tomorrow."

"Then you expect?—" "I expect that the Lawsons will make their attempt tomorrow night."

"And where do I come in on this business, Mr. Tunbridge?"

"You are going to take the plans from Doctor Winn's safe before the Lawsons get to it."

She drew her breath sharply. "That's a pretty large order—"

"I know it, but—of course you'll have the combination of the safe."

"Are you going to give it to me now?"

"Too dangerous. They are quite capable of searching your belongings again—or your person, for that matter—at any time. I'll get it to you with exact instructions just as soon as the Doctor completes that blooming formula and locks it in the safe."

"That's all very well, Mr. Tunbridge. But has it occurred to you that if I steal this paper—I suppose it will be a paper?—"

"Probably several of them—"

"Well, if I take these papers before the Lawsons can get them, how are you going to arrest my uncle and the other men?"

"You," directed Tunbridge, "will simply make a copy and replace the original documents where you found them. This is a safety-first move. We must have a copy in case the originals are destroyed."

"It looks like a very complicated matter to me," Mary Eliska admitted candidly. "Why not put the old gentleman wise? After all, it's his formula, and if he made his own copy it would save us a possible run-in with the Lawsons, and—"

Mr. Tunbridge stood up. "Perhaps you're right," he said, making a brave attempt to stifle a yawn, "but Doctor Winn would never agree to it. For a scientist who dabbles in high explosives, he's the most nervous man I've ever met. He'd give the whole show away. No, that's out of the question. Doctor Winn must be kept in ignorance of the whole proceeding. And now—" a yawn got the better of him this time— "and now to bed. You need sleep even more than advice just now. Good night, or rather, good morning, Mary Eliska. Pleasant dreams, I hope."

He started toward the door and Mary Eliska sprang out of bed and reached for her dressing gown. "I want to see that secret passage, Mr. Tunbridge," she said in a low tone.

"Oh, yes, come along." He opened the door and stepped inside the closet. "It works this way. Press your foot on the board in the farthest right-hand corner, like this, and a panel in the back wall slides up—like that—"

Mary Eliska stared at the gaping black hole, then as the detective-butler snapped on his flashlight she saw that a narrow circular staircase led downward in the wall.

"That stair curves down to the ground floor," he explained. "It comes out through the side wall inside the big fireplace in the hall. To open the panel down there you press a button under the left-hand corner of the mantel. To close either panel you simply put it down, once you're inside."

"Are there any more of these passages in the walls?"

"Very likely, but I haven't found them yet. Winncote is an exact copy of the Doctor's ancestral home in Wales. Those old houses were honeycombed with priest holes, secret passages and whatnot. And Doctor Winn had his architect copy the original Winncote across the water down to the last stone, with modern improvements such as bathrooms and steam heat, added."

"Funny old fellow, isn't he?" commented Mary Eliska sleepily. "Then I'm simply to carry on until I hear from you again?"

"That's right. But whatever you do, watch your step with the Lawson woman. She is fully as heartless as she is beautiful. If you had never heard of that meeting in the Rays' flat, it would be much better for you. She will try to trap you, so please be on your guard continually. Well, good night, again."

"Good night, Mr. Tunbridge."

The panel in the back wall of the closet slid into place, and Mary Eliska went back to bed. She realized now that this matter of impersonating her cousin was not going to prove to be the easy job she had fancied. A slip on her part now would not only put her own life in danger, it would probably ruin all government plans to apprehend these desperate criminals.

At last she fell into a troubled sleep wherein she dreamed that a long circular staircase curved round and round her bedroom, and that Mrs. Lawson, dressed as a butler, had set her to watch every step of it.

Chapter 4.11
GRETCHEN

Mary Eliska awoke from troubled dreams to find that it was another day. Through the open window she saw the swirl of snowflakes driven in a high wind. The bedroom was cold and in the grey light of the winter morning it had lost its cheerful air. She heard a knock on the door. "Who's there?" she called drowsily.

"It's the maid, miss. Mrs. Lawson thought you might be wanting your breakfast now."

Mary Eliska looked at her wrist watch. The hands marked ten-thirty. She jumped out on the rug, which felt cold and clammy under her bare feet, went to the door and unlocked it. Then she scampered back to bed and snuggled under the warm covers.

In walked a trim little figure wearing the small white apron and gray uniform of a chambermaid. Mary Eliska saw a round merry face, and a pair of big blue eyes beneath the white lawn cap, and thick flaxen braids were coiled round the neat head. She was surprised and somehow pleased to discover that this attractive member of the household staff could not be much more than sixteen, just her own age.

The little maid shut the door softly, crossed to the window and closed it, turned on the steam heat and came to the bedside. "Good morning, Marlow Ray." She smiled engagingly. "I'm Gretchen, miss. Will you have your breakfast in bed?"

"Why, thank you, Gretchen—that will be cozy. But if it's going to give you any trouble, don't bother." With the covers drawn up to her eyes, Mary Eliska smiled back at the girl.

"Oh, no, miss—it's no trouble at all." Gretchen was insistent. "It's all ready now. I'll run down and bring it up."

She whisked out of the room and Mary Eliska rolled over for another cat-nap.

"If you'll be good enough to sit up now, Marlow Ray—I have your breakfast here."

Mary Eliska awoke again, yawned and stretched luxuriously. Gretchen stood beside her bed with the breakfast tray. "If you'll be good enough to sit up, miss?" she repeated.

Mary Eliska punched the pillows into position behind her, slipped the quilted gown about her shoulders and leaned back. Gretchen moved nearer—then almost dropped the tray.

"Why—why—miss—"

Mary Eliska leaned over and steadied the tray. "What's the matter, Gretchen?" The little maid was staring at her open-mouthed, her big blue eyes as round as saucers.

"Oh, I—I beg your pardon, but it's—it's the resemblance, miss—Marlow Ray." She set the tray over Mary Eliska's knees and drew back still with that astonished look. "I couldn't see you very well before, miss, with the covers up to your eyes. But when you sat up, it sure did give me a start."

"What do you mean, Gretchen? The resemblance to whom?" Mary Eliska, outwardly calm, fingered her glass of orange juice, but her thoughts raced toward this new complication.

"Why, you look so much like Mary Eliska—the flyer, you know, miss. She's my hero—I mean, heroine, Marlow Ray. I've read everything the newspapers printed about her and Bill Bolton. You must have read about them too, everybody has?"

"Oh, yes, I've heard about them." Mary Eliska hoped her tone sounded indifferent. "But you know, Gretchen, newspaper pictures are often very poor likenesses." The girl smiled and nodded. "I know that, Marlow Ray. I've got them all and there isn't no two of the pictures that looks alike." "Then how—?"

"You see, it wasn't the newspaper pictures I was thinking of, miss, but Mary Eliska herself. You see I know Mary Eliska," she went on proudly, "and you two are certainly the spittin' images of each other, if you don't mind my saying so."

Mary Eliska minded very much, but it was not consistent with the part she was playing to admit it. Here was a contretemps not even Ashton Sanborn had foreseen. Yet, of course, New Canaan was only ten miles away. She had many friends in Ridgefield, and she'd been there hundreds of times. But she simply couldn't remember having seen Gretchen in any of their homes. Her answer was but a feeble stall for time.

"So you know her then?" she said lamely.

"Oh, yes, miss. Not well, you understand. I saw her and Mr. Bill Bolton first when they finished the endurance test on the Conway motor this fall. Then a few days later, I drove over to her house in our flivver—over to New Canaan, you know, and I called on Mary Eliska. I wanted her to autograph a picture of herself I'd cut out of the Sunday paper."

"And you met her?" Mary Eliska remembered the incident perfectly now. But the maid's uniform—and her hair—when she had seen her, Gretchen had worn two braids over her shoulders, very much the schoolgirl. No wonder she hadn't recognized her. But now what should she do? Would it be possible to keep up this camouflage with a girl whom she had met and with whom she would come in daily contact? Gretchen was talking again.

"Yes indeed, I met her. And she was just darling to me, Marlow Ray. She even gave me one of her own photographs and wrote on it, too. You see, us Schmidts came over from Germany about a hundred years ago, but we're honest-to-goodness Americans just the same. Father was in the American army during the war. He was an aviation mechanic. He found one of them Iron Crosses of the Germans on some battlefield in France and kept it for a mascot. And would you believe it, miss, Father never even got wounded once, the whole time he was over there! Perhaps it was the little Iron Cross, and perhaps it wasn't. Anyway, he thought a lot of his mascot. When I was ten years old, he had it fixed on a thin gold chain for me to wear around my neck, and gave it to me on my birthday. Well, when I went to see Mary Eliska this fall, I took it with me. She goes up in her airplane so much and does so many other exciting things, I wanted her to have it. She didn't want to take the cross at first, but I persuaded her to, just the same. And you don't know how nice she was to me, Miss! Took me out to see Will-o-the-Wisp—that's her plane, you know—she calls it Wispy for short. And I had a perfectly grand time. She's my heroine, all right. And you, miss—I hope you'll excuse me for talking so much about it—but you look exactly like her, and your voices are just the same, too. It's wonderful!"

"So you are Margaret Schmidt," Mary Eliska said slowly.

"Yes, miss, that is so, though everybody calls me Gretchen. How did you know my given name, Marlow Ray? Is Mary Eliska a friend of yours? Did she tell you about me? But that's silly—she wouldn't remember me."

Mary Eliska looked the little maid straight in the eyes. "She remembers you, Gretchen. Would you be willing to do something for her—to keep a secret, a very important and maybe a dangerous one? Do you think you could do it?"

Gretchen looked awestruck, then she smiled. "Mother says I'm the closest-mouthed girl she ever saw, miss. They could cut me in pieces before I ever let out any secret of Mary Eliska's. I'd never tell—not me! You can trust me, Marlow Ray."

"I'm sure I can, Gretchen. And I'm going to." Mary Eliska slipped her hand into the V-neck of her pajamas. "Remember this?"

"Why—it's—it's my Iron Cross—that I gave Mary Eliska. How in the world—?"

"I am Mary Eliska." Mary Eliska broke into laughter at the bewildered expression on the girl's face.

"But—but I don't understand!" Gretchen stammered as though her tongue was half-paralyzed. "I knew the resemblance was wonderful—but—they said you were Miss Marlow Ray—and—"

"You sit down on the end of the bed," said Mary Eliska, "I'll go on with my breakfast before it gets cold, and explain at the same time. We won't be disturbed, will we?"

"Oh, no, miss." "How about your work, Gretchen? Will you be wanted downstairs?" "Mr. Tunbridge told me to unpack your trunk, miss—Mary Eliska—and to make myself generally useful." "Fine," smiled Mary Eliska, pouring out a cup of coffee. "But keep on calling me Marlow Ray—otherwise you'll be making slips in the name in front of other people and that would be fatal." "Yes, Marlow Ray," Gretchen grinned happily.

"After this beastly business is over," Mary Eliska went on, "we'll be Gretchen and Mary Eliska to each other." The other girl looked a trifle embarrassed. "But I'm only a chambermaid, Marlow Ray," she said shyly.

"Don't be silly!" Mary Eliska waved away the argument with a sweep of her spoon. "You're proving yourself a real friend—and that's that." "Very well, Marlow Ray."

"Now pin back your ears, Gretchen." Mary Eliska lifted the cover from her scrambled eggs. "I am taking my cousin, Marlow Ray's place as Mrs. Lawson's secretary. Nobody in this house knows who I am except Mr. Tunbridge, nor must they be given the slightest hint that I am anybody but Marlow Ray. As you've probably guessed, Marlow Ray and I look almost exactly alike. Our mothers were twins and that probably accounts for it."

"Gee—" breathed Gretchen. "It's just like a story in a book!"

Mary Eliska bit into a slice of buttered toast. "Maybe it is," she admitted, speaking with her mouth full. "But the point is that you and I are living this story and it may come to a very abrupt and unpleasant ending unless we're both terribly careful. Let's see—where was I? Oh, yes. Mr. Tunbridge and I are working together on this case, working for the United States Government."

"Secret Service?" asked Gretchen in an awed whisper. "Yes."

"Then I'll be working for the secret service too?" Mary Eliska could see that the girl was very much impressed with the idea. "You will, Gretchen—that is, you are—under me. But don't get too pepped up about it. The work we are on is serious and it is extremely dangerous into the bargain. I wouldn't have brought you into it unless I had to. Right now I haven't the slightest notion how you are going to be fitted into the picture. But I couldn't have you going around, talking about how much Marlow Ray looks like Mary Eliska, could I? Doctor Winn and the Lawsons have no idea of either the resemblance or the relationship. If that came out and they got wind of it—well, there's no telling what might happen."

"Especially," chimed in Gretchen, "after all the detective work you did in those three big cases over to New Canaan this summer and fall."

"You've got it," declared Mary Eliska, and sipped her coffee. "A robbery is being planned here, Gretchen, a robbery of some very valuable papers from Doctor Winn's safe. The thieves will probably try to pull it off tonight. These papers, which have to do with an invention of the Doctor are worth a million dollars or more to any number of people. So you see the thieves are playing for big stakes, and I might as well tell you that they aren't the kind that would let a thing like murder stop them. And now that you know the facts, are you willing to go on with it?"

Gretchen seemed horrified that Mary Eliska should doubt her. "Oh, Marlow Ray, I don't want to get murdered any more than anybody else—but, I'm not afraid—honest I'm not!"

"I knew you were true blue," smiled Mary Eliska. "So we'll call it a deal, shall we?"

"You bet!" The two girls solemnly shook hands. "What do you want me to do first, Marlow Ray?" Gretchen asked eagerly.

"Move this tray onto the chair over there, please. Then while I'm taking a bath and dressing you might unpack Marlow Ray's clothes. I'll choose something to wear later."

"Very good, Marlow Ray." The little maid took the tray, then stopped short, her round blue eyes very serious. "But what about the secret service work?"

"Just carry on as usual for the present." Mary Eliska slipped out of bed. "And remember— not a word to anyone about what I've told you—not even Mr. Tunbridge. I don't know myself exactly what I'm to do yet. Mrs. Lawson expects me downstairs in about half an hour, so I've got to hustle. If I need your help later on, I'll get word to you somehow."

"I hope you will need me, Marlow Ray." Gretchen was taking Marlow Ray's frocks from the wardrobe trunk.

"And I hope I shan't!" said Mary Eliska, and she disappeared into the bathroom.

Chapter 4.12
TESTS

Mary Eliska came down the wide staircase a few minutes before eleven-thirty. She wore a dark blue morning frock of her cousin's, its simplicity relieved only by the soft white collar and deep cuffs. Except for being rather tight across the shoulders it fitted her as though she had been poured into it. She had selected this dress because she knew it was just the sort of thing a new secretary would be expected to wear.

She crossed the broad hall to the open door of the library, and there found Mrs. Lawson standing before a window staring into the storm. Although Mary Eliska's footsteps made practically no sound on the thick pile of the handsome Bokhara rug, the woman turned like a flash at her entrance.

"Oh, good morning, Marlow Ray." The frown on her face gave way to a pleasant smile. "I hope you were comfortable last night. Did you sleep well?"

"I dropped off as soon as my head touched the pillow," she answered, taking Mrs. Lawson's outstretched hand. Mary Eliska did not believe in telling a lie unless it was in a good cause; but when necessary, she invariably made the lie a good one.

"I hope the storm didn't wake you," smiled Laura, holding Mary Eliska's hand.

Mary Eliska did not reply at once. Two long fingers were lightly pressing her wrist, and she saw that Mrs. Lawson's eyes had strayed to the grandfather's clock in the corner of the room. "Test number one," she said to herself. "Mrs. du Val, alias Lawson is counting my pulse. Well, I've got a clear conscience, perhaps I can give her a shock." She drew her hand away and answered the woman's question in her normal voice. "Oh, the storm! No, I never heard it, Mrs. Lawson. If that hot lemonade had been drugged, I couldn't have slept any sounder!"

"What makes you say that?" snapped her employer, and beneath the velvet tone, Mary Eliska sensed the ring of steel.

She dropped her eyes, and turning toward the open hearth, held out her hands to the crackling blaze. "Oh, I don't know," she said sweetly and like the clever little strategist that she was, opened her own offensive in the enemy's territory. "I have the bad habit of occasionally walking in my sleep, Mrs. Lawson—and especially when I spend the night in a strange bed. Perhaps it's nervousness—I don't know."

Mrs. Lawson threw her a sharp glance. "Sit down, Marlow Ray," she suggested, pointing to a chair near the fire, and taking one herself across the hearth. "You're—I mean, you don't seem to be at all nervous this morning."

"Good old pulse!" thought Mary Eliska. Then aloud—"No, I feel splendidly, thank you. But, you see, I didn't walk in my sleep last night."

"But surely you can't tell when you do it!"

"Oh, yes, I can." Mary Eliska's manner and tone were those of the simple schoolgirl proud of an unusual accomplishment.

"You don't expect me to believe that you know what you're doing when you walk in your sleep, Marlow Ray. That's impossible!"

"Not while I'm sleepwalking, Mrs. Lawson. That wasn't what I said—but when I have been sleepwalking—there's a difference, you see?"

"Well?" The lady of the house objected to being contradicted and took no trouble to hide it.

"It's really very simple," explained Mary Eliska, painstakingly, as though she were speaking to a rather stupid child. "I found out how to do it. You see, I've been walking in my sleep ever since I was a little thing. When I get in bed at night I leave my slippers on the floor beside it pointed outward—away from the bed. We all leave them that way, I guess. It's the natural thing to do."

"But what have slippers got to do with it?" Laura was becoming impatient.

"Everything, so far as I'm concerned, Mrs. Lawson. When I've been walking at night, I always find them in the morning beside the bed, but pointing *toward* it. I evidently slip them off before I get back into bed, and—"

"I'm beginning to think you are quite a clever girl, Marlow Ray."

"Oh, thank you," said Mary Eliska with a guilelessness that was sheer camouflage. "Has anybody been saying I'm stupid? I've always stood high in my classes at school."

"Oh, not stupid, child—but nervous—perhaps a little unbalanced, especially this past week."

Mary Eliska raised her heavy lashes and looked Mrs. Lawson squarely in the face. This might be a test she was undergoing and it probably was; but here was a heaven sent chance to stir up discord in the enemy's camp. She must work up to it gradually.

"I know that I was nervous and upset past all endurance." She leaned forward, her hands on the arms of the chair. "How would you like your father to lock you in your bedroom for a week, without ever coming to see you, or giving you any explanation for such outrageous treatment? Am I a child to be handled like that? To be shipped up here to strangers, whether I wanted to go or not? How would you feel about it, Mrs. Lawson, if you were me? Don't say you would submit to it sitting down."

"But I am taking you on as my secretary," the lady hedged. "Offering you a good position for which you'll be paid twenty dollars a week. That's not to be thought of lightly, especially in these times."

"But it doesn't seem to strike you that I might like to have something to say about it," Mary Eliska replied calmly. "As for the salary—that's no inducement. My mother left me five thousand a year. I came into the income on my last birthday, so you see I have nearly a hundred dollars a week, whether I work or not."

"I didn't know that, of course," Mrs. Lawson admitted and none too graciously. "Your father wants you to be here while he's away. I hope you aren't going to be difficult, Marlow Ray."

"I hope not, Mrs. Lawson. I shall be glad to stay here for a while and do the work you'd planned for me; but if I do, it must be as a guest and not as a paid dependent."

"But you are a guest, Marlow Ray."

"I shall not accept a salary, Mrs. Lawson."

"Very well, my dear, if you wish it that way."

"Thank you very much."

"To get back to our former topic," Mrs. Lawson said, and lit a cigarette. "I can understand that your father's conduct in confining you to your room might be exasperating—but why should it make you nervous? And my husband tells me that when he visited you in your room you acted as though you were in deadly fear of something or somebody every time he saw you. What was the trouble, Marlow Ray? Was anything worrying you?"

"Yes, there was, Mrs. Lawson."

Mary Eliska looked down at the andirons, and her hands on the chair arms twisted embarrassedly. From the corner of her eye she saw a smile of satisfaction light up the older woman's face. She knew she was playing with fire and that Mrs. Lawson was watching her as a hawk watches its defenseless prey before it strikes. But all unknown to her inquisitor, Mary Eliska had been leading her into this trap as a move forward in her own game. Genuine dislike for the woman as well as a mischievous impulse on her part drew her to make the scene as dramatic and convincing as possible. "Yes—I—I—was afraid," she went on, dragging out the words slowly.

"Then don't you think you'd better tell me about it, Marlow Ray? I'm nearly old enough to be your mother. Let me take your mother's place, dear. Give me your confidence. I feel sure I'll be able to help you, child."

This reference to Marlow Ray's dead mother by a woman who was the vilest kind of a hypocrite swept away Mary Eliska's last compunction. She herself was going to commit justifiable libel. Mrs. Lawson, on the other hand, was attempting to lead Marlow Ray into a confession of shamming sleep at the fateful meeting a week ago. And such a confession meant a sentence of death from this beautiful siren who gazed at her so winningly, who puffed a cigarette so nonchalantly while she waited for an unsuspecting girl to commit herself.

"Well, I don't know—I can't help hesitating to tell *you*, Mrs. Lawson," Mary Eliska began timidly.

"There's no need to be afraid of anything," replied the woman, only half veiling the sneer that went with the words.

"Oh, but you see, there is, Mrs. Lawson!" Mary Eliska's manner was still indecisive. "I don't want—in fact, I hate awfully to hurt you this way."

"Hurt me!" Mrs. Lawson's cigarette snapped into the fireplace like a miniature comet. "Hurt me, child? What in the wide world are you talking about?" "Just what I say, Mrs. Lawson."

Mrs. Lawson sniffed. "Don't be ridiculous, Marlow Ray. Out with it now. What did you fear when you were locked in your room?"

"Your husband, Mrs. Lawson."

"My husband!"

"Yes." "But—why—I don't believe you."

"Oh, very well. You asked the question, I was trying to answer it, that's all." Mrs. Lawson bit her lip. She was furious. "As long as you've said what you have, you'd better go on with it," she said acidly.

"There isn't any more," returned Mary Eliska. "That's all there is."

"But surely he must have given you reasons for your assertion." Mrs. Lawson had walked beautifully into Mary Eliska's trap. Her own plan to snare an unsuspecting girl had been blotted out by the shadow of the Green Goddess, Jealousy. "Tell me what my husband did or said to make you fear him, and tell me at once."

"It wasn't what he did, Mrs. Lawson—it was the way he looked."

"What do you mean—the way he looked?"

Mary Eliska had thrust a painful knife into the mental cosmos of her adversary. Now she deliberately turned it in the wound. "Very probably," she said quietly, looking her straight in the eyes, "you can remember how Mr. Lawson looked when he first made love to you. I don't want to be made love to, and I don't like *him*, Mrs. Lawson."

"What did you do?" "I told him to leave me—and when he would not go, I simply walked into my bathroom and locked the door."

"But what happened the next time he came? Martin went in to see you every day, didn't he?"

"He did. But he talked to me through the bathroom door. Just as soon as I heard the key turn in the lock I'd hop in there." The man she had been talking about must have been listening just outside in the hall, for now he strode into the room and up to Mary Eliska. "That," he said menacingly, "is a deliberate lie, Miss Marlow Ray!"

Chapter 4.13
WINNITE

Mary Eliska looked up and smiled carelessly at the man. "You're very polite, Mr. Lawson. Perhaps it isn't my place to say it to a man old enough to be my father—but eavesdroppers rarely hear good of themselves."

Martin Lawson, who prided himself upon his youthful appearance, grew angrier than ever. "I—I won't stand for such outrageous libel," he thundered. "I've always treated you as though you were my own—well, daughter, if you like."

"I *don't* like it, Mr. Lawson—but that doesn't make any difference," Mary Eliska's tone was one of pained acceptance. "If you listened long enough, you will know that I didn't bring this matter up myself. Mrs. Lawson was asking questions and I was trying to answer them, that's all. If you prefer it, I'll say that it was the wind whistling outside the windows that made me afraid." She looked over at Mrs. Lawson, who was watching them through half shut eyes, as though to say, "—you understand, of course—anything for peace."

Martin Lawson intercepted the glance and became even more furious, if that were possible. "You—you little viper!" he snarled. "Laura, don't you believe a word of it. The whole thing's her own invention—a pack of lies!" "A silly schoolgirl fancy, if you like, Martin." Laura Lawson's tone was expressionless. "But I can understand it just the same. Yes, I can understand it."

"What do you mean—you understand it?"

"I was a girl once myself," she replied in the same colorless tone. "And then, you see, I know you very, very well."

"Oh, you do, do you?"

"He's off again," sighed Mary Eliska, but quite to herself.

"And you have the nerve to insinuate—?" the angry man went on, beside himself with rage. "You know as well as I do, Laura, that this girl was afraid because of what she saw and heard at the meeting. She—"

"That will be quite enough, Martin." His wife interrupted him sharply. "And what is more—you probably have not noticed that since Marlow Ray has been here and with other people, she is very much herself—and afraid of nothing at all."

"What meeting is he talking about, Mrs. Lawson?" Mary Eliska pointedly ignored the angry husband.

Mrs. Lawson stood up. "Never mind that now," she decreed, albeit pleasantly. "Come along with me to my office. I have some typing I'd like you to do for me before luncheon. Martin!" She swung round on her husband. "You will wait here for me. I'll be back in a few minutes—I want to talk to you." She slipped her arm through Mary Eliska's and drew her from the room.

Once in the entrance hall, she led her back and under the gallery to a corridor which opened at the right of the broad stairs. Mary Eliska saw that there were several doors in the right-hand wall. Mrs. Lawson stopped at the second of these and opened it.

They walked in and Mary Eliska saw that they were in the office. It seemed very businesslike and austere after coming from the luxury of the library and spacious hall. Near the one window stood a broad table desk, and opposite that a typewriter desk. Two steel filing cabinets and three plain chairs completed the room's furnishings. The walls were hung with framed blueprints and a large-scale map of Fairfield County, Connecticut.

Mrs. Lawson took some papers from a drawer in the large desk and handed them to Mary Eliska. "This is in longhand, as you see," she explained, "please type it, double space, and I'd like to have a carbon copy." She glanced at a small wrist-watch set with diamonds. "It is just noon now. Luncheon is at one. Do you think you can finish the work by that time?"

Mary Eliska glanced at the manuscript. "This won't make more than four typewritten sheets. I can do it easily in an hour and have time to spare."

"Good!" The older woman patted her lightly on the shoulder. "Take your time about it. Do you think you can read my handwriting?"

"Nothing could be plainer, Mrs. Lawson." Mary Eliska smiled back at her.

"Very well, then. I'll see you at lunch. The dining room is across the hall from the library."

At the door, she stopped and turned as though she had just remembered something.

"Don't let what my husband said bother you, Marlow Ray."

"That's forgotten already," Mary Eliska said easily.

"Like most men, he flies off the handle when irritated. Pay no attention to it."

"I understand."

Mrs. Lawson hesitated for the fraction of a second. "By the way, Marlow Ray," she remarked. "When was the last time you walked in your sleep—that you found your slippers pointed toward your bed in the morning?"

Mary Eliska pretended to think. "Let me see," she said slowly. "Yes—it was the night before Daddy locked me in my room! I found that I couldn't get out in the morning, and naturally, I wanted to know the reason why. I still do, for that matter. Except for some foolishness about my being ill, I'm still waiting for an explanation. As a matter of fact, I was perfectly well. I'm terribly annoyed, of course, and it worries me to think that Daddy should act this way, but so far as my health goes, I've never felt better."

"I'm glad to hear it, dear. We'll check up on your father when he returns. I'm your friend, you know. Don't let the matter prey on your mind."

"Thank you, Mrs. Lawson. I'll try to do as you say." Mary Eliska thought she was going then, but it seemed that the woman had still another question that she had been holding back.

"When you are in this somnambulistic state," she said, "when you are sleepwalking, I mean, doesn't it terrify you to awaken and find yourself out of your bed?"

Mary Eliska frowned and seemed puzzled. "Perhaps it would," she admitted. "But then, you see, I can't remember ever wakening while I was walking during the night. I must sleep very soundly. At school the night watchman or one of the teachers would frequently find me walking about the building. They would lead me back to bed, or just tell me to go there, and I would always obey. Until they told me about it next day, I knew nothing of course. That's how I got onto the business of the slippers, you see."

"Oh, yes. I wondered how you'd been able to check on it. Well, I must trot along now and let you get to work. Until luncheon then, my dear."

She was gone at last and Mary Eliska made a face at the closed door. "Of all the plausible hypocrites I've ever met," she muttered, "you certainly take the well-known chocolate cake!"

She sat down at the typewriter desk, pulled out the machine, and slipped in two sheets of paper and a carbon that she found in one of the drawers. Halfway through a perusal of Mrs. Lawson's first page, she looked up. The door opened quickly and Mr. Tunbridge came into the room.

"I've just a moment," he prefaced hurriedly. "They mustn't find me here. What was the row in the library?"

Mary Eliska explained briefly.

"Fine! Put you through the hoops, eh? I had a good idea she would do something of the kind. You came out of a difficult situation with flying colors, I take it. But be careful about run-ins with Lawson. He's a slick article—in fact, the two of them are a pair of the slickest articles it's ever been my misfortune to run across. And they're going it hammer and tongs in the library right now. I was a bit worried about you, that's why I took this chance."

"When do I get my instructions for tonight?"

"Late this afternoon, probably. I'll get them to you somehow."

"Thanks. And here's something else. This script I'm going to type for Mrs. L. has to do with the properties of a highly explosive gas which seems to burn up everything it comes in contact with and lets off fumes of deadly poison while it's doing that! Shall I make a copy for you?"

"Please do!" His hand rested on the doorknob. "Yes, it's important that we have a copy. That's the stuff Doctor Winn has just invented, without a doubt."

"Awful!" exclaimed Mary Eliska. "Just think what would happen if that were used in a war!"

"That's the government's business, Mary Eliska."

"'Ours but to do—and die—'" she quoted and her tone was deadly serious.

"Quite right. But make the carbon copy just the same—and don't let them catch you at it."

"I won't, Mr. Tunbridge."

"Bye-bye, then. I'll get along now. There may be some home truths floating out of the library that will give me extra dope on the du-Val—Lawson pair."

The door closed, and after slipping an extra carbon and a sheet of very thin copy paper into the typewriter, Mary Eliska read Mrs. Lawson's treatise on "Winnite and Its Properties" from start to finish.

"Horrible!" she murmured, as she finished reading. "Simply horrible!" Again her eyes sought the last paragraph. "The effect is easily estimated of an airplane dropping a single bomb filled with the explosive, inflammable and deadly poison gas, Winnite, upon Manhattan Island, for instance: the bomb would explode upon detonation and within an inconceivably short space of time, not only would the City of Greater New York be in flames, but every living thing within that area would be dead from the poison fumes. This includes not only human, animal and insect life, but all vegetable matter as well."

Mary Eliska sighed. "And I am supposed to help keep this terrible stuff from the hands of thieves so that our government may use it in time of war. Well—we'll see—and that's not that by a long shot!" She put down the manuscript and began to type it.

Chapter 4.14
PROFESSOR

Mary Eliska, upon finishing the article on Winnite, laid the original and first carbon copy of the typewritten sheets on Mrs. Lawson's desk. The almost transparent sheets of the second carbon copy she folded carefully as though she meant to place them in an envelope. But instead of this, her right foot slipped out of its walking pump, the sheer silk stocking followed it. Then she put on the stocking again, but now the soft papers rested between the stocking and the sole of her foot. The pump fitted more snugly than before, although not uncomfortably so. Content with her morning's work, she had closed the typewriter and was studying the effect of a new shade of powder in her compact mirror when Mrs. Lawson came into the room.

"I take it you've finished the work?"

"The original and copy are beside the longhand manuscript on your desk," said Mary Eliska, toning down her efforts with the puff. "I've read it over and I don't think you'll find any mistakes."

Mrs. Lawson ran her eyes over the typewritten sheets. "They are without a fault," she declared, placing them in a drawer. "If you take dictation as accurately as you type, Marlow Ray, you'll be the perfect secretary."

"Thank you," said Mary Eliska demurely and slipped the compact into the pocket of her frock. "It is very nice of you to say that."

"Then we'll go in to luncheon, shall we? That is, if you're ready?"

Mary Eliska stood up. "Quite ready, Mrs. Lawson, and good and hungry, too."

"Splendid!" enthused her hostess, as they walked down the corridor toward the entrance hall. "Doctor Winn declares this Connecticut Ridge country is the most healthful section of the United States. And even if some people have other ideas on the subject, I can testify that it is a great appetite builder."

Mary Eliska smiled, but said nothing. She was wondering how healthful she was going to find this particular spot in the Ridge country after what she had to do tonight.

"Doctor Winn always lunches in his study," continued Mrs. Lawson. "That is the room just beyond my office. My husband has been called to New York on business. He won't be back until after dinner tonight, so we will be alone at luncheon."

For some reason of her own, Laura Lawson had become affability itself. And for this Mary Eliska gave thanks. That she disliked this truly beautiful creature was only natural. But it is much more pleasant to lunch with a person who puts herself out to be charming and affable, no matter what your private opinion of the other's character may be.

The dining room proved to be a low-ceiled apartment paneled in white pine; heavy beams of the satin-finished wood overhead, and on the walls several colorful landscapes in oils, evidently the works of artists who knew and loved this Ridge country. A cheerful log fire burned brightly on the open hearth beneath a high mantelpiece. Outside, the heavy snow continued to drive past frosted window-panes, but within all was warmth and coziness.

Mary Eliska enjoyed the meal thoroughly. Like most girls, she revelled in luxury when it came her way. Not only was her hostess an interesting and entertaining conversationalist, the delicious food served by Tunbridge and a second man in plum-colored knee breeches, added materially to her pleasure. She was really sorry when the butler lighted his mistress' cigarette and Mrs. Lawson rose from the table.

"I have no work for you this afternoon, Marlow Ray," said the lady, as they strolled into the spacious hall with its suits of polished armor and trophies of war and the chase decorating the walls. "I have some work to complete with Doctor Winn, so I won't be free to entertain you. There are periodicals and novels in the library. If it weren't such a beastly day, I would suggest a walk."

"Oh, I don't mind a snowstorm!" Mary Eliska smiled at her. "I'd love to be out in it for a while."

"But I'm afraid you might get lost. The blizzard is driving out of the northeast—and that means something in this country. You'll find it more disagreeable than you think."

"I'm not afraid to walk in a blizzard," Mary Eliska argued, "we used to do it a lot at school—I love it."

"Oh, very well, then," went on Mrs. Lawson. "I used to enjoy that sort of thing myself. Somebody had better go with you, though. Let me see—" She hesitated. "Oh, yes—Gretchen will be just the person. She's a nice little thing—a native of Ridgefield, you know. Gretchen can show you round the place, and there'll be no chance of your getting lost."

Mary Eliska was amused by this pretended concern for her safety. She knew that Mrs. Lawson feared she might take it into her head to walk to the railroad station and board the first train back to town. Gretchen as guide and chaperone would be able to forestall anything like that. Mrs. Lawson was not yet sure of the new secretary!

Mary Eliska's features betrayed no sign of her thoughts. "That will be ever so much pleasanter than going alone," she agreed. "Gretchen seems to be a sweet girl. I saw her this morning when she brought my breakfast and unpacked my clothes. I'm sorry, though, that you can't come too." Deception, she found, was becoming a habit when treating with her hostess.

"Thank you, my dear—I'm sorry, too." Mrs. Lawson went toward the tasseled bell rope that hung beside the fireplace. "Run upstairs now and get into warm things. I'll ring for Gretchen and have her meet you down here in quarter of an hour."

Fifteen minutes afterward, warmly dressed in whipcord jodhpurs, a heavy sweater and knee-length leather coat of dark green, Mary Eliska came out of her room onto the gallery, pulling a white wool skating cap well down over her ears. With a white wool scarf twisted about her throat, the long ends thrown back over her shoulders, she looked ready for any winter sport as she ran lightly down the stairs, the rubber soles of her high arctics making no sound on the broad oaken steps.

Gretchen, well bundled up in sweater and heavy tweed skirt was waiting for her.

"You certainly do look like a picture on a Christmas magazine cover, Marlow Ray," the girl exclaimed, while they walked to the front door. "I'm glad you've got warm gauntlets. It's mighty cold out—you'll need them."

Mary Eliska laughed gaily and swung open the door. "Nothing could be more becoming than your own costume, Gretchen. That light blue skating set is just the color of your eyes."

"That," chuckled Gretchen, "is the real reason I bought it."

They were outside now and standing under the wide porte-cochere of glass and wrought iron.

"It's glorious out here, and not too cold, either." Mary Eliska sniffed the sharp air enthusiastically. "I hate staying indoors on a wild day like this. Look at those big flakes spinning down and sideslipping into the drifts. It makes one glad to be alive."

"You said it, Marlow Ray. I love it myself—though I never thought of snowflakes being like airplanes before. Which way do you want to go?" "You're the leader, Gretchen. Anywhere you say suits me." "Then let's tramp over to the pond, Marlow Ray. The ice ought to be holding. We'll stop at the garage and fetch a broom along. There's too much snow for skating, but we might make a slide."

"That will be fun," agreed Mary Eliska, as they came down the steps and swung along the white expanse of driveway. "I haven't done anything like that since I was a kid. How far's the pond from here?"

"About half a mile. Doctor Winn owns several hundred acres. It's down yonder in a hollow. This time of year when the trees are bare, you can see it plainly from the house. Today there's too much snow."

"There certainly is plenty of it!" Mary Eliska was ploughing through the fluffy white mass nearly up to her knees. "A good eighteen inches must have fallen already and it's drifting fast. If it doesn't stop by tonight, Winncote will be snowed in for a while. What's that building over there, Gretchen—gray stone, isn't it?"

"That's the laboratory, miss. It's really a wing of the house. The stables are just beyond, but this storm's so thick, it blots them out. Well, here we are at the garage. If you'll wait a minute, I'll step inside and get a broom."

"Get two if you can," suggested Mary Eliska. "Then we'll both get some exercise, and they'll come in handy while we're getting through the drifts."

"I'll do my best," said Gretchen. She disappeared through a door in the side of the building.

Mary Eliska looked about her. Rolling clouds of windswept snowflakes made it impossible to see objects more than a few yards away with any distinctness. The dark shadow of low clouds painted the white of her landscape a cold, dull gray. But she noticed, as she waited, that the storm was driving in gusts, that occasionally there would be a short lull when the sun, tinging the sky with rose and yellow, seemed fighting to break its way through to this white-blanketed world. Then Gretchen, a broom in each hand, joined her.

"Whew! that place was stuffy," she said, handing one of the brooms to Mary Eliska, and starting ahead at right angles from the way they had come. "Hanley made a fuss giving me two—he would! It's a wonder the cars don't melt in there. He keeps the place like an oven. All the help from the city is like that. They can't seem to get warm enough, and the way they hate fresh air is a caution! I roomed with Sadie, the other chambermaid, when I first came, and you won't believe it, but that girl had nailed our window shut so it couldn't be opened! I spoke to Mr. Tunbridge next morning, and he gave me a room of my own. I always did like Mr. Tunbridge. He's a real gentleman, he is."

They forged ahead through the drifts to the crossfire of Gretchen's light chatter, and Mary Eliska was given a series of entertaining stories concerning the habits of the Winncote servants and their life below-stairs. It was rough going with the storm in their faces, and Gretchen eventually ceased her gossiping from sheer lack of breath. The ground began to slope gently downward, and finally they came to a belt of trees in a hollow. Fifty yards farther on, a broad expanse of white marked the extent of Winncote Pond beneath its thick, flat quilt of snow.

"Think the ice will hold?" Mary Eliska walked to the brink of the little lake. "I'd hate to go in on a day like this."

"Oh, that's all right. I was down here for an hour yesterday afternoon with my skates before the snow began, and it was much warmer then. The ice was wonderful—slick as glass and solid as a rock."

By dint of considerable exercise they cleared two narrow paths that ran parallel across the ice. Then they commenced a series of sliding contests, each girl on her own ice track. Starting at a line in the snow a few yards above the low bank, they would race forward to the brink and shoot out on the ice, vying with each other to see who could slide the farthest. There were several tumbles at first, but the deep snow along the sides of the tracks prevented bad bumps. Soon, however, they both became adepts at the sport. Mary Eliska, aided by her extra weight, for she was at least twenty pounds heavier than little Gretchen, invariably won.

After a half an hour of this rather violent sport, they cleared the snow from a fallen tree trunk and sat down for a rest. Here in the hollow, surrounded by trees, the wind lost a great deal of its force. But the snow continued to fall unabated, and their hot breath clouded like steam in the cold air. Their cheeks were tingling crimson from the racing, and both felt in high good spirits.

"I can't understand why so many rich people go south every winter," Gretchen said earnestly. "I wouldn't miss out on this fun—the snow and the skating, tobogganing—for anything in the world."

"People like that," decreed Mary Eliska, "just don't know how to live. You can have lots of fun in summer, of course. I don't know which I love the best. But this sort of thing makes you feel just grand. It certainly put the pep into—." She stopped short and sprang to her feet. From somewhere close by and seemingly below her, had come a low, moaning sound.

Gretchen jumped up. Her doll-like face with its round, blue eyes took on a look of startled wonder. "What was that?" she cried. "It sounded as if I—as if I was sitting on it!"

Again came the low cry in a weird, minor key.

"You were. It's coming from the inside of this log. An animal of some kind."

"Why, I guess you're right. Whatever it is, the thing gave me the heebie-jeebies for a minute."

The snow had drifted over the butt of the half-rotted tree. Mary Eliska took her broom and swept it clear.

"The log's hollow!" she exclaimed and bent down. "Yes, there's something in there—I can see its eyes—come here, Gretchen! You can see for yourself."

"Not me!" declared that young woman. "I don't want to get bit—I mean, bitten, miss."

"Oh, never mind the grammar." Mary Eliska was almost standing on her head, trying to get a better view. "But do cut out the polite trimmings when we're alone. You're Gretchen and I'm Mary Eliska—savez?"

"All right—Mary Eliska. But please be careful. That thing may jump out at you."

"I wish it would. Then I'd know what it is. And whatever it is, the animal in there can't be much bigger than a rabbit. The hole isn't wide enough."

"Maybe it is a rabbit." Gretchen came nearer.

"Did you ever hear a rabbit make a noise like that?" Mary Eliska's tone was disdainful.

"Then—maybe it's a wildcat!" said Gretchen fearfully.

"Well, if it is, it's a small one. Here, puss—puss. The silly thing is too far in to reach. She just blinks at me."

"Perhaps she's hurt and crawled in there to die, Mary Eliska."

"Aren't you cheerful! She probably crawled in there to get out of the storm, and is half-frozen, poor thing."

"Well, I don't know what we're going to do about it," sighed Gretchen, still keeping her distance.

Once more the low moan came from the log, but now that the end was free from snow, the sound was much clearer.

"That's no wildcat, either!" Mary Eliska twisted her head, first to the right, then to the left, in an attempt to get a better light on the log's occupant. "There's too much of a whine in that cry. The thing's probably a young fox. How does one call a fox, Gretchen? I'm hanged if I know."

"Nor me, neither, Mary Eliska. It's the first time I've ever heard of anybody wanting to call one."

They both laughed. "You don't seem to know much about foxes," teased Mary Eliska. "Didn't you ever see a fox?"

"No. But my father says the way they steal eggs and suck them is a caution." "Well," admitted Mary Eliska, "we can't stand around here all day, trying to get frozen foxes out of hollow logs. I'll try whistling, and you can make a noise like a sucked egg. If that doesn't work, we'll have to leave him in his lair." With a wink at the giggling Gretchen, she bent down again and whistled shrilly. "Here, boy!" she called. "Come on out to your mama!"

There was a scrambling noise within the log, and Gretchen started for the pond.

"Oh, be careful, Mary Eliska! Do be careful!" she cried, as she saw her friend gather a small creature into her arms. "What is it, anyway—is it a fox?"

"No, a first cousin." Mary Eliska shook the ends of her wool scarf free from snow and wrapped them around the small animal.

"A first cousin?" Gretchen came nearer. "What in the world do you mean by that?"

"Come and take a look," her friend invited. "He won't bite you, will you, boy?"

Gretchen saw her pat a little black nose that poked its way out of the scarf. A long, pointed head, brindle and white, in which were set two snapping black eyes, followed the nose. "Why, why, it's a fox terrier—a fox terrier puppy!" she gasped. "How do you suppose he ever came to crawl into that log?"

Mary Eliska patted the dog's head. "Got lost in the storm, I guess. The poor little chap can't be over three months old. Does he belong up at the house?"

"No, he doesn't. What's more, none of the people who live around here have a fox terrier pup that I know of."

Mary Eliska examined the pup's front paws, but did so very gently. "This little man has come a long way." She covered him again. "The bottom of his feet show it. They're cut and badly swollen. And he's half-frozen and starved into the bargain, I'll bet. Let's go back to the house and make him comfortable."

"I'll carry the brooms," said Gretchen. "You have an armful, with him. By the way, you're going to keep him, aren't you?"

"Surest thing you know! That is, unless someone comes to claim him."

They trudged off through the trees and up the hill, Gretchen shouldering the brooms.

"What are you going to call him?" she asked, after a while.

"What do you think?"

"Why, I don't know. Wait a minute, though—there's a girl who lives over in Silvermine named Dorothea Gutmann. Daddy sometimes does work for her father. Dorothea has a fox terrier pup and she calls him 'Professor.' Do you know why?"

"I give up," said Mary Eliska, floundering through the snow beside her. "Why does Dorothea Gutmann call her fox terrier pup Professor?"

"Because," smiled Gretchen in delight, "he just about ate up a dictionary!"

Mary Eliska laughed merrily, and hugged the warm little bundle in her arms. "And when you've got outside a lot of words like that, even a pup would know as much as the average professor, I s'pose."

"That's the way Dorothea thought about it. I've been over to the Gutmanns a couple of times with Daddy and her dog looks enough like yours to be a twin!"

"We run into doubles nowadays, every day!" Mary Eliska chuckled. "First it's Marlow Ray and me who can't be told apart. Then it's Dorothea's dog and mine. I know her, too, by the way. She's in the New Canaan Junior High. But I haven't seen her puppy. Our names are almost alike, too, but not quite, thank goodness. If any more of this double identity business comes along, I'll just have to give up. A girl's got to have some sort of a personality all her own, you know."

"I wouldn't let that worry me," said Gretchen. "There's only one Mary Eliska, after all."

"Thanks for those kind words, Gretchen. That's really very sweet of you, though. If the pup was a lady, I'd call him 'Gretchen'. Since he isn't, 'Professor' will do very nicely. We'll try him on a dictionary when we get home, that is, after he's had some nice warm bread and milk, and a good sleep."

"If," smiled Gretchen, "what you said just now was meant for a compliment—well, I'm glad Professor is not a lady. You'd better go on to the house, while I drop these brooms in here at the garage. I'll come to your room just as soon as I can slip into my uniform, and I'll bring up the bread and milk."

"I always knew you were a dear," said Mary Eliska, and she continued to push her way on toward the house.

Chapter 4.15
TEA AND ORDERS

After she had changed her clothes and fed the famished pup with a bowl of warm milk and bread, Mary Eliska took him down to the library. Gretchen brought a small open basket and a blanket and they made him a bed near the open fire. Professor promptly went to sleep, and his mistress curled up in a deep chair beside him, reading and dozing for the rest of the afternoon. To amuse Gretchen, she had placed a dictionary near the basket, to see if Professor would follow his double's example and so justify his name. When he awoke, however, about four o'clock, he merely jumped out of his bed on to the book, and up to Mary Eliska's lap, where he went to sleep again.

"Good ole pup!" Mary Eliska rubbed his smooth, warm head between his ears. "You show your intelligence by using the dictionary as a stepping stone to better things, don't you, Prof!"

She yawned, closed her book, and promptly went to sleep again herself.

She awoke with a start, to find Mrs. Lawson smiling down at her. Tunbridge was laying the tea-things on a table at the other side of the fire. "Well, my dear," the lady said, her eyes on the fox terrier, "I see you've found a new friend."

"Oh, yes, isn't he just too darling? I found him out in the blizzard, he was half frozen and almost starved!" She went on to tell Mrs. Lawson about it.

"I'm afraid I'm not very fond of animals, Marlow Ray." Mary Eliska noticed that she did not attempt to touch the puppy. "I don't dislike them, you understand, but somehow they never seem to like me."

"That's too bad," said Mary Eliska. "I do hope you won't mind my keeping him—at least until we learn who his owner is?"

Laura Lawson looked doubtful. "Well, I don't mind. But—this is Doctor Winn's house, you know, and his decision, after all, is the one that counts. You will have to ask him about keeping the dog, Marlow Ray."

"Is Doctor Winn going to have tea with us, Mrs. Lawson?"

"He most certainly is, my dear. That is, if you ladies will pour him a cup."

Mary Eliska glanced up, and beside her stood an old gentleman, very tall and spare, but bowed with the weight of his years. She knew that the scientist was well over eighty. Catching up the fox terrier, she rose to her feet.

"How do you do, Doctor Winn?" She smiled and offered him her hand.

The old gentleman bent over it with courtly grace. "Good afternoon, Miss Marlow Ray. Welcome to Winncote." Merry gray eyes twinkled at her from behind pince-nez attached to a broad black ribbon. An aristocrat of the old school, Mary Eliska thought, as she studied his handsome, clean-shaven face crisscrossed with the tiny wrinkles of advanced age. She had imagined him to be quite a different sort of person. His next words proved that he read her thoughts.

"You expected to see a musty old fellow, with a long white beard, wearing a smock stained by chemicals, eh?" He chuckled softly. "Now, tell me, young lady, isn't that so? Though I admit these flannel slacks and old Norfolk jacket are hardly fashionable habiliments when one is taking tea with ladies!"

He released her hand and smiled a greeting to Mrs. Lawson. The second footman, he of the plum-colored knee-breeches, set the tea table before that young matron, under the supervision of the stately Tunbridge.

Mary Eliska liked this gallant old scientist and his courtly ways. Her own eyes sparkled gaily back at him. "Yes, you did surprise me, Doctor Winn," she confessed. "Please don't think I'm being forward, but—but you seem much more like the English fox-hunting squires I've read about, than the world-renowned chemist you really are, with stacks of letters after your name. But ever so much nicer, and jollier, you know!"

Doctor Winn beamed. "Now that, my dear, is a most charming compliment. Old fellows like me aren't used to compliments from young ladies, either. Do sit down again, please, and tell me how you like Winncote and our New England snowstorms. We old people need young folks around. I can see that we are going to be good friends."

He sat down in a chair the butler drew up for him.

"Mrs. Lawson will tell you," replied Mary Eliska, "that I love it out here in the country." She accepted a cup of tea from Tunbridge and added sugar and a slice of lemon. The butler was followed by his liveried assistant, bearing silver platters of hot, buttered scones and tiny iced cakes. Professor immediately began to show interest in the proceedings. Mary Eliska held him firmly out of harm's way, and placed her tea and eatables on the broad arm of her chair.

Mrs. Lawson looked up from her place behind the shining silver and old china of the tea table. She smiled graciously. "Oh, yes, Marlow Ray loves blizzards, too, Doctor Winn. She went out for a walk this afternoon and acquired a fox terrier puppy, as you see."

"And naturally, she wants to keep him." The old gentleman leaned forward in his chair, the better to look at Professor. "You certainly may, Marlow Ray. And by the way, I hope you'll agree that it's an old man's privilege to call you by your first name?"

"Oh, that is sweet of you!" Mary Eliska cried delightedly, and the Doctor's chuckle echoed her pleasure.

"The dog's got a fine head—a very fine head, indeed. If anybody advertises for him, or comes to claim him, I'll take pleasure in buying the puppy for you."

"Why, you're nicer every minute," declared Mary Eliska. "Isn't he, Professor?"

The pup yawned with great indifference, which set all three of them laughing. His mistress put him in his blanket where he promptly curled up and fell into slumber once more.

"I sadly fear," said Doctor Winn, as he polished his pince-nez with a white silk handkerchief, "that you are a good deal of a flirt Marlow Ray. But inasmuch as I am old enough to be your grandfather, or great-grandfather, for that matter, you are pardoned with a reprimand." He chuckled deep in his throat, a habit he had when pleased. "Now tell me, how you happened to find him out in the snow."

Mary Eliska recounted the story in detail. When she came to the part about Gretchen's fear of the wildcat and the fox, even Mrs. Lawson, who was none too sure she liked the turn things were taking, broke into a merry peal of laughter.

"Capital, capital!" Doctor Winn beamed. "I only wish I'd been there to see it. But why, may I ask, do you call him Professor?"

Mary Eliska explained about the dictionary and Gretchen's idea of the pup's resemblance to Dorothea Gutmann's fox terrier. "Better and better," exclaimed the Doctor. "This is the jolliest tea we've had in this house for ages. We need young people around us to be really happy. You and I and Martin, Laura, have been working too hard of late. 'All work and no play'—We've been bothering too much about things scientific, and neglecting things personal. Well now, we can rest a while, and become human beings again."

Mrs. Lawson leaned forward eagerly. "Then, the formula is complete?" she asked in a low voice, in which Mary Eliska detected the barely controlled tremor of excitement.

"Yes, indeed. Finished and locked in my safe. I added the final figures and quantities three-quarters of an hour ago. Tomorrow, or if the weather doesn't clear by then, the next day at latest, I shall take it on to Washington."

"I congratulate you, Doctor. And I know that once it is in the hands of the government, a great load will be taken off your mind."

"You're right, my dear, you are right. I've been jumpy as a cat with eight of its lives gone for the past year." He turned to Mary Eliska. "Thank goodness, you're young and without responsibilities, Marlow Ray. There are so many unscrupulous people about nowadays. If those papers were lost or stolen, there is no telling what would happen. I dare not think of it. The whole world might suffer if that formula got into the wrong hands!"

Mary Eliska could not help thinking that the world at large would be much better off if the formula were destroyed. She, therefore, merely nodded and looked impressed. How this gentle, kindly old man could have brought himself to invent such a ghastly menace to life, she found it difficult to understand.

Laura Lawson stood up. "Doctor Winn likes to dine early, Marlow Ray, so if we are to be dressed by six-thirty, we had better start upstairs."

"My word, yes!" The old gentleman snapped open the hunting case of his repeater and got stiffly to his feet. "Time flies when one is enjoying oneself. It's nearly six o'clock. This has been very pleasant indeed, the first of many afternoons, I hope." He snapped the watch shut and returned it to his pocket. "You ladies will excuse me, I'm sure." He bowed to them both, and holding himself much more erect than he had formerly, walked stiffly from the room.

"He's simply darling," exclaimed Mary Eliska in a hushed voice.

"Yes, he's a very simple and a very fine old gentleman," said Laura Lawson. She seemed lost in her thoughts and evidently unaware that she uttered them aloud. "Sometimes—I hate to hurt him so.""Why—why, what do you mean?" Mary Eliska could have bitten her own tongue out for speaking that sentence.

"Mean—? Oh, nothing, child. Run along now, and change. But take your dog with you. I'll see that one of the men gives him a run in the stables while we're at dinner."

"Thank you very much," said Mary Eliska. She turned the sleeping pup out of his bed, caught up the basket, and with Professor at her heels, ran lightly from the room. Just outside the door she collided with Tunbridge, and Professor's basket was jerked from her grasp.

"Oh, I'm so very sorry, Marlow Ray!" His acting was perfect. Mary Eliska knew that Mrs. Lawson was close behind them. Then as they both stooped to retrieve the basket their heads came close together. "Under your pillow!" It was hardly more than the breath of a whisper, but Mary Eliska caught the words, nodded her understanding, and stood up.

"I'm afraid I'm to blame, Tunbridge. I didn't see you coming."

"Not at all, Miss. It was my fault, entirely. Very clumsy of me I'm sure!"

From the corner of her eye Mary Eliska caught a glimpse of Laura Lawson watching them from the doorway.

"Don't let it worry you, Tunbridge. I'm not hurt, neither is the basket. Professor will probably park himself on my *pillow* tonight, anyway. Puppies have a way of doing such things, you know. So it really wouldn't matter much if you had smashed it."

She gave him a nod, and picking up the dog made for the staircase.

"So instructions are waiting under my pillow," she mused, as she slowly mounted the broad stair. The afternoon had been a pleasant one, but the evening, with those instructions ahead of her, portended to be something quite different. It had been so nice and cheerful, chatting round the tea table; so cozy sitting before the glowing logs, just talking of jolly things and forgetting all worry and responsibility. Of course, beyond the curtained windows, the blizzard howled. And it whipped the swirling snowflakes into disordered clouds with its arctic lash before it let them seek the shelter of their fellows in the drifts. She felt very much as though she too were a snowflake, tossed hither and thither on the storm of circumstance, to be whipped forward by the secret lash of underlying crime.

If she could only drop down on to her bed and sleep—and awake to find it all a bad dream! She sighed and went toward her door on the gallery. Her pillow held no peace for her tonight—nothing more nor less than detailed instructions as to how Tunbridge wished her to rob a safe. Why didn't the man do his own stealing? Her part was to take Marlow Ray's place out here, and kill suspicion in Laura Lawson. Well, she'd done that, hadn't she? And now they loaded this other job on to her. It wasn't fair. She had done enough—she'd—

"Oh, shucks!" She pulled herself up mentally as her hand fell on the doorknob. "I'll be losing my nerve altogether, if I let my thoughts run on this way. Mary Eliska, you just *must not* funk it!" She turned the knob and entered her room.

Chapter 4.16
CAUGHT IN THE ACT

When Mary Eliska went down to dinner that evening, she knew exactly what she had to do. After reading Tunbridge's note which she found had been slipped between the pillow case and the pillow itself, she had memorized the combination to Doctor Winn's safe, and destroyed the missive as she had his warning of the night before. After a bath and a complete change of clothing, she felt refreshed and in a much better frame of mind. She had selected one of the prettiest gowns in Marlow Ray's wardrobe, a turquoise blue crepe, with a cluster of silver roses fastened in the twisted velvet girdle, put on slippers to match, and surveyed the result in the mirror.

"Decidedly becoming, my girl," she smiled at her reflection, and gave a last pat to her shining bob that she had brushed until it lay like a bronze cap close about her shapely head. "Might as well look my best at my criminal debut!" She made a face at herself, turned and kissed the sleeping puppy in his basket, and went downstairs.

Doctor Winn and Mrs. Lawson were standing talking in the entrance hall, near the fireplace. The old gentleman, dressed in immaculate dinner clothes, looked more than ever like the English squire in his ancestral hall. He came forward to meet her, both hands outstretched. "As charming as an English primrose and twice as beautiful!" he greeted gaily. "Thank you kindly, sir." She dropped him a little curtsey and let him lead her to Mrs. Lawson.

"Our little secretary has blossomed into a very lovely debutante," he beamed.

Mary Eliska bit her lip, remembering her own phrase of a few moments before, then smiled at her employer. Mrs. Lawson was regal in black velvet, trimmed in narrow bands of ermine. She returned Mary Eliska's smile, and lifted her finely penciled brows at the Doctor. "Oh, you men. You are all alike. A pretty gown, a pretty face intrigues you, young or old. Pay no attention to his flattery, Marlow Ray. I can hardly blame him, though. You look lovely tonight. That is an exquisite frock. Did you buy it abroad?"

"Oh, no, at a little place on fifty-seventh street." Of course Mary Eliska had no idea where Marlow Ray had bought the dress. "It is a Paris model, though, Mrs. Lawson."

"I thought as much. Ah, here comes Tunbridge with the cocktails. I wonder which side of the fence you are on?"

"I'm—I'm afraid I don't know quite what you mean, Mrs. Lawson."

"I'll explain," broke in the old gentleman. "I'm the prohibitionist in this house, Marlow Ray. Mrs. Lawson is one of the antis. She likes a real cocktail before dinner. I prefer one made of tomato juice."

Mrs. Lawson had already helped herself to a brimming glass and a small canapé of caviar from the silver tray Tunbridge was holding.

"Oh, I love tomato cocktails," smiled Mary Eliska. She took one from the man and helped herself to the caviar. "Daddy asked me not to drink until I was twenty-one—and I'm not so keen on the idea, anyway."

"I try to keep an open mind about such things," the Doctor said seriously, "but I've never found that the use of alcohol did anyone any good. Well, here's your very good health, ladies!" He raised his glass of tomato juice and drank.

Dinner was announced a few minutes later. Doctor Winn offered his right arm to Mrs. Lawson and his left to Mary Eliska and they walked into the dining room. Mary Eliska did not enjoy that meal as much as she had her luncheon. True, the food was delicious and the panelled room with its cheerful fire on the hearth and the soft glow of candle light was delightfully homey, while Doctor Winn's easy chatter and fund of interesting reminiscence helped to break the tedium of the courses. But Mary Eliska found it difficult to play up to his amusing sallies. The old gentleman appeared to be in very good spirits indeed. Laura Lawson, on the other hand, was unusually quiet. At times she seemed distrait and merely smiled absently when spoken to. She drank several glasses of claret, but hardly touched her food. Mary Eliska felt surer than ever that the Lawsons had planned their coup for tonight. She shrewdly surmised that this cold-blooded adventuress had become fond of the genial, fatherly old man, and realized that at his age the blow she contemplated might very well prove a fatal one.

As the dinner wore on, Mary Eliska felt more and more ill at ease. The sight of Tunbridge, soft-footed and efficient, waiting on table or superintending his satellite of the plum-colored kneebreeches, sent her thoughts to the night's work ahead every time the detective-butler came into the room. She was glad when at last the meal was over and they repaired to the library where after-dinner coffee was served. Mary Eliska rarely drank coffee in the evening, but tonight she allowed Tunbridge to fill her cup a second time. There must be no sleep for her until the wee hours of the morning, and she knew from former experience that the black coffee would keep her awake.

Mrs. Lawson, after wandering aimlessly about the room, finally picked up a technical magazine and commenced to read. Doctor Winn suggested a game of chess to Mary Eliska. She was fond of the ancient game and told him so. Many a tournament she and her father had played with their red and white ivory chessmen. Dr. Winn was a brilliant player, of long experience. Soon he began to compliment Mary Eliska upon a number of strategic moves. But although several times she managed to place his king in check, it was invariably her own royal chessman who was checkmated in the end. As the evening wore on, the beatings became more frequent, for Mary Eliska simply could not keep her mind on the game.

For a while she sat watching the log fire and talking to the Doctor in a desultory way while Mrs. Lawson continued to read. Then as the grandfather clock chimed ten, Laura Lawson laid down her magazine and stood up.

"I think I'll go to bed now, if you don't mind." The half-stifled yawn, sheer camouflage thought Mary Eliska, was nevertheless a masterpiece of deception. "I've a bit of a headache, so I'll say good night."

Doctor Winn and Mary Eliska got to their feet. "I'm for bed myself," announced the old gentleman, "and in spite of the coffee you drank after dinner, I know you're sleepy, Marlow

Ray. Your chess playing toward the end proved it." His eyes twinkled at her. "But in storm or clear weather, there's nothing like the air of this Connecticut Ridge Country to make one eat and sleep. By the way, Laura, when do you expect Martin?"

"Oh, I forgot to tell you, Doctor—he won't be back tonight. He phoned me from town just before dinner, that on account of the blizzard, he had decided to stay in until tomorrow. If you need him sooner, he said to call up the Roosevelt. He always stops there, you know."

"Yes, yes, but I shan't need him, thank you." He turned to Mary Eliska. "The railroad has taken upon itself to discontinue all service to Ridgefield," he explained. "Branchville is our nearest station, and driving will be difficult tonight. There must be very deep drifts by this time."

"I should think it would be mighty unpleasant to get stuck out in a blizzard like this. I'm glad I don't have to go out into it. But in a way I'm thankful for the snow, because we ought to have a white Christmas, and it's ever so much more fun."

"Bless my soul! I'd entirely forgotten that Christmas comes next week. Well, this year we must celebrate the Yuletide in the good old-fashioned way. Thank you, Marlow Ray, for reminding me."

Good nights were said, and a few minutes later Mary Eliska was again alone in the Pink Bedroom. Or so she thought, as she entered. But at once she noticed that a single shaded wall-light sent a pleasant glow from the bay window, and curled up in the cushioned recess, Gretchen was reading.

Mary Eliska stopped short in surprise and the girl sprang to her feet. "Oh, Miss—Marlow Ray, Mr. Tunbridge told me to come and help you undress and get ready for the night. Of course I didn't know if you would want me—" then she added in a whisper, "but he thought you might be sort of blue and I could cheer you up, I guess."

Mary Eliska smiled at Gretchen's pretty, earnest face. "Why, of course I want you, Gretchen. Tunbridge is very thoughtful. I've never had the luxury of a personal maid and I don't know that I'll ever feel helpless enough to need one! But if you want to stay and talk, I'd love it."

"But I can help you, too," Gretchen insisted. "I'm not really a trained maid, you know, but Nanette—that's Mrs. Lawson's French maid—has been teaching me. Gee, I'd certainly love to be *your* personal maid, Marlow Ray."

"Well, you may be, someday, who knows?" she laughed. "But you can help me tonight, though there'll be no bed for me until much later."

Gretchen, who was arranging the pillows and smoothing the covers on the bed, turned her head sharply. "Secret Service Work?" she queried in an excited whisper.

Mary Eliska nodded and tossed her dress on to a chair. She continued speaking in a tone just above a whisper. "At twelve o'clock tonight I've got to go downstairs and commit justifiable burglary in Doctor Winn's office. The real thief will be along later—at least, I hope so, for everybody's sake. In the meantime I want you to do something for me—will you?"

"I sure will, miss—gee, this is exciting!"

"Don't let it cramp your style." Mary Eliska laughed, and pulling off her stocking, she handed Gretchen the packet of thin paper, the manuscript on "Winnite" that she had typed that morning. "When you finish up in here, I want you to find Mr. Tunbridge and give him these papers. You'd better pin it inside your uniform now, and be very careful that nobody sees you giving it to him."

"You can trust me," declared Gretchen, and she put the papers safely within her dress. "Is Mr. Tunbridge really a detective?"

"He certainly is, Gretchen."

"I'd never have guessed it if you hadn't told me. But then, I suppose not looking like one makes him all the better?"

"That's the idea." Mary Eliska put Marlow Ray's quilted satin dressing gown on over her pajamas. "Now that I'm ready for bed, and you've put all my clothes away so nicely, I think you'd better run along, Gretchen. Not," she amended, "that I wouldn't love to talk to you while I'm waiting for twelve o'clock, but we must not let certain people in this house get wise to our friendship."

"And Mrs. Lawson is one awful snoopy lady," Gretchen observed candidly. "Well, good night, Marlow Ray. Thank you a lot for letting me in on this. I'll see that Mr. Tunbridge gets your papers all right. Good night—and take care of yourself." She stood before Mary Eliska with an anxious frown on her honest brow. "I sure do wish you the very best luck!"

Mary Eliska grinned. "Thank you. I certainly need it. Good night."

The door closed upon the little maid and Mary Eliska looked at her wrist watch. It was ten minutes to eleven. For a time she sat on the edge of her bed and stared unseeingly at the rug under her feet. Presently she got up, locked her door, turned off her lights and went over to the window. She drew aside the curtains and was surprised to see that it had stopped snowing. There was no moon, but what sky she could see was fairly a-crackle with stars. The heavy blanket of snow looked silver in the starlight. A remote world and cold. Mary Eliska allowed the curtains to drop back into place, and sat down on the window seat. Lost in thoughts pleasant and unpleasant, she sat there for the next hour, while the faint noises of the big house gradually subsided into stillness.

At exactly five minutes to twelve, Mary Eliska raised the window, letting in the cold night air. Then she turned off the heat and got into bed. After lying there for possibly a minute, she threw back the covers, thrust her feet into the fur-lined slippers she had left at the bedside and moved like a dim shadow to the closet.

It was crowded with Marlow Ray's suits, coats and frocks, and she was careful not to disturb them on their hangers, as she pushed between them in the darkness to the rear wall and pressed her foot on the board in the corner. The panel slid upward with a noiselessness that spoke for well-oiled machinery somewhere in the walls. Mary Eliska stepped cautiously through the opening. Her fingers sought the handle to this sliding door, found it, and she pulled the panel down again.

Then for the first time she made use of the small flashlight which she carried in the pocket of her gown. She saw that she was standing on the top step of a narrow circular stair that wound downward. Off went her light again—she was taking no unnecessary chances tonight—and with her hand on the metal handrail, she felt her way slowly down the stair, holding her free hand well in advance of her body.

When her extended fingers touched a wall that blocked further progress, she felt with a slippered foot out to the right. The board gave slightly, the wall panel moved upward and she stepped forth to find herself in the great fireplace of the entrance hall, just beyond the embers of the dying logs. The hall was illuminated in the dim glow of a night light in the ceiling. As she turned to pull down the sliding shutter, there came a streak of white from the dark passage and Professor bounded into the hall.

Mary Eliska was completely startled, and just as exasperated as she could be. She could not call him, for the slightest sound might bring the wakeful enemy to the spot. The pup, after his long sleep, was playful, and scampered about madly, his bright eyes watching her every move. She attempted to catch him, but he eluded her with an agility that made her still more angry. He seemed to think that this was a splendid game, raced across the floor in high glee, but ever watchful to keep beyond her reach.

Mary Eliska gave it up as a bad job. She dared not pursue him too determinedly, for fear he would bark. She pulled down the sliding shutter in the fireplace, and leaving Professor to his frolic, hurried on to the door of Doctor Winn's office.

Inside the room with the door shut, her flashlight came into play for the second time. It took her but a moment with the memorized combination at her fingertips to open the safe. The door was surprisingly heavy, but at last the interior of the small vault came within her line of vision. From a drawer she took a folded sheet of white paper. Out of her pocket came a pencil and another sheet of paper. In an amazingly short time she copied the formula and replaced the original in the safe drawer. She tucked the copy into the fur lining of her slipper under her bare foot. Then suddenly she sprang up. Her heart leaped into her throat. In the corridor just outside there came the sound of a footstep. There was no time to do more than shut off her torch and drop it, together with her pencil, into the waste paper basket. The door opened, lights flashed on, and Martin Lawson walked into the room.

Chapter 4.17
PROFESSOR MAKES GOOD

In that moment, Mary Eliska knew what she must do. A shiver ran over her slender frame and she blinked as though partly awakened by the flash of lights. Then, with eyes wide open and staring straight ahead, she slowly walked toward Martin Lawson and the open doorway.

"*Stop!*"

The command, though low, was uttered in a tone of deadly menace, and Mary Eliska saw the blue-black muzzle of an automatic revolver pointed at her heart. She stopped on the instant, but continued to stare straight ahead without change of expression. She noted that he wore a soft felt hat pulled over his eyes and a heavy ulster with its broad collar turned up half hiding the lower part of his face. His high arctics bore traces of melting snow. "Sleepwalking, eh! Well, I don't believe it." His sharp eyes took in the open door of the safe. "Snap out of that playacting and tell me what you are doing here!" Mary Eliska did not move a muscle.

Without warning, he grasped her wrist and jerked her savagely toward him. She screamed and went limp in his arms. Lawson clapped a hand over her mouth.

"So you're up to your old tricks again, Martin!"

Mrs. Lawson, fully dressed, and wearing a three-quarters mink coat and brown felt cloche, appeared in the open doorway. "So our little sleepwalker interrupted a very pretty piece of double-crossing!" She pointed toward the safe. Lawson flung the weeping girl into an arm chair where she lay apparently half stunned and shaking in every limb. "Double-cross, nothing!" he snapped at his wife. "How do you get that way, Laura? I came in here just now and found Marlow Ray in the room."

"Was she at the safe?" "No, she wasn't. She was standing in the middle of the floor. Making her getaway without a doubt when I turned on the lights."

"Why do you pretend Marlow Ray opened the safe? The Doctor, you and I are the only ones who know the combination. Laugh that off if you can, my dear!"

They were both fast losing their tempers.

"Combination or no combination, the safe was open when I got here," he snarled. "She was after the formula, of course. That father of hers is in back of it. That Irishman is the double-crosser—and how! Figured on working Winnite into his racket without coughing up a cent for it, either. Call me a sucker if you like, Laura. I qualify, and so do you, for that matter. The other stuff's the bunk."

Mary Eliska stopped her pretended crying and lay back as though utterly exhausted. She knew Tunbridge must be up and about. What in the world could the man be doing?

Mrs. Lawson who seemed to be weighing matters, slowly unbuttoned her coat. "If you are so blameless," she said coldly to her husband, "How do you happen to be here at all? Your part of the job was to bring up the car—or the plane, if it had stopped snowing."

"Well, it's no longer snowing, my dear, and the plane is just where it should be. I got tired of waiting, that's why. Thought there must be a slip-up. You were due out there half an hour ago."

"And I would have been," said Laura Lawson evenly, "if that secret service fool hadn't been snooping outside my door."

"Tunbridge?"

"Who else!"

"What did you do—croak him?"

"No, I didn't. He's not worth burning for."

As they talked, the two dropped their artificial cloaks of refinement as if they had never been.

"It's hanging in this state," sneered Martin.

"What's the difference! I rang for him, instead. When he knocked on the door, I opened up and beaned him with the poker. He'll wake up tomorrow with a headache, but I dragged him into my room and tied him up, just to make sure."

Mary Eliska's heart sank to the very soles of her bare feet.

"Atta girl!" cheered Lawson. "That's the way! And look here, Laura. Just to prove I'm on the straight with you—go over and frisk that kid yourself. She's got the paper."

"Thanks—I intended to." Mrs. Lawson threw a grim smile at her husband and turned to Mary Eliska. "Pass it over, Marlow Ray."

"But, really, Mrs. Lawson! I don't know what you're talking about—"

The woman cut her short. "Stand up and come here!"

Mary Eliska reluctantly obeyed. "I haven't any paper," she protested. "All I know is that I woke up just now and found Mr. Lawson—"

"Hold your tongue!" snapped Mrs. Lawson, and after exploring Mary Eliska's empty pockets, ran her fingers over the quilted gown and the girl's pajamas. In the midst of her search, Professor, still playful, bounded into the room and stood watching them expectantly.

Mrs. Lawson stepped back. "She hasn't got it, Martin." Her tone was acid. "What a hard-boiled liar you are, anyway!"

"Hard-boiled, if you like—but no liar." He strode to the safe and thrust his hand inside. "Here it is," he called, and held up the paper. "I must have got here before she could nab it."

Laura Lawson eyed him appraisingly. "Didn't you say Marlow Ray was in the middle of the room when you switched on the light?"

"Sure—she heard me coming, of course."

"If Marlow Ray heard you coming, why didn't she swing the door shut? Don't try to pull that stuff on me, Martin. Even if the girl knows the combination she couldn't open that safe in the dark. Why lie about the business? I know you opened it yourself—and what's more, while I've been wasting time arguing with you and searching Marlow Ray, the formula was in your pocket the whole time—that is, until you pretended to take it out of the safe, just now!"

Martin Lawson's hard and cruel mouth twisted into a crooked smile. "The world is full of liars," he said equably, "but your husband doesn't play that kind of a racket, Laura—anyway, not to you."

"Then prove it by giving me that paper!" his wife held out her hand.

"Nothing doing, Sweetheart. The formula will be perfectly safe with me." He started to put it in an inside pocket, when Laura Lawson sprang for the paper. She grasped his wrist. There was a tussle and the folded sheet fell to the floor. Professor, seated on his haunches and very interested in these exciting proceedings, dove forward and snapped it up. For half a moment he shook the paper as though he took it for a new species of rat. Then as they went for him, he darted between Martin's legs and scampered out of the room.

"You big goop!" flared his wife. "Why didn't you pot the cur!"

She rushed out of the room after Professor while Martin stared rather stupidly at the gun in his hand. Suddenly his eyes took on a particularly hard glint and he swung round on Mary Eliska.

"This," he rasped, "is the second time you've got me in wrong with my wife, Miss Marlow Ray. And there just ain't going to be no third time, kid!"

"Wha—what are you going to do, Mr. Lawson?" She was still playing the terrified, innocent Marlow Ray, but she no longer feared the man. During the Lawsons' struggle, she had prepared herself for something like this. She had also shifted her position and was standing near the open door, now several yards away.

"You're going to answer my questions, Marlow Ray—and answer them truthfully, or you'll do your sleepwalking in another world after this." He menaced her with the automatic, "It's the bunk, isn't it? The sleepwalking, I mean."

"It sure is, Mr. du Val!" drawled Mary Eliska with a sweet smile.

Lawson was thoroughly surprised and looked it. "Yes—it naturally would be, seeing you know who I really am."

"And all about you."

"Oh, you do, eh? You were awake, of course, at the meeting?"

"Not me—Marlow Ray."

"What do you mean—not you—Marlow Ray?"

"I mean that certain people have been making fools of you and your wife, Mr. du Val."

"Is that so! In what way, may I ask?"

"Why, you see, I'm not Marlow Ray."

"Not Marlow Ray!"

"I wish," said Mary Eliska, "you wouldn't echo my words. No, I am not—most decidedly, not Marlow Ray, although even you have guessed by this time that I look like her. We changed places on you, big boy! Night before last, just before you came into Marlow Ray's room with her father, Marlow Ray was climbing out the window when you knocked the first time. It was rather embarrassing."

"It's going to be even more embarrassing for you in a moment or two, Miss Not Marlow Ray! You know too much to live. Who in thunderation are you—a government dick?"

"That's right, big boy. I also happen to be Marlow Ray's double cousin."

"You're her double, I'll voucher that," agreed du Val alias Lawson. "And all this high-hat cockiness ain't going to do you one little bit of good. What's the moniker, kid? Make it snappy, I'm pressed for time."

"Mary Eliska's my name. And—meet Dash!" Her right hand gave a quick twist and Martin Lawson dropped the exploding automatic with a scream of mingled rage and pain. She sprang for the revolver, covered the man and retrieved the knife from the floor just behind him. "Sit down over there!" She pointed to a chair. "You're not really hurt, you know. Dash only skinned your knuckles. Better tie them up in your handkerchief though. You're ruining the rug."

Gretchen's blond head peered round the door frame. "Oh, Mary Eliska!" she shrilled, and rushed into the room. "Are you hurt? Did he wound you?" She flung herself on her friend in a frenzy of fright and hysterics.

From the hall came Laura Lawson's voice. "Martin!" she called. "They're out in front of the house. They've got the car! Hurry!"

Lawson wasted no time. While Mary Eliska struggled with the excited Gretchen, he nipped out of the room and was gone.

"That tears it!" cried Mary Eliska, freeing herself from the little maid's embrace, and she dove into the passage.

Under the gallery she stopped short. There was nobody in sight, but from the staircase came two sharp detonations of a revolver which were answered by two more from the dining room. Then as she moved warily forward, Bill Bolton ran into the hall with Ashton Sanborn close at his heels. Mary Eliska saw them disappear up the stairs and ran after them.

At the top of the stairs she spied them standing outside a bedroom door. She hurried to join them. "Hello! Gone to cover?"

"You're a great guesser, kid." Bill grinned and nodded.

"Where's Tunbridge?" asked Mr. Sanborn.

Mary Eliska motioned toward the door. "In there. He's got a broken head and he's tied up into the bargain. Laura Lawson did it. That's her room."

"We've got to get the door down," said Bill, and he stepped back for a rush.

"Just a sec, Bill!" Mary Eliska fired three shots from Lawson's automatic into the lock.

"Smart girl!" Ashton Sanborn opened the door to disclose the detective-butler bound and unconscious, lying on the floor. Otherwise the room was empty of occupants. "I thought as much," muttered the secret service man, while Mary Eliska ran to Tunbridge and began to cut his bonds. "They have beat it, all right!"

"Secret passage?" This from Bill. "Yes, the walls are honeycombed with them. But Tunbridge never learned the secret of this room, poor fellow." "Doctor Winn would know," said Mary Eliska. "His suite is right at the end of this corridor. He must surely be awake with all this racket going on."

"I'll get him." Mr. Sanborn was half way to the door. "Look after Tunbridge, you two. Better phone for a doctor." He was gone.

Mary Eliska and Bill lifted the unconscious man on to Mrs. Lawson's bed. Then while young Bolton undressed him, Mary Eliska telephoned. She then gave Bill a hasty account of the night's happenings.

"If Gretchen had only stayed put in her room, I'd have caught Martin Lawson, anyway," she lamented. "Mr. Ray and the bunch outside will take care of that pair," promised Bill. "Fetch a wet towel from the bathroom. This bird is breathing pretty hard."

Mary Eliska sped to obey, talking the while. "Not Uncle Michael!" she called back in astonishment.

"Yep. Uncle Michael showed up in Sanborn's New York office this morning, all on his own."

"What was he doing—wanting to turn state's evidence and peach on his pals?" She brought in the wet towel and laid it on Tunbridge's hot forehead.

"Nothing like that, kid." Bill was grinning. "Give another guess."

"Then he wasn't really a member of that gang with the numbers?"

"Sure he was—in good standing, too."

"Oh, spill it, Bill! What do you think I'm made of, anyway?"

"Snips and snails and puppy dog's tails," said Bill promptly.

"Huh! The story book says 'little boys' belong in that category. Come, Bill, out with it!"

"Well, then, cutie pie,—Uncle Michael is a secret service man."

"And Ashton Sanborn didn't know it! Don't talk rot, Bill!"

"I'm not talking rot, Mary Eliska. Uncle Michael happens to be in the British Secret Service, that's why!"

"Ain't that the nerts!" exploded Mary Eliska.

"You said it, kid! He got on to The Nameless Ones—that's what they call themselves—over on the other side, in Europe, you know—worked his way into their confidence and joined up. Of course, with his government's sanction."

"And what were they up to?"

"Out to blow up the world with Winnite, I reckon. The Lawsons were to get two million plunks for the formula. Martie-boy was Number 1, by the way. The whole thing was financed by the Reds."

"Nice people! What's being done about it?"

"Plenty," returned Bill. "Mr. Ray brought in the goods—letters, confidential papers of the organization, and that kind of thing. All the ringleaders, both in this country and abroad, have been apprehended and jailed by this time."

"Except," she suggested, "the du Vals, alias Lawson."

"That's right! Let's go downstairs and find out about them. Nothing more can be done for Tunbridge until that doctor shows up. He's had hard luck all the way round this evening. The Lawsons fooled him nicely about the time—and then this crack on the nut into the bargain!"

"What do you mean—about the time?"

"Why, he overheard the fair Laura telling her hubby that they would vamoose at two this morning, and that she would nab the formula just before leaving. That's why Tunbridge specified midnight. He thought that two hours leeway would have been plenty of time for you."

"I 'spose they suspected him then, and were just giving him the razz?"

Bill nodded. "Q.E.D., old girl. You're learning, aren't you?"

Mary Eliska made a face at him and pushed him out of the room. "By the way," continued Bill, as they entered the corridor, "I wonder if Mrs. Lawson got the paper away from Professor?"

"She did not!" declared Mary Eliska. "Look!"

They paused on the stairs to view the scene below in the entrance hall. Groups of frightened servants whispered among themselves and here and there a strange man was posted, with somewhat of an air of grim watchfulness. Crouched on the hearth and chewing up the last shreds of some white substance was the puppy.

"The end of a perfect formula," declared Bill. "You'd better call the pup Winnite. He's full of it by this time. Lucky you made the copy, Mary Eliska."

"It certainly is!" A voice spoke behind them and they turned to see Ashton Sanborn descending the broad stair. "Doctor Winn tells me the passageway from the Lawson woman's room comes out into the sunken gardens a quarter of a mile from the house. And I distinctly heard the whirr of an airplane just now from his open window. They've made their getaway in fine style by this time."

"Well—" Mary Eliska breathed a deep sigh. "I can't help being glad of it."

Bill stared at her. "Well!" he mimicked. "I must say you have astonishing reactions!"

"What's the matter, my dear?" asked Mr. Sanborn. "You've done brilliant work on this case, and then, you know, you've saved Winnite." Mary Eliska was not impressed. "That's just it," she retorted. "If I wasn't a government servant for the time being, I'd destroy the copy of that terrible formula myself. As it is, I've got to turn it over to you!"

Ashton Sanborn laid a fatherly hand on her shoulder. "Fortunes of war, Mary Eliska. Sorry, but you must, you know."

"Oh, I know!" She took the sheet of paper from her slipper and handed it to him. "And that," she announced grimly, "spoils all the fun on this racket."

Chapter 4.18
THE CHRISTMAS SPIRIT

Christmas eve was, as Mary Eliska had predicted, a starry night of frost and blanketing snow. Red candles twinkled in every holly-wreathed window of the Dixon home, and a large fir tree before the house glittered with colored Christmas lights.

If old Saint Nick had peeped into the dining room windows, he would have seen a merry company standing round the dinner table, gay with the crimson-berried holly and waxy mistletoe. At the head of the table stood Mary Eliska, appropriately and becomingly dressed in ruby-red velvet. On her right there was an empty place, and beyond it, old Doctor Winn, a boutonniere of holly in the lapel of his dinner coat; Mr. Bolton, Bill's father, was next down the table, and just beyond stood Ashton Sanborn. Facing Mary Eliska at the other end, her father chatted with a bright-eyed Gretchen, who had Bill on her right. Next to Bill came Doctor Winn's ex-butler, John Tunbridge, looking none the worse for his part in the mixup of the fatal night. Beyond Tunbridge stood Mary Eliska's Uncle Michael, and then another empty chair.

"Just a moment, Mary Eliska," said her father as she was about to sit down. "We've a surprise for you."

"Oh, are there more people coming?" She indicated the extra places to her right and left. "I thought our party was as nearly complete as possible. Of course it would have been swell if Marlow Ray and Howard could have been with us."

"Dum—dum—de dum!" hummed Bill, beating time with his hand like an orchestra conductor. From the drawing room a piano crashed into the opening chords of Wagner's beautiful wedding march.

"Here Comes the Bride ..." sang the guests at table, and Mary Eliska's heart skipped a beat.

Through the curtained doorway, walked a blushing girl, leaning on the arm of a tall young man. She wore a bridal gown of white satin, and her smiling face, below the draped tulle veil, was the exact counterpart of the astonished girl at the head of the table.

"Marlow Ray! Howard!" Mary Eliska ran to them and was caught in her cousin's arms. "Where under the sun did you come from? I thought you sailed for South America last week!"

"That," said Howard, grinning broadly, "is a surprise that Mr. Sanborn sprang on us the day after we were married. He persuaded me to give up the South American job and got me a much better one with Mr. Bolton."

"Meet Mr. Howard Bright, the new manager of my Bridgeport plant," cried Bill's father, and everyone clapped.

"Why, that's marvelous!" exclaimed Mary Eliska. "It's only an hour's drive over there from New Canaan. We'll be able to see a lot of each other, Marlow Ray."

Then Uncle Michael, looking very happy and proud, kissed his daughter and led her to the chair between his place and Mary Eliska's.

"Daddy gave me the wedding dress," whispered Marlow Ray. "It's a little bit late for it, but he insisted."

"You look simply darling," began her cousin, then stopped. Doctor Winn, who had pushed in her chair, was addressing the company.

"Ladies, and gentlemen," he said, "before we start on the Christmas cheer which our little hostess and her father have so graciously provided, I would like to propose a toast or two, and may I ask you to stand again while you drink them with me?" He held up his glass of golden cider. "First, let us drink long life and great happiness to our charming bride, Mrs. Howard Bright, and her gallant husband!"

The company drank the toast enthusiastically. Then Uncle Abe, the Stricklins' butler, better known to some of Mary Eliska's friends as "Ol' Man River," grinning from one black ear to the other, laid small leather jewel cases before Marlow Ray and Howard.

"Just a little Christmas gift, my children," explained Doctor Winn.

"Oh, may we open them now?" asked Marlow Ray eagerly. "You most certainly may, my dear."

They snapped open the lids and the company leaned forward to get a better view of the contents.

"I don't know how to thank you, Doctor Winn," began Howard, fingering his handsome gold repeater and chain.

"Nor I—why—my goodness! I never thought I'd have a string of real pearls. They are simply too exquisite for words!"

Doctor Winn laughed and held up a protesting hand. "I'm sure I'm glad you like them, but guests are requested not to embarrass the speaker. Now, I have another toast to propose; and this time we will drink a very Merry Christmas, long life and great happiness to Miss Margaret Schmidt, my new companion-housekeeper!"

Gretchen was overwhelmed and blushed furiously. Uncle Abe placed another jewel case before her, which she opened and found therein a pearl necklace, the counterpart of Marlow Ray's. All she could do was to sit and gaze at it with her wide-open china-blue eyes. Albert Stricklin raised the necklace, slipped it over the embarrassed girl's head, and nodded to the old gentleman.

Doctor Winn took the hint and turned the attention of the table guests to himself. "Third and last, but not in any way the least," he said, "we will drink to the heroine of the already famous case of the Double Cousins. Ladies and gentlemen, I pledge you Mary Eliska—whose bravery and loyalty to her country gained the nation's thanks through its mouthpiece, our President in Washington this week. A very Merry Christmas, my dear, long life and great happiness to you and to our friend Professor, alias Winnite! By the way, where is the pup? I have a little remembrance for him, too."

"He's right here beside me, asleep in his basket, Doctor Winn." Mary Eliska picked up the yawning pup and sat him on her lap.

The old gentleman took a slightly larger morocco case out of his pocket, this time, and laid it on the white cloth before her. With a smile of thanks, she pressed the spring and disclosed, lying on a velvet pad, a double string of gleaming pink pearls. She looked at him, speechless with pleasure, then down again at the necklace. As she did so, she started, for beneath the pearls lay an envelope.

She picked it up and drew forth a paper—"Why! why, it's my copy of the Winnite formula!" she cried.

"The only existing copy, my dear, which I hereby present to your puppy."

"But, Doctor Winn, I don't understand!" "My terms to the government were that Winnite should be used for national defense alone," he said solemnly. "Washington would not agree. Therefore I wish the formula destroyed."

"Oh, what a darling you are!" Mary Eliska leaned over and kissed him. "But let's not give it to Professor this time, please. The last one made him horribly sick."

She held the paper over a lighted candle and watched Winnite burn to charred ash. "I certainly am the happiest girl in the world tonight—but there is just one more toast I'd like to propose before we commence dinner. Here's a long life and a Merry Christmas to Mr. and Mrs. Martin Lawson—if it hadn't been for them, think of all the fun we'd have missed!"

CHAPTER 5

The Air Pilot Mystery

Chapter 5.1
A Dangerous Ride

A blue sports roadster, "Calamity Jane", driven by a girl in a lovely crêpe suit of the same color, threaded its way through the traffic of Spring City's streets to the concrete road that led to the aviation field on the outskirts. Passing the city's limits, the car sped along under the easy assurance of its competent driver, whose eyes were bluer than its paint, deeper than the dress that she was wearing. They were shining now with happiness, for the end of this ride promised the most thrilling experience of her life. That afternoon Mary Eliska was to have her first flight in an airplane!

She parked her car outside of the field and locked it cautiously. Jumping out, she fairly skipped inside the boundary.

A tall, good-looking young man in a flier's suit came from one of the hangars to meet her.

"Mary Eliska?" he said, extending his hand.

"Yes—Mr. Mackay. You see I'm here—a little early, I expect. You haven't forgotten your promise?"

His pleasant face darkened, and he looked doubtfully at the sky.

"I'm afraid it may rain, Mary Eliska. We've suspended pleasure trips for today. But perhaps tomorrow——"

"Oh, no!" she cried in deep disappointment, and the young man believed that her eyes grew moist. "I can't get away tomorrow, or any other day this week. You see I'm a senior at school, and I'm just rushed to death."

"Well, that's too bad," he said, looking again at the sky. "And of course it may not rain after all. But orders are orders, you know."

The girl looked down at the ground, probably, he thought, to hide the tears that would come to her eyes. She was so pretty, so serious, so anxious to go up. It evidently wasn't only a whim with her; she really wanted to fly—like Amelia Earhart, and Elinor Smith. How he hated to deny her!

"Isn't there something you could do?" she finally asked. "Take me up as one of your friends—not as a visitor to the aviation field.... Why, Mr. Mackay, suppose your sister came to see you today, wouldn't you be allowed to take her up?"

"Yes," he replied, smiling. "But that would be on my responsibility, not the school's."

"Then," she pleaded, and she was radiant again with enthusiasm, "couldn't *I* be your responsibility?»

He nodded, won over to her wishes.

"If you put it that way, Mary Eliska, I can't refuse! But I'll have to take you in the plane I'm working on now—making some tests with—and it isn't the most reliable plane in the world. Not one we use to take visitors up in."

"But if it's safe enough for you, it's safe enough for me. I'm satisfied."

"I'm afraid your parents wouldn't be," he objected.

"There I think you're wrong," she asserted. "My father Albert Stricklin believes in taking chances. He has always let me do dangerous things—ride horseback, and drive a car and swim far out in the ocean.... And my mother is dead."

"Very well, then," agreed Mackay. "Please come over here with me. I have been trying to fix up an old biplane, and I think I have her in shape now. But we'll both wear parachutes for precaution."

Her heart fluttering wildly from happiness, but not at all from fear, Mary Eliska accompanied the young flier across the huge field to the runway, where a biplane was resting in readiness for its test. Mackay put her into the cockpit, examined the engine again, and the parachutes, helped her to fasten one of them on, in case of an accident, and started the motor. A minute later the plane taxied forward, faster and faster, until it rose from the ground. "Oh!" cried Mary Eliska, in a tone of deepest joy, although her companion could not hear her for the roar of the motor. "Oh, I'm so happy!"

Up, up, up they went, until they reached the clouds, where the atmosphere seemed misty and foggy. But it did not matter to Mary Eliska that the sky was not blue; nothing could spoil the ecstasy she experienced in knowing that at last she was where she had always longed to be.

Never for a moment was she the least bit dizzy. The sensation of floating through the air was more marvelous than anything she had ever dreamed of.

For some minutes she just allowed herself to dream of the future when she herself would be in control of a plane, sailing thus through the skies. Then she remembered with a start that if she ever expected her ambitions to be fulfilled, it would be necessary to learn how flying was accomplished. She began to examine everything in the cockpit. It was too noisy to ask her companion any questions, but she watched him carefully and tried to figure out what she could for herself. She identified the joystick, which controlled the plane, and she recognized the compass and the altimeter, which registered the height—now sixteen hundred feet—to which they had climbed. All the while she made mental notes of questions she would ask her pilot when they reached the ground.

Up, up they went until, at last, they were beyond the clouds, and saw the bright sunshine about them. It was symbolic to Mary Eliska; she resolved that in after life, whenever she was unhappy or distressed, she would fly on wings to the clear sunlight above. It was almost as if there she would actually find God.

She was so happy that it was some time before she noticed the queer sound the motor was making. Then, glancing questioningly at her companion, she saw a tight, drawn look about his lips, a ghastly pallor in his face. Something was evidently wrong! The motor made an uneven sound, threatening to stall, and the plane went into a tail-spin. Mackay was frantically leaning forward, doing something she did not understand.

"Motor's dying!" he cried, as he managed to right the plane. His voice shook with greater dread than he had ever before experienced. For, fearless though he was for himself, he was scared to death for the pretty girl at his side.

What a fool he had been, he thought, to allow her to come! He would give his own chances of safety that minute if she could be sure of her life! So young, so sweet, so utterly lovely! A great lump rose in his throat, as he took another look at his engine. But he was helpless.

Grim with terror, he pointed to her parachute. And then, to his amazement, he realized how perfectly calm she was!

"You step off first," he said, thankful they both had their parachutes. "I'll stay with the plane as long as I can."

Never in his life did Ted Mackay go through such a horrible moment as that instant when Mary Eliska, at a height of two thousand feet, stepped so bravely from the edge of the plane into the yawning space below. Even if he himself were killed, he could never know sharper agony. Yet the girl herself was gamely smiling!

He managed to pilot the plane a little farther, in the hope that when it did crash, it would not come anywhere near her, and then, when he could no longer keep it from falling, he stepped off himself.

Down he went, and his parachute opened with perfection, but he, in his tenseness, thought only of Mary Eliska, and of her luck with hers. And he prayed as he had never prayed before in his life, not even at his most perilous moments, where death seemed most certain.

No descent ever seemed so slow, so prolonged, but at last he reached the ground. And there, still smiling at him, was lovely Mary Eliska!

Chapter 5.2
Graduation

"Thank Heaven you're safe!" cried Ted Mackay, as he disentangled himself from his parachute. "You certainly are a game little sport, Mary Eliska!"

"I don't see why," returned Mary Eliska. "People jump from planes with parachutes every day!"

"I know. But it was all so sudden. And it is always a pity when anyone's first flight ends disastrously. It makes you feel that you never want to see an airplane again."

"Well, it won't make me feel that way," replied the girl, lightly. "I'd go up again right away if you'd take me."

"I'm afraid I can't. But I'm mighty glad to hear you talk that way. I think you're cut out for a flier. Now let's hunt the wreck."

After they had located the damaged plane, and examined its shattered pieces, they hiked back to the aviation field together, talking all the while about flying. Mary Eliska asked Ted one question after another, which he answered as well as he could without having a plane to demonstrate, and he promised to lend her some books on the subject.

"You must come over and take a course of instruction at our Flying School," he advised. "As soon as you can."

"Oh, I hope to!" she assured him, eagerly. "Maybe after I graduate. Why, I'm almost eighteen! Most boys of my age who cared as much about it as I do would have been flying a couple of years. Because you can get a license when you're sixteen, can't you?"

"Yes.... It's going to be fun to teach you," he added, as they approached the field, and Mary Eliska stopped beside her car. "Good-by! I'll expect to see you soon!"

His hope, however, was not fulfilled until two weeks later, when Mary Eliska again slipped over to the field, between engagements, for another ride in the air. This time she was only one among a group of visitors, and she went up in a plane that was both new and trustworthy.

Her time was so limited—it was a week before Commencement—that she had only chance for a few words with Ted Mackay. She told him that her class-day was the following Friday, and she timidly invited him to a dance which she was giving at her home the night before the event.

"Thanks awfully," he said, more thrilled than he dared tell her at the invitation, "but I couldn't possibly come.... You see, Mary Eliska—I wouldn't fit in with your set."

"Nonsense!" exclaimed Mary Eliska in disappointment, "We're not snobs, just because we go to Miss Graham's school!"

"Well, then, put it this way," he added: "I'm absolutely on my own—and I don't even have evening clothes!"

She smiled at his frankness, but she did not know that he told only part of his story—that he was supporting his mother and helping to put his younger sister through High School.

"All right, then—have it your own way—Ted," she agreed, holding out her hand. "I'll hope to see you some time after class-day."

From that hour on, it seemed as if every moment was filled with more things than she could possibly do. At last Friday came—as hot as any day in mid-summer, though it was still early June.

Soon after two o'clock the audience began to arrive, and at half-past, the twenty-two graduates, in their white dresses, with their large bouquets or American Beauties or pink rose- buds, filed in to take their seats on the flower-decked platform in the garden of the school grounds.

Fans waved, and the flowers wilted visibly, but nobody seemed to notice. For with the exercises the fun began, and everybody listened intently to the jokes and the compliments which came in turn to each and every member of Mary Eliska's class.

After Jax Gray, the president, made her brief speech of greeting, the presenter took charge, and her remarks and her presents were clever without being cruel. Most of the latter she had purchased from the five-and-ten, but they all carried a point. To Mary Eliska she gave a toy car, because she thought that was what the latter was most interested in, and then she asked her to wait a moment, that she had something else for her.

Mary Eliska stood still, smiling shyly, and wondering whether her next gift would have anything to do with airplanes.

"Mary Eliska," continued the presenter, "we have this bracelet for you—in token of our affection. You have been voted the most popular girl in the class."

"Oh!" exclaimed Mary Eliska, and her eyelids fluttered in embarrassment. She was so surprised that she didn't know what to say. Some of the other girls, who had been secretly hoping for this honor, which was always kept as a surprise until class-day, had even prepared speeches. But Mary Eliska had never given the matter a thought.

"I—I—thank you so much," she finally managed to stammer, as she stepped forward to receive the bracelet.

The audience stirred and clapped, for the girl was a favorite with everybody in Spring City.

"She certainly looks sweet today," whispered Mrs. Stricklin, the mother of Mary Eliska's best friend. "There is nothing so becoming as white."

"Yes," agreed her aunt, who had taken care of Mary Eliska ever since her own mother had died when she was only a baby, "but I do wish she hadn't worn those flowers. She had half a dozen bouquets of American Beauties, and she picked out those ordinary pink roses! Sometimes Mary Eliska is queer."

"Yes, but who sent them?" inquired the other woman. "Probably the reason lies there! Ralph Clavering?"

"Ralph Clavering wouldn't buy a cheap bouquet like that—with all his father's mil lions!" exclaimed Mary Eliska. "No; he did send flowers, but Mary Eliska didn't wear them. These had no card."

Their conversation stopped abruptly, for the class prophet was being introduced. Twenty-one girls on the platform leaned forward expectantly, anxious to hear what the future held in store for them. Of course nobody actually believed that this girl could foretell their lives, but it was always fascinating to speculate about their fortunes.

She began with the customary jokes.

"Sara Wheeler" (the thinnest girl in the class), "is going into the food business, but will eat up the profits. However, she'll weigh two hundred pounds before she goes bankrupt....

"Sue Emery, on the contrary, will finally succeed in reducing her weight—when she gets away from these girls and stops talking about it, instead of doing it—until she becomes Hollywood's star dancer...."

"Mary Eliska and Jax Gray—the double I's, we call them, because they are always together—will both marry wealthy men and become the society leaders of Spring City...."

At these words, Mary Eliska's Aunt Polly nudged Jax Gray's mother, and smiled.

"That would suit us, wouldn't it, Mrs. Stricklin?" she asked. "Just what we want for our girls!" nodded her companion, in satisfaction.

It was over at last, the fun and the excitement, the class-day that the girls would keep in their memories for the rest of their lives. Hot, but happy, the graduates came down from the platform to find their friends and their families. Some of them wanted to linger, to talk things over, but Mary Eliska was anxious to get away. It had been wonderful to receive that beautiful bracelet, but somehow it would spoil it to talk about it.

And, in spite of all her happiness, there was a little hurt in her heart. Her father hadn't come home for his only child's graduation!

She came to where her aunt was standing, and put her arm through hers. "Are you ready, Aunt Polly?" she asked.

"Of course, dear—if you want to go so soon. But wouldn't you like to stay and see your friends, and thank them?"

"Oh, I'll write notes," replied Mary Eliska.

"There's Ralph Clavering over there," remarked Mary Eliska, nodding in the direction of a tall, well-dressed young man on the other side of the lawn. "You could thank him for his flowers. He'll probably think it queer if you don't, especially since you didn't wear them."

Mary Eliska smiled carelessly.

"Ralph Clavering probably sent roses to half a dozen girls today," she said lightly. "It's his boast that he's in love with the whole class!... No, I want to go home, Auntie. I'm tired."

"Certainly, dear. We'll go right away."

Nodding to friends as they walked across the beautiful garden where the out-door exercises had been held, they came to Mary Eliska's shining sports roadster, parked just outside the gate. It had been her father's present to her on the day that she was sixteen, and she had taken such care of it that even now, after a year and a half, it looked almost new. "I think it was wonderful for you to receive the bracelet as the most popular girl," Mary Eliska said, as she got into the car. "Everything was really perfect—even the prophecy about your future."

Mary Eliska frowned at the recollection of those words; she hadn't liked that prophecy at all. As perhaps only Ted Mackay realized, her ambition was to fly, to fly so expertly that she could go to strange lands, do a man's work perhaps, carry out missions of importance. She wanted to be known as one of the best—if not *the* best—aviatrix in America!

Ever since she was a child she had had some such longing. Perhaps it was her father who had been responsible for it. Restless and unhappy after her mother's death, he had given his baby to his sister to take care of, and had wandered from one place to another, only coming home every year or so, to see how Mary Eliska was growing. As if to make up to her for his absences, he brought her marvelous presents—presents that were intended rather for a boy than for a girl. Early in life she had learned to shoot a gun, ride a horse, and drive a car. No wonder that she dreamed of airplanes!

Her aunt, on the other hand, disapproved of this way of bringing up a girl. She wanted Mary Eliska to be just like the other fashionable wealthy young ladies in Spring City, to spend her time at parties and at the Country Club, and later to marry a rich man—like Ralph Clavering. Naturally the words of the class prophet pleased her.

Nor had she any idea that Mary Eliska did not agree with her, for her niece had always kept her dreams to herself. There was no use talking about them, Mary Eliska thought, for her aunt would never understand.

"And I guess the prophet was about right," continued Mary Eliska. "Any girl that gets seven bunches of flowers from seven different boys, won't have any difficulty getting married."

"But I don't want to get married, Aunt Polly!" protested Mary Eliska.

"Not yet, dear—of course. Why, you're only seventeen! I couldn't spare you now—just when you're free to be at home with me. Besides, I think every girl should have two years at least to do exactly as she pleases!"

Exactly as she pleases! Why, that would mean learning to fly! Oh, if Aunt Polly could know the fierce longing in her heart to become a really fine pilot, to train herself to make her mark in the world!

"So I want you to have a happy, care-free summer," continued the other, totally unaware of her niece's thoughts. "At first I thought we would go abroad, but on the whole that would be too strenuous, after this hectic year. The other girls' mothers agree with me. Mrs. Stricklin and I were talking about it today, and we've practically decided to go to a charming resort on Lake Michigan that she says is most exclusive. There you can be with all your best friends."

Mary Eliska said nothing; she just couldn't be enthusiastic about wasting three months in that fashion. When she had been hoping to stay at home and enroll for a course at the Spring City Flying School!

"You'd like that, wouldn't you, dear?" persisted Mary Eliska, as Mary Eliska steered her car through the wide gates of their spacious estate. "You could swim and drive and play tennis and dance to your heart's content! With Jax Gray—and—and—the Claverings! Mrs. Stricklin told me they are going there too. Why, you'd meet all the right people!"

Mary Eliska sighed. Aunt Polly's ideas of the right people were not exactly hers—particularly at the present time. She wanted to meet flyers, men and women noted in the field of aviation, not merely wealthy society folk. But she could not say that to her aunt; the latter was afraid of airplanes, and had only grudgingly given her consent that Mary Eliska go up in one. Naturally she had never mentioned her accident.

"Well, we'll talk our plans over later," said Mary Eliska, when Mary Eliska failed to make a reply. "I guess you're too tired to think about anything now. And," she added as she stepped from the car, "don't you want to leave your car here, and let Thomas put it away?"

"No, thank you, Auntie," she replied, for she did not like even so capable a chauffeur as Thomas to touch her precious roadster, Calamity Jane. "It'll only take a minute."

As Mary Eliska walked slowly back to the house, she was thinking of Ted Mackay. For she believed those wilted flowers at her waist were his. There had been no card, but they had come from a small flower shop at the other end of Spring City—not the expensive shop that most of her friends patronized. She would go over to the school soon, and thank him. But she would have to tell him that she was obliged to give up her own plans for the summer! Tears of disappointment came into her eyes, and she wondered if there weren't some way it could be arranged. Maybe if she asked her father....

The thought of her father drove everything out of her mind. He hadn't even bothered to come home! Nothing else seemed to matter.

As she entered the living-room, she found her aunt waiting for her.

"Come in, dear—and get some rest," said Mary Eliska. "You look so tired that you actually seem unhappy."

Mary Eliska forced a smile.

"Is something worrying you, dear? Or is it just the heat and the rush?"

"I don't know," answered the girl, sinking into a deep chair by the window. "I—I— guess I'm just foolish, Aunt Polly." There was a catch in her voice. "But I'm so disappointed that Daddy didn't come for my Commencement. And I wrote to the ranch three times to remind him!"

Mary Eliska nodded; her brother's ways were past her understanding. How anybody could be so indifferent to such a lovely daughter as Mary Eliska! And yet when he was home, no father could be more affectionate. It was just that he was absent-minded, that he hated to be tied down to dates and places. He might be at his ranch in Texas now, or he might have wandered off to Egypt or to South America, without even telling his family. He had been like that, ever since Mary Eliska's mother had died.

"I'm not so surprised at that as I am at his not sending you a present," commented Mary Eliska. "He may never have received your letters—or he may drop in a week late.... But you mustn't let that worry you, Mary Eliska—you have to take your father as he is.... And you must get some rest for tomorrow."

"Tomorrow?" repeated the girl, vaguely. "Yes. The Junior League Picnic. You haven't told me whom you invited."

"Why—I—a——"

"You forgot to invite anybody!" laughed Mary Eliska. "I know you—why, you're something like your father about social engagements, my dear! And of course all the nicest boys will be asked already! I know that Jax Gray is going with Ralph Clavering—Mrs. Stricklin told me today."

"That's fine," commented Mary Eliska, indifferently. "They're great pals."

"But whom will you ask? At this late date?"

"I really think I'd rather stay home, Auntie, if you don't mind. Because—well—Daddy might come—and I'd hate to be so far away. They're going all the way over to Grier's woods, I recall hearing Dot say, and you know that's at least fifteen miles."

"Of course, dear—do just as you like," replied her aunt, putting her motherly arms around her. "Only don't count too much on your father's coming!"

So Mary Eliska went to bed that night, little thinking that her plans would be changed the following morning, and that, in later years, she was to look back upon that day as one of the most wonderful of her whole life!

Chapter 5.3
Her Father's Gift

As Mary Eliska had no plans for the day after her class exercises, she had intended to sleep late. But the arrival of her chum, Jax Gray, accompanied by Ralph Clavering and his Harvard room-mate, Maurice Stetson, changed things for her.

At half-past eight her aunt came into her bedroom, half apologetically, half smiling. "Mary Eliska dear, I want you to wake up," she said. "You have company."

"Yes?" replied the girl sleepily.

"You are rested, aren't you? And it's so much cooler. It's a real June day—the kind the poets write about!"

Mary Eliska sat up in bed, and blinked her eyes. Then suddenly she thought of her father. Did Aunt Polly mean he had come?

"Daddy?" she asked excitedly. "Do you mean he's here?"

Mary Eliska's smile faded; she had not meant to mislead her niece. It was cruel to disappoint her. "No, dear. It's only Jax Gray—with Ralph and another boy. They want you to wake up, and go on the picnic."

"Oh, I see.... But you know I didn't invite anybody, Aunt Polly."

"That's just it. You're to go with this other boy. He's Ralph's room-mate, and he's here on a visit. You will go, won't you, dear?"

"Yes, of course, if Jax wants me to. I'll get dressed right away.... And Auntie, may I have some strawberries up here, to eat after I take my shower? That's all the breakfast I'll want."

"Certainly, dear. I'll send Anna up right away. And how soon shall I tell Jax Gray that you'll be ready?"

"Ten minutes!"

Mary Eliska jumped out of bed, and began to sing as she took her cold shower. It was a wonderful day—a good world after all! Of course the picnic would be fun; she was glad now that she wasn't going to miss it. Jax was a peach to arrange things for her in this way! And it would be exciting to meet a new man. She wondered what he would be like, and hoped she would find him nice. But, even if she didn't, it wouldn't be necessary to stay with him all day. There wasn't much "two's-ing" in their crowd.

Ten minutes later she found her visitors on the porch, singing and amusing themselves, for Mary Eliska had gone to oversee the packing of Mary Eliska's lunch. Ralph introduced his friend, Maurice Stetson, a short, light-haired youth, who was utterly at ease with everybody, and who seemed to think that he was born to be funny. Indeed, he called himself "the prince of wise-crackers." Mary Eliska, who was both sensitive and shy, was afraid she would be made uncomfortable by his comments.

"*Mary Eliska*," he repeated, solemnly shaking her hand. "A potential aviatrix who will follow in the famous Lindy's footsteps?... Let's see—what year was that when he flew the Atlantic? About twenty-seven? Why, you can't be more than three years old!"

Mary Eliska smiled; she really couldn't laugh at the silly remark, though the others seemed to think him exceedingly witty.

"And is your ambition flying?" he asked.

Mary Eliska blushed; she had no desire to admit her dreams and ambitions to the general public.

"Doesn't everybody want to fly now-a-days?" she countered.

"Not your uncle Maurice!" replied the youth, gravely. "My dad gave me a plane, and I wrecked it. I'm through! My flying almost took me to the angels!"

"What's this?" interrupted Mary Eliska, coming out on the porch with a hamper of lunch for the picnic. "You've been in an airplane accident?"

"And how!" he replied, feelingly.

"Now you see, Mary Eliska! You better not go over to that field again! I'm so afraid of planes!"

"All right, Aunt Polly," replied the girl, graciously. "You needn't worry today, anyhow. We're going to the picnic in cars."

But, had Mary Eliska seen Maurice Stetson behind the wheel of his yellow sports roadster, hitting seventy-five miles an hour, and all the while keeping up a conversation not only with Mary Eliska beside him, but with the couple in the rumble-seat as well, she would not have felt so satisfied.

Nevertheless, nothing happened, and the picnic promised to be lots of fun. The girls had selected a beautiful wooded spot outside of the city, where a lovely stream widened into a small lake, deep enough for swimming. Most of the others had already arrived in their cars, when Jax Gray's party drove up. Two large tents, on opposite sides of the lake, had been set up early in the morning for bath-houses.

"Everybody into their suits!" cried Sara Wheeler, who seemed to be managing the picnic, because her mother was the chaperon. "First one into the water gets a prize!"

"Then I get it, without even trying," remarked Harriman Smith, a nice boy, and a particular friend of Mary Eliska's, "because I have mine on now! I got dressed in it this morning, and carried my other clothing."

"Lazy brute!" exclaimed Maurice, enviously, wishing that he had thought of such a labor-saving device.

In fifteen minutes the whole crowd were in the water, diving and swimming, and ducking each other, and finally dividing off into sides for a game of water-polo. It was only when they actually smelled the steaks that Mrs. Wheeler's cooks were broiling, that they were finally induced to leave the lake and get dressed.

A treasure-hunt through the woods was the program for the afternoon. Mary Eliska, who had expected to be coupled with Maurice Stetson for this event, was agreeably surprised to find herself with Ralph Clavering. Jax Gray's doing, in all probability! No doubt she guessed that her chum did not care for Maurice.

They walked along slowly, keeping their eyes on the ground for all possible clues, chatting at intervals about the class-day and the usual gossip, and now and then, when they met other couples, stopping to compare notes. Finally Ralph spoke about his plans for the summer months.

"I'm hoping to persuade your aunt to go to Green Falls with us, Mary Eliska," he said. "There will be quite a bunch of us together. Dot Crowley, Sue, Sally Wheeler, and of course Jax and Kit—from your sorority, and some of the boys from our frat, besides several from Spring City. Harry Smith's going to get a job as a life-guard, and Maurice has promised to go. We ought to be able to make whoopee, all right!"

"Sounds good," admitted Mary Eliska, absently.

"Yes, and I really think we could pull off some serious work there."

"Serious work?" repeated Mary Eliska. As far as she knew, Ralph had never done any real work in his life.

"Yeah. In the competitions, I mean. I think if we go after it tooth and nail, you and I'd make a pretty good team to pull down the cup for the tennis doubles. They have a big meet at the end of the season that's the talk of the whole Great Lakes region.... And Sally swings a mean club in golf. And look at Jax Gray's diving!"

"Yes, that's true," agreed Mary Eliska. She had always liked golf and tennis and swimming, but somehow this year they had all lost their charm. It was different after you graduated, she decided. Then you wanted to make something out of your life—like Ted Mackay. There was no more time to be wasted.

"Promise me you'll go," begged Ralph, leaning over eagerly and putting his hand on her arm.

Instinctively she drew it away, but before she could answer, Jax Gray and Maurice appeared from a cross-path that was hidden by tall bushes.

"Why, there's my little Lindy!" cried Maurice, though Mary Eliska was several inches taller than he was. "Grieving for papa?"

"Shedding tears," laughed Mary Eliska. But the words made her think of her own father, and she grew sober. Suppose he were home now—waiting for her! He never stayed more than a day; how she would hate to miss him!

"Has anybody found the treasure yet?" she inquired.

"I've found *two* treasures,» replied Maurice complacently, looking first at Jax Gray and then at Mary Eliska.

"Forget it!" commanded Jax Gray, tersely, lifting her head. She, like Mary Eliska, was tall, but in that the resemblance ended. Her blond, sleek hair was short and almost straight, and she wore earrings—even in swimming. She said she felt undressed without them—"practically immodest," were her exact words.

"No, but really—?" persisted Mary Eliska.

A wild shout from Dot Crowley, followed by a chorus of "Whoopee!" from half a dozen others, answered Mary Eliska's question immediately. Dot always was lucky. The others ran to the spot where the crowd was gathered, and Dot, a tiny, vivacious blonde, who could take child's parts in the amateur plays, was holding two boxes of golf balls triumphantly up to view.

"Do I have to give one box to that lazy kid?" she demanded, pointing scornfully at her long-legged partner, Jim Valier, who had been languidly following her around. At the time when she had discovered the prize, he was lolling under a tree, resting his "weary bones," as he said, smoking a cigarette. "Sure you do!" he drawled. "Didn't I supply the brains to our combine?"

"Brains!" repeated Dot. "Where did you get 'em? I'll have to have you arrested for stealing 'em, if that's the case! But here—take your box!"

"Couldn't possibly," he said, waving them aside with his cigarette holder. "Besides, I hardly ever play golf. Too fatiguing."

"How about your school-girl figure?" asked Maurice. "Aren't you afraid if you don't exercise, you'll lose it?" Everybody, even Mary Eliska, laughed, for Jim Valier was about the world's thinnest youth.

"He's really afraid somebody will mistake him for a golf-stick, and bang a ball with him," remarked Ralph.

In groups, and some in pairs, the whole crowd went back to the lake. After all that exercise and excitement, everybody wanted another dip to cool off. It was six o'clock by the time they all piled into their cars, and half-past when Mary Eliska reached home.

Hoping to find her father, Albert Stricklin, as she had been hoping every day that week, she dashed up the steps quickly, merely waving good-by to her companions as the sports car shot from the driveway. And then, miraculously, she saw his beloved face at the door!

"Daddy!" she cried rapturously, rushing breathlessly into his arms.

He was taller than Mary Eliska, with a straight, lithe figure like that of a much younger man. His hair was dark, with just a little gray at the temples, and his skin deeply tanned from his out-door life. A sort of habitual smile played about his lips, as if he had made up his mind to find life pleasant, no matter what came.

"My dear little girl!" he said, quietly, patting her hair. "Will you forgive me for coming a day too late? Your Aunt Polly tells me that both Commencement and class-day are over—and you are an old Grad now!"

"Yes, but I don't mind, Daddy, so long as you came today!" she replied, squeezing his hand. "Maybe it's better this way, because I've been so rushed lately that I wouldn't have had much time to see you."

"You must tell me all about everything," he said, drawing her arm through his, and leading her down the steps of the porch. Of course he thought he meant what he said, but Mary Eliska knew from experience that if she did tell him, he wouldn't be listening. A dreamy expression so often came into his eyes when she chattered, and she would wonder what he was thinking of. Strange lands—or his ranch out west—or perhaps her mother?

"Where are we going?" she asked. "I really ought to dress for dinner, Daddy. You know what picnics are."

"Yes, To be sure. But I want to show you your graduation present."

"My present?" There was excitement in her tone; it was sure to be something wonderful—and unusual. All the girls were wild with envy when Kitty Clavering received a real pearl necklace from her father. All—except Mary Eliska. She had no desire for pearls, or for any jewelry, for that matter. She had known that her father's present would be much more thrilling. At least—if he didn't forget!

"You didn't think your old Dad would forget you, did you, Honey?" he asked.

"No—no—of course not.... But, Daddy, where is it? Why are we going out back of the house?"

"We have to walk over to our big field across the creek," he explained, mysteriously.

"The big field? Why?... That's a hot walk, Daddy. No shade at all! If you want a nice walk, we ought to go in the other direction, down towards the orchard, where there are some trees."

"Trees are the one thing we don't want," he replied, solemnly. "You're going to hate trees, after you get my present, daughter."

"Hate—trees?" Mary Eliska's eyes were traveling all over the landscape, scanning it in vain for a clue. And then, as they mounted a slight incline, the thing came into sight. The marvelous, wonderful present! Too good to be true! Her heart stopped beating, her legs shook. She clutched at her father for support.

A beautiful, shining airplane! A superb Arrow Sport! The very kind she had been reading about, had been longing someday to possess! And even a hangar, to keep it in safety!

"Daddy!" she gasped, hoarsely.

He was watching her face, rapturously. "You like it?"

"Oh!" she cried, wrapping her arms around his neck, and suddenly bursting into tears. "How could you know that I wanted it so much?"

He patted her hair, a little embarrassed by her emotion.

"I just tried to imagine what I would want most if I were your age.... You know, dear, you're your father's own girl! You look like your mother, but you're much more like me.... A strange mixture...." He was talking more to himself now, for Mary Eliska was almost running, pulling him along excitedly. "Feminine beauty—with masculine ambition...."

But Mary Eliska was not listening. She had reached the plane now, and was walking around it, enthralled. Touching its smooth surface, to make sure that it was not only a dream. Dashing back to hug her father, and then climbing into the cockpit, to examine the controls, the instruments, the upholstery. If she lived to be a hundred years old, no other moment could hold greater happiness than this!

Her father smiled softly in satisfaction. He wanted her to have all the happiness that he had somehow missed. Money couldn't buy it for him; but money spent for his daughter could bring it to him in the only possible way now.

"You're not a bit afraid?" he asked, though he knew from her shining eyes that his question was unnecessary.

"Dad!"

"And now the question is, who can teach you to fly? Unfortunately, the man who brought it here for me couldn't stay, even to explain things to you—although of course there is a booklet. But I understand there's an air school here at Spring City...."

"Yes! Yes!" she interrupted. "I've been there—been up with one of the instructors. Can we drive over for him tonight?"

"My dear, you can't take a lesson at night," he reminded her. "You know that."

"Oh, of course not!" she agreed, laughing at her own folly. "But tomorrow?"

"Yes, certainly. At least we can see about it. You have to pass a physical examination first, I understand."

"And I want to take the regular commercial pilot's course, Daddy! I want to go to the bottom, and learn all about planes, and flying. May I?"

"I don't see why not.... You needn't stop for the expense."

Mary Eliska blushed; she hadn't been thinking of the expense—she never did. But perhaps she ought to now, for the plane must have cost a lot of money. At the present, however, something else was worrying her. "It was the time I was thinking of," she admitted. "Aunt Polly wants to go away in a week or so. And oh, Dad, I just couldn't bear to leave this!" There were actually tears in her eyes.

"Of course not, dear. Well, we'll see if we can't compromise with your aunt. Stay at home the rest of June and July, be content with a private pilot's license for the present, and then go away *in* your plane in August. Wouldn't that suit you?»

"To the ground—I mean to the skies!" corrected the happy girl. "And now we must get back to dinner," he reminded her. "Aunt Polly's waiting."

Solemnly, tenderly, as a mother might kiss her baby, Mary Eliska leaned over and kissed the beautiful plane. Then giving her hand to her father, she walked back to the house with him in silence, knowing that now her greatest dream was fulfilled.

Chapter 5.4
Summer Plans

The news of Mary Eliska's magnificent present spread like wildfire. She never knew how it got about, for she didn't call anybody. In fact, she would have preferred to keep it a secret for that evening at least, and just spend her time over the booklet, talking things over with her father.

But of course the rest of the crowd couldn't understand that. These young people, who saw their parents every day of their lives, just couldn't believe that a normal fun-loving girl like Mary Eliska would prefer a father's society to theirs. They didn't know that Mary Eliska had always longed to know him better, to understand him, to talk over with him her greatest dreams and ambitions. Because there had been nobody to talk to in that intimate fashion. Aunt Polly never had understood her, and never would. The kind-hearted woman saw, of course, that her niece was pleased with her graduation present, but she could not realize the girl's overwhelming joy in the possession of a plane. To her, even a string of imitation pearls would have been more desirable.

They talked their plans over at dinner, Mary Eliska's father, Albert Stricklin, taking her side in urging that the vacation be postponed until August.

"You don't mind, do you, Polly?" he asked his sister.

"Well, I can't say I don't mind," she replied, a little sharply. "But of course I wouldn't spoil Mary Eliska's fun. But I am wondering whether you have been wise, Albert. Mary Eliska is tired out; instead of going to school and learning some more, she ought to be resting.... But your presents have never shown a great deal of wisdom, I fear."

Her brother laughed.

"Sometimes it's better to be foolish," he remarked.

"Not if Mary Eliska breaks her neck!"

"Which she isn't going to do!" contradicted Mr. Stricklin, confidently. "Mary Eliska's careful—and she's thorough. I know that, from the way she drives her car—and takes care of it."

"Cars and airplanes are different matters!"

"Not so different as you might think. In some ways, cars are more dangerous, because you have to consider traffic—what the other fellow is going to do. And there's so much room in the skies!"

"But if something goes wrong—there's nobody there to help her," objected Mary Eliska.

"Well, Polly, you'd be amazed at the perfection of the airplanes they are putting out now-a-days. They're as different from the old-fashioned ones of the World War, as the first two-cylinder automobiles from the sixes and eights of today."

"But there still are a lot of crashes—and deaths," insisted his sister.

"That doesn't say Mary Eliska will crash! Mary Eliska is going to be a good pilot—learn it all thoroughly!... Why, Polly, you don't think I'd be willing to take any chances with my only child, do you—if I didn't consider it safe?"

He smiled fondly at Mary Eliska, but his sister drew down the corners of her mouth a trifle scornfully. As if his affection could compare with hers, though Mary Eliska wasn't her own child! He saw the girl two or three times a year at the most, while Aunt Polly was with her every day of her life!

"Well," she added, "I'm afraid you'll feel out of the crowd by the time August comes and they have been together all that time at Green Falls!"

"Do you mind missing it, my dear?" her father asked, gently.

"Not a bit!" replied Mary Eliska immediately, her eyes shining at the thought of what she was gaining.

Mary Eliska abruptly changed the subject.

"Do you remember a man named Clavering, Albert?" she asked.

"I remember the name. Connected with oil, wasn't he? Very wealthy?"

"A millionaire, I think," replied Mary Eliska, as if the news were the most important thing in the world. "Well, he has bought an estate just outside of Spring City, and his daughter has just graduated in Mary Eliska's class."

"Yes?" remarked her brother, wondering what possible difference that could make to him.

"Well, the Claverings are planning to spend the summer at Green Falls, on Lake Michigan— the resort that Mrs. Stricklin and I have selected.... And there is a son in Harvard, who is going to be there."

"Yes?" It still didn't dawn on the man what his sister meant. Perhaps that was because he was not worldly, and money and position didn't mean much to him. Or perhaps it was because it had never occurred to him that his little Mary Eliska was old enough to be thinking about getting married.

"You certainly are slow at comprehension at times, Albert," she said, "for a smart man. Do I have to tell you in so many words that young Ralph Clavering is interested in Mary Eliska?"

Mary Eliska blushed, and Mr. Stricklin opened his eyes wide in amazement.

"Well! Well! Well!" he exclaimed.

"Dad!" protested Mary Eliska, nervously. "Don't be so serious! Aunt Polly thinks that because she loves me, everybody thinks I'm grand. But as a matter of fact, Ralph Clavering doesn't like me any better than half a dozen other girls. And I don't believe he likes me nearly so well as Jax Gray—though I haven't given the matter any thought."

"How any boy could fall for Jax Gray is more than I can see!" put in Mary Eliska. "She is a nice girl, but she has ruined what looks she had by cutting her hair off so short, and wearing those dreadful earrings all the time——"

"Aunt Polly!" interrupted Mary Eliska. "Please don't forget that Jax Gray is my best friend!"

"Even so, I don't have to admire her appearance, do I?"

In a man's fashion, Mr. Stricklin was getting very tired of this small talk. He stirred restlessly.

"Well, it's settled then, about the summer, isn't it?" he asked. "I'd like to drive over early tomorrow morning to this Flying School, and make the arrangements about your course. Because tomorrow night I'm taking the sleeper back to the ranch."

"Dad!" cried Mary Eliska, in disappointment. "You don't have to go that soon, do you? Oh, I wanted you to see me fly!"

"I'll be back again, as soon as I can. But just now I'm having trouble with some Mexicans who came over the border and have been threatening us. I've got to be on the job. My help aren't any too reliable."

"You won't be in any danger will you, Daddy?"

He shrugged his shoulders indifferently.

"Guess not," he replied. At the conclusion of the meal, Mary Eliska, who always liked to have Mary Eliska's young friends about, suggested that she call some of them on the telephone and give them her news, inviting them over to celebrate with her. But Mary Eliska shook her head.

"There's only one person I'd like to tell about it," she said, "and I'm afraid I couldn't reach him by phone, for I don't know where he lives. That's a boy over at the school, who has taken me up a couple of times." But, as friends like this did not interest her, Mary Eliska dismissed the subject and went out to consult her cook. Mary Eliska's father, however, felt differently.

"What's his name?" he asked, indulgently. "Maybe we could locate him, if we put in a call at the school. There would probably be somebody about who would know his address."

"Ted Mackay," answered Mary Eliska.

Mr. Stricklin's eyes narrowed suspiciously, and the smile died from his lips. His daughter trembled. What could he possibly have against Ted?

"What's the fellow look like?"

"He's big—with red hair, and blue eyes, Why? Do you know him, Daddy?"

"Think I know his father—to my sorrow. Same name—description fits, too. Likable chap, when you first meet him, isn't he? Looks honest and kind, and all that?"

"Oh yes, Daddy! And he is so nice, too. And so clever!"

"I don't doubt it. So is his father—in his own way. Well, if he's the son of the man I know, you're to keep away from him. Do you understand, daughter?"

"Yes, but Daddy, don't you think it's only fair to give me a reason?" she pleaded.

"I'd rather not. Can't you take my judgment as worth something, Mary Eliska?" He spoke sternly.

The tears came to Mary Eliska's eyes, and she looked away.

"Mayn't I even speak to him?" she asked, finally.

"Oh, certainly. Never cut anybody—it's a sign of a little mind to stoop to such childishness. But don't be friendly with him. I dare say there are other instructors at the field, and I'll arrange for someone else to teach you."

The door-bell rang three times, but before the maid could answer it, Jax Gray dashed into the house, followed by Kitty and Ralph Clavering, and finally, Maurice Stetson.

"Whoopee!" cried Ralph, almost running into Mary Eliska's father, who was standing in the dining-room doorway.

"Darling!" exclaimed Jax Gray, embracing her chum excitedly. "We heard the news! Congratulations!"

"And naturally we couldn't wait to see your plane," added Kitty. "But are you sure you've finished dinner?"

"Yes, indeed," replied Mary Eliska, introducing her father to everybody except Jax Gray, who of course knew him.

"If it only isn't too dark to see it!" exclaimed Jax Gray. "We've all brought flashlights."

"Then we better trail out immediately," laughed Mary Eliska. "And I'll get Aunt Polly. She has only seen it from a distance."

"Better wait for the rest of the crowd," suggested Ralph. "I saw Dot trying to round up some more. They ought to be here any minute."

"Then we might as well wait. Aunt Polly'll be here in a minute."

"What kind of airplane is it, Mary Eliska?" inquired Maurice. "You're 'Lindy' Junior now aren't you—just as I predicted," he added.

"It's a 'Pursuit,'" answered Mary Eliska, ignoring his second remark. "An Arrow Sport."

"Open cockpit?" asked Ralph.

"Yes. See—here's its picture." She waved the folder towards the boys. "It's supposed to be a wonderful little plane for a beginner!"

"From now on, Mary Eliska'll talk of nothing but joysticks and ailerons and—" began Maurice, but he was interrupted by the arrival of Dot Crowley and six other young people, all of whom had been packed in her small car.

It was just as she liked it to be, Aunt Polly thought, as she joined the merry, singing group, and started out with them towards the field beyond the house. Mr. Stricklin did not go with them this time, and later on, Mary Eliska had reason to be thankful for his absence.

It was quite dark now, but both the moon and the stars shone brightly, and the plane was clearly visible. The exclamations of delight and praise from her guests were enthusiastic enough to satisfy any proud owner of such a glorious prize. Mary Eliska was happier than ever.

The boys were naturally interested in the mechanics of the plane, the girls in the upholstery of the seats, the charming, deep cushions, which could be removed if it were necessary to use a parachute. They turned on their flashlights, and walked about the biplane, not a little in awe at the idea of Mary Eliska's piloting it through the skies.

"It only holds two people," remarked Dot, regretfully. "I wonder if we could pile in extras, like I do with my car."

"I'm afraid not," replied Mary Eliska. "But I can take everybody up in turn—after I get my license. I am hoping to bring it to Green Falls in August."

Satisfied at last that they had seen as much as possible for the present, they started to turn back, when Maurice suddenly spied a lonely figure at the top of the incline, some fifty yards away.

"What ho!" he exclaimed. "Who can that be? Yo-ho-ho!" he cried, making a funnel with his hands.

"Not anybody in our crowd," replied Jim Valier, "or he would answer. Hope it isn't a thief—with designs on your new plane."

"We better chase him!" said Jackson Stiles, who was always ready for adventure, "Come on, fellows, let's rush him!"

The boys darted off, all except Jim Valier, who said gallantly that he had better stay as protection for the ladies, though of course everybody knew it was only because he was too lazy to run. The girls laughed and chattered while they were gone—all except Mary Eliska, who waited nervously to find out what success they had had.

In less than three minutes, however, they had returned, shamefacedly admitting defeat.

"Maybe the fellow couldn't sprint!" announced Ralph. "I'll bet he's a track-runner——"

"Or a chicken thief!" suggested Maurice.

"Do you think he is a tramp?" inquired Mary Eliska, relieved that the man had disappeared. Tramps were so dirty, so unpleasant!

"Don't think so. Big fellow—not badly dressed, as far as we could see. Had red hair."

"Too bad we couldn't catch him," remarked Maurice, always ready with his jokes, "for his hair was bright enough to light up the plane. We wouldn't have needed our flashes."

"Might have set the 'Pursuit' on fire!" suggested Jim.

Mary Eliska frowned uneasily. The description sounded like Ted Mackay. But how did he know that she had a plane, and if he had happened to see it, why didn't he come to the house, and ask her permission to examine it? After all, it was on their own property—nobody had any right to intrude. She thought darkly of what her father had said, and hoped that there wasn't anything crooked about Ted. Why, he seemed more of a friend to her than any of these people—except of course her Aunt Polly, and Jax Gray!

By the time they had reached the house, everybody had forgotten the incident, for Jax Gray turned on the radio, and without consulting Mary Eliska, they all decided to dance. Ralph claimed the latter for the first waltz.

"So this will make a change in your summer plans," he said, as if the idea were not wholly to his liking.

"Yes. We're not going to Green Falls 'til August—maybe not then, if I don't succeed in getting a private pilot's license before that."

"But what about me?" he inquired, and the admiring look he gave her would have pleased Mary Eliska, had she noticed it.

Mary Eliska looked puzzled.

"You? Why—you'll never miss me! With all your girlfriends!"

"No; I've decided I'm not going to miss you," he said, quietly. "Because I'm going to stay right here in Spring City, and learn to fly along with you!"

"What?"

"Yes. The thing fascinates me. I want a plane, too! I'm going to touch my Dad for one when I get home tonight!"

"But you've promised everybody you'll go to Green Falls!"

"So I will—August first!" And so, much to Mary Eliska's delight, when the rest of the crowd left Spring City the following week, Ralph Clavering stayed at home with a couple of the servants, and enrolled at the same time as Mary Eliska, at the Spring City Flying School.

Chapter 5.5
The First Lesson in Flying

Early the next morning, Mary Eliska wakened her father and hurried him through his breakfast. There wasn't a moment to be lost, she told him excitedly, like a child waiting to open her Christmas stocking. She had her car under the portico before he had finished his second cup of coffee.

"Don't drive so fast that you are killed on the way," cautioned her aunt. "Remember, dear, you have the rest of your life to fly that plane!"

But the present moment is the only time of importance to young people, and Mary Eliska scarcely took in what she was saying. Besides, the caution was unnecessary; unlike Dot Crowley and Maurice Stetson, she had too much respect for her car to mistreat it by careless driving. Mary Eliska loved her roadster as a cavalry general loves his horse.

"You want to do most of your learning on your own plane, don't you, daughter?" asked her father, as he sat down beside her. "I mean —you'd rather bring your instructor back with us, and fly it, wouldn't you?"

"Of course, if that is possible. But don't you suppose I have to go in a class with others, Daddy?"

"Probably not—for it is a small school. Besides, I can arrange for you to have private lessons. It will hurry things up for you."

"Oh, thank you, Daddy!... But later, I want to go to a regular ground school, if you will let me." Her tone was as eager as any boy's, starting out on his life work. "And study airplane construction, and wireless—and—and——"

He smiled at her approvingly. What a girl!

"You are ambitious, my dear," he said, but there was pride in his words. "I don't see why not, though.... Only, not all at once. As your Aunt Polly reminded you, you have the rest of your life."

"I can't bear to fool!" she exclaimed, impatiently. "Now that I have graduated, I want to get somewhere."

"You're bound to—unless you fly in circles," he remarked, lightly.

"I mean—oh, you know what I mean, Daddy! And you do understand, don't you?"

"Well, not exactly. You don't expect to be one of those independent girls who insist upon earning their own living, do you, dear?"

"I don't know...." Somehow, she couldn't explain. Nobody understood just what she wanted except Ted Mackay, and that was because he had the same sort of goal himself. Ted Mackay! The memory of her father's command hurt her. Must she really give up his friendship? But why? She wanted to ask her father, but he was looking off in the distance, apparently lost in his own thoughts.

So she drove the remainder of the way in silence, absorbed by her own dreams.

The field was outside of Spring City, covering an area of thirty acres, and surrounded by the white fence that was now being used so much by airports. Three large hangars, containing probably half a dozen planes, occupied one side of the field, and, near the entrance was a large building, evidently used as an office and school for the theoretical part of the courses.

"You have been here before, Mary Eliska?" asked her father, as the girl locked her car.

"Yes—a couple of times. I feel almost at home."

Scarcely were they inside the grounds, when Ted Mackay, looking huge and handsome in his flyer's suit, came out of the office building. He recognized Mary Eliska at once, and his blue eyes lighted up in a smile of welcome. Since he wore his helmet, his red hair was not visible, and Mary Eliska, glancing apprehensively at her father, knew that the latter had no idea who Ted was. But, nervous as she was over the meeting that was about to take place, she could not help feeling proud of Ted, and warmed by the frankness of his happy smile.

"Mary Eliska!" he cried. (She had called him Ted the second time she met him, so he reciprocated.) "I owe you an apology—and a confession!"

"Yes?" replied Mary Eliska, glancing fearfully at her father, though she knew that he had not yet realized who the young man was, or his expression would not have been so beneficent. "But first I want you to meet my father," she said. "Dad—this is Ted Mackay."

She was vexed at herself that she was actually stammering. Acting just like a child! Yet she couldn't forget how stern her father could be. She recalled the day that, as a child, she had sneaked off and played with Jax Gray when her chum had whooping cough. Her father happened to come home—and announced that he would take care of her punishment. And what a punishment! For three whole weeks he made her stay in the house, without a single companion except her Aunt Polly! He said he'd teach her to obey.

But he wasn't storming, or even frowning now. Merely looking politely indifferent, perhaps a trifle superior. He made no motion to shake hands with Ted.

"How do you do?" he said. "Would you be kind enough to take us to the man in charge of this field?"

"Certainly, sir," replied Ted.

Immediately, as if he intended to give the young people no chance for personal conversation, Mr. Stricklin began to ask about the courses that were offered.

Ted answered his questions, explaining that Mary Eliska would probably want to become a private pilot at first.

"You have to pass a physical examination," he said, "and get a permit from the Government. Then you must have at least eighteen hours of flying experience—ten with someone else with you, eight of solo flying. There is a written examination, too—all about the rules and regulations that make up the laws of the air. Of course there isn't a lot of traffic, like with the driving of cars," he explained, smilingly, "but you'd be surprised at how many rules there are!"

They had been crossing the field while he talked, and they stopped now at the main building. With a nod of dismissal that was curt, and yet not quite rude, for a muttered, "Thank you," accompanied it, Mr. Stricklin left Ted, and took his daughter inside.

A middle-aged man, dressed in a khaki shirt and breeches, was seated at a desk. He looked up as they entered.

"My name is Stricklin," began Mary Eliska's father, "and this is my daughter. I have bought her a plane, and I have come over to arrange about some lessons in flying."

Lieutenant Kingsberry, a former Army officer, asked them to be seated, and went over about the same explanation that Ted had given, saying that he would be delighted to register Mary Eliska, provided that she passed the physical examination.

"I suppose it is not so unusual now to have girls as students?" inquired Mr. Stricklin.

"Not for many of the schools," replied the lieutenant. "But it just happens that we so far have not enrolled any of the fair sex. Your daughter will be the first. When does she wish to start?"

"As soon as possible," replied Mr. Stricklin.

"Now!" Mary Eliska could not help adding.

"Well, I don't see why not," agreed the lieutenant, leniently. "At least Mary Eliska could take the physical examination, because one of our doctors is here now. And if she passes that, Mackay can give her the first lesson." Mary Eliska's expression of delight suddenly died on her lips. For she glanced at her father, and saw the queer, drawn look about his mouth at the mention of Ted's name.

"This—Mackay—" he said slowly, "he isn't your only instructor?"

"He is our best."

"I prcfcr someone else. Can you arrange it?"

"Why—I suppose so. But if it is only personal reasons, I think you are making a mistake, Mr. Stricklin. Mackay is our most reliable flyer—by far our best instructor. We don't expect to have him here more than a month or so. He's had a good offer from a big company."

Mary Eliska was glancing shyly, pleadingly, at her father, but he did not even see her.

"Unfortunately I found this young man's father to be most unreliable—untrustworthy—during the pcriod that I employed him on my ranch. The fact is, we are not yet through with the trouble that he started. So you can understand why I should refuse to trust my daughter to his son. It is an unpleasant but true fact that children inherit their father's weaknesses. I should not have a comfortable minute, being miles away, and knowing that she was in his hands."

"Of course I will accept your decision, Mr. Stricklin," replied Lieutenant Kingsberry, "and see that your wishes are carried out. I will summon the second ranking instructor—H. B. Taylor."

He called his office boy, a young man learning to fly, and working his way at the same time, and gave the necessary message. A couple of minutes later the man came in, dressed like Ted, but somehow he seemed insignificant to Mary Eliska—as if he were the one who was not reliable. She sighed.

Her father remained with the lieutenant and the instructor while she went into the doctor's office for her physical examination. She knew that her eyesight was good, but she felt a little nervous when the doctor examined her heart. It was fluttering so! Suppose all the excitement had been too much for her—and she did not pass! What good would her lovely plane be to her, if she were never allowed to pilot it herself?

But she need not have been alarmed, for she came through with flying colors. Then young Taylor took her over to one of the planes, and began to explain about the joystick, the rudder, the ailerons, and everything else he could think of, in words of one syllable.

Mary Eliska glanced at him, frowning. Did he think she was a baby. Or was it because she was a girl that his manner seemed so superior, so condescending? Why, he was wasting a lot of time! Ted would have had her up in the air by this time, perhaps letting her guide the plane herself.

"I am familiar with all these terms, Mr. Taylor," she interrupted. "You see I have been up twice—with Mr. Mackay. And I've read a couple of books."

The young man regarded her haughtily.

"It is necessary, Mary Eliska, that you go through the regular lessons, regardless of what you knew beforehand," he answered coldly. "And whatever Mr. Mackay may have shown you—as a friend—has nothing to do with these lessons, so long as I, not he, am your instructor."

"But I want to go up today!" she protested, eagerly.

"It is not our custom to take students up on the first day, Mary Eliska.... Now, have you a notebook and pencil?"

"In my car." She tried to answer naturally, but she was keenly disappointed.

"Then will you please go and get them," he said, seating himself in the cockpit of the plane which he had been using to illustrate his statements. Obediently, but half-heartedly, Mary Eliska started back for the road where her car was parked. She had gone about half-way when she came upon her father, accompanied by Ralph Clavering, dressed like herself, in his riding outfit.

"Hello, Mary Eliska!" he cried. "Passed your physical exam, didn't you?"

"Oh, yes," she answered. "So you're really going to learn, too?"

"I most certainly am. And your father has consented to let us take our lessons together. Won't that be fun?"

"Mary Eliska," interrupted her father, as he saw her start away, "where are you going? I want to tell you something."

"Yes, Daddy?" A wild hope surged in her heart that perhaps he had changed his mind about Ted. It wasn't only that she had taken a dislike to H. B. Taylor—it was rather that she had not confidence in him as a teacher. He might be all right as a pilot, but instructing others was a different matter. And he would never really feel any personal interest in her progress, or understand her, like Ted. His attitude almost said that he thought it was silly of girls to want to fly! But she ought to have known her father better than to think he would change his mind.

"I should like to take your car and go home now, if you don't mind," he said, "because I have some work to do today that is urgent—some people to see about business. And Mr.

Clavering has very kindly offered to drive you home. Is that all right? I know you don't like other people to run your car———"

"Oh, Daddy, you're different," she said, forcing a smile. "Of course I don't mind your driving it.... But I'm sorry you can't wait for us."

Promising to meet Ralph in a couple of minutes, she walked out to the entrance of the field with her father.

"I need not tell you, dear," he said, "that my decision about Mackay is final. And I want you to have as little to do with him as possible, while you are here. It's for your own good, daughter. I can see that girls might find the young man attractive. But it is well to steer clear of such people. Have all the fun you like with your own friends."

"Yes, Daddy," she managed to reply.

"I guess young Clavering will see to it that your time at home, after most of the others go away for the summer, is not dull. And if you pass your course and get your license, you can fly your plane to Green Falls. I will make arrangements about a place to keep it. I dare say they have maps at the school."

"Yes—and thank you so much—for everything, Daddy," she said. She mustn't let him see that she was disappointed, after all he had done for her! He might be right about Ted—but she didn't think so. Whatever Ted's father might be, she felt sure that Ted was one of the finest young Americans that she had ever known.

Securing her notebook, and handing over her keys to her father, she hurried back to the field, and finished her lesson with Ralph at her side. As they walked out together, she looked about shyly for Ted. It wouldn't do any harm for her just to speak to him; after all he did want to tell her something. At last she spotted him, across the field beside one of the planes—in overalls and jumper now, his red hair brilliant in the sunlight.

"Do you know I believe that's the fellow we chased last night!" exclaimed Ralph. "Do you know him?"

"Yes, I've met him. He took me up a couple of times."

"You know him? Then why was he sneaking around so funny last night? Why didn't he come over and speak to you?"

"He's shy," replied Mary Eliska, jumping to the only conclusion that seemed feasible, and her explanation must have been correct, for Ted never looked up from his work as the young couple passed.

Chapter 5.6
Winning Her License

The next few weeks were the most interesting, the most exciting, of Mary Eliska's whole life. Every day she drove over to the Flying School with Ralph, and gained first her theoretical, and then her practical knowledge.

Both she and Ralph were surprised to find that it was so simple a matter to handle a plane. By the middle of July they were accustomed to stepping into the cockpits by themselves, nosing their planes into the wind, and rising to a height of fifteen hundred feet, without even a tremor. Anxiously they counted their hours of solo flying, not only that their licenses would be approved, but because they both wanted to try some stunts. They had studied the principles of loops, Immelman turns, barrel rolls, and falling leaves, and they were wild to try them out for themselves.

Finally, after they had both passed their written examinations, and were only waiting for their licenses to come through, Mr. Taylor allowed them both to try an inside loop and an Immelman turn. Mary Eliska's happiness was so great that she felt she just had to tell somebody, so she went home and wrote to her father. Unfortunately, she thought it wiser to say nothing about stunts to her aunt.

Mary Eliska still insisted that she would never get into a plane, not even Mary Eliska's. "It's too dangerous," she objected, when her niece was begging her to go for a ride. "I might be killed—and then who would take care of you? And besides, I don't see how anybody could learn to fly in the short time you've been at it."

"But Aunt Polly," explained Mary Eliska patiently, "it really is easier than driving a car. Once you are off the ground, the plane practically flies itself. And the higher you are, the safer."

Mary Eliska shuddered.

"I can't believe that, dear. Because the higher you are, the farther you have to fall!"

"But you have all that chance to regain control of your plane," insisted her niece. "Crashes practically always come on the ground—it's very rare indeed that two planes crash in the air, even when they are flying in Army formation."

"How soon do you think you'll get your license?" inquired Mary Eliska, showing that Mary Eliska's words had made no impression at all upon her. She was anxious to get away now; Spring City was becoming very hot.

"Any time now," replied the girl, her eyes shining with anticipation. "I have done all the required solo flying—and more too."

"Solo flying? Do you mean you've been up alone? Without even Ralph?"

"Yes, of course! And I love it, Aunt Polly! Oh, if you could just try it once, you'd never be afraid again. It is the most wonderful sensation—up in the skies, all alone! Free as a bird!" She paused abruptly, smiling at her own enthusiasm. She did not often talk like this to anybody, though there was a great deal of poetry in her make-up.

"Well, dear, I'm glad you like it," said Mary Eliska, in a matter-of-fact tone. "But don't overdo it. And don't go in for any stunts."

Ralph Clavering, who had been making it his habit to come over to see Mary Eliska every evening, now that all his other friends had gone away, arrived on the porch in time to hear Mary Eliska's admonition. He was about to say something, for he was very proud of his successful "acrobatic flying," when he caught Mary Eliska's frown of warning. Of course there was no use of worrying the timid woman, who was worried enough already. He sat on the railing, dangling his legs, and carelessly lighting a cigarette, as if he were very much at home.

"Mary Eliska's little 'Pursuit' is a daisy, Mary Eliska," he said. "It really has a most marvelous motor—and all sorts of safety devices. There's not a thing for you to worry about.... I wish I had one like it!"

Mary Eliska regarded him sympathetically. It was hard luck that his father, with all his money, refused to buy Ralph a plane! But he had been promised one the following year—if he graduated from college without any conditions. Evidently Mr. Clavering was using it as a spur to his son's ambition, for Ralph had never been keen about his studies. Good times came first with him; besides, he argued, what was the use of learning to make money, when his father already had more than they could spend?

"What are you children going to do this evening?" asked Mary Eliska, though it was nine o'clock now, and there wouldn't be much evening left, for Mary Eliska insisted upon going to bed early.

"I'd like to map out our trip to Green Falls," the latter replied. "And then we could show our plan to Lieutenant Kingsberry, and see where the airports are located along the way, in case we have to land."

"Why not Taylor?" inquired Ralph, teasingly, for he knew that Mary Eliska did not care much about her instructor.

She gave the boy a withering look.

"Well, then—Redhead? He ought to know. By the way, I never see you talking to him, Mary Eliska!"

"I never get a chance. He's always busy, and besides, you're usually with me. I guess he's too shy to intrude."

Nevertheless, she decided that she must have one talk with Ted Mackay before she left the school, to clear up matters that had never been discussed. All during the next week she watched for her opportunity, but it did not come until her final day at the school—the day when she received her license as a private pilot.

Wild with joy at her success, she asked where Ted was, and ran over to the hangar where he happened to be working. For once, Ralph was not with her; he had not yet landed the plane he had been flying.

"Mr. Mackay!" she cried joyously—she was afraid to call him "Ted" now, for he seemed like such a stranger. "I'm a real pilot! I can fly my own plane now, wherever I want to go!"

The young man came over solemnly and shook hands with her.

"May I be the first to congratulate you?" he asked.

"Not the first. Lieutenant Kingsberry has done so already. But, of course, in a way he doesn't count."

"And this is only your beginning, I know!" he said, his blue eyes sparkling with enthusiasm. "You're going to a ground school in the fall—as we used to talk about—aren't you?"

"Yes, I hope so." She hesitated, and looked down at the ground, digging the toe of a dainty slipper—entirely feminine, in spite of her flyer's costume—into the dust. She felt shy, and embarrassed; it was so hard to hurt Ted, and yet she didn't dare disobey her father. "Ted," she said, finally, "could I have just one little talk with you, to clear things up—before I go away?"

"I've been longing for it," he confessed, eagerly. "But I'd decided that you were through with me, on account of my actions that night you got your plane—when I sneaked over to see it. One of the boys heard it roaring over our heads, and ran out to see where it was landing. So, when he came back with the news that it was in your field, I knew it must be yours. When I went over to see it myself—I—I was hoping you'd come out alone—and we could gloat over it together! And then all that crowd showed up, and your aunt too—I was sure it was she—and I just lost my nerve and ran. It looked pretty queer, I guess."

"No, only why didn't you come to the house first?" she inquired.

"I was afraid the butler would say, 'Mary Eliska is not at home'—the way the rich young ladies' butlers always do in the novels."

"Only we haven't any butler," laughed Mary Eliska.

"Well, you have a strict aunt—and a father that's made of steel!"

"Don't!" cried the girl, in an offended tone. "You mustn't say a word against my father, or I never will talk to you. But that brings me to what I wanted to say.... My father has no time for you, on account of your father. It seems that a man by the same name worked for him on the ranch in Texas—and was untrustworthy. Could that have been your father?"

"I'm afraid it was," admitted Ted, sadly.

"So you see why he selected Mr. Taylor to teach me to fly...." Tears almost came into her eyes, as she saw how sorrowful Ted was looking. "I think it's absurd, myself," she admitted. "But I suppose Daddy means it for the best.... I'm—not to be friends with you, Ted.... And, oh, I'm so sorry!"

"I'm sorry too, Mary Eliska," the boy said slowly. "But somehow I never believed we could be real friends. I'm not like you—I don't believe in fairy stories."

"What do you mean?"

"I mean that the poor young man, who has a disgrace to live down, isn't likely to be friends with the rich, beautiful girl—in real life.... So I guess it's good-by...." He held out his hand.

"Oh, but I'll at least see you again!" she protested. "Tomorrow I'm going to fly my plane over here and back—all by myself!"

"That's wonderful—I wish I could be here to see you do it," he answered regretfully. "But unfortunately I am leaving myself tomorrow. I'm taking a job as salesman for a plane construction company in Kansas City."

"Congratulations!" cried Mary Eliska, pleased at his advancement. "Well, good luck—and good-by!"

"And, by the way," he added, "I want to thank you for wearing my poor little flowers at your class-day. I saw you—through the fence. I was so glad they held the affair out-of-doors!"

"Then they were from you?" she asked, ashamed that she had forgotten to thank him. "I thought so, but I wasn't sure. I meant to ask you. They were lovely."

"I am going to give you a card of my firm," said Ted, reaching into his pocket. "So that you will know where I am, in case you need any help with your Arrow.... You—you—don't mind?"

"I'll be very thankful to have it," she reassured him. "You know, Ted, I have an awful lot of confidence in you!"

And, with a final pressure of her hand, he turned to go, and she, looking about, saw Ralph Clavering walking towards her.

"What's the big idea?" he asked her, when he reached her side, and Ted had disappeared. "Holding hands with Red?" His tone was irritable.

"I was just saying good-by," she explained. "He's leaving tomorrow for a job in Kansas City."

"Flying?" "Naturally."

"Well, we'll be flying away soon, too," he added, more cheerfully. "I had a letter from Kit this morning, and she wants us surely at Green Falls for July thirty-first. It's the Midsummer Ball, and the big event of the season—socially. She told me to tell you and Mary Eliska to be sure not to miss it."

"Oh, I'll be ready by Saturday," replied Mary Eliska. "Aunt Polly has been doing all the shopping, so I hardly need to do anything.... By the way, did Kit give you any gossip about the crowd?"

"Let me see," muttered Ralph, as he took her arm possessively while they walked across the field, in the hope that Ted Mackay would see them. "She did have quite a bit to say—but it was mostly about Maurry."

"Maurice Stetson? What's he been doing?"

"Rushing Kit, evidently. And she seems to like it.... And she said Harry Smith has a life-guard's job, and is spending all his spare time with Jax."

"I haven't heard from Jax in ages," remarked Mary Eliska. "But I guess it's partly my fault. I haven't had time to answer her letters." Then, changing the subject, as they came out to the road where Mary Eliska's car was parked, "You're going to fly up with me in the 'Pursuit,' aren't you, Ralph?"

"Surest thing! We'll fly everywhere to gether—from now on. Just like Mr. and Mrs. Lindy!"

"Only we won't!" she answered abruptly, laughing at him.

As they stepped up to the roadster, they almost fell over a man who came out from a shabby coupé in front of theirs. He had evidently been leaning over, fixing something.

"Want any help?" asked Ralph, though Mary Eliska knew he hadn't the slightest idea of giving any.

"No, thanks," muttered the man, without looking up. "Engine trouble."

"Engine trouble!" repeated Mary Eliska, sympathetically. Then, turning to Ralph. "Suppose something like that should happen to us—on the way to Green Falls!"

"Well, it won't!" replied Ralph reassuringly. "The motor's just about perfect in that little plane of yours! No—but I tell you what, Mary Eliska, you better bring your gun along. That crazy sister of mine expects me to bring her pearls up for the Midsummer Ball!"

"Real pearls—at a summer resort!" cried Mary Eliska, as she slipped the key into her lock, and started her engine. "She's taking an awful chance!"

"That's what I think. But of course they're insured. And so long as she's succeeded in getting Dad's permission, it's not my business to stop her.... By the way, it's a fancy-dress affair. What sort of costume will you wear?"

"I don't know. I guess I'll leave it to Aunt Polly."

But when she got back home, she forgot all about pearls and dresses and mid-summer balls. Nothing mattered to her, but the glorious fact that at last she was a real flyer!

Chapter 5.7
The Flight to Green Falls

The first thing that Mary Eliska thought of when she opened her eyes the following morning was the glorious fact that she was now a real pilot. She could take her plane anywhere—to Green Falls, to her father's ranch in Texas, wherever she wanted to go—and nobody could stop her. The freedom of the world and of the skies was hers. But she had no intention of taking it any farther than the Spring City Flying School that day. She would spend the morning there, watching one of the licensed mechanics give it a thorough inspection, in readiness for the flight to Green Falls on the following day.

She wished that it might be Ted Mackay who would go over the plane. She had such confidence in his knowledge, his thoroughness. Besides, it would be fun to spend the morning with him, asking him questions, and talking things over.

Naturally, that was impossible. When Mary Eliska reached the field she found that Ted already had gone, and a number of changes had been made. H. B. Taylor was now first-ranking instructor, and the young man who had been acting as office boy, or orderly, or whatever they chose to call him, had passed his course and was promoted to the rank of instructor. Another man took his place—an older man this time, and Mary Eliska thought probably it was the poor fellow who had been having engine trouble with his shabby coupé the preceding day. Everything seemed different, and Mary Eliska was somehow glad that she was leaving. The place would never be the same to her without Ted Mackay.

About noon she received the mechanic's O.K. upon her plane, and flew home in time for lunch. Her aunt had finished packing, and was as excited as a child about going to Green Falls, and again taking up their customary social life among their friends.

"I have bought a new flying suit for you, dear," she said to her niece, as the girl entered the library. "Unwrap it and see how you like it."

Mary Eliska eagerly unfastened the strings and lifted out a pair of white flannel knickers, with a jaunty blue sweater and helmet of knitted silk, just the color of her eyes. The whole costume was charming, and a lovely change from the dark riding breeches she had been using for flying.

"It's perfect, Aunt Polly!" she cried, realizing for the first time that she had never cared for what she was now wearing. "And it was so sweet of you to think of getting it for me!"

"I never could see why girls have to look masculine," replied her aunt. "Of course I can understand that skirts are impractical, but they make these suits so pretty now-a-days. And I want you to look nice the very first minute you arrive at Green Falls. First impressions are always so important and there is sure to be a crowd there to greet you."

Mary Eliska was only too delighted to wear it the next day, which dawned clear and warm for her flight. Mary Eliska left early in the morning, by train, so that she would be at Green Falls in plenty of time to welcome the flyers.

Ralph came over for Mary Eliska about half-past nine. Carrying their lunch, the young people started on their first real adventure in the air.

The young man, too, wore a new suit of spotless white flannel, and, as they walked, tall and slender and straight, they made perhaps the best-looking pair of flyers in America. But neither was conscious of that; both were too much excited about their first trip in the air to give even a passing thought to their appearances.

"Are you sure that you have the precious necklace?" asked Mary Eliska, as they made their way across the field in back of her house. "Yes, indeed," answered Ralph. "I went to the safe-deposit vault this morning to get it. That was one reason why I didn't want to start early. I had to wait for the bank to open."

"Kit would be horribly disappointed if we didn't bring it," returned Mary Eliska. "I honestly think she loves those pearls as much as I do my 'Pursuit'!"

"Queer taste," remarked the boy. "If I had them, I'd sell them and buy a biplane!"

"Of course you would," said Mary Eliska approvingly. "Even if you do insist upon talking baby-talk!"

"Baby-talk?"

"Certainly. 'Buy a biplane'—sounds like 'Bye, Bye, Baby,' doesn't it?"

Ralph smiled, but they both forgot immediately what they were saying, for they were beside the plane now, ready to start on their flight. Mary Eliska was not at all nervous about the journey, only thrilled and happy. She climbed into the cockpit with the same assurance that she entered her car, and her take-off was just as easy, just as natural. It seemed now as if she piloted the biplane by instinct; with the sureness of a bird it rose into the air to a gradual height of fifteen hundred feet. For she had been cautioned again and again that there was safety in height.

They flew along without any attempt at conversation, for it was difficult to hear above the roar of the motor. But Mary Eliska was so happy that she hummed softly to herself, and most of the time she was smiling. Ralph, with a map in his lap, kept a close watch on the compass.

For some time they did not see any other planes in the sky, and then at last one came into view. As it drew closer, it occurred to Mary Eliska to wonder whether she was being followed.

"Who do you suppose that is?" shouted Ralph, above the noise of the motor.

"I think it's somebody from our school—maybe Taylor," she replied. "Perhaps Dad ordered them to follow us—for safety—or maybe it was Ted Mackay's idea."

As the plane drifted off to one side, they thought no more about the matter. But it was noon now; the sun stood high overhead, and both of the young people were astonished to find how hungry they were.

"I want to try a couple of stunts before we eat," Mary Eliska told Ralph. "You're game, aren't you?"

"Surest thing!" replied the boy, with delight. "We've got plenty of height—and a spectator too, for that matter." The other plane had just come back into sight. Mary Eliska's eyes were shining with excitement, yet inside she was perfectly cool. Hadn't she made inside loops and Immelman turns often at school, and didn't she know exactly what to do? With perfect poise, she swung the plane into a loop, and completed it without any difficulty. Pleased with her success, she tried it again and again.

"You must think you're Laura Ingalls!" shouted Ralph, catching his breath. "Trying to beat her record?"

"Hardly," smiled Mary Eliska, for the famous aviatrix he mentioned held the record at that time with nine hundred and eighty consecutive inside loops, at a speed of four and a half loops a minute.

The plane was righted now, but Mary Eliska suddenly noticed that Ralph was acting awfully queer, hanging over the side, and hunting frantically in the pockets of the sweater which he had put over the seat. She believed he must be ill; certainly his face was ghastly white.

"Ralph!" she cried, fearfully. "What's the matter?"

"I've lost the necklace!" he screamed in terror. "Must have fallen out of my pocket!"

"Oh!" wailed Mary Eliska, aghast at the meaning of his words. "Are you sure?"

"Positive!"

"Then we'll land immediately. We're over a field, so we ought to be able to find it. Now—keep your eye on the compass!"

Gradually, and with easy skill, she turned the biplane into the wind and descended, finally coming down into a large flat field, evidently a pasture ground for some horses. Ralph was the first to jump out.

"We went a little south to land," he said, "so it must have dropped up there."

"Was it in a box?" questioned Mary Eliska.

"Yes, fortunately. A white velvet box, inside a larger pasteboard one, with three rubber bands around it. That ought to make it easier to find."

Mary Eliska, however, had her doubts; the field was so big! Besides, what proof had Ralph that he had lost it at that particular minute—when she was making her loops. She remembered that he had taken off his sweater an hour ago, when he felt too warm, and had carelessly hung it over the side, forgetful of the precious box in its pocket. That was the trouble with being so rich! Many times she had noticed how heedless both Kitty and Ralph were about valuables.

They walked silently across the field, their eyes on the ground, their minds filled with remorse. Ten minutes passed, and they had not found it.

"Let's go back and eat our lunch," suggested Ralph, consulting his watch. "It's almost one o'clock, and we'll feel better if we eat. After all, we have plenty of time—Green Falls is only about twenty miles farther. We could search all afternoon, if necessary."

"Yes, only Aunt Polly would nearly die of anxiety. She'd be sure we had been killed, if we didn't arrive before supper."

They went back to the plane and took out the dainty lunch which Mary Eliska's cook had packed that morning for them. But, hungry though they were, the meal was not the pleasant picnic they had been hoping for. Both were too unhappy to enjoy what they were eating.

Presently the noise of a motor overhead attracted their attention, and, looking up, they saw a plane in descent. When it was low enough to identify, they knew that it was the one that had been following them. "It's the 'Waco' from our school!" cried Mary Eliska. "I recognize it now. He must think we're in trouble. I wonder who's piloting?"

The plane made a rather poor landing at the far end of the field, perhaps half a mile away. They could distinguish a man getting out of the cockpit, but of course at that distance they could not identify him. However, he seemed to be coming slowly towards them.

As he advanced nearer and nearer Mary Eliska noticed that he wore an ordinary suit of clothing—not a flyer's uniform, and he kept his hand in his pocket. But she still did not recognize him—unless he was that new man the school had taken on the preceding day. Once he stooped over, as if he were picking something up, and Mary Eliska's heart beat wildly with hope. Could it be that he had found the necklace? Apparently, though, it was only a plant that he had pulled up by the roots, for when he straightened himself, he seemed to be examining its leaves.

"In trouble?" he shouted, as soon as he was within hearing distance.

Ralph jumped up and ran towards him, shaking his head in the negative.

"No trouble with the plane," he replied. "But we've lost a little box—with a necklace in it. You haven't seen it, have you?"

"Why, yes," answered the man slowly, "I did pick up a box." And he put his other hand in his pocket, and drew out the very article. Fortunately it had not been broken; even the rubber bands were still tightly around it. He handed it to Ralph.

"Oh, thank you a thousand times!" cried Mary Eliska, too relieved to believe her eyes. "The necklace was a graduation present to this man's sister, and she values it very highly!"

"Well, if that's all, I'll be off," said the man, as he watched Ralph put the box into his pocket.

"No, I must reward you," insisted the boy, taking out a twenty-dollar bill. "And by the way, you're from the Spring City Flying School, aren't you? We recognized the plane."

The other nodded, and seemed in a hurry to be off. Already he was twenty feet away.

"It was awfully nice of you to follow us, and look after us," called Mary Eliska, "but really we don't need protection. We're getting along finely!"

But the man was running now, and could hardly have heard what Mary Eliska was saying. In a couple of minutes they heard the motor start, and with a clumsy take-off, the plane ascended.

"A queer cuss," remarked Ralph. "And I can't see that he's much of a flyer. You and I are both better—by a long shot.... But anyhow, we've got the necklace!" He put his arms around Mary Eliska and hugged her, and she was too happy to protest. What a miracle it was to have found it!

"That will teach me a lesson," said Ralph, as he helped Mary Eliska gather up the lunch. "I'm going to be more careful now. I've put the necklace in my most inside pocket!"

"And I'm not going in for any more acrobatics for a while," added Mary Eliska. They climbed into the cockpit, and started the motor without wasting any more time. Half an hour later they made a graceful landing at Green Falls' Airport, for a group of a hundred spectators to witness and admire.

Chapter 5.8
The Robbery

"Let's don't say anything about our little mishap," whispered Mary Eliska, as the flying couple got out of their plane. "For one thing, I'd just as soon not boast about stunts in front of Aunt Polly. She would be worried all the more."

"And I'm not any too proud of the fact that I was so careless about a valuable necklace," returned Ralph. "So we'll keep it our secret."

There was no time for further words. Everybody rushed at them, shouting joyous welcomes. Jax Gray was the first to kiss Mary Eliska—then all the others, and finally her aunt.

"Thank Heaven you're safe!" cried the latter. "I couldn't eat a bite of lunch, I was so uneasy."

"Of course we're safe," assured Ralph. "And maybe if we'd come by motor, we should have had an accident. There was a big smash-up—two automobiles—outside of Spring City this morning."

"Isn't the air up here wonderful!" exclaimed Mary Eliska. "After that stuffy town of ours!"

"I think the *airport* is wonderful,» replied Mary Eliska, «for so small a place. But as for the air—well, don›t forget Auntie dear, that Ralph and I have been having marvelous air—up in the skies!»

"Hope you didn't give him the air," remarked Maurice Stetson, solemnly.

Kitty Clavering gave the young man a withering look, and inquired of the flyers when they might hope for rides. "Oh, I don't mean today," she added, "for I know you must both be nearly dead."

"Not a bit of it!" denied Mary Eliska, who still looked as fresh as a flower in her becoming blue and white suit. "But it's supposed to be wise to have a mechanic go over your plane each time you fly. Just a precaution, you see."

"A very good rule to follow," commented Mary Eliska. "Now everybody get into their cars, and we'll go over to our bungalow for some ginger-ale and sandwiches."

"Just a moment, please!" interrupted a voice at her elbow, and everyone turned to see a newspaper man with a camera. "Pictures, please!"

Mary Eliska and Ralph smilingly agreed, and their friends stepped aside. Then they all piled into the three machines that were waiting for them; while the strangers who had been watching commented on the beautiful biplane, and the handsome couple who had been flying it, and wondered whether they were married.

"Did you bring my necklace, Ralph?" asked Kitty Clavering, as he got into her roadster with her and Maurice.

"Surest thing!" he replied, as if nothing at all had happened on the way. Reaching into his pocket, he pulled out the pasteboard box, with the French jeweler's name engraved on the lid.

"Thanks a lot," she replied. "Maurry, you take care of it 'til we get home, so long as you're sitting in the middle. Mind you don't lose it! I think as much of that as Mary Eliska does of her plane."

"But not as much of it as you do of me?" asked the youth, flippantly.

"A thousand times more! Like the old question people always ask married men: 'If your mother and your wife were drowning, which one would you save?' Well, if you and the necklace were drowning, I'd go after my necklace!"

"Righto. Necklaces, no matter how valuable, have never been known to swim. I do."

It was only a five-minute ride from the airport to Mary Eliska's bungalow, so Kitty waited until they had all gone inside the pleasant living-room to open her box, and gaze at her beloved treasure once more. "I'm dying to see it again," she said, as she took the box from Maurice's hand. "If I had my way, I wouldn't keep it in a safe-deposit vault. I like it where I can look at it."

She took off the rubber bands and opened the box, displaying the velvet case inside. But when she unfastened the clasp, her expression of delight changed abruptly to one of horror. The case was empty!

Her exclamation of distress was pitiful to hear. Her dearest possession—gone!

"Ralph!" she cried with torturing accusation. "Ralph! Are you teasing me?" Her brother's face became ghastly white.

"What—what's wrong—Kit?" he stammered.

"My necklace! Oh, what has happened?" She burst out crying.

Everybody crowded around and gazed in consternation at the empty box, looking questioningly at Ralph, to see whether it could possibly be intended as a joke. But he did not need to tell them of his innocence; he looked almost as stricken as his sister. He knew now that it had been stolen by the man who pretended to be a pilot! And he had actually made twenty dollars out of Ralph besides, for the transaction! What fools they had been, never to open the box!

"It's all my fault!" cried Mary Eliska, contritely. "My silly, foolish, childishness, for wanting to show off!"

Nobody of course had any idea what she was talking about—nobody except Ralph.

"No! No! It was mine!" he protested. "My carelessness!"

"Then you both knew!" exclaimed Kitty, raising her head, which she had buried on Mary Eliska's shoulder while she sobbed. "Oh, how cruel, not to prepare me!"

"On my honor, we didn't!" averred Ralph, and from the look on his face, his sister knew that he was telling the truth.

"Explain what you meant, then," she commanded.

"Let me tell you," put in Mary Eliska. "But sit down, Kit dear. You're liable to faint.... You see, we were robbed, and too foolish to suspect it. We even paid the robber twenty dollars for doing the job."

"So you said," Kitty remarked, impatiently. "Do you mean that you saw somebody take it—right under your eyes?" She had dropped down on the couch, and her pale little face was pitiful to see. The tears still ran down her cheeks, washing tiny rivers through the powder. Luckily she was not a girl who used rouge, or she would have looked ridiculous. As it was, she gave the appearance of a very unhappy child.

"Exactly!" explained Mary Eliska. "Or rather, we might have, if we had had sense enough to realize it. I wanted to try a couple of loops, and we started quite high, but by the time we had finished, we were over an open field. It was then that Ralph suddenly realized that the box had dropped out of his pocket when the plane was on its side. So we decided to land, and search the field."

"And somebody had already picked it up?" demanded Dot, excitedly.

"No. Another airplane—I had noticed it before—landed soon after we came down. The pilot walked over and asked us if we were in trouble."

"And you stupids told him all about the fifty-thousand-dollar necklace!" cried Jax Gray, in disgust.

"No, we didn't! We were smart enough to know that wouldn't be wise. We thought we knew him, though—we had seen him at the Spring City Flying School. But we did tell him we had lost a necklace, and he said he had picked something up. As a matter of fact, we had noticed him stoop over."

"And you took it and thanked him, and never looked inside!" cried Kitty.

"I'm afraid you're right," admitted Ralph. "We thought he was a friend, following us for our protection, at the orders of the school."

"Well, then, why was he following you?" demanded Kitty, incredulously.

"He must have overheard us talking about the necklace," answered Mary Eliska slowly, for she was trying to think the thing out. "Yes—that is what I believe he was doing all the time, Ralph. Now I remember—the day we got our licenses!"

"You mean you went around the school shouting the news that you were carrying pearls to Green Falls in an airplane?" asked the unhappy girl.

"Of course not! Only the men at the bank—the safe-deposit vault—really knew about it. And of course they're absolutely trustworthy! Except maybe this one man—who was fixing his car outside the aviation field. We never thought he was listening—why we couldn't even see him!"

"Children," interrupted Mary Eliska, who had been patiently waiting to serve the refreshments, "wouldn't you all feel better if you ate something? Then we can discuss what are the best steps to take to capture the thief."

They agreed, but Mary Eliska and Ralph and Kitty were all extremely nervous; they hated to lose any time. Ralph decided to telephone to a lawyer at once in Spring City, to put expert detectives on the job, and to get in touch with the Flying School.

"Lucky the necklace was insured," remarked Maurice Stetson, as he drank his ginger-ale.

"Yes, but Dad will never get me another!" moaned Kitty, disconsolately. "He'll say I was careless, and invest the insurance in bonds, to be kept in trust 'til I'm older—or something like that." She started to cry afresh. "And I only wore the necklace twice—at graduation and at the class dance!"

Mary Eliska watched her sorrow with more than sympathy—with remorse. It was her fault, she was sure! Of course she couldn't imagine caring so much for a pearl necklace, when such lovely imitations were made, but it wasn't her place to judge. Kitty probably wouldn't understand why she loved her Arrow so much.

Slowly, painfully, she came to her decision. She rose and went over to the couch where Kitty was sitting, and crowded in between the latter and Dot.

"It's my fault, Kit," she said, "and of course I can't pay for it—but I can help. I'm—I'm—going to sell my airplane, and—give you the money. Then you can start buying a new one—a couple of pearls at a time."

Kitty squeezed her hand affectionately.

"You're a dear, Mary Eliska, but I couldn't possibly let you do that. Besides, it was really Ralph's fault."

"Of course it was!" put in the young man, returning from making his telephone call. "But we're going to catch that thief!" he announced, with conviction. "I've just been talking with Lieutenant Kingsberry at the field, and he says that fellow didn't even have a license, that they only took him on temporarily, as sort of errand boy. And he deliberately stole that plane!"

"I thought he was about the poorest pilot I ever saw!" cried Mary Eliska, jumping up excitedly at this piece of news. "He'll probably crash, sooner or later.... Ralph!" Her eyes were shining with inspiration.... "Let's go out after him—ourselves!"

"Lieutenant Kingsberry is broadcasting the news all over—to all the airports," replied the young man. "Everybody will be watching for him. Do you think there would be any use in our going?"

"Yes! Yes! We might be just the ones to spot him! Oh, come on!"

"But haven't you had enough flying for today, Mary Eliska?" inquired Mary Eliska, anxiously.

"We won't go far, Auntie dear," answered the girl. "Just around to the nearest airports, and see if anybody has any information. The practice of landing and taking-off again will be good for us both.... And you needn't worry one bit!... Now, who'll drive us over to our 'Pursuit'?"

"'Pursuit' is right," remarked Maurice. "Your plane has the right name, Mary Eliska!"

Jax Gray immediately offered her services, and in less than five minutes the young pilots had washed their faces and were ready to start. Ten minutes later they climbed into the cockpit on the runway of the airport, and, this time with Ralph at the controls, they took off for the nearest airport.

Ralph was delighted to be piloting a plane again, and in his enthusiasm he almost forgot the seriousness of his mission. A king of the air, he thought, and his lips were smiling. But Mary Eliska could not forget so easily.

Like most young men, he loved going fast, and as soon as he was high enough, he let the plane out to her maximum speed. Over the clouds they sailed, at a rate of seventy miles an hour, yet they did not seem to be traveling fast. Mary Eliska had no sense of danger, yet it was the first flight she had ever made that she did not thoroughly enjoy, for, unlike Ralph, she could not for one moment forget Kitty's tragedy.

Twenty minutes, however, was all that was needed to reach their first port, and Ralph, not quite so skilled or so careful as Mary Eliska, made, nevertheless a pretty landing. It was a large field, evidently designed for amateur sport flyers, and there were a number of licensed mechanics in readiness to greet new arrivals.

Ralph lost no time in telling his story to the first man who came forward. Had they any information so far? he inquired.

"Only of a wreck about fifteen miles away," replied the latter. "That may be your man—if, as you say, he is not an experienced pilot."

"Can you give us directions?" put in Mary Eliska excitedly.

"Certainly," replied the other, taking a map from his pocket, and indicating the position of the wreck. "We've already sent a doctor and a nurse—and telephoned for an ambulance." Marking the spot, he handed the map to Ralph.

Jumping into the plane at once, Mary Eliska took control, for she felt surer of herself than of her companion in an emergency. The boy was so absent-minded, so likely to forget things in his excitement.

Their destination was a field again, but not a large one, this time, and already a small crowd, gathered from passing automobiles, had collected. Here landing was not so easy as in the airports designed for that very purpose. But the girl knew just what she was doing, and she handled the situation with a dexterity that would have brought credit to a far more experienced pilot.

Over against an embankment, its wings smashed to pieces, a plane was lying on its side, mutely testifying to the truth of the mechanic's statement.

"There's the wreck!" cried Ralph, as he and Mary Eliska stepped on the ground. "Do you think it's the Waco?"

Grabbing her companion's arm, Mary Eliska ran forward eagerly. When they were within fifty yards of it, she knew that it was the very plane they were seeking.

"It is! Oh, Ralph! Even the license number—so I'm sure! Remember? Look! Do you suppose that man was killed?"

"Would serve him right!" muttered the boy, resentfully. "Stealing a necklace, and crashing a plane that wasn't his! But let's go over and have a peep at him—there's the ambulance."

The crowd, which was still gathering, although the field was in an isolated spot, was being held back by a policeman, for the ambulance was ready to start. Ralph dashed forward, anxious to get a look at the thief before it departed.

"Not that we could claim the necklace now," he explained to Mary Eliska, whose arm he was holding, "for we haven't any proofs of our ownership. But at least we could warn the cop to look out for it."

"Back! Back!" shouted the officer, for the driver was tooting his horn. "Oh, please wait a minute!" begged Mary Eliska. "Please let me see the man who is inside!"

The policeman regarded the girl doubtfully, but she was so eager in her pleading that he thought perhaps she had a good reason. Perhaps the man inside the ambulance meant something to her; he decided to grant her request.

"Take a look, miss," he agreed. "But be quick about it."

Stepping ahead of Ralph, Mary Eliska climbed upon the back step of the car, and peered anxiously into it, past the white-clad interne, to the unconscious figure on the stretcher. Suddenly she started violently, and clung to the door of the ambulance for support. It was incredible, impossible! Her knees shook, her hands fell to her side, and she swayed backward in a faint. In an instant Ralph's arms were around her; he carried her out of the crowd.

The unconscious man in the ambulance was none other than Ted Mackay!

Chapter 5.9
Suspicions

Someone from the crowd handed Ralph a cup filled with water, and before they had gone half a dozen steps, Mary Eliska had recovered consciousness. She dropped down to the ground and stared questioningly about her.

"What was it, my dear?" asked Ralph gently, as he held the water to her lips. "Was the man hurt so horribly?"

"No—it wasn't that," replied Mary Eliska slowly, remembering all that had happened. "It was just—oh, Ralph! I hate to tell you!"

"Please tell me, Mary Eliska," he begged.

She looked about her for a moment. The ambulance had gone, and the crowd, seeing that the girl was all right, began to withdraw, some to examine the shattered plane, others to go back to their cars parked along the roadside. There was nobody listening now, so she decided to answer Ralph's question.

"It wasn't our thief at all," she said. "It was—Ted Mackay."

"Ted Mackay?" he repeated, as if he could not believe his ears.

"Yes."

"Then how do you explain it? That couldn't have been Mackay we met on that field—Mackay disguised, or anything?"

"No. He wasn't tall enough. And he had black hair. Oh, Ralph, I'm sure of that!"

"Then how do you explain it?"

"I don't explain it," she said weakly.

He said nothing more, but he knew that she was not only terribly disappointed in not being able to trace the necklace, but that she was entertaining grave doubts about Mackay's part in the whole miserable affair. Were he and this thief in partnership, playing a wicked game, and had Ted hired the man because he would not let them know his part in the robbery?

But there was no use talking about that now, for Ralph realized that Mary Eliska was almost ready to collapse. Drawing her arm through his, he led her silently back to the Pursuit, and put her into the cockpit, indicating that he would pilot them back to Green Falls. Not a word did she utter during the entire flight homeward; she drooped listlessly back in her seat, with an expression of disappointment and despair on her face. How she wished that she had not come!

No one was waiting for them at the airport, so they took a taxi to Mary Eliska's bungalow. They found the latter on the porch, with only Kitty and Maurice beside her.

"Any news?" demanded the girl, jumping out of the hammock, and rushing down the steps before the taxi had been stopped.

"Some news, yes," replied Mary Eliska, while Ralph paid the driver. "But I'm afraid it doesn't mean much. Ralph will tell you all about it."

But the young man was not willing to tell his story until he had asked Mary Eliska to take care of Mary Eliska.

"She fainted at the field," he explained. "The hot sun and the crowd, I expect." He did not want to speak of Ted Mackay before her, while she felt so ill. "So if you'll take Mary Eliska up to her room, Mary Eliska, I'll tell Kitty what I know—and tell you later."

The words aroused Mary Eliska's aunt immediately, and she lost interest in the necklace temporarily. What were a few pearls, anyway, in comparison to her precious girl? She hurried her off to bed, and Ralph turned to Kitty and Maurice.

"You see it was this way," he began, and Kitty stamped her foot in exasperation.

"Don't be so slow, Ralph!" she commanded.

"Why, here comes Mary Eliska's father!" interrupted Maurice, as another taxi stopped at the bungalow. "What do you think of that?"

Kitty looked vexed. Another interruption! But Ralph was already on his feet, greeting him, and explaining the absence of Mary Eliska and her aunt.

"And I was just going to tell Kitty about our pursuit of the thief," he added, "so if you care to hear the story, Mr. Stricklin, perhaps you will sit here with us?"

The older man was glad to comply with the request. Naturally, anything that was connected with Mary Eliska's first flights was of paramount interest to him.

So, in spite of Kitty's impatience, her brother began the story with the day that he and Mary Eliska received their licenses, and ended it with the latter's identification of Ted Mackay, unconscious on the stretcher in the ambulance.

"Mackay!" repeated Mr. Stricklin, shaking his head knowingly. "So he was the brains of the crime!"

"I'm afraid so, sir. And I'm afraid that's what made Mary Eliska faint."

"Of course it is! She believed in that fellow. But I warned her not to trust him. You see his father worked for me out in Texas and he's an unprincipled fellow. Stole from everybody— not only myself, but even the rest of the help. And got into a mix-up with some Mexicans, and turned them against me.... Yes, it must run in the family. The father may even be in on this necklace robbery. I don't know where he is now."

"That explains a good deal," mused Ralph, who had been listening thoughtfully. "I never did like Ted Mackay." He would not admit even to himself that jealousy was the main reason for this dislike. "Besides, Mary Eliska probably told him about the Midsummer Ball, and our carrying Kit's necklace to Green Falls. I thought it was funny if that other chap caught on so quickly."

"Did Mary Eliska see much of Mackay while she was at the school?" her father asked, sharply.

"I can't say that, although I wasn't always with her. Towards the end of our time we did so much solo flying, that when I was up in the air I didn't know where she was, although she was usually up too—in another plane. But one time I did find her in a pretty intimate conversation—and that was right before we left. She probably told him then."

"Too bad! Too bad!" muttered Mr. Stricklin, regretfully. He was wishing now that he had sent Mary Eliska to some other flying school.

At this moment, Mary Eliska, having left Mary Eliska asleep in her room, came out on the porch to see her young guests. She showed no surprise at finding her brother; for fifteen years she had been accustomed to having him drop in when least expected, without a moment's notice.

"Well, Albert," was all that she said, as she presented her cheek for his brotherly kiss. "I suppose these children have told you the news."

"Yes, and if you don't mind, Polly, I think I'll drive over with them to see Mr. Clavering," he added, for the young people had all risen, and were showing signs of departure. "I'd like to have a talk with him—at least if you'll excuse me."

"Certainly," replied his sister. "And will you be back in time for dinner?"

"I'll come home in half an hour," stated her brother, laughing, for he always teased her about her insistence upon his promptness. It was natural that he should want to meet Kitty's parents, that he might at least offer to do his part in trying to recover or make good the girl's loss. But Mr. Clavering seemed to take the matter almost lightly.

"Of course it's too bad," he said, "but as long as it is only a theft, and not an injury to one of the children, I think it's foolish to worry. And, after all, we may get insurance."

"*May* get insurance?» repeated Mr. Stricklin, frowning. «Why shouldn›t you get it? I thought that was what insurance was for!»

"I'm afraid ordinary insurance will not cover travel by air," explained the other man. At these words his daughter burst into tears. Her last hope was gone!

"I never thought of that," said Mr. Stricklin, gravely. "That makes a difference.... Well, Mr. Clavering, in that case, I guess we had better divide the obligation. I'll raise my twenty-five thousand—the necklace was worth fifty, I understand—as soon as I can."

"You'll do nothing of the sort!" protested the other, firmly. "Your daughter was not the least bit at fault. It was natural for her to try her stunts—she wouldn't be human if she didn't! I put the whole blame upon Ralph." "No! No———"

"Yes, yes! I won't hear anything else. But we'll wait and give the detectives time. If we have caught the leader, as you and Ralph think, it ought to be an easy matter to locate the accomplice. At least, provided Mackay doesn't die."

"That's true!" exclaimed Ralph. "I never thought of that. We better get over to the hospital to see him as soon as possible."

"How about tomorrow morning?" suggested Mr. Stricklin. "I'd like to go with you, my boy—I've had some experience in dealing with criminals, ever since the episode with Mackay's father."

"I'll be delighted to have you," replied Ralph. "And in the meantime, I'll call my detective and put him on the other man's trail." So while Mary Eliska slept peacefully at home, her father and her best boyfriend made plans to verify their suspicions against Ted Mackay, lying helpless in the hospital, twenty-five miles from Green Falls.

Chapter 5.10
In the Hospital

When Ted Mackay opened his eyes at the hospital the following morning, he did not know where he was. Although he had regained consciousness when the orderlies brought him in from the ambulance the day before, it had not lasted long. An anesthetic was immediately administered, for it was necessary to cut into his arm, and later a drug was given to make him sleep. So, for the moment, he could not understand why he was here—in a ward, undoubtedly, judging from the long row of cots against the wall.

A dull aching pain in his arm and shoulder made him glance suspiciously at his left side. They were bandaged, of course. And then suddenly he remembered.

He had been sent out with a new plane, from his company in Kansas City, to make delivery to a purchaser in Buffalo. Just before he left, a radio message had been received from the Spring City Flying School, asking all pilots and mechanics to look out for a stolen Waco. Naturally, Ted remembered the plane.

He had been flying quite low, to make certain tests with the plane he was delivering, over the fields beyond Green Falls, when he suddenly noticed a wreck. Complying with the regulations of the Department of Commerce, he descended in order to report the casualty and to render assistance, if possible. Smashed as it was, he recognized it immediately as the old Waco, which he had so often piloted at Spring City. He looked about for the pilot, dreading to find his shattered body in the cockpit.

He had been leaning over, peering into the bushes, when a gun went off at his back, hitting him on the left arm, near the shoulder. Reeling about sharply, he just had time to see a shabbily dressed man run for the new plane. And then everything went black; he couldn't recall what happened, or how he got to the hospital.

"The company's new plane!" he suddenly exclaimed aloud, attempting to sit up in his cot. "It's gone!"

He looked about helplessly for the nurse, for anybody, to verify his fears. But nobody came, although down the hall he could hear footsteps of people busy on their early morning duties.

Warned by the pain in his shoulder, he sank back on his pillow to wait, and as he lay there quietly, he went back over the events of the past week that had been so eventful for him. He thought of Mary Eliska, of the pride and joy in her beautiful eyes when she had won her license. And of her farewell! A farewell that might easily be forever! Yet through no fault of his own, merely because his father had disgraced himself.

It had always been like that with Ted; it seemed as if his father had tried to spoil his whole life. Just when the boy was ready to enter High School, Mr. Mackay had been dismissed from his job for stealing from the cash-drawer of the store where he was employed. The judge had let him off, for he knew what a splendid woman Mrs. Mackay was, and Ted and his older sister had gone to work to pay the debt. It was hard sledding after that; Mr. Mackay wandered off, working now in one place and now in another, and Ted put off his hopes of study for a while. Then, just as the family were getting ahead, and Ted had started in at an aviation school, the man came back for more money. The last they heard of him was a year ago, when he had written that he had a real job on a ranch in Texas. But evidently he had done something wrong there, or Mr. Stricklin would not be so bitter against his son.

Ted's shoulder was hurting him badly, and his thoughts were not pleasant, so he uttered a weary sigh.

"Well! Well!" exclaimed a cheery voice at the door. "Is the world as sad as all that?"

Ted's mouth relaxed into a smile, the smile that had won him so many friends at the Spring City Flying School. He had not heard the nurse, a pretty probationer, who just entered the ward.

"How's the shoulder this morning?" she asked him brightly. "You're looking better, Mr. Mackay."

"I'm all right," replied Ted, wondering how she knew his name. "But can you give me any news of my plane?"

"Your plane was wrecked, wasn't it?" she inquired.

"No—I hope not! That was the other fellow's plane. The fellow that shot me."

"Oh, I see. Then there were two planes?"

"Certainly. Didn't you know?... You seem to know my name——"

"There were some letters in your pocket— don't you remember? And the address of a company in Kansas City.... But I don't think anybody realizes that there were *two* planes— that you didn›t wreck yours.»

"Oh, but I wouldn't wreck a plane in that way!" he protested. "I think too much of them!" His face lighted up with the enthusiasm he always showed when he talked about flying. "But I've got to get to a telephone!" he added. "I must notify my company immediately of the loss."

"Probably your company knows all about it," she replied. "Anyway, you can't do anything now—except lie still while I take your temperature. And then eat your breakfast. After your wound is dressed—if the doctor agrees——"

"But I've got to get dressed right away! I want to notify them so that they can catch that bandit!"

"Yes, yes. In due time. You must be patient."

"You say they didn't know about that other fellow!" he cried, excitedly. "I tell you——"

He stopped suddenly, for he saw that his nurse had gone off to another cot. There was no use trying to argue with nurses, he learned, for they had to follow the rules laid down by the doctors and the hospital authorities.

So, for the next two hours he did exactly as he was told, not even making an attempt to dress. For his nurse had informed him that he must stay there at least another day.

He was dozing when a representative from his company called to see him. But the man urged the nurse not to disturb him, saying that he would come again the following morning. She told him what she knew of Ted's story, and of his anxiety over the stolen plane, and he promised to send out scouts in its pursuit.

Ted's next two visitors were not so thoughtful of his welfare. Mr. Stricklin and Ralph Clavering, who made the trip unknown to Mary Eliska, arrived about eleven o'clock, and asked that the young man be awakened at once.

"I think you had better come back tomorrow, if you want to talk to Mr. Mackay," said the nurse, noticing that the two men were not any too friendly towards her patient, for they had not even inquired how he was. "He mustn't be disturbed."

"Then we'll wait until he wakes up," replied Mr. Stricklin, firmly. "It's very important that we speak with him as soon as possible."

"You're from his company?" she asked. "No, we're not."

"Just friends?" "No."

"Then may I ask what reason you have for wishing to see Mr. Mackay at this particular time?"

"Business. Very important business. We think he is involved in the theft of a very expensive necklace." "No!" cried the nurse, aghast. It couldn't be true! Why, she had never seen anybody with franker eyes or a more truthful, honest face than this young man with the wounded arm! There must be some mistake.

"Did he act as if he wanted to get out of the hospital as quickly as possible?" asked Ralph, shrewdly.

"Why, yes—but that was only natural. All men, especially young men, are impatient about staying here. Only last week, the day after a man was operated on for appendicitis, he said he had to get back to his office—he just had to! You should have heard him rave. We laughed at him."

"Well, we'll sit down here in the reception room and read the magazines," announced Mr. Stricklin. "And you send us word when he wakes up."

There was nothing further she could do, but somehow she was against them. Already she was on Ted's side. She didn't believe he was one of those wicked gangsters you read about in the papers. Why, he was only a boy! A boy tremendously interested in aviation. She could see his eyes shine when he talked about flying, and the absolute tragedy he believed it to be because, a fine plane had been wrecked. It seemed worse to him than being shot. Poor fellow! He would get well, of course, but was this going to cripple him so he wouldn't be able to fly?

About twelve o'clock, when it was time for the lunch trays to be brought in, he awakened. But the nurse had no intention of informing those two men in the waiting-room.

However, they did not wait to be informed. Perhaps Mr. Stricklin suspected that the nurse was against him, or perhaps it was merely that he knew that he hadn't much longer to stay— it was imperative that he return to his ranch that night. Anyway, he and Ralph strolled down the hall and found Ted eating his lunch. They walked right into the ward without asking the nurse's permission. "How d'do, Mackay," said Mr. Stricklin, briefly. "How's your wound?"

"Better, thank you, sir," replied Ted, smiling. He had recognized Mary Eliska's father instantly, and a feeling of joy surged through him. What a decent thing for the man to do! Probably Mary Eliska had heard of his accident, and asked him to come to inquire for him. Of course he was totally unaware of the loss of the pearls; he had no idea that the thief who had taken the two planes had done so for the sole purpose of stealing a necklace.

Remembering Ralph, too, he managed to smile at him also.

"You certainly managed to wreck your plane," remarked Mr. Stricklin, not knowing exactly how to begin. "You're in luck that you weren't killed!"

"I didn't wreck *my* plane, sir,» corrected Ted, quietly. «It was the fellow who shot me that wrecked his—or rather the school›s, for he had stolen it from the Spring City Flying School, you know. Then he shot at me, and flew off in my plane.»

"Oh, is that so?" Mr. Stricklin, raised his brows, and his eyes narrowed. He didn't believe a word of it.

"And—er—how did you and this thief happen to be together?" he inquired.

"I was taking a new plane to Buffalo, and flying low, making some tests, when I spotted the wreck. So I brought mine down."

"You knew, then, that he had stolen Miss Clavering's pearls?"

"What?" cried Ted, starting upright in bed, and then, shocked by the pain from his sudden movement, dropping back to his pillow.

"You never heard of a valuable pearl necklace that this young man was carrying from Spring City to his sister, by my daughter's plane?" persisted Mr. Stricklin. His tone was mocking, insulting.

"On my honor, Mr. Stricklin——"

"Come now, Mackay," interrupted Ralph. "Why not make a clean breast of it? We know you—or this other fellow—heard Mary Eliska and me discussing it at the field, and we know you used him as an accomplice. We saw him hanging around outside——"

"You are making a big mistake, Mackay," put in Mr. Stricklin, "if you don't confess everything now. I'd be willing to give you another chance—if you tell us how you can get a hold of that fellow, and get the necklace back. I know you weren't brought up right—it's not exactly your fault if you don't know right from wrong——"

But this was too much for Ted to bear. The man was insulting his mother! If he hadn't been Mary Eliska's father, Ted would have struck him, crippled though he was. Instead, overpowered by nervous exhaustion, he let out a terrific scream that at least stopped the abuse.

"I do know right from wrong!" he cried. "My mother is the finest woman that ever lived, and she knew what to teach her children! What you say is a lie!"

By this time everybody in the ward was looking and listening in breathless interest, and the head nurse, attracted by the noise, stopped in the corridor.

"You men will leave at once," she commanded, from the doorway, and Mr. Stricklin, who was so used to giving orders to others, found that for once he had to obey. He and Ralph picked up their hats and were gone without another word.

After that, Ted was quite ill. His temperature went up, and he became delirious. The little nurse was both angry and remorseful. It was her fault, she thought, for not keeping those dreadful men out. Accusing an innocent boy like her patient!

The visitors, however, went away dismayed. They hadn't proved a thing.

"Unfortunately I have to leave tonight right after dinner," said Mr. Stricklin, as Ralph drove him back to his sister's. "I guess we'll have to turn the whole thing over to the detectives."

"Well, we'll see what Greer and his men can do," replied the other. "One good thing, Mackay can't get away from us, crippled as he is. And the other fellow is such a poor pilot that he'll crash sooner or later."

"If he doesn't get out of the country first," muttered Mr. Stricklin, dolefully.

"What does Mary Eliska think about the affair?" inquired Ralph, for he had not seen the girl since her aunt helped her to go to bed the preceding afternoon.

"I don't know. I haven't seen her. She was still asleep when I left this morning."

"I imagine she believes Mackay guilty. That's what knocked her over so yesterday."

"Well, she'll get over that," returned her father, briefly. And he invited Ralph to come into the house for luncheon.

The young man, however, had the good taste to decline. It would be a ticklish situation at best—and besides, Mary Eliska ought to have some time to be alone with her father, if he were leaving so soon.

"But tell Mary Eliska I'll be over after dinner," he added. "The bunch is planning a canoe party."

Chapter 5.11
An Anxious Day for Mary Eliska

Never in her life did Mary Eliska remember being so exhausted as she had been on the evening of her flight to Green Falls. With her Aunt Polly's help she had somehow gotten into bed, and eaten the supper of milk-toast which the maid had brought to her. Inside of an hour she was fast asleep, not to awaken until eleven o'clock the following morning, although her aunt, still a little worried about her fainting, was in and out of her room three times. It was upon the last occasion that she finally opened her eyes.

"Oh, such a good sleep, Aunt Polly!" she murmured, contentedly.

"Do you feel better, dear?" inquired the other.

"Just fine, thanks. And hungry."

"I'll have Anna bring you up some fruit, and then you can have lunch with us. Or would you rather have a regular breakfast in bed?"

"Just the fruit, please, Aunt Polly," re plied Mary Eliska. How kind, how thoughtful, her aunt always was! No real mother could ever be more so. "You are so good to me, Auntie!" she cried, impulsively catching the older woman's hand.

"And you're always so appreciative, dear," responded her aunt, affectionately. "I don't think most young girls are like you. They just expect their parents to do everything. Older people like thanks."

"I guess everybody likes to be thanked, when they deserve it...." She jumped out of bed, and slipped into a chiffon negligee that hung over the chair. "And now I'll hurry with my bath!"

"Yes, dear—because your father arrived yesterday, after you had gone to bed. He'll be here for lunch, but he has to leave right after supper."

"Is he downstairs now?" asked Mary Eliska, excitedly. "I don't know whether he has come in or not. He went somewhere with Ralph this morning." "With Ralph?"

"Yes. Something about the theft, I believe.... Well, dear, I'll send up some raspberries—or would you rather have cantaloupe?"

"Cantaloupe, I think, Aunt Polly," replied Mary Eliska, as Mary Eliska left the room.

Some of the happiness with which Mary Eliska awoke seemed to vanish at her aunt's statement about her father and Ralph. She had forgotten for the moment about the necklace—

that airplane accident, and the shock of finding Ted Mackay. What could it all mean? Was Ted really involved in the affair?

By this time her father must know about him, since her Aunt Polly said he was with Ralph. What were they up to now? If Ted really were in league with the thief, would they put him in prison too? She hated the thought of such a thing—it did not seem possible. Surely, there must be some explanation. All of a sudden she longed fiercely to see the boy, to hear the story from his own lips. But he was in a hospital, unconscious—perhaps dying!

Anna came in with the cantaloupe as Mary Eliska finished her bath, and she sat on the edge of the bed to eat it. She made a pretty picture, her soft curly hair damp from the water, her cheeks pink with color after the cold shower, her charming blue negligee wrapped about her slender figure. She looked like a lady of leisure enjoying her late breakfast as if it were a regu lar thing; not an aviation student who arose every morning at seven o'clock and put in a hard day's work at school.

When she entered the living-room, she found her father there waiting for her. She was all in white now, white linen sports suit, and white shoes. He held out his arms invitingly, and she leaped gracefully into his lap.

"Daddy dear!"

"Mary Eliska!"

"You didn't mind my not waking up for supper last night, did you?" she asked, after she had kissed him. "I would have been too tired to talk."

"Of course not! It was the wisest thing to do. Sometimes when you force yourself to keep awake after a strain like that, you find you cannot go to sleep again. But you're rested now?"

"Fresh as a freshman," she replied, laughing. "And I'm mighty proud of my little girl," he added, affectionately, "for passing your examination and flying all the way up here without any mishaps." Mary Eliska's face grew sober, and her eyelids fluttered. "But—I didn't, Daddy. You—you heard about the necklace?"

"Yes. That was too bad, but I can't see that it was in any way your fault. You'd be a queer flyer if you didn't want to test your knowledge."

"Then you don't really blame me?" she asked eagerly. Her father's approval had always meant so much to her.

"Of course not. It was the boy's carelessness. He agrees with me, and so do his father and mother. I went over to see them last night."

"Ralph hasn't heard anything more, has he?" she asked anxiously. How she longed for news of Ted! But she was afraid to mention his name to her father.

Mr. Stricklin, however, answered her unspoken wish.

"No," he said. "We drove over to see Mackay at the hospital this morning, and tried to talk to him. But he wouldn't admit a thing. He became hysterical when we accused him, and the nurse had to ask us to go away. We're as much in the dark as ever."

Mary Eliska got up quietly and went over to a chair. Somehow she wouldn't sit on her father's lap when he held such widely different opinions from her own. But Mr. Stricklin did not seem to notice that she had gone. He sat perfectly still, thinking.

"You really believe Ted—Mr. Mackay—had a part in the horrible thing?" she asked, dismally.

"I don't think there is a doubt of it."

"But how do you explain the fact that he was shot? Surely, if he and this thief were working together, one wouldn't shoot the other!"

Her father shook his head, and smiled indulgently. What a child she was! What did she know about the wickedness of criminals?

"I'm sorry to tell you, dear, that in spite of that old proverb about there being honor among thieves, there isn't much. They are so utterly selfish and unprincipled that if one finds that his pal is getting the better of him, he doesn't hesitate to wound—and oftentimes kill— the other. If Mackay was making off with the necklace, and this other fellow saw that all his work had been for nothing, one could hardly blame him for shooting.... No, I'm afraid that doesn't prove a thing."

Mary Eliska sighed; everything seemed hopelessly black for Ted.

"Will they put him in jail?" she asked.

"Whom?"

"Mr. Mackay."

"Of course, when he is well enough. Our detectives will see to that. We can't actually convict him 'til we have more evidence. But we can force him to tell what he knows about this other thief."

A lump came into Mary Eliska's throat, and she felt as if she couldn't talk any more. For the time being, even her interest in her plane was gone. It had brought so much unhappiness— first to Kitty, and now to Ted Mackay.

She was thankful when her aunt came into the room, to take her mind from her morbid thoughts. At the same time, Anna announced luncheon.

"What are you planning to do this afternoon, dear?" inquired her Aunt Polly, as she ate her iced fruit-cup. "Because I want part of your time."

"Certainly, Aunt Polly. But tell me, have you decided you would like to go up in the Pursuit?"

"No, no—nothing like that. I want to live a little while longer, dear—Green Falls is so pleasant! But, seriously," she added, "I do want you to do something for me. I want you to try on your costume for the Midsummer Ball. I had to order it without asking you, dear, for of course you were too busy learning to fly, and it hadn't come when we left Spring City. But I think it is very charming—and I hope you will like it."

"I'm sure I shall. But, Aunt Polly, I could have worn my flyer's suit, and saved you all that trouble."

"You're going to get tired enough of that suit, attractive though it is. Besides, everybody would know you. And I like you to look especially pretty—in fluffy, feminine things. I have chosen the costume of Queen Mab for you."

"Oh, that will be adorable!" cried Mary Eliska, her eyes sparkling with pleasure, for she too loved dainty things.

"And may I see you when you are trying it on?" put in Mr. Stricklin "Your mother once wore something like that in a fairy play—and she was very beautiful. I'd like to see whether you remind me of her."

"Certainly, Daddy. I'll put it on right after lunch. And then I'll do whatever you want. Take you up for a ride, if you would like it."

"I think you're too tired for that," he replied. "No—I'll wait 'til the next time I come. Besides, the mechanics ought to have a chance to go over your motor before you fly it again. Don't forget the promises you made to me."

"I won't forget, Daddy. I'll telephone over to the airport this afternoon."

"By the way, daughter, have you ever tried jumping with a parachute? Did they make you do that at school?" At his question, Mary Eliska suddenly stopped eating and gazed at the girl in terror. Surely Mary Eliska would not do such a hazardous thing as that!

"Yes, Daddy," replied Mary Eliska, blushing, for she did not want to say anything about her jump with Ted Mackay. "Lieutenant Kingsberry himself was with me. Mr. Taylor didn't want to let me try it—I don't think he has much use for girls who want to fly—so I went straight to the Lieutenant. He went up with me himself."

"Wasn't it a dreadful experience?" asked her aunt, with a shudder.

"No—not terrible at all. I felt a little queer before the parachute opened, but after that it was delightful. Just softly floating down from the skies. I loved it."

"Well, I'm glad you did it," remarked her father. "Because now you won't be afraid if you ever have to."

"I am hoping I won't have to—with my Pursuit. Not that I'd be afraid, but because it would be the end of my plane. Think of just leaving it alone, to crash!"

"It would be too bad, of course—but I could buy you another plane. We couldn't buy another daughter, could we, Polly?" he asked his sister.

"Don't talk about it!" begged Mary Eliska, miserably.

"All right," agreed Mary Eliska. "Suppose Daddy tells me what he would like to do this afternoon—after I try on the costume."

"Sure you don't want to be with your young friends?" he inquired.

"I'll have all the rest of the summer for them."

"Then let's go for a little drive in your roadster. Out to some pretty road. And come back in time to go swimming with your crowd."

"I'd love that, Daddy!" she exclaimed. Then, turning to her aunt, "But is my car here, Aunt Polly? Did Thomas bring it up all right?"

It was strange indeed, that she had forgotten to ask about it. Always before she had driven it herself, while Thomas, the chauffeur took charge of her aunt's limousine. This time he had hired a friend to drive the other, and brought hers himself.

"Yes, he drove it up yesterday," replied her aunt.

The hours that followed would have been very pleasant for Mary Eliska, had she not felt underneath her cheeriness, a growing anxiety about Ted Mackay. After their little outing, she and her father put on their bathing-suits and joined the group at the lake. In the diving, the racing, the polo game, Mr. Stricklin proved a match for the young people; indeed he was the ringleader in suggesting tricks to the more daring members of the crowd. Even Jax Gray, who had always stood somewhat in awe of him because he was sterner than her own parents, had to admit that he was a good sport. Ralph, who had not counted upon seeing Mary Eliska until evening, was delighted to find her at the lake, and tried immediately to date her as his partner for the canoe trip of the evening. But Mary Eliska shyly refused, telling him that her aunt was one of the chaperons, and the only partner she was willing to have. She shrank from the thought of talking to Ralph about Ted, or the robbery; she decided not to see him alone.

Early after supper Mr. Stricklin departed in a taxi, and Mary Eliska and her aunt drove over to Jax Gray's bungalow to join the group for the canoe trip. There were a dozen young people besides themselves, and Mr. and Mrs. Stricklin, too. Six canoes had been chartered.

"Canoeing will seem kind of tame after flying, I guess," remarked Dot Crowley, as the young people walked over to the lake. "By the way, how soon will you take me for a fly?"

"Anybody might take you for a fly," remarked Maurice Stetson. "You buzz around so!"

Mary Eliska smiled, but she answered Dot's question immediately. Maybe the latter was as keen about airplanes as she was herself! You never could tell.

"In a few days," she said. "For the time being I want to hold myself and my plane in readiness to chase that thief—if we ever get the chance!"

"You still worrying about those pearls?" inquired Maurice, lightly.

"Naturally," answered Mary Eliska.

"Well, I command you to forget it. Kitty'll soon get over it. Anybody as beautiful as Kit is, doesn't need pearls. Besides, when she marries me, I'll buy her a bigger string!"

"You mean *if*, not *when*, don't you?" countered Kitty. But she was evidently in high spirits again, thanks perhaps to the young man who made no secret of this adoration.

There wasn't much opportunity for conversation, however. Jim Valier had brought his mandolin, and from the moment when the canoes pushed off until they were tied at the opposite side of the lake, where the young people made a fire and toasted marshmallows, everybody sang. Mary Eliska naturally joined in with the music, but only with her lips. Her heart was still heavy with the misfortune the preceding day had brought.

On the way home she made up her mind to telephone the hospital the following morning. At least she could inquire about Ted—and maybe—oh, how she hoped it would be possible— she could speak with him, and hear from his own lips the explanation of his connection with the unfortunate robbery.

Chapter 5.12
The Search for the Thief

For the first time in her life, Mary Eliska was thankful that her father was not at home. He would object to her calling Ted at the hospital, but now it was impossible to ask his permission. Nevertheless, she was trembling when she took off the receiver and gave the hospital's number.

"Mr. Mackay left last night," the attendant told her, "to go to his home. He was very much better."

"Oh!" exclaimed Mary Eliska, hopefully. That was good news indeed. But she wanted to learn more.

"Would it be possible for me to talk to his nurse?" she inquired. "I really have something important to ask."

The attendant hesitated; it was not their custom to call nurses from their duties to answer inquiries about their patients. But Mary Eliska's voice was so eager that the man decided for once to waive the rule.

"If you will hold the line a minute," he said, "I will see whether she is busy. You don't know which nurse it was?"

"No. Probably one of the ward nurses."

Mary Eliska was forced to wait several minutes, but in the end she was rewarded. A cheerful girl's voice informed her that its owner had taken charge of Ted Mackay while he was at the hospital.

"But are you a friend or an enemy of Mr. Mackay, Miss——?" she inquired, cautiously. "Stricklin is my name," answered Mary Eliska. "And I am a friend."

"I'm glad to hear that. Mr. Mackay is such a nice boy that it is a shame he has to have enemies.... Now, what can I do for you?"

"Tell me what you know of his story," replied Mary Eliska. "You see I only know that he was shot and that his enemies are trying to connect him with a thief who stole a valuable necklace. I know it can't be true. It just can't!" She was talking rapidly, excitedly. "I knew if I could see him he could explain everything. But he's gone!"

"Yes, he went home last night. To his mother's. But I can tell you the facts, for he told me the whole story. He was piloting another plane—for his company—and spotted a wreck. It proved to be this thief, who evidently wasn't hurt by the crash, and so shot Mr. Mackay and made off in his new plane. It seems perfectly simple to me. I don't see how anybody could possibly accuse Mr. Mackay, when he was actually wounded himself."

"How does his company feel about it?" asked Mary Eliska.

"Same as we do. He is to go back to his job in a day or two, as soon as he feels rested."

"Thank goodness!" cried Mary Eliska. "Then everything is O.K. Oh, you can't know how thankful I am! And so grateful to you!"

"You're entirely welcome," concluded the young nurse, pleased to have been of some help.

Mary Eliska began to sing as she replaced the receiver, and she went out on the porch in search of her aunt. She just had to tell somebody about Ted's innocence, and the weight which had been taken from her heart at the nurse's reassuring words. Mary Eliska had not heard any particulars about the story; indeed she scarcely knew who Ted Mackay was. So, omitting the parachute jump, Mary Eliska began at the beginning and related everything she knew about him, since that day last April when she had met him at the Red Cross Fair, and he had promised to take her up in an airplane.

"And you don't think he's wicked, just because his father is, do you, Aunt Polly?" she asked, anxiously.

"No, of course not, dear. It wouldn't be fair to jump to any such conclusion as that. Every human being has a right to be judged on his own merits—not his parents'."

"That's what I think," agreed Mary Eliska. "But Daddy says——"

"Hello, everybody!" interrupted a gay young voice from the hedge in front of the bungalow, and, turning about, Mary Eliska saw Ralph Clavering striding up the path.

"Hello!" she answered, trying to make her voice cordial. Such a handsome boy, so charming—why did he have to be so unfair to Ted? Poor Ted, who had never had one-tenth of Ralph's advantages!

"I've got news!" he cried, as he took the steps two at a time, and swung into a chair.

"About the necklace?" demanded Mary Eliska, immediately.

"Yes. From our detectives. They have spotted a gas-station that sold a can of gasoline to a red-headed fellow who said he wanted it for an airplane."

"Really, Ralph!" exclaimed Mary Eliska, scornfully. "You don't call that news, do you? There must be plenty of red-haired pilots in our part of the country."

"I know. But that isn't all. This agent carried the gas over in his car to a field where the plane was waiting, and he says there was another chap in it who answered the description of our thief."

"Was the plane a Waco?" questioned Mary Eliska, keenly.

"The fellow wasn't sure, but when Greer described it, he thought it was."

"And is that all?" Mary Eliska's tone showed disappointment.

"'Is that all?'" repeated Ralph, in amazement. "Why, that's plenty!"

"I don't see how that will help you to catch your thief," remarked the woman.

"But it will! Greer has telephoned the hospital, and located Mackay today. If he really has gone home, as he said, and hasn't run away, he'll be put through a third degree that'll make him tell where the thief is hiding. Because he must be hiding. He couldn't go very far on the gas in that plane, and all the airports and gasoline stations have been warned to watch out for him."

Mary Eliska's eyes were blazing with anger. How could Ralph be so prejudiced, so cruel?

"But Ted doesn't know any more about that thief than we do!" she protested, vehemently. "I talked with his nurse this morning—and she knew all about it. Ted met that thief by accident!"

"By accident is right," remarked Ralph, with a scornful smile. "But never mind, Mary Eliska—don't you worry about it anymore. Let's talk about the masque ball tonight. You're going with me, aren't you?"

"I certainly am not!" announced the girl, haughtily. "I wouldn't go with anybody who could be so unfair——".

"Children!" interrupted Mary Eliska, distressed at their inclination to quarrel. She had been so happy about the friendship between Ralph and Mary Eliska—it was eminently right! When her niece did decide to get married—though she hoped such an event was still far off—she couldn't imagine any young man who would suit her so well as Ralph Clavering. Such family! Such social position! And plenty of money! For Mary Eliska was always afraid that sometime her brother might lose his. He was so careless about it, he spent it so recklessly upon both his sister and his daughter. And, though the older woman had enough of her own securely invested in bonds to take care of her old age, she feared for Mary Eliska. Educated as she had been at that expensive private school, she was in no way trained to earn a living. She did not dream that Mary Eliska would be only too delighted to go into aviation as if she were a boy on her own responsibility—like Ted Mackay!

"If I admit I'm jealous of Redhead, and say I'm sorry," conceded Ralph, "will you forgive me and go to the dance with me tonight?"

His beautiful dark eyes were pleading, and for a moment Mary Eliska almost weakened, thinking of all their experiences together, and especially that moment when they both had thought they were so happy, in regaining the box that supposedly held the necklace. But she remembered Ted, and the cruel grueling he would be subjected to very soon, because of Ralph's suspicions, and she closed her lips tightly.

"Not unless you promise to call off your detectives from Ted Mackay," she pronounced, firmly.

"But I can't do that—couldn't now, even if I wanted to. It's too late."

"Then I'm not going to the party with you."

"But Mary Eliska, dear," put in Mary Eliska, going towards the screen door in her embarrassment at being a witness to the quarrel, "it's too late to arrange to go with anybody else. All the other girls already have their partners!"

"I'll go with you, Auntie!" replied the girl, complacently. "Lots of girls go with their parents."

"Very well," agreed her aunt, disappearing into the living-room, with the unpleasant thought that it was only the unpopular girls who were forced into such a situation. As soon as she had gone, Ralph came over to Mary Eliska's chair. But he was afraid to touch even her hand—she looked so aloof and determined.

"Mary Eliska—after all we've been to each other——" he began.

She stood up, holding her head high.

"I think you'll have to excuse me, Ralph," she said. "I'm very busy."

"All right," he returned, sullenly. "Have it your own way, then! I'll get Jax Gray to go with me."

"Very well. Good-by." Her tone was icy; she did not even offer to shake hands with him.

Ralph turned and hurried down the steps, angry at himself for pleading so hard, angrier at her for being so cold. No girl ever thought of treating him—Ralph Clavering—like that before! The very idea! Most young ladies would be only too delighted at his invitation! And all for the sake of a penniless, dishonest, red-headed pilot! For Ralph had not yet learned that there were some things which he could not buy with his father's millions.

So he strode to the nearest telephone booth, and called Jax Gray who, although she was flattered by the invitation, did not immediately accept. She had already promised Harriman Smith, and she so informed Ralph.

"Well, there isn't any law that says a girl can't go with two men, is there?" he demanded. "If she happens to be popular enough! Can't we all three go together?"

"Why aren't you going with Mary Eliska?" inquired Jax Gray, shrewdly.

"We've quarreled," he admitted. "Then make it up!" she advised. "Pull yourself together, Ralph—and apologize."

"I tried to, but it was no good. No, we're off!"

"Then Mary Eliska hasn't any partner?"

"She says she's going with her aunt," muttered Ralph.

"Oh, that won't do!" exclaimed Jax Gray. "Wait, Ralph, I'll fix everything. I'll get Harry to take Mary Eliska—he's crazy about her anyhow—and then I'll go with you."

"O.K., Jax. You're the little sport!"

"And fixer," added the girl, to herself, as she bade Ralph good-by, and called first Harry and then Mary Eliska.

Jax Gray's suggestion seemed like an act of Providence to the older woman; it would have been mortifying indeed to her to have Mary Eliska appear at the ball without a masculine escort, as if the girl were a mere wallflower. Harriman Smith had been most agreeable about the whole arrangement; anything Jax Gray decided suited him, he told her. And Mary Eliska, too, was delighted with the news.

She came out of her bedroom while her aunt was talking on the telephone, dressed in her flyer's suit.

"Where are you going dear?" inquired Mary Eliska, in anxious surprise.

"I'm going scouting," explained Mary Eliska. "I think I'll fly around—pretty low—and look for wrecks. I have a hunch that that thief has smashed his plane by now. He was such a poor pilot, you know I told you."

"Well, be careful," cautioned her aunt. "But so long as you fly low, I won't worry."

Mary Eliska smiled to herself. If Aunt Polly only realized how infinitely more dangerous it was to fly low than high!

She found her Pursuit in perfect condition, and had it taken to the runway, where she taxied off without the least difficulty. She climbed to about fifteen hundred feet, and flew over past the hospital and the field where the Waco had been smashed. Then she carefully came lower, using her glasses to watch the ground as she flew.

The country was open—there were no buildings and few trees, so she felt safe in keeping within sight of the ground. She was flying along confidently, when suddenly a long pole seemed almost on top of her. Swerving sharply upward, she just avoided striking some wires that the pole was supporting.

"Oh!" she gasped. "What a lucky break! Suppose I hadn't had a foolproof plane!" For she knew that her Arrow had been designed especially for amateurs like herself.

"Crazy of me to fly so near to the ground!" she exclaimed, in self-contempt. "After all the warnings I've had! I deserve a crash!" And she continued to climb upward to safety.

As she flew onward, steadying her thoughts, she decided that it was senseless to try to hunt the thief with a plane. If she wanted to look for him it would be much more reasonable to use her car—or to hike. So she abandoned that project entirely.

But as she continued her flight towards Green Falls, it suddenly occurred to her that she might help Ted in another way. She could establish his alibi for him—by means of his company! That red-haired man that the agent claimed he saw with the thief couldn't have been Ted, and she would take means of proving it. Then, if Ralph's detectives insisted upon throwing him into prison, there would be a way to have him released.

So she flew back to the airport, confident that her morning had not been entirely wasted, and, to her aunt's relief, she arrived home in time for lunch.

Chapter 5.13
The Masque Ball

The gay young set at Green Falls to which Mary Eliska belonged had planned nothing for that afternoon except the regular swim, for the ball would be late, and the donning of their costumes would take a good deal of time. Mary Eliska, however, even passed up the swim in favor of a nap, for she was very tired. Besides, she had no desire to meet Ralph at the lake or anywhere else.

Like all the social affairs at this charming resort, the masque ball—the greatest event of the season, with the possible exception of the field day at the close—began early. Dinner at the Stricklins was over by half-past seven, and, after assuring herself that Mary Eliska's costume was to her satisfaction, Mary Eliska left the bungalow. She was a patroness, of course, and she wanted to get to the Casino early, to pass final judgment upon the decorations and the music.

Harriman Smith arrived at half-past eight, in a taxi, for as one of the poorer members of the crowd, he did not possess a car of his own. Mary Eliska, in the filmy dress of the fairy queen, with a crown of golden stars about her hair, welcomed him into the bungalow.

"Mary Eliska!" exclaimed the young man, in positive awe. "I never saw anyone so beautiful in my whole life!"

She smiled shyly, pleased at the compliment. But of course as yet he had not seen the other girls in their costumes!

"It's the dress," she explained modestly. "If there's any credit, it should go to Aunt Polly. She selected it.... I like your costume, too, Harry. You're Robin Hood, aren't you?"

"Yes—I'm glad you can recognize me, anyway.... But Mary Eliska, seriously, I just know you'll take the prize for the most beautiful woman!"

"I didn't know there was a prize."

"Of course there is. And for the most handsome man. And the best dancers—and the funniest.... Probably some more I don't remember.... But I guess you never think much about prizes."

"I do about some prizes," she admitted. "Cups for endurance flights, and high altitudes—and things like that!"

"Naturally—trust you to be up on anything connected with airplanes. I suppose you'll be winning some of them yourself sometime. But when it comes to social events———"

"Well, you're often the same way, Harry," she teased. "Look at the parties you passed up last winter, just because of your engineering course!"

The boy smiled, not at all displeased by the observation, for he was a youth who took his studies seriously. Unlike Maurice Stetson and Ralph Clavering, who seemed interested only in the fraternities and the sports at college, he went there with the idea of working. And he liked Mary Eliska all the better for recognizing his ambition and understanding it.

"But we oughtn't to stand here talking, forgetting all about your taxi," Mary Eliska reminded her companion. "Why don't you dismiss it, and take my car?"

"A queen mustn't drive!" he protested. "And you wouldn't like me to run your car———"

"I don't mind you, Harry. You're never careless. It's people like Maurice that I can't bear to see handle it."

"I don't blame you one bit," he said, and realizing that she would really prefer to go in her own roadster, he did as she suggested.

All the way to the Casino they both carefully avoided any mention of Kitty Clavering's loss, or, in fact, of anything distasteful—even the quarrel with Ralph and the change of plans which had thrown them together as partners. Mary Eliska asked him how the different members of the crowd had paired off, and Harry told her as much as he had happened to learn at the lake that afternoon. Kit and Maurice were of course going together, and Dot Crowley and Jim Valier—the smallest and the tallest members of their set. Sara Wheeler had promised Jackson Stiles, and Harry seemed to recall that Sue Emery was accompanying Joe Sinclair. He did not mention Jax Gray and Ralph.

It was just a little before nine when they reached the Casino, gayly lighted with Japanese lanterns, and decorated with flowers and streamers. The wide French windows of the dance hall were all thrown open, and the huge verandas were as beautifully lighted as the inside of the Casino. Strains of music floated out from the orchestra, which was already in place. Upstairs there would be bridge tables for the older members of the party and the supper would be served on the roof-garden.

As the couple entered the wide doors of the Casino, a surging of pride swept through the young man because of the girl at his side. In spite of her mask, people must recognize Mary Eliska, so stately, so lovely, so charming! With what wisdom her aunt had chosen that costume! The girl was every inch a queen.

In the dressing-room there was naturally a great deal of excitement, for the girls were all trying to identify each other. Mary Eliska spotted Jax Gray immediately—dressed as an Egyptian Princess. Her costume was unusual, daring; she stood out among all the others as a sunflower might among a bunch of spring blossoms. And of course she wore huge, odd, earrings.

"Mary Eliska, you're sweet!" she cried, starting forward to kiss her chum, and stopping just in time as she remembered the make-up on her lips, and the amount of time she had consumed putting it there.

"Sh!" warned Mary Eliska. "Don't give me away!"

"I won't, darling. But everybody will know you anyhow. Come on—you couldn't possibly improve yourself! And we must hurry. I hear them lining up now for the grand march."

A laughing, happy group, the girls made their way back to the ballroom where their partners claimed them. It amused Mary Eliska—and yet it hurt her a little, too—to see Ralph Clavering lead Jax Gray away without even seeming to notice her. But Harry Smith was right there too, as if to protect his partner from any unpleasantness.

The music of the grand march rolled out triumphantly, and the couples fell into step, circling the big room, and walking past the committee on the raised platform, whose members were to pass judgment on the costumes for the awarding of the prizes. As Mary Eliska walked demurely at Harry's side, past this intent, solemn body of men and women, she never lifted her eyes. She was all the more amazed when, a couple of minutes later, she heard a childish voice cry out above the music.

"Does 'ou fink me cute?" and, turning about, Mary Eliska recognized Dot Crowley, dressed as a little school-girl, and actually calling attention to herself. Of course everybody laughed; you just had to smile at Dot. And her long-legged partner, Jim Valier, dressed appropriately as Uncle Sam, looked so out-of-place at her side.

The costumes were really marvelous; if Mary Eliska had not come for any other reason than to see them, it would have been worthwhile. There were several hundred people at the ball the proceeds of which were given entirely to charity, and though there were naturally many repetitions—numerous George and Polly Washingtons, Pierrots and Pierrettes, clowns and gypsies, there were also many unusual ones. But although she did not realize it, there was no one in that whole assembly so charmingly beautiful as Mary Eliska.

The grand march consumed almost an hour, after which the judges withdrew to make their decisions, and then the dancing began.

The floor was perfect and the music excellent; Mary Eliska fell into step with her partner and gave herself up to the enjoyment the pastime always afforded her. Whenever she had a good partner like Harry—or Ralph—she always experienced a marvelous sensation of floating along to the strains of the music, a sensation that somehow reminded her of flying. And then they passed Ralph and Jax Gray, and Mary Eliska wondered whether the former would ask her to dance.

After that she danced with all the boys she knew, in turn—all except Ralph. Even when Harry managed a dance with Jax Gray, while Mary Eliska was dancing with a stag, Ralph did not cut in. But this did not spoil her good time, for she felt that she had been in the right, championing Ted, even though her father was on the other side.

Ralph's avoidance of her niece had not escaped Mary Eliska's eyes, and she sighed. Why was there always some drawback to rich people, she wondered? But perhaps Ralph would get over his childishness when he grew older. And in the meantime Mary Eliska did not lack for attention.

Just before the party went up to the roof for supper, the prizes were awarded. Mary Eliska won first prize for the women—and, ludicrous as it was, Ralph Clavering, as King Arthur, was selected first among the men. They walked across the floor together, Mary Eliska giving him a shy smile. To Jax Gray and Harry, and Mary Eliska, who knew about the tiff, the coincidence was very amusing.

Two other guests whom Mary Eliska did not know were awarded the prizes for the funniest costumes, and, to their own amazement, Jax Gray and Ralph were called out as the couple who had given the best exhibition of dancing. There was no shyness as these two stepped forward. Ralph, looking roguish, held out his arms and whistled a tune, and as Jax Gray slipped into them, they waltzed across the floor.

The supper was gorgeous in every detail: the food was excellent, the service perfect. Mary Eliska felt that she had never been to quite so magnificent a party before.

"You do like all this, don't you, Mary Eliska?" asked her partner, as they finished their ice-cream, molded in fancy forms, like small dolls or figurines, in pastel colors. "You really like parties? Because I sometimes wonder——"

"I love them," replied the girl, her eyes shining. "That is, when they come once or twice a summer, like this. But I would get awfully tired of them if I had nothing else."

"But next winter," he reminded her, "when you are a débutante—"

"I'm going to try not to be," she interrupted. "If I can slide out of it, without hurting Aunt Polly's feelings. I want to go to a ground school, and study aviation seriously."

"You mean make it your life work?" he asked, respectfully.

"Yes—seriously."

But it was no time to talk; the music had started again, and everybody wanted to make good use of the last, best hour of the party.

And so for all that evening, Mary Eliska was the care-free, popular girl that her Aunt Polly loved her to be.

Chapter 5.14
The Flying Trip

About eight o'clock the following morning while her friends were still sleeping, Mary Eliska, clad in a bathing-suit and a beach robe, dashed down to the lake. She thought an early morning swim before anyone was up would clear her brain and give her a chance to think over her plans and come to a decision. If possible, she meant to get in touch with Ted's company before the detectives arrived at his home to arrest him. She had thought, naturally, that she would find the lake deserted, for everybody ought to be tired out after last night's party. She was therefore amazed and a little annoyed to see someone else already in swimming.

"I'll go in the other direction," she decided, but before she was even in the water she heard a familiar voice calling her.

"Mary Eliska!" cried Jax Gray, waving her arms, and starting to swim rapidly towards her. "Ho—Mary Eliska!" "Jax!" "Yes—me!" shouted the other girl. "But did you say 'Who' or 'You'?"

"I said 'Jax'!" replied Mary Eliska, laughing good-naturedly. It was a relief to find the other bather was her chum.

They were within talking distance now, and Jax Gray hurried to the shore. They sat down together and gossiped about the party, Jax Gray laughing over Ralph's childishness in trying to keep up the quarrel with Mary Eliska.

"To tell you the truth, Mary Eliska," she added, "I'm bored with him. As a matter of fact, I'm fed up with most of the boys. Harry's all right, but he has so little time. All the others are so pleased with themselves. They think we can't get along without them!"

"Well, can we?" teased Mary Eliska.

"Why not? Except for dances——"

Mary Eliska dug her toes into the sand and smiled.

"That's the trouble with us. There's always some 'except.' We ought to make up our minds to stay away from dancing, if we really want them to get over their superiority complex."

"It would be pretty dull in the evenings—we'd have to find something else to take its place...." Jax Gray paused to watch an airplane that was flying overhead. "Mary Eliska!" she cried, abruptly, "I have it! Let's go off on a trip—just the two of us—in your plane! Be gone a week or two!"

Mary Eliska grabbed her chum's hands in delight. What a marvelous idea! The freedom! The adventure of it! And she could link it up with her own errand to Kansas City.

"Oh, I'd adore that, Jax!" she exclaimed. "Would you really trust yourself to me? Honestly? You wouldn't be afraid?"

Jax Gray put her arm about the other girl and hugged her tightly.

"Of course I would! I have an awful lot of confidence in you. And I'd love it!"

Mary Eliska's brow darkened suddenly. For as always, she had to think of others besides herself.

"What's the matter?" demanded Jax Gray, watching her companion's face. "I am thinking of Aunt Polly—and your mother," answered Mary Eliska. "Wondering whether they'd give their consent—and if they did, would they worry themselves to death?"

"Mother would be all right—I can manage her, and Dad too," said Jax Gray confidently. "And, after all, think of the flying that girls do now-a-days. A little picnic like this is tame, compared to flying from England to Australia."

"Yes, I know—but Aunt Polly's so scary about planes."

"Well, I tell you what we could do—we could map out our whole trip beforehand, and decide where we would land each night. We could probably get the names of the hotels where we would stay. And each evening after supper, we could telephone the people at home."

"That's an idea!" agreed Mary Eliska, enthusiastically. "You wouldn't want to camp out, anyway, would you? They would be sure to object to that—just two girls alone."

"No; we'd have to buy a lot of equipment, and I'd hate to load down the plane. But I'm afraid Aunt Polly would even object to our staying alone at hotels. You know how particular she is."

Jax Gray was silent a moment, thinking it was too pleasant an idea to give up at once. She'd have to devise a way out of their difficulty.

"I'll tell you," she announced, finally. "We can plan to stop with people we know each night—or at a hotel where some friend is staying. We surely can round up some relatives and friends!"

"That's it!" cried Mary Eliska, joyfully. "That ought to be easy! And we can send telegrams ahead. But the places will have to have some sort of airports."

"Oh, most every town has some kind of landing place," said Jax Gray. "I don't think that need worry us."

"There's another thing," added Mary Eliska, slowly. "I'd want to start today. Because I must go to Kansas City as fast as I can." And she explained to Jax Gray her plan about establishing Ted's alibi.

Jax Gray leaped into the air in her excitement and approval.

"That's great! You know me, Mary Eliska—I always hate to wait about anything. We can pack our suit-cases and send our wires in an hour if we hustle. Hurry up! Hop in for a dip, and come right back!"

Ten minutes later they dashed breathless and wet into the dining-room of the Stricklin bungalow, where Mary Eliska was eating a leisurely breakfast. In their excitement over their idea they could scarcely explain it. But at last the older woman understood; she heard them out, and gave her rather reluctant consent.

"If you don't make the trip too long," she added.

"A week?"

"Isn't four days enough? Then we would have to arrange only two stopping places—the same one coming back. And I am sure I could do that very easily."

The girls agreed, delighted even with a compromise. Nothing they had ever done promised to be half so thrilling.

They would fly southwest, making their first stop Kansas City, where Ted's firm was located. Searching through her address-book, Mary Eliska remembered that she had a cousin living in a hotel in that city and she wired her immediately to reserve a room for the girls for that night, and to chaperon their visit.

"And then we'll fly to Sunny Hills—as our destination!" cried Jax Gray, with happy inspiration. "It's in Colorado—where my Aunt Margaret and Uncle John live! Oh, we'll have no end of fun there!"

"You're sure they won't mind?" asked Mary Eliska.

"They'll be tickled to death. They have a huge place—sort of a farm—and six children. Of course they're not children now—several of them are married—but they always keep open house. We used to go there a lot when I was a kid."

"All right—you send that wire," agreed Mary Eliska, as she hastily swallowed some food, "and I'll get ready and go down to my plane, and see that it's O.K."

"How about some lunch?" suggested her Aunt Polly.

"Oh, yes, please—if you don't mind!"

In an incredibly short time the girls were dressed, their suit-cases packed, the wires sent, and the lunch in readiness. About half-past ten, without saying a word of good-by to anyone except Mary Eliska and Jax Gray's parents, they took off.

The sky was clear and blue, without even a cloud to threaten them with fog or storm. It was Jax Gray's first ride in a plane, yet she was not a bit afraid. She said she had never been so thrilled before.

"I'm getting the craze, Mary Eliska!" she shouted, above the noise of the motor. "If I only had a suit like yours!"

She was wearing her riding-breeches and a tan sweater-blouse, with a close-fitting hat of the same color—a costume, which though neat and appropriate, had none of the style and charm of her companion's.

"But you can't wear earrings!" teased Mary Eliska, pulling at Jax Gray's ears to make sure that the other girl heard and understood what she was saying.

"In the suit-case!" returned Jax Gray, laughing and pointing towards the article she named.

But neither of the girls wanted to try to talk. They were content to rise higher and higher into the air, to feel the glorious sensation of smooth flying, knowing that everything was just right. Both of them began to sing.

On, on they went, over fields and towns, watching their map and their instruments, dipping now and then to catch a glimpse of the landscape below, climbing back to the heights for safety. As the clock on their plane neared twelve, they realized they were hungry, because breakfast had been such a sketchy affair for them both. Jax Gray untied the box, and they ate joyously. Their first meal in the air!

It was still early when they arrived at Kansas City, and Mary Eliska flew a straight, swift course to the large grounds that were occupied by the company for which Ted Mackay worked. Without the slightest mishap or difficulty Mary Eliska brought her plane to a perfect landing in the large area set aside for that purpose.

A nice-looking young man in a flyer's uniform came to them in welcome. His face showed no surprise; it was evidently an every-day occurrence to meet feminine pilots.

"I would like to speak to the sales-manager," said Mary Eliska, after she had answered his greeting, and made sure that this was the right place. "I want to make some inquiries about Ted Mackay."

"All right," agreed the young man. "I'll take you to Mr. Jordan immediately."

But when they were introduced, Mary Eliska felt suddenly shy. What right had she, she asked herself, to pry into Ted's affairs? She wasn't a relative—or even a friend, if she adhered to her father's command. So it was Jax Gray who came to the rescue, as she always did in emergencies, and proceeded to take charge of the interview.

"You see," she explained, "the people who had that valuable necklace stolen are pretty much perturbed over the whole affair—and naturally they hired detectives. Well, Mr. Jordan—you know what detectives are! They bungle everything."

"Yes?" remarked the man, looking smilingly from one girl to the other, thinking that they, too, were rather excited.

"And just because they found Mr. Mackay by the stolen plane, and because they located a gasoline agent who swears that he sold gas to a red-haired man for that same plane earlier in the day, they're sure Mr. Mackay is a thief."

"And they're going to his home—to arrest him!" put in Mary Eliska, now more at ease.

"But they can't prove anything," Mr. Jordan assured them, calmly.

"Oh, but they say they'll put third degree on him, or whatever it is, and force him to a confession. And—and—think of his poor mother!"

"But what do you girls want me to do?" he asked. "I don't see how I can stop them!"

"We just want you to establish his alibi," explained Jax Gray. "Write down everything Mr. Mackay did from early morning 'til the time he started off in that new plane."

"O.K.!" exclaimed Mr. Jordan, a light breaking over his face. "That's easy! We had a salesmen's meeting at the Winton Hotel, and lunched together. I can swear Mackay was there—and so can half a dozen others. We came back here about three o'clock, and Mackay was looking over the plane and studying his maps for about half an hour. Then he took off— for Buffalo."

"That's just what we want!" cried Mary Eliska, and Jax Gray added, "wonderful!" and squeezed the elderly man's hand. He smiled at her as if she were his daughter.

"And will you dictate that to a stenographer, and send a copy to Ted by air-mail?" urged Mary Eliska.

"Certainly," he agreed.

"And now," added Mary Eliska, "will one of your mechanics look over my plane and put it away 'til tomorrow? We want to get our suit-cases, and taxi to my cousin's hotel."

So, half an hour later, when the girls were making themselves known to the elderly couple who were expecting them, they spoke joyously of the perfect success of their first day's adventure, but they did not mention their mission on Ted Mackay's behalf.

Chapter 5.15
Sunny Hills

The girls' visit with the elderly couple at the hotel at Kansas City was restful, but uneventful. As soon as they arrived, Mary Eliska telephoned to her aunt over long distance, and made a satisfactory report. Dinner and the movies occupied their evening.

Early the next morning they bade their host and hostess a temporary farewell—for they were scheduled to return in a couple of days—and took a taxi to the airplane company where their Arrow was being kept. "It's a little cloudy, girls," observed Mr. Jordan as he came over to meet them. "But I don't think it will actually storm before night. Are you going far?"

"To a place called 'Sunny Hills'," replied Jax Gray, producing her map. "In Colorado."

The man studied it for a few minutes, and then pointed out their best course.

"And your plane's O.K.," he added. "She certainly is a neat little boat."

"I'm fond of her myself!" replied Mary Eliska, her eyes shining as they always did when she spoke of her most precious possession.

"And have you had any word from Mr. Mackay?" asked Jax Gray.

"Yes. He's coming back today," answered Mr. Jordan. "I sent a plane for him, with the letter you suggested. The pilot wired last night that he arrived safely, and both men would be back on the job tomorrow."

"He didn't say anything about the detectives?" "Not a word."

"Then everything must be all right!" breathed Mary Eliska, with a sigh of relief.

"Well, good-by," concluded Mr. Jordan, as the girls stepped into their plane. "And fly carefully. That's rather lonely country you're passing over."

"But the skies are safe!" returned Mary Eliska, as she started her motor. It was indeed a more desolate stretch of land than any they had flown over before. The girls noticed this as they sped on, the miles piling up in rapid succession.

This time they carried no lunch, for they had hesitated to ask at the hotel, and as the hours passed, they grew very hungry. Moreover, the sky was so cloudy that the sun was totally obscured, and they had to be guided entirely by instruments. Two or three times they seemed to get off their course, and it was almost five o'clock when they finally landed at an airport and inquired their way to Sunny Hills.

"It's about five miles north," they were told. "But wouldn't you rather leave your plane and taxi over?" their informer suggested.

"No, thanks," replied Mary Eliska. "Because we want to have our plane there, to use it if we need it, and to show to our friends. But we would love to have something to eat, if you can tell us where there is a stand for refreshments."

While the man was leading them to a sandwich booth, a mechanic came up and filled the plane with gas, and at Mary Eliska's request, looked it over hastily. Fifteen minutes later the girls took off again, having been assured that there was a field for landing at Sunny Hills, because, it seemed, the owner—or possibly the owner's son—had a plane.

As they descended over the field in back of the huge country house that was the home of the Stillmans the girls observed numerous people running out of the doors and from the porches to be on hand to welcome them. By the time they had landed, Jax Gray counted seventeen.

"Hello, everybody!" she shouted, as the noise of the motor died. "Get our wire?"

"Surest thing!" answered a man of about thirty, tall and heavily-built, and smiling.

An elderly woman was pressing through the throng, holding out her arms to Jax Gray.

"Aunt Margaret!" cried the girl, rapturously. "I'm so glad to see you! And I want to introduce my chum—Mary Eliska."

"I am more than delighted to meet you, my dear," said Mrs. Stillman, pressing Mary Eliska's hand—"I am *proud* to meet you!»

"Thank you," murmured the girl, her eyelids fluttering in embarrassment, for she felt that as yet she had done nothing to merit praise.

"And now I'll tell you everybody's name," continued the older woman. "Though I know you can't possibly remember them."

She proceeded to introduce her friends and her children—the latter all younger than Roger, the man who had first spoken to them, and evidently her oldest son. There were four small children among the group, two of them grandchildren of Mrs. Stillman.

"I want you girls to use my hangar," offered Roger, immediately. "My plane's away getting repaired. So shall I put yours away for you?"

"Oh, thanks!" replied Mary Eliska, gratefully. "It's so nice to find another pilot—to do the honors, and the work!"

As the happy, noisy group walked with the two girls back to the house, they asked all sorts of questions at once, about the trip, the plane, the relatives back home. Jax Gray and Mary Eliska answered as fast as they could, but finally gave up, laughing in their confusion.

"Now everybody stop talking!" commanded Mrs. Stillman, and though her tone was jovial, Mary Eliska could see at once that she meant what she said, and that she was used to being obeyed.

"Our brave flyers must be awfully tired, and this is no way to treat them, before they have even had a drink of water. Elsie," she nodded to a girl about Mary Eliska's age, "I want you to take the girls to their room, and I'll send up their suit-cases and some iced tea. And then they are going to have peace until dinner-time!"

"Oh, Aunt Margaret, we're not so tired," protested Jax Gray. Still, the thought of a cool shower, iced tea, and a few minutes for a nap was very pleasant.

Elsie and Jax Gray, who had been great friends when they were younger, spending several long, happy summers together, were both delighted at the chance of renewing their friendship. Mary Eliska, too, found Elsie charming, and the three girls were soon chatting merrily over their iced tea.

"I want you to tell me the news of your family first," said Jax Gray. "And begin in order, so Mary Eliska can get them straightened out. I mean—which ones are married, and which have children, and all that sort of thing."

"Yes, do," urged Mary Eliska. "I only know Roger—because he is a pilot—and you, by name."

A knock at the door interrupted them, and when Elsie answered it, two young men brought in the girls' suit-cases.

"The twins," explained their sister. "Dan and David. It really isn't hard to tell them apart, if you look closely."

"I remember!" cried Jax Gray. "Your hair is curlier, isn't it, Dan? And David has a broken finger."

"Righto," agreed the latter, holding up his finger for inspection, and keeping his eyes on Mary Eliska. He had fallen for her charms already.

"You're excused," said Elsie, tersely.

"With many thanks," added Mary Eliska, graciously.

"Now begin over again," urged Jax Gray, when the boys had gone. She began to open the suit-cases and to pull out the negligees, so that they could be perfectly comfortable.

"Well," continued Elsie, settling back in the pretty cretonne-covered chair that matched all the furnishings of the lovely, yet simple bedroom, "you know Aunt Margaret, of course. Those other two elderly women are friends—no need for you to learn their names.

"Of us, Roger is the oldest—he's thirty-one—and he isn't married. He's had dozens of girls, but I think he loves being a bachelor. He goes in for all kinds of racing—motorboat, automobile, and now airplane. And he adores young girls. You want to watch your step, Mary Eliska, for we're always expecting him to marry all of a sudden sometime. To somebody a whole lot younger!"

Mary Eliska smiled, and Jax Gray shook her head knowingly.

"Mary Eliska's wise," she remarked.

"And Anita's the next oldest," went on Elsie. "I guess you didn't recognize her, did you, Jax Gray? The stout woman, with those two children clinging to her."

"No, I didn't!" exclaimed her cousin. "But remember, it's been ten years since our family were here. I do recall her now—she was a High School graduate that summer. And so thin!"

"Well, she's fat now, and so is her husband. You'll see him tonight—they're spending the summer here. They have two kids.... The twins come next—they're twenty-three, and then my other married sister Jennie. You remember Jen?"

"Naturally!"

"And I'm the baby!" concluded Elsie, cheerfully.

"But does that account for that whole crowd?" asked Mary Eliska. "Jax said she counted seventeen."

"Oh, the others were gardeners, and gardeners' children, and servants. There are twelve of us at dinner every night, with father and Anita's husband. And you girls will make fourteen."

"I always thought it would be wonderful to have a big family," sighed Mary Eliska. "My aunt and I live all alone, except once in a while when my father comes home."

"All the more reason why you should spend a couple of weeks with us!" urged Elsie, cordially.

"We'd love to, but we can't," answered Jax Gray. "But we'll promise to come oftener, now that Mary Eliska has her Arrow."

"And that reminds me," put in Mary Eliska, "that we must call our folks."

Elsie handed her a telephone, which was on a little table beside the bed, and made her excuses and left them alone. It was almost time to dress for dinner.

Before the girls had answered the summons of the gong, the rain, which had been threatening all day long, came in torrents. But it did not dampen the spirits of the happy group that was gathered about the long table.

David Stillman, a starry-eyed young man with a serious expression, had managed to persuade his mother to let him sit next to Mary Eliska on her left, while Roger, the eldest, had naturally preempted the place on her right. The younger man, it seemed, believed her to be the ideal girl he had always dreamed of. He tried almost immediately to make her promise to play tennis with him, to go canoeing and swimming. Roger, on the other hand, saw two days' fun ahead of him, playing with the girls and the plane, and he made up his mind not to give his younger brother a chance.

Sizing up Mary Eliska immediately as a girl seriously interested in aviation, he began to talk on that subject, shutting out poor David completely. He told her about his plane, and the trips he had made, and the races he had won.

"But you are a new pilot, aren't you?" he asked her.

"Yes, why?" she asked. "Did I do anything wrong?"

"No, indeed! You fly like an old-timer. But what I mean is, you haven't gone in for any competitions yet, have you? Air-derbies, endurance flights—height records?"

"No, I haven't had time."

"But you will?"

"I don't know. I want to do something. But just what...."

"You have a wonderful opportunity," continued Roger. "Because you have ambition, and time, and youth—and enough money to back you." He paused to eat a generous slice of roast-beef. Unlike David, who was staring moodily at his plate and playing with his food, Roger ate with enormous appetite. "You see, the trouble with most of us is, that we haven't the time and the money. And the very rich are seldom ambitious."

"I am hoping to do something next year," Mary Eliska announced, slowly. "But not until I study some more."

"Wise girl!" was his comment. "I wish my kid brother—Dan—were of the same opinion. I can hardly keep him out of my plane—and he hasn't even a license. He's a perfect pest."

"Won't you please talk to me?" entreated a voice on the other side, and turning her head, Mary Eliska realized for the first time how she had been neglecting David.

"I'll give you all the rest of the dinner-time!" she said, laughingly. But the conversation at once became so general that she did not have a chance to keep her promise.

After dinner the rain abated, but nobody went out except Dan, who said he was always looking for adventure. But in such a crowd, they did not miss him; the young people danced and sang and played pool and ping-pong in the game-room. They were just finishing some lemonade and cake which Mrs. Stillman had brought out for their refreshment, when a telegram arrived for Mary Eliska. Her mind flew instantly to Ted Mackay, wondering whether he had been arrested in spite of all her efforts to help him.

But the news proved worse than anything she had expected. It was from her aunt.

"Your father seriously hurt. Fly to ranch at once."

Helplessly, she handed the telegram to Mrs. Stillman, who read it aloud to the others. Heroically, Mary Eliska managed to keep from crying.

"Thank Heaven for the Pursuit!" cried Jax Gray, who had her arms about her chum. "We'll get there in no time."

"Let me go with you," suggested Roger.

"No—thank you," stammered Mary Eliska, clinging to Jax Gray. "I need Lou—more than anybody."

"Well, then, I'll map out your course for you," offered the young man. "It's strange country to you?"

"Yes. I've never been to this ranch before. Dad had another one that I used to visit, when I was a child." And she gave Roger the exact location.

Ten minutes later, with their arms still entwined, Mary Eliska and Jax Gray went up to their room, having exacted a promise from Mrs. Stillman to waken them at five o'clock the following morning.

Chapter 5.16
The Accident

At seven o'clock the following morning, after eating the hearty breakfast upon which Mrs. Stillman insisted, the girls entered the Pursuit, and taxied off, waving farewell to Elsie, Roger, and their hostess. Of the large family, only these three—and the cook—had risen in time to say good-by. Even David had overslept; but his eldest brother was on hand to help the girls get their start.

Fortunately, the rain was over, and both Mary Eliska and Roger believed that, barring mishaps, the flyers should reach their destination early in the afternoon. With this hope, both girls kept their spirits high; they refused to worry about Mary Eliska's father until they saw for themselves. For Mary Eliska was likely to look upon the dark side of things, and it was probable too that the help at the ranch were frightened by the accident to their employer.

Tears of gratitude came to Mary Eliska's eyes when she saw the enormous lunch which Mrs. Stillman had been able to provide at such short notice, and she did not know how to thank the kind woman or her son. So she merely smiled gratefully, and waved good-by. Jax Gray kept the map of their course in her lap, and for two hours they flew on, making no attempt to talk, but every once in a while pressing each other's hand in sympathy and affection.

As the sun was growing hotter and higher in the sky, Mary Eliska was beginning to wonder whether they were not somewhat off their course. She examined the map.

"We ought to be nearing that town!" she shouted, pointing to a spot which Roger indicated by a large dot on the map. "And I don't believe that we are."

"Fly lower!" suggested Jax Gray. "Let's see!"

Cautiously the young pilot descended, but though both girls looked eagerly, there were no roofs or other evidences of a town. An almost continuous expanse of shrubbery seemed to cover the ground, and Mary Eliska did not care to land. So she went higher again, and pointed her plane south, trusting that they were right.

For two hours more they continued to fly without seeing any of the landmarks for which they were so eagerly watching. Afterwards Mary Eliska remarked that she believed they had been going in a circle.

The sun was almost directly overhead now, and both girls were feeling hungry, for their breakfast, though substantial, had been an early one. They were just considering opening their box to eat, when Mary Eliska noticed a queer noise in the motor.

"Something's wrong, Jax!" she shouted, trying to smile as if she were not worried. "We'll have to land."

"Here?" gasped Jax Gray, in horror.

"Yes. Watch the ground! We must find a good place."

Jax Gray was gazing about at the sky and the horizon, when, turning around, she happened to glance at her companion's face. A set look had come into Mary Eliska's eyes, her lips were rigid. Uneven, yet deafening, was the threatening sound of the motor. Suddenly it let off a terrific explosion.

"Will we be killed?" screamed Jax Gray, hoarsely.

Mary Eliska did not try to answer. She needed every ounce of brain power, of energy for the test that was ahead of her. She was working frantically with the joystick. So Jax Gray too, kept quiet, and looked over the side of the plane—and prayed.

At first it seemed they were dropping terrifically; but gradually, frightened though she was, she could feel that some safety device was taking hold. The speed was lessening. Down, down they went, but more gradually now.

And then they were close enough to the ground to see it. A woods of stumpy trees stretched under them, but over to the right was a field. Would Mary Eliska be able to guide the plane there, or must they be dashed against the tree-tops, to meet a sickening death?

How would it feel to be dead, Jax Gray wondered. And oh, her poor mother and father! Even in those few seconds, it seemed as if her whole life flashed before her, and although she was really a very sweet girl, she believed herself a monster of ingratitude. Not a bit like Mary Eliska—who was always thinking of her Aunt Polly and her father!

Mary Eliska, on the other hand, had no time for any such thoughts. She was working as she had never worked before, guiding her stricken plane. And—miracle of miracles—they were passing the tree-tops! They were over a field of weeds.

"Thank God!" cried Jax Gray, reverently.

"Wait!" whispered Mary Eliska, not sure yet that they were safe.

The landing was not easy. The plane came down and hit the ground and bounced up again. Suppose it should pancake? Mary Eliska held her breath, suffering greater agony than Jax Gray, who knew less of the dangers. But in a moment the valiant little Arrow came to a stop, in the shrubbery.

In a rapture of relief and thanksgiving, Jax Gray grasped Mary Eliska and kissed her, while the tears ran down the young pilot's face. For a moment the girls sat thus in silent embrace, each too filled with emotion to speak.

"Come, let's get out, Jax," said Mary Eliska, finally, and shakily they both stepped from the plane.

"I wonder where we are," remarked Jax Gray, trying to make her voice sound natural.

"We'll get out our maps and study the situation. But first let's eat. I'm simply famished. It must be noon at least."

They found upon consulting Jax Gray's wrist-watch that it was ten minutes of one.

Resolutely deciding to be cheerful, they opened the hamper which Jax Gray's Aunt Margaret had packed. What a delicious lunch!

There was a whole roast chicken, and tiny dainty lettuce sandwiches—at least a dozen of them. Pears and cherries, and lemonade in a thermos bottle. And a beautiful little layer cake evidently baked just especially for them, though how the cook had managed it, they had no idea. They spread out the paper cloth and attacked the food ravenously.

"It looks pretty desolate around here," remarked Jax Gray, as she nibbled at a chicken leg. "I don't see a house in sight."

"Or a road either, for that matter," returned Mary Eliska. "I wish we could get to a telephone—and send a call for assistance."

They ate silently for a while. How good the food tasted! In spite of their distress and worry, both girls enjoyed that lunch.

"Have you any idea what is wrong with the plane?" asked Jax Gray, as she broke off a piece of chocolate cake. "It was all right yesterday."

"Yes. That mechanic at the airport gave it a hasty examination. Funny he didn't notice anything so serious as this.... Jax Gray, do you suppose that Roger could have done anything to it?"

"No," answered Jax Gray, thoughtfully. "No; I think Roger knows what he's about. But I have an idea, Mary Eliska."

"What?"

"Do you remember hearing a plane very close to the house when we were playing ping-pong last night?"

"Yes. I thought it was the air-mail."

"So did I. But I believe now it was the Pursuit—with Dan piloting!"

"Dan Stillman?"

"Yes. He's a regular daredevil. And you know Roger won't let him fly his plane."

A pained look came into Mary Eliska's eyes, as if she herself had been mistreated.

"Oh, Jax, that seems awful," she said. "He wouldn't do a thing like that, would he?"

"He must have. Remember, he went out right after supper. And he's so conceited. He wouldn't think he could hurt it. But I'll tell you how to find out—look at the gas. You remember you had her filled at that airport."

Holding their cake in their hands, both girls dashed excitedly back to the plane and looked at the dial which indicated how much gasoline was left. And, sure enough, the supply was running low! Too low to be accounted for by the flying they had done that morning. In fact, it was almost gone.

"You're right!" cried Mary Eliska. "Oh, Jax, now we're in a worse pickle than ever. We'll never get to Daddy!" The tears ran down her cheeks.

"Don't!" urged her chum, putting her arms around the other girl. "Don't give up yet! We'll find somebody—on some road—who will send a mechanic to us. And we'll be at the ranch before night!"

"I hope so!" replied Mary Eliska, bravely trying to keep up her courage.

They went back to the spot where their lunch was spread—luckily there was plenty left for supper, in case they needed it—and packed the remainder again. Then, arm in arm, they set out in quest of a road. They walked in an easterly direction; that much they knew from the sun.

What they saw appeared to be a flat country, without even any fences or signs of cultivation. Gazing off in the distance, they could faintly distinguish the outline of a house—but it might be five miles away, or it might be fifteen. Or it might not be a house at all; perhaps just some abandoned building or mill.

For half an hour they walked aimlessly onward, 'til they finally reached a dirt road.

"This is encouraging," said Jax Gray, hopefully. "Let's drop down and wait here 'til something passes. We don't want to get too far from the plane—if we get out of sight, we might not be able to find our way back."

They sat down on some moss by a small tree and consulted the time. It was half-past two.

Everything was extremely still. No noise of motor or traffic anywhere. No voices. So strange after the places they were used to, for even Green Falls was noisy. And the birds were quiet, too—or perhaps there weren't many, for there were no big trees.

Mary Eliska yawned. "I'm so sleepy." "Take a nap," suggested Jax Gray. "You deserve one!"

"Hardly fair," returned the other. "Aren't you sleepy too?" "Not so sleepy as you are. Go ahead! I'll wake you if anything comes along." "And suppose nothing does?" "Then I'll wake you anyway at three o'clock. We'll have to strike out in some other direction."

So Mary Eliska curled up and went to sleep, and Jax Gray, yawning, wondered how she could possibly manage to keep awake. The whole atmosphere was so drowsy—and there was nothing to do. "If only there were a place to swim," she thought, regretfully. "Cold water would make me a different girl!" But there wasn't any water at all, as far as she knew; indeed, she and Mary Eliska didn't dare wash in the small supply they carried with them. For they might need it for drinking.

She never knew how it happened, but soon she too was peacefully asleep. For two whole hours both girls slept the dreamless sleep of fatigue. Then, at a quarter of five they were suddenly awakened by the rattle of an old, tumble-down cart, pulled by a haggard horse. The girls sat up with a start, and looked at each other and laughed. Jumping to her feet in an instant, Jax Gray ran hastily towards the driver. He was staring at them with great curiosity.

"We have been in an airplane accident, and we want to get to a telephone—" began Jax Gray.

But the man only shook his head and grinned. "Nicht versteh'," he replied, helplessly.

"He's a foreigner," said Jax Gray, turning back to where Mary Eliska was standing. "A German, who doesn't understand English."

"I can speak German," said Mary Eliska. "At least, I had some, Freshman year. Let me try him!"

But already he was driving away. "Wo ghen Sie?" called Mary Eliska. "Warte!"

He stopped driving, evidently amazed at her words, and pointed to the road ahead of him.

Encouraged by this display of intelligence, Jax Gray jumped up on the cart, and waved her arms in the direction of the airplane, in the field half a mile away.

"We want *help*!" she cried. Then, turning to Mary Eliska, "What's the German word for help?"

"I don't know," answered the other girl. "But I think he understands. If he does meet anybody, I think he'd send them to us."

So Jax Gray climbed down again, and waved good-by to the man as he continued on with his cart, and, faintly encouraged, the girls went back to the plane to eat their supper.

Chapter 5.17
The Lost Necklace

Many thoughts raced through Mary Eliska's mind, as she and Jax Gray sat beside the airplane, nibbling at their frugal supper. For this time, they had decided to eat sparingly; nobody knew how long they might have to stay there, without any more food.

But all of Mary Eliska's thoughts were regrets. Regret that her father had met with an accident, regret that Dan Stillman had borrowed her Arrow, regret that she was unable to locate the trouble herself and repair it.

Jax Gray, with her usual practical cheerfulness, interrupted these gloomy meditations. "We have three good hours of daylight left, Mary Eliska," she announced, glancing at her watch. "To try another direction. There must be a real road around here somewhere—where automobiles go. Texas isn't the end of the world."

"If we're actually in Texas!" returned Mary Eliska. "It may be Oklahoma, for all we know."

"But Oklahoma has roads, too. Come on, finish your cake! We must hurry."

Taking their coats along, for the night gave promise of being cooler, the girls set off in the opposite direction from the one they had taken that afternoon. This time they had to go right through the shrubbery—the dangerous shrubbery which had threatened disaster to their landing. "This is awful!" exclaimed Jax Gray, pausing to pull a brier from her sweater. "There can't be any road here."

"On the contrary, I think we'll be more likely to find one, once we get through this. The very fact that we can't see beyond is hopeful."

"That's true," admitted Jax Gray, starting on again.

They walked for some time, carefully picking their way through the undergrowth, thankful that they were wearing breeches. At last they came to a more open space, and stopped to look about them.

"No road!" exclaimed Jax Gray, in disappointment.

"But that looks like a stream over there, Jax—between those two banks!" cried Mary Eliska.

"Oh, if it only is! Then we could have a swim!"

"If we ought to take the time."

"I think we might as well, Mary Eliska, because it's going to get too dark for us to take a chance getting lost tonight. Let's have our swim and go back to the plane to sleep. Then tomorrow morning we'll start to hike—if we have to go all the way to the ranch on foot!"

"We won't have to do that, because we have plenty of money," Mary Eliska reminded her. "Once we get back to civilization, our dollars will be some good. And, even if we have to leave the Pursuit, and never see her again, it would be worth it to get to Daddy!"

Having come to this decision, the girls hurried rapidly towards the stream, and then, taking off their flyers' suits carefully, under cover of their coats, in case there should be some human being around, they both plunged in.

The water felt cold, and oh, so refreshing! They swam happily for some minutes, forgetful of all their worries, in the joy of the invigorating pastime.

When they had gone some distance, Mary Eliska suddenly realized how swift the current was, out in the middle of the creek. Already they were several hundred yards downstream.

"Jax!" she called. "We must be careful of this current!"

Her chum did not answer, and Mary Eliska suddenly experienced another sickening moment of dread. Suppose Jax Gray were unconscious! She turned around, but she could not see the other girl.

However, the creek turned sharply at this point, and Mary Eliska reassured herself with the hope that Jax Gray was beyond the bend. She swam in to where it was shallow enough for her to stand up, and cupped her hands and called.

"Jax! Oh, Jax!"

"Yes!" came the instant reply. "Around the bend."

Mary Eliska hurried around the cliff which separated her chum from sight, and there, to her amazement, she beheld a shattered airplane. The wings and the propeller were gone—had evidently been floated out on the stream and swept away on the current, and the plane itself was smashed to pieces. Jax Gray was standing beside it, holding a man's coat in her hand.

"Ye gods!" cried Mary Eliska, shocked by the horror of such a wreck. "How terrible!"

But Jax Gray was searching the pockets of the coat madly, excitedly, as if she had no thought for the man who had been killed.

"Look, Mary Eliska!" she cried triumphantly. "I had an inspiration it might be your thief! I've got it!"

"What?" demanded the other.

"The necklace!"

Both girls held their breath while Jax Gray steadied her nervous fingers and opened the box—a cheap pasteboard affair, totally unlike the original one in which Kitty Clavering's pearls had been sold. To Mary Eliska's unbelieving eyes, she held up the costly jewels. Jax Gray dropped down on the ground, absolutely overcome with emotion, and Mary Eliska sat beside her, examining the necklace for herself, as if she could not believe her eyes. But there was no doubt about it; it was the real thing this time.

"That man didn't know much about flying," remarked Mary Eliska, finally. "I suppose, though, he realized that his only chance of escape lay in getting over the border.... But Jax, if his coat is here, why isn't he?"

"He probably took off his coat before anything happened. But his body may be somewhere in the wreckage. I—I'd just as soon not see it, wouldn't you, Mary Eliska?"

"Of course not," replied the other, with a shudder of repulsion. "Come on, Jax, let's go. But don't let's try to swim with that necklace. I'd rather walk."

"So would I."

Both girls scrambled to their feet, and started back towards their coats. Suddenly Mary Eliska stopped, horrified by what she saw. Over in a little cove, away from the main stream, were not one, but two bodies, half floating, half caught on the shore by the weeds and underbrush.

"It's the thief, all right," she managed to say. "And I wonder who the other man was."

Jax Gray squinted her eyes; she had no desire to go any closer, and in the fading light it was hard to see clearly.

"He looks—as—if—he had red hair," she announced, slowly. "That would explain about the gasoline agent, who tried to put the blame on Ted Mackay."

"Of course!" cried Mary Eliska. "Isn't it all horrible? As if any necklace could be worth this! I wonder when it happened."

"Probably last night, during the storm. That would be too much for an inexperienced flyer."

"Of course."

The girls picked up their clothing and dressed hurriedly, reaching the plane just as it was beginning to get dark.

"Let's make a fire," suggested Mary Eliska, "and tell each other stories 'til we get sleepy. We mustn't try to go to sleep too early on this hard ground, especially after having had naps."

"Are you scared at all, Mary Eliska?" asked Jax Gray.

"No. What of? Ghosts—or tramps?"

"Both."

"Well, I'm not afraid of tramps or robbers because I have my pistol—Daddy made me promise to take it with me on all my flights—and I'm just not going to let myself be worried about ghosts. After all, those two dead men deserved their fate, didn't they? And I mean to forget them. Now, tell me a story!"

"What about?"

"Some nice new novel you've read that I haven't."

So Jax Gray began the story of "Father Means Well"—a very amusing book she had just finished, and the girls kept their camp-fire going until eleven o'clock. Then, when both were certain that they were sleepy, they spread out Jax Gray's raincoat on the ground, and, crawling close together, put Mary Eliska's on top of them. Almost instantly they were asleep, forgetful of accidents and thieves, not to waken until the sun was brightly shining again.

Chapter 5.18
In Pursuit of the "Pursuit"

From the moment that Ted Mackay had been shot by the thief who stole Kitty Clavering's necklace, everything had gone wrong for him. Not only had he been wounded and forced to lose time from work, but the new plane, which was worth thousands of dollars to his company, had been stolen. And, in view of the fact that the robber was not a licensed pilot, it was very unlikely that the plane would stand the test, even if it were ever recovered.

Then, added to his other troubles, Ted had been accused of being in league with the thief! Ralph Clavering believed he was guilty, and so did Mr. Stricklin. But what worried him most was whether Mary Eliska thought so too.

The little nurse at the hospital had been a great comfort, believing in Ted as she did, implicitly, from the first. But when he had gone home, he said nothing to his mother of the suspicions aroused against him. The good woman had enough to worry about, with the unhappy life she led, and the constant menace of his father's returning in trouble or in need of money. But Ted's conscience was clear; all the detective's in the world could not make him a criminal when he knew that he was innocent.

He wasn't surprised, however, when two men arrived at his home the day after he had reached it. Two plainclothes men, with warrants for his arrest.

His first anxiety was of course for his mother. If she should believe that he was following in his father's footsteps! Why, at her age, and after all she had been through, the shock might kill her! Her one comfort in life had always been that her three children were fine, honest citizens, that her teaching and training had been rewarded.

Fortunately when the detectives arrived, she was out in the back yard, working in her little garden. But what could Ted do? To argue with these men would only arouse her attention, bring her hurrying to the front porch to see what was the matter. For she seemed to live in daily fear of trouble between her husband and the law.

"But you have no evidence to arrest me," Ted objected, quietly, in answer to the man's brusque statement.

"You are wrong there! We have evidence. The gasoline agent, who sold you gas for the plane. The description fits you perfectly—a great big fellow, with red hair. Besides, you were caught in the very place where the other thief escaped."

"But I had nothing to do with it! I can prove it!"

"How?"

"By other men in the company——"

"Are they here?" interrupted the detective, with a hard, sneering look.

"No—but——"

"Then you will come with us until such time as you prove your innocence. One of us will go inside with you while you get whatever things you want."

Ted looked about him helplessly. Oh, how could he keep the news from his mother? It would break her heart!

And his career! What would this sort of thing do to that? Did it mean that, just as he was hoping to make his mark in the world, and rendering valuable assistance to his family, all must stop? With a gesture of utter despair he gazed up into the skies, where he heard the noise of an airplane, coming nearer and lower.

For a moment the other men forgot their duties, and likewise looked up into the air. For the plane was certainly flying very low indeed, actually circling over their heads. And its roar was insistent; it would not be ignored.

At last it became plain to Ted that the pilot wanted to land. So the young man held up his arm and pointed to field on the right of his house.

Wondering what its business could be, and interested in the plane as everybody is, although it is a common sight, the detectives waited to find out what would happen.

What they actually saw was certainly worth looking at. The pilot was an experienced flyer, and his landing, in the small area of this field, was as neat as anything they had ever witnessed. Both men watched with admiration and awe.

When the motor had been turned off, and the pilot stepped from the plane, Ted recognized him instantly. Sam Hunter—the best salesman, the most experienced flyer of their company!

"Sam!" he exclaimed with genuine pleasure, for although Ted had been with his firm only a short time, this man was an old friend.

"Ted! Old boy! How are you?" cried the other, clasping his hand in a hearty handshake. "How's the shoulder?"

"Pretty good," replied Ted. "I'm ready to go back to work, if I take it a little easy. But—" he paused and glanced at the two men beside him—"these fellows don't want to let me."

"Doctors?" inquired Sam, though Ted's manner of referring to them seemed queer—almost rude. He hadn't introduced them—a courtesy due them if they were doctors, or men in any way worthy of respect.

"They're detectives," explained Ted. "Sorry I can't introduce you, Sam, but they did not favor me with their names. They've come here with a warrant for my arrest."

"By heck!" ejaculated Sam. "Then the little lady was right! The pretty aviatrix who was so worried about you! And I'm just in time!"

"I don't know what you mean." Sam put his hand into his pocket, and produced the paper which Mr. Jordan had dictated and three of the men had signed. He handed it to the detectives, both of whom read it at once.

"All right," said one of them, briefly, as he handed it back to Sam. "Good-by."

Without another word they turned and fled to their automobile and immediately drove away.

Ted stood gazing at Sam in amazement, unable to understand what his friend had done, how he had been able to accomplish what seemed like a miracle. In a few words the latter told him of Mary Eliska's visit, and her insistence upon the written alibi.

He finished his explanation and Ted had just time to warn Sam not to mention the matter to his mother, when the latter appeared, dressed in a clean linen, beaming at both the boys.

"Are you willing to have me take Ted back again?" asked Sam, after he had been introduced. "Because we need him, if he's well enough to go."

"I'll be sorry to lose him, of course," she answered with a motherly smile. "But I always want Ted to do his duty. And I think he'll be all right if he is careful. But first let me give you an early supper, so that you can do most of your flying by daylight."

Sam accepted the invitation with pleasure, and as the boys sat down at five o'clock to that splendid home-cooked meal, it seemed to Ted that he was perfectly happy again. He knew now that his company believed in his innocence; best of all, he had the reassurance that Mary Eliska shared that opinion!

It was good to be in a plane again, he thought, as they took off, half an hour later. Good to be up in the skies, with Sam—who was a friend indeed!

The whole trip was pleasant, and Mr. Jordan's greeting was just as cordial as Sam's. When the former heard what a life-saver his message had been, he was more impressed than ever with the cleverness of the two girls who had visited him.

"And if you'd like to see them and thank them yourself," he continued, "I'll arrange for you to combine it with a visit to our Denver field. The girls are out there in Colorado, they said—'Sunny Hills', I believe the name of the village is."

"Thank you, sir!" cried Ted, in delight and gratitude. "I don't deserve that—after letting that other plane get away from me!"

"Not your fault a bit!" protested the older man. "We've got insurance. Still—if you could happen to sell one on your trip, it would be a big help to us."

"I'll do my best, Mr. Jordan. Now—when do I start?""Tomorrow morning. At dawn, if you like."

So it happened that when Mary Eliska and Jax Gray were taking off for their trip to Texas, that was halted so sadly, Ted Mackay, at the very same hour, was flying to Denver. He reached his destination without mishap, and went back to Sunny Hills that night. He had some difficulty in finding the place, stopping as the girls had, at the airport to inquire, and reaching the Stillman estate about ten o'clock that night.

Thinking naturally that the airplane was Mary Eliska's, and that the girls were back again for some reason, Roger and his brothers went out to welcome them.

Ted explained quickly that he was a friend of Mary Eliska—it was the first time he had ever made such a statement, and there was pride in his tone—and that, as he had just been to Denver, he wanted to stop over here and see her for a few minutes.

"Shucks! That's too bad!" exclaimed Roger with regret. "Mary Eliska left this morning for her father's ranch in Texas."

Ted's smile faded; the ranch was the one place where he could not visit Mary Eliska.

"But you must come in and make yourself at home. Stay all night—you won't want to fly any more tonight. Why!" he cried, noticing Ted's bandage, "you've been hurt!"

"Last week," replied the other. "It's almost well now. But—really, Mr. Stillman, though I thank you, I have no right to impose on your hospitality!"

"It's a pleasure, I'm sure. Besides, I want to look at your plane by daylight. I'm in the market for a new airplane. My old one's being repaired now, but it's so hopelessly out of date I thought I'd try to trade it in."

Instantly Ted became the business man, the salesman, and while he accepted Roger's invitation to put his plane into the other's hangar, he told of all its merits.

So interested were they that they talked for an hour before they went into the house. Then Roger was all apologies, for he knew Ted had had no supper.

He hunted his mother, who was sitting disconsolately at the telephone.

"I'm worried about the girls," she told them. "They didn't phone from the ranch, as they promised, and I have just finished calling it, by long distance. They haven't arrived." "But they had plenty of time!" insisted Roger. "They started at seven o'clock this morning!"

"Something must have happened," said Mrs. Stillman, anxiously. "Airplanes are so dangerous!"

"I think I know why—if anything did happen," explained Roger, slowly. "It isn't airplanes that are so dangerous as inexperienced pilots. I found out that Dan had Mary Eliska's plane out last night, alone."

"Dan?" Mrs. Stillman was horrified. "But he never flew alone in his life!"

"No, because I saw to it that he didn't. But he admitted that he borrowed the Arrow last night."

"This is serious," put in Ted. "We ought to do something—right away!"

"What can we do? I made the girls a map, but they may be off their course. I have no plane—and your time's not your own, Mr. Mackay."

"But I'll have to do something!" cried Ted, excitedly. "Even if I lose my job on account of it! It may be a question of life or death!"

"I'll tell you what I'll do," decided Roger. "I'll buy that plane of yours. I want it anyhow. And tomorrow morning at dawn we'll go on a search.... Now, mother, can you give Mr. Mackay something to eat—and a room?"

Gratefully the young man accepted the hospitable offers of his new friends and, pleased with the sale he had put through, he fell instantly asleep, not to awaken until Roger both knocked at his door and threw pillows at him the next morning.

He dressed and they left in short order, after a hearty breakfast, however, and armed with a lunch perhaps not so dainty as that provided for the girls, but at least as satisfying. Roger reconstructed the map, like the one he had made for Mary Eliska, and they flew straight for the nearest airport.

Unfortunately, however, they got no information there, no news of a wreck, or of two girls flying in a biplane. But their time was not wasted, for they took the opportunity to question one of the flyers who seemed familiar with the territory around him. They asked particularly about the more lonely, desolate parts of the near-by country, where an airplane accident would not quickly be discovered.

"There's a stretch about ten miles south of here," the man informed them, indicating a spot on Roger's rough map. "Not a farm or a village, as far as I know, except one old shack where a German lives. He hid there during the War, because he didn't want to be sent home, and he has continued to live on there ever since. He has a sort of garden, I believe—just enough to keep him alive—with the fish he catches. And a few apple trees. Once in a while he drives in here with his apples. I could tell you pretty near where he lives, because I was stranded there once myself. You could drop down and ask him if he heard any planes."

Eagerly the two young men marked the spot and set off once more in their plane, flying in the direction indicated. Before nine o'clock they came to the shack, which was the building that Mary Eliska and Jax Gray had spied at a distance. They found the man frying fish on a fire in front of his tumble-down house.

Their landing had been of sufficient distance to avoid frightening him, but near enough for him to hear them. They hurried towards him, Roger almost shouting the question about the girls, before he actually reached him. But, like Mary Eliska and Jax Gray, when they tried to talk to this man, Roger received a shrug of his shoulders in reply, and a muttered, "Nicht versteh." Unlike the girls, however, Roger commanded a good knowledge of German, and he translated the question with ease into the foreign language. To both flyers' unbounded delight, they were rewarded with the information that they so longed to hear. The girls were safe—and not far away!

Chapter 5.19
Rescued

When the girls awakened at practically the same time—for Jax Gray, in stirring, moved against Mary Eliska—they were horrified to see that it was half past eight by their wrist watches. "Two hours wasted!" groaned Jax Gray. "And it's going to be hot today! Oh, Mary Eliska, why didn't we wake up at six?"

"Next time I'll bring an alarm clock," laughed her companion. "Come on, let's straighten ourselves up. I—I—believe I'd rather not swim!"

"No, indeed!" agreed Jax Gray, recalling the horror they had witnessed the night before. "We'll use what water we have—we can't carry much on our hike anyway.... Now, let's see what we have for breakfast."

"There's some fruit left, and a little bit of chicken. With water to drink we'll have a fine meal."

They sat down beside the plane to eat, and both girls seemed to enjoy their breakfast, meager as it was. For each had resolutely made up her mind to be cheerful.

"Are the pearls safe?" asked Mary Eliska, as she gathered up the chicken bones.

"In my pocket!" replied Jax Gray, taking them out for examination. "How about your pistol?"

"O.K.... Jax! Look! A plane!"

Both girls waved their arms and their coats in the air as signals of distress.

Both girls jumped instantly to their feet and waved their arms and their coats in the air as signals of distress. If only the pilot would look down and see them!

He was flying low enough to make this perfectly possible, but a moment later his ascent sent a sickening disappointment into their hearts. He was going away without even seeing them! Useless to yell; no one could possibly hear above the deafening noise. To be so near to a rescue, and then to have it fail them in the end!

It was Mary Eliska, with her knowledge of flying, who was the first to realize that the aviator wasn't really going away, that he was only retreating farther into the field to make a safe landing, clear of them and their plane. In her ecstasy she hugged Jax Gray tightly.

"He's coming down, Jax! To rescue us!"

"How do you know?" demanded the other, incredulously. "He seems to be going farther away to me!"

"No, he isn't! It's only to land clear of us. Jax, it must be Roger!"

"Roger? Why? How!"

"Because he would investigate, when we failed to telephone!"

"But suppose it's another bandit—like—you know! Get your revolver!"

"It's right here. But don't worry, Jax. Look! He's on the ground!"

The pilot brought the beautiful new cabin monoplane expertly to a stop and shut off the engine. To the girls' amazement two men, not one, stepped out. Both of them were old friends!

"Roger! Ted!" cried both the girls at once, in their delight in recognizing them. They felt as if they had been rescued from a desert island.

"You're both safe? Unhurt?" cried Roger, excitedly.

"Thank God!" murmured Ted, reverently.

"Yes—safe, but stranded," replied Jax Gray. "We've only seen one person since noon yesterday—and he couldn't speak English!"

"Nevertheless, he's the one you owe the rescue to!" replied Roger.

"You saw him?" demanded Mary Eliska, incredulously. "But you must have been out hunting for us, first, Roger. Oh, I think you're just wonderful!"

"No—the credit goes to Mr. Mackay," returned Roger, modestly. "And the German fellow, with his apple-cart." And he proceeded to relate in detail everything that had led to their pursuit and discovery.

"Your shoulder is all right, Ted?" inquired Mary Eliska, after she heard that he was back at his job. "Yes, fine, thank you. And I can never thank you enough for what you did for me, Mary Eliska! I'll tell you all about it later."

"Oh, that was nothing!" protested the girl lightly. Then, turning anxiously to Roger, "Have you any news of my father?"

"He is alive, but that is all my mother could learn last night from the housekeeper over the telephone. But don't worry—you'll be there yourself in a few hours!"

"How?" she asked, glancing helplessly at her plane. "There's something wrong with my motor. It may take a long time to fix—and—if I go by train—Daddy might—" she stopped; she just couldn't say "die."

"You're flying in my new plane!" Roger informed her. "Which I have just purchased from Mr. Mackay. We'll leave right away, or as soon as he examines yours, so he can tell me what to send out to him here. We'll stop somewhere and phone for help."

"Roger, would you really do that?" cried Mary Eliska, in relief. "That would be wonderful!"

"A pleasure!" he said. "Now—tell us what happened to you."

"I really don't know, except that the motor acted awfully queer. But I was lucky enough to make a safe landing."

"It was just dreadful," put in Jax Gray. "I was absolutely certain we were going to be killed. Mary Eliska was wonderful."

"She's a fine little pilot," said Ted, admiringly. "Shows she can keep her head in an emergency—and that's one of the most important things for an aviator.... Now, let's have a look at the plane."

They all went with him while he examined it.

"I'm afraid I can't fix it without some new parts, and some special tools," he said, making notes as he spoke. "But it's nothing that can't be repaired quickly. If you'll telephone our Denver field, Mr. Stillman, and read this note to the mechanic, they'll send a man out. And as soon as it's fixed, I'll pilot it to you at the ranch, Mary Eliska.... Be sure to give me the directions.... Now, have you girls had anything to eat?"

"Oh, yes, we had supper last night," answered Jax Gray, "left over from our picnic lunch, and we even saved some fruit and some chicken for breakfast."

"Then you people might as well start," urged Ted. "No use wasting time."

"One thing more," added Jax Gray, while Mary Eliska busied herself writing the directions for Ted, "we almost forgot! We found a wrecked plane last night—two men dead—and recovered the necklace!"

"What?" demanded Ted, in consternation.

Roger, however, did not know what they were talking about, and no one had time to explain.

"The wreck's over by a stream—about half a mile beyond those bushes," Jax Gray informed Ted. "You can explore it while you're waiting."

"And maybe salvage some of it!" added Ted, hopefully.

Five minutes later the other three took off in the new plane, Jax Gray somehow sitting on Mary Eliska's lap. It wasn't very comfortable, but it would not be for far. They would descend at the nearest landing place, Roger getting in touch with Denver, while Jax Gray called Mrs. Stillman and her parents, and then summoned a taxicab, to take her to a railroad station. The rest of the trip was smooth and uneventful. Once only did they make a stop after Jax Gray left—that time to get some lunch at a hotel in Fort Worth. In another hour they reached the ranch and landed right on Mr. Stricklin's field, for Mary Eliska knew from former directions just where the best spot would be.

"Come in with me, Roger," she invited, trying to keep her voice steady.

They approached the house, an old-fashioned, rambling affair, and knocked at the screen door. A middle-aged woman, neatly dressed, came through the hall.

"How do you do, Mrs. Cates," said Mary Eliska. "I am Mr. Stricklin's daughter, and this is Mr. Stillman, who has brought me in his plane."

"Good afternoon," replied the older woman. "Come right in, my dear. I've been expecting you."

Mary Eliska had been watching her face, to try to ascertain from her expression whether the news of her father was bad.

"How—how—is Daddy?" she asked, with trembling lips, as she and Roger followed Mrs. Cates into the big room where her father evidently spent most of his indoor hours. A huge fireplace occupied most of one wall, and there were many book-shelves. A table, a few chairs, and an old couch were all the other furnishings, so that the great room looked almost empty and desolate without its master.

"He is still alive—but unconscious," sighed Mrs. Cates, shaking her head mournfully. Her expression was one of resignation; she felt sure that Mr. Stricklin could not get better.

"Unconscious!" repeated Mary Eliska. "Has he been so, long?"

"Ever since his fall. He was riding a new horse—that he never should have bought—and was thrown down a steep bank. His leg is broken, but worse than that, he suffered severe internal injuries. Dr. Winston is afraid there ain't much hope."

The words were the cruelest Mary Eliska had ever heard; she burst out crying, and hid her face on Mrs. Cates' motherly shoulder. Roger Stillman remained standing, embarrassed. He did not know what to do.

He coughed slightly, and Mary Eliska looked up, ashamed of herself for breaking down.

"Is there anything at all, Mary Eliska, that I can do for you?" he asked. "Or for you, Mrs. Cates?"

"I'm afraid not, thank you, Roger," replied the girl. "But don't you want something to eat before you start back?"

"No, thanks. I ought to be home early this evening, and I'll get supper then. I'm not a bit hungry now." And with a sympathetic handshake, he left her.

"Would you like to go to your room, my dear—or do you want to see your father first?" asked the housekeeper. "I have him here on the ground floor."

"I want to see Daddy!" replied Mary Eliska, wiping the tears from her eyes.

The older woman led her across the hall to a room where the door was open, and she caught sight of her father, lying almost lifeless upon the bed. Impulsively Mary Eliska rushed in to him. It just didn't seem possible that he wouldn't recognize her, and hold out his arms to receive her!

But he continued to lie death-like upon the bed, his head motionless upon the pillow. His eyes were closed. "Daddy! Daddy darling!" she cried, in a voice that shook with pain. Dropping to her knees, she knelt beside his bed, and covered his limp hand with kisses. But there was no response whatever to her greeting!

For some time she stayed there, praying that he would get better. Mrs. Cates had left them alone, but in half an hour she came back.

"Come, my dear, you must get some rest. Take off your clothing, and wash your face and hands and lie down for a while. Then perhaps you will be able to eat some supper."

Obediently Mary Eliska did as she was told, for she realized that the housekeeper was only trying to be kind. And, after a short nap, she had to admit that she felt better.

"Any change, Mrs. Cates?" was her first question, when she sat down to supper with the woman and her husband. The rest of the help ate in the kitchen, but Mrs. Cates realized that this was no time for the girl to be alone.

"No. Not a bit."

"Oughtn't there to be a trained nurse?"

"Dr. Winston didn't think so. I'm doing what needs to be done."

"When will the doctor be back?"

"Tonight, after supper."

Somehow Mary Eliska felt dissatisfied, as if enough were not being done. Another doctor should have been called in—a surgeon, perhaps. And surely a trained nurse.

She spoke of these things to Dr. Winston when he came over about eight o'clock that evening. But he shook his head.

"I'm afraid nothing can save your father, my child," he said. "There's only one chance in a thousand he might get well, if we operated. And there's only one surgeon in the United States who ever had any success with that sort of operation."

"But if there is *one*!" cried Mary Eliska, eagerly jumping to the tiny hope his words suggested. "We must get that surgeon! Who is he? Where is he?" She was talking rapidly, excitedly, almost incoherently.

"He is a Dr. Lineaweaver. A marvelous man. But I happen to know he is away on his vacation now."

"Where does he go?" "That I don't know."

"But you know where he lives?" "Yes. St. Louis."

"Then won't you please call his home and find out where he is, and I'll go for him as soon as I get my plane back."

The doctor shook his head sorrowfully. "I'm afraid it's too late, my child. I—I—doubt if your father will live through the night. And you couldn't fly at night—even if your plane were here."

"I can—and will! And I think I hear my plane now—yes, I'm sure that's it. Get me the address—quick—and you put in the call while I run out and see my plane! And try to get a trained nurse immediately. I'll be back before dawn—unless the surgeon's in Europe or Canada!" And, dashing in to give her father one kiss, she hurried out to find faithful Ted Mackay, alighting from her beloved Arrow.

Chapter 5.20
The Race against Death

"Ted!"

"Mary Eliska!"

"You can't know how thankful I am to see you!" cried the girl. "It—it—may mean that I can save my father's life!" And she told him of her plans. "If I could only go with you!" sighed the young man. "I hate to think of you flying alone at night!"

"But you do believe I'm capable, don't you, Ted?" Mary Eliska's eyes searched his for the truth; she was not asking for flattery, she really wanted his opinion.

"Yes indeed I do!" Ted answered, with assurance. "But it's always safer for two pilots to go together. However, the Pursuit is in fine shape now—and filled up with gas.... Mary Eliska, I have something to tell you."

"Yes?"

"About the wreck—and—those thieves.... The other dead man was my father."

"Your father! Ted!" Every bit of color left the girl's face. What a dreadful, ghastly thing to happen to anybody, and especially to a fine boy like Ted! To come upon his father, dead, in that abrupt fashion, and to know, worst of all, that he had died in disgrace!

Finding no words to express her sympathy, she pressed his hand tightly in silence.

"So you see how much I have to do—why I can't go with you," he continued. "I have reported the wreck to my company, and made arrangements about my father's body. But I must go right home to my mother."

"But how do you explain it all, Ted?" Mary Eliska asked.

"I think my father was paying one of his regular visits to the Spring City Flying School— he came there once in so often to get money from me—and he was disappointed to find I had gone. Whether he knew that other man before, I don't know, but it would seem probable that he did. Together they must have cooked up the scheme to follow your plane and get the necklace.... That is why it is really fortunate the man got the necklace by a ruse. You see he was armed with a gun—as I later found out, and if he had had to fight for the jewels, I'm sure he wouldn't have hesitated to fire on you!"

"And I suppose your father's being involved would explain why you were suspected," added Mary Eliska. "You look like him, I believe."

"Yes. To my regret."

"But perhaps it's better as it is," concluded Mary Eliska. "Don't you feel so, Ted?"

"Yes, I do. It—will be so much easier for my mother.... But Mary Eliska, we mustn't stand here talking. Every minute is precious to you."

"No. I can't go 'til Dr. Winston comes out with the surgeon's address. He's putting in a long-distance call. However, I will go in and change into my flyer's suit, if you don't mind," she added.

Five minutes later she reappeared with the information that Dr. Lineaweaver was in Louisiana—at a small seaport town which Ted instantly located on a map that he gave to Mary Eliska.

"I won't even start off with you," the young man said, "because that would mean an extra stop for you. Now—are you sure you are all right—and that you can stay awake?"

"Yes, I'm sure," replied the girl, forcing a smile. "Mrs. Cates has just given me a thermos bottle full of coffee, and a sandwich, to help me!"

A moment later she climbed into the cockpit and started the motor. The Pursuit, whose engine purred with the smooth even whir of one in perfect order, gained speed until it rose into the air. It was Mary Eliska's first flight at night.

Darkness was all around her, but overhead the stars shone brightly, and the moon came from behind a cloud to light her way. Strange, lonely, mysterious, it seemed to her, as she flew through the night, but nevertheless thrilling. Gradually a sense of peace settled over her, as if a Divine Providence was surely guiding her, and she experienced the firm conviction that everything was right, that she was going to be successful in her mission to save her father's life.

For the first time she realized how much her confidence had to do with Ted Mackay. Because he had repaired and inspected the motor, she felt certain there would be no accident, and a successful flight was a good omen for the operation. Moreover, she had great faith in Dr. Lineaweaver. If he would only promise to come!

The hours passed, the moon set, the night grew darker. But the solitary girl flew on, swift and straight to her course, steadfast in her undertaking. About two o'clock she arrived at the little seaport, found a landing place back of the one big hotel, and went inside.

Fortunately a night clerk was on duty, and he rose immediately to greet her. The flyer's costume identified her so that he had no need to ask what a girl of her age was doing alone at this early hour of the morning.

"Can you tell me where Dr. Lineaweaver, the surgeon, can be located?" she inquired. "I want him immediately—it is a question of my father's life."

Her voice was steady now; there was no danger of tears. She seemed almost mature as she spoke the words.

"Yes," replied the clerk. "He is staying at Dr. Grayson's bungalow—a couple of blocks away. They come over here for their meals."

"Could you get him on the telephone for me?"

"Certainly. I'll let you talk with him."

Although the clerk put in the call immediately, there was no answer for several minutes. A fishing trip had tired both doctors, and they were sleeping soundly. At last, however, there came a reply, and Mary Eliska took the telephone.

In a few words the unhappy girl apologized for the call at that hour, and during the surgeon's holiday, and briefly told her story. Eagerly she pleaded with him to dress and come immediately, informing him that she had her plane waiting.

"You mean you flew from Texas alone—at this hour of the night!" exclaimed the surgeon.

"Yes. But you needn't be afraid, Doctor, to go with me. I'm quite experienced. Oh please, please, say yes!"

"I'll be at the hotel in ten minutes," replied the great man. "And meanwhile, you get something to eat."

Mary Eliska sank gratefully into a chair, thinking that the hardest part of her task was over—the winning of Dr. Lineaweaver's consent to break into his vacation and go back with her. Now, if her father only lived until they returned, all would surely be well!

Still keeping herself in control, she ate her sandwich and drank her coffee, while she waited for the doctor to come. True to his word, he appeared in exactly ten minutes.

The flight back to the ranch was much pleasanter than the one to the seaport. No longer was Mary Eliska alone; it was a comfort to have the great surgeon with her, to know that he would do all in his power to save her father. The darkness gradually faded, giving place to a faint gray, and finally to a beautiful, inspiring sunrise. A dawn that perhaps meant new life to her father!

It did not take Dr. Lineaweaver long to realize that Mary Eliska was an accomplished pilot, and he settled back into his seat in full enjoyment of the ride. His surprise at her youth— she was much younger than he had supposed from the telephone conversation—gradually gave way to admiration of her skill and her poise. He had no fear for his own safety; he was confident that she would make the journey without a mishap.

About seven o'clock she brought the Pursuit to a stop on the field that belonged to her father's ranch. Cates was already there to greet them. "Is my father still alive?" she demanded, with the first indication of any strain in her voice.

"Yes," came the reassuring reply. "He is just the same."

"And did you succeed in getting a nurse?"

"Yes. Dr. Winston's here too.... Now, the Mrs. said to bring you both in for a hot breakfast."

Mary Eliska was so excited that she did not see how she could possibly eat, but when she realized that the surgeon must take time for something, she finally agreed. But first she tiptoed in for a look at her father, and gave him a kiss that was really a prayer. A white-clad nurse smiled at her, and she believed hopefully that all was well.

The inaction, the weary, tense waiting of the next two hours was more difficult for Mary Eliska than her flight to Louisiana, alone in the darkness. She had nothing to do. Sleep was out of the question, yet she was terribly tired. But she could not sit still; aimlessly she followed Mrs. Cates around, begging for work. At last the good woman, realizing that the girl could not rest, set her to washing dishes and preparing vegetables for the noon-day meal.

But finally the operation was over, and Mary Eliska's heart stood still as she heard Dr. Winston coming out of her father's room. Suppose it had all been in vain! She covered her face with her hands, she dared not trust herself to look into his eyes, that would tell her, before he could utter the words, whether her father had lived.

And then came the glorious news that set her heart to singing as if the whole world had been recreated in joy and happiness:

"Your father is doing nicely, Mary Eliska.... Dr. Lineaweaver believes that he will get well."

Now the tears came in floods, tears of thankfulness and gladness, and she hugged Mrs. Cates in her ecstasy. "It was a wonderful operation," continued Dr. Winston. "Dr. Lineaweaver is the greatest surgeon I have ever had the honor to watch."

"Thank God! Thank God!" murmured Mrs. Cates, reverently.... "And now, honey, you must go and get some sleep!"

"Not 'til I've thanked Dr. Lineaweaver!" protested Mary Eliska, and she ran off like a happy child, unmindful of the terrible strain she had just been through.

Chapter 5.21
Honors for Mary Eliska

When Mary Eliska was permitted, the following day, to go in to see her father, she found him conscious, but she knew from his expression that he was suffering severe pain. However, he managed a feeble smile as she entered, that sent a surge of joy to her heart.

"Daddy!" she exclaimed, her voice choked with thankfulness, "you are going to get well!"

He gave an almost imperceptible nod.

"Yes, dear, thanks to you," he managed to murmur.

"You mean thanks to the Pursuit—and to Dr. Lineaweaver," she corrected. She wanted to add Ted Mackay's name to the list, but she felt it would not be wise.

Her father smiled; it was like Mary Eliska to disclaim any credit for herself.

"I phoned Aunt Polly last night," she added, "and she is coming out in a couple of days."

"Well, don't let her make a fuss over me," was his unexpected reply.

Mary Eliska squeezed his hand jubilantly; he was talking like himself again!

She did not stay with him long—the nurse thought fifteen minutes was enough—but she was satisfied. Now that she felt sure he was getting better, time no longer hung heavy on her hands. There was so much to do at the ranch—so many activities that she enjoyed. Hiking, fishing, riding horseback, even helping Cates with the kitchen garden or driving the battered Ford into Fort Worth on errands.

Her aunt arrived a few days later, bringing a trunk as usual. Mary Eliska laughed at the idea of carrying so many clothes to a ranch—she practically lived in her old riding-breeches and khaki shirt-waists—but Mary Eliska could not be comfortable unless she was perfectly dressed. "Mary Eliska, my darling!" exclaimed the older woman, as they kissed each other. "Think how near I came to losing you!"

"Oh, no, Aunt Polly, you mustn't say that! Even though Jax and I were stranded, there was no danger of our dying. We could have hiked the whole way home, if it had been necessary."

"But you *almost* had a serious accident!»

"Well, we didn't. And since my plane saved Daddy's life, you're converted to them now, aren't you?" pleaded the girl.

"I do think they're useful," admitted the other. "And I really believe that you are an exceptionally fine pilot, my dear."

"It's awfully sweet of you to say that, Aunt Polly.... But don't let's talk about it anymore. Come in and see Daddy. He's expecting you."

Mary Eliska was amazed and delighted to find that her brother's progress had been so rapid, and she began to talk immediately about taking him back to Green Falls with her, in a week or so. He could bring his nurse with him, perhaps charter a private car. "Must we go back so soon, Aunt Polly?" asked Mary Eliska. "I love it here!"

"It's too wild for me," replied Mary Eliska. "And too lonely. Besides, we have to be on hand for Field Day. It's the biggest event of the summer at Green Falls."

"All right," agreed Mary Eliska pleasantly. "Whatever you say."

"By the way, did you tell your father about finding the necklace? When Jax Gray came home with it, I thought Kitty Clavering'd go crazy! Such a queer circumstance, too—you girls finding it the way you did!"

"No, I didn't tell Daddy yet," replied Mary Eliska, blushing. She had been afraid to bring Ted's name, or his father's, into the conversation with her father, when he was still so ill.

"You see, Daddy," she explained, turning to him, as he lay there quietly on his bed, "Jax and I were taking a trip in the Pursuit, and something went wrong with the motor, forcing us to land in a desolate spot. After our picnic supper, while Jax and I went swimming, we—

we—came upon a wrecked plane, and—and—two dead men. The two thieves!" She paused, but suddenly remembered that her aunt did not know that one of the men was Ted's father, for that fact had been ascertained after Jax Gray left. "And we got the necklace!"

"Whew!" exclaimed Mr. Stricklin, in amazement at their luck, and horror at the experience. "Pretty sickening for you two girls! But, by the way, did the other fellow have red hair?"

"Yes, he did. Though Jax and I only saw him from a distance. We didn't want to go too near, for luckily the necklace was in the man's coat beside the wreck, and the bodies were some distance away." Seeing that the subject was unpleasant to Mary Eliska, Mr. Stricklin never mentioned it to her again during her entire visit. Three weeks passed happily, and her father was sitting up in his chair, when her aunt's restlessness became so apparent that Mary Eliska was willing to go back to Green Falls.

"You see I'm on the committee for Field Day, my dear," explained Mary Eliska, apologetically. "Besides, I hope you can take part in the events."

"How could I, Aunt Polly? I'm not in practice for golf or tennis, or any of the contests. I'm afraid I'd be a joke."

"I thought perhaps you might enter the airplane competitions," suggested her aunt, to Mary Eliska's consternation.

"Do you really mean it, Aunt Polly?" cried the girl, in delight. "Why, I'd adore that!"

"Well, we'll see what the program calls for. If it isn't anything too dangerous, like parachute jumping.... And another thing—it is very important for you to be on hand, because Jax Gray is planning a surprise that you don't want to miss."

"Is she going to announce her engagement to Ralph Clavering, or Harriman Smith?"

"Not that I know of! She isn't engaged to Ralph, is she?"

"She wasn't when I last saw her. But absence often lends enchantment, you know!"

Mary Eliska looked searchingly into her niece's eyes, but she could see only laughter in them. "Wouldn't you mind a bit, Mary Eliska, if Jax Gray married Ralph?" she inquired.

"Yes, certainly I'd mind," replied the girl seriously, "I don't think Ralph—or any other boy we know—is good enough for Jax!"

"Oh, is that all?"

"Yes, that's all. Marriage is too serious for either of us—yet.... Now tell me, Auntie, what you meant by that surprise!"

"You wait and see! It's something you'll like."

Mary Eliska thought perhaps it was the delightful party that greeted her when she landed, three days later, at Green Falls. All of the old crowd were there to welcome her—Jax Gray and Dot Crowley, the two Claverings, Jim Valier and Harriman Smith, Sara Wheeler, Sue Emery, Maurice Stetson, and Joe Sinclair. They presented her with a beautiful little silver airplane, a model for her desk, which served a useful purpose as a stamp-box. Mary Eliska, who had arrived the day before by train, had arranged an elaborate dinner for the whole party.

There was so much to talk about—the championships the young people were hoping to win, the airplane stunts for which two noted flyers had been engaged, the contests in flying that anyone with a private pilot's license might enter. In this last event they were all hoping to star Mary Eliska.

"Even a race, Mary Eliska," said Ralph, who seemed to have forgotten all about their quarrel. "You'll enter, won't you?"

"Yes, indeed!" replied the girl, her eyes shining with anticipation. "Aunt Polly has already given her consent."

Thinking there had been enough talking and too little dancing, Kitty Clavering suggested that they turn on the radio. She was wearing her pearl necklace, and rushing over every few minutes to kiss Mary Eliska or Jax Gray, in appreciation of their having recovered it. "This is to be our last party, for almost a week," she said. "Ralph says we all have to go in training— though I'd never win anything if I trained for years. But I can't do much, with all the rest of you practicing tennis and golf and swimming every minute, and going to bed at ten o'clock! So let's make this party good!" The evening passed happily, and no one but Kitty seemed to resent the fact that they gave up social activities and late hours for a few days. They all worked seriously at their own particular sports, and Mary Eliska practiced loops and speeding with her plane.

Labor Day dawned, hot but clear—splendid weather for the out-door event of the season. The Casino and the grounds around it were gayly decorated for the fête; a band supplied music whenever there was a lull, and refreshment-booths everywhere offered an opportunity for the guests to eat outside, if they did not prefer the more formal luncheon and dinner served at the restaurant.

Golf tournaments, swimming races and diving contests were on the program for the morning, and the finals in tennis were to be played off soon after lunch. Then came archery and quoits, drills by the Boy Scouts and a pageant by the Girl Scouts. The last thing before supper was the exhibition of flying.

Mary Eliska had decided not to go to the grounds in the morning, for she wanted to have a mechanic inspect her plane, to ascertain that everything was just right before her participation in the most spectacular event of the day. She arrived soon after luncheon in the Pursuit, leaving it at the runway behind the grounds, and strolling over to the tennis matches, watched Ralph capture the men's singles' cup, and Dot Crowley take the women's.

She found the archery contest interesting, and almost wished she had entered, for her father had taught her the art of the bow. However, on the whole she was satisfied to concentrate all her energy upon flying.

The acrobatics came first on the program; two aviators of considerable repute in their profession had been advertised, although their names had not yet been divulged. What was Mary Eliska's amazement, when she heard Edward Mackay and Sam Hunter being introduced by the chairman! This had been her aunt's doing, no doubt, for the latter was on the committee. Was this the surprise she had so mysteriously mentioned, and if so, what was Jax Gray's part in it? A hush fell over the huge throng as they watched the two flyers ascend into the air and demonstrate all sorts of stunts for their amusement. The falling leaf, the

Immelman turn, the inside loop, and the much more difficult outside loop—and a number of others to which even Mary Eliska could not give a name. Then finally, from a height of five thousand feet, Ted Mackay stepped off in a parachute and came safely to the ground.

While she had been watching these skillful yet dangerous performances, Mary Eliska's heart beat fast with excitement, her breath came in little gasps of fear or relief, as the stunt began fearfully or ended in safety. But now that her own turn was coming, she was surprisingly calm and self-possessed.

With five other amateur flyers, all of whom were young men, she taxied along the runway and took off into the air, mounting to fifteen hundred feet, carefully keeping clear of her opponents. The looping began; she completed one inside loop after another, until she had scored six. Then she realized that she was too near the ground to take a chance with another, and it was too late to ascend again. With the wisdom of an Earhart or a Lindbergh, who never sacrifices safety for the sake of foolish publicity, she cautiously landed. A few minutes later the other planes all came down. Only one pilot, a college boy whom she had just met, scored over her by completing ten loops. After a short interval of rest, the signal that was to start the race was given, and a moment later the gun went off, and six planes ascended again, this time aiming for speed.

As the Pursuit soared smoothly upward and then straight ahead, Mary Eliska experienced a great surge of pride—not for herself, but for her wonderful little plane. It was almost as if it were a living thing, like a beloved horse. So light, so easy to guide, so sure of its power! On and on it sped, forging its way ahead, passing now one plane and then another until it came abreast of the leader. The thrill, the intoxication of the race took possession of the young aviatrix, and she urged it on to its fullest speed. Now she was passing the one that had looked like the winner from the first! The shouts of her friends below were inaudible to her, but she could feel their applause in her heart. In another second the gun went off with a loud explosion which even the pilots could hear. The race was over; Mary Eliska, the only feminine entry, had won!

Her friends, even acquaintances and strangers, almost mobbed her when she finally landed. And the college boy who had come in second was nicest of all. He and Ralph, forming a seat with their hands, carried her high above their shoulders, through the crowd to the Casino where the prizes were to be awarded.

Two cups had been provided as a reward for the looping and the racing, and, amid the applause of hundreds, Mary Eliska and her new friend received them. But that was not all; the chairman held up his arm for silence.

"I have another privilege!" he shouted, and the people suddenly became quiet. "Our club, which among other things fosters aviation for useful purposes, and is always on the lookout for deeds of courage which result in the saving of life, wishes to make an award for such an action. We have discovered, entirely unknown to her, that Mary Eliska made a record flight to bring a noted surgeon to her dying father, in time to perform the operation that saved his life. I therefore take great pleasure in awarding this medal to Mary Eliska, of Green Falls!"

A deep wave of color surged over the girl's face as she listened to her own name in connection with the speaker's words. Was it possible that this great honor should come to her, when she had merely performed her duty, and been thankful to be able to do it? Her knees shook, her eyelids fluttered, as she blushingly stepped forward again. But she caught sight of Jax Gray among the crowd—Jax, who had arranged this as her surprise—and then she saw her aunt, with Ted beside her, and she suddenly felt at ease, and smiled. It was over at last, the applause and the con gratulations, and Mary Eliska was walking with these three back to her plane when she noticed a wheelchair, pushed by a white-clad nurse. It must be—it was—her father!

"Daddy!" she cried, pushing her way through the crowd to him. "You are here! How wonderful!"

"It is you who are wonderful, my dear girl!" he returned. "I am prouder than I have ever been in my life!"

"Daddy—" she lowered her voice—"you don't mind my being with Ted Mackay? Because Aunt Polly——"

"Of course not!" he interrupted. "I know all about the boy's part in saving you—your aunt told me. I—I—am ready to admit I was wrong. You will forgive me?"

"Why, of course!" She smiled joyfully; there was so much to be happy about now. "And may I have him for a friend?" she asked, timidly.

"So long as you don't marry him—or anybody else—for a long time!" Her reply was reassuring: "I won't, Daddy dear! My career as a flyer has only just begun!"

CHAPTER 6

The Ocean Flight Mystery

Chapter 6.1
In the Fog

"My girl, you are in perfect physical condition," announced pleasant-faced Dr. Tinsley, who had served as the Stricklin family physician for years. "I can't picture anybody in more radiant health."

"I thought so," smiled Mary Eliska, the pretty aviatrix who had been flying her Arrow biplane for the last three months. "But Aunt Polly wanted to make sure, before I go any further with aviation."

"Yes, of course, she's right. And what are you planning now?"

"A thorough course at a good ground school, so that I can get a transport license—that ranks the highest, you know. I—I haven't decided on any particular school yet, because Aunt Polly still opposes the idea. She wants me to have a coming-out party instead, like the other girls in Spring City. So I'm waiting for Daddy to come home."

"And if I'm a judge your daddy will let you go to the school," said the doctor admiringly. "I heard all about how you saved his life with your plane!"

"Oh, no!" protested Mary Eliska, modestly. "It was that wonderful surgeon—Dr. Lineaweaver—who did that. I was merely lucky enough to be able to get him in time."

The doctor chuckled.

"Well, luck or no luck, you made a long flight alone at night. I think it was marvelous. You can't tell me anything bad about the young people today. To my mind, they're finer and braver than they were in my day! And that's something from an old man...

"Well, good-by, Mary Eliska, and good luck! I suppose you're not flying anywhere today?"

"Oh, no! It's too foggy."

She opened the door of the waiting-room that led to the porch, and it seemed immediately as if the fog rushed right into the house. It was damp and penetrating, and so dense that it hid the doctor's gate from view.

Mary Eliska stepped out on the porch, and almost bumped into a woman with a small child in her arms. The stranger seemed almost to appear from nowhere, out of the obscurity of the fog. "Oh, you must excuse me!" she cried, excitedly. "I'm that worried I can't see where I'm headed!"

"It was just as much my fault," replied Mary Eliska. "Or really, it wasn't either's," she added. "We'll blame it on the fog."

But the other did not seem to be listening, and looking closely at her, Mary Eliska saw how deeply distressed she was. Evidently she was very poor, for her worn blue serge dress hung about her ankles, as if it had been bought for someone else, and her brown straw hat looked about the style of 1900. But she evidently had no concern for her own appearance; she kept her gaze fastened on the doctor's face, and her eyes were filled with terror. Was it possible that the baby was dead—or dying? Mary Eliska paused and waited, wondering whether she might be of any help.

"Doctor!" gasped the woman, frantically. "My baby swallowed a pin! And I'm sure it's in her lungs now. She breathes so queer."

"When did this happen?" asked Dr. Tinsley, gently taking the child in his arms, and motioning Mary Eliska to come back into the house.

"Last week." The woman started to cry, and sympathetically, hardly realizing what she was doing, Mary Eliska put her arm about her.

"But why did you wait all this time to come to a doctor?" inquired the elderly man, trying to soften his disapproval by a kindly tone.

"Because," stammered the other, between her sobs, "because my mother thought it would be all right. One of my brothers swallowed a tack when he was little, and nothing happened. And—we live out in the country, and we're so awful poor!"

"I'm afraid it's too late now," sighed the doctor. "I'll make an examination, of course, but if the pin is lodged in the child's lung, there is nothing I, or anybody else—except that surgeon in Philadelphia—could do. And he's too far away."

The tears rolled down the woman's face, and the tiny little girl—about two years old, Mary Eliska judged—seemed almost to realize the death sentence, for she opened her blue eyes and uttered a pitiful little moan. And, strangely enough, she reached out her tiny hand towards Mary Eliska.

"You precious baby!" exclaimed the tender-hearted girl, touching her hot little fingers. "You are so sweet!"

It seemed almost as if the little girl tried to smile, and at this pathetic effort the distracted mother broke out into convulsive sobs, hiding her head on Mary Eliska's shoulder.

"She's my only girl!" she moaned. "I have three boys, but this baby has always been nearest to me.... My—my little bit of Heaven!"

Silently, sympathetically, the doctor laid the child down on his table in the office, and got out his instruments, while Mary Eliska drew the heart-broken mother to a chair near-by.

"It is as you feared," he said, finally. "There is nothing I can do."

"But—this doctor in Philadelphia——?" began the woman, seizing the one ray of hope he had mentioned. "Is the carfare there very much? Oh, sir, if you could only lend me some money to go, I'd work my fingers to the bone to pay you back!"

Dr. Tinsley shook his head sadly. "I'd be glad to lend you the money, my good woman," he said, "but it wouldn't be a bit of use. The journey would take too long; the child can't live more than a few hours."

A shiver of horror crept over Mary Eliska as she saw the baby's pitiful breathing, and the mother's utter despair. Turning to the window she glanced out at the fog, thinking rapidly.... Should she offer to take them, when it was only a chance at best—a chance in more ways than one? A few hours, the doctor said, were all that the baby had to live.... Suppose Mary Eliska could get through the fog with her Arrow, would the trip be all in vain? Would she be risking her own life, to watch the child die in her mother's arms?... Yet something inside of her compelled her to offer her services; she would be less than human if she didn't try to do something.

"I will take you and the baby in my plane, Mrs.——" she said.

"Beach," supplied the woman, unable to grasp what Mary Eliska meant.

"Oh, no! No, my dear!" protested Dr. Tinsley, immediately. "That would not be wise. It would mean risking two good lives to save one that is almost past hope.... No, you mustn't do that—in this fog."

"I—I don't know what you mean," faltered Mrs. Beach. "An airplane?"

"Yes, yes," explained Mary Eliska, hastily. "I am a pilot, and I have a plane of my own. I will take you and the baby to Philadelphia."

"You mean that?" cried the woman, hysterically.

"Yes, of course I do. Come over to my house with me while I get ready."

"Mary Eliska, I don't approve of this," interrupted Dr. Tinsley. "This fog—your father— your aunt—I thought you had too much good sense to take foolish risks."

"Not when it is a case of life or death," answered the girl, quietly. "Come, Mrs. Beach! There isn't a moment to be lost."

She managed to smile at the doctor, who stood in the doorway, watching their departure, torn between his feeling of fear for Mary Eliska in the fog, and his admiration for her brave, generous spirit.

"Then good luck to you!" he called, as they went cautiously towards the gate.

"My husband is here in the buggy," said Mrs. Beach to Mary Eliska, as they reached the street. "I must stop and tell him."

"You are sure you are not afraid?"

"No! I believe in you, Miss! And, oh, I'd risk anything to save my little girl.... Besides, I've always wanted to go up in an airplane."

After a word of explanation to the astonished man in the rickety old carriage, Mrs. Beach followed Mary Eliska across the street to the girl's lovely home. It was a charming colonial house, much too large for two people, as Mary Eliska, Mary Eliska's aunt, always said. For the girl's father was scarcely ever there, except for over-night visits.

Mrs. Beach, who under ordinary circumstances would have been impressed with its splendor, now hardly noticed the lovely house, or the beautiful room where she waited while Mary Eliska changed into her flyer's suit and helmet, and scribbled a hasty note to her aunt, who happened to be out shopping at the time. In an incredibly short interval she reappeared, her arms laden with woolen clothing—a scarf for the baby, a cap and coat for the mother.

While the gardener rolled the plane from its hangar, Mary Eliska fastened the parachutes on herself and her companion, and explained how to use them.

"You would have a hard time," she said, "with the baby." (She did not say impossible, though she believed that herself.)... "But perhaps we could strap her to you, with this extra belt, here, if an accident occurs.... But don't let's worry! Probably nothing will happen, but we must be prepared at all times."

After a hasty examination of the gas, the compass, the oil gauge, and the other instruments, Mary Eliska started her engine, and listened to its even whir. Sound and steady as an ocean-liner, thank goodness! So she put Mrs. Beach into the companion cockpit beside herself, and with a heart beating faster than it had ever beaten, even on that occasion when she made her first solo flight at school, she took off into the thick grayness all about them.

As the plane left the ground, she carefully pointed it upward in a gradual ascent, hoping that perhaps she could get above the clouds. She must fly high—it would be dangerous crossing the Alleghenies. She hoped she could depend upon her instruments; they had never failed her yet.

Up, up they climbed, but always within the veil of gray that closed upon them so completely. No horizon was visible, it seemed as if they were floating inside a gray ball, with nothing to tell them where they were going. The child was asleep in her mother's arms, and Mary Eliska glanced questioningly at Mrs. Beach. But her expression was all maternal love; no fear of danger for herself seemed to have any part in her feelings.

Everything about the experience seemed queer, so detached from the world, so unreal. A mysterious journey that was no part of everyday life. More than once Mary Eliska wondered whether they were not flying unevenly, perhaps upside down! Oh, if she only had a gyroscopic pilot, that marvelous little instrument that would assure an even keel!... She would ask her father to give her one for Christmas—if she lived 'til then! She smiled in a detached way; she thought of herself almost as another person, in a book or a play.

The plane was evidently dipping. Suddenly, with that sixth sense with which every good pilot is equipped, she felt a stall coming on. It was a sort of sinking sensation; then the ailerons on the end of the wings failed to function. She pushed the stick frantically from side to side—with no response! In that brief moment she glanced again at her companion, so absorbed in her child, and she knew that the mother would not mind going to her death if the baby could not live.

But Mary Eliska meant to do everything in her power to save them all. She had been in difficulties before, and she knew how to overcome them, if it were humanly possible. Fortunately she was flying high, so she immediately pushed the nose of the Pursuit forward and dropped the plane three hundred feet to regain speed. And then, oh, what a gorgeous feeling of relief swept over her, as she succeeded in coming out of that stall! The plane was now flying evenly. Her gasp of thankfulness was audible, but the woman beside her did not even notice. "Maybe I'm not glad Daddy bought me an open plane!" she thought, as she flew steadily onward. "If I couldn't feel the wind in my face.... Oh, you dear Arrow, you have never failed me!"

And then, miraculously, the fog lifted. Everything was clear in the sunlight; all her fears were gone—now she could make speed. Onward they went, over the mountains, and the rivers, through Pennsylvania, flying low enough to see the wonderful beauty of the early autumn in that lovely part of the country. At last they came to Philadelphia, and flew straight to the airport at the southern end of the city, and landed in safety.

"The baby is—breathing!" she asked, as she watched the attendant who came forward to welcome them.

"Yes," replied Mrs. Beach, rapturously. "Oh, I think you must be an angel, Mary Eliska!"

"If we are only in time!" returned the girl. "We taxi from here."

"But I haven't much money——"

"I have. Come! There isn't a moment to be lost!"

Mary Eliska left her plane with the attendant, and helped Mrs. Beach with her baby into the waiting taxicab. In half an hour they were at the hospital.

"You—you will stay with me?" questioned the woman, trembling.

"Of course."

The great surgeon was kindness itself. Mrs. Beach, who had feared that he would be brusque, was delighted. A nurse took the baby immediately into the operating room. Mary Eliska was intensely hungry; it was long past her lunch-time, but she said nothing of it, while they waited tensely in that outer room. She had not failed the poor woman yet, and she would not now, at her most difficult hour.

At last the doctor appeared, his face beaming with smiles.

"Your baby is fine!" he announced. "And one of the sweetest little girls I have ever seen.... The nurse is putting her to bed now."

Mrs. Beach burst into tears of happiness, and rushed forward and clasped the surgeon's hand in rapture.

"Oh, I can never thank you enough!" she cried. Then, drying her eyes, she added, "And how much do I owe you, Doctor?"

The great man had been taking in the woman's appearance, her poor clothing, her work-hardened hands.

"Five dollars," he said, not making the mistake of saying "Nothing," for he realized that she would resent charity.

"The Lord be praised!" she exclaimed, reverently. "Two angels I have met today—you and Mary Eliska! Two utter strangers who do things like this for me!" She buried her head in Mary Eliska's arms and wept hysterically in her joy.

After the bill was paid, the doctor told them that they might stop in to see the baby. Following the nurse, they tiptoed down a corridor and into a children's ward, where they found the little tot in a white crib, breathing naturally, sleeping the dreamless sleep of childhood.

"She had better stay here for a few days," advised the nurse. "You can find a cheap room a couple of doors away from the hospital." And she handed Mrs. Beach a card. It was then, and only then, that the happy mother realized that she had not eaten since the night before. "We'll get something to eat first," she said to Mary Eliska as they left the hospital together. "And then you will want to fly back home?"

"No," replied the girl. "I think I'll stay overnight—to get a good rest, and fly by daylight. And besides, you will not be so lonely."

So, after sending her aunt a telegram to that effect, Mary Eliska treated her grateful friend to the best meal she had ever eaten in her life.

Chapter 6.2
Kitty's Party

Mary Eliska and Mrs. Beach slept soundly that night, in the cheap but comfortable beds in the neat little room not far from the hospital. But both awakened early, the woman because she was longing to see her baby, the girl because she was anxious to fly back to Spring City.

"Do you think that you have enough money, Mrs. Beach?" asked the latter, as they left the house together, after paying the landlady. Mary Eliska had insisted upon taking the room for the week, in order that the child might remain at the hospital as long as was necessary. "Hadn't I better give you some for your ticket home, and for a telegram to your husband?"

"Thank you, Mary Eliska, you have done so much already! But if I could borrow a little?"

"Of course you can," replied the girl, realizing that the other would prefer that arrangement.

"I don't know how soon I can pay it back, but I'll try hard!" promised Mrs. Beach.

"Your husband has a farm, hasn't he?" suggested Mary Eliska. "Why not drive in once a week with vegetables? My aunt would be glad to take them from you."

"The very thing!" agreed the woman, joyfully. It seemed as if all her cares had vanished as completely as the fog of the previous day.

After a hearty breakfast together, Mary Eliska said good-by and went back to her plane at the airport. She found it in perfect condition, inspected and filled with gas, ready for her flight homeward. How she would enjoy it today! How good the clear sunlight would feel, how bracing the air that held the crispness of autumn! She was glad, too, to be alone, after yesterday's nerve-racking experience.

Nor was there any reason for hurry this time. She could land at Pittsburgh, or some other convenient half-way airport, and have a good lunch. And still arrive home long before dark.

It was just about four o'clock when she finally brought her plane down in the field behind her house at Spring City. Gathering her things together, she made her way slowly to the porch, singing as she went along. Her aunt—her father's sister who had taken care of her ever since her mother's death—was nervously waiting for her on the steps.

"Mary Eliska!" she cried, as soon as the girl was within hearing distance. "Do hurry up and tell me what you have been doing!"

"Didn't you get my telegram, Aunt Polly?" she asked, kissing the older woman.

"Yes. But—alone in Philadelphia! I do hope you had a chaperon! You didn't go with any of the boys?" Mary Eliska was old-fashioned and strict; she had done everything in her power to bring up her niece in the most correct manner.

"No, no, Auntie!" She smiled affectionately. "I went with a woman named Mrs. Beach—to rush her baby to the hospital. And I stayed all night with her."

"Oh!" exclaimed Mary Eliska, in relief. "I should have been more worried than I was, except that I didn't find out that you had gone off in your plane until I got your telegram. And by that time the fog had lifted.... But come inside and have some tea and sandwiches, and tell me all about it."

Mary Eliska followed her into the house and briefly related her story, not mentioning the stall at all, for she made it a point never to worry her aunt unnecessarily, because the latter was so timid about airplanes that she had never even gone for a ride in the Pursuit.

"Now I must call Dr. Tinsley," the girl concluded, as she finished the last sandwich on the plate.

"No, dear—I'll call him for you. You must go right upstairs and take a nap. Don't forget that Kitty's dinner is tonight, and Harry is coming for you at half-past seven."

Mary Eliska smiled; of all the boys she knew, she admired Harriman Smith most, although he was the poorest financially of her select social group at Spring City. He belonged to perhaps the finest type of young men in America today—the class who are working their own way through college. Handsome, clean-cut, ambitious, bound to make his mark in the world! And he was head over heels in love with pretty Mary Eliska. But, unlike Ralph Clavering, another of the girl's admirers, he did not often speak of his infatuation. It wasn't fair to a girl to talk love, he believed, until a man had something with which to back it up.

"What will you wear?" inquired Mary Eliska. "Your white chiffon?"

"No," answered Mary Eliska, thoughtfully. "I don't think that would be fair to Kitty. It's Kitty's big party, and of course she'll wear white—with her pearls, so I think all her friends ought to wear colors, to sort of set her off, like a queen.... I believe I'll wear my daffodil. "All right, just as you say. But do run along."

Never in her life had Mary Eliska attended such a gorgeous party as this début of Kitty Clavering. The Claverings were millionaires several times over, by far the richest people in Spring City, and they gave this function in a lavish style. The huge house shone with brilliant lights, the flowers reminded Mary Eliska of a flower show; the caterers had been brought from Chicago, and the music was by Paul Whiteman himself, with his famous jazz orchestra.

It was all so dazzling, so bewildering, that Mary Eliska felt as if she were lost in some tropical island, among strangers. It was some time before she recognized anybody she knew, and she clung tightly to Harry's arm. He pressed her hand gently; it was wonderful to have a chance to protect Mary Eliska, who usually was so fearless.

"I wish we could find Jax Gray," she remarked, mentioning her chum, her dearest friend who had gone through school with her, and graduated in the same class the preceding June. "Jax Gray is so much more at home at this sort of thing than I am."

They were seated at a little table now—there were tables of every size in the dining-room and conservatory and library—and a waiter was serving them with the most delicious food.

Mary Eliska ate hers almost in awe, wondering whether this was the sort of thing her aunt was planning for her. The expense of it! Why, it would cost as much as a whole year's course at a ground school! And where would it get you in the end? It would only lead to more parties—more expense. Mary Eliska sighed. "Why the sigh, Mary Eliska?" inquired Harry, sympathetically.

"I guess it wasn't very polite," replied the girl, flushing. "But I'm afraid my mind is on other things."

"Well, try to bring it back. Here comes our host—with another man. An army officer!"

"I'm not interested in army officers," she whispered, but when she saw from the stranger's insignia that he belonged to the Flying Corps, she changed her mind.

"Hello, Mary Eliska," exclaimed Ralph Clavering, Kitty's brother who had taken a course with Mary Eliska at the Spring City Flying School a few months before. "Been looking all over for you. You too, Harry!... I want to introduce Lieutenant Hulbert, of the U. S. Air Service."

Ralph went on to explain what a marvelous little flyer Mary Eliska was, until Mary Eliska's eyelids fluttered in embarrassment, and she wished he would stop talking so that she could hear some of the Lieutenant's experiences. But the music had started, and Ralph was impatient to dance.

"We mustn't keep Lieutenant Hulbert," he explained. "He's to have Kit's first dance."

With a gracious bow the young officer withdrew, and Ralph turned to Harry.

"Do me a favor, Harry, old man?" he said.

"Did you call him Harriman?" asked Mary Eliska. "Why all the dignity?"

"No. 'Harry—old—man!'"

"So long as you don't call me 'the old Harry,'" laughed the other. "Well, what is it?"

"Lend me your girlfriend for this dance. I have something very important to tell to Mary Eliska."

"All right," agreed the other, pleasantly. "At least if you'll find me another girl."

"Sure I will," said Ralph, and in another minute he came back with Jax Gray Haydock, Mary Eliska's chum.

Jax Gray was just the opposite in type to Mary Eliska. Though not exactly pretty, she was extremely striking-looking; her hair was clipped close, after the manner of Kay Francis, the actress, and she always wore earrings and bright colored dresses. Tonight her dress was a new brilliant shade of green, with trimmings of silver, and silver slippers to match.

"Hello, darling!" she exclaimed, joyfully. "Who'd ever think I'd find you! It's almost as impossible to locate anybody here as on the beach at Atlantic City!"

"I know. And I've been dying to see you!" returned Mary Eliska.

"All your own fault. Where have you been these last two days?"

"Why——"

"Please have your visit later," interrupted Ralph, who still preserved much of the spoiled child in his make-up. "The dance is half over now."

"All right," agreed Mary Eliska, with a wink, meaning, "See you later," to her chum.

Off they started; the floor was perfect, the music excellent, and for a minute or two they both gave themselves up to the joy of the dance. But time was precious; Ralph might not have another dance with Mary Eliska all evening. Besides, nobody cut in during the first dance—that was an unwritten rule with their crowd.

"Who is this Lieutenant?" asked Mary Eliska, as they happened to pass him dancing with Kitty.

"A fine fellow. The kind you girls fall for—uniform, and all that," replied Ralph, somewhat enviously. "But don't you fall for him! He belongs to Kitty!"

"Kitty! But I thought she was practically engaged to Maurice Stetson?"

"That's all off. Stetson made one wisecrack too many, and it cracked Sis's dream of happiness. He isn't even here tonight."

"I can't say I'll miss him a whole lot."

"I always liked the fellow. But I'm rooming with another chap this year. You'll probably meet him at Thanksgiving."

"What's your big news, Ralph?" asked Mary Eliska, wondering whether it had anything to do with flying. "You must have had some reason for taking me away from Harry."

"You're reason enough yourself, my angel," he replied. "You look divine tonight."

"Thanks, Ralph. But that's not quite fair to Harry, is it?"

"All's fair in love and war.... But lest you think too meanly of me, I did have another reason. One that will knock you cold: Kit is taking up flying!"

"Kitty! No! Never!"

Mary Eliska could not imagine anyone less likely to care for aviation than pretty, petite Kitty Clavering, who never had an idea in her head beyond her parties, her pearls, and her boyfriends. Besides, she was so timid. Why, she was even nervous about taking her car into traffic, and almost always used the chauffeur.

"Of course there's a reason," explained Ralph.

"You mean Lieutenant Hulbert?"

"Naturally."

"But what has that to do with me, Ralph? I'm not supposed to teach her, or anything like that, am I?" Mary Eliska had often thought it would be a simple matter to teach Jax Gray, who was naturally air-minded, but Kitty Clavering would be difficult. And she'd simply die if Kitty ever sat at the controls of her Arrow!

"No, of course not. Dad has a big idea—you know how he longs to get me into business? Well, he jumped at the chance of launching Kit. She's to start a Flying Club. You know about them?"

"Yes. They're run something like Country Clubs, aren't they? Only flying is the sport, instead of golf and tennis."

"Exactly. Dad's financing it, and Kit is to take charge. Sell thousand-dollar bonds, get members, arrange about instruction. And she's supposed to run it like a business, and pay interest to Dad."

"Well, of all things!" cried Mary Eliska. Nevertheless, the idea was delightful. Just as flying was ten times better than any other sport, so a flying club would be that much nicer than a country club. "Of course I don't need to tell you that Lieutenant Hulbert is in on this," continued Ralph. "He and Kitty are working hand in hand. He's even hoping to be the instructor for a while, if he can get a short leave from the army."

"So that he can be near Kitty," concluded Mary Eliska. "But suppose Kitty drops him as she did Maurice, then what will happen to the poor people who have invested their money in the club?"

"She can't drop it. There'll be a board of managers to see to that. Besides, Dad'll be back of it. Nobody need worry much, as long as he's behind it."

"That's true," admitted Mary Eliska.

"Of course I'll be at college, but I think I can persuade Dad into giving me a plane of my own, so that I can fly home every week-end. Doesn't it sound thrilling?"

"It surely does. We'll have to get together and talk the whole thing over soon."

"I'll tell the world! I'm going to get the bunch over here tomorrow afternoon. Can you come? It's my last day home."

The music had stopped, but Ralph showed no signs of letting Mary Eliska go back to her escort.

"And will you promise me tomorrow night, Mary Eliska?" he begged. "In case I don't get another dance with you tonight?"

"I don't know," she replied, thoughtfully. "I'm sort of expecting Daddy home this week-end, and I must see him."

"But you can see your father any time!"

"That's just what I can't do! Why Ralph, I see you lots oftener than Daddy. I haven't laid eyes on him since Field Day at Green Falls—three weeks ago!"

"You may not see me for three weeks!"

"And then again, I may.... Here come Jax Gray and Harry.... No, Ralph, I can't promise. If I come tomorrow afternoon, that's all I can say."

"Oh, all right," returned the young man sulkily. He never could get used to Mary Eliska's independence—when he—and everybody else—regarded himself as the biggest catch in Spring City. He'd invite Jax Gray, for spite.

"Jax Gray, will you go riding with me tomorrow night, and paint the town red, because it's my last night home?" he asked.

"O.K.," replied Jax Gray enthusiastically. "But why be so stingy about yourself? Let's make it a crowd!" She turned to Mary Eliska.

"I prefer your society alone," interrupted Ralph, peevishly, and with a wink at her chum, Jax Gray accepted his invitation to dance.

Mary Eliska and Harry started the next dance together, but scarcely had they gone around the floor when Lieutenant Hulbert cut in. Mary Eliska was both proud and delighted; he was an older man, probably twenty-four or five, and she found him most interesting. She made him talk about the army and about flying, and finally of the club. She was keenly disappointed when Joe Elliston cut in and took her away.

She did not dance with the Lieutenant again, although she stayed until midnight. Then she told Harry she wanted to go home.

"But your aunt isn't even thinking of leaving so early, and she's as strict as they come. Besides, I hear that the breakfast we're going to get will put the supper to shame!" Harry was just as anxious as Ralph to have a good time before college opened.

"I know, Harry, and I don't want to be a poor sport. But I'm really awfully tired. I flew to Philadelphia yesterday, and back again today." She didn't say why; Mary Eliska was not a girl to boast of her good deeds. "Besides, tomorrow is a big day for me. If Daddy comes home, we have some momentous questions to talk over—which will decide my whole future."

"Flying?" "Yes.... So, Harry, please take me home, and then you can easily come back again and stay for breakfast."

The young man did as he was requested, but he did not go back. Somehow, the party no longer interested him.

So while her friends still danced far into the night, Mary Eliska slept soundly, that she might retain that radiant health upon which the doctor had complimented her the day before.

Chapter 6.3
The Flying Club

When Mary Eliska came down to breakfast the following morning, she found her father already at the table. He had a way of arriving early in the morning, for he preferred traveling in a sleeper.

"Daddy!" she cried, happily. "Just the person I want to see!"

"Well, that's nice," he said, kissing her affectionately. "I wouldn't want it otherwise. Now sit down and tell me all about your latest experiences while you eat your breakfast."

"No, first you must tell me how you are! Are you all well again after that terrible accident?"

"Much better, but not quite all well," he replied. "I have to stay away from horses, I guess, for the rest of my life. I'm selling the ranch."

"Daddy!" There was the deepest sympathy in her voice; she knew how her father loved his out-door life, almost as much as she loved flying.

"Well, it wasn't paying anyhow. But sit down, dear, and tell me about yourself. I know you were at a party last night—the servants told me, for I haven't seen your Aunt Polly yet."

"Everything's just fine with me," Mary Eliska told him, as she sat down beside him and took a bunch of grapes. "It isn't the past I want to talk about, Daddy—it's the future."

"Of course, of course," murmured her father. "It's always the future with you.... Well, what's on your mind now?"

"I want to go to a ground school. I want to be a commercial pilot—maybe even a 'transport pilot,' the highest of all, you know. And a licensed mechanic." She tried to keep her voice calm, but her blue eyes were shining with excitement.

"What for?" inquired her father, smiling at the idea of a girl with ambitions like these.

"So that I can earn my living in aviation. I want to go in for it seriously, Daddy. Not just play!"

"You're afraid I won't be able to support you, later on?" he asked, half teasingly.

"No, no—not that——"

"Of course such an event is possible. In fact, Daughter, it was that very thing I especially want to talk about to you.... I have decided to go into business."

"Into business?" repeated Mary Eliska, in amazement. "Yes. I want something to do, now that I am selling my ranch. Besides, I have lost a good deal of money in stocks, and I think it's time I made some."

"But what?"

"Importing some very lovely lace-work, and selling it wholesale to the better stores all over the country. This needle-work is made in a convent in Canada, and has never been sold before. But I have been able to persuade the Mother Superior to sell it, because they really are dreadfully in need of money."

"But how did you happen on such a thing as this?" asked Mary Eliska, incredulously.

"Two years ago—the summer you went to camp with Jax Gray in Maine, you remember—Polly and I visited you and went on into Canada. One day your aunt stopped at this convent—it's near Montreal—and one of the nuns took such a fancy to her that she gave her a handkerchief of this work. When we got home, your aunt sent a contribution for the convent, and really the letter of gratitude was touching."

"And they've actually agreed to sell this to you?"

"Yes. All they have. And they are making more. If I hadn't come along, they would have had to give up their convent."

"Of course it's expensive?"

"Yes, and there's nothing like it in America. Nobody in our country would ever have the patience to do it. Of course I have to pay a tax, besides, on every piece. But the stores are enthusiastic, they ordered all I had. Except——" he dug smilingly into his pocket—"except this handkerchief I saved for you."

Mary Eliska opened the small package eagerly, and disclosed the daintiest, loveliest thing of its kind that she had ever seen. Filmy net-work, made with infinite patience, probably as the nuns had learned from their sisters in France. It was exquisite.

"Oh, Daddy, I adore it!" she cried.

"Rather a queer present for a girl who wants to be a licensed mechanic," he remarked, whimsically.

"But I love things like this, too!" she hastily assured him. "And I can appreciate its value. Why, all my friends will be green with envy!"

"Then they can easily buy them in New York," he said. "If you show it to your rich friends, you'll help my business....

"Now, another thing, Daughter, while we're on this subject. As I told you, I've lost some money, and my expenses are pretty heavy. So I'm just taking a precaution, in case I should fail in this business, of putting thirty thousand dollars in bonds aside in your name. Just so you won't be penniless."

"That's awfully sweet of you, Daddy! But can you afford it?"

"Yes, certainly."

"Then—then—instead of a trust fund could I have the money for two purposes?" she asked excitedly. "To pay for my course at a ground school, and—and——" She stopped and flushed; her heart beat so fast with excitement that the words choked her. She was almost afraid to tell her father, for fear of his refusal. It was her most cherished dream, her secret which she had confided only to Jax Gray, her greatest ambition!

"And what, Daughter?"

"Can't you guess, Daddy?"

"No. I never know what you're up to. A new plane? One of those new-fangled autogiros?"

"No—that is, not exactly.... Oh, Daddy, don't think I'm crazy. But if I do well at school, next spring I should like to have a special plane—and—and——" She took a deep breath before she finally blurted out her desire. "And fly the Atlantic! Without a man!" she said.

"All alone?" "No. With Jax Gray. It's never been done by two girls alone. Amelia Earhart did it, but she took a man as co-pilot. But look at Amy Johnson!"

"Where is Amy Johnson?" he asked, glancing at the door.

"*The* Amy Johnson! Daddy, you must know about her! Don›t tease me! She flew alone from England to Australia.»

"Yes, of course. I remember now. But don't expect me to recall all the aviatrixes, and their stunts. I usually skip the flying news."

"But you won't soon!"

"Not if my little girl is going to do public stunts like that! But, seriously, dear, I don't know what to say. It seems too hazardous. Think how many planes have dropped into the ocean, never to be heard of again."

"But planes are being made safer every minute!"

"True. Still, I don't know—I wouldn't like to decide a question like that off-hand. I'll have to think about it."

"But you are willing for me to go to the ground school?"

"Yes. And you can have the money in your own name, invested in bonds that can easily be sold. I know I can trust you not to try the flight without my permission. You'll promise that?"

"Certainly," she agreed. "And by the way, Daddy, don't tell anybody of my plans about the ocean flight—not even Aunt Polly!"

During this whole conversation Mary Eliska had not even touched the fruit that was on her plate, and she realized all of a sudden that her aunt might appear at any minute, and would instantly jump to the conclusion that she was sick, so she resolutely began to make up for lost time. She was just finishing her bacon and eggs when Mary Eliska came downstairs.

"Mary Eliska!" she exclaimed immediately. "What happened to you last night?"

"I got Harry to bring me home early. I was tired."

"No wonder, after that awful trip to Philadelphia." Mary Eliska turned to her brother. "Did Mary Eliska tell you about it?"

"No, we haven't had time yet. But she must tell me all about it after breakfast."

"It wasn't much," remarked Mary Eliska, evasively. She was thinking of Jax Gray now, wondering whether she had succeeded in persuading her parents to let her go to the aviation school too, for the chums wanted to be together.

The first chance she had, she called her on the telephone, and learned that Jax Gray too had been successful. They arranged to go to Kitty's together that afternoon.

They reached the Clavering home about four o'clock, and found the others already there, gathered together in the charming library, about a cheerful open fire. Kitty, her pale face lighted up with unusual color and excitement, was seated on the davenport between Lieutenant Hulbert and an older girl, whose homeliness was increased by the stiff, masculine attire which she wore. The hostess introduced her as Miss Hulbert, the lieutenant's older sister.

All the old crowd were there. Sara Wheeler, Sue Emery, Dot Crowley, Jim Valier, Harriman Smith, Joe Elliston, Ralph and Kitty, and half a dozen others whom Jax Gray and Mary Eliska did not know so well. Everybody seemed to be talking at once. "Now do quiet down!" commanded Kitty, bringing down her little fist upon Lieutenant Hulbert's knee. "We must get to work! We're awfully lucky, girls and boys, to have Miss Hulbert here. She's been flying for three years, and has won two big derbies, and organized flying clubs, and—and——"

"Been in the movies," added the young woman herself, with a smile. "Only that really wasn't worthwhile," she said, condescendingly. "It's not nearly so wonderful after you have been in, as it looks to the outsider!"

There was something about her manner which made Mary Eliska feel very small, very inexperienced, very young. But naturally, she thought, the girl had a right to be proud, with all those records!

"Mr. Clavering is very kindly donating the land—two hundred acres north of Spring City, isn't it, Kitty?" she continued, turning to the girl beside her. "And my brother will write to the Government for a charter. Then we will ask each of you to put in a thousand dollars—or more, if you can afford it—and we will buy a plane or two, and put up a hangar and a rough sort of club-house."

"And will you belong to the club?" asked Kitty, as if it were too great an honor to be expected, as if she were asking Amelia Earhart, or Laura Ingals, or Amy Johnson. "Oh, it will be so wonderful to have your name, Bess!"

"I guess I could work it in," replied the other. "Though I'm usually pretty busy with my own flying. I happen to be out of a job now, but don't forget I'm a working girl!"

"Of course. But just having your name would mean so much to us! If you'd only consent to be president!"

Jax Gray coughed irritably; this wasn't her idea of a business meeting. She had taken an instant dislike to Miss Hulbert, with her conceited manner.

"I'm afraid I couldn't do that," replied the latter. "I might accept a minor office, like secretary or treasurer, just so that you could have *one* experienced flyer on your list. But hardly president—I haven›t time.»

"*One*, indeed!" repeated Jax Gray, scornfully. "I want to tell you, Miss Hulbert, that Mary Eliska is a wonderful aviatrix!"

"Oh, is that so?" smiled the older girl, as one might smile at a child. "I'm sorry, I'd forgotten Kitty did mention that one of you, besides her brother, had been flying a couple of months."

Mary Eliska blushed and Jax Gray opened her mouth to make an angry retort, but Kitty spoke first.

"Two months seems a lot to us, but of course it's nothing to anybody like Miss Hulbert, who has handled all sorts of planes for the last three years. And has actually had instruction from men high up in the Flying Corps!... Now, suppose we elect officers—two boys and two girls."

"I nominate Kitty Clavering for president," said Miss Hulbert, with an affectionate smile.

"And I move the nominations be closed," said the lieutenant. "It was Kitty's idea to have the club, and Kitty's father is making it possible, so I think Kitty is the only person for president."

Everybody seemed to agree with him; the election was unanimous.

Joe Elliston was then made vice-president, and Ralph secretary.

The latter, who had been waiting for a chance to nominate Mary Eliska for an office, spoke up at last, when it was time to choose a treasurer. But she declined.

"I'm afraid I can't stand, Ralph," she said. "You see, Jax Gray and I decided definitely this morning to go away to school."

Miss Hulbert raised her eyebrows.

"But aren't you the young lady who's supposed to be so interested in aviation?" she asked, cuttingly. "If you really cared, I should think you'd give up finishing-school, or college, or whatever it is, for a chance like this. You get a great deal of experience from a flying club."

"Mary Eliska has had plenty of experience!" interrupted Jax Gray, sharply.

"Really? And you got your license when, Mary Eliska?"

"In July," murmured Mary Eliska, in embarrassment. "But I am going to a ground school, Miss Hulbert, to qualify as a mechanic."

"How interesting! But really, Mary Eliska, let me tell you, it's a waste of time. There's no more reason for a girl to learn the engine of an airplane, than for her to know the engine of an automobile. You can't often fix things up in the air anyway."

Mary Eliska shrugged her shoulders; she had no desire to get into an argument. But neither had she any intention of giving up her cherished ambition. Ted Mackay, that wonderful young pilot who had taken her for her very first flight, and who had later rescued Jax Gray and herself from the wilderness, was firm in the belief that this was the next step for her to take.

"Then I nominate Miss Hulbert," said Kitty, immediately. "Now don't forget, Bess, you said you'd consider it!" She looked imploringly at the older girl; it was plain to be seen that she admired her tremendously.

Without further discussion the nomination was made unanimous.

Jim Valier suddenly stood up and stretched. He was so tall and thin that he had been nicknamed "String Bean," and everybody said he was the laziest member of the crowd.

"I'm all tired out with this hard work," he announced. "Let the president do the rest—appointing committees, and what not. Now Kitty, when do we eat?"

Everybody roared. Intimate as they all were with Kitty Clavering, Jim was the only one who would have asked such a question.

"We ate everything they had in the house last night at the party," snapped Dot Crowley.

"Where are your manners, Jim?"

Laughingly, Kitty rang the bell and the usual refreshments appeared. While they were eating, Mary Eliska and Jax Gray had drifted off to a corner of the room, away from Bess Hulbert, whom they both disliked, and Mary Eliska was showing her handkerchief to several of the girls and telling where her father had gotten it. Turning about to put her tea-cup on the tray, she saw Bess beside her, listening intently to her explanation.

"May I see it?" she asked, rather abruptly.

"Certainly," replied Mary Eliska, surprised that a girl like Miss Hulbert would care for such a dainty thing.

"You said outside of Montreal, didn't you?" she inquired. "I believe I know the convent you mean. 'Our Lady of Mercy,' isn't it?"

"Yes, I believe it is," answered Mary Eliska. "Why?"

"Oh, nothing. Only I've been there—I know Canada pretty well."

"Fortunately you don't have to go to Canada to get one. My father is buying them for the finer stores all over the country. You can get them almost anywhere—in any of the big cities."

Miss Hulbert raised her eyebrows.

"Quite an idea," she remarked. "Nobody ever would think of making money from nuns!" It was an insult, of course, to her father, and Mary Eliska would have replied, but just at that moment Lieutenant Hulbert clapped his hands for silence.

"Ladies and gentlemen!" he shouted. "May I say something?"

"If we can go on eating while we listen," said Jim.

"You've had enough, String Bean!" put in Dot. "Go on, Lieutenant Hulbert. All the important people are listening."

"I have an exciting piece of news," explained the young officer. "A wealthy woman by the name of Mrs. Rodman Hallowell has just offered a prize of twenty-five thousand dollars to the first girl, or girls, who fly from New York to Paris, without a man's accompanying them. You know, of course, that this has never been done. Maybe such an undertaking is beyond this club, but anyway it's something to keep in mind. You can never tell how fast you'll progress, once you start flying."

"Oh, Bess!" cried Kitty. "Why don't you do it?"

"I would," replied the girl, coolly, as if she were sure of her ability, "if I had a suitable plane. But there's no use attempting it in the poor old boat I fly."

"Everybody says nobody but Sis could make it go," put in Lieutenant Hulbert, proudly. "It's one the Army gave up."

"I understand its temperament," explained his sister. "It's a Jenny—but somehow I manage her. And I never went to a ground school, either," she added, to Mary Eliska.

"Maybe the club could finance you," suggested Kitty. "Think of the honor it would mean to us!"

"That's awfully sweet of you, Kitty dear. But we'll talk about it later. Nobody will be trying for the prize over the winter, and by spring we'll see how our finances are." Mary Eliska sat perfectly still, drinking in every word. Oh, if she could only win that prize! She and Jax Gray! But how could they hope to, against such an experienced flyer as Miss Hulbert? What a bitter pill it would be to swallow, to watch her money going towards helping a girl like that to win! If it were even Dot, or Kitty—any one of her real friends! Scarcely knowing what she was doing, she said good-by to her hostess, and followed Jax Gray out of the house.

Chapter 6.4
The Ground School

"I certainly don't care for that woman!" announced Jax Gray emphatically, as she got into Mary Eliska's roadster.

"Miss Hulbert?" inquired her chum. "Yes. You might think she were the one and only queen of the air! And it's all so silly. Imagine Lindbergh or Amelia Earhart talking like that!"

"Still, she has a lot of experience on all of us," admitted Mary Eliska. "But I don't believe what she says about ground schools. Why, Ted Mackay——"

"Have you heard from him lately, Mary Eliska?"

"About a week ago. He wants us to go to a school in St. Louis, where he says they give a most thorough course."

"Sure it isn't because that will be near Kansas City—where he is?" teased Jax Gray.

"Oh no, I wouldn't believe that of Ted. He is seriously interested in my career—yours too, for I told him that you might go with me."

"Might!" repeated Jax Gray, settling back in her seat to enjoy the ride, for it was a lovely day, and there was no top over the car. "Nobody could stop me now—after this afternoon! We're going to beat Bess Hulbert to it, and get that prize!"

"Jax Gray, if we only could! You know how I've talked of flying the ocean before. Are you still game?"

"Absolutely! But we wouldn't dare take a chance in your Pursuit, would we?"

"No, of course not. What I'd like to get is a Model J Bellanca—it's made especially for that purpose. Take off early next May—the very day Lindy flew, if the weather happens to be right."

"Where would we ever get the money for such a plane?" asked Jax Gray, incredulously. "It would cost thousands of dollars."

"Yes, I know. I talked to Daddy this morning, and if he decides to let me try it, he won't mind the money. But don't breathe a word of this to anybody! I wouldn't want Miss Hulbert to hear of it; she'd only make all manner of fun of us."

"Suppose she should get that prize," remarked Jax Gray. "Can you imagine her in Paris, Mary Eliska? Representing American Girlhood! Why, it might start a war with the French!"

"Now, Jax Gray, you're exaggerating too much. She isn't as disagreeable as all that."

"She is. She's even worse. But of course I won't say a word about our plan, except to mother and dad. And maybe I won't work hard at school, to get my own license!"

"That's the spirit!" approved Mary Eliska, as she stopped the car at her chum's house.

"Mary Eliska! Look how low that plane's flying!" exclaimed the other, as the girls got out of the car. "And look at the way she's tilting!"

"The pilot must be crazy! Why, that's only a few hundred feet up. Come on, Jax Gray, something is likely to happen! Let's get into the house."

Instinctively Mary Eliska pushed Jax Gray towards the porch, but with a quick glance about, she saw her chum's brother in the next yard, playing with a group of children. Unmindful of her own danger, and the velvet dress she was wearing under her lovely fall coat, she dashed over the hedge and dragged the children into the house.

Nothing happened, however; when she came outside she noticed that the plane was climbing again. With a sigh of relief she went back to Jax Gray.

"That was our friend Miss Hulbert," announced the latter, scornfully. "Doing some stunts for our benefit."

"No! Not really?"

"Absolutely. She waved to me!"

"She certainly doesn't show much judgment. Besides, it's unlawful."

"Let's sue her!"

"Now, Jax Gray! You are positively vindictive. And all because she made fun of my flying." But Mary Eliska gave her chum a hug; it was so comforting to feel her entire loyalty.

"All right, then let's forget her.... Can you stay for dinner, Mary Eliska?"

"No thank you, Jax Gray—I'm afraid not. Daddy's home, and he may leave any minute. You know I told you he's in business now in New York."

"Yes, it seems funny, doesn't it? I never could imagine your father in business. What do you suppose made him do that?"

"Restlessness, I think, and the fact that he can't ride any more. Besides, he told me the ranch doesn't pay, so I guess he has to try something else."

"Well, if you will have airplanes, and expensive courses——" teased Jax Gray.

"Oh, but just wait! We'll be ten-thousand-dollar-a-year women when we finish our education, Jax Gray. It's going to be a good investment."

"I certainly hope so.... Well, so long. I'll call you up tomorrow and we'll go shopping for our overalls."

Mary Eliska drove off, and arrived just in time for dinner. Her aunt, it seemed, had been impatiently awaiting her return, for she had learned from Mary Eliska's father that he had given his consent to the ground school course.

"I simply can't understand you, Mary Eliska," she said when they were at the table. "When you could be having the time of your life this winter! With all the gayety here—and even this new flying club. Why you should want to go off to a school where you will have to mess up your hands with grease and machinery, and practically live in overalls, is beyond me."

"I know, Aunt Polly—I guess I do seem queer. But to me it's just the *only* thing to do. There›s something inside me that makes me feel as if nothing else is so important—for me.» Her eyes shone with ardor. Mr. Stricklin watched her admiringly.

"There isn't anything so great in this world," he said slowly, "as a splendid enthusiasm—a purpose in life. If I were a fairy god-mother, and could give a child only one gift, it would be that. Polly, we should bow down before it in admiration, and thank Heaven that Mary Eliska is so different from most of the young people today—still in their teens and bored with life."

"Oh, thank you, Daddy!" cried the girl. How wonderful it was to be understood!

"But imagine having her away from home all winter!" moaned Mary Eliska. "Or do you think I should close this house and go and board in St. Louis?"

"No, Polly, that won't be necessary," replied Mr. Stricklin. "It would be a shame to take you away from your friends. Besides, Mary Eliska will have her Arrow. I see no reason why she shouldn't fly home every week-end, if she isn't too tired, or too busy."

"Yes, that will be lots nicer," agreed Mary Eliska. "Because then we'll have real Thanksgiving and Christmas just the same as ever. Can you picture those holidays in a boarding-house?"

Mary Eliska looked relieved, but she still disliked the whole idea. She raised another objection.

"Think of Mary Eliska alone in a big city like St. Louis," she said. "She's too young——"

"I'm eighteen now," Mary Eliska hastened to remind her. "I couldn't try to qualify for a transport license if I weren't. Besides, I won't be alone, and I won't be in a big city. The school is quite far out of St. Louis, and Jax Gray expects to go with me."

"Well, that is better, I must say," admitted her aunt, rather grudgingly.

"And you could go out with the girls, Polly," suggested her brother, "and see that they are established in some nice home, with a motherly woman who will look after them. I think the Y. W. C. A.'s keep lists like that, of eminently respectable people, who need to take boarders."

"That is a good idea."

"Then it's all settled?" asked Mary Eliska, excitedly. "When can I start?"

"Next week, I guess," replied her father. "If that is convenient to you, Polly."

So, with no further opposition, Mary Eliska set herself to the pleasant task of getting ready. The next day she accompanied her father to the bank where he deposited the bonds in a safety-deposit box in her name, and opened an account for her. One of these thousand-dollar bonds she reluctantly turned over to Kitty, for although she liked the idea of a flying club for Spring City, she wondered whether she weren't helping to finance her rival on that trip from New York to Paris. But with Harry Smith on the finance committee, she felt somehow safe. He would not willingly allow the club to spend its money for such purposes.

By the tenth of October, everything was in readiness, for Ted Mackay had secured application blanks and mailed them to the girls, and promised to be on hand when they arrived at the school. So, with their suit-cases stuffed with overalls and flyers' suits, they stepped into the Arrow and took off.

The day was so lovely and the country so beautiful that more than once Mary Eliska regretted the fact that her aunt had insisted upon going by train. It would have been such a wonderful chance to show her how safe, yet how fascinating air travel could be. Without the faintest disturbance they flew straight to the school where Ted Mackay had also made arrangements for them to keep the Arrow.

He was the first person they saw when Mary Eliska brought the plane down. He was standing there near a hangar, his helmet off, his red hair shining in the sunlight, and grinning at them delightedly. Beside him was an older man, probably one of the instructors.

As soon as the girls got out of the cockpit, he was beside them, introducing his companion to them.

"This is Mr. Eckers," he said. "He is crazy to meet two girls who want to be mechanics. He never heard of one before."

"Yet we're quite human," laughed Jax Gray. "Almost normal, I think."

"Well, you see," explained Eckers, "we have several young ladies here who are studying to be pilots—even commercial and transport pilots—but we never had a mechanic of your sex before. But that's no reason why you shouldn't succeed."

"I'm not so good myself," remarked Jax Gray. "And I may not take that course after all, because I'm not even any kind of pilot yet. But I'd like to see a man who knows more about the inside of his car than Mary Eliska does. She takes it apart as easily as most girls make fudge."

"Oh, Jax Gray——" protested Mary Eliska, blushing, but Ted changed the subject by asking them about their trip.

After a few preliminaries, such as going into the office and meeting the secretary and a couple of the other instructors, and signing up for their doctor's examination, the girls bade Ted good-by, and took a taxi for the station where they were to meet Mary Eliska.

It was amusing to find that the train was late, whereas they had bettered their own schedule in the airplane. It arrived at last, however, and Mary Eliska hurried anxiously forward, as usual expecting that something had probably happened to her niece. She was relieved to find both girls well and happy.

"We might as well all go to a hotel tonight," she suggested, "and have a good dinner, and take in a picture afterwards. There can't be any rush about your finding your boarding-house, is there?"

"Only that we begin work tomorrow," replied Mary Eliska. "We must be there at nine o'clock for our examinations."

"My, but you are in a hurry!" the older woman remarked. "When I was a girl, fun always came first."

"But it is all going to be fun, Aunt Polly!"

"Still, we might as well have the dinner, and take in an early show," put in Jax Gray. "Mary Eliska would rather stay overnight, anyway, wouldn't you?"

"Yes, of course. And suppose I look up the boarding-house tomorrow, while you're at school. You'd trust to my judgment?"

"Oh, Auntie, we'd be delighted!" cried Mary Eliska, giving her hand a squeeze. "If you don't mind, it would save us a lot of time!" The evening, therefore, was spent just as Mary Eliska desired, dining at the best hotel in St. Louis, going afterwards to the most expensive theater in a taxi. But the girls got to bed early, and left a call for seven o'clock the following morning.

The school was so much bigger, so much more organized than the little one at Spring City that Mary Eliska felt lost at first. After their examinations they made out a roster with one of the instructors, and here they decided to part.

Jax Gray felt that after all, she wasn't particularly fitted to become a mechanic, and she would rather spend her time actually flying, so that perhaps by the end of the term she might win a limited commercial license. Mary Eliska, who had always kept an air-log with the Pursuit—a record of her flights and the number of hours in the air—would not need much more time to complete her two hundred hours solo flying that was part of a transport pilot's requirements. And while Jax Gray was taking only the general course about airplanes, Mary Eliska would study plane structure and rigging, control systems, motors, and everything that had to do with the repair of aircraft. It was a big program; the thought of it was breathtaking. But, as Mary Eliska's instructor informed her, she would go step by step, advancing each day a little.

After that the days flew by all too quickly. The girls liked the house where Mary Eliska had established them, a neat little cottage that was owned by a widow, who lived alone with her two children, and it was near enough to the school for them to walk to and from it each day. They would rise early, eat a hearty breakfast and take their lunch with them, remaining away all day. After supper they were usually too tired to go anywhere; they would sit around the open fireplace in the living-room with the family, Jax Gray reading a novel, Mary Eliska continually poring over some book about aviation. Once or twice Ted Mackay flew over to see them, and took them to dinner and to a show, usually bringing one of his friends with him. But they were too much absorbed to be lonely. Before they scarcely realized it, the Thanksgiving holiday was upon them, and, leaving their overalls and their flyers' suits at St. Louis, they took off in the Arrow for their first visit back to Spring City.

Chapter 6.5
Thanksgiving

In the six weeks that had passed since Mary Eliska and Jax Gray left for the ground school, a great deal had happened at Spring City. Kitty and Ralph Clavering drove over to see Mary Eliska the afternoon that she arrived—the Wednesday before Thanksgiving, to tell her all the news.

"Are you a pilot yet, Kitty?" asked Mary Eliska, as soon as she had kissed the girl and shaken hands with her brother.

"No, not yet. So far only some of the boys have passed the exam—and Dot Crowley. Dot can do anything, you know. But I'm getting along fine."

"Jax Gray has her private pilot's license," announced Mary Eliska proudly. "But do sit down and tell me all about the club."

"There's to be a dance there tomorrow night," replied Kitty, sinking into a chair. "That's the first thing I have to tell you."

"And before the phone has a chance to ring, I want you to promise to go with me," urged Ralph.

"Why, certainly," agreed Mary Eliska. Everything was delightful—and oh, it was so good to be home! "Thanks a lot, Ralph.... But tell me, Kitty, is the club-house all done?"

"Yes. We have seventy-six members, and the most adorable club-house. Oh, nothing pretentious, like the Country Club, but we like it a lot. And we have one plane—a Gypsy Moth. Lieutenant Hulbert flies over twice a week to give the lessons."

"Did seventy-six people actually buy thousand-dollar bonds?" inquired Mary Eliska, incredulously. She couldn't believe there was all that wealth in Spring City, and the surrounding country. "No. Only about twenty. We couldn't keep to that rule. The people who bought the bonds are on the Board of Directors. We let members in for their dues—a hundred dollars a year."

"And do I have to fork out another hundred?" asked Mary Eliska, wearily. She had been spending so much money already; she couldn't begin to live on the interest from her father's gift. Of course she expected to use the principal for her course, but she didn't want it to vanish for trifles.

"I'm afraid you'll have to," said Kitty.

"Well, I'll think it over," replied Mary Eliska, slowly. It was amazing, in the few weeks that she had had charge of her own money, what a business woman she had become. "I may not join this year. My expenses are pretty heavy."

"Why, Mary Eliska!" Kitty laid her hand affectionately upon her friend's arm. "Forgive me if I seem to pry—but—but—your father isn't having money troubles, is he!"

"Oh, no. It's only that I am running my own expenses now, and I don't want to waste money on things that won't do me any good. While I'm away from home it seems sort of foolish to belong to that club, when I have my own Arrow to fly. Especially now that you have enough members, and really don't need me.... I'd rather sell my bond."

"I don't know whether you could sell it now," said Kitty. "Though of course I'll ask Bess—Bess Hulbert, our treasurer, you remember—when she flies back this afternoon. She has our Moth up at Lake Michigan now."

Mary Eliska raised her eyebrows. So this was the way the club was run—for Miss Hulbert's convenience!

"Doesn't she have her own plane anymore?" she demanded.

"No. She smashed it. It wasn't any good anyhow. And she might as well use the Moth, because the club members only need it two days a week."

That arrangement didn't seem fair to Mary Eliska, for the licensed pilots—Dot and Joe and Harry and Ralph—could fly now whenever they wanted.

Noticing that Mary Eliska was not at all pleased with the way things were going, Ralph immediately made her an offer.

"I'll be glad to buy your bond, Mary Eliska," he said, "if nobody else wants it. No reason why you should hang on to it if it's no use to you."

"That's awfully kind, Ralph. I'll think it over, and let you know tomorrow night at the dance."

At this moment Mary Eliska entered, smiling genially because Mary Eliska was home with her again, and because these nice, socially prominent young people were calling upon her niece immediately. She greeted Ralph and Kitty cordially, and rang the bell for tea. Nothing more was said of the club during the call, but as soon as the guests had left, Mary Eliska questioned her niece about their earlier conversation.

"I couldn't help hearing you, dear, and I couldn't imagine what made you suggest a thing like dropping out of that flying club. Why, it's the only thing about flying that I ever heartily approved of."

"I don't like the way the whole thing is run, Aunt Polly. It's too much Hulbert. Did you know, by the way, that Jax Gray refused to buy a bond?"

"No, I didn't. But maybe her father didn't have the money at the time."

"It wasn't that. She never even asked him! She said it was all too unbusinesslike—bossed just like politics! She hates Bess Hulbert."

"Jax Gray always did have strong likes and dislikes.... Of course, I don't know anything about the Hulberts, but I do know the Claverings, and anybody that they like must be all right. Besides, your money is safe with Mr. Clavering in back of the club. And you don't need it now for anything."

Mary Eliska smiled to herself; she still had said nothing to her aunt of her dream of flying across the Atlantic. The older woman could not possibly know how important every dollar would be to her next spring.

But Bess Hulbert was not so unsuspecting. She had returned from her trip while Kitty and Ralph were at Stricklin's, and waited in the girl's bedroom for the former to return. While Kitty dressed for dinner, she told her about her call.

The very moment that Bess heard that Mary Eliska wanted to sell her bond, she jumped to the conclusion that the other girl was determined to try for that twenty-five-thousand-dollar prize. Nor was the idea at all pleasant to her. Much as she might belittle Mary Eliska's aviation ability in public, she was secretly afraid of her as a rival. The very fact that she took almost a year of her life to study at a ground school, that she meant to qualify as a commercial— perhaps even a transport—pilot, neither of which Bess was, showed how seriously Mary Eliska must be going into aviation.

No, Bess did not doubt that Mary Eliska was saving her money for this purpose, if she needed that thousand dollars. Fortunate girl, to be able to raise the money thus easily! At the moment, Bess saw no way for her to buy a plane herself, and compete. The club refused to finance her—unless Mr. Clavering would personally back her up. But, worse the luck, that gentleman didn't seem to care for her at all! Probably he was afraid Kitty would marry her brother; in Mr. Clavering's eyes, no poor young man was worthy of the beautiful heiress.

While these thoughts raced through her mind, she had been listening with only half attention to Kitty's prattle about the dance. Suddenly she interrupted.

"I think I'd better go back to the hotel, Kit," she said. "I couldn't stay to dinner in this costume."

"You could wear one of my dresses," suggested her hostess.

Bess laughed. "Too small, I'm afraid. It's awfully sweet of you to ask me to stay, but I really need some rest—after that trip."

"But Bess!" protested Kitty. "Some of the crowd are coming over tonight———"

"I'll see them tomorrow, at the dance—maybe. Tell them I thank them for the Moth, and that I filled her with gas, and paid for her inspection." She started towards the door.

"Will you come here and go to the dance with us?"

"Maybe.... I'll let you know tomorrow.... So long, dear!"

She closed the door, and ran down the steps, knowing that she had not the slightest intention of going to that dance. If Ralph Clavering had asked her, instead of Kitty, that would have been a different matter. But he had invited Mary Eliska! It seemed as if that snip of a girl was going to take everything she, Bess Hulbert, wanted. It was ridiculous! She hated Mary Eliska. She even went so far as to wonder whether that were her real name. It would be just like a romantic kid like that to persuade her father to change her Christian name in imitation of a hero like Lindbergh.

Bess hurried back to her hotel, conscious now of the fact that she must do some serious thinking, and that she must do it quickly. She just had to raise some money—or rather, a lot of money! She could never save enough from any foolish little job she might take now. No, she would have to make some, as business men do! If she didn't hurry, Mary Eliska would soon have captured that prize.

"Mary Eliska!" she kept repeating, scornfully. "Pampered daughter of a rich man! It isn't fair! All she has to do is ask her 'Daddy' for thousands of dollars, and he comes across!

"Why haven't I a 'Daddy' like that?" Her eyes narrowed with bitterness. "Well, I suppose I can't help that, but, by heck, I'll be the 'Daddy' myself! Nothing to prevent my going into business too!"

A smile crept over her face, as she saw what looked like a solution to her problem, and she settled down into her chair in her hotel bedroom to work over maps and plans.

Meanwhile Mary Eliska entertained no such deep or unpleasant thoughts. It was so nice to be home, that she made up her mind that she wasn't going to worry about a single thing while she was there. Her aunt had bought her some charming new dresses, for the game, for the Thanksgiving dance, for a luncheon Dot Crowley was giving in her honor on Saturday. The whole holiday promised to be so enjoyable, so relaxing after the hard days at school, where she had to concentrate every second upon what she was doing, that she just reveled in the careless freedom of the coming four days. She had learned the secret that many grown people have yet to discover; that good times are sweeter after hard work, just as a delicious dinner tastes far better to the athlete than to the afternoon bridge player.

To add to it all, Mr. Stricklin arrived from New York on Thanksgiving day, in plenty of time for dinner. Mary Eliska could hardly contain her joy.

"Daddy, are you as happy in your new work as I am in mine?" she asked him, when they were seated at the table, and he was carving the turkey.

"Nobody could be as happy as you are, Mary Eliska!" he replied, smiling at his daughter's radiant face. "But I like mine. It's something entirely new to me—and rather fascinating. Besides, it's going well; the stores have practically bought out my supply, and we have to send our agent to Canada for more, in order to fill our Christmas orders."

After dinner he opened his suit-case and took out a lovely bureau-scarf, different from anything Mary Eliska had ever seen, so fine that it seemed as if a silkworm, rather than a human being, must have made it. This he presented to Mary Eliska, at the same time giving his sister a tea-table cloth of the same exquisite work.

"Oh, I adore it!" cried Mary Eliska, delightedly, thinking of her little room in St. Louis, and how the scarf would add to its daintiness. "How the girls will envy me!"

"Will you start a trousseau with it?" asked her aunt, hopefully.

"No, Aunt Polly. I may never get married, and I want to enjoy it now. Things like this help when you're away from home."

Her father pinched her ear, teasingly.

"And why not get married?" he inquired.

"The same old reason: I'm too busy."

He laughed. "And to think," he remarked, "how worried I was last summer about that Mackay boy!"

"Ted's all right," was Mary Eliska's comment. "But I never did want to marry him—only to have him teach me to fly! He never cared for me that way either—I just happened to be the first girl he had ever met who was interested seriously in aviation.... No, if he cares for anybody, it's Jax Gray."

"Jax Gray!" repeated Mary Eliska, in amazement. Yet she was relieved; she liked red-headed Ted, but he was not socially prominent, and she longed to have Mary Eliska make what the world terms "a good match."

"Yes. Oh, nothing is settled, or anything. But whenever Ted flies over to see us, he brings a boyfriend for me."

"And you're going to the dance tonight with Ralph Clavering," was Mary Eliska's satisfied comment.

"Yes, but there's nothing to that, either, Aunt Polly!" protested Mary Eliska. And, changing the subject she began to tell her father all about the ground school, and talked of nothing else until it was time to dress for the dance.

Ralph came for Mary Eliska about nine o'clock, and, dressed in one of her pretty new gowns, she stepped into his machine. "What a glorious night it is, Ralph!" she exclaimed, gazing up at the stars. "It's lovely enough to fly."

The young man frowned as he put his foot on the self-starter.

"I did think of it, Mary Eliska. Thought how pleased you'd be if I could take you for a ride in the Moth. But as usual—Bess Hulbert got it first!"

"You mean she has the Club's plane again?" demanded his companion. "She only brought it back yesterday."

"I know. It's positively sickening the way she grabs it. Yet her brother is a decent sort. If it weren't for him, I'd have raised a row before this."

"Where is she going now?"

"Canada, I believe. On the trail of some job. Well, I hope she gets it. Then maybe we won't see her for a while."

"Or the Moth either, I fear!" added Mary Eliska. Then noticing that Ralph was extremely irritated about the whole thing, she resolved to make him forget it and have a good time.

The dance was an enjoyable affair—all the more so because it lacked the formality of the Country Club functions. Only the members were present, and the crude roughness of the club-house, with its plastered walls, its long wooden window-seats, its huge fireplace, made everybody feel free and easy. Moreover Mary Eliska and Jax Gray found themselves honored guests; everybody made a fuss over them, as if already they had proved themselves heroines. The men were insistent that neither of them dance more than once about the room without an interruption, and the other girls applauded their popularity without the slightest trace of envy. By the end of the evening even Ralph was supremely happy.

The functions that followed during the next three days—the luncheon of Dot's, the dinner-party of Jax Gray's mother, the out-door picnic around a camp fire—were increasingly enjoyable, so that when Sunday came at last, Mary Eliska and Jax Gray stepped into the Arrow with a feeling of regret that they must say good-by to all these good friends until Christmas.

Chapter 6.6
Bad News

The next four weeks at the school opened an entirely new chapter in Mary Eliska's life. Cold weather flying! Figuring on drops in temperature, high winds, sleet and snow! Using instruments as she had never used them before. Practicing landing her plane in small spaces, marked off by the instructor. Learning to repair simple injuries like cuts in the wings and installing new propellers. Never had anything been so fascinating; sometimes, late in the afternoons after regular school hours, she would stay on with Eckers, watching him inspect a motor, or going up in the air with him on a test flight, 'til she would forget all about supper. By the time the holidays had arrived, he told her he would be willing to have her do some testing herself.

Usually as she sat there, watching him intently, and now and then performing some simple service, she would be absolutely quiet. But sometimes she talked of the future, of her hope of securing a good job in aviation, of her dream of flying the Atlantic.

Home, social life—even family life—at Spring City seemed far away from her now. It was with a start that she suddenly realized it was December twentieth, the first day of vacation, when she and Jax Gray were expected home. And they had not even bought a Christmas card!

Only once in those four weeks had she met with the slightest accident. It happened early in the month, one afternoon when, flying a school plane, a sudden shower, a veritable cloudburst, came up, and one of her cylinders cut out. She happened to be rather low—only a few hundred feet above the ground—so it was necessary for her to land. Cutting the throttle, she came down into a soft muddy swamp. The wheels touched the oozy ground, the plane ran a few feet and nosed over. But nothing serious happened; the propeller was badly cracked, and both Mary Eliska and the plane covered with mud, but she stepped out laughing. Minor accidents like that are all in the day's work!

As each succeeding day had passed, she was gaining confidence in her ability to cope with any sort of accident. And now, flying home to Spring City in the clear morning sunlight seemed only like so much play. She suggested that she turn the controls over to Jax Gray, to add to the latter's flying hours.

They came down in the field behind Mary Eliska's house, but Jax Gray refused to stop to go inside with her chum.

"I can run home across the back field by the time you'd have the car out of the garage," she said. "Glad I didn't bring a suit-case—I've nothing to carry but this hand-bag.... So you go on in to your aunt. She's probably waiting breathlessly to see how many broken limbs you have!"

Mary Eliska laughed: it was true that Mary Eliska expected an injury every time anyone rode in an airplane. So she hurried into the house through the back door, and skipped into the library where she knew her Aunt Polly would be waiting.

But she came upon a surprise. Her father was standing beside the table, nervously fingering a magazine. Mary Eliska knew in a glance that something was wrong; he smiled at her in a queer manner as he kissed her, and Mary Eliska's expression was like a person's at a funeral. What were they both trying to hide?

She looked questioningly at her aunt.

"We can't keep anything from you, can we, Mary Eliska?" remarked the latter.

"Please tell me what is wrong, Aunt Polly!"

"Nothing so dreadful. Only—business. I'll let your father tell you while I go to look after the dinner.... You're all right, dear? No accidents?"

"Just fine!" replied Mary Eliska, her eyes still sparkling from the fun of flying in that cold, clear weather.

Mary Eliska left the room, and her brother began almost immediately, without even sitting down.

"I guess I never should have tried going into a new business at my age," he remarked, almost bitterly. "It looked like a good thing, though—a novel thing. But conditions arose that I could never have foreseen. I'm—I'm going to be bankrupt, Mary Eliska, I'm afraid— unless something happens in the next month."

"Bankrupt!" repeated his daughter, in amazement. "But Daddy, why?"

"I'm afraid you wouldn't understand, dear—or rather, it's no use burdening you with unnecessary worries. Your Aunt Polly is willing for me to sell this house, to raise some money. I'm only too thankful that you won't have to give up your school—that that's all paid for, and I put the money aside for you."

"But Daddy, you can have that back again—or most of it! So long as the course is paid for in advance, I'll have very few expenses 'til the end of the term. Only my board—I don't even need clothes."

She had spoken impulsively, but she knew as she said this, that it meant death to her hopes of flying the Atlantic. Yet she did not hesitate; her father's happiness was worth all the prizes and fame in the world.

"And how would you live, after you finish at the school?" he asked. "It's awfully generous of you, dear, but I don't see how I could take it."

"I'm going to get a job—flying. I intended to, anyhow, once I have a commercial pilot's license. Oh, Daddy, please!"

"Well, maybe I will, if I can't see my way clear any other way. But of course it will be only a loan. That is, if the business can be saved." He had forgotten her dream of flying the Atlantic, and she did not remind him.

"I wish you would tell me just what happened," she urged. "I'm sure I can understand.

"Of course I will," he agreed, realizing her genuine sympathy and interest. "Though there is a mystery about it that even I can't understand.

"I sold all my first order to the stores in New York and Philadelphia and Chicago, as I told you at Thanksgiving, and I had a lot more orders. I even took on new salesmen for other cities, and I sent my agent up to Canada, to the convent, to rush me a new supply. I even wrote ahead to ask the Mother Superior to employ some poor women in the village, and teach them the needle-work—at my expense.

"Yesterday the blow came. My agent wired that all the work had been sold to someone else—someone who paid more than I did!"

"But how could they, Daddy?" demanded Mary Eliska. "Didn't they promise you?"

"Well, not exactly. You see I didn't know how well the thing would take, so I didn't have any actual contract. Besides, the Mother Superior probably never noticed the agent—or she may have been led to believe he was one of my men. Anyway, she sold everything. And here is the queer part of the story:

"The stores which bought from me became impatient when I didn't refill their orders, and bought from this other man *at a lower price*! He paid more for the lace-work, and sells it for less!"

It was certainly baffling; Mary Eliska tried hard to see it from every angle.

"Had you marked the goods too high, Daddy?" she asked. "I mean so high that this other man could afford to sell for less, and still make money?"

"No, I hadn't. I was taking a very small profit, because I was afraid to make the work too expensive, for fear it wouldn't sell. And there's a big tax to pay, besides, for bringing it into the United States from Canada. No, every way I figure it out, this man must be losing money."

Suddenly he sighed, and dropped into a chair, as if he were thoroughly beaten.

"So you see, dear, there's nothing I can do," he concluded. "It would be folly for me to go on, because even if the convent would sell to me again, I would have to pay this new high price—and lose more money. The best thing I can do is pay my debts—sublet my offices, if I can, for unfortunately I took a long-term lease—and get out. And be thankful I haven't lost more!"

"But Daddy, aren't you going to even try to solve the mystery?" asked Mary Eliska, her eyes blazing with anger. "Somebody is just planning to kick you out, taking a loss for a few months, so as to get the business! It can't last. Why not take my money and go on—at a loss—for a while?"

"But I couldn't hold out as long as he could. He probably has a lot more capital than I have, and could afford to play a losing game for a long while, until he had wiped me out, and gotten hold of the trade for himself. He's probably begun already to build up a trade all over the country, while so far I've only handled some of eastern cities—as far as Chicago. No, Daughter, I'm afraid I've made a mistake—I'm not the sort of fellow for cut-throat competition, as they all practice in business today."

"Hold on for a little while longer, Daddy, and—investigate!" she urged.

"And use up all your money?"

"Yes. Why not?"

He placed his hand upon hers, and stroked it gently. Then he suddenly remembered her proposed flight over the ocean, and stopped:

"But Mary Eliska, isn't it your greatest hope to fly the Atlantic?" he asked.

She choked a little, but she answered resolutely.

"I think I'll give that up. There are other women flyers so much better and so much more experienced than I am, that they'll be sure to do it next spring."

He could not know how valiantly she was giving up her greatest aspiration.

"Well, if that's the case," he said, "perhaps I will borrow some of your money, and try to go on. But we will sell this house anyway, and take an apartment. Your Aunt Polly says it's too big for her now.... But stop thinking about my troubles, dear, and go find out about your engagements for the holidays. There's a pile of mail on your desk waiting for you."

Mary Eliska dashed off, in the pretense of being interested in her mail, but in reality to get control of herself, to steel herself to the great sacrifice she had just made. She mustn't let her father see how terribly disappointed she was! She mustn't tell him how they had praised her work at the school, how she ranked far above most of the young men who were studying! She must get hold of Jax Gray, and stop her from talking.

Oh, the pain of going back to school, and telling her instructor—Mr. Eckers, who was so much interested in her project that he kept it constantly in mind, the better to prepare her for every emergency that might arise when the time came for the momentous trip! The tears came to her eyes, but she fought them back. There was no good in sacrifice, if one had to be a martyr about it. No; she must pretend to be perfectly satisfied over the affair.

She lay on her bed, her head buried in her pillow, fighting for control of herself. The unopened invitations lay in a tumbled pile beside her.

But it suddenly dawned upon her that her aunt might come in at any moment. She mustn't let her guess anything!

Then, like a refuge in a storm, she again thought of Jax Gray. She would go to her right away. With her chum there would be no need of acting. And though Jax Gray would be almost as disappointed as Mary Eliska was herself, yet the sympathy would help.

So she hurried and changed from her flying suit into a street dress, and hiding her invitations under her pillow so that her aunt wouldn't wonder at her lack of interest, she skipped lightly down the stairs, and, calling good-by to her aunt, ran out to the garage for her little car.

She found her chum lying luxuriously on her bed, sipping tea and reading her mail. Impulsively Mary Eliska threw her arms about her, and started to cry. It was such a relief to weep!

"Darling!" cried Jax Gray, in genuine alarm. "What is the matter? Is your father sick—or hurt?"

"No, no," sobbed Mary Eliska. "Oh, Jax Gray—it's good to cry!"

"Good to cry!" repeated the other girl in utter amazement. Less than an hour ago she had left her in the best of spirits. Besides, it was a rare thing to see Mary Eliska in tears.

"Yes. I can't cry at home. Listen...."

And she told the story of her father's failure.

"So it means giving up our flight—for the prize!" she concluded.

"And let Bess Hulbert win!" added Jax Gray, bitterly. "Not without a struggle, you can make sure of that!"

"But what can we do, Jax Gray?"

"I don't know.... Oh, if Dad only had a lot of money! But I'm sure everything he has is tied up in his business.... Mary Eliska, why aren't we rich like Kitty Clavering?"

"Yes, why aren't we? I never cared much before. I always thought we had enough to be happy."

"So we did. 'til something like this comes along.... We might ask the Flying Club to back us."

Mary Eliska only smiled.

"If they can back anybody, it will be Miss Hulbert. But they can't, unless Mr. Clavering does it personally."

"Well, we'll just have to think up some plan. Maybe the school——"

"No, that's no hope, because every flyer there wants backing for something, some race, or some enterprise. No, that's out."

"Just the same, we're not giving up yet!" announced Jax Gray, with determination. "Your father may pull out, or somebody may stop us on the street and take such a fancy to one of us——"

"Jax Gray, you've been reading dime novels!" teased Mary Eliska. "There are too many good flyers today—good women flyers, too—for anybody to do that now."

"True. But there must be something—some way——"

"If we could only help Daddy in some way," mused Mary Eliska. "Find out who the man is who is trying to kill his business, and persuade him to take Daddy into partnership."

"Now you're on the track, Mary Eliska!" cried the other girl, enthusiastically. "We'll do that very thing! Hunt the mystery! Why, Mary Eliska, we've got over two weeks, and a plane and two cars! Who'd want more?"

"Wonderful! And we don't want to go to all these parties and dances anyhow, feeling the way we do!"

"Righto!"

The girls hugged each other in their ecstasy, and swayed back and forth happily. Then Jax Gray grabbed her invitations, and began to make a list. "We'll go over our mail and decline everything that comes after Christmas day," she said, in a business-like manner.

"And tomorrow morning we'll go to the stores and buy some of this stuff, and get the name of the dealer."

"Then fly to Montreal in his pursuit, if necessary!"

"In our 'Pursuit,'" corrected Mary Eliska.

Chapter 6.7
On the Trail

Although Mary Eliska and Jax Gray were both greatly excited about their plan, they decided to keep it a secret. Once they disclosed it, they would probably meet with all sorts of opposition; Mr. Stricklin would consider it foolish, his sister and Mrs. Haydock, dangerous.

So Mary Eliska went home and opened her invitations, accepting those that were scheduled for before Christmas, and took an active interest in her aunt's preparations for the great day. There was a small afternoon bridge at Sue's which she could attend, and a moonlight skating party which Dot had planned for December twenty-third, and of course she could go to the big Christmas Eve dance at the Country Club with Ralph Clavering.

Nor was her father's misfortune mentioned again after her first afternoon at home. Mr. Stricklin had apparently made his decisions, and wanted his daughter and his sister to forget his troubles in their enjoyment of the holidays. Everything went on as it had at all other Christmas seasons; even the Arrow remained unmolested in its hangar, and Jax Gray and Mary Eliska drove their cars.

It was on one of their shopping tours that they were able to take the first step in carrying out their enterprise. On the twenty-third of December they motored to Columbus and visited the city's largest department store. Going straight to the linen counter, Jax Gray asked to see a handkerchief like the one Mary Eliska was carrying, which she showed to the saleswoman. "Seven dollars!" she repeated, as she examined it. "I'd have to put it in my trousseau at that rate. And then suppose I never got married!"

"You will," returned Mary Eliska, calmly. "But even if you don't, you're sure to be a bridesmaid some time. You could carry it then."

"Your bridesmaid?"

"If I ever need one. Or rather, my maid-of-honor."

The saleswoman coughed irritably; she wanted to hurry the purchase.

"It's the last one we have, Miss," she said. "So if you like it, you had better take it."

Her words recalled to Jax Gray the purpose of their visit.

"The last one? They're hard to get, then?" she inquired.

"Yes. They are made by French women, I believe—in a convent."

Jax Gray suppressed a smile by raising her eyebrows.

"Imported?"

"I think so. We get them through a New York firm."

"What is the name of the firm?" asked Mary Eliska, innocently.

"That I don't know. But if you care to wait, I'll ask the buyer."

"Yes," agreed Jax Gray. "I'll take the handkerchief if you find out the name of the firm."

The saleswoman looked rather puzzled at their interest in the name, but she thought they wanted to make sure their purchase was not an imitation, and she hurried off to comply with the request. In a couple of minutes she returned with the information.

"The name is Carwein," she said, as she handed Jax Gray her package. "J. W. Carwein & Co., Importers, New York City."

Mary Eliska carefully made note of the fact in her tiny shopping book.

"So our first stop is New York," remarked Jax Gray, as they left the store and went to the garage where they had parked her roadster. "Of course we fly?"

"Naturally. We haven't time for any slower conveyance. Besides, we may need the Arrow for further investigation."

"O. K. But Mary Eliska, have you considered snow and sleet? Remember, so far we have had very little experience in cold weather."

"I realize all that. But I've been studying conditions about winter flying, you know, and I have a lot of theory. Of course theory isn't practice, as our friend Miss Hulbert would remind us."

"By the way, where is she? She just seems to have dropped out of existence."

"Probably she has the Club's Moth somewhere, visiting her friends!" replied Mary Eliska. "I can't say I miss her. Still, it is funny her brother isn't around. He seemed so devoted to Kitty."

"Maybe he asked Kitty to marry him, and she refused."

"I don't think so. Kitty was so crazy about him at Thanksgiving."

"Well, you never can tell. But that isn't going to worry me," said the other, laughing. "But here is an idea worth taxing your brain with, Mary Eliska!"

"Yes."

"I think somebody ought to know just what we're doing, and where we're going, so long as we don't want to give our parents the exact information. It ought to be somebody who could fly to our rescue, if necessary.... I am thinking of Ted Mackay."

Mary Eliska nodded, approvingly. Ted was so capable, so dependable, and she knew he would risk his life if need be in an emergency to save them.

"You really think it's necessary?" she asked.

"Maybe not necessary, but prudent. Can't you map out our route to New York tonight, and send him a special-delivery letter? Then we can wire him from New York, if we decide to go on to Canada."

"Yes, that's a fine idea, Jax Gray. Provided, of course, we get Aunt Polly's permission. Daddy leaves Christmas night, and after that I'm under her thumb."

"I'm going to spring it on my family after Christmas dinner," Jax Gray informed her. "Everybody's in such a good humor then, that they probably won't refuse. Besides, we needn't mention Canada. Just say a flying trip."

"I guess I'll do the same thing. And by the way, Jax Gray, let's wire Nancy Bancroft. You know she made us promise to stay with her whenever we flew to New York."

"An excellent plan!" approved her chum, for she liked the girl—a fellow student at the ground school. How much easier it would be to win the older people's permission if they could visit a friend!

Mary Eliska, however, did not wish to tell her father about the flight, for fear he might suspect what she was up to, and forbid her. Accordingly, she waited until almost eleven o'clock on Christmas night to ask her aunt's permission. They were together in the library, Mary Eliska idly gazing at the brightly lighted tree, Mary Eliska looking over the pile of cards on the table. "Here's one from Beatrice Evanston," observed the latter. "Did you send her one, Mary Eliska?"

"I don't believe I did," replied the girl absently. She tapped her fingers nervously. It was difficult to begin. "Aunt Polly!" she finally blurted out, "Jax Gray and I are planning to go to New York tomorrow, if you are willing."

"Why of course," replied the other, to her niece's surprise. "But that's a long trip, and if it's shopping, you can do almost as well in Columbus. Or is it a house-party?"

"Neither. Though we are going to stay all night with a girl from school who lives there. But—we're flying."

"Flying? Oh, Mary Eliska, please don't! We're in for a snowstorm, I'm perfectly sure. I do wish you would put that plane away for the winter!"

"I can't do that, Aunt Polly. A real pilot has to fly in all kinds of weather. I really need the experience, and the Pursuit is in fine shape."

Suddenly her aunt put down the cards she was fingering and frowned.

"You can't, dear! You'd miss the Evanstons' ball, Beatrice's coming-out party. Why, it's the biggest thing in Spring City—after Kitty's!"

"But I had already declined that invitation," Mary Eliska stated coolly. "You didn't? Oh, Mary Eliska, you wouldn't!"

"But I did. The day I got home. Jax Gray and I both did. We wanted to reserve this whole week—between Christmas and New Year's—for ourselves, so we turned down everything." Mary Eliska looked absolutely aghast.

"I never heard of anything so queer!" she exclaimed. "When you and Jax Gray see each other every day in the year!"

"But this is different. This is a lark together.... Oh, Auntie, please understand! We loved this last week with you and Daddy and our friends, but this is important to us now. You won't be hurt?"

She came over and sat on the arm of her aunt's chair, her eyes full of pleading.

"Oh, all right, dear," agreed the older woman with resignation. "I suppose it's about as useless to try to keep you out of the air as it would be to keep Lindbergh.... I wish your mother hadn't named you Mary Eliska!"

Mary Eliska laughed, but she knew that she had won, and, even at this late hour she felt that she must call her chum to tell her the good news.

With sandwiches and hot coffee in their lunch box, and clothing enough to last them for a week, the girls took off the following morning. The air was crisp and cold, but it did not snow. Snug in their leather coats and helmets, they felt ready for any weather. The engine was running smoothly; it was a joy to fly, especially now that they could take turns at the controls.

In her pocket Mary Eliska carried a map which Ted Mackay had sent to her in reply to her letter, so that she found it easy to follow the course he had indicated. Without the slightest deviation, they arrived at their destination late that afternoon.

Leaving the plane to be housed and inspected, the girls made their way across New York to a hotel in the center of the city, where they sent wires to Ted and Mary Eliska and Mrs. Haydock, and changed into street clothing. Then they looked up the firm of Carwein in the telephone book.

"But what shall we say to him?" asked Mary Eliska.

"I don't know," admitted Jax Gray.

Impulsively as they had rushed into this plan, they realized that they hadn't an idea how to proceed.

"Suppose he won't see us!" remarked Jax Gray.

"He probably won't. If we tell the secretary it is private business, she'll think we want to sell him life insurance, or something."

In that strange hotel room, as they sat looking blankly at each other, they knew that they had not thought far enough. Suddenly they were both tired and hungry. "Let's don't do a thing this afternoon," suggested Jax Gray. "Just call up Nancy Bancroft, and say we'll be out there right away. She's expecting us for dinner, anyhow."

Mary Eliska looked immensely relieved.

They found the girl's home without any difficulty, and were welcomed like old friends. Nancy was one of a large family, and the house fairly buzzed with gayety. There were three other guests besides themselves at dinner, and afterwards a dozen more came in for games and for dancing. It was informal and charming; both Mary Eliska and Jax Gray would have liked nothing better than to accept Mrs. Bancroft's invitation to stay until school opened. But that would have meant relinquishing their plan, and this they would not do.

In an interval between dances, Jax Gray drew her chum into the sitting-room where Mr. and Mrs. Bancroft were quietly reading, and asked the former to give them some help on a mystery they were trying to solve.

"Do you happen to know a man named J. W. Carwein—an importer and wholesale dealer in fine linens?" she inquired.

"Why, yes, I know the firm," replied Mr. Bancroft. "I don't know him personally. Why?"

"Well, we want to make an investigation—on the quiet, if possible," explained Jax Gray. "We'd like to find out where and how he's getting hold of a certain kind of very fine lace-work. He's practically smashed Mary Eliska's father's business, and we're trying to discover how he did it."

"From his reputation, I don't believe Carwein goes in for underhand dealing like that. If he is, he probably has had one put over on him. He sells only the most expensive things, and his firm has always had a good name. He'd probably tell you right out where he buys the goods."

"But how could we see him?" asked Mary Eliska. "Girls can't walk right into an office and demand to see the president!"

Mr. Bancroft smiled. "It's been done," he said. "But I don't think it's necessary. I believe you can get the information you want from his secretary. It isn't likely he'd have anything to hide."

Just as simple as that! The girls could hardly believe it was possible, yet next morning, when they put the advice into effect, they found it good.

The secretary informed them that the goods were not imported, that they were made right here in New York state. An agent by the name of Hofstatter had come into the firm's offices and sold them, assuring Mr. Carwein that they were made by a group of French women in the extreme northern part, near the town of Plattsburg. He said he was a traveling man, and that he would return in three months' time for more orders.

When Jax Gray had repeated this conversation to Mary Eliska, they sat looking at each other in despair.

"I'm afraid our trip's been in vain," moaned Jax Gray. "Somebody is imitating the work—somebody right here in New York. Of course they can afford to sell it cheaper than your father—with no tax to pay!"

Mary Eliska's eyes narrowed. She was not convinced.

"There's something fishy about the whole thing!" she said. "Because if this man Hofstatter didn't buy from the Convent, who did? They had nothing left to sell to Daddy!"

"Maybe he lied to Carwein!" exclaimed Jax Gray. "Anybody can see that my handkerchief is exactly like yours."

"Yes! I think this man Hofstatter has smuggled the stuff into the country, avoiding the tax. That's what I believe!"

Jax Gray jumped up energetically. "Now our job is to trap Hofstatter!"

"You mean to try to find him in Plattsburg?"

"I don't believe he's there—Or any lace-makers, either. We might stop and find out—and then go on to Montreal—to the Convent—and try to catch him, or find out something about him there."

"He probably won't be back for a good while, if he has just bought out the supply," remarked Mary Eliska, gloomily.

"True," admitted Jax Gray. "But let's fly to Plattsburg anyhow, and investigate. We've gotten along O.K. here in New York. If we can only do as well there!"

"Well, it's only December twenty-seventh. We have plenty of time before school starts again."

"Now to send Ted a night-letter!" Jax Gray reminded her chum. "New York to Plattsburg—Plattsburg to Montreal—Montreal to the Convent, with the time figured as closely as possible, and a telegram to him each night if we are safe."

"Righto! We'll stay all night at Plattsburg tonight. And we ought to be at the Convent tomorrow—December twenty-eighth."

Chapter 6.8
Eavesdropping

When Mary Eliska and Jax Gray came downstairs in their flying suits, ready to start for Plattsburg, they saw it was snowing. Mrs. Bancroft, entering the living-room with a thermos bottle of coffee, immediately assumed that they would stay with her for another day.

"You girls have never flown in a snowstorm, have you?" she asked.

"No, but we have to begin sometime, Mrs. Bancroft," replied Mary Eliska, cheerfully. She was anxious to be off; the flight promised to be a wonderful adventure.

"I don't see any reason why you should ever have to fly in bad weather," remarked the older woman. "There are so many beautiful days."

"But when we are commercial pilots, we'll have to," Mary Eliska explained. "So we might as well get used to it."

"You don't mean that you expect to take a regular paid position in aviation after you graduate, do you?" she demanded, in amazement.

"Yes. Rather!"

"You young girls certainly are marvelous! I suppose you'll put the idea into Nancy's head too.... Well, if there's no use urging you to stay, I think you had better make your start. You don't want to risk flying after dark."

"Mary Eliska's even done that," boasted Jax Gray.

Hearing the taxi, which was to take them to the airport, they bade a hasty farewell and departed.

"You're not afraid, are you, Mary Eliska?" inquired Jax Gray, as they sped across New York City.

"Not a bit! Only I wish we had as good directions for finding Plattsburg as Ted gave us to follow coming here. It makes it so much easier."

"Maybe we'll find a letter or a wire at the airport," surmised Jax Gray.

What they found, however, was far better than either. Standing beside the Arrow, which had been pushed out in readiness for the flight, was Ted Mackay himself, grinning as usual.

"How do you happen to be here, Ted?" cried Jax Gray, as she jumped out of the taxi.

"I was as far east as Washington yesterday," the young man told her. "And I thought it would be nice to see you."

"Better than nice," laughed Mary Eliska. "Most helpful!"

"Come into the hangar where it's warm," advised Ted, "and we'll figure everything out."

As soon as they were within the shelter of the big building, he reached into his pocket and brought out a map.

"This is your best course," he said. "I've indicated a lot of landings, in case you need them—for it will be impossible to see the ground if this snow keeps on, so you must watch your mileage. Perhaps, though, you'll fly into clearer weather as you go north.

"Look out for Lake Champlain, then you'll know you're right. It's probably frozen over now."

He handed Mary Eliska the map, together with his Washington address, where he said he would be stationed for several days, and where he would expect their telegrams.

"One tonight from Plattsburg," he reminded them. "One tomorrow from Montreal—after you get back from that Convent. You better stay over a day at Montreal and have your plane inspected. Even at that, you ought to get back to Spring City the day before New Year's."

"And then we can go to the dance!" exclaimed Jax Gray. "That will delight your Aunt Polly, Mary Eliska!"

But Mary Eliska was not thinking about social events. Her mind was entirely occupied with her plane and her flight.

"This map is marvelous, Ted," she said, after she had examined it closely. "And how about the Pursuit? Did you give her the once-over yourself? Of course I know the airport made the inspection."

"I did, too. She's absolutely O.K. You have nothing to worry about, except the weather. I want you to make me just one promise, Mary Eliska."

"Yes?"

"You won't fly any longer than you have to through sleet and hail. If ice forms on your wings and propeller, you'll have a tough job. Even the old, experienced pilots—Army men—hate it, and avoid it whenever they can. If it starts, make a landing as soon as possible.... Yes, one other thing: When you get to Montreal, make careful inquiries about the location of this Convent—about the land around it, I mean. They can tell you all about it at the airport, and if there isn't a good big space, don't attempt to go there in the Pursuit. Take a taxi or a train."

"Well, I never had so many instructions in all my life!" laughed Mary Eliska. "But I'm going to take them all seriously, Ted, and follow them to the letter."

"We think you're an old peach, Ted!" put in Jax Gray. "We'd never be able to get along without you!"

He smiled and held out his hand. "Good-by," he said. "And good luck!"

The girls taxied along the snow-covered ground and rose into the air, where the gentle, silent flakes of snow were falling all about them. The atmosphere gave them the queerest sensation; they seemed to float suspended in the sky. It was like fairyland, a region apart from the world, and they gazed at it in awe. Then Mary Eliska climbed higher, until they were well over the cloud line, and the sun shone and the sky was a deep blue.

On and on they flew, now and then shifting controls—first Mary Eliska and then Jax Gray, taking turns sipping their coffee in their intervals of rest. Neither cared to eat. It would be more fun to be terribly hungry and order a grand hot dinner at Plattsburg.

The landing was difficult, for it was hard to see when they flew lower. But Ted's directions had been so accurate that they found the desired airport, and came down gracefully. Giving their instructions to the attendant, the girls left the plane and taxied to the largest hotel.

"Do you think we ought to change our clothing before we order dinner?" asked Jax Gray. "I'm simply starved."

"So am I. No, don't let's bother. We're dry enough, when we take off these leather coats. Let's see what we can get to eat!"

Since it was neither lunch nor supper time, the clerk seemed somewhat doubtful, but the good-natured headwaiter, smiling at their aviation costumes, said he would see to it at once. He put them into a little alcove just off the lobby, behind some big plants, where they would not be stared at, and served them a delicious hot dinner, cooked especially for them.

How good it tasted! It seemed as if nothing had ever been so satisfying. They enjoyed every mouthful. Indeed, the warmth of the atmosphere and the food made them feel so deeply contented that they did not even talk. A radio was playing in the reception room, and the hum of voices in the lobby seemed distant and soothing.

But presently, as they were eating a lovely concoction that was called by a French name, and apparently was a sort of glorified fruit pudding, they heard two voices close to them, near and distinct, yet low. They could not see the speakers, but the voices were somehow familiar, and it was not long before they identified them.

"I think you ought to take that Moth back, Sis," insisted the man's voice. "That club may be wanting to use it."

"Calm yourself," returned the girl, haughtily. "You don't suppose any of those spoiled babies would fly in this kind of weather, do you? Besides, I have important business on!"

"Business?"

"Sure. I'm making money, Bob! Get that under your skin. I've got to have it—and I'm getting it."

"So you can fly over the ocean—after that prize?" "Certainly."

There was silence for a moment, and Jax Gray and Mary Eliska looked at each other breathlessly, hardly daring to move lest they reveal their presence. So this was where Miss Hulbert was—on business! They waited, hoping to hear more.

"Tell me more about your job," urged Lieutenant Hulbert, voicing Mary Eliska's and Jax Gray's wish.

"Can't. It isn't a job.... It's business—and it's a secret.... Oh, not so easy, either. I may be killed, or put in prison. But I've got to have money! And you won't get it for me!"

"How can I, Bess?" demanded the young man, irritably. "I can't work any harder than I'm doing now."

"You know well enough what you could do!"

"You mean marry Kitty Clavering?"

"Now you're talking!"

"Well, I won't!"

"Don't you like her? She's not bad—really quite cute-looking, I think. Now if I asked you to propose to either of those two awful girls that think they know all about flying—you know the ones I mean, one of 'em named after Lindbergh—that would be something else again. But I should think any man could stand a harmless little thing like Kitty Clavering, for the sake of all those millions."

It was all Mary Eliska and Jax Gray could do to keep from bursting out laughing at Miss Hulbert's description of themselves. But they restrained their desire, for the sake of the fun of hearing more.

"That's just it!" the unhappy young officer was protesting. "I'm in love with Kitty—too much so to ask her to marry me when I have nothing to offer her."

"You fool!" exclaimed his sister, in utmost contempt.

"Oh, I'll probably ask her, in the end. I won't be able to help myself. I've been staying away from her—sending that other fellow to give the lessons while I was away—but it doesn't help. I'm all the crazier about her.... But get this, Sis—if I ask her, it will be to live on my pay, until I can make more!"

"Then," announced Miss Hulbert, "I have nothing more to say. But mark this, Bob, and remember it, if I come to any accident or disgrace: remember, it is you who shoved me into it!"

"That's utter rot!" he stormed, forgetting to keep his voice low. "Nobody has to get into disgrace, unless they do disgraceful things!"

"Sh!" warned Bess. "You needn't broadcast your feelings and opinions to the world. No use making anybody suspect me, before it's necessary.... Well, so long! If you ever change your mind, you can wire me at the Flying Club, or at my New York apartment. I shan't be here after tonight."

In another minute they were gone, and Jax Gray and Mary Eliska sat staring at each other in silence, too amazed even to speak.

"Poor boy!" were the first words which Mary Eliska finally uttered. "To have a sister like that!"

"I'm thinking more about 'poor us'," answered Jax Gray. "From her conversation, I take it that Bess Hulbert is rapidly raising money. Money to fly the Atlantic!" "So it sounds."

"I'd like to know how she's doing it," mused Jax Gray.

"She said it might bring disgrace," replied Mary Eliska, thoughtfully.... "Funny she should be here—in Plattsburg.... Jax Gray, do you suppose she could be 'Mr. Hofstatter'—or rather, Mr. Hofstatter's employer?"

"That's an idea, Mary Eliska!" cried Jax Gray, her eyes flashing with excitement. "Only it seems too impossible. How could she have gotten word of your father's business?"

Mary Eliska was silent for a moment.

"Through me," she announced, finally. "Remember the day I showed my handkerchief to the girls, and explained all about where Daddy was getting them? Remember how interested she was—and even knew the name of the Convent?"

"That's right! I do! And she made some nasty remark about making money from nuns!"

"So she did. I was furious.... And the very next day Ralph told me she had gone to Canada in the Moth, in search of a job!"

"It's true! It's true!" exclaimed Jax Gray, jumping up from the table. "No use to hunt Hofstatter now—he's only a pawn in her game—if we are correct in our guess. We must go right to the Convent!"

"Tonight?" asked Mary Eliska, doubtfully.

"No, of course not. Tomorrow. And it's clearing up, Mary Eliska. Oh, we're the luckiest girls in the world!"

Chapter 6.9
Followed

Mary Eliska and Jax Gray went up to their room at the hotel naturally supposing that their presence was unknown to Bess Hulbert.

It happened, however, that she was to hear about them at the desk.

When Bess left her brother in the lobby, she went straight to the clerk and asked for her key. It was a fine day, promising a fine night; she decided to leave for New York as soon as she had packed her bag. But the information caused her to change her mind. "Do you happen to know the young lady flyers, Miss Smith?" inquired the clerk, for Bess had registered as "Anna Smith" at the hotel.

"What young ladies?" she asked, carelessly.

"Two girls who just flew in from New York. Mighty attractive ones, too!" He examined the register. "Mary Eliska and Jax Gray Haydock."

"Hm!" mumbled Bess, wonderingly. What could have brought them up here to Plattsburg?

"I've heard of them," she replied. "How long are they staying?"

"Just over night. Going over to Montreal in the morning, I believe."

Bess was silent a moment, thinking rapidly.

"I guess I'll stay here over night, after all," she concluded. "Night flying isn't so good, if you don't have to do it."

"Wise young lady!" observed the clerk. "If you want to meet these girls, they're still out there in the dining-room, eating. I know flyers always like to get together—for 'ground flying,' as Lindbergh calls it."

"I don't care much about meeting those particular girls," replied Bess, scornfully. "They're only beginners—I dare say this is their first real flight. Yet the way they talk you'd think they had been pilots for years.... No, thank you. I guess I'll go up now, and take a rest. Will you have my dinner sent up to my room?"

She disappeared into the elevator, and when Mary Eliska and Jax Gray came out of the alcove, they thought she had gone back to New York. When they stopped at the desk the clerk made no mention of "Miss Smith" because she had spoken so contemptuously of these young girls. "What's your idea of a way to spend our time here?" asked Jax Gray, as they unpacked their bags. "It's only five o'clock; we can't go to bed yet."

"Let's look for 'Hofstatters' in the phone book," suggested Mary Eliska. "Just for fun, because we probably shan't learn anything, but it wouldn't do any harm."

"O.K. with me. I'm glad his name isn't Smith or Jones, then it wouldn't be so easy."

Jax Gray opened the telephone book on the small table beside the bed, and searched diligently.

"I've found three," she announced a minute later. "Amos, Charles, and Mary. But what shall we say when we call?"

"Say we come from the firm of J. W. Carwein, New York City—it'll be the truth, because we have just come from there—and we want to know when he will have another box of lace-work to sell."

"Great!" approved Jax Gray, smiling at the joke. "And if we should happen to locate the man, what shall we do? Make an appointment?"

"Of course! He would have to tell us exactly where he got the goods, and if he isn't telling the truth and is smuggling them in from Canada, we can have him arrested.... But we'll never meet luck like that!"

"I speak for Amos," said Jax Gray. "I like the name. Besides, nobody with a name like that from the Bible could be crooked."

"And Mary ought to be out of it," remarked Mary Eliska. "Though of course she might have a son or a brother."

They took a few minutes to write down exactly what they would say, and began calling the numbers. But without success—that is, until they came to Mary. Amos Hofstatter grew angry, believing it was another wrong number, and shrieked that he had never heard of anybody named Carwein. Charles Hofstatter, identifying Jax Gray's voice as that of a young girl, tried to make a date with her, but she scornfully replied, "Act your age!" and hung up with a bang.

Mary Eliska took the telephone to give the last call, the number listed for Mary Hofstatter.

A rather feeble voice answered.

"Who? What did you say?" the woman, evidently elderly, asked.

Mary Eliska repeated her message.

"You want my son?" she guessed. "You are Miss Smith?"

"No," replied Mary Eliska, firmly. "But we are from Carwein and Co., linen importers, and we want to see him."

"Oh—I—don't know where he is," stammered the other, nervously. "Miss Smith knows. Anna Smith. Ask her."

"But where is Anna Smith?" persisted Mary Eliska.

"I don't know anything about it at all!" protested the woman. "Good-by!"

Mary Eliska turned excitedly to Jax Gray. "We're on the right track," she said. "But imagine locating an Anna Smith, North America!" She shook her head hopelessly.

"It wouldn't do much good anyway," remarked her chum. "This Hofstatter is probably some weak fellow, who will do anything for money. Our best plan is to strike out for the Convent."

"What do you say if we cut out the stop at Montreal altogether?" asked Mary Eliska, studying her map. "This Convent is between Montreal and Quebec, and I don't see why we shouldn't fly straight to it. We'll save a lot of time."

"Time is precious," agreed Jax Gray. "But remember what Ted said, about inquiring at the Montreal airport for a landing place."

"I know, but we can't always do what Ted says. We're not beginners now, Jax Gray. And I'm sure there will be a good place—the country is so open."

"O.K. with me. If tomorrow is a clear day, as it looks as if it is going to be, we can fly low enough to watch the ground pretty closely."

"Then it's settled," concluded Mary Eliska. "Give me ten minutes with this map, and I'll be finished. Then we can go to the movies, and buy a paper so that we'll have the weather prediction for tomorrow."

The next four hours passed pleasantly for the girls, and they stopped at a drug-store on their return from the early show at the theater, to buy a sandwich and some hot chocolate, which was all the supper they wanted. By ten o'clock their lights were out and they were fast asleep.

Soon after breakfast the following day, which was bright and sunshiny, Mary Eliska and Jax Gray returned to the airport and took off into the bright blue sky. Everything seemed favorable; they had no idea that only a few hundred yards behind them a plane was following them, a plane whose pilot had no love for Mary Eliska or Jax Gray Haydock.

"You didn't bring any coffee, did you?" asked Jax Gray, as they sped on over the frozen country, glimpsing the St. Lawrence as they passed.

"No," returned her companion. "Only some sweet chocolate, matches and about three cans of baked beans, which I always carry. I've read a lot about making fire without matches, but if we ever have another experience like that one last summer, and come down in a lonely spot, I want matches. And something to keep us from starving."

Even in the companion cockpit, which was one of the nicest features of the Arrow Pursuit, conversation was rather difficult, and the girls only talked occasionally. Sometimes they would press each other's fingers just as a joyous signal of their pleasure in flying together.

It was Mary Eliska who first noticed the plane behind her. "See what kind it is, Jax Gray—if you can," she advised.

"Can't very well," replied the other, attempting to lean out and peer through her glasses. But it was too far away to identify. "Hope it's not a thief or anybody like that," remarked Mary Eliska, recalling the other time a plane had followed them, in order that the pilot might steal Kitty Clavering's necklace.

"Don't worry!" returned Jax Gray. "We haven't anything like pearls with us today!"

"You have your earrings! And besides, we must have a couple of hundred dollars between us."

But the plane had disappeared again, and the girls gave their attention to the country beneath them, flying low enough to watch the children on their sleds, and the skaters on the frozen lakes. The winter sports looked so inviting that both Mary Eliska and Jax Gray wished they could stop and join in.

"Maybe we can do that tonight," exclaimed Jax Gray. "If we get back to Montreal safely."

"Aunt Polly wouldn't approve," Mary Eliska reminded her.

"Your Aunt Polly doesn't approve of any of this! But anyway, it's all in a good cause."

"And we've gotten along fine so far...."

For some miles farther they watched the ice-covered lakes and the snow-covered ground, and the thick trees that dotted the landscape. The vastness of the woods was a little terrifying; Mary Eliska shivered when she thought what it would be like to be lost in them, at this time of the year. Their supplies might last them a day—after that they would certainly perish.... She pulled herself sharply from such gruesome thoughts; a pilot was always in a certain amount of danger, and had no right to brood upon it. Prepare for the unexpected, yes—and then forget it!

It was still early in the afternoon when they sighted the Convent. Large and picturesque, like those of the old world, as typical of French Canada as most of Quebec. Mary Eliska gave a cry of Joy. "I'll have to circle awhile," she shouted to Jax Gray, "'til I can find a spot without trees for a landing. But I am sure there must be one—away from these hills."

Soon she was rewarded, for there proved to be a very good place—flat, even ground, covered with only a coating of snow.

Both girls were a little timid about the reception they might get. Were these nuns, living their quiet lives, used to airplanes, or would they resent the noise, breaking in upon their meditations and work? Trembling a little, but remembering their fondness for her Aunt Polly, Mary Eliska brought out her handkerchief which they had made, in readiness to show it to them as proof of her identity. Then she and Jax Gray started towards the Convent, which was the distance of perhaps two city blocks away.

Before they had gone a half of the distance, they saw children running towards them from over the hill, children probably from the village beyond. The girl stopped, smiling.

"Candy! Candy!" cried the youngsters, and Mary Eliska went back to the plane and dug out their supply of chocolate and handed it over to them.

"It was sort of nice to see those kids," remarked Jax Gray, as they again started towards the Convent. "Somehow they make it seem more alive. Oh, Mary Eliska, I do hope we don't interrupt the nuns at a service!"

But she need not have worried, for as soon as the girls entered the building they saw a group in a big room, engaged with their needles. What an opportune time to come!

"You do the talking, Jax Gray!" urged Mary Eliska. "You always know what to say better than I do."

One of the sisters came forward and smiled.

"Welcome!" she said in French. "Come over to the fire and warm yourselves."

Fortunately, both girls had studied this language, and understood what she said. Gratefully they walked over to the old-fashioned stone fireplace, where a frugal fire of fagots was burning, and a kettle, hanging on a crane, was singing and bubbling.

"Merci, beaucoup!" replied Jax Gray, to let the good woman know that she understood her, and appreciated her offer.

"Has anything happened?" asked the sister, still in French.

"Happened? Why?" returned Jax Gray.

"You were here yesterday, and bought everything that we had made. The Mother Superior told us."

"But we weren't here yesterday!" protested Jax Gray.

"Yes. In an airplane."

Mary Eliska and Jax Gray looked at each other knowingly. It must have been Bess Hulbert—in the Moth! That would explain her presence in Plattsburg. They were sure of it now.

"That was somebody else," explained Mary Eliska. "Did you see her?"

"No, we did not see her. The Mother Superior saw her. Instead of sending a man, she said Mr. Stricklin thought we would prefer a lady. And she paid more—and gave the little village children candy. Oh, she is good! We are starting a little school for the village children."

What Jax Gray wanted to say was "She is an impostor!" but she could not think of the French word for "impostor," and besides, what was the use of telling all this to these simple-hearted sisters? Instead, she asked for the Mother Superior.

"She is away, visiting a sick friend, in Quebec. She will not be back until tomorrow."

Jax Gray sighed; there was nothing they could do now. But they had found out what they wanted; it was Bess Hulbert who was smuggling the goods into the country, and stealing Mr. Stricklin's business. It would be an easy thing now to catch her and have her arrested.

"We must go now," said Jax Gray. "Before it gets dark."

"Oh, but have something to eat!" urged the sister. "Some tea and biscuits."

Seeing that these good women might be hurt if they refused, the girls accepted the invitation and sat down to the simple meal. It was plain, but good, and they discovered that they were very hungry, for they had not eaten since breakfast.

"Now let us show you over the Convent," offered another, and while they accompanied several of the nuns about the old, meticulously neat rooms, they heard the roar of a plane, making a landing not far away. Immediately Mary Eliska glanced out of the window, to see whether her Arrow was safe, and she saw another plane landing quite near. But before the girls left the Convent, the latter had disappeared.

"Now back to Montreal for the night—and then hot foot after Bess Hulbert!" cried Mary Eliska, as she started the motor. "If we accuse her of being a smuggler, and she promises to stop, and leave Daddy alone, we won't have to have her arrested."

"But first," qualified Jax Gray, "we must catch Bess Hulbert!"

Chapter 6.10
The Arrow in Flames

Although no definite results had yet been accomplished, Mary Eliska and Jax Gray felt when they left the little French Convent in Canada that they were on the way to victory. All that was necessary now was to get in touch with Mary Eliska's father, who, through his lawyer and detectives, would bring Bess Hulbert to justice.

The facts as they saw them were surprisingly clear and simple, and could not fail to convince the police.

First of all, the firm of J. W. Carwein had declared that they had bought the goods in the belief that they were made in the United States.

Secondly, the firm had been deceived. The goods were not made in this country, but in Canada, as the girls had just proved by their visit to the Convent.

Thirdly, they had been bought by a girl in an airplane, who represented herself as an agent of Mr. Stricklin.

The only missing link in the chain was the actual proof that the girl in the airplane was Bess Hulbert.

Yet all the evidence pointed that way: her visit to Plattsburg, her taking the Moth to Canada, her conversation with her brother, at the hotel, in which she referred to her business as dangerous and liable to end in disgrace, and finally her interest in Mary Eliska's handkerchief a month or so previous.

Surely no one would doubt such evidence as this! But if the police refused to arrest Miss Hulbert, it would be easy enough to send a picture to the Convent for identification. That would prove everything conclusively.

So both girls felt certain, as they stepped into the Arrow, that they had been successful, that they were about to save Mr. Stricklin's business. And this fact meant joy to themselves. Now they could plan again on their flight across the Atlantic; now it would surely be safe to put in the order for the Bellanca which Mary Eliska had set her heart upon having. "Let's don't bother to go back by way of Montreal," said Mary Eliska, exultantly, as she started the motor and taxied along the frozen field. "Let's head straight for Spring City!"

"But do you know the way?" inquired Jax Gray, as the plane rose into the air.

"Yes, I guess so. I have a map—oh, not the kind Ted makes, but good enough. We'll fly across country, and stop when we get tired."

"But it's getting dark, Mary Eliska," objected her companion.

"We can't help that, Jax Gray! It would be getting dark anyway, even if we were headed for Montreal."

"But this is strange country. So many woods, too. A forced landing would be terrible, Mary Eliska."

"Who said anything about a forced landing?" laughed the other girl. She felt thrilled and exhilarated; the cold, fresh air against her cheeks whipped them to a lovely color, and her eyes were shining. She was in the mood for adventure tonight. But when she realized that her chum was dubious, she decided to go easy. Perhaps Jax Gray was tired.

"Jax Gray dear," she shouted, "if you're nervous, we'll go to Montreal, and put up for the night. Say the word—but say it quickly!"

"No! No! I'm for the quickest way home. And I have a lot of confidence in you, Mary Eliska."

"You better have, if you mean to cross the ocean with me. We'll have to get used to night flying, Jax Gray, if we hope to succeed!"

"I know," agreed the other, as she settled down into her seat to try to keep warm.

Darkness came on, but the sky was cloudless, and the stars shone out brilliantly. Mary Eliska kept her eye on her chart, but although she did not tell Jax Gray, she was not sure where they were. Had they crossed into New York state—were they flying in the northern part, or were they still in Canada? Her goal was Syracuse; she hoped to reach it before midnight.

The trees were still thick everywhere, and they were flying about fifteen hundred feet high. All of a sudden, without any warning, the engine missed and sputtered, and stopped dead!

Jax Gray, who for the last five minutes had been peacefully dozing, awoke with a start at the abrupt cessation of noise. Just as a Pullman traveler will sleep while a train is moving, and wake up at a station, so the silence affected Jax Gray. It was positively uncanny.

"What's the matter, Mary Eliska?" she whispered, hoarsely.

"Out of gas," replied the pilot, grimly.

"Then—then—" She clutched her companion's arm, desperately—"Then we jump?"

Before Mary Eliska could reply, the motor took hold again.

"No! Not yet!" she shouted, above the welcome noise. "I have turned on the reserve supply—it's good for about twenty minutes. We'll try to land."

She circled about and came lower, but the prospect was disastrous. Nothing but woods! Trees everywhere! She remembered bitterly the occasion when her father had presented her with the Arrow, as a graduation gift, and had remarked shrewdly that she would get to hate trees. How right he was!

But she must not lose track of the time—the precious twenty minutes that might be all that were left to her in this world. Jax Gray, with the glasses, was peering down towards the ground. But there were no lights, no towns, no signs of civilization anywhere. Nothing but trees.

When only eight minutes remained, Mary Eliska decided in desperation to climb again. If they were to use their parachutes successfully, they must attain a comfortable height.

The ascent only served to make Jax Gray more panic-stricken. She grabbed Mary Eliska's arm, and held to it like a death-clasp.

"Where are you going, Mary Eliska?" she shrieked. "Are you crazy?"

Mary Eliska shook her head. It was surprising how calm she felt.

"Get ready to release your parachute," she commanded. "When we get high enough, we are going to jump. Have you your flashlight handy?"

"Yes. All right, Mary Eliska." Her voice shook with emotion.

"It'll be all right, Jax Gray dear! I've jumped before—it isn't bad. And you've been taught just what to do."

At four thousand feet up in the air, Mary Eliska gave her the signal, and Jax Gray stepped out over the right side of the plane.

Then Mary Eliska turned the nose of the Arrow up, and stepped off herself, falling about a hundred feet, head downward, before she pulled the rip-cord which opened the parachute, and jerked her into an upright position. Off to one side of them, the plane was falling rapidly, in a series of spirals; for a moment Mary Eliska had the tense fear that it might strike her companion or herself. Holding out her flashlight, and watching the ground below, she floated gently away from the plane, landing finally in a clearing perhaps fifty yards away from Jax Gray.

"Jax Gray, are you safe?" she shouted, gasping.

"O.K.!" was the laughing reply, that brought a warm surge of relief to her heart.

With the aid of their flash-lights the girls disentangled themselves from their cords, and ran towards each other. Suddenly they stopped; a blaze of light flashed in the sky, and they saw the beloved Arrow in flames!

"Oh, poor Mary Eliska!" cried Jax Gray, rushing to her chum in sympathy. "What rotten luck!"

Tears came into the young aviatrix's eyes, and she hugged her chum tightly in her grief. It was as if she had lost a very dear friend. For a breathless moment they watched the blazing plane, fearful lest it would drop on them, or set the woods on fire. But gradually the light died, and what was left of the Arrow dropped to the ground at least a mile away.

"I guess we're lucky at that," Mary Eliska finally said, shivering.

"I was sure we'd be killed," Jax Gray admitted. "It seems so much worse to have an accident at night—so much more terrifying."

They stood still for a moment and looked about them. A light covering of snow was on the ground, and on the leafless branches of the trees. In every direction the woods stretched out in desolation. The girls had not the faintest idea where they were.

"Oh, I'm so cold!" complained Jax Gray. "If only we had a fire!"

"My matches!" remarked Mary Eliska, regretfully. "My matches that I packed so carefully! A whole box.... Well, next time I'll see that they are in my pocket. Lucky we have our flashlights—and no sprained ankles. Come on, Jax Gray, we must walk, or we'll freeze to death."

"But where are we going?"

"Anywhere—to keep warm with the exercise, and maybe happen on some hut or house. We daren't sleep tonight, Jax Gray! Oh, if, we only had those blankets!"

"And those baked beans!"

"Shucks!" exclaimed Mary Eliska. "Why didn't I think to throw some stuff out before we left the plane! All the mail carriers do. If they have to jump, they drop their mail bags first."

"Too late now to think of that. But wasn't it lucky we had something to eat at the Convent?"

"It surely was. I wish we had eaten twice as much."

With their arms tightly linked together, the girls were pressing forward now at an even pace, as if they had cheerfully made up their minds to walk all night long. Sometimes they would step into thick piles of dried leaves, but otherwise the ground was hard, except for an inch or so of snow. Often they encountered ice, and their feet grew numb with the cold.

Jax Gray, who had not wanted Mary Eliska to take the unknown course, had said nothing about the cause of the accident, for fear of hurting her chum's feelings. But Mary Eliska's mind had been busily working on the explanation ever since the tank went dry. "Jax Gray," she said finally, as they walked on through the darkness, "I think I have the explanation."

"What explanation? How to get out of these woods?"

"No, no. Of the reason why our gas ran out. I should have had enough to get to Syracuse. But do you remember hearing a plane land near to ours, while we were in the Convent?"

"Yes, of course. We both saw it."

"Well, do you know what I believe? I think that was Bess Hulbert, in the Flying Club's Moth—and it was she who was following us all the way to the Convent."

"Mary Eliska!" cried Jax Gray, in amazement. "But how could she ever know we were here? Not that I'd put it past her—but how could she possibly find out, or guess what we were up to?"

"I don't know, except that she may have seen us—or our names on the hotel register at Plattsburg. People who are committing crimes are always on the watch, you know, expecting to be caught."

"How could she ever dump out our gas, in so short a time?"

"She didn't. She put a little hole in the gas tank, probably, so that the gas would leak out slowly. That would be a much meaner thing to do than to cut a strut, or injure the propeller, because either of those things would keep us from going up in the air without discovering it, and we wouldn't learn our danger from a leak without flying a while. Besides, whatever happened would happen when we were some distance away—so that she couldn't possibly be blamed! And it would be too late to do anything."

"The sneak!" denounced Jax Gray, feeling almost hot for a second in her anger. "You're right, Mary Eliska—I'm sure you are! But really, it was intended murder!"

"Probable murder—if we couldn't make a landing or jump. But she thinks we are so inexperienced that we couldn't do either.... Yes, I really believe Miss Hulbert thinks we're dead now!"

"And won't she get fooled!" exulted Jax Gray. "Once we get back to civilization, we'll do plenty to her!"

"If we get back to civilization," said Mary Eliska, with the first note of despair creeping into her voice. Their feet were so cold, they began to ache dreadfully, and the woods were as dense and as hopeless as when they first began to walk. They slackened their pace, until Jax Gray's feet fairly seemed to drag. She stopped abruptly.

"I just can't go on, Mary Eliska," she sighed. "My feet hurt so terribly!"

"I know," answered her companion, sympathetically. "We might take off our shoes and rub them with snow. But if we once stop, we'll never be able to start again—and then we'll surely freeze."

It was a gruesome alternative; they looked at each other in dismay.

"Let's go very slowly, and hang on to each other," urged Mary Eliska. "The night can't last forever, and the sunshine will bring warmth."

"It's the longest night I ever knew," said Jax Gray, drearily. "But morning will be worse, because we'll be that much hungrier."

Mary Eliska pressed her hand; there was no use trying to cheer the other girl with hopes, that she was in no mood to believe. So they went on doggedly.

For perhaps half an hour they continued in silence; then once again Jax Gray stopped abruptly, her hand rigid in Mary Eliska's. There were footsteps behind them!

"A bear!" she whispered, in fright.

Pulling her cautiously aside, Mary Eliska broke off a stick from a tree, and turned about to face the enemy. There was no use trying to run—why they could hardly hobble. And in the darkness, what hope was there of finding a tree to climb?

To her intense amazement, she saw nothing, and she dared not turn on her flashlight. Tensely she waited, until a shot rang out in the woods and broke the stillness of the night. A gun at least meant a human hand, and both girls immediately let out a piteous cry of "Help!"

"Yo—ho!" came the welcome, answering reply!

Chapter 6.11
Prisoners

When the shot of the gun rang through the woods, the startled girls heard scampering feet behind them, and knew that the animal, whatever it was, had been frightened away. Again they had had a marvelous escape, for they might have been wounded by the unseen hunter's gun. What irony it would have been, to jump from an airplane in parachutes, only to be killed by a human hand!

Desperately they clung to each other, satisfied now by the answering call that there would be more shots until they were located. Rescue was surely at hand; the question now arose: what sort of human being had them at his mercy?

They remained motionless, waiting for their fate, as the footsteps came nearer. At last they were able to distinguish the shaggy outline of a man in a fur coat.

"Who's there?" he called.

Both girls breathed a sigh of relief, as they heard the words in English. Surely they were safe now!

"Two girls—from a wrecked airplane.... Lost," replied Mary Eliska.

"Oh, can you give us shelter, please?" begged Jax Gray.

The stranger came towards them, and they looked into the face of a middle-aged man, rough and hard, but civilized.

"Yes. You can come into my lodge.... This is a cold night to be lost in these northern woods."

"Dreadful!" shivered Jax Gray. "We thought we were done for."

"What happened to your plane?"

"We sprung a leak in our gas tank. We had to jump, and it went up in flames."

"Too bad," muttered the man.

Nothing more was said for a few minutes, and the girls walked painfully on, guided by their companion. At last they came to a small cabin, with an oil lamp lighted inside. It looked like Heaven to Mary Eliska and Jax Gray.

"I'll give you some food, and let you have the place for the night," offered the man, generously. "I was going off anyhow."

"Oh, no!" protested Mary Eliska. "We mustn't drive you out in the cold!" And, seeing that the cabin had two rooms—a living-room and a kitchen, she immediately added, "We can easily sleep in the kitchen."

"No, I expect to be out all night anyway." He went out into the kitchen and made them some hot coffee, and fried bacon and produced crackers and a can of beans.

"Nothing in my life ever tasted half so good!" cried Jax Gray, gratefully, as she ate ravenously, while her host stood there a moment watching both of the girls.

"Now tell me," he said, "what you two young ladies were doing flying a plane up here on the border in the dead of winter?"

"We've been to Canada," explained Mary Eliska, "to visit a Convent where some nuns make this lovely lace-work." She took her handkerchief out of her pocket, and showed it to the man, though she realized it would not be possible for him to appreciate it. "My father buys this, and sells it again."

"Oh, ho!" exclaimed the man, significantly, opening his eyes and his mouth wide, knowingly. "I see."

"What do you see?" asked Jax Gray, sharply. "Nothing—nothing," he muttered. "I must be off—I have to get in touch with a man I know tonight—across the woods." His tone changed abruptly. "I don't want you girls to stir from here 'til I get back! You understand?"

"You mean you want us to go on eating all night?" remarked Jax Gray, ignoring the seriousness of his tone. The coffee had made her feel good; she wanted to laugh and joke.

"No. I mean you're not to leave the cabin, 'til I get back in the morning."

"We won't!" Mary Eliska assured him. "Nothing could induce us to, in all this cold. We'd never find our way, and besides, we want to pay for our lodging. Can you—could you find a way to get us to a train tomorrow?"

"I'll take care of you," he replied, with a queer smile, but neither Mary Eliska nor Jax Gray noticed. They were too tired now for anything but sleep.

As soon as he was gone, they decided to turn in. There was only one narrow cot in the cabin, but there were three blankets, and they knew they would not mind sleeping in close quarters. It was so good to be warm, and fed, alive!

Mary Eliska was the first to awaken the following morning, and for a moment, as she looked about her at the unfamiliar surroundings, she could not recall where she was. The strange little hut, with the big stone fireplace, where now only ashes remained of last night's fire, the crude couch on which she and Jax Gray were huddled so close together, the trophies about the unfinished walls. And outside the icy windows, a desolate country, covered with snow.

"Hurry up, Jax Gray!" she cried, waking her companion. "Let's get washed up before that man comes back! Funny, we never thought to ask him his name!"

"We were too tired," replied the other girl, rubbing her eyes. "Honestly I never was so nearly dead in my life."

"It was because we saw no hope of resting. Just going on and on—or freezing. How do your feet feel this morning?"

"Terrible!" Jax Gray leaned over and examined them. "They're dreadfully swollen. I'll never be able to walk, and how can we get to civilization if we don't?"

"Maybe our friend will dig up some horses. Or an airplane. If there is any place to land."

"An airplane!" repeated Jax Gray, as she laboriously, started to pull on her stockings. "Mary Eliska, do you feel very terrible about losing the Arrow?"

"Of course I'm dreadfully sorry, but I think I should be ungrateful if I thought too much about that—after our lucky escape. Besides, I feel pretty certain I'll get another one now. If Daddy can pull out of his business troubles, we can order that Bellanca."

The girls finished their dressing and set the room to rights, so that everything would be comfortable and neat when their host returned. Then they started a fire in the fireplace with some kindling and logs that were in readiness, and proceeded to the kitchen, to clear up their supper dishes, and to cook some breakfast. Fortunately there was plenty of food, and they enjoyed their hot meal. But they were not so ravenous as they had been the night before. "I wish that man would hurry," remarked Mary Eliska, as she put the clean dishes away. "I'd like to get somewhere to wire Ted. When he didn't get a telegram last night, he probably thought something had happened to us, and maybe he'll send out a searching party today."

"That's true," agreed Jax Gray. "Good old Ted!... But what about your Aunt Polly? Do you think she will worry?"

"Not yet. Because she didn't expect us to wire every night. She probably thinks we're visiting some friends in Plattsburg."

They went back to the living-room, and settled themselves comfortably before the open fire, enjoying the warmth and cheer of the blaze. Mary Eliska's wrist-watch, which was still going in spite of its fall through the air, proclaimed it to be ten o'clock when a knock finally sounded at the door. She sprang up and unfastened the bolt. It was their rescuer, with another man, also in a fur coat. Two horses stood outside, covered with blankets.

"How are you today?" asked the owner of the cabin, genially.

"Just fine!" replied Mary Eliska, gayly. "Thanks to your hospitality!"

"Meet Sergeant Bradshaw," said the man rather brusquely, as he and his companion stepped inside and closed the door. "Your names——?"

"Mary Eliska and Jax Gray Haydock," replied the former.

"Well, Sergeant," explained their host, turning to the other man, "these are the young ladies.... But, as I told you, they've lost their plane now, so they'll probably tell you they are ready to reform."

"Reform?" repeated Jax Gray, thinking that the man was teasing them. But he was not smiling; and his companion was regarding them with a most scornful expression.

"They'll reform all right," sneered the latter. "Under lock and key!"

For the first time a shiver of fear crept over Mary Eliska. Was their rescuer bad, after all? Did he mean to kidnap her and her chum?

"What do you mean?" demanded Jax Gray, in a tone of challenge.

"What I say!" thundered the sergeant, displaying his badge. "I arrest you two young ladies as smugglers! I am going to take you both to jail!"

"Smugglers?" repeated Mary Eliska, aghast.

"Yes. You know all about it. Don't look innocent! We've had wind for over a month of the fact that a plane was taking something from Canada to Plattsburg, but we just found out last week what it was— French lace ! And a girl has been flying it!" Instantly both Mary Eliska and Jax Gray understood what had happened. They were being arrested for Bess Hulbert's crime!

"But neither of us is the girl you're after—the girl that's guilty!" protested Jax Gray. "That girl flew a gray Moth!"

"Yeah? And how do we know your plane wasn't a gray Moth? How are you going to prove that? And didn't you admit you'd just come from that Convent, and didn't you show my friend Marshall here, some of the goods?"

"But those are our own things!" cried Jax Gray. "Bought in Columbus, Ohio!"

"Oh, yeah? Well, I don't happen to believe that.... What I do know, is you didn't stop at the border for the regular search, did you?"

"We didn't know you had to.... We didn't even know the border when we came to it," remarked Mary Eliska, bitterly.

"No? Well, you can tell that to the judge!" replied the sergeant, with a smirk. "I guess you don't even know yet whether you're in the U.S. or not?"

"No, as a matter of fact, we don't."

"Innocent little things!" he sneered, sarcastically. "Rats! What's the use of wasting time? Come on!"

"Won't you even listen to our story?" begged Mary Eliska.

"You can save it for the judge! We've got a couple of horses out here, and we're each taking one of you along. Get your coats on—and hustle!"

Meekly Mary Eliska did as she was told, biting her lips to keep back the tears, but Jax Gray was furiously angry.

"You just wait!" she sputtered. "You'll make a public apology for this, when our fathers hear about it."

"Listen to the little spit-fire!" drawled the sergeant, in a nasty tone. Then, turning to the other man, "Listen, Marshall, I don't think we better try to take these two girls on our horses—especially this little cat here." He pointed rudely at Jax Gray. "She might scratch! And it's none too easy traveling in this kind of weather.... Their trial won't come up for a month or so, anyway, so we might as well lock 'em in here as anywhere 'til we see fit to get 'em. You don't need the cabin, do you?"

"No, I can go over with Hendries."

"Well, the windows are barred. Besides, if they tried to escape, they would only get lost, and freeze or starve to death. Suppose we leave 'em here to think over their crime, and maybe after a few days or so, they'll be more ready to confess."

"But we have to wire our folks!" cried Mary Eliska, in dismay.

"You ought to have thought of that before you tried your tricks. If it's your father you're working for, he knows what to expect. Smuggling's serious business, young woman!"

"But we didn't——"

"So I've heard you say before, but lady, that don't get you anywheres with me.... Marshall, you go and get wood and see that there's enough oil and water and food to last about four days. I'll stay here and watch 'em 'til you get back."

Mary Eliska and Jax Gray did not believe anyone could be so cruel, so inhuman as this man—not even willing to listen to their story. But he was so entirely convinced of their guilt, that he probably thought he was justified. After all, the punishment wouldn't have been too severe if he had caught the right person—Bess Hulbert. But how unfair it was for them!

"Won't you please send my father a telegram?" begged Mary Eliska, with tears in her eyes.

"Are you ready to confess?" countered the sergeant.

"We can't confess what we haven't done!" she protested.

"Then your father will have to wait. He'll know in about four days, when we bring a plane to take you away."

"Oh!" gasped Mary Eliska, realizing the horrible anxiety this decision would cause so many people dear to herself and Jax Gray. Dropping down on the couch, she buried her head in her hands, and did not look up again until the men had gone, and locked and barred the door from the outside. Then she broke into uncontrollable weeping, and Jax Gray, clasping her arms about her, cried too.

"There is only one redeeming thing about it," said Jax Gray, after a moment. "We're together."

"If we weren't," sobbed Mary Eliska, "I think we should lose our minds!"

But already Jax Gray was looking about, trying to figure out some means of escape.

"The thing that makes me maddest," she remarked, "is the delay in catching Bess Hulbert. She'll probably make a get-away before we can notify your father."

"I don't think so," answered Mary Eliska, sitting up and resolutely drying her eyes. "Don't forget, Bess thinks we probably went up in flames with the Arrow. And when nothing is heard of us for five days, she'll be positive.... No, my bet is that she'll go right on with her smuggling and stealing Daddy's business."

Her companion admitted that she was right. And all they could do was sit here and wait for those horrible men to return!

It was a problem of course, how to amuse themselves, for there was no radio, or music of any kind, and there were no books on the shelves. When they had gotten over their first despair, they tried putting their wits together and manufacturing some sort of occupation. And they thought of various things, of giving each other exercises, and playing guessing games, making up new recipes for the ingredients that were in the kitchen store-closet.

But, try as they did to be cheerful, the hours dragged, and four days stretched out as interminably before them.

Chapter 6.12
Waiting for News

As Mary Eliska had surmised, her aunt did not expect her to wire every night, unless something happened, so when December twenty-ninth passed without any message, the latter naturally supposed that the girls were still at Plattsburg with friends. Heretofore, the older woman had known all of her niece's companions, but since Mary Eliska had gone away to school, her circle had naturally widened. Mary Eliska frowned when she recalled that she had neglected to ask the names of the girls Mary Eliska and Jax Gray intended to visit. When she heard nothing from them again on the morning of the thirtieth, she grew anxious and called Mrs. Haydock on the telephone. "I don't want to alarm you, Mary Eliska," answered Jax Gray's mother, "but I am afraid something has happened."

"Why? What makes you think so? Because we haven't heard from them since the twenty-seventh?"

"Not only that," replied Mrs. Haydock. "But I put in a long-distance call for Ted Mackay—Jax Gray said they would keep him informed of their whereabouts, in case they had any difficulties—and I got the message that he had gone to Canada in search of two missing flyers!"

"Canada!" repeated Mary Eliska, aghast. "That couldn't be our girls! They were going to New York."

"So I understood. But they may have gone on to Canada.... Well, let us hope that Ted flew up to search for someone else. All we can do is wait."

"Oh, those dreadful airplanes!" wailed Mary Eliska, hysterically. "I wish they had never been invented.... Well, I'll call my brother," she concluded, for she had no idea what to do.

That, of course, was the difficulty everybody met—every one of Mary Eliska's and Jax Gray Haydock's friends at Spring City, when the news got around that the girls were lost. Nobody knew where they were; nobody had any way of helping find them.

Anxiety for them spread over the little town where they were so popular. Particularly at the Flying Club, where their most intimate friends were gathered that afternoon to play bridge or to dance, as the mood seized them. A skating party which had been planned by Dot Crowley and Jim Valier had to be canceled on account of a heavy snow the night before. Even now the storm was still raging, reminding them all the more of their two friends with the open Arrow.

Dot Crowley, however, resolutely decided to be hopeful, to make an effort to dispel the gloom that threatened to engulf them all.

"No use weeping 'til we hear that something has happened," she said, as she turned on the radio. "I'd stake a good-sized bet on Mary Eliska and Jax Gray! Haven't they always come through with flying colors?"

"If they're still flying colors, or anything else, they're all right," remarked Jim Valier, lazily stretching his legs out toward the blazing fire. But, lazy though he always appeared, he was ready to help Dot in her valiant effort to be cheerful.

"They'll be home yet—in time for the New Year's Eve party!" she asserted, with conviction. "I'm not going to lose faith."

"I'm not either," added Kitty Clavering, who was usually so timid, but who had a deep admiration for Mary Eliska. "I think Mary Eliska is one of the cleverest girls I ever met."

Everybody agreed with her, and somehow they all suddenly felt optimistic. The bridge tables were brought out, the couples began to play and dance in the intervals when they were "dummies." Everybody seemed happy again—everybody except Ralph Clavering. Off in a corner he was smoking a cigarette in doleful silence.

Dot, who still felt the responsibility for the atmosphere of the party, went over to cheer him up.

"What's the matter, Ralph?" she asked half teasingly, half sympathetically.

"Nothing," he muttered, with a frown that plainly said, "let me alone!"

"I know, though," persisted Dot, seating herself beside him. "You haven't any partner for the New Year's Eve dance!"

"Well, I'm not asking you," he replied, rudely.

"You know it wouldn't be any use!" retorted Dot, her chin in the air. "I'm going with Jim."

"O.K. with me." He continued to smoke in silence.

"Well, buck up!" she advised, patting his shoulder. "Mary Eliska may fly home any minute."

"Here comes a plane now!" cried Kitty, jumping up and rushing to the window. "Why, it's our own Moth!"

Everybody dashed to the window, to see Bess Hulbert make her landing, and three or four of the boys slipped into their overcoats to go out and help her put it into the hangar. But Ralph sat stolidly gazing into the fire.

Five minutes later, Miss Hulbert, her cheeks glowing and her eyes flashing with excitement, came into the room.

"Welcome to our famous flyer!" cried Kitty, turning off the radio.

"What's weather to her!" laughed Joe Elliston, admiringly.

"All in the day's work," replied Miss Hulbert.

"Tell us where you've been," urged Kitty.

"Up to the Great Lakes," replied the aviatrix, vaguely. "I bought my own gas and oil, but I feel I owe the Club ten dollars for the use of the plane.... I—I'll pay myself!"

They all smiled, for Bess Hulbert was still treasurer of the club.

"Don't be silly!" protested Kitty. "You're a member of the club."

"But I was using the plane for business—not for pleasure."

"Just what is your business, Miss Hulbert?" inquired Ralph.

The girl colored; she did not like his tone. It was a bitter blow to her pride that this rich young man had never fallen for her charms.

"Fish!" she replied mockingly. "Poor fish!"

Everybody laughed, not knowing whether she was serious or not, and this time the joke seemed to be on Ralph.

"You didn't see Mary Eliska or Jax Gray—in the course of your trip, did you?" asked Dot Crowley.

"Mary Eliska—Jax Gray—?" Miss Hulbert was stalling for time.

"Yes. The two girls who fly in an Arrow Pursuit. They've been missing for two days and Mary Eliska and Mrs. Haydock are almost crazy. We're all worried too, only we try not to be."

"Too bad," murmured Miss Hulbert. "But they really shouldn't be flying in this sort of weather. They haven't had the experience."

"How else would they get it?" demanded Ralph, brusquely.

"Short trips," answered Bess. "It's foolish people like them who do harm to aviation. Make the public think it's so dangerous."

"How do you know they went on a long trip?" questioned Kitty, innocently.

"Oh—er—I don't. I only supposed they did."

"Yes, we're all afraid of that. They were last heard of from Plattsburg—the twenty-seventh."

"And this is the thirtieth," remarked Bess, absently. "I wonder if that wreck that was reported in the early afternoon papers could have been their plane."

"What wreck?" demanded everybody at once.

"The charred wreck of a plane was found by an aviator named Ted Mackay. Up on the border, between New York state and Canada."

"Ted Mackay!" repeated Dot. "That's Mary Eliska's friend—the one who rescued her before."

"Well, he didn't rescue her today," asserted Bess. "There were no bodies in the plane. But then it was almost completely destroyed."

At this gruesome remark, Kitty immediately burst out crying, and even Dot Crowley could find no reason to be hopeful any longer, and wiped the tears from her eyes. Oh, it was dreadful to think of their two lovely friends as dead! Worse still, for them to meet death in such a horrible way!

"It may not have been their plane," Bess reminded her companions, although in her heart she felt sure that it was. "Or, even if it is, they might still be alive, if they had the nerve to use their parachutes."

"They had plenty of nerve!" responded Dot. "But even if they jumped, it isn't likely they'd still be alive in this terrible weather."

"If they were, we should probably have heard from them," said Ralph, glumly.

Nobody spoke for some time; resuming of the games was out of the question now. Finally, to break the silence, and to have something to do, Kitty rang the bell for the club matron to serve tea and sandwiches.

Over the tea-cups a low murmur of conversation finally arose, but it was all in a gloomy undertone. Nothing could have been more depressing than the atmosphere in that room—until the door was suddenly flung open by a small boy—Jax Gray Haydock's brother.

"Whoopee! Whoopee!" he shouted, throwing his hat straight into Ralph Clavering's tea-cup. "The girls are alive and safe!"

"Mary Eliska? Jax Gray?" cried everybody at once. In the excitement all eyes were upon the boy; nobody noticed that Bess Hulbert's face went ghastly white.

"Yeah! Ted Mackay wired just now. He found them on the Canadian border, locked up in a cabin!"

"Locked up? Kidnapped?" demanded Ralph.

"No. Locked up by law. They have to go to jail."

"Jail?"

"It's some joke!" exclaimed Jim Valier.

"No. Honest!" protested the boy. "They're being held for some crime they didn't commit. Smuggling, or something!"

"Oh, they probably brought a bottle of Canadian wine into the United States," laughed Ralph. "They'll just have a little fine to pay——"

"But Mary Eliska doesn't drink—or Jax Gray either!" asserted Dot. "I know they wouldn't think of such a thing."

"Well, so long as they're safe, it'll be an easy matter for them to get free," said Ralph, more relieved than anyone realized. "Why, they may be back in time for the New Year's Eve dance!"

"Not a chance," answered the boy, with a vehement shake of his head…. "Don't forget the Arrow is a thing of the past—they've got to come home by train. Besides, they can't start 'til Dad and Mr. Stricklin get up there to bail 'em out!"

"I wish they had the Moth," sighed Kitty. "If it were only decent weather, Bess could go get them."

Miss Hulbert was horrified at such a suggestion, but she managed to cover her consternation with a smile.

As soon as the excitement died down the party began to break up. But Bess Hulbert continued to sit before the fire, thinking deeply, trying to decide what to do.

So the law had gotten wind of the fact that smuggling was going on, by a girl in an airplane! And had arrested Mary Eliska and Jax Gray Haydock, thinking them guilty. She smiled in a nasty, superior way. What a joke it was on those two upstarts! But her mouth grew grim again; it was only a question of time now, before the officers discovered the right person, before she too was brought to justice. And she wouldn't get off so easily as these two others…. No, there was only one thing for her to do—and that was to leave the country, before anybody thought of accusing her of this crime, or of the more serious one of damaging Mary Eliska's plane….

Lucky thing, she thought, that she had already made some money out of the business! But how she wished she had more!

Kitty Clavering, who was the only person still left at the club, came over and put her arm around Bess, attempting to pull her to her feet.

"What's the matter, Bess?" she asked, noticing that the other girl did not respond to her embrace. "Lots of things, Kitty," replied Bess, soberly. "I've had some pretty bad news today…. Of course I didn't say anything about it in front of the others, especially when I found you all so worried about your young friends."

"Well, we don't have to worry about them anymore! So I can give all my thoughts to you…. Come on home with me, and tell me about it!" urged the younger girl. She did not add that she wanted to hear about Lieutenant Hulbert, whom she had not seen for over a month.

"Oh, all right," agreed Bess, without any enthusiasm. "For a little while…. But I must get back to my hotel. I'll have to go to New York tonight."

Kitty did not question her any further until they were alone in her pretty boudoir, Bess relaxing on the chaise longue, Kitty in the flowered chintz chair.

"Now tell me, my dear," repeated Kitty, sympathetically.

"Well," Bess began slowly, "it's about business. I was joking this afternoon, of course, but the fact is I've been going into something pretty deep—and—and—I'm going to lose. Fail, in other words…. And the worst of it is—I'll have to go to England to get some money, if I can. My brother and I are English, you know."

"Oh, I'm so sorry!" cried Kitty. To the rich young heiress, poverty seemed terrible. And Bess had mentioned her brother—was it possible he had lost money too? Was that the reason he was staying away from her? She put the question to her friend.

"Yes," lied Bess, for she knew that this would draw more sympathy from Kitty, and the latter might even offer to lend her some money. "Yes, I was investing Bob's money, and lost that too."

"How terrible!" Kitty got up and went over beside the older girl. "If I could only help you, dear—financially, I mean."

Bess's eyelids narrowed. This was just what she was hoping for!

"That's good of you, Kit—but I really couldn't accept it!"

"But as a loan? Oh, please! I'd love to!"

"Well—" Bess paused, as if she would need a great deal of persuasion. "My idea would be to borrow enough to order a big plane, and fly the Atlantic and win that twenty-five thousand dollars. Then I could pay you and my brother both back at once."

"And bring glory to our Flying Club!"

"Yes, of course.... But Kitty, have you any idea what a good plane costs? I'm afraid you couldn't raise so much money, could you?"

"About how much?" asked Kitty, vaguely. She was thinking of Bob Hulbert now, wondering whether she couldn't write and tell him she understood why he was staying away from her, and urging him to come back.

"Well, novices like your two friends would probably expect to pay about twenty thousand dollars for their plane.... But I wouldn't have to have that kind. Because, even if I did win the prize, it would hardly pay me.... No, I wouldn't pay more than eight or ten thousand for mine.... But you could never raise that much, could you, Kit?"

The girl shook her head.

"I'm afraid not.... Only by getting a loan on my pearl necklace. Do you suppose that could be done, Bess?"

"Of course it could. But not here in Spring City. We'd have to go to New York."

"I can't go to New York. I'm dated up for a dance tonight."

"I think I could manage it myself," said Bess. "If you care to trust me, and will give me a note authorizing the loan."

"I'll be only too glad to," agreed Kitty, and she produced the necklace and immediately sat down to the desk to write the letter.

So, three hours later, Bess Hulbert stepped into the Pullman for New York, carrying not only the precious pearls, but all of the Flying Club's money as well, which she had pretended to forget to hand over to Kitty. "And now," she said triumphantly to herself, "let the United States courts try to catch me if they can!"

Chapter 6.13
Freedom

Ted Mackay did not sleep well on the night of the twenty-eighth of December. It was one o'clock before he gave up expecting a telegram and finally went to bed. Even then he tossed restlessly.

Something, he thought, had surely happened to Mary Eliska and Jax Gray Haydock. Had they merely been forced down in some lonely spot where there was no means of telegraphing, or had they met with some more serious accident? He was up and dressed at dawn on the twenty-ninth, wiring his firm for leave of absence to go in search of the lost flyers.

He decided not to telephone Mary Eliska or Mrs. Haydock yet; no need to worry them until it was absolutely necessary. Accordingly, he took off early in the morning of December twenty-ninth for Montreal, in his cabin mono-plane, equipped with skis for the snow.

The snow began to fall steadily that afternoon, and continued on through the night. But though Ted reached Montreal before dark, there was no news of two girls at any of the airports. If they had arrived, their plane would have been housed in some hangar in the city or near about it. The snow was falling so fast and thick that Ted realized that night flying would be foolish. Forcing himself to go to bed, he left a call at the hotel desk for four o'clock the following day.

His first stop, at dawn on December thirtieth, was the French Convent. There at least he got some information: the girls had been there, safe and unharmed, two days previous. But where were they now?

Air travel was difficult in the snowstorm, but he shuddered to think of them alone in the woods, if something had gone wrong with their Arrow. How much food were they carrying, and what about blankets? How long could they endure the cold?

Fortunately his plane was built for low flying, and he went carefully, just clearing the tree-tops, looking everywhere for a wrecked plane. About noon he was rewarded. Off on a hill, in a bank of snow, he found the blackened remains of the gallant little Pursuit. But, thank Heaven, no signs of human bodies in the wreckage!

He spent perhaps half an hour searching and calling his lost friends, but when he received no response, he decided that the best thing for him to do was to go back to the nearest town and report the wreck by wire, and send out an S.O.S. for searching parties. It was this account that Bess Hulbert read in the early afternoon papers and announced to the Flying Club members.

Ted lost no time in sending the communication, and returning to the scene of the disaster, resolving to circle the district again and again, watching for signals. There was still hope that the girls were alive.

About two o'clock he sighted the little cabin in the woods and hunted for a spot to land. This might mean protection for Mary Eliska and Jax Gray, from the terrible storm. How he hoped that they had found it, and were now warm and safe inside!

Five minutes later he left his plane and walked excitedly to the hut. But because of the snow his approach was noiseless, and the girls, who happened to be cooking in the little kitchen at the time, had no idea that rescue was at hand.

Ted lifted his fist and banged on the heavy door.

"Who can it be?" gasped Jax Gray, dropping the tin cup she was holding, and spilling flour all over the floor. "If it were that sergeant, he'd open the door. We can't possibly."

"Of course not," replied Mary Eliska. "But let's go see who it is. Those bars won't keep us from looking out."

Breathlessly they dashed to the living-room window, and tapped against the glass, for they could not see the door in their position.

Bliss, oh, bliss! A moment later they recognized the dear familiar form of Ted Mackay!

"Unbar the door!" shouted Jax Gray, giving a leap into the air. "We're locked in!"

Ted's mouth opened in amazement, but he heard what they said, and instantly went over and did what he was told. Then he stepped inside, and, wet and covered with snow as he was, both girls flung their arms around him and cried in rapture.

"Angel!" exclaimed Jax Gray.

"Messenger from Heaven!" added Mary Eliska.

They released him, and made him take off his coat, and come to the fire to get warm.

It took an hour to tell all the details of their hazardous adventure, which had ended in this most surprising way, with imprisonment, and while they talked, they ate the hot-cakes and the coffee which Mary Eliska and Jax Gray were making when Ted arrived. Then the latter glanced at his watch and said they had better be starting.

"Ought we to wash these dishes?" inquired Mary Eliska, when they finished, and went for their coats and leggings and helmets.

"I should say not!" thundered Jax Gray, with a vengeance. "I'd like to smash and dirty everything in the old cabin!"

"Don't forget it saved our lives," Mary Eliska reminded her, laughingly.

But they did not wait. Time was precious now; they wanted to take off before it was any darker, or the snow grew too deep. Opening the door, they stepped outside just as two men on horseback drew up to the cabin. Marshall and the sergeant had returned.

"What's this?" demanded the latter, in a gruff, insulting tone. "Making a get-away, are you?" He glanced suspiciously at Ted. "Maybe you don't know these young women are under arrest!"

"Are they?" retorted Ted. "Well, so are you, for that matter! For not reporting that wreck two days ago! Don't you know it's a government regulation that wrecked planes must be reported as soon as possible?"

The man shuffled nervously, kicking the snow against his horse.

"Well, I'm reportin' it," he asserted, defiantly.

"Today? You bet you'll report it today! It's two days too late, though!"

"They're smugglers," he sneered, scornfully. "Smugglers is enemies to the country, and don't deserve no consideration!"

"We'll see about that!" replied Ted masterfully, as he glowered at the girls' accuser. Mary Eliska and Jax Gray stood quietly by, watching him in admiration. How grand it was to have a friend like this!

"You girls come along with me," snarled the officer. "I'm takin' you to the Court House."

"I'll take them to the Court House," amended Ted. "In my plane. You needn't be afraid I won't show up! I have plenty I want to report myself."

Sullenly the man agreed to the offer, for he still had no desire to take that young spitfire, as he called Jax Gray, on his horse. Waiting only to see the plane take off into the air, he galloped away with his friend, Marshall.

Mary Eliska and Jax Gray felt so gay and happy that they shouted and sang during the entire flight. It was close quarters in the little cabin plane, but who cared? They were free—or soon would be free—once more!

Though Ted smiled at their joviality, he felt more like praying. He was so grateful, so relieved that they were alive and safe, that he was filled with a solemn sense of thanksgiving. For he realized what a terrible fate they had escaped in jumping from that empty plane.

They landed at the little town where the sergeant had directed them, and Ted wired immediately to Mrs. Haydock and to Mr. Stricklin, and to Mary Eliska's aunt. Then they went to the Court House, arriving before the men on horseback.

There, at last, the girls were allowed to tell their story, which a kindly judge listened to in righteous anger. And when Mary Eliska and Jax Gray produced all their evidence, by going into detail about Mr. Stricklin's business, and their own reason for the flight, they had no difficulty in convincing him of their innocence. Things would not go easily with this fellow, who had locked them up without hearing their version, or reporting them immediately to the authorities. The judge said he would see that the man was punished, when he finally arrived.

"Do we need bail or anything?" asked Mary Eliska, who knew nothing about courts or legal matters. "We have wired to our Dads, and they'll probably be right up here, as fast as a train can bring them."

"No, that is not necessary," smiled the judge. "Because I am convinced of your innocence.... You better wire your fathers not to come—it will only delay your return.... But before you go, I should to like to hear more of the real criminal, this woman who, you say, has been smuggling. Tell me her name, and give me a description of her."

"Her name is Bess Hulbert," replied Jax Gray. "But we're pretty sure she goes under an assumed name—possibly 'Anna Smith'." She was thinking of Mary Eliska's conversation in Plattsburg over the telephone, with Hofstatter's mother. "And probably by this time she has changed it again."

"I don't think you'll have to worry about her anymore," added Mary Eliska. "The minute she hears we are safe, she'll know her game is up, and give up the underhand business."

"Just the same, she ought to be caught and punished!" cried Jax Gray, vindictively. She had said nothing about their belief of the cause of their leaking tank, for after all they had no proof, and this judge could do nothing. But for that reason more than any, Jax Gray wanted her punished.

Promising the judge that they would try to get hold of Miss Hulbert's picture, the girls shook hands with him and left, accompanied by Ted Mackay, who was grinning harder than usual now. Everything was so right!

Dusk had set in already, though the storm had passed, and a beautiful sunset was fading from the sky, promising a clear day for the flyers tomorrow.

"I think we had better rest tonight," said Ted, as he followed the girls into a taxicab. "You girls can stay at the hotel—there is only one, for this is a small place—and I'll get a room over near the airport. I want to spend some time checking up on my plane, and I think I'll try to get somebody to help me. It's a long flight back to Spring City."

"Oh!" cried Mary Eliska, rapturously. "Won't it be marvelous to be home? I'm glad we have a couple of days before we have to go back to school!"

"Sure you don't mind flying?" asked Ted. "You're not nervous, after your narrow escape?"

"We've forgotten that," replied Jax Gray. "Forgotten everything except that we are eligible for the Caterpillar Club now."

"Mary Eliska has been for a long time—since her first flight up," Ted reminded them.

The machine stopped at the hotel, and Ted helped the girls to get out.

"You'll come back and have dinner with us, won't you, Ted?" asked Jax Gray anxiously.

"O.K.—if you want me," he promised. "Only I mustn't stay afterwards, or go to the movies with you. I've got to work on that plane."

The girls found their hotel warm and comfortable, though naturally not luxurious like those in the large cities. But after their two days in that cramped little hut, it seemed like a veritable palace. Bathing in a real bathtub was a joy that they had sadly missed, and the dinner seemed like a banquet to them, after doing their own cooking with such a limited supply of food.

But best of all were their conversations with their families that evening, which, as Jax Gray said, were worth all the money in the world to her. Long distance charges meant nothing, compared to the bliss of hearing her mother's voice over that wire. And Mary Eliska felt the same way about her Aunt Polly and her father, who, by this time, was at home.

Finally they brought their conversations to a reluctant end, promising to be home the next night—in time for the New Year's Eve dance!

Chapter 6.14
The New Year's Eve Party

The sun was setting over the snow-covered horizon when Ted Mackay landed his mono-plane at Spring City on the last afternoon of the old year. A trifle stiff from their long ride, but still happy and carefree, the girls stepped out on the field.

At the arrival of the plane several of the men employed at the airport rushed out and greeted Mary Eliska, for they knew her well, from flying her Pursuit over Spring City, and coming there for supplies and inspection. Of course they had read her story in the newspapers.

"But you won't be flying for a while now, will you Mary Eliska?" remarked one of the men, regretfully.

"I shan't be flying the Pursuit," answered Mary Eliska. "But we have planes at school. I am taking a course at a ground school in St. Louis this year."

"What kind of course, Mary Eliska?"

"I am in line for two licenses—a commercial pilot's and a mechanic's."

"Mechanic's!" repeated the man, in consternation. "Are you in earnest?"

"Certainly," smiled Mary Eliska, for she was quite used to people exclaiming over her chosen study. "Will you give me a job here when I finish?"

"I'll say we will! If you'd take it. But you won't. You'll have bigger offers than this."

"Come along, Mary Eliska!" urged Jax Gray, pulling her chum by the arm. "Aren't you cold?"

"No, but I'm dying to see my family," she replied, and followed Jax Gray to the taxi which Ted had engaged.

In contrast to her homecoming before Christmas, when her father and her aunt were plunged in gloom, Mary Eliska found them almost hysterical in their joy. Never had her father seemed so wrought up, so emotional. He kissed her again and again. Tears streamed down her aunt's cheeks.

"Darling child!" she cried, "we thought we should never see you again! Oh, your father and I have never had two such dreadful days as yesterday and the day before!"

"But they're over now," returned Mary Eliska. "And the only sad part of it all is that I have no plane."

"Which is all for the best," was Mary Eliska's comment.

"I wish that I could buy you another," lamented her father.

It was then that Mary Eliska told her story, giving her reasons for the trip, and the events that led up to her suspicions about Bess Hulbert. Only one part she omitted—and that was her own desire to buy a Bellanca and fly the Atlantic. It would be a very poor time to tell her aunt of any such a wish.

Mr. Stricklin listened in amazement; he was sure his daughter was correct in all her surmises.

"We can easily put an end to Miss Hulbert's smuggling now," he said. "With the help of the United States officers.... Why, Mary Eliska, you have saved my business!"

"I hope we have, Daddy. But don't forget the credit goes to Jax Gray too. I never could have done anything without her to help me."

"That's all perfectly lovely," put in Mary Eliska. "But the person I'm most grateful to is Ted Mackay. No knowing what might have happened if he hadn't rescued you when he did. And think of the hours of torturing suspense he saved us all here at home!"

"Yes, that's right," agreed her brother, who now thoroughly approved of the young man. "I'd like to thank him myself. Where is he, Mary Eliska?"

"He went home with Jax Gray. She invited him before I even thought of it. But she asked us all to come over to their house to dinner. How about it, Aunt Polly?"

"I'd be delighted. At least, if you'd rather go there than to the New Year's Eve dance at the Country Club."

"I'd rather go to both," announced Mary Eliska, gayly. "Jax Gray and Ted expect to take that in too, for I heard her saying she'd dig out a costume for him. Could you find something for me, Auntie?"

"Of course I could," replied the older woman, smiling happily. It was just like old times again, she thought—with dinner parties and costume dances to take one's attention.

"I'll go up in the attic right away," she decided. "What sort of thing would you prefer?"

"Anything different from this dirty old flyer's suit. I hate the sight of it, after living in it at that miserable cabin. Why, I haven't had anything else since we left Plattsburg! I'm going to burn it tonight!"

Again Mary Eliska smiled; this was the Mary Eliska she liked best, the dainty girl who looked charming in fluffy, feminine gowns.

"I'm going to hurry and get my bath before anybody comes," added the girl. "And get into a dinner dress."

She left just in time, for no sooner had she reached the top of the stairs than she heard Ralph Clavering's voice in the hall.

"Mary Eliska! Mary Eliska!" he shouted, for her father had told him that she had just gone upstairs to dress.

"Hello, Ralph!" she called back. "I'm dying to see you, but I'm not presentable. Can you wait about twenty minutes?"

"I don't want to," he answered impatiently. "But I must, if you say so. Will you go to the dance with me tonight?"

"O.K.," she replied, joyfully. "I was 'waiting-for-a-partner,' just as we used to sing in that game we played when we were kids. Ted and Jax Gray are going together, and I was left over!"

"As if Mary Eliska would ever be left over!" he muttered to himself, in amusement.

When she came downstairs, fifteen minutes later, arrayed in pink chiffon, he longed so to take her in his arms that it actually hurt to restrain himself. It was so good to see her again—alive and unharmed—more beautiful than ever! He wished she were not so capable, so bent upon having a career. A girl who looked so adorable had no right to possess the keen mind of a man.

But both Mr. Stricklin and his sister were in the room, and Ralph had to content himself with shaking hands with Mary Eliska.

The time was short, however; even as she began to answer his questions, the phone bell rang. Congratulations were pouring in; telegrams and flowers arrived, and finally Ralph gave up hoping to talk to her.

"I'll come for you about ten o'clock," he managed to whisper into her ear while she sat at the telephone. Ever so lightly, without her even realizing it, he touched her hair with his lips.

It was with difficulty that she broke away at last, and went with her father and her aunt to Jax Gray's in the big car that the chauffeur drove. Thanks to Mary Eliska, her aunt Polly would not have to give it up as she had expected.

That dinner party was the noisiest, jolliest affair Mary Eliska had ever attended. No holiday occasion had ever aroused such unrestrained merry-making. Even Ted Mackay, who usually was shy among strangers, felt perfectly at home. Jax Gray's small brother insisted upon sitting next to him at dinner, and regarded him as a favored hero—in the class with Byrd and Lindbergh.

"Ted and I have gone into a conspiracy," announced Jax Gray. "We're going to track down Bess Hulbert tonight, and make her confess everything!"

"At the party?" asked Mary Eliska, in amazement.

"Surest thing! It'll only add to the excitement."

"You'll never catch that baby!" remarked her brother, significantly.

"Go carefully," warned Mr. Haydock. "After all, there is a chance that she isn't guilty."

"A pretty slim chance!" laughed his daughter. "Anyway, it will be fun to spot her among all those rigs and false-faces."

"I thought you were going to say rigs and wigs, Sis!"

"All right, any way you like, Tim. Only I guess we better stop fooling and get dressed. It may take a good while to wiggle into our costumes. Especially yours, Big Boy," she added, to Ted. For he was to wear an old suit of her father's, which was sure to be rather small for him.

The girls, who had been used to these sorts of affairs, found the dance just like all the other parties. Lights, splendid costumes, gayety, color, and music; but to Ted Mackay it was strange and exciting. But he danced well, and his manners were just as good as those of the other boys—if anything he was more courteous than many of them. To his surprise he found that he was being fêted along with Mary Eliska and Jax Gray, who were singled out and congratulated every few minutes, not only by friends, but by mere acquaintances as well, who had read about them in the papers and felt proud to know them. But although Ted was carried away by the fun and the excitement, Jax Gray did not forget the fact that she had a self-appointed duty to perform, to corner Bess Hulbert, and ply her with questions.

She thought she had identified her in a Dutch girl's costume, but she found when they all unmasked for supper that she was mistaken.

"Where's that Hulbert woman?" she asked Kitty Clavering, irritably. Jax Gray just had to be frank; if she felt no respect for a person she made no effort to conceal her opinion.

Kitty flushed. She never could understand why her friends did not care for Bess Hulbert as she did. The young woman was getting to be very unpopular at the Flying Club, and Ralph positively detested her.

"Bess?" she stammered. "She's gone abroad."

"Abroad!" repeated Jax Gray, aghast, wondering whether she and Mary Eliska could have been mistaken all along. "When did she go?"

"She's sailing today. She left here for New York yesterday."

"What for?" demanded Jax Gray, bluntly. But already she had guessed the reason. They had not been mistaken at all: Bess Hulbert was fleeing from justice!

"She's English, you know," Kitty explained. "Her family—except her brother—are all in England."

"Has she given up the idea of competing for that prize?"

"I don't think so. Not if she can get a boat, as she calls it."

"Have her people money?"

"How do I know?" retorted Kitty, in exasperation at this cross-examination. She never had got on well with Jax Gray Haydock; she couldn't understand how such a sweet girl as Mary Eliska could want her as a best friend.

She turned abruptly away, for at that moment Lieutenant Hulbert entered the room, and made straight for Kitty. From that moment on, she had neither eyes nor ears for anyone else.

Jax Gray was thankful to have Ted appear to claim her for another dance, and she told him immediately of Bess Hulbert's sudden departure.

"Just what we might have expected," said Ted. "Well, that is proof enough that she is guilty. Are you going on with the chase?"

"How can I—now? But if she ever dares to set foot in the United States again, and compete for that prize, I'll certainly do everything I can to expose her guilt."

"Don't forget, if you need me, I'm always right there!" Ted reminded her.

"I'll never forget it," Jax Gray replied, wishing that she didn't like him so much. After all, he was Mary Eliska's find—and if her chum cared for him—and wanted him——

But Mary Eliska did not look at this moment as if she wanted anyone or anything more than she had. One partner after another would snatch her away when she had danced only half-way around the ballroom. Ralph Clavering was the most persistent pursuer of them all; he never allowed her a single dance without cutting in at least twice.

At first Mary Eliska took this as a joke, but when it happened for seven dances in succession, she grew a trifle weary, and asked him to stop it.

"If you will give me two whole dances alone—sitting them out in the balcony," he agreed. "Then I'll be satisfied."

"Why two?" she countered.

"Because I have so much to say to you!"

"Oh, all right," she said, and together they pushed through the crowd, up the stairs to the balcony to a spot where a long bench was hidden behind some palms.

She looked at him questioningly.

"Mary Eliska darling, haven't you guessed what it is all about?" he demanded, bending over so close to her that his face almost touched hers. "I love you! I've always loved you! I want you to give up this fool air school, and marry me. Elope with me! Tonight!"

Mary Eliska drew back, in amazement.

"Why, Ralph, you're talking of something impossible!" she said, hurt at the very idea. "Imagine your father—my Aunt Polly—if we eloped!... I never did think elopements were romantic—only selfish, when you consider the folks at home. Besides, you have college to finish——"

"I could chuck it!" he interrupted, putting his arm about her slender shoulders, and drawing her closer to him. "Please! I'll buy you a new plane———"

"Now Ralph!" she laughed, and rose quickly to her feet. "Don't try to bribe me. No—positively no!"

"But you do like me?"

"Yes. Heaps."

"Not love?"

"I don't care for any man in that way," she declared.

"Are you sure you don't love Ted Mackay?" Jealousy was always a part of Ralph's nature.

"Oh, no! I have always admired him for his ability. But I don't love him.... No, I'm only in love with aviation."

He was standing too, looking disappointed, but not heart-broken.

"I may ask you again?" he pleaded.

"When you graduate from college, yes."

"Two and a half years to wait!" he sighed, despondently.

"If I'm not lost in the ocean in the meanwhile," she added, lightly.

"Mary Eliska, that reminds me—" He pulled her down to the bench again. "I know you're counting on trying for that prize—oh, don't deny it, for I saw the excitement in your eyes that day Bob Hulbert made the announcement—but I don't think you can hope to win, even if you do get hold of another plane.... I'm afraid that Hulbert woman is going to beat you to it."

"Why, Ralph?" asked Mary Eliska, seeing that it was useless to deny her desire.

"Because I believe she's planning to fly soon."

"What with?" "She's gone to England to have a special plane made.... I'll tell you a secret, if you promise not to breathe it to Kitty that I told you: Sis lent her her pearls, so that Miss Hulbert could raise a loan for the price of the plane."

"Oh, no!" cried Mary Eliska, shocked for Kitty's sake, as well as for her own and Jax Gray's. "Yes, she did. I saw Miss Hulbert take away a box yesterday, and I questioned Kitty. So she told me why."

"Then," concluded Mary Eliska, dolefully, "I guess that settles it!"

"So you might as well give up aviation and marry me!"

"Forget it, Ralph!" Then, deliberately assuming a light-hearted manner again, she added, "Come on back and dance.... But remember—no more cutting in!"

Chapter 6.15
Plans for the Ocean Flight

The last day of the Christmas vacation—New Year's—passed very quickly for Mary Eliska. The dance had continued until almost dawn, and for once she stayed to the end. For there was no flight in store for her on the morrow, or the day after. She could be as sleepy as she wanted to.

Accordingly, her aunt did not wake her until noon, and only then because her father was taking a late afternoon train back to New York.

"I want to go for a walk with you this afternoon, Daughter," he said, while she ate her combined breakfast and luncheon. "I would like to have a talk with you."

"Yes, Daddy," replied Mary Eliska, trembling inside, lest he intended to tell her that he would forbid the ocean flight.

"Can you spare the time—say about three o'clock—from your social engagements?"

"I haven't any social engagements," she replied. "Jax Gray and I didn't accept anything for after Christmas Day."

"But I heard your aunt tell Mrs. Clavering this morning on the telephone that she'd see that you went to Kitty's dinner party."

Mary Eliska yawned. She had enjoyed the dance the night before, but it was enough to last her for a while.

"Is Jax Gray going?" she inquired.

"I couldn't tell you that, my dear. You can call her up."

"All right. But in any case that wouldn't interfere with our walk, Daddy. I'll be ready at three."

Unlike most of her girlfriends, whose days were spent in constant social activities, Mary Eliska was always punctual about her engagements. As the clock struck three, she appeared in the living-room. Dressed in her gray squirrel coat and matching beret and cloth boots, she presented a beautiful picture of up-to-date winter fashions. Linking her arm affectionately in her father's, she accompanied him out into the crisp, clear air, and started towards the outskirts of the town.

"Wouldn't you rather be sledding, my dear?" he asked, gazing at her in admiration.

"No, indeed!" she hastened to reply. "I'd much rather be with you.... Anyway, I suppose there will be a sledding-party after dinner tonight. Kitty told us to bring our sweaters and riding-breeches."

"Very well.... Have you guessed what I wanted to talk to you about?"

"Yes, I think I have—Daddy," she faltered.

"You have?" he repeated, smiling. "Well, first of all I want to tell you that I am exceedingly proud of your courage and pluck up there on the border, and in Canada, and that I think you have proved your ability to take care of yourself in a plane."

"Daddy!" she exclaimed, in surprise. "I was afraid you and Aunt Polly would say I could never fly again! After all the anxiety I caused you."

"That is what your aunt would like to say—but I feel differently. What happened was due to no fault or carelessness of yours, no lack of skill on your part. A less able pilot would have been killed, I am sure."

"It's awfully sweet of you to say that!"

"Well, I mean it. I'm convinced now that you have a right to go on with aviation. And I am willing for you to order your plane for the ocean flight."

A thrill of emotion ran through Mary Eliska, so intense that she could not speak. Clasping his arm tightly with both her hands, she told him in the only way she could of her great gratitude. Then she remembered his business.

"You won't need the money, Daddy?" she asked, after a moment.

"No—not now that I feel sure that your trip saved me, and that this unfair competition will cease. But just to make sure, I'll go to Canada tomorrow, and visit the Convent myself. I'll wire you results."

"I think," she said slowly, with tears dimming her blue eyes, "that you are the most wonderful father a girl ever had."

He patted her hand gently, not knowing how to reply, and they walked on for some time in silence.

It was not until the short winter afternoon was coming to a close, and they had turned their steps towards home that he mentioned his sister.

"I don't want you to say anything at all of this to your aunt, Mary Eliska," he cautioned her. "She might play on your unselfishness, and make you give it up. It is a risk, of course—I understand that, and I know just how she feels. But we all have to take risks in life; it would be dull indeed if we didn't. So I think I had better handle the thing myself—tell her sometime when I happen to come home when you aren't there. I can win her around to it, I know."

"That would be wonderful, Daddy!" cried the girl, in relief. It had been worrying her for a long time whenever she thought of securing her aunt's consent. She even believed that she might weaken herself, if the older woman used tears and pleading. For Mary Eliska could never forget what a loving foster-mother her Aunt Polly had always been.

"By the way, have you picked out your plane?" her father inquired.

"Yes, indeed! It's a Bellanca—they call it Model J 300. Just built for ocean flights! Oh, Daddy, it has everything to make it perfect! A capacity for carrying one hundred and five additional gallons of gasoline, besides the regular supply in the tanks of one hundred and eighty gallons! And a Wright three-hundred-horsepower engine, and a tachometer, and a magnetic compass——"

"There, that's enough, Daughter!" he interrupted, smiling. "I'm afraid I don't know what all those terms mean. If you're satisfied that it's the best you can buy——"

"Oh, I am! I'm crazy about it. I'm going to put in my order the minute I get your telegram."

"And if anything should happen, so that you had to come down in the water, would it float?" he asked, with an imperceptible shudder. In spite of his bravery, the thought of Mary Eliska over that deep, wide ocean at night made his flesh creep.

"Yes, Daddy. The tanks permit the plane to float. You can be sure it will have every modern invention, every safety device there is today. It will cost about twenty-two thousand dollars!"

"That's right, Daughter," he approved. "If you're going at all, you must do the thing with the utmost care. Don't try to save money. A few hundred dollars might mean the difference between disaster and success."

"I know," she answered, solemnly.

As they were approaching the house, they began to talk of other things, as if by silent agreement. Airplanes and ocean flights were apparently forgotten, for the moment they were inside, Mary Eliska's Aunt Polly was urging her to get ready for the party. Unfortunately, Jax Gray was not going. Like Mary Eliska, she had been invited at first, but once she refused, she was not popular enough with Kitty to be asked again. So Mary Eliska could not talk of her trip with anyone; she would have to wait until the following day, when Jax Gray accompanied her back to the ground school.

It seemed strange indeed, to get up early the next morning and take a train back to St. Louis. Both the girls regretted the loss of the Pursuit, and realized how they were going to miss it, but they resolutely decided to be good sports and to try to joke about it.

"Don't forget we have to buy tickets," Mary Eliska reminded her chum. "Don't go to the window and ask for high-test gasoline!"

"Won't a train seem slow?" returned Jax Gray. "Oh, well, we won't have to care about the weather, that's one good thing! Besides, we can sleep."

"As if you ever made a flight without at least one good nap!" teased the other.

But in spite of their assumed gayety, it seemed like a tiresome, endless journey, with a change of cars and a wait at the station. It was afternoon before they finally arrived at their destination.

Both girls had decided to say nothing about their holiday adventure, but when they reached the school, they found themselves being treated as heroines. Everybody had read all about them in the papers, and knew that they had jumped from parachutes and that they had lost the Pursuit.

"But you'll soon be graduating from here, and making all kinds of money," one of the instructors told Mary Eliska hopefully. "And then you will be able to buy another plane of your own."

(Sooner than you think, Mary Eliska said to herself, for no one but Mr. Eckers at the school knew of her proposed trans-Atlantic flight.)

Both girls plunged headlong into the work, forgetting everything but the studies that were before them. Only, Mary Eliska could not forget to watch eagerly for the telegram that would mean her father's final consent.

It arrived three days later, saying that all his business troubles had vanished, and that he had sold enough of her bonds for her to write a check for her Bellanca.

Wild with joy, she dashed across the flying field to the hangar where Jax Gray happened to be taking some notes from Eckers.

"Everything's O.K.!" she cried, as she burst open the door. "We can fly to Paris, Jax Gray!"

Her chum jumped up and the girls hugged each other in ecstasy, much to the amusement of the elderly instructor.

"So you're ordering a Bellanca long-distance mono-plane?" he asked.

"Yes. Tonight! Oh, Mr. Eckers, from its pictures, from its description, it's absolutely marvelous. And as safe as an ocean-liner!"

"Safer!" amended Jax Gray, "Ocean-liners sometimes sink. But never a Bellanca!"

"We're going to be awfully careful and thorough about our preparations, Mr. Eckers," Mary Eliska explained, as she detached herself from Jax Gray's arms, and sat down on the edge of his desk. "Just like Lindbergh!"

"Well, I hope you have Lindbergh's success," was the instructor's fervent wish. "But tell me, Mary Eliska, have you heard of any others who are planning to try for this prize?"

"Only one so far. She's in England now, having her plane built there, I believe."

Jax Gray gritted her teeth at the mention of Bess Hulbert, but she said nothing.

"Then you'll simply have to beat her!" cried the man, enthusiastically. "It must be an American plane that wins. And American girls!"

"Of course some of our best aviatrixes may compete," put in Jax Gray. "You mean women like Amelia Earhart?" he asked. "Yes."

"Somehow I don't think she will," said Mr. Eckers. "Miss Earhart is too good a sport to take honors from a younger, less experienced flyer. She doesn't go out for sensational glory. She doesn't have to. She has already won her place."

"But of course some of the younger girls may."

"Yes. But you girls have a better chance than anybody, I think. Better prepared. Besides, the difficulty is going to be getting a suitable plane. It would be fool-hardy for anybody to take a chance in a plane that wasn't super-tested, and super-equipped. And few parents are going to give their consent, even if they can provide the money.... I believe your greatest opponent is this English girl."

"Well, we're going to beat her!" announced Jax Gray, defiantly, and she did not add that she meant to take harsh measures if that young woman put in an appearance in the United States.

"When do you expect to go?" questioned Eckers.

"The twentieth of May, if the weather is right," replied Mary Eliska. "I believe in luck, and that was Lindy's lucky day."

"And Mary Eliska's!" added Jax Gray, as the girls went off to send their order.

Chapter 6.16
The Autogiro

Mary Eliska had always been a girl of a single purpose. It was this characteristic that set her apart from Jax Gray Haydock, from her other girlfriends—in fact, from practically all of her sex. In this she was more like a man, with a man's mind.

She never could see the advisability of mixing pleasure with work; when she was determined to accomplish or to learn something, nothing could distract her. Now while she was bending all her energy to the winning of her mechanic's license and the thorough preparation for her trans-Atlantic flight she grew impatient with even her chum for desiring to lead a social life.

One cold night in February, when she was desperately trying to concentrate on a treatise on airplane engines, Jax Gray annoyed her exceedingly by moving restlessly about the bedroom and interrupting her every few minutes with remarks and questions.

"I do wish you'd be more sociable, Mary Eliska!" she exclaimed, taking a dance dress out of the closet, and surveying it mournfully.

"I'm sorry, Jax Gray—I'm busy," replied her companion, without looking up.

"Well, just give me five minutes. Then I'll leave you alone."

"All right," agreed Mary Eliska, trying to be patient.

"Gaze on this dress, please. Don't you think it's an absolute wash-out?"

"I never heard of anybody's washing chiffon," remarked Mary Eliska, facetiously. "Why not try having it cleaned?"

"Don't be smart! You're wasting your precious time.... But seriously, Mary Eliska, could I or couldn't I wear it Saturday night to that dance Ted and his boyfriend are taking us to?"

"I suppose you could. But why not send home for another?"

"There isn't time. Besides, I'd love something new.... Here's my idea, Mary Eliska. Let's take tomorrow off—entirely off—and go on a shopping bat. I'm positively sick for one!"

"For the love of Pete!" cried Mary Eliska, in exasperation. "You don't know what you're asking, Jax Gray. Tomorrow they're going to bring an autogiro to the school, and Mr. Eckers said there was some chance of my being allowed to fly it!"

"Autogiro?" repeated Jax Gray. "What's that?"

"You know, Jax Gray! Get your mind off pink chiffon, and you'll remember. It's that new plane Cierva, the Spaniard, invented—with a windmill sort of thing on top—that can land and take off in a very small space. I'm just crazy to examine one and fly it myself."

Her companion assumed an air of resignation.

"Very well. If you want to go to that dance at the Aviation Club looking like something the cat dragged in, you can! But I'm not. I'm going to get me some raiment."

"I don't want to go to the dance at all."

"What?"

"You heard me, Jax Gray."

"Have you written that to Ted?"

"No. I didn't say positively last week that I'd go. And I haven't time to waste on social correspondence. It's all I can do to get off my weekly letters to Daddy and Aunt Polly. You tell him."

"But Mary Eliska, Ted's boyfriend won't have any girl!"

"You can manage 'em both. I've seen you take care of six or seven on Sunday nights at home."

"That was different."

"Well settle it to suit yourself. Only, remember, I'm not going. I'll be at the school all day Saturday and I'm not going to rush back to a beauty shop to get my hands and fingernails into shape for a dance. I'm staying home!"

Speechless, Jax Gray stood gazing at her chum in utter incomprehension. She was past understanding.

Thinking the conversation ended, Mary Eliska returned to her pamphlet. But her room-mate had not finished.

"Mary Eliska, I want to ask you something—while we're on the subject of Ted Mackay, and these nice parties he is always planning for us. How much do you care for him?"

"Not a rap!" Of course that was not exactly the truth, for Mary Eliska did like the big fellow immensely. But lately she had grown very tired of his regular week-end visits.

"Mary Eliska! You ought to be ashamed of yourself to say a thing like that! After all Ted's done for you."

"Well, I guess I was exaggerating. But I'm fed up with him, Jax Gray. I'm not going out with him any more for a while. And that's that!"

"Do you mind if I do?"

"Certainly not. Go all you please, if you won't try to drag me in!"

Jax Gray sat down, and fingered her dress nervously. There was one more question she just had to ask.

"Mary Eliska, will you tell me the truth about this: Would you mind if I—I—cared a whole lot about Ted?"

At last Mary Eliska was interested. She closed her booklet, and turned about to face the other girl. Seeing how serious, how ardent, yet how confused Jax Gray was, she smiled warmly.

"I think it's lovely, Jax Gray!" she assured her. "If you really care for Ted—because I've known for months that he's head over heels in love with you. Nothing but the real thing could pull him away from his work." Her tone was that of a person much older. "I say, 'Bless you, my children!'" Jax Gray was at her side now, kissing her ecstatically. "I was so desperately afraid you'd mind, Mary Eliska!" Mary Eliska laughed at the mistake. It really was funny. Jax Gray—usually so cocksure of herself in everything—was so modest that she couldn't see Ted's very evident admiration. "You're a goose, Jax Gray, but a dear, foolish goose!" Her brow suddenly darkened. "Does this mean you won't fly with me to Paris?"

"Oh, no! 'Course I'll go. I'm sure Ted wouldn't want me not to."

"I'm not so sure myself," muttered Mary Eliska, remembering how Ralph Clavering had tried to get her to give up the flight. Men were funny when they were in love, she thought; it did not occur to her that girls were funny too.

Jax Gray seemed perfectly satisfied, and did not open her mouth again that evening until Mary Eliska put her work away and suggested that they go downstairs and ask for cookies and milk, which their kind landlady always provided for them.

But Jax Gray did not give up her decision about the shopping trip, and the next day Mary Eliska went to the ground school alone, to forget everything else in her admiration of the autogiro which had arrived.

It was a queer little boat, the motor in its nose, and an ordinary propeller, just like an airplane. Its wings, however, were stubby, and the strangest part of it was the windmill-like arrangement, or rotary wing, mounted right on the top.

Everybody at the school was gathered about it, eagerly examining it, when Mary Eliska appeared, and she lost no time in joining the group. Mr. Eckers was explaining its parts to the students.

"It really is remarkable," he was saying, "the way it can rise vertically right over a given place. It can hover over a spot while it is climbing upward, and can land with almost no forward motion. For this reason a huge landing field is not necessary. I believe it is the plane for the city dweller."

"Everyone can keep an autogiro in his back yard," remarked one of the students. "And make his landing on a postage stamp! Believe—me—I'm going to have one! And I don't mean maybe."

Mr. Eckers continued his explanation, telling them that the autogiro could fly very low, only a few feet from the ground, and then he went on to compare it with the helicopter, another new-fashioned invention somewhat similar.

When he had finished his remarks, he offered to take the students in turn for rides, and they all pressed eagerly forward. All except Mary Eliska, for she was too shy to make her wishes known. Besides, she felt that she did not have to tell Mr. Eckers; he would know how interested she was.

But the time was too short, and the students too many. Closing hour arrived, and Mary Eliska had not had her flight. Stopping in at the instructor's office at five o'clock, she told him wistfully that she had missed out.

"Oh, I'm sorry, Mary Eliska!" he exclaimed, in genuine regret. "But those boys acted just like children, pushing in the way they did. Never you mind, though, you'll get your turn tomorrow."

"Tomorrow?" she repeated. "I thought the autogiro was to be sent to Birmingham, Alabama!"

"So it is. But after a little practice with it, I'm going to let you take it."

"Me?"

"Yes, you! Because you are such a good flyer, and because you are a mechanic besides. There's another job at the end of the trip—taking another plane—not an autogiro—to Nashville, Tennessee. All your expenses will be paid, and there will be twenty-five dollars in it for you. Would you like to do it?"

"Would I?" cried Mary Eliska, her eyes shining with happiness. "I'd just love it."

"Then you can make your plans."

"Could I—take Miss Haydock with me?" she asked, timidly.

"Why, of course. That will make it all the better. I think we can even pay her hotel expenses, though of course she won't make any money. It is because you are a mechanic as well as a flyer that you are in a position to earn the money."

"Because I am a mechanic!" she repeated softly to herself. Her wish was really coming true.

"Be on hand at eight o'clock tomorrow, if the day is clear," the instructor concluded. "And don't wait for that girl friend of yours, if she is late. She cut classes today—isn't sick, is she?"

"No," laughed Mary Eliska. "Playing hookey, I'm afraid."

"Just a typical girl," muttered the man. "We have 'em all the time here—society dames, flying as a fad, school-girls, for the excitement of the thing, married women who are tired of housekeeping…. There isn't one in a thousand who takes it seriously, as you do, Mary Eliska."

"Thank you, Mr. Eckers," replied Mary Eliska, blushing at his praise…. "How long shall I be gone—on this trip, I mean?"

"You ought to be able to get to Birmingham before dark tomorrow. Then you can rest tomorrow night, and start to Nashville Saturday—if the weather is O.K. But don't try to fly too fast with this other plane, and don't attempt it 'til the weather is perfect. The plane's in good condition, but it's an old one, and I wouldn't want anything to happen to you. If you have to stay at Birmingham a week on account of fog, or something, it will be O.K. with me, and your expenses will be paid. You take a train back from Nashville."

"I'll get my map and directions tomorrow?"

"Yes. I'll have them here for you, all ready."

Mary Eliska went back to her boarding-house in an exalted frame of mind, singing as she entered her room. She found her chum equally gay, sitting on the bed amidst a pile of packages.

"Have a good time, Jax Gray?" she asked, merrily.

"And how!"

"So did I! And I've got the best news yet. We fly an autogiro to Birmingham tomorrow."

"Who do?"

"You and I, Jax Gray! Our expenses are to be paid, and we get twenty-five dollars besides!" Mary Eliska did not add that it was she who was earning the money, for she had already made up her mind to share it with her chum.

Jax Gray shook her head.

"Not this baby!" she said. "Tomorrow's Friday, Mary Eliska. I might not get back in time for the dance Saturday night. No, my dear, I'm not taking any chances."

"Do you really mean that, Jax Gray? Give up a wonderful trip like this, just to go to an old dance? You could wire Ted."

"But I don't want to, Mary Eliska. Why, my heart'd break if I couldn't wear these new clothes I just bought…. Gaze on them! How about this cerise taffeta? Would you ever think any trimming could be so clever? It's made of feathers, you see—and look how the slippers match!" Mary Eliska stood perfectly still, gazing at the finery without seeing it. "You really won't go, Jax Gray?" she repeated. "Even if I rush the trip?"

"Oh no, Mary Eliska, I couldn't possibly disappoint Ted." Seeing that it was useless to try to persuade her, Mary Eliska rushed downstairs and called Nancy Bancroft on the telephone, inviting her instead, and this time she was gratified with an acceptance.

Chapter 6.17
Enemies

The day of Mary Eliska's flight to Birmingham, Alabama, was warm and spring-like. It was only a false spring, to be sure, the kind that sometimes comes suddenly in February, making everyone long to be out of doors. How lucky for her, she thought. If it would only last a couple of days!

Nancy Bancroft was already at the school when Mary Eliska arrived, alert and eager for the trip. She had just received her private pilot's license a few days previous, but she did not expect to attempt to guide the autogiro. Nevertheless, she would be company for the more experienced aviatrix.

Half an hour's instruction was all that Mr. Eckers considered necessary, and before nine o'clock the girls took off for the South. Mary Eliska couldn't help singing for joy. The autogiro was so much fun!

"Dad's going to buy me a plane," Nancy informed her companion. "As soon as I get home next week."

"Next week?" repeated Mary Eliska.

"Yes. I'm leaving the school as soon as we get back. I have my license, you know—that's what I wanted."

Mary Eliska was silent, thinking of Mr. Eckers' remark about girls the day before. Yes, he must be right, their ambition usually ended with the government's permission to fly.

"I'll miss you dreadfully, Nance!" was all she said.

"You must fly to New York often," urged the other.

The country over which the girls were flying was beautiful and the air delightful. As they went farther south, they recognized real evidences of spring in the foliage. The little plane hummed gayly on, with never a disturbance in its sturdy motor. Mary Eliska was exceedingly happy.

Noon-time came, and they ate their sandwiches and drank the coffee which Mary Eliska's kind-hearted landlady had insisted upon providing, but they did not stop. Everything was going so wonderfully that they hated to break the spell. At this rate they ought to reach Birmingham long before dark.

It was about two o'clock that they met with a strange adventure. Flying along at an even rate, high enough to span the woods that loomed ahead of them, there suddenly appeared, out of nowhere it seemed, what the girls thought to be a formation of airplanes.

"Go carefully!" warned Nancy. "Don't forget that awful accident a while ago, when several planes were flying in formation!"

Mary Eliska curved to the side, but the planes seemed to be flying straight at her.

"They haven't any sense at all!" she cried, in exasperation, now seriously fearing disaster.

On they rushed, 'til a cold fear gripped Mary Eliska's heart. Try as she might, she couldn't get out of their way! It was all like a dreadful dream, when something menacing rushes inevitably towards you, yet you are powerless to stop. Then, in a flash, Mary Eliska perceived what the formation was.

Eagles! Great, huge, ominous birds, traveling through the air with the speed of machines. Involuntarily, she reached for her gun.

"No use!" shouted Nancy, in terror. "Too many of them!"

Realizing the truth of Nancy's words, Mary Eliska did the only thing possible: swiftly, almost recklessly, she landed on the ground, expecting to be dashed upward again, or the plane turned over, pinning her and her companion beneath. But miraculously, nothing disastrous happened; the autogiro had come down vertically and stopped. That, then, was the wonder of this marvelous little machine! Had it been any other kind of plane, the girls would surely have been injured—and possibly killed!

They had landed in a small clearing between the trees. Shutting off her engine, Mary Eliska turned, gasping, to her friend.

"Would you ever believe, a thing like that if you read it?" she demanded.

"The landing—or the birds?" inquired Nancy, still breathless with excitement.

"I really meant the birds, for I knew that the autogiro was wonderful. I've seen them land and take off before, though of course I never tried anything like this."

"Well, I did read about big birds bothering pilots one time—in a newspaper, I guess. But I didn't think much about it."

They waited quietly for a while until they felt calm again. The birds had flown on immediately; there was nothing to prevent their taking up their journey again. Ordinarily Mary Eliska would have been apprehensive of a take-off in so small a space, but after her landing, she felt confident. The autogiro rose instantly, almost vertically, and they were on their course again.

"I'm going to get Dad to buy me an autogiro!" Nancy announced. "This has decided me."

"Me too!" agreed Mary Eliska.

"But you'll have a big Bellanca!" Nancy said. "Jax Gray told me you put in the order."

"I may not have, after we try that ocean trip," returned the other girl. "We may be ship-wrecked and picked up by some boat——"

"So long as you are picked up, it'll be O.K.... Oh, Mary Eliska, I think you are just marvelous!"

"Thanks, Nance. But I don't deserve the praise yet. Wait 'til I earn it."

Only a short distance stretched between them and Birmingham now, and Mary Eliska covered it in record time. Safe and sound she brought the autogiro down on the airport before four o'clock in the afternoon. Turning it over to the authorities, and giving her instructions about the other plane, which was to be ready the following day, Mary Eliska summoned a taxi and asked to be driven to the best hotel.

The rest of the day was their own, and the girls enjoyed it thoroughly, eating a luxurious dinner, and attending a show afterward. On their way home from the theater, Nancy asked more questions about Mary Eliska's proposed trans-Atlantic flight, and the latter told her everything—even to the story of the enemy whom she and Jax Gray most feared: Bess Hulbert.

"But I don't see why you should worry about her," said Nancy. "She wouldn't dare come back to the United States again."

"I'm not so sure of that. Now that some time has passed, she'll think everyone's forgotten about her crimes."

"I hope not," replied Nancy, optimistically.

Little did the girls think, as they discussed Bess Hulbert, that evening, that they would run into her the following day, just as Mary Eliska was fearing might happen at some time or another. It all happened suddenly, at the field of the airplane construction company in Nashville, Tennessee, where Mary Eliska had delivered the second plane without any mishap.

She had just received the president's signature on the delivery card, and was about to summon a taxi, when the man made a generous suggestion. "If you girls can wait 'til tomorrow," he told them, "I can have you taken north by plane. We are making a delivery at Springfield, Illinois, and St. Louis isn't much out of the way."

"That will be fine!" exclaimed Mary Eliska, gratefully. "Because we both have grown to hate trains. They crawl so."

"Worms instead of birds," remarked Nancy, thinking of the dangerous mistake they had made the previous day.

"Besides," added Mary Eliska, "we will get there so much more quickly, even though we had thought something of taking a sleeper."

"O.K. Then I will introduce you to your pilot, and you can make your arrangements." He turned to a mechanic who was standing by. "Joe, get Miss Mason to come over here." Then, to the girls he explained, "Your pilot happens to be a young lady—one of our saleswomen."

Nancy and Mary Eliska both smiled rather proudly. It was nice to find that women were everywhere taking their places in aviation.

The false name was misleading; Mary Eliska had not a suspicion that "Miss Mason" was Bess Hulbert, although she remembered later that the girl had masqueraded in Plattsburg as "Anna Smith." But the moment the girl came toward them, Mary Eliska recognized her, and had the satisfaction at least of seeing her turn deathly pale.

Noticing Mary Eliska's gasp of astonishment, Nancy turned to her questioningly.

"It's Bess Hulbert!" she whispered, hoarsely. "What's that?" demanded the president of the corporation. "Nothing," answered Mary Eliska. "Only—Mr. Harris—we—we've changed our minds about flying back to St. Louis. We'll go by train."

"But why?" demanded the man, as Miss Hulbert came nearer. "Pardon me, but is it something personal? You know Miss Mason, perhaps?"

"To Mary Eliska's sorrow!" was Nancy's quick and bitter retort. "I think you had better hear all about the kind of woman you have in your employ!"

"No! No!" protested Bess Hulbert, who was now near enough to hear the slur, and who appeared desperately frightened. "Give me a chance to talk to Mary Eliska alone. I don't know this other person!"

At a loss to know what to say, the man looked helplessly at Mary Eliska.

"No. Perhaps we had better go," decided Mary Eliska.

"Please give me a chance!" begged Bess. "Ten minutes—alone." She looked imploringly at Mr. Harris, who nodded immediately, and started towards the building.

Bess reached for Mary Eliska's arm, and clung to it desperately, as a beggar might appeal for alms.

"I know what you think of me," she said. "But I'm so sorry, so frightfully sorry! Won't you have mercy on me—let bygones be bygones, if I give you my word of honor I've reformed?"

Receiving no reply, she continued excitedly: "It's true that I tried to snatch your father's business, but oh, I was desperate! If you could know what it is to be poor—to have an ambition to fly, and not be able to fulfill it! Oh, Mary Eliska, you ought to understand what the longing is! Suppose you didn't have a father to buy you a plane! Remember, I had to fly an old Jenny from the Army, while you piloted an Arrow Sport!"

"But you wrecked my Arrow," Mary Eliska reminded her.

"Yes. In a fit of jealousy. I'm sorry. Oh, please believe that I am truly sorry now! And if you let me go ahead without showing me up, and if I can win that prize for the flight to Paris, I'll buy you a new plane. Honest I will! I'll give you a written promise!"

"But why should I make it possible for you to win the prize, when Miss Haydock and I want to win it ourselves?" countered Mary Eliska.

"To be sporting! Oh, won't you please! You see, I now owe Kitty Clavering ten thousand dollars, and I can never repay her unless I win. I've got a job here, but it would take me years to save that much.... If you throw me into prison, I'll never get out of debt. It will ruin my life."

"Didn't you try to ruin Mary Eliska's life?" put in Nancy.

"No—only the plane. I didn't mean to kill you, Mary Eliska! I'm not so bad as that! I'd never do anything like that again—I've learned my lesson, living these months in a constant dread of arrest and disgrace.... Maybe you haven't heard that my brother is engaged to Kitty Clavering," she added, changing the subject. "But he could never marry her if I brought a terrible disgrace on the family!"

In the face of these arguments and entreaties, Mary Eliska was silent. Never in her life had she been confronted with such a momentous decision.

"When do you plan to fly across the ocean?" she asked, stalling for time.

"April. Early in the month, I hope."

"With another girl?"

"No. Alone."

"No mechanic—no navigator with you?"

"No. I'm relying a lot on luck."

"That's a bad idea. You better get somebody to help you."

Bess Hulbert's eyes lighted up with joy.

"You are going to let me go?" she cried, snatching Mary Eliska's hand in relief. "Oh, you angel!"

"I'm not sure yet," replied Mary Eliska. "I'll have to talk it over with Jax Gray—Miss Haydock. After all, she has a right to some say in the matter.... But meanwhile, my friend and I do not care to go by plane with you to St. Louis."

"You won't trust me! Even now, when you have my confession—when I tell you I've reformed?"

"Sorry," replied Mary Eliska, coldly. "But a burnt child dreads the fire. So I don't feel like risking it.... Now, if we decide to let you off, it is just as you said, because of the sport of the thing—to give you a chance to compete for the big honor. But Miss Haydock and I could never really trust you again."

Bess Hulbert sighed; she was slowly but surely learning that dishonesty did not pay.

"You are going to tell Mr. Harris?" she asked.

"No, I guess not," replied Mary Eliska. "That wouldn't do us any good.... We want to get to a hotel now, and look up our trains, and change our clothing. Can you get us a taxi?"

"Certainly," replied Bess, meekly. How different she was from the haughty girl they had met at the Flying Club in the fall! "And when shall I hear definitely from you?"

"If we decide to take any steps against you, we'll inform the officials this week, and you'll hear from them. But I wouldn't run away this time—you have an even chance of getting free, if you stick to the job. And, if you hear nothing before the tenth of March, say, you can go ahead with your plans."

"Thank you! Thank you!" cried the older girl, rushing off to do as she was told. The taxi appeared in a few minutes, and when Nancy and Mary Eliska were finally alone, the former regarded her friend with wonder and admiration.

"You're actually going to let her go, aren't you, Mary Eliska!" she asked.

"What do you think?" asked the other.

Nancy shrugged her shoulders. "You're doing the big thing, of course, but I don't believe in your place I could do it. I'd want my revenge.... Anyhow, I don't really think she'll win that prize."

"What makes you say that?"

"Not enough preparation. Not a good enough plane—she's spending less than ten thousand dollars, apparently.... And, well, it just wouldn't be right."

Mary Eliska laughed, but she knew that Nancy was absolutely loyal to her.

Chapter 6.18
Rivals

When Mary Eliska got back to the boarding-house on Sunday afternoon, she dashed eagerly up to her room to tell the news to Jax Gray. But her chum was not there.

"Where is Jax Gray?" she called to the landlady.

"Out with Mr. Mackay," replied the woman, smiling.

There was nothing to do but wait, so Mary Eliska tried to busy herself with her studies. But for once she could not get her mind off the subject of Bess Hulbert, and concentrate.

About five o'clock Jax Gray finally arrived. She looked radiantly happy.

"I've got something thrilling to tell you, Mary Eliska!" she exclaimed, giving the other girl a hug.

"And I have something not so thrilling to tell you!" returned Mary Eliska.

"Well, out with it! Let's get the bad news over first!" Jax Gray took off her hat and coat and settled down in the arm-chair beside the window. Her eyes took on a dreamy expression.

"I met Bess Hulbert!" Mary Eliska announced, expecting Jax Gray to jump into the air at the startling fact. But she did no such thing; she took the information with the utmost calm.

"Well, of all things," she remarked. "Where?"

"At an airplane company in Nashville, Tennessee. And Jax Gray, she confessed everything."

"Might as well," muttered her room-mate. "We knew it all anyway."

"She put up a touching plea for forgiveness. Why, she even promised to pay me for the Pursuit, if I didn't turn her over to the authorities."

"And what did you say?"

"That I couldn't decide, without talking to you.... Now, what do you think?"

"I think that she ought to be put into prison, of course!" replied Jax Gray. "But it's up to you, Mary Eliska. I'll be too busy for the next few months to be bothered prosecuting criminals.... You see, I'm engaged to Ted!"

"Engaged!" Though Mary Eliska had expected this to happen, she had no idea it would come so soon. Somehow, she thought Jax Gray would not settle anything definitely until after the flight to Paris.

"Yes, that's my thrilling news! Aren't you pleased, Mary Eliska?"

"Of course I am, darling! I think it's wonderful.... I was just being selfish—wondering whether it would interfere with our flight."

"No indeed it won't! I told Ted I wouldn't consider giving that up. We're not going to be married until June."

"Then I'll have you three months more!" cried Mary Eliska, joyfully. "Whoopee! Long enough to finish our course here. After that we probably should have been separated anyway, because you know I expect to take a job."

"You have to be my maid-of-honor," Jax Gray informed her. "That will be a job for you."

"The kind of job Aunt Polly would approve of. I'll be tickled to death, of course, Jax Gray."

"I'm going home at Easter," continued the other girl, "and Ted is coming too. We'll make all our plans then. You expect to go home for the holidays too, don't you? We have a week."

"I thought something of going over to New Castle, to see how my Bellanca is coming along. Then I'd go back to Spring City for the rest of the time." She did not add that she had been hoping Jax Gray would go with her; such a suggestion was out of the question now.

"Suppose Bess Hulbert beats us, and our trip has to be canceled," remarked Jax Gray. "Aren't you taking an awful chance letting her off?"

"Yes, but I'd hate myself if I prosecuted her just because I was afraid of her as a rival. In fact, that's the very reason I'm inclined to let her off—because of the sporting side of the thing. If she weren't planning to compete for this prize, I'm sure I'd have her held for smuggling, anyway, for it would be a difficult matter to prove that she did something to injure my plane."

"You're a queer girl, Mary Eliska," observed her companion. "You can be so much more impersonal than most of our sex. I admire you for it."

Study was out of the question for that evening, because Jax Gray just had to talk, and this time Mary Eliska humored her, listening in amusement to the girl's praises of Ted Mackay, and her rosy dreams of the future.

In the days that followed Jax Gray tried to settle down to work, but she discovered it to be impossible. Her mind was completely absorbed with her trousseau, her wedding, the little house she and Ted meant to buy and furnish. The only thing about flying that interested her at all was the trans-Atlantic trip; for this she had not lost her enthusiasm.

April arrived, bringing the Easter vacation, for the holiday fell late that year. The girls parted, to meet again at Spring City a day or two later. Mary Eliska considered herself exceptionally fortunate to make the trip to New Castle by air. One of the students who owned a plane happened to be flying east for the week's vacation, and offered to take her with him. The weather was delightful, and her visit wholly satisfactory. The Bellanca would be ready for her by the first week of May.

She boarded a train back to Spring City, and arrived only a day after Jax Gray. But that one day had been sufficient to spread the news of the latter's engagement all over the little town, and in spite of the fact that social affairs had slowed down for Lent, she was being entertained by everyone.

Mary Eliska went directly home and found her Aunt Polly anxiously waiting for her. "There's a tea at the Flying Club, dear," Mary Eliska told her, almost before she had removed her hat and coat. "And Kitty has phoned twice for you."

"Then I'll have to go right away, I suppose," laughed Mary Eliska. "You do love to get me into society, don't you, Aunt Polly?" "Somebody has to keep up that end of it," replied the older woman. "But first, before you go, I want to talk to you…. About that flight to Paris."

Mary Eliska stood perfectly still, unable to keep from trembling. In these three months that had passed since Christmas, neither had ever mentioned the subject, although the girl knew that her father had performed his mission as he promised her on New Year's day. Now, at this late date, was her aunt going to put forth objections? She waited tensely for the latter to continue.

"I gave your father my word that I wouldn't do anything to keep you from going," said Mary Eliska, "and you must admit that I have kept to it. But circumstances have changed. I think I have a right, and a duty, to speak now."

"Why—now?" stammered Mary Eliska. "What has changed?" She was unable to follow her aunt's reasoning.

"Because of Jax Gray's engagement—of course. It wouldn't be fair to Ted Mackay for her to take a risk like that. You must think of him, Mary Eliska."

Mary Eliska fingered her coat nervously, wondering whether she was being selfish. "But Ted is willing for Jax Gray to go," she objected. "And she's crazy about it herself."

"Because she cares so much for you, my dear—not because she cares for the flight itself. If you weren't going, you know she'd never think of attempting it alone." Mary Eliska smiled; how could she tell her aunt, without appearing conceited, that Jax Gray was not capable of such a feat? "Jax Gray hasn't had enough experience, Aunt Polly," she finally said.

"But she has been at school as long as you have. And she accompanied you on most of your flights last summer.... No, dear—she doesn't care the way you do. And I don't want you to be selfish."

"All right, Aunt Polly, I'll talk it over with her," agreed Mary Eliska, as she went up to her bedroom to change into an afternoon dress for the tea. All her joyousness at seeing the almost-completed Bellanca had suddenly vanished at her aunt's warning; she felt blue again, just as she had that day before Christmas when she offered to turn her money over to her father. In a way things were worse now, for she could not go to her chum for sympathy, as on the previous occasion. That would be taking an unfair advantage, literally forcing Jax Gray to accompany her.

She dressed quickly and drove to the Flying Club in her sports roadster, anxious to get away from her own unhappy thoughts.

Kitty Clavering, in a flowered chiffon, and sporting a lovely diamond on her left hand, came to greet her immediately, and in the congratulations and the gayety that followed, Mary Eliska forgot her troubles for the time being. Jax Gray, who was the center of attraction, was completely surrounded by her friends, and it was some minutes before Mary Eliska had a chance to speak to her.

"Have you a date for tonight, Jax Gray?" she asked. "Has Ted come yet?" "No—to both questions," replied Jax Gray. "I promised the family I'd stay home, for some aunts and cousins are coming. Now that I've caught my man, they want to look me over," she added flippantly. "And Ted won't be here 'til tomorrow. Why? What's on?" "I—I'd like to have a talk with you about our flight," said Mary Eliska. "I was going to ask you to come over to our house and stay all night."

"That's O.K. with me. Only you'll have to come to our house instead." The conversation was interrupted by Ralph Clavering, who had spied Mary Eliska for the first time. He took her hand impulsively, and held it so long that she was forced to pull it away. "Where have you been?" he demanded, irritably. "I've been home from college for four days, just waiting for you!"

"I stopped at New Castle to see my Bellanca," Mary Eliska explained, smiling at his impatience. In spite of everything she did and said to the contrary, he always acted as if he owned her. "Mary Eliska! You're not really counting on that ocean trip?" he demanded, making no effort to hide his disapproval.

(Why, oh why, she wondered, is everybody against me?)

"I am, though," she answered. "Jax Gray won't go with you now, will she?" "She fully expected to, when I said good-by to her at school. Of course her family may have changed their minds about letting her." "I shouldn't think Mackay would permit such a thing!" asserted Ralph, masterfully.

"Pull yourself together, Ralph!" teased Mary Eliska. "This isn't Queen Victoria's time— when men say what women can or can't do!"

"Well, if she were my wife—or my fiancée———" "Which she isn't! Come on, Ralph, let's dance. So you'll get over your grouch."

"It isn't a grouch. It's genuine worry.... Listen, Mary Eliska: if you're bound to fly to Paris, take me along with you, instead of Jax Gray. Then at least we could die together."

"Don't be so morbid!" cried Mary Eliska. "Nobody's going to die. Besides, I couldn't take you. The whole point of the thing would be lost. The prize goes to the girl or girls who fly without a man's help."

"You could explain that I wasn't a help, only a hindrance," he suggested. "That I don't know half so much about piloting a plane as you do, and nothing at all about navigating it."

"No good, Ralph. Come on, let's dance, as I suggested before. And talk about something else. How you're going to entertain me tomorrow night, for instance."

The young man's mood changed instantly, and the rest of the afternoon passed pleasantly. Indeed, it was with difficulty that Mary Eliska broke away at six o'clock, in order to have time to dash home to tell her aunt of her plans, and to put some clothing into her over-night bag. Jax Gray's family were just ready to sit down to dinner when Mary Eliska arrived, and as the former had explained, there was an assortment of relatives. But both girls went out of their way to be agreeable, and when they went up to Jax Gray's room a little after ten, they left only the most pleasant impressions. "Now tell me about the Bellanca," urged Jax Gray, thinking this was Mary Eliska's reason for wanting to see her alone.

"Oh, it's marvelous, of course. More wonderful than its pictures." But her tone lacked enthusiasm. "What's the matter, Mary Eliska?" inquired the other girl. "What has gone wrong?"

"Nothing.... Only, Aunt Polly thinks I'm selfish to keep you to your promise. She wants me to urge you to give up the flight."

"Don't you just love it the way other people always want to run your life?" remarked Jax Gray. "With all due respect to your Aunt Polly, you can tell her from me, that I'm going! That's all there is to it. If I were married, it would be different. But I'm not!"

"Oh, Jax Gray, you really want to?" cried Mary Eliska, hugging her joyfully. "I'm not being selfish—and dragging you with me?"

"Absolutely not. We've set the date, and we're going!"

So Mary Eliska went happily to sleep that night, believing that everything was settled. Little did she think that on the following day two momentous events were to take place that would entirely disrupt her plans.

It all happened at the breakfast table, with the abruptness of an electric storm. Mr. Haydock spied the news first, in the paper which lay at his place. His mouth fell open and he stared at the sheet in dismay.

"'Mabel and Joyce Lightcap take off in tri-motored Ford for Paris!'" he read aloud to Mary Eliska and Jax Gray. "What?" gasped his daughter, jumping up from her chair and staring at the headlines over his shoulder.

"'In quest of the twenty-five-thousand-dollar prize offered by Mrs. Rodman Hallowell to the first girls who successfully fly from New York to Paris without a man,'" he continued.

Mary Eliska sat listening, speechless.

Jax Gray went on reading where her father had stopped.

"'The Misses Lightcap, who are sisters, twenty-two and twenty-three years of age, had kept their plans secret until last night, when they arrived at Roosevelt Field in the tri-motored plane. They left at dawn this morning. Weather reports are favorable, and the radio will announce their progress throughout the course of the day and night....'" Jax Gray dropped back into her chair, not daring to show Mary Eliska any sympathy, lest her chum burst out crying. She was probably the only person who realized what that flight meant to Mary Eliska.

"Of course they may not get there," observed Mr. Haydock, soothingly. "You girls may still get your chance."

"Perhaps it's all for the best," observed his wife, unable to conceal her feeling of relief at the knowledge that now Jax Gray probably would not go. Still Mary Eliska said nothing. Silently she ate her grapefruit and drank her coffee. But she believed she would choke if she tried to swallow any toast.

At last the ordeal was over, and she and Jax Gray rose from the table, about to go into the living-room with the newspaper, when a telegram arrived for the latter, containing another startling piece of news, this time from Ted Mackay.

"Transferred to Wichita, Kansas," Jax Gray read aloud. "Beginning May first. Can't we be married now?... Arriving Spring City tonight."

Jax Gray dropped into a chair and burst out laughing. What a relief from the tension! "Might as well do it!" she cried. "Now that these girls have stolen the honors!"

"You really would like to be married next week?" inquired her mother. "Yes, if Ted is going so far away. Of course I'll wait to see if these Lightcap women really arrive, but we ought to hear tonight...." She led Mary Eliska up to their bedroom.

"I really didn't want to go back to school anyway," she explained, when the girls were alone. "I've learned all I wanted to."

"You mean you'll always have Ted, in case things go wrong with your plane?" asked Mary Eliska. It was the first time she had spoken since she had heard the breath-taking news.

"That's about it. I could never hope to learn as much as he knows. Besides, I don't want to. Just have a license to fly—that's my ambition."

Mary Eliska began to put her things into the over-night bag, mechanically, as if she hardly knew what she was doing.

"I think I had better go home now, Jax Gray, because you'll have a million things to do if you want to get married next week. You had better get right to work."

"I will, though I guess mother'll take charge of most everything," she replied, her mind already occupied with the plans for her trousseau and her wedding. The flight to Paris was forgotten.

"I can't have engraved invitations," she muttered, half to herself. "I'll have to telephone everybody. But I guess Miss Bonner can rush my wedding-dress through, she's always so obliging——"

Mary Eliska kissed her good-by, and went downstairs. In another minute she was alone in her roadster.

Alone! Yes, that was the word. Completely alone! Bitterly she thought that there was no one in all the world who would not be thankful that her dream was shattered. Everybody—her aunt, Ralph Clavering, Ted Mackay, her father—yes, and Jax Gray herself—every single person would heave a sigh of relief at the change in the plans.

She entered the house noiselessly, unwilling to see her aunt yet, for fear the latter would gloat over the news. But soon a desire for information of the flyers got the better of her; she must hear the news. After all, she had to admire their spirit; she must not sulk over her own disappointment like a spoiled child. She went into the library and turned on the radio.

Except for her meals, she never left the instrument that day, listening to the reports as they came over the wireless. First the plane was sighted off Newfoundland; then a ship identified it half-way across the ocean. At supper time the bulletin came through that the plane had been seen off the Irish coast, and the newspapers went wild with joy. What a triumph for the feminine sex! Even Amelia Earhart took a man with her! This was new; this was history—great as the moment when the suffrage movement had been won!

By evening Mary Eliska had succeeded in controlling her own feelings, and was able to rejoice with the rest of the world. She even left the radio and went to a dance with Ralph Clavering, and was somehow able to enjoy herself, although she felt like a different person.

The next morning the newspapers blazed forth the story that Mabel and Joyce Lightcap had landed safe and sound in Paris, and would receive their prize that night at a royal reception in their honor.

Chapter 6.19
The Hoax Discovered

It was Harriman Smith who brought Mary Eliska the news that the Lightcap flight was a fraud.

Mary Eliska had not turned on the radio that morning, when the newspaper flashed forth the story of Mabel and Joyce Lightcap's successful arrival in Paris. While they were over the ocean, Mary Eliska had followed their progress with the keenest interest, but now that they were being fêted, it was more than she could bear to listen to the accounts of the celebration.

She was just finishing her coffee when Harry burst in. Good old Harry, whom she hadn't seen since Thanksgiving! Here, she thought, was a friend indeed, who would not rejoice with the others merely because she was safe, even though she had to forfeit her greatest ambition. Deep in her heart she knew that he realized her disappointment and sympathized. "You can still win, Mary Eliska!" he cried exultantly, pulling her from her chair by grasping both her hands. "The Lightcaps are a fake!"

"A fake?" she repeated, in a daze.

"Yes. Joyce happens to be a man! Masquerading as a girl! And he's been discovered, of course."

Wild with excitement, Mary Eliska clutched the boy's hands to steady herself. It was all so impossible, so unbelievable!

"Tell me everything!" she demanded. "Are you sure, Harry?"

"Positive. So would you be, if you'd turned on your radio, instead of saturating yourself with that sentimental newspaper! Everybody knows it now. Needless to say, they are not getting the prize."

Mary Eliska felt almost weak as she listened, and she dropped back into her chair to hear the details.

"It seems that this Joyce Lightcap is an experienced pilot—a mechanic, too—and he got the idea of winning that twenty-five thousand. So for months he and Mabel—she's his wife—have been living in seclusion, while he allowed his hair to grow and practiced acting the part of a girl. Joyce is a girl's name too, you know, as well as a man's, so his license was O.K. Then, when the big moment came, Mabel got backers to buy the Ford tri-motor plane, and they took off for Paris."

"But how did they discover him?" asked Mary Eliska.

"By the simplest method of all. Somebody noticed his beard!"

The answer was so ridiculous that Mary Eliska let out a peal of laughter. "You see," explained Harry, "Joyce relied on paint and powder to cover his cheeks and chin during the flight. From what I understand, Mabel's a wonderful talker, but she can't fly very well, and her husband didn't dare take the opportunity to shave. And some smart Johnnie, who kept shouting that no two girls could possibly fly the Atlantic, found himself challenged. He sneaked up near enough to the pair to rub his hands on their faces. Then, of course their game was up."

Mary Eliska sat silent for a moment, thinking the situation over. At first it appeared impossible, like the plot out of a fantastical musical comedy, but when she remembered how anxious Ralph Clavering had been to go with her, it did not seem so strange. Why, Ralph might have suggested the very thing himself if he had thought of it!

"What made you think of coming to tell me, Harry?" she inquired, after a moment.

"I wasn't coming to tell you, but to rejoice with you!" he amended. "Mary Eliska, dear, you have never been out of my thoughts for a minute these last two days." He paused and looked shyly away from her. "Will you believe it, when I tell you that my heart just bled for you?"

"Harry!" she exclaimed hoarsely. "You really cared—for my sake?"

"More than I can tell you!"

"And I imagined I hadn't a friend," she murmured. "A real friend, I mean, who thought more of my feelings than of my physical safety.... Oh, Harry, I'll never forget this!"

There was a deep silence for a moment, a silence filled with understanding and sympathy. Then Mary Eliska heard her aunt's voice, calling her from the library.

"Can you come in here a minute, dear?" she said. "I want you to look at your new dress."

"Certainly," responded her niece, and as Mary Eliska rose from her chair she felt as if she were walking on air. The whole world had changed for her in that ten minutes since Harriman Smith's arrival.

The young people entered the library together. "Why, good morning Harry," said Mary Eliska, cordially. "I didn't know that Mary Eliska had company."

"It is a queer time to call, I'll admit," replied Harry. "And I guess I even forgot to apologize. But I do now."

"You're excused," smiled the older woman. "At least if you'll be patient while I talk clothes for a moment.... You see, dear," she explained to Mary Eliska, "this dress has just come—I ordered it a couple of weeks ago for you when I was shopping in Columbus—and I think it will do nicely for the wedding. Jax Gray's mother just told me that you will be the only attendant—it's too short notice to worry about bridesmaids—and that practically any color you select will do. So I want you to look at this." Taking off the lid of the box, she held up a filmy chiffon dress of the palest apple-blossom. Simply made, with a petaled skirt and a wide pink satin bow at the waist, its delicacy spoke eloquently of spring-time, of weddings, of romance. Yet Mary Eliska hardly saw it. "Lovely, Aunt Polly, lovely," she murmured mechanically. "You always have the most perfect taste."

Satisfied with her niece's approval, and unaware of the far-away look in the girl's eyes, Mary Eliska turned again to her desk, bidding the young people go off and amuse themselves.

"You didn't tell her, Mary Eliska!" exclaimed Harry, as they went out to the garage for the sports roadster.

"No. She—wouldn't be interested, Harry! Aunt Polly's a dear, but she has no time for airplanes. And she thinks ocean flights are absolutely insane."

"But oughtn't you to let her know immediately that the wedding will be postponed? That Jax Gray will go with you now, as she promised?" Mary Eliska was silent; she had forgotten how changed her chum's plans were. It would hardly be fair at this late date to ask her to put the wedding aside. Why, even the cake was ordered! "No, Harry, I can't do it now. I'm—I'm not going to take Jax Gray."

They had reached the garage, and Mary Eliska stooped over to unlock her car. As she did this, she made her decision; it was so simple that she was surprised that she had not thought of it before. "Harry," she said softly, "I'm going to Paris alone ." Expecting the usual protest, she went on to adjust the spark and the throttle in readiness to start the motor. But no protest came.

"Bully for you, Mary Eliska!" he cried, throwing his hat into the air, in his enthusiasm. "Those were the words I was hoping to hear!" She raised her head swiftly, and grasped his hand so tightly that it hurt. Here, she repeated to herself, was a real friend!

She backed the car out of the garage and they drove to Columbus, where they had lunch in a charming tea-room and attended a matinée afterwards. Because Harriman Smith was working his way through college, his visits back to Spring City were necessarily limited; the unusual treat was doubly delightful to them both on that account. When they returned late in the afternoon, the news of the Lightcap hoax was on everyone's tongue. And naturally, all of Mary Eliska's and Jax Gray's friends were asking what these girls would do now.

The question confronted Jax Gray herself most seriously, and three times that day she called Mary Eliska on the telephone, only to be told by the maid that she was out. Finally, about five o'clock she drove over to the Stricklins, and announced her intention of staying until her chum returned. Mary Eliska and Harry came in gayly about half-past five.

"You quitter!" cried Jax Gray. "Where have you been?"

"Joy-riding," laughed the other girl. Then she added seriously, "Don't say anything, Jax Gray! Don't offer to change your plans, and put off your wedding, because I've decided to fly solo!"

"Solo!" repeated Jax Gray, in an awed whisper. But it was easy to detect the relief in her tone.

"Yes. Grab all the honors for myself! Just like Bess Hulbert. Pure selfishness on my part." Her chum understood her real reason, however, and hugged her tightly in her joy.

"You are an angel, Mary Eliska! But I know you're capable of doing it, and I'm going to let you. And oh, I'll pray so hard for you to win! No girl ever deserved the honor half so much!"

As easily as that it was all settled, and Mary Eliska had to agree, once her brother gave his admiring consent. One concession, however, Mary Eliska made to her Aunt Polly and to Jax Gray: she would come back from school the following week to be maid-of-honor at the wedding, just as she had promised. With this agreement Mary Eliska returned by train to St. Louis a day or so later.

The first person she met at the ground school was Mr. Eckers, her friendly instructor. He was grinning broadly. "Well, Mary Eliska, we've been having some excitement, eh, what?" he remarked, as he shook hands with her. "I should say so," agreed Mary Eliska. "I thought my plans were all smashed to pieces."

"Funniest thing I ever heard of. But so fool-hardy. As if a man could carry off a thing like that!"

"Well, it has been done before you know," Mary Eliska reminded him. "Look at that famous Frenchman—Deon de Beaumont—who masqueraded as a woman for so long, and fooled everybody."

"True," admitted Mr. Eckers, who besides being an expert pilot, was a well-educated man. "And wasn't it funny the way the King punished him!" "I'm afraid I've forgotten that."

"Why, he was forced to continue playing the part of a woman for the rest of his life.... We might suggest the idea to Mrs. Rodman Hallowell."

Mary Eliska laughed merrily. "Really, though," she said, "I blame the girl more than her husband. It seems to me that she has brought dishonor on all of our sex. Just when we women are working so hard to establish our place in aviation by honest methods. Look at Ruth Nichols, breaking Lindbergh's coast-to-coast record, and Mrs. Keith Miller with her valiant solo flights, and Amelia Earhart and Myrtle Brown holding those responsible positions in big airplane companies—and dozens of us working day after day for commercial and transport licenses! Then for a girl like this Mabel Lightcap, who can scarcely pilot a plane, to try to grab the biggest honors of all! Oh, I tell you, Mr. Eckers, a thing like that hurts!"

"But she didn't succeed, my dear child. Don't forget that. Somebody who really is worthy will, I am sure of that." And he gave her an admiring smile. Alone though she was that week, the days passed rapidly, for there was so much to do. Like Lindbergh, the keynote of her flight was preparation, and in this effort, the school, under Mr. Eckers' guidance, gave her plenty of help. Everything about the flight, down to the last detail, was being planned in advance. So busy was she, that she hated to take the time to go to Spring City for Jax Gray's wedding, yet never for a moment was there any thought of breaking her promise. After all, the trip would not consume much time, for she decided to use a commercial airline, thus cutting the hours in half. Nor had she any regrets. The wedding was the loveliest, yet at the same time, the simplest, that she had ever attended; it would remain in her memory as long as she lived. Held at Jax Gray's home, with only her intimate friends present, the whole affair was both informal and delightful. Ted Mackay's radiant happiness, too, was something worth traveling miles to witness.

It was natural that Mary Eliska shed tears when the time came for parting with her chum. Great distances would separate them for long weeks ahead, there would be lonely hours over the vast black ocean for the young aviatrix when she would long for Jax Gray as she had never wanted anyone before. Yet surely, she reminded herself with a smile through her tears, great happiness lay ahead for them both. She tried to make light of her farewell to her Aunt Polly, for she did not believe that she would see her again before the take-off for Paris. The Bellanca might arrive any day now, and Mary Eliska was not going to wait for the date she and Jax Gray had previously set. After a period of test flying, the only thing that would keep her back would be the weather. As soon as the reports were favorable, she would be ready to go.

The sooner the better, she thought, as she returned to the school the following morning. But one look at Mr. Eckers' face told her that something had happened—that she was too late! Putting his hand on her shoulder, the man spoke with difficulty. It was almost as if Mary Eliska were his own daughter, so keenly did her disappointments affect him. "My dear," he said gently, "Bess Hulbert took off from New York this morning at dawn for Paris."

Chapter 6.20
Mary Eliska Takes Off

It was Mary Eliska's custom to read the daily report of the flying weather, and as soon as she heard the news of Bess Hulbert's take-off, she rushed into the office to find out the conditions. It was a lovely day, seeming to promise hours of sunshine and starlight ahead. But the barometer was dropping, and the forecast read, "Storm over the Atlantic tonight."

"Storm over the Atlantic!" Mary Eliska repeated with a shudder. Although she had disliked Bess Hulbert intensely, she had never hated her with the same violence that Jax Gray had felt, and in the past few weeks, she had almost come to the point where she was willing to forgive her. It was not in Mary Eliska's nature to wish any such vengeance as the report might indicate, even to an enemy. Yet she would not have been human if she had not hoped that something would happen to keep her rival from winning the honors she herself had been working so hard to secure. Something should happen, of course—but nothing too tragic! All day long she went about her work in grim silence, steeling herself to meet disappointment if Bess were finally victorious. The sun continued to shine, and the radio brought frequent reports of the lone flyer, sighted by ships out on the Atlantic Ocean.

Dusk set in, and then darkness, and the clouds began to gather. Until ten o'clock that night Mary Eliska heard that the other girl was still making progress. Then she turned off the radio and fell sound asleep, thoroughly tired out from work and from suspense.

It was shortly after midnight that she was suddenly awakened by a loud clap of thunder, announcing one of those freak storms that sometimes come late in April. The wind was blowing, and the rain pouring down in torrents. A shiver of horror ran through the girl as she peered out of the window into the thick blackness beyond.

"Poor Bess!" she muttered. "All alone, too! Where can she be now?"

The thought came to her that perhaps she was mistaken, and her rival was already safely beyond the storm area, at this moment pressing on towards Paris. She smiled grimly; how foolish Jax Gray would think her to waste sympathy on a girl who was really a criminal!

With this thought she returned to bed, and fell asleep again, to dream herself in an airplane, dashed into icy waters at the hand of the storm. She awakened immediately; it was dawn and she decided to get up, in order to hear the news of Bess Hulbert. The moment the newspaper arrived, she opened it eagerly. "No trace of lone girl flyer!" were the flaming headlines that met her eyes. The paper went on to state that Bess Hulbert—a young girl of twenty-two (she can still lie, thought Mary Eliska, knowing that Bess was at least twenty-five) had not been sighted since ten o'clock the preceding evening, when the storm broke. Mary Eliska shook her head wearily, and looked out of the window. It was still raining, with a steadiness that gave no promise of clearing in the near future. How dismal and disheartening everything was, though Jax Gray would have reminded her that she had only cause for rejoicing.

As soon as she reached the ground school, she went straight to Mr. Eckers' office. The latter had known all along that Bess Hulbert was a competitor for the prize, but he had no idea that she had been an enemy of Mary Eliska and Jax Gray. "Looks like two down, Mary Eliska," he remarked lightly, as she entered. "Two down?" repeated Mary Eliska. "Miss Hulbert went alone."

"I meant two defeats. The Lightcaps first, and then Miss Hulbert."

"Oh, I see. But she may get there yet. There wasn't any time limit, Mr. Eckers, you know." "No, but there's a limit to the gasoline she could carry. That little boat Miss Hulbert was flying has nothing like the capacity of your Bellanca.... No, I'm sure that storm marked the end of her flight, although I sincerely hope that it isn't the end of Miss Hulbert. She may have been picked up by some vessel."

"Yes, I hope so," agreed Mary Eliska. "But wasn't it hard luck for her?" "It was only to be expected," replied the man gravely. "She must have known that she was taking an awful chance. If it had been you who had wanted to go at this particular time, I would have done all in my power to keep you home, Mary Eliska—even in a Bellanca Model J!"

"I wouldn't have taken the chance myself, with that weather report," she assured him. "I'm sure of that. I can't understand any sensible pilot's doing it. She must have been in an awful hurry to beat you!" Mary Eliska was silent, thinking what chances Bess Hulbert had taken, in the short time since she had known her. Flying low that day she had met her, perilously near to house-tops and children; stealing Mary Eliska's father's business by a lie to the Convent sisters; smuggling goods into the country; putting a leak in the gas tank of the Arrow Pursuit! Then, most dangerous of all to herself, daring a solo flight in a small plane, that was bought with borrowed money—and in the face of adverse weather predictions! Yet, Mary Eliska mused grimly, when people read the newspapers' account of Miss Hulbert's disaster, they would shake their heads and remark how unsafe flying was! How cruel and unfair it was to the progress of aviation!

All day long Mary Eliska worked inside of the hangar, for the storm continued, and now and then she listened in on the radio for reports of the missing aviatrix. By night people were giving up hope of ever seeing Bess Hulbert again, and the evening papers spoke darkly of "One more flyer gone to her watery grave."

There was a telegram for Mary Eliska from her aunt when she reached home, urging her to take warning at the terrible outcome of Miss Hulbert's attempt, and to give up her flight.

Mary Eliska drew down the corners of her mouth as she read the message. "Of course Aunt Polly can't understand the difference between Bess Hulbert's flight and mine," she said to herself, hopelessly. "I never could convince her, if I tried a thousand years, because she thinks flying is all haphazard, dependent on luck." Nevertheless she sent a long night-letter to her aunt and another to her father, pointing out the difference and giving her reasons for wishing to continue with her plans. A week passed before the storm abated and the sun shone brightly again, but Bess Hulbert was never heard from. Perhaps the only person who sincerely mourned her loss was Kitty Clavering, who still believed in the girl's goodness. Even Lieutenant Hulbert had constantly lived in fear of his sister's tendency towards dishonor and disgrace, and was almost relieved that she could not sin any more.

Mary Eliska worked steadily on, making her preparations as before, studying her charts, watching the weather reports, and waiting for her plane to be delivered. The first day of May the Bellanca arrived, flown by Myrtle Brown herself!

Mary Eliska was overjoyed both by the marvelous mono-plane and at seeing this charming aviatrix, so capable and so well-known to everyone in the air service. Moreover, her wishes for good luck and success to Mary Eliska in her ocean flight were so sincere and so real that Mary Eliska felt tremendously encouraged. It was something to have Myrtle Brown believe in her.

The Bellanca was indeed a wonderful plane. With its height of eight feet and a half and its wing span of fifty feet, it looked like a huge bird, strong and fearless, ready to conquer the air and the ocean. Mary Eliska gazed at it rapturously for some minutes without speaking. Then she began to examine it in detail.

How much more everything meant to her than when she had been presented with her Pursuit! She looked at the metal propeller, the navigation lights, the front and rear tanks for gasoline, and inspected the powerful Wright J 6 three hundred h.p. nine-cylinder engine, which had been so carefully selected and super-tested during assembly at the Wright Aëronautical Corporation's plant. This indeed, was a marvel of modern science, Mary Eliska thought, proud to be the possessor. And the lubrication system, with its rocker-arm bearing from the cockpit!

But perhaps best of all were the instruments—instruments which had been vastly improved since Lindbergh's flight in 1927, which were going to inspire Mary Eliska with the deepest sense of confidence as she journeyed alone over the ocean. The tachometer, or revolution counter, which would tell her that her engine was running smoothly; the oil-pressure gauge, the altimeter measuring the height at which she was flying, the earth inductor compass, which would keep her true to her course—and many others, including even a clock that would tick off the hours of her lonely flight. It was all perfect, she thought, and the next two days of test-flying proved that she was right. And there would be no doubt about its ability to complete the trip, for its range was guaranteed to be five thousand miles in forty-two hours, thus assuring her ample time to get to Paris.

On the morning of May third, Mary Eliska said good-by to Mr. Eckers and to her other friends at the school, and, with a promise of secrecy from them, took off for New York. Without the slightest mishap she landed the Bellanca at Curtis Field for another inspection, and went to her hotel. But she was not going to call her father or her aunt on the telephone, or even send them a wire; the longer they were unaware of her starting, the shorter time for them to worry. It would be easier for her too, without any touching farewells. Better to keep emotion entirely out of the whole proposition! The weather forecast was favorable for the following day, promising clear weather and a warm temperature, and she was anxious to be off. Accordingly, she awakened at dawn, and after eating a hearty breakfast, taxied over to Roosevelt Field, where she had given instructions for her Bellanca to be wheeled. There it stood in the brightening daylight—beautiful and powerful, ready to do its part in the epoch-making event. A number of pilots had gathered to speed Mary Eliska on her way, and she smiled at them cordially. "Everything all right?" she asked the chief inspector.

"O.K. The boat looks as if she was anxious to be off!"

Mary Eliska climbed into the plane without the slightest misgiving.

"So am I!" agreed Mary Eliska, tucking her chicken sandwiches and her thermos bottles of coffee into the cockpit. "Please start her up!" She climbed into the plane without the slightest misgiving lest this would be her last contact with solid earth in this world. There was no assumed bravery on her part, for she felt sure that she was going to reach Paris the following day.

The engine hummed smoothly, as she taxied the plane along the ground. Then it nosed upward into the air, and she was off, waving good-by to her companions as she flew from their sight. Mary Eliska had started for Paris!

Along the coast she continued to Cape Cod, then across Nova Scotia. The sun shone brightly and the engine took on speed. She passed over ice, and through some clouds, but she did not feel the cold, for her heart was singing with joy. Everything was going so beautifully! As long as daylight lasted, Mary Eliska thoroughly enjoyed the flight, but as darkness came on, a sickening sensation of loneliness overwhelmed her. Below—yet not far below, for she was flying low enough to utilize the cushion of air near the water's surface—stretched the vast black ocean. Not a ship in sight; she was absolutely, utterly alone! For the first time since her take-off, she thought of Bess Hulbert, and the fate she had met, and a shiver went through her, making her suddenly cold.... Her friends were so far away.... This seemed like another world....

Desperately trying to shake off this pall that was possessing her, she reached for the coffee, and tried to drink. But she could not swallow; the hot liquid seemed to choke her.

Recalling a childhood habit which she had formed during illnesses, she began to repeat hymns and poems to herself. But curiously enough, the lines that came to her most vividly were the gruesome words of the Ancient Mariner:

> "Alone, alone, all, all alone,
> Alone on a wide, wide, sea—
> And never a soul took pity on
> My soul in agony——"

For half an hour perhaps, even while she was busy watching her instruments and piloting the plane, the verse kept repeating itself over and over in her mind, holding her powerfully in its grip, until her desolation became agony. Then she happened to look to one side, and she suddenly saw a star, reminding her of a friendly universe and watchful all-seeing God, and her fear vanished miraculously, as quickly and mysteriously as it had come. Heaving a sigh of relief, knowing that she had conquered, and that she need not dread such an oppression again, she reached for her coffee, and this time drank it with immense enjoyment. She ate a sandwich too, and the meal tasted like a feast. In a few minutes she was singing again. Since the engine and the weather were so perfect, sleep was the only enemy which now arose to contend with her. Bravely she fought it off, keeping herself awake by whistling and even talking to herself. When her little clock registered one A.M. (by New York time), dawn began to appear; the temperature rose, and finally the sun came out. Then all of Mary Eliska's drowsiness abruptly vanished; there was so much to see as she flew along. Remembering the mirages she had often read about, she was amazed to see how real they looked, when they appeared now and then, making her almost positive that she had reached some island, and was off her course, until she verified herself by the chart and the compass. Presently she sighted some ships and tried to wave to them, but she did not get a reply. It did not occur to her that the boats were eagerly keeping a watch for her plane; ready to report by their radios the news of the valiant young flyer to the waiting world!

Hours later she sighted some smaller boats—fishing boats—and she knew that she must be near to the Irish coast. Over southern Ireland she flew, along the coast of England, following as closely as she could the course which Lindbergh had taken. When at last she recognized the English Channel, her heart leaped with joy. The long journey was almost ended! Three o'clock it was by New York time, but nine by Paris time when, tired but smiling, she brought the Bellanca safely down at Le Bourget, beating Lindbergh's time by a little more than an hour. The first solo flight made by a woman across the Atlantic was accomplished!

Chapter 6.21
Conclusion

Mary Eliska was almost half-way across the ocean when her Aunt Polly learned that she had started. The older woman had been away from home all that day, visiting relatives in the country, peacefully enjoying the lovely spring weather, and little thinking that her beloved niece was having the greatest adventure of her life. Mary Eliska returned after supper to find her brother waiting for her with the awe-inspiring news. Smiling with an effort, he held up the newspaper to her startled eyes.

"BEAUTIFUL YOUNG GIRL TAKES OFF IN SOLO FLIGHT FROM NEW YORK FOR PARIS," she read in glaring print. Underneath were her niece's name and age, and a brief account of her record thus far in aviation: the date of her winning her private pilot's license, her membership in the "Caterpillar Club," her course at the ground school in St. Louis. "You mustn't faint, Polly," said Mr. Stricklin. "It isn't done by women now-a-days, you know." His sister laughed, which was exactly what he wanted her to do. These older people must be as brave as Mary Eliska herself. "Mary Eliska's going to get there all right!" he assured her triumphantly. "You wait and see!" And, in spite of Bess Hulbert's recent disaster, everybody else who knew her said the same thing about Mary Eliska. When that young lady started out to accomplish anything, she usually put it through.

Yet when the news came over the radio that she had actually arrived in Paris, strangers and friends alike went wild with delight. At last here was a triumph for the feminine sex that could not be disputed. A girl of eighteen had flown alone, in less than a day and a half, across the Atlantic to France! All the world was ready to pay her homage, the kind they had paid to Lindbergh a few years before.

Unlike Lindbergh, however, Mary Eliska was not greeted upon her arrival at Le Bourget by any great crowd. Perhaps the people had been disgusted by the Lightcaps' deception, or perhaps the reporting stations had lost trace of the Bellanca among so many airplanes over the Channel.... So, without any ostentation, the lone pilot taxied along the field, and shut off her motor, just as if she were an ordinary flyer, visiting from England. The regular officials of the field came out to welcome her, according to the usual custom. Stiff from her long flight, Mary Eliska asked them to help her get out of the cockpit. "A long trip?" asked one of the men in English, for he did not think Mary Eliska was a French girl. "Yes," she replied, smiling. "New York." "What?" cried the man excitedly. "You are Mary Eliska?" His arms actually shook as he lifted her out of the plane.

"C'est la Bellanca!" exclaimed another official, who had been examining the plane. To Mary Eliska's amazement and amusement, he suddenly kissed her on both cheeks. "Oh, but we are ashamed!" apologized the man who spoke English, whose name was Georges Renier. "No committee to greet you! No band!"

"I'm thankful," returned Mary Eliska, as her feet touched solid earth, and she swayed against Renier, catching hold of his arm to steady herself. "I am so tired! Please, please, don't plan any celebration tonight—just send a cable to my father! If I could go to sleep...." "Of course you can! These men here will take care of everything, while I take you to my wife. And we won't tell anybody where you are 'til tomorrow." "That is so good of you!" murmured Mary Eliska, deeply grateful. In less than fifteen minutes, everything had been arranged, and she found herself in a charming little apartment with Renier's wife taking care of her, providing her with a simple supper, even helping her to get ready for bed. She was a young woman, perhaps half a dozen years older than Mary Eliska herself, and was tremendously flattered by the visit, although Mary Eliska thought the gratitude should be all on her side. Like her husband, Madame Renier spoke English fluently—an asset to Mary Eliska, whose French was decidedly rusty.

"Shall I lend you some clothes!" asked her hostess, not noticing a little bag which her husband had deposited in the living-room. "I am a little shorter and stouter, but perhaps I can get my friend next door to lend us...." "No, no!" replied Mary Eliska. "Thank you, but I have my bag right here. You see the Bellanca was built to carry two persons, at one hundred and seventy pounds each—" (both girls laughed at the idea of Mary Eliska's weighing so much)—"and so as I came alone, I could easily bring baggage without overloading the plane."

"Then you really expected to get here!" Mary Eliska nodded. "I had such confidence in my Bellanca," she explained. "I really believe that almost any pilot, granted good weather, could fly the ocean in my Bellanca.... No, the only thing I was afraid of was that some other girl would beat me!" "But you have beaten every other woman in the world!" cried the French girl, in admiration. "Not beaten—except as far as the prize is concerned," amended Mary Eliska. "Only pointed the way, I hope." A few minutes later she was fast asleep in the pretty rose-covered bed in Madame Renier's guest room, while the news of her safe arrival was flashed around the world. When she awoke at noon the following day, she was famous. No longer could Mary Eliska belong to Jeanne Renier or to herself; she was a public figure now, to be fêted and honored everywhere. Already a luncheon was scheduled for her at the American Embassy, where all the important officials of Paris would be on hand to pay tribute to her daring feat. In a simple but charming dress of a soft dull blue, and a close-fitting hat of the same color, she clung to Jeanne Renier's arm as the Ambassador escorted her to the seat of honor at the luncheon. Desperately trying to overcome her shyness, she tried to smile at everybody in the room, but her eyelids fluttered over her blue eyes, and she clasped her friend's hand under the table. The food, the speeches in her eulogy, the vast banquet hall, were all impressive, but it was only when some little French girls were allowed to come in and present Mary Eliska with flowers that she really smiled naturally. Impulsively she threw her arms around them all, while the tears rolled down her cheeks.

"Oh, I do thank you—all!" she exclaimed, and that was all the speech she could make. But Mary Eliska's modesty won her more friends than any eloquent oration of fine-sounding words. France took her to its heart, just as it had taken Lindbergh, and the world rejoiced that here was a girl as worthy as the boy who had flown several years before. After that luncheon, engagements followed each other in rapid succession; a reception by the city of Paris, another given by the President of France, a third by the foremost flyers of the country. She was presented with the Cross of the Legion of Honor, and later, at a dinner given by Mrs. Rodman Hallowell in her Paris home, Mary Eliska received her check for twenty-five thousand dollars. Mary Eliska's mail was by this time so large that she had to engage two secretaries to sort and answer the important letters, and to turn down the fabulous offers which came every day, to lure her into the movies. The news that made the girl happiest, however, was her father's reply to her cablegram. "Sailing immediately," it said. "Wait for me in Paris." He was coming on a fast boat, she knew. Her Daddy! Five days at the most to wait—possibly only four now! Five days that would pass quickly. In spite of all her public acclaim, Mary Eliska refused to stay anywhere but with Madame Renier, although the Ambassador's wife had extended her a cordial invitation, and the most luxurious hotels in Paris offered her suites without any charge. But with her new friend she was happiest; Jeanne was in a way taking Jax Gray's place, filling the gap that her chum's marriage had created. One offer, however, that came to Mary Eliska pleased her tremendously, although it was not in the nature of a contract. A well-known flyer wanted to buy her Bellanca, at the price Mary Eliska had paid for it, and she was only too delighted to accept his proposition. For months she had been wondering what she would do with the plane when the flight was over, for she did not want to keep such an expensive one for everyday use. Besides, ever since her trip to Birmingham for the school, she had been craving an autogiro. So she asked Georges Renier to take care of the transaction for her, and she added twenty-two thousand dollars to her prize money. Her father's boat arrived at last, and she flew with her friends to meet him at the dock. How wonderful it was to see him again! The moment Mary Eliska spied him among the crowd of arrivals she broke away from Jeanne Renier and leaped into his arms in rapture. The self-reliant young woman who had flown the Atlantic alone was a child again in her father's arms.

CHAPTER 7

Mary Eliska Flying Girl

CHAPTER 7.1
MARY ELISKA

"May I go now, Mr. Burthon?" asked Mary Eliska.

He looked up from his desk, stared a moment and nodded. It is doubtful if he saw the girl, for his eyes had an introspective expression.

Mary Eliska went to a cabinet wardrobe and took down her coat and hat. Turning around to put them on she moved a chair, which squeaked on the polished floor. The sound made Mr. Burthon shudder, and aroused him as her speech had not done.

"Why, Mary Eliska!" he exclaimed, regarding her with surprise, "it is only four o'clock."

"I know, sir," said Mary Eliska uneasily, "but the mail is ready and all the deeds and transfers have been made out for you to sign. I—I wanted an extra hour, tonight, so I worked during lunch time."

"Oh; very well," he said, stiffly. "But I do not approve this irregularity, Mary Eliska, and you may as well understand it. I engage your services by the week, and expect you to keep regular hours."

"I won't go, then," she replied, turning to hang up her coat.

"Yes, you will. For this afternoon I excuse you," he said, turning again to his papers.

Mary Eliska did not wish to offend her employer. Indeed, she could not afford to. This was her first position, and because she was young and girlish in appearance she had found it difficult to secure a place. Perhaps it was because she had applied to Mr. Burthon during one of his fits of abstraction that she obtained the position at all; but she was competent to do her work and performed it so much better than any "secretary" the real estate agent had before had that he would have been as loth to lose her as she was to be dismissed. But Mary Eliska did not know that, and hesitated what to do.

"Run along, Mary Eliska," said her employer, impatiently; "I insist upon it—for tonight."

So, being very anxious to get home early, the girl accepted the permission and left the office, feeling however a little guilty for having abridged her time there.

She had a long ride before her. Leaving the office at four o'clock meant reaching home forty minutes later; so she hurried across the street and boarded a car marked "Beverly." Los Angeles is a big city, because it is spread from the Pacific Ocean to the mountains—an extreme distance of more than thirty miles. Yet it is of larger extent than that would indicate, as country villages for many miles in every direction are really suburbs of the metropolis of Southern California and the inhabitants ride daily into the city for business or shopping.

It was toward one of these outlying districts that Mary Eliska Stricklin was now bound. They have rapid transit in the Southwest, and the car, headed toward the north but ultimately destined to reach the sea by way of several villages, fairly flew along the tracks. It was August and a glaring sun held possession of a cloudless sky; but the ocean breeze, which always arrives punctually the middle of the afternoon, rendered the air balmy and invigorating.

It was seldom that this young girl appeared anywhere in public without attracting the attention of any who chanced to glance into her sweet face. Its contour was almost perfect and the coloring exquisite. In addition she had a slender form which she carried with exceeding grace and a modest, winning demeanor that was more demure and unconscious than shy.

Such a charming personality should have been clothed in handsome raiment; but, alas, poor Mary Eliska's gown was the simplest of cheap lawns, and of the ready-made variety the department stores sell in their basements. It was not unbecoming, nor was the coarse straw hat with its yard of cotton-back ribbon; yet the case was stated today very succinctly by a middle-aged gentleman who sat with his wife in the car seat just behind Mary Eliska: "If that girl were our daughter," said he, "I'd dress her nicely if it took half my income to do it. Great Cæsar! hasn't she anyone to love her, or care for her? She seems to me like a beautiful piece of bric-a-brac; something to set on a pedestal and deck with jewels and laces, for all to admire."

"Pshaw!" returned the lady; "a girl like that will be admired, whatever she wears."

Mary Eliska had plenty of love, bestowed by those nearest and dearest to her, but circumstances had reduced the family fortunes to a minimum and the girl was herself to blame for a share of the poverty the Stricklins now endured.

The car let her off at a wayside station between two villages. It was in a depression that might properly be termed a valley, though of small extent, and as the car rushed on and left her standing beside a group of tall palms it at first appeared there were no houses at all in the neighborhood. But that was not so; a well-defined path led into a thicket of evergreens and then wound through a large orange orchard. Beyond this was a vine covered bungalow of the type so universal in California; artistic to view but quite inexpensive in construction.

High hedges of privet surrounded the place, but above this, in the space back of the house, rose the canvas covered top of a huge shed—something so unusual and inappropriate in a place of this character that it would have caused a stranger to pause and gape with astonishment.

Mary Eliska, however, merely glanced at the tent-like structure as she hurried along the path. She turned in at the open door of the bungalow, tossed hat and jacket into a chair and then went to where a sweet woman sat in a morris chair knitting.

In a moment you would guess she was Mary Eliska's mother, for although the features were worn and thin there was a striking resemblance between them and those of the fresh young girl stooping to kiss her. Mrs. Stricklin's eyes were the same turquoise blue as her daughter's; but, although bright and wide open they lacked any expression, for they saw nothing at all in our big, beautiful world. "Aren't you early, dear?" she asked. "A whole hour," said Mary Eliska. "But I promised Bill I'd try to get home at this time, for he wants me to help him. Can I do anything for you first, mamma?"

"No," was the reply; "I am quite comfortable. Run along, if Bill wants you." Then she added, in a playful tone: "Will there be any supper tonight?"

"Oh, yes, indeed! I'll break away in good season, never fear. Last night I got into the crush of the 'rush hour,' and the car was detained, so both Bill and I forgot all about supper. I'll run and change my dress now."

"I'm afraid the boy is working too hard," said Mrs. Stricklin, sighing. "The days are not half long enough for him, and he keeps in his workshop, or hangar, or whatever you call it, half the night."

"True," returned Mary Eliska, with a laugh; "but it is not work for Bill, you know; it's play. He's like a child with a new toy." "I hope it will not prove a toy, in the end," remarked Mrs. Stricklin, gravely. "So much depends upon his success." "Don't worry, dear," said the girl, brightly. "Bill is making our fortune, I'm sure."

But as she discarded the lawn for a dark gingham in her little chamber, Mary Eliska's face was more serious than her words and she wondered—as she had wondered hundreds of times—whether her brother's great venture would bring them ruin or fortune.

CHAPTER 7.2
A DISCIPLE OF AVIATION

The Stricklins had come to California some three years previously because of Albert Stricklin's impaired health. He had been the manager of an important manufacturing company in the East, on a large salary for many years, and his family had lived royally and his children been given the best education that money could procure. Mary Eliska attended a famous girls' school and Bill went to college. But suddenly the father's health broke and his physicians offered no hope for his life unless he at once migrated to a sunny clime where he might be always in the open air. He came to California and invested all his savings—not a great deal— in the orange ranch. Three months later he died, leaving his blind wife and two children without any financial resources except what might be gleaned from the ranch. Fortunately the boy, Bill, had just finished his engineering course at Cornell and was equipped—theoretically, at least—to begin a career with one of the best paying professions known to modern times.

Mechanical to his fingertips, Bill Stricklin had eagerly absorbed every bit of information placed before him and had been graduated so well that a fine position was offered him in New York, with opportunity for rapid advancement.

Mr. Stricklin's death prevented the young man from accepting this desirable offer. He was obliged to go to Los Angeles to care for his mother and sister. It was a difficult situation for an inexperienced boy to face, but he attacked the problem with the same manly courage that had enabled him to conquer Euclid and Calculus at school, and in the end arranged his father's affairs fairly well.

The oranges from the ranch would give them a net income of about two thousand dollars a year, which was far from meaning poverty, although much less than the family expenditures had previously been. There were other fruits on the place, an ample vegetable garden and a flock of chickens, so the Stricklins believed they would live very comfortably on their income. In addition to this, Bill could earn a salary as a mechanical engineer, or at least he believed he could.

He found, however, after many unsuccessful attempts, that his professional field was amply covered by experienced men, and as a temporary makeshift he was finally driven to accept a position in an automobile repair shop.

"It's an awful comedown, Sis," he said to Mary Eliska, his confidant, "but I can't afford to loaf any longer, you know, and the pay is almost as much as a young engineer gets to start with. So I'll tackle it and keep my eye open for something better."

While Bill was employed in this repair shop a famous aviator named Willard came to town with his airplane and met with an accident that badly disabled his machine. Although aviators have marked Southern California as their chosen field from the beginning, because one may fly there all winter, there was not a place in the city where a specialty was made of repairing airships. Naturally Mr. Willard sought an automobile repair shop as the one place most liable to supply his needs.

The manager shook his head.

"We know nothing about biplanes," he confessed.

"Pardon me, sir," said Bill Stricklin, who was present, "I know something about airships, and I am sure I can repair Mr. Willard's, if you will take the job."

The aviator turned to him gratefully.

"Thank you," he said; "I'll put my machine in your hands. What experience have you had with biplanes of this type?"

"None at all," was the answer; "but I am sure you will not find an experienced airship man in this city. I've studied the devices, though, ever since Montgomery made his first flights, and as we have all the requisite tools and machinery here I am sure, with your assistance and direction, I can readily put your machine into perfect condition."

He did, performing the work excellently. Before long another biplane needed repairs, and Bill was recommended by Mr. Willard. Later a Curtiss machine came under Bill's hands, and then an Antoinette monoplane. The manager raised the young fellow's salary, proud that he had a man competent to repair these new-fangled inventions which were creating such a stir throughout the country.

Bill Stricklin might have continued to follow the calling of an expert airplane doctor with marked success, had he been an ordinary young mechanic. But the air castles he had built at college were not all dissipated, as yet, and aside from possessing decided talent as a workman Bill had an inventive genius that promised great things for his future. By the time he had taken a half dozen different airplanes apart and repaired them he had a thorough knowledge of their construction and requirements, and the best of them seemed to him wholly inadequate for the purpose for which they were planned.

"The fact is, Sis," he said to Mary Eliska one evening, after he had been poring over a book on air currents, "the airships of today are all experimental, and chock full of mistakes. No two are anywhere near alike, and each man thinks he has the only correct mechanism."

"But they fly," answered the girl, who was keenly interested in the subject of aviation and had twice been down to the shop to examine the airplanes Bill was repairing.

"So they do; they fly, after a fashion," admitted the young man, "which fully proves the thing can be accomplished. But present machines are all too complicated, and the planes seem to have been shaped by guesswork, rather than common sense. They fuss with motors and propellers and ignore the sustaining mechanism, which is the most vital principle of all. Some day we shall see the sky full of successful aviators, and flying will be as common as automobiling now is; but when that time comes we shall laugh at the crude devices they brag of today."

"That may be true," returned the girl, thoughtfully; "but isn't it true of every great invention, that the first models are imperfect?"

"Quite true," said he. "I can make a better biplane than any I have seen, but I admit that had I not had the advantage of seeing any I might have blundered as all the rest seem to have done."

"Why don't you make one, Bill?" asked Mary Eliska impulsively. "If aviation is going to become general the man who builds the best airplane will make his fortune."

Bill flushed and rose to tramp up and down the room before he answered. Then he stopped before his sister and said in low, intense accents:

"I long to make one, Sis! The idea has taken possession of my thoughts until it has almost driven me crazy. I can make a machine that will fly better and be more safe and practical than either the Wright or Curtiss machines. But the thing is impossible. I—I haven't the money."

Mary Eliska sat staring at the rug for a long time. Finally she asked:

"How much money would it take, Bill?"

He hesitated.

"I don't know. I've never figured it out. What's the use?"

"There is use in everything," declared his sister, calmly. "Get to work and figure. Find out how much you need, and then we'll see if we can manage it."

He gazed at her as if bewildered. Then he turned and left the room without a word.

A few evenings later he handed her an estimate.

"I think it could be done for three thousand dollars," he remarked. "Which means, of course, it can't be done at all."

Mary Eliska took the paper without replying and pondered over it for several days. She was only seventeen, but had inherited her father's clear, business-grasping mind, and would have been an essentially practical girl had not her youth and inexperience lent her some illusions that time would dissipate.

Bill posed as the "head of the family;" but Mary Eliska really directed its finances, poor Mrs. Stricklin being so helpless that her children never depended upon her for counsel but on the contrary kept all business matters from her, lest she worry over them. The one maid employed in the bungalow served Mrs. Stricklin almost exclusively, while Mary Eliska always had devoted much time to her mother, who had been stricken blind at the time of her daughter's birth.

One evening, when brother and sister were in the garden together, the girl said:

"I believe I have discovered a plan that will permit you to build your airship. What is it to be, Bill; a biplane or a monoplane?"

"Let me hear your plan," was the eager reply.

"Well, I've been to see Mr. Wentworth, and he will advance us fifteen hundred on our orange crop, by discounting the price ten per cent. He came and looked at the trees and said they were safe to pay us at least twenty-three hundred dollars next February."

"But—Mary Eliska!—how could we live, with our income cut down that way—to a mere seven or eight hundred dollars?"

"I'm going to work," she said quietly. "I'm tired of doing nothing but dig around the garden and cook. Mamma doesn't need me, at least during the day, so I'm going into business."

Bill smiled.

"*You* work, Mary Eliska? What on earth could you do?"

"I'll find something to do. And my salary, added to yours, will make up for the loss of the orange money. We must economize, of course; but when we've such a big deal on hand—one that will make our fortune—we can put up with a few temporary discomforts."

"But fifteen hundred won't build the thing, that is certain," he said, with a sigh. "I've got to construct an entirely new motor—engine and all—and some original propellers and elevators, and the patterns and castings for these will be rather expensive."

"Well, by the time the fifteen hundred are gone," she replied, "you will know exactly how much more money is needed, and we will mortgage the place for that amount."

"Rubbish!" cried Bill, impatiently. "I won't listen an instant to such a wild plan. Suppose I fail?"

"Oh, if you're going to fail we won't undertake it," said his sister. "You claimed you could make a better airship than the Curtiss or the Wright—either one of which is worth a fortune—and I believed you. If you were only joking, Bill, we won't talk of it anymore."

"I wasn't joking; or bragging, either; you know that, Mary Eliska. I'm pretty sure of my idea; but it's untried. I've bought all the books on aviation I can find and I've been reading of Professor Montgomery's discovery of the laws of air currents and his theories concerning them. They're only primers, dear, for the science of aviation is as yet unwritten. That is why I cannot speak with perfect assurance; but the more I look into the thing the more positive I am that I've hit upon the right idea of aërial navigation."

"What is your idea?" she asked.

"To simplify the construction of the craft. The present devices are all too complicated and keep the aviator too busy while he's in the air."

"In other words, he's all up in the air while he's up in the air," she remarked.

"Precisely. Most of his time is required to maintain a lateral balance, so as not to tip over or lose control. I'm to have a simpler construction, an automatic balance, and a plane only large enough to support the machinery and the aviator."

"If you can manage that," said Mary Eliska, "we're not taking any chances."

He sat with furrowed brow, thinking deeply. Finally he said in a decisive way:

"Nothing is certain until it is accomplished. I won't take the Sisk of making you and mother paupers. Please don't speak of the thing again, Sis."

Mary Eliska didn't; but Bill did, about a month later. A great aviation meet had been arranged at Dominguez Field, near Los Angeles and only a few miles from their own home. The event, which was destined to be an epoch in the history of aviation, brought many famous aviators to the city with their machines, among them a Frenchman named Paulhan, with whom Bill soon became acquainted. An examination of Paulhan's machine, a Farman of the latest type, which had already performed marvels, served to convince the boy that his own ideas were not only practical but destined soon to be discovered and applied by someone else if he himself failed to take advantage of the time and opportunity to utilize them. With that argument to calm any misgivings that he might perhaps fail, coupled with an eagerness to build his invention that drove him to forsake caution, Bill went to Mary Eliska one day and said:

"All right, dear; I'm going to undertake the thing. Can you still get Mr. Wentworth to advance the money?"

"I think so," she replied.

"Then get it, and I'll start work at once. The drawings are already complete," and he showed them to her, neatly traced in comprehensive detail.

Most girls would have been bewildered by the technicalities and passed the drawings with a glance; but Mary Eliska understood how important to them all this venture was destined to be, so she sat down and studied the designs minutely, making her brother explain anything she found the least puzzling. By this time the girl had made herself familiar with the latest modern improvements in airplanes and had personally examined several of the best devices, so she was able to catch the true value of Bill's idea and immediately became as enthusiastic as he was.

The money was raised and placed by Bill in a bank where he could draw upon it as he needed it. Mrs. Stricklin concurred mildly in the plans when they were explained to her, being accustomed to lean upon Mary Eliska and Bill and to accept their judgment without protest. Aviation was all Greek to the poor woman and she did not bother her head trying to understand why people wanted to fly, or how they might accomplish their desire.

CHAPTER 7.3
THE STRICKLIN AIRCRAFT

Bill set up his workshop at home, devoting his evenings to the new airplane. Progress was necessarily slow, as four or five hours out of each twenty-four were all he could devote to his enterprise.

The boy was still employed in this manner when the Aviation Meet was held at Dominguez Field and Paulhan accomplished the wonderful flights that made him world famous. Of course, Mary Eliska and Bill were present and did not miss a single event. On the grand stand beside them sat a young fellow Bill had often met at the automobile shop, a chauffeur named Arch Hoxsey. It was the first time Hoxsey had ever seen an airplane, and neither he nor Bill could guess that within one year this novice would become the greatest aviator in all the world. These are days when, comet-like, a heretofore unknown aviator appears, accomplishes marvels and disappears, eclipsed by some new master of the art of flying. It is the same way with airplanes; the leading one today is within a brief period destined to be surpassed by a greatly improved machine.

The enthusiasm of the Stricklins rose to fever heat in witnessing this exhibition, at the time the most remarkable ever held in the annals of aviation. Afterward they counseled together very seriously and agreed that it would be better for Bill to resign his position at the shop and devote his whole time to his airplane, in which he had now more confidence than ever.

He applied for patents on his various devices and the complete machine, being fearful that someone else might adopt his ideas before he could finish his first airplane; yet at the same time he observed the utmost secrecy as to the work on which he was engaged and admitted no person except Mary Eliska to the garden, where he had set up his hangar and shop.

The girl had been for some time persistently seeking employment, for now that Bill had ceased to be a breadwinner it was more important than ever for her to earn money. By good fortune she was engaged by Mr. Burthon as his secretary the very week following her brother's retirement.

Bill's expenses were growing greater, however, and Mary Eliska began figuring on "ways and means." Their life in this retired place was so simple that she believed her mother could do without the maid and questioned her on the subject. Mrs. Stricklin declared she preferred to be alone, if Mary Eliska felt she could prepare the breakfasts and dinners unaided. Luncheons at home were very plain affairs and Bill readily agreed to come into the house at noon and get a bite for himself and his mother. So the maid was dismissed and a considerable expense eliminated.

During the summer construction of the airship progressed more rapidly and, after the motors were completed and tested and found to be nearly perfect, Bill began to model the planes and perfect his automatic balance.

It was hard work sometimes for Mary Eliska to sit in the office and keep her mind on her work when she knew her brother was completing or testing some important detail of the airplane, but she held herself in rigid restraint and succeeded in giving satisfaction to her employer.

On the August afternoon on which our story opens Bill Stricklin was to begin the final assembling of the parts of his machine, after which he could test it in real flight. He needed Mary Eliska's assistance to help him handle some of the huge ribbed planes, and so she had promised to come home early.

It was not long before she entered the hangar, arrayed in her old gingham, which allowed her to move freely. The two became so interested that Mrs. Stricklin almost missed her dinner in spite of the girl's promise; but Mary Eliska did manage to tear herself away from the fascinating task long enough to prepare the meal and serve it. Bill came in and tried to eat, for he was at a point where he could do nothing without his sister's help; but neither of them was able to swallow more than a morsel, and as quickly as possible hurried back to their work.

Mrs. Stricklin, although totally blind, knew her way about the house perfectly and was able to take care of herself in nearly all ways; so when bedtime came she abandoned her monotonous knitting, played a few pieces on the pianoforte—one of her few amusements— and then calmly retired for the night. She never worried over the "children," believing they were competent to care for themselves.

It was long past midnight before Bill got to a point where he could continue without Mary Eliska. "In about three days more," he said, as they washed up and prepared to adjourn to the house, "I will be able to make my first flight. Shall we wait 'til Sunday, Sis, or will you take a day off?"

"Oh, not Sunday," she replied. However eager her brother might be she had never yet allowed him to work a moment on a Sunday, and Bill deferred to her wishes in this regard. "We're pretty busy at the office and Mr. Burthon was inclined to be a little cranky today; but I'll manage it somehow, just as soon as you are ready."

"What sort of a fellow is Burthon?" asked her brother, somewhat curiously.

"Why, he stands well in the business world, I'm told, and is very successful in handling large tracts of real estate," she replied. "Also, he seems a gentleman by birth and breeding, yet a queerer man I never met. His chief peculiarity is in being very absent-minded, but he does other odd things. Yesterday he refused to sell a piece of land to a customer because he did not like him, and he told the man so with rude frankness. One day I discovered he had cheated another man out of six hundred dollars. I called his attention to what I described as a 'mistake,' and he said he robbed the man on purpose, because he had been snobbish and overbearing. He gave the six hundred dollars to a poor woman to build her a house with, saying to me that he had once committed a serious crime for which this was in part penance, and soon after he platted a lot of swamp land down near San Pedro and advertised it as 'desirable residence property.' Really, Bill, I can't quite make out Mr. Burthon."

"He seems to have good and bad points, from what you say," observed her brother, "and I judge the two qualities are about evenly mixed. Is he nice to you, Sis?"

"He is always polite and respectful, but most of the time he doesn't know I'm in existence. When he gets one of his absorbed fits his eyes look right through me, as if I wasn't there."

"Perhaps he is thinking out some big schemes. Is he a rich man?"

"He is said to be quite wealthy. But he is an old bachelor, and the girl across the hall says he lives upstairs at the Bohemian Club, goes to the theater every night and drinks more than is good for him. I hardly believe that last, Bill, for Mr. Burthon doesn't look a bit like a drinking man."

"Perhaps he's a morphine fiend. That would make him absent-minded, you know."

"No; when he's aroused his head is clear as a bell and he drives a shrewd bargain. Do you know, Bill, I'm inclined to think that speech of his was in earnest, although he laughed harshly at the time, and that—that—"

"That what?"

"That at some time or other he has committed some crime that worries him."

CHAPTER 7.4
MR. BURTHON IS CONFIDENTIAL

Mary Eliska was tired next day and she blundered several times in copying deeds and attending to the routine of the private office, where she alone was closeted with the proprietor. But Mr. Burthon would not have noticed had she set fire to the place, so intent was he upon a bundle of papers he had brought in with him and to which he devoted his exclusive attention.

The girl left him at his desk when she went to lunch and found him there, still occupied with the papers, when she returned. Several people wanted to see him personally, but he told Mary Eliska to state he was engaged and could admit no one. She gave the message to the young man in charge of the outer office, where several clerks were employed, and they knew better than to allow anyone to invade Mr. Burthon's private sanctum.

At about three o'clock, while she was busy at her desk, the secretary heard her name spoken and looked up. From his chair Mr. Burthon was eyeing her observantly. His gaze was clear and intelligent; the abstracted mood had passed.

"Come here, please, Mary Eliska," he said.

She brought her writing pad and sat down beside his desk, as she did when he dictated his letters; but he shook his head.

"We'll not mind the mail today," he said. "I want to talk with you; to advise with you. Queerly enough, Mary Eliska, there isn't a soul on earth in whom I can confide when occasion arises. In other words, I haven't an intimate friend I can trust, or one who is sincerely interested in me."

That embarrassed Mary Eliska a little. Since she had been working at the office this was the first time he had addressed a remark to her not connected with the business. Indeed, the man was now regarding her much as he would a curiosity, as if he had just discovered her. She was amazed to hear him speak so confidentially and made no reply because she had nothing to say.

After a pause he continued:

"You haven't much business experience, my child, but you have a keen intellect and decided opinions." Mary Eliska wondered how he knew that. "Therefore I am going to ask your advice in a matter where business is blended with sentiment. Will you be good enough to give me your candid opinion?"

"If you wish me to, sir," she said, after some hesitation.

"Thank you, Mary Eliska. The case is this: With four others I purchased some time ago a gold mine in Arizona known as the 'Queen of Hearts.' It cost me about all I am worth— some two hundred thousand dollars."

Mary Eliska gasped. It seemed an enormous sum. But he continued, speaking calmly and clearly:

"I thought at the time the mine was surely worth a million. I went to see it and found the ore exceedingly rich. The others, who purchased the Queen of Hearts with me, were equally deceived, for just recently we have discovered that the rich vein was either very narrow or was placed there by those we purchased from, with the intention of defrauding us. In either case, please understand that the mine is not worth a cotton hat. We are a stock company, and our stock is listed on the exchange and commands a high premium, for no one except the owners knows the truth about it. The general idea is that the mine is still producing largely—and it is—for, to protect ourselves until we can unload it on to others, we have secretly purchased rich ore elsewhere, dumped it into the mine, and then taken it out again."

He paused, drumming absently on the desk with his fingers, and Mary Eliska asked:

"What is the object of that deception, sir?"

"To maintain the public delusion until we can sell out. And now I come to the point of my story, Mary Eliska. Gold mines, even as rich as the Queen of Hearts is reputed to be, are not easy to sell. I have exhausted all my resources in keeping up this deception and the time has come when I must sell or become bankrupt. The other stockholders have smaller interests and are wealthier men, but each one is striving hard to secure a customer. I have found one."

He looked up and smiled at her; then he frowned.

"The man is my brother-in-law, Thatcher Allen" he added.

Mary Eliska was getting nervous, but waited for him to continue.

"This brother-in-law is a man I detest. He married my only sister and did not treat her well. He is a notorious gambler and confidence man, although perhaps he would not admit that is his profession. At all events he had the assurance to sneer at me and abuse my sister, and I was powerless at the time to interfere. Fortunately the poor woman died several years ago. Since then I have not seen much of Thatcher Allen, for he lives in the East. He came out here last month on some small business matter and has gone crazy over the Queen of Hearts mine. He hunted me up and asked if I'd sell part of my stock. I told him I would sell all or none. So he has been getting his money together and has raised two hundred and fifty thousand dollars—the sum I demanded."

Mary Eliska was looking at him wonderingly. The story seemed incredible. Perhaps Mr. Burthon saw the dismay and reproach in her eyes, for he asked:

"What do you think of this deal, Mary Eliska? Am I not fortunate?"

"But—would you *really* sell a worthless property to this man—your own brother-in-law—and—and steal a fortune from him?" she inquired.

The man flushed and shifted uneasily in his seat.

"He abused my sister," he said, as if defending himself.

"The property is worthless," she persisted.

"He can hustle around and sell it again, as I am doing."

"Suppose he fails? Suppose he refuses to do such a wicked thing?"

Mr. Burthon stared at her a moment. Then he laughed harshly.

"Thatcher Allen would delight in such a 'wicked' game," he replied. "And, if he failed to sell, the scoundrel would be ruined, for I believe this two hundred and fifty thousand is about all he's worth."

"It's dreadful!" exclaimed the girl, really shocked.

"It is done every day in a business way," he rejoined.

"Then why did you ask my advice?" demanded the girl, quickly. Before answering he waited to drum on the desk with his fingers again.

"Because," said he, speaking slowly, "I dislike this man so passionately that I have wondered if the hatred blinds my judgment. He may be dangerous, too, yet I think he is too much of a fool to be able to injure me in retaliation. I don't know him very well. I've not seen him before for years." He paused, taking note of the horror spreading over the girl's face. Then he smiled and added in a gentler voice: "Perhaps my chief reason, however, for seeking your advice is that I find I have still a conscience. Yes, yes; a troublesome conscience. I have been suppressing it for years, yet like Banquo's ghost it will not down. My business judgment determines me to unload this worthless stock and save myself from the loss of my entire fortune. I must do it. It is like a man taking unawares a counterfeit coin, and then, discovering it is spurious, passing it on to some innocent victim. You might do that yourself, Mary Eliska."

"I do not believe I would."

"Well, most people would, and think it no crime. In this case I'm merely passing a counterfeit, that I received innocently, on to another innocent. If the fact is ever known my business friends will applaud me. But that obstinate conscience of mine keeps asking the question: 'Is it safe?' It asserts that I am filled with glee because I am selling to a man I hate—a man who has indirectly injured me. I am to get revenge as well as save my money.

Safe? Of course it's safe. Yet my—er—conscience—the still small voice—keeps digging at me to be careful. It doesn't seem to like the idea of dealing with Thatcher Allen, and has been annoying me for several days. So I thought I would put the case to a young, pure-minded girl who has a clear head and is honest. I imagined you would tell me to go ahead. Then I could afford to laugh at cautious Mr. Conscience."

"No," said Mary Eliska, gravely, "the conscience is right. But you misunderstand its warning. It doesn't mean that the act is not safe from a worldly point of view, but from a moral standpoint. You could not respect yourself, Mr. Burthon, if you did this thing."

He sighed and turned to his papers. Mary Eliska hesitated. Then, impulsively, she asked:

"You won't do it, sir; will you?"

"Yes, Mary Eliska; I think I shall."

His tone had changed. It was now hard and cold.

"Thatcher Allen will call here tomorrow morning at nine, to consummate the deal," he continued. "See that we are not disturbed, Mary Eliska."

"But, sir—"

He turned upon her almost fiercely, but at sight of her distressed, downcast face a kindlier look came to his eyes.

"Remember that the alternative would be ruin," he said gently. "I would be obliged to give up my business—these offices—and begin life anew. You would lose your position, and—"

"Oh, I won't mind that!" she exclaimed.

"Don't you care for it, then?"

"Yes; for I need the money I earn. But to do right will not ruin either of us, sir."

"Perhaps not; but I'm not going to do right—as you see it. I shall follow my business judgment."

Mary Eliska was indignant.

"I shall save you from yourself, then," she cried, standing before him like an accusing angel. "I warn you now, Mr. Burthon, that when Thatcher Allen calls I shall tell him the truth about your mine, and then he will not buy it."

He looked at her curiously, reflectively, for a long time, as if he beheld for the first time some rare and admirable thing. The man was not angered. He seemed not even annoyed by her threat. But after that period of disconcerting study he turned again to his desk.

"Thank you, Mary Eliska. That is all."

She went back to her post, trembling nervously from the excitement of the interview, and tried to put her mind on her work. Mr. Burthon was wholly unemotional and seemed to have forgotten her presence. But, a half hour later, when he thrust the papers into his pocket, locked his desk and took his hat to go, he paused beside his secretary, gazed earnestly into her face a moment and then abruptly turned away.

"Good night, Mary Eliska," he said, and his voice seemed to dwell tenderly on her name.

CHAPTER 7.5
BETWEEN MAN AND MAN—AND A GIRL

That night Mary Eliska confided the whole story to Bill. Her brother listened thoughtfully and then inquired:

"Will you really warn Thatcher Allen, Sis?"

"I—I ought to," she faltered.

"Then do," he returned. "To my notion Burthon is playing a mean trick on the fellow, and no good business man would either applaud or respect him for it. Your employer is shifty, Mary Eliska; I'm sure of it; if I were you I'd put a stop to his game no matter what came of it."

"Very well, Bill; I'll do it. But I don't believe Mr. Burthon means to be a bad man. His plea about his conscience proves that. But—but—" "It's worse for a man to realize he's doing wrong, and then do it, than if he were too hardened to have any conscience at all," asserted Bill oracularly.

"And if I let him do this wrong act I would be as guilty as he," she added.

"That's true, Sis. You'll lose your job, sure enough, but there will be another somewhere just as good."

So, when Mr. Burthon's secretary went to the office next morning she was keyed up to do the most heroic deed that had ever come to her hand. Whatever the consequences might be, the girl was determined to waylay Thatcher Allen when he arrived and tell him the truth about the Queen of Hearts.

But he did not come to the office at nine o'clock. Neither had Mr. Burthon arrived at that time. Mary Eliska, her heart beating with trepidation but strong in resolve, watched the clock nearing the hour, passing it, and steadily ticking on in the silence of the office. The outer room was busy this morning, and in the broker's absence his secretary was called upon to perform many minor tasks; but her mind was more upon the clock than upon her work.

Ten o'clock came. Eleven. At half past eleven the door swung open and Mr. Burthon ushered in a strange gentleman whom Mary Eliska at once decided was Thatcher Allen. He was extremely tall and thin and stooped somewhat as he walked. He had a long, grizzled mustache, wore gold-rimmed eyeglasses and carried a gold-headed cane. From his patent leather shoes to his chamois gloves he was as neat and sleek as if about to attend a reception.

Observing the presence of a young lady the stranger at once removed his hat.

"Sit down, Thatcher Allen," said Mr. Burthon, carelessly.

As he obeyed, Mary Eliska, her face flaming red, advanced to a position before him and exclaimed in a pleading voice:

"Oh, sir, do not buy Mr. Burthon's mine, I beg of you!"

The man stared at her with faded gray eyes which were enlarged by the lenses of his spectacles. Mr. Burthon smiled, seemed interested, and watched the scene with evident amusement.

"Why not, my child?" asked Thatcher Allen.

"Because it is worthless—absolutely worthless!" she declared.

He turned to the other man.

"Eh, Burthon?" he muttered, inquiringly.

"Mary Eliska believes she is speaking the truth," said the broker jauntily.

"Oh, she does. And you, Burthon?"

"I? Why, I'm of the same opinion."

Thatcher Allen took out his handkerchief, removed his glasses and polished the lenses with a thoughtful air. Mary Eliska was trembling with nervousness.

"Don't buy the Queen of Hearts, sir; it would ruin you," she repeated earnestly.

He breathed upon the glasses and wiped them carefully.

"You interest me," he remarked. "But, the fact is, I—er—I've bought it."

"Already!" "At nine o'clock, according to agreement. Burthon sent word he'd come to my hotel instead of meeting me at his office, as first planned."

"Oh, I see!" cried Mary Eliska, much disappointed. "He knew I would prevent the crime."

"Crime, miss?"

"Is it not a crime to rob you of two hundred and fifty thousand dollars?"

"It would be, of course. I should dislike to lose so much money."

"You have lost it!" declared the girl. "That mine has no gold in it at all—except what has been bought elsewhere and placed in it to deceive a purchaser."

Thatcher Allen replaced his glasses, adjusting them carefully upon his nose. Then he stared at Mary Eliska again.

"You're an honest young woman," he said calmly. "I'm much obliged. You interest me. But—ahem!—Burthon has my money, you see."

Mr. Burthon's expression had changed. He was now regarding his brother-in-law with a curious and puzzled gaze.

"You're not angry, Thatcher Allen?" he asked.

"No, Burthon."

"You're not even annoyed, I take it?" This with something of a sneer.

"No, Burthon."

Both Mary Eliska and her employer were amazed. Looking from one to another, Thatcher Allen's waxen features relaxed into a smile.

"I've placed my Queen of Hearts stock in a safety deposit vault," he remarked blandly.

"I have deposited your money in my bank," retorted Mr. Burthon, triumphantly.

"Excellent!" said the other. "The thing interests me—indeed it does. You couldn't purchase that stock from me at this moment, Burthon, for twice the sum I paid you."

"No? And why not?"

"I'll tell you. I had not intended to refer to the matter just yet, but this young woman's exposé of your attempted trickery induces me to explain matters. You have always taken me for a fool, Burthon."

"I've tried to place a proper value on your intellect, Thatcher Allen."

"You have little talent in that line, believe me. Before I came out here I had heard such glowing reports of the Queen of Hearts that I stopped off in Arizona to see the wonderful mine. The manager was very polite and showed me about, but somehow I got a notion that all was not square and aboveboard. I've always been interested in mines; they fascinate me; and if this mine was as rich as reported I wanted some of the stock. But I imagined things looked a little queer, so I sent a confidential agent—fellow named Brewster, who has been with me for years—to hire out as a miner and keep his eyes open. He soon discovered the truth—that the mine was being 'salted' or fed with outside gold ore in precisely the way this girl has stated."

He turned to Mary Eliska with a profound bow, then looked toward Burthon again. "The thing interested me. I wondered why, and wired my man to stay on a little longer, 'til I had time to think it over. I—er—think very slowly. Very. In a few days Brewster telegraphed me the startling intelligence that the mine had actually struck a new lead, with ore far richer than the first showing, although that had made the Queen of Hearts famous. My man had been sent to the telegraph office with messages from the manager to Mr. Burthon and the four other stockholders; but poor Brewster's memory is bad, and he forgot to send a telegram to anyone but me. Of course the great strike—er—interested me. I instructed Brewster over the telegraph wire. At a cost of five thousand dollars we bribed the manager to keep the valuable strike secret for ten days. He's an honest man, and I shall retain him in the office. The ten days expire tonight. Meantime, I've purchased the stock."

Mr. Burthon sprang to his feet, white with anger.

"You scoundrel!" he shouted.

"Don't get excited, Burthon. This is a mere business incident, between man and man—and a girl." Another bow toward Mary Eliska. "You tried to rob me, sir, and sneered when you thought you had succeeded. I haven't robbed you, for I paid your price; but I've made a very neat investment. My stock is worth a million at this moment. Interesting, isn't it?"

Mr. Burthon recovered himself with an effort and sat down again.

"Very well," he said a little thickly. "As you say, it's all in the way of business. Good day, Thatcher Allen."

The other man arose and faced Mary Eliska, who stood by wholly bewildered by this unexpected development.

"Thank you again, my child. Your name? Mary Eliska Stricklin. I'll remember it. You tried to do me a kindness. Interesting—very!"

Without another glance at Mr. Burthon he put on his hat, walked out and closed the door softly behind him.

Mary Eliska looked up and found the broker's eyes regarding her intently.

"I—I'm sorry, sir," she stammered; "but I had to do it, to satisfy my conscience. I suppose I am dismissed?"

"No, indeed, Mary Eliska," he returned in kindly tones. "An honest secretary is too rare an acquisition to be dismissed without just cause. Having told you what I did, I could expect you to act in no other way."

"And, after all, sir," she said, brightening at the thought, "you did not rob him! Yet you saved your fortune."

He made a slight grimace, and then laughed frankly.

"Had I taken your advice," he rejoined, "I should now be worth a million."

CHAPTER 7.6
A BUCKING BIPLANE

Bill Stricklin had scarcely slept a wink for three nights. When Mary Eliska came home Thursday evening he met her at the car with the news that his airplane was complete.

"I've been adjusting it and testing the working parts all the afternoon," he said, his voice tense with effort to restrain his excitement, "and I'm ready for the trial whenever you say."

"All right, Bill," she replied briskly; "it begins to be daylight at about half past four, this time of year; shall we make the trial at that hour tomorrow morning?"

"I couldn't wait *longer* than that," he admitted, pressing her arm as they walked along. "My idea is to take it into old Marston's pasture."

"Isn't the bull there?" she inquired.

"Not now. Marston has kept the bull shut up the past few days. And it's the best place for the trial, for there's lots of room."

"Let's take a look at it, Bill!" she said, hastening her steps.

In the big, canvas covered shed reposed the airplane, its spreading white sails filling the place almost to the very edges. It was neither a monoplane nor a biplane, according to accepted ideas of such machines, but was what Bill called "a story-and-a-half flyer."

"That is, I hope it's a flyer," he amended, while Mary Eliska stared with admiring eyes, although she already knew every stick and stitch by heart.

"Of course it's a flyer!" she exclaimed. "I wouldn't be afraid to mount to the moon in that airship."

"All that witches need is a broomstick," he said playfully. "But perhaps you're not that sort of a witch, little sister."

"What shall we call it, Bill?" she asked, seriously. "Of course it's a biplane, because there are really two planes, one being above the other; but it is not in the same class with other biplanes. We must have a distinctive name for it."

"I've thought of calling it the 'Stricklin Aircraft,'" he answered. "How does that strike you?"

"It has an original sound," Mary Eliska said. "Oh, Bill! couldn't we try it tonight? It's moonlight."

He shook his head quickly, smiling at her enthusiasm.

"I'm afraid not. You're tired, and have the dinner to get and the day's dishes to wash and put away. As for me, I'm so dead for sleep I can hardly keep my eyes open. I must rest, so as to have a clear head for tomorrow's flight."

"Shall we say anything to mother about it?"

"Why need we? It would only worry the dear woman unnecessarily. Whether I succeed or fail in this trial, it will be time enough to break the news to her afterward."

Mary Eliska agreed with this. Mrs. Stricklin knew the airship was nearing completion but was not especially interested in the venture. It seemed wonderful to her that mankind had at last learned how to fly, and still more wonderful that her own son was inventing and building an improved appliance for this purpose; but so many marvelous things had happened since she became blind that her mind was to an extent inured to astonishment and she had learned to accept with calm complacency anything she could not comprehend.

Brother and sister at last tore themselves away from the fascinating creation and returned to the house, where Bill, thoroughly exhausted, fell asleep in his chair while Mary Eliska was preparing dinner. He went to bed almost immediately after he had eaten and his sister also retired when her mother did, which was at an early hour.

But Mary Eliska could not sleep. She lay and dreamed of the great triumph before them; of the plaudits of enraptured spectators; of Bill's name on every tongue in the civilized world; and, not least by any means, of the money that would come to them. No longer would the Stricklins have to worry over debts and due bills; the good things of the world would be theirs, all won by her brother's cleverness.

If she slept at all before the gray dawn stole into the sky the girl was not aware of it. By half past four she had smoking hot coffee ready for Bill and herself and after hastily drinking it they rushed to the hangar.

Bill was bright and alert this morning and declared he had "slept like a log." He slid the curtains away from the front of the shed and solemnly the boy and girl wheeled the big airplane out into the garden. By careful manipulation they steered it between the trees and away to the fence of Marston's pasture, which adjoined their own premises at the rear. To get it past the fence had been Bill's problem, and he had arranged to take out a section of the fencing big enough to admit his machine. This was now but a few minutes' work, and presently the airplane was on the smooth turf of the pasture.

They were all alone. There were no near neighbors, and it was early for any to be astir.

"One of the most important improvements I have made is my starting device," said Bill, as he began a last careful examination of his aircraft. "All others have a lot of trouble in getting started. The Wright people erect a tower and windlass, and nearly every other machine uses a track."

"I know," replied Mary Eliska. "I have seen several men holding the thing back until the motors got well started and the propellers were whirling at full speed."

"That always struck me as a crude arrangement," observed her brother. "Now, in this machine I start the motor whirling an eccentric of the same resisting power as the propeller, yet it doesn't affect the stability of the airplane. When I'm ready to start I throw in a clutch that instantly transfers the power from the eccentric to the propeller—and away I go like a rocket."

As he spoke he kissed his sister and climbed to the seat.

"Are you afraid, Bill?" she whispered, her beautiful face flushed and her eyes bright with excitement.

"Afraid! Of my own machine? Of course not."

"Don't go very high, dear."

"We'll see. I want to give it a thorough test. All right, Ris; I'm off!"

The motors whirred, steadily accelerating speed while the airplane trembled as if eager to dart away. Bill threw in the clutch; the machine leaped forward and ran on its wheels across the pasture like a deer, but did not rise.

He managed to stop at the opposite fence and when Mary Eliska came running up, panting, her brother sat in his place staring stupidly ahead.

"What's wrong, Bill?"

He rubbed his head and woke up.

"The forward elevator, I guess. But I'm sure I had it adjusted properly."

He got down and examined the rudder, giving it another upward tilt.

"Now I'll try again," he said cheerfully.

They turned the aircraft around and he made another start. This time Mary Eliska was really terrified, for the thing acted just like a bucking broncho. It rose to a height of six feet, dove to the ground, rose again to plunge its nose into the turf and performed such absurd, unexpected antics that Bill had to cling on for dear life. When he finally managed to bring it to a halt the rudder was smashed and two ribs of the lower plane splintered.

They looked at the invention with dismay, both silent for a time.

"Of course," said Bill, struggling to restrain his disappointment, "we couldn't expect it to be perfect at the first trial."

"No," agreed Mary Eliska, faintly.

"But it ought to fly, you know."

"Being a flying machine, it ought to," she said. "Can you mend it, Bill?"

"To be sure; but it will take me a little time. Tomorrow morning we will try again."

With grave faces they wheeled it back into the garden and the boy replaced the fence. Then back to the hangar, where Bill put the Stricklin Aircraft in its old place and drew the curtains—much as one does at a funeral.

"I'm sure to discover what's wrong," he told Mary Eliska, regaining courage as they walked toward the house. "And, if I've made a blunder, this is the time to rectify it. Tomorrow it will be sure to fly. Have faith in me, Sis."

"I have," she replied simply. "I'll go in and get breakfast now."

CHAPTER 7.7
SOMETHING WRONG

All that day Mary Eliska was in a state of great depression. Even Mr. Burthon noticed her woebegone face and inquired if she were ill. The girl had staked everything on Bill's success and until now had not permitted a doubt to creep into her mind. But the behavior of the aircraft was certainly not reassuring and for the first time she faced the problem of what would happen if it proved a failure. They would be ruined financially; the place would have to be sold; worst of all, her brother's chagrin and disappointment might destroy his youthful ambition and leave him a wreck.

Somehow the girl managed to accomplish her work that day and at evening, weary and despondent, returned to her home. When she left the car her step was slow and dragging until Bill came running to meet her. His face was beaming as he exclaimed:

"I've found the trouble, Sis! It was all my stupidity. I put a pin in the front elevator while I was working at it, and forgot to take it out again. No wonder it wouldn't rise—it just couldn't!"

Mary Eliska felt as if a great weight had been lifted from her shoulders.

"Are you sure it will work now?" she asked breathlessly.

"It's bound to work. I've planned all right; that I know; and having built the aircraft to do certain things it can't fail to do them. Provided," he added, more soberly, "I haven't overlooked something else."

"Are the repairs completed, Bill?"

"All is in apple-pie order for tomorrow morning's test."

It was a dreadfully long evening for them both, but after going to bed Mary Eliska was so tired and relieved in spirit that she fell into a deep sleep that lasted until Bill knocked at her door at early dawn.

"Saturday morning," he remarked, as together they went out to the hangar. "Do you suppose yesterday being Friday had anything to do with our hard luck?"

"No; it was only that forgotten pin," she declared.

Again they wheeled the aircraft out to Marston's pasture, and once more the girl's heart beat high with hope and excitement.

Bill took a final look at every part, although he had already inspected his work with great care. Then he sprang into the seat and said:

"All right, little sister. Wish me luck!"

The motor whirred—faster and faster—the clutch gripped the propeller, and away darted the aircraft. It rolled half way across the pasture, then lifted and began mounting into the air. Mary Eliska stood with her hands clasped over her bosom, straining her eyes to watch every detail of the flight.

Straight away soared the aircraft, swift as a bird, until it was a mere speck in the gray sky. The girl could not see the turn, for the circle made was scarcely noticeable at that distance, but suddenly she was aware that Bill was returning. The speck became larger, the sails visible. The young aviator passed over the pasture at a height of a hundred feet from the ground, circled over their own garden and then began to descend. As he did so the aircraft assumed a rocking motion, side to side, which increased so dangerously that Mary Eliska screamed without knowing that she did so.

Down came the airplane, reaching the earth on a side tilt that crushed the light planes into kindling wood and a mass of crumpled canvas. Bill rolled out, stretched his length upon the ground, and lay still.

Mary Eliska Stood with Hands Clasped.

The sun was just beginning to rise over the orange grove. The deathly silence that succeeded the wreck of the aircraft was only broken by the irregular, spasmodic whirr of the motors, which were still going. Mary Eliska, white and cold, crept in among the debris and shut down the engines. Then, slowly and reluctantly, she approached the motionless form of her brother.

To be alone at such a time and place was dreadful. A few steps from Bill she halted; then turned and fled toward the garden in sudden panic. Away from the horrid scene her courage and presence of mind speedily returned. She caught up a bucket of water that stood in the shed and lugged it back to the pasture.

Was Bill dead? She leaned over him, dreading to place her hand upon his heart, gazing piteously into his set, unresponsive face.

Pat—pat—patter!

A rush across the springing turf.

What was it?

Mary Eliska straightened up, yelled like an Indian and made a run for the fence that did full credit to her athletic training.

For Marston's big bull was coming—a huge, tawny creature with a temper that would shame tobasco. He swerved as if to follow the fleeing girl, but then the draggled planes of the aircraft defied him and he changed his mind to charge this new and unknown enemy—perhaps with the same disposition that Don Quixote attacked the windmill.

Mary Eliska shrieked again, for the enormous beast bounded directly over Bill's prostrate body and with bowed head and tail straight as a pointer dog's rushed at the airplane. The sails shivered, collapsed, rolled in billows like the waves of the ocean, and amid them the struggling bull went down, tangled himself in the wires and became a helpless prisoner.

The girl, who was sobbing hysterically, heard herself laugh aloud and was inexpressibly shocked. The bull bellowed with rage but was so wound around with guy-wires that this was the extent of his power. Turning her eyes from the beast to Bill she gave a shout of joy, for her brother was sitting up and rubbing his leg with one hand and his head with the other, while he stared bewildered at the wreck of his airplane, from which the head of the bull protruded.

Mary Eliska ran up, wringing her hands, and asked:

"Are you much hurt, dear?"

"I—I've gone crazy!" he answered, despairingly. "Seems as if the aircraft was transformed into the mummy of a—a—brute beast! Don't laugh, Sis. Wh—what's wrong with me—with my eyes? Tell me!"

She threw herself down upon the grass and laughed until she cried, Bill's reproachful glances having no particle of effect in restraining her. When at last she could control herself she sat up and wiped her eyes, saying:

"Forgive me, dear, it's—it's so funny! But," suddenly grave and anxious, "are you badly hurt? Is anything—broken?"

"Nothing but my heart," he replied dolefully.

"Oh; that!" she said, relieved.

"Just look at that mess!" he wailed, pointing to the aircraft. "What has happened to it?"

"The bull," she answered. "But don't be discouraged, dear; the thing flew beautifully."

"The bull?"

"No; the aircraft. But as for the bull, I'm bound to say he did his best. How in the world shall we get him out of there, Bill?"

"I—I think I'm dazed, Sis," he murmured, feeling his head again. "Can't you help me to—understand?"

So she told him the whole story, Bill sighing and shaking his head as he glared at the bull and the bull glared at him. Afterward the boy made an effort to rise, and Mary Eliska leaned down and assisted him. When he got to his feet she held him until he grew stronger and could stand alone.

"I'm so grateful you were not killed," his sister whispered. "Nothing else matters since you have so miraculously escaped."

"Killed?" said Bill; "why, it was only a tumble, Ris. But the bull is a more serious complication. I suppose the aircraft was badly damaged, from what you say, before the bull got it; but now it's a hopeless mess."

"Oh, no," she returned, encouragingly. "If he hasn't smashed the motor we won't mind the rest of the damage. Do you think we can untangle him?"

They approached the animal, who by this time was fully subdued and whined apologetically to be released. Bill got his nippers and cut wire after wire until suddenly the animal staggered to his feet, gave a terrified bellow and dashed down the field with a dozen yards of plane cloth wound around his neck.

"Good riddance!" cried Mary Eliska. "I don't think he'll ever bother us again."

Bill was examining the wreck. He tested the motors and found that neither the fall nor the bull had damaged them in the least. But there was breakage enough, aside from this, to make him groan disconsolately.

"The flight was wonderful," commented his sister, watching his face anxiously. "Nothing could work more perfectly than the Stricklin Aircraft did until—until—the final descent. What caused the rocking, Bill?"

"A fault of the lateral balance. My automatic device refused to work, and before I knew it I had lost control."

She stood gazing thoughtfully down at the wreck. Her brother had really invented a flying machine, of that there was no doubt. She had seen it fly—seen it soar miles through the air— and knew that a certain degree of success had been obtained. There was something wrong, to be sure; there usually is with new inventions; but wrongs can be righted.

"I've succeeded in a lot of things," her brother was saying, reflectively. "The engines, the propeller and elevator are all good, and decided improvements on the old kinds. The starting device works beautifully and will soon be applied to every airship made. Only the automatic balance failed me, and I believe I know how to remedy that fault."

"Do you suppose the machine can be rebuilt?" she asked.

"Assuredly. And the automatic balance perfected. The trouble is, Mary Eliska, it will take a lot more money to do it, and we've already spent the last cent we could raise. It's hard luck. Here is a certain fortune within our grasp, if we could perfect the thing, and our only stumbling block is the lack of a few dollars."

Having reviewed in her mind all the circumstances of Bill's successful flight the girl knew that he spoke truly. Comparing the aircraft with other machines she had seen and studied at the aviation meet she believed her brother's invention was many strides in advance of them all.

"The question of securing the money is something we must seriously consider," she said. "In some way it will be raised, of course. But just now our chief problem is how to get this ruin back to the hangar."

"That will be my job," declared Bill, his courage returning. "There are few very big pieces left to remove, and by taking things apart I shall be able to get it all into the shed. The day's doings are over, Sis. Get breakfast and then go to your work. After I've stored this rubbish I'll take a run into town myself, and look for a job. The aviation jig is up—for the present, at least."

"Don't do anything hurriedly, Bill," protested the girl. "Work on the aircraft for a day or two, just as if we had money to go ahead with. That will give me time to think. Tonight, when I come home, we will talk of this again."

CHAPTER 7.8
MR. BURTHON'S PROPOSITION

Saturday was a busy day at the office. They did not close early, but rather later than on other days, and Mary Eliska found plenty of work to occupy her. But always there remained in her thoughts the problem of how to obtain money for Bill, and she racked her brain to find some practical solution.

Mr. Burthon was in a mellow mood today. Since the sale of his mining stock he had been less abstracted and moody than before, and during the afternoon, having just handed Mary Eliska several deeds of land to copy, he noticed her pale, drawn face and said: "You look tired, Mary Eliska."

She gave him one of her sweet, bright smiles in payment for the kindly tone.

"I *am* tired," she returned. "For two mornings I have been up at four o'clock."

"Anyone ill at home?" he asked quickly. "No, sir."

Suddenly it occurred to her that he might assist in unraveling the problem. She turned to him and said:

"Can you spare me a few minutes, Mr. Burthon? I—I want to ask your advice."

He glanced at her curiously and sat down in a chair facing her.

"Tell me all about it," he said encouragingly. "Not long ago it was I asking for advice, and you were good enough to favor me. Now it is logically your turn."

"My brother," said she, "has invented an airship."

He gave a little start of surprise and an eager look spread over his face. Then he smiled at her tolerantly.

"All the world has gone crazy over aviation," he remarked. "I, myself, witnessed the flights at Dominguez Field and became strongly impressed with the desire to fly. I suppose your brother contracted the fever, too, and has made a model he thinks will float in the air."

"Oh, it is not a model," she gravely replied. "Bill is an expert mechanic and has worked on many of the most famous airplanes in the country. He has recently built a complete airship of his own, and this morning I watched him make a very successful flight in it."

"Indeed?" he exclaimed, the eager look returning. "There is money in a good airship, Mary Eliska. This is the psychological moment to forge ahead in aviation, which will soon become the world's popular mode of transit. It is easy to build an airship; yes. Perhaps I could build one myself. But where many will try, many will fail." "And some will succeed," she added, smiling. He examined her expressive face with interest. "Please tell me all about it," said he.

So Mary Eliska gave him the history of the aircraft, from its conception to the final triumph and wreckage and its conquest by the bull. Incidentally she told how they had mortgaged their home and the orange crop to get the needed money, and finally explained the condition they were now in—success within their grasp, but no means of taking advantage of it.

Mr. Burthon was very attentive throughout, his eyes fixed upon Mary Eliska's lovely face and watching its shades of anxiety and exaltation as the story progressed. While she enthusiastically described Bill's aircraft, her eyes sparkling and a soft flush mantling her cheeks, the man scarcely heard what she said, so intent was he in admiring her. He did not permit his fair secretary to notice his mood, however, and the girl was too earnestly engaged to heed her employer's intent gaze. At the conclusion of her story she asked:

"Tell me, sir, is there any way in which we can raise the money required?"

Mr. Burthon roused himself and the hard business expression settled upon his features again.

"I think so," he returned, slowly. "What your brother needs is a backer—what is called an 'angel,' you know—who will furnish the necessary funds for the perfection of the invention and to place it upon the market and properly exhibit it."

"Would anyone do that?" she inquired. "For a consideration, yes. Such a party would demand an interest in the invention, and a share of the profits."

"How much, sir?" "Perhaps a half interest." She considered this statement.

"That is too much to give away, Mr. Burthon. The aircraft is already built and tested. It is a proved success, and the best airplane in all the world. Why should we give a half interest in return for a little money?"

He hesitated; then replied coldly:

"Because the invention is useless without the means to publicly demonstrate it, and establish it on a paying basis. At present your airship is without the slightest commercial value. Once exploited, the half interest you retain would make your fortune."

Her brow wrinkled with a puzzled look.

"I'll talk to Bill about it," she said. "But, if he consents, where could I find such an—an 'angel'?"

"In me," he answered coolly. "If, on investigation, I find your brother's airship to be one half as practical as you represent it, and doubtless believe it to be, I will deposit ten thousand dollars in the bank to exploit it—in return for a half interest—and agree to furnish more money whenever it is required."

"Thank you, sir," said Mary Eliska, doubtfully. "I—I'll talk with my brother."

"Very well," he replied. "But beware of confiding in strangers. I am your friend, and will guard your interests faithfully. Talk with your brother, but with no one else."

Mary Eliska did talk with Bill, that very evening, and the boy frowned at the suggestion just as his sister had done.

"I know that is the way business men do things," he said, "and it's a good deal like robbery. Burthon sees that we must have money, and he's driving a shrewd bargain. Besides that, I'm not sure he's honest."

"I don't see how he could defraud us, though," mused Mary Eliska. "There are two things for us to consider. One is, whether we can raise the money in any other way; and then, whether a half interest in a business with plenty of money behind it would not pay better than the whole thing, with a constant struggle to make both ends meet."

"Perhaps it might," he replied, hesitatingly. "But I've done all this alone, so far, and I hate to let anyone else reap the benefit of my ideas. I suppose if I had not proved the thing, but merely begun work on it, Burthon wouldn't have invested a dollar in it."

"I suppose not," she agreed. "But think it over, dear. We have all day tomorrow to talk of it and consider what is best to be done. Then, when I go to the office Monday morning, I can tell Mr. Burthon our decision."

They talked considerably more on this subject after dinner, and worried over it during a sleepless night. After breakfast on Sunday morning they went quietly to church, Mrs. Stricklin accompanying them, as was her custom. But Mary Eliska had hard work to keep her mind on the service and Bill found the attempt impossible. The return home, including a long car ride, was passed in silence, and then Mary Eliska had to busy herself over the dinner.

It was the middle of the afternoon before brother and sister found time to meet in the hangar, which was now strewn with parts of the aircraft. Bill looked around him gloomily and then seated himself beside Mary Eliska upon a bench.

"I suppose we must settle this thing," he said; "and there's no doubt we must have money, or we shall face ruin. The thing has cost too much for us to withdraw from it without a heavy loss that would mean privation and suffering for you and mother. If we go to anyone but Burthon we may not get as good an offer as he makes, for men with money are eager to take advantage of a poor fellow in need. I can't blame Burthon much. I don't suppose there's a rich man living who wouldn't hold us up in the same selfish way. And so—" He paused, shrugging his shoulders.

"So you think we'd better accept Mr. Burthon's proposition and give him a half interest?" she asked.

"Beg pardon," said a cold voice; "am I intruding?"

CHAPTER 7.9
THE OTHER FELLOW

Bill and Mary Eliska both sprang to their feet, startled by the interruption. A tall man, having a stoop to his shoulders, had parted the entrance curtains and stood looking at them. He wore blue goggles, an automobile cap and duster, and heavy shoes; but Mary Eliska recognized him at once.

"Thatcher Allen!" she exclaimed.

"Dear me!" said the man; "it's the young lady from Burthon's office—and my friend." He laughed, lightly, as if amused by the recollection; then added: "I've run out of gasoline and my car is stranded a quarter of a mile off. Think you could furnish me enough of the elusive fluid to run me into town?"

Bill walked silently to his gasoline tank. He was excessively annoyed to have a stranger spy upon his workshop and resolved to get rid of the man in short order. Mary Eliska also was silent, fearing Thatcher Allen might linger if she entered into conversation with him. The spot was so retired that until now no one but themselves had ever entered the hangar, and the secret had been well kept.

"Here's a two-gallon can," said Bill, surlily. "Will that do you?"

Thatcher Allen nodded, set the can upon the ground and walked over to the bench, where he calmly seated himself beside the girl.

"What are you up to, here?" he asked.

"Our own especial business," retorted Bill. "You will pardon me, sir, if I ask you to take your gasoline and go. This is private property."

"I see," said Thatcher Allen. "I'm intruding. Never mind that. Let's talk a bit; I'm in no hurry."

"We are very much occupied, sir," urged Mary Eliska, earnestly.

"No doubt," said the man. "I overheard a remark as I entered. You were wondering whether to accept Burthon's offer and give him a half interest. Eh? That interests me; I'm Burthon's brother-in-law."

He glanced around him, then calmly took a cigarette from his pocket and offered one to Bill.

"I can't allow smoking here, sir; there's too much gasoline about," said the boy, almost rudely.

"True. I forgot." He put the case in his pocket. "You're building some sort of a—er—er—flying machine, I see. That interests me. I'm a crank on aviation. Is this the thing Burthon wants a half interest in?"

Bill scowled. When Thatcher Allen turned to Mary Eliska she slightly nodded, embarrassed how to escape this impertinent questioning.

"I thought so. Then you've really got something?"

Bill laughed. His annoyance was passing. The man had already seen whatever there was to see, for his eyes had been busy from the moment he entered. And Bill remembered that this was the person who had outwitted Mr. Burthon in the mine deal.

"I have something that will fly, if that is what you mean," he replied.

"Yes; that is what I mean. Tried the thing yet?"

"Oh, yes," said Mary Eliska eagerly. "It flew splendidly yesterday morning, but—but Bill had an accident with his airplane, and a bull demolished what was left of it."

"Ah; that interests me; it really does," said Thatcher Allen. He looked at Bill more attentively. "Your brother, Mary Eliska?"

"Yes, sir."

"And you need money?"

"To rebuild the machine, and perfect it; yes, sir."

"And Burthon will furnish the money, for a half interest?"

"Yes, sir," repeated the girl, uneasy at his tone.

"Too much," asserted Thatcher Allen, positively. "Burthon's a rascal, too. You know that, Mary Eliska. Tried to rob me; and you tried to prevent him. I haven't forgotten that; it was a kindness. I've had to fight a cold, hard, selfish world, and fight it alone. I've won; but it has made me as cold, as hard and selfish as the others. You're different, Mary Eliska; the world hasn't spoiled you yet. I can't recollect when anyone ever took the trouble to do me a kindness before. So I, your direct opposite, admire you for your originality. I'm a scoundrel and you're a—an honest girl."

There wasn't a particle of emotion in his voice, but somehow both Mary Eliska and Bill knew he was in earnest. It was difficult to say anything fitting in reply, and after a brief pause the man continued:

"I can see that your airship is at present something of a wreck. How much money do you need?"

"I ought to have at least a thousand dollars," answered Bill, reflectively glancing around the shop. Thatcher Allen's eyes followed his.

"Will two thousand do it?"

"Of course, sir."

"I'll lend you three," said the man. "I don't want a half interest. I won't rob you."

Both boy and girl stared at him in amazement.

"What security do you require?" asked Bill, suspiciously.

"Eh? None at all. The thing interests me. If you make a lot of money, I'll let you pay me back some day. That's fair. If you fail, you'll have worries enough without having to repay me. But I attach two conditions to my offer. One is that you have nothing to do with Burthon. The other is that I have permission to come here and watch your work; to advise with you at times; to help you map out your future career and to attend all the flying exhibitions in which you take part. Agree to that, and I'll back you through thick and thin, because I'm interested in aviation and—because your sister was good to me."

"I'll do it, sir!" cried Bill, excitedly.

"Oh, thank you! Thank you, Thatcher Allen," added Mary Eliska, in joyful tones.

"It's a bargain," said Thatcher Allen, smiling at them both. He took out a fountain pen and wrote a check on Montecito Bank and Trust in Santa Barbara for three thousand dollars in favor of Bill Stricklin. But he handed it to Mary Eliska.

"Now then," said he, "tell me something about it."

CHAPTER 7.10
A FRESH START

When Mary Eliska appeared at the office Monday morning she went quietly about her work, feeling very happy indeed. The astonishing generosity of Thatcher Allen had relieved all her worries and brought sunshine into her heart.

Mr. Burthon came at his usual time and on taking his place at the desk looked inquiringly at Mary Eliska, but said nothing. Neither did she mention the subject of the aircraft. Her employer, watching her stealthily from behind his desk, could not fail to note the joy in her face and was undoubtedly puzzled to account for it—unless, indeed, she and her brother had decided to accept his proposition. He had an idea that they would accept; that they must accept; it was the only way they could carry on their experiment. But he waited for her to refer to the subject.

Mary Eliska managed to escape that night while a customer was engaging Mr. Burthon's attention. She disliked, for some unexplained reason, to tell him they had decided not to take him for a partner. Arriving home she found Bill busily at work rebuilding his airship, and it pleased her to hear his cheery whistle as she approached the hangar. The young fellow was in capital spirits.

"You see, Sis," said he, "with all this money to use I shall be able to make an entirely new automatic balance. I've come to the conclusion the first one doesn't work smoothly enough to be entirely satisfactory. I shall also provide a store of extra ribs and such parts as are liable to get damaged, so that the repair work will be a matter of hours instead of days. How lucky it was Thatcher Allen ran out of gasoline yesterday."

"He's a queer man," replied Mary Eliska, thoughtfully. "I can't make up my mind yet whether I like him or not."

"I like his money, anyhow," laughed Bill; "and we didn't have to give him a half interest to get it, either. I imagine the man was really touched by your endeavor to save him from what you thought was a bad bargain, and certainly his magnanimous act could have been prompted by nothing but kindness."

"It saved our half interest, at least," she said, evasively. "Has he been here today, Bill?"

"Haven't seen even his shadow," was the reply. "I don't imagine he'll bother us much, although he has reserved the right to look around all he wants to. He must be a busy man, with all his wealth."

The next morning, however, after Mary Eliska had gone to her work, Thatcher Allen's car spun up the lane and he came into the hangar, nodded to Bill and sat down quietly on the bench.

For a time he silently watched the young man shave a Cyprus rib into shape; then got up and carefully examined the motor, which was in good order. Bill knew, when first Thatcher Allen began asking questions, that he understood machinery, and the man was quick to perceive the value of young Stricklin's improvements.

"It interests me," he drawled, after starting the engines and watching them work. "As a boy I longed to be a mechanic. Got sidetracked, though, and became a speculator. Needs almost as much ingenuity to succeed in that as in mechanics. Pays better, but ruins one's self-respect. Stick to mechanics, Stricklin."

"I will," promised Bill, laughing.

"This new profession," continued Thatcher Allen, "will throw you in with a lot of 'queer' people—same sort that used to follow the races and now bet on automobile contests. Keep your sister away from them."

"I'll try to," returned Bill, more soberly. "But Mary Eliska is crazy over aviation, and she'll have to go everywhere that I do."

"That's all right; I like the idea. But don't introduce her to every fellow you are forced to associate with. Girls are queer, and your sister is—beautiful. I've a daughter myself." "Oh!" exclaimed Bill, not knowing just how to take this remark.

"My daughter is not—beautiful. No. And she's a demon. I'll bring her here to see you and your sister, some day."

"Thank you," said Bill, turning red. Certainly this new acquaintance was odd and unaccountable in some ways. Bill wondered why he should bring a "demon" to the hangar, and why he described his own daughter in such uncomplimentary language.

Thatcher Allen smoked a cigarette thoughtfully. "Your sister," he said, "interests me. She's a good girl. Must have a good mother." "The best in the world," asserted Bill, proudly.

"My daughter," resumed Thatcher Allen, "takes after her mother. Girls usually do. Her mother was—well, she was Burthon's sister. Catch the idea? It was all my fault, and Sybil—that's my daughter—blames me for her parentage. With apparent justice. Not a joke, Stricklin. Don't laugh."

"I'm not laughing, sir." "Speaking of Burthon reminds me of something. I don't like the idea of your sister working there—in his office."

"He has always treated her very nicely, I believe," said Bill, "and Mary Eliska feels she must earn some money."

"Not necessary. You've a fortune in your airship. Take the girl away from Burthon. Keep her at home." Bill did not reply to this, but he decided it was not a bad suggestion. "How old is she?" inquired Thatcher Allen, presently. "Just seventeen." "Too young to work in an office. Finished her education?" "All we are able to give her, sir." "H-m-m. Take my advice. Burthon's unreliable. I know him. Gorilla inside, man outside. I—I married a Burthon."

These brief sentences were spoken between puffs of his cigarette. Sometimes there would be a very definite pause between them, while the man smoked and reflected upon his subject. Bill continued his work and answered when required to do so.

Thatcher Allen stayed at the hangar until nearly noon, watching the boy work, bearing a hand now and then when a plane rib was awkward to handle alone, always interested in everything pertaining to the airplane. He made Bill explain the changes he proposed to apply to the lateral balance and offered one or two rather clever suggestions, showing his grasp of the subject. But he did not refer to Mary Eliska again and finally slipped away without saying good-bye.

Bill thought him queerer than during their first interview, but liked him better.

CHAPTER 7.11
MARY ELISKA RESIGNS

Meantime Mary Eliska was having a hard time at the office endeavoring to avoid a personal conversation with Mr. Burthon. When he came in at nine o'clock he smiled upon her and asked:

"Anything to tell me, Mary Eliska?"

She shook her head, flushing a little, and he went to his desk without another word. He seemed abstracted and moody during the forenoon—a return of his old puzzling manner—and Mary Eliska regretted she had not been brave enough to tell him of their decision to reject his offer when he gave her the opportunity.

Nothing more passed between them until after luncheon, but when she reëntered the office Mr. Burthon, who had not gone out, suddenly roused himself and said:

"Come here, please, Mary Eliska."

She obeyed, meekly seating herself in the chair beside his desk.

The man looked at her a long time; not impudently, with direct gaze, but rather speculatively and with an expression that seemed to penetrate far beyond her and to consider many things beside her fair face. Finally he asked:

"What conclusion have you reached in regard to your financial matters, of which we spoke Saturday?"

"I've talked with my brother, sir, and he dislikes to give up a half interest in his invention."

"Did you tell him I would furnish all the money that might be required?"

"Yes, sir."

"And he refused?"

"This airplane is very dear to my brother, Mr. Burthon. He cannot bear to transfer a part ownership to another, who would have the right to dictate its future."

"Pshaw!" exclaimed the broker, impatiently; "the boy's a fool. There's scarcely an inventor in the world who hasn't had to sacrifice an interest in his creation in order to raise money."

"Bill won't do it," declared Mary Eliska, positively, for she resented the speech.

Mr. Burthon fell silent, drumming on the desk with his fingers, as he always did when in deep thought. Mary Eliska started to rise, thinking the interview closed.

"Wait a moment, please," he said. "How old are you, Mary Eliska?—your name is Mary Eliska, isn't it?"

"Yes, sir. I am seventeen."

"So young! Why, you ought to be in school, instead of at work."

She made no reply. He watched her awhile, as she sat before him with bent head, and then continued, in the kindly tone he so often used when addressing her:

"Mary Eliska—Mary Eliska—I will give your brother all the money he needs, and he may retain the entire interest in his airship. The payment may come from you alone."

She started and became alert at once, raising her head to look at him inquiringly.

"In other words," he added, "I'm not especially interested in your brother or his invention; but I am greatly interested in you."

"Mr. Burthon, I—"

"Listen to me, Mary Eliska, and let me explain. I'm a lonely man, for I have never married—or cared to. You are the only member of the fair sex who has ever attracted me except my sister, whom I regarded with warm affection. When she married that scoundrel Thatcher Allen we became separated forever, and in a few years she died. Since then I have thought of nothing but business. I am now thirty-eight years of age, and in my prime. I have amassed a fortune—something more than a quarter of a million, as you know—and have no one to leave it to when I pass away. I should like to leave it to you, Mary Eliska."

"To me, sir!" she exclaimed, amazed.

"Yes. Your presence here in the office has transformed the place from a barren den to a cozy, homelike apartment. I like to see your sweet face near me, gravely bending over your work. Your personality has charmed me; your lack of affectation, your sincerity and honesty, have won my admiration. I cannot say to you, as a younger man would, that I love you, for I will not take an unfair advantage of one who is as yet a child. But you will become a woman soon, and I want to make you a splendid woman—and a happy one. This is my proposition: place yourself in my hands unreservedly, and let me direct your future. I will send you to a famous finishing school in the East and supply you with a liberal allowance. In two years you will return to me, old enough to become my wife."

"Oh, Mr. Burthon!"

"Meantime I'll finance your brother's airship proposition until it either fails or finally succeeds."

Mary Eliska was greatly distressed. She felt at the moment like giving way to a flood of tears, for she realized that this absurd, astonishing proposal would deprive her of her position. He saw her agitation and felt intuitively she would not consider his offer. So he said, with grim insistence:

"You may answer me with one word, my child; yes or no."

"Oh, Mr. Burthon, it is impossible! I have a home, a mother and brother, and—I—I could not think of such a thing."

"Not to save those relatives from disaster—from misery—from ruin, perhaps?"

The implied threat hardened her heart, which had begun to pity the man.

"Not even to save them from death!" she replied firmly.

"Am I so distasteful to you, then? Is my money of so little account?"

With cold dignity Mary Eliska rose from her chair. He saw the look on her face and became a little alarmed.

"Please forget all I have said," he added, hastily. "I—I am not myself today. You may get the mail ready, Mary Eliska, and I will sign the letters before I go."

She went to the wardrobe and took down her things. He sat silently watching her as she put them on, a slight frown upon his face. The girl hesitated a moment, then walked straight to his desk and said:

"Of course I cannot stay here a moment after what you have said. But I think you—you meant to be good to me—in your way. Good-bye, Mr. Burthon."

"Good-bye, Mary Eliska."

His voice was cold and hard. She did not look at him again, but walked out of the office and quietly left the building, so she did not see that the frown had deepened to a scowl, nor hear him mutter:

"Both lost—the girl and the airplane! But I'll have them yet, for the Stricklins are too simple to oppose me successfully."

At three o'clock Mary Eliska surprised Bill by coming into the hangar in her working dress.

"Why, what's the matter, Sis?" he demanded. "I've left Mr. Burthon," she said quietly. "What's up?" Mary Eliska thought it unwise to tell her brother all that had transpired. "He was angry because we refused to give him a half interest in the aircraft," she explained. "So I simply quit and came home."

Bill sat down and stared at her a moment. He had been thinking of Thatcher Allen's warning ever since that strange individual had gone away, and Mary Eliska's "resignation" afforded him distinct relief.

"I'm glad of it, Sis," he said, earnestly. "There's no necessity for you to work now, for we have plenty of money to see us through. Besides, I need you here to assist me." "Really, Bill?"

"It's a fact. I don't like to employ outside assistance at this stage of the game; it might be fatal. But you are nearly as well posted on airplanes as I am, Mary Eliska, and you're clever enough to be of real help to me. I don't need brute strength, you know."

"Why, I'm terribly strong!" she said with a gay laugh, baring her round arm and bending her elbow to show how the muscle bunched up. "I can lift as much as you can, Bill, if it is necessary."

"It won't be necessary," replied her brother, delighted to find how easily she adopted his suggestion. "Just grab the end of that bow and hold it steady while I shave a point to it. That's it. Don't you see how awkward it is for me to handle these things alone?"

She nodded.

"You're right, Bill. I'll stay at home and help you finish the aircraft," said she.

CHAPTER 7.12
THE SPYING OF CULLEY MAY

Mr. Burthon was like many other men accustomed to modern business methods: he believed there was always an indirect way to accomplish whatever he desired. Also, like many others who have little or no use for such a contrivance, he owned a motor car. His chauffeur was a little, wizen featured man named Culley May, familiarly called "Culley" by his chums, a chauffeur who knew automobiles backward and forward and might have progressed beyond his present station had he not been recognized as so "tricky" that no one had any confidence in him.

About two weeks after Mary Eliska had left the office Mr. Burthon said to his man one morning:

"Culley May, would you like to do a little detective work?"

"Anything to oblige, sir," answered Culleyham, pricking up his ears.

"Have you ever met a fellow around town named Stricklin?"

"Bill Stricklin, sir? Oh, yes. He used to be foreman of Cunningham's repair shop. Quit there some time ago, I believe. Clever fellow, sir, this Stricklin."

"Yes; he has invented a new sort of airplane."

Culley May whistled, reflectively. All motor car people have a penchant for flying. As Thatcher Allen would have said: it "interests them."

"Stricklin is keeping the matter a secret," continued Mr. Burthon, "and I'm curious to know what he's up to. Find out, Culley May, and let me know."

"Very good, sir. Where is he working?"

"At home. He lives out Beverly way. Take a Beverly car and get off at Sandringham avenue. Walk north up the lane to the first bungalow."

"Ever been there, sir?"

"No; but Stricklin's sister has described the place to me. When you get there, try to hire out as an assistant, but in any case keep your eyes open and observe everything in sight. I'll pay you extra for this work, according to the value of the information you obtain."

"I understand, sir," answered Culley May, wrinkling his leathery face into a shrewd smile; "I know how to work a game of that sort, believe me."

In pursuance of this mission the little chauffeur came to the Stricklin residence that very afternoon. As he approached the bungalow he heard the sound of pounding upon metal coming from the canvas covered hangar; otherwise the country lay peacefully sunning itself. An automobile stood in the lane. On the front porch a woman sat knitting, but raised her head at the sound of footsteps. Culley May touched his cap, but there was no response. Looking at her closely he saw the woman was blind, so he passed her stealthily and tiptoed up the narrow path toward the hangar. The top canvas had been drawn back on wires to admit the air, but the entrance was closed by curtains. Culley May listened to the hammering a moment, and summoning his native audacity to his aid boldly parted the curtains and entered.

"Hello, Stricklin!" he called; then paused and took in the scene before him at a glance.

Bill was at the bench pounding into shape an aluminum propeller-blade; a tall man with a drooping mustache stood near, watching him. A young girl was busily sewing strips of canvas. On its rack lay a huge flying machine—its planes spread, the motors in place, the running gear complete—seemingly almost ready for action.

But Culley May was not the only one with eyes. Stricklin paused with uplifted hammer and regarded the intruder with a frown of annoyance; Mary Eliska stared in startled surprise; the tall man's spectacles glittered maliciously.

"Burthon's chauffeur!" he muttered; "I remember him." Swiftly his long arm shot out, seized Culley May's shoulder and whirled him around. The square toe of a heavy shoe caught the little man unprepared and sent him flying through the entrance, where he sprawled full length upon the ground.

In an instant he was up, snarling with rage. The curtains were closed and before them stood his assailant calmly lighting a cigarette.

"Thatcher Allen, sir," gasped Culley May, "you shall smart for this! It's actionable, sir. It's—it's—assault 'n' battery; that's what it is!"

"Want any more?" asked the man coolly.

"Not today, thank you. This'll cost you plenty."

"Then go back to Burthon and tell him we know his game. You're trespassing, sir. I could wring your neck—perhaps I will—and the law would uphold me. If you want to escape alive, make tracks."

Culley May took the hint. He walked away with as much dignity as he could muster, considering his anatomy had so recently been jarred; but he did not take the car home. Oh, no. There was much more to discover inside that hangar. He would wait until night, and then take his time to explore the place fully.

With this end in view the chauffeur secreted himself in the outskirts of the orange grove, creeping underneath a tree with thick branches that nearly touched the ground. He could pick ripe fruit from where he lay, and was well content to rest himself until night came.

An hour later Thatcher Allen whirled by in his motor car, headed for the city. Culley May shook his fist at his enemy and swore effectively to relieve his feelings. Then he sank into a doze.

The approaching chug of an engine aroused him. He found it was nearly dark, so he must have slept for some hours. Here was Thatcher Allen, back with his car and speeding up the lane so swiftly that Culley May could only see a cage-like affair occupying the rear section of the automobile.

The chauffeur wondered what this could be, puzzling his brain for a solution of the problem. Even while considering the matter Thatcher Allen passed him again, smoking his eternal cigarette and running the car more deliberately, now, toward the city.

"All right," mumbled the chauffeur; "he's out of the way for the night, anyhow. But he left the cage somewhere. What the blazes could he have had in it?"

He ate a few more oranges for his supper, smoked his pipe, snoozed again and awoke to find it was nearly midnight.

"Good!" said he; "now's my time. I don't mind a bit of a wait if I get the goods in the end; and here's where I get 'em. It takes a pretty good man to outwit Culley May. They'll agree to that, by'm'by."

He crept down the lane and kept on the south side of the hedge until he came opposite the hangar, thus avoiding the house and grounds. The canvas top of the shed showed white in the moonlight, not twenty feet from where he stood, and the chauffeur was pressing aside the thick hedge to find an opening when a deep bay, followed by a growl, smote his ears. He paused, his head thrust half through the foliage, his blood chilled with terror as there bounded from the hangar a huge bloodhound, its eyes glaring red in the dim light, its teeth bared menacingly.

Culley May thought he was "done for," as he afterward told Mr. Burthon, when with a jerk the great beast stopped—a yard from the hedge—and the clank of a chain showed it could come no farther.

Culley May caught his breath, broke from the hedge and sprinted down the lane at his best gait, followed by a succession of angry bays from the hound.

"Confound Thatcher Allen!" he muttered. "The brute was in that cage, and he went to town to get it, so's to keep me out of the hangar. That's two I owe this guy, an' I'll get even with him in time, sure's fate."

There was no car at this hour, so the discomfited chauffeur had to trudge seven miles to the city, where he arrived at early dawn.

The man was not in an amiable frame of mind when he brought Mr. Burthon's automobile to the club, where his master lived, at nine o'clock. As he drove the broker to the office he related his news.

"Thatcher Allen!" cried Mr. Burthon. "Are you sure it was Thatcher Allen?"

"Yes, sir; I remember him well. Took him to your office and the bank, you know, the time you had some deal with him; and he tried to tell me how to run the car. Me! I spotted him right away for a fresh guy from the East, an' now he's kicked me out of Stricklin's hangar an' set a dog on me. Oh, yes; I know Thatcher Allen."

"So do I," said Burthon, grimly.

Culley May caught the tone.

"I'll do him yet, sir. Leave it to me. I couldn't get much of a pointer on Stricklin's airplane; hadn't time, you know; but it looked like a rosebud an' I guess he's got something good. I'm going to find out. I'll take out a dose for the dog that'll put him to sleep in a wink, and then I'll go all over the thing careful."

"Never mind the airship," said Mr. Burthon. "I've found out what I wanted to know."

"What! you have, sir?" exclaimed the chauffeur, amazed.

"Yes," was the quiet reply. "That is, if you're positive the man at the Stricklins was Thatcher Allen."

"Sure? Why, I'd stake my life on it, sir."

"Then I'll follow the clue in my own way," said Mr. Burthon, alighting from the car.

The discovery made by Culley May necessitated a change in the proposed campaign. The broker entered his office, sat down at his desk and fell into one of his fits of deep abstraction. The new "secretary," noting this, chewed her gum reflectively a moment and then began to read a novel, keeping the volume concealed behind her desk.

"If Thatcher Allen was in the hangar," Mr. Burthon mused, "he has undertaken to back Stricklin's airplane, and I'm too late to get hold of the machine in the way I planned. I suppose the fool offered better terms than I did, to blind those simple children, and so the Stricklins turned me down. Never mind. Thatcher Allen has beaten me on two deals, but the third trick shall be mine. I must get hold of the designs of Stricklin's airplane in some way; perhaps I may find them at the patent office. Then I'll regulate things so the boy's invention will prove a failure. The result ought to satisfy me: it would cause Thatcher Allen serious loss, ruin young Stricklin, and—bring Mary Eliska to me for assistance. But Culley May can't manage the job; I must have a man more clever than he is, and direct the intrigue in person."

The secretary read and chewed most of the day. When she quit "work" at five o'clock, Mr. Burthon was still thinking.

CHAPTER 7.13
SYBIL IS CRITICAL

Bill was now progressing finely with the work on the Stricklin Aircraft and believed he would be able to overcome all the imperfections that had disclosed themselves during the first trial. Thatcher Allen came to the hangar nearly every day, now, and Bill and Mary Eliska began to wonder how he found time to attend to other business—provided he had any. On the day of Culley May's visit he had announced it was his last trip to see the Stricklins, as he had been summoned to Chicago to attend a directors' meeting and from there would go on to New York. But having discovered that Burthon was intent upon some secret intrigue, which could bode no good to his protégés—the Stricklins—he promptly changed his mind and informed Bill on a subsequent visit that he had arranged affairs at home and was now free to spend the entire winter in Southern California.

"My daughter likes it here," he added, "and kicks up fewer rows than she does at home; so that's a strong point in favor of this location. Aviation interests me. I've joined the Aëro Club out here and subscribed for the big meet to be held in January, at Dominguez Field. That's when we are to show the world the Stricklin invention, my lad, and I think it will be an eye opener to most of the crowd present."

"How does your mine, the Queen of Hearts, get along?" asked Mary Eliska.

"It continues to pay big—even better than I had hoped. Burthon must be pretty sore over that deal by this time. Speaking of my sainted brother-in-law, I've just made a discovery. He owns the mortgage on your place."

"Why, we got the money from the Security Bank!" exclaimed Mary Eliska.

"I know. I went there. Thought I'd take up the mortgage myself, but found Burthon had bought it. Now, the question is, why?"

Neither brother nor sister could imagine; but Thatcher Allen knew.

"He hopes you won't be able to meet it, and then he'll foreclose and turn you out," he said. "But you're not the principal game he's after; he's shooting me over your heads. Burthon is miffed because I let you have the money, but believes I haven't any financial or personal interest in you beyond that. If he can prevent your aircraft from flying he'll make me lose my money and also ruin you two youngsters. That's doubtless his game. That's why he sent his man here to spy upon you."

"But that is absurd! Burthon can't prevent our success," declared Bill. "Even if some minor parts go wrong, the aircraft will fly as strongly and as well as anything now in existence."

"Don't be too sure," cautioned Thatcher Allen. "You and your machine may be all right, but that's no reason why Burthon can't push failure at you, or even prevent you from flying. We must watch him."

"I do not believe the man hates us," observed Mary Eliska, thoughtfully. "Mr. Burthon is a little queer and—and unscrupulous, at times; but I don't consider him a bad man, by any means."

"I know him better than you do, and he hates me desperately," replied Thatcher Allen.

"He says that—that you abused his sister," doubtfully remarked the girl.

"Well, I did," said Thatcher Allen, calmly. "I pounded her two or three times. Once I choked her until it's a wonder she ever revived."

"Oh, how dreadful!" exclaimed Mary Eliska, shrinking back.

"Isn't it?" he agreed, lighting a cigarette. "Only a brute would lift his hand against a woman. But Burthon's sister—my wife—had a fiendish temper, and her tantrums aroused all the evil in my nature—there's plenty there, I assure you. It was the time I choked her that Burthon had me arrested for cruelty. She had put poison in my coffee and I took the fluid into court with me. Burthon said I was lying and I asked him to drink the coffee to establish his sister's innocence. But he wouldn't. Pity, wasn't it? The judge begged my pardon and said I ought to have choked her a moment longer. But no; I'm glad I didn't, for she died naturally in the end. My dear daughter, whom I sincerely love, is like her lamented mother, except that I can trust her not to poison me."

"Doesn't she love you in return?" asked Mary Eliska.

"Sybil? Why, she's tremendously fond of me. My daughter," and his voice grew suddenly tender, "has been for years—is now—the only person I live for. We're chums, we two. The poor child can't help her inherited tendencies, you know, and I rather enjoy the fact that she keeps me guessing what she's going to do next. It—er—interests me, so to speak. I like Sybil."

Sybil interested Mary Eliska, too. Her father's reports of her were so startlingly condemnatory, and his affection for her so evident, that Mary Eliska's curiosity was aroused concerning her. Thatcher Allen, in spite of his peculiarities and deprecating remarks concerning himself had won the friendship of both Bill and Mary Eliska by this time; for whatever he might be to others he had certainly proved himself a friend in need to them. It was evident he liked the Stricklins and sought their companionship, for the aircraft could scarcely account for his constant attendance at the hangar.

"I would like to meet your daughter," said the girl, thoughtfully.

"Would you, really?" he asked, eagerly. "Well, I'm sure it wouldn't hurt Sybil to know you. I'll bring her out here tomorrow, if she'll come. Never can tell what she will do or won't do, you know. Interesting, isn't it?"

"Quite so," she concurred, laughing at his whimsical tone.

Because of this conversation the Stricklins awaited Thatcher Allen's arrival next day with keen curiosity. Bill advanced the opinion that the girl wouldn't come, but Mary Eliska thought she would. And she did. When the motor car stopped in front of the bungalow there was a girl in the back seat and Mary Eliska ran down the path to welcome her.

A pale, composed face looked out from beneath a big black hat with immense black plumes. A black lace waist with black silk bolero and skirt furnished a somber costume scarcely suited to so young a girl, for Sybil Allen could not have been much older than Mary Eliska, if any. Her father was right when he claimed that Sybil was not beautiful. She had high, prominent cheek bones, a square chin and a nose with a decided uplift to the point. But her brown hair was profuse and exquisitely silky; her dark eyes large, well opened and far seeing; her slight form carried with unconscious grace.

Mary Eliska's critical glance took in these points at once, and intuitively she decided that Sybil Allen was not unattractive and ought to win friends. That she had a strong personality was evident; also the girl whom her father had affectionately called a "demon" was quiet, reserved and undemonstrative—at least during this first interview.

She acknowledged the introduction to Mary Eliska with a rather haughty bow, alighting from the car without noticing Mary Eliska's outstretched hand.

"Which way is the airplane, Daddy?" she asked, speaking not flippantly, but in low, quiet tones.

"I'll lead the way; you girls may follow," he said.

As they went up the path Mary Eliska, anxious to be sociable and to put the stranger at her ease, said brightly:

"Don't you think the ride out here is beautiful?"

"Yes," responded Sybil.

"The orange groves are so attractive, just now," continued Mary Eliska.

There was no response.

"I hope you enjoyed it, so you will be tempted to come again," resumed the little hostess.

Miss Thatcher Allen said nothing. Her father, a step in advance, remarked over his shoulder: "My daughter seldom wastes words. If you wish her to speak you must address to her a direct question; then she will answer it or not, as she pleases. It's her way, and you'll have to overlook it."

Mary Eliska flushed and glanced sidewise to get a peep at Sybil's face, that she might note how the girl received this personal criticism. But the features were as unemotional as wax and the dark, mysterious eyes were directed toward the hangar, the roof of which now showed plainly. It was hard to continue a conversation under such adverse conditions and Mary Eliska did not try. In silence they traversed the short distance to the shed, where Bill met them, a little abashed at receiving a young lady in his workshop.

But Thatcher Allen's daughter never turned her eyes upon him. She gave a graceful little nod when presented to the inventor, but ignored him to stare at the aircraft, which riveted her attention at once. "This, Sybil," said her father, enthusiastically, "is the famous airplane to be known in history as the Stricklin Aircraft. It's as far ahead of the ordinary biplane as a sewing machine is ahead of a needle and thimble. It will do things, you know. So it—er— interests me."

It seemed to interest her, also. Examining the details of construction with considerable minuteness she began asking questions that rather puzzled Thatcher Allen, who retreated in favor of Bill. The inventor explained, and as all his heart and soul were in the airplane he explained so simply and comprehensively that Sybil's dark eyes suddenly flashed upon his face, and clung there until the young fellow paused, hesitated, and broke down embarrassed.

Mary Eliska, smiling at Bill's shyness, picked up the subject and dilated upon it at length, for the girl had every detail at her tongue's end and understood the mechanism fully as well as her brother did. The visitor listened to her with interest, and when she had no more questions to ask stood in absorbed meditation before the airplane, as if in a dream, and wholly disregarded the others present.

CHAPTER 7.14
THE FLYING FEVER

Thatcher Allen said frankly to Bill and Mary Eliska: "Don't expect too much of Sybil, or you'll be disappointed. She's peculiar, and the things that interest her are often those the world cares nothing for. Anything odd or unusual is sure to strike her fancy; that's why she's so enraptured with the aircraft."

The word enraptured did not seem, to Bill, to describe Sybil's attitude at all; but Mary Eliska, watching the girl's face, decided it was especially appropriate. They left her standing before the machine and went on with their work, while Thatcher Allen ignored his daughter and smoked cigarettes while he watched, as usual, every movement of the young mechanic.

"Saw Burthon this morning," he remarked, presently.

"Did he say anything?" asked Bill.

"No. Just smiled. That shows he's up to something. Wonder what it is."

Bill shook his head.

"I don't see how that man can possibly injure me," he said, musingly. "I've gone straight ahead, in an honest fashion, and minded my own business. As for the machine, that's honest, too, and all my improvements are patented."

"They're what?"

"Patented, sir; registered in the patent office at Washington."

"Oho!"

Bill looked at him, surprised.

"Well, sir?"

"You're an irresponsible idiot, Bill Stricklin."

"Because I patented my inventions?"

"Yes, sir; for placing full descriptions and drawings of them before the public until you've startled the aviation world and are ready to advertise what you've done."

Bill stared, a perception of Thatcher Allen's meaning gradually coming to him.

"Why, as for that," he said a little uneasily, "no one ever takes the trouble to read up new patents, there are so many of them. And, after all, it's a protection."

"Is it? I can put another brace in that new elevator of yours and get a patent on it as an improvement. The brace won't help it any, but it will give me the right to use it. I'm not positive I couldn't prevent you from using yours, if I got mine publicly exhibited and on the market first."

Bill was bewildered, and Mary Eliska looked very grave. But Thatcher Allen lighted another cigarette and added:

"Nevertheless, I wouldn't worry. As you say, the patent office is a rubbish heap which few people ever care to examine. Is everything covered by patent?"

"Everything but the new automatic balance. I haven't had time to send that on."

"Then don't."

"The old one is patented, but it proved a failure and nearly killed me. The one I am now completing is entirely different."

"Good. Don't patent it until after the aviation meet. It's your strongest point. Keep that one surprise, at least, up your sleeve."

As Bill was considering this advice Sybil Allen came softly to her father's side and said:

"Daddy, I want to fly."

"To flee or to flew?" he asked, banteringly, at the same time looking at her intently.

"To fly in the air."

Thatcher Allen sighed.

"Stricklin, what will a duplicate of your aircraft cost?"

"I can't say exactly, sir," replied the boy, smiling.

"Shall we order one, Sybil?"

She stood staring straight ahead, with that impenetrable, mysterious look in her dark eyes which was so typical of the girl. Thatcher Allen threw away his cigarette and coughed.

"We'll consider that proposition some time, Bill," he continued, rather hastily. "Meantime, perhaps my daughter could make a trial flight in your machine."

"Perhaps," said Bill, doubtfully.

"Will it carry two?"

"It would support the weight of two easily," replied the young man; "but I would be obliged to rig up a second seat."

"Do so, please," requested Miss Thatcher Allen, in her even, subdued voice. "When will it be ready?"

"The aircraft will be complete in about ten days from now; but before I attempt to carry a passenger I must give it a thorough personal test," said Bill, with decision. "You may watch my flights, Miss Thatcher Allen, if you wish, and after I've proved the thing to be correct and safe I'll do what I can to favor you—if you're not afraid, and still want to make the trial."

"Thank you," she said, and turned away.

"I'll go myself, some time," observed Thatcher Allen, after a pause. "Flying interests me."

Mary Eliska was much amused. She had not known many girls of her own age, but such as she had met were all commonplace creatures compared with this strange girl, who at present seemed unable to tear herself away from the airship. Sybil did not convey the impression of being ill-bred or forward, however unconventional she might be; yet it seemed to Mary Eliska that she constantly held herself firmly repressed, yet alert and watchful, much like a tiger crouched ready to spring upon an unsuspecting prey. In spite of this uncanny attribute, Mary Eliska found herself powerfully drawn toward the peculiar girl, and resolved to make an attempt to win her confidence and friendship.

With this thought in mind she joined Sybil, who was again examining the airplane with rapt attention. While she stood at her side the girl asked, without glancing up:

"Have you ever made a flight?"

"No," replied Mary Eliska.

"Why not?"

"I haven't had an opportunity."

"Don't you like it?"

"I imagine I would enjoy a trip through the air," answered Mary Eliska; "that is, after I became accustomed to being suspended in such a thin element."

"You seem to understand your brother's invention perfectly."

"Oh, I do, in its construction and use. You see, I've been with Bill from the beginning; also I've examined several other modern airplanes and watched the flights at Dominguez Field. Naturally I'm enthusiastic over aviation, but I haven't yet considered the idea of personally attempting a flight. To manage a machine in the air requires a quick eye, a clear brain and a lot of confidence and courage."

"Is it so dangerous?" asked Miss Thatcher Allen quietly.

"Not if you have the qualities I mention and a bit of experience or training to help you in emergencies. I'm sure an airplane is as safe as a steam car, and a little safer than an automobile; but a certain amount of skill is required to manage even those."

The girl's lips curled scornfully, as if she impugned this statement; but she remained silent for a while before continuing her catechism. Then she asked:

"Do you mean to try flying?"

"Perhaps so, some day," said Mary Eliska, smiling; "when airplanes have become so common that my fears are dissipated. But, really, I haven't given the matter a thought. That is Bill's business, just now. All I'm trying to do is help him get ready."

"You believe his device to be practical?"

"It's the best I have ever seen, and I've examined all the famous airplanes."

"What has my father to do with this invention?"

Mary Eliska was surprised. "Hasn't he told you?" she asked.

"Only that it 'interests him;' but many things do that."

"We needed money to complete the aircraft, and Thatcher Allen kindly let us have it," explained the girl.

"What did he demand in return?"

"Nothing but our promise to repay him in case we succeed."

Sybil shot a swift glance toward her father.

"Look out for him," she murmured. "He's a dangerous man—in business deals."

"But this isn't business," protested Mary Eliska, earnestly; "indeed, his act was wholly irregular from a business standpoint. As a matter of fact, Thatcher Allen has been very generous and unselfish in his attitude toward us. We like your father, Miss Thatcher Allen, and—we trust him."

The girl stood silent a moment; then she slowly turned her face to Mary Eliska with a rare and lovely smile which quite redeemed its plainness. From that moment she lost her reserve, toward Mary Eliska at least, and it was evident the praise of her father had fully won her heart.

Day by day, thereafter, Sybil came with Thatcher Allen to the hangar, until the important time arrived when Bill was to test the reconstructed aircraft. By Thatcher Allen's advice the trial was made in the early morning, and in order to be present both father and daughter accepted the hospitality of the Stricklins for the previous night, Sybil sharing Mary Eliska's bed while Bill gave up his room to Thatcher Allen and stretched himself upon a bench in the hangar.

Mrs. Stricklin knew that her son was to make an attempt to fly at daybreak, but was quite undisturbed. The description of the Stricklin Aircraft, which Mary Eliska had minutely given her, seemed to inspire her with full confidence, and if she had a thought of danger she never mentioned it to anyone. The Thatcher Allens were very nice to Mrs. Stricklin, while she, in return, accepted their friendship unreservedly. Mary Eliska knew her mother to be an excellent judge of character, for while her affliction prevented her from reading a face her ear was trained to catch every inflection of a voice, and by that she judged with rare accuracy. Once she said to her daughter: "Thatcher Allen is a man with a fine nature who has in some way become embittered; perhaps through unpleasant experiences. He does not know his real self, and mistrusts it; for which reason his actions may at times be eccentric, or even erratic. But under good influences he will be found reliable and a safe friend. His daughter, on the contrary, knows her own character perfectly and abhors it. As circumstances direct she will become very bad or very good, for she has a strong, imperious nature and may only be influenced through her affections. I think it is good for her to have you for a friend." This verdict coincided well with Mary Eliska's own observations and she accepted it as veritable. Yet Sybil was a constant enigma to her and seldom could she understand the impulses that dominated her. The girl was mysterious in many ways. She saw everything and everyone without looking directly at them; she found hidden meanings in the most simple and innocent phrases; always she seemed suspecting an underlying motive in each careless action, and Mary Eliska was often uneasy at Sybil's implied suggestion that she was not sincere. The girl would be cold and silent for days together; then suddenly become animated and voluble—a mood that suited her much better than the first. Bill said to his sister: "You may always expect the unexpected of Sybil." Which proved he had also been studying this peculiar girl.

CHAPTER 7.15
A FINAL TEST

It was the morning of the tenth of December that the eager little group assembled at dawn on Marston's pasture to witness the test of the Stricklin Aircraft. Bill was so occupied with his final adjustments and anxiety lest he should overlook some important point, that he never thought of danger. He would not have remembered even his goggles had not Mary Eliska handed them to him and told him to put them on.

This was the first time Thatcher Allen had witnessed a performance of the airplane, yet he was much less excited than his daughter, who could not withdraw her gaze from the device and was nervously attentive to every move that the young aviator made. Mary Eliska, confident of the result, was most composed of all.

When all was ready Bill took his seat, started the motors, and when they had acquired full speed threw in the clutch. The airplane ran less than fifty feet on its wheels before it began to rise, when it steadily soared into the air and mounted to an elevation of several hundred feet. By this time the aviator, who had kept a straight course, was half a dozen miles from the starting point; but now he made a wide circle and, returning, passed over Marston's pasture at the same high altitude.

The speed of the aircraft was marvelous. Thatcher Allen declared it was making a mile a minute, which estimate was probably correct. After circling for a while Bill descended to a hundred feet in a straight dive, holding the device in perfect control and maintaining at all times an exact balance. At a hundred feet he tested the rudders thoroughly, proving he could alter his course at will, make sharp turns and circle in a remarkably small space. Then, having been in the air twenty-seven minutes by the watch, he descended to the ground, rolled a hundred feet on his running gear and came to a halt a few paces away from the silent, fascinated group of watchers.

Not a hitch had occurred. The Stricklin Aircraft was as perfect a creation as its inventor had planned it to be. Mary Eliska gave Bill a kiss when he alighted, but said not a word. Sybil impulsively seized the aviator's hands and pressed them until he flushed red. Thatcher Allen lighted a fresh cigarette, nodded approvingly and said: "All right, Bill. It—interests me."

"It almost seemed alive," remarked Bill, with pardonable exuberance. "Why, I believe it would fly bottom-side-up, if I asked it to!"

"Any changes necessary?" inquired Thatcher Allen.

"Only one or two, and those unimportant. The steering-wheel is too loose and needs tightening. The left guy-wires are a bit too taut and need to be relieved. Half an hour's tinkering and the aircraft will be as perfect as I know how to make it."

As they were wheeling it back to the hangar, Sybil asked:

"Weren't you frightened, Mr. Stricklin, when you were so high above the earth?"

"Oh, no; it is far safer a mile up than it is fifty or a hundred feet. There are no dangerous air currents to contend with and the machine glides more smoothly the more air it has underneath it. When I am near the earth I sometimes get a little nervous, but never when I'm far up."

"But suppose you should fall from that distance?"

"Fall? Oh, but you can't fall very easily with this sort of a biplane. At any angle it's a kind of a parachute, you know, for the hinged ends automatically spread themselves against the air pressure. And as for a tumble, you know that a fall of fifty feet would kill one as surely as a fall of several hundred feet. If a fellow can manage to stick to his airplane he's pretty safe."

"It seems such a frail thing," observed Sybil, musingly.

"Just wooden ribs and canvas," laughed Bill; "but anything stronger would be unnecessary, and therefore foolish."

"Now, then," said Thatcher Allen, when the aircraft rested once more upon its rack, "I've something to tell you, Stricklin. I've known it for several days, but refrained from speaking until you had made your trial."

There was an ominous suggestion in the words. Bill turned and looked at him questioningly.

"Any bad news, sir?"

"Time will determine if it's bad or good. Anyhow, it's news. Burthon is building an aircraft."

"An airplane?"

"I said an aircraft."

"But that word designates only my own machine."

"Burthon is building your machine."

"It—interests me."

Bill stared at him, doubtful if he heard aright. Mary Eliska stood motionless, growing white and red by turns. Sybil's lips curled in a sneer as she said:

"My clever uncle! What a resourceful man he is."

"I—I don't believe I understand," stammered Bill.

"It's simple enough," replied Thatcher Allen. "Burthon sent to Washington for copies of your plans and specifications, has built a hangar and workshop over South Pasadena way, and employed a clever mechanic from Cleveland to superintend the construction—already well under way."

"How do you know this, sir?" inquired Bill, breathless.

"The clever mechanic from Cleveland is my own man, who has been my confidential agent for years."

"And you permit him to do this work!" cried the young man, indignantly.

"To be sure. If Brewster loses the job, someone will get it who is *not* my agent. It is the only way I can keep accurate account of what Burthon is up to."

They were all silent for a time while they considered this startling information. By and by Thatcher Allen said:

"Burthon has joined the Aëro Club, has donated a handsome cup for the best endurance flight during the coming meet at Dominguez, and in some way has made himself so popular with the officials that he has been appointed a member of the committee on arrangements. I dropped in at the Club yesterday, for I'm a member, and made this discovery. My scheming brother-in-law has some dusky, deep-laid plan, and is carrying it out with particular attention to detail."

"Do you think it concerns us, sir?" asked Mary Eliska, anxiously.

"Yes. It isn't extraordinary that Burthon should take a fancy to aviation. He is full of fads and fancies, and such a thing is liable to interest him. It interests me. But the meat in the nut is the fact that he is building a copy of the Stricklin Aircraft, merely adding a few details which he will declare are improvements."

"Can't we issue an injunction and stop him?" asked Bill.

"I've seen a lawyer about that. We can't prove infringement at this stage of the game and it would be folly to attempt it. Burthon's plan is to exhibit his machine first, then keep yours off the field during the meet and afterward claim that you are infringing upon his rights. He has organized a stock company, keeping most of the stock himself, has entered his device in all the aviation tournaments throughout the country, and is issuing a circular offering the machines for sale. I have a hand proof, fresh from the printer, of this circular."

"Who will be his aviator?" asked Bill, with puckered brows.

"His former chauffeur, Mr. Culley May, is one. He is now looking for another, also."

Bill drew a long breath.

"What can we do?" he asked in a bewildered tone.

"Checkmate him," was the composed reply.

"How, sir?"

"Well, we know pretty well all Burthon's plans. He doesn't suspect we know a thing; believes he will be able to keep his secret until his airplane is ready and he can announce it in the newspapers and create a sensation. He has concocted a very pretty trick. Until this date no one has ever heard of the Stricklin Aircraft. After the Burthon Improved Biplane is exploited and its praise on every tongue, you won't be able to get even a hearing with your invention, much less a chance to fly it."

Bill sat down and covered his face with his hands. His attitude was one of despair.

"When will Mr. Burthon's machine be finished?" asked Mary Eliska, thoughtfully.

"He expects to make the first trial a week from tomorrow. He has kept a force of expert men at work, and they haven't attempted to make the Stricklin engines, but are using a type that has worked successfully in many biplanes. So his machine has grown into existence very quickly."

"A week from tomorrow," repeated Mary Eliska, softly. "And Bill is ready today."

Bill looked up quickly. Sybil laughed at him.

"You silly boy," said she. "Can't you understand what Daddy means by a checkmate?"

Bill turned to Thatcher Allen, who was lighting a fresh cigarette.

"If you will place the matter in my hands," said that gentleman, "I will proceed to put a spoke in Burthon's wheel, so to speak. Heretofore, Bill, I have been a mere onlooker, a—an interested friend, I may say. At this juncture you'd better make me your manager."

"Would you accept the position?" asked the boy.

"Yes; there isn't much else to interest me just now, and—I hate Burthon."

"Poor uncle!" sighed Sybil.

"On what terms will you undertake this, sir?" Bill inquired, with anxiety.

"Why, I may have to spend a lot of money; probably will; and my time's valuable; when I'm not here I'm moping at the Alexandria Hotel; so I propose you give me ten per cent of your profits for the first three years."

"That is absurd, sir," declared Bill. "There will be little profit at first, and ten per cent of it wouldn't amount to anything."

Thatcher Allen smiled—a grim smile that was one of his peculiarities.

"It'll do, Bill. I'll make it pay me well, see if I don't. But you may add to the demand, if you like, by promising to present my daughter the fourth complete Stricklin Aircraft your factory turns out."

"The first!" cried Bill.

"No, the fourth. We want the first three to go where they'll advertise us. Is it a bargain, Mr. Stricklin?"

Bill grasped his hand.

"Of course, sir," he replied gratefully. "I'm not sure we can defeat Mr. Burthon's conspiracy, but I know you will do all that is possible. And thank you, sir," he added, again pressing the elder man's hand.

Mary Eliska took Thatcher Allen's hand next. She did not express her gratitude in words, but the man understood her and to hide his embarrassment began to search for his cigarette case. As for Sybil, she regarded the scene with an amused smile, and there was a queer look in her dark eyes.

"Now," said Mary Eliska, "let us go in to breakfast. You must all be nearly famished."

"Yes; let us eat, so that I can get back to town," agreed Thatcher Allen, cheerfully. "The campaign begins this very morning, and it may take a few people by surprise. Remember, Bill, you're to stand ready to carry out any plans your manager makes."

"I understand, sir."

CHAPTER 7.16
THE OPENING GUN

Sybil rode with her father into town. On the way she said:

"You puzzle me. One would imagine you are playing fair with the Stricklins."

"Mere imagination," he returned, gruffly.

"Yes," she agreed; "your nature is to plot and intrigue. The deeper, the more stealthy and unsuspected the plot, the more characteristic is it of my subtle parent."

"True," he said.

"But here is a condition that puzzles me, as I have remarked. I understand how you won the confidence of the Stricklins by posing as generous and unselfish. That was quite like you. But today you had them in your power. You might have demanded anything—everything— yet you accepted a mere ten per cent. Now I'm really wondering what your game is."

It was evident he did not relish his daughter's criticism, for his usually placid brow bore a heavy frown. Still, he answered lightly:

"You're stirring too deep; you're roiling the pot. Why don't you look on the surface?"

"Oh! how stupid of me," she said in a relieved voice.

"To be a diverse scoundrel," announced her father, "is the acme of diabolic art. From complication to simplicity is but a step, yet requires audacity. Most rascals fail to realize that an honest act, by way of contrast, affords more satisfaction than persistent chicanery will produce. We must have variety in our pleasures in order to get the most from them."

"To be sure," said Sybil.

"Meantime, you are forgetting your Uncle Burthon."

They rode in silence for a time. Then the girl nestled a little closer to her father's side and murmured:

"I'm mighty glad, Daddy. I like the Stricklins."

"So do I," he responded.

"And isn't Bill's airplane marvelous?"

"I consider it," said he, "the cleverest and most important invention of the age."

By eight o'clock a skillful photographer was on his way to Bill Stricklin's hangar to get pictures of the aircraft, while Thatcher Allen sat in the office of a noted advertising expert and bargained for an amount of publicity that fairly made the man's head swim. The city editors of all the morning papers were next interviewed and interested in the Thatcher Allen campaign, so that half a dozen reporters who were noted for their brilliant descriptive writing attended a luncheon given by Thatcher Allen at the Aëro Club and listened to his glowing accounts of the Stricklin Aircraft and the wonderful flight made by its inventor that very morning.

For fear Mr. Burthon might drop into the Club during this session, the cautious "manager" of the aircraft had taken the precaution to have Brewster telephone him to come to the South Pasadena workshop, and to keep him there by some pretext 'til late in the day. This was done. Mr. Burthon spent the entire afternoon with his imitation aircraft, returning to Los Angeles for a late dinner at his club. Then, being very tired, he went early to bed.

At breakfast next morning he picked up a newspaper, started as his eye fell upon the lurid headlines, and nearly fainted with chagrin and anger.

Upon the first page was a large picture of the Stricklin Aircraft, with a vignette of its inventor in an upper corner and columns of description and enthusiastic comment regarding his creation, which was heralded as a distinct forward stride in practical aviation. Bill's remarkable flight was referred to and promise made of an exhibition soon to be held at Dominguez Field where the public would be given an opportunity to see the aircraft in action.

Mr. Burthon, as soon as he could recover himself, read every word carefully. Then he smoked his cigar and thought it over. Half an hour later he was making the rounds of the evening papers, but found he was unable to "kill" the articles prepared to exploit the Stricklin Aircraft. The morning papers having devoted so much space to the subject, the afternoon papers could not possibly ignore it, and finding he was helpless in this attempt he followed another tack.

Entering the office of the secretary of the Aëro Club he said:

"I believe our contract with the owners of Dominguez Field provides that the Aëro Club may have the use of the grounds whenever it so desires, regardless of any other engagements by outsiders."

"Certainly," replied the secretary. "I remember you yourself insisted upon that condition, as chairman of the committee on arrangements."

"Please notify the manager that we require Dominguez Field, for Club purposes, every day for the next two weeks."

"But—Mr. Burthon! Think of the expense."

"I shall personally pay all charges."

"Very well."

The secretary telephoned, and was informed that the Field had been engaged that morning for the coming Saturday by a Thatcher Allen, an Aëro Club member. But Mr. Burthon insisted on the rights of the Club, as an organization, and the manager agreed to cancel Thatcher Allen's engagement.

From there Mr. Burthon went to the managers of the Motordrome, the baseball parks and Luna, engaging every open date for two weeks to come. Then having practically tied up every available place where the Stricklin Aircraft might be publicly exhibited, he sighed contentedly and went to his South Pasadena workshop to hasten the completion of his own airplane.

Thatcher Allen was annoyed when he received notice that he could not have Dominguez Field for any day previous to the aviation meet. He was further annoyed by the discovery that Burthon had engaged every public amusement park in the vicinity of Los Angeles. But he was not the man to despair in such an emergency; the contest between him and his hated brother-in-law merely sharpened his wits and rendered him more alert.

He found a broad vacant field on the Santa Monica car line; arranged with the street railway company to carry the people there for a five-cent fare, and tied up his deals with contracts so that Burthon would be unable to interfere. Then he ordered a large grand stand to be built and instead of fencing in the grounds determined to make the exhibition absolutely free to all who cared to attend.

These arrangements completed, Thatcher Allen announced in glaring advertisements the date of the exhibition, and decided he had won the game.

Mr. Burthon tried to enjoin the exhibition, claiming that Bill Stricklin's aircraft was an infringement on his own device; but Bill personally appeared before the judge and convinced him there was nothing in the assertion. Of course Thatcher Allen saw that the newspapers had full accounts of these proceedings, and so public interest was keyed up to the highest pitch when Saturday arrived. The cars on that day were taxed to their fullest capacity to carry the crowds to Stricklin Park, as the new aviation field was called.

A large and attractive hangar had been constructed on the field, and Bill, on the morning of the exhibition, flew his airplane from Marston's pasture to Stricklin Park, alighting successfully just before the hangar. Mary Eliska, Sybil and Thatcher Allen were there to receive him, and after placing the aircraft safely in the new hangar they all motored to town for breakfast at the Alexandria.

It was no longer possible for Bill to take entire personal charge of his invention, so Thatcher Allen, having made a careful search, was finally able to secure two men, who until that time had been strangers to one another, as assistants. These men were skilled mechanics and recommended as honest and reliable—which perhaps they were under ordinary circumstances. Their names were Wilson and Reed. As they had already been two days in Bill's workshop and were now thoroughly conversant with their duties, these two men were left at the hangar in charge of the airplane, with instructions to watch it carefully and allow no one to enter or to examine it.

Bill needed rest, for he had worked night and day preparing for this important public test. The exhibition was to be held at two o'clock, so he reluctantly acceded to Thatcher Allen's request that he lie down in a quiet room at the hotel and sleep until he was called to lunch.

CHAPTER 7.17
A CURIOUS ACCIDENT

Mary Eliska had not been at all nervous over the event at Stricklin Park until the hour when she entered the field and noted the tremendous throng assembled to witness her brother's much heralded flight. The band was playing vigorously and many gay banners waved over the grand stand and the big hangar wherein the aircraft was hidden. Then, indeed, she began to realize the importance of the occasion, and her heart throbbed with pride to think that Bill was the hero all awaited and that his name would be famous from this time forth.

This was the th of December, and on January first the great International Aviation Meet was to be held at Los Angeles, with such famous aviators present as the Wright Brothers, Glenn Curtiss, Hubert Latham, Arch Hoxsey, their old friend Willard, Parmalee, Ely, Brookins, Radley and many others. Thatcher Allen had entered Bill Stricklin for this important meet and the young man was booked to take part in the endurance and speed tests and to make an attempt to break the world's record for altitude—all in his own flyer, the Stricklin Aircraft. So swift a transition from obscurity to popularity—or at least to the attention of the civilized world—was enough to turn the head of anyone; but as yet Bill seemed all unaware of his own importance.

Disregarding the crowds, which were eagerly seeking a glimpse of the young aviator but did not know him, he quietly made his way to the hangar and was admitted by Wilson, who guarded the doorway from an insistent group demanding a peep at the airplane.

Bill took off his coat, made a thorough inspection of all the working parts, and then put on his close-fitting cap and goggles, buttoned a sweater over his chest and nodded to his men to throw back the entrance curtains.

Two policemen cleared the way and as the aviator drew back his lever the aircraft rolled out of the hangar into full view of the multitude. A shout went up; handkerchiefs were waved and the band played frantically. On its big wheels, which were almost large enough for a motor car, the airplane sped across the field, turned, passed the grand stand, and with accelerating speed dashed away to the farther end of the field.

A murmur arose, in which surprise and disappointment were intermingled. One fat gentleman, who had been patiently waiting for two hours, exclaimed: "Why, it's only a sort of automobile, with crossed airplanes set over it! I thought they claimed the thing could fly." Those who knew something of aviation, however, were the ones astonished at Bill's preliminary performance. They realized the advantage of being able to drive an airplane on its own wheels, as an automobile goes, in case of emergencies, and moreover the "crossed planes"—a distinct innovation in construction—gave them considerable food for thought. Usually the two surfaces, or floats, of a biplane are exactly parallel, one above the other; but in Bill's machine the upper plane ran fore and aft, while the lower one extended sidewise. At a glance it was possible to see the advantage of this arrangement as a duplex balance, which, with the swinging wing-ends, comprised the safety device that the inventor believed made his airplane superior to any other.

From the far end of the field Bill swung around and started back, straight for the grand stand. He had nearly reached it when he threw in the clutch that started the propellers and at the same time slightly elevated the front rudder. Up, like a bird taking wing, rose the aircraft, soaring above the grand stand and then describing a series of circles over the field. Gradually it ascended, as if the aviator was ascending an aërial spiral staircase, until he had mounted so far among the clouds that only a grayish speck was discernible.

The spectators held their breaths in anxious suspense. The speck grew larger. Swooping down at a sharp angle the aircraft came suddenly into view and within a hundred feet of the ground resumed its normal position and began to circle around the field again.

Now a mighty cheer went up, and Mary Eliska, who had been pressing Sybil's hand with a grip that made her wince, found herself sobbing with joy. Her brother's former flights had been almost as successful as this; but only now, with the plaudits of a multitude ringing in her ears, did she realize the wonderful thing he had accomplished.

But on a sudden the shout was stilled. A startled, frightened moan ran through the assemblage. Women screamed, men paled and more than one onlooker turned sick and faint.

For the Stricklin Aircraft, while gracefully gliding along, in full view of all, was seen to suddenly collapse and crumple like a pricked toy balloon. Airplane and aviator fell together in a shapeless mass toward the earth, and the sight was enough to dismay the stoutest heart.

But Bill's salvation lay in his altitude at the time of the accident. Fifty feet from the earth the automatic planes asserted their surfaces against the air and arrested, to an appreciable extent, the plunge. Had it been a hundred feet instead of fifty the young man might have escaped without injury, but the damaged machine had acquired so great a momentum that it landed with a shock that unseated young Stricklin and threw him underneath the weight of the motor and gasoline tank.

A dozen ready hands promptly released him from the wreck, but when they tried to lift him to his feet he could not stand. His leg was broken.

CHAPTER 7.18
THE ONE TO BLAME

Thatcher Allen locked the doors of the hangar and refused to admit anyone but his own daughter. Even Reed and Wilson, having assisted to drag the wreck to its shed, were ordered peremptorily to keep out. Wilson obeyed without protest, but Reed was angry and said it was his duty to put the aircraft into shape again. Thatcher Allen listened to him quietly; listened to his declaration that he had had nothing to do with the construction of the airplane and therefore could in no way be held responsible for the accident; and after the man had had his say his employer asked him to come to his hotel in the evening to consider what should be done. He also made an appointment with Wilson. Then he shut himself up in the hangar with Sybil.

Mary Eliska had gone with Bill in the ambulance to the hospital, where she remained by his side until the leg was set and the young man felt fairly comfortable. The injury was not very painful, but Bill was in great mental distress because his accident would prevent his taking part in the aviation meet. All their carefully made plans for the successful promotion of the Stricklin Aircraft were rendered futile by this sudden reverse of fortune, and the youthful inventor constantly bewailed the fact that Burthon would now have a clear field and his own career be ignominiously ended.

Mary Eliska had little to say in reply, for her own heart was aching and she saw no way to comfort her brother. When he was settled in his little white room, with a skillful nurse in attendance, the girl went home to break the sad news to their blind mother.

Meantime Thatcher Allen was busy at the hangar. In spite of his usual nonchalance and obtuse manner—both carefully assumed—the man had a thorough understanding of mechanics and by this time knew every detail of young Stricklin's airplane quite intimately. Also, he was a shrewd and logical reasoner, and well knew the accident had been due to some cause other than faulty parts or inherent weakness of the aircraft. So he took off his coat, rolled up his shirt sleeves and began a careful examination of the wreck.

It was Sybil, however, who stood staring at the airplane, always fascinating to her, who first discovered the cause of Bill's catastrophe.

"See here, Daddy," she exclaimed; "this guy-wire has been cut half through, in some way, and others are broken entirely."

Thatcher Allen came to her side and inspected the guy-wire. The girl was right. It was certainly odd that several strands of the slender but strong woven-wire cable had parted. Her father took a small magnifying glass from his pocket and examined the cut with care.

"It has been filed," he announced.

Sybil nodded, but she seemed absent-minded and to have lost interest in the discovery.

"From the first I suspected the guy-wires," she said. "When the aircraft collapsed I knew the wires had parted, and then—I thought of my clever uncle."

Thatcher Allen rolled down his sleeves and put on his coat.

"Three of the wires gave way," he observed, "and it's a wonder young Stricklin wasn't killed. Come, 'Bil; we'll go back to the hotel."

They found the field deserted, their motor car being the last on the grounds. During the ride into town Sybil remarked:

"This affair will cause you serious loss, Daddy."

"Why?"

"Bill can't exhibit his device at the meet, and Uncle Burthon will be on hand to win all the laurels."

"Don't worry over that," he said grimly. "We've ten days in which to outwit Burthon, and if I can't manage to do it in that time I deserve to lose my money."

Wilson came to the hotel promptly at eight o'clock for his interview with Thatcher Allen. Said that gentleman:

"Tell me all that happened at the hangar after we left you and Reed there this morning."

The man seemed reluctant at first, but finally decided to tell the truth. He appeared to be an honest young fellow, but knew quite well that his testimony would injure his fellow assistant.

"It was quite early, sir, when an automobile came into the field and a gentleman asked to see the aircraft. Mr. Reed was at the door, at the time, and I heard him reply that no one could be admitted. Then the gentleman said something to him in a low voice and Reed, after a little hesitation, turned to me and told me to guard the door. I did so, and the two walked away together. I saw them in close conversation for quite a while, and then Reed came back to the hangar and said: 'The gentleman is having trouble with his motor car, Wilson, and one of his engines is working badly. You understand such things; go and see if you can help him, while I guard the door.'

"I thought that was queer, sir, for Reed is as good a mechanic as I am; but I took a wrench and walked over to the automobile, which was not a hundred yards distant. A little dried-up chauffeur was in the driver's seat. The gentleman asked me to test the engines, which I did, and found there was nothing wrong with them at all. I hadn't been a bit suspicious until then, but this set me thinking and I hurried back to the hangar. I hadn't been away ten minutes, and I found Reed standing in the doorway quietly smoking his pipe. Everything about the aircraft seemed all right, so I said nothing to Reed except that his friend was a ringer and up to some trick. He answered that the man was no friend of his; that he had never seen him before and was not likely to see him again. That is all, sir. I didn't leave the hangar again until Mr. Stricklin returned and took charge of it."

Thatcher Allen had listened intently.

"Do you know the name of the man with the automobile?" he asked.

"No, sir."

"Describe him, please."

Wilson described Burthon with fair accuracy.

"Thank you. You may go now, but I want you on hand tomorrow morning to assist in getting the machine back to Stricklin's old hangar."

"Very well, sir."

Reed came a half hour after Wilson had left. His attitude was swaggering and defiant. Thatcher Allen said to him:

"Reed, your action in filing the guy-wires is a crime that will be classed as attempted manslaughter. You are liable to imprisonment for life."

The man grew pale, but recovering himself replied:

"I didn't file the wires. You can't prove it."

"I'm going to try, anyway," declared Thatcher Allen. "That is, unless you confess the truth, in which case I'll prosecute Burthon instead of you."

Reed stared at him but, stubbornly made no reply.

"How much did he pay you for the work?" continued Thatcher Allen.

No answer.

Thatcher Allen touched a bell and a detective entered.

"Officer, I accuse this man of an attempt to murder Bill Stricklin," said he. "You overheard the recent interview in this room and understand the case perfectly and the evidence on which I base my charge. You will arrest Mr. Reed, if you please."

The officer took the man in charge. Reed was nervous and evidently terrified, but maintained a stubborn silence.

"Confession may save you," suggested Thatcher Allen; but Reed was pursuing some plan previously determined on, and would not speak. So the officer led him away.

Next morning the wrecked airplane was transferred to the workshop in the Stricklin garden, where Wilson, under the supervision of Mary Eliska and Thatcher Allen, began taking it apart that they might estimate the damage it had sustained. Mary Eliska's face bore a serious but determined expression and she directed the work as intelligently as Bill could have done. Thatcher Allen, who had brought a pair of overalls, worked beside Wilson and in a few hours they were able to tell exactly what repairs were necessary.

"The motors are not much injured," announced Mary Eliska, "and that is indeed fortunate. We need one new propeller blade, five bows and struts for the lower plane, new wing ends and guy-wires and almost a completely new running gear. It isn't so very bad, sir. With the extra parts we have on hand I believe the aircraft can be put in perfect condition before the meet."

"Good!" exclaimed Thatcher Allen. "Then our greatest need is to secure a competent aviator."

"To operate Bill's machine?"

"Of course. He's out of commission, poor lad; but the machine must fly, nevertheless."

Mary Eliska's blue eyes regarded him gravely. She had been considering this proposition ever since the accident.

"Our first task," said she, "is to get my brother's invention thoroughly repaired."

"But the question of the aviator is fully as important," persisted her friend. "Wilson," turning to the mechanic, "do you think you could operate the aircraft?"

"Me, sir?" replied the man, with a startled look; "I—I'm afraid not. I understand it, of course; but I've had no experience."

"No one but Bill Stricklin can claim to have had experience with this device," said Thatcher Allen; "so someone must operate it who is, as yet, wholly inexperienced."

"Can't you find an aviator who has used other machines, sir?" asked Wilson. "The city is full of them just now."

"I'll try," was the answer.

Thatcher Allen did try. After engaging another mechanic to assist Wilson he interviewed every aviator he could find in Los Angeles. But all with the slightest experience in aërial navigation were engaged by the various airplane manufacturers to operate their devices, or had foreign machines of their own which were entered for competition. He was referred to several ambitious and fearless men who would willingly undertake to fly the Stricklin invention, but he feared to trust them with so important a duty.

Returning one day in a rather discouraged mood to Mary Eliska, who was busy directing her men, he said:

"I have always, until now, been able to find a man for any purpose I required; but the art of flying is in its infancy and the few bold spirits who have entered the game are all tied up and unavailable. It looks very much as if we were going to have a winning airplane with no one to develop its possibilities."

Mary Eliska was tightening a turnbuckle. She looked up and said with a smile:

"The aviator is already provided, sir."

"What! You have found him?" exclaimed Thatcher Allen.

"I ought to have said 'aviatress,' I suppose," laughed the girl.

"My daughter? Nonsense."

"Oh, Sybil would undertake it, if I'd let her," replied Mary Eliska. "But I dare not trust anyone but—myself. There is too much at stake."

"You!"

"Just Mary Eliska Stricklin. I've been to the hospital this morning and talked with Bill, and he quite approves my idea."

Thatcher Allen looked at the slight, delicate form with an expression of wonder. The girl seemed so dainty, so beautiful, so very feminine and youthful, that her suggestion to risk her life in an airship was positively absurd.

"You've a fine nerve, my child," he remarked, with a sigh, "and I've no doubt you would undertake the thing if I'd give my consent. But of course I can't do that."

"Why not?"

"You're not fit."

"In what way?"

"Why, er—strength, and—and experience. Girls don't fly, my dear; they simply encourage the men to risk their necks."

"Boo! there's no danger," asserted Mary Eliska, scornfully. "One is as safe in the Stricklin Aircraft as in a trundle-bed."

"Yet Bill—"

"Oh, one may be murdered in bed, you know, as well as in an airplane. Had those guy-wires not been tampered with an accident to my brother would have been impossible. Have you stopped to consider, sir, that even when the planes separated and crumpled under the air pressure Bill's device asserted its ability to float, and dropped gently to the ground? Bill managed to get hurt because he fell under the weight of the motors; that was all. Really, sir, I can't imagine anything safer than the aircraft. And as for brawn and muscle, you know very well that little strength is required in an aviator. Skill is called for; a clear head and a quick eye; and these qualities I possess."

"H-m. You think you can manage the thing?"

"I know it—absolutely. I've talked over with Bill every detail from the very beginning, and have personally tested all the working parts time and again, except in actual flight."

"And you're not afraid?"

"Not in the least."

"You won't faint when you find yourself among the clouds?"

"Not a faint, sir. It isn't in me."

Thatcher Allen fell silent and solemn. He began to seriously consider the proposition.

CHAPTER 7.19

PLANNING THE CAMPAIGN

That evening the secretary of the Aëro Club telephoned Thatcher Allen to ask if he wished to withdraw his entry from contest in the coming aviation meet.

"By no means," was the reply.

"But you state that Bill Stricklin is to be the aviator, and we are informed that Bill Stricklin has a broken leg."

"Leave the entry as it stands: 'Stricklin, Aviator,'" said Thatcher Allen, positively.

"Very well, sir," returned the secretary, evidently puzzled.

But his friend Burthon, who had suggested his telephoning, was highly pleased when he learned Thatcher Allen's decision.

"All right," he observed, with satisfaction; "we'll leave the Stricklin Aircraft on the program, for everyone is talking of the wonderful device and the announcement of its competition will be the greatest drawing card we have. But the entry of 'Stricklin, Aviator' will disqualify anyone but Stricklin from operating the aircraft, and I happen to know his leg is in a plaster cast and he cannot use it for months to come."

"Won't it hurt us to disqualify the Stricklin Aircraft and have it withdrawn at the last moment?" inquired the secretary, doubtfully.

"No; for I'm going to spring on the crowd the biggest surprise of the century—Burthon's Biplane."

"Are you sure of its success, sir?"

"Absolutely. Bill Stricklin copied his machine from mine, as I have before explained to you, and in addition to all the good points he has exhibited I have the advantage of a perfect automatic balance. If Stricklin's device had been equipped with it he wouldn't have fallen the other day."

Perhaps Mr. Burthon was sincere in saying this. He had had no opportunity to examine Bill's latest creation at close quarters, but on the day of the trial at Stricklin Park he had observed the fact that Bill had abandoned the automatic balance he had first patented, and now had recourse to crossed planes. Both Burthon and his mechanics considered the original device the best and most practical, and they depended upon it for the biggest advertisement of Burthon's Improved Biplane, having of course no hint that Bill had tested it and found it sadly lacking.

Once the Burthon flyer was ready for trial, and Culley May, after several attempts, got it into the air and made a short flight that filled the heart of Mr. Burthon with elation.

"Curtiss and the Wrights will do better than that, though," observed the ex-chauffeur, "to say nothing of those daredevils Latham and Hoxsey. I'll improve after a few more trials, but I can't promise ever to do better than the other fellows do."

"That isn't to be expected," returned Burthon. "I'm not backing you to excel the performances of the old aviators; that isn't my point. The improvements and novelties we have to show will take the wind out of the sails of all other airplanes and result in a flood of orders. Comparing machine for machine, we're years in advance of the Wrights and Curtiss— and centuries ahead of those foreign devices."

"Perhaps," admitted Culley May. "But Stricklin's airplane is practically the same as your own, and it is still on the programme."

"It won't fly, though," declared Burthon, with a laugh. "Don't worry about anything but your own work, Culley May. Leave all the rest to me."

The man knew his employer was playing a hazardous game and that he had stolen outright the Stricklin Aircraft, and while the knowledge did not add to Culley May's nerve or assurance he was gleeful over the prospect of "doing" his enemy, Thatcher Allen. The little fellow was bold enough—even to the point of bravery—and fully as unprincipled as his employer. His hatred of Thatcher Allen was so acrid that he would have gone to any length, even without pay, to defeat his plans, and Burthon found him an eager and willing tool. Nevertheless, the little man scented danger ahead of them and had an idea that trouble was brewing from some unknown source.

By this time Burthon had begun a campaign of widespread publicity, and in spite of the long list of famous aviators in the city the newspapers were filled with pictures of the Burthon device and accounts of the marvelous flights of Culley May. Nothing more was heard of the Stricklin Aircraft, but the public had not forgotten it and many were puzzled that two local airplane makers should be exhibiting identically the same improvements, each claiming to have originated them. As for the visiting aviators, they were interested, but held their peace. The performances at the coming competition would tell the story of supremacy, and whatever good points were displayed by the local inventors could doubtless be adapted to their own craft. They waited, therefore, for proof of the glowing claims made in the newspapers. Many promising inventions have turned out to be failures.

The public was, to an extent, in the same doubting mood. Stricklin's magnificent public flight had ended with an accident, while Culley May's preliminary exhibitions were in no way remarkable as compared with records already established. The meet would tell the story.

Meantime Mary Eliska completed her repairs. On the day that Bill came home from the hospital in an ambulance she wheeled him in an invalid chair to the hangar and allowed the boy to inspect a perfect aircraft. The young man suffered no pain, and although he was physically helpless his eye and brain were as keen as ever. Being wheeled around the device, so that he could observe it from all sides and at all angles, he made a thorough examination of his sister's work and declared it excellent.

"Think you can manage it, Sis?" he asked, referring to her proposed venture.

"I am sure I can," she promptly replied. "You must understand—all of you," turning to confront Thatcher Allen and Sybil, who were present, "that I am not undertaking this flight from choice. Had Bill been able to exhibit his own airplane I might never have tried to fly alone; but it seems to me that our fortune, my brother's future career, and our friend Thatcher Allen's investment, all hinge upon our making a good showing at Dominguez Field. No one but me is competent to properly exhibit the aircraft, to show all its good points and prove what it is capable of doing. Therefore I have undertaken to save our reputation and our money, and I am sure that my decision is proper and right."

"I agree with you," said Bill, eagerly. "You're a brave little girl, Sis."

"I have but one request to make, Thatcher Allen," she added.

"What is it, Mary Eliska?" he inquired.

"Do not advertise me as 'The Girl Aviatrix,' or by any other such name. I prefer people should remain ignorant of the fact that a girl is operating the Stricklin Aircraft. Can't you keep quiet about it?"

"I can, and will," he asserted. "Indeed, my dear, I much prefer that course. It will be all the more interesting when—when—the discovery is made."

"I do not wish to become a celebrity," she said, seriously. "One in the family is enough," glancing proudly at Bill, "and I'm afraid nice people would think me unmaidenly and bold to become a public aviatrix. I'm not at all freakish—indeed, I'm not!—and only stern necessity induces me to face this ordeal."

"My dear," said Thatcher Allen, looking at her admiringly, "your feelings shall be considered in every possible way. But you must not imagine you are the first female aviatrix. In Europe—especially in France—a score of women have made successful flights, and not one is considered unwomanly or has forfeited any claim to the world's respect and applause."

"The most successful aviatrixes of the future," remarked Bill, thoughtfully, "are bound to be women. As a rule they are lighter than men, more supple and active, quick of perception and less liable to lose their heads in emergencies. The operation of an airplanc is, it sccms to me, especially fitted to women."

"Ah!" exclaimed Sybil, with a whimsical glance at the speaker, "I have discovered my future vocation. I shall aviate parties of atmospheric tourists. When the passenger airships are introduced I'll become the original sky motoress, and so win fame and fortune."

Bill laughed, but shook his head.

"The airship of the future will not be a passenger affair," he predicted, "but an individual machine for personal use. They'll be cheaper than automobiles, and more useful, for they can go direct to their destination in a straight 'air-line.' Men will use them to go to business, women to visit town on shopping expeditions or to take an airing for pleasure; but I'm sure they will be built for but one person."

"Then I'll have one and become a free lance in the sky, roaming where I will," declared Sybil.

This unconventional girl had developed a decided fancy for the inventor, and while in his presence it was noticed that she became less reserved and mysterious than at other times. Bill liked Sybil, too, although she was so strong a contrast to his own beautiful sister. When she cared to be agreeable Miss Thatcher Allen proved interesting and was, Bill thought, "good company." Mary Eliska observed that Sybil invariably presented the best side of her character to Bill. While he was in the hospital the girl visited him daily, and now that he had come home again she passed most of her time at the hangar.

Thatcher Allen was greatly annoyed to learn that the Stricklin headquarters at Dominguez Field had been given a location in the rear of all the others, where it would be practically unnoticed. Of course this slight was attributed to Burthon's influence with the committee of arrangements, of which he was a member. Burthon's own hangar, on the contrary, had a very prominent position. From his man Brewster, as well as from others, Thatcher Allen also learned that Burthon had hinted he would prevent the Stricklin Aircraft from taking any part in the contests.

All these things worried the Stricklin party, whose anxieties would have been sufficient had they not been forced to encounter the petty malice of Burthon. Sybil, silently listening to all that was said, assumed a more mysterious air than usual, and on the day previous to the opening of the great aviation meet she informed her father that she would not accompany him to Dominguez, where he was bound to attend to all final preparations. The decision surprised him, but being accustomed to his daughter's sudden whims he made no reply and left her in their rooms at the hotel.

CHAPTER 7.20
UNCLE AND NIECE

When her father had gone Sybil addressed a note to Mr. Burthon which read:

"I will call upon you, at your club, for a private interview at twelve o'clock precisely. As all your future depends upon this meeting you will not fail to keep the appointment."

She signed this message with the initials "S. C." and Mr. Burthon, receiving it as he was about to start for Dominguez in his motor car, for the messenger had had a lively chase over town to catch him, read and reread the epistle carefully, was thoughtful a moment, and then ordered his man to drive him to the club.

"'S. C.,'" he mused; "who on earth can it be? A woman's handwriting, of course, crude and unformed. When women intrigue there is usually a reason for it. Better find out what's in the wind, even at the loss of a little valuable time. That's the safest plan."

He reached his club at exactly twelve o'clock and heard a woman inquiring for him of the doorkeeper. He met her, bowed, and without a word led her to his own private sitting room, on the third floor. The woman—or was it a girl?—was, he observed, heavily veiled, but as soon as they were alone she removed the veil and looked at him steadfastly from a pair of dark, luminous eyes.

Mr. Burthon shifted uneasily in his chair. He had never seen the girl before, yet there was something singularly familiar in her features.

"Be good enough to tell me who you are," he said in the gentle tone he invariably employed toward women. "I have granted this interview at your request, but I am very busy today and have little time to spare you."

"I am your niece," she replied, slowly and deliberately.

"Oh!" he exclaimed; then paused to observe her curiously. "So, you are my sister Marian's daughter."

"Exactly."

"I knew she had a child, for often she wrote me about it; but her early death and my estrangement with your father prevented me from seeing you, until now. Your mother, my dear, was a—a noble woman."

"You are not telling the truth," said Sybil, quietly. "She was quite the contrary."

He started and flushed. Then he replied, somewhat confused by the girl's scornful regard:

"At least, I loved her. She was my only sister."

"And your accomplice."

"Eh?" He stared, aghast. Then, quickly recovering himself, he remarked:

"You were rather too young, when she died, to judge your mother's character correctly."

"It is true; but I remember her with abhorrence."

"Your father, on the other hand," observed Mr. Burthon, his face hardening, "might well deserve your hatred and aversion. He is a scoundrel."

"I have heard him say so," replied Sybil, smiling, "but I do not believe it. In any event his iniquity could not equal that of the Burthons."

"We are complimentary," said her uncle, returning the smile with seeming amusement. "But I regret to say I have no time to further converse with you today. Will you call again, if you have anything especial to say to me?"

"No," replied Sybil. "You must listen to me today."

"Tomorrow—"

"Tomorrow," she interrupted, "you may be in prison. It is not easy to interview criminals in jail, is it?"

He looked at her now with more than curiosity; his gaze was searching, half fearful, inquiring.

"You speak foolishly," said he.

"Yet you understand me perfectly," she returned.

"I confess that I do not," he coldly persisted.

"Then I must explain," said she. "When my mother died I was but eight years of age. But I was old for my years, and on her deathbed your sister placed in my hands a sealed envelope, directing me to guard it carefully and secretly, and not to open it until I was eighteen years of age—and not then unless I had in some way incurred the enmity and persecution of my uncle, George Burthon. She said it was her *confession*."

He sat perfectly still, as if turned to stone, his eyes fixed full upon the girl's face. With an effort he said, in a soft voice:

"Have I persecuted you?"

"Indirectly; yes."

"But you cannot be eighteen yet!"

"No," she admitted; "I am only seventeen."

He breathed a sigh of relief.

"Then—"

"But I am half a Burthon," Sybil continued, "and therefore have little respect for the wishes of others—especially when they interfere with my own desires. I kept the letter my mother gave me, but had no interest in opening it until the other day."

"And you read it then?"

"Two or three times—perhaps half a dozen—with great care."

"Where is that letter now?"

"Where you cannot find it, clever as you are. I may say I have great respect for your cleverness, my dear uncle, since reading the letter. How paltry the story of Dr. Jekyl and Mr. Hyde seems after knowing you!"

He moved uneasily in his seat; but the man was on the defensive now, and eyed his accuser steadily.

"You seem much like your mother," he suggested, reflectively.

"But you are wrong; I am more like my father."

He shrugged his shoulders.

"What matter, my child? You have a rare inheritance, on either side."

They sat in silence a moment. Then he said:

"You have not yet confided to me your errand."

"True. I have a request to make which I am sure you will comply with. You must stop annoying the Stricklins."

He smiled at her.

"You have marked them for your own prey—you and your precious father?"

"Yes. Your persecution must cease, and at once."

He seemed thoughtful.

"I have an end in view," said he; "an important end."

"I know; you want to force Mary Eliska to marry you. But that is absurd. She is scarcely half your age, and—she despises you."

He flushed at this.

"Nevertheless—"

"I won't have it!" cried Sybil, sternly. "And, another thing: you must withdraw your airplane from the aviation meet tomorrow."

"Must?"

"I used the word advisedly. I have the power to compel you to obey me, and I intend to use it."

He sat watching her with his eyes slightly narrowed. Sybil was absolutely composed.

"Your mother, my dear," he presently remarked, "was a—charming woman, but inclined to be visionary and imaginative. I have no idea what she wrote in that letter, but if it is anything that asperses my character, my integrity or fairness, it is not true, and can only be accounted for by the fact that the poor creature was driven insane by your father, and did not know what she was doing."

"Oh, indeed!" the girl retorted. "Is it not true, then, that you were convicted in Baltimore, twenty years ago, of a dastardly murder and robbery, and sentenced by the court to life imprisonment? Is it not true that my mother at that time contrived your escape and secreted you so cleverly that the officers of the law could never find you?"

"It is not true," he declared, speaking with apparent effort.

"The letter states that you were arrested and convicted under the name of Harcliffe; that when active search for you was finally abandoned you went with my mother to Chicago, and there began a new life under your right name of Burthon; that there your sister met and married my father, although you opposed the match bitterly, fearing she would betray your secret to her husband. But she never did."

"It is not true," he repeated. "The whole story is but a tissue of lies."

"Then," said Sybil, "I will telegraph to the police of Baltimore that the escaped prisoner, Harcliffe, whom they have been seeking these twenty years, is here in Los Angeles, and ask them to send at once someone to identify him. You need not be afraid, for the story is false. They will come, I will point you out to them, and they will declare you are not the man. Then I will believe you—not before."

He sat a long time, his head upon his hand, looking at her reflectively. At the same time her dark eyes were fixed upon him with equal intentness.

By and by she laughed aloud, but there was no mirth in the sound.

"Not that, dear uncle," she said, as if he had spoken. "Am I not my mother's daughter, and my clever uncle's own niece? You cannot quiet me by murder, for in that case my revenge is fully provided for. I know you, and I did not venture upon this disagreeable errand unprepared. There is a plain clothes man at the street door, who, if I do not emerge from this club in—" she looked at her watch—"in fifteen minutes, will summon assistance, guard every exit, and then search your rooms for my body. The doorkeeper has my name and knows that I am here. Therefore, to injure me now would be to thrust your head into the hangman's noose. Afterward you will be very considerate of my welfare, for from this day any harm that befalls me will lead to your prompt arrest and the disclosure of your secret."

He threw out his hands with a despairing, helpless gesture.

"What a demon you are!" he cried.

"I believe I am," said Sybil, slowly. "I hate myself for being obliged to act in this dramatic fashion—to threaten and bully like a coward—but being blessed with so unscrupulous an uncle I cannot accomplish my purpose in a more dignified way."

"State your demands, then," said he.

"I have stated them."

"To withdraw my airplane from the aviation meet would mean my ruin. I have sold my real estate and brokerage business and invested my money in aviation; I positively cannot withdraw now."

"You must. To whine of ruin is absurd. I know that my father paid you a quarter of a million for your mine. You also obtained, without doubt, a good sum for your business. So far you cannot have invested more than a few thousand dollars in your attempt to steal Bill Stricklin's invention. My advice, sir, is to get away from here as soon as you can. Go to London or Paris, where there is more interest in aviation than here, and make a business of flying, if you will. But the Stricklin device is fully protected by foreign patents, and any infringement will be promptly prosecuted."

"You are merciless," he complained.

"You will find me so."

"I am a member of the Aëro Club. I cannot, without arousing suspicion, withdraw my airplane from the meet."

"If you do not I will telegraph to Baltimore."

The threat seemed to crush him and still any further remonstrances.

"Very well," he returned; "if you have finished your errand please leave me. I must—consider—my—position."

She rose, cast one scornful glance at him and walked out of the room, leaving him seated with bowed head, dejected and utterly defeated.

CHAPTER 7.21
MR. H. CHESTERTON RADLEY-TODD

There lived in Los Angeles at that time one of those unaccountable individuals whom nature, in fashioning, endows with such contradictory qualities that their fellow creatures are unable to judge them correctly.

He was a young man, fresh from college, whose name was engraved upon his cards as H. Chesterton Radley-Todd, but whom his new acquaintances promptly dubbed "Chesty Todd." Having finished his collegiate course he had been at a loss what to do next, so he drifted to the Pacific coast and presently connected himself with the Los Angeles *Tribune* as literary critic, society reporter and general penistic roustabout.

Mr. Radley-Todd had a round, baby face; expressionless and therefore innocent blue eyes that bulged a little; charmingly perfect teeth; an awkward demeanor; a stumbling, hesitating mode of speech and the intellectual acumen of a Disraeli. He was six feet and three inches tall and dressed like a dandy. People estimated him as a mollycoddle at first acquaintance; wondered presently if he possessed hidden talents, and finally gave him up as a problem not worth solving. No one believed in his ability, even when he demonstrated it; because, as they truly said, he "did not look as if he amounted to shucks."

That such a callow youth, predoomed to adverse judgment, should be able to secure a position on a daily paper seemed remarkable. But the *Tribune* loves to employ green and budding "talent," which can be had at a nominal salary. The managing editor shrewdly contends that these young fellows work with an enthusiasm and perseverance unknown to older and more experienced journalists, because they have a notion that the world is their oyster and a newspaper job the knife that opens it. When they discover their mistake they are dismissed and other ambitious ones take their places. Mr. H. Chesterton Radley-Todd was at present enjoying this fleeting prominence, and occasionally the editor would read his copy with genuine amazement and wonder from what source he had stolen its brilliance and power.

So, when the great aviation meet approached and every man, woman and child in Southern California was eager for details concerning it and demanded pages of description of the various participating airplanes and aviators, in advance of their exhibition, and when Tom Dunbar, the *Tribune's* expert on aviation, was suddenly stricken with pneumonia, "Chesty" Todd was assigned to this important department.

"Dig for every scrap of information that can possibly be unearthed," said the editor to him. "Spread it out as much as you can, for the dear public wants a cyclone of aërial gossip and will devour every word of it. When there isn't any broth don't fear to manufacture some; any 'mistake' in the preliminaries will be forgotten as soon as the big meet is in full swing."

Chesty nodded; stumbled against a chair on his way out; stepped on the toe of the private stenographer and slammed the door to muffle her scream. Then he made his way to Dominguez Field; strolled among the hangars with his hands in his pockets and imbibed unimportant information by the column.

Two things, however, really interested the reporter. One was the popular interest in the Stricklin Aircraft, which was now in its hangar and invited inspection. Wilson and Brewster, the latter now openly in the employ of Thatcher Allen, guarded the local airplane and explained its unique features to an eager throng. For, although the Stricklin hangar was in a retired location—"around the corner," in fact—a bigger crowd besieged it, on this last day preceding the official opening of the meet, than visited the older and better-known devices. Bill Stricklin's remarkable flight at Stricklin Park, which was followed by his peculiar accident, was of course responsible for much of the interest manifested in his machine; and this interest was shared by the experienced aviators present, who silently examined the novel improvements of the young inventor and forbore to discuss them or their alleged merits.

"What do you think of it?" Chesty Todd asked an aviator of national prominence.

"Looks good," was the evasive reply. "Thatcher Allen, who is managing the Stricklin campaign, has been trying hard to get a man to fly it, but so far without success. Pity the thing can't be exhibited. Young Stricklin, who was entered as the aviator, broke his leg and is now out of it."

The reporter made a mental note of this; he would find out the plans of the Stricklin party and make a two-column story of their hope or despair.

Later in the afternoon another thing puzzled him. Burthon, the direct competitor of Stricklin, suddenly and without explanation withdrew his airplane from the meet and actually took it from the field, closing his hangar. The officials and others interested were amazed, and the action aroused considerable comment.

Chesty Todd scented a story. He secured an automobile and followed Burthon and Culley May at a distance, until they placed the airplane in the old workshop at South Pasadena. He crept up to the shed unobserved and found half a dozen men busily putting the parts together again and preparing the device for use. Why, since it had been withdrawn from the aviation meet?

Todd and Burthon walked out and went to a nearby restaurant, where the reporter found them seated in a corner engaged in earnest conversation. Chesty made signs to the waiter that he was deaf and dumb, secured a seat at a table within hearing distance of Burthon and his chauffeur, and overheard enough to give him a clue to their latest conspiracy. Then he went away, regained his automobile and drove straight to the Alexandria Hotel.

Thatcher Allen had insisted on the Stricklins taking rooms at the hotel during the meet, and all three were now established there, Mrs. Stricklin having decided to go each day to Dominguez, where Bill and Sybil could tell her of the events as they occurred. In a way the blind woman would thus be able to participate and avoid the anxiety and suspense of remaining at the bungalow while her daughter undertook the hazardous feat of operating Bill's airplane. The Thatcher Allen automobile was placed at the disposal of mother and son, and the young inventor could watch the flight of his machine while propped among the cushions, Sybil being at his side to attend him and his mother.

The party had just finished dinner and assembled in the Thatcher Allen sitting room when Chesty Todd's card was brought in. It was marked "Tribune" and Thatcher Allen decided to go down to the office and see the reporter, as it was not his purpose to snub the press at this critical juncture. However, the young man discouraged him at first sight. His appearance was, as usual, against him.

"Will the Stricklin Aircraft take part in the contests?" he inquired.

"Certainly," replied Thatcher Allen.

"You have secured a man to—er—run the thing?"

"We have secured an operator."

Chesty stared at him, his comprehensive mind alert. Why did Thatcher Allen turn his reply to evade the "man" proposition? Could a woman operate an airplane? Perhaps none but an inexperienced youth would have dreamed of the possibility.

"Has Bill Stricklin any family?" he cautiously asked.

"A mother and sister. He is unmarried."

"How old is the sister?"

"Seventeen."

"Oh!" The age seemed to eliminate her. "And the mother?"

It was Thatcher Allen's turn to stare.

"The mother is blind," he said.

Mr. Radley-Todd's thoughts took another turn.

"Have you a family, sir?"

"I have a daughter, an only child. Mrs. Thatcher Allen is not living."

"And your daughter's age, sir?"

"Seventeen. She is the same age as Mary Eliska Stricklin."

"Are the young ladies—er—interested in airships?"

Thatcher Allen did not like these questions. He knew that a reporter is akin to a detective, and began to fear the youth was on the track of their secret. So he answered rather stiffly:

"Fairly so. Everyone seems interested in aviation these days. It interests me."

Chesty saw he would not confess; so he tried another tack.

"Mr. Burthon is your brother-in-law, I believe."

Thatcher Allen nodded.

"You are—eh—enemies?"

"Mr. Radley-Todd, or whatever your name is," angrily glancing at the card, "I do not object to being interviewed on the subject of the Stricklin Aircraft, or the coming aviation meet. But your questions are becoming personal and are wide of the mark. You will please confine yourself to legitimate topics."

The young man rose and bowed.

"Excuse me," he said in his halting way; "a reporter is often forced to appear impertinent when he does not intend to be so. At present I am—er—face to face with a curious—er—complication. I have discovered—eh—unintentionally—that your er, er—aviator will be in great danger tomorrow. If it's a man, I don't care. I don't like you, Thatcher Allen, and I wouldn't lift a finger to save the Stricklin Aircraft from going to pot. Why should I—eh? It's nothing to me. But if one of those girls—your daughter or Stricklin's sister, is to fly the thing, I feel it my—cr—duty to say: look out!"

He started to go, but Thatcher Allen grabbed his arm.

"What do you mean?" he demanded sternly.

"Is it a girl?"

"You won't betray us? You won't publish it?"

"Not at present."

"Mary Eliska Stricklin will operate the aircraft."

Chesty looked at his boots reflectively.

"Don't let her undertake it, sir," he said. "If you can't find a man, follow Burthon's example and withdraw your—eh—airship from the meet. Better withdraw it, anyhow—that's the best move—if you don't wish to court disaster."

"Explain yourself, sir!"

"I won't. I'm not going to spoil a good story for my paper—and a scoop in the bargain—to satisfy your curiosity. But Mary Eliska—May I see her a moment?"

Thatcher Allen reflected.

"If you warn her of danger you will take away her nerve. She's the only person on earth competent to operate the Stricklin Aircraft, and to withdraw the airplane would mean the ruin of her brother's fortune and ambitions."

"I don't know her brother; I don't care a fig for him. If I see the girl I shall warn her," said the reporter.

"Then you shall not see her."

"Very good. But you will tell her to look out?"

"What for?"

"For danger."

"When?"

"At all times; especially during her flight."

"There is always danger of accident, of course."

"This won't be an accident—if it happens," said Chesty Todd, decidedly.

"But who would wish to injure Mary Eliska?" asked Thatcher Allen, wonderingly.

"Think it over," said the reporter. "If you've one deadly enemy—a person who will stick at nothing, being desperate—that's the man."

With this he coolly walked away, leaving Thatcher Allen considerably disturbed. But he thought it over and decided to say nothing to Mary Eliska. The warning might refer to Burthon, who was the only person they might expect trouble from, although to Thatcher Allen's astonishment Burthon had quit the field at the last moment and abandoned the contest. Knowing nothing of Sybil's interview with her uncle, that action seemed to indicate, to Thatcher Allen's mind, that Burthon had weakened.

Under no circumstances would he have permitted Mary Eliska to face an unknown danger, but it occurred to him, after thinking over the interview, that Mr. H. Chesterton Radley-Todd was a fair example of a fool.

CHAPTER 7.22
THE FLYING GIRL

The morning of the first day of the long-heralded aviation meet dawned bright and sunny, as only a Southern California January morning can. By seven o'clock vast throngs were hurrying southward to Dominguez—a broad plain midway between Los Angeles and the ocean—where much important aviation history has been made.

By nine o'clock the grand stand was packed and "automobile row" occupied by hundreds of motor cars, filled with ladies in gay apparel, their escorts and imperturbable chauffeurs. The crowd was beginning to circle the vast field, too, and nearly every face bore an excited, eager expression.

The events scheduled might well arouse the interest of a people just awakened to the possibilities of aërial navigation. Important prizes had been offered by wealthy men and corporations for the most daring flights of the meet. Ten thousand dollars would go to the aviator showing the most skillful and adroit handling of an airplane; five thousand for the longest flight; another five thousand for an endurance test and a like sum to the one attaining the greatest height. In addition to these generous purses, two thousand dollars would be given for the best starting and alighting device exhibited and two thousand for the best safety device. For speed several huge purses were donated, and altogether the aviators present would compete for more than fifty thousand dollars in gold, besides various medals and cups and the priceless prestige gained by excelling in a competition where the most successful and famed airships and aviators of the world congregated.

Therefore, it is little wonder public interest was excited and every aviator determined to do his best. Many thronged the hangars, asking innumerable questions of the good-natured attendants, who recognized the popular ignorance of modern flying devices and were tolerant and communicative to a degree.

The morning events were of minor importance, although several clever exhibitions of flying were given. But at two o'clock the competition for skillful handling of an airplane in midair was scheduled, and at that time the appetite of each spectator was whetted for the great spectacle.

The day seemed ideal for aviation; the sky was flecked with fleecy clouds and scarcely a breath of air could be felt at the earth's surface.

Now came the first appearance of the Stricklin Aircraft. It had not been brought from the hangar during the forenoon and, in watching such celebrated airplanes as the Bleriot, Farman, Antoinette, Curtiss and Wright, manned by the greatest living aëronauts, those assembled had almost forgotten that a local inventor was to enter the lists with them. The secretary of the Aëro Club and others interested had expected Mr. Burthon to protest against allowing the Stricklin device to be operated, on the ground that Stricklin was entered to operate it and was unable to do so; but for some unaccountable reason Burthon remained silent, not even appearing at the field, and Thatcher Allen's explanation that the "Stricklin" in this instance meant the young man's sister, satisfied the officials perfectly. Naturally they were surprised and even startled at the idea of a girl taking part in the great aviation meet, but hailed the innovation with keenest interest.

Suddenly, while the field was clear and half a dozen airplanes hovered in the air above it, the Stricklin Aircraft rolled into the open space, circled before the grand stand and then, gracefully and without effort, mounted into the air.

Those who had witnessed Bill's prior performance were not astonished at this unassisted rise from earth to air, but all were delighted by the grace and beauty of the ascent and a roar of applause burst spontaneously from the crowd. The peculiar construction of the aircraft so diverted attention from its aviator that few marked the slender form of Mary Eliska, or knew that a girl was making this daring flight.

There were some, however, whose eyes were eagerly rivetted on the indistinct figure of the flying girl and utterly disregarded the machine. Bill, comfortably propped among the cushions of the motor car with his mother seated behind him and Sybil opposite, divided his attention between his sister and his creation. Thatcher Allen, knowing what the machine would do, watched Mary Eliska through a powerful glass and decided from the first that she was cool and capable. Chesty Todd also watched the girlish figure, with a more intense interest than he had ever before displayed during his brief and uneventful lifetime.

The reporter had been worried lest Thatcher Allen neglect to warn the girlish operator of the Stricklin Aircraft of danger; so he pushed through the crowd about the hangar and just as Mary Eliska passed the doorway, seated in her airplane, he said in a low voice: "Look out—for a collision!"

She started and cast an inquiring look at him, but there was no time to reply. The machine had been drawn by the assistants to a clear space and she must devote her attention to her work. As she threw in the lever Thatcher Allen, who stood beside the aircraft, hurriedly whispered: "Be careful, Mary Eliska—look out for danger!" Then she was off, facing the thousands on the field, with nerve and brain resolutely bent upon the task she had undertaken.

It was no indifferent thing this brave girl attempted. Until now her acquaintance with an airplane had been wholly theoretical; it was her first flight; yet so thoroughly did she understand every part of her air vehicle—what it was for and how to use it—that she had implicit confidence in herself and in her machine. Naturally level-headed, alert and quick to think and to act, Mary Eliska was no more afraid of soaring in the air than of riding in an automobile. Aside from her desire to operate the aircraft so skillfully that her brother's invention would be fully appreciated she was determined to attempt the winning of the ten-thousand-dollar prize, which would establish the Stricklin fortunes on a secure basis. Enough for one untried, seventeen-year-old girl to think of, was it not? And small wonder that she absolutely forgot the impressive warnings she had received.

The air is a mighty thoroughfare, free and untrammeled. The little group of airplanes operating over Dominguez—darting here and there, up and down—had little chance of colliding, for there was space enough and to spare. Mary Eliska knew all about air currents and their peculiarities and she also knew that her greatest safety lay in high altitudes. With a feeling of rapturous exhilaration she began to realize her control of the craft and her dominance of the air. A masterful desire crept over her to accomplish great deeds in aviation.

Those who were watching from below—judges, friends and spectators—saw her steadily mounting, higher and higher, until she seemed to fade out of sight like the figure in a moving picture, with nothing but a little iron-and-wood skeleton and the chugging of a tiny engine to ward off death. Then she came into sight again, a little smudge of grayish white against the shifting clouds. To see her up there, a mere speck dodging among the storm clouds, reminded the observers, as nothing in aviation has ever done before, of the awful audacity of man in building these mechanical birds. As they watched they found themselves hoping—as a child might—that in some way the brave little speck would manage to escape those gigantic sky monsters. Then one seized the aircraft, and just as the sun caught and flung back to earth a flash from one of the busy propeller-blades a huge cloud swallowed up machine and aviator and they vanished like mist.

It was odd how the terror of the spectators increased at this sudden disappearance; they knew that somewhere in that awesome, infinite firmament a frail thing made by the hand of man was battling with nature's most mysterious forces for supremacy. And man won. In less than a minute there was another flash of sunlight and the little gray speck emerged saucily from behind the cloud and made a dive for another.

Then the speck in the sky began to grow larger, and Mary Eliska attempted an amazing dive earthward that caused the throng to fall silent, motionless, gazing with bated breaths and startled eyes at the thrilling scene. It was a long swoop out of space and into being; a series of dives half a mile long and each nearly straight down.

The girl glided earthward until the aircraft nearly touched the ground; then she adroitly tilted it up again and tore away around the course in great circles, while the spectators, roused to life, thundered their applause.

Her control of the airplane was really wonderful. Again, encouraged by her success, she shot up into the air, rising to the height of half a mile and then performing the hazardous evolution known to aviators as the "spiral dip." She began by circling widely, at an even elevation, and then dipping the nose of the aircraft and narrowing the circles as she plunged swiftly downward with constantly accelerating speed. It was a bewildering and hair-raising performance, and no one but Walter Brookins had ever before undertaken it. A dozen feet from the ground Mary Eliska reined in her Pegasus and glided over the group of hangars on her inclined ascent—the third she had made without alighting. There were other airplanes doing interesting "stunts." Each aviator seemed to be exercising his ingenuity to excel all others, yet the eyes of the crowd followed the Stricklin Aircraft with an absorbed fascination that relegated other contestants to the rear.

CHAPTER 7.23
A BATTLE IN THE AIR

The Rescue.

"What is she doing now?" asked Mrs. Stricklin, anxiously.

"Soaring in the air about half a mile high and a half mile to the northward," replied Bill.

"And performing wonders," added Sybil, with enthusiasm. "I had no idea the aircraft could be controlled so perfectly."

"Nor I," admitted the young inventor, modestly. "It really seems like a thing of life under her management, and I am sure I could not have exhibited its good points half as well as little Sis is doing."

"Are any other airplanes flying?" Mrs. Stricklin inquired.

"Oh, yes," said Sybil. "There are several in the air, doing really marvelous things; but all seem to keep away from Mary Eliska and are more to the south of us. There's one, though!" she added suddenly. "Isn't that an airplane coming from the far north, Bill?"

He looked carefully through the field glasses he held.

"Why—yes! It surely is an airplane. But how did it get over there?" he exclaimed. "I've been watching the other contestants, and they're all nearby. Who can it be?"

Sybil had glasses, too, and she focused them on the approaching airship. "It looks very much like Uncle Burthon's imitation of the aircraft," she murmured.

"By Jove! That's what it is!" cried Bill. "How dare he fly it, after it has been withdrawn?"

"Uncle Burthon will dare anything," she retorted, coldly. "But he is making the mistake of his life today—if that is really his airplane."

"Why, he's driving straight toward Mary Eliska," said Bill, indignantly. "What is the fellow trying to do—bump the aircraft?"

Sybil laid a warning hand on his arm and glanced into the blind woman's startled face.

"Mary Eliska is all right," she announced in calm tones.

But Mary Eliska did not seem all right to Bill, who was growing excessively nervous; nor even to Sybil, whose face was stern and set as she watched the maneuvers of the two craft through her powerful glasses.

"It's Culley May," she said softly, meaning that the little chauffeur was operating Burthon's device. Bill nodded, and thereafter they were silent.

Swift as a dart the Burthon airplane approached Mary Eliska, who was deliberately circling this way and that as she glided through the air. She saw it coming, but at first paid little heed, thinking Culley May intended to pass by. But he altered his course to keep his machine headed directly for her and in gravely examining the approaching craft the girl noticed two slender steel blades projecting from his front elevator, like extended sword blades. They were slightly upcurved at the points, and while Mary Eliska marveled to see such things attached to an airplane the thought occurred to her that if those blades struck her planes they would rend the cloth to shreds and destroy their sustaining surfaces. In that case one result was inevitable—a sudden drop to earth, and death.

Even as this thought crossed her mind the Burthon airplane came driving toward her at full speed. Filled with dismay she could only stare helplessly until the thing was so near that she could distinctly see the scowling face and glaring eyes of Culley May, intent on mischief. Then, without realizing her action, she caused the aircraft to duck, and the other swept over her so closely that Culley May's running gear almost scraped her planes.

Mary Eliska's machine rolled alarmingly a moment, but she quickly regained control and then looked to see where Culley May was. He had turned and again was swooping toward her, at a slight downward angle. Mary Eliska ascended to escape him, now realizing the man's wicked determination to destroy the aircraft, and Culley May, displaying unexpected skill, altered his course to follow her.

The girl, thoroughly alarmed, now turned to flee, scarcely realizing what she did. Culley May followed like some huge bird of prey and, curiously enough, gained upon the Stricklin Aircraft. The two sets of engines were chugging away steadily, all the propellers revolving like clockwork, while the two rival airplanes answered obediently the slightest movements of their rudders.

Finding a straight flight would not permit her to escape her enemy, the girl swerved and began circling widely. After her came Culley May, the wicked looking blades that protruded from his elevator gleaming menacingly in the sunlight, his features distorted by hate and murderously determined.

In the circles Mary Eliska seemed able to keep her distance, but the poor child was so bewildered by this pitiless attack that her head was in a whirl and only by instinct could she handle the levers and wheel to guide her flight.

Culley May now observed several airplanes approaching at full speed, and realized he must end the chase quickly or be driven from his prey and prevented from carrying out his diabolical design. He made a quick turn to head off Mary Eliska's circle and the dreadful blades almost touched her lower plane as she dodged them. Culley May swept round again, but in his eagerness forgot his balance. Perhaps the man relied too much on the automatic device that had once brought Bill to grief; anyway his airplane developed a side motion that nearly shook him from his seat. He tried in vain to restore the balance. The jar caused the motors to slip; the engines stopped dead; with a rending sound the huge planes collapsed and the wreck of Burthon's biplane began to sink downward. Culley May was pitched headlong from his seat, but caught a rail and clung to it desperately as with ever increasing speed the fall to earth continued.

Mary Eliska had witnessed the accident and with the sudden transition from danger to safety the girl's wits returned and she regained her coolness. As she saw Culley May falling to his death, a quick conception of the situation inspired her to action. The Stricklin Aircraft suddenly tipped and began one of those tremendous dives through space which it had accomplished earlier in the day. Mary Eliska's airplane was absolutely under control, even at this thrilling moment, while the wreck to which Culley May clung was somewhat restrained in its fall by the mass of fluttering canvas and splintered bows. Although the weight of its engines and tanks dragged it swiftly down, Mary Eliska's aircraft dove much more rapidly. Five hundred feet above the earth she overtook Culley May, guided her airplane dangerously close to the man, and cried out to him to seize it. He may not have heard or understood her, but an instinct of self-preservation such as leads a drowning man to grasp at a straw induced him to clutch her footrail, and at the same moment Mary Eliska turned the machine, so as not to become entangled in the wreck, and began a more gradual descent, the little chauffeur dangling from her footrail while, alert and masterful, the girl controlled her overladen craft.

Down, down they came, and thirty thousand pair of startled, wondering eyes followed them as if entranced. Mary Eliska had not looked to see where she would land, for until this moment she had been so thoroughly occupied with the chase and the rescue of her enemy that she never once glanced toward the ground. But the hand of fate was guiding our brave young aviatrix. Her aircraft, maintaining a safe angle, settled directly upon Dominguez Field, where Culley May released his hold and rolled unconscious upon the ground. Mary Eliska's machine sped forward on its running gear and came to a stop just before the crowded grand stand.

No one who witnessed that exciting event will ever forget the mad shouts that rent the air when the Stricklin Aircraft, safe from its battle in the clouds, came to rest just in front of the gasping throng that had watched it with a fascination akin to horror. A hundred eager onlookers surrounded the machine, plucked the aviatrix from her seat and held her aloft for all to see, while the discovery that a young girl was the heroine of the terrible adventure caused them to marvel anew.

The applause redoubled; men shouted until they were hoarse; women wept, laughed hysterically and waved their handkerchiefs; everyone stood up to applaud; thousands crowded the field about Mary Eliska, who by this time was herself softly crying, until Bill, white as a ghost, directed his man to run the motor car through the crowd to his sister's side and assist her aboard.

Thatcher Allen took no part in this ovation. He was rushing about the field, flinging everyone out of his way with mad excitement and asking continually: "Where is he? Where is Culley May? What has become of him?"

No one heeded him for a time, as every eye was on Mary Eliska, every individual striving to get near her, to touch her—as if she had been a goddess whose hand could confer untold blessings and remedy the ills of the world. But after a while Thatcher Allen found a man who deigned to give him the desired information.

"The fellow who was rescued?" he said. "Oh, he fainted dead away the minute he touched solid ground."

"And what became of him?" demanded Thatcher Allen.

"Why, the crowd wanted to mob him, it seemed, and I guess that faint was the only thing that saved him from being torn to pieces."

"Well—well! What then?"

"Then a tall young fellow grabbed him up, chucked him into an automobile and got away with him."

"Where?"

"How the blazes do *I* know, stranger? I only saw them get away, that's all."

This information was later confirmed by several others, but Mary Eliska's manager was unable to learn who had taken Culley May away or where they had gone. Thatcher Allen was in an ugly mood, his heart throbbing with a fierce desire for vengeance. Culley May had escaped him for the moment but he vowed he would never rest until both Burthon and his chauffeur were behind the bars.

He was still pursuing his futile inquiries when Brewster approached him and said his daughter, with Bill, Mary Eliska and their mother, awaited him at the hangar, which was besieged by an excited throng. Directing the man to look after the aircraft and get it safely housed, he hurried away and managed to squeeze through the mass of humanity surrounding the hangar and gain admittance.

Within he found Mary Eliska the center of a group of aviators who were earnestly congratulating the girl on her escape and flooding her with compliments and praise for her skillful handling of the airplane. They were noble fellows, these professional aviators, and unselfish enough to be honestly enthusiastic over Mary Eliska's performances. The girl's beauty and modesty won them at once, and adding these charming qualities to her cleverness and bravery, today fully proven, it is not difficult to understand why Mary Eliska Stricklin from this moment became a prime favorite with every disciple of aviation.

Just now, however, Mary Eliska was embarrassed and a little distressed by all this laudation, following the spirited ovation tendered her by the public at large, so her nerves were beginning to fail her when by good fortune Thatcher Allen appeared. He saw at once her condition and without stopping to add a word of praise or congratulation managed to hurry her out of the back entrance, past the surging crowd that was even here in evidence, and into their automobile. The others of the party followed with less difficulty and soon they were all headed for town and speeding swiftly along the roadway.

CHAPTER 7.24
THE CRIMINAL

As soon as Sybil reached her room at the hotel she wrote a line to her uncle, Mr. Burthon, which said: "I have wired to Baltimore." Summoning a messenger she instructed him to search for Mr. Burthon until he found him and then place the message in his hands. She delayed sending the telegram just then, but was so angry and indignant that she was fully resolved to do so during the evening.

Meantime Mary Eliska, who to an extent had recovered from her excitement, was being petted by the family party in the sitting room that had been reserved for them. Poor Mrs. Stricklin, having hugged and kissed her child and wept over her terrible danger and miraculous escape, now held the girl's hand fast in her own and could not bear to let it go. Bill was full of eager praise and, ignoring for the time the final incident of the flight, led Mary Eliska to talk of her aërial exhibition and the admirable behavior of the aircraft, together with its perfect adjustment and obedience under all conditions.

"You've won the prize, dear," he asserted confidently. "No one else did half as much or did it as well, to say nothing of your skillful dodging of that scoundrel Culley May. But I can't let you make another flight, little sister. You are too precious to us all for us to let you risk your life in this way. The aircraft will have to stand by its record for that one flight—at least for this meet."

"Oh, no," protested Mary Eliska; "I'll go again tomorrow, Bill. I want to. The sensation is glorious, and I'm sure that monster, Culley May—or his master, Burthon—will be unable to get another airplane to chase me. I shall be perfectly safe, for your aircraft was from first to last like a thing with life and intelligence. I understand it, and it understands me."

"I wonder if Burthon really sent Culley May on that murderous errand," said Bill, thoughtfully.

"Of course he did!" declared Thatcher Allen, entering the room in time to hear the remark. "Here's a letter for you, Mary Eliska, just left at the office, and I'm pretty sure it's Burthon's handwriting."

Mary Eliska took the letter, opened it, and read aloud:

> *"Do not, I beg of you, my dear Mary Eliska, accuse me of inciting that fool Culley May's mad attack upon your airplane. The man stole the machine from its hangar and, crazed by my withdrawal from the meet, which deprived him of the chance of becoming famous, and inspired by anger toward Thatcher Allen, who had at one time maliciously assaulted him and whom he thought responsible for my withdrawal, he made a desperate attempt to wreck your airplane without knowing who was operating it. As soon as I found my machine gone I hurried to Dominguez and arrived in time to see the terrible result of Culley May's madness and your noble rescue of him. I am leaving the city tonight and may never see your sweet face again, but I do not wish you to misjudge me and have, therefore, made this explanation, which is honest and sincere. I trust you will remember me only as a true and loyal friend who would willingly sacrifice his unhappy life to save you from harm. Now and always faithfully yours,*
>
> "George Burthon."

During the reading Sybil had entered and quietly seated herself, listening with lip scornfully curled to her uncle's protestations of innocence. For a moment after Mary Eliska finished the letter all were silent. Then said Mary Eliska, gently:

"I'm so glad Mr. Burthon had no hand in it!"

"Bah!" sneered Thatcher Allen; "Burthon is a liar. I don't believe a word of his lame excuse."

"Nor I," added Bill, gravely. "Culley May is a hired assassin, that's all. I think Burthon is frightened, and wishes to throw us off the track and put the blame on his tool, before running away."

"I hope that is a lie, too—about his running away," said Thatcher Allen. "If Burthon escapes scot-free I shall be greatly disappointed. But the fellow is so tricky that if he says he is going you may rest assured he means to stay."

"I think not, Daddy," remarked Sybil, in her cold, even tones. "My uncle is in earnest this time and I doubt if you ever see or hear of George Burthon again."

A knock at the door startled the little group. Thatcher Allen stepped forward and opened it to find a tall, blue-eyed young man standing in the hall. He recognized Mr. Radley-Todd—the *Tribune* reporter—at once, and said stiffly:

"You are intruding, sir. I left word at the office that Mary Eliska and I would see the newspaper men at eight o'clock, but not before."

He started to close the door, but Chesty Todd inserted one long leg into the opening, smiling pleasantly as he said:

"This isn't a newspaper errand; let me in."

Thatcher Allen let him in, throwing wide the door, for there was an earnest ring in the young fellow's voice that could not be denied.

After Chesty Todd had entered, stumbling over the rug and bowing low to the ladies, another form shuffled silently through the doorway in his wake—a little, dried-up, withered man with tousled hair, his cap under his arm, a woebegone and hopeless expression on his leathery face.

"Culley May!" cried a surprised chorus.

The ex-chauffeur did not acknowledge the greeting. Chesty, extending one arm toward the man as if he were exhibiting a trained animal, said sternly:

"Down on your knees!"

Culley May bumped his kneecaps upon the floor in an attitude of meek humiliation.

"Now, then!"

"M-m-m—pardon," gurgled the little chauffeur, not with contrition but rather as an enforced plea for mercy.

Chesty kicked his shins.

"Get up," he commanded.

Culley May slowly rose, surveyed the group stealthily from beneath his brows and then dropped his eyes again, standing with bowed shoulders before them and nervously twirling his cap in his hands.

"Here," announced Chesty, pointing impressively to the culprit, "stands the murderous ruffian known to infamy as Culley May. He is at your mercy, prepared to endure any amount of torture or to die ignominiously at the hands of those he has wronged."

All but Mrs. Stricklin were staring in amazement first at Culley May, then at his captor. Said Bill to the latter, curiously:

"You are a detective, I suppose!"

"Merely as a side line," was the cheerful rejoinder. "Primarily I'm a newspaper reporter, and whenever I strike for a higher salary they tell me I'm a mighty poor journalist. Let me introduce myself. My name is Havely Chesterton Radley-Todd, quite a burden to carry but it all belongs to me. This is my first experience as an imitator of the late lamented Sherlock Holmes, and I may point with pride to the fact that I've unraveled the supposed plot to murder Mary Eliska Stricklin."

Culley May growled incoherently.

"True," said Chesty, looking at the man thoughtfully; "the plot was not to murder Mary Eliska, but Thatcher Allen, whom his loving brother-in-law supposed would operate the

Stricklin airplane. Incidentally it was planned to so wreck the aircraft—is that what you call it?—that it would be out of commission during the rest of the meet.”

“Why?” asked Bill.

“To satisfy his petty malice. If Burthon couldn’t fly he didn’t want you to fly, and he hoped to obtain revenge for being driven into exile.”

There was a murmur of surprise at this.

“Who drove Burthon into exile?” asked Thatcher Allen.

“I did,” said Sybil, indifferently.

“Have you seen him, then?” demanded her father.

“Oh, yes; but my uncle is unreliable. Before he obeyed my command to leave this country forever he decided on a final coup, which has fortunately failed.”

“Burthon,” announced Chesty Todd, “boarded an east-bound train an hour ago. I tried to head him off, but he was too slick and escaped me. That is the reason I am now here. I want you to listen to Culley May’s story and then decide whether to wire ahead and have Burthon arrested or let the matter drop. It is really up to you, as the interested parties. So far the police have not had a hand in the game.”

“Please sit down, Mr. Todd,” requested Mary Eliska, shyly. In the tall youth she had recognized the man who had tried to warn her on Dominguez Field, and was grateful to him.

Chesty bowed and sat down. Then he turned to his prisoner and said:

“Fire away, Culley May. Tell the whole story—the truth and nothing but the truth so help you.”

Culley May opened his mouth with effort, mumbled and gurgled a moment and then looked at his captor appealingly.

“Oh; very well. The criminal, ladies and gentlemen, seems to have lost, in this crisis, the power of expressing himself. So I shall relate to you the story, just as I extracted it—by slow and difficult processes—from the prisoner in my room, a short time ago. If I make any mistakes he will correct me.”

Culley May seemed much relieved.

“This creature,” began Chesty, “has previous to this eventful day been known to mankind as a good chauffeur and a bad citizen. He was employed by Burthon as an unscrupulous tool, his chief recommendation being a deadly hatred of Thatcher Allen, who at one time indelicately applied the toe of his boot to a tender part of Mr. Culley May’s anatomy. Burthon also hated Thatcher Allen, for robbing him of a million or so in a mine deal, and for other things of which I am not informed—or Culley May, either. Thatcher Allen owns a controlling interest in the Stricklin Aircraft, and—”

“That’s wrong,” interrupted Bill.

“I imagine Mr. Culley May’s story is wrong in many ways,” returned Mr. Radley-Todd, composedly. “I am merely relating it as I heard it.”

“Go on, sir.”

"Thatcher Allen had also maligned Mr. Burthon to Mary Eliska Stricklin, a young lady for whom Burthon entertained a fatherly interest and a—er—hum—a platonic affection. Is that right, Culley May?"

Culley May growled.

"Therefore Burthon decided to get even with Thatcher Allen, and Culley May agreed to help him. The first plan was to steal the design of Bill Stricklin's airship and by cleverly heading him off in some aëro-political manner put the firm of Thatcher Allen & Stricklin out of business. This scheme was approaching successful fruition when a saucy, impudent schoolgirl—Culley May's description, not mine—appeared on the scene and spiked Mr. Burthon's guns. Burthon explained to Culley May that in bygone days he had saved his sister, Thatcher Allen's wife, from going to prison for a crime Thatcher Allen had urged her to commit, but in doing this he had been obliged to defy the law, and the officers are unfortunately still on the generous man's trail. Thatcher Allen's daughter, knowing the situation, threatened to have Burthon arrested—to betray him to the bloodhounds of the cruel law—unless he withdrew his machine from the aviation meet and made tracks for pastures new."

The Stricklins were now regarding Sybil with amazement and her father with suspicion if not distrust. The girl stared back at them haughtily; Thatcher Allen shrugged his shoulders and stroked his drooping, grizzled mustache. Chesty Todd, observing this pantomime, laughed pleasantly.

"Culley May's story—told to me—of Burthon's story—told to Culley May," he observed, his eyes twinkling. "There's pitch somewhere, and I've not been favorably impressed by Mr. Burthon during my slight acquaintance with him. I make it a rule," speaking more slowly, "to judge people by their actions; by what they do, rather than by what people say of them. Judging Burthon by his actions I should have little confidence in what he says."

"You are quite right," declared Bill, eagerly. "I'll guarantee, if necessary, that Burthon lied about both Thatcher Allen and his daughter. No man ever had a truer friend than Thatcher Allen has been to me."

Thatcher Allen scowled; Sybil gave Bill one of her rare smiles.

"Anyhow," continued the narrator, "Culley May was in despair because the airplane he was booked to operate was withdrawn from the meet. Burthon told him if they wanted revenge they must act quickly. Their sources of information—erroneous, as the event proved—led them to believe their enemy Thatcher Allen would fly the rival airplane, and Culley May needed little urging to induce him to undertake to wreck it. Burthon paid him a thousand dollars in advance, to make the attempt, and promised him four thousand more if he succeeded."

"Five more," growled Culley May.

"I stand corrected; but it won't matter. Culley May made the attempt, as you know. He had no idea Mary Eliska was in the airship he was trying to demolish until the last moment, when by a clever turn he intercepted her airplane and was on the point of running it down. Just then, to his horror and dismay, he saw the girl plainly and made a desperate effort to check the speed of his machine—to avoid running her down. That was the cause of his mishap, he claims, and his desire to save Mary Eliska nearly cost him his life. While he was descending a mile or so through the air, clinging to the footrail, he fiercely repented his wicked act, so that by the time he struck the ground he was a reformed criminal, and, for the first time since he cut his eye teeth, an honest man. So he says, and he expects us to believe it.

"I happened to be near the spot where Culley May rolled and picked him up unconscious—dazed by his repentance, I suppose. The mob wanted to disjoint him and remove his skin, which was not a bad idea; but I decided he could be of more use to Mary Eliska alive—for the present, at least—because he might untangle some threads of the mystery. So I threw him into my car, got him to my room at Mrs. Skipp's boarding house, restored him to consciousness, applied the thumbscrews, got his deposition, lugged him here to you, and now—please have the kindness to take him off my hands, for I'm tired of him."

Mary Eliska laughed, a little nervously. They were all regarding Chesty with unfeigned admiration and Culley May with pronounced aversion.

Mrs. Stricklin was the first to speak. Said the blind woman, softly:

"Mary Eliska, you alone can judge this man. You alone can tell whether from the beginning he knew you were in the airplane or whether his claim is true that he discovered your identity at the last moment—and tried to save you. If he speaks truly, if he repented at the moment and risked his life to save you, it will have a great influence upon his fate. Speak, my child; you two were together in the air a mile above the earth, a mile from any other human being. Does the man speak truly?"

Mary Eliska paled; suddenly she grew grave and a frightened look crept into her clear eyes.

CHAPTER 7.25
THE REAL HEROINE

Chesty Todd had spoken so lightly, in a serio-comic vein, and had so belittled the "reformed villain" and contemptuously made him appear pitiful and weak, that he had somewhat disarmed his hearers and led them to forget the seriousness of the contemplated crime. But Mrs. Stricklin, listening intently to the story, found no humor in the situation, and the blind woman's gentle remark promptly recalled to every mind the full horror of the dastardly attempt.

She was quite right in declaring that Mary Eliska alone could approve or condemn Culley May's statement. If he spoke truly he was entitled to a degree of mercy at their hands; if, knowing that a girl was operating the Stricklin Aircraft, he had still persisted in his frantic attempt to wreck it and send her to her death, then no punishment could be too great for such a cowardly deed.

This was instantly appreciated by all present. Even Culley May, seeing that his fate hinged on Mary Eliska's evidence, ventured to raise his head and cast at her an imploring glance.

Chesty Todd dropped his flippant air and earnestly watched the girl's face; the others with equal interest awaited her decisive statement.

As for Mary Eliska, the gravity of the situation awed her. Recalling the dreadful moments when she battled in the air for her life she saw before her the scowling, vicious face of her enemy and remembered how his eyes had glared wickedly into her own time and again as he attacked her airplane, determined to destroy it at all hazards. There was no question in her mind as to the truth of Culley May's claim; she knew he had recognized her and still persisted in his purpose. She knew the accident to his machine was caused by his own carelessness and its faulty construction, and not by any desire of his to arrest its speed. Culley May had deliberately lied in order to condone his cowardly act, and she experienced a feeling of indignation that he should resort to such an infamous falsehood, knowing as he must that her evidence would render it impotent.

Mary Eliska contemplated her erstwhile assailant with reflective deliberation. She noted his miserable appearance, his abject manner, the moods of alternate despair and hope that crossed his withered features. An enemy so contemptible and mean was scarcely worthy of her vengeance. It seemed dreadful that such a despicable creature had been made in man's image. Could he possess a soul, she wondered? Could such an one own a conscience, or have any perception, however dim, of the brutal inhumanity of his offense? Being in man's image he must have such things. Perhaps in his nature was still some element of good, dormant and unrecognized as yet, which might develop in time and redeem him. To send him to prison, she reflected, would not be likely to correct the perversity of such a nature, while generous treatment and the forbearance of those he had wronged might tend to awaken in him remorse and a desire to retrieve his past. Without knowing it the girl was arguing on the side of the world's most expert criminologists, who hold that to destroy an offender cannot benefit society so much as to redeem him.

Whether Culley May's ultimate redemption was probable or not, Mary Eliska did not care to assume the responsibility of crushing him in order to avenge the shameful attempt, made in a moment of frenzy, to destroy her life. While those assembled hung breathless upon her words she said with assumed composure:

"The man knows better than I whether he speaks the truth. Could one be so utterly vile as to try to murder a girl who had never injured him? I think not. It is more reasonable to suppose that in his excitement he forgot himself—his manhood and his sense of justice—and only at the last moment realized what he was doing. I believe," she added, simply, "I shall give him the credit of the doubt and accept his statement."

Culley May stared at her as if he could scarcely believe his senses, while an expression of joy slowly spread over his haggard face. Radley-Todd gave Mary Eliska a quiet smile of comprehension and approval. Thatcher Allen said, musingly: "Ah; this interests me; indeed it does." But Bill exclaimed, in an impatient tone: "That does not clear Culley May of his attempt to murder Thatcher Allen and destroy the aircraft. He admits that such was his design and that Burthon paid him to do it. He is not less a criminal because Mary Eliska happened to be in the airplane. Therefore it is Thatcher Allen's duty to prosecute this scoundrel and put him in prison."

Culley May cast a frightened look at the speaker and began to tremble again. Said Chesty Todd, leaning back in his chair with his hands thrust into his pockets:

"That's the idea. The prisoner belongs to Thatcher Allen."

Thatcher Allen sat in his characteristic attitude, stooping forward and thoughtfully stroking his grizzled mustache.

"Did I hurt you very much when I kicked you, Culley May?" he meekly asked. "No, sir!" protested the man, eagerly.

"Would you have thought of such a revenge had not Burthon suggested it, and paid you to carry it out?"

"No, sir!"

"M—m. Would you like to murder me now?" "No, sir!"

"What will you do if I set you at liberty?"

"Clear out, sir," said Culley May earnestly.

"Ah; that interests me," declared Thatcher Allen.

"It doesn't interest me, though," Bill said angrily. "The brute tried to wreck my aircraft."

"But he failed," suggested Thatcher Allen. "The aircraft is still in apple-pie order."

"My son," said the boy's mother, in her gentle voice, "can you afford to be less generous than Thatcher Allen and—your sister?"

Bill flushed. Then he glanced toward Sybil and found the girl eyeing him curiously, expectantly.

"Oh, well," he said, with reluctance, "let him go. Such a fiend, at large, is a menace to society. That is why I wished to make an example of him. If airplanes are to be attacked in mid-air, after this, the dangers of aviation will be redoubled."

"I wouldn't worry about that," carelessly remarked Todd. "This fellow is too abject a coward to continue a career of crime along those lines. He's had his lesson, and he'll remember it. I don't say he'll turn honest, for I imagine it isn't in him; but he'll be mighty careful hereafter how he conducts himself."

"I—I'll never step foot in an airplane again!" growled Culley May, hoarsely but with great earnestness.

"Suppose you meet Burthon again?" suggested Bill, distrustfully.

"If I do," said the man, scowling and clinching his fists, "I—I'll strangle him!"

"A nice, reformed character, I must say," observed Bill, with fine contempt.

"But he interests me—he interests me greatly," asserted Thatcher Allen. "Let him go, Bill."

Radley-Todd looked round the circle of faces with an amused smile, which grew tender as his eye rested upon the placid features of Mrs. Stricklin. The boy loved to study human nature; it had possessed a fascination for him ever since he could remember, and here was a fertile field for observation. Reading accurately the desire of those assembled to be rid of the abhorrent creature he had brought before them, the young man slowly rose and opened the door.

"Culley May," said he, "you've saved your skin. Not by your whining falsehoods and misrepresentations, but because these people are too noble to be revenged upon one so ignoble and degraded. But I'm not built that way myself. I'm longing to kick you 'til you can't stand, and there's a mighty power to my hamstrings, I assure you. I refrain just now, because ladies are present, but if I ever set eyes on your carcass again you'll think Thatcher Allen's kick was a mere love-pat. Get out!"

Culley May cringed, turned without a word and shuffled through the doorway.

Mary Eliska came forward and took the young fellow's hand in her own, impulsively.

"Thank you, Mr. Todd!" she said.

He held the hand a moment and looked admiringly into her upturned face.

"It is I who should give thanks, and I do," he answered reverently. "I thank God today, as I have had occasion to do before, for his noblest creation—the American girl."

"Good!" cried Thatcher Allen, with approval. "That interests me."

CHAPTER 7.26
OF COURSE

Mary Eliska did fly the next day, as she had declared she would. The morning papers were full of her achievement, with columns of enthusiastic praise for her beauty, her daring, her modesty and skill. The attempt of a rival airplane to interfere with her flight and her clever rescue of her enemy when he came to grief made a popular heroine of the girl, yet no one seemed to know the true history of the astonishing affair. The *Tribune* had glowing accounts of the day's events from the pen of Mr. H. Chesterton Radley-Todd, but this astute correspondent refrained from making "a scoop," as he might have done had he bared his knowledge of the conspiracy that ended with Mary Eliska Stricklin's aërial adventure.

One of the other papers suspected Burthon of being the instigator of the wicked plot to wreck Mary Eliska's airship and, discovering the fact that he had fled from the city, openly accused him. Culley May could not be found, either, for the little ex-chauffeur had wisely "skipped the town" and his former haunts knew him no more.

The judges awarded the Stricklin Aircraft the ten-thousand-dollar prize, and singularly enough not a word of protest came from the competing aviators. Those who had attended the meet the day before, and thousands who read of Mary Eliska Stricklin in the newspapers, eagerly assembled at Dominguez to witness her further exhibitions on the next day. It was estimated that fully fifty thousand people were in attendance, and when the Stricklin Aircraft appeared, decked with gay banners and ribbons, and made a short flight above the field, the girl aviatrix met with a reception such as has never before been equaled in the annals of aviation.

Later in the day Mary Eliska took part in the contest for speed and although she did not win this event the girl aëronaut managed her biplane so gracefully and pressed the leader in the race so closely that she was accorded the admiring plaudits of the spectators.

Bill was a little disappointed in the result, but Thatcher Allen reminded him that his employment of crossed planes was sure to sacrifice an element of speed for the sake of safety, and assured him it was not at all necessary for his invention to excel in swiftness to win universal approval.

In other events that followed during the progress of the meet Mary Eliska captured several of the prizes, with the final result that the Stricklins were eighteen thousand dollars richer than they had been before. Crowds constantly thronged the Stricklin hangar, inspecting the wonderful machine and questioning the attendants as to its construction and management, while so many orders for the aircraft were booked that Thatcher Allen assured Bill they would be justified in at once building a factory to supply the demand.

Throughout the meet Mary Eliska Stricklin remained the popular favorite and the wonderful performances of the young girl were discussed in every place where two or more people congregated. Had Bill been able to operate his own machine he would not have won a tithe of the enthusiastic praise accorded "The Flying Girl," and this was so evident that Mary Eliska was instantly recognized as the most important member of the firm.

Naturally she was overjoyed by her success, yet she never once lost her humble and unassuming manner or considered the applause in the light of a personal eulogy. Devoting herself seriously and with care to every detail of her work she strove to exhibit Bill's aircraft in a manner to prove its excellence, and considered that her important aim.

There was nothing reckless about Mary Eliska's flights; her success, then and afterward, may be attributed to her coolness of head, a thorough understanding of her machine and a full appreciation of her own ability to handle it. The flattery and adulation she received did not destroy her self-poise or cause one flutter of her heart, but when anyone praised the merits of the Stricklin Aircraft, she flushed with pleasure and pride. For Mary Eliska firmly believed she basked in the reflected glory of her brother's inventive genius, and considered herself no more than a showman employed to exhibit his marvelous creation.

"You see," she said to Chesty Todd, who stood beside her in the hangar on the last day of the meet while she watched Thatcher Allen and his assistants preparing the aircraft for its final flight, "Bill has a thorough education in aëronautics and knows the caprices and requirements of the atmosphere as well as a gardener knows his earth. The machine is adjusted to all those variations and demands, and that is why it accomplishes with ease much that other airplanes find difficult. A child might operate the Stricklin Aircraft, and I feel perfectly at ease in my seat, no matter how high I am or how conflicting the air currents; for Bill's machine will do exactly what it is built to do."

"The machine is good," observed Chesty, "but your sublime self-confidence is better. You're a conceited young lady—not over your own skill, but over that of your brother."

She laughed.

"Haven't I a right to be?" she asked. "Hasn't Bill proved his ability to the world?"

The boy nodded, a bit absently. He was thinking how good it was to find a girl not wrapped up in herself, but unselfish enough to admire others at her own expense. A pretty girl, too, Chesty concluded with a sigh, as he watched her prepare to start. What a pity he had lived all of twenty-one years and had not known Mary Eliska Stricklin before!

By some sleight-of-hand, perhaps characteristic of the fellow, Chesty had attached himself to the "Stricklin-Thatcher Allen Combination," as he called it, like a barnacle. At first both Bill and Thatcher Allen frowned upon his claim to intimacy, but the boy was so frankly attracted to their camp, "where," said he, "I can always find people of my own kind," that they soon became resigned to the situation and accepted his presence as a matter of course.

Sybil treated this new acquaintance with the same calm indifference she displayed toward all but her father and, latterly, Bill Stricklin. Chesty found in her the most puzzling character he had ever met, but liked her and studied the girl's vagaries from behind a bulwark of levity and badinage. Perhaps the reporter's most loyal friend at this time was Mrs. Stricklin, who had promptly endorsed the young man as a desirable acquisition to their little circle. In return Chesty was devoted to the afflicted woman and loved to pay her those little attentions she required because of her helplessness.

Thatcher Allen celebrated the closing day of the meet by giving a little dinner to the Stricklins in his private rooms at the hotel that evening, and Chesty Todd was included in the party. Bill attended in a wheeled chair and was placed at one end of the table, while Mary Eliska occupied the other. The central decoration was a floral model of the Stricklin Aircraft, and before Mary Eliska's plate was laid a crown of laurel which her friends tried to make her wear. But the girl positively refused, declaring that Bill ought to wear the crown, while she was entitled to no more credit than a paid aviatrix might be.

The next morning's developments, however, proved that she had been too modest in this assertion. A telegram arrived from the directors of the San Francisco Aviation Club asking Mary Eliska Stricklin's price to attend their forthcoming meet and exhibit her airplane. Accounts of her daring and successful flights had been wired to newspapers all over the world and public interest in the girl aviatrix was so aroused that managers of aerial exhibitions throughout the country realized she would be the greatest "drawing card" they could secure.

Thatcher Allen, as manager for Mary Eliska as well as for Bill and the aircraft, telegraphed his terms, demanding so large a sum that the Stricklins declared it would never be considered. To their amazement the offer was promptly accepted, and while they were yet bewildered by this evidence of popularity, a representative of the New Orleans Aëro Club called at the hotel to secure Mary Eliska for their forthcoming meet. Thatcher Allen received him cordially, but said:

"Unfortunately, sir, your dates conflict with those of the San Francisco meet, where Mary Eliska has already contracted to appear."

"Is there no way of securing her release?" asked the man, deeply chagrined at being too late. "Our people will be glad to pay any price to get her."

"No," replied Thatcher Allen; "we stand by our contracts, whatever they may be. But possibly we shall be able to send you a duplicate of the Stricklin Aircraft, with a competent aviatrix to operate it."

The man's face fell.

"We will, of course, be glad to have you enter the Stricklin machine, on the same terms other airplanes are entered; but we will pay no bonus unless 'The Flying Girl' is herself present to exhibit it. To be quite frank with you, the people are wild to see Mary Eliska Stricklin, whose exploits are on every tongue just now, but all airplanes look alike to them, as you can readily understand."

When the emissary had departed, keenly disappointed, Thatcher Allen turned to Mary Eliska and Bill Stricklin, who had both been present at the interview, and said:

"You see, Mary Eliska should have worn the laurel crown, after all. 'The Flying Girl' has caught the popular fancy and I predict our little heroine will be in great demand wherever aviation is exploited. As a matter of truth and justice I will admit that she could not have acquired fame so readily without Bill's superb invention to back her. In coming years your principal source of income will be derived from the Stricklin Aircraft; but just now, while aviation is in its infancy, Mary Eliska will be able to earn a great deal of money by giving exhibitions at aviation meets. If she undertakes it there is, we all know, much hard work ahead of her, coupled with a certain degree of danger." He turned to the girl. "It will be for you to decide, my dear."

Mary Eliska did not hesitate in her reply.

"I will do all in my power to exhibit Bill's machine properly, until he is well enough to operate it himself," she said. "Then he will become the popular hero in my place, and I'll retire to the background, where I belong."

Even Bill smiled at this prediction.

"I'll never be able to run the thing as you can, Sis," he replied, "and you mustn't overlook the fact that your being a girl gives you as great an advantage over me, as an aeronaut, as over all other aviators. I think Thatcher Allen is right in saying that the advertising and prestige you have already received will enable you to win a fortune for us—provided you are willing to assume the risk and exertion, and if mother will consent."

"I love the moil and toil of it, as well as the pleasure," exclaimed the girl. "It will be joy and bliss to me to fly the aircraft on every possible occasion, and if you'll leave me to manage mother I'll guarantee to secure her consent."

At this juncture Chesty Todd came in. His face was solemn and dejected.

"What's up?" asked Bill.

"Lost my job, that's all," said Chesty. "Our editor thinks I didn't run down that Burthon affair as well as the other fellows did and that I neglected some of the famous aviators to gush over Mary Eliska. That's his excuse, anyhow; but my private opinion, publicly expressed, is that I was predoomed to be fired, whatever I did."

"Why so?" inquired Mary Eliska.

"I'm getting too good. They're afraid if they kept me on I'd demand more wages."

There was a shout of laughter at this.

"Of course I didn't expect sympathy," observed Chesty, dolefully. "I see starvation ahead of me, and as there's a good deal of Mr. Radley-Todd to starve it's bound to be a tedious and trying experience."

"This interests me," remarked Thatcher Allen, musingly.

"Me, also," said Chesty.

Thatcher Allen related the engagement made that morning for Mary Eliska's San Francisco exhibition and the demand of the New Orleans representative.

"The promoters of every aviation meet, hereafter, will want to secure Mary Eliska," he added, "and so we are about to organize a campaign to advertise 'The Flying Girl' and the Stricklin Aircraft throughout the United States. Possibly we may take her to Europe—"

"Oh!" exclaimed Mary Eliska, excitedly. "Don't you think the people of Mars would like me to visit them?"

"I see," said Chesty, nodding. "You need a press agent."

"It might not be a bad idea," admitted Thatcher Allen.

"I'm engaged from this moment," declared the young man. "I've had my breakfast, thank you, but I shall require three square meals a day from this time on. Any further emolument I leave to you. As for promoting Mary Eliska, you'll find me thoroughly capable and willing— provided the young lady proves flighty and goes up in the air occasionally, as young ladies are prone to do. This may be a soar subject to discuss just now, so I'll end my aëroplaintive lay."

"If you put that bosh in the papers you'll ruin us," said Bill.

"Trust me," returned Chesty, earnestly. "I'll stick to the most dignified facts, merely relating that Mary Eliska is to make an ascension for the purpose of picking air currants to make jam of."

"All right," announced Thatcher Allen; "you're engaged."

CHAPTER 8

Flying Girl and Her Chum

CHAPTER 8.1
THE GIRL WITH THE YACHT

Perhaps they call them "parlor" cars because they bear so little resemblance to the traditional parlor—a word and a room now sadly out of style. In reality they are ordinary cars with two rows of swivel seats down the center; seats supposed to pivot in every direction unless their action is impeded by the passenger's hand baggage, which the porter promptly piles around the chairs, leaving one barely room to place his feet and no chance at all to swing the seat. Thus imprisoned, you ride thoughtfully on your way, wondering if the exclusive "parlor car" is really worth the extra fee. However, those going to San Diego, in the Southland of California, are obliged to choose between plebeian coaches and the so-called "parlor" outfit, and on a mild, sunny morning in February the San Diego train rolled out of the Los Angeles depot with every swivel seat in the car deluxe occupied by a passenger.

They were a mixed assemblage, mostly tourists bound for Colorado, yet quite unknown to one another; or, at least, not on speaking terms. There was a Spanish-looking gentleman in white; two prim, elderly damsels in black; a mamma with three subdued children and a maid, and a fat man who read a book and scowled at every neighbor who ventured a remark louder than a whisper. Forward in the car the first three seats were taken by a party from New York, and this little group of travelers attracted more than one curious glance.

"That," murmured one of the prim ladies to the other, "is Madeline Dentry, the famous heiress. No one knows how many millions she has just inherited, but she is said to be one of the richest girls in America. The stout lady is her chaperon; I believe—she's a distant relative—an aunt, or something—and the thin, nervous man, the stout lady's husband, is Madeline Dentry's financial manager."

"I know," replied the other, nodding; "he used to be her guardian before she came of legal age, a month or so ago. His name is Tupper—Martin J. Tupper—and I'm told he is well connected."

"He is, indeed, to have the handling of Madeline's millions." "I mean in a family way. The Dentrys were nobodies, you know, until Madeline's father cornered the mica mines of the world and made his millions; but the Tuppers were a grand old Baltimore family in the days of Washington, always poor as poverty and eminently aristocratic."

"Do you know the Tuppers?"

"I have never met them. I strongly disapprove of their close association with Miss Dentry—a fly-away miss who kept Bryn Mawr in a turmoil while she was a student there, and is now making an absurd use of her money."

"In what way?"

"Haven't you heard? She has purchased Lord Tweedmonk's magnificent yacht, and has had it taken to San Diego harbor. I was told by the bell boy at the Los Angeles Ambassador Hotel—bell boys are singularly well-informed, I have observed—that Madeline Dentry is to take her new yacht on a cruise to Hawaii and Japan. She is probably now on her way to see her extravagant and foolish plaything."

"Dreadful!" said the other, with a shudder. "I wonder how anyone can squander a fortune on a yacht when all those poor are starving in China. What a pity the girl has no mother to guide her!"

"Tell me about the beautiful girl seated next to Madeline."

"I do not know who she is. Some stranger to the rich young lady, I imagine. They're not speaking. Yes, she is really beautiful, that girl. Her eyes are wonderful, and her coloring perfect."

"And she seems so modest and diffident."

"Evidence of good breeding, whoever she may be; quite the opposite of Madeline Dentry, whose people have always been rapid and rude."

The fat gentleman was now glaring at the old ladies so ferociously that they became awed and relapsed into silence. The others in the car seemed moodily reserved. Mr. Martin J. Tupper read a newspaper. His stolid wife, seated beside him, closed her eyes and napped. Madeline Dentry, abandoning a book that was not interesting, turned a casual glance upon her neighbor in the next chair—the beautiful girl who had won the approval of the two old maids. Madeline herself had a piquant, attractive countenance, but her neighbor was gazing dreamily out of the window and seemed not to have noticed her. In this listless attitude she might be inspected at leisure, and Madeline was astonished at the perfect profile, the sheen of her magnificent hair, the rich warm tintings of a skin innocent of powders or cosmetics. Critically the rich young lady glanced at the girl's attire. It was exceedingly simple but of costly material. She wore no jewels or ornaments, nor did she need them to enhance her attractiveness.

Perhaps feeling herself under observation, the girl slowly turned her head until her eyes met those of Madeline. They were gloriously blue eyes, calm and intelligent, wide open and fearless. Yet with a faint smile she quickly withdrew them before Madeline's earnest gaze.

"Will you have a chocolate?"

"Thank you."

The strong hand with its well-shaped fingers did not fumble in Madeline's box of bonbons. She took a chocolate, smiled again, and with a half shy glance into her neighbor's face proceeded to nibble the confection.

Madeline was charmed.

"Are you traveling alone?" she asked.

"Yes. I am to meet my brother and—some friends—in San Diego."

"I am Miss Dentry—Madeline Dentry. My home is in New York."

"And mine is in Los Angeles. I am not straying very far away, you see."

Madeline was piqued that her hint was disregarded.

"And your name!" she asked sweetly.

The girl hesitated an instant. Then she said: "I am Miss Stricklin."

Mr. Tupper looked up from his newspaper.

"Stricklin?" he repeated. "Bless me! That's the name of the Flying Girl."

"So it is," admitted Miss Stricklin, with a little laugh.

"But flying is not in your line, I imagine," said Madeline, admiring anew the dainty personality of her chance acquaintance.

"At present our train is dragging, rather than flying," was the merry response.

Mr. Tupper was interested. He carefully folded his paper and joined in the conversation.

"The idea of any girl attempting to do stunts in the air!" he remarked disdainfully. "Your namesake, Miss Stricklin, deserves to break her venturesome, unmaidenly neck—as she probably will, in the near future."

"Nonsense, Uncle!" cried Madeline; "Mary Eliska, so far as I've read of her—and I've read everything I could find—is not at all unmaidenly. She's venturesome, if you like, and manages an airplane better than many of the bird-men can; but I see nothing more unwomanly in flying than in running an automobile, and you know *I* do that to perfection. This Flying Girl, as she is called, is famous all over America for her daring, her coolness in emergencies and her exceptional skill. I want to see her fly, while I›m out here, for I understand there›s to be an aviation meet of some sort in San Diego next week, and that Mary Eliska is engaged to take part in it.»

"Flying is good sport, I admit," said Mr. Tupper, "but it would give me the shivers to see a girl attempt it. And, once a machine is in the air, you can't tell whether a man or woman is flying it; they all look alike to the watcher below. Don't go to this aviation meet, Madeline; you've seen girls fly. There was Miss Moissant, at Garden City——"

"She barely got off the ground," said Miss Dentry.

"And there was Blanche Scott——"

"They're all imitators of Mary Eliska!" declared Madeline impatiently. "There's only one real Flying Girl, Uncle, and if she's on the program at the San Diego meet I'm going to see her."

"You'll be disappointed," averred the gentleman. "She's a native of these parts, they say; I presume some big-boned, masculine, orange-picking female——"

"Wrong again, sir! The reporters all rave about her. They say she has a charming personality, is lovely and sweet and modest and—and——" She paused, her eyes dilating a little as she marked the red flush creeping over Miss Stricklin's neck and face. Then Madeline drew in her breath sharply and cast a warning glance at her uncle.

Mr. Tupper, however, was obtuse. He knew nothing of Madeline's suspicions.

"Have you ever seen this dare-devil namesake of yours, Miss Stricklin?" he asked indifferently.

"Yes, sir," she answered in a quiet tone.

"And what did you think of her?"

Madeline was powerless to stop him. Miss Stricklin, however, looked at her questioner with candid eyes, a frank smile upon her beautiful face.

"She has a fine airplane," was her reply. "Her brother invented it, you know. It's the Stricklin Aircraft, the safest and speediest yet made, and Bill Stricklin has taught his sister how to handle it. That she flies his Aircraft successfully is due, I am sure, to her brother's genius; not to any especial merit of her own."

Mr. Tupper was staring now, and beginning to think. He remembered reading a similar assertion attributed to Mary Eliska, the Flying Girl, who always insisted on crediting her brother with whatever success she achieved. Perhaps this girl had read it, too; or, perhaps——

He began to "put two and two together." Southern California was the favorite haunt of the Flying Girl; there was to be an aviation meet presently at San Diego; and on this train, bound for San Diego, was riding a certain Miss Stricklin who answered to Madeline's description of the aërial heroine—a description he now remembered to have often read himself. Uncertain what to say, he asked haltingly:

"Do you call it 'aviatrix' or 'aviatrice'? The feminine of 'aviator,' you know."

"I should say 'aviatress,' now that you appeal to me," was the laughing reply. "Some of the newspaper men, who love to coin new words, have tried to saddle 'aviatrice' on the girl aviator, and the French have dubbed her 'aviatrix' without rhyme or reason. It seems to me that if 'seamstress,' 'governess' or 'hostess' is proper, 'aviatress' is also correct and, moreover, it is thoroughly American. But in—in the profession—on the aviation field—they call themselves 'aviators,' whether men or women, just as an author is always an 'author,' regardless of sex."

Mr. Tupper had made up his mind, by this time. He reasoned that a girl who talked so professionally of aviation terms must be something more than a novice, and straggled to remember if he had inadvertently said anything to annoy or humiliate Miss Stricklin. For, if the little maid so demurely seated before him was indeed the famous Flying Girl, the gentleman admitted he had good reason to admire her. Madeline was watching his embarrassment with an expression of amusement, but would not help him out of his dilemma. So Mr. Tupper went straight to the heart of the misunderstanding, as perhaps was best under the circumstances.

"Your first name is Mary?" he inquired, gently.

"It is, sir."

"Won't you have another chocolate!" asked Madeline.

Mary Eliska took another chocolate, reflecting how impossible it seemed to hide her identity, even from utter strangers. Not that she regretted, in any way, the celebrity she had gained by flying her brother Bill's Aircraft, but it would have been so nice to have ridden today with these pleasant people without listening to the perfunctory words of praise and adulation so persistently lavished upon her since she had acquired fame.

"I knew Thatcher Allen some years ago," continued Mr. Tupper, rather aimlessly. "Thatcher Allen's your manager, I believe!"

"Yes, sir; and my brother's partner."

"Good chap, Thatcher Allen. Had a queer daughter, I remember; an impossible child, with the airs of a princess and the eyes of a sorceress. She's grown up, by this time, I suppose."

Miss Stricklin smiled.

"Sybil Allen is my chum," she replied. "The description applies, so far as the airs and eyes are concerned; but the child is a young lady now, and a very lovable young lady, her friends think."

"Doubtless, doubtless," Mr. Tupper said hastily. "If Thatcher Allen is in San Diego I shall be glad to renew our acquaintance."

"You are bound for Coronado, I suppose," remarked Mary Eliska, to change the subject.

"Only for a few days' stay," Madeline answered. "Then we expect to make a sea voyage to Honolulu."

"That will be delightful," said the girl. "I've lived many years on the shores of the Pacific, but have never made a voyage farther to sea than Catalina. I'm told Honolulu is a fascinating place; but it needs be to draw one away from Coronado."

"You like Coronado, then?"

"All this South Country is a real paradise," declared Mary Eliska. "I have had opportunity to compare it with other parts of America, and love it better after each comparison. But I am ignorant of foreign countries, and can only say that if they excel Southern California they are too good for humans to live in and ought to be sacred to the fairies."

Madeline laughed gayly. "I know you now!" she exclaimed; "you are what is called out here a 'booster.' But from my limited experience in your earthly paradise I cannot blame you."

"Yes, we are all 'boosters,'" asserted the younger girl, "and I'm positive you will join our ranks presently. I love this country especially because one can fly here winter and summer."

"You are fond of flying?"

"Yes. At first I didn't care very much for it, but it grows on one until its fascinations are irresistible. I have the most glorious sense of freedom when I'm in the air—way up, where I love best to be—but during my recent exhibitions in the East I nearly froze making the high flights. It is a little cold even here when you are half a mile up, but it is by no means unbearable."

"They call you a 'dare-devil,' in the newspapers," remarked Mr. Tupper, eyeing her reflectively; "but I can scarcely believe one so—so young and—and—girlish has ventured to do all the foolish aërial tricks you are credited with."

Mrs. Tupper had by this time opened her eyes and was now listening in amazement. "Yes," she added, reprovingly, "all those spiral dips and volplaning and—and—figure-eights are more suited to a circus performer than to a young girl, it seems to me."

This lady's face persistently wore a bland and unmeaning smile, which had been so carefully cultivated in her youth that it had become habitual and wreathed her chubby features even when she was asleep, giving one the impression that she wore a mask. Now her stern eyes belied the smirk of her face, but Mary Eliska merely smiled.

"I am not a 'dare-devil,' I assure you," she said, addressing Mr. Tupper rather than his wife. "I know the newspapers call me that, and compare me with the witch on a broomstick; but in truth I am as calculating and cold as any aviator in America. Everything I do is figured out with mathematical precision and I never take a single chance that I can foresee. I know the air currents, and all their whims and peculiarities, and how to counteract them. What may seem to the spectators to be daring, and even desperate, is often the safest mode of flying, provided you understand your machine and the conditions of the air. To volplane from a height of five or ten thousand feet, for example, is safer than from a slight elevation, for the further you drop the better air-cushion is formed under your planes, and you ride as gently as when suspended from a parachute."

Madeline was listening eagerly. "Are you afraid?" she asked.

"Afraid? Why should I be, with my brother's wonderful engine at my back and perfect control of every part of my machine?"

"Suppose the engine should some time fail you?"

"Then I would volplane to the ground."

"And if the planes, or braces, or fastenings break?"

"No fear of that. The Stricklin Aircraft is strong enough for any aërial purpose and I examine every brace and strut before I start my fight—merely to satisfy myself they have not been maliciously tampered with."

Then Madeline sprung her important question: "Do you ever take a passenger?"

Mary Eliska regarded Miss Dentry with a whimsical smile.

"Sometimes," she said. "Do you imagine you would like to fly?"

"No—no, indeed!" cried Mr. Tupper in a horrified voice, and Mrs. Tupper echoed; "How absurd!" But Madeline answered quietly:

"If you could manage to take me I am sure I would enjoy the experience."

"I will consider it and let you know later," said the Flying Girl, thoughtfully. "My chum, Sybil Allen, has made several short flights with me; but Sybil's head is perfectly balanced and no altitude affects it. Often those who believe they would enjoy flying become terrified once they are in the air."

"Nothing could terrify Madeline, I am sure," asserted Mrs. Tupper, in a rasping voice; "but she is too important a personage to risk her life foolishly. I shall insist that she at once abandon the preposterous idea. Abandon it, Madeline! I thought your new yacht a venturesome thing to indulge in, but flying is far, far worse."

"Oh; have you a yacht?" inquired Mary Eliska, turning eagerly to the other girl. "Yes; the *Salvador*. It is now lying in San Diego harbor. I've not seen my new craft as yet, but intend it shall take us to Honolulu and perhaps to Japan."

"How delightful," cried Mary Eliska, with enthusiasm.

"Would you like to join our party?"

"Oh, thank you; I couldn't," quite regretfully; "I am too busy just now advancing the fortunes of my brother Bill, who is really the most clever inventor of airplanes in the world.

Don't smile, please; he is, indeed! The world may not admit it as yet, but it soon will. Have you heard of his latest contrivance? It is a Hydro-Aircraft, and its engines propel it equally as well on water as on land."

"Then it beats my yacht," said Madeline, smiling.

"It is more adaptable—more versatile—to be sure," said Mary Eliska. "Bill has just completed his first Hydro-Aircraft, and while I am in San Diego I shall test it and make a long trip over the Pacific Ocean to exploit its powers. Such a machine would not take the place of a yacht, you know, and the motor boat attachment is merely a safety device to allow one to fly over water as well as over land. Then, if you are obliged to descend, your aircraft becomes a motor boat and the engines propel it to the shore."

"Does your brother use the Gnome engines?" inquired Mr. Tupper. "No; Bill makes his own engines, which I think are better than any others," answered Miss Stricklin.

By the time the train drew into the station at San Diego, Madeline Dentry and her companions, the Tuppers, knew considerably more of airplanes than the average layman, for Mary Eliska enjoyed explaining the various machines and, young and unassuming as she appeared, understood every minute detail of their manufacture. She had been her brother's assistant and companion from the time of his first experiments and intelligently followed the creation and development of the now famous Stricklin Aircraft.

At the depot a large crowd was in waiting, not gathered to meet the great heiress, Madeline Dentry, but the quiet slip of a girl whose name was on every tongue and whose marvelous skill as a bird-maid had aroused the admiration of every person interested in aërial sports. On the billboards were glaring posters of "The Flying Girl," the chief attraction of the coming aviation meet, and the news of her expected arrival had drawn many curious inhabitants of the Sunshine City to the depot, as well as the friends congregated to greet her. First of all a tall, fine looking fellow, who limped slightly, sprang forward to meet Mary Eliska at the car steps and gave her a kiss and a hug. This was Bill Stricklin, the airship inventor, and close behind him stood a grizzled gentleman in a long gray coat and jaunty Scottish cap. It was Thatcher Allen, the "angel" and manager of the youthful Stricklins, the man whose vast wealth had financed the Stricklin Aircraft and enabled the boy and girl to carry out their ambitious plans. This strange man had neither ambition to acquire more money nor to secure fame by undertaking to pilot the Aircraft to success; as he stood here, his bored expression, in sharp contrast to the shrewd gray eyes that twinkled behind his spectacles, clearly indicated this fact; but a little kindness had won him to befriend the young people and he had rendered them staunch support.

On Thatcher Allen 's arm was a slender girl dressed all in black, the nodding sable plumes of whose broad hat nearly hid Mary Eliska from view as the two girls exchanged a kiss. Sybil Allen had no claim to beauty except for her dark eyes—so fathomless and mysterious that they awed all but her most intimate friends, and puzzled even them.

And now an awkward young fellow—six feet three and built like an athlete—slouched bashfully forward and gripped Mary Eliska's outstretched hand. Here was the press agent of the Stricklin-Thatcher Allen alliance, Mr. H. Chesterton Radley-Todd; a most astonishing youth who impressed strangers as being a dummy and his friends as the possessor of a rarely keen intellect. Mary Eliska smiled at him; there was something humorous about Radley-Todd's loose-jointed, unwieldy personality. Then she took her brother's arm and passed through the eager, admiring throng to the automobile in waiting.

Beside Thatcher Allen 's car stood a handsome equipage that had been sent for Miss Dentry's party, and as Mary Eliska nodded to her recent acquaintances Sybil Allen inquired: "Who is that girl?"

"A Miss Dentry, of New York, with whom I exchanged some remarks on the train. She has a yacht in the bay here."

"Oh, yes; I've heard all about her," returned Sybil, indifferently. "She's dreadfully rich; rather snubbed New York society, which was eager to idolize her—says she's too young for the weary, heart-breaking grind—and indulges in such remarkable fancies that she's getting herself talked about. I hope you didn't encourage her advances, Mary Eliska?"

"I fear I did," was the laughing reply; "but she seemed very nice and agreeable—for a rich girl. Tell me, Bill," she added, turning to her brother, "what news of the Hydro-Aircraft?"

"It's great, Mary Eliska! I put the finishing touches on it night before last, and yesterday Thatcher Allen and I took a trial spin in it. It carries two beautifully," he exclaimed, his eyes sparkling with enthusiasm.

"Did you go over the water?" asked Mary Eliska.

"Nearly half a mile. Then we dropped and let the engine paddle us home. Of all the hydro-airplanes yet invented, Sis, mine will do the most stunts and do them with greater ease."

They were rolling swiftly toward the ferry now, bound for the Hotel del Coronado, a rambling pile of Spanish architecture that dominates the farther side of San Diego Bay. Presently the car took its place in the line of vehicles on the ferry and Thatcher Allen, who was driving, shut off the power and turned to Mary Eliska.

"You are advertised to exhibit the new Hydro-Aircraft the first day of the meet—that's Monday," he announced. "Do you think you can master the mechanism by that time?"

"Is it the same old engine, Bill?" she inquired.

"Exactly the same, except that I've altered the controlling levers, to make them handy both in the air and on water, and balanced the weight a little differently, to allow for the boat attachment."

"How did you do that?"

"Placed the gasoline tanks in the rear. That makes the engine feed from the back, instead of from directly overhead, you see."

Mary Eliska nodded.

"I think I can manage it, Thatcher Allen," she decided. "Will Bill go with me on Monday?"

"Why—no," returned the manager, a trifle embarrassed. "Our fool press agent had an idea the event would be more interesting if two girls made the flight out to sea, and the trip back by boat. Sybil has been crazy to go, and so I let Chesty Todd have his own way."

"You see, Miss Stricklin," added Mr. H. Chesterton Radley-Todd, who was seated beside Thatcher Allen, while Bill and the two girls rode behind, "the management of the meet couldn't get another aviatress to take part, because you had been engaged to fly. The other air-maids are all jealous of your reputation and popularity, I guess, so the management was in despair. The dear public is daffy, just now, to watch a female risk her precious life; it's more thrilling than when a male ventures it. So, as they're paying us pretty big money, and Miss Allen was anxious to go, I—er—er—I——"

"It is quite satisfactory to me," announced Mary Eliska quietly. "I shall enjoy having Sybil with me."

"I knew you wouldn't object," said Sybil.

"The only thing I don't like about it," observed Bill, reflectively, "is the fact that you have never yet seen my Hydro-Aircraft. It's safe enough, either on land or water; but if the thing balks—as new inventions sometimes do—there will be no one aboard to help you remedy the fault, and the invention is likely to get a black eye."

"Give me a tool bag and I'll do as well as any mechanician," responded Mary Eliska, confidently. "And your Hy is not going to balk, Bill, for I shall know as much about it as you do by Monday."

CHAPTER 8.2
THE GIRL WITH THE AIRPLANE

The morning following Mary Eliska's arrival, which was the Saturday preceding the meet, she went with her brother Bill to his hangar, which was located near the Glenn Curtiss aviation camp on a low bluff overlooking the Pacific. There the two spent the entire forenoon in a careful inspection of the new Hydro-Aircraft.

As she had told Madeline Dentry, the Flying Girl never wittingly took chances in the dangerous profession she followed. The remarkable success of her aërial performances was due to an exact knowledge of every part of her airplane. She knew what each bolt and brace was for and how much strain it would stand; she knew to a feather's weight the opposition of the planes to the air, the number of revolutions to drive the engine under all conditions and the freaks of the unreliable atmospheric currents. And aside from this knowledge she had that prime quality known as "the aviator's instinct"—the intuition what to do in emergencies, and the coolness to do it promptly.

Bill Stricklin, who adored his pretty little sister, had not the slightest fear for her. As she had stood at his side during the construction of his first successful airplane and learned such mechanical principles of flying as he himself knew, he had no doubt she could readily comprehend the adaptation he had made to convert his Aircraft into the amphibious thing that could navigate air and water alike.

"It seems to me quite perfect, Bill," was Mary Eliska's final verdict. "There is no question but the Hydro-Aircraft will prove more useful to the world than any simple airplane. If we could carry gasoline enough, I would venture across the Pacific in this contrivance. By the way, what am I to do on Monday? Must I carry Sybil in any certain direction, or for any given distance?"

"I'll let Chesty explain that," said Bill, turning to the youthful press agent, who had just then entered the hangar in company with Thatcher Allen and Sybil.

"Why, er—er—a certain program has been announced, you know," explained Chesty Todd; "but that doesn't count, of course. We'll say that owing to high winds, contrary air currents, or some other excuse, you had to alter your plans. That'll satisfy the dear public, all right."

Mary Eliska frowned slightly.

"You mustn't compromise me in such ways, Mr. Todd," she exclaimed. "The Stricklin-Thatcher Allen Camp has the reputation of fulfilling its engagements to the letter; but if you promise impossible things of course we cannot do them."

The young man flushed. In the presence of Mary Eliska this big fellow was as diffident as a schoolboy.

"I—I didn't think I promised too much," he stammered. "There are two or three islands off this coast, known as the Coronado Islands. The big one—you can see it plainly from here—is named Sealskin. No one knows why. There are seals there, and they have skins. Perhaps that's the reason. Or they may all be related, and the seals' kin play together on the rocks."

"Be sensible, Chesty!" This from Thatcher Allen, rather impatiently.

"I'm quite sensible of Miss Stricklin's annoyance," resumed Mr. Radley-Todd, "but I hope she will find her task easy. She has merely to fly to Sealskin Island, a dozen or fifteen miles—perhaps twenty—and alight on the bosom of the blue Pacific. Mighty poetical in the advertisements, eh? Then she'll ride back in motor boat fashion. When she approaches the shore she is to mount into the air again, circle around the hotel and land on the aviation field before the grand stand. If any part of this program seems difficult, we can cut it out and tell the reporters——"

"Bill," interrupted Mary Eliska, "can I rise from the water into the air?"

"Of course. That's my pet invention. While skimming along the water you lift this lever, free the propeller, then point your elevator and—up you go!"

"Run out the machine. We will make a trial and you shall show me how it is done. The rest of Chesty's program seems easy enough, and if I master this little trick of rising from the water we will carry out our contract to the letter."

"All right. Your costume is in that little dressing room in the corner, Sis."

While his sister donned her short skirt, leggings and helmet, Bill Stricklin called his mechanicians and had the Hydro-Aircraft rolled out of the hangar and headed toward the ocean. For himself, he merely put on a sweater and his cap and visor, being ready long before Mary Eliska appeared.

The inventor seldom flew his own craft, for an accidental fall had lamed him so that he was not as expert an aviator as his sister had proved to be. He was recovering from his hurt, however, and hoped the injured leg would soon be good as new. Meantime Mary Eliska was doing more to render the Stricklin Aircraft famous than any man might have done.

A wire fence encircled the Stricklin-Thatcher Allen Camp for some distance, except on the ocean side, where the bluff protected it from invasion. There was an entrance gate adjoining the beach road, and while the assembled party awaited Mary Eliska's appearance Bill noticed that a motor car stopped at the gateway and a man and woman alighted and entered the enclosure, leisurely approaching the spot where the Hydro-Aircraft stood.

"Oh!" exclaimed Sybil, whose dark eyes were far-seeing; "it's that girl who owns the yacht, Madeline what's-her-name."

"Dentry," said Bill. "I wonder if Mary Eliska invited her here. Go and meet them, Chesty, and find out."

Mr. Radley-Todd promptly unlimbered his long legs and advanced to meet Madeline and Mr. Tupper. The press agent had an unlimited command of language when driving his pen over paper, but was notably awkward in expressing himself conversationally. He now stopped short before the visitors, removed his hat and said:

"I—er—pardon me, but—er—was your appointment for this hour?"

"Is Miss Stricklin here, sir?" asked Madeline, unabashed.

"She is, Miss—er—er——"

"Dentry."

"Oh; thank you."

"Then I will see her," and she took a step forward. But Chesty Todd did not move his huge bulk out of the way. So many curious and bold people were prone to intrude on all aviators, and especially on Miss Stricklin, that it was really necessary to deny them in a positive manner in order to secure any privacy at all. The press agent, in his halting way, tried to explain.

"We—er—Miss Stricklin—is about to—er—test the powers of our new Hydro-Aircraft, and I regret to say that—er—er—the test is private, you know."

"How fortunate that we came just now!" cried Madeline, eagerly, as she flashed her most winning smile on the young man. "Please lead us directly to Miss Stricklin, sir."

"Yes; of course; please lead us to Miss Stricklin," echoed Mr. Tupper pompously.

Chesty succumbed and led them to the group surrounding the machine, just as Mary Eliska emerged from the hangar. Recognizing her recent traveling companion, the Flying Girl ran up and greeted her cordially, introducing her and Mr. Tupper to the others present.

"I'm going to try out our new Hy," she said, with a laugh. "'Hy,' you must know, is my abbreviation of the Hydro-Aircraft—too long a word altogether. If you will promise not to criticize us, in case we foozle, you are welcome to watch our performance."

"That will be glorious," returned Madeline. "We have been to the bay to inspect the *Salvador*, my new yacht, but being anxious to see your new Aircraft and hoping to find you here, we ventured to stop for a few minutes. Forgive us if we intruded."

She spoke so frankly and was so evidently unconscious of being unwelcome that the entire group accepted her presence and that of her uncle without murmur.

Bill took his place in the "Hy" and Mary Eliska sat beside him.

The motor boat attachment, which took the place of the ordinary running gear, was of sheet aluminum, as light and yet as strongly built as was possible for a thing intended to be practical. Adjustable wheels, which could be folded back when the boat was in the water, were placed on either side, to give the craft a land start. The huge engine was beautiful in appearance, while the planes—a crossed arrangement peculiar to the Stricklin Aircraft—were immaculately white in their graceful spread.

"This upper plane," said Bill, proud to explain the marvels of his latest mechanical pet, "is so arranged that its position may be altered by means of a lever. If you're on the water and want to save gasoline you adjust the plane as a sail and let the wind drive you."

"Clever! Very clever, indeed," observed Mr. Tupper. "I had no idea these flying machines had been improved so much since I last saw an aviation meet, some six months ago."

"The art of flying is still in its infancy, sir," replied Thatcher Allen . "It is progressing with wonderful strides, however, and young Stricklin is one of those remarkable geniuses who keep a pace ahead of the procession."

Even as he spoke Bill started the engine, and as the first low rumble of the propeller increased to a roar the machine darted forward, passed the edge of the bluff and, rising slightly, sped over the placid waters of the Pacific, straight out from shore.

He did not rise very high, but half a mile or so out the aviator described a half-circle and then, as gracefully as a swan, sank to the surface of the ocean. Instantly a white wake of foam appeared at the rear of the boat, showing that the propeller was now churning the water. And now, with speed that to the observers appeared almost incredible, the Hydro-Aircraft approached the shore. A few yards from the bluff it abruptly rose from the water, sailed above the heads of the spectators, and after a circle of the field, came to a halt at almost the exact spot from which it had started.

This remarkable performance had taken place in so brief a space of time that those on the bluff had scarcely moved during the entire period. They now hastened forward to congratulate the inventor. Thatcher Allen 's grim features were for once wreathed in smiles; Chesty Todd capered like a schoolboy and flung his hat into the air as he yelled "Hooray!" while Sybil impulsively grasped Bill's hand in both of her own. As for Madeline Dentry, she eyed the young man wonderingly, asking herself if the marvel she seemed to have witnessed had actually occurred.

"Do you know," said Mr. Tupper, his voice trembling with excitement, "I wouldn't much mind a ride like that myself!"

Mary Eliska was much pleased with this successful test of the new machine's powers. As the men wheeled the Hydro-Aircraft back to its hangar she turned to Chesty and said:

"I forgive you, sir. Really, you were too modest in your promises. Sybil and I will carry out your program to the entire satisfaction of the management and the public, I am positive."

"I can hardly wait for Monday, Sis," exclaimed Sybil. "If father wasn't so afraid, I would learn to navigate the Hy myself."

"Ah, you interest me, my dear," returned her father, blandly; "you do, really. But as your talents will never enable you to rival Mary Eliska it will be well for you to curb your ambitions. I've conceded a lot, to allow you to go with her on that long jaunt Monday."

"You have, indeed," laughed Mary Eliska. "But Sybil and I will have a real joy ride, and be perfectly safe in the bargain. How long a time will the trip take us, Bill?"

"Oh, a couple of hours, or so; it will depend on whether the current is favorable to your paddling back. In the air you can do forty miles an hour, easily."

"We will take some lunch with us," said Sybil. "Don't forget to order it, Daddy."

Thatcher Allen nodded. Unimpressionable as this strange man seemed, his daughter was verily the "apple of his eye" and he was not likely to forget anything that might add to her comfort. Sybil's desire to aviate had been a constant source of disturbance to her father. He had worried a good deal over Mary Eliska, during her first attempts to fly, but was now convinced of the girl's capability and, although he exhibited nervousness every time she gave one of her exhibitions, he had by degrees acquired supreme confidence in her skill. Still, being thoroughly experienced in all aviation matters, through his connection with the Stricklin Aircraft, Thatcher Allen realized that flying is always accompanied by danger, and whenever an aviator met with an accident on the field he was wont to inform Sybil that on no account could she ever accompany Mary Eliska again in a flight. He would even urge Mary Eliska to abandon the dangerous work; but she answered him gravely: "This accident, as well as all others I ever heard of, was the result of carelessness and inexperience. The more flights I make the less liable am I to encounter accident. Perhaps I realize better than you do, Thatcher Allen, the elements of danger, and that is the reason I am so careful to avoid every hazard."

Flying was an intoxication to Sybil. She never had enough of it and always complained to Mary Eliska that their flights were of too short duration. Each time she was obliged to plead and argue with her father for days, before obtaining his consent to let her go, and even now, when he had given his reluctant permission to Chesty Todd to advertise Sybil as the companion of the Flying Girl, he was frequently impelled to forbid the adventure. His only consolation was that the new invention seemed very safe and practical, and with Mary Eliska's guiding hands at the levers his beloved daughter would be as well guarded as possible under such conditions.

As a matter of fact, protests from Thatcher Allen had little value, as Sybil possessed a knack of getting her own way under any and all circumstances. She had really no great desire to operate an airplane herself, being quite content to remain a passenger and enjoy the freedom of riding, untrammeled by the necessity of being alert every instant to control the machine.

Mary Eliska, excusing herself, retired to the hangar to change her costume, and the young inventor was left to listen to the enthusiastic comments of his friends.

"When will your Hydro-Aircraft be on the market, Mr. Stricklin?" asked Madeline.

"In the course of the next three months we expect to complete two other machines," he replied.

"I want one of them," she said quickly. "Will you teach me how to operate it?"

"Of course," he answered. "That is part of the bargain. But you have not asked the price, and for all business transactions I must refer you to Thatcher Allen ."

"Madeline, my dear! My dear Madeline!" protested Mr. Tupper; "what in the world are you thinking of?"

"That I would give Thatcher Allen a check at once," she calmly answered.

"But I—we—that is, I can't permit it; I—I really can't allow it, my dear!" asserted the gentleman, evidently alarmed by her positive attitude.

Madeline's slight form stiffened and her eyes flashed defiantly.

"Mr. Tupper," said she to her uncle, "do I employ you to advise me, or to manage my business affairs?"

That he was greatly humiliated by this attack was evident. His face grew red and he half turned away, hesitating to make reply. Then Thatcher Allen came to Mr. Tupper's assistance.

"Your—eh—friend—is quite right, Miss Dentry; quite right to oppose your—eh—reckless impulse, if I may put it that way. Your enthusiasm interests me; it—eh—interests me greatly; but for your own welfare and the comfort of mind of your friends, I should advise you to—eh—curb your adventurous spirit, for the present. You have what is known as the 'Flying Fever,' which attacks the most conservative people when on the aviation field. Let it alone and it will dissipate, in time; but if you nurse it you—eh—buy a flying machine and become a slave. We have machines to sell, you know; we are anxious to dispose of all we can; but kindly keep your check for three months, and if at the end of that time you are still disposed to purchase, I will deliver the machine to you promptly."

"How can you do that? The demand will be greater than your ability to build the Hydro-Aircraft, after the exhibition of next Monday," she affirmed.

Thatcher Allen regarded her thoughtfully.

"I believe you are right," said he. "Anyhow, I hope you are right. But I'll promise to reserve a machine, pending your decision. Young ladies who are seriously determined to become aviators and who—eh—have the means to indulge the fad to any extent, are rare; very rare. Therefore, my dear Miss Dentry, you—eh—interest me, and I'll keep my promise."

Madeline could not refuse to admit the fairness of Thatcher Allen 's proposition, and Mr. Tupper was grateful to him for his efficient support, so harmony was once more restored. Sybil, indeed, smiled derisively as she exchanged a meaning glance with Madeline—a glance that said as intelligently as words: "How clever these men think themselves, and how helpless they really are to oppose us!"

Then Miss Dentry invited them all, including Chesty Todd, to dine on board her yacht the next day, which was Sunday, and the invitation being promptly accepted they all motored back to the hotel.

CHAPTER 8.3
A PRODIGY IN AERONAUTICS

San Diego Bay is always interesting, with its shipping from all ports of the world, but on this gorgeous Sunday afternoon there was no prettier sight among the scattered craft than the trim yacht *Salvador*, lying at anchor just north of the ferry path. The Stricklin-Thatcher Allen party found a small launch awaiting them at the pier, which quickly took them aboard the big white yacht, where Madeline, attired in appropriate sailor costume, cordially welcomed them.

"This affair is fully as great a novelty to me as it must be to you," she explained, as they cast admiring glances over the decks. "I bought the boat of an Englishman several months ago, with the understanding it should be delivered to me here; but I only arrived to claim it the day before yesterday. It has a crew of seven, besides the chef, who, I must admit, is my own selection, as I feared to trust the English taste in cookery. The English crew, however, seems capable and every man jack wants to stay with the boat; so I've agreed to keep them. I'll introduce you to the skipper presently. He rejoices in the title of 'Captain' and has quite awed me with his superior manner and splendid uniform. But I'll introduce you to the creations of my chef, first, for dinner is waiting. Forgive Monsieur Champetre, if he falls down occasionally; he is as unused to the kitchen—or is it scullery? Oh, I know; the 'galley'—as I am to the cabin."

Really the chef needed no excuses, and after the meal they made a thorough inspection of the beautiful craft, peeping into the state-rooms, the men's quarters and even into the sacred galley. Everyone aboard, including the big, bluff skipper, was so proud of the boat that he delighted to have it exhibited, and when it was understood that the slim, beautiful young lady guest was the famous Flying Girl the deference shown Mary Eliska was amusing.

"I had intended to test the *Salvador* tomorrow and make a short run to sea in it," said Madeline; "but I am so eager to witness the aërial exhibitions that I shall postpone the voyage until later. My yacht is permanent, but this Aviation Meet is temporary."

The visitors returned to their hotel early in the afternoon, for Mary Eliska and Sybil had still a few preparations to make for the morrow's trip, while Bill and Thatcher Allen decided to pay a visit to the aviation field, to which both the Stricklin Aircraft and the Stricklin Hydro-Aircraft had been removed by the mechanicians in charge of them. Chesty Todd's labors that Sunday evening were perhaps more onerous than those of the others of his party, for he had to meet an aggressive band of newspaper reporters and load each one to the brim with material for a double-header next morning. Having served as a journalist—and an able one—himself, Mr. Radley-Todd understood exactly the sort of priming these publicity guns required.

The home of the Stricklins was a delightful orange ranch near Los Angeles, where the blind mother of Bill and Mary Eliska—their only parent—lived surrounded by every comfort and devoted attendants, while her boy and girl were engaged in the novel and somewhat hazardous exhibitions of the new Stricklin Aircraft. Mary Eliska had remained at home with her mother while Bill was perfecting his latest machine at San Diego, and had not left there until it was necessary to prepare for the Meet, in which she had engaged to take part. Mrs. Stricklin, perhaps because of her blindness, seemed to have little anxiety on account of her daughter's ventures, although at the time of Mary Eliska's first flights her nervousness had been poignant. Assured of her girl's skill and coolness, the mother had come to accept these occasions philosophically, as far as the danger was concerned, and she was naturally interested in Bill's inventions and overjoyed at the financial success which Thatcher Allen 's business ability had already insured the firm.

This Sunday evening Mary Eliska wrote a long letter to her mother, telling how perfectly her brother's new machine worked, and assuring Mrs. Stricklin of her confidence in winning new laurels for Bill on the morrow. "The latest engine, made for the Hy, is more powerful than were the others," she added, "but its operation is practically the same and while the combination of boat and aircraft necessitated a more complicated arrangement of the control, I have easily mastered all the details and could take the whole thing apart and put it together again, if obliged to do so."

The girl slept peacefully that night and neither she nor Sybil were in the least nervous when they went to the aviation field, overlooking the sea, after an early luncheon on Monday.

They found the Stricklin Hydro-Aircraft reposing majestically in its hangar, in perfect order and constantly surrounded by a group of admiring and interested spectators. The little band of professional aviators present at the Meet welcomed Mary Eliska very cordially, for every one of them knew and admired the brave girl who had so often proved her ability to manage her brother's machines.

The grand stand was packed with spectators, and long rows of automobiles lined the edge of the enclosure reserved for the exhibitors.

The "Stricklin Event," as it was called, was early on the program of the day, for it was understood that the flight over the ocean and the voyage back would consume much of the afternoon. Many had brought binoculars and other powerful glasses to watch the Flying Girl and her chum during their progress.

Sealskin Island lay a little to the south of the aviation field and was one of a group of barren rocks jutting out of the sea and plainly visible from the mainland. The Coronado Islands, which have little or no value, belong to Mexico, as the Mexican boundary is only twelve miles south of San Diego, and this group, although not appearing to be so far south, is below the line claimed by the United States. Therefore Mary Eliska's flight would be in a southwesterly direction and most of her journey made in plain view of every spectator.

As the "Hy" was run out to the center of the field Bill said to Mary Eliska:

"I've anchored an aluminum chest just back of your seats, at the suggestion of Thatcher Allen . In it are all the tools you could possibly need in case of emergency, a couple of warm blankets to use if your return trip proves chilly, and enough 'lunch'—which I think Sybil pleaded for—to last you both a week. The chest enables you to carry all this safely and comfortably, and it won't be at all in your way. Personally, I think such a precaution wholly unnecessary, but Thatcher Allen is a good deal of an old woman where Sybil is concerned and it is easier to give up to him than to try to argue him out of an idea. Take the trip easy, Sis; we don't need to make time. What we want to demonstrate is the practicability of the machine, and we ourselves already know that it is thoroughly practical, and we therefore ought to be able to convince the world of the fact."

Mary Eliska nodded.

"How about gasoline?" she asked.

"Both tanks are filled. There's enough to run you a hundred miles in air and fifty miles in water, which is far more than you will require. Be gentle with the steering gear; it is such a long connection that it doesn't respond as readily as the old one, and I guess I've made the rods a trifle too light. I mean to rig up a more substantial device as soon as I get time, but this will do you all right if you don't jerk it. Put a little more strength to the wheel and turn it gradually, that's all."

"I understand," she replied. "Are you ready, Sybil?"

"Waiting on you, Sis."

"And I think the crowd is waiting on us."

The band was at this moment playing its loudest and most stirring tune and as the two venturesome girls, dressed in appropriate aërial costume, appeared on the field, wildly enthusiastic shouts rose from ten thousand spectators. Chesty Todd had decorated the braces of the machine with bunches of fresh violets and the aluminum and nickeled parts shone gloriously in the sun.

"Be good, Sybil," said Thatcher Allen. "Take care of her, Mary Eliska."

The girls laughed, for this was the old gentleman's customary parting warning.

"All right, Sis," said Bill.

She applied the power and one of the mechanicians gave the propeller a preliminary whirl. Then Mary Eliska threw in the automatic clutch that started the machine and it ran forward a few feet and promptly rose into the air. A moment later it was speeding straight out to sea, at an altitude of a hundred feet, and the wonderful voyage of Bill Stricklin's new Hydro-Aircraft was begun—a voyage destined to vary considerably from the program mapped out for it.

CHAPTER 8.4
THE ALUMINUM CHEST

Mary Eliska realized quite perfectly that Sealskin Island was much farther away from the mainland than it appeared, so on leaving the shore she pursued a direction straight west for several miles, intending to make a turn and proceed south to the island which was the terminus of her flight. That prolonged the trip somewhat, but she figured it would prove more interesting to the spectators, since for a part of the journey she would be flying parallel with the coast. On the return she planned to run straight back from the island.

When she decided they had reached a point about as far out as was the island, she attempted to make the turn—a mere segment of a circle—but in spite of Bill's warning Mary Eliska was surprised at the stiffness of the steering gear. The engines were working beautifully and developing excellent speed, but the girl found she must apply all her strength to the wheel to make the turn.

She succeeded, and brought the head to bear directly upon the island, but the gear grated and stuck so persistently that Mary Eliska's effort sent the entire craft careening at a steep angle. Sybil gave a gasp and clung to the supporting rods and both girls heard a loud "chug" that indicated something was wrong; but the Stricklin balancing device was so perfect that almost immediately the machine righted itself and regained its equilibrium, darting swiftly and in a straight line in the direction of the island.

"What was it?" asked Sybil, putting her head close to Mary Eliska's to be heard above the whir of the motors behind them.

"The steering gear binds; that's all," was the quiet response. "I think it will work better when we are in the water."

"But what made that noise? Didn't something give way?" persisted Sybil.

"Glance behind us, dear, and see."

Sybil carefully turned so as to examine the parts of the airplane.

"Oh!" she exclaimed.

"Well?" said Mary Eliska.

"That chest that Bill loaded us with. It has broken away from its fastenings and is jammed edge downward against your gear."

Mary Eliska thought about it.

"That's unfortunate," said she. "I suppose the bolts broke when we tipped so badly. But it hasn't interfered with our engines any."

"No," answered Sybil, still examining the conditions; "but it has interfered seriously with your control, I fear. Both your levers are thrown out of position and even the front elevator bars are badly bent."

For the first time a worried expression appeared on Mary Eliska's face.

"If that is true," she said, "our best plan is to return at once."

"Do," urged Sybil, her dark eyes very serious.

Mary Eliska tried to turn the wheel. It resisted. She applied more strength. Something snapped and the released wheel whirled so freely that the girl nearly lost her seat. Recovering instantly she turned a pale face to her companion and said:

"We're wrecked, Sybil. But don't worry. With the boat under us and in this quiet sea we shall be quite safe."

"I'm not worrying—especially—Sis," was the reply; "but it occurs to me to wonder how you're going to get down to the ocean."

"Why?"

"You can't stop the engines, unless one of us crawls back over the planes."

"I can cut off the spark." She tried it, but the engines chugged as merrily as before. "Guess there must be a short circuit," gasped Mary Eliska.

"And you can't depress your elevator, I'm sure."

"I'll try it," announced Mary Eliska, grimly.

But the fatal chest balked her attempt. The elevator was steadfastly wedged into its present position; the engines were entirely beyond control and the two helpless girls faced one of the most curious conditions ever known in the history of aviation.

At an altitude of perhaps a hundred and fifty feet from the water the airplane sped swiftly on its way, headed a trifle to the west of south. It passed Sealskin Island even while the girls were discussing their dilemma, and stubbornly maintained its unfaltering course. The air conditions were perfect for flying; scarcely a breath of wind was felt; the sky above was blue as azure.

Suddenly Sybil laughed.

"What now?" demanded Mary Eliska.

"I was thinking of the consternation on shore at about this moment," explained Miss Allen. "Won't they be amazed to see us continue this course, beyond the island? Not understanding our trouble, Daddy will think we're running away."

"So we are," replied Mary Eliska. "I wish I knew where we are running to."

"I suppose we can't stop 'til the gasoline gives out," said Sybil.

Mary Eliska shook her head.

"That's what scares me," she admitted. "Even now the Mexican shore is a mere line at the left. We're gradually diverging to a point farther out at sea, and when at last we alight, drained of the last drop of gasoline, how are we to run the boat back?"

"We can't. Bill's wonderful Hy will become a mere floating buoy on the bosom of the rolling blue," responded Sybil lightly. "Oh, I'm so glad I came, Sis! I'd no idea we were going to have such fun."

Mary Eliska did not return her chum's smile.

"Sit still and balance her, Sybil," she said. "I'm going to make an investigation."

Exercising the necessary caution she turned and knelt upon the foot bar, clinging to the seat rail and in this position facing the Aircraft so she could examine its mechanism. Sybil had described the condition of things quite accurately. The engine control was cut off and as the gasoline tanks fed from the rear Mary Eliska had no way of stopping the flow. The steering gear was broken and the front elevator firmly wedged in position by the chest.

"I wonder if we could manage to move this thing," she said, and getting a hand on one corner of the aluminum chest she gave a tug and tried to raise it. It proved solid and unyielding. Not heavy in itself, or perhaps in its contents, the thing was caught between the rods in such a manner that no strength of the girls, limited in movement as they were, could budge it a particle.

Realizing this, and the folly of leaving the seats to get at the gasoline feed, Mary Eliska resumed her place and faced the inevitable as bravely as she could.

"Bill told me," she said to Sybil, "that the gasoline would last a hundred miles in air and fifty in water; that's at least two hundred miles in an air line. Have you any idea where we shall be by that time?"

"Not the slightest," responded her companion, cheerfully. "Ocean, of course; but latitude and longitude a mystery—and not important, anyhow."

Sybil Allen was a reserved and silent girl on most occasions. Few were attracted toward her, on this account. Her dark eyes seemed to regard the world with critical toleration and she gave one the impression of considering herself quite independent of her fellows. Moreover, Sybil was eccentric in character and prone to do and say things that invoked the grave displeasure of her associates, seeming to delight in confusing and annoying them. But there was a brighter side to this queer girl's nature, which developed only in the society of her trusted friends. On any occasion that demanded courage and resourcefulness she came to the front nobly, and at such times Sybil Allen became vivacious, helpful and inspiriting.

Here was such an occasion. Danger was the joy of Sybil's heart and the "breath of her nostrils." Indifferent to the ordinary details of life, any adventure that promised tribulation or disaster was fervently welcomed. Then the girl's spirits rose, her intellect fairly bristled and she developed an animation and joyous exhilaration entirely at variance with her usual demeanor.

So now, as Mary Eliska, a girl of proved courage and undaunted spirit, grew solemn and anxious at the perilous condition that confronted them, Sybil Allen became gay and animated.

"It's such an unusual thing, and so wholly unexpected!" she said blithely. "I'm sure, Sis, that no two girls who ever lived—in this world or any other—ever found themselves in a like dilemma. We're as helpless as babes, chummie dear; only no babes were ever forced to fly, willy-nilly, for hundreds of miles through the air to some forlorn spot in the dank, moist ocean."

Mary Eliska let her chatter. She was trying to realize what it might mean to them and how and when, if ever, they might be rescued from their difficulties.

"Our great mistake," continued Sybil, as they swept along, "was in not rigging the machine with a wireless outfit. To be sure, neither of us could operate it; but a wireless, in such a case—if we understood its mysteries—would solve our problem."

"How?" asked Mary Eliska.

"We could call up the shore at San Diego and tell them what's happened, and give them the direction in which we are flying; then they could send a fast steamer for us, or perhaps Madeline Dentry would loan her yacht."

"They may follow us with a steamer, anyhow," said Mary Eliska, thoughtfully. "If we manage to land safely, Sybil—which means if we drop to the water right-side-up—we could float for some days, until we were found and rescued."

"Thirst is a terrible thing, at sea; and hunger is almost as bad."

"But in that dreadful chest, which has caused all our trouble, Bill told me he had packed provisions. Probably there is water there, too," asserted Mary Eliska, hopefully.

"Yes, Dad said there was lunch for two. Well, that's one good feed we shall have, anyhow, provided the chest doesn't get away from us entirely, and we can manage to open it. In its present position, neither event is at all probable."

She seemed to love to discover and point out the gloomy side of their adventure, that she might exult in the dangers that menaced them.

Meantime, swift and straight as an arrow the Aircraft continued on its course. Not a skip to the engines, not an indication of any sort that the flight would be interrupted as long as a drop of gasoline remained in the tanks. They could only be patient and await the finale as bravely as possible.

CHAPTER 8.5
THE LAST DROP OF GASOLINE

Hour after hour they flew, while each hour seemed, to Mary Eliska, at least, a month in duration. Sybil chatted and laughed, refusing to take their misfortune seriously.

"But," said she, "I'm getting famished. An air-trip always stimulates the appetite and that lunch of Bill's is so very near to us—and yet so far! I How did he expect us to get at the repast, anyhow?"

"Why, in water," replied Mary Eliska, "the chest and its contents would be handy enough. I do not think it would be safe for us to creep into the boat underneath us now, for we must maintain the aërial balance; but, even if we could get below, we couldn't open the chest while it is wedged crosswise among the braces and levers."

"All true, milady," commented Sybil, her usually pale cheeks now flushed with excitement. "Our present stunt is to 'sit still and take our medicine,' as the saying goes."

By this time the Mexican coast had vanished entirely and only the placid blue waters of the Pacific remained visible, even from the altitude of the Aircraft. Once or twice they sighted a small island, bleak and bare, for this part of the ocean is filled with tiny islets, most of which are unfertile and uninhabited. Farther along, in the South Pacific, such islands have verdure and inhabitants.

At about four o'clock a change occurred in the atmospheric conditions. A brisk wind arose, blowing steadily for a time from the southwest and then suddenly developing puffs and eddies that caused the Aircraft to wobble dangerously. One powerful gust seized the helpless flying-machine and whirled it around like a toy balloon, but failed to destroy its equilibrium because the girls balanced it with their bodies as well as they might. When their craft was released, however, it pointed in a new direction—this time straight west. An hour later a similar gust swept its head to the southward, and in this direction it was still flying when the red sun dipped into the water and twilight fell.

"I don't like this, Syb," said Mary Eliska, anxiously. "If the gasoline holds out much longer it will be dark, and when we drop our danger will be doubled."

"What will be the fashion of our dropping, anyhow?" asked Sybil. "We can't volplane, with no control of the rudder. Chances are, dear, the thing will just tip over and spill us in the damp."

"Hold fast, if it does that," cautioned Mary Eliska. "If we become separated from the boat we will drown like rats. The engine may swamp the boat, in any event, but it has air compartments which will keep it afloat under any favorable conditions, and we must trust to luck, Sybil—and to our own coolness."

"All right, Sis. A watery grave doesn't appeal to me just now," was the reply. "I'm too hungry to drown comfortably, and that's a fact. On a full stomach I imagine one could face perpetual soaking with more complacency."

"Huh!" cried Mary Eliska. "Listen!"

Sybil was already listening, fully as alert as her chum. The speed of the engine was diminishing. Gradually the huge propeller slackened its rapid revolutions, while its former roar subsided to a mere moan.

"Thank goodness," said Sybil, fervently, "the gasoline is gone at last!"

"Look out, then," warned Mary Eliska.

With a final, reluctant "chug-chug!" the engine stopped short. Like a huge gull the frail craft remained poised in the air a moment and then a sudden light breeze swept it on. It was falling, however, impelled by its own weight, and singularly enough it reversed its position and proceeded before the wind with the stem foremost.

Splash! It wasn't so bad, after all. Not a volplane, to be sure, but a gentle drop, the weight of the heavy engine sustained by the "air-cushions" formed beneath the planes.

Mary Eliska wiped the spray from her eyes.

"That would have been a regular bump, on land," Sybil was saying affably, "but the old ocean has received us with gracious tenderness. Are we sinking, Sis, or do we float?"

How suddenly the darkness was falling! Mary Eliska leaned from her seat and found the water had turned to a color nearly as black as ink. Beneath her the bow of the aluminum motor boat was so depressed that it was almost even with the water and as it bobbed up and down with the waves it was shipping the inky fluid by the dipperful.

She scrambled out of the seat, then, to step gingerly over the unlucky chest and crouch upon a narrow seat of the little boat, near the stern.

"Come, Sybil," she called; "and be very careful."

Sybil promptly descended to the boat, which now rode evenly upon the waves. In this position the propeller was just under water and the engine rested over the center of the light but strong little craft. But propeller and engine were alike useless to them now. Overhead the planes spread like huge awnings, but they carried so little weight that they did not affect the balance of the boat.

"Bill planned well," murmured Mary Eliska, with a sigh. "If only he had never thought of that dreadful chest, we would not be in this fix."

As she spoke she kicked the chest a little resentfully with her foot, and it seemed to move. Sybil leaned forward to eye it as closely as the gathering darkness would allow.

"Why, Sis," she exclaimed, "the thing has come loose. Help me to tip it up."

Between them they easily raised the chest to its former position, where it rested just before them. Bill had bolted it at either end, but one of the bolts had broken away and the other had bent at almost a right angle. Perhaps this last bolt would have broken, too, had not the chest, in falling, become wedged against the braces.

"This horrid box has heretofore been our dire enemy," remarked Sybil; "but let us be forgiving and encourage it to make amends—for it holds eatables. How does the cover open, Sis?"

Bill had shown Mary Eliska how to work the sliding catch and in a moment the girl had the lid open and held it upright while Sybil searched within.

"Hooray! We've discovered a regular cafeteria," said the latter, jubilantly, as she drew out a number of parcels. "I was afraid we'd have to nibble, Mary Eliska, so as not to gorge ourselves tonight and starve tomorrow; but I reckon there's enough to last two delicate girls like us a week. What shall we tackle first?"

"Let us plan a little, dear," suggested Mary Eliska, restraining her own eagerness, for she was hungry, too. "We cannot possibly tell tonight what this precious chest contains or how much food there really is. We must wait for daylight to take an inventory. But here are some tins, we know, which will keep, and that package of sandwiches on your lap is perishable; so I propose we confine our feast to those for tonight."

"Perishable it is, Cap'n," answered Sybil, consuming half a sandwich at a single bite. "If there's only a pickle to go with these breadspreads I shall be content. It's not only luncheon that we're indulging in, you know; it's our regular dinner, as well, and there ought to be two courses—pickles and sandwiches—at the least."

"You must feel for the pickles, then," returned Mary Eliska, intent upon her own sandwich, "for it's too dark to use eyes just now."

Sybil found the pickles—who ever put up a lunch for two girls without including pickles?—and declared she was quite content.

"If we hadn't discovered the eats, my dear Cap'n," she remarked with cheery satisfaction, "I think I could have dined on my own shoes. That's a happy thought; we'll keep the shoes in reserve. I'd no idea one's appetite could get such an edge, after being tantalized for a few hours."

"Do you realize, Sybil," asked Mary Eliska in a grave tone, as she took her second sandwich, "that we must pass the night in this wiggly, insecure boat?"

"What's insecure about it?" demanded Sybil.

"It won't stand much of a sea, I fear. This attachment to the Aircraft was intended for pleasant weather."

"All right; the weather's delightful. Those long, gentle rolls will merely rock us to sleep. And—Oh, Sis!—we'll have rolls for breakfast."

"Do be serious, Syb! Suppose a storm catches us before morning?"

"Then please wake me up. Where do you suppose we are, anyhow?"

"I've no idea," answered Mary Eliska, soberly. "We must have traveled a couple of hundred miles, but it wasn't in a straight line, by any means. Let's see. Perhaps a hundred miles on our first course—over Sealskin Island and nearly south—then forty or fifty miles north——"

"Oh, no; west."

"Yes; so it was. Then twenty-odd miles south, ten miles or so east, a couple or three miles west again, and then—and then——"

"Dear me! Don't bother your head with it, Mary Eliska. We zigzagged like a drunken man. The only fact we can positively nail is that we were getting farther away from home—or our friends, rather—every minute. That's a bad thing, come to think of it. They'll never know where to search for us."

"True," responded Mary Eliska. "But I am sure they will search, and search diligently, so we must manage to keep afloat until they find us. What shall we do now, Sybil?"

"Sleep," was the prompt reply. "If we lift this seat off—it seems to be removable—I think there is room enough for us both to cuddle down in the bottom of the boat."

"Oh, Sybil!" This from Mary Eliska, rather reproachfully.

"Well, I can't imagine anything more sensible to do," asserted her chum, with a yawn. "These air-rides not only encourage hunger, but sleep. Did you cork that bottle of water? I want another drink."

"I—I think we'd better economize on the water," suggested Mary Eliska, "at least until morning, when we can find out if there's any more in the chest."

"All right. Help me bail out this overflow and then we'll cuddle down."

"Bill said there were two blankets in the chest," said Mary Eliska, presently, when the bottom of the boat was dry. "I'll search for them."

She found the blankets easily, by feeling through the contents of the chest. Offering no further objection to Sybil's plan, she prepared their bed for the night. Neither of these girls had ever "roughed it" to any extent, but in spite of the peril of their situation and the liability of unforeseen dangers overtaking them, they were resourceful enough and courageous enough to face the conditions with a degree of intrepid interest. Afloat on an unknown part of the broad Pacific, with merely a tiny aluminum boat for protection, with final escape from death uncertain and chances of rescue remote, these two carefully nurtured young girls, who had enjoyed loving protection all their lives, were so little influenced by fear that they actually exchanged pleasantries as they spread their blankets and rolled themselves in the coverings for the night.

"The lack of a pillow bothers me most," remarked Sybil. "I think I shall rest my head on one of those cans of baked beans."

"I advise you not to; you might eat them in your sleep," was Mary Eliska's comment.

"May I rest my head upon you, chummie dear?"

"You may not. Try the engine."

"That's hard. And there are enough wheels in my head already, without pounding my ear with them. Suggest something else."

"Your own elbow, then."

"Thanks, dear. Where's that slab of aluminum that used to be a seat?"

It was a happy thought and furnished them both with a headrest. The seat was not an ideal pillow, but it answered the purpose because there was nothing better.

CHAPTER 8.6
CASTAWAYS

"Well, I declare!" exclaimed Mary Eliska, sitting up.

After a moment Sybil said, sleepily:

"Go ahead and declare it, Sis. Only, if we're drowned, please break the news to me gently!"

"How strange!" muttered Mary Eliska, still staring.

Sybil stirred, threw off the blanket and also rose to a sitting position.

"If it's a secret," she began, "then—Oh, goodness me!"

During the night the boat with its great overhead planes had gently floated into a little bay, where the water was peaceful as a millpond. Two points of black rock projected on either side of them, outlining the bay. Between these points appeared an island—a mass of tumbled rocks guiltless of greenery. There was a broad strip of clean, smooth sand on the shore, barely covering the slaty ledge, but back of that the jumble of rocks began, forming irregular hillocks, and beyond these hillocks, which extended for some distance inland, there seemed to be a great dip in the landscape—or rockscape—far back of which arose a low mountain formed of the same unlovely material as all else.

"It's an island!" gasped Sybil, rubbing her eyes to make sure they were working properly. "Now, see here, Cap'n Sis, I want it understood right now which one of us is to be Robinson Crusoe and which the Man Friday. Seems to me, I being the passenger and you the charioteer, the prestige is on my side; so I claim the Crusoe part. I can't grow whiskers, and I'm not likely to find a parrot to perch on my shoulder, but I'll promise to enact the part as well as circumstances will permit."

"I can't see a sign of life," announced Mary Eliska, regretfully. "There isn't even a bird hovering over the place."

"Lizards and snakes among the rocks, though, I'll bet," responded Sybil, with a grimace. "All these rocky Pacific islands are snaky, they say. I wonder if I can learn to charm 'em. You don't object to my being Crusoe, do you?"

Mary Eliska sighed; then she turned to her cheery comrade with a smile.

"Not at all," said she. "But I'll be Columbus, the Discoverer, for I've discovered a desert island while you were peacefully dreaming."

"There's no desert about your island," stated Sybil. "A desert would be a relief. What you've discovered, Miss Sis Columbus—or what's discovered us, rather—is a rock heap."

"Desert or not, it's deserted, all right," maintained Mary Eliska.

"And you may not have discovered it, after all," said Sybil, musingly examining the place. "These seas have been pretty well explored, I guess, and although no nation would particularly care to pin a flag to this bunch of rocks, the maps may indicate it clearly."

"Ah, if we only had a map!" cried Mary Eliska eagerly.

"What good would it do us?" asked Sybil. "It couldn't help us to find ourselves, for we don't know what especial dot on the map we've arrived at. With Muggins' Complete Atlas in hand, and a geography teacher thrown in, we wouldn't be able to pick out this island from the ones that litter these seas."

"That is, unfortunately, quite true," sighed Mary Eliska; "and anyhow it's not worth an argument because we have no map. But we must be up and doing, Sybil. If we are to keep ourselves alive, we must take advantage of every favorable circumstance."

"What time is it?" yawned Sybil.

Mary Eliska looked at her watch.

"A little after six."

"Call me at eight. I can't get up at six o'clock; it's too early, entirely."

"But you went to bed at about seven."

"Did I? Well, how about breakfast?"

"We must inspect our stores and take inventory. Then we must plan to make the provisions last as long as possible."

"How dreadful! Why, this is a real adventure, Sis—threatened famine, and all that. We're regular castaways, like we read about in the fifteen-cent story magazines, and I wouldn't be surprised if we had to endure many inconveniences; would you?"

"Sybil," said Mary Eliska earnestly, "we are face to face with privation, danger, and perhaps death. I'm glad you can be cheerful, but we must understand our terrible position and endeavor to survive as long as possible. We know very well that our friends will have a hard time finding us, for they cannot guess what part of the ocean we descended in. It may take days—perhaps weeks—for them to discover us in this dreary place, and meantime we must guard our safety to the best of our ability."

"Naturally," agreed Sybil, duly impressed by this speech. "Your head is clearer and better than mine, Mary Eliska; so you shall take command, and I'll gladly follow your instructions.

You mean to land, don't you? I'm tired of this cramped little boat and even a rocky island is better than no refuge at all."

"Of course we must land," replied Mary Eliska; "and that, I think, must be our first task. The shore is only a stone's throw from here, but we're fast on a sand bar, and how to get off is a problem."

Sybil began to take off her leggings, then her shoes and stockings.

"We'll wade," she said.

Mary Eliska peered over the side.

"It's very shallow. I think we can wade to shore, Syb, and pull the Hy in after us. We must get the whole thing high and dry on the beach, if possible."

Sybil plumbed the water by tying a can of sardines to a cord from around one of the parcels.

"I guess we can make it all right, Cap'n," she said. "It's not very deep."

"It may be a lot deeper closer in. But I guess we'll have to take a chance on it. And if the worst comes to the worst we *can* dry our clothes on the beach.»

The sun was showing brilliantly above the horizon as the two girls stepped into the water. Both could swim fairly well, but where the boat was grounded on the sand bar the water was scarcely knee-deep. They dragged Bill's invention over the bar with little difficulty, the wheels materially assisting their efforts. Beyond the bar the water deepened in spots, and once, as they drew the wrecked Hy after them, the waves reached perilously high. Then they struck the shelving beach and found hard sand under their feet.

By pushing and hauling energetically they managed to run the boat, with its attached planes, to the shore, where the wheels on either side enabled them to roll it up the slope until, as Mary Eliska said, it was "high and dry."

"Seems to me," remarked Sybil, panting, "we ought to have breakfasted first, for all this exercise has made me ravenous. That'll diminish our precious store of eatables considerably, I fear."

With the machine safely landed they proceeded to dress themselves, after which Mary Eliska arranged upon the sand the entire contents of the aluminum chest. A kit of tools, adapted for use on the Aircraft, together with some extra bolts, a strut or two and a coil of steel wire were first placed carefully on one side.

"With these," said the girl, "I can easily repair the damage to our machine."

"But what's the use, without gasoline?" asked Sybil.

Mary Eliska had no reply to this. She proceeded to inspect the provisions. Thatcher Allen had a way of always providing enough for a regiment when he intended to feed a few, so in ordering lunch for two girls on an aërial voyage his usual prodigality had been in evidence. Perhaps with an intuition that a delay or even an accident might occur to Sybil and Mary Eliska, the old gentleman had even exceeded his record, in this instance. A big box of dainty sandwiches had been supplemented by three cartons of biscuits, a whole Edam cheese, a bottle of pickles, two huge packages of cakes and eighteen tins of provisions, provided with keys for opening them. These consisted of sardines, potted ham and chicken, baked beans, chipped beef and the like. In another parcel was a whole roasted duck, in still another an apple pie, while two jars of jam completed the list of edibles. For the voyagers to drink Thatcher Allen had added two half-gallon jars of distilled water, a bottle of grape juice, two of ginger ale and one of lemonade.

The girls examined this stock with profound gravity.

"I wish," said Mary Eliska, "there had been more bread and biscuits, for we are going to need the substantials rather more than the delicacies."

"Thank goodness we have anything!" exclaimed Sybil. "I suppose we must breakfast on the cakes and jam, and save the other truck until later."

"That's the idea," approved Mary Eliska. "The cakes won't keep for long; even the sandwiches will outlast them, I think."

"True, if I eat all the cake I want," added Sybil. "Cakes and jam make a queer breakfast, Mary Eliska. In New England the pie would be appropriate."

"Let's save the pie—for lunch."

"Agreed. Breakfast isn't usually my strong point, you know."

As they ate, seated together upon the sands, they cast many curious glances at the interior of the island—a prospect forbidding enough.

"Do you know," said Mary Eliska, "the scarcity of food doesn't worry me so much as the scarcity of water. Grape juice and ginger ale are well enough in their way, but they don't take the place of water."

"We may possibly find water on this island," replied Sybil, after a little thought.

"I don't believe it. I've an idea that, hunt as we may, we shall find nothing more than rocks, and rocks, and rocks—anywhere and everywhere."

"That's merely a hunch, and I distrust hunches. It will be better to explore," suggested Sybil.

"Yes; I think we ought to do that. But—the snakes."

"Ah, the exclusive rock theory is already exploded," said Sybil, with a laugh. "Yet even snakes can't exist without water, can they? Just the thought of the wrigglers makes me shudder, but if they are really our co-inhabitants here we won't be safe from them even on this shore. Have we anything in the way of clubs?"

Mary Eliska considered the question. Then she went to the machine and with a wrench unfastened the foot-bar, which was long enough to extend across both seats and was made of solid steel. She also took the bolts out of one of the levers, which when released became an effective weapon of defense. Thus armed, and feeling somewhat more secure, the girls prepared to move inland to explore their new habitation.

They found the climb over the loose rocks adjoining the shore to be quite arduous, and aside from the difficulties of the way they had to exercise constant caution for fear of snakes. They saw none of these dreaded reptiles, however, and when they came to the hillocks they selected a path between the two most promising and began the ascent, keeping close together. So jagged were the tumbled masses of rock and so irregular in their formation that it was not a question of walking so much as crawling, but with their leggings, stout shoes and thick cloth skirts they were fairly protected from injury.

The silence throughout the island was intense. The girls spoke in hushed tones, awed by their uncanny surroundings. From a clear sky the sun beat down upon their heads and was refracted from the rocks until the heat was oppressive. Added to this a pungent, unrecognized odor saluted their nostrils as they progressed inland. "Reminds me of the smell of a drug store," asserted Sybil; but Mary Eliska replied: "It's more like the smell of a garage, I think."

After a long and weary climb they reached the brow of the rock hills and were able to look down into the "dip" or valley which lay between them and the mountain. The center of the depression, which was three or four miles across, appeared to be quite free from rocks except in a few places where one cropped up in the form of a hummock. Elsewhere the surface seemed smooth and moist, for it was covered with an oozy, stagnant slime which was decidedly repulsive in appearance.

Looking beyond this forbidding valley they discovered the first interesting thing they had yet observed. At the right base of the far-away mountain, lying between it and the sea, was a patch of vivid green, crowning an elevation that distinctly separated it from the central depression of the island. It might be grass or underbrush, this alluring greenery, but in any event it proved a grateful sight to eyes wearied by the dull waste of rocks. From the point where the girls stood they could also see the top of a palm tree which grew around the edge of the mountain.

"Well!" said Mary Eliska, drawing a long breath, "there is the first sign of life—animal or vegetable—we have found in this wilderness. That tree must indicate water, Sybil."

"Whatever it indicates," was the reply, "yonder bluff is a better place for our camp than the bay where we floated ashore. How shall we get to it, though? It will be a heart-breaking climb cross-lots over these interminable rocks."

"An impossible climb," Mary Eliska agreed. "I think our best plan will be to go around the island, following the sandy beach. It seems from here as if that bluff drops sheer down to the sea, but it will be much easier for us to climb a bluff than to navigate these rocks. Let's go back and try it."

Cautiously and laboriously they made their way back to the beach, feeling considerably cheered by what they had seen and reassured by the total absence of the dreaded "wigglers." After resting a little from their exertions they prepared for the more important journey of discovery. Sybil carried some food and the bottle of lemonade, while Mary Eliska secured two straps from the airplane and the coil of wire. Then, still armed with their steel bars, they set out along the beach.

Their first task was to climb the rocks of the point which formed the bay, where it jutted out from the shore. This being accomplished they encountered another stretch of smooth beach, which gradually circled around the north end of the island. Here it was easy walking and they made good progress, but the coast line was so irregular that it wound in and out continually, and in places huge boulders interrupted their passage and obliged them either to climb or wade, whichever seemed the most desirable.

"Already," sighed Sybil, "we have tramped a thousand miles. Did you mark that place, Mary Eliska, so we will know when we come to it?"

"Yes; I can tell it by the position of the sun. That side of the island faces the northwest."

"And we haven't passed it?"

"No; but we must be drawing near to it. I've been looking for the bluff the last half hour. The green place was quite elevated, you remember, and must be well above the sea level. Look ahead; you'll notice the rocks are gradually rising, from here on."

Sybil nodded and again they trudged on. As the rocks grew higher at their left, the girls kept to the narrow strip of beach, which was beginning to be washed by an occasional wave.

"The tide is Sising," announced Mary Eliska; "but we shall be at the bluff very soon, and can then climb above this moisture. Feet wet, Syb?"

"Pickled in brine. Wet feet signify a cold; cold signifies la grippe; la grippe signifies a doctor; the doctor signifies a depleted bank account. Science of deduction, Sis. It's only a step from wet feet to poverty."

"I prefer a doctor to an undertaker," said Mary Eliska, "but as neither profession is represented here I advise you to forego the pleasure of taking cold."

"Right you are, Cap'n Columbus. No doctor, no cold. Banish the thought! We can't afford the luxury of illness, can we? Oh, here's the bluff."

There it was, indeed; but absolutely unclimbable. It was sixty feet high, at least, and overhanging the sea like a shelf, the waves having cut it away at the base.

"Now, then," said Mary Eliska, after a careful inspection, "we must either go back or go on, in order to find a way up. As we haven't passed any steps or easy inclines, I propose we advance farther and see what the west end looks like."

"I'll follow the leader; but the waves are already covering the beach," asserted Sybil, with a grimace.

"Then let us wade; and don't lose any precious time, for the tide will come in faster every minute. Shoes off, Crusoe!"

"Aye, aye, Columbus."

With shoes, leggings and stockings in hand they began the advance, hugging the wall of rock and proceeding as swiftly as they could. At times one or the other would cry out as she stepped on a sharp bit of rock, but this was no time to shrink from petty trials and they bore up with admirable fortitude.

CHAPTER 8.7
TWO GIRLS AND ONE ISLAND

Plodding along the narrow ledge of beach and constantly soused by the waves, the girls began to fear, as afterward proved to be fact—that the bluff covered the entire west end of the island. The water beneath their feet grew deeper and the undertow stronger with every step they advanced, but fortunately for their safety they finally came to a crevasse that split the bluff in twain, and down this rift trickled a rill of pure water.

They both exclaimed with delight as they crept into the shelter of the crevasse. The fissure was not level, but extended upward at an acute angle, yet there was room enough at its mouth for the girls to creep above the wash of the waves. Examining the place carefully, Mary Eliska thought they might be able to follow the rift up to the top of the bluff, and so at once they began the ascent. The two walls were so close together that they could touch both by extending their arms, and there was room, by stepping occasionally into the shallow brook, for them to climb from shelf to shelf without much difficulty. At the very top, however, they were brought to an abrupt halt. A waterfall leaped from the edge of the bluff, dropping a good ten feet to the point they had now reached, from whence there seemed no way of gaining the top.

Mary Eliska and Sybil looked at each other and laughed, the spray from the waterfall wetting their cheeks, which were now rosy from exercise.

"Trapped, Cap'n!" cried Sybil, merrily. "What next?"

"We can't go back, you know."

"Not unless we prefer Davy Jones' locker to this stronghold—which I, for one, don't. Therefore, let's eat."

"That seems your resource in every emergency, Sybil."

"Naturally. Feasting stimulates thought; thought develops wit; wit finds a way."

Mary Eliska raised herself to a seat upon a projecting crag and then, swinging her feet, proceeded to think while Sybil brought out the food.

"Could you climb a wire, Syb?"

"Not without years of practice. Have you positively decided to establish a circus in these wilds, Sis?"

Mary Eliska stood upon the crag, examined the face of the rock and then drove the end of the bar she carried into a small fissure that was nearly on a level with her head. Sybil observed the horizontal bar and laughed gleefully.

"Have a sandwich, chummie, and curb your imagination," said she. "I catch your idea, but respectfully decline to accept the hazard."

Mary Eliska ate her sandwich and drank from the bottle of lemonade. Then she rinsed her fingers in the brook, dried them on her handkerchief and again mounted the crag.

"Listen, Crusoe: I'm going to make an attempt to break out of jail," she said impressively. "If I can reach to the top I'll find some way to get you up. As soon as I get my feet on that bar, you are to come up on this crag and hand me your lever. If I can find a pocket to stick that into, the deed is done.”

“Bravo, Sis! What a pity you haven’t any spangles on your skirt. If you fall, fall gradually, for I’ll be afraid to catch you.”

Mary Eliska’s fingers clutched at the rough projections of rock and with some difficulty she gained a footing on the bar. Then, still clinging to the face of the rift, she made a further examination. There seemed a small hole at the right, about breast high, and she called for the lever. This Sybil promptly passed up. Mary Eliska thrust in the lever and the next instant nearly lost her footing, for with a bewildering hoot a white owl of monstrous size fluttered out and tumbled almost at Sybil’s feet, who uttered a shriek like an Indian war whoop. The creature was blinded by the glare of day and went whirling down the incline of the crevasse until it was lost to sight.

“First sign of life,” called Sybil. “Don’t look so scared, Sis; there’s nothing more harmless than an owl.”

“Did you yell because *I* was scared?» inquired Mary Eliska.

“No, I was reproving the owl, who has a voice like a steam calliope. It would take more than a blind bird to scare either of us; wouldn’t it, Cap’n?”

“I—I wish it hadn’t been so—so unexpected,” muttered Mary Eliska, feeling her way up to the second projection. With her feet on the lever she found her head well above the edge of the precipice and the first glance showed her a good hold for her hands.

Mary Eliska was no skilled athlete, but her experience in Bill’s workshop, together with her aërial exercises and constant outdoor life, had given her well-developed muscles which now stood her in good stead. She drew herself up, got her knee on the edge of the rock, and a moment later was on level ground at the top of the bluff. Then she leaned over and called to Sybil:

“Can you manage it?”

“What a question!” retorted Sybil, indignantly. “I stood below to catch you in case you slipped; but who is there to catch *me*, I beg to inquire?”

“The owl,” said Mary Eliska. “Will you try it?”

“Is it worthwhile? Tell me what you’ve found up there.”

Mary Eliska turned and examined the scene now spread before her.

“Better come up, Syb,” she said. “But wait a moment and I’ll help you.”

She attached one of the straps to the coil of steel wire and passed the end down to her chum.

“Buckle the strap around you—just under your arms,” she called. “I’ll hold fast the wire at this end. You can’t fall, then; but be careful, just the same.”

With this support Sybil gained confidence. Exercising extreme caution she followed Mary Eliska’s example in scaling the cliff and as fast as she mounted her companion took up the slack in the wire and kept it taut. As soon as Sybil stood on the upper bar Mary Eliska grasped her arms and drew her up beside her in safety.

"There!" she exclaimed triumphantly. "Where there's a will, there's a way. It wasn't such a difficult feat, after all."

"There isn't enough money in the world to hire me to do it again," panted Sybil, trembling a little from the giddy experience.

"That may be true, but if our safety requires it we may repeat the performance more than once," declared Mary Eliska. "Unfortunately, we have lost our weapons of defense."

"Can't we recover the bars?"

"Not without going down for them. If you think you could lower me over the edge——"

"I just couldn't, Sis. Don't mention it."

"Very well; then we will proceed unarmed. Look, Sybil! Isn't it a glorious prospect?"

"In point of comparison, yes," admitted Sybil, speaking slowly as she gazed around her.

They were standing on a level table-land which lay between the base of the mountain and the sea. The "mountain" was really a great hill of rock, rising only a hundred and fifty feet or so from the table-land. The level space before them was clothed with a queer sort of verdure. It was not grass, but plants with broad and rather crinkly leaves, so tender that wherever the girls stepped the leaves were broken and crushed. Nor was the color an emerald green; it was rather a pale pea-green and the plants grew not in soil but sprang from tiny cracks and fissures in a sort of shale, or crushed slate, which was constantly kept moist by the seepage of the little stream.

The island here made an abrupt curve to the west and a little farther along the girls saw patches of bushes and several small groups of tall, tropical trees, resembling plantains, or palms. There were vines, too, which grew in rank profusion among the rocks and helped relieve the dismal landscape by their greenery. But nowhere appeared any earth, or natural soil; whatever grew, grew among the crushed rock, or shale, which seemed to possess a certain fertility where moisture reached it.

"This part of the island seems by far the best," asserted Sybil. "Let us explore it thoroughly."

They set out to skirt the edge of the bluff and on reaching the first group of trees found they were bananas. Several bunches of plump fruit hung far up among the branches, quite out of reach.

"We'll find a way to get at them if we are detained here long enough to need them," said Mary Eliska.

A half mile beyond the place where they had so laboriously climbed the bluff they came upon a broad ravine which led directly down to the water's edge. It appeared as if a huge mass of rock had at some time become detached from the mountain and, sliding downward, had cut away the bluff and hurled itself into the sea, where it now lay a few rods from the water's edge and formed a sort of breakwater. The swirl of the waves around this mass of rock had made a small indentation in the shore, creating a tiny bay with a sandy beach.

"Ah," said Mary Eliska, examining this place, "here is where we must establish our camp; there is room enough to float our boat into the bay, where the water is calm, and on that smooth beach I can repair the Hy at my leisure."

"Also, from this elevation," added Sybil, "we can fly a flag of distress, which would be seen by any ship approaching the island."

Mary Eliska nodded approval.

"Here is also water and food," said she. "If we can manage to navigate the Hy to this place we have little to fear from a temporary imprisonment."

"We must wait for low tide before we start back," observed Sybil. "Meantime, let's run down to the beach and see how it looks."

The descent to the water's edge was easy, and they found the little bay ideal for their purpose. But they could hear the waves breaking with some force against the face of the cliff, just outside their retreat, and it would be hours before they might venture to return to the other side of the island.

So again they ascended the bluff and selected a place for their camp, beneath the spreading foliage of the tall bananas. Afterward they sought the source of the little brook, which was high up on the mountain and required a difficult climb to reach it. A spring seemed to well up, clear and refreshing, from a cleft in the rock, but even at its source there was no more water than would run from an ordinary house faucet.

"Isn't it astonishing," said Mary Eliska, "how much moisture is dispersed from this tiny stream? I think it never rains here and this spring of water supplies all the island."

"This part of it, anyhow. It's mighty lucky for us the babbling brook is here," declared Sybil, drinking deeply of the cool water and then bathing her heated brow with it. "But what stumps me, Sis, is the lack of any life on the island. With water and green stuff both animals and birds might thrive here—to say nothing of bugs and lizards and serpents galore—yet aside from that great white owl we've not seen a living thing."

"It really *is* curious,» admitted Mary Eliska. Then, turning her gaze seaward, she exclaimed: «See there, Sybil! Isn›t that another island?»

"It surely is," was the reply; "and only a few miles away. It's a big island, too, Sis—far bigger than this. Did you bring along your glasses?"

"No; they are in the boat."

"When we get them we can inspect that island better. Perhaps we could manage to get to it, Sis."

"We'll see," was the doubting answer. "I imagine, if that island is so much larger, and proves to be more fertile than this, that we have discovered the reason why the live things, such as birds and animals, prefer it as a place of residence."

They made their way back to the bluff and waited patiently for the tide to ebb. According to Mary Eliska's watch it was quite four o'clock before they deemed it safe to venture on the sands, and even then they went barefooted, as an occasional wave still crossed their narrow path.

By the time they reached the bay and their boat the two girls were very tired with their long tramp and as it was nearly sundown they decided to spend the night in this location and make the attempt to shift camp next day.

CHAPTER 8.8
AN OWL CONCERT

While daylight lasted Mary Eliska was busy examining the injury to the Aircraft and attempting a few preliminary repairs. Her long mechanical experience in the workshop with her brother enabled her to determine accurately what was required to put the machine into proper working order, and she thought she could accomplish the task.

"I can't see that it matters, anyhow," said Sybil, watching her chum from a seat upon the sands. "We can't fly, and the boat is our only refuge. Even that we must manage to row or sail in some way."

"All very true," returned Mary Eliska, "but I can see no object in neglecting these repairs when I am able to make them. I can take off the bent elevator rods and straighten them, after which the elevator and rudder may assist us in sailing, as we can oppose them to the wind. The engine control is a more serious matter, for the wheel connection was broken off short. But I shall take a rod from a support and fit it in place and then replace the support with our steel wire. That is a sort of makeshift and will require time and nice adjustment, but I can do it, all right. The tools Bill supplied were quite complete; there's even a box marked 'soldering outfit.'"

"Is there?" asked Sybil, eagerly. "See if any matches are in it, Sis."

"Matches?"

"Yes. The lack of matches has disturbed me considerably."

"Why, Syb?"

"We can't cook without them."

"Cook! why, I never thought of such a thing," said Mary Eliska, truly astonished. "What is there to cook, in this place?"

"Fish," answered Sybil.

"And what would you use for fuel?"

"Fuel?"

"Yes; what is there to make a fire with?"

"Never mind that. Just see about the matches."

Mary Eliska opened the soldering case and found an alcohol torch, a flask of alcohol, solder, acid and a box of matches.

"Good!" cried Sybil, joyfully. "Don't you dare do any wasteful soldering, Mary Eliska. Save every drop of that alcohol to cook with."

Mary Eliska laughed.

"I have nothing to solder, just yet," said she. "And you've nothing to fry."

"I soon shall have, though," was the confident reply. "We've assured ourselves of one thing, Miss Columbus, and that is that we can sustain life, in case of necessity, on bananas and spring water. So I propose we have one good, luxuriant square meal this evening by way of variety. We've done nothing but lunch for two whole days and I want something hot."

"I'm willing, Sybil. Can you catch a fish?"

"If there's one in our neighborhood. I'll try it while you are tinkering."

Among the tools was a ball of stout cord, and for hook Sybil cut a short length of wire and bent it into shape with a pair of nippers, filing a sharp point to it. Then she opened a can of chipped beef and secured a couple of slices for bait. Going to the point of rock she found a place on the ocean side where a projecting shelf afforded her a seat above fairly deep water, and here she dropped her line.

Thatcher Allen was an enthusiastic fisherman and while Sybil had never cared particularly for the sport she had accompanied her father on many a piscatorial expedition.

A tug. The girl hauled in, hand over hand, and found she had captured a large crab, which dropped from the hook to the rocks and with prodigious speed made for the water and disappeared.

"Good riddance, old ugly!" laughed Sybil.

Scarcely had she thrown her line when another tug came. A second crab floundered upon the rocks, but fell upon his back and lay struggling to turn himself.

Sybil ruefully contemplated the empty hook.

"I can't feed all our good beef to horrid crabs," she exclaimed; "but the beef seems a good bait and I'll try again."

Another crab. Mary Eliska came clambering over the rocks to her friend's side. The sun was sinking.

"What luck, Syb?"

"Only three crabs. I'm afraid it's too shallow here for fish."

Mary Eliska leaned over the still struggling crab—the only one that had not escaped.

"Why, we pay big money in Los Angeles for these things," said she. "They're delicious eating; but they have to be boiled, I think, and then cracked and newburged or creamed."

"Keep an eye on the rascal, then," said Sybil. "Can't he be eaten just boiled?"

"Yes; with mayonnaise."

"There's none handy. Let the high-brow go, and we'll fish for something that doesn't require royal condiments."

But Mary Eliska weighted the crab with a heavy stone, to hold him down. Then she sat beside Sybil and watched her.

"I'm afraid our fish dinner must be postponed," began Miss Allen, sorrowfully; but at that moment the line jerked so fiercely that she would have been pulled from her seat had not Mary Eliska made a grab and rescued her. Then they both clung to the line, managing to draw it in by degrees until there leaped from the water a great silvery fish which promptly dove again, exhibiting a strength that nearly won for him his freedom.

"Hold fast!" gasped Sybil, exerting all her strength. "We mustn't let him escape."

The fish, a twelve-pound rock cod, made a desperate fight; but unfortunately for him he had swallowed the entire hook and so his conquest was certain if the girls could hold on to the line. At last he lay flopping upon the rocks, and seeing he was unable to disgorge the hook, they dragged him to the beach, where Mary Eliska shut her eyes and beheaded him with a hatchet from the tool chest.

In the outfit of the chest, which had evidently been intended by Bill and Thatcher Allen for regular use in connection with the Hydro-Aircraft, they had found two aluminum plates, as well as knives and forks and spoons. Sybil cut two generous slices from the big fish and laid them upon one of the metal plates. Then they opened a can of pork and beans and secured a lump of fat to use in frying. Mary Eliska lighted the alcohol torch and Sybil arranged some loose rocks so that they would support the plate suspended above the flame of the torch. The intense heat melted the fat and the fish was soon fried to a lovely brown. They ate it with biscuits and washed it down with ginger ale, confiding the while to one another that never had they eaten a meal so delicious.

They let the torch flicker during the repast, for night had fallen, but when from motives of economy Mary Eliska had extinguished the flame they found a dim light suffused from a myriad of stars. Later a slender crescent moon arose, so they were able to distinguish near-by objects, even with the shadow of the bleak mountain behind them.

They had arranged their blankets in the boat and were sitting upon them, talking together in the starlight, when suddenly an unearthly cry smote their ears, followed by an answering shriek—then another, and another—until the whole island seemed echoing with a thousand terrifying whoops.

"Ku-whoo-woo-oo-oo! Ku-whoo! Ku-whoo-oo!"

The two girls clung together tremblingly as the great chorus burst upon them; but after a moment Sybil pushed her companion away with a nervous little laugh.

"Owls!" she exclaimed.

"Oh!" said Mary Eliska, relieved as the truth dawned upon her. "I—I thought it was savages."

"So it is. I challenge any beings to yell more savagely than those fearful hoot owls. Something must have happened to them, Sis, for they've never made a mutter all day long."

"Because they have been asleep," answered Mary Eliska. They had to speak loudly to be heard above the turmoil of shrieks, although the owls seemed mainly congregated upon the distant mountain. The rocks everywhere were full of them, however, and hoots and answering hoots resounded from every part of the island. It was fairly deafening, as well as annoying and uncanny. They waited in vain for the noise to subside.

"There must be thousands of them," observed Sybil. "What's the row about, do you suppose!"

"Perhaps it's their nature to, Syb. I wonder why we didn't hear the pests last night. When we wakened this morning all was silent as the grave."

"I think we floated into the bay about daylight, when all the big-eyes had ducked into their holes. Do you know, Sis, the owls must be responsible for the absence of all other life on the island? They dote on snakes and lizards and beetles and such, and they'd rob the nests of any other birds, who couldn't protect themselves in the nighttime. So I suppose they've either eaten up all the other creatures or scared them to death."

"That must be so. But, oh, Sybil! if this racket keeps up every night how are we going to be able to sleep?"

"Ah. Just inquire, Cap'n, and if you find out, let me know," replied Sybil, yawning. "I got up so early this morning that I'm dead for sleep this blessed minute."

"Lie down; I'll keep watch."

"Thank you. This lullaby is too entrancing to miss."

The air grew cool presently, as it often does at night in the semi-tropics, and the two girls crouched down and covered themselves to their ears with the blankets. That deadened the pandemonium somewhat and as the owls showed no tendency to abate their shrieks, an hour or two of resigned submission to the inevitable resulted in drowsiness, and finally in sleep. As Sybil said next morning, no one would have believed that mortal girl could have slumbered under the affliction of such ear-splitting yells; but sleep they did, and when they wakened at daybreak profound silence reigned.

CHAPTER 8.9
MISS COLUMBUS AND MISS CRUSOE

Sybil cooked more fish for their breakfast, although Mary Eliska objected to the extravagant waste of alcohol. But her chum argued that they must waste either the alcohol or the fish and as they had a strenuous day before them a substantial breakfast was eminently desirable.

They now packed the aluminum chest and made arrangements for the voyage, for the sea in the bay was smooth as glass and the ocean seemed nearly as quiet outside. Mary Eliska had straightened and repaired the elevator rods and firmly bolted the chest in its original position, but the control must be a matter of future tinkering, the rod needed for its repair being at present stuck in the side of the bluff.

It was easy to roll the machine down the beach into the water and set it afloat, but the difficult matter was to propel their queer, top-heavy craft through the water. A quiet sea meant no wind, nor could they feel the slightest breath of air stirring. Oars they had none, nor any substitute for such things; nor could they find anything to pole the boat along with.

"There's just one thing to be done," announced Mary Eliska, gravely, "and that is for us to take turns wading behind the thing and pushing it along. By keeping close to the shore we ought to be able to accomplish our journey in that way."

"Suppose we strike deep water?" suggested Sybil.

"We'll stay close to shore. There seems to be a beach all the way."

"I'm game to try," declared Sybil, in a brisk tone, "but it seems at first sight like an impossible task. I'm glad, Miss Columbus, that under these circumstances your island is uninhabited—except by owls who can't see in the daytime."

"Were there other inhabitants," returned Mary Eliska, "we would not be undertaking such a thing. The natives would either eat us or assist us."

"True for you, Cap'n. I'm going to keep my stockings on. They'll be some protection against those sharp rocks which we're liable to tread on."

"I shall do the same," said Mary Eliska. "Take your seat in the boat, Syb, and I'll do the first stunt shoving. After we get around the point I will give you a chance to wade."

"Unanimously carried," said Sybil.

This undertaking did not appear nearly so preposterous to the two castaways as it may to the reader sitting quietly at home. Except that circumstances had made Mary Eliska and Sybil aëronauts at a time when few girls have undertaken to fly through the air—as many will do in the future—they were quite like ordinary girls in all respects. A capricious fate had driven them into a far-away, unknown sea and cast them upon an uninviting island, but in such unusual circumstances they did what any girls would do, if they're the right sort; kept their courage and exercised every resource to make the most of their discouraging surroundings and keep alive until succor arrived.

So far, these two castaways had shown admirable stamina. Had either one been placed in such a position alone, the chances are she might have despaired and succumbed to girlish terrors, but being together their native pride forbade their admitting or even showing a trace of fear. In this manner they encouraged and supported one another, outwardly calm, whatever their inward tremors might be.

Mary Eliska was habitually dainty and feminine in both appearance and deportment, yet possessed a temperament cool and self-reliant. Her natural cleverness and quickness of comprehension had been fostered by constant association with her mechanical, inventive brother, and it seemed to her quite proper to help herself when no one was by to render her aid. To wade in the warm, limpid water of the Pacific, at a place far removed from the haunts of humanity, in order to propel the precious craft on which her life and that of her companion might depend, to a better location, seemed to this girl quite the natural thing to do. Sybil's acute sense of humor led her to recognize the laughable side of this queer undertaking; yet even Sybil, much more frail and dependent than her beloved chum, had no thought of refusing her assistance.

The aluminum boat rode lightly upon the surface of the sea, the broad, overhanging planes scarcely interfering with its balance. Indeed, the planes probably assisted in keeping the boat upright. Mary Eliska, knee-deep in the water, was not called upon to exert herself more than to wade; but this was a slow and tedious process and required frequent rests. At such times she would sit in the back of the boat and let her feet dangle in the warm water.

Gradually the Hy was propelled around the point of rock into the open sea, and by keeping close to shore the girl seldom found herself out of her depth, and then only temporarily.

Sybil kept up a constant chatter, inducing Mary Eliska frequently to laugh with her, and that made the task seem more an amusement than hard labor. They took turns at the wading, as had been agreed upon, but because Mary Eliska was much the stronger her periods of playing mermaid were longer than those of her chum.

In this manner they made good progress, and though Sybil made a great deal of fun of what she called her "patent propeller," she took her turn at wading very seriously and pushed the strange craft through the water at a good rate of speed. By midday they reached the point where the bluff began to rise and here they sat together in the boat, shaded by the planes, and ate their luncheon with hearty appetites. They found it high tide, yet the water was more quiet than on the preceding day, and when they resumed their journey their progress was much more rapid than before.

By two o'clock they had cautiously propelled the boat around the huge boulder that marked the ravine they had found and soon after had rolled it upon the sandy beach and anchored it securely beyond the reach of the tide.

"If it would fly," said Mary Eliska, "I think we could push it to the top of the bluff; but if we use it at all, before our friends arrive, it must be as a boat, and not an airplane."

"Then," returned Sybil, "let's remove the canvas from the lower plane and make a tent of it."

"I've been thinking of that," said Mary Eliska, "and I'm sure it is a wise thing to do. I know how to take the clips off, and it won't injure the cloth in the least."

"Then get busy, and I'll help you."

So, after a good rest on the beach in the sun they resumed their clothing. The wet stockings were thoroughly dried by the sun by the time they were ready for them, and presently they set to work removing the cloth from the lower plane. The task was almost completed when Sybil suddenly exclaimed:

"How about a frame for our tent?" Mary Eliska looked puzzled.

"Come up on the bluff," she proposed.

The incline was not at all difficult and they soon stood on top the bluff. A thorough examination of the place disclosed no means of erecting the tent. A few dead branches that had fallen from the banana trees lay scattered about and there was a quantity of anæmic shrubbery growing here and there, but there was nothing to furnish poles for the tent or to support it in any way.

"Stumped, Columbus!" laughed Sybil, as they squatted together in the shade of the trees. "We shall have to drag up the airplane, after all, and use the plane-frame for our ridge-pole."

Mary Eliska demurred at this. "There is always a way to do a thing, if one can think how," she said.

"In this case, chummie dear, magic or legerdemain seems the only modus operandi," maintained Sybil. But Mary Eliska was thinking, and as she thought she glanced at the trees.

"Why, of course!" she exclaimed. Sybil's eyes questioned her gravely.

"Come on!" cried Mary Eliska, jumping up.

"Not a step, Miss Columbus, until I'm enlightened."

"Oh, Crusoe, can't you see? It is so extremely simple that I'm ashamed of our stupidity. We've but to stretch our coil of wire between these two trees, throw the canvas over it and weight the bottom with rocks to hold it in place."

Sybil sighed.

"It was *too* easy,» she admitted. «I never *could* guess an easy conundrum; but give me a hard nut to crack and I›m a regular squirrel.»

They returned to the beach for the canvas and wire and Mary Eliska took several of the clips, with which to fasten together the ends of their tent. Ascending once more, this time heavily loaded, to the group of bananas on the bluff, they proceeded to attach the wire to two of the trees. The plane-cover was large enough to afford a broad spread to their "A" tent and when the lower edges were secured by means of heavy stones, and the scattered rocks cleared away from the interior, their new domicile seemed roomy and inviting.

Their next task was to fetch the aluminum chest from the beach, and after they had lightened its weight by leaving in the boat all the tools except the hatchet and a small hack saw, they were able to carry the chest between them, although forced to make frequent stops to rest.

"The lack of a bedstead worries me most," remarked Sybil. "I don't like the idea of sleeping on the bare ground. How would it do, Sis, to build a stone bed—something like an altar, you know, with a hollow center which we could fill with sand?"

"That is a capital idea, Crusoe, and will help clear our front yard of some of those flat stones. They are mostly slate, I think, instead of rock formation. Heave-ho, my hearty, and we'll do the job in a jiffy."

The girls lugged into the tent a number of stones of such size as they could comfortably move, and then Mary Eliska, who could put her hand to almost any sort of work, planned and built the extraordinary bedstead. It was laid solid, at first, but when about a foot from the ground she began to extend the sides of the pile and leave a hollow in the middle. This hollow they afterward filled with sand, carrying it in their dress-skirts from the beach. When finally the "Altar to Morpheus"—as Sybil persisted in calling it—was completed, they spread their blankets upon it and it made a very comfortable place to sleep.

They also erected a small rock stove, for there was enough firewood to be gathered, in the way of fallen branches, dead leaves and "peelings" from the tree-trunks, to last them for several days. The hatchet and hack saw helped prepare these scraps to fit the stove and by sundown the girls felt quite settled in their new residence.

"We ought to fly a flag of distress from some place high up on those trees," observed Mary Eliska; "but we've no flag and no way to shin up the tree."

"Couldn't any ship see our white tent from the ocean?" asked Sybil. "Yes; I think so."

"As for climbing the tree," continued Sybil, "I wish your creative brain would evolve some way to do it. Those fat, yellow bananas look mighty tempting and they would serve to eke out our larder. Supplies are beginning to diminish with alarming rapidity, Sis. Only a box and a half of those biscuits left." "I know," said Mary Eliska, soberly. "Tomorrow we will see what may be done to capture the bananas."

After a time Sybil said, softly: "By tomorrow we may begin to look for Daddy and Bill. Of course it will take them some time to find us, but——Don't you think, Mary Eliska, they're quite certain to find us, in the end?"

Mary Eliska looked at her companion with a gleam of pity in her deep blue eyes; but she had no desire to disturb Sybil's confidence in their rescue, whatever misgivings oppressed her own heart.

"I believe they will find us," she affirmed. "It may not be tomorrow, you know, nor in a week, nor—perhaps—in a month——"

"Oh, Mary Eliska!"

"But they'll cover the entire Pacific in their search, I am positive, and sooner or later they'll come to this island and—take us away." "Alive or dead," added Sybil, gloomily.

"Oh, as for that, we are perfectly safe, and healthy—so far—and I imagine we could live for a long time on this island, if obliged to." Again they sat silently thinking, while twilight gave way to darkness and darkness was relieved by the pale moonlight. Suddenly a shriek sounded in their ears. A great white bird swooped down from the mountain and passed directly between their two heads, disappearing into the night with another appalling cry. This shriek was answered by another and another, until the whole island resounded with the distracting "Ku-whoo-oo!" "The owls are awake," said Mary Eliska, rising resignedly. "Come into the tent, Sybil. I'm not sure they wouldn't attack us if we remained in the open."

CHAPTER 8.10
MADELINE DENTRY'S PROPOSITION

At the aviation field the crowd had watched the departure of the two girls, flying the famous Stricklin Hydro-Aircraft, with eager interest but assured confidence in their making a successful trip. The Flying Girl never indulged in accidents, and her skill was universally admitted. To be sure, there was an added risk in flying over the water, but with a motor boat to sustain them when they alighted, the danger was reduced to a minimum and, in the minds of nearly all the spectators, a triumphant return was unquestioned. Hundreds of glasses followed the flight and although the management sent several bird-men into the air to amuse the throng the real interest remained centered on the dim speck that marked the course of the Flying Girl.

No sooner had Mary Eliska and Sybil started on their voyage than Bill Stricklin and Thatcher Allen ran to the bluff overlooking the sea, where with powerful binoculars they could obtain an unobstructed view of the entire trip to the island and back again. Presently Madeline Dentry joined them, in company with Mr. and Mrs. Tupper, all standing silently with leveled glasses.

"She's working beautifully," muttered Bill, referring to his invention with boyish delight. "I'm sorry Sis didn't make a straight line of it, but she always likes to give the dear public the worth of their money…. Ah-h!"

"By Jove! that was an awkward turn," cried Thatcher Allen, as they saw the Aircraft keel at a dangerous angle and then slowly right itself. "I'm surprised at Mary Eliska. She usually makes her turns so neatly."

"I've an idea that blamed steering gear stuck," said Bill, ruefully. "I've been a little afraid of it, all along. But the girls are all right now. They're headed dead for the island and if Mary Eliska makes a neat drop to the water the rest is easy."

No one spoke again for a time, all being intent upon the flying-machine. When it had seemed to reach the island, and even to pass over it, without a halt, there was an excited hum of amazement from the grand stand.

Madeline glanced at Bill Stricklin's face and found it as white as a sheet. He was staring with dilated eyes toward the Aircraft.

"What in the mischief is Mary Eliska up to now?" questioned Thatcher Allen, uneasily. "Wasn't she to alight this side of the island?"

"Yes," answered Bill hoarsely. "Then——She can't be joking, or playing pranks. It isn't like her. Why, they haven't swerved a hair's breadth from the course, or even slackened speed. They they——"

"They're in trouble, I'm afraid," said Bill in trembling tones. "The control has failed them and they can't stop."

"Can't stop!" The little line of observers on the bluff echoed the thrilling words. From the grand stand came a roar of voices filled with tense excitement. Some thought the Flying Girl was attempting a reckless performance, with the idea of shocking the crowd; but Bill Stricklin knew better, and so did Thatcher Allen . As the two men held their glasses to their eyes with shaking hands, straining to discover a sign that Mary Eliska had altered her course and was coming back, Madeline Dentry turned to look earnestly at the brother and father of the girls, knowing she could read the facts more truly from their faces than by focusing her own glasses on that tiny speck in the sky.

The moments dragged slowly, yet laden with tragic import. The powerful lenses lost the speck, now found it again—lost it for good—yet the men most affected by this strange occurrence still glared at the sky, hoping against hope that their fears were unfounded and that the Aircraft would come back.

Someone plucked Bill's sleeve. It was Chesty Todd, his big body shaken like an aspen.

"It—it has run away with 'em, Bill. It's gone wrong, man; there's danger ahead!"

"Eh?" said Bill, dully. "Wake up and do something!"

Bill lowered his glasses and looked helplessly at Thatcher Allen . Thatcher Allen returned the stare, glowering upon the inventor.

"That's right; it's up to you, Stricklin. What are you going to do?" he asked coldly.

"There's no other hydro-airplane on the grounds," said the boy brokenly.

"Then get an airplane," commanded Thatcher Allen, sharply.

"It would mean death to anyone who ventured to follow our girls in an airplane—not rescue for them."

Thatcher Allen moaned, as if in pain; then stamped his foot impatiently, as if ashamed of his weakness.

"Well—well! What then, Bill Stricklin?" he demanded.

Bill wrung his hands, realizing his helplessness.

"Gentlemen," said Madeline Dentry, laying a gentle hand on Thatcher Allen 's arm, "let me help you. There is no reason for despair just yet; the condition of those girls is far from desperate, it seems to me. Did I understand you to say, Mr. Stricklin, that your sister is unable to stop the engine, or to turn the machine?"

Bill nodded. "That's it," he said. "Something has broken. I can't imagine what it is, but there's no other way to explain the thing."

"Very well," rejoined Madeline, coolly, "let us, then, try to consider intelligently what will happen to them. Will they presently descend and alight upon the surface of the water?"

"I'm—I'm afraid not," Bill answered. "If that were possible, Mary Eliska would have done it long ago. I think something has happened to affect the control, and therefore my sister is helpless."

"In that case, how long will they continue flying?" persisted Madeline.

"As long as the gasoline lasts—three or four hours." "And how fast are they traveling, Mr. Stricklin?"

"I think at the rate of about forty-five miles an hour."Miss Dentry made a mental calculation.

"Then they will descend about a hundred and fifty miles from here, in a straight line over that island," said she. "Having a boat under them, I suppose they will float indefinitely?"

Again Bill nodded, looking at the girl curiously and wondering at her logic.

"If—if they manage to alight upon the water in good shape," he replied more hopefully, "they'll be safe enough—for a time. And they have food and water with them. The only danger I fear for them, at present, is that when the gasoline is exhausted the machine will be wrecked."

"Don't you aviators often shut off your engine and volplane to the ground?" asked Madeline.

"It—it has run away with 'em Bill. It's gone wrong, man; there's danger ahead!"

"Yes, with the elevator and rudder in full control. But that isn't the case with Mary Eliska. I'm certain her elevator control has bound in some way. Were it broken, and free, the Aircraft would have wobbled, and perhaps tumbled while we were looking at it. The elevator is wedged, you see, and my sister can't move it at all. So, when the gasoline gives out, I—I'm not sure how the machine will act."

"Anyway," exclaimed Madeline, with sudden determination, "we are wasting valuable time in useless talk. Follow me at once.""Where to?" asked Bill, in surprise.

"To my yacht. I'm going after the girls. Please come with us, Thatcher Allen —and you, too, Mr. Todd. Aunty," turning to Mrs. Tupper, "if you require anything from the hotel for the journey I will send you there in the car; but you must hurry, for every moment is precious."

Thatcher Allen straightened up, animated and alert, while his face brightened with a ray of hope.

"We will take my car to the bay," said he, eagerly, "and Mr. and Mrs. Tupper can use your own car to visit the hotel. Will you accompany us, or ride with your aunt?"

"With you," decided Madeline. "I must have the captain get up steam and prepare to sail. It won't take long; I've ordered them to keep a little steam all the time, in case I wish to take a party out for a ride."

Even as they were speaking all walked rapidly toward the long line of motor cars. Mrs. Tupper, who had not ventured a remark or made any protest—quite contrary to her usual custom—now astonished her niece by saying:

"Never mind the hotel; let us all go directly to the yacht. With those two poor girls in danger I couldn't bear to think I had caused a moment's delay. It is very comfortable on the yacht and—we'll get along all right for a day."

"To be sure; to be sure," agreed Mr. Tupper, nervously. "I shall be seasick; I'm bound to be seasick; I always am; but in this emergency my place is by Madeline's side."

Of course no protest would have affected Madeline's determination, and the worthy couple recognized that fact perfectly; hence they diplomatically abetted her plan.

Captain Krell had attended the exhibitions at the aviation field, but while there he kept one eye on Miss Dentry. During the panic caused by the runaway airplane he saw Miss Dentry in earnest conversation with Thatcher Allen and Stricklin and marked their hurried departure from the field. So the gallant captain scuttled back to the yacht at his best speed, to find Miss Dentry already aboard and the engineer shoveling in coal.

Both Thatcher Allen and Bill knew that the *Salvador* was by odds the fastest ship in the bay, and Madeline›s prompt offer to go to the rescue of their imperiled daughter and sister awakened hope in their breasts and aroused their lively gratitude.

After all it did not take the yacht long to get under way. It was so perfectly manned and in such complete readiness that steam was the only requisite to begin a trip instantly. Madeline could scarcely wait while with aggravating deliberation they hoisted anchor, but she became more composed as the yacht slowly headed out of the bay, the crew alert and the big captain as eager as any of them to rescue the daring bird-maids.

By the time the *Salvador* reached the open sea the shore was lined with thousands of spectators, and the sight of the graceful yacht headed in chase of the two girls raised a cheer so lusty and heartfelt that it reached Madeline›s ears and caused her to flush with pleasure and renewed determination.

CHAPTER 8.11
A GAME OF CHECKERS

"Nine o'clock!" cried Mary Eliska, giving Sybil a nudge. "Are you going to sleep all day, Crusoe, like those dreadful owls?"

"I'd like to," muttered Miss Allen, regretfully opening her eyes. "My, what a blessed relief from that night of torture! Don't you think, Sis, that those feathered fiends only stopped the concert because they'd howled until their throats were sore?"

"I fear we made a mistake in changing our camp," returned Mary Eliska, busy with her toilet. "The shrieks sounded much louder than they did the night before."

"Question is," said Sybil, rolling off the improvised bed, "how long we are to endure this imprisonment. If it's to be a mere day or so, don't let's move again. However, if you think we're here for life, I propose we murder every owl and have done with them."

"We can't read the future, of course," remarked Mary Eliska thoughtfully, as she stroked her beautiful hair with her back-comb—the only toilet article she possessed. "Bill may get to us any day, or he may have a hard time finding us. He will never give up, though, nor will your father, until our retreat is located and—and—our fate determined."

"Poor Daddy!" sighed Sybil; "he'll be worried to death. I've led him a dog's life, I know; but he's just as fond and faithful as if I'd been a dutiful daughter."

"I hope they won't tell mother," said Mary Eliska. "The anxiety would be so hard for her to bear. *We* know we›re fairly comfortable, Syb; but they can›t know that, nor have any clear idea what›s become of us.»

They fell quiet, after this, and exchanged few words until they were outside the tent and had made a fire of twigs and leaves in the rock stove. Sybil warmed the last of the baked beans, adding a little water to moisten them. With these they each ate a biscuit and finished their breakfast with a draught of cool water from the spring.

After the meal they wandered among the queer greenery they had before observed and Sybil called attention to the fact that many of the broad, tender leaves had been nibbled at the edges.

"The owls did that, of course," said Mary Eliska, "and if it is good food for owls I'm sure it wouldn't hurt us."

"Doesn't it look something like lettuce?" asked Sybil.

"Yes; perhaps that is what it is—wild lettuce."

She plucked a leaf and tasted it. The flavor was agreeable and not unlike that of lettuce.

"Well," said Sybil, after tasting the green, "here's an item to add to our bill-of-fare. If only we had dressing for it a salad would be mighty appetizing."

"There's the vinegar in the bottle of pickles," proposed Mary Eliska. "It won't go very far, but it will help. Let us try the new dish for luncheon."

"And how about the bananas?" asked Miss Allen.

"I'll proceed to get them right now," promised Mary Eliska, walking back to the group of trees.

The bare, smooth trunks extended twenty feet in the air before a branch appeared. The branches were broad, stout leaves, among which hung the bunches of fruit.

"I hate to ruin a perfectly good tree," declared Mary Eliska, picking up the hatchet, "but self-preservation is the first law of nature."

"Goodness me! You're not thinking of chopping it down, I hope," exclaimed Sybil.

"No; that would be too great a task to undertake. I've a better way, I think."

She selected a tree that had three large bunches of bananas on it. One bunch was quite ripe, the next just showing color and the third yet an emerald green. Each bunch consisted of from sixty to eighty bananas.

First Mary Eliska chopped notches on either side of the trunk, at such distances as would afford support for her feet. When these notches rose as high as she could reach, she brought two broad straps from the Aircraft, buckled them together around the tree-trunk, and then passed the slack around her body and beneath her arms. Thus supported she began the ascent, placing her feet in the notches she had already cut and chopping more notches as she advanced.

In this manner the girl reached the lower branches and after climbing into them removed the strap and crept along until she reached the first bunch of bananas.

"Stand from under!" she cried to Sybil and began chopping at the stem. Presently the huge bunch fell with a thud and Sybil gleefully applauded by clapping her hands.

"The lower ones are a bit mushy, I fear," she called to her chum, "but that can't be helped."

"We will eat those first," said Mary Eliska, creeping to the second bunch.

She managed to cut it loose, and the third, after which she replaced the strap around her body and cautiously descended to the ground. The two girls then rolled over the ripest bunch and found the damage confined to a couple of dozen bananas, the skins of which had burst from the force of the heavy fall. A moment later they were feasting on the fruit, which they found delicious.

"I've read somewhere," said Sybil, "that bananas alone will sustain life for an indefinite period. They are filling and satisfying, and they're wholesome. We needn't worry any longer for fear of starvation, Sis."

"I imagine we'd get deadly tired of the things, in time," replied Mary Eliska; "but, as you say, they'll sustain life, and just at present they taste mighty good."

They drew the ripest bunch into the tent, but left the others lying in the bright sunshine.

"Now," announced Mary Eliska, "we must make an expedition to that crevasse and rescue the bar and the lever, which we left sticking in the rocks. The tide is low, so we may go around by way of the shore."

A leisurely walk of fifteen minutes brought them to the crevasse, down which tumbled the tiny brook. Mary Eliska, as the most venturesome, climbed to the bar, from whence she managed to pull the lever out of the owl's nest into which she had formerly thrust it. If the owl was hidden there now it failed to disclose its presence and on descending to the rocks Mary Eliska easily released the bar. So now, armed once more with their primitive weapons, the girls returned to their camp.

"I can attach these to our machine at any time," said the air-maid, "so I think it may be best to keep them beside us, to use in case of emergency. I haven't felt entirely safe since we lost them."

"Nor I," returned Sybil. "We haven't encountered anything dangerous, so far, but I like to feel I've something to pound with, should occasion arise."

That afternoon Mary Eliska worked on the Aircraft, repairing the damage caused by the sliding chest. She also took apart the steering gear, filed the bearings carefully, and afterward replaced the parts, fitting them nicely together and greasing them thoroughly. As a result of this labor the gear now worked easily and its parts were not likely again to bind.

"Bill made it altogether too light for its purpose," said the girl. "On the next machine I must see that he remedies that fault."

Sybil had been lying half asleep on the sands, shaded by the spreading plane of the Aircraft. She now aroused herself and looked at her companion with a whimsical expression while the other girl carefully gathered up the tools and put them away.

"All ready to run, Sis?" she asked.

"All ready."

"I suppose with the gasoline tanks filled we could go home?"

"Yes; I think so. With the wind in our favor, as it was when we came, we ought to cover the same distance easily."

"Very good. I hope you are now satisfied, having worked like a nailer for half a day, getting a machine in order that can't be utilized. Gasoline doesn't grow on this island, I imagine— unless it could be made from bananas."

"No; it doesn't grow here."

"And none of the department stores keep it."

"True."

"But we've got a flying-machine, in apple-pie order, except that we're using one of the plane coverings for a tent and a lever for a weapon of defense."

"Absolutely correct, Crusoe."

"Hooray. Let's go to sleep again, dear. Those screechers will keep us awake all night, you know."

She closed her eyes drowsily and Mary Eliska sat beside her and looked thoughtfully over the expanse of blue ocean. There was nothing in sight; nothing save the big island at the west, which seemed from this distance to be much more desirable than the bleak rocks on which the adventurers had stranded.

Mary Eliska got her binoculars and made a careful inspection of the place. Through the powerful glasses she could discover forests, green meadowland and the gleam of a small river. It was a flat island, yet somewhat elevated above the surface of the sea. She judged it to be at least four times bigger than the island they were now on. The distance rendered it impossible to discover whether the place was inhabited or not. No houses showed themselves, but of course she could see only one side of the island from where she sat.

Mary Eliska did not feel sleepy, in spite of her wakeful night, so she took Sybil's fishline and baited the hook with a scrap of beef. Going to the top of the bluff she began to fish, and as she fished she reviewed in mind all the conditions of their misfortune and strove to find a way of relief. Being unsuccessful in both occupations she finally came back to the little bay and waded out to the big rock that guarded the mouth of the inlet. On the ocean side there was good depth of water and in the course of the next half hour she landed a huge crawfish, two crabs and a two-pound flat fish resembling a sole. This last is known as "chicken-halibut" and is delicious eating.

She aroused Sybil, and the two girls built a fire, using dry twigs from the brushwood, a supply of which they had gathered and placed near their tent. In the fat taken from the crawfish they fried the halibut for supper. Then among the coals and hot stones they buried the crabs, keeping a little fire above them until they were sure the creatures were thoroughly roasted. Next day they cracked the shells and picked out the meat, deciding they might live luxuriously even on an island of rocks, provided they exercised their wits and took advantage of all conditions Nature afforded them.

At dark thousands of great owls came from their retreats among the rocks and flew ceaselessly about the island, uttering their distracting cries. Nor was there a moment's peace again until daybreak. The birds were evidently in search of food, and found it; but what it consisted of the girls could not imagine. Singularly enough, the castaways were growing accustomed to the deafening clamor and as they felt quite safe within their enclosed tent they were able to sleep—in a fitful, restless way—a good part of the night.

The following day they began to find the hours dragging tediously, for the first time since their captivity. Arm in arm the two girls wandered around the elevated end of their island, exploring it thoroughly but making no new discoveries of importance. The barren, slimy hollow that lay inland had no temptations to lure them near it and so there remained little else to do but watch the ocean and prepare their meals.

"This is our fourth day of isolation," announced Sybil, in a tone more irritable than she was wont to use. "I wonder how long this thing will last."

"We must be patient," said Mary Eliska, gently. "Our dear ones are making every effort to find us, I'm sure, and of course they will succeed in time. We are at some distance from the usual route of ships; that is evident; and for this reason it will be more difficult for our friends to locate us. I suppose that a few days more may easily pass by before we catch sight of a boat coming to get us. But they'll come, Syb," she repeated, confidently, "and meantime we—we must be—patient."

Sybil stared across the water.

"Do you play checkers?" she asked abruptly.

"Bill and I used to play, long ago. I suppose I could remember the game, and it might amuse us; but we have no checkerboard, nor men for it."

"Pah! and you the sister of an inventor!" cried Sybil scornfully. "I'm astonished at you, Miss Stricklin. Haven't you enough reflected ingenuity to manufacture a checkerboard?"

"Why, I think so," said Mary Eliska. "The idea hadn't occurred to me. I'll see what I can do."

"You make the board, and I'll find the men," proposed Sybil, and springing to her feet she ran down to the beach, glad to have anything to occupy her and relieve the dreary dragging of the hours.

Mary Eliska looked around her, pondering the problem. Material for a checkerboard seemed hopelessly lacking, yet after a little thought she solved the problem fairly well. First she ripped the flounce from her black silk petticoat and with the jackknife from the tool kit she cut out thirty-two black squares, each two inches in diameter. Then she took a tube of prepared glue that was in the outfit and walked up the incline to their tent, in the center of which stood the aluminum chest. This chest, being of a dull silvery color, and quite smooth on all its sides, was to be the groundwork of the checkerboard squares, as well as the board itself and the elevated table to play on. Mary Eliska glued the squares of black silk to the cover of the chest, leaving a similar square space on the aluminum surface between each one. When this was accomplished she pasted a narrow edge of black around the entire sixty-four squares, thus marking their boundary.

She was very proud of this work and was regarding it admiringly when Sybil entered.

"How clever!" cried her chum, genuinely enthusiastic. "Really, Miss Columbus, you have done better than I. But here are the checker-men, and they'll do very nicely."

As she spoke she dumped from her handkerchief upon the board twenty-four shells which she had carefully selected from those that littered the beach. Twelve were dark in color and twelve pearly white and being of uniform size they made very practical checkers.

"Now, then," said she, squatting beside the chest and arranging her shells in order, "I'll play you a series of games for a box of bonbons, to be purchased when we return to civilization."

"How many games?" asked Mary Eliska, seating herself opposite.

"Let us say—the best three in five. If that's too rapid we will make the next bet the best six in ten, or twelve in twenty. Agreeable, Columbus?"

"Entirely so, Crusoe."

It was really a capital diversion. Sybil played very well and it required all Mary Eliska's cleverness to oppose her. At times they tired of the play and went for a stroll on the bluff; and always, no matter how intent they were upon the game, they kept watchful eyes on the ocean.

And in this manner the days dragged on their weary lengths and the nights resounded to the shrill cries of the owls. One morning Sybil asked:

"Isn't today Tuesday, Mary Eliska?" "Yes," was the quiet reply. "We've inhabited this wilderness just a week."

CHAPTER 8.12
THE QUEST OF THE SALVADOR

On the roomy forward deck of the *Salvador* an earnest conference was held.

"How fast are we going?" asked Bill.

"The captain says about fifteen miles an hour. That's our best clip, it seems," replied Madeline.

"And very good speed," added Captain Krell, proudly.

"So it is, for an English yacht," agreed Thatcher Allen .

"In that case," said Bill, "we are moving one-third as fast as the Aircraft did, and we were about two hours later in starting. Provided the girls exhaust their gasoline in flying, they will make a hundred and fifty to two hundred miles, requiring five-or-six-hours' time. Then they will alight, bobbing upon the water and helpless to move in any direction except where the current carries them. It will take us eighteen hours to reach that same spot, and we will therefore be twelve hours behind them. Do you all follow me?"

They nodded, listening intently.

"Now, the girls left at about one thirty this afternoon. If my calculations are correct, they'll take to the water anywhere from six thirty to seven thirty this evening. We shall overtake them at about the same hour tomorrow morning. Unless they drift considerably out of their course we shall see the white planes at daybreak and have no trouble in running alongside. But there's always the chance that through some cause they may manage to drop to water sooner, and perhaps run the boat toward home. Mary Eliska is a very clever girl, as you all know; calm and resourceful; quick-witted and brave. She will do all that anyone could do to bring the Aircraft under control. So the one danger, it appears to me, is that we may pass them during the night."

"That danger, sir," said Captain Krell, "may be reduced to a minimum. We carry a very powerful searchlight, which shall be worked by my men all night, illuminating not only the course ahead, but the sea for miles on every side. As you say, Mr. Stricklin, the white planes may be easily seen against the blue water, and we positively cannot miss them during the night."

"You—er—interest me," said Thatcher Allen, looking more cheerful. "We seem to have everything in our favor, thanks to Miss Dentry's generosity."

"I'm *so* glad I bought this yacht!» exclaimed Madeline, fervently, «for it enabled me to go to the assistance of those poor girls. I›m sure it was all providential.»

"Let us hope," said Mr. Tupper pompously, "the young women will survive until we reach them. However, we shall learn their fate, in any event, which will afford us a certain degree of satisfaction."

That speech was like a douche of cold water, but although the gentleman received various indignant and reproachful looks he had "sized up the situation" with fair accuracy.

Thatcher Allen, however, since those first despairing moments on the aviation field, had recovered command of his feelings and seemed hopeful, if not confident, of his daughter's ultimate escape from serious mishap. He was exceedingly fond of Mary Eliska, too, and even had not Sybil been with her it is certain that he would have been much worried and eager to go to her assistance.

Bill Stricklin, on the contrary, grew more nervous as time passed. Better than the others he knew the dangers that threatened the girls if, as he suspected, the steering gear had broken and the elevator and engine control been rendered useless. He racked his brain to think what could have caused the trouble, but never a hint of the truth dawned upon him.

The third member of the Stricklin-Thatcher Allen party, Mr. H. Chesterton Radley-Todd, had maintained a discreet silence ever since Miss Dentry had invited him to join the rescue party. This she had been led to do by the look of abject misery on the boy's face, and he had merely pressed her hand to indicate his thanks. Chesty Todd was never much of a conversationalist and his appreciation of his own awkwardness rendered him diffident unless occasion demanded prompt and aggressive action, when he usually came to the front in an efficient if unexpected manner.

Madeline Dentry, seeing Chesty Todd merely as he appeared, wondered in a casual way why such a blundering, incompetent booby had been employed by the Stricklin-Thatcher Allen firm, but as the big boy was a part of the "camp" and was so evidently disturbed by the accident, she was glad to relieve him to the extent of adding him to the party.

Very soon after the *Salvador* started, however, nearly everyone on board began to feel the presence of the youthful press agent. It was Chesty Todd who discovered the searchlight aboard and long before the conference on the deck he had primed the captain to use it during the coming night. It was Chesty Todd who sat on a coal-bunker in the hold, swinging his long legs and inspiring the engineer, by dark insinuations concerning the *Salvador's* ability to speed, to give her engines every pound of steam she could carry. It was Chesty who pumped the steward to learn how well the boat was provisioned and supplied the deck hands with choice cigars until they were ready to swear he was a trump and imagined him quite the most important personage aboard, after Miss Dentry.

The chef served an excellent dinner in the cabin, to which no one did full justice except Mr. Tupper. All were loth to leave the deck long enough to eat, although they knew a watch was stationed in the "crow's nest" with powerful glasses. When night fell the searchlight came into play and the entire party sat huddled forward, eagerly following the sweep of light across the waters. It was ten o'clock when Mr. and Mrs. Tupper retired, and midnight when Madeline went to her room, leaving orders to call her if the Aircraft was sighted.

Bill Stricklin, Thatcher Allen and Chesty Todd sat by the rail all night, wide-eyed and alert. Once the searchlight caught the sails of a ship and they all leaped up, thinking it was the Aircraft. Again, something dark—a tangled mass of wreckage—swept by them and set their hearts throbbing until they held the light steadily upon it and discovered it to be a jumble of kelp and driftwood. Daylight came and found them wan but still wakeful, for now they were getting close to the limit of flight possible to the Aircraft.

Captain Krell was a skillful navigator and, having taken his course in a direct line from Sealskin Island, following the flight of Mary Eliska's Hydro-Aircraft, had not swerved a hair's breadth from it the entire voyage.

"You see," said Bill, peering ahead in the strengthening daylight, "the *Salvador* hasn›t dodged a bit, and the Aircraft couldn›t. So we›re bound to strike our quarry soon.»

"Wind," suggested Chesty.

"Yes; the wind might carry them a little out of their course, to be sure," admitted Bill; "but I think—I hope—not far enough to escape our range of vision."

At about seven o'clock, at Chesty Todd's suggestion, the engines were slowed down somewhat, that the lookout aloft might have better opportunity to examine the sea on all sides of the ship. The yacht still maintained fair speed, however, and the call to breakfast finding no one willing to respond, Madeline ordered coffee and rolls served on deck, where they could all watch while refreshing themselves.

"What's your run, Captain?" asked Bill, nervously.

"Hundred and forty miles, sir."

"Indeed! Go a little slower, please."

The captain rang the bell to slow down. Presently the *Salvador* was creeping along at the rate of ten miles an hour.

"The gasoline," said Bill, "may have carried them farther than I figured on. It's a new machine and I haven't had a chance to test the exact capacity of the tanks."

The moments dragged tediously. Every person aboard was laboring under tense excitement.

"What's the run, Captain?"

"One fifty-two, sir."

"Ah."

Nothing was in sight; only an uninterrupted stretch of blue sea. Hour after hour passed. At noon the run was two hundred and twenty miles and the airplane had not been sighted. Bill turned and faced those assembled.

"It's no use going farther in this direction," he said, the words trembling on his lips. "I'm very sure they couldn't have made this distance."

"Evidently their course has been altered by the wind," added Thatcher Allen .

"Gusty, at times, last night," asserted Chesty.

Bill nodded.

"A strong wind might do what the girls couldn't," said he. "That is, it might alter the direction of their flight. How did it blow?"

"At four o'clock, from the north; at five fifteen, from the west; at six, due south," said Chesty.

There was silence for a few minutes. The engines had been shut down and the boat lay drifting upon the water.

"I think it will be well to examine the charts," suggested Mr. Todd, "and find out where we are."

"I know where we are," said Captain Krell. "Wait a moment; I'll get the chart, so you may all study it."

He brought it from his cabin and spread it upon a folding table on the deck. A penciled line ran directly from the port of San Diego to a point south by southwest.

"A few more hours on the same course and we'd sight the little island of Guadaloup, off the Mexican coast," explained Captain Krell. "But the airplane couldn't go so far; therefore we must search on either side the course we've come."

They all bent their heads over the map.

"What are those unmarked dots which are scattered around?" inquired Thatcher Allen .

"Islands, sir. Mostly bits of rock jutting out of the sea. They're not important enough to name, nor do they appear on an ordinary map; but a seaman's chart indicates them, for unless we had knowledge of their whereabouts we might bump into them."

"They're mostly to the south of us, I see," remarked Mr. Tupper.

"Yes, sir."

"And it's south we must go, I think," said Bill, looking at Chesty Todd for the youth to confirm his judgment. "There was no wind to take them to the west of this course, I believe."

"That's my idea," declared the press agent. "I would suggest our doubling back and forth, on the return trip, covering forty or fifty miles at each leg. Seems like we couldn't miss 'em, that way."

After much consultation this plan was finally agreed upon. The captain outlined his course and followed it, so that during the next four days not a square yard of ocean escaped their search. But it was all in vain and at the end of the fourth day, with the California coast again in sight, there was scarcely a person aboard who entertained the slightest hope of finding the missing girls.

CHAPTER 8.13
CAPRICIOUS FATE

A wireless was sent to the shore, reporting the failure of the *Salvador* to locate the runaway airplane and asking if any tidings had been received of Mary Eliska and Sybil Allen.

There was no news.

Madeline called her passengers together again for a further consultation.

"What shall we do?" she asked.

Neither Bill nor Thatcher Allen could well reply. Miss Dentry had generously placed her splendid yacht at their disposal and in person had conducted the search, neglecting no detail that might contribute to their success. But failure had resulted and they could not ask her to continue what appeared to be a hopeless undertaking. Bill, who had had ample time to consider this finale, tried to answer her question.

"We are very grateful to you, Miss Dentry," he said, "and both Thatcher Allen and I fully appreciate the sacrifice you have made in so promptly trying to rescue our girls. That we face failure is no fault of yours, nor of your crew, and I realize that you have already done all that humanity or friendship might require. Of course you understand that we cannot give up until my sister's fate, and that of Miss Allen, is positively determined. Therefore, as soon as we reach shore we shall organize another expedition to continue the quest."

"You are doing me an injustice, sir," returned the girl gravely. "Whatever my former plans may have been I am now determined not to abandon this voyage until we have found your sister and her companion. I was greatly attracted by Mary Eliska, and grieve over her sad fate sincerely. Moreover, I do not like to put my hand to the plow without completing the furrow. Unless you believe you can charter a better boat for your purpose than the *Salvador*, or can find a crew more devoted to your interests, I shall order Captain Krell to turn about and renew the search."

That, of course, settled the matter. The *Salvador* put about and returned to a point where the see-sawing must be renewed and extended to cover more expanse of ocean.

Chesty Todd, coming to where Madeline stood beside the rail, looked into her piquant face with frank admiration.

"Excuse me, Miss Dentry," said he, "but you're what I'd call a brick. I knew, of course, you'd stick it out, but there's no harm in congratulating a girl on being true blue. I'm awfully glad you—you had the grit to tackle it again. I'll never be myself again until those girls are found."

She looked up at him reflectively.

"Which of the young ladies are you engaged to?" she asked.

"Me?" blushing like a schoolboy; "neither one, if you please. They—they're only kids, you know."

"Then which one do you love?"

"Both!" said Chesty Todd, earnestly. "They're splendid girls, Miss Dentry; *your* sort, you know.»

She smiled.

"Then it's the 'sort' you love?" she asked.

"Yes, if you'll allow me. Not the individual—as yet. When I love the individual I hope it'll be the right sort, but I'm so humbly unlucky I'll probably make a mistake."

For the first time since their acquaintance Madeline found the big boy interesting. She knew very little of the history of the Stricklins and Allens, but found Chesty eager to speak of them and of his past relations with them, being loud in his praise for the entire "combination."

Thatcher Allen was an eccentric fellow, according to Mr. Radley-Todd, but "straight as a die." Bill was chock full of ability and talent, but not very practical in business ways. Mrs. Stricklin, Mary Eliska's blind mother, was the sweetest and gentlest lady in the world, Sybil Allen a delightful mystery that defied fathoming but constantly allured one to the attempt, while Mary Eliska——

"Mary Eliska is a girl you'll have to read yourself, Miss Dentry, and the more you study her the better you'll love her. She's girl all over, and the kind of girl one always hopes to meet but seldom does. Old-fashioned in her gentleness, simplicity, truth and candor; up-to-the-minute in the world's latest discovery—the art of flying. Modest as Tennyson's dairymaid; brave as a trooper; a maid with a true maid's heart and a thorough sport when you give her an airplane to manage. Excuse me. I don't often talk this way; usually I can only express myself in writing. But a fellow who wouldn't enthuse over Mary Eliska could only have one excuse—total dumbness."

"I see," said Madeline, slyly. "Miss Stricklin is the type of the 'sort' of girl you love." "Exactly. But tell me, since you've started on such an indefinite cruise, is the *Salvador* well provisioned?»

"From the sublime to the ridiculous! We have stores to last our party six weeks, without scrimping." "Good. And coal?"

"Enough for a month's continuous run. I had intended a trip to Honolulu—perhaps as far as Japan—and had prepared for it even before I was privileged to lay eyes on my yacht."

"How fortunate that was, for all of us! Somehow, I've a feeling we shall find those girls, this time. Before, I had a sort of hunch we were destined to fail. Can you explain that?""I shall not try."

"We didn't allow enough for the wind. A sudden gust might have whirled the Aircraft in any direction, and it would jog along on that route until the next blow."

"Do you believe they are still alive?" she asked softly.

"Yes; I've never been able to think of them as—as—otherwise. They are wonderfully clever girls, and Mary Eliska knows airplanes backwards and forwards. She's as much at home in the air as a bird; and why shouldn't the machine fall gently to the water, when the gasoline gave out? If it did, they can float any length of time, and the Pacific has been like a mill pond ever since they started. According to Thatcher Allen, they have enough food with them to last for several days. I've an idea we shall run across them bobbing up and down on the water, as happy and contented as two babes in the wood." The big fellow sighed as he said this, and Madeline understood he was trying to encourage himself, as well as her.

In spite of Chesty Todd's prediction, day followed day in weary search and the lost airplane was not sighted. Captain and crew had now abandoned hope and performed their duties in a perfunctory way. Bill Stricklin had grown thin and pale and deep lines of grief marked his boyish face. Thatcher Allen was silent and stern. He paced the deck constantly but avoided conversation with Bill. Madeline, however, kept up bravely, and so did Chesty Todd. They were much together, these trying days, and did much to cheer one another's spirits. Had a vote been taken, on that tenth dreary day, none but these two would have declared in favor of prolonging what now appeared to be a hopeless quest.

"You see," said Chesty to Madeline, yet loud enough to be heard by both Thatcher Allen and Bill, "there's every chance of the girls having drifted to some island, where of course they'd find food in plenty; or they may have been picked up by some ship on a long voyage, and we'll hear of 'em from some foreign port. There are lots of ways, even on this trackless waste, of their being rescued."

This suggestion was made to counteract the grim certainty that the castaways had by now succumbed to starvation, if they still remained afloat. Several small islands had already been encountered and closely scanned, with the idea that the girls might have sought refuge on one of them. The main thing that kept alive the spark of hope was the fact that no vestige of the Aircraft had been seen. It would float indefinitely, whether wrecked or not, for the boat had enough air-tight compartments to sustain it even in a high sea.

On the evening of this tenth day the *Salvador* experienced the first rough weather of the trip. The day had been sultry and oppressive and toward sundown the sky suddenly darkened and a stiff breeze caught them. By midnight it was blowing a hurricane and even the sturdy captain began to have fears for the safety of the yacht. There was little danger to the stout craft from wind or waves, but the sea in this neighborhood was treacherous and full of those rocky islets so much dreaded by mariners. Captain Krell studied his chart constantly and kept a sharp lookout ahead; but in such a night, on a practically unknown sea, there was bound to be a certain degree of peril.

There was as little sleep for the passengers as for the crew on this eventful night. The women had been warned not to venture on deck, where it was dangerous even for the men; but Madeline Dentry would not stay below. She seemed to delight in defying the rage of the elements. Clinging to the arm of Chesty Todd, the huge bulk of whose six-feet-three stood solid as a monument, she peered through the night and followed the glare of the searchlight, now doubly useful, for it showed the pilot a clear sea ahead. Mr. Tupper bumped into them, embraced Chesty for support and then bounded to the rail, to which he clung desperately.

"Why are you on deck?" asked Madeline, sternly. "Go below at once!"

Just then a roll of the yacht slid him across the deck, tumbled him against the poop and then carried him sprawling into the scuppers. When he recovered his breath Mr. Tupper crawled cautiously to the companionway and disappeared into the cabin.

Bill and Thatcher Allen had lashed themselves to the rail and in spite of the drenching spray continued to peer into the wild night with fearful intensity. Both were sick at heart, for they knew if the girls had managed to survive 'til now, their tiny boat would be unable to weather the storm. Every shriek of the wind, which often resembled a human cry, set them shivering with terror.

It was toward morning when the glare of the searchlight suddenly revealed a dark peak just ahead. Bill Stricklin and Thatcher Allen saw it, even as the warning scream of the lookout rang in their ears. Captain Krell saw it, and marveling at its nearness, sprang to the wheel.

Madeline and Chesty saw it, too, and instinctively the big fellow put his arms around her as if to shield her.

Wild cries resounded from the deck; the bells rang frantically; the engines stopped short and then reversed just as a huge wave came from behind, caught the *Salvador* on its crest and swept her forward in its onward rush. Two men threw their weight upon the wheel without effect: the propeller was raised by the wave above the water line and whirred and raced madly in the air, while beneath the gleam of the searchlight a monstrous mass of rock seemed swiftly advancing to meet the fated ship.

Past the port side, where Madeline and her escort clung, swept a jagged point of rock; the yacht bumped with a force that sent everyone aboard reeling forward in a struggling heap; then it trembled, moaned despairingly and lay still, while the wave that had carried it to its doom flooded the decks with tons of water and receded to gloat over the mischief it had caused.

The searchlight was out; blackness surrounded the bruised and bewildered men and women who struggled to regain their feet, while in their ears echoed a chorus of terrifying shrieks not of the wind, but so evidently emanating from living creatures that they added materially to the panic of the moment.

Chesty Todd released Madeline, gasping and half drowned, from the tangle of humanity in the bow, and succeeded in getting her to the rail. The bow of the yacht was high and it lay over on one side, so that the deck was at a difficult angle.

"Are—are we sinking?" asked the girl, confused and unnerved by the calamity.

"No, indeed," replied Chesty, his mouth to her ear. "We can't sink, now, for we're on solid ground and lying as still as a stuffed giraffe."

"Oh, what shall we do?" she cried, wringing her hands. "If we are wrecked we can't save Mary Eliska—perhaps we can't save ourselves! Oh, what shall we do?—what shall we do?"

The boy saw that the shock had destroyed her usual poise and he could feel her trembling as she clung to him.

"My advice," he said quietly, "is that we all get to bed and have a wink of sleep. It has been a long and exciting day for us, hasn't it?"

CHAPTER 8.14
ON THE BLUFF

Sybil clapped her hands gleefully and looked at Mary Eliska in triumph.

"The rubber is mine!" she cried. "You now owe me sixteen boxes of chocolates, nine of caramels and twelve of mixed bonbons—enough to stock a candy store. Tell you what I'll do, Commodore Columbus; I'll pit my desert island and my man Friday against your fleet of galleys and the favor of Queen Isabella, and it shall be the best three out of five games. Are *you* game, my dear Discoverer?»

Mary Eliska laughed.

"You ought to give me odds, Crusoe, for you are the more skillful checker player," she replied. "But I won't play any more today. This heat is dreadfully oppressive and from the looks of the sky I'm afraid a storm is brewing."

"What? A rain storm?" asked Sybil, jumping up to go outside the tent and examine the sky.

"Rain, hail, thunder, lightning and tornadoes; anything is likely to follow a storm in this latitude," declared Mary Eliska, following her. "I think, Sybil, we ought to make all as safe and secure as possible, in case of emergency, while we have the time."

"What can we do?" asked Sybil. "I won't mind the storm very much, if it doesn't have lightning. That's the only thing I'm afraid of."

Mary Eliska examined the sky critically.

"I predict high winds," she presently said, "and high winds might endanger our property. Let us get to the beach, first, and see what may be done to protect the Aircraft."

They found the flying-machine fairly well protected by the walls of the ravine in which it lay, but as the big upper plane offered a tempting surface to the wind Mary Eliska set to work and removed it, a task that consumed two full hours. Then she wired the framework to a big rock, for additional security, and carrying the canvas from the plane between them, the girls returned to their tent.

"Will our house stand much of a wind?" asked Sybil.

"It is rather exposed, on this bluff," replied Mary Eliska, doubtfully. "I think it will be wise for us to pile more rocks upon the edges. The wire will hold, I'm sure, for it is nickel-steel, and if we close the ends of the tents securely we may escape damage."

"All right; I'm glad to have something to do," cried Sybil, picking up a rock. "We'll build a regular parapet, if you say so."

This was exactly what they did. In spite of the oppressive heat the two girls worked faithfully piling the rocks around the tent, until they had raised a parapet nearly half its height. They were inspired to take this precaution by the glowering aspect of the sky, which grew more threatening as the afternoon waned.

Finally Mary Eliska wiped the perspiration from her brow and exclaimed: "That'll do, I'm sure, Syb. And now I'm ready for dinner. What's to eat?"

Sybil made a grimace.

"Bananas and jelly," she replied. "Could you conceive a more horrible combination?"

"Meat all gone?"

"We've part of a baked crab; that's all."

"And the lettuce. I shall have crab salad, with bananas for dessert."

"A salad without lemon or vinegar is the limit," declared Sybil. "I shall stick to bananas and jelly."

Their appetites were still good and Mary Eliska really enjoyed her salad, which she seasoned with salt which they had obtained by evaporating seawater. The bananas were getting to be a trifle irksome to the palate, but as food they were nourishing and satisfying. Neither of the castaways grumbled much at the lack of ordinary food, being grateful at heart that they were able to escape starvation.

The storm burst upon them just after dark and its violence increased hour by hour. There was little rain, and no lightning at all, but the wind held high revel and fluttered the canvas of the tent so powerfully that the girls, huddled anxiously in bed, feared the frail shelter would be torn to shreds.

But the plane-cloth used by Bill Stricklin was wonderfully strong and had been sized with a composition that prevented the wind from penetrating it. Therefore it resisted the gale nobly, and after a time the fears of the two girls subsided to such a degree that they dozed at times and toward morning, when the wind subsided, sank into deep sleep. The hooting of the owls no longer had power to keep them awake, and on this night the owls were less in evidence than usual, perhaps deterred from leaving their nests by the storm.

Weather changes are abrupt in the semi-tropics. The morning dawned cool and delightful and the sun shone brilliantly. There was a slight breeze remaining, but not more than enough to flutter Mary Eliska's locks as she unfastened the flap of the tent and walked out upon the bluff to discover if the Aircraft was still safe.

It lay at the bottom of the ravine, in plain sight from where she stood, and seemed quite undisturbed. Mary Eliska turned her eyes toward the distant island, let them sweep the tumbling waves of the ocean and finally allowed them to rest upon the bay at the east, where they had first landed. Then she uttered an involuntary cry that echoed shrilly among the crags.

A ship lay stranded upon the shelving beach—fully half its length upon dry land!

The cry aroused Sybil, who came running from the tent rubbing her eyes and with an anxious face.

"What's up, Sis?" she demanded.

Mary Eliska pointed a trembling finger across the rock-strewn plain to the bay, and Sybil looked and gave a gasp of delight.

"Oh, Mary Eliska, we're saved—we're saved!" she murmured. Then, sinking upon the sand, she covered her face with her hands and began to cry.

But the air-maid was too interested to weep; she was looking hard at the boat.

"Isn't it Madeline Dentry's yacht?" she asked. "Yes; I'm sure it is. Then they've been searching for us and the storm has wrecked them. Sybil, your father and Bill may be on that ship, alive or—or———"

Sybil sprang up.

"Do you see anyone?" she asked eagerly.

"No; it's too far away, and the sun interferes. I'll get the glasses."

She was quite composed now and her quiet demeanor did much to restore Sybil's self-possession. Mary Eliska brought the binoculars, looked through them for a time and then handed the glasses to her chum.

"Not a soul in sight, that I can see," she remarked. "Try it yourself."

Sybil had no better luck.

"Can they all be drowned?" she inquired in horrified tones.

"I think not. They may have abandoned the wreck, during the storm, or they may be hidden from us by the side of the boat, which lies keeled over in the opposite direction from us."

"Can't we go there, Mary Eliska, and find out?"

"Yes, dear; at once. The tide is out, and although there is quite a sea left from last night's hurricane I think we can manage the trip, by way of the sands, with perfect safety."

Each tore a couple of bananas from the bunch and then they ran down the incline to the beach. Knowing every turn in the coast and every difficult place, they were able to scorn the waves that occasionally swept over their feet, as if longing to draw them into their moist embraces.

CHAPTER 815
BOAT AHOY!

The first indication of dawn found anxious faces peering over the side of the *Salvador*. Passengers and crew gathered at the lower angle and inspected the position of the boat with absolute amazement.

"Never, in all my experience," said Captain Krell, "have I heard of so remarkable a wreck. We struck the only channel that would have floated us; a few yards to either side and we would have been crushed to kindling wood. As it is, we lie high and dry on this shelf—a natural dry dock—and not a timber is cracked."

"Are you sure of that?" asked Madeline.

"Quite sure, Miss Dentry. We have made a thorough investigation. But I do not wish to create any false hopes. Our condition is nearly as desperate as if we were a total wreck."

"You mean we can't get the yacht off again?"

"I fear not. Even a duplicate of that gigantic wave which hurled us here would be unable to float us off, for our tremendous headway carried us beyond the reach of any tide. This island is of rock formation. I know at a glance that a solid bed of rock is under us. Therefore we cannot dig a channel to relaunch the *Salvador*."

"Couldn't we blast a channel?" asked Mr. Tupper.

The captain merely gave him a reproachful glance.

"To be sure," replied Chesty Todd, seriously. "We'll have Stricklin invent a sort of dynamite that will blast the rocks and won't hurt the ship. Good idea, Mr. Tupper. Clever, sir; very clever."

Mr. Tupper glared at the boy resentfully, but his wife said in a mild tone of rebuke: "Really, Martin, my dear, the suggestion was idiotic."

The steward came crawling toward them with a coffeepot, followed by a man juggling a tray of cups. It was quite an acrobatic feat to navigate the incline, but they succeeded and everyone accepted the coffee gratefully.

"This place is nothing but a rock; an extinct volcano, probably," remarked Madeline, gazing thoughtfully over the island.

Chesty, having finished his coffee, climbed to the elevated side opposite.

"Here's a far better view of the place," he called. "It's quite a——" He stopped short, staring fixedly at a white speck far up on the bluff beside the low mountain.

They waited breathlessly for him to continue. Then Bill, reading the expression on Chesty's face, quickly clambered to a place beside him. As he looked he began to tremble and his face grew red and then pallid.

"Thatcher Allen," called the press agent, "bring your glasses, please."

"What is it?" pleaded Madeline.

"Why, something—just—curious, Miss Dentry. We can't say what it is, as yet, but——"

They were all scrambling up the incline by this time and soon all eyes were directed upon the white speck. Thatcher Allen focused his glasses upon the spot.

"Ah," said he presently; "this interests me; it does, indeed!"

"Is it a—a—tent?" inquired Bill, a catch in his voice.

"Looks like it," was the reply; "but not a regulation tent. Seems more like—like——Here, see for yourself, Bill."

Bill seized the binoculars.

"I think—it's—the—plane-cloth!" he gasped.

Mr. Tupper lost his balance and slid down the deck, landing with a thud against the opposite rail. That relieved the tension and a laugh—the first heard on the *Salvador* since she left port—greeted the gentleman's mishap.

"Why—if it's the plane-cloth, the girls are alive!" cried Madeline.

"To be sure," added Chesty, with joyful intonation, "and doubtless enjoying their outing."

The discovery changed the current of all thoughts and led them to forget their own calamity. The *Salvador* carried a small gasoline launch and two life-boats, all of which were in good condition.

"May we take the launch, Miss Dentry?" pleaded Bill.

"I was about to order it lowered," she said. "Can you run it, Mr. Stricklin?"

"Certainly," he replied.

"Then I shall go with you. It will carry six comfortably, and more uncomfortably; but as we may have passengers on our return trip only four had better go."

Bill ran to assist in lowering the launch. It had to be unlashed from its rack, first of all, and the tank filled with gasoline, the engine oiled and the boat prepared for action. The men worked with a will, however, and within half an hour the launch was lowered to the rocks and slid safely into the water. The landing-steps being impracticable, a rope ladder was lowered and by this means Madeline easily descended to the launch. Thatcher Allen followed, as a matter of course, but Chesty Todd modestly waited to be invited to make the fourth voyager.

"Come along, sir," said Miss Dentry, and he eagerly obeyed.

"How about food?" he suggested.

The chef, a fat little Frenchman who was much interested in the fate of the Flying Girl and her chum, had foreseen this demand and now lowered a hamper.

"Any water in it?" asked Chesty.

"Certainmente, monsieur."

"All right. Let 'er go."

Bill started the engine and the little craft quickly shot out of the bay into the open sea and took the long swells beautifully. Bounding the point, Stricklin kept as close to the shore as he dared, making for the place where the bluff began to rise.

"Boat ahoy!" cried a clear voice, so suddenly that they nearly capsized the launch in their first surprise. And there were the two lost damsels prancing and dancing up and down the beach, waving their handkerchiefs and laughing and crying with joy at beholding their friends

CHAPTER 8.16
AN ISLAND KINGDOM

It was a merry reunion, in spite of the dangers that were past and the tribulations that threatened. Because the yacht's deck afforded precarious footing they all landed on the flat rocky shore, where the breakfast, hastily prepared by the chef, was served to the united company.

"My greatest suffering," said Sybil, nestling close to her father, "was for want of coffee. I've dreamed of coffee night after night, and hoped I would be privileged to taste it again before I was called to the happy hunting grounds."

"Ah; that interests me; it does, really," said Thatcher Allen, filling her cup anew. "But—who knows, dear?—you might have reached the happy coffee-grounds."

They laughed at any absurd remark just now, and when Mary Eliska related how they had subsisted of late on bananas and jelly you may be sure the castaways were plied with all the delicacies the ship's larder afforded.

Most of the day was spent in exchanging stories of the adventures both parties had encountered since the Hydro-Aircraft ran away. Everyone wanted to add an incident or tell some personal experience, and it was all so interesting that no one was denied the privilege of talking.

But afterward, when an elaborate dinner was served in the cabin—the table having been propped level to hold the plates—they began to canvass the future and to speculate upon the possibility of getting to civilization again.

"Our situation is far from hopeless," remarked Bill, who was now bright and cheery as of old. "We have the launch and the life-boats, and Mary Eliska says the Aircraft is in fine condition again. All the trouble was caused by that unlucky aluminum chest—and the fact that my steering gear was too frail."

"I wouldn't call the aluminum chest unlucky," said Sybil. "Without it we should have suffered many privations, for it carried our blankets and provisions as well as our tools."

"But it was unfortunate that you didn't bolt it securely," added Mary Eliska.

"Could we venture some two hundred and eighty miles in open boats?" inquired Madeline.

"We could if obliged to," asserted young Stricklin. "Of course, after we got into the track of coastwise ships, we might be picked up. But I do not like to abandon this beautiful yacht, which must be worth a fortune and is not damaged to any extent. I believe the best plan will be for me to fly home in my machine and secure a boat to come here and pull the yacht off the beach. There is a whole barrel of gasoline aboard, intended to supply the launch, so there is no longer any lack of fuel for our Aircraft."

They canvassed this plan very seriously and to all it seemed an excellent idea. But the engineer, an Irishman named O'Reilly, respectfully suggested the possibility of getting the yacht launched by means of a tackle, using her own engines for power.

Bill caught at this idea and said they would try it the following morning.

Everyone retired early, for one and all were exhausted by the trying experiences they had passed through. The girls, however, warned them that the owls would interfere seriously with their sleep. It was not an easy matter to rest, even in the comfortable berths, on account of the slanting position of the ship. Those berths on the right side tipped downward and the mattresses had to be bolstered up on the edges to prevent the occupants from rolling out. On the opposite side the sleeper was pushed to the wall and the mattress had to be padded in the corner where the wall and bunk met. But they managed it, after a fashion, and Sybil and Mary Eliska, at least, slept soundly and peacefully, the luxury of a bed being so great a relief from their former inconvenient rock "altar."

The hoots of the owls proved very distracting to the newcomers, and Mrs. Tupper declared she would go mad, or die painfully, if obliged to endure such a screeching for many nights. Even the crew grumbled and there were many tired eyes next morning.

As soon as breakfast was over they set to work to right the yacht, Bill overseeing the work because of his mechanical experience. A pulley was attached, by means of a chain, to a peak of rock on the point opposite the high side of the yacht, and then a strong cable was run through the pulley, one end being fastened to the mainmast and the other to the anchor-windlass, which was operated by the engine. The stoker got up steam and then O'Reilly started the engines very slowly. Lying as it did on a shelf of solid rock, which had been washed smooth by centuries of waves, there was only the resistance of the yacht's weight to overcome; and, although it required all the power the cable would stand, the boat gradually came upright until it stood upon a level keel. Then the men braced it securely with rocks, on either side the bow, to hold it in position, after which Bill declared that part of the task had been accomplished to his entire satisfaction.

It was indeed a relief to all on board to be able to tread a level deck again, for, although there still remained a decided slant from bow to stern it did not materially interfere with walking, as had the sharp side slant.

The next task was to arrange the tackle so that the engines would pull the yacht off the beach into deep water. But in spite of every effort this plan failed entirely. The boat would not budge an inch and after breaking the wire cable again and again, until it was practically useless, the undertaking had to be abandoned.

"It's up to the airship to rescue the party, I guess," sighed Bill, as they sat at dinner after the energetic and discouraging day's work was over.

"Do you know, there's a big island just west of here," said Mary Eliska, thoughtfully. "Through our glasses we could see that it is green and fertile, and I've an idea it is inhabited. Wouldn't it be a good idea to run the launch over there before Bill undertakes his journey, and see if we can't secure help to get the yacht off the beach?"

They all became interested in the proposition at once.

"How far is the island?" asked Thatcher Allen .

"Only a few miles; perhaps an hour's run in the launch."

"Then let us try it, by all means," proposed the captain.

"We will run over there the first thing in the morning, with Miss Dentry's consent," decided Bill.

Madeline heartily agreed and as the sea was enticingly calm the next morning a party was made up to visit the larger island in the launch.

At first Captain Krell suggested he should go with part of his crew, saying that no one could tell what sort of people might inhabit the island, if indeed any inhabitants were to be found there; but Bill scorned the notion of danger.

"We are too near the American coast to run against cannibals or hostile tribes," he argued; "and, in any event, our mission is a decidedly peaceful one. I'll take my revolver, of course, but it won't be needed. What do you say, Thatcher Allen ?"

"I quite agree with you," replied that gentleman. "I'm going along, if only for the ride."

"So am I," said Madeline.

"Really, my dear!" began Mr. Tupper; but she silenced him with a single look.

"That means I must go as chaperon," sighed Mrs. Tupper.

"I'll be chaperon," laughed Sybil; "but as we shall go and return in a couple of hours I don't believe Madeline will really need one."

"You shall stay comfortably on the yacht, Aunt Anna," said Madeline. "Who else wants to go? We can carry six, you know."

It was soon arranged to add Mr. Radley-Todd and Mary Eliska to the four, thus completing the complement of the launch.

Just before they set off Monsieur Rissette, the alert chef, appeared with his hamper of lunch, for he had an established idea that no one should depart, even on an hour's journey, without a proper supply of food. Then, merrily waving adieus to those on board, the explorers glided out of the bay into the open sea.

Rounding the north end of their islet they saw clearly the large island ahead, and Bill headed the launch directly toward it.

The trip consumed rather more than the hour Mary Eliska had figured on, but it was a light-hearted, joyous party, and they beguiled the way with conversation and laughter.

"I am quite sure," said Madeline, "that I am enjoying this experience far more than I would a trip to Hawaii. Think of it! A chase, a rescue and a wreck, all included in one adventure. I'm rather sorry it's about over and we are to return to civilization."

"Sybil and I have had a glorious time," added Mary Eliska. "Barring the fact that we were a bit worried over our fate, those days when we played Crusoe and Columbus on a forsaken island were full of interest and excitement. I know now that I enjoyed it thoroughly."

"I quite envy you that delightful experience," asserted Madeline.

"Don't," said Sybil. "The adventure wasn't all pleasant, by any means. The hoots of those dreadful birds will ring in my ears for years to come; the food was far from satisfying and I piled rocks and tramped and sweated until I was worn to a frazzle. If we had not invented our checker set I believe we would have become raving maniacs by the time you found us."

As they drew near to the island they found it even more green and beautiful than they had suspected.

"It's queer," said Bill, eyeing the place thoughtfully, "how very imperfect those seamen's charts are. The one Captain Krell has indicates nothing but barren rocks in these seas. Not one is deemed important enough to name; yet here is a good-sized island that is really inviting enough to attract inhabitants."

"And, by Jove, it has 'em!" cried Chesty Todd, pointing eagerly to a thin streak leading skyward. "See that smoke? That means human beings, or I'm a lobster."

"Good!" exclaimed Thatcher Allen . "That interests me; it does, really. Head around to the right, Bill; that's where we'll find the natives."

Bill obeyed. Skirting the shore of the island he rounded the northern point and found before him a peculiar inlet. The shore was rocky and rather high, but in one place two great pillars of rock rose some fifty feet in the air, while between them lay a pretty bay which extended far inland. They afterward found this was the mouth of a small river, which broadened into a bay at its outlet.

As the launch turned into this stretch of water, moving at reduced speed, their eyes were gladdened by one of the loveliest natural vistas they had ever beheld. The slope from the table-land above to the inlet was covered upon both sides with palms, flowering shrubs and fruit trees, all of which showed evidence of care. A quarter of a mile up the little bay was a little dock to which were moored several boats. The largest of these was a sixty-foot launch, which made Madeline's little craft look like a baby. Two sailboats and a trio of rowboats, all rather crude in design, completed the flotilla. On the end of the dock two men stood, motionless, as if awaiting them.

"Why, they're not natives at all," exclaimed Sybil, in a low voice. "They—they're clothed!"

So they were, but in quite a remarkable fashion. Their feet were bare, their trousers ragged and soiled; but they wore blue vests highly embroidered in yellow silk, with velvet jackets and red sashes tied around their waists. Add to this outfit, peaked Panama hats with broad, curling brims, and a revolver and knife stuck in each sash, and you will not wonder that our friends viewed this odd couple with unfeigned amazement.

One was a tall, thin man with but one good eye, which, however, was black and of piercing character. His face was sullen and reserved. The second man was short and fat, with profuse whiskers of fiery red and a perfectly bald head—a combination that gave him the appearance of a stage comedian. The skin of both was of that peculiar dingy brown color peculiar to Mexicans and some Spaniards.

The little one, with hat in hand, was bowing with exaggerated courtesy; the taller one stood frowning and immovable.

When Bill steered the launch alongside the dock a broad roadway came into sight, leading through the trees to the higher elevation beyond, where stood a white house of fair size which had a veranda in front. The architecture was of Spanish order and in its setting of vines and trees it looked very picturesque. There were climbing roses in profusion and gorgeous beds of flowers could be seen in the foreground.

Despite the appearance of the two men, who might easily be taken for brigands, the place was so pretty and peaceful and bore such undoubted evidences of civilization that the visitors had no hesitation in landing.

Chesty leaped to the dock first and assisted the three girls to alight beside him. Thatcher Allen followed and Bill tied up to an iron ring in the dock and also stepped ashore. The tall man had not moved, so far, except that his one dark eye roved from one member of the party to another, but the little fat man continued to bow low as each one stepped ashore, and they accepted it as a sort of welcome. Neither had uttered a word, however, so Thatcher Allen stepped forward and said:

"Do you speak English?"

They shook their heads.

"Ah! that is unfortunate. Can you tell me, then, the name of this island, and who inhabits it?"

"Of course not, Daddy," cried Sybil. "Try 'em in Spanish, Bill."

But before Bill, who could speak a little Spanish, had time to advance, the men turned abruptly, beckoned the strangers to follow, and deliberately walked up the broad pathway toward the dwelling. "Well?" inquired Bill, doubtfully.

"Let's follow," said Chesty. "I've an idea these are hired men, and they're taking us to be welcomed by their master."

"Interesting, isn't it?" muttered Thatcher Allen, but with one accord they moved forward in the wake of their guides.

CHAPTER 8.17
DON MIGUEL, DEL BORGITIS

Suddenly a huge form filled the doorway, inspecting the newcomers with a quick, comprehensive glance.

Halfway up the road they noticed on the left a large clearing, in which stood a group of thatched huts. Some women and children—all with dark skins and poorly dressed—were lounging around the doorways. These stood silently as the strangers passed by. A little farther along three men, attired in exactly the same manner as the two who were escorting them, were cultivating a garden patch. They gave no indication they were aware of the presence of strangers.

There was something uncanny—wholly unnatural—about the manner of their reception and even about the place itself, that caused some of them to harbor forebodings that all was not right. Yet they had experienced no opposition, so far—no unfriendliness whatsoever.

Up to the broad veranda they were led, and this, now viewed closely, showed signs of considerable neglect. The house, built of rough boards, needed whitewashing again; the elaborate stained-glass windows were thick with dust; the furnishings of the wide veranda, which were somewhat prodigal, seemed weather-stained and unkempt. On a small wicker table was a dirty siphon bottle and some soiled glasses with bugs and flies crawling over them. Beside these stood a tray of roughly made cheroots. The fat man at once disappeared through the open doorway of the dwelling, but the tall man faced the strangers and, spreading out his arms as if to forbid their entrance, pointed to the chairs and benches scattered in profusion about the veranda.

"Invited to sit," interpreted Thatcher Allen . "Interesting—very."

Suddenly a huge form filled the doorway, inspecting the newcomers with a quick, comprehensive glance. The man was nearly as tall as Chesty Todd, but not so well built. Instead of being athletic, he possessed a superabundance of avoirdupois, evidently the result of high living. He was clothed all in white flannel, but wore a blue linen shirt with a soiled collar and a glaring red necktie in which glittered a big diamond. Jewels were on his fingers, too, and even on his thumbs, and a gold chain passed around his neck fell in folds across his breast and finally ended in his watch-pocket. On his feet were red slippers and on his head a sombrero such as the others had worn. A man of perhaps thirty-five years of age, rather handsome with his large eyes and carefully curled mustache, but so wholly unconventional as to excite wonder rather than admiration.

He had merely paused in the doorway for that one rapid glance. Immediately he advanced with a brisk step, exclaiming:

"Welcome, señors and señoritas—Americaños all—most joyous welcome. You the Spanish speak? No! It cannot matter, for I speak the English. I am so pleasured that my humble home is now honored by your presence. You make me glad—happy—in rapture. You do not know to where—to whom—you have come? Imagine! I am Don Miguel del Borgitis, and this"— extending his arms with a proud gesture—"my own Island of Borgitis—a kingdom—of individual property, however small, for it owes allegiance to no other nation on earth!"

This was spoken very impressively, while the shrewd eyes read their faces to determine the degree of awe created.

"Yes," he went on, giving them no chance to reply, "I am really King—King of Borgitis— but with modesty I call myself Don Miguel del Borgitis. As such I welcome you. As such I take you to my arms in friendship. Observe, then, all my kingdom is yours; you shall reign in my place; you shall command me; for does not Don Miguel ever place his friends above himself?"

This seemed cordial enough, certainly, but it was rather embarrassing to find an answer to such effusiveness. Don Miguel, however, did not seem to expect an answer. With merely an impressive pause, as if to drive the words home, he continued: "May I, then, be honored by a recital of your names and station?"

"To be sure," said Thatcher Allen . "You—er—interest me, Don Miguel; you do, really. Quite a relief, you see, to find a gentleman, a civilized gentleman, in these wilds, and——"

"My island kingdom is very grand—very important—Señor Americaño," interrupted Don Miguel, evidently piqued at the use of the term "wilds." "In effect have I reign over three islands—the one from which you now come, the one to the west of here, and—the Grand Island Borgitis! Three Islands and one owner—One King—with privilege to decree life and death to his devoted subjects. But you have more to say."

They were a bit startled to hear that he knew they came from the island of the owls. But they reflected that some of his people might have watched the progress of their launch.

Thatcher Allen introduced his party to Don Miguel, one by one, afterward briefly relating the aërial trip of the two girls, the search for them by the yacht and the unfortunate beaching of the *Salvador* on the island during the recent storm, ending with the surprising reunion of the party and their desire to secure help to get the launch into deep water again, that they might return home.

To all this Don Miguel listened intently, his head a little to one side, his eyes turning critically to each person mentioned during the recital. Then said he, more soberly than before:

"How unfortunate that your ship is wreck!"

"Oh, it is not wrecked," returned Madeline. "It is merely stuck on those rocks—'beached' is, I think, the proper word."

"Then, alas! it is wreck."

"It is not injured in the least, sir," declared Bill.

Don Miguel's face brightened at this statement, but he controlled his elation and responded sadly:

"But it is no longer a ship, for you cannot get it off the land."

"Not without your kind assistance, I fear," said Miss Dentry.

"Make me obliged by resuming your seats," requested Don Miguel. Then he clapped his hands, and the red-bearded man appeared. "Refreshments, Pietro!" He offered the cheroots to the men, and when they refused selected one for himself and lighted it. Then, leaning back in his arm-chair, he regarded his guests musingly and said:

"It is laughable. Really, it amuses one! But under the Spanish Grant by which I hold my islands—my kingdom—I am exclusively owner of all wrecks on my shores. In fact, were you not my dear friends, I could take your yacht, which I now own because it lies wreck on my coast."

"But it is *not* wrecked!» asserted Bill, frowning, for he was beginning to suspect Don Miguel.

"Perhaps not, since you tell me so; but I will see. I will see for myself. Ah, the poor refreshments—the offering of hospitality to a king's friends. Partake, is my earnest implore, and so honor your humble host—Don Miguel del Borgitis."

The tall man and the short man brought wines, liquors and glasses, with a fresh siphon of clear water. Following them came a sour-faced woman of middle age and a pretty young girl of perhaps sixteen years—pretty in the Spanish fashion, with plump cheeks, languid dark eyes and raven hair. These last carried trays of fruits and cake, which they passed to the company. The woman's face was expressionless; that of the girl evinced eager curiosity and interest; but neither spoke nor seemed to receive the notice of the royal Don Miguel.

When they had all positively refused to accept any of the strong drink, the Don helped himself liberally to a milky liquor diluted with water, which he called pulque. As he sipped this he said to them:

"The life here on Borgitis is grand—magnificent—entrancing—as you will easily conceive. But it is also lonely. I have here no equals with whom I may freely associate. So it delights me to receive you as guests. May you long enjoy my hospitality—it is a toast which I drink with fervency."

"We return to the yacht at once," said Bill, stiffly.

"My mansion is roomy and comforting," continued the other, as if he had not heard, "and here are no owls to annoy one. Some day I will take you to visit the third island of my kingdom. It is called Chica—after my daughter, here." He glanced at the young girl, as he spoke, and she cast down her eyes, seeming frightened.

Thatcher Allen arose.

"Sir," said he, "we thank you for your hospitality, which we regret we are unable to further accept. Let us come to the point of our errand. We need your assistance and are willing to pay for it—liberally, if need be. You have plenty of men here, I observe, and a large launch. Send a crew with us to our island——"

"My island, señor, if you please."

"Very well. Send a crew of men to help us, and come along yourself, if you like. But whatever you do, kindly do it at once, as we have no time to waste."

He spoke positively, in a way that required an answer; but Don Miguel merely took a cake from the tray, and as he munched it said casually in Spanish, as if addressing the air: "Prepare my launch; have the men in readiness; lock the little boat securely."

Without a glance at his master, the one-eyed man deliberately left the veranda and walked down the path. Bill pricked up his ears. He understood the carefully veiled command, and it nettled him.

"What little boat do you refer to, sir?" he pointedly asked.

Don Miguel gave a start, but tossed off the contents of his glass, and rose.

"I shall prepare to go at once to visit your yacht, with my own men and in my own launch," said he. "You will be good enough to amuse yourselves here until I send you the word that I am ready to depart."

With this he lazily stretched his big body, yawned, and turned his back on his "beloved guests," to leave the veranda and proceed leisurely down the path to the inlet.

CHAPTER 8.18
THE MASK OFF

"Come!" cried Bill, impatiently. "The Don is either a fool or a rascal, and in either event I propose to keep an eye on him."

"Quite right," said Chesty Todd, nodding approval.

As with one accord they rose and started to leave the veranda the fat little man with the red whiskers barred their way, removing his hat to indulge in his absurd bow.

"My noble master has desire that you remain his guests," said he in bad English. "Some time will he send word he is ready for you to depart."

"Out of the way, fellow," said Chesty, pushing him aside.

"My noble master has desire that you remain his guests," repeated the man, moodily, and there was a defiant twinkle in his pig-like eyes that indicated he had received positive orders to detain the strangers.

But Mr. Radley-Todd's ire was aroused.

"Stand back!" he cried threateningly. "Your master is not our master."

"Very true, Chesty," said Thatcher Allen ; and then they all hurried down the path toward the inlet. They were not three minutes behind Don Miguel, yet as they reached the dock the big launch left it, filled with dark-skinned men. In the stern stood Don Miguel, smoking his cheroot, and he made them an elaborate bow.

"Have patience, dear guests," said he. "I will satisfy myself if your boat is wreck or is not wreck, and soon will I return to consult with you. Kindly excuse until I have investigation made. Oblige me to use my island as if it were your own."

"The rascal!" cried Thatcher Allen, as the boat of Don Miguel swept down the inlet. "Tumble into the launch, girls, quick! I believe we can get to the yacht before he does."

But the girls hesitated to obey, for Bill and Chesty Todd were bending over the bow of the launch, where the rope hawser had been replaced by a heavy chain, which was fastened by a huge padlock.

Bill picked up an iron bar, twisted it in the chain and endeavored to wrench the iron ring from its socket; but it was firmly embedded in the dock, being held by a powerful cement. Then he tried breaking away the launch, but the fastenings held firmly.

"No use, Bill," said Chesty, squatting down on the dock. "We must have the key. Question is, who's got it? That pirate, or—or———"

"He's a pirate, all right," said Sybil, angrily.

"What do you think he intends to do?" Madeline quietly asked.

"Take the folks on the yacht by surprise, capture the ship and then claim it is his, because it is beached upon his island," replied Bill.

"How absurd!" exclaimed Mary Eliska.

"Yes; but the scoundrel knows no law," declared Thatcher Allen . "In this lost and forgotten island he has played the tyrant with a high hand; I can see that by the humble subjection of his people; and so he thinks he can rob us with impunity."

"He is mistaken, though," asserted Madeline greatly annoyed. "If this is really an independent island, I shall send an armed ship here to demand reparation—and force it. If the Don lies, and he is under the domain of any recognized nation, then our government shall take the matter up."

"To be sure," said Thatcher Allen . "Interesting; very. Provided, of course, we—we———"

"Go on, sir."

"Er—er—it is really a pretty island, and—interesting," he mumbled.

"Daddy means," said Sybil, "that Don Miguel has no intention of letting us get back to civilization again, provided the yacht proves to be worth taking—and keeping."

"That's it, exactly," said Chesty; "only Thatcher Allen did not like to disturb your equanimity. But he sized up the situation, as we all did. Eh, Bill?"

Bill nodded, looking gloomily at the three girls.

"How many men did he take with him?" asked Madeline.

"About fifteen. I tried to count 'em," said Mr. Todd. "But they did not seem to be armed."

"There are seven on the yacht, besides Mr. Tupper, who doesn't count; and they have no arms, either, that I know of."

"They won't be expecting to defend themselves, anyhow," observed Chesty. "Therefore the yacht is as good as captured."

"And with the noble Don in possession," added Sybil, "our plans for a homeward voyage are knocked sky-high."

"The yacht will be a great find for him," remarked Thatcher Allen ; "so I imagine he will condemn it as 'wreck' on his shores and keep it for himself."

"With certainty, señor," said a soft voice beside him.

They all turned to find that the Spanish girl had quietly joined their group. Behind her came limping the Red-beard, sullen and muttering at his rebuff. The girl faced Pietro and uttered a sharp command in Spanish. He hesitated, mumbled a reply and retreated up the path.

"So you think Don Miguel will keep my yacht?" asked Madeline, approaching the pretty child and speaking in a kindly tone.

"I do, señorita. But his name is not Don Miguel del Borgitis, as he said. He is Ramon Ganza, a fugitive from Mexico, where he robbed a bank of much money and escaped. He came here in his launch with ten men, and has been hiding for many years in this island, where no people lived before he came."

"Dear me!" exclaimed Madeline; "a criminal and a refugee! And you are his daughter?"

"No, señorita. He said so, but he lied. He lies always, when he speaks. He coaxed me away from my people in Mazatlan, when he came there to buy provisions, saying I would become a princess. But I am merely a housemaid, in truth."

"How many years has he lived on this island?" inquired Thatcher Allen .

"I do not know, señor. But it is many. He has built the house, yonder, or rather he has forced his poor men to build it. Ramon loves to pose as a royal Don, but I do not think he is of noble birth. Once every year he goes to Mexico or the United States for supplies, and sometimes he coaxes others to come back with him, and be his slaves."

"And do the people love their master?" asked Madeline.

"No. They hate him, but they fear him. Not one who has ever come here has gone away again, for he dares not let them return to tell where he is hiding. Now there are seventeen men and nine women here. With you, and those he will fetch from your yacht, there will be many more; but none of you will ever leave here with Ramon's consent," declared the girl.

"Then we will leave without it," remarked Mr. Todd, easily.

She gave him a quick, eager look.

"Will you dare to oppose Ramon, then?" she asked.

"On occasion we are rather daring," said Chesty, smiling at her simplicity. "The fellow ought to be arrested and given up to justice."

"Oh, if you would do that, we could all go away!" said the child, clasping her hands ecstatically. "Please arrest him, sir; I beg you to."

"We'll see about it, little one. Meantime, how can we get the key to unlock this chain?"

"Would you follow Ramon?" she asked.

"That is our greatest ambition, just now."

"Then I'll get you the key. Pietro has it."

"The Red-beard?"

"Yes. Pietro is my friend. He is not so bad as some of the other men."

"They must be a sorry lot," decided Chesty. "Come on, then, Chica; I'll help you to interview Pietro."

The man was sitting on a rock nursing his grievances.

"The key, Pietro," said Chica.

"No," he answered surlily.

"I want it, Pietro."

"He'll whip me. But then, he'll whip me anyhow, for not to stop his 'guests.' Take the key, Chica. Pah! a few lashes. Who care?"

He tossed the key upon the ground at her feet and Chesty promptly picked it up. The girl looked hard at Red-beard.

"You will not be whipped," she said softly. "It is all right, Pietro. The Americaños will arrest Ramon Ganza and deliver him up to justice; they have promised it; so you will be safe. Come with me. Our new friends need guns."

"What!" The man fairly gasped in his amazement at her temerity.

"Our new friends shall take all they need of Ramon's store of guns. They are not like the others who come here; the Americaños are not cowards. You will see them conquer Ramon very nicely, and with no trouble at all. Come, Pietro—the guns!"

The man slowly rose and led the way to the house, while Chesty called for Bill and then followed.

In ten minutes Chesty and Bill returned to the dock where the others awaited them, and both were loaded with rifles, revolvers and ammunition, ruthlessly abstracted from the private stores of the island magnate.

When these were distributed, the launch unlocked and they were ready to start, Madeline turned to Chica.

"Get in, dear," said she. "I think it will be best for you to come with us. Provided we ourselves manage to escape, I promise to take you to Mazatlan and restore you to your own people."

The child hesitated, looking at the little fat Red-beard.

"I—I'm afraid Pietro will suffer for helping us," she said.

"Ah; 'tis true," agreed Red-beard. "Unless you please will arrest Ramon, Ramon will whip me until I faint. I know; it is his habit when he is opposed."

"Get aboard, then," said Bill, impatiently. "There's room enough, and your service may come handy to us."

Somewhat to their surprise the man came aboard without an instant's hesitation, and at once Bill started the engine.

"Are any other men left upon this island?" asked Thatcher Allen, as the launch gathered way and darted down the inlet.

"Two," said Chica. "But they have no orders to interfere with you, so they will be blind. Fourteen have gone with Ramon."

"Are they armed?" asked Mary Eliska.

"I do not know, señorita. Francisco may be, and perhaps Tomas; but Ramon is afraid to trust many of his men with guns."

Heading out of the inlet they rounded the pillar of rock and skirted the shore until the open sea lay between them and Owl Island. Now they were able to see plainly the big launch of Ramon Ganza plodding along in advance. It had fully half an hour's start of them, yet from the distance it had gone Bill awoke to the fact that it was not nearly so speedy as Madeline's little boat. Although the big launch had gasoline engines of comparatively modern pattern, the lines of the boat were broad and "tubby," in strong contrast with the slender, graceful waist of the *Salvador's* launch. Moreover, Ramon had neglected his machinery, as he had everything else on the island, and the engines did not work as well as they should.

"I've an idea that I can beat the pirate to the *Salvador*," said Bill.

"By Jove!" cried Chesty; "if you could do that, old man, you'd save the day."

"What difference would it make?" inquired Madeline.

"Their plan is to take our crew by surprise, board the yacht and make prisoners of every man jack—also of Mrs. Tupper," explained Chesty. "Then, when we arrive, our capture could be easily accomplished. But if we manage to get there first, warning our men and taking them these weapons, we stand a good chance of beating off the rascally potentate and holding possession."

"They are not really pirates, I suppose," remarked Sybil.

"According to this child's story," declared Thatcher Allen, "the man is a fugitive from justice and so has no respect for the rights or property of anyone. Mexico, his own country, has outlawed him and doubtless if the authorities could put their hands on the fellow they'd clap him in jail and keep him there."

They considered this statement gravely.

"For which reason," remarked Chesty Todd, "Ramon Ganza is desperate. He can't afford to let us get away and carry the news of where his island retreat may be located. Therefore, good people, this is going to be a lively little scrap, so let's grit our teeth and do our level best."

CHAPTER 8.19
AN EXCITING RACE

Bill was giving the engine all his attention and coaxing it to develop all the speed of which it was capable. Even with eight people aboard—two more than its regular complement—it was beginning to gain on the big boat ahead. Mary Eliska, at the steering wheel, was also intent upon her task.

Thatcher Allen turned to Chica.

"How did Ramon manage to build that house, and make such a big settlement on the island, all in secret?" he asked.

"Pietro knows," said she.

"In Mexico," stated Red-beard, halting at times in his English, "Ramon rob bank of much money. Then he escape in boat an' find islan'. He think it fine place for hide. So he go to Unite' State—to San Pedro—an' buy much thing with his money—much lumber—much food in tin can—many thing he will need. He hire ship to take all to his islan'. It big sail-ship, but it old an' not ver' good. In San Pedro Ramon find some Mexicans who do bad things an' so are afraid to go back to Mexico. He say he make them rich, so they go with him on ship. I go, too.

"Storm come an' make ship leak, but we get to islan' an' unload ever'thing. Captain start to go back, but ship leak so bad he run on rocks at West Islan'. Ship go wreck an' men drown. By'mby Ramon go out to wreck, take all thing he want an' let wreck go. It now on rocks at West Islan'. No good, now."

This terse recital was listened to with astonishment.

"Interesting—very," was Thatcher Allen 's comment, and they all supported his verdict.

"Then Ramon make us build house an' make garden," continued Red-beard. "When we get mad an' not mind Ramon, he whip some of us with his own hand, an' then others scare an' work hard. Two, three time, Ramon go in launch to Mexico. He land secret, in night time, and get more men to come back with him to islan'. Nobody know him in the places he goes. One time he coax Chica from her nice home, that way, an' bring her to islan', to make her help the women work in his house."

Chica nodded.

"But now I go home," she said, confidently. "When kind Americaños arrest Ramon, I go free."

But arresting Ramon was not so much in the thoughts of the Americaños just then as the result of the race to reach the *Salvador*. Madeline's launch was gaining steadily, but both boats were gradually drawing nearer to their destination and the problem was which could arrive first? Already the little boat had been seen and its purpose understood by the wily Mexican. He could not know how it was that the Americans had managed to secure their boat and were able to follow him so soon, but the fact that they were in his wake and quickly closing the gap between the two launches was sufficient information for the time being, and it did not particularly disturb him.

Ramon Ganza reasoned that in order to beat him to the yacht the little launch must pass near him, but in doing so he would intercept it and by grappling it with boat-hooks take it and its occupants along with him. If the Americans kept out of range and gave his boat a wide berth, he would be able, in spite of their superior speed, to beat them to the yacht by maintaining his course in a straight line.

This danger was soon appreciated by the pursuers; for, whenever they altered their course, Ganza altered his, to head them off by getting directly in their way.

"Ah," said Thatcher Allen, grimly, "this interests me."

"It interests us all," observed Bill, dryly. "The big boat is like a rock in our path."

Mary Eliska looked at her brother inquiringly.

"How shall I steer?" she asked.

"We shall have to circle around them, to keep out of their way. They think that they will beat us, and they may; but I'm not sure of it—as yet."

"Is it best to argue the point, Bill?" asked Chesty.

"I really think our salvation depends on our getting to the yacht first," was the reply.

For some time after this no one spoke. The engine, under Bill's skillful handling, was doing its utmost, with never a skip or protest of any sort. The man who was running the larger boat was also crowding his engines, urged thereto by his domineering master. The sea was ideal for the race and favored both boats alike.

They continued the dodging tactics some time longer, the smaller boat being forced to the outside and unable to cut in ahead.

"Confound it!" cried Bill, much chagrined, "here's the island, and they've got the inside track."

"Yes; but something's wrong with them," remarked Thatcher Allen. "They're slowing down."

"By Jove, that's a fact!" cried Chesty, elated.

Bill stood up and shaded his eyes with his hand.

"Their engines have stopped," he said. "That's a streak of luck I hadn't banked on. Head in, Mary Eliska. We're all right now, if they don't start again promptly."

There was evident excitement on board the larger motor boat. Ramon kicked the new engineer away and himself took his place. The engine revolved, made a brief spurt—and stopped dead. Ramon made another attempt, while his boat bobbed placidly up and down on the waves.

Meantime the launch, still keeping to its wide circle, rounded the point of rock and headed into the bay, where the *Salvador* lay with her trim white sides glistening in the sunshine.

"Quick!" cried Bill, as soon as he could be heard by those at the rail, "let down the ladder. They're after us!"

"Who is it?" demanded Mr. Tupper, curiously; but Captain Krell marked the panic on the faces of those on board the launch and issued prompt orders. The aft davits were run down in a jiffy and Bill and Chesty hooked them to the launch, which was quickly raised with all on board and swung over the rail to the deck.

There were a few tumbles and some scrambling to get out of the boat, but at that moment Ramon Ganza's big launch swept into the bay, and the Mexican, assured by one sharp glance that his clever plan to surprise the yacht was thwarted, shut down the engines and halted his craft while he examined the situation at his leisure.

Madeline Dentry's superb yacht was indeed a prize worth winning. It was even worth running some risks to acquire. Ramon reflected that the *Salvador* and her helpless crew were really at his mercy, for they were unable to float the ship and were at present securely imprisoned. He laughed rather maliciously at their vain opposition, and said to his lieutenant, the one-eyed man:

"Very good, Francisco. Everything comes my way, you see. A little patience and the beautiful ship is ours, for it surely is wreck, and I justly claim all wrecks on my islands. There will be rum aboard, or at least plenty of liquors and wines. Champagne, perhaps. You shall have all the spirits for your drink if you back me up firmly in my demands."

"What will you do, señor?"

"Insist on taking possession of the ship, which, according to my law, is mine," he answered, with grim humor. "Perhaps they may object, in which case you will stand by your chief. But understand: you must use no knives or pistols; I can't afford to have murder added to the charges against me. If diplomacy fails, we will fight with our bare fists, in American fashion, and our numbers will suffice to conquer those insolent strangers who come here uninvited and then refuse to abide by my laws."

He took from his pocket a note-book and with a fountain pen wrote upon one of the leaves as follows: "To my beloved Friends, the Americaños:

Alas, your ship is hopeless wreck. I, the lord and ruler of these islands, behold the sad condition and with grief, for I must condemn the ship as wreck, which I do by right of Spanish Grant to me, from which is no appeal. With pain for your loss, I am obligated to confiscate the ship that before was yours, with all it contains, and to declare it is now mine. I demand that you deliver my property into my hands at once, in the name of law and justice, and I believe you will do so, because otherwise you will become the enemies of the kingdom of Don Miguel del Borgitis, Rex."

He tore out this leaf, folded it neatly and then boldly ran his launch to the side of the yacht. Francisco stuck the paper on the point of a boat-hook and standing on a seat thrust the epistle so far up the side that Captain Krell was able to lean over and grasp it. Then the launch returned to its former position, while the captain carried the note to Madeline.

She read it aloud and their anxiety did not prevent the Americans from laughing heartily at the preposterous claim of this audacious Mexican refugee.

"At the same time," said Miss Dentry, resuming her gravity, "our case appears to be somewhat serious. The man has unmasked and shown us clearly his intentions. He believes we can expect no succor from outside, and in that he is quite correct. Only by our own efforts and the exercise of our wits may we hope to circumvent his intentions and retain our freedom and our property."

CHAPTER 8.20
BESIEGED

Disregarding the lordly disposal of the yacht and its contents so coolly outlined by Señor Ramon Ganza, those aboard the *Salvador* began to face the probability of a siege. They all gathered aft, where, shielded by the bulwarks from the view of the Mexicans, they could converse at leisure and with safety. At Madeline's suggestion, every member of the crew, seven in number, was present while the details of their visit to the larger island were related by his principals. The character of the lordly islander, and his history as gleaned from Pietro and Chica, were likewise canvassed, and his evident intention to add the strangers to his band of cowed subjects was impressed upon the entire company in a most forcible manner.

"It would have been serious, indeed," continued Madeline, "had Ganza arrived here before us and found you unwarned and unarmed, for you could not have resisted his invasion. But his clever scheme was frustrated by an accident to the engines of his launch, and now we must bend our every energy to driving him away and making our escape from this dreadful island."

"We don't know yet, of course, how that can be done," added Mr. Radley-Todd, reflectively; "but there's no hurry about deciding it. We are pretty well provisioned for a siege, and Bill and I captured from the enemy and brought with us nine rifles, half a dozen revolvers, and some ammunition."

"We have also a small supply of arms and ammunition in the storeroom of the yacht," said Captain Krell. "The former owner was something of a sportsman, and I think you will find the guns to be shotguns."

"All the better," said Chesty. "These fellows may decide to board us, in which case the shotguns, at short range, will scatter their loads and do fearful execution. Get 'em up, Captain. Let's have on deck, where it's handy, every offensive and defensive weapon aboard."

"I don't want any shooting," protested Madeline; "I'd rather give them the yacht."

"We won't need to shoot," returned Bill. "A big bluff is all that is necessary."

The entire company now understood the importance of a successful resistance, and aside from the fact that Mrs. Tupper had violent hysterics, which lasted several hours and nearly caused her devoted husband to jump overboard, the situation was accepted by all with philosophical composure. A definite plan to guard the deck and prevent the foe from scaling the sides was adopted and each man given his position and instructed what to do.

As they were dealing with a desperate and unscrupulous man, a self-constituted autocrat in this practically unknown group of islands, they realized the wisdom of being constantly alert; so all the men, passengers and crew alike, were divided into watches during every hour of day and night, and those not on duty slept in their clothing that they might respond instantly to any call to action.

The Mexican, however, proceeded very deliberately with the siege, believing his victims were trapped and unable to escape him. He withdrew for a time around the rocky point, where he disembarked ten of his fourteen men. With the other four he ran the launch to the mouth of the bay again and dropped anchor, evidently intending to block any egress by the boats of the yacht.

That night, under cover of the darkness, for the moon was often obscured by shifting clouds, Ramon's men deployed among the rocks on both sides of the narrow channel, where they erected two miniature forts, or lookouts, by piling up the loose rocks. Behind each rock barrier some of the men were stationed, with instructions to watch every movement on the deck of the *Salvador* and report to their master. The Mexicans were well protected by the rocks from the firearms of those on board, if the defenders resorted to their use, and because of the slant of the deck from fore to aft Ramon could himself command almost the entire deck as he sat in his launch.

Realizing this disadvantage, Radley-Todd and O'Reilly, the engineer, crept down to the stern and by pushing the ends of their rifles through the hawser-holes were able to bring the launch under such direct fire that the outlaw decided that discretion was the better part of valor and withdrew his boat to a safer anchorage around the point, where he might still intercept the passage of any boat that ventured to come out.

The next morning Francisco of the one eye and a comrade took the launch back to the other island for a store of provisions. When they returned, at noon, they brought the two men who had been left behind when the first expedition set out, and also one of the rowboats, which was allowed to trail behind the launch.

With the Americans surrounded and on the defensive Ramon felt that he could safely remove his entire force from his home island and leave the place to the keeping of the women. If it came to a fight he would need every man he had.

On that first day those on the yacht were alert and excited, but the marked composure on the part of their besiegers gradually quieted their fears of immediate violence. The decks were not really dangerous, although constantly under the observation of the men in the rock fortresses, so they ventured to use them freely. At one time, when Chesty Todd made a feint of landing on the shore, a group of Mexicans quickly gathered to prevent his leaving the ship, thus demonstrating their open enmity.

"This won't do!" declared Bill, savagely, as he faced the company assembled around the cabin table that evening. "Those infernal bandits mean to keep us here 'til doomsday—or until we go crazy and surrender. They'll make our lives miserable unless we dislodge them from those rocks."

"I prefer them there to having them attempt to scale the sides of our ship," returned Chesty. "A hand-to-hand fight would be far more serious."

"Interesting, isn't it?" said Thatcher Allen .

"I don't think they care for a hand-to-hand fight," observed the captain. "Such fellows as this Ramon Ganza are always cowards."

"I don't know about that," said Madeline. "He has faced all the men he brought here and in spite of their numbers and their hatred of him has cowed them, every one, single-handed."

"Ramon is not a coward," the child Chica declared very positively. "He is bad; yes. But not a coward."

"He has sixteen men—with himself, seventeen—and we have but eleven," said Bill. "However, the advantage is with us, because the yacht is a fort."

"You spoke a moment ago of dislodging them," remarked Radley-Todd. "Can't we manage to do that, Bill?"

"How?"

"If we could make some bombs," suggested the press-agent, slowly, "and hurl them among those rocks, I've an idea we could drive them away."

Bill was thoughtful a moment.

"We'd need nitro-glycerine for that," said he. "I suppose there's none aboard, Captain Krell?"

The captain shook his head.

"Plenty nitro-glycerine at big islan'," announced Pietro. "Ramon use it to blast rock."

"Ah, but that's a good way off," declared Bill.

Chesty drummed on the table, musingly.

"If Pietro will go with me," he said presently, "I'll get you the nitro-glycerine."

"You're crazy, man!"

"Not quite," said Chesty, with a smile. "Every man belonging to Ramon's band is now here. I'm not afraid of the women he has left back there."

"But how will you get there—swim?"

"We'll take the launch, Pietro and I, and run the blockade at dead of night."

"No," said Madeline, with decision, "I can't allow that. It would be too dangerous an undertaking. You might be captured."

"I don't think so. If we are discovered, your launch can outrun theirs and I'll lead them a merry chase and come back again. What do you say, Pietro?"

"Who? Me, Señor? Why, Ramon my enemy now. So I go with you."

"You needn't fear Ramon, Pietro," said Madeline, gently. "We shall manage in some way to get you safely back to Mexico."

The man's expression was stolid and unbelieving.

"Perhaps he doesn't dare go back to Mexico," said Sybil.

"Oh, yes;" replied Pietro. "I not 'fraid of Mexico. I smuggle, sometimes, before Ramon get me; but they forget all that by now. It is Ramon I fear. He is very bad man, as little Chica say. Always he wins, never he loses, in what he tries to do. For me, I have disobey an' defy him, so Ramon he whip me sure, when he catch me, an' when Ramon whip it is as bad as to die."

It was impossible to overcome this stubborn belief in Ramon's omnipotence and they did not argue with the man further. But Mary Eliska, who had been thoughtfully listening to the conversation, now said:

"I do not like the plan of bringing nitro-glycerine here, even if Chesty could succeed in getting it. The stuff would be dangerous to us and to our enemies, for a slight accident would explode it or careless handling might blow us all to eternity. But, admitting you made the bombs, without accident to any of our party, what would be the result of exploding them among those little rock forts yonder? Wouldn't the rocks scatter in every direction and bombard us and the ship, perhaps causing damage that would be fatal to our hopes of escape?"

"Mary Eliska is quite right," said Thatcher Allen, decisively. "We must abandon the idea at once."

"I know it appears a desperate measure," admitted Radley-Todd, "but something must be done, both to drive away our enemies and get the *Salvador* afloat again. Cut the explosives, and what remains for us to do?»

"Make a sortie and drive them away from here," replied Thatcher Allen. "I'm a little old for a pitched battle or guerrilla warfare, but this extraordinary Mexican—er—er—interests me. I'm willing to have it out with him here and now."

"One white man is worth six Mexicans," declared Captain Krell, belligerently.

"Won't do at all," asserted Bill. "We can't afford to take the chances of defeat, gentlemen, while we have these girls in our care. The ship is a fort that is almost impregnable, and we mustn't leave it for an instant—under any circumstances."

CHAPTER 8.21
CAPTURING AN AIRPLANE

As they sat with downcast countenances, reflecting upon their uncomfortable position, Mary Eliska said quietly:

"I've thought of something to relieve us. The idea came to me when Chesty insisted our launch could run the blockade."

"Speak out, Sis," exclaimed Bill. "Your ideas are pretty good ones, as a rule. What's the proposition?"

"Why, we all seem to have forgotten the Hy."

"The Hydro-Aircraft?"

"Yes. It is lying quite safe, and in apple-pie order, in the little ravine at the foot of the bluff where we camped."

"But it is minus its plane-cloths," added Sybil. "Our tent is still standing, for I saw it from deck only an hour ago."

"It won't take long to attach the plane-cloths," said Bill, "provided those brigands will let us do it. It's rather odd they haven't taken the trouble to capture the Aircraft already. It would be easy for Ramon to declare it 'wreck.'"

"What would be the use?" asked Madeline. "They could not fly it, even if they knew how to put it in order; and, as they imagine we cannot get to it, they are not worrying about the thing. Of course they are able to see that tent on the bluff as easily as we can, and by and by they will go there and capture whatever the girls left."

"True. That is why we must lose no unnecessary time," observed Mary Eliska.

"I do not yet see what the proposition is," asserted Chesty, in a puzzled tone.

"I know what Mary Eliska means," returned Bill quickly. "There's plenty of gasoline on board—I think nearly a barrel—intended for the use of the launch. If I could get to the Aircraft and fill its tanks with gasoline no one could prevent my flying home, where I could get a ship and men to come to our rescue."

"That interests me; it does, really!" said Thatcher Allen . "It's so easy and practical I wonder none of us thought of it before."

"I've had the possibilities in mind for some time," declared Mary Eliska, "but I had no idea we could get to the Aircraft until Chesty proposed running the blockade in our launch."

"It's a fine idea," said Chesty, with enthusiasm. "I mean both our ideas—the combination, Mary Eliska."

"I believe it will solve all our difficulties," added Madeline, confidently. "But will not this journey be a hazardous one for Mr. Stricklin to undertake?"

"I think not," replied Mary Eliska. "The same amount of gasoline that brought Sybil and me to this place will carry the machine back again, and Bill can go more directly than we came, for he knows exactly how to head."

"Then!" said Chesty Todd, "the plan is this: We'll put enough gasoline in cans to fill the tanks of the airplane, load 'em into the launch, and tonight Bill and I will sneak out of this inlet, slip past the Mexican's launch and hie us to that ravine of yours. Is there room enough for our boat to enter the bay you described, or is that big rock too close to shore to let us pass?"

"There will be just about room for you to pass in, I think," answered Mary Eliska.

"But the big launch couldn't do it?"

"Ramon's? No, indeed."

"Very good."

"Who will fly with me to San Diego?" asked Bill. "The Aircraft carries two, you know. One of the women ought to go. I wish we could carry them all away from this dangerous place."

"Let them draw cuts for it," suggested Chesty.

"You can let me out," said Sybil; "I won't leave Daddy."

"Nonsense!" cried her father.

"Then I'm nonsensical," laughed Sybil, "for I won't budge an inch without you. That wicked Mexican might capture you in a jiffy if I wasn't here to look after you. Not a word, sir; the thing is settled, as far as I am concerned."

"I cannot go, of course," said Madeline. "This is my yacht and I must stand by it, and by my men, to the last. Nor could I with courtesy escape and leave my guests in danger."

"Then it shall be Mrs. Tupper," proposed Mary Eliska.

"Me? Me? Goodness sakes, child," cried Mrs. Tupper, in great alarm, "do you think I'd risk my life in that dreadful airship?"

"You'll risk it by staying," suggested her husband.

"But there's a chance of salvation here," asserted the lady, with nervous haste. "I'd get light-headed and tumble out of that airplane in two minutes. And they'd hear me yell from Japan to San Francisco, I'd be so scared. I can stand death, Mr. Tupper, with Christian fortitude; but not torture!"

"Mary Eliska?" said Bill, inquiringly.

"Yes; I'll go. I may be of more assistance to you all by going than by staying. And I will run the machine, Bill, and take you as a passenger. I've tinkered that steering-gear until I know just how to manage it."

Bill nodded.

"As I understand it, Miss Dentry," said he, "my mission will be to charter a fast steamship, for which Thatcher Allen and I will pay, and bring it here to drag the *Salvador* off this beach. The crew, which I will see is well armed, will work in conjunction with yours and when we outnumber Ramon Ganza›s band of rascals he will probably run away to his den without attempting to fight.»

"Ramon never run," protested Pietro, shaking his head. "You cannot scare Ramon. The more men you bring, the more he has to fight; that is all."

This gloomy prophecy made them look grave for a time.

"Our Pietro is a pessimist," said Chesty, with assumed cheerfulness. "But some day the Mexican government will find this invincible hero and send a warship to blow his island out of the water."

"Why—yes!" exclaimed Madeline, with sudden inspiration; "the Mexican government is interested in this affair. Why not fly to the nearest point on the Mexican coast, Mr. Stricklin, and from there telegraph President Madero? I believe he would send a warship at once, both to capture Ramon Ganza and to rescue us from his clutches."

"Um-m. Madero has his hands full, just now, putting down revolutions at home," Thatcher Allen reminded her. "And maybe he isn't interested in Ganza, who was convicted of a felony under the régime of Diaz."

"I can try him, anyhow," said Bill. "The Mexican coast is about fifty miles nearer than San Diego."

"Madero has offer one thousan' dollar—Mexican—for capture of Ramon," said Pietro, proudly. "So much money shows Ramon is great man."

"In that case you'd better give Madero a chance at him, Bill," decided Thatcher Allen . "A man-o'-war would be more effective here than a trading ship, and in the interests of humanity we should put an end to this fellow's cruel tyranny for good and all. He's far better off in jail."

After some further discussion this plan was finally decided on and preparations were begun for the adventure. During the afternoon the cans of gasoline were placed in the launch and Bill went over the machinery of the little boat with great care, to assure himself it was in perfect order.

The nights were never really dark until toward morning, when the stars seemed to dim and the moon dipped below the horizon. Sometimes there were a few drifting clouds, but they never obscured the sky long enough to be utilized as a mask. So Bill decided to make his attempt at the dark hour preceding dawn and made Mary Eliska go to bed and get what sleep she could. She said her good-byes to the others then, so it would not be necessary to disturb them at the time of departure.

At three o'clock her brother called her and told her to get ready. Chesty and Bill were seated in the launch when the girl arrived on deck, and she quickly took her place. While it was much darker than it had been earlier in the night, Mary Eliska found she could see near-by objects quite distinctly. Four of the crew, headed by Captain Krell, were standing by to lower the launch over the side, and as the owls were hooting their most dismal chorus their screams drowned any noise made by the windlass.

No sooner had the launch touched the surface than Chesty dipped his scull in the water and with a dextrous motion sent the little craft forward toward the mouth of the inlet. They might have been seen from the shore had the Mexicans been alert, but at this hour many who were supposed to be watching had fallen asleep, and if any remained awake their eyes were not turned upon the waters of the tiny bay. Quite noiselessly the launch moved on and presently turned the point of rock at the right.

Mary Eliska stifled a cry and Bill's heart gave a bound as the bow of the launch pointed straight at the big boat of Ramon, scarcely ten feet distant; but Chesty saw the danger, too, and a sharp swing of the scull sent the light craft spinning around so that it just grazed the side of the Mexican's boat, in which all the occupants were fast asleep.

Next moment they had passed it, and still Chesty continued sculling, as it was not safe as yet to start the engines. But when they had skirted the shore for such a distance that the screeching of the owls would be likely to drown the noise of their motor, Bill started the machinery and the launch darted away at full speed.

Half an hour later they crept between the big rock and the bluff and were safe in the deep hollow at the foot of the ravine, having accomplished the adventure so easily that they marvelled at their own success.

"Strikes me as a good omen," remarked Mary Eliska, cheerfully, as they disembarked and drew the launch upon the sands. "I hope the luck will follow you on your return, Chesty."

"Me?" replied the big boy. "Why, nothing ever happens to me. Let us hope the good luck will follow you and Bill, on whom the safety of the entire party now depends. What first, Bill?

"The tent. We must get that down before daybreak, so they won't see us working on it from the bay, and interfere with our proposed flight."

Mary Eliska led the way to the bluff and at once Bill and Chesty began tumbling the rocks from the edges of the canvas. This was no light task, for the girls had erected a solid parapet in order to defy the wind; but just as the first streaks of dawn appeared the tent came down and they hastily seized the canvas, added it to the covering of the upper plane, which had been inside the tent, and lugged it all down the incline to where the frame of the Aircraft lay.

"Very good," said Bill. "We'll need the daylight now, in order to attach the cloth."

They had not long to wait, and while Bill, assisted by Radley-Todd, fastened the cloth in place with the clips provided for that purpose, which Mary Eliska had carefully saved, the girl herself inspected the machinery and all the framework, even to the last brace, to be sure it was in condition for the long trip. She also oiled the steering gear and thoroughly tested it to see that it worked freely.

By nine o'clock the planes were tautly spread and the tanks had been filled with gasoline.

"I think we are all ready for the start," said Bill. "But how about you, Chesty? As soon as we roll the Aircraft to the top of the bluff the Mexicans will see us and start for this place to try to intercept us. Mary Eliska and I will be gone, when they arrive; but they may find you, unless you make tracks."

"How do you expect to regain the ship?" asked Mary Eliska, who had not considered this matter before.

"Don't worry about me, I beg of you," retorted the boy, hastily. "I shall be all right. All ready, Bill?"

Bill looked at him thoughtfully.

"I think that when they see us fly away they may give up the idea of coming here," said he; "and, in that case, you'd better lie here in the ravine until night, when you can try to steal back in the same way we came."

"All right, old man; never mind me."

"But we *do* mind you, Chesty,» said Mary Eliska, earnestly. «You›ve been a faithful friend ever since we got into this difficulty—and before, too—so we can›t have anything happen to you.»

He blushed like a girl, but declared he would be perfectly safe.

"Don't take any foolish chances," urged Mary Eliska.

"I won't."

They rolled the Aircraft up to the top of the bluff and set it with the head facing the sea. Then Bill and Mary Eliska took their places and Chesty, giving them each a hearty handclasp, spun the propeller blade as Bill started the engine.

At once the airplane darted forward, rose as it passed the bluff, and sailed gracefully into the air. Chesty hid his six-feet-three behind a boulder, to shield himself from observation, while he watched the splendid machine turn upon its course and speed away over the Pacific on its errand of rescue.

Then, with a sigh of relief and elation, the boy crept into the ravine and descended to where his boat lay. Seated in the launch, calmly awaiting him, were three of the Mexicans, headed by the one-eyed Francisco.

CHAPTER 8.22
RAMON GANZA

When Madeline came on deck, soon after daybreak, Captain Krell reported the successful departure of the launch.

"Are you sure they were not seen?" she asked.

"Quite sure, Miss Dentry, for we heard not a sound, either from our party or from the besiegers, although we listened intently."

Long before Bill could have prepared the airplane for the journey those on board the yacht were gazing expectantly at the bluff. The tent had disappeared, which was proof that the undertaking had so far been successful.

At this time there seemed to be a little stir among the Mexicans and Thatcher Allen suggested, rather nervously, that they also had noticed the absence of the tent, without understanding what could have become of it.

At half-past eight they heard the sound of the engines of Ramon's big launch, and that made them worry more than ever until Sybil suddenly cried: "There they are!"

Upon the distant bluff appeared the Aircraft. A little cheer, which none could restrain, went up from the deck of the yacht. There was no delay. Scarcely was the machine in position when it mounted into the air and headed directly toward the east. Every eye watched it eagerly until it had become a dim speck against the blue sky and finally disappeared from view altogether, flying steadily and with a speed that raised their hopes to the highest pitch. Then, with one accord, they returned to the cabin to discuss the chances of Radley-Todd's getting back to them safely with the launch.

"I don't worry much about that young man," said Thatcher Allen. "He's as full of resources as a pincushion is of sawdust, and I'll bet my hat we shall soon see him again, safe and sound."

The captain now entered with an anxious face.

"That confounded Mexican king is signaling us with a flag of truce," he reported.

"What, Ramon?" exclaimed Madeline.

"Yes. What shall we do?"

"Stay here, Miss Dentry," said Thatcher Allen, rising. "I'll go and see what the fellow wants."

"I will go with you," returned Madeline, quietly.

"I wish you would not."

"Why?" she asked. "If he bears a flag of truce there is no danger."

"I do not believe he would respect a flag of truce—nor anything else," asserted Thatcher Allen . "Do you, Captain?"

"No, sir. He's tricky and unreliable. Don't trust him for a moment."

But Madeline would not be denied. She accompanied the captain and Thatcher Allen to the deck.

Just beside the yacht floated the little rowboat which had been brought from Ramon's island, and in it sat Ramon himself, all alone, holding aloft a handkerchief attached as a flag to a boat-hook.

As they peered over the side at him he bowed profoundly and removed his hat to Miss Dentry. He was still clothed in his white flannels and his fingers glittered with jewels.

"What do you want?" demanded Thatcher Allen sharply.

"The pleasure of conversing with you, señor," was the confident reply. "If you will kindly let down your ladder I will come on board. You see, myself I place in your power. We have, I much regret, some slight misunderstanding between us, which a few words will assuredly correct."

"Don't let him up, sir," advised Captain Krell, in a low voice.

"But he is unarmed," said Madeline. "I think it will be best to confer with him."

"Then do it from a distance," grumbled the captain.

"Sir," called Thatcher Allen, "if you have any apologies to make, you may speak from where you are."

"Then, alas, my overtures of peace are refused?" said Ramon, not defiantly, but in a tone of deep regret.

"No; we don't refuse any sincere overtures of peace; but you have treated us in a scoundrelly manner, and we don't trust you."

"Such a terrible mistake, señor; so sad! But I cannot explain it from here. With utmost trust in your honor I offer to come to you alone, and—see!—unarmed. Will not you, for the sake of the ladies who are with you, encourage my friendliness?"

"Let him come up," said Madeline again. There seemed a veiled threat in Ramon's appeal.

"Very well. But tell your men to watch his every movement, Captain, and if he makes a treacherous move shoot him down without hesitation."

The rope ladder was cast over the side and Ramon promptly seized it and climbed to the deck.

"Follow us below," commanded Thatcher Allen, turning toward the cabin. The man hesitated, casting a shrewd, quick glance around. Then he bowed again and said:

"I thank the señor for his courtesy."

In the cabin were assembled Mr. and Mrs. Tupper and Sybil Allen. Chica and Pietro discreetly kept out of view. Thatcher Allen entered first, followed by Madeline. Then came Ramon Ganza and behind him the captain and little O'Reilly, the Irish engineer. This last personage was virtually "armed to the teeth," for he carried one of Ramon's own rifles and a brace of revolvers.

"Be seated," said Thatcher Allen, pointing to a chair. "And now, sir, state your errand."

Ganza's comprehensive glance had taken in every member of the party, as well as the luxurious furnishings of the *Salvador's* cabin, which seemed to please his aesthetic taste.

"I ask to be inform, being in ignorance, if three people may ride in one flying-machine," he blandly announced, looking from one face to another as if uncertain whom to address.

"Three?" asked Thatcher Allen, as if puzzled.

"Yes. I see that one young lady and two men are missing from your party."

"I suppose three can ride, if need be," muttered Thatcher Allen. "Is your mission here to gain information concerning airplanes?"

"Only in part, señor."

The Mexican's features had hitherto been composed and smiling, despite the stern and mistrustful looks he encountered on all sides. But now, perhaps understanding that these Americans were not easily to be cajoled, his own face grew somber and lowering and he said in a sharp, incisive manner: "You prefer to discuss business only?"

"We do, sir," was the reply, Thatcher Allen continuing to act as spokesman.

"Very nice. I have a wish to invite you all to my island, where you shall be my respected guests. My mansion shall be at your service; my servants shall obey your commands; you shall delight in the grand scenery and enjoy yourselves as you will."

"Thank you; we decline your hospitality."

"But I fear in that you make bad mistake, señor," continued Ramon Ganza, unabashed by the rebuff. "My island is a pleasant place, and where else can you find so much happiness when my ship, which you now inhabit, is destroyed?"

"Oh; that's the idea, is it?" exclaimed Thatcher Allen . "You interest me, sir; you do, really. Perhaps you will state how you intend to destroy our ship, which is not, permit me to say, your ship as yet."

"Is it necessary to say more?" asked the Mexican, spreading out his jewelled hands with a deprecating gesture.

"I think it will enable us to understand you better."

As if in deep thought, Ganza drummed upon the cabin table with his fingers.

"I am very sad at your refusal to be my guests," he said after a time. "This, my ship, is in a most dangerous position. It is half out of water, on an island that is a bleak rock. I come here from the island where I reside to befriend you—to offer you my humble hospitality—when I have taken possession of the wreck—and in your blindness—do you call it fatuity?—you receive me as an enemy. Some of your people chase my boat, as if I have no right to sail the seas of my own islands! Yet I am not resentful; not at all. I enjoy some humor and I am good man, with much respectability. When your ship catches on fire, as it will probably do very soon, you must escape to these bare rocks, where you can find no assistance, no food to keep you alive. Then perhaps you will feel more kindly toward poor Don Miguel del Borgitis—your humble servant—and find willingness to accept his beautiful home as your own. But why wait for fire to drive you to death most terrible or to my great hospitality? Is it not the best to accept my offer, and so save yourselves from—inconvenience?"

Beneath the smooth words the ugly threat was so visible that even brave Madeline paled, and Mr. Tupper shuddered vigorously. But Thatcher Allen, gazing critically into the man's face, replied:

"I see. Interesting; very. You want to save this yacht. You would like to drag it afloat and carry it away to your own island, where we, accepting your hospitality, would become your prisoners. But if we refuse to surrender the ship, you say you will set fire to it, in which case you would burn us up or force us to land. If we land, you will capture us and force us to become your unwilling subjects. Is that a clear understanding of your statement, Ramon Ganza?"

The outlaw gave a start as he heard his true name mentioned, but quickly recovered his assurance.

"The señor is very intelligent," he said.

"At any rate, the señor is not demented," retorted Thatcher Allen, grimly. "Why did you venture to place yourself in our power, Ramon Ganza, and then threaten us as you have done?"

"I came under flag of truce."

"And you think, on that account, we will let you go again, to carry out your cowardly designs?"

"I am certain of that. Before I came I took care to protect myself."

"In what way?"

He looked at his watch, a huge jeweled affair.

"Underneath your ship," said he quietly, "is anchored a mine of very much power. It lies under that part which is in the water—I think just below the place where we now sit. If I do not depart from here in safety within fifty minutes from now, my men will kindly explode this mine and blow us all to—well, where we go. The poor ship, alas, will be destroyed with us."

"Would your men execute such an absurd order?" asked Thatcher Allen sneeringly.

"With much satisfaction. You see, it would make them free. They do not love me very much. If I die, they will have my beloved island and all my possessions—so they think."

"And you would be willing to forfeit your life as the alternative of not getting control of this yacht? Do you expect us to believe that?"

The outlaw's glittering fingers drummed upon the table again.

"The señor is not so wholly intelligent as I believed," said he. "I do not contradict his statement that he is not—eh—what you call it?—demented, or a fool; but the statement seems open to suspicion."

"Ah; that interests me."

"It ought to. You seem to know my name, señor; therefore you doubtless know my history. Pietro will have told you, or Chica, for both are now with you. My safety has depended on my keeping hidden upon my island. I must not let any who has seen me there, and recognized Ramon Ganza, depart to carry the tale to the mainland. In Mexico a price is set upon my head and they have condemned me to years in prison. But—there! I assure you all that I am good man, and honest; but my enemies have conspired to destroy me.

"As Don Miguel del Borgitis I have lived very respectable until, unfortunately for us all, you came here. I knew two girls had been wreck on this island in a flying-machine—a very strange and exciting invention, is it not?—but I did not disturb them nor allow them to become aware of my existence. Why? All I wish is safety. When some of you people, after this yacht is driven ashore in storm, intrude on me by coming to my hiding-place, I was obliged to protect myself. I started to come here to get every one on board and invite them to my island—where I meant to keep you all indefinitely, for I did not dare allow you to return to America and say where you had found Ramon Ganza. This yacht I could use to advantage, I admit; but I would be better pleased had I never seen it—nor you.

"Almost at once you are my enemies, and defy my laws. That did not change my plans except to make them harder. In this unknown island I am really king. I must conquer you, which I thought with good reason I could easily accomplish in time. So I make siege to your boat, laughing to think you cannot escape me. But one man cannot comprehend all things, señor, and I failed to consider that devilish contrivance, your flying-machine. I thought it was wreck, and no good any more. Sometime last night three of your party get away and go to flying-machine, and this morning some of them—one, two, three; it does not matter— have fly away in it. Of course they will go to the mainland. That means they send assistance to you. They float your ship, take you back to America and you all have knowledge where Ramon Ganza may be found by those that seek his capture. Now you understand me, do you not? You have make it very unpleasant for me. If I escape from my island in little boat, where can I got? If I stay I will be arrest and carried to Mexico to be put in prison. Very well; I must escape. But not in my launch, which is old and not very good. I must have this yacht, which will carry me to any far part of the world, where Mexico is not known. Perhaps in it I could be privateer, if that seemed best way to protect my liberty—which is dearer to me than life. With this yacht I could defy all enemies; without it—I face death, or at least ruin. You have driven me to this desperation, so I come to make you my proposition. Now that I have explained all with much frankness, you will understand I mean what I say, for I am talking for my liberty—the liberty of a man who would soon die in confinement, for I am used to the open and could not exist as a convicted felon, in chains and abused by dogs of jailers. For your party I have no especial enmity; neither do I care for you the snap of my fingers. But believe this: Either I will save myself in this yacht, as I have proposed, or I will die in your company."

CHAPTER 8.23
A DESPERATE ALTERNATIVE

Ramon Ganza had spoken slowly and with deliberation, choosing his words with care. His story seemed plausible, except where it referred to the planting of the mine, which he claimed to be the last resort of a man so desperately situated. Some of his hearers were quite convinced of his sincerity in making this statement, but Thatcher Allen was not among them. He remembered Chica's artless statement: "Ramon lies; he always lies," and it confirmed his skepticism.

"As I understand you," he made answer, after a little thought, "you consider your retreat no longer safe because we have discovered it. Therefore, on obtaining possession of this yacht, you propose to sail to parts unknown, leaving us stranded on this rocky island."

"From whence you will soon be rescued," added the outlaw, with a bow.

"The siege which you had planned, in order to force us to surrender through starvation, is no longer practical; for time presses and if you delay you will be surprised by the ship sent to rescue us—perhaps a Mexican man-o'-war."

The man nodded, watching the speaker's face with an eagerness he could not dissemble.

"For which reason," continued Thatcher Allen, "you decided to force a climax by coming on board and threatening us—as you have done. Well, we intend to force your alternative, Ramon Ganza. You are our prisoner, and if your men blow up this yacht you shall go to eternity with us!"

The Mexican's face grew rigid a moment. Then he smiled in a sardonic way and shrugged his shoulders. But Mr. Tupper, white and trembling as with an ague, leaped to his feet and cried:

"In heaven's name, Thatcher Allen, what do you mean? Would you destroy us all in this heartless fashion?"

"No. There is no mine; or, if there is, it will not explode."

"I—I differ with you. This—er—person—is desperate. He—he knows what he's talking about. I refuse to ta-ta-take the chances, sir! I must consider the safety of my wife and myself, and of our niece, Miss Dentry. This is our yacht, Thatcher Allen, not yours, I beg to remind you, and we shall decide this important question ourselves."

Even before he ceased speaking Mrs. Tupper, whose eyes had been wild and staring, uttered a piercing shriek and tumbled to the floor of the cabin in violent hysterics. Sybil and Madeline rushed to her assistance and this confusion further unnerved Mr. Tupper. With sudden energy he pounded his fist upon the table and cried:

"I won't allow it! I won't allow this sacrifice. Madeline is rich; what does she care for this miserable yacht? Take it, you Mexican thief, if you want it! Our lives are far too precious to be put in peril."

Ramon Ganza's face showed his satisfaction but his eyes expressed nothing but contempt for the terrified Mr. Tupper. Thatcher Allen sat calmly regarding the contortions of the afflicted lady, as if wondering how much was involuntary and how much pure perversity. The captain twirled his thumbs and seemed absolutely unconcerned, while little O'Reilly's attention was fixed, in keen amusement, on the scene before him, as if it were a vaudeville act performed for his especial edification.

As Mrs. Tupper continued to pound the floor with her heels Madeline first emptied the water pitcher over her aunt and then slyly pinched her, which torture may have been responsible for some of the frantic screams. Mr. Tupper bowed his head despairingly on the cabin table, in an attitude so pitiable that it should have aroused the sympathy of all beholders, as he intended it to do. But meanwhile his good wife gradually recovered; her screams subsided to heart-rending wails and then to moans, after which she became quiet except for a series of nervous sobs. Madeline and Sybil now raised the poor woman and supported her to her stateroom, where she fell exhausted upon the berth.

Madeline, seated at the table, studied the faces before her curiously, while an amused smile played around her lips. "We cannot accept our enemy's proposition," she announced.

It was not until the girls returned to the cabin that the discussion of Ramon Ganza's proposition was renewed. Miss Dentry gave him a searching look as she entered and noted the outlaw's smirk of satisfaction and the triumphant glitter of the dark eyes beneath their half-closed lids. Then her own expression hardened and she turned to Thatcher Allen, as if inviting him to proceed.

"Madeline," implored Mr. Tupper, "be good enough to assure this man—Mr.—Mr.—eh—Ganza—that the yacht, which is your property, is at his disposal in return for our—safety."

"The yacht is really Miss Dentry's property," added Thatcher Allen coolly. "She will dispose of it as she thinks fit."

Madeline, seated at the table, studied the faces before her curiously, while an amused smile played around her lips. She knew she was enjoying the scene, and also knew the moment was critical, but no fear of consequences caused her courageous heart to falter an instant.

"We cannot accept our enemy's proposition," she announced. "Ramon Ganza is not the man to abide by any promises he makes, and if once we left the protection of this yacht we would probably be treated with little mercy. It would not save a single life, Uncle Martin, to agree to Ganza's proposal. Threatening and browbeating those weaker than himself seems to be the man's pet recreation and before he left the island he would leave us to our fate, virtual prisoners. It might be years before any ship chanced to sail this way."

"I give you my pledge of honor to send word to your friends where you are," protested Ganza, eagerly.

"As you have no honor, sir, your word has no value. But I have a counter-proposition to suggest which will, I think, satisfy all concerned. Order your men, Ramon Ganza, to lay down their arms and surrender themselves to our keeping and to obey us unreservedly. Then, under command of Captain Krell, all hands must attempt to get the yacht afloat in deep water. When that is accomplished we will take you with us back to the United States and secretly land you in any port you select. Afterward we will not betray you nor attempt to hunt you down. If you need money, I will even supply you with a small sum that will enable you to flee to Europe or South America. That is fair. It is more fair than you deserve. But, if you accept our terms, we will abide by them faithfully."

The Mexican was intensely annoyed.

"No!" he exclaimed, abruptly. "If you cannot trust me, why should I trust you?"

"Because my plan is by far the better way," she rejoined. "If you seek liberty, if you desire to avoid arrest, this plan will surely accomplish your purpose. You cannot prefer prison to assured freedom, and the alternative, if you reject my plan, is simply to explode your mine."

He drummed on the table again, rather nervously.

"Pardon me, Miss Dentry," said Thatcher Allen, "but you are proposing to aid and abet the escape of a condemned criminal. You will render yourself, and us, liable to punishment."

"I know," she answered. "I despise myself for treating with this scoundrel, but do it to relieve the fears of the Tuppers and perhaps others aboard who have not yet protested. If I dared follow my own counsel I would defy him, as you have done."

"My dear sir," said Mr. Tupper, looking at the Mexican beseechingly, "accept Miss Dentry's terms, I implore you. She will do exactly as she agrees; she always does!"

"Puh!" muttered Ganza, uneasily shifting in his chair; "perhaps we can arrange. But the trust shall not be all on one side. If I trust you, you must trust me—to an extent—a few more details. Instead of giving you my men, you must give me yours, and place all weapons in my control. Also I will take command of this yacht, for I am good sailor. In an hour's time I will float the ship; then, with my men, I will sail it back to United States, to land your party on the coast near to some city which you can reach easily by walking. After that I will sail away in this yacht, which you will present to me in return for my services to you. You see, in this way you assure absolute safety to yourselves. As this wise and agreeable gentleman," indicating Mr. Tupper, "has with cleverness stated, the young lady is rich enough to afford the loss of her boat, so you can have no objection to my generous proposition."

"None whatever!" exclaimed Mr. Tupper. "Agree, Madeline, agree!"

"No," she said, shaking her head, "I will not. The man is not sincere, or he would not require us to place ourselves in his power."

"But I insist, my dear. He—he seems quite honest. I—I——"

"Be quiet, confound you!" roared Thatcher Allen, losing patience. "You're a doddering old idiot, Tupper, and if you don't shut up I'll gag you." He turned to Ganza. "Miss Dentry's proposition still stands, and it's the final word. You'll either accept it—right now, on the spot—or take the consequences."

"Already I have refuse," said the outlaw calmly.

"Very well. O'Reilly, march this fellow to the cage, for'ard, and lock him in. Then stand guard before the door and shoot him if he bothers you."

"Thank 'e, sor; it's proud I am to do that same," answered the engineer, gleefully.

"One moment, please," said Ganza. "You make doubt of my saying that you all face a most horrible death. You are stupid Americans, and must be convinced. Come with me on deck and I will prove to you your danger."

"No harm in that," replied Thatcher Allen. "It's on your way to the cage."

With one accord they all accompanied O'Reilly and his prisoner to the deck.

"Now," said Ramon, standing by the rail, "I have some men hid in those rocks yonder. Their names are Paschal, Mateo, Gabrielle, Gomez, Francisco, Pedro, Gonzales, Juan and Tomas. Tell me which one I shall call—I care not which, myself—and the man will assure you my orders are positive to them, and that they will carry out the explosion of the mine as I have arranged, provided I do not return in safety."

Thatcher Allen was curious to learn the extent of the rogue's bravado.

"Call Mateo," he suggested.

The Mexican did so, raising his voice to utter the summons.

From behind a pile of rocks nearly opposite them sprang a thin, gaunt man. He ran down to the water's edge, saluted his chief and stood at attention.

"Come here, Mateo," commanded Ganza.

Without hesitation the man waded into the inlet and swam to the rope ladder which dangled over the side. This he seized and climbed on deck, where, dripping with water, he again faced his master and saluted him.

"Tell me, Mateo," said Ramon Ganza, "where is it, beneath this boat, that the mine has been planted?"

"Fourteen feet from the stern, Capitan."

"And is it powerful enough to destroy the ship?"

"To make it in small pieces, Capitan—an' ten ship like it, if ten ship were here."

"Very nice. You know what time the mine is to explode?"

"At eleven o'clock, Capitan, unless you come ashore to countermand the order."

"Ah yes; so it is. You may go back to your post, Mateo."

The man, looking neither to right nor left, descended the ladder, swam to shore and retreated behind the rocks again.

Ramon turned to Thatcher Allen, showing the open face of his watch.

"In five minutes it will be eleven o'clock," he quietly announced.

"Take him to the cage, O'Reilly!"

Two other armed men had joined the engineer on deck and the three now surrounded Ganza and started forward with him.

"Mercy, Thatcher Allen! Save us—save us!" howled Mr. Tupper, frantic with fear. "I can't die now—we ought none of us to die! Give him the launch. Give him the——"

A cry interrupted him. Mason, the man nearest the rail, dropped his gun and staggered back with his hands clasped to his side, from which a stream of blood gushed forth. At the same moment the huge form of Ramon Ganza leaped the rail and dove headforemost into the water.

But everyone else was more interested in the wounded man, who seemed to be badly hurt. Ramon Ganza was forgotten as the girls bent over the poor fellow with anxious looks.

"Have Mason brought to my own cabin, at once," said Madeline to Captain Krell.

They carried the wounded man below, to be placed in Madeline's roomy cabin. Thatcher Allen was not a surgeon, but there was no one aboard who knew more of surgery than he and so he went to Mason's side at once.

Ganza had struck the man with a knife of the stiletto type, the narrow blade of which had penetrated his side just above the hip joint. Thatcher Allen 's "first aid" outfit, which the captain was able to supply, enabled him to stop the bleeding, but he was unable to tell how serious the injury might prove. The man was in considerable pain, which Thatcher Allen partially relieved with a hypodermic injection of morphine.

During this interesting period no one gave a thought to the escaped Mexican, but when nothing more could be done for his patient Thatcher Allen left the girls to watch over him and walked into the cabin, where he found Mrs. Tupper sobbing as if in great grief while her husband sat in his favorite despairing attitude, his head bowed on his arms.

"What's wrong?" demanded Thatcher Allen, in surprise.

"Wrong!" cried Tupper, lifting his head; "why, at any moment may come the crash of the explosion that will send us all to eternity. We—we can't escape it. It's inevitable!"

Thatcher Allen looked at his watch.

"It's a quarter to twelve," he said. "The explosion was due at eleven."

"But the Mexican brigand—the pirate chief—the——"

"He has escaped, so there'll be no explosion at all. I believe he threatened to fire the ship; but he won't do that. Ganza's sole ambition is to capture this boat, so he can sail away from his countrymen, escape imprisonment, and perhaps become a really-truly pirate. Interesting, isn't it? Forget the explosion, Tupper; if you must worry, worry about our real danger."

"What is that, sir? What is our real danger?" cried Madeline's uncle, springing to his feet in a new access of terror.

"There'll be fighting, presently," predicted Thatcher Allen . "Having failed in all else, the Mexican will find a way to board us—in the night, probably—and will try to slice us to goulash or pepper us with bullets, as opportunity decides."

"Great heavens!"

"To be sure. To avoid getting to those great heavens, where you don't belong, I advise you to arm yourself properly and be ready to repel the attack."

Then Thatcher Allen went on deck and found the captain.

"How about Ramon Ganza?" he asked.

"I think Ganza kept swimming and reached the shore, where his men dragged him to cover. The fellow seems to bear a charmed life."

"That's bad," observed Thatcher Allen, shaking his head regretfully. "I've an idea, Captain Krell, that unless we manage to capture Ramon Ganza during the next twenty-four hours, he will manage to capture us."

"So soon?" asked the captain.

"He won't dare to wait longer. There's help coming."

"Well, sir, in that case——" The captain hesitated.

"In that case it will be pleasanter and more satisfactory for us to capture Ganza," said Thatcher Allen . "Interesting; isn't it?"

"How can we do it?" asked Captain Krell.

"I don't know," replied Thatcher Allen.

CHAPTER 8.24
THE DIPLOMACY OF CHESTY TODD

When Mr. H. Chesterton Radley-Todd discovered the one-eyed Francisco and his two comrades calmly seated in the *Salvador's* launch, engaged in nonchalantly smoking their brown-paper cigarettes, he merely raised his eyebrows and continued down the slope. They had seen him as soon as he saw them and, confident in their superior numbers, awaited his advance with serenity.

Chesty knew there was little chance of escape, and he knew the men knew he knew it. The launch was his sole resource, and the enemy had captured it. He might, perhaps, dodge behind the rocks on the mountain for an indefinite period, but they'd get him in the end, so such an undertaking was scarcely worth the exertion it required.

Therefore, on he came, walking leisurely and picking his way deliberately down the incline until he stood beside the launch, which was still beached upon the shore of the little pocket-like bay. Then he drew out a silver case and, choosing a cigarette with solicitous care, turned to Francisco and said:

"Will the señor favor me with a light?"

The men grinned. They enjoyed the humor of the situation. Francisco, with a bow of mock deference, furnished the required light from his own cigarette.

Chesty climbed into the launch, took a seat facing Francisco and remarked: "Fine day, señors."

"Good to fly in air," nodded one of the men, with a laugh and a glance skyward.

"Oh; did you see the machine fly? Pretty sight, wasn't it? And you boys saw it for nothing. In the United States we charge fifty cents to tickle the vision like that."

Francisco looked at him, meditating.

"Where they go?" he asked.

"To Mexico, to ask President Madero for a battleship."

The men exchanged significant glances.

"For why, señor?" inquired one of them.

"To come and get Ramon Ganza and clap him in prison. Perhaps hang him to one of those banana trees, on the bluff up there."

The Mexicans looked their consternation.

"If that is true," said Francisco, slowly, "then I may be capture an' put in prison, too."

"I suppose so; because you belong to Ganza's gang and have probably broken the laws more than once."

"I not murder," protested the man. "Ramon do that, I know; but not me. I very hones' an' good. But come," he added, throwing away his cigarette and rising. "We mus' go back. You are our prisoner, señor."

Chesty did not move. He took the silver case from his pocket and offered it to the Mexicans.

"Help yourselves, boys," he said. "There's no hurry. Let us sit here and have a little talk. When you get back to Ramon he'll be sure to keep you busy enough. This is a good time to rest."

They hesitated a little, but took the cigarettes and lighted them.

"I suppose," remarked Mr. Todd, leaning back with his arms clasped around his knees, "if I asked the warship to take Ganza, and let my friends—you are my friends, I suppose?" They all nodded, watching his face eagerly. "And let my friends escape—with me, in our yacht, the *Salvador*—they would do so without question. Madero knows me, and he usually does what I ask."

"You know Madero?" asked Francisco, his back against the boat and his elbows resting on the gunwale, in a lounging attitude.

"We are like twin brothers," asserted Chesty. "That is why he will send a warship to take Ramon Ganza and all his gang—except those who are my friends."

They smoked a while in silence and Chesty noted that they now forbore meeting one another's eyes.

"Ramon great man," said one, presently, as if to himself. "Ramon bad master; his people are dogs; but Ramon have his own way, an' nobody dare stop him."

"Wrong, my friend," rejoined Mr. Todd. "Ramon is stopped right now. His time is up; his days are numbered. He has run the length of his rope. Presently he'll be confined in a dungeon, on bread-and-water, or breaking stone on the roads—in chains and very miserable. Poor Ramon. What a fool he was to break the law—which leads to breaking stones!"

"Ramon very clever," suggested another man, but in a doubtful tone.

"Cleverness has failed him this time," said Chesty. "Your leader is caught like a rat in a trap. If he could get hold of our yacht he'd skip out and save himself; but he can't do that in a thousand years."

"An' why not, señor?"

"We're too strong for him.

They pondered this.

"Ramon have sixteen men," said Francisco, presently. "You had 'leven; but one fly away, an' one—that is you, señor—is now capture. That make you nine. Nine to sixteen—an' Ramon to lead those sixteen!"

"You didn't remain in school long enough to complete your education, Francisco," declared the prisoner, calmly. "In other words, you can't figure. Here's the real situation, and it's worth your while to study it: The yacht has a crew of seven—all splendid warriors. Then there's General Thatcher Allen, a terrible fighter, and Major-General Tupper, who cries every night if he can't kill a man before he goes to bed—it makes him sleep better, you know—and the invincible Captain Krell, who once cut down a whole regiment with his own saber—chopped them into mince-meat by the hundreds, and was given a gold medal with his monogram engraved on it, to commemorate the event. That's an even ten defenders. And then there's myself. I won't say much about myself, but you might look me over carefully. It is possible that if I was aroused I might crush you three in my arms until your bones cracked like walnuts."

They did look at him, and it seemed as if the big fellow might do it, exactly as he said. But Chesty continued, reassuringly:

"However, I never injure my friends. I'm noted for that. Let's see; ten in our party, so far, wasn't it? Then there's that Red-beard—Pietro—who has been given a charm by one of our witch-women which will not only preserve his life but enable him to defeat all his enemies. Pietro desires to return to civilization, a free man, and we will allow him to do so."

They were much impressed by this statement. Chesty's idea of the "witch-woman" was destined to prove his most forceful argument.

"Pietro makes eleven," he continued, "and you three bring the number up to fourteen, which leaves Ramon but thirteen followers to be arrested with him—unlucky number, thirteen. Haven't you noticed it?"

"You think we join you, then?" asked Francisco, curiously.

"I'm sure of it. You are no longer afraid of Ramon, for his jig is up. You don't want to go to prison with him, because it is very disagreeable to break stone on the roads, I'm told, and in prison they deprive a man of even his cigarettes. I know you have been bad boys, all three of you, and until now the law has threatened you. But you have reformed. Remember, señors, you have reformed, and are now honest men. I will tell Madero, my friend the president, what honest men you are, and how you have helped to defy Ramon, the outlaw, and give him up to justice. Madero will then reward you, and you will live happy ever after."

It was an enticing picture. The men looked grave and undecided. In their hearts they hated Ramon; but they also feared him. For years they had lived in daily terror of the tyrant who ruled them with an iron hand, who whipped a man brutally if he incurred his anger, who dominated them so utterly that they grovelled at his feet like the curs they were. If they could be sure of Ramon's downfall; if they could believe this big American boy, who was fully as powerful of frame as Ramon himself, then they would gladly desert the tyrant and save themselves by joining his enemies. It was only their inbred fear of Ramon and their confidence in his cleverness in defying justice, that made them hesitate.

Chesty saw this. He racked his brain to find other arguments.

"You have witch-women?" asked one of the men, in an awed tone.

"Three of them, all very bewitching."

"One has fly away."

"Yes; to cast a spell over the captain of the Mexican battleship, and make him hurry. The two most powerful are still here on this island."

"Then why they not use their witchcraft to push your ship into deep water!" inquired Francisco, his one eye flashing triumphantly. "Why the witch-women let Ramon make trouble for you? Eh? Tell me, señor."

Chesty looked at the man reproachfully.

"How stupid you are, Francisco. Must we not keep Ramon busy, to hold him here until the warship comes? Why do you suppose we came to this island at all, and ran our ship high on the beach, without hurting it in any way! Did we lay a trap for Ramon? Did we coax him to come and try to capture us, that we might prove he is a wicked law-breaker? We do not seem much afraid of your Ramon, do we? Am I frightened? Do I grow pale, and tremble? Here—feel my pulse—does my blood beat faster in my veins because Ramon Ganza, the trapped criminal, is waiting here to be captured, and thinks he is making us worry?"

The two men exchanged a few sentences in Spanish. Francisco listened to them and nodded approvingly.

"The case is this, señor," he announced, addressing Mr. Todd. "We would like to leave Ramon. We would like to join your ship an' go back to Mexico, an' have pardon. But Ramon is not trap yet. Ramon great man. Many time he escape. If we leave him, an' he then capture your ship, Ramon flog us with whip, which make great pain in us."

"True, that might be the result if Ramon captures the ship; but he can't do that—not in a century of Sundays, which is a long time. And if you stay with Ramon you will surely be made prisoners when the warship comes, which will be in another day or two. You must make up your minds which is the most powerful—we and our witch-women, with the Mexican government and its warships to back us, or poor Ramon, who is caught in a trap. I like you, all three—but not too much. You are fine men—unless I am lying—and I would grieve to see you imprisoned with Ramon. But otherwise I do not care what you decide to do. Come with me and I will save you, just as I intend to save myself, from Ramon's anger. But if you stick to your old master I cannot say one good word for you when you face the Mexican authorities. Now I am tired talking. Make up your minds and let me know."

He carelessly rose, lighted another cigarette and strolled down to the water's edge, where he stood with his back to them. The three rascals took advantage of the opportunity and argued among themselves for half an hour.

"Señor!" called Francisco, who, as a trusted lieutenant of Ramon Ganza, was the more important of the three.

Mr. Radley-Todd came back to the launch.

"It is this way," explained Francisco. "We desire to be save, señor, but we have caution. We believe you speak true, but not yet have you conquer Ramon; not yet has the warship come to take him to prison. So we think of a way to be safe if Ramon win, an' safe if you win. It is but just to us, as honest men, that we do that way."

Chesty smiled, really amused.

"How childlike and bland you naughty, naughty men are!" he exclaimed. "But let me hear your clever plan to play both sides and win hands down."

"When we find you escape from ship," began Francisco, "then Ramon think you have come here, for the tent is gone from the top of the bluff. So Ramon tell us to come here in big launch, to see what you do, an' he say capture you an' bring you back to him. When we get here we find this boat; but two fly away in air-machine, an' only one is left to capture. But Ramon not know if we come before the two fly away or not; he not know if we three, who come to capture, get capture ourselves. So that is what we mus' do. We get capture. You tie up our arms an' our legs an' put gag in our mouth. Then you put us in boat an' take us away to your ship. If Ramon stop us, we say we have been capture. If Ramon see you take us on your ship, he think we have fight hard an' been capture, an' he sorry but not mad. Then, if he take your ship, he set us free; if warship come an' capture Ramon, we safe on your ship an' be hones' men, like you say, an' get reward from Madero. Is it not good way, señor?"

Chesty's sentiments wavered between indignation and admiration. Such a combination of low cunning, cowardice and absence of all shame he had never encountered in any being of human origin. But his cue was not to quarrel with the men at this time. It was enough to realize that instead of becoming a prisoner he was to carry his three captors, bound, to the ship, and so deprive Ramon of that many assistants.

In the outlaw's big launch, which was anchored just outside the tiny bay in the open sea, were plenty of stout ropes. Francisco waded out and got a supply, and then he proceeded deftly to bind his two comrades, trussing their arms to their bodies and their legs together, so that they were helpless. The fellows grinned with delight at this experience, thinking how cleverly they were fooling Ramon Ganza, and when they were laid side by side on the beach Chesty stuck a lighted cigarette in the mouth of each, to afford them comfort and render them patient. Then Francisco bound his own legs and turned to Mr. Radley-Todd, who at once completed the operation and fastened Francisco's arms to his body—not too tightly, but in a very secure manner.

When this was done the big boy breathed a sigh of contentment and set himself down beside his captives.

"Now," said Francisco, "you mus' put us in big boat an' go back to ship with us."

Chesty shook his head.

"Not yet, old man," said he.

"Not yet?"

"No; I shall wait for night. It will be safe in the darkness."

"Then you are 'fraid of Ramon?"

"Not much. Just a little."

The prisoners wriggled uneasily.

"Listen, then, Señor American," observed Francisco. "If we not go before night, then release our bonds—make loose the ropes—so we will rest more easy. When night come you will again tie us up."

Mr. Todd was unresponsive.

"Too much trouble, Francisco," he remarked, with a yawn. "Why do the work twice?"

"But—to lie here all day? San Sebastian, it is too horrible!"

"Fortunes of war, my dear boy. Ramon might appear unexpectedly, you know. We made a bargain, to ensure your safety, and we're going to keep it."

All three turned their heads to regard him with interest. There were sparks of glowering resentment in their dark eyes. Presently one of them said in humble tones:

"With your kind permission, Señor Americaño, I think I will change my mind."

"Certainly," replied Chesty; "do anything you please with your mind. It's yours, you know."

"I think, then, señor, I will not be your prisoner—until night."

"Don't think any such thing. It's wicked of you. Try to guide your thoughts into right channels. Make up your mind to be true to your bargain, because—you have to be."

Francisco groaned.

"All masters are cruel," he muttered. "This Americaño is as bad as Ramon!"

"But he's going to preserve your liberty and keep you out of jail," Chesty reminded him.

"And now, boys, try to sleep, for I'm going to take a little walk and stretch my legs."

CHAPTER 8.25
SCUTTLED

A modicum of truth had been included in Ramon Ganza's recital of falsehoods during his interview with those on board the yacht. The outlaw was really in a tight place and only by forcing, in some way, the capture of the yacht could he hope to escape in a manner at all agreeable to his requirements.

By this time he was fully aware of the situation that confronted him. The flying-machine, if it encountered no accident, would reach the mainland and secure assistance for the stranded Americans. Perhaps it was true that President Madero would send a warship to capture him. Like most fugitive criminals, he had an exaggerated idea of his own importance. In any event he must abandon his island kingdom and seek another hiding place. His first intention—to make every one of these intruders prisoners and subjects, so they could not betray him—was frustrated by the escape of the two in the airplane. It would be useless to capture the others when these two had already carried the news to the authorities who were seeking him.

Two courses of procedure were, open to Ganza. One was hastily to outfit his sixty-foot launch and run it to the South Pacific in search of some other island that was uninhabited, taking with him enough men and women to start a new colony. The other was to capture the yacht, put his most cherished possessions on board and then make off in it before any help could arrive from the mainland. The first was by far the most sensible course, but the beauties of the *Salvador* had so enraptured him and he was so well aware of the value a yacht would prove to him that he could not bring himself to abandon the idea of securing it until the last moment of grace had arrived.

This led him to consider how much time remained to him in which to carry out his intentions. He figured that at least thirty-six hours must elapse before any ship could possibly arrive. It was unlikely that the messengers would find a ship prepared to sail at a moment's notice, and therefore three or four days might pass before he would be disturbed by any outside foe.

Ramon had hoped to frighten the Americans into surrender and therefore had arranged the little drama so lately enacted; but the finale had disappointed him. There was no mine planted beneath the yacht, but he had instructed one of his men to answer to his call, no matter what name he cried out, and to make the statement to the Americans which he had so cleverly invented. He made a mistake in thinking the flag of truce would protect him, for these strangers were not so simple as he had believed; so he had been forced to attempt a desperate escape, which succeeded because it was so bold and unexpected.

Recovering his breath as his white flannels dried upon the rocks, Ramon Ganza carefully considered his next move in the game. The yacht was a glorious prize. He must certainly have it for his own. The people on board seemed unequal to a successful defense. There might be half a dozen determined men among them, but the rest were women and cowards. He laughed as he recalled Mr. Tupper's terror at his threats.

The outlaw decided to carry the ship by assault. A night attack would be best. As soon as Francisco returned with the launch he would call his men together and instruct them what to do. Being informed of every movement on the part of the besieged, Ganza was aware that three people had escaped in the small launch to the bluff where the flying-machine lay. As soon as he discovered that the tent was gone he had dispatched Francisco with two men to capture the three, or as many as he could find. When the airplane ascended Ganza watched it carefully and decided it contained but two people; therefore Francisco would find the other and presently return.

But Francisco failed to put in an appearance, to his master's great annoyance. That old tub of a launch was precious to him, for if all else failed he must use it to make good his escape. Also he needed the three men to assist in boarding the yacht in the night attack. His men were unarmed, while the yacht's crew seemed well provided with weapons of defense.

As the day wore on he considered sending the rowboat to search for Francisco's party, but decided not to risk it. Of course Francisco would come, in time; doubtless he was delayed because he experienced difficulty in capturing his man.

Evening came, but no Francisco. Ramon Ganza was perplexed; he was even somewhat troubled. He must defer the attack until the launch arrived, for he intended to use it to carry his men to the side of the yacht. His plan was to have the launch run up to one side and make a noisy attack, to create a diversion and concentrate the attention of those on board, while he and a party of picked men stole silently to the other side in the rowboat, climbed to the deck and overcame all who opposed them. The bow was too high to scale, where it rested on the beach; the attack must be made near the stern, which sat low in the water.

Therefore the launch was quite necessary, as were the three men who were absent with it, so Ramon was angry with Francisco for not returning more promptly.

The outlaw paced up and down the rocks in the starlight and cursed his dilatory lieutenant most heartily.

But the launch was coming. In fact, two launches were coming to the bay.

As soon as night had really settled down, Mr. Radley-Todd quit loafing and suddenly became active. He carried his trussed and helpless prisoners, one by one, to the small launch and laid them gently along the bottom. He had already, during the afternoon, waded out to the larger launch of Ganza, bored a large hole in its bottom and then stopped the inrushing water with a plug. He chuckled while doing this, being greatly pleased by what he called his "foxy plan to fool the pirate."

With his prisoners aboard, the boy shoved the *Salvador's* launch into the water and cautiously paddled it between the rocks and to the side of the big launch, to which he attached it by means of a rope.

"I think I shall gag you boys, as you suggested," he said to the prisoners, who by this time had become sullen and decidedly unfriendly.

"No!" cried Francisco, partly in anger and partly in fear; "it is not necessary. We know what to do."

"Will you promise not to cry out and attract Ramon's attention?"

"We swear it!" they all cried eagerly.

"Then I think I shall gag you. Not because I doubt your word but because I've whittled out three lovely gags and I'm anxious to see how they work."

They began to protest vigorously at such unkind treatment, but Chesty gagged them, by turns, and they were effectually silenced.

"You boys are splendid actors," he told them, admiringly, "and you are performing your parts with great credit to us all. No one would guess this was your plan, would he? Ramon least of all. If we are not captured, you will make an important addition to our party on the yacht. If we are, you will lie gloriously to Ramon and say I sneaked up behind you and sandbagged all three before you saw me. Eh? Never mind answering, for you can't."

As he spoke, Chesty climbed into the big launch and started the engines. They grumbled and refused to act, at first, but finally overcame their reluctance and the boat chug-chugged on its way to the south bay, making such a racket that the owls thought it was defying them and redoubled their frantic screeches.

"Ramon will be certain to hear me coming," reflected the boy as the boat swept on. "He's a clever scoundrel, that Mexican; exceptionally clever; but if he guesses this riddle he's a wizard."

He kept the launch well out from the shore and as it approached the points of rock behind which the yacht lay hidden he set the steering wheel to carry the boat a couple of hundred yards past the entrance to the bay, lashing it firmly in place. Then, while the engines continued their monotonous "chug-chug," he pried the plug out of the bottom of the boat, crept aboard the *Salvador's* launch and unfastened the rope, cutting the two craft apart. The big launch quickly forged ahead and Chesty sat down and let the smaller boat drift peacefully where it lay.

Ramon Ganza had heard his boat coming, as Chesty had intended he should. Greatly relieved, but still angry with Francisco, he ran as far out upon the point as the rocks would permit and peered through the starlight to catch sight of the approaching launch.

Presently it appeared, making good time, the old engines working steadily and doing their full duty. But it did not turn into the bay, for some extraordinary reason; instead, it kept straight on and headed for some indefinite point out at sea.

"Francisco!" shouted Ganza, in a rage; "Francisco—villain—fool! What are you doing? Wake up, Francisco! The idiot is asleep."

As the precious launch did not halt, the outlaw ran along the shore, following its track and shaking his fist at the perverse Francisco with vengeful energy. Most of his men, attracted by their chief's excitement, left their posts to join him on the shore; the others gazed wonderingly in the direction of the disappearing launch.

Meantime, Chesty Todd cautiously paddled his little boat into the bay, crept to the side of the yacht and uttered a low whistle—the signal agreed upon. Those on board, who had been interested in Ramon's shouts and suspected something was about to happen, lost no time in lowering the davits and Chesty promptly attached the grappling hooks. A few moments later the launch and its occupants were safely on deck and the boy stepped out to be greeted by hearty handshakes and congratulations on his safe return.

"You'll find three prisoners in the launch, Captain Krell," he said. "When you remove their gags they'll protest they are our friends; but I wouldn't trust 'em. Better lock 'em in the cage until this cruel war is over."

"What has become of the Mexican's launch?" asked Thatcher Allen . "The pirates seem to be having some trouble over it."

"It won't bother 'em for long," replied Mr. Todd, complacently. "The boat is headed out to sea, all by its lonesome; but there's a hole in the bottom and it's fast filling with salt water. I imagine that within the next fifteen minutes it will go to Davy Jones's locker, and be out of commission."

CHAPTER 8.26
MARY ELISKA RETURNS

If ever man was thoroughly perplexed it was Ramon Ganza the outlaw. He heard his launch proceed for a distance out to sea, then listened while the engines hesitated and stopped, and saw the boat on which his liberty might depend whirl slowly around and disappear beneath the waves. What could it mean? Were his men on board, and had they met with some astonishing accident, or had they deliberately committed suicide? The curses died on his lips; the affair was too startling and too serious for mere raving; he must try to think of a logical solution of the problem.

The loss of the launch, his last refuge from captivity and imprisonment, left him caught like a wolf in a trap—in case he failed to get possession of the yacht. All night long he sat on a rock by the sea, smoking his black cheroots and thinking—thinking—thinking. Neither he nor his men knew that Chesty Todd had returned to the yacht; but if Ramon had known it he would not have attached especial importance to the fact. It would merely mean one more person to capture during the assault.

Morning found Ganza still deep in thought. He glanced rather uneasily at the ocean and at times swept the horizon with his glasses, which were slung by a strap to his shoulder. His men brought him food and a cup of hot coffee, but dared not speak to him in his present mood.

They suspected his case was growing desperate, yet they still retained confidence in their resourceful, clever master, who had never yet failed to accomplish whatever he undertook.

In this crisis of his career the fugitive, usually irritable and quick to act, proved his strength of mind by taking time to consider his position from all points and to weigh carefully the merits of the different plans that suggested themselves. He realized that an error at this time would prove fatal.

The hours wore on until, at about the middle of the afternoon, as Ganza made one of his periodic inspections of the horizon, his glasses caught a speck in the sky—a speck that moved and grew larger. At first he thought it a gull or an eagle; later he changed his mind, for the speck rapidly increased in size and took form, and the form was that of an airplane.

Those on the yacht saw it now and great was the wonder and excitement it caused. Here was a messenger from the great world, bringing them hope of succor or black disappointment. Presently the broad spreading planes bore down upon the island and circled gracefully over the ship.

"It's Mary Eliska!" they cried in chorus and Chesty Todd added: "She wants to land on deck. Clear a space—quick!"

They did the best they could. It seemed like a tiny place for that great sweeping thing to land on and even Sybil exclaimed: "She'll never make it in the world!" But Mary Eliska, hovering above them in her Aircraft, observed carefully the conditions below and shutting off her engine began to volplane.

The huge machine settled quietly down and alighted fairly upon the deck. One rail caught the lower plane and tipped it, but the girl leaped lightly from her seat and was caught by Thatcher Allen, whose gray eyes sparkled with joy from behind their spectacles.

You may be sure the brave girl received a glad welcome, but as soon as her safety was assured she was deluged with questions. The ping of a rifle ball warned them to scuttle below to the cabin, where Mary Eliska tried to explain.

"Why on earth did you venture to come back?" demanded Madeline. "We had told ourselves that you, at least, were safe from the dangers that menace us, and it pleased us to know that. But where is your brother?"

"Did you get to land?" cried half a dozen voices, eagerly. "What did you do? Tell us!"

Mary Eliska laughed and held up both hands, imploring silence.

"I came to bring you good news," she began. "And now that you are assured of that, please let me tell the story my own way, or I shall bungle it."

"Go ahead," they answered and settled themselves to listen.

"We followed the route Captain Krell had mapped out for us," said Mary Eliska, "and in four hours after leaving here we sighted the Mexican coast. Fifteen minutes' run to the north brought us to the village of San Blas, where there is a telegraph office. We landed and had some difficulty in satisfying the authorities that we were harmless Americans, but finally they agreed to escort us to the telegraph office under guard. We wired our story direct to President Madero, putting it as briefly as possible and asking him for a warship to rescue our friends and capture Ramon Ganza. There was no answer until evening, when we received a message from the Secretary of the Navy saying he had conferred with the President and Secretary of State and would be glad to accede to our request. In eight or ten days he thought he could spare a warship to go to the island for Ganza. Unfortunately, the entire navy was in use at the present time.

"That dashed our hopes, you may be sure, for we feared you couldn't hold Ganza at bay for so long; so Bill and I determined to fly to San Diego and secure help there. The Secretary of the Navy had wired the authorities of San Blas to afford us every consideration and hospitality, so we filled our tanks with gasoline and slept at a little inn until daybreak. Then we were off for the north, and in two hours met the United States torpedo fleet, on its way to Magdalena Bay for target practice. We made out the flagship and dropped to the water beside it. Commodore Davis at once laid to and sent a boat to us. Bill went aboard and explained fully to the commodore our story and the need for immediate help. As a result the *Mermaid* was signaled and its captain presently came aboard and received his orders. He was to take us directly to this island, drive off Ganza or fight him, as circumstances might require, and then assist in getting the *Salvador* afloat again. If he captures Ganza he is to carry him away a prisoner and turn him and his men over to the Mexican authorities at Magdalena.

"Captain Swanson undertook the adventure gladly and is now on his way here with the *Mermaid*, with Bill to guide him. My brother and I thought it best for me to come on ahead and tell you the good news, for we have worried about you and knew that with rescue at hand you would have courage to hold out, no matter how desperate your condition. So here I am, and the *Mermaid* will arrive either tonight or early in the morning."

They were indeed delighted with this assurance and it put new heart into the most timorous of those aboard.

"However," said Chesty Todd, "we seem to be in no danger, just now, and since our clever enemy has failed to scare us into surrender he has remained quiet and behaved himself as well as could be expected."

They told Mary Eliska all that had transpired in her absence and the conversation continued all during the dinner—on which the chef exercised his best talents, in honor of Mary Eliska's return—and even until bedtime, there was so much to say.

Chesty went on watch at eleven o'clock, and as he leaned silently over the rail at a point near the bow of the launch he detected a series of queer sounds coming from below. This part of the yacht was high on the shelving beach and it was here that they had arranged huge piles of rock, on either side, to hold the keel level. It sounded to Mr. Todd as if someone was at work near these rocks, for on account of the swell of the boat's side it was impossible to see, from the deck, anyone below, in case he kept close to the keel.

So Chesty crept aft, held a whispered conversation with Captain Krell, and quickly divested himself of his clothing. At the stern, which was settled quite close to the surface of the water, the boy let himself down by means of a rope, descending hand under hand, and silently dropped into the dark water. Swimming was one of Radley-Todd's principal accomplishments and he scarcely made a ripple as he crept alongside the boat until the bow came into full view. The night was somewhat darker than usual, but the American had sharp eyes and it did not take him long to discover that the besiegers were employed in removing the rocks from the right hand side of the keel.

Instantly comprehending their purpose in this, Chesty turned and quickly regained the stern, climbing to the deck. His report to Captain Krell seemed so serious, because it meant a desperate attack presently, that it was promptly decided to arouse the entire party and warn them that a crisis was at hand.

CHAPTER 8.27
FACING THE CRISIS

Consternation reigned in the cabin when the principals assembled there with white and startled faces. On deck Captain Krell was instructing his men how to act in the threatened emergency. Pietro was among them, accepting his rifle and his instructions willingly, but shaking his head at what he considered a vain attempt to resist Ramon Ganza.

"Ramon great man!" he said to Captain Krell. "Ramon always win; nobody can conquer him. I knew Ramon would win this time, an' when he does he will capture me an' whip me hard. All right; I know I am to be whipped at the time Chica tell me to leave Ramon. Never min'. Pietro can stand it, for others have been whipped by Ramon an' lived—with marks like a zebra's on their skins."

In the cabin Chesty was trying to explain the situation.

"It's this way," he said; "when the rocks are all removed the yacht will fall over on her side, as she was at first, with the rail quite near to the water. You remember how she lay before we propped her up. Well, that means we have no secure footing on deck and that the pirates can easily climb aboard and have the best of the argument. If we slip, we fall into their arms; if we stick to the deck—like flies to a ceiling, they'll rush and get us."

"We can't fight from the deck," declared Thatcher Allen. "Tell Captain Krell to come here."

The captain arrived and after a consultation it was decided to gather all hands in the cabin and fortify it as strongly as possible. The roof projected a few feet above the deck and there was a row of small windows on either side, but these were supplied with heavy shutters designed for use in case of storms, when the shutters were readily fixed in place. The stairway might be well guarded by one man, and above the windows were small ventilators through which several rifles could be pointed. By standing upon the cabin table the defenders could command the deck in this way. They were instructed not to shoot, however, unless absolutely obliged to. All the hatches were battened down, so that if Ganza gained the deck he could not get below and was welcome to remain aboard until the rescuers arrived.

Mary Eliska, who had listened silently, now approached Thatcher Allen and said:

"When the yacht tips, our Aircraft will be ruined, for the chances are it will slide overboard. Even if it doesn't, those scoundrels will wreck it completely, for it will be quite at their mercy.

So I've decided, while there is yet time, to fly it across to the bluff, where I can remain until you are rescued."

"Can you manage to get away from the deck?"

"Easily."

"Then I think it best for you to go."

"May I take Sybil with me?"

He hesitated a moment; then replied: "Yes. It will be a good thing to have you girls away from here when the attack is made. Here you could be of no service whatever, and your absence will—eh—give us more room to defend the cabin."

"You will have to act quickly, Miss Stricklin," suggested Chesty.

"I know. Come, Sybil."

They drew on their jackets as they went on deck, both girls realizing that no time must be lost if they hoped to get away. Once the yacht tipped on her side it would be impossible to fly the machine.

As they took their places Mr. Radley-Todd inquired: "Plenty of gasoline?"

"I think so," said Mary Eliska. "I'm not sure how much is left in the tanks, but it ought to be enough to get us to the bluff. Whirl the propeller, Chesty."

He did so, and the engine started with a roar. Thatcher Allen and Chesty steadied the Aircraft until the motor had acquired full speed and then Mary Eliska threw in the clutch and the big airplane rose as easily as a bird takes flight and ascended into the starlit sky at a steep angle. This feat is what is called "cloud climbing" and Mary Eliska understood it perfectly.

It seemed a bold thing to undertake such a flight in the nighttime, but the Flying Girl's friends had so much confidence in her skill that they never considered the danger of the undertaking. Across the barren island to the bluff was so unimportant a flight to one of Mary Eliska's experience that when she was once away they believed her quite safe.

While the men stood watching the Aircraft mount into the dim sky the yacht suddenly trembled and keeled over, throwing them all flat upon the deck. With one accord they scrambled up and dashed into the cabin, which they reached just as Ramon Ganza and his men swarmed over the rail.

CHAPTER 8.28
THE PSISONER

"What's wrong, Sis?" asked Sybil, as the engine skipped and wavered.

"Gasoline," was the brief answer.

"Oh. Can you get to the bluff?"

"I—don't—know. There!" as the propeller ceased to whirl; "now I'll volplane. It's a long reach, Syb; but we'll land somewhere—right side up."

The dim mountain seemed far ahead of them; below was the "dip," or valley, which lay between the rock ridges and the mountain. As they had casually glanced toward it in former times, it seemed a forbidding place, slimy and moist, devoid alike of any green thing or living creature. Even the owls shunned the "dip."

Tonight, when everything was obscure, they seemed gliding into a black pit. Mary Eliska had to manipulate her levers cautiously, for she could not tell just when they would reach the ground. As it was they bumped, bounded forward, bumped again and brought up suddenly between two boulders that topped a rugged knoll.

"Any damage?" asked Sybil, catching her breath.

"Not much, I'm sure," replied her chum. "But here we are; and here we'll stay until someone comes with gasoline. Can you see anything, Syb?"

"The mountain, over there against the sky. It seems so near I could almost touch it. It wouldn't have taken but a few drops more to have landed us on the bluff, drat the luck!"

"See anything else?"

"Where?"

"Around us."

"No; but I can smell something. Smells like spoiled gasoline. Does gasoline ever spoil, Sis?"

"Not to my knowledge. But come; let's crawl into the boat and get the blankets out. Wherever we are, it's our hotel, and we must make the best of it."

Skyward, there could be distinguished the mountain at the west and the rock hills at the east; but the pocket in which they lay was black as ink. From the boat Mary Eliska managed to open the aluminum chest and take out the blankets. They then arranged a temporary bed in the bottom of the boat and covered themselves up.

"Anyhow, I managed to save the Aircraft," sighed Mary Eliska, contentedly. Then she sat bolt upright and cried: "Listen!"

"The battle's on," answered Sybil, as a succession of wild shouts reached their ears. It was very aggravating to be so ignorant of what was happening to their friends. The shouts continued, at intervals, but there was no sound of firearms. Evidently the Mexicans had gained the deck but had found it a barren victory. On the mountain the owls were hooting and flying about as usual, but the shouts that had come from the bay were of such a different nature that the shrieks of the night-birds did not drown them.

Suddenly a broad streak of light shot over them, rested a moment on the mountain, swayed to right and left and then sank below the ridges of rock. Above the bay where the *Salvador* was beached thin shafts of white light radiated, illuminating the sky like an aurora borealis.

"A searchlight!"

"The torpedo boat!" the girls cried in one breath; and then they sat trembling and straining their ears to listen.

A dull, angry "boom!" rent the air and echoed from the mountain. It was a warning gun from the *Mermaid*. The shouts became screams of fear. Then silence followed, complete and enduring.

Mary Eliska breathed heavily. "It's all over, Sybil!" she gasped.

"I—I wonder if—anyone was—hurt."

"Any of our people?"

"Of course."

"I think not. That gun was merely a signal and I imagine the Mexicans ran like rats. How fortunate it was that Captain Swanson arrived with the *Mermaid* so soon!»

"How unfortunate he didn't come sooner. We wouldn't have been in this awkward predicament. It will take them hours to get to us over those sharp rocks."

Mary Eliska did not reply. She was trying to understand the events transpiring around the *Salvador*. Had there been a tragedy? Or had the torpedo boat merely frightened the outlaws, as she had imagined, and driven them away?

There was no sleep for the isolated girls during the brief hours preceding the dawn. As it gradually lightened they peered about them to see where they were, and by degrees made out their surroundings. There were fewer rocks in this cup-shaped hollow than in other parts of the island. On the knoll where the Aircraft rested were the two big rocks which had arrested its progress, and between these the body of the aluminum boat was tightly wedged. At intervals throughout the valley were similar rocky hummocks, but all the space between consisted of an oozy, damp soil of a greenish-brown color, with glints of red where the sun caught it prismatically. Looking at this ooze critically, as the light strengthened, it seemed to the girls to shift somewhat, showing here and there a thick bubble which slowly formed and disappeared.

Mary Eliska put her hand over the side of the boat and withdrew it again.

"Look, Sybil," she exclaimed. "It's oil."

"Hair or salad oil, Sis?"

Mary Eliska sniffed at her dipped finger.

"Petroleum. This is the crude article, and seeps up from some store of oil far down in the earth. There would be a fortune in this find, Syb, if it happened to be in America. Out here it is, of course, valueless."

"Don't they make kerosene and gasoline of it?"

"Yes; of course."

"Then make some gasoline and let's fly away."

Mary Eliska laughed.

"If you will furnish the distillery, Syb, I'll make the gasoline," she said; "but I believe it's a long, slow process, and——"

"Look!" cried Sybil, with a start, as she pointed a slim finger toward the east. From a far distant ridge a man came bounding over the rocks, leaping from one to another with little hesitation in picking his way. He was a big man, but as the light was still dim they could see no more than his huge form. Presently he paused to look behind him; then on he dashed again. He had come from the direction of the bay and was at first headed toward the mountain, but in one of his pauses, whether to regain his breath or look behind, he caught sight of the airplane and at once turned directly toward it.

"Do you think," asked Sybil, uneasily, "it is one of our people come to look for us?"

"No," returned Mary Eliska, positively. "That man is a fugitive. He has escaped over the rock hills and is trying to find some hiding place."

"Then I wonder he dares come in our direction."

"It is *strange*," agreed Mary Eliska, with a shudder as she remembered how helpless they were.

Then, with fascinated gaze, the two girls fell silent and watched the approaching fugitive. As he neared that part of the valley where the oil seeped up he proceeded more cautiously, leaping from one point of rock—or hummock—to another. Once, when forced to step on the level ground, the oil tripped him. He slipped and fell, but was instantly up again and bounding on his way. It seemed no easy task to make speed over such a rough and trackless way, yet here it was easier to proceed than back in those almost impassable hills. It was wonderful that he had succeeded in crossing them at all.

"I think," said Mary Eliska, as she sat cold and staring, "it is Ramon Ganza."

"The outlaw? But he wears white flannels."

"Not now. He probably changed them for the night attack; but I can see the rings glitter on his fingers, and—none of the other Mexicans is so big."

Sybil nestled a little closer to her friend.

"Have you a revolver, Sis?"

Mary Eliska shook her head.

"No arms at all—not even a hatpin?"

"Nothing whatever to use for defense."

The man was quite near now. Yes; it was Ramon Ganza. His clothes were torn by the rocks and hung around him in rags, and where he had fallen the thick, slimy oil clung to them. His face was smeared with dust and grime and the whole aspect of the outlaw was ghastly and repulsive—perhaps rendered more acute by the jewelled rings that loaded his fingers.

He was obliged to step with more care as he neared the airplane, in which crouched the two girls, and finally he came to a halt on a hummock a few paces away. The oil lay more thickly around the Aircraft than elsewhere, and Ramon Ganza eyed it suspiciously. Then he spoke, resting his hands on his hips and leering insolently at Sybil and Mary Eliska.

"So, I have caught you, then," he cried. "Why did you try to escape?"

"For the same reason you are trying to escape, perhaps," retorted Mary Eliska, summoning what courage she could command. "But I warn you that our friends will presently come for us, and—you may not care to meet them."

He uttered an angry snarl and cast a quick glance around the valley. In all its broad stretch not a person other than themselves was visible.

Ramon sat down on his knoll, breathing heavily from his long run.

"Yes, I have run away," he admitted, bitterness and hate in his tone. "I can fight ten—or twenty, perhaps—with my single hand; but not fifty. They have come to put me in prison, those fiends over there," jerking his thumb toward the bay, "and seeing they were too strong for me to oppose, I came away. It is what you call discreet—eh?—which is more safe, if less noble, than valor. But they have the island and they will hunt me down. And once more I shall laugh at them—once more Ramon Ganza will defy them all!"

"How?" asked Mary Eliska, curiously.

"Have you not the flying-machine—the airship?" he asked, simply. "And are you not here alone, and in my power? It carries but two, I see, so one of you shall stay here. The other must fly with me to my own island, where I will take a sailboat and—vanish from the dogs who are hounding me."

"That," said Mary Eliska, with forced calmness, for her heart was beating wildly, "is impossible."

He uttered a fierce growl.

"It is *not* impossible,» he cried. «I have seen your machine fly, and know it can fly when you want it to. It must fly now, or by San Filippe I will tumble you both out and fly it myself. It is best that you not arouse my anger, for Ramon Ganza is desperate and will not be denied. Get ready, girl! We will fly to my island, or——» He laughed harshly. «Or you will both ruin your beautiful toilets, and—the mire is dangerous,» he added.

"We have no gasoline," pleaded Mary Eliska.

"Pah! a trick to deceive me."

"No; it is true," cried Sybil, who grew more quiet as fear possessed her.

He hesitated, a look of despair flashing across his features. Then he said with grim determination: "I will see for myself," and stepped recklessly into the pool of oil that lay between him and the hummock where the airplane perched.

The slime reached to his ankle, but he kept doggedly on. The second step sent him knee-deep into the ooze and he had to struggle to wade farther in. But now he sank nearly to his waist and the sticky soil held him fast. Then suddenly the man seemed to realize his peril and uttered a shrill cry of terror.

"Help, young ladies! For the love of humanity—help! Will you see me die like this?" he screamed.

Mary Eliska and Sybil, both horrified, had risen to their feet. The sinking outlaw was fully five yards distant and there seemed no possible way to aid him. But it was terrible to allow a human being to perish in such a way, even when it was a confessed enemy who stood in peril. Mary Eliska caught up a blanket and hurled it toward him, and he seized it eagerly and spread it around him for support. Next moment Sybil had hastily folded the second blanket and cast it with all her strength toward Ganza. One corner he caught and in a moment had added it to the first, now becoming saturated with oil. Yet the blankets would not have availed much had not Ramon's feet now rested upon a rock far beneath the surface, effectually preventing him from sinking any lower. Almost waist-deep in the putty-like mire he stood a fast prisoner, for no effort of his own could enable him to free himself.

He realized, presently, that he was not fated to be entombed in the mire, so part of his old assurance returned to him. As he stared at the girls and they returned his gaze with horrified looks, he remarked:

"Well, I am caught, as you see; but it was no officer of the law that did it. Ramon Ganza can defy mankind, as he has often proved, but he bows to Nature. Also, young ladies, I beg to point out that—if you have spoken truly—you are likewise caught, and alas! we cannot assist one another. What, then, shall we do for amusement?"

"I think," said Sybil gravely, "you ought to pray."

"I? I have forgotten how. What then? Shall we sing songs? If you will accompany the chorus I will delight your ears with my excellent tenor voice."

This bravado, coming from a man stuck fast in the mire, was so gruesome that it made the girls shudder with aversion. But Sybil, happening to glance up, cried with sudden animation: "Look, Mary Eliska!" and pointed with a trembling finger.

In the distance a group of men had appeared over the edge of the rock hills. They saw the stalled airplane and waved their arms encouragingly.

Ganza screwed his head around with some difficulty and also observed the rescue party.

"It cannot matter," he said coolly. "As well one prison as another, and no Mexican dungeon could hug me tighter than this."

He fell silent, however, and no further remarks were exchanged as the distant party drew nearer. They were forced by the treacherous nature of the valley to move cautiously and when they entered the area of oil seepage more than one slipped in the slimy pools. But gradually they approached the spot where the airplane rested and now Mary Eliska and Sybil could make out Bill Stricklin, Thatcher Allen, Captain Krell, Chesty Todd and an unknown man in uniform, who were accompanied by several seamen.

The girls stood up and waved their handkerchiefs and then cried out warnings to beware the mire. Not until the rescuers were quite near to the place did they perceive the upper half of Ramon Ganza protruding from the imprisoning slime.

"Dear me," cried Thatcher Allen ; "this is interesting; very! How are you, girls? All right?"

Through the bombardment of eager questions they assured their friends that they had suffered no serious discomfort because of the accident to the Aircraft. "But," added Sybil, "we had a good fright when Ramon Ganza threatened us, unless we assisted him to escape in our airplane. Fortunately the mire came to our assistance, for he stepped into a soft place and it held him fast—as you see."

All eyes turned upon the helpless outlaw, who nodded his head with astonishing nonchalance.

"I bid you good morning, señors," said he. "When you are sufficiently rested from your walk, be kind enough to pull me out of this loving embrace; but gently, or you may dislocate my bones."

"Who is this?" asked the officer in uniform, a fine featured young man.

"The rascal who has so boldly annoyed us, regardless of consequences," replied Thatcher Allen, frowning upon the Mexican. "He escaped us last night, but we have him now, sure enough, and I intend to see he is handed over to the authorities of his country, whose laws he has defied."

"What did he do?" the officer inquired, gazing at Ganza curiously.

"Permit me to explain that I robbed a bank—a bank engaged in robbing others under government sanction," said Ganza. "To rob is a small thing, señors; but it is a crime to be discovered robbing. That was my fault. Others in my native land, who are more successful embezzlers than I, are today respected, rich and happy."

"Was that your only crime?"

"So far as is known, señor. Otherwise I am very good man and quite respectable."

"He is a tyrant and a bully, and whips his men if they disobey him," declared Bill.

"Pah! they are curs. The whip is less than they deserve," retorted Ganza. "But permit me to remind you of my present discomfort, señors. I will gladly exchange this bog for a Mexican prison."

They managed to drag him out, none too gently, and the seamen scraped the oily slime from his legs and body so that he could stand erect.

Then they turned to examine the condition of the airplane.

CHAPTER 8.29
MARY ELISKA DECIDES

Only by taking the Aircraft entirely apart, decided Bill, might he hope to remove it to the bay, for it could not be flown from the hummock where it was wedged between the rocks. But they could not wait to do that now. The girls were very near one of those feminine crises so familiar to Mrs. Tupper, and their friends realized the nervous strain they had endured and made haste to lead them back to the yacht. The seamen looked after Ramon Ganza, who was so physically exhausted by his late experience that he made no endeavor to escape.

It was a tedious climb, by no means devoid of danger, but so anxious were Mary Eliska and Sybil to escape from the dread valley that they energetically persevered until the last rock hill was passed and they descended the slope to the inlet.

There lay the *Salvador*, keeled over, indeed, but safe and sound. Just without the bay floated the *Mermaid*, and one of her boats was run upon the beach and another clung to the *Salvador's* side.

A hearty cheer greeted the return of the rescue party when Mary Eliska and Sybil were observed approaching with them, and Captain Swanson himself came forward to offer his congratulations.

On their way, Bill had briefly related the events of the night attack and told how the defenders, fortified within the cabin and below decks, had been quite safe from Ganza until the arrival of the torpedo boat relieved the situation. Then the Mexicans fled and made frantic attempts to escape, hiding themselves in the wilderness of rocks that littered the island.

When Captain Swanson learned of the capture of Ramon Ganza and the rescue of the young ladies he decided to attempt no pursuit of the scattered Mexicans but to apply himself promptly to the task of floating the yacht, which he succeeded in doing before night.

The *Salvador* was in no way injured and as soon as she had anchored outside the bay was again in commission and fully able to care for herself.

Madeline invited the officers of the *Mermaid* to dine aboard her yacht and Monsieur Risette prepared a repast that surprised even his employer, so elaborate and delicious it proved.

As they conversed together afterward, commenting upon the exciting experiences of the yacht and her company and the daring flights of the Stricklin Hydro-Aircraft, Madeline said to Captain Swanson:

"What shall we do with Ramon Ganza?"

"Where is he, Miss Dentry?"

"Locked up in our cage. But I don't want him aboard. Won't you take him to Magdalena and turn him over to the Mexican police?"

"I am not sure I have authority to arrest the man," replied the captain gravely. "I will send a wireless to the fleet tonight and endeavor to get the admiral and receive his instructions concerning Ganza."

He wrote out a message at once and dispatched it to his ship by one of his men, that the wireless operator aboard might repeat it a number of times in the attempt to reach the ship for which it was intended. A wireless message travels farther by night and is more distinct.

Madeline now urged Captain Swanson to carry Chica and Pietro to Magdalena, which would enable them to reach their homes quickly and he agreed to do this. Miss Dentry supplied the two with sufficient money for their needs and the Red-beard and the child said their good-byes and were rowed to the *Mermaid*.

The yacht party, now reunited and safe from further molestation, thoroughly enjoyed the evening and expressed their gratitude again and again for the prompt assistance rendered them by their fellow countrymen. Madeline had already written a nice letter to the admiral, which she entrusted to Captain Swanson.

As Mary Eliska and Sybil, as well as many others of the party, had passed a trying and sleepless night, the officers thoughtfully retired early, returning to their quarters on the *Mermaid*.

Breakfast was in progress on the *Salvador* next morning when a note was brought from the captain of the torpedo boat.

"I was fortunate in reaching the admiral," it said, "and I beg to enclose you a copy of the message I have received from him in reply. I further regret to state that I am ordered to rejoin the fleet without delay and must therefore bid you all adieu."

The wireless read: "President Madero proclaimed a general amnesty to Mexican refugees some three months ago. On the list of pardons appears the name of Ramon Ganza."

Madeline drew a long breath.

"I'm sorry for that," she said. "Ramon Ganza has escaped the penalty of breaking his country's laws and we are powerless to punish him ourselves—even though he struck poor Mason with a knife."

"How is Mason getting along?" asked Mary Eliska.

"Very nicely," stated Thatcher Allen . "It was a deep cut, but reached no vital organs and the man will soon be as good as new."

"That does not alter the fact that Ganza is a wicked desperado," said Sybil.

"It's a shame to allow him to escape," exclaimed Mr. Tupper, indignantly. "Can't we arrest him for disturbing the peace, and trying to capture our yacht, and attempting to murder one of the crew?"

"No," replied Thatcher Allen . "This island doesn't belong to the United States. I believe it is Mexican territory. But if we can prove damages we might be able to recover from the Mexican government—and then, again, we might not."

"I'll never put in a claim, for my part," said Madeline, laughing. "But what are we to do with Ramon Ganza—and those three rascals imprisoned with him, whom Chesty captured and brought to us?"

"Let Chesty get rid of them; they're his prisoners," suggested Sybil.

"The chief bandit is your own prisoner—and Mary Eliska's," declared Chesty. "What do you intend to do with him, Miss Allen?"

Sybil laughed.

"It's a problem," she confessed. "Can you solve it, Miss Dentry?"

"I fear not," answered Madeline, indeed puzzled. "Our prisoners are likely to prove white elephants on our hands. To carry them to America would involve us in endless difficulties, and—I have other plans, wherein their presence is better dispensed with."

"Then," said Chesty, after due reflection, "let us leave them all behind us, on the island. Not this island, where they would be prisoners and perhaps starve, because I have sunk their gasoline launch and they cannot get away, but on Ramon Ganza's own island. Then the fellow may decide his future as he deems best and we may wash our hands of the whole disagreeable affair."

"I hope you won't inform him that he is pardoned," said Mr. Tupper, earnestly.

"Why not?" asked Madeline. "Let us return good for evil. Perhaps, when Ramon Ganza is no longer a refugee and can face the world a free man, he will redeem his past and become honest."

"I doubt it," declared Thatcher Allen ; "but I think you are right to give him the chance."

It was so decided. There remained on Owl Island but one of Ganza's rowboats which would be available for use by the men hidden among the rocks, but at the larger island was a small sailboat in which, during calm weather, the chief might go for his men and transport them to their former quarters.

Next morning a party accompanied Bill into the valley once more, where the Aircraft was taken apart and brought with considerable labor to the bay, from whence it was conveyed to the yacht and compactly stored away below decks.

"There's no use putting it together until we get back home," said the inventor; and his partner, Thatcher Allen, agreed with him.

This task had consumed the entire day, during which Mary Eliska and Sybil had kept to their state-rooms, trying to quiet their nerves and get some much-needed sleep. Madeline, in the meantime, had ordered a store of provisions placed on the beach for the use of the band of Mexicans until they were rescued by their leader, as she did not wish them to suffer for lack of food, however mischievous and lawless they might be.

The following day Captain Krell hoisted anchor and headed for the larger island, and it was good to all to feel the water slipping along underneath the *Salvador's* thin keel again.

Ramon Ganza accepted his liberty with the same stoical indifference that characterized all his actions. He strutted a bit when Chesty told him of his pardon, but declared he would continue to inhabit the island where he was virtually a king.

"With no fear of a prison to haunt me," he said, "I can make the island a paradise. Many Mexicans will settle there and become my subjects."

"You'll have to cut out the flogging, then," suggested Chesty.

"It will gratify me to do so. Before, I have the obligation to flog the disobedient ones because I dared not send them away; but now, if they prove obstinate, I may send them back to Mexico."

He took off his hat with an elaborate bow as the *Salvador's* boat left him standing with his three men on the little dock below his residence; but Francisco and the other two scowled fiercely at Mr. Todd, whom they reproached for deceiving them about Madero›s reward, although they had elected to remain with their old master rather than be taken to America.

"It's a good thing for civilization that those villains are sequestrated on a far-away, unknown island," remarked Chesty, when he had regained the yacht's deck. "I suppose anyone can reform, if he tries hard, but I'll bet a hat that Francisco and his comrades never make the attempt."

"We are well rid of them, in any event," asserted Thatcher Allen .

Mary Eliska and Sybil appeared at dinner, both considerably improved in spirits after their long rest.

"When do we sail for San Diego?" Sybil asked Madeline.

"Captain Krell is ready. I am waiting for Mary Eliska and you to decide," was the reply.

Mary Eliska looked up in surprise.

"What have we to decide?" she inquired.

"Merely which way we shall proceed. My yacht hasn't had a fair trial yet and I had in mind a trip to Honolulu before we went in chase of two runaway girls. We still have on board enough coal and supplies for such a trip and I have resolved to invite you all to make it in my company—in which case we will head directly for Hawaii from here."

Mary Eliska was thoughtful for a time and looked inquiringly at Bill, who smiled in return.

"I think such a trip would do us all good," he suggested.

"The Flying Girl has no important engagements, at present," added Mr. Todd, the press agent.

"If she had, I think she deserves a little recreation after her late trying experiences," said Thatcher Allen .

"Why, Mary Eliska, it has all been decided in advance," exclaimed Sybil. "They're merely asking our consent out of politeness."

Mary Eliska turned to Madeline and pressed her hand gratefully.

"You've really been our guardian angel, Miss Dentry," she said. "We can never repay your great kindness and generosity, nor properly thank you for what you have done for us."

"Why should you?" asked Madeline. "Think what a splendid time I've had during this adventure, all due to the Flying Girl and her chum—and to a defect in the famous Stricklin Aircraft. But if you sincerely wish to please me, come with me on the trip to Honolulu."

"Of course I will," Mary Eliska responded. "I've always longed for an ocean voyage, and in such company, and on the dear old *Salvador*, the trip will be delightful."

The others of the Stricklin-Thatcher Allen party, who were every one eager to go, rapturously applauded this decision.

CHAPTER 9

The Hollywood Flight

CHAPTER 9.1
A FLASH ON THE SCREEN

A bright red sports-roadster, loaded to overflowing with young people of both sexes, turned in at the gate of the Carltons' home in Spring City and whizzed up the driveway to the porch steps. As it stopped at the entrance, Jax Gray, who was Mary Eliska's best friend, disentangled herself from the group and jumped out.

"Hello, Aunt Sally!" she called to the middle-aged woman sitting on the porch. "Any news of the world's most famous aviatrix?"

"You mean Mary Eliska?" returned Aunt Sally, smiling. Jax Gray nodded. "Of course. Have you heard from her?"

"No, I haven't, Jax Gray. But then, I didn't expect to. You know, of course, that Mary Eliska has set her heart on taking some sort of flying position, and she had several prospects to interview."

"But she's been gone a week!" protested Jax Gray. "This is the twenty-second of September."

"I know, but she expected to be gone a week. She ought to be home sometime today. If she doesn't come, I think she will let me know."

"Well, we miss her just fearfully," concluded Jax Gray. "And we want to hear the very minute she gets back. You know Ralph leaves for college tomorrow, and he's all hot and bothered about going off without even a good-bye from Mary Eliska."

Aunt Sally smiled at the mention of Ralph Clavering's devotion to her niece. The young man, whose father happened to be the wealthiest citizen of Spring City, made no attempt to keep his admiration for Mary Eliska a secret.

"I'll have her call you the minute she arrives. At least—if she doesn't come home in an ambulance."

Jax Gray laughed at the absurdity of such a suggestion and turned to go. In her haste she almost bumped into a messenger-boy, who at that very moment was coming up the porch steps with a telegram.

Aunt Sally rose from her seat and stepped forward excitedly.

"Oh, I'm afraid something dreadful has happened!" she exclaimed, ominously.

Jax Gray remained motionless, and even the young people in the car grew silent. An awful tenseness seemed to hang over the peaceful September day, as Aunt Sally received the message into her trembling hands.

"Why, it's *for* Mary Eliska—not *from* her!" she cried in sudden relief. "So she must be all right."

Scarcely were the words out of her mouth when the drone of a motor attracted everybody's attention to the skies. A plane—yes, with the rotors that proclaimed it an autogiro—was approaching from the west, until it seemed to hover over the very house itself.

"There she is!" screamed Jax Gray, joyously, and in another moment the six young people in the roadster had all jumped out and were racing towards the field beyond the house, where Mary Eliska always landed her plane.

"Thank goodness!" exclaimed Aunt Sally, grateful that once again the girl who had been through so many catastrophes in her zeal for flying would be safe on the ground.

Linking her arm with Jax Gray's, she accompanied the young people to the field beyond the house.

With the ease of a cat settling down to take her nap, the Ladybug, Mary Eliska's famous autogiro, descended to the earth, and the slender, pretty girl in a flier's suit and helmet, climbed out of the cockpit.

"Darling!" cried Jax Gray, dashing forward for the first embrace.

Mary Eliska tried to hug everybody at once, with an especially tender caress for her Aunt Sally, who had mothered her ever since she was a baby.

"Were you kidnapped?" inquired Ralph Clavering, the tall, good-looking young man who considered Mary Eliska his special property.

"Or in a burning house?" suggested Kit Hulbert, Ralph's married sister.

Mary Eliska shook her head laughingly.

"Just taking a good week's rest, I'll bet!" surmised long-legged Jim Valier, whose idea of bliss was to sleep. "Don't blame you a bit, Mary Eliska. A fellow can't get a decent nap with this snappy bunch around, let alone a full night's rest!"

"You're surely all right, dear?" inquired Aunt Sally, anxiously. "No bones broken?"

Again Mary Eliska smiled.

"I'm fine, and I had a most successful trip. I'll tell you all about it later—if anything materializes," she added, mysteriously.

"We want to go to the movies," explained Kit, as they all turned back towards the house. "Can you make it, Mary Eliska?"

"Yes, if you will give me fifteen minutes for a shower, and five for a bite to eat," she replied. "And if Aunt Sally will come along too," she added affectionately.

She made even better time than she had promised, and inside of a quarter of an hour, a different Mary Eliska came down the stairs. Clad in a blue silk suit the color of her eyes, her beautiful blond hair showing under her turban, she looked more like a society girl than the world's most famous aviatrix.

In the meanwhile, Jax Gray had gone into the garage and brought out Mary Eliska's roadster, for Ralph Clavering's car, elastic as it seemed to be, could not be stretched to accommodate two extra passengers. Since Aunt Sally had graciously accepted their invitation, they wanted her to be comfortable.

"So you won't ride with me!" complained Ralph, as he watched Mary Eliska take her place at the wheel of her own car.

"I'll sit beside you in the movies," she promised,

"And you even take Jax Gray away from us!" protested Jim Valier, pretending to be angry.

"You'll be glad of my space!" returned Jax Gray, as she squeezed into Mary Eliska's car, between her chum and Aunt Sally.

"We'll miss the wise-cracks," remarked Ralph. "But I can't say that you occupy much room, Jax Gray." He started his engine. "Hurry up, now, or we'll miss the news reel, and think how ignorant we'll be!"

"WORLD'S MOST FAMOUS AVIATRIX SIGNS CONTRACT WITH THE APEX FILM CORPORATION!" thundered the voice of the announcer.

The theatre was already darkened when the group entered ten minutes later, so they all walked quietly, in order to make as little disturbance as possible. Even Sara Wheeler, who giggled on every occasion, managed to suppress any outburst with her handkerchief.

But their good behavior lasted only a moment. No sooner were they comfortably seated than the most extraordinary piece of news was flashed on the screen. As if the manager had been waiting for the dramatic moment to make his announcement.

"As if any other girl could be as famous as you, Mary Eliska!" whispered Jax Gray resentfully. "I'd like to know who—"

The words died on her lips as the actual picture of the famous aviatrix was shown. Why— it looked like—it must be—Mary Eliska herself!

The girl, in a flier's costume, smiled and turned aside to sign a contract.

"MISS MARY ELISKA, THE FIRST GIRL TO FLY FROM NEW YORK TO PARIS ALONE, ACCEPTS PART IN 'BRIDE OF THE AIR,' A PICTURE NOW BEING FILMED IN HOLLYWOOD," continued the calm voice of the announcer.

"So that's where you've been!" exclaimed Jax Gray, just a little bit hurt that Mary Eliska had kept this a secret from her. They had shared all their joys and secrets ever since their experiences in the Okefenokee Swamp together, and it did not seem possible that Mary Eliska would deliberately shut her out of such an important event. Besides, Mary Eliska had always refused to go into the movies. Why the sudden change?

"You cagey thing!" muttered Ralph, as amazed at the revelation as Jax Gray, and even more hurt than the latter that he had been excluded from her confidence.

Mary Eliska made no attempt to answer; she sat rigid in her seat, staring at the screen with unseeing eyes. The girl whom the announcer had proclaimed to be Mary Eliska was tall and slender, and in her flier's suit and helmet, had resembled Mary Eliska to a remarkable degree. But of course it wasn't Mary Eliska. Why, she hadn't been near Hollywood!

"It's not true," she finally whispered to Jax Gray. "That's somebody else, posing for me."

"Now, Mary Eliska!" returned Jax Gray, unconvinced. "Don't try to play innocent!"

"You'll make a stunning heroine, Mary Eliska," whispered Kit, leaning over from her seat beside Ralph. There was sincere admiration in her tone.

Then the whole party grew excited, and all talked at once, shooting questions at Mary Eliska without any regard to the fact that they were supposed to keep quiet. People around them showed perceptible signs of annoyance, until Ralph, sitting back in sullen silence, admonished them all to keep still.

The talk subsided, and the crowd's attention was diverted during the feature, but Mary Eliska did not even see it. Inside she was seething at the very idea of anything so preposterous. Usually a peaceful girl, she felt as if she would like to tear that impostor to pieces.

Yet there was no use trying to tell the young people after the show that it wasn't true. Hadn't Mary Eliska been away for a number of days, on some mysterious errand connected with flying! Didn't the girl look like her—why, they were sure it was Mary Eliska! And they were thrilled, too. It was great fun to have one of their own group a famous actress, as well as a famous aviatrix. All of them—except Jax Gray and Ralph.

"I want you to stay at our house for supper, Jax Gray," urged Mary Eliska, as the other car drove off after the show. "Can you phone?"

"Yes, of course," agreed her chum, wondering what kind of explanation Mary Eliska was going to make for her secrecy in the affair.

Neither girl mentioned it until they were inside the Carltons' house. They did not stop on the porch, but followed Mary Eliska's Aunt Sally into the living-room.

"I suppose your telegram was from Hollywood, Mary Eliska?" inquired Aunt Sally, as if to lead up to the all-exciting topic.

"No, it wasn't, Aunt Sally," replied Mary Eliska, decidedly. "It was from Mr. Eckert—you remember, the head of the Air School at St. Louis, where I took my course?... He wanted me to take a position teaching there this year."

"Why, that sounds very attractive, dear," replied Aunt Sally. "Safer and more dignified than all this stunt flying you'll have to do for the pictures." A look of distress passed over her face.... "Mary Eliska, I don't like your accepting that contract without consulting either me or your father," she added, gently.

Mary Eliska dropped into a chair with a groan.

"Please sit down, Aunt Sally—and Jax Gray. I have a lot to say."

Not knowing what was coming next, they both complied with her request.

"Haven't you both always found me pretty truthful?" she asked, seriously.

"Of course we have, dear," answered the older woman, immediately. "Nobody ever doubts your word. But you never promised me that you wouldn't go into the films. I never asked you not to, for I thought you wouldn't consider it."

"No, Aunt Sally, I wouldn't. And I *haven't*! You and Jax Gray must believe me. *That girl you saw today impersonating me is a fake.* I never signed a contract, with any picture producer, and I haven't been near Hollywood!"

Jax Gray jumped to her feet joyfully, and, dashing across the room, wound her arms about her chum.

"I'm so glad, Mary Eliska!" she cried.

Aunt Sally breathed a long sigh of relief.

"But think of the impudence of that girl!" she exclaimed. "To dare to do a thing like that—"

"Expecting that she can get away with it!" added Jax Gray.

"Well, she can't!" announced Mary Eliska, her eyes shining with indignation. "I'm going to fly right out there and grab her by the collar—and—and—"

"Why, Mary Eliska, I never heard you talk so!" remarked her aunt in amazement. "Not even when you were a child."

"I never had such occasion to do so before. You know what Shakespeare says about stealing your good name. That's just what that girl's doing. Making me cheap. As if I were in aviation for publicity, or for personal gain! Oh, I'm stirred up, all right!"

"I don't blame you one bit, dear!" agreed Aunt Sally, soothingly.

"But what are you going to do?" demanded Jax Gray, realizing that Mary Eliska must have already formulated a plan during that moving-picture show. "Going to wire the Corporation?"

"Indeed I'm not!" she replied, emphatically. "They wouldn't believe me."

"'How could they believe you?'" quoted Jax Gray, from the old song of "The Girl from Utah."

"Exactly! If all my own friends—Ralph, and Kit and Jim and everybody—yes—even you and Aunt Sally—actually thought I was fooling, how could I convince a strange director by merely sending a telegram? He'd think I was the impostor, of course, and their Mary Eliska was the real thing."

"Yes, that's logical," admitted Aunt Sally. "But what can you do, dear?"

"I'm going to fly right out to Hollywood tomorrow, after I give the Ladybug a thorough inspection."

Aunt Sally sighed, this time not in relief.

"Then you'll be home only one night!"

"I can't help that, Aunt Sally. I must go. I just have to. I'll stop and see Mr. Eckert at St. Louis, on my way."

Jax Gray's eyes lighted up with sudden inspiration.

"May I go with you, Mary Eliska?" she asked.

"May you!" Mary Eliska repeated. "Oh, Jax Gray, would you? I'd just love it!"

"And I'd feel safer," put in her Aunt Sally.

"It's decided, then," announced Jax Gray. "I'm thrilled to death!... Oh, Mary Eliska, think of seeing Hollywood. The movies being made—and the stars themselves! We'll have a marvellous time."

"Be sure to take plenty of clothes," cautioned Aunt Sally. "You know how much they dress out there."

"We'll outshine Lilyan Tashman herself!" promised Mary Eliska, thankful that her aunt was not raising any objection to the trip.

"Going to tell Ralph about it?" inquired Jax Gray, as she rose to telephone to her mother.

"What's the use?" returned Mary Eliska. "He wouldn't believe me. He'd think I was going back to complete my contract. No; he's peeved—let him stay peeved. I'd rather spend my evening planning our trip."

"Flying comes first, as always," observed Aunt Sally, in a resigned tone, as she, too, left the room, to do her part in making the trip comfortable for the two girls.

CHAPTER 9.2
A DANGEROUS LANDING

Early after lunch the following afternoon—another clear, bright fall day typical of late September—Mary Eliska and her chum Jax Gray climbed into the Ladybug, ready to take off for Los Angeles. Smiling and waving good-bye to Aunt Sally and Mrs. Gray, who were standing on the side of the field, Mary Eliska gave her the gun. The plane taxied only a short distance, then with her nose headed upward, she began to climb almost vertically. It was a pretty, graceful take-off, and even Aunt Sally, frightened as she was of airplanes, had to admit that the autogiro seemed almost human.

"We ought to make St. Louis before dark," said Mary Eliska, through the speaking-tube. "I know the way so well—I flew it so often when I was going to the Air School."

"I remember," replied Jax Gray. "You and Louise."

Louise Haydock had been Mary Eliska's inseparable chum all through high school. Then, when they had graduated, and Mary Eliska's father had given the latter an Arrow Sport plane, the two girls had spent a year at a ground school in St. Louis. Louise's marriage to Ted Mackay had finally separated them, for the Mackays went to Kansas City to live. Ever since that time Jax Gray had shared in most of Mary Eliska's flying adventures.

"I'll tell you what," suggested Mary Eliska. "Let's send Lou a wire tonight, and plan to stop in Kansas City tomorrow for lunch. I'm wild to see her."

"Great!" agreed Jax Gray. "If she and Ted aren't off on some flying trip."

The autogiro soared up into the clear, tingling air, colder above than it had been on the ground, and the old exhilaration of flying took possession of Mary Eliska and made her heart sing. Poor people down there on the earth, looking like ants crawling about on their humdrum affairs, when she was flying joyously through the heavens! Poor Aunt Sally, who would never know the thrill of this higher, freer, purer world!

Even her anger against this impostor was temporarily forgotten. Nobody could be angry long in the sky. And, no matter what happened later, she and Jax Gray were going to enjoy this trip to the coast. It would be the experience of a lifetime to an ordinary girl.

The motor continued to hum evenly and the Ladybug averaged a hundred miles an hour. Over rivers and valleys and flat country, through Ohio, past Indiana, on to Illinois. The sun was setting as the girls sighted the broad waters of the Mississippi, and they knew that their first goal was in sight.

A huge beacon light was already glowing, guiding the fliers on their way to the airport, and then on to the Air School. But Mary Eliska could have found her way without any guide, even in the fast-increasing darkness.

Mary Eliska decreased her speed and hovered over the field. Some of the attendants recognized the famous Ladybug, and by the time the autogiro descended to earth, quite a crowd had gathered to greet her.

"Hello, Mary Eliska! We knew it was you!"

"Glad to see you back, Mary Eliska!"

Mary Eliska and Jax Gray jumped out and Mary Eliska spoke to all her friends and asked them to put the Ladybug away for the night, and to tell her where to find Mr. Eckert.

"He's gone home, but you can get him on the telephone," answered one of the attendants, writing the number down for her.

"We saw you in the movies, Mary Eliska!" announced another. "You didn't look half pretty enough, though. But we're sure goin' a see that picture when it comes to town!"

Mary Eliska frowned. She didn't want to take the time to deny the false impression, but she certainly did hate this sort of thing.

The girls found a taxi at once, and, leaving their bigger box in the autogiro, they took out an overnight bag and went to a hotel that had been familiar to Mary Eliska during her year at St. Louis.

"That's what I'm going to be up against all the time!" she remarked, with distaste, as she and Jax Gray settled back in the taxi.

"You mean about the movies?" questioned her companion. "I was wondering why you didn't deny it right off."

"I haven't time to go about the world denying things. And it seems so useless. Until I have proof, I mean. They wouldn't believe me any more than the crowd at home did."

"I suppose you're right. Oh, well, don't let's worry. We can clear the whole thing up in no time."

They reached the hotel, made an appointment with Mr. Eckert over the telephone, and changed their costumes for dinner. It was after seven o'clock when they sat down to the table, and they did full justice to the meal.

Mr. Eckert's first remark when he greeted Mary Eliska was practically the same as that of the boys on the field.

"I hear you are going into the movies, Mary Eliska," he said, trying to hide his disapproval. "If I had known that, I shouldn't have wasted your time offering you this position at the school."

Mary Eliska sighed. "That's a false rumor, Mr. Eckert," she explained.

"But it wasn't a rumor. It was a fact," he persisted. "Sam and Jeff told me they saw your picture, signing the contract."

"I know. I saw it too. But it's a fake. Some girl is impersonating me. For the sake of the money, I suppose."

The elderly man leaned forward, staring incredulously.

"Do you really mean that, Mary Eliska?" he demanded.

She nodded. "I'm on my way to the coast now, to clear it all up. Naturally, I'm furious."

"You won't take over the contract yourself?" the man asked, with apparent satisfaction. What a joy this girl was, he thought! She was made for far greater things than moving-picture acting. Hers was a name that ought to go down in history, among the daring pioneers of aviation.

"Of course not," she assured him. "You know, Mr. Eckert, that that sort of thing doesn't appeal to me—publicity and acting—and all that stuff. I'm happiest when I'm up in the skies with nobody else but my chum—Jax Gray."

"That is what I always thought," he said. "So I must say I was somewhat disappointed in the news when I heard it."

Mary Eliska smiled. Mr. Eckert had always understood her, and admired her—not as Ralph Clavering admired her, for her beauty and feminine charm,—but for her knowledge and skill as a flier.

"Then you might consider my proposition after all?" he inquired, hopefully.

"Yes, indeed. If you are willing to make it more or less temporary. I mean I could sign up for the duration of one course—say until next spring. The other offers I have had have all been so far away, that I'd rather accept yours, so that I could fly home every week-end. My aunt is practically alone, you see, for my father's business is in New York."

"That's splendid, Mary Eliska!" he cried, and he proceeded to go into detail about the work that he wanted her to teach. Jax Gray sat back in her chair, gazing out of the window, and vainly trying to suppress a yawn.

"I'm afraid, Mr. Eckert," remarked Mary Eliska, when the former had finished his explanation, "that I may not be back in time to start when the school opens. Would you be willing to wait for me—'til, say, the first of October? I ought to be here by then, though you never can tell."

At these words Jax Gray sat up and laughed.

"You surely can't!" she agreed, heartily. "We have a habit of not showing up when we're expected, Mr. Eckert—when Mary Eliska goes on her wild adventures."

"Oh, but this is different," put in Mary Eliska, sincerely believing that there were no wild adventures in store for her this time. "Hollywood isn't like the Okefenokee Swamp. It's the most civilized spot in the world."

"But we haven't promised to stay in Hollywood," Jax Gray reminded her.

"True," admitted Mary Eliska.

Mr. Eckert rose.

"I'll tell you what I'll do, Mary Eliska," he said. "I'll teach the class myself until the first of October. Then, if you can't come, I'll get another instructor. Is that all right with you?"

"Fine," agreed the girl, delighted to have it all settled, and at a salary that was by no means small. For Mary Eliska was a drawing-card, and Mr. Eckert knew that her name would bring new students to the school, and add prestige to the fine faculty which they already had.

The last several days had been glorious weather—too good to last, Mary Eliska knew—for about the middle of September the fall rains usually set in. So she was not surprised to waken the following morning to find a dismal downpour, and what was worse, a bad wind. It was one of the equinoctial storms, so common at that time of the year.

Jax Gray looked dismayed, but she had no idea that Mary Eliska would postpone the flight. For you couldn't tell how long such a rain might last, and time was important.

She watched Mary Eliska get into her flying-suit, as if the mere matter of weather were nothing—all just part of the day's work.

"Hurry up, Jax Gray. If we are to make Kansas City by lunch time."

"O.K.," agreed the smaller girl, cheerfully.

They were back at the field by half-past seven, ready to start.

But the field was horribly muddy. Other planes had encountered severe difficulty in taking off, and the attendants looked doubtful.

"Looks as if you're not going after all," remarked Sam, stepping close to the Ladybug, as Mary Eliska started the rotor blades in motion. "It's a beastly day."

Mary Eliska smiled.

"My rotor blades are going to help me to rise," she returned, gaily. "Just watch 'em!"

Two minutes later the autogiro left the rain-covered field, and soared into the murky skies. Almost immediately the ground and the landmarks became invisible to the girls in the cockpits, and the plane seemed to be wrapped in a great gray blanket of clouds and rain. The wind was blowing furiously, as if it were determined to get the better of the gallant Ladybug, but the rotor blades of the autogiro succeeded in keeping her on an even keel. But she rocked furiously, until Jax Gray felt sure that she was going to be seasick.

Mary Eliska's gas was growing a little low—plenty, she felt sure, to get to Kansas City— but not any to waste, so she was keeping low. But she could not see anything, and she was thinking that at times like these flying could even be monotonous, when, all of a sudden, as if in a hideous dream, she saw a nineteen-story building rushing madly at her. Not that she realized that it was exactly nineteen stories—indeed it looked taller than that at the moment.

It was huge, too big to avoid, as it loomed there in her path, like some tremendous, horrible monster, shutting out everything else in her sight, waiting to annihilate her.

In the seat ahead Jax Gray suddenly let out a sharp cry of terror, and Mary Eliska, realizing in a flash that she could not hope to clear the building now, pushed the joy-stick forward and nosed the plane into a dive. What was she heading for? A street, where she would dash down on top of pedestrians and motor-cars, killing others as well as herself and Jax Gray?... But no, the speed was reducing; she was right over another office building—a shorter one, only about six stories in height—with—oh, joy of joys—a flat roof! As if she had planned it, she selected her spot, banked the autogiro to the left, cleared the wire fence around the edge, and landed right in the center of the roof! Making it look all the world as if she had planned a demonstration.

With a grin of incredulity she turned exultantly to Jax Gray.

"Mary Eliska, you're priceless!" shouted her chum. "Anybody'd think it was a stunt for the movies."

Mary Eliska frowned, and Jax Gray was sorry the instant the words were out of her mouth. She had forgotten all about the reason for the flight, in her excitement at this narrow escape. At this moment half a dozen people appeared on the fire-escape, and a freckle-faced youth of about eighteen climbed immediately to the roof.

"Pretty neat!" he exclaimed. "Is it a stunt?"

"It was a life-saver," explained Jax Gray. "We nearly crashed on top of that big office building over there, and this one just loomed up in time."

"Know what building this is?" asked the young man.

Mary Eliska shook her head.

"It's a newspaper building! Biggest newspaper in Kansas City!"

"I never heard of a building made of newspapers," returned Jax Gray. "Funny we didn't crash through!"

The young man grinned; his specialty was wise-cracks. "I'm a reporter," he announced. "My slogan's 'First on the spot, to get news while it's hot.'—so please give me your names and addresses." He took out his notebook, prepared to write.

Mary Eliska looked displeased, but Jax Gray was equal to the occasion.

"Sallie Slocum and May Manton, from Toonerville," she replied, briskly. "Two society buds."

The reporter solemnly wrote down the names.

"Toonerville—where—what state?" he asked.

"Toonerville, Trolley," answered Jax Gray, without blinking an eyelash.

This time the young man didn't know whether to smile or not.

"You're kidding me! That's a name in Fontaine Fox's cartoon."

"Sure it is," agreed Jax Gray. "But it's a place, just the same. Just write and ask Mr. Fox, if you want to know."

Mary Eliska, meanwhile, had been examining her gasoline supply. It was sufficient to take them to the suburbs, where Ted and Louise lived, and she was anxious to be off.

"Come on, May," she said to Jax Gray, managing with a great effort to keep her face straight. "We're off—if the young man will be kind enough to get out of the way."

The reporter went back down the fire-escape, and Mary Eliska took off, but as the girls flew away they could distinguish faces peering at them from every window in sight. After all, they had afforded a pleasant diversion to a dull, work-a-day world, and Mary Eliska was thankful that it had all turned out so happily.

"And how clever of you to think of giving fictitious names, Jax Gray," she said, through the speaking-tube. "Now if it gets into the papers, Aunt Sally will never guess that it was my Ladybug. It might worry her dreadfully if she thought I was dropping out of the skies all the time on top of office buildings. She's dreamt about my being pinned on a church steeple, dangling in mid-air."

Fifteen minutes later, without further mishap, they landed at the Mackays' field, and saw Louise waiting for them with an umbrella.

"Darlings!" she shouted, above the noise of the engine and the rotors, and dashed across the muddy field like the impulsive girl she had always been. "I'm just wild about this!"

Mary Eliska and Jax Gray jumped out of the cockpits and hugged her joyfully.

"Now come on in and get warm and dry," said Louise. "Pity we can't take the Ladybug inside too. But Ted'll look after her comfort when he gets home."

"Does Ted get home for lunch?" asked Mary Eliska. "Oh, I hope he does, for I haven't seen him in ages."

"No, darling, he doesn't. But he gets home for supper, and you two are going to stay all night."

"We can't, Lou—honestly—"

"There's no use arguing. You just have to. Didn't my Ted save your life a couple of times at least, Mary Eliska? Don't you owe him a debt of gratitude?"

Mary Eliska laughed; there was no use arguing with Louise. After all, there was no great hurry—and it was bad weather for flying. One night more or less wouldn't make much difference, she thought.

So the young people spent a pleasant afternoon and evening together, talking aviation, swapping stories and gossip, and laughing heartily over the newspaper story about their strange landing, which appeared on the front page that night. Little did they think at the time that Jax Gray's prank was to cause them serious trouble later!

CHAPTER 9.3
THE CROSS-COUNTRY FLIGHT

"How do you go from here?" inquired Louise the next morning at breakfast, which had been arranged for seven o'clock so that the girls could make an early start. The skies were still dark, and it was raining, but the wind had died down, and with it the worst of the storm.

"From here to Wichita, and then on to Albuquerque by tonight, I hope," replied Mary Eliska. "We'll be following the regular air-line. I think that is really the safest and best way. By tomorrow night I expect to land at Los Angeles."

"Do you have to cross Death Valley?" asked Louise.

"Fly over it—not cross it," corrected Mary Eliska. "But that has no terrors for me. And we shall miss the worst of the Rockies, following such a southern course."

"Take plenty of water and gas, in case you come down in the desert!"

"That reminds me, Ted," said Mary Eliska, turning to the big, red-haired young man at the head of the table. "Did you fill my Ladybug up?"

"Yes, and gave her a hasty inspection, too," he replied. "She looks O.K. to me."

"Then I'm not expecting any trouble," returned Mary Eliska, for she had great confidence in Ted Mackay's judgment and knowledge of airplanes.

While Mary Eliska took time to call Aunt Sally on the long-distance telephone, Louise insisted upon packing a lunch, and filling the thermos bottles with water and coffee. For she had never forgotten Mary Eliska's first long flight when they had been stranded on a lonely prairie, far from food and civilization, and how grateful they had been then for the elaborate picnic lunch with which their hostess had supplied them.

"You're a brick, Lou!" Mary Eliska cried, as she kissed her good-bye.

"Don't forget to stop next week, on your way home!" Louise reminded her.

The Ladybug's engine roared, and she taxied a short distance, soaring soon into the skies. To her joy Mary Eliska found that flying conditions had considerably improved since the previous day. The storm was clearing, and up above the clouds, the sun was shining. Mary Eliska's way lay straight before her, and she flew on and on, keeping a sharp watch all the time for other planes, until the clouds beneath her had completely dispersed. Passing over Kansas, she left Wichita behind long before noon time, and pressed on through the northern part of Oklahoma—into Texas, the state in which her father's ranch had been located, when she took that daring night-flight for the surgeon who saved his life. At last, by consulting her map, she felt certain she had reached New Mexico.

Both girls had been so thrilled in watching the country beneath them—so strangely different from the East—that they had not realized how late it was growing. Hunger finally drove Jax Gray to consult her watch. To her surprise she found that it was after three o'clock.

"Let's eat!" she said to Mary Eliska, through the tube. "I'm starved!"

"Where?" shouted Mary Eliska, surveying dubiously the ground beneath them, covered with dry bushes. There wasn't a sign of civilization or cultivation anywhere about, and she had no desire to land.

"Right here in the plane," returned Jax Gray. "You haven't forgotten the lunch Lou packed for us?"

"Good idea! And we'll get to Albuquerque all the sooner. Something tells me that we're not far off—if my calculations are correct."

"Well, we can't be lost," replied Jax Gray. "For we've been following the beacon lights straight along the way. O. K., then. I'll unpack. Thank goodness Lou fixed a lunch."

The sandwiches and coffee were delicious, and all the while Mary Eliska kept right on flying. But it was still light when the spires and buildings of Albuquerque loomed up in the distance.

They landed at the airport and went to a hotel for the night, thankful that the day, though uneventful, had passed so pleasantly, and hopeful for clear weather to continue for the rest of their journey.

The sun was shining brightly and the day was already hot when the girls took off from Albuquerque the following morning. For hours they flew over this hot, dry plateau region, where the water supply was scanty, and where they could see, even from their height in the air, the bare earth shining between the scattered clumps of grasses and shrubs.

"We have to miss the Grand Canyon," Mary Eliska told Jax Gray as they came down at a small airport town in Arizona, to rest and get their lunch. "It lies up in the north-western part of the state, you know, and if we follow the most direct course to Los Angeles, we miss it."

"Maybe we can fly over it on our way back," suggested her companion. "We'll have more time to enjoy the scenery when we have settled with this impostor."

"Yes, that's just what I think. So long as we get home before the first of October, I'm a free woman."

They continued their flight without any interruptions or disasters all that afternoon. They left Arizona behind and crossed into the great state of California, over the San Bernardino Mountains, where the climate was lovely. Orange groves blossomed everywhere, the air was sweet and delicious; they felt a great envy of the people who could always live in this beautiful region. At last they reached the city of Los Angeles, and spotted the new white city hall, as it rose in its majestic splendor, gleaming in the brilliancy of its electric lights.

"Good old Ladybug!" exclaimed Jax Gray, as the autogiro came to the ground at the airport, and she stiffly climbed out of the cockpit. "Never lets us down!"

"Always lets us down—when we want her to," corrected Mary Eliska, laughingly.

"You're going to leave her here at the airport while we go on to Hollywood?" asked Jax Gray.

"Yes, I think so. I'll have the mechanics give her a thorough inspection in the meanwhile. But I don't want to go tonight. Let's have a good dinner and get some sleep and start out fresh tomorrow morning. We'll have our box taken with us this time, and dress for the occasion. We don't want to look like hicks from a small town."

While Mary Eliska turned to give her instructions to an attendant, a strange young man strolled up to the girls and stopped, evidently waiting for an opportunity to speak to them. It was growing dark, but the beacon searchlight at the airport was bright enough for them to see him perfectly. He looked at the autogiro, and then peered almost rudely into the faces of the two girls. Mary Eliska ignored him, but Jax Gray was furious.

"Pardon me, ladies," he said finally, "but aren't you the two girls who landed on the top of that newspaper building in Kansas City?—Miss Slocum and Miss Manton, I believe the names were?"

Jax Gray giggled. She couldn't deny the fact.

"So you've been taking a cross-country flight in this boat," he continued. "I have a friend who is a reporter—he's around here somewhere, for he stops here every day at the airport for news—and he'd like that story, if you'd give me a few facts."

"We don't want publicity," Jax Gray said, immediately. "So please don't let him print anything at all about us."

"Besides," added Mary Eliska, "there's nothing new in what we've done. Girls fly all over the country every day alone. It really doesn't mean much more than driving a motor-car now-a-days."

"You're right about that," agreed the attendant. "It was a stunt to fly the Atlantic once, but now it seems rather common-place. The first person to go from here to Australia by plane will sure get a head-line."

"We don't expect to try that!" returned Jax Gray, laughingly. "That's a little too far."

"By the way," remarked the stranger who had looked so keenly at the girls, "did you girls know that Mary Eliska is here at Los Angeles—or rather, at Hollywood? You remember her—the first girl to fly from New York to Paris alone?... She has a contract with the Apex Film Corporation."

Mary Eliska and Jax Gray looked at each other in distress. This was a fine situation indeed. What could they say?

"My name is Mary Eliska," the aviatrix finally announced, quietly.

"Go on! Your name's Sallie Slocum!" insisted the young man.

"As you please," shrugged Mary Eliska, turning to the attendant. "Nevertheless, I want this autogiro registered here as belonging to Mary Eliska, of Spring City, Ohio." "O. K., Miss," agreed the attendant, making note of the fact.

Summoning a taxi, the girls stepped into it and closed the door without even so much as good-bye to the young man who had forced a conversation with them.

"What gets me," observed Jax Gray, "is the way reporters seem to bob up anywhere and everywhere—just when they're not wanted."

"True, but they have to get news, I suppose. And it was really my fault in the first place, for landing on a newspaper building. I would have to pick that out!"

"Oh, well, who cares?" returned Jax Gray. "It'll blow over, and be forgotten.... What hotel are we going to?"

"The Ambassador. I've heard so much about their 'Cocoanut Grove' that I want to see it."

A few minutes later the taxi stopped at the luxurious hotel, and the girls secured a room. They engaged it for only a couple of days, little thinking that they would have to remain in Los Angeles for a longer period of time.

It was lots of fun to dress in evening gowns and sweep into the dining-room as if they were actresses. Even Mary Eliska admitted that she enjoyed taking off her flier's suit at times, and just being a "regular girl."

"For tonight we'll be absolutely care-free," she said. "As if we hadn't a thing to worry about!"

"Which we really haven't," added Jax Gray.

They ordered an elaborate dinner and ate slowly, watching the people in the dining-room, hoping to catch a glimpse of a famous star or a celebrated flier. But if there were actors and actresses there, neither Mary Eliska nor Jax Gray recognized them.

"I wish there were a 'first-night' performance that we could attend," remarked Jax Gray, when, after dinner, they summoned a taxi to go to a moving-picture show.

"Yes, it would be nice. But then, we probably couldn't get in, anyhow. Unless I pretended to be the Mary Eliska who is in 'Bride of the Air'."

Jax Gray laughed.

"That would be a mix-up. The other girl doubling for you—and then your pretending to be the other girl!"

"Sounds kind of like 'Alice in Wonderland' to me."

In spite of the fact, however, that nothing unusual happened, the girls spent a pleasant evening, and were glad of the chance to get to bed early.

"For," remarked Mary Eliska, as she undressed in the charming bedroom, "I am tired, even though we didn't break any records crossing the country."

"It was fast enough for me," agreed Jax Gray. "I'd rather rest now and then, than dash off like Frank Hawks. And when you compare it to the way they used to cross the United States, it's no less than miraculous."

"I know," yawned Mary Eliska. "What was it that that movie said—twenty-four days in ?"

"Yes, that was it, I think. Only I'm too sleepy to remember much now.... Wake me up early tomorrow, Mary Eliska. For it's HOLLYWOOD!"

CHAPTER 9.4
HOLLYWOOD

"It certainly seems queer to be riding along the ground," remarked Mary Eliska, as she and Jax Gray stepped into a bus for Hollywood the following morning. "But we can see so much more."

"And it's only eleven miles," Jax Gray reminded her. "Oh, aren't you thrilled, Mary Eliska?"

"Of course I am. What girl wouldn't be?"

"If they offer you the contract now, won't you change your mind and go into pictures?" inquired Jax Gray.

"No," replied the famous aviatrix, decidedly. "I love the movies, and of course I'm keen to see the stars face to face, but I still haven't the slightest desire to act. I guess I'm too shy. I get so fussed."

"But it'll be kind of a mean trick to haul that girl out of the picture after the Film Corporation have advertised it, and then not take her place. The producer may lose a lot of money."

"That's his fault. They should have been more careful about looking up her credentials."

"Suppose you can't convince them that you're the real Mary Eliska?" suggested Jax Gray.

"I'll have to stay there 'til I do. But I have my licenses with me. I only wish I had my Distinguished Flying Cross, but unfortunately Daddy put it away in his safe-deposit box."

The bus was luxurious and the girls settled down in delighted comfort. All the other passengers looked prosperous and well dressed; from their appearance they might easily be moving-picture stars. But of course they weren't, the girls decided, for even the humblest star has her own car.

The country through which they were travelling was lovely, and as they approached Hollywood, the girls noticed charming, well-kept bungalows and homes of every description. As if everyone who lived there were wealthy. The fresh green lawns, the tall palm trees shading the streets, the vivid blue sky above formed a striking picture. No wonder most girls were wild to go to Hollywood!

Mary Eliska and Jax Gray went on to Culver City, where most of the studios were located, and found the Apex Film Corporation, housed in a large and imposing building. As they ascended the steps Mary Eliska became exceedingly nervous, almost to the point of wishing that she hadn't come.

"Suppose they take us for extras—applying for jobs—and throw us out!" she whispered, fearfully.

"Don't be silly, Mary Eliska! Your name would get you in anywhere!"

"I'm not so sure of that. We fliers aren't much here, where they have a world of their own and so many celebrities."

The girls walked through a hall to a beautiful reception room, where a "publicity" girl, who looked like an actress herself, took Mary Eliska's card and passed into an office to the right.

In a moment she returned with the information that the girls might go into the office.

"Mr. Von Goss is out, but his secretary will see you," she said. "Mr. Leslie Sprague."

"You do the talking, Jax Gray," begged Mary Eliska, as they left the room.

"Be yourself!" commanded her companion. "You can fly over the Atlantic Ocean alone, and you're afraid of an insignificant little secretary!"

Mary Eliska laughed. What would she ever do without Jax Gray to restore her courage whenever a fit of shyness overtook her? Holding her head high, she marched into the office where the secretary was sitting.

The latter, a young man of medium height, with a blond moustache, stood up as the girls entered. He opened his mouth to speak—but continued to keep it open without saying anything for a moment.

"There's some mistake," he finally managed to stammer.

Mary Eliska laughed, quite at ease. "There's been a *big* mistake," she said. "And your director, Mr. Von Goss, I believe his name is, has made it. I am the real Mary Eliska, and he has signed up an impostor for the flying part in his picture!"

A slight sneer spread over the young man's features.

"I suppose you have proof, Miss—er—?" he asked in a tone that plainly showed that he did not suppose anything of the sort. How nasty he was, not even to call Mary Eliska by her name and at least give her the benefit of the doubt!

Jax Gray's chin shot up in the air.

"You don't suppose we'd come here, without some proof, do you, Mr. Sprague?" she demanded, haughtily. "Aunt Sally is a very busy person, as you'd know if you read the newspapers."

The man flushed at Jax Gray's high-handed manner; he was not used to being rebuked by others. Little as she was, Jax Gray had a masterful way of driving straight at the mark.

Mary Eliska opened her handbag and held out her licenses.

"Just have these verified," she said, calmly.

The young man stared at them.

"Where did you get hold of these?" he asked, slyly. "Find Mary Eliska's handbag?"

Mary Eliska made no reply, but turned her face aside in haughty disdain, as Sprague rang a bell and summoned a young woman from another office, to whom he made a slight explanation.

"And now," he continued after the girl had left with the cards, "what do you propose to do about it—if your identity should be established?"

"Simply have proof that you will remove my name from the pictures, and print a statement saying that you had been misled."

Mr. Sprague smiled sarcastically. "You want the part yourself, I suppose?"

"I do not," replied Mary Eliska, firmly. "I have neither time nor inclination to go into the moving pictures. Your actress can play the part—under her own name, whatever it is."

"Mr. Von Goss would never consent to that. The girl isn't much of an actress. He just engaged her for the value of the publicity. And, if she should prove to be an impostor, I'm sure he wouldn't want her."

"Well, that's not my affair," concluded Mary Eliska, rising. "Please get my licenses back for me now, Mr. Sprague, and when you have proof, Mr. Von Goss can communicate with me at the Ambassador Hotel in Los Angeles."

"Wait a minute—wait a minute," cautioned Sprague, smugly. "We can't verify that license in five minutes. The other girl also had licenses in the name of Mary Eliska, and the two will have to be compared, in order to find out which is a counterfeit!" "Why, that's ridiculous!" exclaimed Jax Gray. "People can't counterfeit U. S. Government licenses!"

The secretary smiled in his superior manner.

"Real counterfeiters can counterfeit anything," he informed them.

"Then let me have mine back until we can place them side by side with this other girl's," demanded Mary Eliska.

Sprague shook his head. "I'm sorry, but it's too late to do that now. They have already been handed over to our private detective, I'm sure."

"How soon will he give them back?" asked Jax Gray.

"Tomorrow, probably."

"Where is this double of mine?" questioned Mary Eliska, with astonishing directness. "On the lot?"

"No. She's at Spring City now—or rather, on her way to the coast. She's due here tomorrow afternoon, flying into the Los Angeles airport, to begin her part in the rehearsals."

"We'll be there to meet her," announced Mary Eliska, with determination. "What time?"

"Three o'clock. I'll—meet you."

Reluctantly the girls left the building, for they hated to go without the licenses, and walked out into the bright sunshine.

"What a pest that man is!" exclaimed Jax Gray. "Of all the smug, self-satisfied, little tin-gods, he's the worst I ever met."

"He was rather unpleasant," agreed Mary Eliska. "But he probably likes the false Mary Eliska, and believes in her. So he treats us as criminals."

"I suppose that's it. But he didn't have to be so nasty about it. And the ridiculous way he tried to trip you up, asking where you got hold of Mary Eliska's licenses. It made my blood boil."

"He's not worth getting excited over, Jax Gray, for after all, it will be Mr. Von Goss who will decide the thing. Let's forget him now, and go to one of these spiffy restaurants for lunch. Don't you hope we see some of the stars?"

They sauntered along leisurely, looking at the people they passed, wondering whether they were actors and actresses. But it was confusing, for every girl here seemed to be pretty, and every man handsome. Indeed, the stenographers and waitresses were no doubt girls who had won beauty contests at home, only to come to Hollywood to find that beauty was as common as blades of grass, and that there was more to getting into the films than that. But of course these girls with the jobs—any jobs—were the lucky ones. Thousands of others must have returned home penniless.

The restaurant Mary Eliska and Jax Gray selected was a charming one, not far from several of the studios, and the girls entered it with subdued excitement. Although it was crowded, the head waiter succeeded in finding them a little table by the wall, where they could eat and watch their fellow-diners.

For a few minutes, while they sipped their tomato cocktails, their eyes wandered about the softly lighted room, recognizing nobody in particular. Then, all of a sudden, Jax Gray pinched Mary Eliska's arm.

"That's Joan Crawford!" she whispered.

"Where?"

"Over there—to the left."

"That girl with glasses?"

"Yes. She wears them a lot in public, they say, so that people won't recognize her. But I'm sure it's she. And there's her husband, sitting down beside her now. Anybody'd know him."

Mary Eliska nodded, and feasted her eyes on one of Hollywood's most celebrated and charming couples.

"And here comes Marlene Dietrich!" exclaimed Mary Eliska. "With that director she's so fond of. She is pretty, isn't she?"

"Yes, only I like our own actresses better than those foreigners. They always seem so affected."

"How about Claudette Colbert? You like her, don't you?" asked Mary Eliska, jealously. She had a great admiration for the French ever since her delightful reception in Paris.

"Yes, of course.... Oh, look, Mary Eliska—there's Dimples!"

"Dimples? You mean June Collyer?"

"No, Stupid! A masculine Dimples. Gable, of course."

"So it is! Wouldn't Sara Wheeler be thrilled if she were here? She's wild about him."

"I heard he was getting a divorce. If you stayed around here, Mary Eliska, and took that part, you might have a chance."

Mary Eliska laughed. "The last thing I'd ever want to do is marry a movie actor!"

"I guess you're right at that," agreed Jax Gray, sensibly. "Their marriages don't often take."

The girls made their lunch last as long as they could, and when they had finished they decided to go to a movie. For although Hollywood is the town where they make pictures, they also have many gorgeous picture palaces. Both Mary Eliska and Jax Gray felt proud to know that they were having first chance at seeing a show which their friends in Spring City probably could not view until many months later.

After the performance was over they took the bus back to Los Angeles and went straight to their room to dress elaborately for dinner. They were almost ready when the telephone on the tiny table between their beds jingled impatiently.

It was Mr. Von Goss, the director of the Apex Film Corporation, the man whom they had hoped to see instead of that unpleasant secretary.

"May I come over and see you right after dinner, Miss—er—Stricklin?" he asked. "Sprague has just told me the news, and I want to learn all I can about it at once."

"Certainly," agreed Mary Eliska. "I shall be glad to see you as soon as possible."

Mary Eliska replaced the receiver and turned to Jax Gray.

"You know what I've been thinking? This girl can't look exactly like me, or Mr. Sprague wouldn't have noticed the difference at once. Instead, he'd have greeted me more like a friend. But you remember—he opened his mouth in surprise."

"That's right. Of course we couldn't judge much from her picture, with that helmet on. She was your build and your type, Mary Eliska. Light curly hair, and the same kind of nose."

"I'm dying to see her."

"So am I. But we shall tomorrow."

"Well," continued Mary Eliska, "it's going to be interesting to get Mr. Von Goss's reaction. At any rate, he was a lot more polite over the telephone than his secretary."

The man arrived about nine o'clock, and Mary Eliska heard herself being paged just as she and Jax Gray came out of the dining-room.

"Hadn't I better slip off?" suggested the latter, in a whisper.

"No, indeed!" protested Mary Eliska. "I need your moral support."

Mr. Von Goss was a stout man of past middle-age, heavy set, with a big jaw and a pair of keen blue eyes—obviously a man of power in his own field. Nevertheless, he looked thoroughly disturbed over the matter which had just been brought to his attention by his secretary.

"You claim to be Mary Eliska?" he inquired, as Mary Eliska came up to him in the hotel lobby.

"Yes," replied Mary Eliska. "And this is my friend, Jax Gray. Shall we go into one of those little parlors where we can talk?"

The director nodded, and Mary Eliska led the way into a small room that was unoccupied at the moment.

"Er—will you have a cigarette, Miss—er—Stricklin?" he inquired.

"No, thank you," answered Mary Eliska. "But you go ahead and smoke, Mr. Von Goss."

The man lighted a cigar.

"This is bad business," he said. "If what you claim is true, and we have signed up the wrong young lady."

"You are satisfied with my proofs?" asked Mary Eliska, hoping that he had brought back her licenses.

"Can't tell yet. The other girl certainly looks like all the newspaper pictures I've ever seen of the famous aviatrix. If she isn't Mary Eliska, she certainly fooled me—and my secretary, too."

"Do I look like my pictures?" inquired Mary Eliska, demurely.

Mr. Von Goss surveyed her critically. "Not so much as the other girl," he replied, with a smile. "But of course you're in evening dress, and the other girl always wears flying suits."

"She would," put in Jax Gray, cryptically.

"And, as Mr. Sprague suggested," added Mr. Von Goss, "there's the possibility that the real Mary Eliska's licenses were stolen—and that by you—or anyone else!"

"Oh, that Mr. Sprague!" exclaimed Jax Gray, with the utmost disdain.

"There are two things to do," announced Mary Eliska, who had already come to a definite conclusion. "Get the two of us together, and have someone who knows us in aviation pick out the real Mary Eliska—or—"

"But Mr. Sprague, and some fliers he knows, have already identified our Mary Eliska," interrupted the director. "It was Sprague who looked her up, and brought her into the production."

"Then we'll have to resort to the only other suggestion I have, if you can't decide on our license cards.... It so happens that I am the only woman in the United States to hold an airplane mechanic's license.... Now, my cards could be stolen, but not my knowledge. So my idea is this: Have some good airplane mechanic give us both an examination, and only the real Mary Eliska will pass."

The director smiled broadly at the suggestion. It was an ingenious plan, and it appealed to his sense of the dramatic.

"I believe you, Mary Eliska. I think you must be the right girl, or you would never make such a suggestion. We'll try the thing out tomorrow. When the other girl arrives at two o'clock, as she wired, I'll take you to the airport to meet her."

"Two o'clock?" repeated Mary Eliska. "But Mr. Sprague said 'Three'!"

"He must have made a mistake. He told me two.... Now, how would you girls like to go to a reception with me? One of the stars is giving a house-warming at her new place at Beverly Hills, and I think I can ring you in on it, if you'd care about it."

"We'd love it!" cried Jax Gray, jumping up excitedly. "But please wait until we put on our very best dresses, Mr. Von Goss."

CHAPTER 9.5
THE VANISHING "DOUBLE"

The home of the star where the reception was held was the most gorgeous place that Mary Eliska and Jax Gray had ever seen. It was more like a palace than a home—out in the rich, exclusive Beverly Hills section, among those of other famous actors and actresses whose salaries soared into the thousands. Compared to it, the Claverings seemed almost paupers, yet they were the wealthiest people Mary Eliska had ever known.

"It's just like a fairy-tale," whispered Jax Gray, as the girls left their evening cloaks in a beautiful blue satin boudoir. "But what is there for a girl like this to look forward to? Why, she has everything!"

"Almost too much," said Mary Eliska.

"But her fame probably won't last more than ten years at the most. I read somewhere that even that is a long time for an actress. After that she has to take character parts, and 'what have you'."

"That seems tragic—giving up what you like to do best. I expect to fly 'til I die."

"That's just what your Aunt Sally says—only she means it differently. That you'll meet your death in the air."

Mary Eliska laughed, and she and Jax Gray hastened to join Mr. Von Goss, who was waiting for them at the foot of the marble staircase.

"I sort of feel as if we were butting in," whispered Mary Eliska. "Do I look terribly countrified—or small-townish?"

"My dear, you're as pretty as any star here, and lots prettier than some," replied Jax Gray, reassuringly.

"Well, you surely look sweet in that peach chiffon, Jax Gray. You look like Paris itself."

"Of course I do!" laughed the other girl. "I'm not going to have any inferiority complex. And don't you, either, Mary Eliska!"

Taking them into his charge, Mr. Von Goss led the girls about the luxurious rooms, introducing Mary Eliska to everybody as the most famous girl flier in the world. It was evident from his manner that he was entirely convinced that she was the real Mary Eliska.

The effect of the reception as a whole was startling, overpowering. Mary Eliska felt almost as if she wanted to gasp for breath, so overcome was she by the brilliancy of it all. It was only when she met Ann Harding, her favorite actress, that she really felt at home.

Miss Harding was amazingly beautiful—far lovelier than she seemed on the screen, if such a thing were possible. Her rich, low voice was charming, her complexion perfect, her golden hair like the pictures of a fairy queen. Yet there was something sad in her beautiful brown eyes. She and her husband had recently parted.

"Oh, I am so thrilled to meet you, Mary Eliska!" she said, holding Mary Eliska's hand in hers. "I am only an amateur flier, but I love it so. And I have read about every single thing you have ever done."

Mary Eliska blushed deeply at the praise; she wished she could summon courage to tell Miss Harding that she was her favorite star, but she was too shy to utter the words. She was afraid it might sound like idle flattery, thought up on the spur of the moment.

Jax Gray, however, came to her rescue.

"You're Mary Eliska's favorite actress, Miss Harding," she announced, calmly. "She goes to see all your pictures—two or three times. Especially the one where you played a character named 'Mary Eliska.' Do you remember?"

"Indeed I do," replied Miss Harding. "And I loved that part."

The three girls sat down in a corner and actually were able to talk flying without any interruption for about ten minutes. Then someone came to claim Miss Harding, and Mr. Von Goss appeared for his protegees.

Nothing was said, during the entire reception, of the trouble Mary Eliska was in, or of the fact that another girl was actually playing her part. The director had asked the girls not to mention the fact, and they were glad to accede to his wishes.

He took them to another room, a spacious hall with a beautiful shiny floor and a marvelous orchestra, and introduced some younger men to them, so that they could enjoy the dancing. Then a sumptuous supper was served, and the party broke up before midnight.

"I never thought the reception would be over so early, Mr. Von Goss," remarked Jax Gray, as the director drove the girls back to their hotel in his car. "I always thought Hollywood went in for wild parties."

The man shook his head.

"No. If anything, the stars keep earlier hours than ordinary people. Many of them have to be on location early in the morning, and their work is long and tiring. All the considerate hostesses arrange for their parties to be early affairs."

"One more mistaken idea shot to pieces," laughed Jax Gray.

"We've had a marvelous time, Mr. Von Goss," said Mary Eliska, as the car stopped at the Ambassador Hotel where her father Albert Stricklin and mother shared their honeymoon. "We never can thank you enough. And I'm so glad we could go tonight, for we'll probably be flying home tomorrow."

The man raised his eyebrows.

"I'm not so sure we can clear things up by then. But I hope so. At any rate, I'll meet you both at the airport at two o'clock in the afternoon."

The girls said good night to Mr. Von Goss and went to their room, but they found that they were not sleepy. The party had been too exciting to settle down and forget it so soon.

"It does kind of get into your blood," remarked Mary Eliska, as she took off her most elaborate evening gown. "All the rush and splendor and excitement, I mean."

"Weakening?" teased Jax Gray.

"You mean go into pictures myself, if I had the chance? No—never! Why, you can't tell me Ann Harding's happy. Or Joan Crawford.... No, it's not satisfying, like flying. I know what I love best, and I mean to stick to it!"

"Wise girl!" was the comment. "But you surely have Mr. Von Goss worried."

"No wonder. He says he advanced that other girl fifteen thousand dollars, just for the use of my name, and he's already spent at least a hundred thousand on the story and the sets."

"It seems as if you just couldn't let him down, Mary Eliska."

"I'm not letting him down. I never made any promises to him. He's being let down because he was so careless."

For at least an hour the girls continued to discuss the party and the stars, until, at last, they settled down to sleep, thankful that they had no need to get up early in the morning.

They combined breakfast and lunch the following day at noon, and went to the flying field a little before two o'clock to be on hand when the false Mary Eliska should arrive.

Mary Eliska was intensely excited. She tried over and over to picture to herself what this meeting would be like, whether the girl would be humble and sorry, whether she would try to work on Mary Eliska's sympathies by telling of some pressing need she had for money, or whether she would be flippant and self-assured, still insisting that she was the real Mary Eliska.

Mr. Von Goss's car appeared shortly after Mary Eliska and Jax Gray arrived, and they recognized Mr. Leslie Sprague in the back seat. Both men nodded to the girls, who had dismissed their taxi and were standing beside one of the hangars, talking to an attendant.

"See your names in the paper, girls?" he was asking them.

"No. When?" inquired Jax Gray.

The mechanic picked up a newspaper and handed it to them. There was a picture, somewhat poor, to be sure, of Mary Eliska and Jax Gray in their flying suits and an account of their arrival, recalling the incident of their strange landing at Kansas City. Underneath were the names, "Miss Sallie Slocum and Miss Savannah Manton."

"How did they ever get that picture?" demanded Jax Gray.

"Snapped it when you weren't looking. Those newspaper reporters are up to all sorts of tricks. The beacon light is bright, and he had a special camera."

Mary Eliska looked serious.

"This may make trouble for us, Jax Gray," she said, in a low voice.

The director and his secretary got out of the car and advanced toward the girls just as an airplane loomed into view. Mary Eliska stared excitedly at the sky, trying to make out what kind of plane it was. It was not an autogiro.

"There she is!" shouted Mr. Von Goss, and Mr. Sprague took off his hat and waved it violently into the air.

"The secretary's pretty keen about the false Mary Eliska, or I miss my guess," whispered Jax Gray, in her companion's ear. "Look how excited he is! How wildly he's waving!"

The aviatrix, who was just overhead, suddenly banked her plane, and made a turn to the left. Then she nosed her plane higher into the air.

"Doing some stunts for us!" exclaimed Mr. Von Goss. "She's a great little flier, all right—"

"She's—she's going away!" faltered Mary Eliska, in deepest disappointment.

"Probably forgotten something," remarked Leslie Sprague, casually. "I was almost certain, anyhow, that she said three o'clock—not two. She'll most likely be back at three."

"You mean to say we'll have to wait a whole hour?" demanded Jax Gray, as the plane disappeared in the distance.

"That's up to you," returned Sprague, nonchalantly.

Mr. Von Goss reached into his pocket and extracted a clipping. It was the newspaper picture of Jax Gray and Mary Eliska, with the fictitious names under it.

"Sprague showed me this," he said, handing the clipping to Mary Eliska, with a suspicious look in his eyes.

Mary Eliska trembled in spite of herself, but Jax Gray immediately explained how it had happened. Mr. Von Goss, however, looked doubtful of the truth of the story, and Sprague listened with a nasty grin on his face.

"We'll have to talk this over later," the director said finally. "I have an appointment now. As soon as the girl arrives, you better all come straight to the studio, where we can compare licenses, and so on."

"Where is mine?" demanded Mary Eliska.

"Sprague's keeping it. He'll hand it over when the time comes."

With a brief nod of good-bye, the two men drove away together, and the girls stood watching them in dismay.

"Something tells me that that young lady won't be back here," Jax Gray said dismally.

"I'm afraid not. Maybe she even saw us, for her plane was pretty low. And if she had glasses—"

"Of course she had glasses! No girl who plays a tricky game like this one is going to go about unprepared. It would be like a gangster without a gun."

They waited impatiently for over an hour, but nothing happened, and even the men did not return. Other planes flew into the busy airport, landed and took off, but there was no sign of Mary Eliska's "double."

Bored with the inactivity, they strolled over to the hangar where the Ladybug was housed, and looked her over.

"I'd fly over to the studio if I only had my licenses," said Mary Eliska. "But I hate to break laws—even though it isn't my fault."

"That man has no right to keep them!" stormed Jax Gray. "I'll bet Sprague's at the bottom of this."

"He's still trying to protect his girl-friend, I'm sure of that.... Well, Jax Gray, we may as well go back to the hotel, for if she should arrive, I feel confident that Mr. Von Goss would call us there."

Mary Eliska's confidence, however, was sadly misplaced. For no one at the studio called to inform her that the other girl landed her plane right on the set a little after three o'clock.

With the neatness of a born flier, she brought her plane to the ground, climbed out of the cockpit and strolled into Mr. Von Goss's office. The director had not yet returned, but Sprague was sitting at his desk. In a few words he explained the situation, but before the girl could make any reply, Mr. Von Goss walked in.

"You've heard the story, Miss—Stricklin?" he asked, hesitating a little over the name.

The girl, who really resembled Mary Eliska to a remarkable degree, laughed and shrugged her shoulders.

"I'm used to things like that," she said. "It used to worry me at first, but I never pay any attention to them now. Why, Mr. Von Goss, you can see for yourself how absurd the claim is! The girl's real name—Sallie Slocum—has been printed in the newspaper twice."

"Yes, of course that's true. But how about those license cards?"

"Your detective will soon prove them counterfeits. And the signatures forged."

Still, the man hesitated.

"The other girl said something about taking a test. Said she was the only licensed mechanic in the country. That made it sound pretty genuine to me."

Again the girl laughed.

"That was a clever ruse," she said. "But probably Miss Slocum has passed that test since I did, and thinks she knows more than I would.... No, Mr. Von Goss, I haven't time to fool around here taking tests. I've got to be on my way tomorrow. So if you want me in the picture, you'll have to let me go through my stunts now."

"I don't see how it can be done—" began the director.

"Very well, then," agreed the girl. "I'd better give you back your check, because I'm really too busy to wait around here. After all, the money doesn't mean much to me—and I don't need the publicity!"

Mr. Von Goss looked at her keenly. She must be the real Mary Eliska, he thought, or she certainly wouldn't talk like this. It never occurred to him that she was acting.

"No—I don't want to give up now. We'll go through with your part of the show.... Sprague, get the people on the wire...."

And so, while Mary Eliska and Jax Gray were patiently waiting for their telephone call at the Ambassador Hotel, the impostor almost completed her part in the picture, promising to return for only a couple of hours' work in the morning.

CHAPTER 9.6
THE FORGED SIGNATURE

"Good morning, Miss Slocum," said Mr. Sprague, smugly, as Mary Eliska and Jax Gray entered the studio at Culver City the following day.

Mary Eliska winced at the bogus name, and looked around her, to see whether another girl could be entering at the same time. But there was no one except a strange young man sitting in the corner, who couldn't possibly be "Miss Slocum." The secretary was evidently giving her a dig; perhaps he was trying to trap her by calling her by the name which Jax Gray had manufactured on the spur of the moment at Kansas City, and which had been repeated by the newspapers.

"Trying to be funny, Mr. Sprague?" inquired Jax Gray, scathingly.

The stranger in the corner arose from his seat.

"This is Mr. Bertram Chase, of the police," Sprague announced, calmly. "Miss Slocum and Miss Manton."

The girls regarded the young man questioningly. He was in plain clothes—not an ordinary policeman.

"A detective," explained Sprague, simply.

Jax Gray became impatient; she wanted to get to the point of their visit.

"We should like to meet the aviatrix who calls herself Mary Eliska," she announced, in a business-like tone. "Has she come in yet?"

"She is on the set now," replied Sprague. "Going through her stunts. She has only a small part in the picture, so it can all be done at once."

"Will you kindly take us out where she is?" asked Mary Eliska.

"In a minute, sister," returned the man, condescendingly. "But we have some business with you first."

Mary Eliska's expression became freezing. She could not bear this insolent young man. He smiled in an irritating manner.

"We have examined your licenses, Miss Slocum," he said. "And we believe the signatures have been forged. The real Mary Eliska brought hers today, and we compared the two. There is no doubt that hers is genuine."

"What?" demanded Mary Eliska, in horror.

"Let us see them!" demanded Jax Gray, entirely unconvinced.

Mr. Sprague nodded.

"Our friend, Mr. Chase, has them now. He will let you look at them."

The young man, who could not have been a day over twenty-five, looked extremely embarrassed. Not like a hard-boiled detective at all, Mary Eliska thought. Indeed, he flashed her a look of sympathy, as if he did not share in Sprague's accusation. Still, it was his business, and he had to go through with it.

He fumbled in his pockets and produced two cards, identical at a glance. The same numbers, the same printing—and what looked like the same signatures.

"Don't let them out of your hands, Chase," warned Sprague, evidently determined to be as nasty as possible.

"You see, ladies," Chase said, almost apologetically. "This signature is forged." He held up one of the cards. "Look at the capital 'L'. It hasn't been copied quite right."

"Of course it hasn't!" cried Jax Gray. "But the other one is yours, Mary Eliska."

"Yes," agreed Mary Eliska, trembling in spite of her innocence, "I remember that mud-spot on mine. I got it on that treasure-hunt that Mr. Clavering planned, from Green Falls last summer."

"Odd," remarked Sprague, sarcastically. "That is the very mud-spot the real Mary Eliska identified her card by!"

"What do you propose to do?" demanded Jax Gray, now thoroughly exasperated.

"Hold Miss Slocum under bail," replied Sprague. "For forgery."

Jax Gray burst into a peal of laughter.

"It's too absurd!" she exclaimed.

The young detective looked exceedingly uncomfortable.

"Shall we go out on the lot?" he suggested. "And see the stunts?"

"O. K. by me," agreed Sprague.

"Are we to wear hand-cuffs?" inquired Jax Gray, flippantly.

Sprague gave her a withering look.

"You are not being held at all, Miss Manton," he said. "We're not concerned under what names you care to travel."

The young detective fell back and walked across the lots with the girls.

"I believe you are innocent, Miss—Stricklin," he said, his brown eyes already showing devotion to Mary Eliska. "Of course I have to take your money for bail, but I'm sure it will be all cleared up soon. I think that the other girl is the impostor."

"Oh, thank you, Mr. Chase!" cried Mary Eliska, the tears dangerously near to her eyes at this expression of sympathy.

The group reached the lot, where the picture was being rehearsed. It looked so interesting, so thrilling,—had it been under any other circumstances, the girls would have only been too delighted at the opportunity. But now they could think only of the horrible fix they were in, with not a friend in this strange city to vindicate them.

Mr. Von Goss, who was buzzing busily about the lot, paid no attention at all to Jax Gray and Mary Eliska—not even a formal nod of greeting as he passed them by. He had evidently decided that they were impostors, who had cleverly deceived him, thereby securing for themselves an evening's unusual entertainment at his expense. Therefore, he preferred not to recognize them at all. The deliberate cut hurt Mary Eliska, for she had liked and admired the older man, and had found him exceedingly interesting.

The moving-picture aviatrix, however, was going through all sorts of stunts in a silver Moth, which had been brightly painted and decorated. Mary Eliska stood still, gazing at her enviously. Not that she wanted to be in the picture, but she would always rather be in the air than on the ground. And it looked now as if she were to be chained to the earth for several days to come, unless she or Jax Gray could think of a way out of their difficulties.

"The girl's too low!" cried Chase suddenly, in horror.

Mary Eliska watched her; she certainly was dangerously near to the ground. The roar of her motor was deafening. But, by a stroke of luck, she regained control, and abruptly pointed her plane upward, climbing without disaster.

"She's good," admitted Mary Eliska, in all fairness.

"Not so good as she looks," remarked Chase. "I happen to know that plane and it will take a lot of punishment. But she'll do that little stunt once too often."

"You're a flier too, Mr. Chase?" inquired Mary Eliska.

"Yes," he replied. "I'm a secret-service man, on the air force of the police."

He looked right into Mary Eliska's eyes, as if to tell her that his love of flying was another bond of sympathy between them.

"How did you happen to be called in—on an unimportant case like ours?"

"I'm here on something else. Connected with another case. And I know Mr. Von Goss personally, so he asked me to help him out."

"I see.... I suppose I shouldn't ask you for advice, Mr. Chase—but—I feel as if you would help me, if possible. What would you do if you were in my place?"

"Wire to somebody well-known in aviation circles, who can come and identify you as *the girl who flew the Atlantic alone*. Because that is the important thing. That's why Von Goss is paying the aviatrix thirty thousand dollars for a small part in one picture. Just because of that one fact!"

"Then friends wouldn't help—in establishing my identity?"

"No. They ought to be people in aviation."

Jax Gray interrupted this conversation, by suddenly grasping Mary Eliska's arm. "Look at Sprague!" she cried. "Look at the way he's waving that hat of his to his girl-friend! Now what do you suppose the idea of that is?"

At the mention of his own name, the secretary turned to the girls.

"Mary Eliska is supposed to fly away—be lost to sight now," he informed them, calmly. "It isn't likely she'll come back and land here, for that finishes her part."

"You mean we're not to see her?" demanded Jax Gray. "That looks suspicious to me!"

"Oh, yeah?" returned Sprague. "Well, don't flatter yourselves that Miss Mary Eliska has time to waste on a couple of upstarts from Toonerville, or wherever it was you came from. She's a busy girl!"

Mary Eliska sighed deeply as she watched the airplane disappear entirely from view. There was nothing to do now; Sprague and Von Goss were both against her. She might as well go back to the hotel.

"Come to the Ambassador Hotel this afternoon for that check for bail," she said to Chase. "I'll have it ready."

Then, with a nod of farewell, she and Jax Gray left the lot and went into a restaurant at Culver City for their lunch. But this time they were not interested in seeing the stars. Their own problems were too pressing.

"If I could only get in touch with Daddy," said Mary Eliska, as she nibbled at her salad. "But I don't know where he is, and I should hate to alarm Aunt Sally by telling her that I am being held under bail. No ... I guess the best idea is to wire Mr. Eckert."

"That's the stuff!" approved Jax Gray. "Why not go over to that telephone and do it now, while I order something for dessert?"

Mary Eliska took the suggestion, and fifteen minutes later the girls started back for their hotel in Los Angeles. They felt like prisoners, unable to come and go at will. As a matter of fact, Jax Gray was still as free as air, but she had no thought of deserting Mary Eliska.

They bought the afternoon paper on their way back to the Ambassador Hotel, and when they reached their room, Jax Gray spread it out on her bed to read. But the first item that met her eye made her stare in horror. It was Mary Eliska's picture, right on the front page, with the caption "Miss Sallie Slocum, impersonating Mary Eliska," and underneath it, the whole dishonest story.

She read it in rising anger, determined to destroy it before Mary Eliska should see it. But her companion, noticing the look on her chum's face, crossed the room and saw it for herself.

"Not a soul will believe it is really I!" she exclaimed. "Because it doesn't look a whole lot like me."

"No, it certainly doesn't. It must be that same picture the reporter took of us both at the airport, the day we landed here in Los Angeles. Only I'm cut off. I'm not news anymore."

"No, you're free, Jax Gray."

"Yet it's all my fault!" She wound her arms around Mary Eliska. "Darling, I just can't tell you how sorry I am for that silly prank!"

Mary Eliska patted her hand.

"Don't think of it as your fault, Jax Gray. That name business is only a side-issue. That girl would have gotten away with it, no matter what we did. She'd have thought up something else if she hadn't had that to play on."

"But I played right into her hands."

"Perhaps. Only, any girl who would go to all this trouble to invent such a dishonest scheme would have succeeded somehow. Why, the licenses were really the most important thing. But how she ever managed to get them exchanged without that smart Sprague noticing, is more than I can account for."

"Well, you must remember he wasn't prejudiced against her as he was against you. He trusted her, so he probably wasn't watching her closely." "I detest that man," said Mary Eliska.

"So do I," agreed Jax Gray.

"Well, this isn't getting us anywhere," remarked Mary Eliska, with a yawn. "I think a nap would do us good."

So, wisely acting upon the suggestion, the girls slept until Mr. Chase called at five o'clock for Mary Eliska's check for one thousand dollars for bail.

"Which I hate to have to take," he said, apologetically. "But I expect to give it back to you soon!"

CHAPTER 9.7
STOLEN!

Mary Eliska and Jax Gray both felt terribly depressed, in spite of their luxurious surroundings. Indeed, both girls had showed more spirit on that deserted island in the Atlantic Ocean, where they had been stranded without any plane during the early summer. When both their food and their water supply were limited, and the chances of survival were small. But now there was nothing to do but wait—wait in this strange, lonely city, where their only friends— Mr. Von Goss and Mr. Chase—had turned out to be enemies. And now Mr. Chase was going away, flying south on important business, so that even he would be lost to them.

"But you will soon be free," he had said, after he had heard that Mary Eliska had wired for Mr. Eckert.

"In time to stop that picture's being shown, do you think?" inquired Mary Eliska. "I understand that the rest of it was completed, and that all that had to be filmed was my double's part."

"Yes, I believe that's what Von Goss said. But surely it won't be released for a month or so. I shouldn't worry. You do hate publicity, don't you?" he asked, sympathetically.

"I have always tried to shun it," answered Mary Eliska. "But it seems that I am being punished now."

But the young man had gone, and the girls were feeling very blue.

"We've got to pull ourselves together!" announced Jax Gray, after a few minutes of somber silence. "Let's step out and go to a show tonight! After all, you paid that thousand dollars bail, and we might as well get some fun out of it."

"True," admitted Mary Eliska.

"Not a picture this time. A theater. I'm sick of movies."

"So am I."

"And let's make a rule, with a forfeit of five dollars, if either of us mentions that aviatrix, or Sprague, or any other vermin we have met around the studio, we have to pay the other! Is it a go?"

"Does that include Mr. Chase?" asked Mary Eliska, slyly. Jax Gray poked her companion under the chin.

"I suppose not," she agreed. "You couldn't exactly describe him as 'vermin'…. And besides, I can see that you were rather smitten. And did he fall for you? Whew!"

Mary Eliska blushed.

"He is a nice young man, don't you think so, Jax Gray?"

"Of course I do. But poor Ralph! How jealous he'd be, if he only knew!"

"Ralph will be furious because I didn't wire to him to help us out. But after all, he's only a personal friend, and of course his assertions about my innocence wouldn't carry much weight."

"We're agreed, then," said Jax Gray, as she began to dress for dinner, "that the tabu subjects are Von Goss, movies, Sprague, and your double. At five dollars apiece!"

Mary Eliska laughed, but she felt much better. Trust Jax Gray to find some fun in every situation, no matter how unpleasant or dangerous it seemed. They were able to get seats at a very good play, and in the excitement of the mystery involved, they forgot all about their own troubles, and had no need to worry about the forfeit.

It was lucky indeed that they were able to enjoy their evening, for the next morning held a most unpleasant surprise for them. They had gone for a walk after breakfast and returned to the hotel about eleven o'clock, hoping for some word from Mr. Eckert.

The telephone rang and Mary Eliska picked it up gaily, expecting it to be the message. But it proved to be a message of a very different sort a summons from a police-court in Los Angeles!

"The officer wants you to come downstairs immediately, Mary Eliska," the operator told her.

"I'm going too," announced Jax Gray, following her companion into the elevator.

A uniformed policeman was waiting for Mary Eliska in the lobby. He was a rough, uneducated person of the lower class, evidently accustomed to bullying his suspects into submission. He did not return Mary Eliska's feeble "Good morning," but merely extended a piece of paper with his right hand.

"Your bum check!" he snarled. "For bail. You had no right to sign the name of 'Mary Eliska' anyhow, but besides that, there ain't no funds to cover it—even if you say you are the real 'Mary Eliska'."

"No funds!" gasped Mary Eliska, staring incredulously at the man. "Why, I keep five thousand dollars in my check account—just to be ready for any kind of emergencies that may come up when I'm flying about the country!"

"That's just the amount that was took out yesterday. By the real Mary Eliska." His tone was jeering, as if he were enjoying the situation as he would a play.

"Oh!" cried Mary Eliska. "This is terrible!"

"I'll say it is," agreed the policeman. "Now get your hat, and come along with me. You're goin' to jail."

The girls looked at each other in speechless amazement. This was too dreadful for words.

"Let me wire for the money," suggested Jax Gray, suddenly. "I can get it from my father."

"Do as you like. But this here forger goes to jail—even if she is a pretty girl. That ain't a gonna help her none now!"

"Oh!"

The tears came to Mary Eliska's eyes, in spite of her effort to hold them back. She felt dizzy and weak. It was all like a hideous nightmare, from which, try as she might, she could not awaken. She opened her mouth to speak, but only a stifled sob came. Then, with a hopeless gesture of powerlessness, she decided to do as she was told.

She turned about desperately and walked towards the elevator like a criminal going to the electric chair. Jax Gray, still trying to think of some way to save the situation, waited, hesitating, breathing hard. It was a tense and horrible moment—until Mary Eliska walked right into the arms of her dear old friend, Mr. Eckert!

"Mary Eliska, I'm here!" he said, putting out his arms to catch her, for he could see that she was blinded by tears. "Dear child, you're not going to faint?"

Mary Eliska looked up in a daze, too astonished to believe that he was true. Had her imagination conjured up his kindly presence? But no; Mr. Eckert's hands were on her shoulders, supporting her, keeping her from falling. And beside him was a large, fine-looking man in a blue uniform.

"Oh!" she gasped, in joy and relief, clinging desperately to the elderly man's hand.

"What are you doing to Mary Eliska?" demanded the stranger in uniform, of the policeman. "Hounding her with abuse?"

"This here young lady forged a name and passed a bum check," he whimpered.

"What name?" asked the other man.

"Claims she's Mary Eliska, with five thousand bucks in a bank, where she's already overdrew her account."

"She is Mary Eliska!" announced Mr. Eckert. "I can testify to that—your superior officer, James A. Brenan, can testify to my knowledge, for he knows me well. He is Chief of Police in St. Louis."

"How did you get here so soon, Mr. Eckert?" asked Jax Gray. "We only wired yesterday."

"We started immediately, sensing your trouble. And flew day and night. But I see that we got here just in time."

"Ten minutes later I'd have been wearing prison stripes!" returned Mary Eliska, now almost herself again. "Oh, Mr. Eckert, I can never thank you enough."

"I was only too thankful to be of use, my dear child," said the kind-hearted man.

"What shall we do first?" inquired Jax Gray, as the policeman made a move to slip away.

"Catch the thief," announced Chief Brenan. "If she has forged a check for five thousand dollars already, she must have gone away as fast as she could." He turned to the Los Angeles policeman. "Go and inform your station of this as fast as you can.... And meanwhile, we'll go straight to the studio of the Apex Film Corporation and find out what we can about her from the director."

The policeman departed, and Mary Eliska asked Mr. Eckert whether he weren't terribly hungry and tired.

"Hungry, yes, but I haven't had time to think about being tired yet. I want to get things all straightened out for you first, before I consider sleeping. We will arrange for a couple of rooms and order a meal before we go to Hollywood."

In an incredibly short time the men reappeared from their rooms and ate a hasty meal that was both breakfast and lunch. Then the whole party, the two girls, and the two older men chartered a car for Culver City.

"Won't it be fun to stick out our tongues at that Sprague insect?" laughed Jax Gray, now enjoying herself hugely. "He was so condescending—so sure that the other girl was the real thing!"

"And I'm going to insist that they don't show the picture under my name!" added Mary Eliska.

"It'll serve Mr. Von Goss right. I'm glad he's losing money. Remember how snippy he was to us yesterday, on the lot?"

"He certainly was. Wouldn't even speak to us!"

"He may get his money back when we catch the impostor," remarked Chief Brenan. "She can't have had a chance to spend much of it."

"I'll wager she bought that plane that she was doing stunts with," observed Mary Eliska. "It certainly was speedy. And she'd want to get out of the country as soon as possible."

The short distance to Culver City was covered quickly in the high-powered car. Jax Gray was the first to run into the studio when they arrived. She wanted to have the fun of saying, "I told you so," to that "fresh Sprig," as she liked to call him.

The same "publicity girl" took their cards. But, though Mr. Von Goss was in, she informed them that Mr. Sprague was no longer with the Apex.

"Fired?" asked Jax Gray, hopefully.

"No, I believe not. He left yesterday—to be married to Miss Mary Eliska."

"No, he didn't!" contradicted Jax Gray. "This is Miss Mary Eliska right here, and she'd rather be dead than married to that shrimp. Your actress wasn't Mary Eliska at all—as we're just about to prove."

"Really?" remarked the girl, only slightly interested. It was a practice of hers never to frown or show emotion, lest she encourage wrinkles.

They passed on in to the director's office, and Mary Eliska introduced the two men and told her story. When she had finished, Mr. Von Goss looked extremely worried, crestfallen, even defeated. For now Mary Eliska's identity was established beyond a doubt.

"How then do you account for this license?" he asked, extending the one with the forged signature to Mary Eliska.

"Sprague's doing, of course!" cried Jax Gray, before Mary Eliska had a chance to answer. "He was in league with that girl. We just heard that they were married."

"But how could he manage these licenses?" demanded Von Goss.

"He got hold of a blank somehow, and forged the name. Then when he had the chance to get hold of the real Mary Eliska's, of course he exchanged them."

The Chief of Police was listening to Jax Gray's logic with admiration.

"You're a bright girl," he said. "And you've figured it out just about right." He turned to Mary Eliska. "You should never have let your own licenses get out of your hands."

"I had no idea Mr. Sprague was dishonest," she said. "But the worst part of it is, that now I have to fly with a false license."

"We'll get yours back when we catch that couple!" promised Von Goss. "Because we've got to catch them. Why, I paid her thirty thousand dollars for her part in the picture—and if my picture is not shown, I'll lose thousands more...."

He looked terribly discouraged.

The Chief of Police rose.

"We must go back now and get to work. Have you any idea, Von Goss, where this couple went, or what kind of plane they flew in?"

"I heard Sprague say something about South America for a honeymoon," the man replied. "He told us to keep his mail for him, 'til he came back, as he wouldn't have any definite address. But I haven't any idea whether they expected to fly, or what kind of plane they used if they did."

"The girl didn't buy your plane—or steal it?" asked Mary Eliska.

"No. It's still out there. We needed it today for some stills."

"What kind of plane did she own when she came to the studio?"

"She didn't own any. She told me that she had left her autogiro at Spring City, and had flown west wit

"And you believed every word of it!" was Jax Gray's taunt. "And never even asked to see her license, until we showed up and made it necessary."

"It's all true," agreed the director. "I've been a fool."

"If we only knew what kind of plane, it would be so much easier to follow and catch her," remarked Mary Eliska, sadly.

Mr. Von Goss rose from his desk, and followed the group to the door, lingering beside Mary Eliska, as if he were trying to get up courage to say something to her. For such a self-possessed man, he seemed unusually nervous.

"Mary Eliska," he said, in a humble tone, "won't you please do that part of the picture for me?" It seemed strange that a man who could tell stars what to do, should speak so deferentially to Mary Eliska.

"Oh, no, Mr. Von Goss," she replied immediately. "I couldn't possibly. I'm all keyed up for a chase. I want to catch this girl, if it's the last thing I ever do!"

"Then let me pay you, say fifty thousand dollars for the use of your name, and let me show the picture as it is. Nobody would ever guess that it isn't you. For she does look astonishingly like you."

"Wouldn't I love to see that girl!" said Jax Gray.

Again Mary Eliska shook her head. "I don't want my name in moving-pictures, Mr. Von Goss," she said with quiet determination. "Besides, I shouldn't like people to think I flew in the dangerous, spectacular way that girl did. It is harmful to the whole cause of aviation. No; you cannot use my name in connection with your picture."

Von Goss knew that she meant what she said, and there was no use of any further argument. But he was in a terrible fix, and he didn't know how to get out of it without losing a great deal of money. Certainly he couldn't use the name of the girl—whatever it was—for when she was caught, the whole world would know that she was a criminal.

A solution of his problem, however, suddenly suggested itself to Mary Eliska.

"I have it, Mr. Von Goss!" she cried, turning about. "Use Ann Harding! She's a flier, and a popular actress besides. She can do the stunts, and probably will prove more of a drawing card to the public than I could hope to be."

"Ann Harding!" repeated the man. "But she belongs to another studio."

"Borrow her! Pay her! You'll save your picture."

"I believe you're right, Mary Eliska," he admitted, with a sigh of relief. "That ought to save the situation."

The four visitors left the studio and hurried in their car back to the hotel. But no news of the couple had been received by any of the Los Angeles police. Mary Eliska therefore determined to pack a box of supplies and to set out, that very afternoon, on the search, inquiring at the airports they passed as they flew towards Mexico.

Just before sitting down to her late lunch with Jax Gray, she wired the news to her aunt, informing her of her plans, and asking that additional funds be put into her checking account. Then she called the airport on the telephone.

"This is Mary Eliska," she said. "I want you to have my autogiro in readiness for a long trip. Plenty of gas and oil. I will call for it inside of an hour."

"Mary Eliska?" repeated the voice at the other end of the wire. "Autogiro?... Must be some mistake.... Mary Eliska flew away in her autogiro last night, about eight o'clock. She paid the bill, and said she wouldn't be back!"

CHAPTER 9.8
IN HOT PURSUIT

Mary Eliska replaced the telephone receiver and sat motionless, staring at the wall of the hotel bedroom. The worst had happened. The autogiro was stolen. The Ladybug! Her dearest possession.

"What's the matter?" asked Jax Gray, realizing that her chum must have heard bad news.

In a few words Mary Eliska explained the situation.

"And the worst of it is, that girl evidently didn't have any difficulty at all about doing it. Just walked into the airport at night and demanded the plane. They handed it over to her without so much as a question."

For once in her life, Jax Gray remained speechless. There was not a single word of comfort she could think of to offer to her companion.

"She's had almost a whole day's start," Mary Eliska added dismally. "Here it is three o'clock, and she must have pulled out at dark last night. She's probably out of the United States by this time. And nobody even on her trail yet!"

"Our police always catch the wrong person, anyway," remarked Jax Gray, grimly.

"Don't be too hard on them, Jax Gray. They're not all like that dreadful specimen that came for me this morning. And in a case like this, they would probably put the air-force on duty. Men of a much higher type."

"Like Mr. Chase, for instance."

"Yes."

"What are you going to do, Mary Eliska?"

"Call the police headquarters first. Tell them to get in touch with all the airports possible, so that any autogiros can be reported. But I'd like to go after that girl myself, too!"

"In what?"

"'In what?' is right! Oh, if I only had a plane! If Ted Mackay were only here—or even Ralph, with his autogiro! But do you realize, Jax Gray, that I'm bankrupt? I can't buy an airplane, nor even hire one, now that that girl took everything I had in the bank."

Her companion nodded. "If somebody would only lend you one," she said. "Maybe Mr. Eckert—"

"I've thought of him. But he has to get back to the school immediately. Why, Jax Gray, this is the twenty-ninth of September! We've wasted a whole week, just to establish the fact that I am Mary Eliska! Isn't it just too absurd!"

"It's the craziest thing I ever heard of. And now you'll lose your chance at that teaching position, unless you give up trying to get your Ladybug back."

"I can't do that. I couldn't give up now. No, I'll call the police headquarters, and then I'll wait around until Mr. Eckert wakes up from his nap. We'll surprise the men by having dinner with them."

It was indeed a surprise, as Mary Eliska expected, when she and Jax Gray met Mr. Eckert and Chief Brenan in the lobby of the hotel that evening at seven o'clock. Naturally, both men thought that the girls had flown away early in the afternoon.

"I'm tied to the earth again," Mary Eliska announced immediately. "But not by the law this time.... That girl flew off in my autogiro!"

"No!" cried Mr. Eckert, incredulously. "Why, there isn't anything she won't steal!" He smiled grimly. "Did she leave you your own clothing, Mary Eliska?"

"Yes," replied the girl. "But that's about all."

"You should have had me awakened the minute you heard the news. If you had done that, you might have been on your way by this time."

"You mean—?" gasped Mary Eliska.

"In my airplane, of course. Take it and welcome, my dear child!"

Mary Eliska seized his hand and tried to stammer out her thanks. But she was too much moved by his generosity to say anything.

"How will you get back to St. Louis in time for the opening of your school?" inquired Jax Gray.

"By the commercial air-line," replied Mr. Eckert. "Now come in and eat some dinner, and after that, you can make your plans."

It seemed to Mary Eliska almost too good to be true. To have the privilege of flying that new, fast biplane, which she had admired so much that morning. It had a cruising speed of a hundred and fifty miles an hour! Surely, in it, she could catch her own Ladybug.

"You'll start early tomorrow morning, I suppose?" asked Mr. Eckert, as they seated themselves in the dining-room.

"Yes," answered Mary Eliska. "The police are already on the job, in communication with all the airports, which are to keep a watch out for all autogiros that pass overhead or land for gas. We'll find out what reports have been turned in, before we take off in the morning."

"And will you go along, Jax Gray?"

"Certainly," replied Jax Gray. "I'm just as anxious to recover the Ladybug as Mary Eliska is."

"It may mean dangerous business."

"It's bound to be exciting!"

After dinner Chief Brenan telephoned to the police headquarters to find out what information had been gained. Three autogiros, he learned, had been spotted, but only two of them had been stopped. Neither of these was the Ladybug. The third, it seemed, had been seen early in the day, flying southeast across California toward Arizona. Two secret-service planes had already been sent out in that direction.

With Mr. Eckert's help, Mary Eliska sketched out a course to follow. She would head straight for the city of Yuma, in the extreme southwest of Arizona, stopping there for the first night. Then she would go over the border into Mexico.

Jax Gray, in the meanwhile, took charge of the practical preparations for the trip. She arranged to leave their box of clothing at the hotel, and packed all the supplies for the trip. Water in gallon jugs and thermos bottles, canned food, blankets in case they were forced to camp out at night, field glasses and first-aid kit—and finally, upon Mr. Eckert's suggestion—a revolver.

The whole party breakfasted at dawn the following morning, and Mr. Eckert accompanied the girls to the airport, to sign the necessary papers for the release of his plane, the Sky Rocket. It was a beautiful new biplane, of the latest model. Painted yellow, with a companion cockpit, it stood in readiness on the runway, as if inviting Mary Eliska to climb in and fly.

Her eyes were shining in happy anticipation as she skipped forward and climbed into the cockpit to peer at the instruments. Everything for convenience and comfort seemed to be provided. Altimeter, clocks, compass, parachutes—even a wireless, with transmitting radio wires placed inside the wings, so that messages could be sent and received.

"It's marvelous, Mr. Eckert!" she exclaimed, as she seated herself at the controls, her hand fingering the joy-stick.

"Aren't you even going to give her a trial flight, Mary Eliska?" inquired the mechanic, skeptically.

"Mary Eliska can pilot any plane that's made!" replied Mr. Eckert, proudly. "She never needs any instruction. But," he added, coming closer to Mary Eliska, "don't forget that this isn't an autogiro. Don't try to land her on top of a building!"

Mary Eliska smiled.

"I only wish I had my own license," she said.

"I shouldn't worry about that," returned Mr. Eckert. "The police aren't going to make any more mistakes about arresting you."

"I should hope not!" exclaimed Jax Gray.

A minute later the mechanic started the motor, and Mary Eliska taxied along the runway, waving good-bye to Mr. Eckert. A few hundred feet farther, and the Sky Rocket rose into the air like a bird, soaring up to the skies. The usual fog common to the early morning climate of California had lifted, and the sun shone brightly as Mary Eliska directed her course towards the mountains. She let out the throttle to its maximum as soon as she reached a good safe height; a hundred and fifty miles an hour did not seem an abnormal speed, but it was a thrilling experience. Mary Eliska loved her own Ladybug, but after all, this was an exciting change.

Over the orange groves of southern California they passed again, then, even higher up in the air to clear the San Jacinto Mountains, over the city of Imperial—on towards Yuma. The flight was nearly four hundred miles, but Mary Eliska covered it in less than four hours. At noon she landed the Sky Rocket at the airport of Yuma, Arizona.

Being a large airport, the men had already been informed by radio of the stolen autogiro, and the attendant who came out to greet the Sky Rocket was prepared to answer Mary Eliska's questions.

"A giro stopped here yesterday for gasoline and oil," he said. "And we filled her up. Put a patch on one wing, but the couple wouldn't wait long enough to have it done right. That must have been about three o'clock in the afternoon. We got the radio soon after that, to take the licenses of all the giros we got a look at."

"What did the people look like? Were they a man and a girl?" demanded Jax Gray, excitedly.

"Yeah. A married couple, I believe."

"On their honeymoon?"

"Can't tell you that. They didn't act mushy."

Mary Eliska smiled.

"Did they give you their names?" she inquired.

"And did the girl look like—Mary Eliska?" put in Jax Gray, before the man could answer Mary Eliska's question.

"Couldn't say she did, except that all you girl fliers look something alike. But her face was pretty dirty, and her helmet was pulled down low.... Yeah, they gave their names. A Mr. and Mrs. Bower, of Texas."

"Oh!" gasped Mary Eliska, in disappointment. "We're looking for people named Sprague."

"They wouldn't be likely to give their right names, Mary Eliska," Jax Gray reminded her. "Why, that girl thinks nothing of swiping a new name to fit her fancy!"

"True," admitted Mary Eliska.

"And another thing," added the attendant. "There was a secret-service flier here this morning already. After them. A nice-looking chap, in a gray monoplane."

"Could it have been Mr. Chase?" demanded Jax Gray.

"Yeah. I think that was the name.... Well, he crossed the border, hot on their trail. Shouldn't be surprised if he had 'em by now, for he flew a fast plane!"

The news was encouraging, so after a bite of lunch and a hasty inspection, the girls flew away again, heading south now, avoiding the Gulf of California, and crossing over into Mexico.

They passed over the California river and continued an easterly course, avoiding the mountains near the coast, and pointing inland before they turned southeast again. From their height in the air they could not see the ground without glasses, but as Mary Eliska dipped lower, they could distinguish how barren and desolate it was. There were no trees; only short, stumpy underbrush scattered about, with big patches of bare, hard earth between. A most unattractive part of the country.

The engine of the plane continued to throb evenly; it was in perfect condition. At least, Mary Eliska thought, her plane was giving her no worry. But then, planes were more like automobiles now; the accidents were oftener due to the pilots themselves than to faulty motors.... But thus far, she had accomplished nothing. There had been no sign of an autogiro, or indeed of any kind of plane, since they left Arizona.

"We may be flying too high," she remarked, as the hours passed without any success. "I'm afraid to dip too low with this plane."

"Yes, that must be the trouble," responded her companion. "They could come down amongst those bushes and camp for the night, and we'd never see them. It seems like a wild-goose chase to me."

"You don't want to give up?"

"No, not as long as we can get any news at all. And they can't go on forever without gas. They'll have to stop at airports every once in a while to refuel, and then they'll be caught."

"Some of these little Mexican places may not have been informed," observed Mary Eliska. "If they didn't speak English—or didn't have a radio."

On and on they flew, over this hot, deserted land, so uncultivated and barren. The sun sank and twilight came on—and still no sign of a town or an airport where the girls might land.

"I'm afraid I'm lost," Mary Eliska admitted to Jax Gray, when it became too dim to distinguish the ground even with the aid of glasses. "I'll have to fly lower, and look for a landing. I think remember a place a couple of miles back."

She circled about and began flying in the opposite direction, cautiously gliding a little nearer to the ground.

"Do you mind sleeping out tonight, Jax Gray?" she inquired.

Her companion made a face. She had read enough about Mexican bandits not to relish the prospect.

"I suppose we'll have to," she said. "Anyway, we have plenty of food."

Darkness was coming on fast; there was nothing to do but take a chance at landing. Beyond them stretched great black mountains, deep and forbidding, inhabited, they felt sure, by all sorts of wild animals. These must be avoided at any cost; so Mary Eliska went back to the spot she had selected and prepared to make a dangerous landing. How thankful she was that she had had plenty of experience in spot landings!

Keeping the plane still high enough to maintain the glide to the spot, she combined maneuvers to accomplish her purpose. From a glide, she went into a side-slip until she lost altitude, then, as she approached the landing-mark, she gradually reduced speed with the forward slip, straightening out just as she reached the ground. And landed on the exact spot she had selected!

"Good work, Mary Eliska!" cried Jax Gray, admiringly.

Mary Eliska grinned.

"I was afraid I might be out of practice," she said. "Spoiled by my Ladybug. It's a satisfaction to know I can still land an ordinary plane. I guess she'll be all right, just here.... Now for some food! I'm starved."

"So am I. And thirsty too.... Where shall we make our camp?"

They looked all about them. In spite of the gathering darkness, they could see bare ground everywhere; only a few clumps of dry bushes in the distance. It was not exactly the spot one would select to camp out, if given a choice.

"Not too near the plane," said Mary Eliska. "Though I guess we don't need to build a fire. I don't believe we could find any wood. No; let's just open a can or two, and eat oranges and biscuits for tonight. Anything would taste good now."

They prepared their meal and ate it almost in silence, for they were too weary to talk. Then, crawling into their blankets, although the night was exceedingly mild, they went to sleep under the stars.

The first faint rays of light were appearing when Mary Eliska was abruptly awakened by a familiar sound over her head. She sat up, reaching instinctively for her revolver at her side, and looking about her for some animal which might be the cause of the noise. But the sound, now more loud than before, was not that of an animal. It grew nearer, almost deafening—over her head. An airplane, of course! Now fully awake, she looked up into the skies. The plane was descending; a flashlight was turned into her face. Blinded for an instant, she looked away. Then, as she turned her gaze upon it again, she saw it on the ground. And, wonder of wonders, it was an autogiro!

Excitedly she turned to her companion. But Jax Gray was still sleeping peacefully. That wasn't surprising; it had always been hard to waken Jax Gray. Alarms right beside her bed never had any effect.

"Jax Gray!" she whispered, disentangling herself from her blanket, and edging up nearer to her chum. "Jax Gray! Wake up!"

But Mary Eliska stopped suddenly; she couldn't say anything more. With the speed of a bolt of lightning, a man ran at her, and, grasping both Mary Eliska's hands with one of his, he clapped a wet rag over her face with the other. She had just time enough to identify her attacker as Sprague, when she fell to the ground unconscious. And, although she did not see what happened next, the same fate was accorded to Jax Gray.

Both girls had been chloroformed!

CHAPTER 9.9
THE LADYBUG!

Jax Gray was the first of the two girls to come to consciousness. With a gasp for breath, she pushed the cloth from her face and sat up. For a moment or two everything swam about her; she didn't know where she was.

She thought at first that she and Mary Eliska were on that deserted island in the Atlantic Ocean where they had been stranded early in the summer. But no; the ground was hard and dry—not a bit sandy—and there was no ocean in view. That couldn't be the explanation. For there was the Ladybug within a few hundred yards!

She glanced at Mary Eliska and saw that she was lying motionless beside her on the barren ground, her blanket thrown aside. With a cloth over her face! In sudden panic Jax Gray pulled it off desperately. Oh, suppose Mary Eliska were dead!

"Mary Eliska! Darling!" she implored piteously, but there was no reply, no movement from the inert figure. With a tremendous effort Jax Gray forced herself to rise and bend over her chum.

"Tell me you aren't dead, Mary Eliska!" she begged, hysterically.

A faint flutter of her companion's eyelids came as a response.

With a tremendous effort, Jax Gray reached for the thermos bottle and held water to Mary Eliska's lips. At last the color came faintly back to the aviatrix's face, and she smiled faintly.

"I'm—all right—Jax Gray," she managed to whisper. "But what happened?"

"I don't know."

Jax Gray took a drink of the water herself, and felt more revived.

"Where are we?" asked Mary Eliska.

"Somewhere in Mexico. Don't you remember? We were flying after that girl, in Mr. Eckert's Sky Rocket, and we came down for the night."

Mary Eliska rubbed her eyes and looked about her. And caught sight of the Ladybug, whose appearance had so amazed Jax Gray a moment before. And rubbed her eyes, and stared again.

"Am I crazy, Jax Gray—or is that really an autogiro over there? Or am I seeing things?"

"It's the Ladybug," replied Jax Gray. "I'm positive. We couldn't both be dreaming."

"But how did it get here? Is that girl around?"

"I don't hear her. Unless she's hiding." Jax Gray lowered her voice to a whisper. "Have you got your revolver handy, Mary Eliska?"

Mary Eliska felt at her side, where she had put it the previous night when she went to sleep, and sure enough, it was there. And, with the touch of that revolver, memory of the scene that preceded unconsciousness returned.

"I remember now!" she cried triumphantly. "I was wakened just as it was getting light, by a big noise. I finally identified it as a plane. At first I thought it was bandits, and I recall reaching for my revolver.... Yes.... Then I saw it was an autogiro. It landed ... and a man ... it was Sprague, I'm sure ... came and clapped that rag over my face. That's all."

"How ghastly!" cried Jax Gray. "I can't seem to remember a thing myself. I must have been sound asleep when he did it to me. But where is he now?"

"I know!" exclaimed Mary Eliska, with a sudden flash of understanding. "They must have made off in Mr. Eckert's plane! In the Sky Rocket—for it's gone."

"Of course that's it!" agreed Jax Gray. "But how do you suppose they ever spotted us?"

"Well, you see, the Ladybug can fly much lower than we could in the Sky Rocket," Mary Eliska explained. "They probably saw us in the air—when we didn't see them—and followed us about 'til they saw where we made our landing. Then they waited for us to get to sleep, and for early morning light to help them in landing and taking off, and then descended on us with the chloroform."

"Why do you think they wanted to swap planes?" asked Jax Gray. "Because the Sky Rocket is faster?"

"Yes. And it wouldn't be so easy to spot in the sky as an autogiro. Besides, by doing this, they know they will be throwing the police off the clue. Pretty clever, I'd say."

"Those two are about the slickest pair of schemers I've ever heard of. There's nothing they don't think of."

"And with each new trick they make a gain. Mr. Eckert's plane is faster, newer, and more expensive than the Ladybug."

"True. But aren't you glad to have the dear old Ladybug back again?" asked Jax Gray.

"I surely am. If she will fly. That's another thing, Jax Gray. You know that man at the airport said that she had a damaged wing. So naturally, the Spragues would be glad to get hold of a fresh plane."

"I wonder whether they had trouble taking off," observed Jax Gray. "It's not any too easy."

"No, but the ground's very hard. I guess they haven't had any rain here all summer.... Come on, Jax Gray, if you're able to walk, let's go over and see the Ladybug. I'm dying to get a look at her again."

"So am I," agreed her companion.

Walking a trifle shakily at first, and feeling extremely weak and queer after their experience, the girls went slowly to the spot where the autogiro was resting. Like her owner, she, too, looked in bad condition, as if she had been mistreated, and had travelled a great distance. And, as Mary Eliska expected, the patch on the wing was split open again.

"No wonder they swapped planes!" exclaimed Mary Eliska. "I guess that girl was pretty desperate. Well, thank goodness, I keep stuff on hand for repairs."

"And thank goodness you know how to do it!" added Jax Gray, with admiration. "Any other girl would be in a fine picnic in a fix like this!"

"Speaking of picnics, don't you think we'd feel better if we ate something? I don't feel a bit sick at my stomach—only terribly weak. Breakfast might help. They didn't take our food and water, did they?"

"They didn't take what we left out for breakfast," replied the chum. "But unfortunately we left most of our stuff in the plane."

"Well, we'll have to eat sparingly. But if I work fast, I ought to be able to get off by noon, and we can surely fly 'til we find a place to eat."

"Have we gasoline?"

"Yes, I just looked. Enough to go a couple of hundred miles."

Arm in arm they went back to their little encampment and ate the food which Jax Gray had reserved for breakfast and drank the coffee in one of the thermos bottles. The remainder of the water they decided to keep for their flight, and they still had half a dozen oranges which Jax Gray had purposely left out of the Sky Rocket, expecting to eat them during the morning.

Mary Eliska wasted no time. As soon as she had finished eating she set right to work on the damaged wing. It was not hard for her, for she knew every tiniest detail of the construction. How thankful she was that it was her own Ladybug that she had to repair, and not a strange plane!

Much to her delight, she found her own license cards on the seat of the cockpit. Evidently the girl had no further use for them.

After the repairs had been made to the outside of the plane, Mary Eliska tested the engine. It was not running so smoothly as she liked to hear it. A spark plug was missing. With a sigh, she set to work again.

Jax Gray, who had cleaned up all evidence of their camp, watched her in dismal silence. The day grew hotter and hotter, the sun poured down mercilessly on Mary Eliska, bending patiently over her work while the perspiration streamed from her face. But it was fixed at last; everything was to her satisfaction.

"Let's have an orange," she suggested, wiping her face with her handkerchief. "Oh, maybe I wouldn't like a good swim right now!"

"And we haven't even water enough to wash our faces!" lamented Jax Gray.

"If we only had that gallon jug we put into the Sky Rocket!"

"Oh, well, we will soon find a town, now that it is light enough to find our way."

Jax Gray brought the oranges, and they tasted good, although they had become exceedingly warm from the hot sun.

"Think we'll have any trouble taking off?" she inquired, as they finished the fruit.

"I guess not. If the Sky Rocket could get off—and she evidently did—I'm sure the Ladybug can make it. It's good hard ground all about."

Mary Eliska sounded confident, but Jax Gray's heart was in her mouth until she saw the Ladybug actually rise from the earth and soar up into the skies—wherein lay safety.

Once again Mary Eliska's heart was singing with rapture. She had enjoyed piloting that swift plane of Mr. Eckert's, but after all, there was nothing like her beloved Ladybug. Why, the thing was almost human, the way it responded to her touch!

Another great advantage at the present time, when the girls had lost their way, was the autogiro's ability to fly low. Now they could watch the landscape for towns and airports and landing-fields. Oh, it was good to have the Ladybug back again, if she couldn't make a hundred and fifty miles an hour!

The country was so strange, so different from anything they were used to, that, in spite of its barrenness, they watched it in fascination. They came to the mountains and Mary Eliska nosed her plane upward, over the steep slopes covered with pine forests, until she was rewarded by seeing little villages on the other side. Straw-roofed houses Jax dotted the landscape; there was evidence of farm-life, of some kind of civilization, though just what, the girls couldn't make out from their height in the air.

Mary Eliska consulted her map, and familiarized herself with the names of several of the towns near the mountains, determined to fly on until she could find a good landing. She noticed the tracks of a railroad in the distance, and this she decided to follow, until it should lead to a station, and be identified as a town. Her gas was growing low, but she had no fear of a forced landing. In country like this there would be plenty of opportunities for an autogiro.

Half an hour later she hovered over a small Mexican town that provided an airport, and brought the Ladybug to earth.

A man who was obviously a Mexican came forward to meet them.

"Do you speak English?" asked Mary Eliska.

The man nodded, smiling.

Reassured, the girls climbed out of the cockpit, and Jax Gray proceeded to tell their story, asking how she could notify the police in Los Angeles in the quickest time, so as to have them pursue the Sky Rocket instead of the autogiro.

"You can send a wire immediately, right from here," the man replied. "At least—you can when the operator comes back. He's off for supper now."

"I am a wireless operator," announced Mary Eliska, calmly. "If you are willing to trust me, I can send my own message."

"O. K.," agreed the man, who was beginning to decide that girls could do almost anything now-a-days.

"And I want to leave the autogiro here for the night, and have her filled with gasoline and oil," she continued. "And go to some hotel for a meal. Can you recommend one for us?"

"There are several hotels," he replied, proudly. "But I will send you to the best."

It proved to be strangely unlike any hotel the girls had ever visited. It was a long, low stucco building, with stone floors on the first story, and bare boards above. The supper, too, was unlike American food, but it tasted good to the hungry girls who had had nothing but a couple of oranges since their breakfast. And the prospect of a roof over their heads, after their disastrous adventure of the night before, was extremely pleasant. After their hearty supper they sat out on the wide, roofless veranda until the night grew cool enough for sleep.

"But where do we go from here?" asked Jax Gray, wondering whether Mary Eliska had had enough by now, and was ready to go back to Los Angeles.

"More pursuit," returned her companion. "I feel under greater obligations than ever to catch that thief now—for she has Mr. Eckert's plane. I'm responsible for it. We'll fly around to all the airports for news. Their gas supply ought to be getting low, and they'll have to stop somewhere to fill up. That's the clue we'll have to follow."

"I wish we could get back into the United States," remarked Jax Gray. "I don't like the bugs here in Mexico."

"I don't think we can hope for that, 'til we catch them. They're going to steer clear of our police."

"I suppose you're right," yawned Jax Gray. "Well, let's go get some sleep. We can't tell what adventures may be in front of us tomorrow."

"No, we can't possibly tell," agreed Mary Eliska.

CHAPTER 9.10
A CLOSE CALL

"I think," announced Mary Eliska at the breakfast table in the Mexican hotel the following morning, "that we'll have to cross the mountains today."

Jax Gray groaned.

"What a pleasant little ray of sunshine you are, Mary Eliska!" she said.

"I don't see why you object so to the mountains—in broad daylight, I mean. If there are bears and snakes in the mountains, they can't attack us in the air, can they?"

"So long as we just stay up in the air, it's all right. What I don't care about is camping out in these wild spots."

"I don't expect we'll have to," Mary Eliska assured her. "But I am taking an extra tank of gasoline, in case we can't find a place to refuel. Meanwhile, what I want you to see about is the food, if you will."

"I'm to make a visit to the kitchen, I suppose?" inquired Jax Gray. She made a wry face at the cereal she was eating. "Do you know, Mary Eliska, I could bear most anything if only we never had to eat another mouthful of this hotel's cooking."

Mary Eliska laughed.

"I know it's not exactly like the Ambassador. Still, it's a lot better than nothing, and we might be very glad to have it."

Jax Gray did as she was asked and raided the hotel kitchen, ignoring the indignant protests of the servants. Inside of half an hour the girls were back at the airport where they had left the autogiro, and Mary Eliska was giving the Ladybug a thorough inspection, for she did not have much confidence in the mechanic's knowledge.

"Any news of the Sky Rocket?" she asked, as she completed her work to her satisfaction.

"No, not a thing," replied the man.

Somewhat discouraged, the girls climbed into the cockpits and Mary Eliska taxied a short distance along the runway, but left the ground so quickly that the mechanic stood there staring at the autogiro with his mouth wide open.

Mary Eliska directed her course south, aiming to reach a larger airport before noon. Here she made a landing, refueled, and again inquired for news. A yellow biplane, it seemed, had been sighted that morning, flying low, going west towards the coast of the Gulf of California. Whether it was the Sky Rocket or not, no one could say. But at least it was a clue to follow.

"I told you we'd have to cross those mountains," remarked Mary Eliska. "But please don't start to worry about them yet."

Mary Eliska changed her direction and headed the ship west, and they flew a monotonous course for a couple of hours. The sun glared down upon them, and the earth below looked parched and barren. So different from their own Ohio country in the month of October.

They reached the mountains at last, and after assuring herself that there was plenty of gas in her reserve tanks, Mary Eliska flew dauntlessly towards them. As she approached, she noted a heavy cloud bank hovering directly above the mountains, and extending so far on either side that she gave up all thought of going around it. Instead she put the ship into a sharp climb and headed resolutely into it. She held the climb until she was several thousand feet higher to make sure of clearing the mountain safely, but as they had failed at this height to rise above the cloud, she leveled off.

Grayness was all about them, enveloping them like a blanket, and cutting off their view of either the mountains or the sun. In her powerlessness to see in this unknown region, Mary Eliska suddenly experienced a queer choking sensation, brought on by her helplessness. Scolding herself for this momentary weakness, she pulled back the joy-stick and nosed the Ladybug still higher up. But climb as she might, she could not get away from that cloud.

Jax Gray, however, did not appear to be frightened at all. Wasn't Mary Eliska always able to get the best of almost any bad situation, even if it were an unknown mountain range in a mist? She was singing cheerfully to herself, when all of a sudden, the words died on her lips.

Another plane was approaching—was almost on top of them! They had not been able to see it, because of the cloud, or to hear it, because of the noise of their own motor. But there it was, rushing headlong at them with the relentless speed of an infuriated animal. Jax Gray held her breath and shut her eyes.

Mary Eliska saw it too, and flashed on her lights as a signal. But it was too late for signals; only a miracle could save them. With a sudden sharp turn she banked to the left, and went into a side-slip, dropping the plane fifty feet. The other plane passed over their heads, barely missing the rotor blades.

The perspiration had collected on her face in beads, and her hands were hot and moist. It had been a narrow escape!

But it evidently wasn't over. Or could it be another plane? For the thing was almost upon her again, as if it, too, had dropped on purpose. She couldn't believe her ears. Was it that girl—and had she recognized the rotor blades of the autogiro, and was trying to force Mary Eliska to land?

Her heart in her mouth, she banked again, dropping for the second time, determined to land now at any cost. The strain had been awful the first time, but now it actually unnerved her. Inside of that cloud—on the dangerous mountain side! No; she could not take another chance, not only with her own life, but with Jax Gray's. Wherever she came down, it couldn't be as dangerous as this.

Gradually throttling her engine down to a slower speed, she began her descent by a series of glides. All the while watching for a glimpse of the solid earth beneath her.

Down, down they came, but still there was no ground visible. They must have passed over the mountains, she decided, and were descending into a valley. Or level ground, perhaps. That thought was encouraging.

"There it is!" shouted Jax Gray, almost hysterically. "The earth, I mean!"

Mary Eliska breathed a deep sigh of relief. Never before had she been so thankful to see it, unless perhaps the first time she had made a parachute jump.

"It must be the plateau!" she cried, joyfully. "We must have passed over the mountains!"

Gently the autogiro settled down to a landing on the level ground beneath them. It was a fertile spot in comparison with the other places in Mexico where they had landed. The earth was not nearly so parched or barren, and here and there, between the underbrush and the bare spots, a kind of coarse grass was growing. Perhaps, Mary Eliska thought, the land was used by someone for grazing.

"Quite a pleasant spot," remarked Jax Gray gaily, as if they had been on a picnic instead of face to face with death.

"See the mountains over there?" asked Mary Eliska, for they were out of the range of the cloud through which they had just passed.

"Yes. But they're far enough away that I really don't mind. If a bear wanders over to visit us, we'll feed him some Mexican food."

They climbed out of the cockpits, carrying their box of provisions in their arms, when they saw a sight that made them stand breathless in horror. About five hundred yards away they beheld a great mass of flame, shooting up to the sky.

"It's a plane!" exclaimed Mary Eliska. "It must be the one we almost crashed against."

With one thought in mind, the girls both dropped their box and started to run. Oh, if a human being were caged in that burning cockpit! It was too dreadful to think of—a death like that.

But before they had covered fifty yards of the intervening distance, they saw a parachute floating down to the earth. They stopped instantly, waiting in breathless suspense. Suppose it were Sprague, with his supply of chloroform? Tensely alert, Mary Eliska pulled her revolver from her belt.

But it was not Sprague. The man who floated down let out a cry of horror when he recognized Mary Eliska and Jax Gray. Though why he should be so horrified, the girls did not know.

The man was Bertram Chase!

He disentangled himself from his ropes, glanced at his burning plane, and let out a groan.

"You!" he cried. "And to think, I almost killed you!"

"You couldn't help that," said Mary Eliska gently. "It seems we almost did for you, too. If you hadn't jumped."

"That wasn't your fault. My plane caught on fire somehow—a leak, I think, in the gas feed. That's why I jumped.... But that had nothing to do with you.... But I actually tried to force you down—the second time, I mean. The first was accident."

"But why?" asked Jax Gray, incredulously.

"I saw your rotors, the first time I passed over you. And knew it was the autogiro. And thought that girl was piloting it, of course. How did you girls ever get hold of it again?"

"Then you didn't get the report from the Los Angeles headquarters?" inquired Mary Eliska.

"What report?"

"That we exchanged planes. My double stole our Sky Rocket, and left us the Ladybug instead."

"And got away with it?" demanded Chase.

"Yes. We're still after them. But where have you been in the meanwhile?"

"Flying around these mountains, without any touch of civilization. I even made a search on foot, but it proved to be a false clue that I was following. But tell me the story, while we take a walk over and examine my poor ship."

Briefly Jax Gray related the facts of the night-adventure with Sprague and his wife, as the three young fliers approached the burning mass. The flames had somewhat subsided, and only a smoking, blackened frame remained.

"Was it yours, Mr. Chase?" asked Mary Eliska sympathetically, thinking how dreadful she would feel if it were the Ladybug.

"No," he replied. "It belonged to the secret service. It was an old boat, but I was fond of it. And I've lost a lot of my things.... I think," he added, gloomily, "that I'd better hunt about for some water, to put the fire entirely out. I don't want to start a prairie fire, or whatever you call it."

"Do you suppose there is a stream anywhere about?" asked Mary Eliska.

"I hope so. If we've got to stay here for the night."

"Then come back to the Ladybug and get a can to fill, in case you do find water. Bring some back to us, if possible, and then we'll give you some supper. Real Mexican food—if you like it." It was Jax Gray who made this offer, and she winked slyly at Mary Eliska as she concluded.

The young man wandered off, and the girls turned to their preparations for supper. The food had already been cooked, so they decided to eat it cold.

It was some time before Chase returned with the can of water and the announcement that he had found a stream, and had succeeded in putting out the fire. He sat down gloomily beside the girls, but he made no motion to eat.

"Don't look so sad, Mr. Chase," said Jax Gray. "They'll give you another plane."

"It isn't that," he replied, morosely. "It's my foolhardiness. When I think of what I did to you, I'd like to shoot myself."

He looked so pathetic, so utterly downcast, that Mary Eliska didn't know what to say. But Jax Gray, in her characteristic manner, tried teasing him. Very solemnly she handed him Mary Eliska's pistol.

"If you really want to shoot yourself, go off away from us, where you won't clutter up the landscape!"

The young man laughed in spite of himself.

"Snap out of it, Bert!" she commanded, using his first name on purpose. "And have some of this delicious Mexican food. I don't know its name, but it tastes like week-old hash to me."

Smiling again, Chase accepted the paper plate she held out to him.

"Just imagine, Bert," Jax Gray continued, afraid to stop talking lest he become sad again, "that we're here on a picnic, with the autogiro, and this delicious supper. And you're lucky enough to be the young man chosen—out of hundreds of admirers of Miss Mary Eliska! Why, you have no idea how many young men in this country would give their best hats to have your chance!"

Mary Eliska flushed at this remark.

"Now, Jax Gray," she protested. "You're being silly!"

"I am not. I'll enumerate them, if you like. There's Ralph Clavering, and Harriman Smith, and—"

"Hush, Jax Gray!" cried her chum, putting her hand over her mouth. "That's about enough out of you!"

Chase, who by this time was grinning broadly, bowed in acknowledgment.

"All joking aside," he said, "I realize what an honor it is. And that's just why I feel so rotten about doing those two mean things to you, Mary Eliska." He was so in earnest that he did not realize that he had used her first name. "Accusing you of forgery the first time I saw you, and then almost killing you. You, who have never done anything wrong in your whole life!"

"Come now, that's putting it on a little bit too thick!" remonstrated Jax Gray. "Mary Eliska's not such a saint as that. I remember many a time that she climbed cherry trees that didn't belong to her, and skinned out of school—"

"That's enough about me," interrupted Mary Eliska. "It's getting so dark, I think we ought to make our plans for the night."

"I suppose we have to stay here," remarked Jax Gray, with a sigh.

"Why the sigh?" asked Chase. "Oh, I don't care for camping out—in Mexico."

"I don't blame you—after being chloroformed," sympathized Chase. "But you don't have to, tonight. For I found a straw-covered shack over near the stream where I got our water. You girls can have that. I'll stay up here, beside the autogiro."

"You have redeemed yourself, Bert!" exclaimed Jax Gray, jumping to her feet, and shaking his hand. "For one night at least, we'll be safe!"

CHAPTER 9.11
FLIRTING WITH DEATH

The little Mexican adobe house which Bert Chase had discovered was the funniest Mary Eliska and Jax Gray had ever seen. A one-room affair, with a slanting straw-covered roof, and no windows. Only two doors, opening back and front.

"I'd almost rather sleep under the stars," remarked Mary Eliska. "For there are probably all sorts of bugs in the corners and cracks."

Jax Gray shivered. "Still, bugs are better than bears and snakes, that might come wandering down from those mountains," she said. "And besides, it would be ungrateful not to use the house after Bert found it."

"It will be protection from the sun in the morning," added Mary Eliska. "Because this Mexican climate gets pretty hot."

So, spreading their blankets on the floor and propping the doors open with sticks, they lay down on their hard bed and fell fast asleep, not to awaken until quite late the following morning.

"Fog again!" yawned Jax Gray, as she finally got up stiffly and walked to the door. "I'm sick of these fogs."

"It'll probably clear up soon," Mary Eliska reminded her. "I've read that early morning fogs are the common thing in this part of the country."

"Let's hunt that stream Bert was talking about, and get a good wash," suggested Jax Gray. "Before we go back to the autogiro."

They found it not far from the little house, and although it was shallow and narrow, the water was clear and refreshing. They felt much better as they made their way back to the spot where the Ladybug had landed.

For several minutes they could see nothing because of the fog, and they began to feel worried. Suppose something had happened to Chase or to the autogiro during the night! What a desolate place to be stranded!

Before these dismal thoughts could really take hold of them, they spied the dim outlines of the Ladybug, shadowy in the fog. She was still there! Their means of escape.

Jax Gray placed her hands at her mouth, and gave a war-whoop for Chase.

"Yo-ho-ho-ho-Bert!" she shouted.

"Yo-ho, girls!" came the reassuring reply. "This way!"

Then they distinguished a fire, and a moment later, came upon him, contentedly cooking a fish.

"Where did you get it?" demanded Jax Gray.

"Caught it. Early this morning," he replied. "I felt guilty about eating so much of your food last night, so I tried to get a contribution. That stream widens out about a mile below your little house, so I went down and tried my luck."

"You're a peach!" exclaimed Jax Gray. "Because all we have left is coffee and that terrible Mexican bread. It's a wonder they don't learn how to bake in Mexico."

"It surely smells good," observed Mary Eliska. "How soon can we eat?"

"As soon as you girls make the coffee. I brought up a fresh supply of water this morning. We'll boil some of it, to take along with us for drinking, while we have the chance to do it."

It turned out to be a delicious as well as a merry meal. While they ate, the fog gradually lifted, bringing a clear, if hot day, for their flight.

"We must be pretty near the coast of the Gulf of California," said Mary Eliska. "So I think perhaps our best plan would be to fly across to the peninsula. I have an idea that girl is going to abandon the Sky Rocket as soon as she can, for it's pretty conspicuous."

"What would she do to get away, if she hadn't a plane?" demanded Jax Gray.

"Hide somewhere, or take a boat for South America perhaps. Now that she and her husband are out of the United States, it would be easy enough for them to book passage on a small steamer—without being noticed."

"Is your autogiro in good condition?" inquired Chase. "I mean—I didn't damage it yesterday, did I?"

"No. You know you never touched me. But I'll look her over before we start. And put in that tank of extra gas I was carrying in the passenger's cockpit."

"Perhaps I could help you?" suggested the young man. "I don't know much about the inside workings of a plane, but maybe two heads are better than one."

Jax Gray let out a peal of laughter.

"Mary Eliska is a graduate airplane mechanic," she said. "She is the only woman in the country with a mechanic's license!"

Chase stared in open-mouthed amazement.

"Whew!" he exclaimed. "I do take off my hat to you, Miss Mary Eliska!"

"You'd better!" laughed Jax Gray.

"Oh, don't be so silly," put in Mary Eliska, anxious to be off. "Let's all go over to the Ladybug now."

While Jax Gray put the equipment into the autogiro, Chase filled the gasoline tank and Mary Eliska gave the boat a hasty inspection. Apparently everything was ship-shape.

They climbed into the cockpits and Mary Eliska started the rotors in motion. It was Chase's first experience in an autogiro, and he watched her with absorbed interest. The ease with which the Ladybug rose into the air seemed nothing short of miraculous to him, accustomed as he was to the prolonged taxi-ing of a fast plane.

With the aid of her maps and compass, Mary Eliska was able to judge their location pretty definitely, and she flew westward to the Gulf of California, aiming to stop first at an airport to make inquiries about the Sky Rocket, and to refuel. They passed over the plateau, and caught glimpses of several Mexican villages, which, however, seemed too small to boast of airports. At last, however, about noon, she spotted a town of some size, with beacon sign-posts, pointing to an airport. Here she made her landing.

"We'll be out of luck if they don't speak English," remarked Jax Gray.

"Don't worry about that," returned Chase. "I can speak Spanish, and they all understand that down here."

But it wasn't necessary, for one of the attendants at the field spoke English perfectly.

"Have you seen a yellow biplane?" demanded Jax Gray, as the man came out of the hangar. "A fast plane?"

The attendant nodded.

"Yes," he replied. "I did. We got a radio yesterday, telling us to be on the look-out for a stolen plane. I'm pretty sure I saw her yesterday, but she didn't stop here."

"She wouldn't," remarked Jax Gray, bitterly.

"What direction did she take?" asked Mary Eliska.

"Straight across the Gulf. Due west."

"Due west for us, then," announced Mary Eliska. "Fill up my tanks, for we want to leave with all possible speed."

Inside of ten minutes they were off again, more encouraged than they had been since the beginning of their pursuit. It looked now as if they really might catch those criminals.

In their eagerness to follow hot on the trail, not one of the three fliers even thought of lunch. Later in the day they were to regret this omission sorely.

An hour of flying brought them to the coast, but Mary Eliska did not stop. Out over the water she flew, her heart beating rapidly with the expectation of victory ahead.

But in her excitement, she had not realized how wide the Gulf of California was at this southern part. Two hundred miles, at least, if she kept her course straight. She had covered only a little more than half of this, when she saw to her horror that her main tank was exhausted. Twelve gallons of gas in the emergency supply, and almost a hundred miles to go!

What a fool she had been, not to put an extra tank into the cockpit! To think that after all her experience, she should be endangering three lives by her carelessness! To be forced down in the water! To meet death in a way she had not thought of, since her flight across the Atlantic Ocean!

She slowed down her speed and gazed all about her at the limitless expanse of water beneath them. No land in sight—not even a boat to which she could signal. Parachute jumping would be of no use, and she did not carry life-preservers.

She glanced again at the indicator; conserving gas as well as she could, it was nevertheless rapidly disappearing. Ten minutes more, perhaps—and then a watery grave! She grew panicky, more for her companions than for herself. She would have to tell them of their fate.

Trying to keep her voice from shaking, she called into the speaking-tube:

"We're out of gas. We have to come down. Be prepared to jump clear of the ship!"

Chase and Jax Gray looked at each other in incredulity. The young man thought Mary Eliska was joking, but the girl knew that it was not her chum's habit to make ghastly jokes. If Mary Eliska said danger, she meant it. Desperately Jax Gray reached for the glasses and peered anxiously about them in all directions.

Mary Eliska, her lips tight and her heart tense, continued to guide the plane and to watch the indicator. Five minutes more, perhaps—and then—what? The hungry waves, tossing beneath her, seemed to make their greedy answer.

A sudden hysterical cry from Jax Gray sounded above the roar of the motor.

"Land!" she shouted, wildly. "Bank to the right!" And then, fearing that Mary Eliska had not heard her, she repeated her message through the speaking-tube.

Although Mary Eliska could still see nothing with her naked eye, she did as she was told, thankful that she was high enough in the air to gain considerable distance by gliding. Two minutes passed; the gas ran dry, but now the island was in sight. By careful manipulation, Mary Eliska thought she could make it.

With a series of side-slips, she gradually made her approach, coming nearer and nearer to the land as she descended, until she was actually over it. Then, with a dead-stick landing, so much easier with an autogiro than with an ordinary plane, she slowly came down on the sandy soil of the beach!

"Oh, thank Heaven!" cried Jax Gray, in an ecstasy of relief. "A miracle, if there ever was one."

Chase said nothing for a moment; he was speechless with admiration.

"Pretty tight squeeze," admitted Mary Eliska, as she wiped the perspiration from her face. "If it hadn't been for you, Jax Gray, I'd never have seen it."

Still trembling from their experience, the girls climbed out of the cockpits with Chase's assistance. At last the young man found words to express his admiration to Mary Eliska. But she was too ashamed of her lack of foresight to accept any praise. She was still terribly vexed with herself.

"Now we'll have to explore," announced Jax Gray. "Do you suppose anybody lives on this island?"

"I'm afraid not," replied Chase. "Or they'd have been here to see us by this time. It looks pretty barren and forsaken to me."

"No trees! No shade at all!" added Jax Gray.

Nothing, indeed, but a dry underbrush, and the sort of weeds that grow in sandy soil. The little group walked all around the island, and found it to be very small. Probably it was not even shown on most maps, though Mary Eliska did recall seeing some Jax Grays in the southern part of the Gulf. And of course nobody lived there.

Dismally they came back to the beach where the Ladybug was resting.

"Is there any food left at all?" asked Chase, trying not to appear too eager.

"Not a crumb," replied Jax Gray. "Though we do still have about a gallon of water."

"The first thing to do," he said, "is to climb up on the plane and hoist a signal of distress. So we'll catch a ship, if one goes past. If you'll get me something to put...."

He glanced shyly at the girls. As they were both in khaki flying-suits, there was no chance of using a white skirt or petticoat, as he had so often read of, in books about ship-wreck. But Mary Eliska immediately procured a large square of canvas which she kept on hand for repair, and he did the climbing at once.

When he came down again, he produced the fishing-line which he had improvised that morning and set about to try to catch a fish. Mary Eliska spent her time inspecting the plane, and Jax Gray went about gathering underbrush for a fire, in case Chase was lucky enough to secure a catch.

Each of the three had taken a deep drink of water, resolutely trying to stave off their hunger by that means.

An hour passed, and another, without any sign of a boat, and the girls began to wonder whether they would have to spend the night on this tiny island, without any food. They were sitting back on the beach, near to the autogiro, talking a little, and searching the waters often with the glasses for the sight of a ship. The sun was already low against the horizon.

"I wonder how far we are from the peninsula," remarked Jax Gray. "Maybe we could swim."

"Not on an empty stomach," returned Mary Eliska. "Besides, we must be pretty far. According to my figures.... Oh, look, Jax Gray!" She jumped gaily to her feet. "What! A boat?" cried her companion.

"No. Only Bert—with a fish! But it surely does look good."

"Light your fire, Jax Gray!" the young man called as he approached. "The fish is cleaned— all ready to fry."

"You're an ace!" returned the girl, looking admiringly at the young man in his flier's suit, and his rumpled hair and cheery smile. How different he looked from the first time the girls had seen him—as a stern detective in Von Goss's office. It didn't seem possible that they had known him only a few days.

She lighted the fire, and half an hour later they ate their scanty supper. If anyone had ever told them that fish without any bread, or even salt, would taste good, they would not have believed it. But now they found it extremely satisfying.

"I'm going right back again," said Chase, when they had finished eating. "If I have to fish all night, I'm determined to get something for your breakfast!" "You—won't—have—to," announced Mary Eliska, slowly, handing her glasses to Jax Gray. "I'm sure I see a boat!"

CHAPTER 9.12
THE ENEMY PLANE

The three young fliers stood on the beach, waiting for the approaching boat in excited suspense. She was nearer now; there was no doubt that she was answering their signal.

It was a large, flat steamboat with wide decks, which were packed with passengers who were peering at the lonely little island, and waving cheerily at the three survivors. It approached rapidly; when it was within calling distance of the island it stopped and let down a life-boat, which two men rowed to the shore.

"Shall we all get aboard?" inquired Jax Gray, turning to Mary Eliska.

"I think I'd rather not," replied Mary Eliska. "If they can supply us with some food, I think I'd better stay here. You see, I don't like to leave the Ladybug alone."

"What do you suggest, Mary Eliska?" asked Chase, as if he, too, considered her the guide in this situation.

"That you go to the mainland, Bert—or to the peninsula, whichever the boat happens to be headed for—and bring me back some gas."

"You mean leave you two girls here alone?" he asked. "It'll mean all night—before I can get back."

"Yes. Why not? We'll be safe, unless a shark comes to shore and bites us. But for goodness' sake, don't forget us!"

"I'll never forget you," replied the young man solemnly.

The life-boat had reached the island by this time, and two men jumped out and leaped to shore.

"This is wonderful of you!" cried Jax Gray. "We certainly are grateful."

"Glad to do it," replied one of the men, a big, brawny sailor. "But do tell me what that thing is." He pointed to the autogiro. "It looks like a plane, but I never seen a plane like that before."

"It's an autogiro," explained Chase. "And we ran out of gas—almost dropped down in the Gulf.... So, if you can take me to shore, I'd like to get some and bring it back here."

"Sure," replied the man. "But what about the ladies?"

"We've decided to stay here," replied Jax Gray. "At least, if you can supply us with some food to keep us 'til tomorrow morning. We're nearly starved."

"Sure," repeated the man, "anything you say!"

Chase and the two sailors climbed into the rowboat and pushed off immediately. Inside of ten minutes they returned, bringing a box of food with them, and a tank of ice-water.

"How much do we owe you?" inquired Mary Eliska, taking a bill from her pocket.

"Nothin'!" answered the man. "The Captain says it's a present, with his compliments."

"I think that's awfully good of him," said Jax Gray, lifting the lid of the box and peering hungrily inside. "And it looks like real American food, too. Biscuits—and ham—and eggs!"

"Mexican chickens lay the same kind of eggs that American chickens do," observed Chase, dryly.

"That'll be enough out of you!" retorted Jax Gray, trying to look scornful, but laughing in spite of herself.

"Be sure to get something to eat for yourself, right away, Bert," put in Mary Eliska.

"We'll take care of that," the sailor assured her, as the men returned to the boat.

"And come back soon!" added Jax Gray.

The rowboat went back to the steamer, and the girls remained on the beach watching it, all the while waving and smiling to their rescuers. At last the steamboat pulled off, and disappeared from view; then they returned to their fire and built it up again.

"This is going to be a meal worth eating!" exclaimed Jax Gray, as she unpacked biscuits and butter, ham, eggs, and coffee. "Even oranges and bananas!" she added, hardly able to wait until they should begin to eat.

They sat about their fire talking until long after darkness came on, and the stars appeared in the sky. Both girls felt happy now—only anxious to be after their enemy again.

"I'm so sorry for the delay," remarked Mary Eliska. "More on Mr. Eckert's account than my own. If I could only get his plane back, I shouldn't worry so much about that forged check for five thousand dollars."

"It's the idea of what that girl got away with that exasperates me," said Jax Gray. "Making all that money on your name. It's maddening."

"But she's sure to be caught sometime, by the police. And then she'll have to pay up."

"Yes, but I want her caught soon—and by us, if possible."

"Well, tomorrow's a new day," said Mary Eliska hopefully. "And you never can tell what will happen. Now—let's get some sleep."

So, wrapping up in their blankets, they lay down in the sand, far inland, lest the tide should rise, and slept until the sun awakened them. A delightfully cool breeze was blowing from the ocean, reminding the girls of pleasant days at the seashore.

"Only it reminds me more of that island off the coast of Georgia," returned Jax Gray, when Mary Eliska made this observation.

"It does look something like it. But oh, such different circumstances now. We're not Robinson Crusoes here. We've got everything we want—food, and the Ladybug, and Bert Chase to rescue us."

"Speaking of Bert," put in Jax Gray, "let's get a good swim before he gets back."

They acted upon the suggestion immediately, and enjoyed their dip immensely. What a thrill it gave them to bathe for the first time in the Gulf of California! Almost like going into the Pacific Ocean. But they did not venture out far, or stay long in the water. They wanted to be all ready for Chase when he returned, so that they could be on their pursuit again as quickly as possible.

"I like your boy-friend, Mary Eliska," said Jax Gray, taking up the conversation where they had left it when they went in to bathe. "But it's nice to have him out of the way for a while."

"I don't see why you call him *my* boy-friend," returned the other girl. "He's just as much yours."

"He is not! Haven't you noticed how he's always watching you? As if he couldn't take his eyes from you. Pure devotion, I'd call it."

Mary Eliska laughed and began to run a comb through her wet hair, arranging the ringlets in place. She had a lovely natural wave—a gift which saved her a great deal of time at hairdressers'. No matter where she was, or how she was dressed, she always looked pretty.

"I think you're exaggerating, Jax Gray. He's never said anything to make me think he especially likes me."

"All the more credit to him! But just the same, I'll bet Ralph Clavering wouldn't feel any too easy about him."

Suddenly Mary Eliska sighed.

"What's the matter?" demanded Jax Gray. "That wasn't a sigh of hunger!"

"No, it wasn't. The mention of Ralph made me feel just a little bit homesick. Not for him especially—but for the whole crowd, and for Aunt Sally and Daddy. We've only been gone about ten days, but it seems ages and ages!"

"Because so much has happened."

"Yes, and because we have been in such strange places. And the days have been long too."

"What do you suppose everybody is doing by now?" inquired Jax Gray.

"Most of them are at college, I suppose. Sue Emery and Sara Wheeler are rooming together. And Jim and Ralph both must have gone back. I don't know about Harriman Smith. The last letter I had from him, he said he wasn't sure whether he'd have enough money."

"He's a nice boy," was Jax Gray's comment.

"One of the best," replied Mary Eliska, with unusual enthusiasm for her. "But Jax Gray," she continued, as they began to make their fire for breakfast, "don't you regret not going to college?"

"No, not a bit. I get lots more thrills batting about the country on adventures with you. If I were at college, and learned that you were suddenly off to California—or to the North Pole, I'd be absolutely sick with jealousy. I'd probably drop everything and go. And then, of course, college would drop me."

"You're an old peach, Jax Gray!" exclaimed Mary Eliska, giving her chum a hug. "But some day I 'spose I'll have to lose you, as I did Lou. Jim'll decide that he just won't wait any longer, and you'll be going up the aisle to the tune of Lohengrin!"

Jax Gray dimpled, but shook her head.

"You needn't worry about that, Mary Eliska," she said. "But if the time ever comes, I'll tell you what you can do: Get married yourself! And then you'll have a chum who won't ever desert you!"

"I'm not so sure about that—these days.... Now, shall we have our breakfast?"

"I'm all for it," agreed Jax Gray, sitting down to the pleasant meal they had just cooked.

The boat bringing Chase with the gasoline did not arrive until eleven o'clock. It took some little time to get the tanks of gasoline into shore, for the men dared load only one at a time on the rowboat. And Chase had brought three.

"Greetings!" he called to the girls, as the small boat approached. "You're still alive? Nothing happened during the night?"

Jax Gray laughed merrily.

"You sound like Mary Eliska's aunt, Bert. She always expects the worst."

"Well, I didn't really think there was anything much you girls couldn't conquer. Only something like a big tide, that would sweep the whole island away."

He filled the empty tanks of the autogiro, and put the other two cans into the passenger's cockpit. As soon as the rowboat pulled off, the young man turned excitedly to the girls.

"I've got hot news!" he announced. "A yellow biplane was sighted yesterday, flying with all possible speed towards the Pacific Ocean. I got that from Los Angeles headquarters last night."

Mary Eliska's eyes sparkled with excitement.

"We'll be right after them," she said. "Oh, if we're only not too late!"

"It's a peach of a day," commented Jax Gray. "If it is hot."

"Heat doesn't bother me," returned Mary Eliska, climbing into the cockpit, and setting the rotors in motion. "Get in—if you're coming with me!"

Mary Eliska gave her the gun, and the Ladybug left the beach a minute or so later, soaring triumphantly into the skies.

"We're going to fly high, now!" shouted Mary Eliska. "And we're going to make speed!"

The outlines of the island faded and disappeared from their sight; even the water was lost to their view. The Ladybug flew as if she were on a test flight, to prove her ability to take part in any kind of service. Mile after mile disappeared as Mary Eliska watched her instruments and her map closely, for now she could figure just about how far she had to go to reach the coast of the peninsula. All the while Jax Gray scanned the air with the glasses, looking for a flash of yellow in the sky.

"We are over an airport town now," Mary Eliska announced about one o'clock. "Shall we come down for lunch?"

"No! No!" returned her companions. "We'll dig out something from the box, and eat as we go. On to the coast!"

They continued onward for an hour or so, landing once to refuel from an extra tank of gas. Now Mary Eliska dipped lower, anxious to watch the landscape, for she knew that she must be very near to the Pacific Ocean. She identified the roofs of a village—a little seaport town, probably—and yes—there was the ocean beyond!

"I'd go south for a while, Mary Eliska!" Chase advised. "The report was that the Sky Rocket was headed southwest."

So Mary Eliska banked and directed her course along the coast to the southward. Flying low, and watching the ground for an airport. From the air they were able to identify scattered seaside huts, and even fishing boats out on the ocean. But no town of any size, and no sign of an airport.

"We ought to land and make inquiries," Mary Eliska was thinking to herself, when Jax Gray suddenly let out a piercing scream. Terrified, Mary Eliska looked all about her, thinking they must be rushing headlong into some awful peril.

"I see the plane!" Jax Gray cried, frantically. "Over there on the beach—to the left!"

Mary Eliska peered out to the side her chum indicated, but she could distinguish nothing but a blurred outline of green.

"The Sky Rocket!" screamed Jax Gray. "Bank to the left!"

Though she still failed to see it with her naked eye, Mary Eliska's heart beat rapidly with the thrill of success, and she took the direction Jax Gray indicated. She dipped lower, and banked to the left, approaching the spot slowly. And then, sure enough, she saw it for herself. The Sky Rocket!

The beach was wide and the plane stood erect, as if all ready for a take-off. Suppose it sailed off this moment! Before Mary Eliska could get to it! The Sky Rocket was bigger, faster, newer than the Ladybug—wouldn't it be sure to get away in a race?

While these thoughts were running through her head, she kept her eyes glued upon the plane, approaching it cautiously. Nearer and nearer she came—but still the Sky Rocket did not move. What was Sprague's game now? Would he wait for her to land, and shoot from under cover?

Down—down the Ladybug came. To death? Or at least a struggle? Reaching instinctively for her revolver, Mary Eliska landed the autogiro on the beach, about a hundred yards from the enemy plane.... And—waited!

CHAPTER 9.13
HOT ON THE TRAIL

Chase, his hand on his revolver, climbed out of the autogiro and slipped cautiously around the side. He kept his eyes riveted on the Sky Rocket, but there was no movement whatsoever.

"They're probably hiding," he whispered, as the noise of the rotors died out. "You girls stay right here, and creep up on them."

Jax Gray and Mary Eliska did as they were told. In tense silence they watched the young man advance nearer and nearer to the Sky Rocket, expecting every moment to hear a shot ring out from the underbrush that grew along the beach.

It was a deserted spot; there were no cottages or boathouses about. The only sound was the breaking of the waves, with monotonous regularity, upon the shore.

Chase got nearer and nearer; he actually came up to the yellow plane, and peered all around it. Still there was no sign of human life anywhere. He looked into the cockpit; then he sauntered towards the scattered bushes on the beach, examining them with his glasses. And still nothing happened.

Unable to bear the suspense any longer, the girls came out from behind the Ladybug and started to advance towards the Sky Rocket. At the same time Chase, satisfied that the enemy was nowhere about, proceeded slowly back to meet them.

"We're too late again," he observed, gloomily. "They've abandoned it, there's no doubt of that. Evidently got scared and decided to leave it."

Running up to the plane, Mary Eliska began to examine it eagerly.

"It seems to be in good condition," she said. "And that certainly is a lucky break. If I couldn't get both, I'd rather have the plane than the girl!"

Chase regarded her in amazement.

"But she has your money!" was his comment.

"I know. But I care more about Mr. Eckert's plane—it's worth a whole lot more than five thousand dollars. And he was such a good sport to lend it to me. I can just imagine how dreadfully he'd feel, if he thought he'd never see it again. I know how I felt when I lost the Ladybug."

"But where do you suppose they have gone?" asked Jax Gray. "The Spragues, I mean."

Mary Eliska dropped down to a sitting position on the sand and fished in her pocket for a map.

"They must have taken a boat from somewhere near here," she said. "So if we can find out where we are, and the nearest seaport town, we might be able to catch them before they sail."

"We're pretty far south on this peninsula," put in Chase, looking over Mary Eliska's shoulder at the map.

"Yes, I think so…. You know what I believe would be best, Bert? If the Sky Rocket is in good condition—we'll look her over in a minute and find out—one of us could fly her south along the coast, and another take the Ladybug north. In that way we ought to pick up news of our honeymooners pretty quickly."

"Good idea!" returned Chase, immediately. "Which plane do you want, Mary Eliska?"

"I think I'd rather have the Sky Rocket," returned the girl. "If you can manage the Ladybug. Because if I should find out that the Spragues have sailed somewhere in a boat, I might like to pursue them. And the Sky Rocket can go so much faster, and carry enough gas for a trip across the United States."

"It's all one to me," agreed Chase. "If you'll trust me with the Ladybug."

"Certainly," Mary Eliska assured him. "Now I think I'll go look the Sky Rocket over, and tighten some of those wires that I see out of 'stream-line'. That makes a lot of difference, you know."

Mary Eliska finished her job in less than an hour, and after they had eaten the remainder of their food supply, she gave Chase a few instructions about flying the autogiro. Satisfied that he knew how to manage it, the girls insisted that he take off first, flying back north along the sea-coast.

"And when you're through, you can park the Ladybug at the Los Angeles airport," concluded Mary Eliska. "I'll pick her up there, after the girl has been caught—by us, or somebody else."

She and Jax Gray stood watching the young man take off and soar into the air, until he was finally lost to sight. Once again they were alone, but with more hope of success than they had had before. Now both planes had been regained, and they had the Sky Rocket to rely on. They felt, with it, that they had the world—or better still, the air—at their command.

"There must be a seaport pretty near here," said Mary Eliska, as she and Jax Gray climbed into the powerful yellow plane. "If the Spragues haven't left from there, they at least ought to be able to find out by wire what vessels have left the coast."

She flew straight down to Cape San Lucas, a seaport town, which boasted of a sizable airport. It was terribly hot here, when she brought the plane to the ground; the heat seemed to rise in waves to hit them in the face as the girls climbed out of the cockpits. For the airport was located behind the town, and that morning no ocean breezes brought cooling refreshment to landward.

It was a large airport, and it kept attendants who could speak all the principal languages. The man who came forward, a Mexican, surprised the girls by speaking perfect English.

Briefly Mary Eliska told him the facts of her story—about the stolen planes, which had since been regained, and the forged check for five thousand dollars. But she said nothing about the part in the talking-picture, or of the girl's having taken her name. There was no reason, she felt, for emphasizing that point or drawing publicity to herself.

"So we think this couple have sailed," she concluded. "Though under what name, we don't know. Probably neither Sprague nor Bower, but something else, to fool us, and throw the police off the track. Our first desire is to find out what big vessels have left this vicinity today or yesterday."

"I'll get in touch with the docks immediately," the man assured her. "Though I think can tell you myself. A vessel named the 'Mona' left here yesterday for Hawaii. There isn't another until day after tomorrow, which sails for South America."

Mary Eliska's eyes shone with excitement.

"Hawaii!" she exclaimed. "I always did want to fly the Pacific!"

"You wouldn't try it!" he cried, in horror.

"Why not?" she demanded. "It's only a matter of about two thousand miles—less than a non-stop flight across the United States. And I have a marvellous plane."

"You mean—this?" he asked, pointing to the Sky Rocket.

"Yes. She's a marvel, even if she has only one motor. She can make a hundred and fifty miles an hour, and is equipped with all the newest inventions and improvements."

"I can see that.... But the danger—in any kind of plane," he remonstrated. "No woman has ever attempted it, and plenty of airmen have found a watery grave in the Pacific."

"Well, some woman has to be first," returned Mary Eliska. "I'll think about it, anyway. In the meanwhile, I think I'll go down to have a talk with the men at the docks.... By the way, have you an expert mechanic?"

"The very best!"

"Then please have him give the Sky Rocket a thorough inspection. Doubly thorough, for tell him what I am contemplating. And have him take a look at the wireless that is already installed. And fill her up with gas and oil."

"O. K.," agreed the man, shaking his head as if he thought Mary Eliska were crazy.

"Oh, yes—and could you get me a rubber life-boat?" she inquired.

"At considerable cost."

"Well, get me one if you can, and have it put in," said Mary Eliska, as if she were ordering an ice-cream soda.

"Then you really are serious about going?" asked the man, unable to believe she meant what she was saying.

"If I find good reason to think that couple sailed for Hawaii," she replied. "But not if I don't. It isn't a stunt, you see."

The girls left immediately in a taxicab for the dock. Here they saw numerous small boats and yachts, and it occurred to Mary Eliska to wonder whether the missing couple might not have gone off in a pleasure boat. But after all, they couldn't get far in the Pacific in a yacht, unless it were one specially built for the purpose, and the idea seemed improbable.

They made their inquiries about the couple of a sailor.

"Yes, there were several young couples among the passengers that left for Hawaii yesterday," he informed them. "About thirty passengers, all told."

"But did one of the young couples look like honeymooners?" demanded Jax Gray.

"Can't say as I noticed. But you can look at the list of passengers in the office. That ought to tell you."

He led the girls through an open door, where they found the book on the desk with the name of the boat, the "Mona," and the list. But, as they had expected, neither the name of Bower nor of Sprague occurred.

"If that girl were using her own maiden name, we shouldn't even know what it was," remarked Jax Gray, gloomily.

"True," admitted Mary Eliska, thinking how strange it was that once again they were involved in complications with a nameless girl. But, unlike poor little Helen Tower, who had been nameless because of a cruel accident wherein she lost her memory, this girl was deliberately, criminally, nameless.

"Were there any couples in flying costumes?" asked Jax Gray, thinking perhaps that if the Spragues had hiked from the plane, and speed were their object, they wouldn't have had time to change.

But such a course would have been too obvious, and would have given them away immediately. As she expected, the sailor shook his head to the question.

"Any with hand-luggage?" suggested Mary Eliska.

"Yeah. A couple of couples."

"Now we're getting there! Can you describe them?"

"Can't say as I could. Didn't look at 'em, to tell you the truth. Only I do recollect our baggage man sayin' he was gipped out of two tips, so these two guys must of carried their bags theirselves."

"Let's go see him," suggested Jax Gray.

"He's a Mexican. Don't speak English. But maybe I can explain to him what you want."

They walked about the dock until they found a man who was sprawled on a truck-van, smoking a pipe. The sailor explained what the girls wanted, and the man sat up and stared at them.

Mary Eliska could hardly restrain a shudder. She thought that she wouldn't care about meeting this man alone in the dark, or in the desert. But he seemed pleasant enough. And, to their delight, he gave them the information they wanted. Pointing abruptly at Mary Eliska, he told the sailor in Spanish that one woman looked like that girl!

Before the sailor had even interpreted his meaning, Mary Eliska and Jax Gray had jumped to the correct conclusion and were wild with excitement. Nothing could keep them back now, short of a cyclone. If the weather held like this on the morrow, they would be on their way to Hawaii!

"That settles it!" announced Mary Eliska. Then, turning to the sailor, she inquired the exact destination of the "Mona."

"Honolulu," was the reply.

"Then I'll send a wireless there now," she said, and proceeded to write out a message.

"Hold all passengers of the 'Mona' for identification at Honolulu dock. Two criminals aboard.... Signed, Mary Eliska."

"The Captain ought to pick up that message, too," she remarked, turning to Jax Gray as soon as the words had been sent. "And the thing for us to do now, is to make sure that we beat that boat to Honolulu!"

Realizing their need for rest and food, the girls went back to their taxi and directed the driver to take them to the best hotel the seaport afforded. Here they engaged a room for the night and proceeded to make themselves comfortable. After they had their baths, they stretched out on the bed in their room, shaded and darkened by awnings from the hot sun, and began to discuss the proposition seriously. They realized now how suddenly they had plunged headlong into what really might be the experience of a lifetime—an undertaking that took most fliers months and months to prepare for.

"Do you think we ought to go, Jax Gray?" asked Mary Eliska, over-awed for the first time at the dangers of the project, when she considered them for somebody besides herself.

"I'm dying to go!" cried the other girl, her eyes sparkling with anticipation. "There's only one thing that might hold me back."

"What's that? You mean consideration for your parents?"

"No. They'd be willing to let me do anything you considered safe. It's just that if I didn't go with you, you could take a more experienced flier in my place—or a mechanic or a navigator. And that would be better and safer for you."

"Nonsense!" laughed Mary Eliska. "I can do those things, and if anything goes wrong, you can take the controls. You certainly fly well—I'd trust you a lot farther than a good many boys I know—like Ralph Clavering, for instance. You're air-minded—you have air sense, to put it another way—and you never get rattled. You can take charge if I want to rest—though it isn't nearly so far as Paris, and I flew that alone."

"That's true," agreed Jax Gray. "It isn't even as far as if we were taking off from Los Angeles." She was pleased, more than she could say, at her chum's praise, for Mary Eliska never said anything she didn't mean.

"Yes, we're a lot farther south than Los Angeles—almost in a direct line westward."

"Are you going to tell your Aunt Sally?" inquired Jax Gray, after a moment of silence.

"No, I think not. I don't believe I'll tell anybody except the people at this airport. Then, if anything goes wrong, we shan't have a lot of unpleasant publicity. Besides, it's all the better for our cause to keep it a secret. It's not an aviation feat this time, like flying the Atlantic. The main object is to catch those two criminals."

"Then we won't call Spring City on the telephone?"

"No. Let's send wires, assuring our families of our safety, and telling them not to expect us home for several days. That will put their minds at rest, and won't disclose anything."

"What about food?"

"Enough for a day. I figure that if we start before dawn tomorrow, we ought to land early in the morning of the following day. So, while I am mapping out our course, you can go visit the chef and see about packing sandwiches and fruit and coffee. That ought to be enough. And we'll eat an early breakfast before we start."

"What are the predictions for weather?" "Favorable and warm."

"It doesn't seem possible that we're going so soon," observed Jax Gray. "It's the way I like to do things," returned Mary Eliska. "With a snap—and we're off! Let's have an early supper, about six o'clock, and get in bed by nine. And leave a call for three o'clock tomorrow morning."

"Three o'clock! The time lots of young people are getting home from dances!"

"Well, this is going to be more thrilling than any dance you ever attended, Jax Gray!"

"It's going to be the thrill of a lifetime!"

"I hope it is. I really believe it will end happily, or I shouldn't be taking you along, for I am the one who's responsible. The Sky Rocket can carry a good load, and we're both so light that I can easily put in a big extra tank of gas for emergency, in case we get off our course."

"And if that runs out, or anything else happens, we'll go to sea in a rubber life-boat!"

"I hope we shan't have to," said Mary Eliska.... "But now we really must get to work. I'm going to get out my maps. It'll be a pretty hard job to locate those little islands in that vast expanse of ocean."

"If we only don't run into a fog!" commented Jax Gray.

"But if we do, there's the good old earth-inductor compass to guide us. And besides, our course lies pretty straight westward."

For the next few hours the girls scarcely exchanged a word, so busily were they employed upon their duties. Jax Gray sent the wires and interviewed the chef of the hotel, and Mary Eliska pored over maps and diagrams, running her fingers through her hair, marking her course with her pencil. At six o'clock she telephoned to the airport with final instructions. Then, dressed as they were, for all their dresses were still at the Los Angeles hotel, they went down to dinner.

The dining-room was warm in spite of the fans, and it seemed exactly like midsummer to the girls, although it really was October by the calendar. But San Lucas was much farther south than Spring City, Ohio.

There were not many people in the dining-room, for it was an early hour to dine. How thankful the girls were that they were not at the Ambassador, crowded as it always was with motion-picture people and visitors! They ate their meal slowly, then retired to their room to work quietly until bed-time.

And so, at nine o'clock they prepared to go to sleep, conscious that their next night would probably be spent on the ocean—an adventure which would either end in disaster, or would make a story that would go down in history, of the first young women to fly the Pacific Ocean.

Only time could answer that question!

CHAPTER 9.14
OVER THE PACIFIC

The gray dawn of early morning found Mary Eliska and Jax Gray at the airport of Cape San Lucas, all ready to take off on their momentous journey. More than two thousand miles over the biggest ocean in the world, without a single stop!

The Sky Rocket was already on the runway, in perfect condition for the trip. Her high-powered Wright engine was performing as excellently as an expensive watch; her instruments were in tune, her tanks filled. The wireless had been tested, and found to be working, and the rubber life-boat which Mary Eliska had ordered was tucked away in the plane.

"What are the weather predictions for this morning?" Mary Eliska inquired of the mechanic, as Jax Gray put the lunch into the cockpit.

"Good for at least twenty-four hours," he replied. "But that's not the only danger, Mary Eliska." He shook his head ominously. "This is sure suicide," he predicted.

"Why?" demanded Jax Gray. "Isn't the motor in perfect condition? There isn't anything wrong, is there?"

"No. She's O.K. Oiled her up a bit, and tightened a few screws. It isn't that. But you'll run into a typhoon, or lose your way—"

"It's a pretty straight course," said Mary Eliska. "We're on the Tropic of Cancer now, and Hawaii is just a little below it. It looks like pretty easy navigating to me."

"You're welcome to it. And—happy landing!"

Mary Eliska and Jax Gray lost no time in getting started. Five minutes later the Sky Rocket was triumphantly rising into the air, heading straight towards the ocean. Over the weeds and rough seashore growth on the beach, past the waves breaking on the shore of the Pacific! The sun had not yet risen, but it was light enough to see where they were going. On they flew; now the waves seemed higher, but the air was calm.

There was little wind, so Mary Eliska continued to fly low, so that they could make use of the cushion of air on top of the water. And it was thrilling to watch the ocean—more exciting than seeing it from the deck of a boat.

"It does seem calmer than the Atlantic," observed Jax Gray, in a loud tone. Seated side by side as they were in the companion cockpit, it was not necessary to use the speaking-tube, and for this advantage they were grateful. "They say that's why it was called the 'Pacific.'"

"It's beautiful, anyway," returned Mary Eliska, admiringly.

On and on they flew, ever westward, as the sun rose in its full glory behind them. Soon the land was lost to view; there were no vessels in sight—only limitless sky and ocean, and two girls alone in that vast, empty universe. But both girls were in high spirits; neither was the least bit afraid.

Climbing a little higher, Mary Eliska opened her throttle to its maximum, and found themselves travelling at a speed of a hundred and fifty miles an hour. The girls laughed and sang at the joy of the exhilarating motion, but they did not attempt to talk. There was so much to think about—the fun of the flight, and the triumph of landing in Hawaii, ahead of that boat, the "Mona." Oh, if they only made it!

Water everywhere—and the sky overhead. Noontime came, with the sun right above them, and the girls realized that it had been a long time since they had eaten. Jax Gray made a dive for the coffee and sandwiches, divided off as they were in portions for lunch and supper and breakfast, and both girls ate ravenously. When they had finished she insisted that Mary Eliska take a rest.

With a yawn and a stretch, Mary Eliska willingly complied, and gave the controls over to the other girl. It would afford her not only an opportunity to relax, but a chance to study the maps as well.

"We've covered eight hundred miles already," she shouted in Jax Gray's ear. "And we're sticking straight to our course."

"How's the gas holding out?" returned her companion.

"Fine. I think we'll have some left over, at this rate.... Now Jax Gray, if you're all right, I think I'll take forty winks. Even that blazing sun doesn't seem to keep me from being sleepy."

The other girl nodded, and Mary Eliska slipped off to sleep. Even the bumps in the air seemed to have no effect upon her slumbers; for an hour perhaps, she slept soundly, while Jax Gray continued on the flight. Then, all of a sudden she was abruptly awakened by a terrified cry from her companion. The plane was dropping—it seemed to be diving right into the ocean—into the very jaws of death!

For one brief moment Mary Eliska thought of the life-boat, but that did not seem feasible now. Instinctively she grabbed the stick, and pulled it back sharply. The Sky Rocket wobbled almost on the surface of the water, and at that very moment a hideous, terrifying shark poked its head above the surface!

For one awful second death stared them in the face. Not the easy death of drowning, but a horrible torturing agony at the jaws of a ferocious fish. The plane seemed to hover uncertainly for a moment; then with a sudden lightning speed it gathered control and started to climb upward—to safety!

Mary Eliska let out a gasp of relief, and Jax Gray sobbed in contrition as the Sky Rocket soared into the air.

"I don't know how I could have done it," wailed Jax Gray. "All of a sudden, it seemed as if we were headed straight for the ocean, and nothing could stop us. If you hadn't taken hold that very instant, we'd have been killed."

"It was a lucky escape," returned Mary Eliska. "And from now on we'll make it a point to fly higher, even if we can't use the wind to such advantage, as we could right over the water."

The afternoon passed, with the motor still functioning perfectly. The wind increased somewhat, but not enough to disturb Mary Eliska greatly. She was continuing to fly high, for she didn't want to run any risk of hitting that deep, terrifying ocean again. A little before sunset they sighted a ship.

"I'm going a little lower," she shouted to Jax Gray. "Get your glasses. We'll see whether that's the 'Mona.'"

"It is!" exclaimed Jax Gray, a few minutes later. "I suppose we're too far south to meet the regular Los Angeles-Hawaii lines. But we must be following about the same course as the 'Mona.'"

"Keep a watch-out for the girl-friend!" advised Mary Eliska.

Down they glided, keeping the ship in sight until they were about a hundred feet over the water. It was a small boat—not nearly so large as the regular San Francisco-Hawaii line; and they could see the people hurrying to the deck, peering through their glasses, and waving and shouting in greeting. Jax Gray, too, did her share of the searching.

"I don't see them," she said.

Mary Eliska looked intently, but she could not distinguish the passengers' faces. However, she did not think it was likely that Sprague or his wife would be waving to them. They would surely recognize the plane.

"Probably they've been keeping off the decks," she said. "Hiding, as much as possible, without arousing suspicion."

"Maybe the girl's seasick," observed Jax Gray. "I only hope she doesn't pass out and get buried at sea, before we ever have a look at her, or a chance to collect that five thousand," remarked Jax Gray.

Mary Eliska regained her height, and sped onward, determined to get to Hawaii well in advance of the boat, and to lie in wait for the criminals. The blood was rushing through her veins, and she was thrilled with the chase, but she resolutely kept calm. The worst of the trip—the black night—was ahead of her, and she needed every ounce she had of energy and nerve.

The plane was still doing well over a hundred miles an hour, and going forward with mighty gains, eating up the miles. The sun set and once again the girls ate some sandwiches and drank more coffee.

"I'm almost afraid to offer to take the controls and let you rest," said Jax Gray, humbly. "After the way I fell down before."

"It was the Sky Rocket that did the falling," laughed Mary Eliska. "But I guess that wouldn't happen again. You'll stay up high, I'm thinking."

"You'll trust me again?"

"Certainly, Jax Gray. Don't be so foolish. Besides, I want to do a little calculating."

Relaxing back in her seat, Mary Eliska consulted her maps and her sextant, when suddenly she heard a queer noise. The motor was knocking in a strange, ominous way that almost made the girls' hearts stop beating. Was it going dead? Panic-stricken, Jax Gray looked down on the ocean, hoping that she could see the "Mona," or some other ship that might rescue them, and Mary Eliska's thoughts turned to the wireless.

The tapping was growing worse; the engine seemed to be dying. Mary Eliska racked her brain for a reason; surely the gas hadn't given out. Telling Jax Gray to keep on guiding the plane, she examined the feed-valve. And here she located the trouble!

A broad smile of relief spread over her face. "I can fix that, easily," she assured her companion. "Just hang on for a couple of minutes."

She was as good as her word; soon the knocking ceased, and the engine was running as smoothly as when the Sky Rocket left Cape San Lucas. And Mary Eliska herself was back at the controls, urging Jax Gray to avail herself of a nap while she had the chance.

It was entirely dark now, and the stars were shining in the sky, and reflected in the ocean, making a beautiful picture for the girls as they flew on. Phosphorescent lights, too, played through the water, reminding Mary Eliska of the dangerous life beneath.

Towards ten o'clock, while Jax Gray was taking her nap, they had one more terrifying experience. Suddenly, for no reason at all, they started to fall. Yet the engine was not dead, nor was their motion slow enough for a stall. There was only one explanation, of course: an air-pocket. Down, down they came, like an elevator whose cords have been broken. Jax Gray wakened up with a scream and the beads of perspiration stood out on Mary Eliska's forehead, for she believed that this time the sea was really about to swallow them.

But she had been flying high, and this proved to be her salvation. She tried banking the plane, first on one side and then on the other, breaking the fall, but making both herself and Jax Gray dizzy with the sickening motion. Her head swam; she hardly knew what she was doing, and there was the black water beneath them. But at last a current of air swept under the wings, assuring her that she was out of danger once more. Making a sharp turn away from the air-pocket, she found her plane responding to the stick as she started to climb back again to the height she had lost.

The girls breathed freely again, and Jax Gray, now wide awake, produced coffee from the thermos bottle, for they felt in need of a stimulant. But, as the plane flew fearlessly on, and the flight again became monotonous, Jax Gray fell asleep once more, and Mary Eliska continued, waking and watchful.

She watched the stars fade gradually from the sky, and the first gray light play over the sea. Tensely alert, she glanced eagerly at her speedometer. If her calculations were correct, there were only three hundred miles more to go!

It was considerably lighter when Jax Gray finally opened her eyes.

"Fine companion I am!" she exclaimed, in shame. "To go to sleep like that. Leaving you as lonely as you were on your Atlantic flight!"

Mary Eliska reached over and touched her hand affectionately.

"Don't you believe it, Jax Gray!" she said. "It makes a big difference, having you here.... And if you're awake now, I'd like to have you take control. I want to do some figuring. Now that we're getting so near, I want to locate the islands. Suppose we'd miss them, after coming all this distance!"

"Suppose we would!" repeated Jax Gray. "And never realize it 'til we landed on the coast of Australia!"

"We'd know it before then. Our gas would give out somewhere in the middle of the ocean."

"Well, we're not going to miss them!"

It was, as Mary Eliska said, one of the most difficult parts of the flight, to locate those tiny Jax Grays of islands in the vast expanse of ocean. But Mary Eliska was a good navigator, and she made her calculations correctly. They were, she discovered, only about fifty miles off their course—an error which was easily remedied, since their gas supply was adequate.

"A hundred miles more!" she announced, when she finally resumed control. "Now we can watch for the sea-gulls!"

Nearer and nearer to their destination they came. Now Jax Gray spied some fishing craft with her glasses, and that fact told her that the shore must be near. Her excitement was so intense that she could hardly sit still. The end of her first ocean flight! Her first landing from over the water!

"We're coming!" she shouted, in wild exultation.

Mary Eliska was almost equally thrilled, although her pulse was calmer. It had been less terrifying, less difficult, less nerve-racking than the solitary, long flight over the Atlantic. But she was nevertheless excited.

Now the cliffs rose from the ocean, and the waves broke against the shore, showing their white-caps. And, as if to stage a dramatic arrival, the sun rose in all its glory, shedding its beams over the land and water.

The green island of Molokai was beneath them!

But this was not their destination, and Mary Eliska pressed on.

"Aren't you going to land?" cried Jax Gray, in disappointment.

"No," returned Mary Eliska. "We are making for the island of Oahu. I must come down in Honolulu."

On they flew, past Molokai, directing their course southwest, over the indigo waters of the Pacific, now so beautiful in the sunlight, then swinging north towards the capital city of the Hawaiian Islands. Now they saw speed boats and launches on the waves; they passed the great Diamond Head, and Waikiki beach, and hovered at last over the Rogers Airport on the coast. "Honolulu!" cried Mary Eliska, joyously. "We are here!"

As the girls looked beneath them, it seemed for a moment as if the airport were a bed of flowers. Garlands of leis and gardenias filled the air with a strange and wonderful fragrance. Then, as Mary Eliska dropped lower, she realized that these flowers were all in the arms of people standing about the ground. People of every race and color.

"Who are all those people?" demanded Jax Gray. "Do you suppose there's been an accident?"

"Oh, I hope not!" replied Mary Eliska. "I'll keep on flying over the field until they scatter. I mustn't hurt anybody." She brought the Sky Rocket lower, and gave a signal that she wanted to land.

But already policemen were busily pushing the crowd back, making a clear runway for the plane. When Mary Eliska thought it was safe, she gracefully glided to the ground.

Even above the noise of the engine, the girls heard the wild shouts of the multitude. "Hello, Mary Eliska! Hello, Jax Gray!" seemed to rise from every direction, and flowers were strewn in their path. "Welcome to Oahu!"

The girls stared at each other a moment in consternation, not understanding how these people could possibly be informed of their names. But only a moment, for the crowd rushed in, and it took all the policemen's efforts to hold them in check. A small and select group of half a dozen or so were admitted close to the plane. From this group, a couple of young fliers stepped forward and lifted the girls right out of the cockpit.

"Congratulations to the first girls to cross the Pacific!" they cried, as they put garlands of leis around their necks. Then, with Mary Eliska and Jax Gray on their shoulders, high over the heads of the crowd, the boys carried them to a waiting car.

"Aloha!" shouted everyone as they passed. "To our heroines of the air!"

CHAPTER 9.15
THE ISLAND OF OAHU

"But how did you know about us?" gasped Jax Gray, as she found herself miraculously seated in a shining, low car at the edge of the flying field. "We didn't tell anybody about it."

Both the young men grinned broadly.

"A special late edition came out last night with the announcement," explained one of the boys. "A Los Angeles paper. And every newspaper in the United States and Hawaii will run the story this morning. Besides, a ship you flew over yesterday sent a radio that you had been sighted!"

The car moved slowly through the space blocked off by the policemen, and Mary Eliska and Jax Gray smiled and waved to the crowd as they passed.

"Where are we going now?" asked Mary Eliska.

"To the Governor's mansion. There's a big breakfast waiting for you. Then there will be a reception tonight. Did you know that you will receive an award of ten thousand dollars, to be shared between you?"

Mary Eliska and Jax Gray looked at each other in amazement. They had undertaken the flight with no thought of glory or reward, and they were winning applause from the whole world. It was nothing short of miraculous!

But what would their own relatives think? Aunt Sally, and Mr. and Mrs. Gray—and Mary Eliska's father, who hadn't even been informed of the project? Was it too late now to send them telegrams?

"We each get five thousand dollars?" repeated Jax Gray, incredulously. "But why? Who is giving it?"

"A wealthy woman in Honolulu promised that amount some time ago to the first woman to fly to Hawaii from the coast of America. The only point she stipulated was that there was to be no man in the plane. So, if two girls made the flight, she said she would divide the prize."

"So you'll get the five thousand back that you lost, Mary Eliska!" exclaimed Jax Gray. "Now you won't have to catch that girl."

"But I'm going to catch her," Mary Eliska insisted. "Not for the money, especially, but because I've made up my mind to do it."

The automobile threaded its way through the streets of Honolulu, on to the Governor's mansion. Here the girls were received with the greatest cordiality by the chief executive's wife. A lovely breakfast, to which all the important aviators of the island were invited, was served on the wide veranda, and a suite of rooms had been set aside for the girls' visit.

"I suppose you will want to take a nap first," said their charming hostess. "Then, after you have rested, perhaps you would like to go down to our beach and bathe."

"We'd love it!" cried Jax Gray, eagerly. "Think of the thrill of going in bathing in October!"

"Then this evening," continued the older woman, "is the banquet, followed by a reception in your honor at the hotel. And Mrs. Dinwitty, the donor of the award, will present you with your checks."

"It's all just too wonderful!" exclaimed Jax Gray. "But what shall we do for clothes? We can't attend receptions in flying-suits!"

"I'll see that they are provided," promised the other. "We have marvellous shops in our city, and now that I know your sizes, it will be easy enough to order a supply."

As soon as she had left them, Mary Eliska went to the telephone in her room.

"I must call the police before we go to sleep," she said to Jax Gray. "We might miss our criminals."

The reply, however, was reassuring.

"The 'Mona' doesn't dock 'til noon tomorrow," an official assured her. "And we have detailed men to help you. We got in touch with the Los Angeles police after we got your wireless, and we made out a warrant for the arrest of the girl. We'll call you when the ship docks."

Reassured now, and at ease for the rest of the day, the girls slept all morning in the beautiful bedroom set aside for their visit, and after luncheon they were driven to the famous Waikiki beach, and lay on the sand and later rode the waves of the Pacific on the long, narrow boards which they had so often seen pictured in the movies. There was so much to do and see and enjoy that they wished that they might spend at least a month in this Paradise of the Pacific, as the Hawaiian Islands are so often called.

"It's hard to think of crime and criminals in a spot like this," remarked Mary Eliska, as she lay on the sand and gazed at the deep blue sky above her. "I purposely haven't mentioned them to our hostess—because I didn't want to spoil things. Today has been so perfect."

And perfect it continued to be, until the girls finally closed their eyes in sleep that night. The dinner and the reception were gorgeous affairs, yet the kindness of the Governor and his wife prevented them from becoming stilted and formal. Even Mary Eliska felt no embarrassment when she was called out and presented with the check. For Jax Gray was at her side, equal to the occasion with a clever little speech of acceptance and thanks.

Excitement had kept the girls going during the first day, but the next morning reaction set in and they felt as if they wanted to sleep forever. Their thoughtful hostess, realizing just what they had been through, decided not to have them wakened. Telegrams and flowers began to arrive, but she saw no need of disturbing Mary Eliska and Jax Gray. She did not know that they were counting on meeting the ship that was scheduled to dock at noon.

At last, however, Mary Eliska opened her eyes and reached for her wrist-watch that lay on the tiny table between her bed and Jax Gray's. It said twenty minutes after twelve!

She picked it up and examined it closely, unable to believe her eyes.

"Jax Gray!" she cried. "We've overslept! Do you suppose the police have called? And we've missed them?"

"Missed—who—whom—I mean?" inquired her companion, sleepily.

"The couple we're after! Sprague and that girl! Oh, Jax Gray, wake up!"

"What shall we do?" asked Jax Gray, realizing at last the seriousness of the situation.

"Get dressed at once!" replied Mary Eliska, as she rang the bell for the maid.

Almost miraculously the latter appeared in answer to the summons, with fresh sports-clothing for both the girls. And bringing telegrams and boxes of flowers.

"Have the police telephoned?" asked Mary Eliska, to the maid's amazement.

"Police? Oh, no, ma'am. There's been some calls for you, but not from the police. Are you expectin' them?" She eyed the girls suspiciously, as if she thought they might be criminals.

"Yes," replied Mary Eliska, her fingers already on the telephone, giving the number to the operator.

"This is Mary Eliska," she announced. "Has the 'Mona' docked yet?"

"No, ma'am. But she's due any minute now at Aloha Tower, just across Nimitz Boulevard from where your father Albert Stricklin was project manager and part owner of the twenty-stories twin towers Amfac Center, and the Chief gave me orders to call you. We've got a warrant ready for Mrs. Leslie Sprague—is that right?"

"That's it!" replied Mary Eliska, grinning with satisfaction. "And we'll be right over—so hold all the passengers until we get a look at them."

"O.K., Mary Eliska. See you later!"

Mary Eliska replaced the receiver, and turned to the maid, who was still awaiting her orders.

"Do you think we could have our breakfast right away—and then have a car take us to the flying field?" she asked. "Please ask your mistress—and tell her that it's terribly important."

"Aren't you even going to read those telegrams?" asked Jax Gray, a trifle disappointed. After all, it was her first big air triumph, and she wanted to enjoy the victory to its utmost. But, instead, Mary Eliska must be rushing off immediately.

"When we come back!" returned Jax Gray, as she put on the pretty white linen suit with which her hostess had provided her.

Jax Gray sighed, and proceeded to dress. There was no stopping Mary Eliska, once she had made up her mind to do something.

"I could go alone, Jax Gray," Mary Eliska remarked, as they started for the dining-room. "Then you'd have a chance to enjoy yourself this afternoon."

"No," replied her chum. "It isn't going to take long, and I wouldn't miss it for the world. You know how I despise that man Sprague—I want to gloat over his capture."

They ate a hasty meal that was both breakfast and lunch, and got into a car with a native chauffeur, that was waiting for them in the driveway. A few minutes later they arrived at the Aloha Tower dock, just as the passengers from the "Mona" were about to be discharged.

It would have been difficult to press through the crowds of native children, with their flowers of welcome for the arriving visitors, had the girls not had the aid of the Chief of Police. Clearing a passage for himself and his companions, he led them right on board the "Mona." The Captain came forward to meet them, beaming proudly at the two brave aviatrixes, as he shook their hands.

"Congratulations, Mary Eliska and Jax Gray!" he exclaimed. "You did a valiant thing!"

"Thank you so much," replied Mary Eliska, modestly. She had no desire to talk of her flight over the Pacific; her one absorbing interest now was the capture of the girl whom she had pursued so far.

"Stand here," continued the Captain, "and you can watch the passengers as they go by."

Two by two the people on board the "Mona" walked over the gangplank to the pier, as Mary Eliska and Jax Gray, their hearts beating fast with excitement, peered intently into their faces.

A dozen couples hurried by, then three lone passengers straggled along as if in no haste at all. But still no girl that even remotely resembled Mary Eliska. And no sign of Leslie Sprague.

"Is—that—all?" faltered Mary Eliska, unable to believe that they really had not come.

"Here's one more couple. They're still awful seasick," explained the Captain, and Mary Eliska and Jax Gray strained their necks to catch the first glimpse of these last people, just emerging from the cabin.

But their hopes were immediately dashed to the ground. The couple were elderly; their hair gray, their faces wrinkled.

"Maybe it's a disguise," whispered Jax Gray, suspiciously.

The Captain shook his head.

"No. I know these people well. Cousins of mine, by the name of Rankin. Lived on Oahu all their lives."

Mary Eliska heaved a deep sigh of disappointment.

"And you're sure that's positively all the passengers who sailed from Cape San Lucas?" she asked.

"All except a couple that docked at the island of Lanai. A planter who lives there part of every year—and often makes the trip. I know him well—have brought him across half a dozen times. He had a new bride with him this trip."

"A new bride!" repeated Mary Eliska. "Did she look like me?"

The Captain regarded her closely.

"Believe she did.... But that man's not a criminal. He couldn't be the fellow you want."

"Well, whether the man is or not, the girl is!" cried Mary Eliska. "What name did they give?"

"Steve Long is the man's name. He didn't have to give it—I know him."

"Light hair—light moustache?" she questioned.

"Sissy-looking!" added Jax Gray.

The Captain smiled.

"That must be your man," he agreed.

"So we have to fly to Lanai," muttered Mary Eliska, turning to the Chief of Police. "Can you help me out?"

"You mean go with you?"

"No, not necessarily. I'd rather not overload the plane.... Isn't there somebody on the island who would help us?"

"Of course there is. I can send a wireless to our agent over there, and you can report to him. He can give you native police, if you need them. And give you the warrant for the girl's arrest."

They completed their arrangements, and had the chauffeur drive them immediately to the airport, where the Sky Rocket had been resting since their landing the preceding morning. Here they dismissed the car, asking the driver to make their explanations to his mistress, assuring her that they would be back in time for dinner. Mary Eliska then went in search of her plane.

"What sort of shape is she in?" she asked, as she spied the Sky Rocket in a hangar, with a mechanic beside her.

"Fine!" replied the man. "We did some overhauling on her yesterday—a few minor repairs, and filled her up with gas and oil. She's fit as a fiddle now.... But why? You girls aren't thinking of flying back over the ocean, are you?"

"No!" laughed Mary Eliska. "Once is enough. But we want to go to one of the islands—Lanai, to be exact—to do some scouting. We're after a criminal."

"A criminal?"

"Two criminals, rather. Forgers—thieves. They came across on the 'Mona,' and we thought they'd dock here—but they got off at Lanai instead."

"By heck!" exclaimed the mechanic in amazement. "What will modern girls take up next?"

"Can you tell us what that island is like?" asked Jax Gray.

"Well, it's not like Oahu," he replied. "Not a place that tourists visit much. No hotels and stores—or cities. Mostly pineapple plantations there—not many white people, except some of the owners.... But I'll get you a map, and show you just where to land if you want to go to the agent's office first. He can tell you all about it."

He disappeared into an office, and returned with the map in question, marking the best spot on the beach for Mary Eliska to make her landing. Then he had the Sky Rocket pushed out on the runway, and the engine started.

"Watch the planes that arrive and leave here," Mary Eliska shouted into his ear as she climbed into the cockpit.

"I'll be on the job!" the man assured her. "And happy landings to you!" The Sky Rocket taxied along the runway, and left the ground a minute later, as if it, too, were eager to be in the skies again, on the chase. Over the beach of Waikiki, past Diamond Head, southeast over the Pacific Ocean again, Mary Eliska directed her course, sure that at last she was within sight of her goal.

CHAPTER 9.16
MISSING!

The girls had been away from Spring City for ten days when Albert Stricklin, Mary Eliska's father, returned from his trip abroad and arrived at Aunt Sally's home, expecting, naturally, to see his daughter.

"Hello, Sally!" he exclaimed, walking in as he so often did, without any notice, and kissing his sister nonchalantly, as if he had been absent a week instead of six months. "Where's Mary Eliska?"

"Hollywood," was his sister's reply.

"No!" exclaimed the man, in a tone of deepest disappointment. It had always been a matter of extreme satisfaction to him that Mary Eliska had never been carried away by the lure of fame and fortune, and accepted a motion-picture contract.

"Don't look so horrified, Tom!" laughed Aunt Sally. "I only wish she were safely acting for the movies. Instead of that, she's chasing wildly around Mexico after a couple of criminals."

"Mexico!"

"Yes. And I'm so afraid of bandits there."

"Now, Sally, you're judging Mexico by the movies. That sort of stuff has gone out long ago. Mexico City is as civilized as New York."

"Mexico City—yes. But that isn't where Mary Eliska's telegram is from, and that isn't where she'll be. Trust her to find some lonely wilderness! Oh, I'm so worried. In fact, I'm packing now to go out to Los Angeles."

Albert Stricklin sat down and lighted a cigar.

"You might as well tell me the story," he said.

Aunt Sally made it as brief as possible and showed her brother the telegrams she had received thus far. The man listened quietly, more worried than he cared to admit to his sister, but then and there he decided to go with her.

He would have preferred to fly by the commercial air-line, in order to save time, but since Aunt Sally stubbornly refused to get into a plane, he agreed to take the fast train on which she had already engaged passage.

A few hours later, just as they were about to leave the house, a very excited young man rushed into the living-room, without even waiting to ring the doorbell. It was Ralph Clavering, who always had the right to come and go as he pleased.

"I've just heard the news about Mary Eliska and Jax Gray!" he exclaimed. "And so Jim Valier and I are flying to the coast in my autogiro immediately."

"What news?" demanded Aunt Sally, turning pale. Did he know more than she did—and had something terrible happened to her darling niece?

"About chasing off to Mexico. Jax Gray's mother showed me the telegrams. Believe me, I'm scared this time. Those girls may be dead by now."

"Now—now—Ralph, please be a little more tactful!" urged Albert Stricklin. "Don't scare my sister to death with your gloomy conjectures."

"I'm scared to death myself," muttered the boy, sullenly. "That's why I'm going. There's nobody out there to help her—not even Ted Mackay, or that young reporter that saved her from burning to death. I've got to go!"

"Of course, that's fine of you," agreed Albert Stricklin. "But don't get all worked up about it. I'm betting on Mary Eliska and Jax Gray every time!"

"How about your college work?" questioned Aunt Sally.

"I can't be annoyed with classes when my best girl's in danger," replied Ralph. "And Jim feels the same way about Jax Gray."

"We're just ready to go too," announced Aunt Sally. "But not by plane."

Ralph smiled; he did not need to be told that.

And so that morning in early October four people departed from Spring City to go to the rescue of those two daring young fliers, who never expected help from anyone.

When the news came that Mary Eliska and Jax Gray had safely reached Honolulu, Ralph and Jim had already arrived at the Los Angeles airport, and Aunt Sally and Albert Stricklin were well on their way to the West.

Their train had stopped at Santa Fe for a few moments, and newsboys were shouting the story.

"Two girls fly the Pacific!" they screamed. "All about the flight to Hawaii!"

Albert Stricklin looked at Aunt Sally. "Could it be Mary Eliska and Jax Gray?" he demanded. Aunt Sally nodded.

"Of course. They would. I knew it. The Pacific Ocean would be too much of a temptation to Mary Eliska, once she was out here. I've been fearing it all along."

"But you don't have to fear it any longer—if it really is they who did it. It'll be over by now—and the danger past."

He stepped to the platform and bought a paper. And, sure enough, his daughter's and Jax Gray's pictures stared at him from the front page.

There was no hiding his pride now. His eyes shone with happiness; he looked like a small boy who sees his favorite pitcher win a baseball game.

"Look! Look! Sally!" he cried, as he came back to her chair. "Read what it says for yourself!" And she noticed that his hands were actually shaking.

A wave of pride and admiration surged over Aunt Sally as she read about the two dauntless girls. The first of their sex to make this flight over the gigantic ocean—from the United States to Hawaii. They had evidently made up their minds in a hurry, and had not told anyone except the people at the airport from which they took off.

But the feat had evidently not been accepted so casually by others, for already, they read, the girls were being feted. Entertained by the Governor of Hawaii—a reception planned in their honor—and five thousand dollars apiece to be presented to them!

"And to think we came out to rescue them!" laughed Aunt Sally.

"I wonder what Ralph and Jim will think of this news," remarked her brother.

"Ralph will probably be jealous because he didn't make the flight with Mary Eliska— instead of Jax Gray. But Jim will just be filled with admiration."

"I like Jim," observed Albert Stricklin.

"Yes, so does everybody," agreed his sister. "He's so good-natured, even if he is lazy. But he's really true-blue, all the way through. And if Jax Gray marries him, she'll certainly keep him stepping."

"Do you still want Mary Eliska to marry Ralph, Sally?" inquired the other. "I remember how excited you were at her graduation, because he had evidently fallen so hard for her. With all his wealth and social position."

The woman smiled a little and shook her head.

"I've learned my lesson, Tom," she said, "in this year and a half since Mary Eliska's been out of school. I had expected her to have a year of parties—to 'come out,' you know—and then marry some nice young man. But Mary Eliska has plans of her own, and I realize now that I might as well save my time as to try to arrange anything for her.... And, as for wealth and social position—well, they simply mean nothing in her life. Besides, she doesn't need them; I can see that. Mary Eliska could go anywhere, be accepted at Court, if she wanted to, because of what she has accomplished herself."

"I'm glad you've got so much sense, Sally! Lots of women of your age wouldn't see that at all."

"I didn't at first. But I do now. And so I think, when she marries, it must be somebody as big as herself. It won't be Ralph Clavering—unless he does cave-man stuff, and actually kidnaps her."

"Even then, she'd probably find a way to escape. She always does get out of the most difficult situations."

"Yes. When Mary Eliska marries, I think it will be love at first sight—on the spur of the moment, just as she evidently decided to take this flight to Hawaii. It will seem to her to be the one, the only thing to do—and she'll do it. I'm sorry, for I'd love a big wedding for her—she'd make such a beautiful bride—but I'm not going to count on it."

Albert Stricklin nodded approvingly. Like most men, he couldn't see the use of the big fuss a formal wedding entailed. But though he knew Mary Eliska was tremendously interested in aviation, he didn't want her to miss the happiness that marriage would bring her. His own had been blissfully happy during its short duration, until his wife died at her baby daughter's birth.

"Yes, Mary Eliska will decide for herself," he muttered. "I only hope that the man will be worthy of her."

"He couldn't be. No mere man could possibly equal Mary Eliska," remarked Aunt Sally.

"How you love to tease, Sally!" retorted Albert. "But I guess you're right at that."

The rest of the journey seemed longer than ever, now, to the impatient couple who longed to be with the girls to celebrate their great triumph with them. Never did a train seem to move so slowly. But, at last, it arrived at Los Angeles, about seven o'clock of the night on which Mary Eliska and Jax Gray came down in the wilds of Oahu, at the cabin of their enemies.

"We'll take a boat to Honolulu tomorrow," announced Sally. "I only wish we could take it right away—if there were only one sailing."

From out of the crowd on the platform two young men, hatless and sun-burned, edged their way toward the girls. Both were tall, so that they could easily be seen above the heads of the other people around.

"Greetings, Mary Eliska!" called Ralph Clavering, before he had even reached them. "We've got bad news."

"Bad news!" repeated Albert Stricklin, in consternation. "But we read in the papers that the girls arrived safely in Honolulu!"

"Yes. They did, sir. But they're lost again!"

Aunt Sally seized Ralph's arm, to steady herself, and looked into his face.

"You're not joking, Ralph? You wouldn't—joke about a thing like this?" Her voice was trembling.

"Indeed I'm not, Aunt Sally," replied the boy, earnestly. "I'm worried sick."

Albert Stricklin, however, looked less troubled than Aunt Sally.

"No, I know you're not joking, Ralph," he said. "But you probably are exaggerating. You always see the black side of everything. You and Aunt Sally are just alike.... But let's go over here and sit down, and suppose Jim tells us the story."

They went to one of the waiting-rooms in the station and sat down together, Aunt Sally struggling hard to get herself under control. Suppose Mary Eliska had taken it into her head to fly back—and she and Jax Gray were now lost at the bottom of the Pacific! Suppose—But Jim was already explaining.

"Well, we don't know much that you haven't read in the papers," he began. "The girls went to the dinner and the reception in their honor last night, and were staying at the

Governor's mansion. We were going to sail for the island this morning, but there was no boat 'til tomorrow, so we called them on the telephone.

"That was about eleven o'clock this morning, and we were told that they were still asleep. We phoned again at one, and they had gone out.

"So we sent a couple of telegrams and waited. We asked them to call our hotel here at Los Angeles. But by seven o'clock there was no message, and we sort of got mad. At least, Ralph did. I thought maybe they had too much to do, but Ralph thought some new bird like that Englishman Mary Eliska fell for last summer was taking her time, and he resented it.

"But I persuaded him to give them another chance, and we phoned again. This time the Governor himself talked to me. And he was really scared.

"It seems Mary Eliska and Jax Gray had gone to the airport right after they got up about noon, and had taken the Sky Rocket for a flight—"

"The Sky Rocket?" interrupted Albert Stricklin. "Has Mary Eliska a new plane?"

"Temporarily—yes. The Ladybug is here at Los Angeles.... But that's another story.... Well, anyhow, the girls promised to be back early, for a dinner that had been planned in their honor but they haven't been heard from!"

"Murdered! Attacked by some tramps, of course!" cried Aunt Sally. "And no man with them to protect them!"

"Nonsense, Sally!" returned Albert Stricklin. "They probably ran out of gas—or damaged a wing. Or had a missing spark-plug. Mary Eliska will fix that, and those two girls will show up tomorrow morning."

"I wish I could think that, sir," said Ralph. "Gosh, if I only had my bug over there on that island! But I haven't the nerve to fly it."

"No, don't!" pleaded Aunt Sally. "It would only add another disaster to our troubles. No, we'll sail together tomorrow morning."

"In the meanwhile, let's go to our hotel and wash and have dinner," suggested Albert Stricklin. "Then things may look brighter. I positively refuse to worry 'til I have just cause!"

"Wise man!" commented Jim Valier, as he picked up Aunt Sally's bag.

So the little group had dinner together at the Ambassador, waiting all the time tensely for news. But none came. And the newspapers duly reported the story that the dinner for two famous aviatrixes had been postponed!

CHAPTER 9.17
CAPTURE

The flight across the Pacific from Oahu to Lanai took less than two hours. Early in the afternoon Mary Eliska brought the Sky Rocket to a landing on the beach of the lonely island, near to the spot indicated on her map.

"That must be the agent's shack over there," she said, as she and Jax Gray climbed out of the cockpit. "I hope he's there."

The girls walked along the beach a short distance. How different it was from Waikiki! How deserted! Yet just as beautiful in the bright sunlight. Before they reached the shack, however, a man in a linen suit came out to meet them.

"Mary Eliska and Jax Gray, I suppose?" he inquired, holding out his hand. He was a pleasant-faced man of middle age, with a tanned complexion and eyes as blue as the waters of the Pacific. "My name is Jardin. I have the wireless from Honolulu."

"Then you know all about us," said Mary Eliska. "Can you take us to Steven Long's plantation?"

"Yes, I can. But it doesn't seem possible that that man is a criminal. What are the charges against him?"

Briefly, Mary Eliska told the facts of her story.

"But those are all charges against the girl," Jardin pointed out. "You haven't anything against Long."

"He stole two planes," insisted Jax Gray.

"You mean his wife stole them. I don't think that man can fly."

Mary Eliska and Jax Gray looked at each other in disappointment. How awful it would be if they couldn't bring Sprague to justice! For they believed that he was responsible for the whole affair.

"Well, we've got plenty against the girl—if she is the one you're seeking," concluded Jardin. "So I'll get my runabout and drive you over to their plantation."

"Wait!" interposed Jax Gray. "A plane's coming! Who can it be?"

"Probably only some of the coast guards," explained Jardin, gazing up at the approaching monoplane. It was the type used by the U. S. fliers in their patrol about the islands.

Nearer and nearer it whirred; a moment later it swooped down on the beach a short distance from them. The pilot climbed out of the cockpit, and the girls, recognizing him instantly, uttered a wild cry of joy. It was Bertram Chase!

"Bert!" they both cried at the same time, as he rushed forward and seized their hands. "What miracle brought you here?"

"I found out about your flight at the Honolulu airport," he replied. "You might know I'd come after you, no matter where you went!"

"But what are you doing in Hawaii?" demanded Jax Gray.

"I sailed from Los Angeles the very night I left you—after I put the Ladybug into the airport. We're on the track of a counterfeiter, and a clue pointed to Honolulu. Money turned in at a bank there. So I was sent to Hawaii. Lucky break for me!" He looked admiringly at Mary Eliska.

"That's great!" exclaimed Jax Gray. "Leave your plane here and come along with us in Mr. Jardin's car. We think we're going to nab Mary Eliska's double at last."

Mr. Jardin took the wheel of his runabout and Mary Eliska sat beside him. In the rumble-seat behind, Jax Gray and Bert Chase laughed and talked excitedly of the adventure.

Over the beach, through lanes that could hardly be called roads, the little car threaded its way into the heart of the island. Fifteen minutes later, within sight of a low, straw-covered bungalow, it came to a stop.

"This is Long's place," announced Jardin. "Do you all want to come in with me?"

"Certainly," replied Jax Gray, her eyes sparkling with anticipation.

Along a path overgrown with ferns and flowers, in thick profusion, the little party went single file to the veranda of the bungalow. Not a person was in sight; the place looked empty. Had Sprague and his wife run away again—or were they only hiding?

Jardin stepped boldly up to the door and rapped. A Hawaiian boy answered his summons in a minute or two.

"Meester Jardin," he said, with a grin of welcome.

"Is your master about?" asked the agent.

The boy nodded and beckoned for them to come inside.

The room to which the door opened was deserted. A plain, bare room, with only a few rough chairs, a table, and a hard cot. Not exactly the kind of place a woman would enjoy.

"I get him," said the boy, indicating for the visitors to be seated, and going out of the front door again.

Mary Eliska and Jax Gray sat down upon the hard chairs, but Chase wandered aimlessly around the room, examining its scanty contents with curiosity. Another Hawaiian boy came in with a pitcher of water, and Jardin inquired for Mrs. Long.

"She sick," he explained, briefly, pointing to another room beyond, and he, too, disappeared.

They drank their water, and waited tensely. Why didn't the man come? Did he suspect something? Chase continued to walk about the room, peering with interest, at the closed door where the girl was supposed to be lying, stopping now at the table beside a window, and picking up a little tool that looked like a nut-pick, that was lodged in a crack between the table and the window-sill.

"What's that, Bert?" asked Jax Gray idly, not because she cared about knowing, but just for something to say.

"Looks like a dentist's drill to me," remarked Jardin, with a shudder.

But Chase was holding it up, examining it closely, his eyes staring with unbelief. He had made a discovery!

"I'm going to investigate this place!" he announced, putting the little instrument into his pocket. "See you later." And he went out of the front door.

"Now what do you suppose—?" began Jax Gray, but she stopped abruptly, for at that moment a door at the back opened and Long came into the room. He, like Jardin, was wearing a linen suit, and a big hat, but there was no mistaking the man. As Mary Eliska and Jax Gray had insisted, he was none other than Leslie Sprague!

If he was startled by the sight of the two aviatrixes, he did not betray the fact by his expression. Whatever he felt, he covered his surprise by a grin.

"Afternoon, Jardin," he said, calmly shaking hands. "How are you?"

"Afternoon, Long," replied the agent, looking questioningly at the girls.

"How do you do, Mr. Leslie Sprague?" asked Jax Gray, triumphantly.

Sprague shrugged his shoulders and laughed.

"A name I used in connection with moving-pictures," he explained to Jardin.

"Where is your wife, Long?" asked the agent, desirous of getting this business over as quickly as possible. "If she is the girl these young ladies believe her to be, we have a warrant for her arrest."

"Poor Fanny's sick," replied Sprague. "Too bad to arrest her now, when she feels so rotten.... Besides, it was only a prank." He looked understandingly at Jardin.

"A prank!" repeated Jax Gray, in disdain. "A prank to steal two planes, chloroform both of us, and forge a check for five thousand dollars!"

Sprague laughed uncomfortably.

"You must be mistaken, Miss—er—Manton." He remembered Jax Gray's assumed name, and took pleasure in using it. "Probably Mexican bandits did that."

"Mexican bandits can't fly planes!" returned Jax Gray, defiantly.

"We will have to take your wife, Long," interrupted Jardin. "Go in and get her."

"Can't we arrest him?" demanded Jax Gray, resentfully.

"I don't see how we can, until we have something more definite," replied Jardin, who was evidently an easy-going person, who hated to suspect anybody. "We can hold him as accessory while his wife is being tried...."

He stopped abruptly, for Chase suddenly opened the door and walked into the room, dragging a man with him. A hard-looking fellow, with a sullen expression and a slinking gait.

"I have found my counterfeiter!" Chase announced triumphantly to Jardin. "And this is his accomplice!"

Still holding the man by the arm, the detective swung about and pointed his finger at Sprague.

"Steven Long is the criminal the U. S. Government has been searching for -- for a year! Long, alias Logman, alias Sprague—" He stopped, and laughed. "To think that I saw this man in the studio of the Apex Film Corporation—even tried to help him out—and never knew who he was! The joke is on me!"

"But you've got him now!" cried Jax Gray, unable to restrain her delight.

All eyes were turned upon Sprague. He was not laughing now. Rather, he was cowering, deathly pale, holding on to a chair for support. He did not even demand how Chase had discovered his secret. But Jardin asked immediately.

"It was this little instrument I picked up out of the crack," explained the young detective, producing the tool that resembled a nut-pick. "I recognized it as an engraver's tool. I wondered why it should be here. And then I had an inspiration to search the place. Where could a counterfeiter work better than here on this lonely island? Under the guise of a pineapple planter?"

"But is that all the proof you have, Chase?" demanded Jardin, impatiently.

"Not by any means. That was only the beginning. I wandered about the place 'til I found another shack, hidden almost completely by camouflage. But I got in. And caught this fellow—" he shook his captive's arm—"in the act of engraving fifty-dollar bills!"

Deliberately, then, he reached into his pocket for two pairs of handcuffs, which he calmly proceeded to fasten upon the wrists of the two men. A tense silence lasted while he performed this operation, a silence which was suddenly broken by the hysterical wail of a girl.

In a second the closed door of the bedroom was flung open, and Mary Eliska's double dashed into the room. Sobbing with fright, she threw herself at Mary Eliska's feet.

"I didn't know I was married to a criminal!" she wailed. "Oh, this is the end—the end of everything! I wish I was dead!"

Leaning over, Mary Eliska gently raised the girl to her feet, and for the first time, looked into the face of her double. The same blue eyes, and blond, curly hair; a nose not unlike her own, and a lovely, flower-like complexion. But oh, how different she looked, with that expression of terror and misery on her face, and the tears streaming from her eyes! Like Mary Eliska, and yet totally unlike her!

"Sit down,—Fanny," whispered Mary Eliska. "And try to control yourself."

The girl did as she was told, and Chase turned to Jardin.

"Let's take these men away in your car, Jardin," he suggested. "And come back for the girls. We'll send a wireless for a boat to come over from Honolulu and put them into the jail there."

"Is that all right with you, Mary Eliska?" inquired Jardin. "Can you manage Fanny 'til we get back?"

"Yes, that suits me," agreed Mary Eliska.

"Do you want to say good-bye to your husband, Mrs. Long?" asked Chase.

"I never want to see him again!" was the impassioned reply. "I hate him!"

So the four men went out, leaving Mary Eliska and Jax Gray alone at last with the girl who had made so much trouble for them. The girl who had pretended to be Mary Eliska!

CHAPTER 9.18
FANNY'S STORY

The three girls sat silently for a few minutes after the men had left. They heard the car start, and Fanny heaved a sigh of relief.

"Of course you hate me," she said, in a pathetic voice, turning her face towards Mary Eliska. "But I don't believe you can hate me half so much as I hate Les!"

Both Mary Eliska and Jax Gray looked at the girl in surprise.

"But you didn't have to marry him!" Jax Gray pointed out.

"I know. But I hadn't found him out then. I—I didn't know anybody could be so awful!"

Mary Eliska stood up.

"Suppose," she suggested, "we go outside where it is so much more beautiful—and hear your story, Fanny. I'd like to know just what did lead up to your pretending to be me."

The girl jumped to her feet. She didn't seem sick at all now; in all probability it had only been nerves.

"Wait," she said. "I want to get you something first." And she disappeared into the bedroom.

In a moment she returned, carrying a heavy bag in her hands.

"It's your money, Mary Eliska," she said. "That check I cashed. Les made me get it in gold—I guess he didn't want the bank numbers traced. Anyhow, I hid it, and never let him have it."

And she dropped the bag at Mary Eliska's feet.

"Why, thank you, Fanny," said Mary Eliska, in surprise. "I'll just leave it here 'til Mr. Chase comes back for us."

"Aren't you going to count it?"

"Oh, no. I believe you," replied Mary Eliska.

Tears came into Fanny's eyes. She seized Mary Eliska's hand gratefully.

"It's sweet of you to say that," she said. "But you better not leave it here just the same. You can't trust those native boys."

"True," admitted Jax Gray, and picking it up, she carried it for Mary Eliska out of the bungalow.

The girls walked along the path and settled themselves on the ground amongst the bright flowers and soft ferns. Now that Fanny had stopped crying, it was astonishing how much she resembled Mary Eliska. Both Mary Eliska and Jax Gray watched her intently, eager to hear her version of the story.

"Well," she began, finally, "I'll tell you first of all that I'm an orphan. I was brought up in a children's home—I don't remember my parents at all. But I had a pretty good education, and took a business course after I finished high school. My first job was with an airplane construction company."

"You mean you had a flying job?" interrupted Mary Eliska, with interest.

"No. I was a stenographer. But the boss did give me a chance to learn to fly—on the side. But there wasn't any hope of a job in aviation—I just worked inside the office for twenty-five dollars a week. And, like every other girl in the world, I never had enough money."

"Where did you work?" asked Jax Gray. "What city, I mean?"

"San Francisco. That was the trouble, I suppose. Too near Hollywood. I got the craze to go into pictures. Everybody told me I was pretty—and other girls succeeded—so why shouldn't I?"

"Naturally," commented Jax Gray.

"Well, I had some money saved up," continued Fanny, "and I tried to register at all the studios as an extra. But I soon learned how impossible it is to get into the movies in times like these. I couldn't land a thing—not even a part in a crowd!"

"I've heard they're using old actresses and actors for those parts—people who used to be stars—and even ex-directors," remarked Mary Eliska.

"It's true! And even some of those people can't get anything at all! People with years of experience go absolutely broke!... Well, my money dwindled and dwindled until I finally met Mr. Sprague. Not in a studio—but at a party. That was last June—only a little while after you made your famous Atlantic Ocean flight."

Mary Eliska nodded, wondering whose idea the masquerade had been. She asked the question.

"It was Mr. Sprague's," replied Fanny. "He saw the resemblance immediately to your newspaper pictures, and when he found out I could fly a plane, he told me I ought to cash in on it. I thought he was only joking, but he told me he was serious, and explained how you had refused movie contracts at enormous salaries.... Well, he kept after me, and when I found that I wasn't getting any parts, and that my money was all gone and even my old job in San Francisco, I gave in and promised to try it.

"Les planned everything—even rehearsed with me how I was to talk to Mr. Von Goss. And it was he who pushed through the aviation picture.

"Mr. Von Goss was lovely—he never asked me for any proofs of my identity at all, just signed me up for the picture, and it was Les who made me insist on the enormous salary. I acted stubborn, like Greta Garbo, and I got it.

"And then Les proposed to me. Told me that he'd invest my money, and give up his job at the studio and come over here to Hawaii to live after we were married. He said he had a plantation here, and that I'd never be discovered as the girl who pretended to be Mary Eliska. Oh, Les can be very charming if he tries, and he made me think we'd live on this island paradise in a perpetual honeymoon."

"Then you had no idea that he was also involved in anything that was crooked?" asked Mary Eliska.

"No. Absolutely none. I just thought that the masquerade was a clever trick, that wouldn't really hurt anybody, because you had refused movie contracts.... Well, to get back to the story.... Everything went well 'til you girls appeared. Of course we were prepared for that— Les had thought it all out ahead of time, in case you ever did show up. I came back to Los Angeles, as you know, in a hired plane, and was just about to land when Les gave me the pre-arranged signal not to come down. You remember—waving his hat on the field?"

Mary Eliska nodded, though she had hardly noticed it at the time.

"I flew off and landed an hour later at Culver City. And he pushed the rehearsals right through, and the next morning he told me to go right to the Los Angeles airport and demand your autogiro. We'd only borrow it, he said, to get away. I believed him, and did it, for I was anxious to be married and out of the country. We flew to Mexico, as you know, and got married.

"And I guess you know the rest. How we circled about you when we found out you were chasing us—and how we changed planes. But you don't know that Les made me fly that

Sky Rocket at the point of a pistol. He seemed to change then and there into a demon, and he had me frightened to death. Of course I realized what a horrible mistake it had been to marry him.

"Then he seemed nice again when we sailed on that boat, but when I actually saw you girls fly over the Pacific Ocean, it was too much for me. We recognized the Sky Rocket, and knew you were after us. I wanted to give up then, but Les said nobody would ever find us here at Lanai...."

"But didn't you know that he was a counterfeiter, after you lived here?"

"No, of course not. I never knew 'til this afternoon. Of course I'd often seen that man before—the one that the detective caught—but I thought he was just the overseer. Les has always been away from here most of the time, so he needed somebody to manage the plantation."

"Is there much of a plantation?" asked Mary Eliska, suspiciously.

"I guess not," admitted Fanny. "We do raise a few pineapples. But I never saw any great quantities. And there are only a couple of native boys working here."

"Well, you won't have to worry about your marriage, anyhow. So long as Sprague married you under a false name, and in Mexico besides, I guess it can easily be annulled. You won't have to see him again."

Fanny was silent, worn out with the tension of telling her story. Stretching back, she buried her face in the ferns. Mary Eliska and Jax Gray looked at each other in hopeless dismay. Here was the girl whom Mary Eliska had threatened to prosecute to the uttermost, completely in her power, and she felt only sympathy for her!

"You poor kid!" said Jax Gray, feelingly, as if Fanny were years younger than she was.

"Oh, I know it's my own fault," said Fanny, with a suppressed sob. "It was acting a lie in the beginning. But I never dreamed it would lead to anything like this. I thought if you—the real Mary Eliska—ever did appear, I'd just hand over the money, and maybe you'd give me back part of it for my work in the picture."

"I suppose," said Mary Eliska, "that we have to learn for ourselves that deceit never pays. But somehow, I can't be hard on you, Fanny. And I'll tell you why. It's because of the very first thing you told us—that you are an orphan. It's so much more difficult if you haven't parents to teach you. I—haven't a mother—but I have a wonderful father and a loving aunt.... So, somehow, I just feel as if I hadn't the right to judge you...."

Without raising her head from the ground, Fanny groped blindly for Mary Eliska's hand. And found it and pressed it gratefully.

The sound of a motor in the distance made the girls glance towards the lane. The car was returning.

"What are you going to do with me?" asked Fanny, plaintively.

"Take you with us, of course," replied Mary Eliska. "You can fly with Mr. Chase."

"And—when we get to Honolulu—shall I have to go to jail?"

Mary Eliska hesitated a moment and looked at Jax Gray. But her companion, usually so relentless in seeing that justice was done, had evidently softened too. She, also, felt a great sympathy for Fanny.

"I don't think so," said Mary Eliska. "I think you've suffered enough, Fanny. You've returned my money, and both planes, and if you'll return Mr. Von Goss's—"

"I can't!" interrupted the girl. "Les took that."

"Well, he'll be made to return it. So—if you'll promise to be good, I think we'll let you go free—if Mr. Chase can fix it up with the police."

The girl's blue eyes opened wide with appreciation.

"You really mean that, Mary Eliska?"

"Yes, I do."

"Oh, you are wonderful! So generous! So clever, too!" She lowered her eyelids. "And to think I ever dared to pretend I could be you!"

Mary Eliska flushed in embarrassment at this praise—from the girl she had been regarding as her worst enemy. Luckily she did not need to say anything, for the car had stopped now, and Jardin, who had returned alone, was getting out.

"I left Chase with the two prisoners," he explained. "Now you girls climb in."

"Oughtn't we to say something to the native boys who work here?" asked Fanny.

"I'll come back and talk to them later," replied Jardin. "After Long tells me what he wants to do with the plantation."

The ride back to the beach consumed only fifteen minutes, but Mary Eliska realized when she got there that the afternoon was gone. So much time had been spent at the plantation, waiting around, first for Sprague, and then for the return of Jardin. Though it was still bright sunlight, her watch indicated six o'clock.

"We had better send a wireless to our hostess," she said to Jax Gray. "To let her know that we can't be back in time for dinner."

Her chum nodded dismally. Another festivity passed up! But it had been worth while this time, for, at last, their purpose was accomplished.

Mary Eliska proceeded to send the wireless from the Sky Rocket, and then returned to the agent's shack, where Chase was still sitting.

"Will you take Fanny," she asked, "and when you get to Honolulu see whether you can have that warrant for her arrest nullified? We are dropping the charges."

The young detective stared at Mary Eliska in incredulous amazement.

"You don't really mean it?" he gasped. Mary Eliska laughed.

"I do, though. Fanny returned the money—and is sorry, so we're forgiving her. That's all there is to it."

"You stand there and tell me you're letting that girl off, after flying four thousand miles, over land and ocean, to capture her?" he demanded. Mary Eliska nodded.

"But why?"

"Because Mary Eliska's a Christian!" retorted Jax Gray, exasperated at the delay. Mary Eliska believes "to err is human, to forgive, divine." "But I warn you, Bert, I won't show Christian spirit towards you, if you don't stop talking and get a move on pretty soon. Do you realize we're starved—and we've got almost two hours' flight before we get any food?"

Chase grinned, and started towards the door.

"If you're willing to wait an hour," suggested Jardin, "I can take you all to my bungalow for supper."

"No, thank you, Mr. Jardin," replied Mary Eliska. "We want to be on our way—and fly while it is light. We'll set off immediately. Fanny, you go with Mr. Chase. Come on, everybody!"

"What's your other name, Fanny?" asked Chase, as the group walked along the beach to the planes.

"Preston," replied the girl, with a sigh of relief at the thought of dropping the name of Sprague—or Long—forever.

The Sky Rocket took off first, and five minutes later Chase's monoplane left the island. Within sight of each other, the two planes flew across the Pacific in the glorious light of the sunset, and arrived at the Honolulu airport without any disaster, a little after eight o'clock.

CHAPTER 9.19
CONCLUSION

Leaving the planes at the airport, the four young people ate supper together at a quick-lunch restaurant in Honolulu. Here they discussed their plans concerning Fanny Preston.

Mary Eliska insisted that the girl live at one of the smaller hotels, on some of the gold pieces which she had returned that afternoon, and though Fanny protested, she had no money of her own, and no place to go, so she finally had to agree. In the meantime, Chase promised to work for her release.

"And then we'll take you back to Los Angeles with us when we go," Mary Eliska concluded. "And try to find you a job."

There were tears in Fanny's eyes when Mary Eliska and Jax Gray finally left her at the hotel and took a taxi to the Governor's mansion. Here they offered profuse apologies to their hostess—apologies which she dismissed with a smile. She was delighted to learn that the counterfeiting menace had been checked, for news of this crime had been in the papers for more than a year. She felt that Mary Eliska and Jax Gray had helped in a big service for both Hawaii and the United States, but the girls insisted that the honors were for Bertram Chase.

"Now for our telegrams!" exclaimed Mary Eliska. "Oh, I do so hope there is one from father!"

"I received one from Albert Stricklin, your father, Mary Eliska," announced her hostess. "From Los Angeles. He and your aunt are sailing tomorrow for Honolulu. And two young men are with them—I have forgotten their names."

"Was one of them Jim—I mean James—Valier?" asked Jax Gray, eagerly.

The older woman smiled.

"I believe so," she said. "And a Ralph somebody. Would that be right?"

"Absolutely," agreed Jax Gray, with immense satisfaction.

"So, in view of that news," continued the Governor's wife, "I think we will plan a big dinner for the night they arrive. It takes four days, you know, from Los Angeles. I hope we can keep you amused until then."

"Oh, we love it here!" cried Mary Eliska. "It's the most beautiful spot in the world!"

So, although Mary Eliska was anxious to see her own family and the two boys, the time nevertheless passed pleasantly. They went to the famous Waikiki beach every morning, and swam in the water that seemed like velvet, or rode in the launches and speed boats. After luncheon they drove about the beautiful island visiting the Stricklin family home at 2400 Round Top Drive that Albert Stricklin had constructed, seeing the marvelous aquarium, with its gorgeous fish of all colors and descriptions, or viewing the mountains and the coral formations; and in the evening they would watch the glorious sunsets over the ocean and then dance or bathe in the moonlight. One lovely afternoon Mary Eliska and Jax Gray took Fanny and flew to the island of Kauai, and saw the Waimea Canyon and the Barking Sands, and the rocky, jagged cliffs, and the beaches and parks in all their beauty. One evening Bert Chase went with them on another flight, for he had managed to have his stay at Hawaii extended, since he had successfully completed his work.

And so the great day came when the boat from Los Angeles docked at Pearl Harbor. Mary Eliska and Jax Gray were at the wharf half an hour before it was scheduled to arrive, so impatient were they to see their folks from home. A great surging joy swelled up in Mary Eliska's throat at the sight of her father Alert Stricklin as he came forward to meet her at Aloha Tower. It was so suffocating that for a moment she couldn't say a word of greeting. Breathless, she flew into his arms. "Daughter!" he said, in a tone filled with emotion.

"Daddy, darling!" she managed to stammer, and then, recovering herself somewhat, she kissed her Aunt Sally and shook hands with the boys.

"Congratulations, congratulations, and then some!" exclaimed Jim, to both of the girls.

"It was great, Mary Eliska!" cried Ralph.

"'Mary Eliska *and* Jax Gray,' if you please," corrected Mary Eliska. "Jax Gray did every bit as much as I did!"

"In fact, I flew nearer the ocean," added her chum, mischievously. "So near that I almost drowned us both!"

"Don't tell us about the dangers—now that you have miraculously escaped with your lives!" begged Mary Eliska, with a shiver.

And then everybody talked at once, asking questions, making explanations, accounting for all the time since they had seen each other. The girls drove right to the hotel with the party, and here Mary Eliska dragged out Fanny and introduced her, much to Mary Eliska's amazement. And then she actually asked her aunt to look after the girl for the rest of the visit, until they should all go back to Los Angeles together.

The dinner at the Governor's mansion that night was another gorgeous affair. All the celebrities of the island were invited, as well as Mary Eliska's friends. Even Fanny Preston was included, and Bertram Chase was accorded a seat of honor on Mary Eliska's right, with Ralph Clavering on her left—an arrangement which made Ralph exceedingly jealous, for Chase managed to absorb most of her attention. "I want you to go into the secret service, Mary Eliska," he said, earnestly. "You'd be a marvelous detective. Have you signed up for anything for the winter?"

"I had expected to teach," replied the aviatrix. "But I guess it's too late for that."

"No, no, don't do that."

Chase wasn't eating at all, instead he was fumbling with his fork, as if he were terribly nervous. Mary Eliska noticed his queer actions, and wondered what could be the cause of them, for he had always seemed to have such easy, pleasant manners. But his next question, abrupt as it was, offered the explanation.

"It's a funny place—and a funny time—to ask you, Mary Eliska," he began, very low "but I'm so afraid you'll fly away and I'll never see you again.... You see—I'm crazy about you. I love you! I want you to marry me, and fly everywhere with me!"

Faltering as his speech was at first, he ended it very fast, as if he had to finish with one breath. Out of the corner of her eye, Mary Eliska could see his hand trembling; this fearless flier, who dared all sorts of dangers! Why, he seemed to be afraid to look in her face!

Mary Eliska, too, was embarrassed; she didn't know what to say. She liked him so much that she couldn't bear to hurt his feelings, yet marriage was out of the question at this time.

"I appreciate it a lot, Bert," she finally replied, softly. "But—I couldn't. Not now, anyway," she added, so as not to seem too abrupt. "But there's no reason why you shouldn't see me often. Distance isn't anything to fliers. And I'll talk to you later about the secret service." She paused, nodding in Ralph's direction.... "This impatient boy on my left is having a fit. I must talk to him now."

She turned to Ralph, sulking as usual. "Old friends are a nuisance when we have a new crush, aren't they?" he asked, bitterly.

"Ralph, behave yourself!" she commanded. "Don't spoil my party by getting peeved!"

"I'm sorry, Mary Eliska," he said, penitently. "I didn't mean it. Only I just know that guy has fallen for you. What was he talking to you so long about?"

Mary Eliska blushed. "He wants me to go into secret service flying," she explained.

"He would! And then get you to marry him!"

Mary Eliska laughed, as if to imply that what Ralph suggested was nonsense. If he only knew how near to the point he had come!

"Well, are you going to do it?" he persisted.

"I don't know. First I'm going to get my Ladybug at Los Angeles—and fly home!"

"Ladybug, Ladybug, fly away home!" quoth Ralph.

"We will!" promised Mary Eliska, smiling. But she did not say how long she would stay there.

CHAPTER 10

Gypsies of the Air

CHAPTER 10.1
The *Skybird* Hops Off

With a loud sputtering roar, something like Mary Eliska's own feelings at that moment, *Skybird*, her little blue-and-gold airplane sprang forward and taxied over the flying field, taking the air gracefully as a leaping horse, under the guidance of its youthful pilot.

Mary Eliska was working off steam. Half angry, half frightened, the girl knew that a flight in her plane was the quickest way to get hold of her nerves and make her head clear for thinking what was to be done.

"Those boys!" she muttered between close-pressed lips. "What's happened to them *now*? Starting out for a flight to Paris and not even getting to Newfoundland!"

Over and over again that terrifying report, "Missing," kept ringing in her ears. Liam McAdams and Syd missing! She could picture a crack-up easily for the two boys. While they knew how to handle their planes skillfully, they were inclined to be reckless and were always taking chances.

Pulling back on the stick, Mary Eliska sent the plane zooming, one thousand feet, two thousand! Far beneath her she could see her father's flying field at Elmwood, and from that distance it looked as if the hangars had been flattened against the ground. Beyond was the Sound, a broad strip of water with what appeared to be toy boats on its glassy smooth surface.

Far to the right were estates, wooded tracts of land, small towns and villages connected by tiny thread-like highways to the large city in the distance.

Mary Eliska loved to fly. She was never so happy as when she was zooming to a lofty height. Her blue eyes were glowing, her ivory skin was flushed to rose as she handled the controls of her little plane. Mary Eliska claimed that the higher she flew above the earth, the better she could think and plan. But today Mary Eliska's brain was in a whirl. She could think of a dozen different kinds of accidents, any one of which might have happened to the boys.

Liam McAdams and Syd Ames had started out on the first lap of their transatlantic flight. They had been reported all along the route until well over the Canadian border. Then they had disappeared, been swallowed up.

And at Albert Stricklin Flying Field, their friends anxiously awaited word.

Twelve hours overdue at Harbor Grace!

Then it was that Mary Eliska took her plane into the clouds to think out a way to help. What could she do?

Her white face told how much she cared for those two young friends, her father's first student flyers. At the thought that there might be two more names added to the long list of missing aviators, Mary Eliska's heart sank with fear. She could see Liam McAdams's tall figure, his clear blue eyes and his thatch of unruly blond hair. Mary Eliska never knew how dear Liam McAdams was to her until that report had come, "Missing!" And Syd Ames had been like a brother to her. She liked this boy with the laughing brown eyes. His fun-loving disposition had saved them from utter despair at times, when everything was going wrong. A groan escaped Mary Eliska's lips as she thought of these boys who might at that very moment be lying crushed and needing help.

But Mary Eliska had not come aloft to moan over the imaginary fate of her friends. She knew they must have had an accident or they would have reached the airport long before this. They might be injured.

What could she do?

What would her father, Albert Stricklin, have done if he had not been crippled and left helpless by a fall in his plane, two years ago?

"Why Dad would go out and find them!" she exclaimed to herself. "And that's what I'll do. I'll go to Newfoundland and look for them."

This decision was natural for the daughter of a flyer. And the idea once fixed in her mind Mary Eliska did not waste time in further plans. She put her plane into a fast dive. The girl found it hard to come down in her usual way. She wanted to do reckless things. Take chances! But Mary Eliska was well trained by her father. She took the long dive with open throttle. She straightened out, banked and spiraled but not for a second did she take a chance with her plane. She would need *Skybird* to help her in her search.

As she headed toward the flying field she remembered with satisfaction that she had just overhauled her plane the previous day. It seemed that, even then, she must have known that it would be needed. As soon as she put in a supply of gasoline and oil, it would be ready for the long trip north.

Mary Eliska set her plane down neatly on the field in front of the hangar. *Skybird* settled down like a great seagull with outspread wings. Stepping lightly over the cowling, Mary Eliska ran to the veranda of the cottage adjoining the flying field where Albert Stricklin sat in a wheel chair. His face was deathly pale, stern and drawn with suffering. His hands opened and then clutched at the arms of his chair, nervously.

"Dad, dear," said Mary Eliska, quietly yet with determination in her voice. "I'm starting out to find the boys."

Albert Stricklin looked into his daughter's face. He seemed to be measuring the girl, deciding whether she was equal to the task ahead of her. What he saw assured him that Mary Eliska would not fail. He could trust her not to take big chances. He held out his hand.

"When do you start?" he asked. "Within an hour!" said Mary Eliska simply. "*Skybird* is in shape, I've been all over her!"

The father nodded his head. Between him and Mary Eliska there was no need for many words. They understood each other.

"I wish to goodness Bud Hyslop hadn't chosen this time to go off on a vacation," exploded Mary Eliska, her big brown eyes snapping. "When we want that fellow around, he's never here, and when we don't want him he sticks like a burr. He isn't much good at any time but now he could take care of the field while I'm away. I hate to leave you alone, Dad."

"Don't worry about me, Mary Eliska." Albert Stricklin put out his hand and let it rest for a moment on his daughter's curly blond locks. "The boys' safety is more important than business. If they are in trouble, they'll need us. Why, oh why do I have to be tied to this chair when...!"

"Now Dad, just you thank your stars that you are getting well! Six months ago it looked pretty hopeless. Now the doctor says that inside of a year you can walk and be back in the flying game again. Think of that, Dad! Won't that be fine?"

"Yes, I know, Mary Eliska, but it's hard to sit here, just a useless lump, when Liam McAdams and Syd are out somewhere...."

"I'm on my way, Dad. I'll find them somehow. Probably they have been forced down with engine trouble. You know those boys are frightfully reckless."

"Yes, that's what makes me so worried about them. I never could teach them to be cautious. If it were you, Mary Eliska, I would feel almost certain that you'd find a way out of your trouble."

"Thanks, Dad!" The girl stooped and kissed her father tenderly. Then with a smile she ran into the house.

While Albert Stricklin assented to Mary Eliska's plan with very few words, her mother wanted long explanations. Where and how was Mary Eliska to carry out her plans? What would she do if she found the boys injured? How would she get them home?

"I don't know yet," replied Mary Eliska. "Ask Dad, he'll explain everything!" Mary Eliska hurried to the stairway and called, "Martha, come here. Get into your flying togs. Pack food and water and the first-aid outfit. We are going to find Liam McAdams and Syd and they may be in bad shape."

Mary Eliska delivered orders like a general and Martha, her older sister obeyed like a private in the ranks. She did not stop to ask questions. Mary Eliska's commands were always important—or interesting.

Albert Stricklin, the father of the girls was an former airmail pilot. He had taught both girls to fly. The home-loving Martha had become a good pilot but she was not as fond of the sport as her younger sister. Mary Eliska was a pretty blonde, brilliant as a girl detective and easy-going as a companion, while Martha tended to be more serious, high strung and nervous. Mary Eliska loved to fly and now that her father was crippled from a recent airplane crash and still unable to leave his wheel chair, she was trusted with many important air jobs.

To Mary Eliska it was not half so venturesome to cut up antics in the air as it would have been to race in a motor boat or automobile. She always felt perfectly safe and perfectly happy when she could put a thousand feet of air between her plane and the earth.

Martha, in spite of her protests, had perfect confidence in her younger sister's ability to handle her plane and whether she was stunting or flying straight. Martha could feel sure of a happy landing and enjoy herself. She sort of balanced her sister's temper, for Martha was easy-going, practical and diplomatic. She could get along with any one, while Mary Eliska with her quick tongue was always getting into trouble and making enemies. The two sisters were chums. They loved to be together. They liked to do the same things, and while Martha would never make the expert flier her sister was, she enjoyed the sport and was always ready to follow Mary Eliska's lead.

Mary Eliska's decision to go north and hunt for the boys did not come as a surprise to Martha. She had been half expecting it. Her whole heart was crying out with the need to do something for these boys whom they loved, and now she wondered why Mary Eliska had not thought of it at once.

Martha needed no instructions regarding her part of the work to be done. A thermos bottle of hot coffee, bandages and food were packed into the plane, then Martha ran to get into her flying outfit. It was a jaunty flying suit, a white fleece-lined jacket, and baggy breeches, high white boots and helmet to match. Martha was fond of dress and her white togs were always in order. Mary Eliska had chosen a more practical outfit of brown leather. It was trim and smart and Mary Eliska carried it well. She had style.

Mary Eliska had left the details of supplies to Martha, knowing that her sister's part would be done well. She hurriedly examined her plane, looked over the instrument board to see that everything was in order, tested the engine, took on a supply of gasoline and oil and in less than an hour was all set and ready to go.

Mrs. Stricklin could never see any of her three daughters, Sarah, Martha or Mary Eliska, take-off without a feeling of dread. She had none of the confidence of the flyer. Although she had flown with her husband ever since her marriage she could never be persuaded to take the controls herself and learn to fly.

"I'm just an old-fashioned housewife and why try to make me into anything else?" she pleaded with Albert Stricklin when he tried to urge her. The fearlessness of her modern daughters frightened her. She was always afraid when she was in the air, much preferring to stay on the ground.

Mary Eliska saw her look of anxiety now. "Come on, Mother. Send us away with a smile. I know you're going to wish us luck, but we need your confidence as well. We're perfectly safe. And remember, if there is any message for us, telegraph to Harbor Grace."

With a smile and a wave of her hand, Mary Eliska stepped into the plane. Martha spun the propellor and the motor roared. With a bound Martha jumped into the rear cockpit.

Skybird headed into the wind as she taxied along the field and Mary Eliska, pulling back gently on the stick, sent the little plane into the air. She circled the field twice for goodbye, then she began to climb and took her course northward.

Mrs. Stricklin slipped into the chair beside her husband. Her face was white. Her hands were trembling.

"Do you suppose it's all right for them to go?" the mother asked, her voice husky with anxiety.

"I'd trust Mary Eliska anywhere in a plane," Albert Stricklin answered confidently. "And if anyone can find the boys, she can."

Long after *Skybird* had disappeared, the couple sat gazing into the clouds, as if they could follow their daughters all the way to their journey's end.

Albert Stricklin was calm and hopeful and patted his wife's hand reassuringly as she voiced her fears.

If the father could have foreseen the danger and treachery that was awaiting the girls, he might not have been so serenely confident of their success.

CHAPTER 10.2
Thwarted Plans

Albert Stricklin had started as a flyer when the game was new. For years he had been an air mail pilot and then had established a field of his own for training and commercial flying.

The Albert Stricklin Flying Field began with great promise, for Albert Stricklin was acknowledged to be one of the best aviators in the country and people had confidence in him.

At first, before the birth of his sons Bill and John, Albert Stricklin had been terribly disappointed that he had no son to follow him in his glorious profession. But one Christmas Mrs. Stricklin gave Mary Eliska and her older sisters Sarah and Martha, each a rosy-cheeked doll while Albert Stricklin presented them with toy airplanes. Mary Eliska, then only six months old, took one look at the doll and thrust it aside carelessly, but the airplane she hugged in her tiny arms, and squealed with delight. The less demonstrative Sarah and Martha calmly laid aside the plane and rocking back and forth sang a lullaby to their dolls.

"Mary Eliska's a chip off the old block," said her mother with a laugh. "You'll be trying to make a flyer out of her."

"That's an idea!" replied Albert Stricklin as he watched the child intently. "There's a great future for women flyers, I'm sure of it."

"Don't be ridiculous, Albert Stricklin! I was only saying that in fun. One flyer in the Stricklin family is plenty. Besides women will soon get tired of this dangerous sport."

"Don't be too sure of that, my dear. I'd like to have Mary Eliska learn to fly and know all there is to know about airplanes. That is if she takes to it."

And Mary Eliska really started her training the next day. Albert Stricklin put her into his big plane and placed her tiny hands on the controls. Although the motor was still, the child screamed with delight and pulling back on the stick cried, "Up, up!"

Albert Stricklin hugged her to him. "You've got a great life ahead of you, little daughter," he said. "That's right, you *are* a chip off the old block. You're like your Dad, you're a born flyer." And from that time on, Mary Eliska played in Albert Stricklin's big airplane whenever her father could spare the time necessary to watch her play.

Sarah and Martha were their mother's girls, more home-loving, and not nearly so full of flying spirit.

"We'll make flyers of both of them, too," declared Albert Stricklin, not wanting to be partial. "But I doubt if they'll take to it the way Mary Eliska does. I think Mary Eliska has a talent for flying."

Mrs. Stricklin laughed heartily at this joke, for how could Albert Stricklin tell at that age whether Mary Eliska would be able to fly a plane or not?

But Albert Stricklin was right. As the girls grew older, Mary Eliska took to flying as a duck takes to the water, but with Sarah and Martha it was always hard work and while each had done the necessary solo flying to entitle them to a pilot's license, Albert Stricklin was never quite sure of Sarah or Martha. Neither loved flying as Mary Eliska did. But to Mary Eliska flying was the breath of life. She had the air sense which her two older sisters lacked.

At sixteen Mary Eliska not only was an expert flyer but was a good mechanic as well. And in the venture of the flying field, Albert Stricklin called her his "right hand man" and declared that she could do more work and understood more about planes than Bud Hyslop, his helper.

Liam McAdams and Syd Ames had been Albert Stricklin's first student flyers. And for that reason he felt as if they belonged to him. Syd was an orphan, the son of a flying buddy of Albert Stricklin's, and the boy spent most of his time in the Stricklin household.

Liam McAdams was the son of a wealthy business man and the boy had persuaded his father to back Albert Stricklin financially. Bennett McAdams only half believed in the plan. He didn't like flying and he wished with all his heart that Liam McAdams would choose some other profession. He even blamed Albert Stricklin for encouraging the boy to continue against his will.

However Liam McAdams, this sturdy, broad shouldered youth, usually got his own way. And what he wanted now from his father was a partnership in the Albert Stricklin Flying Field.

Albert Stricklin had secured an option on a large tract of land belonging to Sean Hall, a man who lived at his small silver mine in Peru. He had given little thought to this strip of land that he owned, for it had been considered waste until the airplane brought about a new use for it.

With the option settled, Bennett McAdams finally put up money for transport planes and agreed financially to stand back of Albert Stricklin's venture until success was certain.

As Albert Stricklin had been a lucky pilot, he had no difficulty in getting contracts for his airplane transportation service. Everything looked good. Success was certain.

Then had come the crash!

Albert Stricklin had gone over his plane thoroughly before starting out on an important trip. The airplane was in order, the engine running true. Then half an hour later Albert Stricklin had crashed.

At the hospital his wife and daughters looked on his still form and were given no hope of his recovery. "And if he lives, he'll be a cripple for the rest of his life," the doctors had predicted. "A wheel chair is all he can hope for."

"Pray, Liam McAdams, pray that Dad will die," Mary Eliska whispered with a sob as Liam McAdams put his arm tenderly about her. "Death would be better, far better, than a broken body. He mustn't live! I could never bear to see Dad live out the rest of his whole life in a wheel chair!"

Liam McAdams caught her meaning. He could understand. A flyer who had piloted a plane through the sky, had shot up above the clouds and been alone in the heavens, would never be happy in a wheel chair. Looking down at the death-like face of his friend, Albert Stricklin, Liam McAdams too prayed that he might die.

But Albert Stricklin did not die. His recovery was like a miracle, so the doctors said, and while he stormed at the wheel chair, even that was only to be for a little while. A famous specialist at the University of California San Diego, La Jolla, California, Dr. Michael Madani, M.D., selected by Dr. Kirk Peterson, M. D., of the UCSD Sulpizio Center, gave Albert Stricklin promise of being able to walk and get back to flying within a few years.

Liam McAdams and Syd Ames carried on the business as well as they could, but new contracts did not come as rapidly as when Albert Stricklin was in charge.

Then, for some reason, after the accident, Bennett McAdams suddenly lost what little enthusiasm he had and refused any further help, even intimated that he wanted to withdraw his offer of standing financially behind Albert Stricklin's field.

Liam McAdams pleaded with his father. But it was no use. Then the father, in his turn, tried to persuade the son to leave the Stricklin Field.

"Break loose and I'll start you in a field of your own," promised the father. "You've nothing to gain by sticking to Albert Stricklin. He's down and out, a failure, a cripple, and it's my opinion that he'll never be any better."

"No!" answered Liam McAdams. "I couldn't break away now. Anyway I want to work with him. I want to make the field a success. I'm his partner."

"If you want a partnership, why not go in with a promising young business man like Thatcher Allen whose field is next to Albert Stricklin's?" suggested Bennett McAdams. "Thatcher Allen's a good flyer and all he needs is more room out there."

Liam McAdams snorted in disgust. "Thatcher Allen! I hate that fellow! He's not a square-shooter. No one on our field has any respect for him."

"That's jealousy. It's well known that Thatcher Allen is making a lot of money and will be a big man in the aviation field someday. Think it over and don't let a big opportunity like this slip by. If you decide to go in with Thatcher Allen I'll back you for any amount you need, but I have no more faith in Albert Stricklin."

Liam McAdams thought over his father's refusal for a long time then went straight to the point.

"What's the matter with Albert Stricklin? What have you got against him? You seem to have no confidence in him."

"That's right, son. I have lost faith in him. I've had some very unfavorable reports about him."

"What have you heard?" Liam McAdams demanded. "It's only fair to tell me."

"It's something serious, you may be sure, or I would never take the stand I do. But at the present time I do not care to say what it is. Enough for you to know is that he is incompetent."

"That's nonsense. Father. You know that his record in the air service has been almost perfect. This is the first serious accident. And it's the first plane he ever crashed since he got his license."

But even Liam McAdams could not deny that since Albert Stricklin had established his field one thing after another had happened that might have come from carelessness. There had been minor accidents, forced landings with engine trouble that had delayed delivery of goods. A plane had burned on the field under suspicious circumstances.

Bennett McAdams reminded the boy of these mishaps.

"But you know well enough that it was not from any carelessness of Albert Stricklin's that the plane was burned," retorted Liam McAdams.

"Why wasn't it? How do you explain the matter? You said yourself the circumstances were suspicious. How do you clear Albert Stricklin of responsibility?" asked his father.

"Albert Stricklin had nothing whatever to do with that fire. And if he'd listen to me and discharge Bud Hyslop, that good-for-nothing mechanic he has, there wouldn't be so many accidents. I'm certain of that."

"I've also made inquiries about young Hyslop," returned the father. "He's a rough chap but I've heard nothing against him. It looks as if your friend Albert Stricklin was the incompetent one."

"I know one thing," declared Liam McAdams excitedly. "If I were the boss out there, I'd fire Bud. He's always making trouble. I'm half afraid of what he may do next." Liam McAdams stormed out of the room, angry and disappointed. The boy could not bear to have his friend Albert Stricklin criticized, especially now that he was down and out and needed him. Albert Stricklin was the best-hearted man in the world and a real pal to all boys. That accounted for his unwillingness to let Bud Hyslop go. He kept hoping that with kindness Bud Hyslop could be persuaded to do his work properly.

Mary Eliska and Martha had never cared for Bud Hyslop and it was due to Bud that Mary Eliska had become the expert mechanic she was.

"Women haven't any business around an airplane," Bud had told Mary Eliska the first day he had come on the field. "The kitchen is where they belong, and they should be made to stay there. And if they *must* fly, let them do their own repair work. That's what I say, and I'll stick to it."

And stick to it he did, which made Mary Eliska take up the challenge and getting into cover-alls, which were soon well daubed with grease, she mastered every detail of her plane. And she loved the work. This was in the days when she had flown one of Albert Stricklin's planes to which they had given the name of *The Crate*. It was an old model, patched and re-patched, but Albert Stricklin declared that it was still a fine craft.

Mary Eliska and Martha had liked *The Crate*. It was an old friend. But they were the proudest girls in Elmwood when their father presented them with *Skybird*, the little blue-and-gold monoplane, a tiny amphibian. This gift was a reward of merit. Albert Stricklin had been criticized for allowing his daughters to spend so much time on learning to fly, so he had talked it over with the three girls and promised them that if they led their class in at least two subjects and graduated with honors they were to have a plane of their own, and would be allowed to take out their pilot licenses.

Two of the girls buckled down to work and made good. Mary Eliska led in three subjects and Martha graduated first from Punahou, then from Harvard University with honors.

Their knowledge of planes stood them in good stead. After Albert Stricklin's accident when contracts did not come, Mary Eliska took matters into her own hands and advertised for women flying students. Albert Stricklin from his wheel chair directed the lessons and Mary Eliska demonstrated and took them up for flying instruction. This had come to be their chief source of income.

Liam McAdams decided that he would make a record by flying the Atlantic and in this way bring distinction to Albert Stricklin's training school. And as a famous flyer, he would be able to draw down big contracts for the field.

Mary Eliska liked to teach others to fly but she had higher ambitions than that for herself. She longed to take that flight across the ocean, and there had been a secret struggle as to whether she would start out on her own or remain with her father in his misfortune.

It was hard to give up all the time. She also had the feeling that she could make more money by getting out and doing something to bring her fame quickly.

It was with a bitter heart that she listened to Liam McAdams and Syd when they announced their intention to make the flight to Paris. Mary Eliska hastened to her room to fight it out with her rebellious heart. Why was it that Liam McAdams always got everything he wanted? He and Syd both were lucky. All they had to do was desire a thing and the way was smoothed out for them to get exactly what they wanted, while she only had to wish and all the powers in the world combined to keep her from getting it, or at least so she thought.

"I always have bad breaks! I'm out of luck! Everything is against me!" she declared one day.

Yet when Liam McAdams and Syd leaped into their plane, *The Comet*, ready to start out for their great adventure, Mary Eliska bade them goodbye with a smile. Not for worlds would she show anyone how much she wanted to go. And she was especially careful not to let her father get any hint of her disappointment. Only her older sister Martha guessed at the truth. She was close to Mary Eliska in thought, and understood. Slipping her hand in her sister's, she said: "Someday Mary Eliska, we'll take that little jump together!" The forced smile left Mary Eliska's face and tears started to her eyes but only for a second. Then she shouted as she waved her hand toward *The Comet*: "Good luck and happy landing!"

CHAPTER 10.3
Skybird **to the Rescue**

High up near the clouds Mary Eliska kept her plane at top speed. Now that she was on her way to find Liam McAdams and Syd most of her nervousness left her. She was hopeful. She even expected to hear when she made her first stop for gasoline and oil, that the boys had been reported.

But in this she was disappointed. "Still missing!" said the manager of the field. "Nothing's been heard of them, and now I guess nothing will. They've disappeared. They've crashed!"

Mary Eliska's heart sank. She looked at Martha, whose anxious face was turned away to hide her feelings.

"Don't let us give up, Martha," said Mary Eliska in a low voice. "It isn't as if they were forced down away out at sea. I wouldn't be a bit surprised if they had engine trouble and came down in the woods a hundred miles from a telegraph office."

"Of course, I know," replied Martha. "They're probably safe enough. I do wish they had a radio on their airplane. In my heart I feel as if nothing *could* happen to Liam McAdams and Syd." Martha's comforting words brought a smile to Mary Eliska's face.

"All right, let's go!" she said impulsively. "We'll find them."

As Mary Eliska climbed once more into the air, sending her plane zooming for a high altitude, she thought of her own hopes. How different this trip to Harbor Grace was from the one she had mapped out for herself. Instead of a triumphant, adventurous flight that might bring her fame, she was simply out scouting to find her friends. Always duty stood in her way. She allowed her mind to play with the idea that she and Martha were on their way to Europe, she yearned for the applause of the crowd that would welcome her back to her own country.

Above the rugged wilds of Canada, Mary Eliska brought her plane lower and Martha kept her eyes strained toward the ground, hoping to see the stranded *Comet*. But there was no sign of a plane. Flying low over a vast forest, Mary Eliska circled back and forth, fearing to see a tangled mass of wings in the tree tops.

"Let's go on to Harbor Grace. Perhaps there is word from them now," cried Martha through the earphones.

Far below them now was the Gulf of St. Lawrence. It was hardly likely that the boys had been forced down there. They would certainly have been sighted and picked up by a passing steamer. Yet Martha watched the water for any sight of the wreck.

Straight over the vast waste land of Newfoundland Mary Eliska kept her plane headed toward the distant airport. Great stretches of uninhabited country spread out below them, marshes, forests and rocky hills.

"Look Mary Eliska! Is that a plane? Down there in that rocky field?"

Mary Eliska made a steep dive. She circled and banked over the rugged land. "I see it. It is a plane! Oh Martha, I do believe we've found the boys!" From the air they could not be sure whether anyone was near the plane. Mary Eliska circled low to find a safe landing place. As she shut off the motor for a landing, the plane bounced and jumped over the uneven ground, threatening to tear the wheels off. But as soon as it stopped the two girls sprang from the cockpits and ran toward the stranded plane, frightened at what they might find.

Martha was ahead and let out a sharp cry.

"Oh, what is it, Martha? What's the matter?"

Then Mary Eliska stood speechless, for the plane beside them was *The Crate*, her father's old air craft which Bud Hyslop had borrowed for his trip to Florida. Yet Bud was nowhere to be seen.

What did it mean?

"What's *The Crate* doing up here when Bud went south with it?" exclaimed Mary Eliska indignantly.

"Perhaps Bud came up to find the boys, the same as we did," said Martha, but the girl did not believe her own words. Both of them were well aware that Bud hated the boys, they knew that he had done them many a bad turn. And there was no likelihood that he had flown from Florida in the time since the boys were reported missing.

"What's the answer?" asked Mary Eliska. "Let's find Bud Hyslop and ask *him* that question," replied Martha.

Mary Eliska made a quick examination of *The Crate*. There was plenty of gasoline and oil. There was no leak in the fuel tank. Mary Eliska got into the plane, and Martha turned the propellor. The engine roared. It was working perfectly.

Mary Eliska shut it off and remarked with a shrug, "Well, one thing is certain. Bud wasn't forced down with engine trouble. It's my opinion that he's up here on some mischief."

"Mary Eliska," said Martha quietly, "I don't think any more of Bud Hyslop than you do. But we oughtn't to accuse him before we are certain and I don't believe he'd harm the boys in any way."

"I'm not so sure, even about that. But what's he doing up here when he said he was going to Florida?"

"I don't know, Mary Eliska. Don't let us waste time by standing here thinking mean thoughts about Bud Hyslop. We'll never find the boys that way."

"You're right, Martha. Only I'm mad clear through! Come on!" The girls climbed into the plane. There was a brisk wind blowing and Mary Eliska headed into it for a quick take-off. *Skybird* bumped over the rocky field, then with a flirt of the tail, the little plane cleared the boulders and nosed upward.

Mary Eliska and Martha looked around them for landmarks in order to locate the position of *The Crate* when they wanted it. She judged it was a mile back from the rocky shore line of the island. A great cliff rose like a castle. Stretching out from the summit was a broad plateau. At its base was a collection of fishermen's huts. Consulting her map, Mary Eliska decided that Harbor Grace was twenty miles away. She took a straight course and half an hour later put her plane down on the field in a perfect three-point landing.

Before the girl could step from the cockpit a mechanic came toward her.

"Are you Mary Eliska?" he asked. "There's a telegram here for you. Please call at the office!"

Mary Eliska and Martha ran toward the office of the airport. "They're safe! I'm sure of it! I could scream with joy!" said Mary Eliska.

Tearing open the telegram she read:

THE BOYS HAVE BEEN KIDNAPPED FOR LARGE RANSOM. TROUBLE HERE. COME. STRICKLIN.

"Kidnapped! Now we understand! Bud Hyslop is at the bottom of this business, you can be sure of that," stormed Mary Eliska, as she made her way back to the airplane.

"But what does mother mean by 'trouble here. Come'?" asked Martha. "Do you suppose Dad is sick? Maybe we'd better start home right away, Mary Eliska."

"If Dad were sick, Mother wouldn't just say, 'trouble here,' she'd say very decidedly, 'Your father ill, come at once!'"

Martha laughed and the nerve tension relaxed. "I guess you're right, Mary Eliska. She wouldn't beat about the bush where Dad is concerned. Then what does she mean? What can be wrong?"

But neither of the girls foresaw that their father would be suspected of the kidnapping and that their absence from home would be taken as a sign that they were mixed up in the plot.

When Bennett McAdams received a ransom note, telling him that his son had been kidnapped and demanding the sum of fifty thousand dollars, the man was almost beside himself with anxiety. Threats were made against the two boys and Bennett was making arrangements to have the sum paid over. Then he received a mysterious telephone message which hinted that Albert Stricklin and his daughter, Mary Eliska, were responsible for the kidnapping. He was told that Albert Stricklin was in with a gang of criminals and that they would stop at nothing.

It was well known that Albert Stricklin was having a hard time financially, that his doctor bills had taken every cent he possessed and that he needed money desperately at this particular time. To Liam McAdams's father this seemed motive enough for the kidnapping.

Bennett McAdams snapped the receiver of his telephone into place and without waiting to think things over calmly he raced his car toward the Albert Stricklin Flying Field.

Here he found Albert Stricklin in his wheel chair and before the cripple could speak, Liam McAdams's father burst out with a storm of abuse.

"Where is my son? You kidnapper!"

Albert Stricklin stared at the man for a full minute before he could realize that Bennett McAdams was accusing him.

"*I* kidnap Liam McAdams and Syd? Why, what are you talking about? Have you lost your reason?"

Suddenly Bennett McAdams became calm. "Albert Stricklin, you may as well own up. Of course I know you couldn't go out and kidnap the boy yourself. But your gang!"

"My gang! The only gang I have is your son and his friend Syd Ames. They are good boys and I'm proud of them. No one feels worse about this matter than I do."

"What is your price, Albert Stricklin? What do you want? Is this your way of getting even with me for withdrawing my support from your field?"

As Albert Stricklin did not answer, the man went on, "I've been hearing about you from different sources. I'm on to you, and you must know it. Now tell me where the boy is! I'll pay you. Yes, even the fifty thousand dollars, if you return him safely."

"I don't want your money that way, Bennett McAdams! And if I knew where Liam McAdams is, I'd tell you."

"Where's Mary Eliska?" demanded Bennett. "She knows all about this deal. She thinks that fifty thousand dollars will finance the field here!"

"Stop! Not another word! Mary Eliska and Martha went north to try to find your son and Syd Ames. They started before they heard that the boys had been kidnapped."

"Listen here, Stricklin, for the last time I ask you to bring back my boy. I've been told that Mary Eliska and Syd Ames are both in this scheme to get money out of me. Don't force me to have you arrested." The old man rose to his feet walked up and down excitedly then came and stood over Albert Stricklin's chair.

"Where is Mary Eliska, I ask again?"

"I told you all I know. The girls started out for Harbor Grace. We are expecting word from them any time now."

Suddenly the man turned to Albert Stricklin. "If I give you the money will you bring Liam McAdams back safely? Can you be sure that your gang will not kill him?"

Albert Stricklin's eyes flashed with anger.

"Listen to me, Bennett McAdams," he finally said. "If I could get up from this chair you would never dare to talk to me like this. I say again, I do not know where your son is. Tell me exactly what you have heard about me. Who has been talking? I must know."

But Bennett McAdams was too agitated to be reasonable. His eyes flashed angrily. Rising he strode without another word to his car. His lips were set in firm determination. If Albert Stricklin would not talk, then the law must take its course.

"He's hard hit, poor man," said Mrs. Stricklin, coming on to the veranda in time to see Bennett McAdams leave. "But you'd think by the way he glared at us that he thinks *we* kidnapped the boys."

"That's just what he thinks," said Albert Stricklin. "He accused me to my face of kidnapping Liam McAdams for ransom money. Fifty thousand dollars!"

Mrs. Stricklin stood for a moment, as if in a trance. She could hardly believe Albert Stricklin's statement. Then she burst into an hysterical laugh. "Of all the ridiculous things I've ever heard, this is the limit! *You* a kidnapper! That's a joke!"

"I'm afraid it's not a joke," replied Albert Stricklin. "Bennett McAdams seems determined to ruin me. Ever since my accident he is like a stranger. One would think that he was my worst enemy."

"Then let's not have anything more to do with the man," his wife exclaimed angrily.

"That's easier said than done, my dear. He has threatened to have me arrested."

"Let him try and see what will happen!" stormed the woman. And an hour later she had sent the telegram to Mary Eliska demanding that she return.

And Mary Eliska and Martha, reading it through in Harbor Grace and knowing what they did about Bud Hyslop, decided that they must stay on. Bud was a treacherous enemy. They might have trouble, but when the lives of Liam McAdams and Syd Ames were at stake, they had no choice. They had to see it through.

Mary Eliska's answer to her mother's telegram was flippantly worded in an effort to cheer her up.

EVERYTHING JAKE HERE. HAPPY OUTCOME OF TRIP EXPECTED. MARY ELISKA.

Little did the girl realize that the foolish message was to be taken as an acknowledgment of guilt and would bring still further suspicion and suffering upon her father.

CHAPTER 10.4
Plots and Counter-Plots

After a wakeful night in Harbor Grace the girls arose for an early start. It was scarcely dawn when Mary Eliska and Martha took off from the airport and headed toward the big rock from which point they could see *The Crate*. They had no doubt in their minds that Bud Hyslop was responsible for the disappearance of Liam McAdams and Syd. They must find Bud and make him talk. No one had seen or heard of him at Harbor Grace. Where was he hiding? The girls decided to keep watch.

"He's apt to come back to *The Crate*," said Martha.

"I'm not so sure of that," answered Mary Eliska. "If he has *The Comet*, he's not particular what happens to the old plane. What I'd like to know is, what did he do with the boys?"

Mary Eliska kept the plane at high speed. Suddenly she looked around. "The fog, Martha. Look at that great mountain of fog behind us."

"What will we do, Mary Eliska?" asked Martha.

"Nothing to do but run," said Mary Eliska with a shrug. "We'll put *Skybird* down on the plateau by the big rock."

"Can't we get back to Harbor Grace?" asked Martha anxiously.

But Mary Eliska was already circling for a landing and did not answer her sister. The little plane bumped over the rocky surface and then stood still. With the motor stopped, Mary Eliska turned to her sister.

"I had to come down, it's not safe to fly in this fog! And as you see, there wasn't a chance of getting back to the airport. It's like a thick blanket in that direction."

"And it's closing in on us. There's nothing to do but make the best of it here," answered Martha. "But we may freeze to death. This fog is like an icy wind, it goes clear through you." Mary Eliska walked up and down to get warm, as the fog pierced her thick coat.

"How long will it last, Mary Eliska?" asked Martha. "This is terrible!"

"There's no telling. This Newfoundland fog often hangs around for days," replied her sister.

"That's a cheerful prospect," said Martha dolefully. "In that case we'd better make our way to that little fishing village. It's near this rock. At least it looked that way from the plane."

But Mary Eliska interrupted. "No, let's stick it out as long as we can by ourselves. I don't like to mix with people."

"You'd better get over that idea, Mary Eliska. What's the matter with you anyway, why don't you like everybody the way I do? And let me tell you one thing right now. We may have to go down there to find out about Liam McAdams and Syd—or we may find Bud Hyslop there. There's no telling. So don't you put on that superior air."

"I won't Martha, truly, I won't. I guess it's more bashfulness than anything else. I really like people but I never know what to say to them," responded Mary Eliska.

"Then think up a good line of talk right now, and make it nice and friendly. We don't want any more enemies. Bud's plenty!"

The practical Martha was already looking about the plateau for a suitable place to build a fire.

"Go get some dry twigs, Mary Eliska!" she said.

"Where will I find anything dry in this fog? Why not use the alcohol stove?" asked Mary Eliska.

"We'd better save that. You don't know how long we'll have to stay out here and in another hour things will be still wetter. You can hardly see *Skybird* now, the fog is so thick." Mary Eliska scrambled around the rocks, digging into crevices for dry roots and twigs. Martha broke them into tiny bits and made a neat little pile.

"Some fire!" teased Mary Eliska. "Just big enough to heat something in a spoon."

"You needn't laugh, Mary Eliska! You know well enough I'm a champion fire builder and I say that the smaller your fire is, the better. You only want blaze enough to cover the bottom of your kettle. If it comes out beyond that it's apt to make your food smoky."

"All right, have it your own way," said Mary Eliska with a laugh. "I leave it all to you. Just as long as you don't ask me to cook, I'll let you do anything you want to do. Here's the tin egg box."

Soon the smell of bacon and eggs made them ravenous. They found a shelter under a wind-stunted tree and spread out their meal.

"Isn't it delicious!" exclaimed Martha. "I don't believe food is as good when cooked over a gas fire. I'm sure I never tasted anything like these fried eggs."

"No need to ask me if I enjoy them. Just watch my speed," returned Mary Eliska, buttering a slice of bread. "That's one nice thing about aviators, they never pick over their food. They're always hungry!"

At that moment the crackling of brush was heard below the cliff. Martha grabbed Mary Eliska's arm.

"Oh what is it, Mary Eliska? I'm frightened. Maybe it's a wild animal!"

"Hush, Martha. Keep still. It's a man."

"Then hide and he won't see us," whispered Martha.

"We can't hide *Skybird*. I'm not afraid," replied Mary Eliska as she rose to her feet just as the dim figure of a man came up the trail to the summit. The girl took a few steps toward the intruder.

"Who's there?" she demanded sternly.

The next moment she stood face to face with Bud Hyslop.

Bud stared as if he were seeing ghosts, then he demanded with an angry glare, "What are you doing here, Mary Eliska? What brought you to Newfoundland?"

"I might ask *you* the same question, Bud Hyslop," replied Mary Eliska, flaring with anger.

But the sensible Martha came to the rescue. "Why, we came up to find Liam McAdams and Syd. They're missing. They must have been forced down on the island."

"Then we're on the same errand," replied Bud. "I started to go to Florida but was delayed, so when the word came that the boys were missing, I just turned around and came on up here to help find them. I've scoured the country everywhere for them. But they're gone! Disappeared without any clue."

Mary Eliska watched Bud. She was almost certain that the boy was not telling the truth. She felt sure that he knew the whereabouts of Liam McAdams and Syd.

But the story he told half convinced Martha. "Maybe he *is* telling the truth, Mary Eliska," she whispered at the first opportunity. "Maybe his intentions are good."

"Good intentions!" stormed Mary Eliska in a low voice. "I wouldn't trust that fellow as far as I could see him."

Bud was talking once more. "You haven't a chance of getting back to Harbor Grace today in this fog. You'd better come down to Jim Heron's place where you can keep warm and get something to eat."

"We've had our breakfast," answered Mary Eliska, her head high, her nose in the air.

Martha gave her a dig with her elbow. Mary Eliska understood and when her sister agreed to the plan, Mary Eliska followed without a word. "Martha is always so sensible," thought Mary Eliska. "Whatever would I do without her? She's my balance wheel."

"It's warm there and it's only a few hundred feet down the cliffside by the shore," said Bud as he led the way.

Mary Eliska and Martha scrambled down the trail to the narrow inlet called Fish Cove, where rude shelters had been put up to house the fishermen and their families. A sickening odor of salted fish came to them long before they could see the houses in the sheltered canyon.

Bud took the girls by a round-about trail leading to Jim Heron's house. It was the largest building in Fish Cove and stood there like a fortress, a two storied stone building, grim and forbidding in the fog.

Mary Eliska grabbed her sister by the arm. "What a house! It looks like a prison."

Martha was trembling. "I don't want to go in there. It's spooky! I'd rather be cold outside in the fog."

But at that moment a girl opened the door. From her face and figure one could not have told whether she was a boy or girl. Her straight hair was cut short and plastered down close to her head. Her face was angular with large features. Only her torn gingham dress proclaimed her a girl. Over her thin shoulders she wore a man's coat, which added to the boyish appearance.

The girl's face was pitifully sad. And when she saw Bud Hyslop, a look of distrust made her frown but this changed to a smile when she caught a glimpse of the two girls. She started forward as if to greet them, then hesitated as she looked once more at Bud.

But through the wide-open door Mary Eliska and Martha caught sight of a glowing, old-fashioned fireplace.

"I've brought some friends of mine," explained Bud. "They came on the same errand I did. Got caught in the fog and were forced down. This is Sally Wyn, girls. Now I'll leave you to get acquainted and go and see Jim Heron."

"I'm Mary Eliska, and this is my older sister, Martha," announced Mary Eliska. "I'm so glad to find a girl of our own age around here."

Sally led the girls inside and offered them a chair, while she hurried to steep some tea over the glowing coals. In the gloomy interior the fire lit up Sally's face. Her features were good. She looked kind and sweet. But the lines about her mouth were sad and bitter. The girls pitied her.

When Mary Eliska explained that they had just had their breakfast on the plateau, Sally looked so disappointed that they were forced to eat more. The tea and doughnuts tasted good.

While they were eating, a complaining voice called from the next room, "Get to work, Sally. What you doing now? Bring me a cup of tea."

Sally jumped up. "She's awfully cranky since she's been laid up with a broken leg. Keeps at me all the time," said the girl in a weary voice. "I don't know what to do to please her."

"Who is she, anyway?" asked Mary Eliska.

"She's Nancy Heron, that's Jim Heron's wife. They live here," answered the girl as she went about her work.

Mary Eliska and Martha wanted to question her further, but Sally's lips had drawn together in a bitter line. They feared that they had offended her.

Who was this girl? And what was that old woman to her? Mary Eliska longed to know, but now was not the time to ask.

As Sally leaned over the fire, the girls watched her intently. She did not seem to belong to this sinister looking house. Even with the blazing wood fire the room felt damp and uncomfortable. They shuddered at the thought of any girl living here and calling it home.

While the tea was preparing for Nancy, Sally flew about the kitchen, tidying up and whenever her footsteps paused, the voice always called her to account.

"Such a life!" thought Mary Eliska. "I'm glad I'm not Sally Wyn."

Yet this was the only home that Sally knew. A few minutes later she said, "I just happened to be home this week. Mrs. Heron broke her leg and Mrs. Armes, the lady I work for, let me come to help."

"That's nice!" said Mary Eliska. "I'm glad you're here."

Sally looked up quickly. Most people didn't care where Sally was. She was not used to appreciation and now she wondered if Mary Eliska really meant it. Sally smiled. Her whole face changed with that smile. She was almost pretty, thought Mary Eliska.

Suddenly Mary Eliska jumped up. "Wonder why Bud doesn't come back," she said in a whisper to Martha. "I don't trust that fellow. I think we'd better see if our plane is all right," Mary Eliska said aloud.

"Let me go up with you and see your plane," pleaded Sally. "I can be ready just in a minute, as soon as I take this tea to old Nancy."

"Take your time, Sally, we'll wait," said both girls together.

A few minutes later the three girls left the cabin. Outside they met Jim Heron, a tall, ungainly man who glared at them with piercing eyes. He carried a shotgun across his shoulder, which added to his fierce appearance.

"Git back there!" he shouted. "Where do you think you're going?"

"I wonder what Jim's doing with that shotgun," said Sally "This isn't shooting weather."

Jim beckoned them to come back then suddenly he turned aside. "All right, go! The harm's done!"

"What does he mean by that, Sally? What harm?" asked Mary Eliska.

The girls ran swiftly up the trail. At the summit they understood Jim Heron's remark. As they stepped on the plateau *Skybird* was just leaving the ground. Bud Hyslop at the controls guided the little craft straight out into a bank of fog. Mary Eliska screamed. "Oh, Martha! Bud's stolen our plane! He's taken *Skybird!*" she cried.

"Keep quiet, Mary Eliska. Nothing can be done by getting angry and shouting. Maybe he'll bring it back," said Martha.

"No he won't! He's stolen *Skybird!* He'll crash in this fog! Oh, Martha, what can we do?"

Martha was just as worried as Mary Eliska over the danger to their little plane, but she controlled herself. Mary Eliska was trembling with anger. Martha took her arm.

"Don't worry so, Mary Eliska. Maybe things will come out all right."

At that moment the tall form of Jim Heron appeared. He had suddenly decided that he had better keep his eyes on the girls. Mary Eliska ran to him.

"Bud Hyslop has stolen our plane," she cried indignantly, looking to the old man for sympathy.

"Don't you worry none, Miss," replied Jim Heron. "Bud's all right. He'll bring your plane back. He just went over to Harbor Grace on an errand. He's just borrowed that plane."

Mary Eliska wanted to ease her mind by expressing her honest opinion about Bud Hyslop but a look from Martha quieted her. She frowned, then held her lips tight-pressed. With her head high she started down the trail after Jim Heron. Her manner was very angry, superior and haughty.

Martha grabbed her by the arm: "Mary Eliska behave yourself. If we are ever going to find Liam McAdams and Syd, we've got to keep in with these people. Maybe the old man knows something about the boys."

Mary Eliska asked Jim Heron, but the old man shook his head. "I never saw the boys at all. Bud says his two friends crashed up here somewhere and he's hunting them. And you're doing the same thing, he told me. You're working together like partners."

Mary Eliska laughed outright, then walked on without a word. As they were coming down the cliff, they heard Nancy Heron calling in her cracked and peevish voice: "Sally Wyn! Where are you? Get to work! I'll have no idling in my house!"

"Now Martha, there is one thing sure," Mary Eliska whispered to her sister. "Bud Hyslop has proven that he is our enemy. We know now where he stands. I wish I knew whether Jim Heron is in on Bud's scheme."

As they neared the house Mary Eliska thought of a plan. She approached Jim Heron and asked him to take them to Harbor Grace. "Surely there's a launch in Fish Cove," she said.

"What do you want to go to Harbor Grace for?" demanded Jim suspiciously. "What are you going to do there?"

"I want to telegraph my father so he'll know we're all right."

Jim Heron refused flatly and firmly. Mary Eliska insisted and Jim was not used to arguments with women. He lost his patience and stormed at them. "Into the house you go!" he said, as he thrust them ahead of him through the door. "Now don't you step your foot across the sill until I give you leave. And that won't be until Bud returns. That's his order!"

"Oh, now I see. Bud Hyslop told you to watch us and not let us get away. Is that it?" demanded Mary Eliska.

"Right you are, Miss! You caught my meaning. You're my prisoners! And do you hear that, Sally Wyn? We're not to let the girls out of our sight!" Sally looked at the girls, her face was flushed, fear was in her dark eyes. She did not answer the man.

"Do you hear me?" Jim Heron shouted at her.

"Yes sir!" replied Sally, not daring to meet the glances of her new friends. Jim Heron went outside and sat down on a rude bench before the door. He held his shotgun in his hand.

"Prisoners!" said Mary Eliska under her breath. "What do you know about that!" She looked around the room and what she saw was not reassuring for the old stone house looked very much like a prison. But Mary Eliska was game. Her lip curled disdainfully.

"Prisoners, indeed!" she said with a shrug. "Just wait and see, Bud Hyslop!"

CHAPTER 10.5
Captives in the Old Fort

Although Mary Eliska was confident that it would be an easy matter to escape from the old stone house, she soon saw her mistake. For the building was originally a trading post of the early French explorers and had been built like a fort to withstand the raids of hostile Indians.

Mary Eliska examined the windows but the openings in the solid stone wall were nothing but narrow loopholes through which the shooting had been done in the early days. They were far too small for anyone to crawl through. And the only door to the structure was the one which they had foolishly entered. Outside that door Jim Heron kept his eagle eyes alert.

"We're in a nice trap!" whispered Martha. "How did we ever happen to get into a jam like this?" Martha's face was deathly pale.

"Now Martha, don't get panicky! There must be a way out!" comforted Mary Eliska. "It isn't reasonable to think that we can be kept here as prisoners. And look at that old man," exclaimed the girl, pointing through the narrow opening. "He's grinning as if he'd done something smart. That's what makes me wild. I hate to have anything put over on me!"

The girls stood with their arms around each other as they watched Jim Heron whose broad grin displayed his brown snaggle teeth.

"I wish he'd scowl," said Martha. "He doesn't look half as mean and sly as when he laughs. I wonder what he's thinking about?"

"I can tell you that!" exploded Mary Eliska. "He's thinking that we're just a couple of dumb-bells, walking right into the trap that he and Bud Hyslop set for us. There is only one thing to do, Martha. We must get out of here!"

"But how, Mary Eliska?" asked her sister anxiously. "Don't take chances. You know Dad wouldn't like that."

"Well, what's to prevent us from just walking out past the old man? He wouldn't *dare* to shoot us. It's worth trying. Come on!"

"Don't, Mary Eliska! Please don't do that. It isn't safe!"

"I'm going to try it, anyway. Now listen, Martha, I'll go ahead and you follow. Don't lag, keep right on my heels."

With head held high, Mary Eliska walked boldly to the door and threw it open. But Jim Heron had leaped to his feet and stood facing her. With an angry snarl he commanded, "Get back there. In you go!"

Mary Eliska stood her ground. "I just wanted to stay outside where the air was cool. Anyway I want to talk to you!" But Jim Heron thrust out a horny hand and shoved the girl inside. Raising his gun to his shoulder he pointed it menacingly at Mary Eliska as the girl started once more toward the open door. Sally dragged the girl back and shut the door.

"Don't go, Mary Eliska! Come here! You don't know Jim Heron," Sally whispered. "He'd just as soon shoot you as not. Bud Hyslop probably gave him money to keep you locked up and after that he'd kill you rather than let you go. He'd do anything for money."

Mary Eliska obeyed. She sat down but her eyes were blazing and her jaw was set in determination. "All right, Sally, I'll not make any more fuss. But I'll watch my chance. What's more I'll get away!"

Martha looked around anxiously: "I don't see how it can be done, Mary Eliska," she said. "We're prisoners, all right. Just as much as if we were locked in a cell."

"Don't do anything to get him angry," pleaded Sally Wyn. "He's terrible when he gets started." Suddenly Mary Eliska faced the girl. "Sally, is that old man any relation to you? Why are you in this terrible place?" Mary Eliska blurted out.

Tears came to the girl's eyes. "He's no relation to me. But I've been with them ever since I was ten years old. I can't find my people. The one that is left is an uncle and he has disappeared."

"Where are your father and mother?" asked Mary Eliska.

"They're dead!" said Sally bitterly. "They're both dead. I have no one now."

"Who were they, Sally and why do you live here with Nancy Heron and Jim?"

Sally gave a gulp then turned to Mary Eliska and Martha.

"We were shipwrecked off the coast near here. My father was Captain David Wyn of the *Riverside*, a small coast steamer running between St. Johns and American ports. Whenever we could, mother and I always went with father. That's what we liked best. It was lots of fun to go on the ship." Sally paused, her voice choked with a sob.

"There, there dear, don't talk about it if it hurts you, Sally!" said the sympathetic Mary Eliska, and Martha clasped the girl's hand. "I'm so sorry for you. But I knew from the first that you didn't belong to these dreadful people. You couldn't."

"Don't cry," Martha soothed her.

"I want to tell you. I want to talk about it. That terrible, terrible storm! Sometimes I dream about it, even yet. And I see my father carried away by a big wave when the ship smashed on the rocks. It was horrible. I'll never forget!"

Martha and Mary Eliska had tears in their eyes as the girl continued.

"Mother and I were picked up by a lifeboat, and brought to land. Then mother took pneumonia from the exposure, and she died the next week. She had a brother much older than she, he was wealthy but lived like a hermit, she told me. She wrote to him asking him to look after me."

"But how did you get in with Nancy Heron?" asked Mary Eliska impatiently.

"She was looking after my mother and after her death Nancy thought she saw a way to make some money. She sent my mother's letter with one of her own to my uncle John Wentworth in Westhaven, hoping that the rich old man would pay her for her trouble."

"What a terrible woman!" exclaimed Mary Eliska. "How she must have loved money!"

"Yes, but it didn't do her any good," answered Sally. "For the letter was returned unclaimed. No one knew anything about John Wentworth. He had left Westhaven years before and there was no address or means of finding him."

"Then what happened, Sally? What did you do then?"

"Nancy was disappointed and took out her spite on me. She put me to work and I've been at it ever since, slaving and giving her all my pay," Sally confided in a low voice.

"Have they been kind to you in any way, Sally?"

"Not what I call kind. But they seem to *think* they've done a lot for me. That's what they tell people."

"You poor girl!" exclaimed Martha. "Haven't you got any friends at all?"

"Yes, I've got one friend. His name is Dan. Dan Brent! He lives down in Fish Cove with his uncle. He's a dear boy, and the truest friend a girl could have. He'd do anything for me."

"But the people for whom you work, Sally? Are they kind?" asked Martha.

"Yes, they're kind enough, but of course I can't expect them to take an interest in me. I work hard for all I get."

"You poor darling!" Mary Eliska impulsively threw her arms about the girl. "Martha and I will find a home for you where you won't have to work hard, won't we Martha?"

"I should say so," agreed Martha. "The idea of a girl of your age having to work so hard. It's downright cruel!"

"Sally!" came a voice from the adjoining room. "Are you working?"

"Yes, Mrs. Heron, I'm mending."

"That's right. Keep working."

Mary Eliska's lips set in a determined line. "That's a job for us. Martha," she whispered as Sally left the room. "We'll come up and get her soon, and maybe we can find her uncle."

"Yes, we'll do that. But first we must find Liam McAdams and Syd. And we don't seem to be making any headway. Do you think that Sally knows where the boys are?"

But Sally knew nothing about Liam McAdams and Syd. She had suspected when she saw Bud Hyslop and Jim Heron with their heads together that they were hatching a plot, but she could not find out what it was.

"I wish I could help you," said Sally anxiously. "Then I'd know that you would help me with *my* problem."

"We'll help you anyway, Sally, and since you're an American you'd have no trouble in getting back to your own country. Only how are we going to prove that?"

"I can prove it," said Sally. "I have a little box of my mother's things and my birth certificate is among them. I was born in Boston."

"Then everything is fine. And as soon as we get the boys safely home, we'll come up here and get you. Let me see your birth certificate," said Mary Eliska.

"I can't now, Mary Eliska. It's hidden so Mrs. Heron can't find it. Now that I bring her my wages she wants to keep me. And she thinks if she could destroy my birth certificate, I could never go back to the States. That isn't true, is it?"

"Of course it isn't," said Mary Eliska. "But I'd like to see that paper just the same. It might help us find your uncle."

"All right, Mary Eliska, I'll go and get it now." The girls watched from the tiny window as Sally slipped out of the door, stood for a moment and talked to Jim Heron, then started down the trail toward the Cove. But once out of sight she took the opposite course, climbing up the hill behind the town and over to the next low ridge. Burrowed into the hillside was an old abandoned mine tunnel. Sally entered the passage timidly. Far in the black depths she pried with her fingers in a deep crevice and brought forth a small copper box. Clasping it tightly in her hand she ran from the tunnel as if pursued. The tunnel was the safest place she knew about. It ran into the hill for fifty feet or more and was said to be haunted. Sally didn't believe in ghosts but still she never felt quite comfortable in that long dark burrow in the hill.

As Sally emerged into the daylight she heard a familiar whistle.

The girl started violently then gave a cry of joy.

"Why Dan Brent, where did you come from?"

"Come here, Sally. I want to show you something!" said Dan as he led the girl along the trail to the clearing. At one side of this space grew trees with overhanging branches and under them stood an airplane. It was placed so that it could not be seen by an aviator flying overhead.

Sally let out a little cry of surprise. "Why Dan Brent, where did you get that airplane?"

"I'm being paid to guard it," answered Dan. "Gee, isn't it a beauty? It's called *The Comet*, and I bet it goes as fast as a comet. The fellow said I wasn't to let anyone near, not even to look at it, but you're all right. You won't tell."

"Tell what?" asked Sally, looking up at the tall boy beside her. His freckled face was frank and he beamed down at Sally in a protecting way.

He stammered, "Why, you won't tell you saw the plane."

"But Dan, what are you doing with it and what is all the mystery about? You aren't doing anything wrong, are you, Dan?" asked Sally, searching her friend's face earnestly.

Dan laughed aloud and slapped his pants pocket, making the silver coins jingle. "Nothing like that, Sally. I'm earning an honest living. A fellow by the name of Bud Hyslop gave me a dollar. What's more he's going to give me a lot of money. Just think, Sally, I'm getting paid good money for doing nothing. Pretty soft, eh?"

"But *what* are you doing, Dan? I don't understand," asked Sally with a puzzled frown.

"Didn't I just tell you? I'm guarding this plane. It belongs to two bank robbers, who escaped from the States and are hiding away in Newfoundland. Bud Hyslop has them cornered and wants to give them up and get the reward. That's why we're not supposed to talk or know anything about it. But Gee, Sally I just had to tell you. We're friends."

"But where is Bud Hyslop keeping these crooks?" asked Sally.

"It's not likely that he'd give his secret away to me. He wants that reward. He's not telling *anybody*."

Sally drew near to the boy and after making sure that no one was around she said in a whisper, "Dan, there's something crooked going on around here. I don't believe those fellows that are hidden away are thieves, at all. I think they've been kidnapped."

"Kidnapped! What makes you think that, Sally?" asked the boy.

"I heard my girls talking and that's what they said," replied Sally.

"*Your* girls? What do you mean by your girls?"

Sally laughed at the boy's puzzled look. "You needn't think, Dan, that you're the only one to have aviator friends. I just wish you could see Mary Eliska and Martha. They are exactly like the pictures I've seen in the paper, all dressed up in smart flying suits. Mary Eliska's is brown leather and Martha is all in white. They're beautiful, Dan. And someday they are going to come and take me back to the States with them. Then I'll try to find Uncle John."

Dan's face fell. "What are they doing up here? Why don't they stay where they belong? Trying to coax you away? Don't go, Sally. I don't want you to go. Where are these girls?"

"Jim Heron is keeping them prisoners in the old house. They're being guarded by Jim Heron and me."

"What did they do? Did *they* rob a bank?" asked Dan.

"Of course not. And it's my opinion that the two flyers who came in this *Comet* plane, aren't thieves either. Mary Eliska says they are two splendid boys. I'm almost afraid for you to guard this plane. You might get into serious trouble."

"I'm not afraid of trouble, but I don't want to help out a man if he's crooked. If I thought that this Bud Hyslop wasn't straight, I wouldn't guard this plane even for the fifty dollars."

"Fifty dollars!" cried Sally. "Why Dan Brent, do you mean to tell me that you're getting fifty dollars for doing nothing? It almost seems wicked. Gee, some people have all the luck!"

"Maybe those girls will pay you to look after their plane," suggested Dan.

"No, it's gone. Bud Hyslop took it without asking. I think he stole it!" Sally said with venom in her voice. "I don't like Bud Hyslop."

"I'd have guessed as much, Sally. But never mind about the money. When I get the fifty dollars, I'm going to ask you to go on the excursion to St. Johns with me. We'll spend every cent of it on a good time."

"But what I want more than anything else is to find out where those two flyers are, and why they are held by Bud Hyslop," said Sally. "Can't you make Bud talk when he comes back? I wish you'd help me, Dan. It will mean a lot to me if I can help these girls."

"I'll do what I can, I'd do anything for you."

"All right Dan, that's a promise," and Sally smiled up at the tall boy beside her, then hurried away down the trail.

Once out of sight of Dan's camp, Sally sat down and opened the little copper box with its strange markings. Her birth certificate was safe, and the little bag of trinkets. She poured them into her lap. A baby necklace of her own, her mother's tiny gold watch, and wedding ring, and a garnet necklace and bracelet. Sally often looked at them and cried over the trinkets, but today she smiled. She was proud that she had something pretty to show the girls.

Hastily putting them back into the box, Sally ran toward home. The first thing she heard as she came near was Nancy Heron's voice. "Sally Wyn, where are you? Get to work!"

"She's been calling you all the time you've been away," whispered Mary Eliska. "Did you get the birth certificate?"

"Yes, here it is, Mary Eliska," returned Sally.

Mary Eliska examined the paper. "It doesn't tell much, does it? Well, put it carefully away, Sally, and soon we'll get you out of here. Have patience."

But Sally did not appear to be listening, her eyes were bright as if she were burning up with fever. Mary Eliska looked at the girl in surprise.

"What's the matter, Sally?" she asked.

"I've got something to tell you. I know where the plane is. I've found *The Comet*!"

"Sally!" Mary Eliska's voice rose in excitement but Martha laid a hand on her arm.

"Hush, Mary Eliska! Everything depends on keeping quiet." She turned to Sally. "Where is the plane?"

"Over the hill a little ways. It isn't far. It's being guarded by Dan Brent, that boy I was telling you about," whispered Sally, trembling with excitement.

"But where are Liam McAdams and Syd? Did you see them?" demanded Martha anxiously.

"They're not there. Bud Hyslop has them hidden away somewhere."

"Did you tell Dan that Bud is a crook? That he is keeping the boys hidden, hoping to get a reward?" asked Martha.

"No, that would spoil everything. Dan thinks they are bank robbers. Bud told them that he was holding them for the law and expects to get a reward."

"There, I just knew that Bud had fixed up a plot against Liam McAdams and Syd, and that settles it! Doesn't Dan know where they are?"

"No, he didn't know but he's going to try and find out. He promised to help us."

Mary Eliska turned to the girl impulsively. "Help us, Sally, if you can. You and Dan will never be sorry. We'll do anything for you! Bud Hyslop has kidnapped Liam McAdams and Syd and we must find them at once!"

Late that afternoon Sally slipped away once more. She wanted to see Dan and find out if he had heard anything further from Bud. As she neared the *Comet's* hiding place something made her tiptoe softly along the trail. When she came in sight of the clearing she stopped short, with a gasp of surprise. Two other planes were standing near *The Comet*. Sally crept close, keeping under cover of the low growing bushes. Bud Hyslop and a stranger were talking together a little apart from Dan. The stranger was a slightly built man, very trim in his flying suit and helmet.

"There's a mystery here," said Sally to herself. "Somebody else besides Bud Hyslop is interested in that reward."

She looked at the planes. She knew *Skybird*, the little blue-and-gold amphibian. Mary Eliska had described it to her. But this other one. Where did it come from and what was the matter?

Dan Brent was standing between the trail and the flyers. Sally picked up a pebble and threw it at the boy's foot. It struck. Dan looked in Sally's direction, frowned, then turned carelessly away.

"Stupid!" said Sally to herself. "He's awfully slow to take a hint."

But Dan had understood. Thrusting his hands deep in his pockets, he sauntered away in the opposite direction, then doubled back. Sally saw his intention at last and went to meet him.

"What are those men talking about, Dan? What is their scheme?"

"They're hatching plots. I don't dare go near enough to catch what they are saying. I heard plenty to prove to me that they are crooks. Bud Hyslop plans to do me out of my fifty dollars. I heard him telling the other guy, that he never planned to pay more than the dollar he gave me. Said that was plenty and I could whistle for the rest."

"And what did the other man say?" asked Sally.

"He laughed, and his squint eye looked worse than ever. I don't like that fellow!"

"But it proves what I told you, Dan. Bud is a crook."

"And another thing I found out, Sally. Those bank robbers are just boys, not more than eighteen or twenty years old."

"There now, Dan Brent, didn't I tell you that! Now I guess you believe my girls. And from now on, you'll help us in every way you can."

"I'll say I will. I'll go right back there now and listen and get all the information I can," Dan moved toward the trail leading to the clearing.

Sally looked after him. "Gee, I'm proud of Dan," she said softly. "I want the girls to see him."

Running at full speed down the hill, Sally determined to help the girls escape.

"It's tonight or never," she said. "But how is it to be done?"

CHAPTER 10.6
The Menacing Stranger

Mary Eliska and Martha had been racking their brains, feverishly trying to plan some way of escape from their prison. But late that afternoon their hopes were dashed to the ground. Just as Sally returned to the house and before she could tell them of her discovery, Jim Heron ordered his captives upstairs into a rear room under the roof. In one gnarled fist he held a key, a rusty antique fully eight inches long, which looked as if it had been meant for a dungeon.

Mary Eliska pleaded with the old man for she had a horror of being locked up. She frantically promised him money; more money than Bud Hyslop was giving him if he would let them go, but Jim Heron shook his head.

"Nothin' doin', young lady! You can't raise as much money as Bud has promised; that I'm sure of. Anyhow I promised Bud Hyslop that I'd keep you under lock and key, and I'm goin' to do it. I'm a man of my word. What I promise, I stick to!"

Jim threw out his chest as he boasted of his honesty, then he added sharply, "Look here, if you girls hadn't wanted trouble, you shouldn't have come all the way up here huntin' for it. You should have stayed at home where girls belong."

Then Mary Eliska threatened him with the law, when her friends found out what he had done to her, but Jim Heron only sneered and showed his yellow fangs. "Into the room you go!" he snarled. "I'm not afeared of the law. In Fish Cove, *I'm* the law! All the law there is!"

A glimpse of Sally's excited face was the last thing that Mary Eliska and Martha saw before the oaken door closed on them and the key grated in the lock. The next moment the sisters were facing each other with puzzled and angry looks, for Sally's voice came to them through the closed door. She was saying to Jim Heron, "That's fine! Now we've got them where we want them. You can have your night's sleep now. Just leave it to me; I'll see that they don't escape." And Jim Heron growled in reply, "I'm going to keep the key under my pillow tonight. You keep watch, for if they do get loose, I'll skin you alive."

"So that's that!" stormed Mary Eliska. "Sally's our jailer. And we thought we could trust that girl!"

Martha was on the verge of tears, and Mary Eliska continued wrathfully, "Aren't we a couple of saps to be taken in by that lying little cat! We listened to her sad story and swallowed it all. How she must have laughed at us! Probably there wasn't a word of truth in it. If you ask me, I think she's Jim Heron's daughter."

"I'll say we're dumb!" replied Martha. "What makes me feel sore is that we told her a lot of our plans, thinking she was our friend. This ought to be a lesson to us, never to trust anybody again."

But while Martha was raging, her sister suddenly burst out laughing. It was real laughter this time. There was nothing forced about it. She pointed to the roughly plastered wall opposite the windows where hung a framed motto worked in brightly colored wool yarn. It read, "Home, Sweet Home."

Even in her anger, Martha had to smile at that innocent text. "So this is Home, Sweet Home!" she chuckled. "Can you tie that! Let's see what it is like."

The room was extremely plain, bare and ugly. Against the wall under the motto stood a broad, old-fashioned four-poster bed. There was a small table with a lamp on it and in one corner stood a shabby wash stand with a cracked mirror above it.

"We can thank our stars they gave us a lamp," said Martha. "I'd be scared here in the dark. It's a wonder they trusted us with a light. You'd think they would be afraid we would set fire to the house."

"If the place were wood, I'd do that very thing," declared Mary Eliska angrily. "Then they'd *have* to unlock the door!"

"Mary Eliska! Aren't you ashamed to talk like that? You know well enough you'd never do such a thing. Anyway, you'll never get a chance. This house is built of stone all through."

"Worse luck! How are we ever going to get out? Are we to stay here for weeks and weeks until Bud Hyslop gets the ransom money out of Bennett McAdams? It would take a long time to make the old skinflint part with his bankroll. In the meantime Syd and Liam McAdams may be injured, or even killed."

"You shouldn't say such things about Liam McAdams's father. Bennett McAdams will pay the money in a day or two. He just worships Liam McAdams. You know that. So there is nothing for us to do but wait and see what happens. We're locked in this old prison, and here we will have to stay until everything is over." Martha dusted a chair and sat down as if she were settled.

"Wait and see!" echoed Mary Eliska scornfully. "That kind of talk makes me mad! And I'm blue as can be, when I think of being kept prisoner in this terrible place."

But Mary Eliska was not the kind of girl to stay depressed very long when she might think out a plan. "Now, Martha," she exclaimed, "What's to be done? The door is locked, the windows are too narrow to climb through. What will we do now?"

"Let's count our blessings," said Martha. "Mother says there is always *something* to be thankful for."

"All right. Let's begin." Mary Eliska looked about the room. "Here's a big bed. That's something. It's hard as a rock, but who cares! Let's see what is under these home-made quilts. No wonder they were called crazy quilts. It makes you crazy just to look at them."

While she chattered, Mary Eliska examined the bed. It was clean and spotless, and the mattress was filled with fresh straw.

"Things might be much worse," answered Martha. "Look what the mattress rests on. No wonder it's hard, for there are no springs at all but just a network of ropes stretched crisscross. It's a real antique."

Mary Eliska exclaimed, "A rope! Just what a prisoner needs—in stories, that is! We might tie somebody with it while we escape. Or we might make a rope ladder and go out through the window. Rope is awfully useful in stories."

"But in real life it's not so good," answered her sister. "As we can't squeeze through these slits of windows, a rope ladder is no use. Let's think of something else, Mary Eliska. There must be a way out if we could only find it."

"Who says so? You needn't overdo the business of being cheerful on my account." Mary Eliska gave a toss of her head.

"We have the lamp to be thankful for," insisted Martha. "Maybe you can find some old books in the closet, and we can read all evening and forget our worries." But her teasing brought no smile from Mary Eliska, who remained steeped in gloom. Martha turned on her sharply. "Snap out of it, Mary Eliska! A girl like you ought to be able to think herself out of any kind of a scrape," she cried. "If you are in the air and get into a jam, you always think fast and find a way out. Many a time I've seen you pull your plane out of a tailspin and make a perfect landing. And that is lots more dangerous than just being locked in this room. Now quit your nonsense and do some headwork."

"All right," answered Mary Eliska. "I'll try, even if it does look hopeless." She went once more to examine the windows. It was no use. Escape was impossible that way. The door was solid as a rock. Then she opened the door of the closet, which was dark and hung with old clothes. As her eyes got used to the darkness, she gave a little cry of excitement.

"Look up there, Martha. See that little crack of light. There must be a trap-door to the roof. Quick, give me a chair to stand on. No, the table is better. Quiet! Don't let them hear us!"

Climbing on the table, which was dragged to the closet, Mary Eliska could reach the square trap-door and loosen the rusty iron latch that held it. She raised it a few inches and daylight streamed into the closet like a ray of hope.

"There's our way to freedom!" exclaimed Mary Eliska. Quietly she lowered the trap-door and sprang to the floor. "Now let's see about that rope," she said. "First we'll put the table back in its corner, in case Jim Heron comes back."

The girls threw the mattress to the floor and examined the network of rope, which seemed good and strong. Quickly they removed it, leaving just enough strands to hold the mattress, and Martha coiled it neatly and hid it in the closet. There was nothing more to do until darkness fell. They sat close together discussing in whispers what they would do, once they were free. Where would they go first? What would they do? They agreed that their best hope of escape was to get to the *Comet.*

Suddenly a scratching sound at the door attracted their attention, followed by the patter of retreating footsteps. A paper had been shoved under the crack of the door and Mary Eliska snatched it up and read the message in a childish handwriting:

"Bud came back with another man in another plane. Don't worry. When Jim is asleep tonight, I'll try to get you out. Burn this letter. Sally."

Mary Eliska sniffed disdainfully. "Nothing doing, you little cheat! We heard you talking to Jim Heron, and we know you're a traitor."

But Martha asked anxiously, "Who could that other man be? He came in a plane. Could it be Liam McAdams or Syd?"

"No such luck! It's another enemy. The mystery grows every minute, but we're going to win. We've *got* to win!"

They were interrupted by Jim Heron, who passed some food through the door. He looked around suspiciously but said nothing, only grinned in triumph and showed his snaggle teeth as he left.

The girls were too nervous to eat much. Carefully they made a parcel of the remaining food for future use. If they escaped, they might need it badly.

After hours of suspense, darkness came at last and then Mary Eliska whispered, "Let's get out of here. I'll choke if I stay another minute."

As Mary Eliska dragged the table under the trap-door and raised it, her sister cried, "Oh do be careful!" but Mary Eliska answered, "Everything's O. K. I'm on the roof already. Throw me the rope and I'll help you up." With a vigorous tug, she pulled Martha through the narrow door.

The girls breathed in the cool night air with relief. The fog had lifted. Stars were shining overhead.

"So far, so good!" Mary Eliska whispered. "Now help me fasten the rope to the chimney."

Moving carefully on the steep roof, the girls made fast the rope, then Mary Eliska let herself to the eaves and looked over. It was a long drop to safety, for the rear of the house was built above a ravine, with only a narrow ledge of rock for a foothold. Yet escape from the front was impossible. Jim Heron might come out of the door and seize them.

"Are you game to try it?" asked Mary Eliska.

"I'm scared already, but I'll go through with it," Martha replied.

"I'm scared too. But it's the only way," said Mary Eliska.

"You're never scared when you're flying," answered Martha. "You do loops and side-slips and all kinds of stunts, and you never seem to worry."

"That's different. In a plane I feel safe. I guess it's because I'm a born flyer. Come on, Martha, let's go!"

"Wait, Mary Eliska. We must go down hand over hand. Let's tie knots in the rope for a hand hold."

"Of course. Wasn't I stupid to forget that!" Hastily the girls tied big knots at intervals, then let the rope down at the rear of the house. It seemed like a terrible distance to the ledge, and the ravine below it was dark and terrifying. Martha gasped:

"Oh, Mary Eliska. Let's turn back. If you lose your grip, you'll be killed."

But for answer Mary Eliska swung off, over the eaves and began letting herself down, hand over hand. Without the knots she would have been lost and even as it was, the pain in her hands was terrible, but in a minute her feet touched the ground, and she gave a low whistle as a signal for Martha.

Mary Eliska waited for her sister with outstretched arms, and Martha almost fell the last ten feet, sinking limply into Mary Eliska's arms.

"It was terrible," she gasped. "I wouldn't try that again for a thousand dollars."

"Brace up," whispered Mary Eliska. "We're all right now. But Gee, I thought I was a goner!"

"So did I— Hush. What was that noise?"

A window had been raised in the house. Mary Eliska and Martha hugged the wall, hardly daring to breathe. Footsteps were heard in the house and someone opened the front door.

"Now we're in for it!" whispered Martha. "Let's run. It's Jim Heron."

But Mary Eliska looked around the corner of the wall and said softly, "It's that girl, Sally Wyn. The little traitor! Keep still, she may not see us. If she does, we'll fight her off and run."

The sisters remained motionless and quiet while Sally went to an old shed and back, dragging something heavy. After she was out of sight, and the house was quiet, Mary Eliska pressed Martha's hand, and said:

"Now is our chance. Come on."

Tiptoeing along the hard ledge, the girls reached the front of the house. No one was in sight. They slipped along the path to the road, and Mary Eliska muttered, "Safe at last. We're free!"

But at that moment a figure rose from the bushes beside them with a startled cry. It was Sally Wyn.

Mary Eliska flung herself upon the girl. "Little sneak!" she cried.

Holding one hand over Sally's mouth to silence her, Mary Eliska dragged her to the road, and then she and Martha hurried away, with the girl between them. When they were some distance from the house, they stopped running and Mary Eliska took her prisoner by both arms, shaking her violently. "Why did you double-cross us?" she demanded angrily. "Why did you pretend to be friendly when you were helping Jim Heron? You little traitor!"

"I'm not a traitor. I'm not against you. I was out getting a ladder from the shed, to help you down from the roof," Sally cried.

"Don't tell me any more lies. We heard you telling Jim Heron it was a good thing he locked us up. You promised to stand guard over us. And before that you pretended to be our friend."

"But Mary Eliska, I *am* your friend! I had to say that to Jim, so he would go to sleep tonight and leave me on guard. Can't you see?"

Martha looked at the girl, who was now sobbing in distress, and said gently, "I believe you, Sally. You are telling the truth."

Mary Eliska voiced her disapproval at first, but finally owned up that she had been mistaken. "I'm sorry, Sally," she said. "Shake hands and forgive me. Now let's get away from here."

"I'll take you to where the *Comet* is hidden," said Sally. "Come on."

In the darkness she led them up the trail and at the summit she whispered, "Not a sound!" and peered through the bushes. A small campfire glowed not far away, and beside it two men were sleeping.

While she watched, the stranger leaned forward to stir the campfire and as the blaze leaped up they saw a smartly dressed man of slight build whose black eyes glittered in the firelight. One of those jet-black eyes had a cast, which gave him a crafty and dangerous aspect. His thin lips denoted a cruel and grasping character. Mary Eliska clutched her sister's arm in dismay.

"It's Thatcher Allen! Thatcher Allen!" she gasped. "Dad's worst enemy!"

CHAPTER 10.7
A Perilous Take-Off

The girls knew that Thatcher Allen was an enemy far more dangerous than Bud Hyslop or Jim Heron, for he was their superior in brains and experience, and was quite as unscrupulous. Thatcher Allen, they knew was their father's rival and would do anything to injure Albert Stricklin, to discredit him and ruin his business. And now here was Thatcher Allen before them.

The sisters tiptoed back down the hill where they could talk without being heard, taking Sally with them. The three girls clung together. These were desperate men, taking desperate chances, therefore they might do terrible things, even commit murder to get what they wanted.

There was silence for a long time then Mary Eliska spoke in low tones. "Listen, Martha. I'm certain that *Skybird* is all ready to take-off. So is Thatcher Allen's plane. But I must get the *Comet*."

"Mary Eliska, don't be ridiculous. We can't get any of the planes with those men there."

"We'll have to take a chance. We've got to do it!" said Mary Eliska.

"But Dad says that there is never any excuse for taking chances," cautioned Martha.

"That's all right. Dad will change his mind when he knows what we know."

"But what do you want me to do, Mary Eliska? I'll do anything you say!" agreed Martha.

"First, I want you to be game. I'm going down the hill and take a look at *The Comet* and see if there is plenty of gasoline and oil. Don't speak, no matter what. I'll be all right!"

"I'll be game, only I wish you wouldn't go. It's too dangerous, Mary Eliska. Please give it up!" Martha clutched her sister's sleeve.

"Don't hold me back, Martha. I've got to go! It's the only way out. Now that the fog has lifted, everything is in our favor. It's now or never."

As Mary Eliska slipped quietly down the hill, Sally and Martha returned cautiously to the crest where they could see what was going on. Mary Eliska was gliding about among the planes, keeping herself hidden from the man, who was sitting with his back toward her. Mary Eliska reached *The Comet* unobserved. It stood to reason, she thought, that Bud Hyslop would have the planes ready for a quick take-off at any moment. With a tiny flashlight that she always carried in the pocket of her leather coat, she looked over the plane. Everything was set.

Just as Mary Eliska was starting to return, Thatcher Allen threw away his cigar, rose, stretched and took a leisurely turn around the planes. Mary Eliska crouched low and scarcely breathed. Martha, on the hill above, almost screamed in fear as the man walked within a few feet of the hidden girl. It seemed hours to Mary Eliska and her sister before he turned away and strode over to Dan. He gave the boy a poke in the ribs.

"You take a turn," he said. "I'll try and get a wink of sleep," and Thatcher Allen stretched himself on the ground.

Sally pressed her companion's hand. "Luck is with us, Martha," she whispered.

"But what's keeping Mary Eliska so long? Why doesn't she come?" asked Martha anxiously. For Mary Eliska was slipping once more between the planes. She crossed a space near the campfire and busied herself about Thatcher Allen's aircraft, then went noiselessly up the hill to safety.

Dan Brent was restless. He walked up and down anxiously, looking toward the trail as if he suspected that someone was watching. Finally Sally could stand it no longer; she picked up a pebble and threw it at the boy's feet. Dan understood and without a bit of hesitation, walked up the trail.

Mary Eliska and Martha stepped back to let Sally talk with Dan alone.

"What are those men planning to do, Dan? Have you found out anything?" demanded Sally.

"I heard them say they were soon going to take the boys back to the States. They talk straight enough. I don't know which to believe, these fellows or the girls you have."

"If you're wise, you'll believe what *I* tell you. The idea of your being taken in by *them*! A lot of crooks!"

"I'm not taken in by them, Sally. I have their number. They're not playing fair, I know that. If they were, they wouldn't try to cheat me out of that fifty dollars they promised. But are your girls on the level?"

"You bet they are," said Sally.

"Then I'll throw in with you and tell you everything those fellows said. I heard them talking and I have a tip about where those kidnapped boys are."

"Where?" demanded Sally. "Tell me, quick! Don't keep us waiting!"

"*Us!* What do you mean?" demanded Dan. "You mean your friends?"

"Come and talk to them yourself. The girls are right here. They escaped," said Sally as she drew the boy down the trail.

"I don't exactly know where those kidnapped flyers have been taken," he explained to Mary Eliska and Martha. "But they are out with the fishermen. Bud told Thatcher Allen that he had hired a launch to take them out. I think the boys are safe enough. The fishermen are all decent people, they wouldn't do them any harm."

"Oh, is that so, Dan? What about old Mackey Jones? He isn't exactly what I'd call decent!"

"That's right, Sally. He doesn't amount to much, but we don't know whether the boys are on his boat. How could Bud Hyslop be able to pick out the only crook among the fishermen?" asked Dan.

"I guess Jim Heron could tip him off to anything of that sort that was needed. But how are we going to find out where Mackey Jones is fishing? Sometimes they're miles and miles away. What we want to find out is whose launch took them out."

Dan jumped to his feet. "I have it," he exclaimed. "Why didn't I think of it before? Old Spencer was the man who told me to come up here and get this job. Likely as not he took them out in his motor launch. I'll go and see him right now."

"All right, Dan," said Mary Eliska quietly. "You go and see if you can get the information out of this man, Spencer. Here's five dollars. Promise more, if you have to and get back as soon as you can. We want to take-off in the planes before these men wake up."

The boy hurried away and in half an hour had returned with the information. He also had the five dollars which he offered to Mary Eliska but she refused it. Old Spencer had taken the boys out to Mackey Jones' fleet and as Bud had short-changed him he said he'd have nothing more to do with the scheme. And Dan could not persuade the stubborn old salt to make the trip and bring the boys back.

"That's all right, Dan," said Mary Eliska. "Thatcher Allen might have caught on and beat him there. You come along with us and we'll fly out to that fishing fleet and bring the boys back ourselves."

"Gee!" exclaimed the astonished Dan. "I don't know about that! I've always wanted to go up in one of them planes, but lots of them crash around here."

"If we're going to go, Mary Eliska, let's get started. Thatcher Allen and Bud will be waking up soon," said Martha.

Mary Eliska took command at once. "Now Dan, you're coming along! You have to! Go down there and get into the rear cockpit of *The Comet*. Don't make any mistake! And Martha, you hop off with *Skybird*!"

At that moment Sally threw her arms about Mary Eliska's waist. "Take me with you, Mary Eliska, please! Don't leave me here. I don't want to stay another day. Please, Mary Eliska. I'm frightened of Jim Heron. You heard him threaten me. He'll see the ladder and think I helped you escape."

Mary Eliska looked at the frightened face staring up at her in the darkness. She hesitated for a moment then said: "All right, go with Martha. Now be quiet. And when you hear me give a loud whistle start your engine, Martha, and get out of here in double quick time. Fly straight to Harbor Grace."

They crept down the hillside slowly, fearing that the sound of their footsteps might awaken the men. There was not a move from the sleepers. Everything was still.

Then suddenly from the woods came the report of a gun, then another. Somebody had let off both barrels of a shotgun, as a signal. The next moment Jim Heron came crashing through the brush, his white hair flying, his eyes wild, and yelling at the top of his voice.

"Wake up, Bud Hyslop. Watch out for trouble!" he shouted. "Those two girls got away and they are trouble-makers, sure enough!"

Jim Heron's warning came too late.

A loud whistle from Mary Eliska rent the air followed by a deafening roar of the two airplane motors. Bud Hyslop and Thatcher Allen jumped to their feet. Thatcher Allen made a dash toward *The Comet* as it started to move forward. He grabbed the cowling.

"Not so fast, Mary Eliska. You may be smart, but you've met your match. Shut off that engine!"

Mary Eliska's heart sank. It was hard to be so near to freedom, and then to lose out!

Dan Brent saw the danger. He grabbed up a wrench and brought it down with all his force on the knuckles of the man. Thatcher Allen gave a howl of pain and anger. His hand dropped, and Mary Eliska sent her plane taxiing across the bumpy surface of the ground to a quick take-off. As she pulled back the stick to send the plane upward, the engine sputtered and for an anxious second the girl felt that all was over. Then *The Comet* took the air and followed the *Skybird*.

As Thatcher Allen saw them climbing into the sky, he sprang to his own plane and worked the controls. Something was wrong. The ignition had been tampered with.

"It's Mary Eliska' work! I know her," cried Bud Hyslop. "She's too smart for us, Thatcher Allen."

"Keep quiet. Who's asking your opinion?" With an oath he turned to Jim Heron and cried, "Why didn't you guard those girls? You were paid to watch them! You old fool!"

"Don't talk to me like that," retorted Jim in a rage. "Who are you, anyhow?"

For answer Thatcher Allen drove his fist into the old scoundrel's face and Jim Heron fell backward in a heap. This was a dose of his own medicine!

Bud interfered and the three rascals quarreled violently, calling each other names until finally Thatcher Allen cried:

"Come on, Bud, we're wasting time. Get busy and repair that ignition, quick. Maybe we can catch those two Stricklin girls before they do any more damage."

"You're on," said Bud. "Let's go!"

Jim Heron rose from the ground and shouted, "Where's my pay for guarding them girls?"

"You can whistle for it!" said Thatcher Allen. "Just keep on whistling!"

Half an hour later the Stricklin girls set down their planes on the landing field of the Harbor Grace airport, taking on a supply of oil and gasoline. As Mary Eliska watched the men at work, Martha suddenly ran to her sister thrusting a torn newspaper into her hand.

"Oh Mary Eliska, read this. They've arrested Dad! They are going to grill him to find out if he knows anything about the kidnapping. Oh Mary Eliska, what will we do?"

Mary Eliska's face turned pale as death. Then determination to win once more came to her aid.

"Martha, there's only one way in which we can help Dad. We must get those boys back to Elmwood. Let's go. Martha, you take Sally in *The Comet* and when you get one of the boys aboard make a straight shoot home. Don't even wait for me, if I lag behind. Get back to Dad!"

The girls lost no time in getting their airplanes started.

"You're in luck," cried Dan through the earphones. "It's not often that the sea is as smooth as it is today. Sometimes the wind howls around here like all furies—that's when some of the fishermen's boats get lost. And you're in luck again because Mackey Jones' fleet is headed home."

Mary Eliska kept her plane down toward the water and a moment later Dan again called, "I'm sure that's Mackey Jones' fleet below you." Mary Eliska banked and circled over the boats. She was answered by a vigorous waving of arms from the bow of the largest vessel.

"There they are! There's your friends. How are you going to get them into the plane?" cried Dan.

But at the moment, other figures ran to the boys and the pair disappeared. They had been thrust down the hatchway.

Mary Eliska circled and banked and finally landed on the water within hailing distance of the boat. Mackey Jones, himself, in one of the smaller craft, rowed close and demanded to know what she wanted.

"I want those two young men you have there," said Mary Eliska, with decision in her voice.

"We haven't seen any young men," answered the fisherman.

Mary Eliska laughed. "Then you've got poor eyesight. We saw them from the air. We also saw you shove them down the hatchway. You'd better bring them out quickly, if you don't want trouble."

"Nothing doing! I've got my orders."

"Who from?" asked Mary Eliska. "What will he pay you?"

"He'll pay a good price. I work hard for my money, and fifty dollars isn't picked up so easy."

"Fifty dollars? Did he give it to you?" called Dan.

"No, but he promised he would. Anyway I've got the boys and he won't get them 'til he gives me the fifty dollars."

"I'll pay you sixty," said Mary Eliska, "and all you'll have to do for that extra ten spot is to row the boys from your boat to the plane. That's easy money. Is it a bargain?" The old man took a moment for thought. "You'll pay me sixty dollars now, cash in hand?" he asked.

"Yes sir, cash in hand just as soon as the boys are alongside this airplane. No promises, but good hard cash!"

"It's a bargain," said Mackey Jones. Turning to his men, he ordered, "Row for your lives, men! Hurry! That girl may change her mind!"

A few minutes later Mary Eliska saw the hatch being opened and the two boys scrambled out. They were hustled without ceremony into the boat and Mackey Jones and his men rowed for dear life.

While Mackey Jones was bringing the boys toward the plane, Dan said, "You can drop me here, if you like. I'll go back with the fleet."

"All right, Dan, and thank you for your help." The girl passed him a roll of bills but Dan shook his head. "You've already paid me five dollars, that's plenty for what I did."

But Mary Eliska pressed the money into his hand. "No Dan, take it, you earned it. Someday we'll see you again. You'll want to see Sally and you'll always be welcome at Elmwood."

The boy had no time to answer for Mackey Jones hailed them.

"Here you are, Miss! Now where's my money?"

Mary Eliska wrapped the bills in her handkerchief and dropped them into the boat as Liam McAdams and Syd shouted a greeting.

"Why Liam McAdams, what's the matter?" cried Mary Eliska as she saw his bruised face and his arm done up in a sling. "Are you hurt badly?"

"It's nothing serious, Mary Eliska. I broke my arm. I had a set-to with Bud Hyslop and another old villain. I'll tell you about it some other time," returned Liam McAdams.

"Want an extra hand, Mackey Jones?" called Dan.

"Sure, climb out!" said the old man.

Dan and Syd helped Liam McAdams into the rear cockpit of *Skybird*. "Syd, you're to go with Martha in *The Comet*. She's to come down as soon as I'm out of the way."

"*The Comet!*" cried Liam McAdams. "Mary Eliska, where did you get my plane?"

"I stole it!" she said with a toss of her head. "But that story can wait until later,—and Syd, you'd better take the controls. Martha is tired out!"

"O. K. Chief!" Syd's brown eyes were full of fun once more as he gave a mock salute.

"And Syd, make a bee line for home. The plane is all set, gas and oil and everything. Our next stop is The Albert Stricklin Flying Field!"

"That's the best trade I ever made," said Mackey Jones, as he pocketed the money.

The boys laughed heartily. "That's what he thinks of us," said Liam McAdams as he settled in the seat.

With a wave of her hand to the fishermen, Mary Eliska started her engine, throwing up a shower of water in front of the plane as she gained speed for the rise.

Mary Eliska sent the *Skybird* into the air, nose tilted for a sharp rise. Then she leveled out and began circling, waiting to be certain that Mackey Jones was playing fair and would allow Syd to go with Martha.

As she brought her plane once more over the fishing boats, Syd was climbing into the *Comet*. The boy looked up and waved his hand to indicate that everything was all right.

Mary Eliska soared high into the air, straight up into the glorious morning sunlight. She felt fine! She had accomplished what she had set out to do. Liam McAdams and Syd were safe.

And now for home!

Finally Liam McAdams spoke. "There's another plane coming our way. Maybe it's our dear friend Bud Hyslop. Wants to see if I have been looked after properly!" said Liam McAdams with a laugh. "He's so thoughtful of my comfort!"

Mary Eliska glanced at the far speck in the sky. "It may be an enemy."

"That's what I just said. It may be Bud Hyslop. But I'm not afraid of that fellow."

Mary Eliska headed her plane straight for Elmwood. "We'll get away from here," cried the girl.

"What's all the hurry! Let's take our time and enjoy the scenery," the boy answered, still in a happy mood.

But Mary Eliska was sending her plane forward with wide open throttle. "We haven't any time to lose, Liam McAdams. That plane is coming, and coming fast. I can't be sure who it is but I'll make a guess. It's Thatcher Allen! And he's after us. He's a dangerous man!"

CHAPTER 10.8
Happy Landing

But the tiny speck in the distance did not gain on them. Mary Eliska decided that it was just a cruising airplane and had no connection with them whatever.

"Did you say that Thatcher Allen was up here?" asked Liam McAdams through the earphones. "What do you think he's up to?"

"Didn't he help kidnap you two boys?" Mary Eliska countered.

"No, that was Bud Hyslop's little scheme to spoil my trip to Paris—At least I thought it was all Bud's idea. But if Thatcher Allen had a hand in it, then it's no joke."

"I'll say it isn't, Liam McAdams. I saw a newspaper in Harbor Grace this morning. They've arrested Dad!"

"Arrested Albert Stricklin! What for?" demanded Liam McAdams. "What did he do?"

"He's supposed to have kidnapped you and Syd. The paper says he's trying to get fifty thousand dollars out of your father as ransom money."

Liam McAdams shouted with laughter. "Fifty thousand dollars for me!" cried Liam McAdams. "Gee, I never heard of anything so funny in my life. And I never guessed that I was worth fifty thousand dollars."

"Poor Dad, it will be terrible for him. He isn't well yet," said Mary Eliska. "And you know how they question people in a case like this. They may even give him the third degree!"

"But who is responsible for all this, Mary Eliska? Surely no one believes it!" said Liam McAdams with a frown of contempt.

"The newspapers said that your father believes that Albert Stricklin is the man who arranged the kidnapping. They speak of Albert Stricklin's gang!"

"Mary Eliska, somebody's crazy, but who is it? Let's head for home as fast as we can go. I'll soon unravel the mystery," said Liam McAdams.

Ahead of them, far in the distance they could see *The Comet*. Syd was evidently challenging them to a friendly race.

"Now tell me what happened to you, Liam McAdams. What's the matter with your arm? Did you crash?"

"Nothing like that, Mary Eliska! The day we arrived in Newfoundland, we got stranded in the fog, and followed another plane that we thought had been sent out from Harbor Grace to guide us to the airport. But when we landed and I walked over to thank the pilot for showing us a good field to land in, I was face to face with Bud Hyslop. He pulled a gun on us and said, 'Hands up!' in a businesslike way. At first we thought he was kidding but we soon saw that he was in earnest."

"Bud Hyslop did that? Why he's a regular gun man. Then what did he do, Liam McAdams? Did he shoot you?" asked Mary Eliska.

"No, he just shot in the air as a signal and soon a man came running with a shotgun. In the fog he looked like a giant."

"That was Jim Heron," explained Mary Eliska. "We've met that man. Go on, what next? How did you hurt your arm?"

"I got into a little scrap. The old man grabbed Syd and tied him up. Syd was no match for such a gorilla. I got mad clean through to see them rough-handle my flying buddy. I couldn't stand it, so I started something."

"I bet you did, Liam McAdams," cried Mary Eliska. "And I don't blame you. I think I'd have done the same."

"So I got fighting mad. Bud didn't shoot after all, but he reversed his gun and hammered me with the butt of it. Jim Heron joined in and the two of them pressed me back to the edge of a cliff which I couldn't see in the fog."

Mary Eliska interrupted. "They backed you over the cliff! Oh Liam McAdams, it's a wonder you weren't killed."

"I might have been if I hadn't caught at a bush and saved myself. It was just luck that I got off with some bruises and a broken arm."

"Then they took you out in a launch to Mackey Jones' fishing fleet," said Mary Eliska. "I know about that."

"How did you trace us, Mary Eliska?" asked Liam McAdams. "How did you get wise to where we were?"

"That story can wait until we get to Elmwood—until I've had a good long sleep."

Liam McAdams looked at the girl anxiously.

"Mary Eliska, I hate this business. You're tired out! You're all in and here I am not able to take the controls."

"Don't worry, boy, I never felt better in my life. I'm on the top of the world! I could do anything this minute. I'd even feel able to tackle Thatcher Allen!"

If Mary Eliska had flung this challenge in Thatcher Allen's face, he could not have answered with more speed. For out of the fog bank that hung over the sea, Thatcher Allen's plane had suddenly appeared. It swooped upon them without warning, driving so close that Mary Eliska was thoroughly frightened. Two men were in the plane that was bearing down upon her, and desperately she put *Skybird* into a swift sideslip to avoid a collision.

Thatcher Allen was there to fight! And the fight had started!

"Watch out, Mary Eliska," called Liam McAdams through the ear phones. "Be careful. Bud Hyslop is at the controls and Thatcher Allen is in the rear cockpit. He's got a sub-machine gun. We're up against the real thing!"

Thatcher Allen's plane was climbing to get above *Skybird*. Mary Eliska sensed his plan and dropped her plane into a tail spin.

Liam McAdams gasped. What had happened? Were they falling? Had Mary Eliska lost her nerve. Poor girl, she was tired out and wasn't responsible! The boy tried to speak and ask her what had happened but the whirling plane made him dizzy.

"Mary Eliska!" he called, anxiously. But if the girl heard she made no sign. Grim faced and silent she kept her hand on the controls and strained her eyes to watch her enemy's movements.

Once in a while Liam McAdams caught a glimpse of Thatcher Allen's plane circling above them as if he were gloating over their fate. It looked to the boy as if the ocean were running madly up to snatch at them, while the heavens whirled about in a dizzy dance. It seemed that no power on earth could save them. If only he had been able to fly the plane himself, this accident would never have happened! In his brain flashed the thought, "No girl should attempt to fly when there is trouble ahead. That is man's work!"

But in the midst of his dismay, he felt the plane cease its mad spinning and come back to an even keel. Mary Eliska skillfully brought her plane out of the spin and leveled off like an expert stunt flyer. It was not for nothing that she was the daughter of Albert Stricklin. She had inherited her father's air sense.

Mary Eliska fumed inwardly at the unsportsmanlike action of her enemy. To attack a plane with machine gun fire when he knew that *Skybird* was unarmed! That seemed to the girl to show the base character of her father's business rival.

Mary Eliska let her plane out to the limit of its power. She tried her best to outdistance her enemy but the scheming attacker brought his plane to landward of the girl's and was now deliberately forcing her out to sea.

"He's trying to wear me out," thought Mary Eliska. "I see his plan now. He'll drive me out over the ocean and keep me there until my fuel is gone!"

But in face of this peril she did not lose her courage. Determination to win was written in every line of the girl's face. "He'll not get me," she said as she pressed back on the stick and sent her plane zooming. "I'll fight! I'll win!"

The tension was relieved. Her nerves were tingling with excitement. Every sense was alert to catch the meaning of her enemy's moves.

Then Bud Hyslop let the powerful motor loose. It zoomed at tremendous speed until it was carried once more above the *Skybird*. Thatcher Allen thought now that he had *Skybird* at his mercy. Bud put the plane into a loop so as to come down behind Mary Eliska's plane where he would have every advantage. Then Thatcher Allen's sub-machine gun spoke. A stream of bullets zipped through the wings of Mary Eliska's plane. For a moment she thought they had been torn to pieces.

Straight out to sea a huge fog bank was rolling landward. Mary Eliska headed her plane toward its protecting folds. Blindly she flew sending her plane soaring, then came down in a spiral. She levelled her plane and flew in a zig-zag course to spoil her enemy's aim. His bullets whistled harmlessly to right and left and so by good luck and good flying she escaped destruction.

No one knew better than Mary Eliska that she was playing the most dangerous game in the world. Beneath her was five thousand feet of thin air and below that the cold waters of the Atlantic. She dived into the cloud bank and suddenly she saw the angry billows close beneath her.

"Steady, girl!" she heard Liam McAdams's voice speaking. "You're flying like an ace. Keep it up and we'll win!"

Hastily consulting her compass, the girl flew low, heading her craft toward land. She had a wild hope that Thatcher Allen would think she had been lost in that mountain of fog and would give up his pursuit.

Rising gradually, she came out at last through the fog and into the sunlight. Beneath her the fog stretched for miles like a fleecy texture glistening in the sun.

Thatcher Allen was nowhere to be seen. "Safe at last!" gasped Mary Eliska as she took a long breath. She searched the horizon for signs of land but as far as the eye could reach there was nothing but the expanse of dazzling white.

Trembling with excitement she looked in every direction to see if her pursuer was in sight, and gasped, "We've fooled Thatcher Allen! He'll never catch us now!"

She turned to Liam McAdams with a reassuring smile. At that moment she heard Liam McAdams's voice in the earphones. "He's coming, Mary Eliska. Behind us! And far above." Mary Eliska's heart sank. She nodded to show that she had heard.

Then she began a slow spiral down. Liam McAdams held his breath. Had the girl gone crazy? What was she doing?

Mary Eliska might have been having a joy ride, a romp in the air, by the way she was banking so carelessly, circling and levelling off. Above, Thatcher Allen's plane had gone into a steep dive. It was coming straight at *Skybird* and Mary Eliska seemed to be making no effort to get out of the way.

Just as the powerful plane drew near, Thatcher Allen let out a burst of fire. Then he leaned far over to see Mary Eliska's plane falling in a mass of flames.

But *Skybird* was not there. His fire had missed. The girl had side-slipped and then straightened out, while Bud at the controls had allowed his plane to shoot past and into the bank of fog.

Mary Eliska made the most of that breathing time. She did not wait to see whether Thatcher Allen's plane had dived into the sea, but with throttle wide open she headed for land.

The girl kept her plane high above the glistening floor of fog. Half an hour slipped by and still no sign of the pursuing plane.

Again Mary Eliska zoomed skyward and found what she was looking for. Far below her to the right was a break in the fog and through it she could see the green earth below.

Mary Eliska headed for the opening and slipped through. Below that thick bank of cloud stretched the green fields dotted with towns and villages. It looked good. "Where are we Liam McAdams?" she cried.

Liam McAdams studied the terrain. "We're near home," he said as he recognized the different landmarks. "That's Beacon Hill to the right!"

Mary Eliska laughed with relief. "Oh boy, let's go!" she cried.

With the tense nerve strain over, Mary Eliska suddenly felt herself go weak. The plane wobbled under her control but only for the fraction of a second. Then Mary Eliska went straight for home.

Never had the Albert Stricklin Flying Field looked so good to her as it did when she banked and circled for a landing.

With steady hand she brought her plane down in a three-point landing, neat and clean. On the field was the *Comet* and she saw Martha and Sally Wyn running to meet her.

As Mary Eliska stepped from her plane, Martha threw both arms about her.

"We beat you by a full hour, Mary Eliska. What's kept you so long?" she cried, laughing hysterically now that the danger was over.

Mary Eliska kissed her then ran across the field to her father and mother.

"Good girl, Mary Eliska!" her father said in a husky voice. "You're...."

But he did not have a chance to finish the sentence. At that moment Bennett McAdams with one arm about Liam McAdams's shoulders advanced with outstretched hand.

"I want to thank you, Mary Eliska. You dear, brave girl! You saved Liam McAdams!" he exclaimed in a voice choking with emotion.

Mary Eliska's head was high, her eyes flashed fire. "I don't want your thanks, Mr. Graham!"

Albert Stricklin raised his hand reprovingly to his daughter, "Don't, Mary Eliska!" he said. "Mr. Graham has explained everything. It was all a mistake."

But Bennett McAdams broke in: "I don't blame her, Albert Stricklin. The girl is right. I've been a fool! But I've been well punished. Can you forgive me, Mary Eliska?"

"Oh, come on Mary Eliska, be a sport!" Liam McAdams advanced toward the girl and took her hand. "Dad's just as sorry as he can be. Shake hands with him and let's be friends."

Mary Eliska drew back, her heart was still bitter. Her father's face showed how he had suffered. It was hard to forgive.

"And listen, Mary Eliska," said Liam McAdams. "Dad says he's going to give you that fifty thousand dollars that was asked for ransom. It's for a reward."

"No, he's not!" snapped Mary Eliska. "I wouldn't *touch* his money!" Her face was scarlet, anger blazed in her eyes. "There are two things that money cannot buy! Loyalty and friendship!"

Bennett McAdams sadly turned away.

"Someday Mary Eliska, I'll prove my loyalty and friendship. Just give me time."

Mary Eliska's heart softened at sight of the old man's sorrow. She turned and offered her hand.

"Then let's begin right now," said the girl.

"Now tell us everything that happened," cried Mary Eliska's mother, hugging and kissing her daughter in an excess of joy. "Goodness knows I never expected to see you come back alive, after all you've been through."

"Hasn't Martha told you?" asked Mary Eliska. "She and Syd have been here an hour."

"Yes, but I want to hear it all over again," exclaimed Mrs. Stricklin.

"All right. But first I must have a hot bath and a cold shower and a change of clothes. Then I'll tell you at the table. I'm just simply starved."

An hour later the whole party gathered at Albert Stricklin' dinner table, not only the flyers but Bennett McAdams as well, for Albert Stricklin had urged him to stay.

Breathlessly they listened as Mary Eliska told about the flight to the rescue and when she came to the story of Thatcher Allen's attack on her plane with a sub-machine gun, they were so excited that they forgot to eat.

"I knew Thatcher Allen was unscrupulous, but I never dreamed he would go as far as murder," cried her father. "He and Bud Hyslop shall suffer for this!"

"But I *think* they have both been lost," said Mary Eliska. "The last I saw of their plane it was diving straight to the sea. Then the fog swallowed them up, and the chances are that they hit the water, and went under."

"I certainly hope so," said Bennett McAdams. "To think that I advised Liam McAdams to go into business with that scoundrel! It's unbelievable!"

Syd, who was sitting beside Martha, remarked quietly, "Well, that's the end of our attempt to fly the Atlantic. It will be a long time before we set out again."

"I'm not so sure," said Bennett McAdams. "I'm going to give Liam McAdams a new plane. He can pick it himself and you two boys can try again when Liam McAdams's arm is well."

"Thanks, Dad," said Liam McAdams. "I'll accept on one condition."

"Name it." "That is that these two girls are given a mate of the plane I pick. But for them, we would be still in Thatcher Allen's clutches."

"I'll be only too glad," cried the old gentleman. "That is if Mary Eliska and Martha will accept the plane." He turned to Mary Eliska and Martha, adding, "Please do. It will show that you have forgiven me."

The two sisters extended their hands impulsively and once more friendship was restored. The meal progressed happily.

"And now," said Mary Eliska, "we'll have a nice restful summer, playing about in our new airplanes and teaching the students how to win their pilot's licenses. No more adventure for a long time!"

"And you've got to teach Sally to fly!" exclaimed Martha.

"That will be a joy, for Sally has shown that she's one grand little sport, the stuff that will make a flyer," replied Mary Eliska.

They all smiled happily then went outside on the veranda for their coffee.

If only they had foreseen what the next months would bring into their lives, they would not have been so happy, for Martha and Mary Eliska were destined to set out upon an even more perilous air cruise, far in the southern seas. Amid the tropic splendors, the two girls were to encounter thrills they had never dreamed of among the denizens of the isles of mystery.